Tami Hoag: Three Great Novels

Also by Tami Hoag

Cry Wolf
Still Waters
Lucky's Lady
Sarah's Sin
Magic
Dark Paradise
Ashes to Ashes
Dust to Dust

Tami Hoag: Three Great Novels

NIGHT SINS
GUILTY AS SIN
A THIN DARK LINE

TAMI HOAG

ORION

First published in Great Britain in 2001 by
Orion
An imprint of Orion Books Ltd
Orion House, 5 Upper St Martin's Lane
London WC2H 9EA

ISBN: 0 75284 757 0

A CIP catalogue record for this book is available
from the British Library

Typeset by Deltatype Ltd, Birkenhead, Merseyside
Printed and bound in Great Britain by
Clays Ltd, St Ives plc

Contents

NIGHT SINS

To Andrea for opening doors. To Nita for pushing me through them. I owe you both so much.

To Irwyn for your support and your genius.

To Beth for another fine job, and to Kate Miciak for going above and beyond the call of duty.

And to Dan, who is patient enough and understanding enough to put up with all my characters – real and imagined – and with my artistic temperament, which is all too real. You are my anchor, my support, and the one who lifts me up to help me reach for stars. I love you.

.

Acknowledgments

My sincere thanks to Special Agent in Charge Don Peterson of the Minnesota Bureau of Criminal Apprehension for graciously taking time out of your busy schedule to answer my endless questions and give me the grand tour. Your generosity in sharing your expertise was greatly appreciated. I followed procedure as closely as fiction allows and hope that any dramatic license taken will not be held against me. (And for those who will inevitably ask, no, Don was not the model for SAC Bruce DePalma. Don is far more charming and bears no resemblance whatsoever to Richard Nixon.)

Additional thanks go to Amy Muelhbauer for serving as research assistant, and Elizabeth Eagle for sharing your experience and knowledge of migraine and medications. Also to Dr Karen Bjornigaard for answering what had to be the weirdest questions ever put to you in your professional life.

To Trisha Yearwood and Jude Johnstone – your words and music made me see what had been missing. You touch the most tender of hidden-heart secrets simply and beautifully. I stand in awe.

And last, but certainly not least, thanks to my sister-in-crime, drinking buddy, and pub singer extra-ordinaire, the notorious suspense diva Eileen Dreyer, for tutoring me in trauma lingo and gizmos, and for sharing all the weird stuff. May all your royalty checks have commas.

And much of Madness, and more of Sin,
And Horror the soul of the plot.

Edgar Allen Poe
The Conqueror Worm

Prologue

They found the body today. Not nearly as soon as we expected. Obviously, we gave them too much credit. The police are not as smart as we are. No one is.

We stood on the sidewalk and watched. What a pitiful scene. Grown men in tears throwing up in the bushes. They wandered around and around that corner of the park, trampling the grass, and breaking off bits of branches. They called to God, but God didn't answer. Nothing changed. No lightning bolts came down. No one was given knowledge of who or why. Ricky Meyers remained dead, his arms outflung, his sneakers toes-up.

We stood on the sidewalk as the ambulance came with its lights flashing, and more police cars came, and the cars of people from around town. We stood in the crowd, but no one saw us, no one looked at us. They thought we were beneath their notice, unimportant. But we are really above them and beyond them and invisible to them. They are blind and stupid and trusting. They would never think to look at us.

We are twelve years old.

5

1

Prologue

January 12, 1994. Day 1
5:26 p.m. 22°

Josh Kirkwood and his two best buddies burst out of the locker room, flying into the cold, dark late afternoon, hollering at the tops of their lungs. Their breath billowed out in rolling clouds of steam. They flung themselves off the steps like mountain goat kids leaping from ledge to ledge and landed hip-deep in the snow on the side of the hill. Hockey sticks skittered down, gear bags sliding after. Then came the Three Amigos, squealing and giggling, tucked into balls of wild-colored ski jackets and bright stocking caps.

The Three Amigos. That was what Brian's dad called them. Brian's family had moved to Deer Lake, Minnesota, from Denver, Colorado, and his dad was still a big Broncos fan. He said the Broncos used to have some wide receivers called the Three Amigos and they were really good. Josh was a Vikings fan. As far as he was concerned, every other team was just a bunch of wusses, except maybe the Raiders, 'cause their uniforms were cool. He didn't like the Broncos, but he liked the nickname – the Three Amigos.

'We are the Three Amigos!' Matt yelled as they landed in a heap at the bottom of the hill. He threw back his head and howled like a wolf. Brian and Josh joined in, and the racket was so terrible it made Josh's ears ring.

Brian fell into a fit of uncontrollable giggles. Matt flopped onto his back and started making a snow angel, swinging his arms and legs in wide arcs, looking as if he were trying to swim back up the hill. Josh pushed himself to his feet and shook like a dog as Coach Olsen came out of the ice arena.

Coach was old – at least forty-five – kind of fat and mostly bald, but he was a good coach. He yelled a lot, but he laughed a lot, too. He told them at the beginning of hockey season that if he got too cranky they were to remind him they were only eight years old. The team had picked Josh for that job. He was one of the co-captains, a responsibility that pleased him a lot even though he would never say so. Nobody liked a bragger, Mom said. If you did your job well, there wasn't any reason to brag. A good job would speak for itself.

6

Coach Olsen started down the steps, tugging down the earflaps of his hunting cap. The end of his nose was red from the cold. His breath came out of his mouth and went up around his head like smoke from a chimney. 'You guys have rides home tonight?'

They answered all at once, vying for the coach's attention by being loud and silly. He laughed and held his gloved hands up in surrender. 'All right, all right! The rink's open if you get cold waiting. Olie's inside if you need to use the phone.'

Then Coach jumped into his girlfriend's car, the way he did every Wednesday, and off they went to have dinner at Grandma's Attic downtown. Wednesday was Grandma's famous meat loaf night. All-U-Can-Eat, it said on the menu. Josh imagined Coach Olsen could eat a lot.

Cars rumbled around the circular drive in front of the Gordie Knutson Memorial Arena, a parade of minivans and station wagons, doors banging, exhaust pipes coughing. Kids from the various Squirt League teams chucked their sticks and equipment in trunks and hatches and climbed into the cars with their moms or dads, talking a mile a minute about the plays and drills they had worked on in practice.

Matt's mom pulled up in their new Transport, a wedge-shaped thing that to Josh looked like something from *Star Trek*. Matt scrambled for his gear and dashed across the sidewalk, calling a good-bye over his shoulder. His mother, wearing a bright red stocking cap, buzzed down the passenger window.

'Josh, Brian – you guys have rides?'

'My mom's coming,' Josh answered, suddenly feeling eager to see her. She would pick him up on her way home from the hospital and they would stop at the Leaning Tower of Pizza to get supper and she would want to hear all about practice. *Really* want to hear. Not like Dad. Lately, Dad just pretended to listen. Sometimes he even snapped at Josh to be quiet. He always apologized later, but it still made Josh feel bad.

'My sister's coming,' Brian called. 'My sister, Beth Butt-head,' he added under his breath as Mrs Connor drove away.

'You're the butt-head,' Josh teased, shoving him.

Brian shoved back, laughing, three big gaps showing in his mouth where teeth had been. 'Butt-head!'

'Butt-breath!'

'Butt-face!'

Brian scooped up a mitten full of snow and tossed it in Josh's face, then turned and ran up the snow-packed sidewalk, bounded up the steps, and dashed around the side of the brick building. Josh let out a war whoop and bolted after him. Immediately they were so involved in their game of Attack, the rest of the world ceased to exist. One boy hunted the other to deliver a snowball up close in the face, in the back, down the neck of the jacket. After a successful attack the roles reversed and the hunter became the hunted. If the hunter couldn't find the hunted in a count of a hundred, the hunted scored a point.

Josh was good at hiding. He was small for his age and he was smart, a combination that served him well in games like Attack. He smashed Brian in the back of the head with a snowball, whirled and ran. Before Brian had shaken the snow off his coat, Josh was safely tucked behind the air-conditioning units that squatted beside the building. The cylinders were covered with canvas for the winter months and blocked the wind. They sat well back along the side of the building, where the streetlights didn't quite reach. Josh watched as Brian ventured cautiously around a Dumpster, snowball in hand, pouncing at a shadow, then drawing back. Josh smiled to himself. He had found the all-time best hiding place. He licked the tip of a gloved forefinger and drew himself a point in the air.

Brian homed in on one of the overgrown bushes that lined the edge of the parking lot and separated the ice rink grounds from the fairgrounds. Tongue sticking out the side of his mouth, he crept toward it. He hoped Josh hadn't gone farther than the hedges. The fairgrounds was the creepiest place in the world this time of year, when all the old buildings stood dark and empty and the wind howled around them.

A car horn blared and Brian swung around, heart pounding. He groaned in disappointment as his sister's Rabbit pulled up around the curve.

'Come on, hurry up, Brian! I've got pageant practice tonight!'

'But –'

'But nothing, twerp!' Beth Hiatt snapped. The wind whipped a strand of long blond hair across her face and she snagged it back behind her ear with a bare hand white with cold. 'Get your little butt in the car!'

Brian heaved a sigh and dropped his snowball, then trudged toward his gear bag and hockey stick. Beth the Bitch raced the Rabbit's motor, put the car in gear, and let it lurch ahead on the drive, as if she might just leave him behind. She had done that once before and they had both gotten hollered at, but Brian had gotten the worst of it because Beth blamed him for getting her in trouble and spent four days tormenting him for it. Instantly forgetting his game and the remaining amigo, he grabbed his stuff and ran for the car, already plotting ways to get his sister back for being such a snot.

Behind the air-conditioning units, Josh heard Beth Hiatt's voice. He heard the car doors slam and he heard the Rabbit roar around the circle drive. So much for the game.

He crawled out of his hiding spot and went back around the front of the building. The parking lot was empty except for Olie's old rusted-out Chevy van. The next practice didn't start for an hour. The circular drive was empty. Packed over the asphalt by countless tires, the snow gleamed in the glow of the streetlights, as hard and shiny as milky-white marble. Josh tugged off his left glove and shoved up the sleeve of his ski jacket to peer at the watch Uncle Tim had sent him for Christmas. Big and black with lots of dials and buttons, it looked like something a scuba diver might wear – or a commando. Sometimes Josh pretended that he was a commando, a man on a mission, waiting to meet with the world's most dangerous spy. The numbers on the watch face glowed green in the dark: 5:45.

Josh looked down the street, expecting to see headlights, expecting to see the minivan with his mom at the wheel. But the street was dark. The only lights glowed dimly out the windows of houses that lined the block. Inside those houses, people were having supper and watching the news and talking about their day. Outside, the only sound was the buzz of the street lamps and the cold wind rattling the dry, bare branches of winter-dead trees. The sky was black.

He was alone.

5:17 p.m. 22°

She nearly escaped. She had her coat halfway on, purse slung over her shoulder, gloves and car keys clutched in one hand. She hurried down the hall toward the west side door of the hospital, staring straight ahead, telling herself if she didn't make eye contact, she wouldn't be caught, she would be invisible, she would escape.

I sound like Josh. That's the kind of game he likes – what if we could make ourselves invisible?

A smile curved Hannah's lips. Josh and his imagination. Last night she'd found him in Lily's room, telling his sister an adventure story about Zeek the Meek and Super Duper, characters Hannah had made up in stories for Josh when he was a toddler. He was passing on the tradition, telling the tale with great enthusiasm while Lily sat in her crib and sucked her thumb, her blue eyes wide with astonishment, hanging on her brother's every word.

I've got two great kids. Two for the plus column. I'll take what I can get these days.

The smile faded and tension tightened in Hannah's stomach. She blinked hard and realized she was just standing there at the end of the hall with her coat half on. Rand Bekker, head of maintenance, shouldered his way through the door, letting in a blast of crisp air. A burly man with a full red beard, he pulled off a flame-orange hunting cap and shook himself like a big wet ox, as if he could shake off the chill.

'Hiya, Dr Garrison. Decent night out there.'

'Is it?' She smiled automatically, blankly, as if she were speaking with a stranger. But there were no strangers at Deer Lake Community Hospital. Everyone knew everyone.

'You bet. It's looking good for Snowdaze.'

Rand grinned, his anticipation for the festival as plain as a child's eagerness for Christmas morning. Snowdaze was big doings in a town the size of Deer Lake, an excuse for the fifteen thousand residents to break the monotony of Minnesota's long winter. Hannah tried to find some enthusiasm. She knew Josh was looking forward to Snowdaze, especially the torchlight parade. But it was difficult for her to feel festive these days.

For the most part, she felt tired, drained, dispirited. And stretched over it all was a thin film of desperation, like plastic wrap, because she couldn't let any of those feelings show. People depended on her, looked up to her, thought of her as a model for working women. Hannah Garrison: doctor, wife, mother, woman of the year; juggling all the demanding roles with skill and ease and a beauty queen smile. Lately the titles had felt as heavy as bowling balls and her arms were growing weary.

'Rough day?'

'What?' She jerked her attention back to Rand. 'I'm sorry, Rand. Yeah, it's been one of those days.'

'I better let you go, then. I got a hot date with a boiler.'

Hannah murmured good-bye as Bekker pulled open a door marked Maintenance Staff Only and disappeared through it, leaving her alone in the hall. Her inner voice, the voice of the little goblin that kept the cling wrap pulled tight over her emotions, gave a shout.

Go! Go now! Escape while you can! Get away!

She had to pick up Josh. They would stop and get a pizza, then go on to the sitter's for Lily. After supper she had to drive Josh to religion class. . . . But her body refused to bolt in response. Then the great escape was lost.

'Dr Garrison to ER. Dr Garrison to ER.'

That selfish part of her prodded once more, telling her she could still get away. She wasn't on call tonight, had no patients in the hundred-bed facility who were in critical need of her personal attention. There was no one here to see her escape. She could leave the work to the doctor on duty, Craig Lomax, who believed he had been set on earth to rush to the aid of mere mortals and comfort them with his cover-boy looks. Hannah wasn't even the backup tonight. But guilt came directly on the heels of those thoughts. She had taken an oath to serve. It didn't matter that she'd seen enough sore throats and bruised bodies to last her one day. She had a duty – a bigger one now that the hospital board had named her director of the ER. The people of Deer Lake depended on her.

The page sounded again. Hannah heaved a sigh and felt tears warm the backs of her eyes. She was exhausted – physically, emotionally. She needed this night off, a night with just herself and the kids; with Paul working late, keeping his moods and his sarcasm in his office instead of inflicting them on the family.

A wavy strand of honey-blond hair escaped her loose ponytail and fell limply against her cheek. She sighed and brushed it back behind her ear as she stared out the door to the parking lot that looked sepia-toned beneath the halogen lights.

'Dr Garrison to ER. Dr Garrison to ER.'

She slipped her coat off and folded it over her arm.

'God, there you are!' Kathleen Casey blurted out as she skidded around the corner and hustled down the hall, the tails of her white lab coat sailing behind her. The thick, cushioned soles of her running shoes made almost no sound on the polished floor. Not a fraction of an inch over five feet, the nurse had a leprechaun's features, a shock of thick red hair, and the tenacity of a pit bull. Her uniform consisted of surgical scrubs and a pin that proclaimed No Whining. She drew a bead on Hannah that had all the power of a tractor beam.

Hannah tried to muster a wry smile. 'Sorry. God may be a woman, but she's not *this* woman.'

Kathleen gave a snort as she curled a hand around Hannah's upper arm. 'You'll do.'

'Can't Craig handle it?'

'Maybe, but we'd rather have a higher life form with opposable thumbs.'

'I'm not even on call tonight. I have to pick up Josh from hockey. Call Dr Baskir – '

'We did. He's in bed with your friend and mine, Jurassic Park flu, also known as tracheasaurus phlegmus. That's one butt-kicking virus. Half the staff is down with it, which means I, Kathleen Casey, queen of the ER, may press you into service against your will. It won't take long, I promise.'

'Famous last words,' Hannah muttered.

Kathleen ignored her and started to turn as if she had every intention of towing all five feet nine inches of Hannah in her wake. Hannah's feet moved of their own accord as the wail of an ambulance sounded in the distance.

'What's coming in?' she asked with resignation.

'Car accident. Some kid hit a patch of ice on Old Cedar Road and spun into a car full of grandmas.'

Their pace picked up with each step, the low heels of Hannah's leather boots pounding out a quick staccato rhythm. Her fatigue and its companion emotions slipped under the surface of duty and her 'doctor mode,' as Paul called it. Power switches flipped on inside her, filling her brain with light and energy, sending a rush of adrenaline shooting through her.

'What's the status?' Hannah asked, her speech taking on a sharper, harder quality.

'They flew two critical to Hennepin County Medical Center. We get the leftovers. Two grandmas with bumps and bruises and the college kid. Sounds like he's banged up pretty good.'

'No seat belt?'

'Why bother when you haven't lived long enough to grasp the concept of mortality?' Kathleen said as they reached the area that served as a combination nurses' station and admissions desk.

Hannah leaned over the counter. 'Carol? Could you please call the hockey rink and leave word for Josh that I'll be a little bit late? Maybe he can practice his skating.'

'Sure thing, Dr Garrison.'

Dr Craig Lomax arrived on the scene in immaculate surgical greens, looking like a soap opera doctor.

'Jesus,' Kathleen muttered half under her breath, 'he's been watching *Medical Center* reruns again. Get a load of the Chad Everett hair.'

Strands of black hair tumbled across his forehead in a careless look he had probably spent fifteen painstaking minutes in front of a mirror to achieve. Lomax was thirty-two, madly in love with himself, and afflicted with an overabundance of confidence in his own talents. He had come to Deer Lake Community in April, a reject from the better medical centers in the Twin Cities – a hard truth that had not managed to put so much as a dent in his ego. Deer Lake was just far enough out-state that they couldn't afford to be choosy. Most doctors preferred the salaries in the metro area over the chance to serve the needs of a small rural college town.

Lomax had arranged his features in a suitably grave expression that cracked a little when he caught sight of Hannah. 'I thought you'd gone home,' he said bluntly.

'Kathleen just caught me.'

'In the nick of time,' the nurse added.

Lomax sucked in a breath to chastise her for her attitude.

'Save it, Craig,' Hannah snapped, tossing her things on a waiting area couch and moving forward as the doors to the ER slid open.

A stretcher was rolled in, one paramedic at the rear, one bent over the patient, talking to him in a soothing tone. 'Hang in there, Mike. The docs'll have you patched up in no time.'

The young man on the stretcher groaned and tried to sit up, but chest and head restraints held him down on the backboard. His face was taut and gray with pain above the cervical collar that immobilized his neck. Blood ran down across his temple from a gash on his forehead.

'What have we got here, Arlis?' Hannah asked, shoving up the sleeves of her sweater.

'Mike Chamberlain. Nineteen. He's a little shocky,' the paramedic said. 'Pulse one twenty. BP ninety over sixty. Got a bump on the noggin and some broken bones.'

'Is he lucid?'

Lomax cut her off on the way to the stretcher with a move as smooth as glass. 'I'll handle it, Dr Garrison. You're off duty. Mavis.' He nodded to Mavis Sandstrom. The nurse exchanged a glance with Kathleen, her expression as blank as a cardshark's.

Hannah bit her tongue and stepped back. There was no point in fighting with Lomax in front of staff and the patient. Administration frowned on that kind of thing. She didn't want to be there anyway. Let Lomax take the patient who would require the most time.

'Treatment room three, guys,' Lomax ordered, and ushered them down the hall as a second ambulance pulled into the drive. 'Let's start an IV with lactated ringers ...'

'Dr Craig Ego strikes again,' Kathleen growled. 'He has yet to grasp the notion that you're his boss now.'

'No biggie,' Hannah said calmly. 'If we ignore him long enough, maybe he'll stop trying to mark territory and we can all live happily ever after.'

'Or maybe he'll flip out and we'll find him in the parking lot, peeing on car tires.'

There wasn't time to laugh. A heavyset EMT from the second ambulance charged into the reception area.

'We've got a full arrest! Ida Bergen. Sixty-nine. We were bringing her in with cuts and bruises, and as we pulled into the drive, *bam*! She grabs her chest and goes −

The rest of her words were lost as Hannah, Kathleen, and another nurse bolted into action. The emergency room erupted into a whirlwind of sound and action. Orders shouted and relayed. Pages sounding for additional staff. The stretcher wheeling into the reception area and down the hall. The trauma cart and crash cart thundering into the treatment room.

'Standard ACLS procedure, guys,' Hannah called out. 'Get me a 6.5 endotracheal tube. Let's get her bagged and get some air into her lungs. Do we have a pulse without CPR?'

'No.'

'With CPR?'

'Yes.'

'BP forty over twenty and fading fast.'

'Start an IV. Hang bretylium and dopamine and give her a bristoject of epinephrine.'

'Goddammit, I can't get a vein! Come on, baby, come on, come to Mama Kathleen.'

'Allen, check for lung sounds. Stop CPR. Angie, run a strip. Is respiratory coming?'

'Wayne's on his way down.'

'Gotcha!' Kathleen slipped the line onto the catheter and secured it with tape, her small hands quick and sure. A tech handed her the epinephrine and she injected it into the line.

'Fine v-fib, Dr Garrison.'

'We need to defibrillate. Chris, continue CPR until my word. Allen, charge me up to 320.' Hannah grabbed the paddles, rubbing the heads together to spread the gel. 'Stand clear!' *Paddles in position against the woman's bare chest.* 'All clear!' *Hit the buttons.* The old woman's body bucked on the gurney.

'Nothing! No pulse.'

'Clear!' She hit the buttons again. Her eyes went to the monitor, where a flat green line bisected the screen. 'Once more. Clear!'

The woman's body convulsed. The flat line snapped like a cracking whip and the monitor began to bleep out an erratic beat. A cheer went up in the room.

They worked on Ida Bergen for forty minutes, pulling her out of the clutches of death, only to lose her again ten minutes later. They worked the miracle a second time, but not a third.

Hannah delivered the news to Ida's husband. Ed Bergen's chore clothes emanated the warm, sweet scent of cows and fresh milk with a pungent undertone of manure. He had the same stoic face she had seen on many a Nordic farmer, but his eyes were bright and moist with worry, and they brimmed with tears when she told him they had done their best but had been unable to save his wife.

She sat with him and led him through some of the cruel rituals of death. Even in this time of grief, decisions had to be made, etc., etc. She went through the routine in a low monotone, feeling on autopilot, numb with exhaustion, crushed by depression. As a doctor, she had cheated death time and again, but death wouldn't let her win every time and she had never learned to be a gracious loser. The adrenaline that fueled her through the crisis had vaporized. A crash was imminent. Another familiar part of a routine she hated.

After Mr Bergen had gone, Hannah slipped into her office and sat at the desk with the lights off, her head cradled in her hands. It hurt worse this time. Perhaps because she felt perilously close to loss for the first time in her life. Her marriage was in trouble. Ed Bergen's marriage was over. Forty-eight years of partnership over in the time it took a car to skid out of control on an icy road. Had they been good years? Loving years? Would he mourn his wife or simply go on?

She thought of Paul, his dissatisfaction, his discontent, his quiet hostility. Ten years of marriage was tearing apart like rotted silk, and she felt powerless to stop it. She had no point of reference. She had never lost anything, had never developed the skills to fight against loss. She felt the tears building – tears for Ida and Ed Bergen and for herself. Tears of grief and confusion and exhaustion. She was afraid to let them start falling. She had to be strong. She had to find a solution, smooth over all the rough spots, make everyone happy. But tonight the burdens weighed too heavily on her slender shoulders. She couldn't help thinking the only light at the end of the tunnel was the headlight of a big black train.

Knuckles rapped against her door and Kathleen stuck her head in. 'You know she'd been seeing a cardiac specialist at Abbott-Northwestern for years,' she said quietly.

Hannah sniffed and flicked on the desk lamp. 'How's Craig's patient?'

Kathleen slid into the visitor's chair. She crossed a sneaker over one knee and rubbed absently at an ink mark on the leg of her scrub pants.

'He'll be fine. A couple of broken bones, a slight concussion, whiplash. He was lucky. His car was turned sideways at the moment of impact. The other car hit him on the passenger side.'

'Poor kid. He feels terrible about the accident. He keeps going on and on about how the road was dry and then suddenly there was this big patch of ice and he was out of control.'

'I guess life can be that way sometimes,' Hannah murmured, fingering the small cube-shaped clock on her desk. The wood was bird's-eye maple, smooth and satiny beneath her fingertips. An anniversary gift from Paul four years ago. A clock so she would always know how long it would be before they could be together again.

'Yeah, well, you've hit your patch of ice for the night,' Kathleen said. 'Time to pick yourself up, dust yourself off, and get home to the munchkins.'

A chill went through Hannah like a dagger of ice. Her fingers tightened on the clock and tilted the face up to the light. Six-fifty.

'Oh, my God. Josh. I forgot about Josh!'

Journal entry
Day 1

The plan has been perfected.
The players have been chosen.
The game begins today.

2

Day 1
6:42 p.m. 22°

Megan O'Malley had never expected to meet a chief of police in his underwear, but then again, it had been that kind of day. She had not allotted enough time for moving into the new apartment. Rather, she had not allowed for as many screwups as she had encountered before, during, and after the move. She kicked herself for that. Should have known.

Of course, there were things that couldn't have been foreseen. She couldn't have foreseen the key breaking off in the ignition of the moving van yesterday, for example. She couldn't have foreseen her new landlord hitting it big on the pull tabs at the American Legion hall and skipping town on a charter trip to Vegas. She couldn't have imagined that tracking down the keys to her apartment would involve a manhunt into the deepest, darkest reaches of the BuckLand cheese factory, or that once she got into the apartment, none of the utilities that were to have been turned on two days before were operational. No phone. No electricity. No gas.

The disasters and delays clustered together in a spot above her right eye. Pain nibbled at the edge of her brain, threatening a full-blown headache. The last thing she needed was to start her new assignment with a migraine. That would establish her all right – as weak. Small and weak – an image she had to fight even when she was in the best of health.

As of today she was a field agent for the Minnesota Bureau of Criminal Apprehension, one of the top law enforcement agencies in the Midwest. As of today she was one of only eleven field agents in the state. The only woman. The first female to crash the testosterone barrier of the BCA field ranks. Someone somewhere was probably proud of her for that, but Megan doubted that sentiment would extend to the male bastions of outstate law enforcement. Feminists would call her a pioneer. Others would use words omitted from standard dictionaries for the sake of propriety.

Megan called herself a cop. She was sick and tired of having gender enter into the discussion. She had taken all required courses, passed all tests – in the classroom and on the streets. She knew how to handle herself, knew how to handle anything that could shoot. She'd done her time on patrol, earned her stripes as a detective. She'd put in the hours at headquarters and had been passed over twice for a field assignment. Then finally her time had come.

Leo Kozlowski, the Deer Lake district agent, dropped dead from a heart attack at the age of fifty-three. Thirty years of doughnuts and cheap cigars had finally caught up with him and landed poor old Leo facedown in a plate of post-Christmas Swedish meatballs at the Scandia House Cafe.

When the news of his demise swept through the warren of offices at headquarters, Megan observed a moment of silence in honor of Leo, then typed yet another memorandum to the assistant superintendent, submitting her name for consideration for the post. When the day for decision-making drew near and she had heard nothing encouraging, she gathered her nerve and her service record and marched to the office of the special agent in charge of the St Paul regional office.

Bruce DePalma went through the same song-and-dance he'd given her before. There were reasons all the field agents were men. The chiefs and sheriffs they had to work with were all men. The detectives and officers who made up their network were nearly all men. No, that wasn't discrimination, that was reality.

'Well, I've got another dose of reality for you, Bruce,' Megan said, plunking her file dead center on his immaculate blotter. 'I've got more investigative experience, more class time, and a better arrest record than any other person in line for this assignment. I've passed the agent's course at the FBI academy and I can shoot the dick off a rat at two hundred yards. If I get passed over again for no other reason than the fact that I have breasts, you'll hear me howling all the way to the city desk of the *Pioneer Press.*'

DePalma scowled at her. He had a Nixonesque quality that had never endeared him to the press. Megan could see him playing the scene through his mind – reporters calling him evasive and uncooperative while the cameras focused on his deep-set, shifty eyes.

'That's blackmail,' he said at last.

'And this is sex discrimination. I want the assignment because I'm a damn good cop and because I deserve it. If I get out there and screw up, then yank me back, but give me the chance to try.'

DePalma slumped down in his chair and steepled his fingers, bony shoulders hunched up to his ears, a pose reminiscent of a vulture on a perch. The silence stretched taut between them. Megan held her ground and held his gaze. She hated to stoop to threats; she wanted the job on merit. But she knew that the brass was especially skittish of words like *harassment* and *gender bias*, was still smarting from the sexual harassment charges several female employees had made against the outgoing superintendent months before. It may have been a risk, but the reminder might be just enough to make DePalma pay attention.

He scowled at her, jowls quivering as he ground his teeth. 'It's an old-boy network out there. That network is essential to successful police work. How do you expect to get in when everyone else thinks you don't belong?'

'I'll make them see that I do belong?'

'You'll hit a stone wall every time you turn around.'

'That's what jackhammers are for.'

DePalma shook his head. 'This job calls for finesse, not jackhammers.'

'I'll wear kid gloves.'

Or *mittens*, she thought as she fiddled with the car's heater setting. Frustrated and cold to the bone, she smacked the dashboard with a fist and was rewarded with a cloud of dust from the fan vents. The Chevy Lumina was a nag from the bureau's stable. It ran, had four good tires, and the requisite radio equipment. That was it. No frills. But it was a car and she was a field agent. Damned if she was going to complain.

Field agent for the Bureau of Criminal Apprehension. The BCA had been created by the state legislature in 1927 to provide multijurisdictional investigative, lab, and records services to the other law enforcement agencies in the state, a scaled-down version of the FBI. Megan was now the bureau's representative to a ten-county area. She now served as liaison between the local authorities and headquarters. Consultant, detective, drug czar – she had to wear many hats, and as the first woman on the job, she would have to look damn good in all of them.

Being late for her first meeting with the chief of police in the town that would be her base of operations was not a good beginning.

'Should have made the appointment for tomorrow, O'Malley,' she muttered, climbing out of her car, struggling with what seemed to be twenty yards of gray woolen scarf.

The scarf was like a python twisting itself around her neck, around her arm, around the handle of her briefcase. She snatched at it and pulled at it, cursing under her breath as she made her way across the skating rink that passed for a parking lot behind the Deer Lake city hall and law enforcement center. Getting hold of the end of the scarf, she flung it hard over her shoulder – and threw herself off balance. Instantly, her feet went out from under her and she scrambled in a mad tap dance to keep from going down. The heels of the boots she had chosen to give herself the illusion of height acted like skate blades instead of cleats. She danced another five feet toward the building, then fell like a sack of bricks, landing with teeth-rattling impact smack on her fanny. The pain shot up her spine from her butt to her brain and rang there like a bell.

For a moment Megan just sat there with her eyes squeezed shut, then the cold began to penetrate through the seat of her black wool trousers. She looked around the parking lot for witnesses. There were none. The afternoon had been crushed beneath the weight of darkness. Five o'clock had come and gone; most of the office personnel had already left for the day. Chief Holt was probably gone as well, but she wanted it on the log that she *had* shown up for their appointment. Three hours late, but she had shown.

'I hate winter,' she snarled, gathering her legs beneath her, and rose with little grace and confidence, slipping, stumbling, finally grabbing hold of a car door to steady herself. 'I *hate* winter.'

She would rather have been anywhere south of the snow belt. It didn't matter that she had been born and raised in St Paul. A love for arctic temperatures was not part of her genetic makeup. She had no affinity for down jackets. Wool sweaters made her break out in a rash.

If it hadn't been for her father, she would have been long gone to friendlier climes. She would have taken the FBI assignment that had been offered when she'd been at the academy in Quantico. Memphis. People in Memphis didn't even know what winter was. Snow was an event in Memphis. Their thermometers probably didn't have numbers below zero. If they'd ever heard the words *Alberta clipper*, they probably thought it was the name of a boat, not a weather system that brought wind-chill factors cold enough to freeze marrow in the bones of polar bears.

I stay here for you, Pop.

As if he cared.

The teeth of the headache bit a little harder.

The Deer Lake City Center was new. A handsome V-shaped two-story brick building, it testified to the growing tax base brought about by professional people moving out from the Cities. The town was just within commuting distance of the south end of the metro area. With crime and crowding on the rise in Minneapolis and St Paul, those who could afford to and didn't mind the drive sought out the quaint charm of places like Deer Lake, Elk River, Northfield, Lakefield.

The city offices were housed in the south wing of City Center, the police department and the office of the late lamented Leo Kozlowski in the north, with the city jail on the second floor. Additional jail facilities were available across the town square in the old Park County courthouse and law enforcement center, where the county sheriff's offices and the county jail were located.

Once inside the building, Megan hung a left and marched down the wide hall, ignoring the pretty atrium with its skylights and potted palms and pictorial history of Deer Lake. Catching a glimpse of her reflection in the glass of a wall-mounted display case, she winced a little. She looked as if she'd just pulled a gunnysack off her head. That morning – seemed like a month ago – she had swept her dark mane back into a low ponytail and secured it with a small, no-nonsense bow in a dark Black Watch plaid. Neat. Businesslike. Now, strands fell like fine silk thread across her forehead and along her cheeks and jaw. She tried to sweep the stragglers back with an impatient gesture.

The reception desk at the head of the police wing had been abandoned for the day. She marched past it and on to the security doors that kept the city council safe from criminals and cops, and vice versa. She punched the buzzer and waited, looking into the squad room through the bulletproof glass. The room was bright and clean – white walls, slate-gray industrial-grade carpet that had yet to show any signs of wear. A small platoon of black steel desks squatted in two rows. The desks, for the most part, were not neat. They were piled with files and paperwork, crowded with coffee mugs and framed photos. Only three of them were manned, one by a massive uniformed cop talking on the phone, the other two by men in plainclothes, eating sandwiches while they tackled paperwork.

The uniform hung up the phone and rose to a towering height, big, drowsy eyes on Megan as he lumbered to the door, unwrapping a stick of Dentyne. He looked thirty and Samoan. His hair was dark and unruly, his body as thick as the trunk of an oak tree, and probably just as strong. His name tag said NOGA. He popped the gum in his mouth and punched the intercom button.

'Can I help you?'

'Agent O'Malley, BCA.' Producing her ID, Megan held it up to the glass for his inspection. 'I had an appointment with Chief Holt.'

The cop studied the photo with mild interest; he looked half asleep. 'Come on in,' he said with a casual wave. 'Door's open.'

Megan gritted her teeth and willed herself not to blush. She didn't care to be made a fool of, especially not at the end of a day like this one or by a man who was a part of her network. Noga pulled one of the doors open and she marched in, fixing him with a steely look.

'Shouldn't this area be secured?' she asked sharply.

Noga appeared unperturbed by her manner. He shrugged his shoulders, a move that looked like an earthquake going through a small mountain range. 'Against what?' When she just glared at him, he smiled a crooked half-smile, his thick lips tugging upward on the right side. 'You aren't from around here, are you?'

Megan was getting a crick in her neck from looking up at him. Hell of a trick, trying to do imperious on someone a full foot taller than you. 'Are you?'

'For long enough. Come on back.' He led the way through the rows of desks to a hall with private offices off it. 'Natalie's still around. No one sees the chief without seeing Natalie first. She runs the place. We call her the Commandant.' He eyed her with mild curiosity. 'So what are you here for? Filling in until they find a replacement for Leo?'

'I *am* the replacement for Leo.'

Noga arched a thick brow, schooling a look of shock and dismay into something that more resembled indigestion. 'No shit?'

'No shit.'

'Huh.'

'You got a problem working with a woman?' Megan worked to keep the edge out of her voice. But she was tired and her temper was running on a real lean mix. She could feel it simmering just beneath the surface of her control.

Noga played innocent, eyes wide. 'Not me.'

'Good.'

21

He ducked into an office, drumming his knuckles on the open door as he went. 'Hey, Natalie! The BCA guy – er – gal –' Noga cast a self-conscious glance at Megan.

'Agent O'Malley,' she said stiffly.

'– is here,' he finished.

'Well, it's about damn time.'

The churlish line came from an office beyond the one in which they were standing. Stenciled on the frosted glass was MITCHELL HOLT, CHIEF OF POLICE, but it was not Mitchell Holt who came to the door with black eyes blazing.

The infamous Natalie was no taller than Megan's five feet five, but considerably more substantial of body. She had a certain squareness about her that suggested immovability, but she draped that squareness in a rust and purple ensemble that more than suggested taste. Her skin was the color of polished mahogany, her face as round as a pumpkin and crowned with a fine cap of tight black curls that looked like the wool of a newly shorn sheep. One hand propped on a hip, the other braced against the doorjamb, she gave Megan a hard once-over from behind the lenses of huge, red-rimmed glasses.

'Girl, you are *late*.'

'I'm well aware of that,' Megan replied coolly. 'Is Chief Holt still in?'

Natalie made a sour face. 'No, he isn't *in*. You think he'd just be sitting here, waitin' on you?'

'I *did* call to say I'd be late.'

'You didn't talk to me.'

'I didn't know that was necessary.'

Natalie snorted. She pushed herself away from the door and bustled around her desk, adding papers to a file, filing the file in one of half a dozen black file cabinets behind her. Every move was efficient and quick. 'You *are* new. Who'd you talk to? Melody? That girl would forget her own behind if some man didn't always have his hand on it to remind her.'

Noga edged his way toward the door, trying to be unobtrusive. 'Noogie, don't you try to sneak out on me,' Natalie warned, not bothering to look at him. 'Have you finished that report Mitch asked for?'

He made a pained face. 'I'll finish it in the morning. I've got patrol.'

'You got trouble, that's what you got,' Natalie grumbled. 'That report is on my desk by noon or I take the electric stapler after your ass. You hear me?'

'Loud and clear.'

'And don't forget to drive by Dick Reid's place twice. They've gone to Cozumel.'

Megan heaved a sigh and wished she were gone to Cozumel. A faint tic had begun in her right eyelid. She rubbed at it and thought about food for the first time since breakfast. She needed to eat something or the headache would take a stronger hold and she wouldn't be able to keep medication down.

'If Chief Holt is gone for the day, then I'd like to reschedule our appointment.'

Natalie pursed her thick lips and fixed Megan with a long, measuring look. 'I didn't say he was gone. I said he wasn't *in*,' she qualified. 'What kind of cop are you, you don't listen to nuances?' She made a sound of disgust and led the way out of the office. 'Come on, *Agent* O'Malley. You're here, you might as well meet him.'

Megan marched along beside the chief's secretary, careful not to step ahead, well aware the woman was taking her measure.

'So you're here to fill Leo's spot.'

'I couldn't hope to fill Leo's spot,' Megan said, deadpan. 'I don't eat enough fried food.'

A muscle ticked at the corner of Natalie's mouth. Not quite a smile. 'Leo could pack it away, that's for sure. Now they've packed Leo away. I told him to watch his cholesterol and quit smoking those damn cigars. He wouldn't listen to me, but that's a man for you. Look up *obtuse* in the dictionary – they ought to have a picture of a man beside it.

'Everybody liked Leo, though,' she added, her gaze sharpening on Megan once more. 'He was a hell of a guy. What are you?'

'I'm a hell of a cop.'

Natalie snorted. 'We'll see.'

When she first heard the music, Megan thought she was imagining it. The sound was faint, the tune something from the Christmas season. Nobody played Christmas music in January. Everybody had OD'd on it by the middle of December. But it grew louder as they went down the hall. 'Winter Wonderland.'

'The cops and the volunteer firemen put on a show for Snowdaze and give the proceeds to charity,' Natalie explained. 'Rehearsal goes on till seven.'

A roar of male laughter drowned out the music. Natalie tugged open a door marked CONFERENCE 3 and motioned for Megan to precede her. Half a dozen people lounged in chrome-and-plastic chairs that had been set up in two haphazard rows. Another half dozen stood along the paneled walls. All were in various states of hysteria – laughing, slapping thighs, doubled over, tears streaming. At the front of the room a Mutt and Jeff team lumbered through a soft-shoe routine in red longjohns while from the speakers of a boombox a man with an overdone Norwegian accent sang, 'Itch a little here. Scratch a little dere. Valkin' in my vinter undervear . . .'

Megan stared openly at the spectacle. The man on the right had a build like the Pillsbury doughboy and wore a red plaid Elmer Fudd cap. The one on the left was a different story altogether. Tall and trim, he had Harrison Ford's looks and an athlete's body. The underwear fit him like a second skin, announcing his gender in no uncertain terms. Megan fought to drag her gaze to less provocative details of his anatomy – his sculpted chest, narrow hips, long legs as muscular as a horseman's. Whoever had meant for the outfit to make him look ridiculous was obviously without hormones.

The headgear was another matter. The Minnesota Vikings stocking cap sported yellow felt horns and long braids made of yellow yarn. The braids bounced as he shuffled and hopped through the steps of the dance. His expression was one of disgruntled indignity, but he was having a hard time maintaining it.

When the routine ended, the performers took exaggerated bows, laughing so hard they couldn't straighten. He had a wonderful laugh, Harrison. Warm, rough, masculine. Not that it affected her, Megan thought, attributing the wave of warmth to being overdressed. She didn't have involuntary physical reactions to men. She didn't allow it. It wasn't smart – especially when the man was a cop.

Harrison straightened, and a wide grin lit up his face; an interesting, lived-in face that was a little bit rough, a little bit lined, not exactly handsome, but utterly compelling. An inch-long scar hooked diagonally across his chin. His nose was substantial, a solid, masculine nose that might have been broken once or twice. His eyes were dark and deep-set, and even though they gleamed with good humor, they looked a hundred years old.

Megan hesitated and Natalie bumped her forward, then stepped past her.

'Have you no pride at all?' she demanded of her boss, tugging hard on one of his yellow braids. She shook her head, and her black eyes sparkled as she fought a smile.

Mitch Holt blew out a big breath. 'You're just jealous because I've been asked to model in *Victoria's Secret*.' He grinned down at the woman who ran his professional life. *Secretary* was far too lowly a title for Natalie Bryant. He considered her an administrative assistant and had bullied the city council into paying her accordingly, but he thought her nickname suited her best. She was a commandant in pumps.

Natalie made a sound like a horse blowing air through its lips. '*Farmer's Almanac* is more like it. You look like a reject from the rube factory.'

'Don't spare my ego,' he drawled, giving her a cranky look.

'I never do. You got company. *Agent* O'Malley from the BCA.' She swung a hand toward the woman who had come in with her. '*Agent* O'Malley, meet Chief Holt.'

Mitch leaned forward to offer his hand, sending a yellow braid swinging. He snatched the stocking cap off his head and tossed it to his dance partner without looking. 'Mitch Holt. Sorry you're catching me out of uniform.'

'I apologize for being so late,' Megan said, stepping forward to shake his hand.

His hand engulfed hers, broad and strong and warm, and she felt a little involuntary jolt of something she would neither name nor acknowledge. She looked up at Mitch Holt, expecting to find something smug in his expression, finding instead confidence and the keen gleam of awareness. The word *dangerous* came to mind, but she dismissed it. She tugged her hand back, trying to break the contact. He held on just a second longer, just long enough to let her know they would do things his way. Or so he thought. Business as usual . . .

'I ran into some unforeseen complications moving in,' she said crisply. 'I'm ordinarily very punctual.'

Mitch nodded. *I'll bet you are, Agent O'Malley.* He kept his gaze steady on hers, searching for a reaction to the physical contact. Her gaze was cool green ice. He could almost feel the shields go up around her.

'It wasn't a problem,' he said, absently combing a hand back through his thick tawny hair in an attempt to tame the havoc wreaked by the stocking cap.

'So you're Leo's replacement.' He cocked a brow and tried to visualize her without the mega-parka. 'Well, God knows you'll be easier to look at.'

The remark struck like flint against steel, sparking off Megan's frayed nerves. 'I didn't get the job because I look good in panty hose, Chief,' she said, cutting him a wry look.

'Neither did Leo, thank Christ. There are some things I can go my whole life without experiencing. Leo Kozlowski in lingerie is right up there on the list. He was a hell of a guy, though, Leo. Knew every good fishing hole for a hundred miles.'

Megan had never felt that was one of the more crucial talents a field agent should possess, but she kept her opinion to herself.

Rehearsal had been declared officially over. The participants drifted out the door, Natalie bringing up the rear like a shepherd. A couple of men called good-byes back to Mitch. He raised a hand to acknowledge them, but kept his attention on Agent O'Malley.

He wondered if she realized the tough-cookie act was more intriguing than if she had been skittish. It made him wonder what was behind the shields. A thread to play with just to see how it might unravel. It was his nature to work at puzzles, a compulsion that suited his profession. He let the silence hang, to see how she would react.

She held his gaze and waited him out, her head cocked to one side. Casually she brushed back the wisps of dark hair that had escaped her ponytail. Its color made him think of cherry Coke – nearly black with a hint of red. Exotic in this land of Swedes and Norwegians. Aside from the stubborn set of her chin, she most resembled an escapee from a convent school. Her face had that earnest quality usually reserved for CPAs and novice nuns. A pale oval with skin like fresh cream and eyes as green as the turf in Killarney. Pretty. Young. Mitch suddenly felt about ninety-three.

'Well,' Megan started. What she needed was to end this conversation, retreat, regroup, come back tomorrow, when she was feeling stronger and he was dressed in something more than long underwear. 'It's late. I can come back tomorrow. We'll have more time. You'll have pants on . . .'

He grinned the crooked grin. 'Are you uncomfortable with this situation, Agent O'Malley?'

Megan scowled at him. Her eyelid ticked, ruining the effect. 'I'm not in the habit of doing business with men in their underwear, Chief Holt.'

'I'll be happy to take it off,' he said, scratching his arm. 'It itches. Come on back to my office and I'll climb out of this sausage skin.'

He started for the door of the conference room, reaching a hand out as if he meant to sling it around her shoulders. Megan shied sideways. Her temper boiled up, rattling the lid on her control. She was feeling tired and testy, in no mood to deal with yet another come-on or innuendo.

'I am an agent of the Bureau of Criminal Apprehension, Chief,' she said, fighting to hang on to her last scrap of humor. 'I served two years on the St Paul police force, seven years on the Minneapolis force – five of them as a detective. I've been a narc. I've worked vice. I have a degree in law enforcement and have passed the agent's course at Quantico. I really don't think the taxpayers would be getting their money's worth if I came here in the capacity of sex toy.'

'Sex toy?' Mitch leaned back, brows raised, caught somewhere between amusement and insult. 'Perhaps I should rephrase my suggestion,' he said. 'You may wait in Natalie's office while I change into my clothes. Then I will be glad to escort you – in a strictly businesslike fashion – to one of the finer dining establishments in our fair town, where we might partake of a meal.' He held his hands up to ward off potential protest. 'Feel free to pay for your own, Agent O'Malley. Far be it from me to threaten your feminist sensibilities. You can accept or decline this offer. I make no attempt at coercion, but, if you'll pardon my candor, you look like you could use a little meat loaf.

'For the record, I have no problem with an agent who happens to be a woman. I'm a reasonably enlightened nineties kind of guy. So you can take the chip off your shoulder and put it in your briefcase, Agent O'Malley. Believe me, there will be plenty of guys in line to knock it off, but I won't be one of them.'

Megan felt herself shrinking with each sentence. She wished fervently for a break from the laws of physics so she could melt down into the tight fibers of the carpet and disappear.

'Way to go, O'Malley,' she muttered to herself. Her eyelid ticked furiously. She reached up to rub it, took a deep breath, and swallowed what pride she had left. 'I'm sorry. I don't usually jump to insulting conclusions. I don't know what to say other than this hasn't been one of my better days.'

Two years in St Paul, seven in Minneapolis. A detective, a narc. Impressive record, especially for a woman. Mitch knew what a fight it was for a woman to make it in this business. The odds stood against women, shoulder to brawny shoulder, in the form of a fraternity as old as dirt. Equal opportunity quotas notwithstanding, Ms O'Malley had to be tough and she had to be good. It looked as though the effort was costing her today.

Her efforts would cost him, too, he thought irritably. He ran a department and a life that were equally well ordered and calm. He sure as hell didn't need some woman charging in, waving her bra like a banner, spoiling for trouble where there was none to be had.

'If I need a sex toy, I'll consult a mail-order catalogue,' he said darkly. 'Don't rock my boat, Agent O'Malley. I don't like troublemakers – whether they look good in panty hose or not.'

He drew in a breath as he stepped back from her and wrinkled his nose as he caught an odd scent. 'Interesting perfume you're wearing. Cheddar?'

Her cheeks bloomed pink. 'I spent half the afternoon in the cheese factory, tracking down my apartment keys.'

'You *have* had a rough day. I prescribe meat loaf.' he declared. 'Maybe a glass of wine. Definitely a piece of carrot cake . . . God, I'm starving.' he muttered, rubbing a hand over his flat belly as he headed for the door.

Megan followed hesitantly, trying to decide if dinner with him would be a chance to start fresh or a continuing exercise in conversational combat. She wasn't sure she had the steam left for either, but she wouldn't let Mitch Holt see that. Despite his professions of enlightenment, she knew he would be both colleague and adversary. She had learned long ago to show no weaknesses to either.

3

Day 1
7:33 p.m. 21°

He didn't look bad with his clothes on, either. Just a casual observation, Megan told herself as Mitch hung their coats in the cloakroom at Grandma's Attic. He had dressed in dark pleated trousers, an ivory broadcloth shirt, and dark tie with a small print she couldn't make out. He'd combed his hair – or tried to. Tawny brown and thick, it stubbornly defied the stylish cut that was short on the sides and longer on top. He parted it on the left and had a habit of brushing it back with his fingers. Not a vain gesture, but an absent one, as if he were used to having it fall in his eyes.

Megan had made her own repairs, slipping into the ladies' room at the station. The hair got a quick brushing back into its simple ponytail. The lips got a slicking with gloss. She tried to rub the mascara smudges out from under her eyes, but discovered to her dismay the marks were natural, the telltale signs of fatigue. Her face was chalk white, but there was nothing to be done about it. She didn't wear much makeup as a rule and carried nothing with her.

No matter, she told herself as she glanced around the restaurant. This wasn't a date, it was a business dinner. She wasn't out to impress Mitch Holt as a woman, but as a cop.

The restaurant was crowded and noisy, the air thick with conversation and the warm, spicy smell of home cooking. Waitresses in ruffled muslin aprons and high-necked blouses with puffed sleeves wound through the array of mismatched wooden tables with heavy stoneware plates and trays laden with the special of the day. Grandma's was housed in a section of a renovated woolen mill. Its walls were time-worn brick, the floors scarred wood, and the ceiling beams exposed. A row of tall, arched windows had been installed on the street side of the main dining room. Lush ferns in brass pots hung from an old pipe that ran from wall to wall parallel to the windows.

Household antiques decorated every available spot – copper kettles, graniteware coffeepots, china teapots, kitchen utensils, butter churns and wooden butter molds, salt boxes and blue Mason jars. Steamer trunks were strategically located around the dining room to be used by the waitresses as serving tables. In addition to the more mundane items, there was a marvelous collection of ladies' hats that dated back a century. Broad-brimmed hats wound and draped with yards of sheer fabric. Pillbox hats and hats trimmed with ostrich plumes. Driving hats and riding hats and hats with black lace veils.

Megan took it all in with a sense of delight. She loved old things. She enjoyed hunting through flea markets for items that might have been heirlooms, things passed down from one generation of women to another. There were no such things in her family. She had nothing of her mother's. Her father had burned all of Maureen O'Malley's things a month after she had abandoned the family when Megan was six.

The hostess greeted Mitch by name, eyed Megan with interest, and led them back to a booth in a raised section of dining room where things appeared less hectic and the noise level was cut by the high walls of the booths.

'It's the usual madness,' she said, smiling warmly at Mitch. She looked mid-forties and attractive, her pale blond hair cut in a pageboy she tucked behind her ears. 'And then some, with everybody gearing up for Snowdaze. Denise said she might come for the weekend.'

Mitch accepted a menu. 'How's she doing at design school?'

'She loves it. She said to tell you thanks again for encouraging her to go back – and to look her up sometime when you're in the Cities. She's dating an architect, but it isn't serious,' she hastened to add, her gaze darting Megan's way with a gleam of sly speculation.

'Nnnn,' Mitch said through his teeth. 'Darlene, this is Megan O'Malley, our new agent from the BCA. She's taking over Leo Kozlowski's job. It's her first night in town, and I thought I'd introduce her to Grandma's. Megan, Darlene Hallstrom.'

'Oo-oh!' Darlene cooed, the exclamation spanning an octave as she gave Megan a plastic smile and a once-over that scanned for signs of matrimony. 'How nice to have someone new in town. Is your husband working in Deer Lake as well?'

'I'm not married.'

'We-ell, isn't that interesting.' She ground the words through the smile as she thrust a menu out. 'We all sure liked Leo. Have a nice dinner.'

Mitch heaved a sigh as Darlene swept away, skirt twitching.

'Who's Denise?' Megan asked.

'Darlene's sister. Her *divorced* sister. Darlene had ideas.'

'Really? What did your wife have to say about that?'

'My –?'

Her gaze pointed a straight line to the hands that held the menu. The gold band on his left ring finger gleamed in the soft light. He wore it for a variety of reasons – because it helped to ward off prowling females, because it was habitual, because every time he looked at it he still felt the sting of grief and guilt. He made the excuse that he was a cop and cops were perverse by nature and Catholic in their guilt if not in any other way.

'My wife is dead,' he said, his voice a hard, cold whisper, the emotional shields coming up around him like iron bars. Nearly two years had passed and the words still tasted like the glue of postage stamps, bitter and acrid. He hadn't gotten any better at saying them. He fielded sympathy as awkwardly as a shortstop with a catcher's mitt.

'I don't talk about it,' he said flatly, mentally drawing a line in the sand and chasing her back to her side.

His pride and sense of privacy shunned the sympathy of virtual strangers. And simmering beneath that boar's nest, feeding on it, was the anger, his constant companion. He contained it, controlled it, ruthlessly. Control was the key. Control was his strength, his salvation.

'Oh, God, I'm sorry,' Megan murmured. She could feel his tension across the table. His shoulders were rigid with it, his jaw set at an angle no sane person would challenge. She felt as if she had trespassed on sacred ground.

She propped her elbows on the table and rubbed her hands over her face. 'You're batting a thousand, O'Malley. If there's a pile of shit to be found today, you'll step in it with both feet.'

'I hope you're not referring to the cheese factory,' Mitch said dryly. He forced a wry smile. 'I'd hate to have to send the health inspector down there again.'

Megan peeked out at him from between her fingers. 'Again?'

'Yeah, well, last year there was a minor incident involving a mouse tail and a brick of Monterey Jack . . .'

'Gross!'

'Les Metzler assures me that was a one-time thing, but I don't know. Personally, I make it a policy not to buy cheese from a place where the gift shop also features taxidermy.'

'They don't,' she challenged.

'They do. I can't believe you didn't see the sign when you were out at the factory. *Metzler's BuckLand Fine Cheese and Taxidermy*. Les's brother Rollie does the taxidermy. He got hit in the head with a rolling pin as a child and became obsessed with roadkill. He's not quite right,' he said in an exaggerated whisper, twirling a forefinger beside his temple. Leaning across the table, he glanced around for eavesdroppers and whispered, 'I buy my cheese in Minneapolis.'

Their gazes locked and Megan felt something she didn't want or need to feel. She jerked her eyes down and studied the pattern in his necktie – a hundred tiny renditions of Mickey Mouse.

'Great tie.'

He glanced down as if he'd forgotten what he was wearing. All the cynicism melted out of his smile. The rough edges of his face softened as he ran the strip of burgundy silk between his fingers. 'My daughter picked it out. Her tastes run a little off the *GQ* scale, but then, she's only five.'

Megan had to bite her lip to keep from sighing. He was the chief of police, a big tough macho guy whose main fashion accessory was probably a nine-millimeter Smith & Wesson, and he let his little girl pick out his neckties. Sweet.

'A lot of cops I know don't have the fashion sense of a five-year-old,' she said. 'My last partner dressed like a bad parody of a used car salesman. He had more plaid polyester pants than Arnold Palmer.'

Mitch chuckled. 'You didn't list fashion police in your oral résumé.'

'I didn't want to overwhelm you.'

They both ordered the meat loaf. Megan declined the suggestion of a glass of wine, knowing it would aggravate her headache. Mitch asked for a bottle of Moosehead beer and made a point of noticing the waitress – a blond girl of eighteen or nineteen – had had her braces removed. The girl smiled shyly for him and went away blushing.

'You seem to know everyone here,' Megan said. 'Is this one of those hometown boy-makes-good stories?'

Mitch pulled apart a dinner roll, steam billowed up from the center of it. 'Me? No, I'm a transplant. I put in fifteen years on the force in Miami.'

'No way!' She gripped the edge of the table as if the shock had knocked her loopy. 'You moved *here* from *Miami*? You gave up *Florida* to live in this godforsaken tundra?'

Mitch arched a brow. 'Am I to assume you don't like our fair state?'

'I like summer – all three weeks of it,' she said, her voice crackling with sarcasm. 'Fall is pretty, provided it isn't prematurely buried under ten feet of snow. That's as far as my love goes, despite the fact that I'm a native. In my opinion, life is too damn short to have half of it be winter.'

'Then why do you stay? With your qualifications, you could probably have your pick of jobs in a warmer climate.'

He recognized the defenses the instant they switched on. They were a mirror image of his own – built to protect, to deflect, to keep outsiders from moving in.

'Family complications' was all she said, turning her attention to a dinner roll. She picked a chunk out of it and played with the bread between her fingers. Mitch didn't probe, but he wondered. What family? What kind of complications would make her duck his gaze? Another loose thread for him to worry at. Another puzzle piece to define and fit.

She tossed the conversational ball back in his court. 'So what'd you do in Miami?'

'Homicide. Did a stint on the gang task force. My last two years were on the major case squad. Tourist murders, socialite drug busts – high-profile stuff.'

'Isn't life around here a little slow for you?'

'I've had enough excitement to last me.'

Another answer with a past, Megan thought, glancing at him through her lashes as he took a long pull on his beer. Another reason to steer clear of him in all ways but the professional. She didn't need anyone else's emotional baggage. She had enough of her own to fill a set of Samsonite luggage. Still, the curiosity itched and tickled, the need to solve riddles and uncover secrets. She attributed the need to her cop instincts and denied that it had anything to do with the guarded shadows in his eyes or with some convoluted desire to comfort a man in pain. If she had a brain in her head, she wouldn't think of Mitch Holt as a man.

Fat chance, O'Malley, she thought as he took another swallow of Moosehead, his eyes narrowed, firm lips glistening with moisture as he set the bottle down. In the subdued light of the booth, his five o'clock shadow seemed darker against the lean planes of his cheeks, the scar on his chin looked silver and wicked.

'So how did you end up in the frozen North?' She ripped another chunk from her roll.

Mitch shrugged, as if it had been a random thing of little consequence, when that was about as far from the truth as any lie. 'The job was open. My in-laws live here. It was a chance for my daughter to spend time with her grandparents.'

Their salads arrived, along with a member of the Moose Lodge, who wanted to remind Mitch that he was to speak at their Friday luncheon. Mitch introduced Megan. The Moose man looked at her and chuckled as if to say 'great joke, Mitch.' He shook the hand Megan offered him, giving her a patronizing smile.

'You're Leo's replacement? Well, aren't you cute!'

Megan bit down on a caustic reply, reminding herself she had asked for this assignment.

Mr Moose departed and was quickly replaced by one of the organizers of the Snowdaze torchlight parade, who went over details regarding the barricading of the streets involved. The introduction ritual was a near replay of the one before it.

'She's Leo's replacement? Easier on the eyes than ol' Leo, eh?'

Megan gritted her teeth. Mitch diplomatically refrained from comment. The meat loaf arrived and parade man took his leave, winking at Megan as he went.

She stared down at her plate. 'If one more person calls me cute, I'm going to bite them. Is it 1994 or have I fallen through a time warp?'

Mitch chuckled. 'Both. This is small-town Minnesota, Agent O'Malley. You ain't in the big city anymore.'

'I realize that, but this is a college town. I expected attitudes to be more progressive.'

'Oh, they are,' he said, dumping pepper on a mountain of scalloped potatoes. 'We no longer require women to hide their faces or walk three steps behind men.'

'Very funny.' Megan cut into her meat loaf and thought the aroma of herbs and spices might just induce her to fall face-first on her plate and inhale everything on it.

'Seriously, Deer Lake is very progressive as small towns go. But the men you're likely to meet in the line of duty are going to be from the old school. There are still plenty of guys around who believe the little woman should stay home darning holey socks while they're off whooping it up at the NRA meeting. You can't tell me you haven't run up against your share in the departments you've worked.'

'Sure I did, but in the city the threat of lawsuits means something,' Megan replied. 'You seem to have made the adjustment to small-town life without any trouble. What's your secret? Besides having a penis, I mean.'

'Gee, honey, I'm flattered you noticed,' Mitch drawled.

Poor choice of words there, O'Malley. 'It was kind of hard to miss, considering what you were wearing when we met.'

'I feel so cheap.'

She made the mistake of giving him a look, and her gaze locked onto his again like iron drawn to a magnet. God, of all the rotten luck. Attraction. A rare phenomenon in the life of Megan O'Malley. Naturally, it would strike when she least expected it, least needed it. Naturally, it would be sparked by a man she couldn't touch. Old Murphy and his laws of irony had nothing on her.

Mitch Holt felt it, too. Chemistry. His gaze drifted to her mouth. The moment stretched into two.

'I thought you said you weren't one of them,' she murmured, mustering all defenses.

'One of who?'

'The gun-toting, flag-waving, Neanderthal rednecks who consider anything in a bra to be fair game for their I'm-God's-gift-to-women brand of charm.'

Mitch sat back and sighed, forcing the tension out of his shoulders. He could have argued, but there didn't seem to be any point in it at the moment.

'You're right,' he admitted grudgingly. 'I let my testosterone run away with me there for a minute. Temporary hormone psychosis. Really, I'm enlightened enough to pretend I'm not attracted to you, if that's what you want.'

'Good. That's what I want.' Megan turned back to her meat loaf and discovered her appetite had gone south. 'Because that's my number one rule: I don't date cops.'

'A wise policy.'

A matter of survival was what it was, but Megan kept that information to herself. She couldn't afford to be vulnerable in any way. Not in police work. The ranks were too heavily dominated by men who didn't want her there. Her gender was a strike against her. Her size was a strike against her. If she let her sexuality be used as a strike against her, she'd be out. That would be the end of her career, and her career was all she had.

'Yeah.' Mitch recovered his sense of humor as the madness receded. 'There's a certain wisdom in not letting the people you work with see you naked.'

'The underwear was close enough,' Megan said dryly.

'But now you've got me at a disadvantage,' Mitch pointed out. 'You've seen me in my underwear. It would be only fair for you to return the favor. Then we'd be even.'

'Forget it, Chief. I'll take all the advantages I can get.'

'Hmmm . . .'

Across the room he caught sight of one of his patrol officers winding his way awkwardly through the maze of tables, struggling to keep from conking some unsuspecting diner in the back of the head with the revolver strapped to his hip. He clomped up the steps, his eyes on Mitch.

'Hey, Chief, sorry to interrupt your dinner.' Lonnie Dietz pulled a stray chair up to the end of the booth and straddled it. 'I thought you'd want to hear the update on that accident out on Old Cedar Road.'

'I'm Leo's replacement,' Megan said, offering her hand.

Dietz ignored the hand. His eyebrows disappeared beneath the black Moe Howard wig that crawled down over his forehead. He looked fifty and intolerant, lean everywhere but his beer belly. 'I thought all the field agents were men.'

'They were,' she said sweetly. 'Until me.'

'So what's the latest?' Mitch asked, forking up a mouthful of potatoes.

Dietz tore his gaze away from Megan and flipped through a notebook he pulled from his shirt pocket. 'Two fatalities. Ethel Koontz was DOA at Hennepin County Medical Center – massive trauma to the head and chest. Ida Bergen passed away at Deer Lake Community – heart attack on her way in for treatment of minor injuries. Mrs Marvel Steffen is critical but stable – she's at HCMC too. Clara Weghorn was treated and released. Mike Chamberlain – the kid who lost control – he's banged up but he's going to be okay. Pat Stevens took his statement and I've been over the scene.'

'And?'

'And it's like the kid said. The road was bare until just after that curve by Jeff Lexvold's place. There's a patch of glare ice about ten feet long, goes across both lanes of the road. This is where it gets odd,' Dietz confided, looking troubled. 'I figure there's no reason for ice there, right? The weather's been good. God knows it hasn't been warm enough for anything to melt and run down the hill from Lexvold's. So I go have a look. You know Jeff and Millicent are gone to Corpus Christi for the winter, like always, so there's no one home. But it looks to me like someone snaked a garden hose down the driveway from the faucet on the front side of their house by the garage there.'

Mitch set his fork down and stared hard at his patrolman. 'That's crazy.

You're saying someone ran water across the road and made that ice slick on purpose?'

'Looks like. Kids playing around, I suppose.'

'They got two people killed.'

'Could have been worse,' Dietz pointed out. 'There's some kind of music recital going on at the college tonight. Seems like more people use that back way onto the campus than the front. We could have had a real pileup.'

'Have you questioned the neighbors?' Megan asked.

Dietz looked at her as if she were an eavesdropper butting in from the next booth. 'There aren't any close by. Besides, Lexvolds, they've got all them overgrown spruce trees along the front of their place. You'd have to be right there to see anyone screwing around.'

'Well, Jesus,' Mitch muttered in disgust. 'I'll have Natalie write up an appeal for the media tomorrow, asking for anyone with information to call in.'

Megan trespassed a second time into the conversation. 'Was there any sign of a break-in?'

Dietz looked at her sideways, scowling. 'No. Everything was locked up tight.' He turned back to his chief as he rose from his chair. 'We got a DOT crew out to scrape and sand the slick spot. Hauled the cars in – one to Mike Finke's and one to Patterson's. That's it.'

'Good. Thanks, Lonnie.' Mitch watched the officer weave his way back through the tables, what little he'd eaten of his supper sitting like gravel in his stomach. 'What the hell do kids think about, pulling shit like that?'

Megan considered the question rhetorical. The wheels of her brain turning, she stared at the Mickey Mouse figures on Mitch's tie until they started to swim in front of her eyes.

Mitch's gaze drifted to the restaurant entrance, where people were still coming in from the wide hall of the old warehouse-turned-mini-mall. Half a dozen people from the Snowdaze pageant committee were waiting to be seated. Here for after-practice pie and coffee. Hannah Garrison came in and pushed her way past them. Strange.

She looked harried. Her coat was open and hanging back off one shoulder. Her blond hair was a mess, curling ropes of it falling across her face as her eyes scanned the dining room with a wild look. She waded through the sea of chairs and faces, bumping into people, nearly colliding with Darlene Hallstrom. The hostess reached out to steady her, smiling, bemused. Hannah shoved her away and lunged ahead to the table where John Olsen and his girlfriend were lingering over coffee. Damn strange.

Mitch kept his eyes on her like a bird dog on point, pulling his napkin off his lap. He crumpled the heavy green cloth and dropped it blindly on the table.

'So where's the hose?' Megan muttered. She looked up as Mitch started to rise.

35

'Excuse me,' he mumbled, sliding out of the booth.

He couldn't hear the conversation going on at John Olsen's table. The din in the restaurant drowned out individual words. But he could see the expression on Hannah's face, the wild gestures of her long, graceful hands. He could see John's look of shocked surprise, watched him shake his head. Mitch descended the steps and strode toward the table. A fist of instinctive tension curled in his gut.

Hannah was one of the first people he had met when he and Jessie had moved to Deer Lake. Hannah and her husband, Paul Kirkwood, and their son had lived across the street then. Hannah, pregnant with her second child, had dropped by that first day on her way to work to welcome them to the neighborhood with a pan of brownies. She was one of the most capable, unflappable people he knew. Grace under fire personified. She ran the emergency room at Deer Lake Community Hospital with skill, volunteered for community causes, and still managed a house with a husband, son, and baby daughter. All with a dazzling smile and sweet good humor.

But Hannah didn't look cool or unruffled now. She looked on the brink of hysteria.

'What do you mean, you don't know?' she demanded, her voice loud and raw. She slammed a fist down on the table. John's girlfriend squealed and jumped up out of her chair as coffee sloshed out of her cup and splashed across the tabletop.

'Dr Garrison, calm down!' John Olsen pleaded, coming up out of his chair. He reached out for Hannah's arm. She jerked away from him, her eyes blazing.

'Calm down!' she shrieked. 'I won't calm down!'

Everyone in the restaurant had stopped to watch. The air was electric with tension.

'Hannah?' Mitch said, approaching her side. 'Is something wrong?'

Hannah wheeled at the sound of his voice. The floor seemed to tilt beneath her feet. Heat pressed in on her like an invisible blanket, burning her skin, choking her. *Is something wrong?* Everything was wrong. She could feel a hundred pairs of eyes on her. She could feel the darkness creeping down from the rafters and in through the high, arched windows.

She was caught in a nightmare. Wide awake. Like being buried alive. The thoughts and impressions zoomed across her brain, too many, too fast. *Oh, God. Oh, God. Oh, God!*

'Hannah?' Mitch murmured, gently sliding his fingers over her shoulder. He eased a little closer. 'Honey, talk to me. What's wrong?'

Hannah stared at him, at the concern in his eyes. He moved closer. *What's wrong?* Something inside her burst and the words came rushing out, screaming out.

'*I can't find my son!*'

4

'What do you mean, you can't find Josh?' Mitch asked calmly.

Hannah sat in the manager's chair, shaking uncontrollably, tears leaking from her big blue eyes. Mitch dug a clean handkerchief out of his hip pocket and offered it to her. She took it automatically but made no effort to use it, crumpling it in her hand like a wad of paper.

'I m – mean I c – can't find him,' she stammered. She couldn't find Josh and no one seemed to grasp what she was trying to tell them, as if the words coming out of her mouth were nonsense. 'Y – you have to help m – me. *Please,* Mitch!'

She started to come up out of the chair, but Mitch pressed her back down. 'I'll do everything I can, Hannah, but you have to calm down –'

'Calm down!' she shouted, gripping the arms of the chair. 'I can't believe this!'

'Hannah –'

'My God, you've got a daughter, you should understand! You of all people –'

'Hannah!' he barked sharply. She flinched and blinked at him. 'You know I'll help, but you have to calm down and start at the beginning.'

Megan watched the scene from her position by the door. The office was a claustrophobic cube of dark, cheap paneling. Certificates from the chamber of commerce and various civic groups decorated the walls in plastic frames that hung at slightly drunken angles. Nothing about the filing cabinets or battered old metal desk suggested the success or the quaint charm of the restaurant. The woman – Hannah – slumped down in the chair, squeezing her eyes shut, pressing a hand over her mouth as she fought to compose herself.

Even in her current state – crying, hair disheveled – she was a strikingly attractive woman. Tall, slim, with features that belonged on the pages of a magazine. Mitch positioned himself directly in front of her, back against the desk, but leaning forward, his concentration completely on Hannah, waiting, patient, intent. Without saying anything, he reached out and offered her his hand. She took it and squeezed hard, like someone in extreme pain.

Megan watched him with admiration and a little envy. Dealing with victims had never been her strong suit. For her, reaching out to someone in pain meant taking on some of that pain herself. She had always found it smarter, safer, to keep some emotional distance. Objectivity, she called it. Mitch Holt, however, didn't hesitate to reach out.

'I was supposed to pick him up from hockey practice,' Hannah began in little more than a whisper, as if she were about to confess a terrible sin. 'I was leaving the hospital, but then we had an emergency come in and I couldn't get away on time. I had someone call the rink to tell him I'd be a little late. Then one of the patients went into cardiac arrest and –'

And *I lost the patient and now I've lost my son.* The sense of failure and guilt pressed down on her, and she had to stop and wait until it seemed bearable again. She tightened her hold on Mitch's big, warm hand. The sensation only built and intensified until it pushed the dreaded words from her mouth.

'I forgot. I forgot he was waiting.'

A fresh wave of tears washed down her cheeks and fell like raindrops on to the lap of her long wool skirt. She doubled over, wanting to curl into a ball while the emotions tore at her. Mitch leaned closer and stroked her hair, trying to offer some comfort. The cop in him remained calm, waiting for facts, reciting the likely explanations. Deeper inside, the parent in him experienced a sharp stab of instinctive fear.

'When I g-got to the rink he w-was g-gone.'

'Well, honey, Paul probably picked him up –'

'No. Wednesday is *my night.*'

'Did you call Paul to check?'

'I tried, but he wasn't in the office.'

'Then Josh probably got a ride with one of the other kids. He's probably at some buddy's house –'

'No. I called everyone I could think of. I checked at the sitter's – Sue Bartz. I thought maybe he would be there waiting for me to come pick up Lily, but Sue hadn't seen him.' And Lily was still there waiting for her mother, probably wondering why Mama had come and gone without her. 'I checked at home, just in case he decided to walk. I called the other hockey moms. I drove back to the rink. I drove back to the hospital. *I can't find him.*'

'Do you have a picture of your son?' Megan asked.

'His school picture. It's not the best – he needed a haircut, but there wasn't time.' Hannah pulled her purse up onto her lap. Her hands shook as she dug through the leather bag for her wallet. 'He brought the slip home from school and I made a note, but then time just got away from me and I forgot.'

She whispered the last word as she opened to the photograph of Josh. I *forgot.* Such a simple, harmless excuse. Forgot about his picture. Forgot about his haircut. Forgot him. Her hand trembled so badly, she could barely manage to slip the photograph from the plastic window. She offered it to the dark-haired woman, realizing belatedly that she had no idea who she was.

'I'm sorry,' she murmured, dredging up ingrained manners and a fragile smile. 'Have we met?'

Mitch sat back against the edge of the desk again. 'This is Agent O'Malley with the Bureau of Criminal Apprehension. Megan, this is Dr Hannah Garrison, head of the emergency room in our community hospital. One of the best doctors ever to wield a stethoscope,' he added with a ghost of his grin. 'We're very lucky to have her.'

Megan studied the photograph, her mind on business, not social niceties. A boy of eight or nine dressed in a Cub Scout uniform stared out at her with a big gap-toothed grin. He had a smattering of freckles across his nose and cheeks. His hair was an unruly mop of sandy brown curls. His blue eyes were brimming with life and mischief.

'Is he normally a pretty responsible boy?' she asked. 'Does he know to call you if he's going to be late or to get permission to go to a friend's house?'

Hannah nodded. 'Josh is very levelheaded.'

'What did he wear to school today?'

Hannah rubbed a hand across her forehead, struggling to think back to morning. It seemed as much a dream as the last few hours, long ago and foggy. Lily crying at the indignity of being confined to her high chair. Josh skating around the kitchen floor in his stocking feet. Permission slip needed signing for a field trip to the Science Museum. Homework done? Spelling words memorized? A call from the hospital. French toast burning on the stove. Paul storming around the kitchen, snapping at Josh, complaining about the shirts that needed ironing.

'Um – jeans. A blue sweater. Snow boots. A ski jacket – bright blue with bright yellow and bright green trim. Um . . . his Vikings stocking cap – it's yellow with a patch sewn on. Paul wouldn't let him wear a purple one with that wild coat. He said it would look like Josh was dressed by color-blind gypsies. I couldn't see the harm; he's only eight years old. . . .'

Megan handed the photograph back and looked up at Mitch. 'I'll call it in right away.' Her mind was already on the possibilities and the steps they should take in accordance with those possibilities. 'Get the bulletin to your people, the sheriff's department, the highway patrol –'

Hannah looked stricken. 'You don't think –'

'No,' Mitch interceded smoothly. 'No, honey, of course not. It's just standard procedure. We'll put out a bulletin to all the guys on patrol, so if they see Josh they'll know to pick him up and bring him home.

'Excuse us for just a minute,' he said, holding up a finger. He turned his back to Hannah and gave Megan a furious look. 'I need to give Agent O'Malley a few instructions.'

He clamped a hand on her shoulder and herded her unceremoniously out the door and into the narrow, dimly lit hall. A round-headed man in a tweed blazer and chinos gave them a dirty look and stuck a finger in his free ear as he tried to have a conversation on a pay phone outside the men's room door. Mitch hit the phone's plunger with two fingers, cutting off the conversation and drawing an indignant 'Hey!' from the caller.

'Excuse us,' Mitch growled, flashing his badge. 'Police business.'

He shouldered the man away from the phone and sent him hustling down the hall with a scowl that had scattered petty drug pushers and hookers from the meanest streets in Miami. Then he turned the same scowl on Megan.

'What the hell is wrong with you?' she snapped, jumping on the offensive, knowing it was her best defense.

'What the hell is wrong with me?' Mitch barked, keeping his voice low. 'What the hell is wrong with you – scaring the poor woman –'

'She has reason to be scared, Chief. Her son is missing.'

'That has yet to be established. He's probably playing at a friend's house.'

'She says she checked with his friends.'

'Yes, but she's panicked. She's probably forgotten to look in an obvious place.'

'Or somebody grabbed the kid.'

Mitch scowled harder because it took an effort to dismiss her suggestion. 'This is Deer Lake, O'Malley, not New York.'

Megan arched a brow. 'You don't have crime in Deer Lake? You have a police force. You have a jail. Or is that all just window dressing?'

'Of course we have crime,' he snarled. 'We have college students who shoplift and cheese factory workers who get drunk on Saturday night and try to beat each other up in the American Legion parking lot. We don't have child abductions, for Christ's sake.'

'Yeah, well, welcome to the nineties, Chief,' she said sarcastically. 'It can happen anywhere.'

Mitch took a half step back and jammed his hands at his waist. The president of the Sons of Norway lodge went into the men's room, smiling and nodding to Mitch. A cloud of chokingly sweet air freshener escaped the room as the door swung shut. Mitch blocked it out just as he tried to block out what Megan was telling him.

'The people in St Joseph didn't think it could happen there, either,' Megan said quietly. 'And while they were all standing around consoling themselves with that lie, someone made off with Jacob Wetterling.'

The Wetterling case in St Joseph had happened before Mitch had moved to Minnesota, but it was still in the hearts and minds of people. A child had been stolen from among them and never returned. That kind of crime was so rare in the area that it affected people as if someone from their own family had been taken. Deer Lake was nearly two hundred miles away from St Joseph, but Mitch knew several men on his force and in the sheriff's department had worked on the case as volunteers. They spoke of it sparingly, in careful, hushed tones, as if they feared bringing it up might call back whatever demon had committed the crime.

Swearing under her breath, Megan grabbed the telephone receiver. 'We're wasting time.'

'I'll do it.' Mitch reached over her shoulder and snatched the phone from her.

'A little rusty on our telephone etiquette, aren't we?' she said dryly.

'Our dispatcher doesn't know you' was all the apology he offered.

'Doug? Mitch Holt. Listen, I need a bulletin out on Paul Kirkwood's boy, Josh. Yeah. Hannah went to pick him up from hockey and he'd gone off somewhere. He's probably in somebody's basement playing Nintendo, but you know how it is. Hannah's worried. Yeah, that's what women do best.'

Megan narrowed her eyes and tipped her head. Mitch ignored her.

'Let the county boys know, too, just in case they spot him. He's eight, a little small for his age. Blue eyes, curly brown hair. Last seen wearing a bright blue ski jacket with green and yellow trim and a bright yellow stocking cap with a Vikings patch on it. And send a unit over to the hockey rink. Tell them I'll meet them there.'

He hung up the phone as the Sons of Norway leader emerged from the men's room and sidled past them, murmuring an absent greeting, his curious gaze sliding to Megan. Mitch grunted what he hoped would pass for an acknowledgment. He could feel Megan's steady gaze, heavy, expectant, disapproving. She was new to this job, ambitious, eager to prove herself. She would have called out the cavalry, but the cavalry wasn't warranted yet.

The first priority in a missing persons case was to make certain the person was actually missing. That was why the rule with adults was not to consider them missing until they had been gone twenty-four hours. That rule no longer applied to children, but even so, there were options to consider before jumping to the worst conclusion. Even levelheaded kids did stupid things once in a while. Josh might have gone home with a friend and lost track of time, or he might have been intentionally punishing his mother for forgetting him. There were any number of explanations more probable than kidnapping.

Then why did he have this knot in his gut?

He dug another quarter out of his pants pocket. He dialed the Strausses' number from memory and murmured a prayer of thanks when his daughter answered on the third ring with an exuberant 'Hi! This is Jessie!'

'Hi, sweetheart, it's Daddy,' he said softly, ducking his head to elude Megan's curiosity.

'Are you coming to get me? I want you to read me some more of that book when it's bedtime.'

'I'm sorry, I can't, sweetie,' he murmured. 'I've got to be a cop for a while longer tonight. You'll have to stay with Grandma and Grandpa.'

There was a heavy silence on the other end of the line. Mitch could clearly picture his little daughter making her mad face, an expression she had inherited from her mother and perfected by imitating her grandmother. An eloquent look, it could provoke feelings of guilt in the blink of a big brown eye. 'I don't like it when you're a cop,' she said.

He wondered if she had any clue how badly it hurt him when she said that. The words were a knife slipped into an old wound that wouldn't heal. 'I know you don't, Jess, but I have to go try to find somebody who's lost. Wouldn't you want me to come find you if you were lost?'

'Yeah,' she admitted grudgingly. 'But you're *my* daddy.'

'I'll be home tomorrow night, honey, and we'll read extra pages. I promise.'

'You better, 'cause Grandma said she could read with me about Babar, too.'

Mitch clenched his jaw. 'I promise. Give me a kiss good night, then let me talk to Grandpa.'

Jessie made a loud smacking sound over the phone, which Mitch repeated, turning his back to Megan so she couldn't see the color that warmed his cheeks. Then Jessie turned the phone over to her grandfather and Mitch went through the ritual explanation that wasn't an explanation – police business, hung up on a case, nothing major but it might drag on. If he told his in-laws he had to see about a possible kidnapping, Joy Strauss would burn up the phone lines whipping the town into a frenzy.

Jurgen didn't press for details. A born-and-bred Minnesotan, he considered it rude to ask for more information than the caller was willing to give. Aside from that, the routine wasn't unfamiliar to him. Mitch's job dictated a late night from time to time. The standing arrangement was for Jessie to remain with her grandparents, who looked after her every day after school. The routine was convenient and provided stability for Jessie. Mitch might not have been enamored of his mother-in-law, but he trusted her to take good care of her only grandchild.

He hated to miss seeing Jessie, to miss tucking her in and reading to her until her eyes drifted shut. His daughter was the absolute center of his universe. For a second he tried to imagine what it would feel like if he couldn't find her, then he thought of Josh and Hannah.

'He'll turn up in no time,' he murmured to himself as he hung up the receiver. The knot in his gut tightened.

Megan's temper dropped from a boil to a simmer. For a second there Mitch Holt had seemed vulnerable, not tough, not intimidating. For a second he was a single father who sent his little girl kisses over the phone. The word *dangerous* floated through her head again and took on new connotations.

Kicking the thought aside, she gave him a no-nonsense look. 'I hope you're right, Chief,' she said. 'For everyone's sake.'

5

The last of the senior league hockey players were limping and shuffling their way out of the Gordie Knutson Memorial Arena when Mitch pulled his Explorer into the drive. Fifty or older, the senior leaguers still displayed an amazing amount of grace on the ice, as if they somehow shed the cumbersome stiffness of age in the locker room as they laced on the magic skates. They skated and passed and checked and laughed and swore. But when the game was over, the skates came off and the realities of age settled in with a vengeance. They inched their way down the steps, faces contorted in grimaces of varying degrees.

Noogie watched them with a grin as he stood leaning against his patrol car parked in the fire lane in front of the building. He gave them a thumbs-up, then laughed when Al Jackson told him to go to hell.

'Why do you keep playing when it does this to you, Al?'

'What kind of stupid question is that?' Jackson shot back. 'Oh, yeah, I forget – you used to play football; too many knocks in the head.'

'At least we had sense enough to wear helmets,' Noogie goaded.

'You mean there's no excuse for that face?'

Noga growled and waved them past.

'What's going on, Noogie?' Bill Lennox asked, hiking up the strap on his duffel bag. 'Caught Olie speeding on the Zamboni machine?'

They all laughed, but their gazes slid past Noogie to Mitch and Megan as they came up the sidewalk.

'Evening, Mitch,' Jackson called, raising the end of his hockey stick in salute. 'Crime wave at the ice rink?'

'Yeah. We've had another complaint that your slap shot is criminal.'

The group roared. Mitch kept an eye on them until they were well out of earshot, then turned to his officer.

'Officer Noga, this is Agent O'Malley –'

'We've met,' Megan said impatiently, tapping a foot against the snowpack on the sidewalk for the dual purpose of releasing energy and trying to keep the feeling in her toes.

Her gaze scanned the area. The ice rink was at the end of a street, set

43

well back from the residences. Located at the southeast edge of Deer Lake, it was half a mile off the interstate highway. Beyond the island of artificial light that was the parking lot, the night was black, vaguely ominous, certainly unwelcoming. On the other side of a wall of overgrown leafless shrubbery, the Park County fairgrounds stretched out across a field, an array of old vacant buildings and a looming grandstand. It looked abandoned and somehow sinister, as if the shadows were inhabited by dark spirits that could be chased away only by carnival lights and crowds of people. Even looking in the other direction, toward the town, Megan felt a sense of isolation.

'Is this about the missing kid?' Noga asked.

Mitch nodded. 'Hannah Garrison's boy. Josh. She was supposed to pick him up here. I figured we'd take a look around, talk to Olie –'

'We should have uniforms canvassing the residential area,' Megan interrupted, drawing a narrow look from Mitch and owl eyes from Noga. 'Find out if the neighbors might have seen the boy or anything out of the ordinary. The fairgrounds will be the likely place to start the search once we've secured this area.'

Mitch had tried to stick her with baby-sitting detail, suggesting she stay with Hannah and offer moral support while they waited for word of Josh. She had informed him that moral support was not part of her job description, then suggested they call a friend to come stay with Hannah and help make another round of phone calls looking for Josh among his friends. In the end Mitch called Natalie, who lived in Hannah's neighborhood.

His gaze hard and steady on her, he took a deep breath and spoke to his officer in a tone too even to be believed. 'Go on inside and round up Olie. I'll be there in a minute.'

'Gotcha.' Noga hustled off, clearly relieved to be out of the line of fire.

Megan braced herself for a skirmish. Mitch stared at her, his jaw set, his eyes dark and deep beneath his brows. She could feel the tension coming off him in waves.

'Agent O'Malley,' he said, his voice as cold as the air and deceptively, dangerously soft, 'whose investigation is this?'

'Yours,' she answered without hesitation. 'And you're screwing it up.'

'How diplomatically put.'

'I don't get paid for diplomacy,' she said, knowing damn well that she did. 'I get paid to consult, advise, and investigate. I advise that *you* investigate, Chief, instead of dragging your butt around, pretending nothing's happened.'

'I didn't ask for your consultation or your advice, *Ms* O'Malley.' Mitch didn't like this situation. He didn't like the possibilities and what they could mean to Deer Lake. And at the moment he was nursing a strong dislike for Megan O'Malley just because she was there and witnessing everything and poking at his authority and his ego. 'You know, old Leo wasn't much to look at, but he knew his place. He wouldn't stick his nose into this until I asked him to.'

'Then he would have been dragging his butt, too,' Megan said, refusing to back down. If she backed away from him now, God knew she would probably end up sitting around the squad room monitoring the coffeepot. It wasn't just a question of turf, it was a matter of establishing herself in the pecking order. 'If you don't call in uniforms to question the neighbors, I'll question them myself as soon as I've had a look around.'

The muscles in his jaw flexed. His nostrils flared, emitting twin jet streams of steam. Megan held her place, gloved hands jammed on her hips, the muscles in the back of her neck knotting from looking up at him. She had ceased to feel her smaller toes as the cold leeched up through the thin soles of her boots.

Mitch ground his teeth as that fist tightened a little more in his belly and a voice whispered in the back of his mind. *What if she's right? What if you're wrong, Holt? What if you blow this?* The self-doubt made him furious, and he readily transferred that fury to the woman before him.

'I'll call for two more units. Noga can start looking around out here,' he said tightly. 'You can come with me, Agent O'Malley. I don't want you running unchecked in my town, spooking everyone into a panic.'

'I'm not yours to keep on a leash, Chief.'

His lips curled in a smile that was feral and nasty. 'No, but it's a great fantasy.'

He stalked off down the sidewalk and up the steps, denying her the chance for rebuttal. She hurried after him, cursing the slippery footing with every breath she didn't use to curse Mitch Holt.

'Maybe we ought to set some ground rules here,' she said, coming up alongside him. 'Decide when you'll be enlightened versus when you'll be an asshole. Is that a matter of convenience or a territorial thing, or what? I'd like to know now, because if this is going to degrade into a fence-pissing contest, I'm going to have to learn how to lift my leg.'

He shot her a glare. 'They didn't teach you that at the FBI academy?'

'No. They taught me how to subdue aggressive males by ramming their balls up to their tonsils.'

'You must be a fun date.'

'You'll never know.'

He pulled open one of the doors that led into the ice arena and held it. Megan deliberately stepped to the side and opened another for herself.

'I don't expect special treatment,' she said, stepping into the foyer. 'I expect equal treatment.'

'Fine.' Mitch pulled his gloves off and stuffed them into his coat pockets. 'You try to go over my head and I will be as equally pissed off with you as I would be with anyone else. Make me mad enough and I'll punch you out.'

'That's assault.'

'Call a cop,' he tossed over his shoulder as he jerked open a door into the arena and strode through it.

Megan cast a glance toward heaven. 'I asked for this, didn't I?'

Olie Swain had done most of the grunt work at the Gordie Knutson Memorial Arena for the better part of five years. He worked from three till eleven six days a week, keeping the locker rooms in order, sweeping trash from the seating areas, resurfacing the ice with the Zamboni machine, and doing whatever odd jobs needed doing. His real name was not Olie, but the nickname stuck with him and he made no effort to lose it. He figured the less anyone knew about the real him, the better – an attitude he had developed in childhood. Anonymity was a comfortable cloak, truth a neon light that directed unwanted attention on the unhappy story of his life.

Mind your own business, Leslie. Don't be proud, Leslie. Pride and arrogance are the sins of man.

The lines that had been hammered into him in childhood with iron fists and pointed tongues rang dully in the back of his head. The mystery had always been what he could possibly have to be proud of. He was small and ugly with a port wine birthmark spreading over a quarter of his face like a stain. His talents were small and of no interest to anyone. His experiences were the stuff of shame and secrets, and he kept them to himself. He always had, shrugging off what few concerns were expressed on his behalf, denying bruises and scars, excusing the glass eye as the result of a fall from a tree.

He had a clever mind, a head for books and studies. He had a natural aptitude for computers. This fact he kept mostly to himself as well, cherishing it as the one bright spot in an otherwise bleak existence.

Olie didn't like cops. He especially didn't like men. Their size, their strength, their aggressive sexuality, all triggered bad feelings in him, which was why he had no real friends his own age. The closest he came to having friends at all were the hockey boys. He envied their exuberance and coveted their innocence. They liked him because he could skate well and do acrobatics. Some were cruel about his looks, but mostly they accepted him, and that was the best Olie could ever hope for.

He stood in the corner of the cramped storage room he had converted into an office of sorts, his nerve endings wiggling like worms beneath his skin as Chief Holt's tall frame filled the doorway.

'Hey, Olie,' the chief said. His smile was fake and tired. 'How's it going?'

'Fine.' Olie snapped the word off like a twig and tugged on the sleeve of the quilted flight jacket he'd bought at an army-navy store in the Cities. Inside his heavy wool sweater, perspiration trickled down his sides from his armpits, spicy and sour.

A woman peeked in around the chief's right arm. Bright green eyes in a pixie's face, dark hair slicked back.

'This is Agent O'Malley.' Holt moved no more than a fraction of an inch to his left. The woman glanced up at him, her jaw set as she wedged herself through the narrow opening and into the little room. 'Agent O'Malley, Olie Swain. Olie's the night man here.'

Olie nodded politely. Agent of what? he wondered, but he didn't ask. *Mind your own business, Leslie.* Good advice, he'd found, regardless of the source. Early in life he had learned to channel his curiosity away from people and into his books and his fantasies.

'We'd just like to ask you a couple of questions, Mr Swain, if that's all right with you,' Megan said, loosening the noose of her scarf in deference to the heat of the room.

She took in everything about Olie Swain in a glance. He was jockey-size with pug features and mismatched eyes that seemed too round. The left one was glass and stared straight ahead while the other darted around, his glance seeming to bounce off every surface it touched. The glass eye was a lighter shade of brown than the good eye and ringed in brighter white. The unnatural white was accentuated by the scald-red skin of the birthmark that leeched down out of his hair and across the upper left quadrant of his face. His hair was a patchwork of brown and gray and stood up on his head like the bristles of a scrub brush. He was probably in his late thirties, she guessed, and he didn't like cops.

That was, of course, a hazard of the job. Even the most innocent of people became edgy when the cops invaded their territory. And then again, sometimes it turned out to be more than routine jitters. She wondered which explanation applied to Olie.

'We're trying to find Josh Kirkwood,' Mitch said, his tone very matter-of-fact. 'He plays on John Olsen's Squirts team. You know him?'

Olie shrugged. 'Sure.'

He offered nothing else. He asked no questions. He glanced down at his Ragg wool half-gloves and smoothed his right hand over his left. Typical Olie, Mitch thought. The guy possessed no social graces to speak of, never had much to say, and never said anything without prompting. An odd duck, but there was no law against that. All he seemed to want in life was to do his job and be left alone with his books.

From his position in the doorway Mitch could see Olie and the whole room without moving his eyes. An old green card table with a ripped top and a paint-splattered wooden straight chair took up most of the floor space. On top of and beneath the table were piles of outdated used textbooks. Computer science, psychology, English literature – the books ran the gamut.

'Josh's mom was late coming to get him,' Mitch went on. 'When she got here he was gone. Did you see him leave with anyone?'

'No.' Olie ducked his head. 'I was busy. Had to run the Zamboni before Figure Skating Club.' His speech was a kind of linguistic shorthand, pared down to the bare essentials, just enough to make his

47

point, not enough to encourage conversation. He stuck his hands in his coat pockets and waited and sweat some more.

'Did you take a call around five-fifteen, five-thirty from someone at the hospital saying Dr Garrison would be late?' Megan asked.

'No.'

'Do you know if anyone else did?'

'No.'

Megan nodded and ran the zipper of her parka down. The little room was located next door to the furnace room and apparently absorbed heat in through the walls. It was like a sauna. Mitch had unzipped his parka and shrugged it back on his shoulders. Olie kept his hands in his jacket pockets. He rolled his right foot over onto the side of his battered Nike running shoe and jiggled his leg.

'Did you notice if Josh came back in the building after the other boys had gone?'

'No.'

'You didn't happen to go outside, see any strange cars?'

'No.'

Mitch pressed his lips together and sighed through his nose.

'Sorry,' Olie said softly. 'Wish I could help. Nice kid. Don't think something happened to him, do you?'

'Like what?' Megan's gaze didn't waver from Olie's mismatched eyes.

He shrugged again. 'World's a rotten place.'

'He probably went home with a buddy,' Mitch said. The words sounded threadbare, he'd said them so often in the past two hours. His pager hung like a lead weight on his belt, silent. In the back of his mind he kept thinking it would beep any minute and he'd call in to hear the news that Josh had been found eating pizza and watching the Timberwolves game in a family room across town. The waiting was eating at his nerve endings like termites.

Megan, on the other hand, appeared to be enjoying this, he thought. The idea irritated him.

'Mr Swain, have you been here all evening?' she asked.

'That's my job.'

'Can anyone verify that for you?'

A bead of sweat rolled down Olie's forehead into his good eye. He blinked like a deer caught in a hunter's crosshairs. 'Why? I haven't done anything.'

She offered him a smile. He didn't buy it, but it didn't matter. 'It's just routine, Mr Swain. Have you –'

Mitch caught hold of a belt loop on the back of her parka and gave it a discreet tug. She snapped her head around and glared at him.

'Thanks, Olie,' he said, ignoring her. 'If you think of anything at all that might help, would you please call?'

'Sure. Hope it works out,' Olie said.

The feeling of claustrophobia lifted from his chest as Holt and the woman backed away from the door. As their footsteps faded away, Olie's sense of solitude began to return. He moved around the room, running his fingertips over the block walls, marking his territory, erasing the intrusion of strangers. He slid into the chair and ran his hands over his books, stroking them as if they were beloved pets.

He didn't like cops. He didn't like questions. He wanted only to be left alone. *Mind your own business, Leslie.* Olie wished other people would take that advice.

'I didn't appreciate the little gaff hook gag,' Megan snapped. Walking beside Mitch, she nearly broke into a jog to keep up with him. Their footfalls against the concrete floor echoed through the cavernous building. Lights shined down on the sheet of smooth white ice. The bleachers that climbed the walls were cloaked in heavy, silent shadows, a cold, empty theater.

'Pardon me,' Mitch said sardonically, gladly picking up the hostilities where they had left off. 'I'm used to working alone. My manners may need a little polish.'

'This doesn't have anything to do with manners. It has to do with professional courtesy.'

'Professional courtesy?' He arched a brow. 'Seems a foreign concept to you, Agent O'Malley. I don't think you'd recognize it if it bit your tight little behind.'

'You cut me off −'

'Cut you off? I should have thrown you out.'

'You undermined my authority −'

Something hot and red burst behind Mitch's eyes. The flames burned through his control for the first time in a very long time. He wheeled on Megan without warning, grabbed her by the shoulders, and pinned her up against the Plexiglas that rose above the hockey boards.

'This is *my* town, *Agent* O'Malley,' he snarled, his face an inch from hers. 'You don't have any authority. You are here to *assist upon request.* You may have degrees out the wazoo, but apparently you were in the ladies' room when they gave that particular lecture at the bureau.'

She stared up at him, her eyes impossibly huge, her mouth a soft, round O. He had meant to frighten her, shock her. Mission accomplished. Her heavy coat hung open, and Mitch could almost see her heart racing beneath her evergreen turtleneck.

Fascinated, he let his gaze slide downward. With her shoulders pinned back, her chest was thrust forward and her breasts commanded his attention. They were small round globes, and even as he stared at them, the nipples budded faintly beneath the fabric of the sweater. The heat within him altered states, from flames of indignation to something less civilized, something primal. His intent had been to establish professional dominance, but in the heat the motivation melted and shifted, sliding down from the logical corners of his mind to a part of him that had no use for logic.

Slowly he dragged his gaze up to the small chin that jutted out defiantly. Up to the mouth that quivered slightly, betraying her show of bravado. Up to the eyes as deep and rich a green as velvet, with lashes short and thick, as black as night.

'I never had this kind of trouble with Leo,' he muttered. 'But then, I never wanted to kiss Leo.'

Megan knew better than to let him. She knew every argument against it by heart – had repeated them over and over in her mind tonight like chants to ward off evil spirits. *It's stupid. It's dangerous. It's bad business. . . .* Even as they trailed across her brain she was lifting her chin, snatching a breath. . . .

She flattened her hands and shoved at him, succeeding only in breaking Mitch's concentration. He pulled his head back an inch and blinked, his head clearing slowly. He had lost control. The thought was like a bell ringing between his ears. He didn't lose control. *Contain the rage. Control the mind. Control the needs.* Those dictates had gotten him through two long years, and in the time it took to draw a breath Megan O'Malley had driven him to the verge of breaking them.

They stared at each other, wary, waiting, breath held in the cool of the dark arena.

'I'm going to pretend that didn't happen,' Megan announced without any of the authority or righteous indignation she had intended. The announcement came out sounding like a promise she knew she couldn't keep.

Mitch said nothing. The heat abruptly died to a glow. He lifted his hands from her shoulders and stepped back. She wanted to usurp his authority, then rob him of his sanity, then pretend it hadn't happened. A part of him bridled at the thought. But that wasn't an intelligent part of him.

It wasn't smart to want Megan O'Malley. Therefore, he would not want Megan O'Malley. Simple. She wasn't even his type. Pint-size and abrasive had never done anything for him. He liked his women tall and elegant, warm and sweet. Like Allison had been. Not at all like this little package of Irish temper and feminist outrage.

'Yeah,' he muttered, digging deep for sarcasm. 'Good move, O'Malley. Forget about it. Wouldn't want to get caught with your femininity showing.'

The words stung, as he had intended them to, but the hit brought no satisfaction. All that stirred within him was guilt and a hint of regret that he had no desire to examine more closely.

An entrance door banged open, the sound bounced around the quiet like a rubber ball.

'Chief!' Noga bellowed. 'Chief!'

Mitch bolted, that knot in his stomach doubling, tripling, as he ran along the back side of the boards. *Please, God, let him say they found Josh. And let him be alive.* But even as he made the wish, cold dread pebbled his skin and closed bony fingers around his throat.

'What is it?' he demanded, rushing up to his officer.

The look Noga gave him was pale and bleak, the face of fear. 'You'd better come see.'

'Jesus Christ,' Mitch whispered desperately. 'Is it Josh?'

'No. Just come.'

Megan brought up the rear as they ran from the building. The cold hit her with physical force. She zipped her jacket, dug her gloves out of her pockets, and pulled them on. Her scarf trailed off one shoulder, fluttering like a banner behind her and finally falling off as she dashed across the parking lot.

Mitch sprinted ahead, running across the rutted ice in dress shoes, as surefooted as a track star. Midway down the lot, along the far edge, three more uniformed officers stood huddled together by a row of overgrown leafless hedges.

'What?' he barked. 'What'd you find?'

None of them spoke. Each looked to another, mute and stunned.

'Well, fuck!' he yelled. 'Somebody fucking say something!'

Lonnie Dietz took a step to the side, and a ray of artificial light fell on a nylon duffel bag. Someone had written across the side of it in big block letters: JOSH KIRKWOOD.

Mitch dropped to his knees in the snow, the duffel sitting before him with all the potential of a live bomb. It was partially unzipped and a slip of paper stuck up through the opening, fluttering in the breeze. He took hold of the very edge of the paper and eased it slowly from the bag.

'What is it?' Megan asked breathlessly, dropping down beside him. 'Ransom note?'

Mitch unfolded the paper and read it – quickly first, then again, slowly, his blood growing colder with each typed word.

a child has vanished
ignorance is not innocence but SIN

6

Day 1
9:22 p.m. 19°

'Kids do the damnedest things,' Natalie said. She worked at the kitchen counter, building turkey sandwiches while the coffeemaker hissed and spit. 'I remember Troy pulling a stunt like this once. He was ten or eleven. Decided he was going to go door to door, selling newspaper subscriptions so he could win himself a remote-control race car. He was so caught up in winning that prize, he couldn't think of anything so minor as calling from school to tell *us* what he was doing. *Call my mother? Why should I call her when I see her every day?*'

She shook her head in disgust and bisected a sandwich corner to corner with a bread knife the size of a cross-cut saw. 'This was when we lived in the Cities and there was starting to be a lot of gang activity going on in Minneapolis. You can't imagine the things that went through my head when Troy hadn't come home yet at five-thirty.'

Yes, I can. The same thoughts were trailing through Hannah's mind in an endless loop, a litany of horrors. She paced back and forth on the other side of the breakfast bar, too wired to sit. She hadn't been able to bring herself to change out of the clothes she'd worn to work. The bulky sweater held the faint tang of sweat from the exertion and stress of working on Ida Bergen. Her black hose bit into her waist, and her long wool skirt was limp and creased. She had taken her boots off at the door only out of habit.

She walked back and forth along the length of the counter, her arms crossed in a symbolic attempt to keep herself together, her eyes never straying from the phone that sat silent beneath a wall chart of phone numbers. *Mom at the hospital. Dad at his office. 911 for emergency.* All printed by Josh with colorful markers. A home project for safety week.

The panic rushed up inside her again.

'I tell you, I was a wild woman,' Natalie went on, pouring the coffee. She added a drop of skim milk to each and set them on the bar next to the plate of sandwiches. 'We called the police. James and I went out looking for him. Then we damn near ran over him. That's how we found

52

him. He was riding around in the dark on his bike, so obsessed with winning that damned toy, he couldn't be bothered to look out for traffic.'

Hannah glanced at her friend as the silence stretched and she realized this was where she was expected to interject. 'What did you do?'

'I went tearing out that car before James could put it in park, screaming at the top of my lungs. We were right outside a synagogue. I screamed so loud, the rabbi came running outside, and what does he see? He sees some crazy black woman screaming and shaking this poor child like a rag doll. So he goes back inside and calls the cops. They came flying with the lights and sirens and the whole nine yards. 'Course by then I had my arms around that boy and I was crying and carrying on – *My baby! My baby boy!*' She shrieked at the ceiling in a hoarse falsetto, waving her arms.

Rolling her eyes, she pursed her lips and shook her head. 'Looking back on it, we probably didn't have to punish Troy. The embarrassment was probably enough.'

Hannah had zoned out again. She stared at the phone as if she were willing it to ring. Natalie sighed, knowing there was really nothing she could do that she wasn't already doing. She made coffee and sandwiches, not because anyone was hungry but because it was a sane, normal thing to do. She talked incessantly in an attempt to distract Hannah and to fill the ominous silence.

She went around the end of the counter, put her hands on Hannah's shoulders, and steered her to a stool at the breakfast bar. 'Sit down and eat something, girl. Your blood sugar has to be in the negative digits by now. It's a wonder you can even stand up.'

Hannah perched a hip on one corner of the stool and stared at the plate of sandwiches. Even though she hadn't had a bite since lunch, she couldn't work up any desire to eat. She knew she should try – for her own sake and because Natalie had gone to all the trouble to make them. She didn't want to hurt Natalie's feelings. She didn't want to let anyone down.

You've already managed to do that today.

She'd lost a patient. She'd lost Josh.

The phone sat silent.

In the family room, where the television mumbled to itself, Lily woke up and climbed down off the couch. She toddled toward the kitchen, rubbing one eye with a fist, the other arm clutching a stuffed dalmatian in a headlock. A fist squeezed Hannah's heart as she watched her daughter. At eighteen months Lily was still her baby, the embodiment of sweetness and innocence. She had her mother's blond curls and blue eyes. She didn't resemble Paul in any way, a fact Paul did not care to have pointed out to him. After all the indignities he'd had to suffer in the long effort to conceive Lily, he seemed to think he deserved to have his daughter look like him.

Thoughts of Paul only made Hannah more aware of the mute

telephone. He hadn't called, even though she had left several frantic messages on his machine.

'Mama?' Lily said, reaching up with her free hand in a silent command to be picked up.

Hannah complied readily, hugging her daughter tight, burying her nose against the little body that smelled of powder and sleep. She wanted Lily as close as possible, hadn't let her out of her sight since bringing her home from the sitter's.

'Hi, sweetie pie,' she whispered, rocking back and forth, taking comfort in the feel of the warm, squirming body clad in a purple fleece sleeper. 'You're supposed to be sleeping.'

Lily deflected the remark with a beguiling, dimpled smile. 'Where Josh?'

Hannah's smile froze. Her arms tightened unconsciously. 'Josh isn't here, sweetheart.'

The panic hit her like a battering ram, smashing the last of her resistance. She was tired and terrified. She wanted someone to hold her, to tell her everything would be all right – and mean it. She wanted her son back and the fear gone. She clutched Lily to her and shut her eyes tight against the onslaught of tears. As scalding as acid, they squeezed out and ran down her cheeks. A low, tortured moan tore free of her aching throat. Lily, frightened and unhappy at being held so tightly, began to cry, too.

'Hannah, honey, please sit down,' Natalie said softly, leading her to the camelback love seat. 'Sit. I'll bring you something to drink.'

Outside the house, the dog barked and a car came up the driveway. Hannah swallowed back the rest of the tears, though Lily made no similar attempt. The suspense was as thick as smoke in the air. Would Josh come bursting in the kitchen door? Would it be Mitch Holt with news she couldn't bear to think about?

'Why isn't Gizmo in the backyard, where he belongs?'

Paul stepped into the kitchen, a petulant frown turning his mouth. He didn't look across the room to Hannah, but went about his nightly ritual as if nothing were wrong. He went into his small office off the kitchen to put his briefcase on the desk and hang up his coat. Hannah watched him disappear into the room that was his sanctuary of perfect order. Fury boiled up inside her. He cared more about hanging his coat perfectly in line with his other coats – arranged left to right from lightest weight to heaviest, casual to dress – than he cared about his son.

'Where's Josh?' Paul snapped, striding back into the kitchen, tugging loose the knot in his striped tie. 'That dog is his responsibility. He can damn well go out and put him away.'

'Josh isn't here,' Hannah answered sharply. 'If you would bother to return my phone calls, you would have known that hours ago.'

At the tone of her voice, he glanced up, his hazel eyes wary beneath the heavy line of his brow. 'What –?'

'Where the hell have you been?' she demanded, unconsciously squeezing Lily harder. The baby made a fist and hit her shoulder, wailing. 'I've been frantic trying to get you!'

'Jesus, I've been at work!' he shot back, trying to take in the scene and make some sense of it. 'I had a hell of a lot more important things to do than answer the damn phone.'

'Really? Your son is missing. Do you have a client more important than Josh?'

'What do you mean, he's missing?'

Natalie stepped between them and reached up to rescue Lily. The baby went gratefully into her arms. 'Let me put her to bed while you and Paul sit down and discuss this *calmly* and *rationally*,' she said firmly, her eyes hard on Hannah's.

'Missing?' Paul repeated, hands jammed at the waist of his fashionable brown trousers. 'What the hell is going on here?'

Natalie wheeled on him. 'Sit, Paul,' she ordered, swinging an arm in the direction of the kitchen table. His eyes widened, his frown deepened, but he obeyed. She turned back to Hannah, her fierce expression softening. 'You sit, too. Start at the beginning. I'll be right back.'

Cooing to Lily, she headed across the plush carpet of the family room for the short flight of steps that led up to the bedrooms. Hannah watched her go, guilt rising at the way Lily laid her head on Natalie's shoulder and blubbered a watery, 'No, no, Mama,' her big eyes full of accusation as she stared at Hannah.

God, what kind of mother am I? Goose bumps turned her skin the texture of sandpaper, and she pressed a hand over her mouth, afraid an answer might come out that she didn't want to hear.

'Hannah, what's going on? You look like hell.'

She turned back toward her husband, wondering bitterly why the effects of stress seemed to lend character to a man's appearance. Paul had just put in better than twelve hours at the accounting firm he was partners in with his old college friend Steve Christianson. He looked tired, the lines that fanned out from the corners of his eyes and bracketed his mouth were a little deeper than usual, but none of that detracted from his attractiveness. Just an inch taller than she, Paul was trim and athletic, with a lean face and a strong chin. His pinstripe shirt had lost its starch, but with the tie hanging loose at his throat, he looked sexy instead of rumpled. She glanced down at herself as she sank onto a chair and felt like something that had crawled out of the depths of the clothes hamper.

'We had an emergency at the hospital,' she said softly, her eyes on her husband's. 'I was late picking up Josh. I had Carol call the rink to leave word, but when I got there he was gone. I looked everywhere but I couldn't find him. The police are out looking now.'

Paul's face hardened. He sat up, shoulders squared. 'You *forgot* our son?' he said, his voice as sharp as a blade.

'No —'

'Christ,' he swore, pushing to his feet. 'That damn job is more important to you –'

'I'm a doctor! A woman was dying!'

'And now some lunatic has made off with our son!'

'You don't know that!' Hannah cried, hating him for voicing her fears.

'Then where is he?' Paul shouted, bracing his hands on the tabletop and leaning across into her face.

'I don't know!'

'Stop it!' Natalie barked, storming into the kitchen. 'Stop it, both of you!' She gave them both the ferocious glower that had cowed more than one cop on the Deer Lake force. 'You have a little girl upstairs crying herself to sleep because her parents are fighting. This is no time for the two of you to be sniping at each other.'

Paul glared at her but said nothing. Hannah started to speak, then turned her back on them both when the front doorbell rang. She ran across the family room, stumbled into the hall, and flung herself at the door, her heart hammering wildly in her chest.

Mitch Holt stood on the front step, his face grave, his eyes deep wells of pain.

'No,' she whispered. 'No!'

Mitch stepped inside and took her arm. 'Honey, we'll do everything we can to find him.'

'No,' she whispered again, shaking her head, unable to stop even as dizziness swirled through her brain. 'No. Don't tell me. Please don't tell me.'

No amount of training could prepare a cop for this, Mitch thought. There was no protocol for shattering a parent's life. There were no platitudes adequate, no apology that could suffice. Nothing could stem the pain. Nothing. He couldn't be a cop for this, couldn't detach himself even if it would have lessened his own pain. He was a father first, a friend second, and memories and guilt assaulted whatever professional reserve he might have had left. Behind Hannah, he could see Paul and Natalie standing in the hall, waiting, their faces bleak, stricken.

'No,' Hannah whispered, her lips barely moving, her tear-filled eyes brimming with desperation. 'Please, Mitch.'

'Josh has been abducted,' he said, the words tearing his voice into a low, hoarse rumble.

Hannah crumpled like a broken doll. Mitch wrapped his arms around her and held her tight. 'I'm sorry, honey,' he murmured. 'I'm so sorry.'

'Dear God,' Natalie murmured. She stepped past them and shut the front door against the bitter chill of the night, but the cold that had come into the house had little to do with the weather. It cut to the bone and could not be shaken off.

Paul stepped forward and pried loose one of Mitch's hands from around Hannah's shoulders. 'She's *my* wife,' he said. The bitterness in his tone caused Mitch to lift his head.

Paul pulled Hannah away as Mitch dropped his arms. But he made no real effort to offer her the same kind of comfort or support. Or perhaps it was just that Hannah drifted away from him when he would have tried. Either way, it seemed odd, but then, what about this night hadn't been surreal? Children weren't abducted in Deer Lake. The BCA didn't have any female field agents. Mitch Holt never lost control.

Christ, what a lie.

The anger flared inside him, saved him, as ironic as that seemed. It gave him something to focus on, something familiar to hold on to. He pulled in a deep breath, pulled himself together. He rubbed a hand across the stubble on his jaw and looked to his assistant. Behind the big lenses of her glasses Natalie's eyes were swimming with tears. She looked nearly as lost as Hannah, who stood hugging the archway into the living room, her face pressed hard against the wall.

'Natalie,' he said, touching her shoulder. 'Is there any coffee made? We could probably all use some.'

She nodded and hustled off to the kitchen, glad for the task.

Mitch herded Hannah and Paul into the family room. 'We need to sit down and talk.'

'Talk?' Paul snapped. 'Why the hell aren't you out trying to find my son? My God, you're the chief of police!'

Mitch gave him an even look and the benefit of the doubt. 'Every officer I have available is on the case. We've called the sheriff's department, the state patrol, and the BCA is here. We're organizing search parties at the ice rink. Helicopters are coming with infrared sensors that will pick up anything that gives off heat. In the meantime, Josh's description is being sent out to all surrounding law enforcement agencies and it's being entered into the system at the National Crime Information Center. He'll be registered as a missing child all across the country. I'll be coordinating efforts on the search myself, but first I've got to ask the two of you some questions. You might be able to give us a starting point, something to work with.'

'We're supposed to know what madman grabbed our son? Jesus, this is unbelievable!'

'Stop it,' Hannah snapped.

Paul gaped at her, feigning shock. 'Or maybe Hannah can shed some light on the situation. She's the one who left Josh there–'

Hannah gasped, reeling as if he'd struck her across the face.

Mitch hit Paul Kirkwood hard with the heel of his hand, knocking him backward and dumping him unceremoniously into a wing chair. 'Knock it off, Paul,' he ordered. 'You aren't helping anyone.'

Paul slumped in the chair and scowled. 'I'm sorry,' he murmured grudgingly, leaning heavily against one arm of the chair, his head in his hand. 'I just got home. I can't believe any of this is happening.'

'How do you know–?' Hannah couldn't bring herself to finish the sentence. She wedged herself into one corner of the love seat as Mitch shrugged off his parka and sat on the other end.

'We found his duffel bag. There was a note inside.'

'What kind of note?' Paul demanded. 'For ransom or something? We're hardly rich. I mean, I make a good living, but nothing extravagant. And Hannah, well, I know everyone thinks doctors are rolling in it, but it's not like she's working at the Mayo Clinic . . .'

He let the thought trail off. Mitch frowned at him, wondering just how careless the remark had been. It tilted the blame in Hannah's direction again. She began to cry silently, tears rolling down her cheeks, her hand pressed over her mouth.

'It wasn't a ransom note, but it made it clear Josh had been taken,' Mitch said. The words were branded in acid on his brain, an eerie message that pointed to a twisted mind. He wished he could give them the confidential evidence line, tell them it might be crucial to keep the information secret, knowledge only the guilty party would have, et cetera, but he couldn't. They were Josh's parents and they had a right to know. 'It said, "ignorance is not innocence but SIN."'

A chill shot through Hannah. 'What does it mean? What–'

'It means he's nuts,' Paul declared. He raked his fingers back through his hair again and again. 'Oh, Jesus . . .'

'It doesn't ring any bells with either of you?' Mitch asked. They shook their heads, both looking too stunned to think at all. Mitch let out a measured sigh. 'What we need to concentrate on now is coming up with possible suspects.'

Natalie brought the coffee in on a tray and set it on the cherrywood trunk, where remote controls lay like abandoned toys. She handed Mitch a cup, took another, and pressed it into Hannah's hands, leaving Paul to fend for himself while she coaxed her friend to take a sip. Paul didn't miss the slight. He shot the woman a glare as he leaned forward to add sweetener to his.

'You can't honestly think anyone we know would do this?' he said.

'No,' Mitch lied. The statistics scrolled through the back of his head like a news bulletin crawling along the bottom of a television screen. The vast majority of child abductions were not perpetrated by strangers. 'But I want you both to think. Have any clients or patients gotten mad at either of you? Have you noticed any strangers in the neighborhood lately, any strange cars driving by slowly? Anything at all out of the ordinary?'

Paul stared into his coffee and heaved a sigh. 'When are we supposed to notice strangers hanging around? I'm at the office all day. Hannah's hours are even worse than mine now that she's been named head of the emergency room.'

Hannah flinched as another small barb struck its target. It occurred to Mitch to ask them how long they'd been having problems, but he held his tongue. For all he knew, the stress of the situation was bringing out Paul's cruel streak.

'Has Josh said anything about someone hanging around the school or approaching him on the street?'

Hannah shook her head. Her hand trembled violently as she set her mug back on the tray, sloshing coffee over the rim. Ignoring the mess, she folded herself in two, hugging her knees, dry sobs racking her body. Someone had stolen her son. In the blink of an eye Josh was gone from their lives, taken by a faceless stranger to a nameless place for a purpose no mother ever wanted to consider. She wondered if he was cold, if he was frightened, if he was thinking of her and wondering why she hadn't come for him. She wondered if he was alive.

Paul pushed himself up out of the wing chair and paced the room. His face was drawn and pale.

'Things like this don't happen here,' he muttered. 'That's why we moved out of the Cities – to live in a small town where we could raise our kids without worrying about some pervert – ' He slammed a fist against the fireplace mantel. 'How could this happen? How could this happen?'

'There's no way to make sense of it, no matter where it happens,' Mitch said. 'The best thing we can do is focus on trying to get Josh back. We'll get a tap and a tracer on your phone in case a call comes in.'

'Are we just supposed to sit here and wait?' Paul asked.

'Someone has to be on hand if the phone rings.'

'Hannah can stay by the phone.' He'd volunteered his wife without consulting her or even considering her mental state, Mitch thought, his patience wearing thin. 'I want to help with the search. I have to do something to help.'

'Yeah, fine,' Mitch murmured, watching as Natalie knelt at Hannah's feet and tried to offer her some words of comfort. 'Paul, why don't we go out in the kitchen and discuss this, all right?'

'What can I bring to the search?' he asked, trailing after Mitch, his mind completely absorbed with planning a course of action. 'Lanterns? Flashlights? We've got some good camping gear –'

'That's fine,' Mitch said curtly. He looked Paul Kirkwood in the eye, giving him a moment to realize this conference wasn't about the search. 'Paul, I know this is a tough situation for anyone,' he said softly, 'but could you show your wife a little compassion here? Hannah needs your support.'

Paul stared at him, incredulous and offended. 'I'm a little angry with her at the moment,' he said tightly. 'She left our son to be abducted.'

'Josh is a victim of circumstance. So is Hannah, for that matter. She couldn't foresee an emergency coming into the hospital the exact time she was supposed to be picking up Josh.'

'No?' He gave a derisive snort. 'How much you want to bet she was late leaving as it was? She has regular hours, you know, but she doesn't keep them. She hangs around the place just waiting for something to go wrong so she can have an excuse to stay later. God forbid she should spend any time in our home, with our kids —'

'Put a cork in it, Paul,' Mitch snapped. 'Whatever problems you and Hannah are having in your marriage go on the shelf this minute. You got me? The two of you need to be together — for Josh's sake — not taking potshots at each other. You need to be angry with someone, be angry with God or with me or with lenient courts. Hannah has enough on her conscience without you climbing on top of the pile.'

Paul jerked away from him. Mitch was right — he wanted to lash out at someone. Hannah. His golden girl. His trophy bride. The woman who didn't have a clue about how to make him happy. She was too busy basking in the glow of everyone's adoration to be there for him or for their children. This was Hannah's fault. All of it.

'Bring whatever equipment you have,' Mitch said wearily. 'Meet me at the ice arena.' He started for the hall and brought himself up short. 'Bring some clothing of Josh's,' he added quietly, his eyes on Hannah, curled into a ball of misery on the love seat. 'We'll need something for the dogs to scent.'

Natalie followed him to the front hall. 'That man needs more than a talking-to. He needs a good swift kick in the pants — right where his brain is.'

'That's assault,' Mitch said. 'But if you want to go in there and get him, tiger, I'll swear in court I didn't see a thing.'

'I can't believe that little number-twiddling twerp,' she grumbled. 'Let that poor girl sit there and cry. Stick pins in her from across the room like she was a voodoo doll. God almighty!'

'Did you know they were having trouble?'

She made one of her faces. 'Hannah doesn't talk about personal things. She could be living with the Marquis de Sade and she wouldn't say a word against him. I'm the wrong person to ask, anyway,' she admitted ruefully. 'I always thought Paul was a stuck-up little prick.'

Mitch rubbed at the knots of tension in the back of his neck. 'We should cut him a little slack, Nat. No one's at their best in a situation like this. Everyone reacts differently and not always admirably.'

'I'd like to react all over his head,' she muttered.

'Can you stay with Hannah? Is James home with the kids?'

Natalie nodded. 'I'll call some other friends. We can pull shifts here. And I'll get the tuna casserole brigade rolling.'

'Use my cellular phone. That way you won't tie up the line here. Someone will be coming over to get the phones wired. If anything happens, I'm on the beeper.' He gave her a long look as he shrugged into his parka. 'You're worth your weight in gold, Miz Bryant.'

'Tell it to the town council,' she quipped, struggling for a scrap of humor in this nightmare. 'They can start cleaning out Fort Knox.'

He slipped the small portable phone from his coat pocket and handed it over. 'Call the priest while you're at it. We're going to need all the help we can get.'

7

From a distance, the parking lot of the Gordic Knutson Memorial Arena resembled a giant tailgate party – cars and trucks in makeshift rows, men milling around portable heaters, their voices carrying on the cold night air. But there was no party atmosphere. Tension and anger and fear hovered like a cloud, like a drift of noxious fog.

If there had been any hope of picking up a trace of evidence from the lot itself, it was gone now. That was the risk of working crime scenes with large groups. The attention to small detail was lost in the hunt for larger clues. The sense of urgency fed on itself and grew, making the mob difficult to control.

Control. A prized word in Megan's vocabulary. She had been left in charge, but at the moment she had no control. The men turned to one another for guidance and instruction. They looked for their chief. They paid no attention whatsoever to Megan. She tried twice to raise her voice above the din. No one listened and she turned to Noga.

He gave her a rueful look and shrugged. 'Maybe we should just wait for the chief.'

'Noga, a child has been abducted. We don't have time to piss around with this male pecking-order bullshit.'

Scowling, she went around to the trunk of the Lumina and rummaged through the dusty junk heap for a bullhorn, then went around to the front of the car and scrambled up on the hood, the heels of her boots denting it like hailstones.

'Listen up!' she bellowed.

The sound echoed off across the fairgrounds. As if a switch had been flipped off, the men fell silent and turned to stare at her.

'I'm Agent O'Malley with the BCA. Chief Holt has gone to speak with the parents of the missing boy. In his absence, I'm going to organize you into teams and get you started on the search. Deer Lake cops: I want three teams of two doing house-to-house on this block, asking if anyone saw anything going on between five-fifteen and seven-fifteen. We don't have a photo of the boy to give you at this point, but he was last seen wearing a bright blue ski jacket with green and yellow trim and a yellow stocking cap with a Vikings patch on it. If anyone saw Josh Kirkwood or saw anything odd or suspicious going on, we want to hear about it. The rest of you cops and county boys divide into –'

'I'll direct my own men, if you don't mind, Miss O'Malley.'

Megan's gaze dropped like an anvil onto the head of the Park County sheriff. He stood with his hands on his lean hips, a half-smile twisting his nonexistent lips. Somewhere in the vicinity of fifty, he was tall with a lean, bony face and an aquiline nose. The lights of the parking lot gleamed off dark hair that he wore slicked straight back à la basketball coach Pat Riley. His voice boomed, carrying farther than hers did with the bullhorn.

'I want my deputies on the fairgrounds. We'll do a complete sweep – every plowed road, every building. If you find something, call it in to me. Art Goble's coming with his dogs. As soon as Mitch gets back with something for them to scent off, they'll be in business. Let's go!'

Half a dozen deputies started toward the fairgrounds, flashlights bobbing in their hands. The Deer Lake cops shuffled around, uncertain who to send where or if they should do anything at all on the orders of a woman they had never seen before. Megan shot a look at Noga, and he hustled off to get them moving. She hopped down off the hood of the Lumina, landing squarely in front of the sheriff.

'It's *Agent* O'Malley,' she said, sticking a gloved hand out in front of her.

Russ Steiger gave her a patronizing once-over with his big dark eyes, blatantly ignoring her token gesture of courtesy. 'What'd they do? Run out of men in St Paul?'

'No.' Her smile was as sharp as a scimitar. 'They decided on a novel idea and sent the most qualified person instead of the one with the biggest dick.'

The sheriff blinked as if she'd hit him in the forehead with a mallet. Christ, DePalma would have her head on a pike if he heard her talk that way to a county sheriff. Never mind that she knew male agents who had vocabularies that could singe the hair in a sailor's ears. That was guy stuff, locker-room bravado. She had been given explicit instructions to make a good impression, not to offend, not to step on toes. But she knew too well what would happen if she kept her mouth shut and bowed to the local potentates. She'd end up sitting in her office, filling out forms and trimming her cuticles. It didn't take a genius in human behavior to see that this particular potentate was like a big bull moose – a polite tap on the shoulder would not get his attention; he needed something more along the lines of a sharp whack between the ears with a Louisville Slugger.

The sheriff snorted. 'Russ Steiger, Park County sheriff. Leo was a hell of a guy.'

'Yeah, well, he's dead now and we've got a job to do,' she said, fed up to her back teeth with Leo accolades. 'Let's get to it before the press shows up.' She deliberately turned her back on him, then turned around in calculated afterthought. 'Your men find something on the fairgrounds, Sheriff, you call it in to me. I'll be coordinating the effort at the command post.'

She blew out a long breath. Fatigue pressed down on her like a millstone. These were hardly the ideal circumstances for her to establish a rapport with the local boys. She would have to be on the offensive every second or get trampled beneath a herd of size-twelve boots – a distraction she didn't need. Every time she closed her eyes, she could see Josh Kirkwood grinning out at her from his third-grade photo. She could see his mother, the elegant beauty of her face twisted with guilt and a terrible fear Megan could only imagine.

Pain stabbed as sharp as an ice pick above her right eye. She had a bad feeling about this one. Abductions seldom ended happily. The message they had found in Josh's duffel bag rang like a bell of doom in her head: *ignorance is not innocence but SIN*.

That the note was typed suggested premeditation, and the whole idea of abduction reeked of a seriously disturbed mind. She wondered if they were dealing with a local or a drifter, someone already familiar with the community or someone who had hung around just long enough to get down the town routines. Or maybe the perp was someone who prowled the interstate highway systems, pulling off when the mood or opportunity hit to grab a kid and go. Maybe he had a whole glove compartment full of typed notes composed to strike terror into the hearts of those left behind. The possibilities were multifarious, the probabilities chilling.

Every step of the way a cop was taught not to become emotionally involved in a case. Good advice, but damn hard to follow when the victim was a child. Megan's heart wrenched at the idea of a small boy dragged into God knew what terror. She knew what it was to be small and alone and afraid, to feel abandoned. Those memories of her own childhood swirled like oil on water down in the pit of her soul.

A shout went up off to Megan's right, snapping her back to the moment just in time to see a pair of coon hounds bearing down on her with bright eyes and long pink tongues lolling out the sides of their mouths. At the last second one darted right and one left, their big, muscular bodies glancing off her legs, knocking her flat in the driveway.

'Aw, damn, they're after a rabbit!' A man who looked like one of the Keebler elves in a snowmobile suit looked down at Megan in disgust, then offered his hand. 'Sorry, miss.'

'Agent O'Malley, BCA,' she said automatically, grimacing as she let him help her up.

'Art Goble. Excuse me, miss, while I round up Heckle and Jeckle.'

'Heckle and Jeckle?' She watched him trundle off after the dogs, her heart sinking as she stepped up onto the sidewalk. 'Jesus, Mary, and Joseph.'

'They're the best we can do on short notice,' Mitch said. He had parked his Explorer in the fire zone in front of the arena. 'I called the volunteer canine search and rescue club, and the canine unit in Minneapolis. They'll have dogs here inside two hours.'

The challenges of law enforcement in the hinterlands. Megan sighed. 'The mobile lab is on its way and the choppers should be here within the hour. How are the parents?'

He shook his head, his expression bleak. 'Hannah is despondent. Paul is angry. They're both scared. I left Natalie in charge at the house to deal with your techs.'

'Good. It'll go more smoothly that way.'

'Paul is coming down to help with the search.'

Megan squeezed her eyes shut and groaned.

'I know, I know,' Mitch muttered. 'But I couldn't stop him. He needs to feel like he's taking some kind of action.'

'Yeah, well, if we knew where *not* to look for Josh, we could send him thataway.' She could sympathize with a parent's need to do something proactive in a situation like this, but no one wanted a father to discover his child's body or a civilian to unwittingly miss or destroy evidence.

'I'll let him bring up the rear with the county boys. They've started?'

'Oh, yeah. Me and Wyatt Earp got them all whipped into a frenzy,' she replied sarcastically.

'So you met Russ?'

'A charming fellow. Were I a fish, he would have thrown me back in disgust.'

'Don't say I didn't warn you.'

'I'll be hearing that in my sleep,' she muttered. 'If I ever get any. This is liable to be a long night.'

'Yeah, and it's about to get longer,' Mitch snarled as a *TV* 7 news van rolled up to the curb in front of them. 'Here comes the sideshow. There ought to be a law against civilians owning scanners.'

'Would that apply to the media? They only appear to be humanoid.'

The newspeople piled out of the van like the troops landing at Normandy. Technicians grabbed equipment, flipped on blinding portable strobes, tossed coils of electrical cord out onto the sidewalk. The passenger door opened and the star emerged, glamour-girl looks and too-blue contact lenses, thick sandy hair spray-starched into a helmet impervious to weather. She wore a stylish blue ski jacket open over an equally stylish sweater, and navy leggings tucked into tall leather boots. The latest outfit for reporters on the go tracking down misery and tragedy in the dead of winter.

'Oh, shit,' Mitch growled through his teeth. 'Paige Price.'

While he had no great love for any reporter, he knew only too well this one was hungry, ambitious, and ruthless in her pursuit of a story. She would do anything for a scoop, for a fresh angle, for an edge against the competition.

'Chief Holt!' The smile that graced Paige Price's mouth was small, appropriate, businesslike. The gleam of excitement in her eyes was not. 'Can we get a few words from you about the abduction?'

'We'll hold a press conference in the morning if necessary,' he said curtly. 'We're very busy right now.'

'Of course. This will take only a moment,' she said smoothly. 'Just a sound bite.'

She turned toward Megan, her reporter's eyes glinting with shrewd speculation, but she quickly arranged her features into perfect concern touched with sympathy. 'Are you the boy's mother?'

'No. I'm Agent O'Malley with the Bureau of Criminal Apprehension.'

'You must be new,' she said, the speculation sharpening.

'To the bureau, no. To the Deer Lake area, yes. This is my first day here.'

'Really? What a terrible way to start a new job.' Paige mouthed the platitudes automatically while she scanned the files of her brain, ferreting out pertinent kernels of information. 'I don't recall ever hearing of a female agent in the field. Isn't that unusual?'

'You might say that,' Megan said dryly. 'If you'll excuse me, Ms Price, I have work to do. This is Chief Holt's investigation, at any rate,' she added, tossing the ball into Mitch's court and not missing the narrow look he shot her. She kept her focus on the reporter, however, knowing better than to turn her back on a viper poised to strike. 'Any help we can get from the media in achieving the safe return of Josh Kirkwood will be greatly appreciated.'

On that note, she abandoned Mitch, heading for the relative warmth of the ice arena to await the arrival of the crime scene unit. Relief flooded through her for escaping Paige Price's manicured claws. Bureau policy was to remain in the background of investigations, leaving the publicity and the credit to fall on the shoulders of the local chief or sheriff, where it belonged. The BCA was a workhorse at the disposal of local authorities, not an organization of grandstanders looking to bask in the limelight.

The policy suited Megan fine. She wanted to be a cop, not a celebrity. She could imagine the minor strokes touched off in the bureau hierarchy if Paige Price latched on to her for an exclusive. *BCA's First Female Field Agent Fields Sensational Child Abduction Case.* She had no desire to be held up by Paige Price or anyone else as a curiosity or an icon for the women's movement. All she ever wanted was to do her job.

She climbed the stairs into the darkened bleachers and settled in an aisle seat two-thirds of the way up, grateful for the silence. It wouldn't last long. The mobile lab would arrive to collect what pitifully meager evidence they had – the duffel bag, the note. She would send the techs to the Kirkwood house to wire the phones. Then she would work with Mitch to establish a command post where searchers would report any findings, where a telephone hotline would be set up to receive tips from the public. A million details flew around inside her head like a swarm of fireflies, threatening to overwhelm her.

This was the kind of responsibility she had asked for. This was as close as she would come to FBI work as long as her father was alive. *Careful what you wish for, O'Malley.*

Punchy with exhaustion, she tried to imagine what Neil O'Malley would have done if she had been abducted as a child. Pretend paternal outrage and hoist a bottle of Pabst in private, glad to be rid of the daughter he never wanted.

'There's a million stories in the Naked City,' she mumbled absently, dismissing her own as she glimpsed movement down in the shadows near the doors to the locker rooms. Olie Swain? Uneasiness danced across her nerve endings as she pictured his ugly face and remembered the sour smell of sweat in his little cubbyhole next to the furnace room. 'A million stories in the Naked City. What's yours, Olie?'

Mitch stood scowling into the glare of the *TV 7* portable lights and gave a terse, much-abridged version of the abduction of Josh Kirkwood, assuring the ten o'clock news audience that everything possible was being done to find the boy, asking them to come forward with any information they might have.

A lot of people in Deer Lake watched KTVS, channel seven out of Minneapolis. If there was any chance that one of them had even a scrap of information, Mitch was more than willing to beg for it. It galled him to give Paige Price the exclusive, but he couldn't let personal feelings enter into the picture. He would use whom he could, however he could. If it meant getting Josh back, he would deal with the devil himself – or the devil's sister.

Paige stood beside him, looking grave and glamorous. The scent of her perfume seemed intensified by the heat of the lights – something thick and expensive. Choking. Or was that his own temper rising up in his throat and pounding between his ears? When he finished his statement, she was right there with a question, deftly heading off his escape.

'Chief Holt, you're calling this an abduction. Does that mean you have proof that Josh Kirkwood was kidnapped? And if so, what kind of proof?'

'I'm not at liberty to divulge that kind of information, Ms Price.'

'But it's safe to say you fear for Josh Kirkwood's life?'

Mitch gave her a cold look. 'Someone has taken Josh Kirkwood. Any rational person would be concerned for Josh's safety. We're doing everything we can to find him and bring him home to his family, unharmed.'

'Is that a realistic hope, considering the outcome of such cases as the Wetterling abduction or the Erstad disappearance? Or the cases gaining national prominence at the moment – Polly Klaas in California and Sara Wood in upstate New York? Isn't it true that with every moment that passes, the chances of a child's safe return diminish?'

'Cases are individual, Ms Price.' He mentally cursed her for trying to sensationalize an already terrible situation. Unprincipled bitch. But then, he knew that firsthand, didn't he? 'There's no reason to frighten people by connecting either the crimes themselves or their outcomes to this incident.'

Paige didn't bat an eyelash at the reprimand. She forged onward – straight for the jugular. 'Does this case hold a special significance for you, Chief Holt, considering your own personal –'

Mitch didn't wait for a conclusion to the question. He ended the interview for her, turning on his heel and stalking off toward the arena, shrugging off the hand that reached for his arm. The rage seethed inside him, hissed like steam in a pressure cooker. Behind him he could hear Paige saving herself gracefully, tying up the story with a neat, touching bow of words.

'. . . first on the scene as a big-city horror strikes at the heart of this quiet small town, this is Paige Price, *TV 7 News*.'

Someone called out, 'And . . . we're clear! That's it for the moment, folks.'

He heard the technicians bitching about the cold, then the sharp clack of boot heels on the sidewalk, rushing up behind him.

'Mitch, wait!'

He jammed his hands in his coat pockets and continued up the steps without sparing her so much as a glance. Not that she was the least daunted by his ignoring her. Paige Price didn't dignify subtle hints.

'Mitch!'

'Nice save, Paige,' he said flatly. 'A touch of sensationalism, a touch of sympathy, let the viewers know you're the first vulture to roost. Very professional.'

'It's my job.' Somehow she managed to sound both apologetic and proud of herself.

'Yeah, I know all about it.'

'You're still angry with me.'

Mitch jerked open a door with more force than was necessary and stepped into the dimly lit foyer. His temper surged at the false note of hurt in her voice. She had a hell of a nerve playing the part of the wounded party. He was the one who had been sliced and diced in public, dissected by the cold metaphorical scalpels of Paige Price's shrewd mind and sharp tongue.

She had told him she wanted to do a piece on the native Floridian relocating to Minnesota, the big-city cop adjusting to small-town life. A harmless public interest story. What had aired was an exposé of his life. She had callously exhumed the past he had buried and broadcast it all over the state, the crowning jewel for her first prime time special for *TV 7 News*. The tragic tale of Mitchell Holt, soldier for justice, his life shattered by a random act of violence.

'Score another point for the investigative reporter.' His sarcasm echoed harshly. The smile that twisted his mouth was mocking and bitter. He turned it on her like a spotlight. 'Congratulations on once again discerning the obvious.'

Her mouth tightened. She stared up at him, her eyes luminous. 'What I reported was a matter of public record.'

Just doing my job. Common knowledge. The public has a right to know. The excuses throbbed in his brain like hammers hitting at his sense of decency. The pressure hit the red line and his control snapped like brittle old metal.

'No!' Mitch bellowed, charging her a step. She backpedaled, eyes wide, and he pursued, leading with a finger that pointed at her like the lance of justice. 'What you reported was *my life*. Not *background*. Not *color*. *My life*. I prefer *my life* to remain *my own*. If I wanted everyone in the state of Minnesota to know *my* life story, I'd be writing a fucking autobiography!'

She was against the wall now, the top of her head just below the photograph of Gordie Knutson shaking hands with Wayne Gretzky. No amount of professional polish could hide the fact that she was trembling. Even so, her gaze was steady on his, reading everything, soaking it all in and storing it away in that calculating brain. Mitch could all but see her searching for a way to use this, to gain something, to add a shade of 'close personal knowledge' to her angle on the story. It made him sick. He'd known plenty of reporters over the years. All of them were a nuisance, but most of them played by a set of rules everyone understood. Paige Price disregarded rules as casually as most people disregarded the speed limit. Nothing was out of bounds.

She gathered her cool expertly, bent her perfect mouth into an arc of contrition. 'I'm sorry if the story upset you, Mitch,' she said quietly. 'That wasn't my intent.'

Mitch pulled himself back, his face twisting at the acrid taste of disgust. He wanted to wrap his hands around her slender, lovely throat and shake her like a rag doll. He envisioned banging her beautiful head against the block wall until Gordie's picture fell down, in an attempt to physically knock some sense of propriety into her. But he couldn't do that and he knew it.

With an extreme effort he carefully packed the rage into that little room in his chest and slammed the door.

'I know your intent, Ms Price,' he said tightly. 'Touch some hearts and win yourself the local news pissant version of an Emmy. I hope it looks good on your trophy shelf. I could suggest several more creative places for you to put it, but I'll leave them to your imagination.'

She put her hand on his arm. 'Mitch, I'd like us to be friends.'

'Christ.' He laughed. 'I'd hate to see how you treat your enemies!'

'Okay,' she admitted, her voice soft, her sapphire gaze steady and earnest, 'I should have been more up front with you about the background for the story. I can see that now.'

'Twenty-twenty hindsight.'

She ignored his sarcasm. 'Don't I get a second chance? We could have dinner. Sit down together and clear the air – when this case is over, of course.'

'Of course,' Mitch sneered. 'And as you dangle that promise out in front of me like a carrot on a stick, I'm supposed to give you little scoops on the case, right? Isn't that how it works?' His eyes narrowed with revulsion. 'I had dinner with you once, Paige. Once was enough.'

She blinked as if he'd hurt her. As if I could, Mitch thought.

'It could have been more than dinner,' she whispered, her expression softening, the hand on his arm moving in a subtle caress. 'It still could be. I like you, Mitch. I know I made a mistake. Let me make it up to you.'

She didn't seem to feel it necessary to point out her own appeal. Her ego probably let her believe any man with feeling below the waist would want her, regardless of the less attractive aspects of her personality.

Mitch shook his head. 'Amazing. You'd literally do anything, wouldn't you?' Turning a pointed look on her hand, he lifted it from his arm and dropped it. 'Frankly, Ms Price, I'd sooner stick my dick in a meat grinder. Now, if you'll excuse me, I have a stolen child to find. Impossible as it may be for you to comprehend, he's a hell of a lot more important than you.'

8

'Old girlfriend?' Megan asked carefully as Mitch stormed up the steps.

He automatically shot a look in the direction of the lobby. From her vantage point she had probably witnessed the entire scene. For that matter, the *TV 7* camera and sound people looking in from the outside had probably seen it as well. Great.

He dropped into the seat beside her, glowering. 'Not in this lifetime.'

'What happened? She burn you on a case?'

'Dismembered might be a better description,' he muttered to himself, his gaze shifting to the ice below.

He had no desire to talk about the story, no desire to satisfy Megan O'Malley's curiosity about his past. His eyes landed on the spot along the boards where he had pinned her. It seemed a year ago, and yet he could still taste the desire to kiss her, still smell the faint aroma of cheese that clung tenaciously to her coat. He wished they could have been suspended in that moment indefinitely. Dangerous thinking for a man who wasn't looking for a relationship and a woman who didn't date cops. They were going to have problems enough with the matter of who was in charge without adding sex to the equation.

'Let's just say Paige Price should have her promo photo taken with an ax in one hand and a butcher knife in the other,' he grumbled.

While wearing black lace underwear and stiletto heels. Megan kept the thought to herself. A catty remark might be misconstrued. *And just how would you mean for it to be construed, O'Malley?* She didn't care to answer that question. She didn't care to think how Paige Price – so tall and elegant and model-perfect – made her feel short and plain and unkempt. Glamour looks were not a prerequisite of her job. And the job was all that mattered here.

'So where do you want to set up the command post?' she asked.

'The old fire hall. It's on Oslo Street, half a block from the station and half a block from the sheriff's department. The garages are being used for parade floats, but there are a couple of large meeting rooms that will serve the purpose, and a bunk room upstairs. I've already called the phone company, and Becker's Office Supply is hauling in copy and fax machines. CopyCats are working on the fliers.'

'Good. What information we have is already going out on the bureau teletype. I've been in touch with the National Center for Missing and Exploited Children. They're sending a support person down from the Cities. So is Missing Children Minnesota. They'll be a big help with getting the fliers distributed regionally and nationally. They'll also offer support for the family.'

Mitch thought of Hannah sitting on the love seat, alone, in misery, and his heart ached. 'They'll need it.'

'I've got Records compiling a list of all known child molesters in a hundred-mile radius and a list of all reports of attempted abductions and suspected child predator situations in that same radius.'

'That's like building a haystack in which to find our needle,' Mitch said glumly.

'It's a starting place, Chief. We've got to start somewhere.'

'Yeah. If only we knew where we were going.'

They sat in silence for a moment. Mitch leaned ahead in his seat, his elbows on his knees, shoulders sagging beneath the weight of it all. No crime of any note had taken place in Deer Lake since he'd come on the job. Burglaries, fights, domestic disputes – those were the stock crimes of a small town. Drug deals were as heavy-duty as it got, and what they had here didn't hold a candle to what he'd seen on a daily basis in Florida.

He'd grown complacent, maybe even a little lazy. He'd let down his guard. A far cry from his days on the force in Miami. He'd been like a racehorse then – all taut muscles and nerves strung as tight as violin strings, instincts and reflexes like lightning, running on adrenaline and caffeine. Every day had brought a crisis of magnitude, dulling his sensitivity until murder and rape and robbery and kidnapping seemed normal. But those days were long behind him. He felt rusty now, slow and clumsy.

'Have you done an abduction before?' he asked.

'I've been in on a couple of searches. But I know the procedure,' she added defensively. She sat up a little straighter in her seat. 'This is all SOP. If you want to waste our time checking –'

'Whoa, Fury!' Mitch held up a hand to check her tirade. 'Innocent question. I wasn't impugning your abilities.'

'Oh. Sorry.' She shrunk down, heat rising into her cheeks.

Mitch dismissed her embarrassment, looking back out onto the ice. His eyes were bleak, the lines of strain beside them etching deeper into his skin.

'I've done four.'

'Did you find the kids?' She wished instantly she hadn't asked. Her sixth sense – her cop sense – twisted uneasily inside her.

'Twice.' A simple one-word response, but his face spoke volumes about tragedy and disappointment and the hard life lessons cops had to suffer again and again with the families of victims.

'They don't all end that way,' Megan asserted, pushing herself to her feet. 'This one won't. We damn well won't let it.'

They would have damn little say in the matter, Mitch thought as he rose. That was the bald, ugly truth. They could launch an exhaustive search, utilize incredible manpower, use every tool modern technology had to offer, and it still came down to luck and mercy. Someone in the right place at the right time. The whim of a warped mind and a twisted conscience.

She knew it, too, he thought, but she wouldn't say so. She wouldn't jinx them and she wouldn't give in to the fear. Her jaw was set at a stubborn angle, her brows pulled tight and low over her jewel-green eyes. He could feel the determination rolling off her in waves and he wanted to pull her close and absorb some of it because all he was feeling at the moment was tired and disillusioned. Not a smart idea. Still, he reached out and brushed a thumb across a streak of dirt on her cheek, picked up no doubt in the close encounter with Art Goble's hounds.

'Let's hit the bricks, O'Malley,' he said. 'See if we can't make good on that promise.'

The mobile lab and technicians from Special Operations arrived almost simultaneously with the BCA helicopter. The chopper set down in a parking lot on the fairgrounds and Mitch hustled to meet them. Megan led the other agents into the ice arena to brief them.

'What have you got for us, Irish?'

Dave Larkin was an evidence tech, thirty, cute in a beachboy sort of way. He loved his job, if not the crimes that made it necessary, and always came to the scene eager to dig in. He was a good guy and a good cop, one of Megan's first friends when she had joined the bureau. If it hadn't been for his badge and his string of amiable ex-girlfriends, she might have taken him up on one of his many offers for a date.

'Not much,' she admitted. 'We assume the boy was taken off the sidewalk out front, but we have no witnesses at the moment to substantiate this, therefore, no true crime scene. In any event, there's been a parade of cars over the drive and in the parking lot, so we're screwed there. In the way of evidence, we've got Josh Kirkwood's duffel bag – which we left where we found it – and we have this note, which was sticking up out of the bag.'

She handed Dave a glassine bag with the note inside. He read it and frowned. 'Christ, a head case.'

'Anyone who grabs a little boy off the street is a head case, whether he leaves a note or not,' said Hank Welsh, a still photographer for Special Operations. The others nodded gravely.

Dave went on studying the note, looking displeased. 'This ain't much, kiddo. Looks like a laser printer on ordinary copy paper. We'll run Ninhydrin and argon-ion laser tests, but our chances of getting a decent fingerprint off this . . .? You'd get better odds on the Mets winning the next World Series.'

'Do what you can,' Megan said. 'Our priorities now are to get the

Kirkwoods' phones wired and to get the command post up and running. You graphics guys – I know it might seem pointless at the moment, since we haven't been able to preserve a scene, but I'd like you to shoot stills and video outside. It might come in handy later on.'

'You're the boss,' Hank replied archly, coming to his feet.

Megan's gaze sharpened on him. Welsh was heavyset with a ruddy face left pitted by a long-over adolescent battle with acne. He was closer to fifty than forty and he looked none too pleased to be there. Megan wondered if it was the case or her that gave him that look of a man with chronic heartburn.

The techs moved toward the doors, but Dave Larkin hung back, planting a hand on Megan's shoulder. 'Rumor has it Marty Wilhelm was up for Leo's job,' he said in a low voice. 'Do you know him? He's a Spec Op guy.'

Megan shook her head.

'Marty is engaged to Hank's daughter, et cetera, et cetera . . .'

'Oh, swell.'

'Don't sweat it. Hank knows his job and he'll do it.' He flashed her one of his beach-bum grins. 'For what it's worth, I'm glad you got the assignment. You deserve it.'

'At the moment, I'm not sure if that's a compliment or a curse.'

'It's a compliment – and I'm not making it for the sole purpose of getting you to go out with me. That will just be a bonus.'

'In your dreams, Larkin.'

Impervious to put-downs, he went on as if she hadn't spoken. 'I'm not the only one rooting for you, either, Irish. A lot of people think it's great you got the nod. You're a pioneer.'

'I don't want to be a pioneer; I want to be a cop. Sometimes I think life would be so much easier if we were all gender neutral.'

'Yeah, but then how would we decide who leads when we dance?'

'We'd take turns,' she said, pushing open a door. 'I have no desire to spend my whole life dancing backward.'

As they stepped out into the cold, his grin faded. 'How many guys will they spare you from Regional for the investigation?'

'Maybe fifteen.'

'You'll get at least another ten volunteers. This kind of thing rings a lot of bells. You know, if kids aren't safe on the streets of a town like this . . . And if we can't catch the scumbags who pull this kind of shit, what kind of cops are we?'

Desperate cops. Scared cops. Megan kept the answer to herself as she looked around. Down the block, porch lights burned bright. She could see a couple of Mitch's uniforms tramping from one house to another. In the other direction, the beams from flashlights bobbed and darted like fireflies across the dark fairgrounds. Overhead, the eerie thump of helicopter rotors broke the calm of the night. And somewhere out there a faceless person held the fate of Josh Kirkwood in his hand.

Desperate and scared barely began to cover the feelings that thought inspired.

Day 2
4:34 a.m. 12°

Paul pulled his Celica into the garage, killed the engine, and just sat there, numb, staring straight ahead at the bicycles he had hung up on the wall for winter. Two mountain bikes and the new dirt bike Josh had gotten for his birthday. The dirt bike was black with splashes of neon-bright purple and yellow. The wheels were like big blank eyes staring back at him.

Josh. Josh. Josh.

They had called the ground search at four A.M. and told everyone to regroup at the old fire hall at eight o'clock. Cold to the bone, exhausted, disheartened, the deputies and patrolmen and volunteers had trooped back to the ice arena parking lot.

Paul could see himself as if he were watching a movie – arms gesturing angrily, his face contorted as he'd railed at Mitch Holt.

'What the hell is going on? Why are you calling this off? Josh is still out there!'

'Paul, we can't push people beyond human endurance.' They stood beside Holt's Explorer and Holt tried to put himself between Paul and any onlookers lingering around the lot. 'They've been at it all night. Everybody is frozen and tired. It's best if we call it now, get some rest, and regroup when we have daylight to work with.'

'You want to sleep?' Paul shouted, incredulous, wanting the whole world to hear him. Heads turned their way. 'You're leaving my son out there with some madman so people can go home and sleep? This is incredible!'

Those lines had struck the ears of the press people who hadn't left for warm motel rooms, and they had descended like a swarm of mosquitoes smelling blood. Holt had been furious with the impromptu mini press conference that transpired, but Paul didn't give a shit what Mitch Holt liked. He wanted his outrage on the record. He wanted his grief and desperation on videotape for all the world to see.

Now he felt drained, empty. His hands were trembling on the leather-wrapped steering wheel. His heart beat a little faster, seeming to rise up to the base of his throat until he felt as if he couldn't breathe. Somewhere in the distance a helicopter passed over the rooftops.

Josh. Josh. Josh.

He bolted from the car, walked around the hood of Hannah's van, up the steps, and into the mud room. The kitchen lights were on. A stranger sat at the table in the breakfast alcove, bleary-eyed, paging through a magazine and drinking coffee out of a giant stoneware mug from the

Renaissance Festival. He came to attention as Paul stepped into the room, shrugging out of his down coat.

'Curt McCaskill, BCA.' Stifling a yawn, he held up an ID.

Paul leaned across the table and studied it, then gave the agent a suspicious look, as if he didn't quite trust the man to be who he said he was. McCaskill endured the examination with stoic patience. His bloodshot eyes were primarily blue, his hair a thick shock of ginger red. He wore a multicolored ski sweater that looked like a television test pattern.

'And you are . . .?' the agent prompted.

'Paul Kirkwood. I live here. That's my table you're sitting at, my coffee you're drinking, my son your colleagues would be out looking for if they weren't too lazy to bother.'

McCaskill frowned as he came around the table and offered Paul his handshake. 'Sorry about your son, Mr Kirkwood. They've called the search off for the night?'

Paul went to a cupboard, pulled down a mug, and filled it with coffee from the pot on the warmer. It was bitter and strong and swirled in his stomach like discarded crankcase drippings.

'Left my son out there to God knows what fate,' he mumbled.

'Sometimes it's better if they can regroup and start fresh,' McCaskill said.

Paul stared at the pattern in the vinyl floor. 'And sometimes they're too late.'

In the silence, the refrigerator began to hum and the ice maker chattered.

Josh. Josh. Josh.

'Ah . . . I'm here to monitor the phones,' McCaskill explained, avoiding the topic of outcomes. 'All calls will be taped, in the event the kidnapper makes a ransom demand. And we'll be able to trace them.'

Kirkwood didn't seem to have any interest in the technology. He went on staring at the floor for another minute, then brought his head up. He looked like a junkie in need of a fix. His eyes were red-rimmed, his face drawn, skin ashen. His hand was shaking as he set his cup down on the counter. Poor guy.

'Why don't you go take a hot shower, Mr Kirkwood. Then get some rest. I'll call you and the missus if anything comes in.'

Without a word Paul turned and went into the family room, where a single ginger-jar lamp burned low. He started past the couch and jumped when Karen Wright sat up, blinking and disheveled. A blood red afghan dropped into her lap as she braced her arm against the back of the couch and looked up at him. Her other hand automatically combed back through her fine ash-blond hair. It fell into place like a silk curtain, a classic bob cut that fell just short of her slender shoulders.

'Hi, Paul,' she murmured. 'Natalie Bryant called me to come sit with Hannah. I'm so sorry about Josh.'

He stared at her, still trying to adjust to her sudden appearance in his living room. Nausea swirled through him like water sucking down a drain.

'All the neighborhood women are taking turns.'

'Oh. Fine,' he mumbled.

She frowned prettily, her lips a feminine bow set in a fine-featured oval face. From the corner of his eye he could see McCaskill sliding back down into his chair at the kitchen table, his attention already on his magazine.

'Are you all right?' she asked. 'You should probably go lie down.'

'Yes,' Paul murmured. His heartbeat stuttered and pumped as his brain swam dizzily. *Josh. Josh. Josh.* 'Yes, I'm going.'

He was turning as the words came out of his mouth, struggling to keep himself from running out of the room. He was sweating like a horse, even as chills raced through him. He peeled his sweater off over his head and dropped it on the floor in the hall. His fingers fumbled over the buttons of his Pendleton shirt. The shakes went through him like the tremors before an earthquake. His heart raced. His head pounded.

Josh. Josh. Josh.

The shirt was hanging from one arm as he stumbled into the bathroom. He fell to his knees in front of the toilet and retched, his whole body convulsing with the effort to vomit. On the third attempt the coffee came up, but there was nothing else in his stomach to be discarded. Clutching the bowl, he dropped his head on his forearm and closed his eyes. The image of his son pulsed behind his eyelids.

Josh. Josh. Josh.

'Oh, God, Josh,' he whimpered.

The tears came, scalding and scarce, squeezing out of him. When they were spent, he pushed himself up off the floor and finished undressing, folding his clothes neatly and dropping them into the hamper on top of half a dozen tangled wet towels. Shaking like a palsy victim, he climbed into the tub and turned the shower on full blast, letting the hot water pound the cold out of his bones. It pelted his skin like hailstones, washed away the sweat and tears and the faint tang of sex that clung to him.

After he had dried himself off and hung the towel on the bar, he slipped into the thick black terry robe that hung on the back of the door and went out into the hall. The door to Lily's room was ajar, letting a sliver of the hall light fall across the rose-pink carpet. Farther down the hall, the door to Josh's room stood open.

Everything about the room said *boy*. A friend of Hannah's had painted murals on each wall, each mural depicting a different sport. A poster of Twins outfielder Kirby Puckett held a place of honor on the baseball wall. A miniature desk sat between two windows, piled with books and toy action figures. Bunk beds were stacked along another wall.

Hannah sat on the bottom bed, her long legs curled beneath her, her arms wrapped tight around a fat stuffed dinosaur. She watched Paul as he turned on the small lamp on the bedside table. She wanted him to grin at her and hold his arms out as he told her they had found Josh safe and sound, but she knew that wouldn't happen. Paul looked old and drawn, a preview of how he would look in twenty years. With his wet hair slicked back, the bones of his face stood out prominently.

'They called off the ground search until morning.'

Hannah said nothing. She didn't have the energy or the heart to ask if they had found any clues. Paul would say if they had. He just looked at her. The silence spoke for itself.

'Have you slept?'

'No.'

She looked as if she hadn't slept in days, he thought. Her hair frizzed around her head; mascara and fatigue had left dark smudges beneath her eyes. She had changed out of her clothes into another of his bathrobes, a cheap, garish blue velour job his mother had given him for Christmas years before. Paul refused to wear it. He had worked hard to be able to afford better than the junk Kmart had to offer. But Hannah refused to throw it out. She kept it in her closet and wore it from time to time. To irk him, he thought, but tonight he ignored it.

She looked vulnerable. *Vulnerable* was a word Paul seldom used to describe his wife. Hannah was a nineties woman – intelligent, capable, strong, equal. She didn't need. She could have lived just as well without him as with him. She was exactly the kind of woman he had dreamed of marrying. A wife he could be proud of instead of embarrassed by. A woman who was someone other than her husband's shadow, slave, and doormat.

Be careful what you wish for, Paul . . . His mother's mousy voice whispered in the back of his mind. He shut it out as successfully as he had always managed to shut her out.

'I've just been sitting here,' Hannah murmured. 'I wanted to feel close to him.'

Her chin quivered and she squeezed her eyes shut. Paul sat down on the edge of the bed, reached over, and touched her hand. Her fingers were as cold as ice. He covered them with his, thinking that it used to be easy to touch her. There had been a time when they couldn't get enough of each other. That seemed ages ago.

'About – When you told me –' He broke off and sighed, then tried again. 'I'm sorry I jumped on you. I wanted to blame somebody.'

'I try,' she whispered almost to herself, tears squeezing out between her lashes. 'I try *so hard*.'

To be a good wife. To be a good mother. To be a good doctor. To be a good person. To be everything to everyone. She tried so hard and thought she succeeded most of the time. But she must have done something wrong to be made to pay this way.

'Shh . . .' Paul pried the dinosaur from her grasp and pulled her into his arms, letting her cry on his shoulder, letting her lean on him. He rubbed her back through the cheap velour robe and felt needed. 'Hush . . .'

He kissed her hair and breathed in its scent. He listened to her soft weeping, absorbed the feel of her clinging to him, and desire drifted through him like smoke. Hannah needed him now. Superwoman. Dr Garrison. She didn't need his income or his friends or his social position. God, she didn't even need his name. He was chronically superfluous to her life. He was the shadow, the nobody. But she needed him now. She wrapped her arms around him and hung on tight.

'Let's go to bed,' he whispered. Hannah let him help her up from Josh's bed and walk her down the hall to their own room. She made no protest as he slipped the robe from her shoulders and kissed the side of her neck. Breath shuddered out of her lungs as his hands cupped her breasts. She had felt so alone all night. Emotionally abandoned. Exiled. She needed so badly to feel loved, comforted, forgiven.

She turned her head and brushed her mouth across his, inviting his kiss, rising into his kiss, her breasts pressing into his chest, her back arching as his hand settled low along the valley of her spine. The need burned out the fear for a few moments. It suspended time and offered a refuge. Hannah took it gladly, greedily, desperately. She pulled Paul down to the bed with her, wanting his weight on top of her. She opened herself to him as he pressed his erection between her legs, needing to feel him inside her. She held him while he arched into her again and again, wanting nothing more than the contact, the illusion of intimacy. And when it was over, she closed her eyes and lay her head on his shoulder, wishing against the hollow ache in her chest that the sense of closeness could last. But it wouldn't. Not even on this night, when she longed so desperately for something to cling to.

What happened to us, Paul?

She didn't know how to ask. She still couldn't believe it was real, this distance and anger that hung between them. It seemed all a bad dream. They had been so happy. The perfect couple. The perfect family. The perfect life of Hannah Garrison. Now her marriage was falling apart like a cheap tapestry and her son had been stolen. *Stolen . . . taken . . . abducted. God, what a nightmare.*

Her eyes drifted shut on that terrible thought, the exhaustion winning out at last, and she slid from the nightmare into blessed blackness.

Paul knew the instant she fell asleep. The tension went out of the arm she had banded across his chest. Her breathing deepened. He lay there, staring up at the skylight, feeling caught in the middle of some surreal play. His son was gone. By this time tomorrow Josh Kirkwood would be a household word all over the state. Newspapers would splash his picture all over their front pages, along with the impassioned plea Paul had made in the parking lot of the ice arena at four A.M. *Please bring my son back! Josh. Josh. Josh.*

His eyes burned as he stared up at the starless sky. And the play went

79

on. Act Two. His wife lay naked in his arms hours after his mistress had done the same. Overhead, helicopter blades beat the night air.

5:43 a.m. 12°

Mitch climbed out of his truck, his gaze automatically scanning the alley behind his house for signs of reporters, skittish after the debacle in the ice arena parking lot. He wouldn't have put it past any of them to follow him. *Get a shot of the failure of a police chief as he drags his sorry ass home. Lets child predators snatch kids off the streets of his town. No big surprise. Look what happened in Miami.*

It settled on his aching shoulders like a cloak – the guilt, edged in anger, dyed black by his mood. He threw it off with a violent swing of his arm, snarling in self-contempt.

What a jerk you are, Holt. This isn't about you. It isn't about Miami. Hold the old rage inside where it belongs, and rage anew for Josh.

Easier said than done. The anger, the sense of impotence and loss and betrayal, were echoes from his past. And as much as every cop knew better than to personalize a case, he couldn't stop himself from feeling as if this crime had been perpetrated in part against him. This was his town, his haven, the safe little world he could control. These were his people, his responsibility. He represented safety to them, and they were his extended family.

Family. The word hung with him as he went up the path to the back door, the snow squeaking beneath his feet in the icy stillness of the early morning. He let himself into the house and toed off his heavy Sorel boots in the back hall.

In the kitchen Scotch, the old yellow Labrador who was his only roommate in Jessie's absence, cracked open one eye and looked at him without raising his head from his cushioned dog bed. At twelve, Scotch had officially retired from guard duty. He filled his time sleeping or wandering around the house, carrying in his mouth whatever object struck his fancy en route on his travels – a shoe, a glove, a throw pillow from the couch, a paperback book. One of Jessie's Minnie Mouse dolls was wedged between his head and his paws for a pillow.

Mitch let him keep it. The old scoundrel might have stolen it out of her bedroom, but it was just as likely Jessie had put him to bed with it. The Strausses lived across the alley, and every day after school Jessie came over with her grandfather to let Scotch outside and to play with him. She adored the old dog. Scotch patiently suffered through dress-up games and tea parties with her, faithful, gentle, returning the little girl's love unconditionally.

The images striking on tender feelings, Mitch padded into the kitchen in his stocking feet. The light above the sink cast the room in amber and shadow. His gaze wandered aimlessly. The house dated back to the

80

thirties. A nice, solid story-and-a-half with hardwood floors and a fireplace in the living room and big maple and oak trees in the yard. A house with character that remained mostly repressed because of his lack of decorating skills.

That had been Allison's forte. She was a nest builder with an eye for style and a love of small detail. She would have converted this kitchen into a place of warmth and charm with framed prints and strings of peppers and old Mason jars filled with cinnamon-scented potpourri. Mitch had left the room exactly as it was when he moved in – the walls mostly bare, the curtain at the window above the sink an old rummage sale reject left by the last owners. The only things Mitch had added were drawings Jessie had done for him. Those he mounted on the refrigerator with magnets and stuck up on the wall with tape. Somehow, the bright, childish images in the otherwise vacant room served only to point out how bleak and empty the house was.

He felt hollow as he stared at the pictures. Alone. Lonely. God, sometimes the loneliness ached so badly he would have given anything to escape it – including his life. He would have died as penance, but then, living was a harsher punishment.

Crazy thoughts. Irrational thoughts, the department psychiatrist had told him. Logically, he knew it wasn't his fault. Logically, he knew he could not have prevented what happened. But logic had little to do with feeling.

Leaning back against the sink, he squeezed his eyes shut and saw his son. Kyle was six. Bright. Quiet. Wanted a two-wheeler for Christmas. Took his dad to school during job week and beamed while Mitch told the first grade about being a policeman.

'Policemen help people and protect them from the bad guys.'

He could hear the words, could look out on the small sea of little faces, his gaze homing in on Kyle's expression of shy pride. So small, so full of innocence and trust and all those things the world had ground out of his father.

'Policemen help people and protect them from the bad guys.'

A hoarse, tortured sound wrenched out of Mitch's throat. The feelings ripped loose, the bars of their cage weakened by fatigue and memory and fear. He clamped a hand over his mouth and tried to swallow them back. His whole body shook with the effort. He couldn't let them loose; he would drown in them. He had to be strong. He had to focus. He had a job to do. His daughter needed him. The excuses came one after another. Deny the feelings. Ignore them. Put them off. His town needed him. Josh Kirkwood needed him.

He forced his eyes to open. He stared out the kitchen window at the velvet gray of the day before dawn, and still in his memory he could see Kyle. His vision doubled, the image splitting, the face of the second body going out of focus and coming back as Josh.

God, please no. Don't do that to him. Don't do that to his parents.

Don't do that to me.

Shame washed through him like cold water.

Across the alley a light came on in the Strauss kitchen. Six A.M. Jurgen was up. He had been retired from the railroad for three years, but kept his schedule as regular as if he were still going down to the Great Northern switching yard every day. Up at six, start the coffee. Drive down to the Big Steer truck stop on the interstate to pick up the *StarTribune* because paperboys were unreliable. Home for coffee and a bowl of hot cereal while he read the paper. His quiet time before Joy emerged from their bed to begin the recitation of her daily litany – a deceptively soft, deceptively mild running commentary on all that was wrong with the world, the town, the neighbors, her home, her health, her son-in-law.

As badly as Mitch wanted to avoid his in-laws, the sudden need to see Jessie was stronger. To look at her and hold her and see that she was real and alive and warm and sweet and safe. He stepped back into his boots and trudged outside without bothering to lace them.

Jurgen came to the back door of the neat Cape Cod house in his daily uniform of jeans and a flannel shirt, neatly tucked in. He was a stocky man of medium height with piercing Paul-Newman-blue eyes and military-cropped gray hair.

'Mitch! I was just making the coffee. Come on in,' he said, his expression a mix of surprise and annoyance at having his regimen interrupted. 'Any word on the Kirkwood boy? Cripes, that's a terrible business.'

'No,' Mitch replied softly. 'Nothing yet.'

Jurgen swung the basket out on the coffeemaker and dumped in a scoop of Folger's. Too much, as usual. Joy would comment on it being too strong, as always, then drink it anyway so she could later complain about the heartburn it gave her.

'Have a seat. You look like hell. What brings you over at this time of day?'

Mitch ignored the chairs arranged neatly around the kitchen table. 'I came to see Jessie.'

'Jess? It's six o'clock in the morning!' The older man glowered at him.

'I know. I've only got a little time,' Mitch mumbled. Going into the dining room and up the stairs, he left Jurgen to think what he wanted.

Jessie had the room her mother had grown up in. The same bed, same dresser, same ivory wallpaper strewn with mauve tea roses. Jessie, being Jessie, had, of course, added her own touches – stickers of the Little Mermaid and Princess Jasmine from *Aladdin*. Joy had scolded her, but the stickers were the variety that did not peel off without a fight, and so they had remained. Because she spent so much time there, the dresser drawers were filled with her clothes. On the toy shelves, the place of honor was given over to figurines of Disney characters – Mickey and Minnie, Donald Duck and nephews, a broken alarm clock with Jiminy Cricket perched on top with his cricket hands clamped over his ears.

The clock had been Kyle's. Seeing it never failed to bring Mitch a stab of pain.

He crept into the room, closed the door softly behind him, and leaned back against it. His daughter slept in the middle of the old double bed, her arms curled around her teddy bear. She was the picture of childhood lying there asleep, dreaming sweet dreams. Her long brown hair was plaited in a thick loose braid that disappeared beneath the covers. The frilly collar of her flannel nightgown framed her face and her dark lashes curled against her cheek. Her plump little mouth was pursed in a perfect O as she breathed deeply and regularly.

He couldn't look at her like this – when she seemed most precious, most vulnerable – without having emotion kick him in the belly with all the strength of a mule. She was everything to him. She was the reason he had never given in to the desperate wish to end his pain after Allison and Kyle had been taken from him. His love for her was so deep, so fierce, it sometimes scared him. Scared him to think what he would do if he ever lost her, too.

Carefully he lifted the layer of blankets and quilt and eased himself down, resting his back against the carved oak headboard. Jessie's eyes blinked open and she looked up at him, smiling a sleepy smile.

'Hi, Daddy,' she murmured. She wriggled herself and her bear onto his lap and snuggled against him.

Mitch tugged the covers up beneath her chin and kissed the top of her head. 'Hi, cuddlebug.'

'Whatcha doing here?'

'Loving you up. Is that okay?'

She nodded, burrowing her face into the thick cotton sweater that spanned his chest. Mitch just wrapped his arms around her and held her, listening to her breathe, breathing deep the scents of warm child and Mr Bubble.

'Did you find the lost boy, Daddy?' she asked in a drowsy voice.

'No, honey,' he whispered around the ache in his throat. 'We didn't.'

'That's okay, Daddy,' she assured him, hugging him tight. 'Peter Pan will bring him home.'

Journal entry
Day 2

Act I: Chaos and panic. Predictable and pathetic. We watched, amused by their pointless sense of urgency. Going nowhere at a breakneck pace. Grasping at the dark. Finding nothing but their own fear.

> *But is there any comfort to be found?*
> *Man . . . loves what vanishes;*
> *What more is there to say?*

9

The old fire hall in downtown Deer Lake was overflowing with law
enforcement officers, volunteers, media people, and locals who had come
out of fear and morbid curiosity. Mitch arrived, freshly showered and
shaved and running on a giant mug of coffee grabbed at Tom Thumb and
drunk en route.

He had expected the place to be in a state of chaos, had wondered
where he was going to find the patience to deal with it, but there seemed
to be a sense of order to the madness. The command post had been set up
in one of the two community rooms used mainly for the senior citizens'
card club and 4-H meetings since the fire department had been moved
into snazzier quarters on Ramsey Drive. The hotline telephones had been
set up – six of them spaced apart on a long bank of tables. Two of the
phones were already manned and busy. Copy and fax machines sat along
the opposite wall. At another long table volunteers were stacking up the
fliers that had been run off during the night with Josh's picture and vital
statistics.

Mitch moved on to the room down the hall where those who would
be resuming or joining the search milled around, drinking coffee and
eating doughnuts. This room would serve as meeting place and makeshift
media center. The walls were painted a moldy shade of green – a
clearance color from Hardware Hank in 1986. The sickly hue went well
with the musty smell of old linoleum and dust. Two dozen dismembered
construction-paper hands decorated the wall behind the podium at the
front of the room, the 4-H pledge scrawled on them in crayon. Each
macabre masterpiece was signed by the artist and marked with his or her
age.

Already the room was crowded with reporters and photographers and
cameramen from newspapers, radio and television stations all around the
state. A photographer stood three feet back from the wall, killing time
taking artsy shots of the hands. A television reporter stood along another
wall, beside the wall plaque of Boy Scout knots, staring gravely into the

lens of a video camera as he oozed platitudes about Norman Rockwell towns and all-American families.

The ranks of those who had come to document the tragedy would only grow as the search continued. At least for the next week – if it lasted that long. While the search was at its most intense, they would be constantly underfoot, looking for a scoop, an exclusive, an angle no one else had.

Damn bunch of parasites, Mitch thought as he shouldered his way through the throng of reporters, scowling and snarling in answer to their shouted questions.

At the front of the room Megan was overseeing the setup for the press conference, directing the placement of the podium, a screen and overhead projector. Her small mouth set in a tight line, she wheeled on a reporter who ventured too near.

'For the sixty-ninth time, Mr Forster, the press conference will not begin until nine,' she said sharply. 'Our first concern is to find Josh Kirkwood. If he is still in the vicinity, that means we have to get these people organized and resume the search.'

A reporter for the *StarTribune* since the days of Linotype, Henry Forster had the face of a bulldog, a balding head adorned with liver spots, and long, weedy strands of gray hair he wore in a classic horizontal comb-over. His trademark dirty horn-rimmed bifocals sat crooked beneath a pair of bushy eyebrows that should have had their own zip code. He was a big old warhorse with hips that had splayed out in his later years to provide a good base for his medicine-ball belly. Megan would have guessed he had slept in his brown trousers and cheap white dress shirt, but she knew from past acquaintance Henry always looked that unkempt.

The eyebrows crawled up his forehead. 'Does that mean you think the boy has been taken out of this area?'

Two of his cohorts perked up and inched forward away from the wall, like rats venturing forth to sniff at some promising crumb.

Megan stopped them in their tracks with a look that had incinerated humans. She turned the look on Henry, who stood close enough that the fumes of his Old Spice burned her nasal linings. He didn't retreat. He kept staring at her as if he fully expected an answer.

No doubt he did, Megan thought. Forster had seniority and a track record that had littered his office with awards, which he allegedly used as paperweights and ashtrays. Politicians cowered at the mention of his name. The BCA brass cursed the day he was born – one of the original seven. Henry Forster had been the man who'd blown the lid off the sexual harassment charges in the bureau the previous fall. He was the last man Megan wanted sniffing after her heels. The pressure of this case would be enough without Henry Forster's grimy bifocals magnifying her every move.

Show no fear, O'Malley. He can smell fear – even through that aftershave.

'That means Officer Noga is going to escort you out of this room if you don't get out of the way,' she told him without flinching.

She turned her back on Forster as he snorted his affront. One of the other reporters who had been standing in his considerable shadow hoping for a scrap muttered, 'Little bitch.' Megan wondered if they would dare make slurs behind Noga's broad back. She caught hold of the patrolman's sleeve and he looked down at her, his dark eyes bloodshot and bleary.

'Officer Noga, would you please herd these press weasels out of the way before I rip out their windpipes and have them for breakfast?'

He scowled at the reporters. 'You got it, Miss – Agent.'

'No offense,' Mitch muttered, easing into the spot Noga vacated, 'but I don't think you have much of a shot at Miss Congeniality today.'

'Miss Congeniality is a wimp,' Megan returned. 'Besides, neither one of us is beauty pageant material. You look like I feel.'

Mitch made a face. 'Gender confusion. Don't let the boys from the *Pioneer Press* hear that.'

'I think they already have their theories.'

'Did you get any sleep?'

The question seemed perfunctory. It looked to Mitch like she had gone through the same minimal morning routine as he had. She had changed into a pair of snug black ski pants and a heavy Irish fisherman's sweater over a turtleneck. Her dark hair was clean and brushed back into a utilitarian ponytail. Her makeup was scant and did nothing to hide the violet smudges beneath her eyes.

She shot him a look. 'Who needs sleep when you can take an ice cold shower? I have an apartment with no utilities. I shaved my legs by lantern light, fed my cats, and came back here. How about you?'

'I have a dog and hot water,' he said, moving around the end of the table. 'And I'll keep my legs hairy, thanks. Has anything come in from your people?'

'Besides ten pages of known pedophiles? No.'

Mitch shook his head, his stomach turning at the idea that there were so many scumballs preying on children within a hundred miles of his town – and his daughter. Christ, the world was turning into a cesspool. Even out in rural Minnesota he could feel the muck seeping up around his shoes. It was as if overnight someone had opened the floodgates on the sewer.

He looked out over the crowd as he stepped behind the podium – men from his own office and the sheriff's department, volunteer firemen, concerned citizens, Harris College students who had stayed in town for their winter break. What he saw in their faces was determination and fear. One of their own had been taken and they were there to get him back. Mitch wanted to believe they would do it, but in his experience hope didn't get the job done.

Still, he drew himself up and put on the game face. He addressed the troops and issued orders and sounded like a leader. He narrowed his eyes against the glare of the television sun-guns and thought he probably looked determined and purposeful instead of blind.

The cameras rolled film, not willing to wait for the official press conference, not wanting to miss out on any of the drama. Flash strobes went off at irregular intervals as the newspaper photographers shot stills of the cops and the crowd. The reporters scribbled. In one of the front row chairs Paige Price sat with her long legs crossed and a notebook on her lap. She gazed up at Mitch with an earnest expression while her cameraman knelt at her feet and got a reaction shot of her. Business as usual.

A map of Park County went up on the projection screen, the area cut into sections by red lines Mitch and Russ Steiger had drawn at five A.M. Teams of searchers were numbered and assigned areas. Instructions were given as to technique, what to look for, what to call to the team leader's attention. Mitch gave the mike over to Steiger, who added orders and details for the SO deputies, the mounted posse volunteers and snowmobile club members who would be searching the fields and densely wooded areas outside of town.

As fliers were passed out to all those present, media people included, Josh's photograph went up on the projection screen. The room went still. The murmured conversations died. The rustle of paper faded away. The silence was as heavy as an anvil, the soft whir of video cameras underscoring and somehow amplifying it. Every eye, every thought, every prayer, every heartbeat, was focused on the screen. Josh stared out at them with his sunny, gap-toothed smile, his hair a tangle of soft brown curls; every freckle was a mark of innocence, as much a symbol of boyhood as the Cub Scout uniform he wore so proudly. His eyes were bright with excitement for all life had to offer him.

'This is Josh,' Mitch said quietly. 'He's a nice boy. A lot of you have little boys just like him. Friendly, helpful, a good student. A happy, innocent little kid. He likes sports and playing with his dog. He has a baby sister who's wondering where he is. His parents are good people. Most of you know his mother, Dr Garrison. A lot of you know his dad, Paul Kirkwood. They want their son back. Let's do everything we can to make that happen.'

For a moment the silence hung, then in a gruff voice Russ Steiger ordered his men out and the search parties began filing from the room. Mitch wanted to go with them. The burden of rank prevented him. It was his job to deal with the press and the mayor and the city council. The position of chief often had less to do with the kind of in-the-trenches police work he had once thrived on and more to do with politics than he had ever cared for. He was a cop at heart. A damn good one once upon a time.

His gaze cut involuntarily to Paige Price. She caught the action as quickly as a trout snagging a fly, and rose gracefully, coming toward him while her colleagues remained seated, furiously jotting notes and mumbling into microcassette recorders.

'Mitch.' She reached across the podium, deftly flicking off the switch of the microphone. Her expression was perfect – contrition and regret with just the right touch of caring. 'About last night . . . I don't want cross words between us.'

'I'm sure you don't,' Mitch said coldly. 'Keeps you from getting an edge.'

Paige gave him the wounded look she had used to melt more than one wall of male resistance. But Mitch Holt wasn't buying and she called him a son of a bitch in her mind. Her exclusive of the night before had won her words of praise from the news director and station manager. Her agent had two words for the scoop – dollar signs. If she could keep ahead of the pack on this story, it would mean serious money, maybe even an offer from one of the larger network affiliates. She was shooting for L.A. Warm, sunny L.A. Regardless of where she went, it would beat this godforsaken icebox. But Mitch Holt stood in her way, a tarnished, battered knight upholding antiquated ideals.

'I'm sorry you think that's my only motivation,' she murmured. 'I'm not a barracuda, Mitch. Yes, I want a story out of this, like every other reporter in this room. But my first concern is this poor little boy.'

Mitch didn't blink. 'Save it for the Nielsen families.'

Paige bit down on the tip of her tongue. From the corner of her eye she could see Henry Forster from the *StarTribune* shoving past people to reach them. She could feel his angry stare burning into her. Forster hated nothing more than being scooped by someone in television, unless it was being scooped by a woman in television. But before Forster could intrude on her moment, Agent O'Malley stepped into the picture.

'The press conference will begin shortly, Ms Price,' she said, steering Paige away from the podium. 'Why don't you help yourself to a cup of coffee and a nice fat doughnut?'

The suggestion came with a smile etched in steel. Paige looked down at Megan O'Malley, amused that this slip of a woman was coming to the aid of a man who dwarfed her. She flicked a glance between them, speculating. Neither face gave anything away, which, to Paige's way of thinking, gave away much. She backed off toward the coffeepot, a hand raised in a false gesture of surrender.

'And may it all go straight to your hips,' Megan muttered under her breath, moving back to her position behind the front table. She caught the wry look Mitch sent her and scowled at him. 'Lack of sleep makes me uncharitable.'

He raised an eyebrow, shuffled his papers, and flicked the microphone back on.

The press conference was woefully short on information. They had no suspects. They had no witnesses. They had no leads but the note the kidnapper had left behind and Mitch would not divulge the contents on the excuse that to do so might compromise the investigation later on. His official statement was that the Deer Lake Police Department, along with the other agencies involved, was taking every possible step to find Josh and apprehend his abductor.

Russ Steiger added that the sheriff's department would work around the clock. He would be overseeing the search himself in the field – a statement made with a bravado borne of self-importance. Park County attorney Rudy Stovich made the requisite statement about prosecuting to the full extent of the law. Megan gave the usual bureau line, offering investigative support, lab and records assistance at the request of the police and sheriff's departments.

Then began the feeding frenzy. The reporters clamored for attention, blurting out questions, each trying to shout the next one down.

'Is it true you're looking for a known pedophile?'

'Will the parents be giving statements?'

'Has the FBI been called in?'

'They're aware of the situation,' Mitch said, fielding the last of the barrage. 'We already have three agencies working on the case. We have all the resources of the BCA at our disposal. At the moment we don't believe Josh has been taken out of the immediate area. If the prospect of interstate flight arises, then by all means the FBI will be called in. In the meantime, I believe the agencies involved are best equipped to deal with the situation.'

'Is it common practice for eight-year-olds to be left unsupervised at the ice arena?'

'Have there been any previous incidents of child molestation in Deer Lake?'

'Is it true the boy's mother simply forgot him at the ice rink?'

His face tight with anger, Mitch drew a bead on the *Pioneer Press* reporter. 'There's nothing *simple* about this. Dr Garrison was trying to save a life in the emergency room. She did *not simply* forget her son and should in no way be made to feel responsible for his abduction.'

'What about the father's statement that rink management and the hockey coach should be held responsible?'

'What about you, Chief Holt?' Paige stood. 'Do *you* hold yourself responsible?'

He met her eyes without blinking. 'In a manner of speaking, yes. As chief of police, it is ultimately my responsibility to keep the citizens of this town safe.'

'Is that strictly your professional philosophy or are your feelings tainted by the guilt related to your personal –'

'*Ms* Price,' he ground out her name between his teeth. 'I believe I made it perfectly clear last night that this case should in no way be tied to any other. We're here to talk about Josh Kirkwood and the efforts being made to find Josh Kirkwood. Period.'

Megan watched the exchange, her attention focused on Mitch. She thought she could feel the anger vibrating in the air around him. Something about the defensive set of his shoulders, the taut line of his mouth, made her feel as if Paige Price had hit below the belt. Megan told herself it was just her sense of justice that responded, nothing more than the loyalty she would feel toward any other cop. She pushed to her feet to draw the fire away from him.

'On behalf of the BCA I would like to put extra emphasis on what Chief Holt is saying. It is essential that we keep the focus here on Josh Kirkwood. It is essential that we keep the focus of your readers, listeners, and viewers on Josh. We need him in the hearts and minds of everyone we can reach. We ask especially that his photograph receive maximum exposure. For you radio people – detailed descriptions of Josh and what he was last seen wearing. If there's a chance that anyone has seen him, we need to do everything possible to make certain those people recognize Josh as the victim of an abduction.'

'Agent O'Malley, is it true yesterday was your first day on the job in Deer Lake?'

She gave Henry Forster a cool look and cursed herself for volunteering that information to Paige Price the night before. 'I fail to see how that pertains to what I've just said.'

He shrugged without apology. 'That's news, too.'

A number of heads nodded agreement. Not to be outdone by her rival, Paige rose again.

'Miss O'Malley, can you tell us how many women hold positions as field agents with the BCA?'

'*Agent* O'Malley,' Megan corrected her firmly. This was all she needed – a bitch with nightly airtime on her case. She could already imagine Bruce DePalma's blood pressure skyrocketing. She drew in a slow breath and struggled to find a diplomatic way of saying fuck off.

'There are a good number of female agents with the bureau.'

'At headquarters, in office jobs. What about in the field?'

Mitch nudged Megan away from the mike. 'If none of you have any more questions in direct reference to the abduction of Josh Kirkwood, we'll have to end this now. I'm sure you all can appreciate the fact that we have a great many more important duties to attend to. We've got a child missing, and every second we waste could make a difference. Thank you.'

He switched off the mike and nodded Megan toward a side door that would get them out of the room without having to pass through the swarm. Megan went readily, noticing that both Steiger and the county attorney remained behind to catch any leftover attention. The reporters rushed forward to snatch one more statement, one more sound bite. Paige snagged the sheriff, beating Forster to the punch. She turned her big phony blue eyes up at Steiger with an expression of interest-touched-with-awe, and the sheriff's chest puffed up a notch.

'She didn't waste any time catching herself a consolation prize,' Megan muttered as Mitch opened the door.

'Better him than me.'

'Ditto.'

They both heaved a sigh. Megan leaned back against the wall, grabbing a moment's peace. They had escaped into the garage that had once housed Deer Lake's entire fleet of fire trucks, all three of them. One remained, a round-fendered antique. Taking up most of the floor space now were a pair of hay wagons tricked out as parade floats. The near one featured a gigantic fiberglass trout leaping from a puddle of blue fiberglass water. Chicken wire had been stapled around the sides of the wagon and stuffed with blue and white paper napkins to form a decorative border. The glittering sign that rose at the back of the wagon invited one and all to CATCH SOME FUN at Trout Days, May 6, 7, 8.

The creation of the Deer Lake Trout Unlimited club was a far cry from the professionally designed floats of St Paul's Winter Carnival. It was quaint and tacky and the club members who had put it together in their spare time were probably enormously proud of it. The thought struck Megan unexpectedly, hitting a vulnerable spot, reminding her of the innocence and naïveté of small towns. Things that had been shattered in a single ruthless act.

ignorance is not innocence but SIN

Josh's image floated up in her memory, and she blinked it away before it could undermine her focus on the job.

'Steiger isn't going to be a problem, is he?' she asked, glancing at Mitch.

He mimicked her pose – shoulders back against the wall, arms crossed. He looked weary and dangerous despite the fact that he had obviously showered and shaved before coming back in. The rugged lines of his face were set like stone, deeply etched, weathered and tough. He looked at her sideways, his dark eyes narrowed.

'How do you mean?'

'That I-am-the-field-general shit. He isn't going to go territorial on us, is he? We don't need a loose cannon on a case like this.'

He shook his head a little, pulled a roll of Maalox tablets from his pants pocket, and thumbed one off. 'Russ is okay. He has to worry about the next election, that's all. He'll grab press time and I'll be glad to let him. I thank God daily my job isn't decided in a voting booth.'

But his reins were held by the town council, and Mitch had the sinking feeling that he would have to answer to each and every member before the day was out.

He rolled onto his left shoulder and gave Megan a wry look. 'I thought you were the loose cannon.'

Green eyes blinking innocence, she touched a hand to her chest. 'Who, me? Not me. I'm just doing my job.'

Mitch frowned at the reminder. 'Yeah. And I should have listened. Maybe if I'd moved as fast as you wanted to –'

'Don't,' Megan ordered, reaching out as if she meant to lay her hand on his arm.

The gesture was out of character and she caught it and pulled it back quickly. She wasn't a touchy-feely person. Even if she had been, the job would have cured her of it. She couldn't afford to make overtures that might somehow be misinterpreted. Image was everything to a woman in this business – her edge, her armor, her command for respect. Still, she couldn't simply dismiss the guilt in Mitch's face. In the back of her mind she could hear Paige Price's honey-smooth voice – *are your feelings tainted by the guilt related to your personal* . . . What? she wondered, and told herself it didn't matter. She couldn't let another cop second-guess himself when it wouldn't matter, that was all. Really.

'We were too late before we even knew,' she said. 'Besides, it's your town. You know it better than I do. You reacted accordingly. You did your best.'

Their voices had softened to whispers. Their gazes held fast. She looked so earnest, so sure that what she said was the absolute truth. Her green eyes glowed with it, and with the determination to make him see it. Mitch wanted to laugh – not with humor, but with the cynicism of someone who was too intimate with life's more twisted ironies. Apparently Megan hadn't seen enough to be jaded, hadn't failed enough to quit trusting herself. She would believe that good was good and bad was bad with no gray zone in between. He had believed that, too, once. Live by the rules. Do the job right. Fight the good fight. Toe the line and reap the rewards of a righteous man.

His mouth twisted in a sad parody of a smile. One of life's crueler jokes – there were no rewards, only random acts of good and madness. A truth he had tried to run from, but it had found him here, found his town, reached out and struck at Josh Kirkwood and his parents.

He touched Megan's cheek and wished he could lean down and kiss her. It would have been nice to taste some of that sweet certainty, to believe he could drink it in and heal the old wounds. But at the moment he felt he was tainting her enough as it was, so he tried to content himself with the feel of her skin warming beneath his palm.

'My best wasn't good enough,' he murmured. 'Again.'

Megan stared after him as he walked away, her fingertips brushing the side of her face, her heart beating a little too hard. Just a show of support for a fellow officer. Nothing personal. The covers slipped off to show those lies for what they were. Somewhere in that moment the lines of distinction had blurred. That was a dangerous thing for someone who needed to maintain a clear vision of the world and her place in it.

'Just so it doesn't happen again, O'Malley,' she whispered, refusing to acknowledge her lack of hope as she started for the door.

The office of the late lamented Leo Kozlowski resembled Leo as much as a room can resemble a person. Square and plain, it was an unkempt mess of rumpled papers and coffee stains, ripe with the aromas of stale cigars and Hai Karate.

'Jesus, Mary, and Joseph,' Megan muttered. She ventured slowly into the room, wrinkling her nose at the state of the place and at the vicious-looking dust-covered northern pike mounted on the wall with a cigar stuck in the corner of its toothy mouth. A monument to Leo's fishing skills and Rollie Metzler's taxidermy talents, she guessed.

Natalie scrunched her entire face into a look of utter disgust as she pulled the key from the lock. 'Leo was a hell of a guy,' she reiterated. 'Didn't know shit about housekeeping, but he was a hell of a guy.'

Megan reached into an abandoned doughnut box with a pencil and stabbed a cruller that was well on its way to petrification. She lifted it out and dropped it into the wastebasket. It sounded like a shotput landing in an oil drum. 'Good thing he didn't die in here. No one would have noticed.'

'I would have sent the cleaning people in after Leo passed on,' Natalie said. 'But we didn't want anyone touching anything until the new agent was assigned.'

'Lucky me.'

Megan pulled a brass nameplate out of her briefcase and set it along the front edge of the desk, staking her territory with the present she had bought herself to celebrate her new assignment. Her name was engraved in bold Roman type on the front: AGENT MEGAN O'MALLEY, BCA. On the back side was the motto TAKE NO SHIT, MAKE NO EXCUSES.

Natalie eyeballed both sides. She gave a crack of laughter as loud and abrupt as an air horn. 'You might just be all right, *Agent* O'Malley.'

'If the fumes don't get me first,' Megan said dryly.

She started sifting through the debris on the desk, shoving the paperwork into haphazard piles; discarding candy wrappers, enough empty foam coffee cups to put a hole in the ozone the size of Iowa, two glass ashtrays overflowing with cigar stubs, and a half-finished Slim Jim. She unearthed the telephone just as it began to ring.

Natalie laid the key on a square inch of bare space on the corner of the desk and backed out the door, promising to send someone from maintenance with a Dumpster and a case of air freshener. Megan waved her thanks and snatched up the receiver.

'Agent O'Malley, BCA.'

'The ink hasn't even dried on your transfer and already we've had no less than a dozen calls from reporters asking about you.'

At the sound of DePalma's voice, she closed her eyes and thought uncharitable thoughts about reporters and what they should do with their laminated press passes.

'The issue is the abduction, Bruce,' she said, sinking down into the old snot-green desk chair. The seat had been beaten into a sorry state by Leo's big behind, and listed sharply to the left. The upholstery was worn smooth in some spots, nubby in others, and spotted all over with stains of dubious origin that made Megan grimace. 'I'm doing everything I can to keep the reporters focused on the case instead of on me.'

'You had damn well better be. The superintendent doesn't want a spotlight put on the bureau. He sure as hell doesn't want you making headlines. Is that understood?'

'Yes, sir,' she answered with no small amount of resignation. The ghost of her headache was coming back to haunt her. She reached up and rubbed at it with two fingers.

'How's the search coming?'

'Nothing yet. We're praying for a lead. I don't expect the note to get us anywhere.'

'It's a tough deal – a child abduction,' DePalma said quietly, the professional concern melting into something personal. DePalma had three boys, one of them not much older than Josh. Megan had seen the family photograph on his desk many times. They all looked like Bruce, poor kids, miniature Nixon masks on gangly bodies of varying heights. 'I worked the Wetterling case,' he continued. 'It's tough on all concerned.'

'Yeah, it is.'

'Do your best and keep your head down.'

Mitch's words echoed in her mind as she hung up the phone and sank down into Leo's battered chair – *my best wasn't good enough . . . again.* She couldn't allow herself to wonder what he had meant by *again.* Their collective best had to be good enough for Josh.

The line from the note came back to her. She found a clear spot on the blotter between the coffee stains and phone numbers for local takeout restaurants and printed the message out in ink: *ignorance is not innocence but SIN.* Ignorance of what? Of whom? The quote was from Robert Browning. Was that significant? Her mind shuffled possibilities like a deck of cards. Ignorance, innocence, sin, poetry, literature – Books. She stopped on that card as the memory came and a dozen other questions rapidly branched off from it.

Her brain buzzing, she grabbed the phone and punched out the number for BCA records division. Sandwiching the receiver between her shoulder and her ear, she dug through her briefcase for the printout of known offenders and began scanning the list of names and addresses.

'Records. This is Annette speaking, how may I help you?'

'Annette, it's Megan O'Malley. Can you run one for me yesterday?'

'Anything for our conquering heroine. What's the grease spot's name?'

'Swain. Olie Swain.'

The morning was an endless barrage of phone calls and impromptu appointments. As predicted, Mitch had the town council members calling and Don Gillen, the mayor, in his office, all of them expressing their horror, their outrage, and their blind faith in Mitch's ability as chief of police to make it all better.

With the start of Snowdaze just a day away, there was much discussion over whether the event should be cancelled or postponed. On the one hand, it seemed ghoulish to proceed with the festivities. On the other were economic considerations, courtesies to the high school bands bussing into Deer Lake and the tourists who had already booked the hotels and B&Bs full. If they cancelled the event, would they be surrendering to violence? If they went on, would it be possible to use the event to the benefit of the case by amassing fresh volunteers and holding rallies to show support and raise money?

After twenty minutes with the mayor, Mitch washed his hands of those decisions. Don was a good man, capable, concerned. Mitch appreciated his problems but made it clear that his time had to be spent on the case.

In addition to Josh's disappearance, there were daily duties that couldn't be ignored – rounds of the jail, logs to review, paperwork to be dealt with, an ongoing investigation into a series of burglaries, a bulletin from the regional drug task force, a call from the administrator at Harris College about the criminology course Mitch was to help teach this semester. The tasks were the ordinary daily course of life for a small-town police chief. Today each one felt like a stone in an avalanche, all coming down on him at once.

Natalie stormed in and out of his office, relieving him of as much of the menial stuff as she could. He could hear her phone ringing almost without cease and silently blessed her for passing through only the most pressing of the calls to him. At twelve-fifteen she delivered a takeout bag from Subway. At two-fifteen she scolded him for not having opened it.

'You think the calories are going to jump out that bag and be absorbed into your body through the air?' she demanded, snapping a pen against the bag. 'You and my Troy ought to get together. He thinks just being in the same room with his advanced algebra book will be enough to make him into a mathematical genius. You all could start a club – the Osmosis Gang.'

'Sorry, Nat.' Mitch rubbed a hand across his eyes as he paged through six months' worth of reports of prowlers and Peeping Toms, looking for anything that might connect to Hannah or Paul or Josh or children in general. 'I just haven't had two seconds.'

'Well, take two now,' she ordered. 'You won't get through this day running on empty.'

'Yes, Mother.'

'And share some of those potato chips with *Agent* O'Malley,' she said, pulling the door open. Megan stood waiting on the other side. 'She looks like a stiff wind would blow her to Wisconsin.'

'I brought my own, thanks,' Megan said, holding up a banana.

Natalie rolled her eyes. 'A whole banana? How will you ever finish it?'

'I'll be lucky if I get to peel it, let alone take a bite,' she muttered, slumping down into the visitor's chair. She dropped a sheaf of computer paper onto the desk and deposited the banana on top of the pile.

'A little light reading?' Mitch asked, digging a turkey sandwich out of the Subway bag. He took a big bite and chewed aggressively, his eyes on Megan.

Her gaze fixed on his mouth, and a strange heat crept through her, which she put down to being overdressed. He ate like he didn't want to waste calories chewing, devouring the sandwich in huge bites. A small comma of mayonnaise punctuated his chin, shadowing his scar. He wiped it away impatiently and licked it off the pad of his thumb, an action that seemed to have too much influence over her pulse.

Disgusted with herself, she jerked her gaze away and did a quick survey of the office. Neat and tidy, it was devoid of mounted fish and bowling trophies. More curious, there was no ego wall of certificates and commendations. A cop of Mitch's stature and longevity would have accumulated a boxful by now. But the only frames that hung on the walls contained photographs of a little girl with long dark hair and a big yellow dog with an in-line skate in its mouth.

'Earth to O'Malley,' he said, waving a hand. 'What's the printout?'

'The known offenders,' she replied, kick-starting her brain. 'I've been trying to cross-reference with reports of recent incidents in the vicinity and DMV records when there was a vehicle sighted or involved on the off chance that something might eventually match up. Narrow down the possibilities, then if we get a break . . .'

'Find anything?'

'Not yet. I also called Records and ran a check on your boy Olie Swain – or tried to. They don't have anything on him. The guy doesn't have so much as a traffic ticket.'

Mitch took another bite out of the sandwich and wolfed it down. 'Olie? He's harmless.'

'You're that close, you and Olie?' she asked, holding up crossed fingers.

'No, but he's been here longer than me and we've never had a serious complaint against him.' He washed the turkey down with warm, flat Coke and grimaced.

Megan sat up straighter. 'Does that mean you've had complaints that *weren't* serious?'

He shrugged. 'One of the hockey moms got a little bitchy about him hanging around the kids at the rink, but it was nothing. I mean, hell, his job is at the rink. What's he supposed to do – hide out in his cubbyhole all day and night?'

'Did she allege anything specific?'

'That Olie gave her the creeps.'

97

'Gee, imagine that.'

'She also accused the Cub Scout leader of the same thing, told me I ought to send someone undercover into St Elysius because everyone knows priests are homosexual pedophiles and accused her son's second-grade teacher of subverting the minds of children by reading Shel Silverstein books aloud to the class and displaying the illustrations – which any Christian person can see are filthy with phallic symbols.'

'Oh.' She sank back down in her chair, chagrined.

'Right. The kids have never complained about Olie. The coaches have never complained about Olie. What set you off?'

'He gave me the creeps,' she said sheepishly, scowling at her banana as she peeled back the skin. She took a bite and chewed, regrouping mentally. Olie Swain still gave her the creeps. Unfortunately, that was not considered probable cause for running someone in and taking their fingerprints. 'He seemed evasive last night. Nervous. I got the impression he didn't like cops.'

'Olie's always nervous and evasive. It's part of his charm,' Mitch said, practicing a few evasive maneuvers of his own, shuffling papers as an excuse to keep from watching her wrap her lips around that banana. 'Besides, I ran a check on him myself when Mrs Favre made her complaint. Olie keeps his nose clean.'

'If no other part of his anatomy.' Megan wrinkled her nose at the remembered aroma of ripe body odor. 'You don't think he had anything to do with Josh disappearing?'

'He'd never have the balls to steal a kid, then stand there and look me in the eye and tell me he didn't know anything about it.'

'He looked you in the eye? With his real eye or the fake one?'

He shook his head at her as he leaned over to hit the button on the buzzing intercom. 'Yes?'

'Christopher Priest to see you, Chief,' Natalie announced. 'Says he might be able to help with the investigation.'

'Send him in.'

Mitch dumped the remnants of his lunch in the trash and scrubbed his hands with a napkin as he came around the desk. Megan stood, too, and tossed the last of her banana. Adrenaline shot through her at the possibility of a lead.

The man who let himself into the office didn't look like anyone's savior. He was small, slight, his body swallowed up by a blue and white varsity jacket from Harris College. Even with the jacket, no one would ever have mistaken him for a jock. Nothing short of a truckload of steroids could have delivered the professor from his computer-geek looks. Christopher Priest had the pale, fragile look of a man whose most dangerous sport was chess. Megan put him in his late thirties, five feet nine, mousy brown hair, dirt brown eyes behind a pair of glasses too big for his face. Unremarkable.

'Professor,' Mitch said, shaking hands. 'This is Agent O'Malley with the BCA. Agent O'Malley, Christopher Priest, head of the computer science department at Harris.'

They shook hands – Megan's firm and strong, a hand that could hold a Glock 9-mil semiautomatic without wavering; Priest's a thin, collapsible sack of bones that seemed to fold in on itself. She had to fight the urge to look down and make certain she hadn't hurt him. 'Your name seems familiar to me,' she said, scanning her brain for filed information. 'You do some work with juvenile offenders, right?'

Priest smiled, a mix of shyness and pride. 'My claim to fame – the Sci-Fi Cowboys.'

'It's a great program.' Mitch motioned Priest into a vacant chair as he went back around behind his desk. 'You should be proud of it. Taking kids off the wrong track and giving them a shot at getting an education and having a future is more than commendable.'

'Well, thanks, but I can't take all the credit. Phil Pickard and Garrett Wright put in a lot of time with the kids as well.' He settled into the chair, his oversize jacket creeping up around his earlobes, making him look like a cartoon turtle ready to pull his head into his shell. 'I heard about Josh Kirkwood. I feel so terrible for Hannah and Paul.'

'Do you know them well?' Megan asked.

'We're neighbors of a sort. Their house is the last one on Lakeshore Drive. Mine is behind them, in a manner of speaking, a quarter of a mile or so to the north through Quarry Hills Park. Of course, I know Hannah. Everyone in town knows Hannah. We've been on several charity committees together. Has there been any word?'

Mitch shook his head. 'You thought you might be able to help – in what way?'

'I heard you had set up a command post. That serves as a clearing-house for leads and information, right?'

'Yes.'

'Well, I remember reading the newspaper reports during the search for that young girl in Inver Grove Heights. The police talked about the volume of information they had to deal with and how cumbersome it was. Things got left out, some jobs were repeated several times due to lack of communication, it was time-consuming to cross-reference facts and so on.'

'Amen to that,' Megan said, fanning the pages of her known-offenders printout.

'I'd like to offer a solution,' Priest said. 'My department has plenty of personal computers available. With winter break, I'm short on students at the moment, but I know those who are still in town would be more than willing to help out. We can put everything you want on our computers, give you the ability to pull specific information, cross-reference, whatever you need. We can also scan in Josh's photo and send it across the United States and Canada on electronic bulletin boards. It would be a good project for my students and save you guys a lot of headaches.'

Mitch sat back and swiveled his chair as he thought. One of the things he missed most about being on a big-city police force was the access to equipment. The Deer Lake town fathers had seen a need for a pretty new building to house their jail and police department, but they were having a harder time seeing a need for up-to-date computer equipment. At present the department had half a dozen PCs from the Stone Age. Natalie brought in her own personal laptop to do her work.

'I don't know,' he said, scratching a hand back through his hair. 'The students might be privy to confidential information. They're not sworn personnel. That could be a problem.'

'Couldn't you deputize them or something?' Priest asked.

'Maybe. Let me check with the county attorney and I'll get back to you.'

The professor nodded and pushed himself up out of his chair. 'Just give me a call. Moving the equipment is no problem; we have access to a van. We'd be set up in no time.'

'Thanks.'

They shook hands again and Priest moved toward the door. He hesitated with his hand on the doorknob and shook his head sadly. 'This has been a bad week all the way around. Josh Kirkwood abducted. Now I'm off to the hospital to visit a student who was involved in that terrible car accident yesterday. My mother always said trouble comes in threes. Let's hope she was wrong.'

'Let's hope,' Mitch murmured as the professor went out, closing the door behind him.

'It would be great to have those computers,' Megan mused. 'It'd be even better if we had a lead or two to put in them.'

'Yeah. I haven't heard anything but lame excuses all day,' Mitch grumbled. 'I wish I were out there myself. Sitting around here is getting old in a hurry.'

'So let's go,' Megan said impulsively. She kicked herself mentally the instant the words came out. There was plenty of work to be done in the office, and it made no sense to pair herself with a man who could distract her by doing something so innocuous as chewing his lunch.

'I mean, I thought I'd go over to the command post and then join one of the teams for a couple of hours,' she back-pedaled smoothly. 'You could do that, too. Not *with* me, necessarily. In fact, it would probably be better if we split up.'

Mitch watched the color rise in her cheeks. His sense of humor was running low, but a smile of wry amusement curled up a corner of his mouth. It was a relief to think of something besides the case for a minute. The cool and collected Agent O'Malley blushing seemed as good a diversion as any.

He rose and strolled around the desk with his hands in his trouser pockets, his gaze pinning Megan to her chair. 'You're blushing, Agent O'Malley.'

'No. I'm just hot.' She winced mentally at the implications. 'It's warm in here.'

He prowled a little closer. 'You're hot?'

He looked into her eyes, his gaze shrewd and predatory. It seemed a prudent time to snap off a sharp retort and get her ass away from this fire. But no retort formed, no words came out of her dry mouth. Her muscles tightened, but she didn't move quickly enough. He read her thoughts and in a heartbeat was leaning down over her, his big hands gripping the arms of the chair as she jerked her own hands back.

'What's making you hot?' he whispered, forgetting his pledge to not want her. He liked the little rush of excitement. It made him feel alive instead of weary, made him feel anticipation instead of dread. 'Are you afraid to ride in the same car with me, Agent O'Malley?'

'I'm not afraid of you,' Megan whispered, grabbing ahold of her pride and wielding it like a sword. She didn't like this insidious desire that drifted in and out of their relationship like smoke. Elusive and intangible, it obscured boundaries, altered expectations. She didn't trust it, and she didn't trust herself when it came over her like a boiling tide. 'I'm not afraid of anything.'

Mitch watched her resolve harden in the deep green of her eyes. She would let him pursue the attraction just so far and then she started pushing back. Just as well, he told himself. Just as well for both of them. Wrong time, wrong place, wrong people. She had a chip on her shoulder the size of Gibraltar.

'Don't sell yourself short,' he murmured as the old weariness came washing back through him, dousing the spark. 'We're all afraid of something.'

10

Through the long hours of the day Hannah gained a new sympathy for the family members who sat in the hospital lounge waiting while their loved one underwent surgery. She could do nothing but wait and pray. There was no control. There was no participation. There was no energy to distract herself with menial chores – not that anyone would have allowed her to attend to menial chores. All she could do was wait and listen to the unearthly sound of helicopter blades beating the air as the search choppers passed slowly back and forth over the town. Giant vultures hovering over the rooftops, scanning the ground with electric eyes for any sign of her son . . . or his body.

Her house was full of interlopers. Strangers from the BCA, watching her telephone as if waiting for a vision. Friends from the neighborhood and from around town, watching *her* as if they all had money riding on the exact time she would have a nervous breakdown. They attended her tag-team fashion, one person hovering and fussing, denying her even the small comfort of tending to Lily's needs, while another did her laundry or scrubbed the soap scum out of her bathtub. Every hour or so they would switch jobs, and Hannah caught herself wondering which was considered the worst duty.

She knew which *she* hated most. She would rather have been cleaning her tile grout than sitting in the family room with watcher number two, a truth that clearly demonstrated how desperate she was feeling.

Paul would have readily testified that she had no affinity for housework. She managed the basics, but took no enjoyment in them. They were nothing but chores that seemed to need doing again the moment she had finished them. They took away time she would rather have spent with her children. She cursed every second she had spent vacuuming the carpet instead of playing with Josh. She cursed Paul for guilting her into continuing the thankless jobs. She would have long ago hired someone to come in and do the cleaning and the laundry and bake fresh cookies once a week if it hadn't been for Paul and his little digs about her lack of domesticity.

His mother's house always smelled of lemon oil and wax from polishing the furniture. His mother always spent Saturday baking bread and sweet rolls and cookies. Hannah had pointed out to him once that he hated his mother, never went to see his mother, had married his mother's opposite and therefore had no right to complain.

'At least I knew she was my mother. At least my father knew she was a woman –'

'You'd know I was a woman, too, if I weren't so exhausted from trying to keep this house up to your lofty standards –'

'The house? You're never in the damn house! You're at the hospital day and night –'

'I happen to think saving lives is a little more important than dusting and baking coffee cakes!'

It was a wonder she remembered the angry words so well; there had been so many of late.

Sighing, she rose and crossed the family room to the big picture window that looked out over the lake. A crooked arm of ice, Deer Lake was seven miles long and a mile across with half a dozen small fingers reaching into the wooded banks. Normally the view brought her a sense of peace. Today it only made her feel more restless and alone.

Cars hung precariously on the snow-packed shoulder of Lakeshore Drive. Reporters camped like hyenas on the fringe of a lion's fresh kill. Waiting for any scrap of news. Waiting for her to emerge so they could pounce on her and tear at her with their questions. A green and white patrol car sat parked in the driveway, a guardian sent by Mitch, God bless him. A mile to the north, ice-fishing huts dotted the public access area of the lake like multicolored mushrooms. No one had come to fish today. What little light the day had offered was fading away. Lights winked on in the houses that ringed the banks. School was out. There should have been children out on the ice, on the end of the lake that had been cleared of snow for skating. There were no children tonight. Because of Josh.

Because of me.

Like ripples in a pond, the effects reached out and touched the lives of people she didn't even know. Everyone was paying for her sin. It seemed such a small thing, a moment's slip, a forgivable lapse. But no one would forgive her, least of all Hannah herself. Josh was gone and she was sentenced to this punishment – to stand and do nothing while her neighbors cleaned her house and a cop sat at her kitchen table reading a paperback novel.

'The waiting is the worst.'

Hannah turned and stared at the woman from the missing children's group. Another of the unwanted entourage. She didn't know which was worse – pity from friends or from strangers. She hated the woman's I've-been-where-you-are-and-emerged-a-better-woman-for-it look. The woman stood beside her, the picture of upscale suburbia in a knit ensemble of hunter and rust, accessorized in brass, her deep red hair cut in a smooth shoulder-length bob.

'I went through this two years ago,' the woman confided. 'My ex-husband stole our son.'

'Were you frightened for his life?' Hannah asked bluntly.

The woman frowned a little. 'Well, no, but —'

'Then I'm sorry, but I don't think you can possibly know what I'm feeling.'

Ignoring the woman's expression of shock, Hannah walked past her and into the kitchen.

'It was still a trauma!' the woman exclaimed, outrage ringing in her voice.

The cop glanced up from his book, looking as if he wanted no part of this scene. Hannah didn't blame him. She wanted no part of it, either.

'I have to get some air,' she said. 'I'll be just outside if the phone rings.'

In the mud room she pulled on the old black parka Paul used for weekend dirty work. As she grabbed mittens off the shelf she visualized the sniping match that would go on if he came home and caught her wearing his coat.

'*You have coats of your own.*'

'*What's the difference? You weren't wearing this one.*'

She wouldn't try to explain to him that it somehow made her feel safer, protected, loved to wear something of his. It made no sense — would certainly make no sense to Paul — that she could draw more comfort from his clothing than she could from him. She could never explain to him that the clothes were like memories of what they had once shared, of who he had once been. They were the shrouds of ghosts, and she wrapped herself in them and ached for what had died in their marriage.

She pulled open the door to the garage and gasped at the dark figure of a man standing on the stoop with his fist raised.

'Hannah!'

'Oh, my God! Father Tom! You nearly gave me a heart attack!'

The priest offered a sheepish smile. He was young — mid-thirties — tall with an athletic build. Her nurse and friend from the ER, Kathleen Casey, always teased him that he was too good-looking to have taken himself out of the eligible bachelor pool — a joke that never failed to bring a little blush to Tom McCoy's cheeks. Hannah didn't think of him as handsome. The word that came to her when she looked at Father Tom was *kind*. He had a strong, kind face, kind blue eyes. Eyes that offered understanding and sympathy and forgiveness from behind a pair of round wire-framed glasses.

He had been the priest at St Elysius for two years and was enormously popular with the younger parishioners. Hardliners found him a little too unconventional for their tastes. Albert Fletcher, St Elysius's only deacon, was a vocal opponent to what he called 'this New Age Catholicism,' but then, Albert was also against women wearing slacks and often hinted that Vatican II was the work of the Antichrist. Paul derisively called Father Tom's off-the-cuff homilies his 'lounge act,' but Hannah found them refreshing and insightful. Tom McCoy was a bright, articulate man with a degree in philosophy from Notre Dame and a heart as big as his home state of Montana. On a day as black as this one, she couldn't think of anyone she would rather have as a friend.

'I thought it would be better if I came in this way.' A hint of the West accented his warm voice. 'There are an awful lot of people watching your front door.'

'Yes, it's Eyes-on-Hannah-Garrison Day,' she said without humor. 'I was just trying to escape for a few minutes.'

'Would you rather I left?' He stepped down to the garage floor, showing his sincerity, giving her the chance to answer honestly. 'If you need to be alone –'

'No. No, don't go.' Hannah walked out onto the stoop and listened to the soft hiss of the storm door as it closed behind her. 'Alone isn't really what I want, either.'

As her eyes adjusted to the faint gray light, her gaze wandered the cavernous garage, hitting on Josh's bike. Hanging on the wall. Abandoned. Forgotten. A fist of emotion slammed into her diaphragm. She had managed to cocoon herself in numbness all day, as the watchers and well-wishers and sympathizers came and went. But the sight of the dirt bike punched a hole in the gauze, punched a hole in her heart, and the pain came pouring out.

'I just want my son back.'

She sank down on the cold concrete step, her legs buckling as her strength drained away. She might have fallen to the floor if not for Father Tom. He was on the step beside her in an instant, catching her. He slid an arm around her shoulders and held her gently. She turned her face into his shoulder and wept, the tears soaking into the heavy wool of his topcoat.

'I just want him back. . . . Why can't I have him back? Why did this have to happen? He's just a little boy. How could God do this? How could God let this happen?'

Tom said nothing. He let Hannah cry, let her ask the questions. He thought she didn't really expect answers, which was just as well, because he didn't have any answers to give. He himself had asked all the same questions of a higher power, and his ears still rang with the silence. He didn't know a better person than Hannah. So gracious, so caring, dedicated to her children and to helping others. Her soul was as good as they came. In a just world, bad things wouldn't happen to people like Hannah or innocent children like Josh. But the world was not a just place. It was a hard place full of random cruelty, a truth that always brought him to question God. *If the world is an unjust world, then is God therefore an unjust God?* The guilt that accompanied the question was heavy and cold inside him. Blind faith remained beyond his reach. Doubt was his cross to bear.

He couldn't offer Hannah answers, only comfort. He couldn't take away her pain, but he could share it with her. So he sat on the hard, cold step with his arms around her and let her cry, his heart aching for her, his own tears rolling down into the thick tangle of her honey-blond hair. When she had cried herself out he pulled a handkerchief from his pocket and pressed it into her hand.

'I'm sorry,' she whispered, edging away from him, lifting her face from his shoulder and turning it away. 'I don't cry on people. I don't fall apart and make other people pick up the pieces.'

'I'll never tell,' he promised, gently stroking the back of her head. 'I'm a priest, remember?'

Hannah tried to laugh, but the sound caught in her throat. She stared down at the handkerchief, her brows drawing together.

'It's clean,' he teased, giving her shoulders a squeeze. 'I promise.'

She sniffed and tried to smile. 'I was looking at the monogram. F?'

'Christmas gift from a parishioner. F for Father Tom.'

The naïveté of the gesture struck her as sad and sweet and squeezed another pair of tears from her eyes. She wiped them away with the linen and blew her nose as delicately as she could manage. They sat in silence for a while. Night had fallen. The temperature was noticeably dropping. The front security light outside had come on automatically and burned brightly against the dark, warding off danger. What a joke.

'You're entitled to fall apart, Hannah,' Tom said softly. 'The rest of us are supposed to lift you up and hold you together. That's the way it works.'

He didn't understand, she thought. The lifting and the holding had always been her jobs. Now that she was the one in pieces, everyone just stared at her and didn't know what to do.

'Has there been any word?'

Hannah shook her head. 'I feel so helpless, so useless. At least Paul can go out with the search party. All I can do is wait . . . and wonder . . . This must be what hell is like. I can't imagine anything worse than what's gone through my mind in the last twenty-two hours.'

She rose slowly, went down the steps to the door that opened to the backyard, and stared out the window into the dark. Weak yellow light seeped out the kitchen window, staining the snow. Gizmo lay in the amber rectangle, a huge immobile lump of shaggy hair. Beyond the dog, the shadow of the swing set stood out, black on white, then the yard melted into the thick woods that wrapped around the north end of the lake, giving the neighborhood a sense of seclusion.

'I did my residency at Hennepin County Medical Center,' she said, her voice a flat monotone. 'That's a tough ER, a tough part of town, you know. I've seen things . . . the things people can do to one another . . . the things people can do to a child. . . .'

The words faded. She stared out through the window, but Tom could tell she was seeing another place, another time. Her face was strained and pale. He stood beside her and waited quietly, patiently.

'. . . Unspeakable things,' she whispered. Even with the oversize coat, he could tell she was breathing hard, trembling. 'And I think of Josh –'

'Don't,' he ordered.

She looked at him sideways and waited. There was no expectation in her eyes, no hope that he would say something that could brighten her perspective. Seldom in his years as a priest had he felt so impotent, so ill equipped to give anything of worth to someone who was suffering. She stared at him and waited, her eyes big and fathomless in the absence of light, her lovely face cast in shadows.

'It won't help,' he said at last. 'You're only torturing yourself.'

'I deserve it.'

'Don't say that.'

'Why not? It's true. If I'd been there to pick him up, he would be with us now.'

'You were trying to save a life, Hannah.'

'Kathleen told you that, didn't she?' He didn't answer. He didn't have to; she knew Kathleen too well. 'Did she tell you I went zero for two last night? Ida Bergen died and I lost Josh in the bargain.'

'They'll find him. You have to believe that, Hannah. You have to have faith.'

'I had faith that this would never happen,' she said bitterly. 'I'm all out of faith.'

He couldn't blame her. He supposed he should have tried to prod her into retracting the statement. He could have wielded that favorite old Catholic club of guilt, but he didn't have the heart for it. In times like these he had enough trouble hanging on to his own faith. He wasn't hypocrite enough to castigate someone else.

The fire went out of Hannah abruptly. She heaved a sigh and rubbed her mittened hands over her face and back through her hair. 'I'm sorry, Father,' she whispered. 'I shouldn't –'

'Don't apologize for how you feel, Hannah. You're entitled to react.'

'And rail at God?' Her mouth twisted up at one corner as a new sheen of tears glazed across her eyes.

'Don't worry about God. He can take it.'

He reached out and tenderly brushed a tear from her cheek with the pad of his thumb. For the first time Hannah noticed he wasn't wearing gloves. His thumb was cold against her skin. Father Tom, the absentminded. He routinely forgot little things like wearing gloves in freezing weather, eating meals, and getting his hair cut. The trait brought out the maternal qualities in all the women of St Elysius Parish.

'You forgot your gloves again,' she said, drawing his hand down and holding it between hers to warm it. 'You'll end up with frostbite.'

He shook off her concern. 'More important things on my mind. I wanted to let you know I'm here for you – for you and Paul.'

'Thank you.'

'I've organized a prayer vigil for Josh. Tonight at eight. I'm praying we won't need it by then,' he added, squeezing her hand tight.

'Me, too,' Hannah whispered. She couldn't tell him that she had the sick, hollow feeling her prayers weren't going anywhere, that the pleas did nothing but bounce around inside her head. She clung to his hand a second longer, desperate to absorb some of his strength and faith.

'Would you like to stay for supper?' she asked, scraping together her manners again, and again need and honesty cut through them. 'I have a house full of women who don't know what to do except stare at me and thank their lucky stars they aren't in my shoes,' she confided. 'It would be nice to break that up. On the menu we have a variation on the miracle of the loaves and fishes – the miracle of the tuna casseroles. I can't imagine there's a can of tuna left in town.'

'Did Ann Mueller bring the kind with the fried onions on top?' he asked, giving her a gentle comic look of speculation, giving her something other than pity.

'And a pan of crème de menthe brownies.'

He grinned and draped an arm around her shoulders, steering her toward the kitchen door. 'Then I'm all yours, Dr Garrison.'

5:28 p.m. 17°

Mitch walked alone down the hall of Deer Lake Elementary School. Immune to his teasing, Megan had gone off with two of his officers for round two of questioning Josh's hockey buddies and the youth team coaches. Had they seen anything at all? Had Josh talked to them about being afraid of somebody? Had Josh been acting differently? The questions would be asked again and again by this cop, that cop, the next cop, all of them hoping to shake loose a memory. All of them hoping to find some small piece of information that might seem insignificant in itself but fit together with another piece to form a lead. It may have seemed tedious to the people being questioned, and it certainly created mountains of paperwork, but it was necessary.

Mitch had chosen to meet with the schoolteachers and other school personnel for the same purpose. One of his men had already questioned Josh's teacher, Sara Richman. Mitch addressed the entire staff in the cafeteria, conducting the meeting as an informal question-and-answer session. He told them what little he knew, tried to stem the flow of wild rumors, asked them for any information they had. Had anyone been hanging around the school? Had any of the children reported being approached by a stranger?

Mitch studied the faces in the room – the teachers, the cooks, the janitors, the office help – wondering, as a cop, if any one of them could have done this; wondering, as a father, if any of the people who came into contact with his daughter every day could have been a danger to her.

After nearly two hours, he left them to their own discussion of plans for a schoolwide safety assembly, and headed down the long hall for the side door. His head felt like a walnut in a vise. Questions chased each other around and around his brain. Questions with no answers. He had his own staff meeting at six, to talk with his men about what the day had yielded in terms of information, and to brainstorm for ideas. With no real leads and no real suspects, it was difficult to focus the investigation.

As he walked, Mitch couldn't help but notice the miniature lockers that made him feel like a giant, the artwork taped to the walls at his hip level. He caught glimpses of classrooms with pint-size desks. All of it served only to make him more painfully aware of the vulnerability of children.

He had asked to look inside Josh's locker. One of O'Malley's evidence techs had beat him to it, cleaning out Josh's desk and locker of notebooks and textbooks, leaving behind a stash of Gummi Bears and Super Balls and a glow-in-the-dark yo-yo. The detritus of boyhood. Evidence of nothing more than Josh's normalcy and innocence.

Every day this hall was filled with little kids just like Josh, just like his Jessie. It pissed him off to think that all of them would be touched by this crime. Their innocence would be marred like a clean white page streaked by dirty fingers.

Mitch didn't bother to zip his coat as he stepped outside, but he dug his gloves out of his pockets and pulled them on. Day had yielded to night. Security lights shone against the brick walls of the school and illuminated the parking lot at intervals.

The school had been built in 1985 to educate the children of baby boomers and the influx of new families into Deer Lake. The site was on Ramsey Drive, in a newer part of town, just two blocks from the even newer fire station, ensuring disruptions of class every time a fire truck rolled out for duty. The parking lot stretched out before Mitch, edged on two sides by thick rows of spruce trees. The playground sprawled across three acres just to the west. A handy arrangement for parents picking up their kids – or for anyone looking to steal a kid.

Now everywhere Mitch looked he saw hazards, potential for danger, where before he had seen only a nice, neat, quiet town. The knowledge served only to darken his mood. Fishing his keys out of his pocket, he headed for the Explorer.

The truck sat alone in the second row, just out of reach of a light. Mitch stuck the key in the lock of the door, his mind already on the meeting to come and the night beyond that. He wanted to make it to his in-laws before eight o'clock, before Joy could get Jessie into pajamas. He wanted his daughter home with him tonight. A brief oasis of normalcy before another day of madness and frustration.

As he moved to open the truck's door, something caught his eye, something out of place, something on the hood.

Even as he turned, the reaction began – the rush of adrenaline, the tightening of nerves, the instincts coming to attention. Even as he reached for the spiral notebook, his heart was pounding.

He picked it up gingerly, pinching the wire spine between left thumb and forefinger, lifting the opposite edge with the tip of his right forefinger. The cover was dark green, decorated with the image of Snoopy as Joe Cool. Printed in Magic Marker across the top was 'Josh Kirkwood 3B'.

Mitch swore. His hands were shaking as he eased the book back down on the hood. He went into the truck and returned with a flashlight and a slim gold pen. Using the pen, he opened the notebook and turned the pages.

Nothing remarkable, just a little boy's doodling. Drawings of race cars and rocket ships and sports heroes. Notes about kids in his class. A boy named Ethan who puked during music – *He herled chunks all over Amy Masons shoes!* A girl named Kate who tried to kiss him at his locker – *gross! gross! gross!* On one page he had carefully traced the Minnesota Vikings' logo and drawn a jersey with the number twelve and the name KIRKWOOD in block letters.

A little boy's dreams and secrets. And tucked in before the final page, a madman's message.

i had a little sorrow, born of a little SIN

11

Hannah took one look at the notebook, turned chalk white, and sank into the nearest chair. It was Josh's, no question. She knew it well. He called it his 'think pad.' He carried it everywhere – or had.

'He lost it,' she murmured, rubbing her fingers over the plastic evidence bag, wanting to touch the book. Something of Josh. Something his kidnapper had tossed back at them. A taunt. A cruel flaunting of power.

'What do you mean, he lost it?' Mitch asked, kneeling beside her, trying to get her to look at him instead of the notebook. 'When?'

'The day before Thanksgiving. He was frantic. I told him he must have left it at school,' she said. 'But he swore he hadn't. We tore the house apart looking for it.'

She remembered that all too well. Paul had come home from racquetball and blown up at the sight of the mess. His family was coming for Thanksgiving. He wanted the house to be perfect, to rub it in to his relatives how well he had done. He hadn't wanted to waste time looking for a stupid notebook he thought could be easily replaced.

Hannah looked down at that 'stupid notebook' now and wanted to hug it to her chest and rock it as if it were Josh himself. She wanted to turn to Paul and ask him how he felt about Josh's stupid notebook now, but Paul had yet to come home. She imagined he had gone straight from the search to the prayer vigil – something she couldn't think of facing. Father Tom had understood. Somehow she knew Paul would not.

'He was upset for days,' she murmured. 'It was like losing a diary.'

Megan exchanged looks with Mitch. 'He must have found it again, though,' she said. 'He must have had it with him last night.'

Hannah shook her head, never taking her gaze off the book lying in her lap. 'I never saw it again. I can't believe he wouldn't have told me if he found it.'

Lily peeked around the side of the chair, turning an impish smile up at her mother, her blue eyes wide, her golden curls tousled around her head. The notebook caught her eye and she gave a little squeal of delight, pointing a finger at the figure of Snoopy on the cover.

'Mama! Josh!' she declared. Giggling, she reached for the notebook.

Mitch caught the end of the plastic bag and lifted it away from her. Megan took the bag from him. 'I'll give this to my guy,' she murmured. 'It'll be in the lab first thing in the morning.'

Mitch remained behind to offer empty words of little comfort and less hope. Hannah seemed dazed. A blessing, he supposed. He left her sitting in the wing chair with Lily on her lap and a cop in her kitchen.

Megan waited for him in the Explorer. She had come to the elementary school in a squad car with Joe Peters, the officer who had been helping her interview the youth hockey crowd. They had yet to return to City Center, where her Lumina was parked.

The search of the school grounds had been an exercise in futility and frustration. The notebook could have appeared by magic for all anyone could discern. The school staff had all been in the cafeteria with Mitch – no witnesses. It would have been simple enough to drive up alongside the Explorer and place the book on the hood. The perpetrator wouldn't have even had to get out of his car. Slick, simple, diabolical.

Fury curdling like sour milk in his stomach, Mitch climbed into the truck and slammed the door shut.

'Mother-fucking son of a bitch!' he snarled, pounding a hand against the steering wheel. 'I can't believe he just plunked it down on the hood of my truck. *Here, chump, get a clue!* Fuck!'

Like throwing down the gauntlet, he thought, and the thought sickened him. It turned a crime into a game. *Catch me if you can.* A mind that worked that way had to be black with rot and soaked with arrogance. So sure of himself he believed he could drop evidence in their laps and calmly slip away – which was exactly what he had done.

'I want this bastard,' he growled, twisting the key in the ignition.

Megan took his temper and his language in stride. Neither were anything new to her. In his position she imagined she would have been saying the same things. The kidnapper had shown him up, made him feel like a fool. It was difficult not to take that personally, but personal couldn't enter into the picture. There was too much potential for distorting perceptions.

The notebook was the only lead they'd picked up since the night before. Nothing had been turned up by the teams in the field. The volunteer ground search had been called for the day. Teams of Deer Lake police, the county boys, and Megan's agents-on-loan from the St Paul regional district continued on, checking vacant and abandoned buildings, warehouses, the railroad yard; patrolling the streets and side roads for signs of anything remotely suspicious; following up on anything promising picked up by the flyboys in the search choppers, scrambling from point to point like participants in a macabre scavenger hunt.

The BCA and State Patrol helicopters would continue through the night, creeping over every inch of Park County again, their rotors breaking the quiet peace of the winter night. But unless they found something to go on, they would not be coming back the following day. They had covered a territory of two hundred square miles with nothing to show for it and no clue as to which direction to expand the search.

At the command post the hotline phones had been ringing off the hooks – mostly calls from concerned citizens wanting to check up on the progress of the search or express their fears and anger about the abduction. No one had seen a thing. No one had seen Josh. It was as if an unseen hand had reached out of another dimension and plucked him off the earth.

And the clock was ticking. Twenty-six hours had passed, the sense of urgency and desperation increasing with every one of them. Twenty-four was the magic number. If the missing person wasn't found in the first twenty-four hours, the odds against finding the victim went up with every passing minute.

Night had fallen around them like a black steel curtain. The wind was starting to pick up, whipping mare's tails of snow along the white-blanketed ground. The temperature kept dropping, aiming for a nighttime low of ten degrees. Cold, but January nights could get colder. Ten below zero, twenty below, thirty below. Brutal cold. Deadly cold. In the back of everyone's mind was the fear that Josh's abductor might have left him somewhere, alive only to die of exposure before anyone could get to him.

'We need to go over these pages,' Megan said, looking down at the stack of photocopies on her lap, copies of every page in Josh's think pad. 'I can't imagine the kidnapper would have left anything truly incriminating in it, but who's to say.'

Mitch turned toward her. In the glow of the dashboard lights, his lean face was all rough angles and shadowed planes, the deep-set eyes hard and unblinking.

'What about the big question?' he asked. 'Where and when did our bad guy get the book? It's been missing nearly two months. If he's had it all that time, we're looking at a crime with a lot of premeditation.'

'And where did he get it from? Josh's locker? That could implicate a school employee –'

'Anybody can walk into that school at any time of the day. The halls aren't monitored. There are no locks on the lockers.'

'Josh might have dropped the notebook walking home,' Megan offered. 'Anybody walking down the street could have picked it up. Anybody coming into the Kirkwood house might have taken it, for that matter.'

Mitch said nothing as he backed the Explorer out of the drive and headed it south on Lakeshore, then east on Ninth Avenue. He ran through the mental list of new complications created by the notebook.

'We'll have to find out if any school employees were missing from that meeting tonight, find out if anybody's been fired in the last six months, get a list of everyone who has been through Hannah and Paul's house since mid-November – friends, neighbors, service people . . .'

The idea of the manpower, the tedium, the paperwork, was daunting. The irony made him see red – that their perpetrator had handed them a clue and in doing so had built a bigger haystack to hide the needle in.

Mitch swore. 'I need some food and a bed.'

'I can offer the first,' Megan said cautiously. 'You're on your own for the bed.'

It wasn't that she wanted his company, she told herself. It had nothing to do with the hollow feeling that came with the thought of sitting alone in her apartment that night. She had spent most of her life alone. Alone was no big deal.

Josh's image floated through her mind like a specter as the glowing green numbers of the dashboard clock marked another passing minute. Alone was a very big deal. Like most of the cops on the case, she would have worked around the clock if she could have forgone food and rest, but the body needed refueling. So she would pull herself off the streets for a few hours and lie in bed staring at the dark, brooding about Josh while the clock ticked. And Mitch would do the same.

'We can go over these pages without any distractions,' she said.

'Do you have utilities?' Mitch asked, his thoughts following the same line.

'I'm hopeful, but as a born cynic I took the precaution of calling for a pizza on your cellular phone while you were talking to Hannah.'

He arched a brow. 'Using police equipment for personal business, Agent O'Malley? I'm shocked.'

'I consider the need for pizza a police emergency. And so will the delivery boy if he knows what's good for him.'

'Where are you living?'

'Eight sixty-seven Ivy Street. Drop me off at my car and I'll lead the way.'

'We go back to the station now, we've got reporters to face,' Mitch said. 'My temper is too short for one more asinine question.'

'Then I guess I won't ask you if you're a mushroom man or strictly a pepperoni guy.'

'My only requirement tonight is that it isn't alive and it doesn't have hair. We'll eat, take a look at these pages. With any luck, by the time we get back to the station the press people will have given up for the night.'

They rolled past the turn for downtown and City Center. Mitch hit the blinker when they reached Ivy Street and eased the Explorer in along the curb. The three-story house on the corner was a huge old Victorian that had been cut up into apartments. The wraparound porch was lit up invitingly, the lack of natural light hiding the fact that the house was in need of a coat of paint. A Christmas wreath still hung on the front door.

They climbed the creaking old staircase to the second floor and wound their way down a hall. The sounds of television sets and voices drifted out of apartments. Someone had fried onions for supper. A mountain bike was propped in the hall with a sign taped to the handlebars – RIGGED TO BLOW. THIEVES, TAKE YOUR CHANCES. Then they turned onto another flight of stairs and left the neighbors behind.

'I've got the third floor to myself,' Megan explained, digging her keys out of her coat pocket. 'It's big enough for only one apartment.'

'What made you pick this place instead of one of the apartment complexes?'

She shrugged off the question a little too easily. 'I just like old houses. They have character.'

A blast of heat hit them as she opened the door. Light banished the darkness as she hit the switch.

'Behold utilities!'

'God, it must be eighty degrees in here!' Mitch declared, peeling his coat off and tossing it over the back of a chair.

'Eighty-two.' Megan gasped for breath and gave the thermostat a twist. 'Guess there's a trick to this. I had it set for seventy-two.' She sent Mitch a wry look as she shrugged out of her parka. 'You ought to like this, you're from Florida.'

'I've acclimated. I own snowshoes. I go ice fishing.'

'Masochist.'

She tossed the stack of photocopies on the table and disappeared down the hall and into what Mitch guessed was a bedroom. He stood in the center of the living room and surveyed the apartment, trying to find clues to Megan O'Malley as he rolled up his shirtsleeves.

The kitchen and living area flowed together, divided only by an old round oak table surrounded by mismatched antique chairs. The kitchen cupboards were painted white and looked as though they had been salvaged out of another old house. The walls were a soft rose pink and, while he knew Megan couldn't have had time to paint them herself, he thought they suited her. He also thought she would deny it if he said so. The color was too feminine. That was a side she didn't show to the public. But he had caught glimpses of it.

The furniture in the living room was all old, and what he could see of it was lovingly well kept. Boxes were piled on every available surface. Books, dishes, quilts, more books. It looked as if nothing but the bare essentials had been unpacked.

'Just move the boxes anywhere if you want to sit down,' she called.

She emerged from the bedroom rolling up the sleeves of a flannel shirt three sizes too big for her. The heavy sweater and turtleneck were gone. The black leggings remained, hugging her slim legs like a second skin. A pair of shorthaired cats wound themselves around her ankles, begging for attention. The larger one was black with a white bib, white paws, a crooked tail, and a complaining voice. The smaller one, a gray tabby, flung himself on the rug in front of her and rolled on his back, purring loudly.

'Beware the watchcats,' she said dryly. 'If they mistake you for a giant hunk of Little Friskies, you're a goner.' She turned for the kitchen and they trotted after her with their tails straight up. 'The black one is Friday,' she said, popping open a can of food. 'The gray one is Gannon.'

Mitch smiled to himself. She would name her cats after the characters on *Dragnet*. Nothing soft and fuzzy, no Puff, no Fluff. Cop names.

'My daughter would love them,' he said. Guilt nipping him, he checked his watch and realized he'd missed Jessie's bedtime for the second night in a row. 'We've got a dog and that's enough animal life for our house. She's been begging her grandparents to get a kitten, but her grandfather is allergic.' Or at least that was Joy's excuse. Dump the blame on Jurgen. Mitch suspected it was more a matter of Joy being allergic to changing litter boxes and brushing hair off her furniture.

'You're lucky to have someone to look after her,' Megan said. She tossed the empty can in the trash and bent to dig through a brown Coleman cooler on the floor next to the refrigerator.

'Yeah, I guess,' Mitch said, taking the bottle of Harp she handed out to him. 'I'd rather be with her myself.'

'Really?'

'Yeah, really,' he answered defensively, trying to decipher the expression in her eyes. Surprise? Vulnerability? Wariness? 'Why wouldn't I? She's my daughter.'

She lifted a shoulder but dodged his eyes, dropping her gaze to her hands as she twisted the cap off her beer. 'Raising a child alone is a burden a lot of men wouldn't want.'

'Then there are a lot of men who shouldn't be fathers.'

'Well . . . that's a fact.'

Mitch stood with the beer bottle dangling from his fingers, his attention sharp on Megan as she tossed the cap in the wastebasket and took a long drink. The offhand remark had a sting of truth in it, an old thread of experience.

'You said your dad was a cop.'

'Forty-two years in the blue.' She leaned back against the counter, crossing her ankles, crossing her arms. 'Got his sergeant's stripes and never went any higher. Never wanted to. As he says to anyone who will listen, all the *real* cop work is done in the trenches.'

The touch of humor didn't quite cover the bitterness. She heard it, too. He saw the flash of caution in her eyes. Setting her beer aside, she turned to the window above the sink, opened it a crack, then stood back and stared out at nothing. Mitch moved to the end of the counter, just close enough to read her, just close enough to feel her tension.

'Got any brothers?'

'One.'

'He a cop, too?'

'Mick?' She laughed. 'God, no. He's an investment broker in L.A.'

'So you followed in Dad's footsteps instead?'

He didn't know how true that was, Megan thought, staring out at the night as its cool breath whispered in through the open window. It had begun to snow lightly, fine, dry flakes sifting down from the clouds, shimmering like sequins under the streetlight. She had spent much of her life dogging her father like a shadow, unknown, unseen. What a sad, stupid cycle of life.

In the corner of her eye she could see Mitch standing there, tie loose around his neck, top two buttons of his shirt undone, sleeves rolled up neatly, exposing muscular forearms dusted with dark hair. The pose was nonchalant, but there was a certain tension in the broad shoulders. His expression was pensive, expectant, the dark, deep-set eyes locked on her, studying, waiting.

'I like the job,' she said flatly. 'It suits me.'

It suited the image she presented the world, Mitch thought. Terrier-tough, tenacious, all business. It suited the image she was trying to present to him. He should have taken it at face value. God knew, she was trouble enough as the first female field agent the bureau had ever inflicted upon the unsuspecting county cops of rural Minnesota. He didn't need to look deeper. He didn't need to understand her.

Still, he caught himself moving toward her, close enough so he could feel the electrical field come to life between them, close enough that she narrowed her eyes in subtle warning. But she didn't back away. She wouldn't. He was probably a fool to let that please him, but he didn't seem to have any say in the matter. His response to her was elemental, instinctive. She was a challenge. He wanted to crack the tough-cookie façade. He wanted . . . and that surprised him. He hadn't wanted a woman since Allison. He had *needed* and he had succumbed to that need, but he hadn't *wanted*. It amazed him to want now, to want her.

'Yeah, the job suits you,' he murmured. 'You're a tough cookie, O'Malley.'

Megan lifted her chin a proud notch, not taking her eyes off him. 'Don't you forget it, Chief.'

He was standing too close. Again. Close enough that she could see the shadow of his evening beard on his hard jaw. Close enough that some reckless part of her wanted to lift a hand and touch it . . . and touch the scar that hooked across his chin . . . and touch the corner of his mouth, where it pulled into a frown of concentration. Close enough that she could see into the depths of the whiskey-brown eyes that looked as though they had seen far too much, none of it good.

Her heart beat a little harder.

'We have a case to discuss,' she reminded him. He raised a hand and pressed a finger against her lips.

'Ten minutes,' he whispered, lifting her chin with his thumb. 'No case.' He leaned down and touched his lips to hers. 'Just this.'

He parted her lips and slid his tongue between them, into her, as if he had every right; plunging deep and retreating slowly in a rhythm that was primal and unmistakable, blatantly carnal. She rose in his arms, into the kiss, answering with a hunger of her own.

His hands slid over her back and he pressed closer, trapping her between the cupboards and his body. For just this sliver of time there was nothing but need between them. Simple. Strong. Burning. His body was hot and hard, muscle and desire, undeniably male. And she was melting against him, on fire.

With his hands at her waist, Mitch lifted her easily and set her on the counter. She let her knees part, let her stocking feet hook around behind his thighs as he stepped in close. As he found her mouth again, she speared her fingers back through his thick hair and ran them down the muscles of his neck to his big, hard shoulders. He cradled her face in his hands as the kiss grew wilder, more urgent. Her barrette clattered into the sink and her hair spilled around her shoulders, mahogany silk he sifted through his fingers and combed back from her face.

Even as the cool night air streamed in through the window, the heat around them and between them intensified. The back of his shirt was damp with it. It burned the breath from her lungs. A bead of perspiration pooled in the hollow at the base of her throat and trickled down. He chased it with his lips. Her head fell back. Her eyes drifted shut. She could feel his knuckles against her chest as he thumbed the buttons of her shirt free. Then the flannel dropped back off her shoulders and his mouth was on her breast.

She gasped as he took her nipple between his lips and caressed it with his tongue. The need exploded. Tore through her. Shocked her back to sanity.

Mitch knew the instant it happened. He heard her sharp intake of breath, felt the muscles of her back go rigid beneath his hands. And he thanked God she had a better warning system than he did, or in another five minutes he would have taken her right there without benefit of a bed or any other consideration. He wanted her too badly and for reasons he couldn't quite fathom. Need pounded through his body, throbbing relentlessly in his groin.

Slowly he raised his head, raised his heavy-lidded gaze to meet hers. Just as slowly he pulled the halves of her shirt together over her small, plump breasts and held them there.

'You're sure you won't reconsider on the offer of the bed?' he asked, his voice a low, husky rasp.

'I'm sure,' she murmured.

He let her slide down from the counter but held her there, trapped her there with his legs on either side of hers. Leaning down, he feathered slow, soft kisses along her hairline and drew her up against him, pressing his erection against her belly, letting her know just what he wanted, just what she did to him.

Megan trembled at the feel of him hard against her, at the mental image of the two of them together, naked in the bed in the next room. She trembled at the ache of desire and at the consequences that desire could bring. He could ruin her, ruin the career she had worked so hard to build. And even knowing that, she wanted him. The wind blew in through the open window behind her and chilled the sweat on her skin.

'Not that it isn't tempting,' she admitted with as much cool as she could scrape together as a fist hammered against the apartment door and the smell of pizza crept in through the wood. 'But our ten minutes are up.'

9:16 p.m. 15°

Paul sat in the leather executive's chair behind his desk. Beyond the puddle of light from the brass gooseneck lamp, his office was dark. The accounting firm of Christianson and Kirkwood rented a suite in the Omni Complex, an overnamed two-story brick building that also housed a real estate agency, an insurance agency, and a brace of small law firms. Every other office in the building was empty at this time of night. All the lawyers and agents and secretaries had gone home.

The idea cut into Paul like a dull blade.

His family was broken, torn. Even before last night it had been skewed, fractured. Because of Hannah. The great Dr Garrison, savior of the unwashed masses. The town darling. The model of modern womanhood. Because she was selfish, because she valued her job more than her marriage, the whole structure of their family life had cracked and eroded. Because of her he didn't want to go home. Because of her he was having an affair. Because of her Josh was gone.

Hours after coming in from the search, his hands and feet were still cold. Adrenaline continued to race through him, pushing him up out of his chair to pace. Scenes ran through his mind on fast forward. The volunteers, hundreds of them, tramping through the knee-high snow; the air fogged with their breath, electric with their tension. The pounding of helicopter blades. The baying of bloodhounds and barks of police dogs. The motor drives of cameras and the whine of audio equipment. The glare of lights. The urgency of reporters' questions.

'*Mr Kirkwood, do you have a comment?*'

'*Mr Kirkwood, would you like to make a statement?*'

'*I just want my son back. I'll do anything – I'll give anything to get my son back.*'

It seemed unreal. As if life had fallen out of sync. As if this existence were the mirror image of reality, cast in shadows and sharp relief. It made him uneasy, uncomfortable, made him feel as if his skin didn't fit. He was a man who needed order, craved order. Order had gone out the window.

'Paul, sit down. You need to rest.'

The voice came from the shadows. He had almost forgotten her. She had followed him from the prayer vigil, careful not to come into the building right behind him. That was one of the things he liked most about her – her sense of discretion, her sensitivity to his needs. She did part-time secretarial work in the State Farm office. Not a career, just a small job for pin money. Her husband taught at Harris College. He had lost interest in her and in her desire for a family, totally immersing himself in his work in the psychology department. His work was important. His work was essential. Like Hannah's.

Paul lowered himself on the upholstered couch and sat leaning forward, elbows braced on his thighs. She was beside him instantly, her legs curled beneath her, her hands on his shoulders, kneading the knotted muscles through his L. L. Bean wool shirt.

'There were volunteers from all over in the command post,' she said softly. She always spoke softly, the way he believed a woman should. He closed his eyes and thought of how feminine she was, what a fool her husband was to turn his back on her. 'Just at my table there was a woman from Pine City and two from Monticello. They came all that way just to help label fliers.'

'Can we not talk about it?' Paul said tersely.

Images whirled in his brain faster and faster. The volunteers, the cops, the reporters; fliers, bulletins, police reports; lights, camera, action. Faster and faster, out of control. He pressed his thumbs against his eyes until colors burst behind the lids.

He shrugged off her touch, standing once again. 'Maybe you should just go. I need to be alone.'

'I only want to help, Paul.' She laid her head against his hip. Sliding her arms around his legs, she stroked her hands lightly up and down the fronts of his thighs. 'I only want to give you some kind of comfort.' Her touch grew firmer, bolder, sliding upward. 'Last night I wanted so badly to come to you, to lie down with you and just hold you.'

While he had been lying naked with Hannah . . . He closed his eyes again and pictured her coming to him, pictured himself making love to her in his own bed while Hannah watched from the corner. Shame and desire twisted inside him, a potent, bitter mix as he turned to face her and she undid his pants.

As he always did, he began the petition of excuses. He deserved this. He deserved comfort. He was entitled to a few moments' release. Closing his eyes, he gave himself over to it. He tangled his hands in her silken hair and moved his hips in rhythm with her. He lost himself in the pleasure for a few brief moments. Then the end came in a rush and it was over, and the feeling of vindication faded into something dirty.

He didn't see her to the door. He didn't tell her he loved her. He let her assume the grief had swamped him again and went to stand at the narrow window behind his desk, looking down on the parking lot. He listened to his office door close, then the door to the hall. Automatically, he checked his watch so he would know when ten minutes had passed and he would be free to go.

Free.

Somehow, he didn't think he would feel free tonight. In a dim corner of his mind, where primitive fears stirred, he wondered if he would ever feel free again. He watched Karen Wright get into her Honda two stories below, pull out onto Omni Parkway, and drive off into the dark, taillights glowing like a pair of demon-red eyes.

Slowly he turned and went back to his desk, staring down at the answering machine that took all calls to his personal line. A cold, clammy sweat broke over his body. The images of the day whirled and spun crazily in his head, making him dizzy. His stomach cramped and his finger shook as he reached down and punched the message button. His legs buckled. He sank down into his chair, cradling his head in his hands as the tape played.

'Dad, can you come and get me from hockey? Mom's late and I wanna go home.'

12

They paged through Josh's private thoughts with Phil Collins singing something melancholy in the background. Here were Josh's personal drawings and doodlings, not something meant for strangers to paw over and pick apart. Megan let that fact run off her like rain against glass, concentrating instead on anything that seemed to indicate unhappiness or fear or dislike for an adult.

There were careful drawings of race cars and notes bemoaning the tenacity of a little girl named Kate Murphy who had set her sights on making Josh her boyfriend. He had a crush on his teacher. Brian Hiatt and Matt Connor were his best buddies – Three Amigos. There was mention of hockey and one page with a cartoonish image of Olie Swain, recognizable by the dark smudge of his birthmark, doing a flip on skates. Beside the picture Josh had written *Kids tease Olie but that's mean. He can't help how he looks.*

He knew his parents were having problems. There was a drawing of his mother facing one way, a stethoscope hanging around her neck, and his father facing the other way, his eyebrows dark, angry slashes of black. A big storm cloud hung over their heads, spitting down raindrops the size of bullets. At the bottom of the page he had printed: *Dad is mad. Mom is sad. I feel bad.*

Megan turned the page over and rubbed her hands over her face.

Mitch stared at the note the kidnapper had slipped into the back of the book. It looked just like the one that had been left behind in the duffel bag. Laser print on cheap office paper.

i had a little sorrow, born of a little SIN
ignorance is not innocence but SIN

SIN. This was the second reference to sin. Josh had been an altar boy at St Elysius. He would have gone to religion class Wednesday night if he hadn't vanished. Someone had already interviewed his instructor, asking if there had been any call saying Josh would be late or absent, asking all the same questions that had been asked of all the adults who came into contact with Josh on a regular basis. But there were other people connected with the church, a few hundred parishioners, for instance. Or it could be that the kidnapper had nothing to do with St Elysius at all; he could have been a member of any one of the eight churches in Deer Lake – or none of them.

Mitch's beeper went off. He dropped a half-eaten slice of pepperoni and mushroom back into the cardboard box as he rose from the table. Heedless of the grease on his fingers, he dug a hand into his coat pocket, fished out his portable phone, and punched out the number.

'Andy, what's up?' he asked, his eyes on Megan. She rose from her chair slowly, as if a sudden move might ruin their chances of good news.

'We've got a witness!' The excitement in the sergeant's voice sang over the airwaves. 'She lives over by the ice arena. She thinks she saw Josh last night. Says she saw him get in a car.'

'Well, Christ, what took her so long to call?' Mitch barked. 'Why didn't anyone talk to her last night?'

'I dunno, Chief. She's coming into the station. I figured you'd want to be there.'

'I'll be right in.' He snapped the phone shut, his eyes still on Megan. 'If there's a God in heaven, we've got a break.'

9:54 p.m. 14°

'I feel so terrible about this, Mitch.'

The fluorescent lights of the conference room washed down on Helen Black, giving her a haunted look that seemed appropriate to the circumstances. Helen was forty-three and divorced, preserved – in her own words – by treadmill torture, Elizabeth Arden, and SlimFast. In kinder lighting she was not unattractive, but tonight the lines of strain and time were too evident beside her eyes and mouth; the shade of blond she had chosen at the Rocco Altobelli Salon had taken on a brittle, brassy cast that only accentuated her pallor.

Helen ran her own portrait photography studio on the second floor of a renovated building downtown. She had taken the shot of Mitch and Jessie that sat on his desk in his office. She had a talent for capturing the personalities of her subjects that brought her business from miles around. Successful and single, Helen was one of the many women Mitch's friends had tried to steer him toward in the past two years. He had ducked the fixup, deflecting Helen's attention elsewhere.

'I was getting ready to leave for the Cities. Your friend from the wildlife art gallery in Burnsville, Wes Riker, asked me to *Miss Saigon*. I was rushing around the house like a chicken with its head cut off, and I just happened to look out the front window –'

'What time was this?' Megan asked, pen poised above a legal pad.

She sat across the imitation walnut table from Helen Black. Russ Steiger had pulled out the molded plastic chair to Megan's left and planted his heavy winter boot on it. Melting snow and dirt dripped out of the treads to pool in the deepest part of the seat. Mitch sat next to the witness, his chair turned to face her. He had a pad and pen as well, but they lay on the table untouched. Helen Black had his complete attention.

Helen made a helpless motion with her hands. 'I couldn't say exactly. It had to be before seven, and it had to be later than when the boys usually get picked up or I wouldn't have thought anything of it at all. I *didn't* think anything of it. It just stuck in my mind because I thought. Here's someone running as late as I am.'

'Can you swear it was the Kirkwood kid?' Steiger asked.

She looked even more distressed, her brows tugging together, digging a deep furrow into her forehead. 'No. I wasn't paying that much attention. I know he had on a light-colored stocking cap. I know he was the only boy on the sidewalk.' Tears welled up in her eyes. She gripped a tattered tissue in her fist but made no move to use it. 'If I'd known – If I'd had any idea – God, that poor kid! And Hannah – she must be going crazy.'

She pressed her fist against her mouth and still the tears came. Mitch reached out and covered her other hand on the table.

'Helen, it wasn't your fault –'

'If I'd thought – If I'd paid closer attention – If I could have called someone then –'

Unmoved, Steiger chewed a toothpick. He shot a glance at Megan, but only to check for cleavage. She glared at him, resisting the urge to button her shirt up to her throat.

'It would have been nice to hear this twenty-some hours ago,' he muttered.

'I'm so sorry!' Helen cried, apologizing to Mitch. 'I just didn't think. I went into Minneapolis for the play, and stayed over to shop. I spent the whole day at the Mall of America. I never heard a word about Josh until I got home tonight. My God, if I'd known!'

As she dropped her head down into her hand and sobbed, Mitch sent the sheriff a scathing glare. 'Helen,' he said softly, patting her shoulder. 'You had no reason to think anything was wrong. What do you remember about the car?'

She sniffed and swiped at her dripping nose with the disintegrating tissue. 'It was a van. That's all. You know me – I don't know one end of a car from the other.'

'Well, was it full-size?' Steiger asked impatiently. He pulled his foot down off the chair and paced like a Doberman on a short leash. 'Was it a panel van, a conversion van? What?'

Helen shook her head.

Megan bit down on a suggestion for the sheriff to go pass the time attempting the anatomically impossible and leave the interview to her and

Mitch. She focused instead on the witness. 'Let's try this another way, Ms Black,' she said evenly. 'Do you remember if the van was light-colored or dark?'

'Um – it was light. Tan or maybe light gray. It might have been dirty white. You know, the lighting around that parking lot has an amber cast to it. It distorts color.'

'All right,' Megan said, jotting *color: light* on her notepad. 'Did it have windows – like a minivan or a shuttle-type van?'

'No. No big windows. There might have been small ones on the back doors. I'm not sure.'

'That's okay. A lot of people couldn't tell you if they had back windows on their own van, let alone the make and model of someone else's.'

Helen managed a wry smile. 'My ex was a car nut,' she confessed with a woman-to-woman look. 'He could remember the day the odometer in his four-by-four turned over on 100,000 miles. Couldn't remember our anniversary, but he knew to the minute how long it had been since his precious 'vette had its lube job. All I want to know is can it get me where I want to go.'

'And does it have a heater,' Megan said, winning another watery smile.

Helen brushed her bangs back out of her eyes, relaxing visibly. 'It wasn't the kind of van I'd want to run around town in. It was more the kind of thing a plumber would drive.'

Steiger scowled. 'What the hell does that mean?'

'I know exactly what you mean,' Megan said, and noted *panel van.* 'A scuzzy plumber or a good one?'

'Scuzzy. It looked older. Dirty or maybe rusty in spots.' She hesitated, considering. 'Plumber,' she murmured. 'You know, I wasn't sure why I said that, but now that I think about it, the shape of it was the same as Dean Eberheardt's van. He came to fix my shower and tracked mud all over the house. I remember watching him drive away, thinking, My God, I wonder what kind of pigsty that van is.'

'Are you saying Dean Eberheardt is the kidnapper?' Steiger said, incredulous.

'No!' Helen looked horrified at his conclusion.

Megan gritted her teeth and looked to Mitch.

'Ford Econoline, early eighties,' he said, ignoring the sheriff. 'Dean snaked out my kitchen sink. It took a whole bottle of Mr Clean to do the floor.'

'Relative of yours, Sheriff?' Megan muttered, rising with notepad in hand. She gave Steiger a pointed look and directed his gaze to the muddy puddle his boot had left in the chair.

'Did you notice anything else, Helen?' Mitch asked. 'Anything that struck you as odd or stuck in your mind for any reason.'

'The license plate, for instance,' Steiger grumbled.

Helen gave him a narrow look. 'I would have needed binoculars. I don't know about you, Sheriff, but I don't keep them handy in my living room.'

'I'll get this on the wire right away,' Megan told Mitch. 'Thank you so much, Ms Black. You've been an enormous help.'

Fresh tears glazed across Helen's eyes. 'I just wish I could have helped sooner. I hope it's not too late.'

That was everyone's hope, Megan thought as she went out into the hall and headed toward her office. The bulletin had to go over the teletype to BCA headquarters. From headquarters the information would go out immediately to every agency in Minnesota and to surrounding states.

'What are you going to put in the bulletin?' Steiger asked, striding up alongside her. 'Someone saw a kid get into a van a plumber might drive?'

'It's more than we had an hour ago.'

'It's shit.'

Megan bristled. 'You think so? I've already got a printout of recent incidents involving possible and known child predators in a hundred-mile area. If one of them was driving a light-colored, older, full-size van, we've got a suspect. What have you got, Sheriff?'

Indigestion, if his expression was anything to go by. He scowled down at her, his face a weathered roadmap of lines, his nose so sharply aquiline, it was nearly a vertical blade protruding from his lean face. He caught hold of Megan's shoulder and stopped her. The overhead lighting gleamed against the oil slick in his dark hair.

'You think you're pretty smart, don't you?' he rasped.

'Is that a rhetorical question or would you care to see my diplomas?'

'You can get by on that smart mouth in the Cities, but it won't fly out here, honey. We have our own way of doing things –'

'Yes, I took note of your style in the conference room. Badgering a cooperative witness to tears. What do you do for an encore – take a rubber truncheon to Josh's playmates?'

Heat flared in Steiger's eyes, and he raised a finger in warning. 'Now, listen –'

'No. *You* listen, Sheriff,' Megan said, stabbing him in the chest with a forefinger, backing him off a step. 'We've all been working around the clock and tempers are wearing thin, but that's no excuse for the way you treated Helen Black. She gave us a lead, now you want to blow it off because it doesn't spell out the crook's name in big capital letters –'

'And you're going to crack the case with it,' he sneered.

'I'll damn well try, and you'd better, too. This investigation is a cooperative effort. I suggest you go look up *cooperative* in the dictionary, Sheriff. You don't seem to grasp the concept.'

'You'll be out of here inside a month,' he growled.

'Don't count on it. There are plenty of people who bet against me ever getting this job. I'm planning to feed them the crow myself. I'll be more than happy to add your name to the guest list.'

She turned to go, knowing she was making an enemy of Steiger, too angry to care. But she whirled back toward him for a parting shot. 'One other thing, Steiger – I'm not your honey.'

10:58 p.m. 14°

The image of Olie Swain's ugly pug face hovered at the back of Mitch's mind like a gremlin from a bad dream as he drove out of the parking lot. Olie Swain drove a beat-up, rusted-out 1983 Chevy van that had once been white. Olie, who was strange by anyone's standards. Olie, who had access to nearly every little boy in town. Olie, whom Mitch had sworn was harmless.

'This must be especially hard for you,' Helen said softly.

Mitch glanced at her sitting in the passenger seat of his truck, wrapped in a goofy-looking faux leopard jacket. The jacket suited her sense of humor, but there was no trace of that humor in her expression. There was pity, something Mitch had seen enough of to last him a lifetime.

'It's hard on everybody,' he said. 'You might want to give Hannah a call. She's really hurting. She blames herself.'

'Poor kid.' Helen called anyone more than a month younger than her 'kid,' a habit that made her seem world-weary. 'Mothers aren't allowed to make mistakes anymore. A generation ago everyone just assumed they would screw up their kids. Now they've got to be Wonder Woman.' Her tone hardened and chilled as she said, 'I don't suppose Paul is taking any of the burden of guilt.'

'He was working. It was Hannah's night to pick up Josh.'

'Uh-huh. There but for the grace of God goes Paul.'

Mitch glanced at Helen again. Her mouth was pinched tight. 'You and Paul don't get along?'

'Paul is a horse's ass.'

'For any particular reason?'

Helen didn't answer. Mitch let it drop. 'Helen, would you be willing to take a look at a couple of vans, tell me if any of them resemble the one you saw last night? Just so I can get an accurate description?'

'Of course.'

They drove out to the car dealerships on the east side of town, where flags and giant inflatable animals enticed people to turn off the interstate and buy a different car. At Dealin' Swede's Helen pointed out a gray Dodge utility van and said 'sort of but not quite.' On the way back across town, Mitch slowed beside several parked vans, giving her a chance to look at a number of vehicles. On her own block he drove past her house and into the parking lot at the ice arena. He slowed to a stop thirty feet away from Olie's van, saying nothing.

Helen's brows knitted. She nibbled her lower lip. Mitch's stomach twisted.

'More like this one,' she said slowly.

'But not *just* like this one?'

She turned her head to one side and then the other as if a memory might shake loose. 'I don't think so. Something's different – the color or the shape – but it's close. . . . I don't know.' She faced him, shaking her head, her expression apologetic. 'I'm sorry, Mitch. I saw it for only a few seconds. I just got an impression, is all. I wish I could say it looked exactly like this one, but I can't.'

'It's okay,' he murmured, swinging the Explorer around and driving back to Helen's house. 'Did you have a good time at the play?' he asked as she picked her purse up off the floor.

'Yeah,' she said with a small smile. 'Wes is nice. Thanks for the introduction. You're a good guy, Mitch.'

'That's me – the last of the good guys.'

The tag struck him as ironic. Yeah, he was a great guy – deflecting the interest of women onto his friends so he wouldn't have to deal with them.

You weren't exactly dodging Megan tonight, were you, Holt?

A memory of heat and softness and the cool breath of night air stole into his consciousness. The taste of sweetness. Odd how someone with a tongue as tart as hers could taste sweet. She had been the one to pull back. He would have taken them past the point of no return.

'Your timing stinks, Mitch,' he muttered, turning south. At the next corner he turned east and drove down the street that ran behind the ice arena.

The case demanded all their energy. And he would be the one dodging when Megan found out Olie Swain drove a van, that he had been to Olie's house without her. She already had her suspicions about Olie. She would jump on this van connection like a she-wolf on a rabbit – and spook Olie in the process. Mitch knew even the most harmless of women made Olie uncomfortable. Mitch couldn't afford to have Olie bolt if he did have something to do with Josh's disappearance.

Olie's house was a converted single-car garage that sat on the last property on the block. The main house on the lot was owned by old Oscar Rudd, who collected junker Saabs and parked them on every available inch of ground in the yard and on the street, in violation of three city ordinances, leaving no room for Olie to park his van. Olie left the van in the lot at the rink and walked back and forth, tramping through the snow, slush, mud – whatever the season left for him in the vacant lot between his home and the arena.

Like the main house, the garage was covered with brown asphalt-coated tar paper designed to look like brick. It fooled no one. A stovepipe stuck up through the roof at a crooked angle, venting the smoke from the woodstove that was the main source of heat. Light glowed out through the single window in the side of the building. Mitch could hear the chatter of a television as he walked up the shoveled path toward the door. *Letterman*. He wouldn't have given Olie credit for having a sense of humor. He knocked and waited. The television went mute. He knocked again.

'Olie? It's Chief Holt.'

'What'd you want?'

'Just to talk. I have a couple of questions you might be able to answer.'

The door cracked open and Olie's ugly face filled the space, his eyes round and wary. 'Questions about what?'

'Different things. Can I come in? It's freezing out here.'

Olie backed away from the door, as much of an invitation as he was willing to give. He didn't like people coming into his place. This was his safe spot, like the old shed he had stumbled across as a kid. The shed sat on an abandoned piece of land, not far from his house out on the edge of town where the trashy people lived. The land backed onto a city park, but the paths in that part of the park were overgrown and so no one came near the shed. Olie had pretended the shed was his own, his place to hide to avoid a beating or to hole up after a bad one. In the shed he was safe.

He had transferred that feeling of safety to this place. The garage was small and dark. A cubbyhole. He filled it with his books and the stuff he bought at junk shops. He invited no one inside, but he couldn't say no to the chief of police. He stepped back to his makeshift desk and absently stroked the top of his computer screen, petting it as if it were a cat.

Mitch had to duck a little to come in the door. He took in the state of Olie's domain with a seemingly casual glance. There was only one room. One dark, cold room with dirty blue indoor-outdoor carpet covering the concrete floor. The kitchen consisted of an ancient refrigerator and a cast-off olive green electric range. The bathroom was partitioned off by a pair of mismatched curtains hanging from a wire. The curtains gaped, offering a glimpse of a tin shower stall.

'Cozy place you got here, Olie.'

Olie said nothing. He wore the same green flight jacket, the same dark wool sweater, the same Ragg wool half-gloves he had worn the night before. Mitch wondered if he bothered to change clothes all winter. For that matter, he wondered if he ever bothered to use that shower stall. The place smelled like dirty feet.

He looked for a place to sit, hoping to put Olie at ease, but settled for leaning against the back of a ratty old recliner. There were books everywhere. Shelves and shelves of books. Piles and piles of books. What furniture there was seemed to serve only as another place to pile books. What room wasn't taken up by books was taken up by computer equipment. Mitch counted five PCs.

'Where'd you get all the computers, Olie?'

'Different places. In the Cities. Businesses throw 'em out 'cause they're out of date. I didn't steal them.'

'I didn't think you did. I'm just making conversation here, Olie.'

Mitch offered him a smile. 'Businesses throw them out? That's quite a deal. How'd you find out about that?'

Olie eased down into his chair, his good eye darting from the computer screen to Mitch and back. The glass eye stayed on Mitch. 'Professor Priest.' His hand darted over the keyboard to hit a button. 'He lets me sit in on some classes.'

'He's a nice guy.'

Olie didn't comment. He hit another button and the screen before him went blank.

'So what do you do with all these machines?'

'Stuff.'

Mitch forced another smile and let out a measured sigh between his teeth. That Olie, master of small talk. 'So, Olie, did you work tonight?'

'Yeah.'

'Anything going on at the rink around five-thirty?'

He shrugged. 'Skating club.'

'Practicing for the big show Sunday, I suppose.'

Olie took it for a rhetorical statement.

'I wanted to ask you a couple of questions about last night,' Mitch said.

'You haven't found that boy.'

It seemed more a statement than a question. Mitch watched him carefully, his own expression impassive. 'Not yet, but we're looking real hard. We've got a couple of leads. Did you think of anything that might help us?'

Olie's good eye looked down at his keyboard. He flicked a lint ball off one of the keys.

'Someone thinks they saw Josh get into a van last night. A van that looked something like yours – older, light-colored. You didn't see a van like that, did you?'

'No.'

'You didn't loan your van to someone, did you?'

'No.'

'You leave the keys in it?'

'No.'

Mitch lifted a book from the pile on the seat of the recliner and studied the cover idly. *Story of the Irish Race*. He wondered if Olie was Irish or just curious. He'd never thought of Olie as being anything but weird.

Olie popped up from his chair. His brows pulled low over his mismatched eyes, seeming to tug at the port wine birthmark on the left side of his face. 'It wasn't my van.'

'But you were inside the arena,' Mitch said. He set the book aside and slid his hands into his coat pockets. 'Running the Zamboni, right? Maybe someone used your van without asking.'

'No. They couldn't.'

'Well ...' Yawning hugely, Mitch pushed away from the decrepit recliner. 'People do strange things, Olie. Just to be safe, we should probably take a look inside. Would you mind showing me?'

'You don't have a warrant.' Olie immediately regretted the words. Mitch Holt's gaze sharpened like a gun scope coming into focus.

'Should I get one, Olie?' His soft, silky voice raised the short hairs on the back of Olie's neck.

'I don't know anything!' Olie shouted, shoving at a stack of books on a TV tray. They tumbled to the floor, sounding like bricks as they hit the concrete. 'I didn't do anything!'

Mitch watched the outburst stonefaced, his expression giving away nothing of the tension tightening inside him like a watch spring. 'Then you don't have anything to hide.'

His mind was racing. If Olie consented to a search of the vehicle now and something turned up, would a judge later toss out the evidence on the argument of no warrant, consent given under duress? Without a positive ID on the vehicle, Mitch didn't have enough cause to obtain a warrant, and he doubted he could get Olie to sign a consent form. Goddamn technicalities. What he had was a missing child and a need to find him that far outstripped the needs of the courts.

If Olie let him take a look and he saw something in the van, he could have the vehicle towed in on the grounds that overnight parking was technically not permitted in the Gordie Knutson Memorial Arena lot. Upon impounding the vehicle, they would be able to inventory the contents, and anything suspicious listed on the inventory would give them probable cause to ask for a warrant authorizing seizure of it as evidence of a crime.

Okay. He had a plan. His ass was covered. The next move was Olie's.

Olie glared at him, his small mouth puckered into an angry knot. The birthmark that spilled down his forehead seemed to darken, and the rest of his face paled. His hand was trembling as he raised it and pointed a finger at Mitch.

'I don't have anything to hide,' he said.

The eye staring defiantly at Mitch was made of glass. The other one slid away.

Journal entry
Day 2

Round and round and round they go. Will they find Josh? We don't think so.

13

Day 3
5:51 a.m. 11°

Megan overslept, dreaming dark, sensuous dreams about Harrison Ford. As she slowly blinked her eyes open, the feelings lingered – forbidden needs and a lush, heavy sense of pleasure; guilt and gratification; the taste of Mitch Holt's kiss, the feel of his hands on her body, the feel of his mouth on her breast . . .

She stared at the hairline cracks in the ceiling plaster. The predawn light seeped into the room through sheer curtains, casting everything in shades of gray, like a dream. She lay beneath the tangled sheets and quilt, her heart beating slowly, strongly, her body warm, nerve endings humming. She could feel Gannon curled against her, the cat tucked into his favorite spot behind her knees. Friday would be in the kitchen, prowling for breakfast.

Megan's mind wandered into forbidden territory, and she wondered if Mitch might have dreamed about their kiss, wondered if the sensations hung around him like a heavy, sultry cloud as he lay in his bed.

Not a smart thing to wonder. He should have been just another cop, just someone she had to work with. But she had the feeling there was nothing simple about Mitch Holt. The Everyman façade hid a complex core of anger and need and pain. She had glimpsed those things in his eyes, tasted them in his kiss, and the hidden mysteries drew her in. She could have resisted mere sex appeal, but a mystery . . . Her mind was naturally geared to solving mysteries.

There was a more pressing mystery to solve. The reminder was a poke in the conscience that drove Megan out of bed and into the shower. She let the water beat down on her in an attempt to pound out the numbness of sleep. Her head seemed as heavy and dense as an anvil. Her eyes felt as if they had grown a coat of fur. Five hours of sleep in forty-seven was not enough. She could have slept for a day, but she didn't have that luxury and wouldn't until this case was over. Even then she would be behind in her duties. All appointments with the other chiefs and sheriffs of her territory had been put on hold, but crime in those other counties and towns didn't stop just because Deer Lake had been hit with a big one. There was no balance maintained at the courtesy of lowlifes.

Friday jumped up on the edge of the old clawfoot tub and stuck his head inside the shower curtain. He wore a disgruntled expression on his round black face, golden eyes glowering at Megan, white whiskers twitching in annoyance as water droplets pelted him. He yowled at her in his complaining voice and swiped at his whiskers with his paw.

'Yeah, yeah, you want breakfast. You want, you want – what about what I want, huh?'

As he hopped down from the tub, he made a sound that indicated he was patently disinterested in her needs. A typical male attitude, Megan thought, cranking the faucet off and reaching for a towel.

After pulling on sweats, she fed the cats, then fed herself an English muffin. Sitting at the table, she stared unseeing at the depressing mess in her living room, the unpacked and half-unpacked boxes. She didn't let herself think about the need to build herself a nest and surround herself with the things she had collected – other people's heirlooms and memories, the false sense of belonging and family she had attached to her flea-market finds.

Her mind sorted tasks into a priority list and tumbled bits of information over and over in an attempt to sift out anything useful. Helen Black's statement played in the back of her mind like a videotape, and she strained to see something, hear something that might trigger an idea. She had found nothing encouraging in the reports she had gone through the night before, her share of the reports of recent incidents and known offenders. But then her eyes had given out before she could get through everything. One of her men may have had better luck.

Licking strawberry jam off her fingers, she grabbed her portable phone and punched the speed dial button for the command post.

'Agent Geist. How may I help you?'

'Jim, it's Megan. Any word?'

'Nothing yet, but the news about the van is just hitting the airwaves. I expect the hotline phones to light up like Christmas trees in another hour or so. Every third person in the state probably knows someone with a junker van.'

'What about those listings? Anything turn up?'

'Close but no stogie. We've got a couple of aborted attempts to pick up kids in Anoka County in a brown van, a convicted pedophile in New Prague who drives a yellow van –'

'It's worth checking out. Did you call the chief in New Prague?'

'He's not in yet, but he'll call back as soon as he gets there.'

'Good. Thanks. I'm going over to talk to the parents. Page me if anything goes down.'

She dried her hair and brushed it back into the usual pony-tail. Makeup amounted to a touch of blusher and two swipes with the mascara wand. In the bedroom she dug through her suitcase for a pair of burgundy stirrup pants and a bulky charcoal turtleneck. The cats found perches on the boxes in the living room and watched her shrug into her parka and struggle with her scarf.

'You guys feel free to unpack and decorate while I'm out,' she told them.

Gannon curled his paws beneath him and closed his eyes. Friday gave her a look and said, 'Yow.'

'Yeah, well, be that way. You don't have any sense of style anyway.'

The Lumina started grudgingly, growling and coughing. A belt somewhere in the inner workings squealed like a stuck pig when she cranked the knob for heat. The air that blasted out of the vents was like a breath from the Arctic.

To distract herself from the fact that her fingertips were going numb and the hair inside her nose was frosting over, Megan studied the town as she cruised the tree-lined streets from the east side to the west side. The established, older part of Deer Lake was a Beaver Cleaver kind of town – comfortable family homes, dogs peeing on snowmen built by the children being trundled off to school in minivans. She saw no children walking to school. Was it the cold or Josh Kirkwood that kept them off the sidewalks?

Downtown looked like a movie set for the all-American town. The city park square in the center with its quaint old bandshell and statues to long-forgotten men, the old false-front brick shops, the courthouse built of native limestone. The Park Cinema theater with a vintage 1950s marquee jutting out, heralding the showing of *Philadelphia* at 7 & 9:20, and the grand old Fontaine Hotel, five stories of renovated Victorian splendor.

North and west of downtown, the old neighborhoods gave way to sixties ramblers, then seventies split-level homes, then the latest upscale developments – expensive hybrid homes on lots of an acre or more. Pseudo-Tudors and pseudo-Georgians, saltboxes with attachments, and yuppie-rustic homes like the Kirkwoods', sided in split cedar and landscaped with river birch and artfully arranged boulders. The builders had gone to great pains to make it seem as if the houses had been there for decades. Strategic sites, mature trees, and winding lanes gave the impression of seclusion.

The Kirkwood house faced the lake, an expanse of snow-dusted ice dotted with ice-fishing huts. In the early morning gray it looked desolate. Beyond the western bank, the buildings of Harris College squatted like a crop of dark mushrooms among the leafless trees. South of the college lay what had once been a town called Harrisburg. In the last century it had competed with Deer Lake for commerce and population, but Deer Lake had won the railroad and the title of county seat. Harrisburg had faded, had eventually been annexed, and now bore the indignity of the nickname Dinkytown.

Megan parked, cringing as the Lumina's engine knocked and rattled before going silent. Maybe if she solved this case the bureau would give her a better car. Maybe if she solved this case there would be a little boy playing in the half-finished snow fort on the Kirkwoods' front lawn.

Hannah Garrison answered the front door herself, looking drawn and thin. She wore a faded Duke sweatshirt, navy leggings, and baggy wool socks, and still somehow managed to project an air of elegance.

'Agent O'Malley,' she said, her eyes widening at the possibilities Megan represented standing there on her front stoop. She gripped the edge of the door so hard, her knuckles turned white. 'Have you found Josh?'

'No, I'm sorry, but we may have a lead. Someone may have seen Josh getting into a van Wednesday night. May I come in? I'd like to talk to you and your husband.'

'Yes, of course.' Hannah backed away from the door. 'Let me catch Paul. He was just leaving to go out on the search again.'

Megan stepped inside and closed the door behind her. She drifted after Hannah, staying far enough behind to remain unobtrusive, to observe without seeming to take in anything at all.

In the family room a fire crackled in the fieldstone fireplace, closed off from the room by glass doors and a safety screen in deference to the baby, who was curled up dozing on the back of a huge stuffed dog on the floor. The *Today* show was playing on a television set into a cherry armoire. Katie Couric needling Bryant Gumbel, Willard Scott laughing like an imbecile in the background. A petite woman with big brown eyes and an ash-blond bob silenced them with a remote control and looked up at Megan expectantly.

'Can I help you?' she asked in a hushed voice. 'I'm Karen Wright, a neighbor. I'm here to help Hannah.'

Megan gave her a cursory smile. 'No, thank you. I need to speak with Mr and Mrs – um, with Mr Kirkwood and Dr Garrison.'

Karen made a sympathetic face. 'Awkward, isn't it? Life was simpler when we were all less liberated.'

Megan made a noncommittal sound and moved on toward the kitchen, where Curt McCaskill was pouring himself a cup of coffee and reading the *StarTribune*. The agent glanced up with an exaggerated show of surprise.

'Hey, O'Malley, I was just reading about you. Did you really crack a kiddie porn ring when you were in vice?'

Megan ignored his question, zeroing in on the article spread out on the kitchen table. *Female Agent Fighting Crime and Gender Bias*. The byline was Henry Forster's, the jerk. 'Oh, Jesus, Mary, and Joseph, DePalma will shit a brick when he sees this!'

The piece detailed her service record and her struggle to gain a field post at the bureau. There were no direct quotes from her, but 'sources in the bureau' had made several uncharitable remarks about her ambition. The article went on to recount the sexual harassment brouhaha of the previous fall, which had not involved her at all but had made life at headquarters unpleasant for everyone for a month or two. Battle lines had been drawn between the sexes and hard feelings still lingered. Forster's article would poke a stick at that old hornet's nest, but no one would turn on Forster. They would turn on her.

She groaned when she finished reading.

'You want a cup of coffee?' McCaskill asked.

'No, thanks. I need something stiffer than caffeine.'

'I could make a joke here, but it might seem inappropriate, all things considered.'

Megan laughed. She had always liked Curt. He had a sense of humor, something in increasingly short supply in the world at large.

His blue eyes twinkled. With his thick shock of ginger hair he looked like a leprechaun on steroids. 'What brings you to this neck of the woods?'

'We have a witness who may have seen Josh getting into a van. I want to talk to the parents about it. Nothing happening on your end of things?'

The smile faded. He shook his head and lowered his voice to a confidential murmur. 'I gotta tell you, thirty-nine hours and no word . . . If we haven't heard anything by now, we're not liable to. What we've got here is an abduction by a predator, not a kidnap for ransom.'

Megan didn't answer him, but the weight of truth pressed down on her just the same. Just because she didn't give it voice didn't make it any less real. She pulled in a hard, deep breath, trying like hell to hang on to her determination. 'You want to take a break? I'll be here half an hour or better.'

He rose from his chair, trying to work the kinks out of his shoulders. 'Thanks. I could use some fresh air.' He made a fist and scuffed it against her upper arm. 'You're okay – for a chick.'

She rolled her eyes at him, but the sound of sharp voices coming from the other side of the kitchen door drew her attention. The door swung open and Hannah stomped in, hugging herself against the cold that drifted in from the garage beyond. Her wide mouth was drawn in a thin, angry line, and her eyes gleamed with tears or temper or both. Paul stalked in behind her, looking irritated.

Megan had taken an instant dislike to Paul Kirkwood and she chided herself for it. The poor man had lost his son, he had every right to behave in any way he wanted. But there was just a certain petulant arrogance about Paul Kirkwood that rubbed her the wrong way.

He looked at her now, his mouth set in an expression that was more pout than frown. 'What's this about a van?'

'A witness thinks she may have seen Josh getting into an older, light-colored van Wednesday night. I was wondering if either of you knows anyone with a van that matches that description or if you might have seen one in the neighborhood recently.'

'Did they get a license plate?'

137

'No.'

'A make and model on the van?'

'No.'

He shook his head, not bothering to hide his impatience with her incompetence. 'I told Mitch Holt neither of us is here enough to notice anyone hanging around. And if we knew anyone sick enough to steal our son, don't you think we would have said so?'

Megan bit down on her temper.

Hannah gave her a brittle, sour smile. 'Paul is in a hurry,' she said sarcastically. 'God knows, they can't start the search without him. Heaven forbid he should be held up by something as trivial as a real lead –'

Paul cut her a narrow look. 'Someone thinks they *might have* seen a boy who *might have been* our son getting into a van they can barely describe. Big fucking lead, Hannah.'

'It's more than anyone else has come up with,' she shot back. 'What have you found out there tramping around in the snow? Have you found Josh? Have you found anything at all?'

'At least I'm doing something.'

He might as well have slapped her. Hannah pulled back, chin up, mouth quivering as she tightened it against the sobs that ached in her throat. 'Implying that I'm not?' she whispered. 'I'm not in this house by choice. You want to stay here with Lily and wait for the phone to ring? I will gladly trade places with you.'

Paul rubbed a hand over his face. 'That's not what I meant,' he said softly, knowing it was exactly what he had meant. He had meant to hurt her. This was all her fault in the first place. If it hadn't been for Hannah and her all-important career . . . Hannah this, Hannah that, Hannah, Hannah, Hannah . . .

Megan watched the exchange, uncomfortable with being a spectator to something that should have been private.

'Mr Kirkwood,' she said, drawing his attention away from his wife, trying to diffuse the tension between them and get their focus back on the task at hand. 'You're telling me you don't know anyone with a van that fits that general description – eighties model utility van, tan or light-colored?'

He shook his head absently. 'No. If I think of anyone, I'll call Mitch.'

'Do that.' She ignored the slight. It didn't matter as long as the job got done.

Without a word to his wife, Paul turned and left. The tension hung in the air as they listened to his car start and back out of the drive. Hannah closed her eyes and pressed the heels of her hands against them. Karen Wright came in, wide-eyed. Bambi in the headlights, Megan thought. What an ugly little scene to play out in front of the neighbors.

'I know this is hard on both you and Paul,' Megan said, her attention on Hannah. 'And this lead probably doesn't seem like much, as vague as it is. I can understand he feels more useful physically searching for Josh –'

'I'm sure it makes Paul feel useful,' Hannah snapped. 'Just as I'm sure nothing could make anyone feel more use*less* than sitting around this house all day with people staring at them.'

Karen blinked her big doe eyes, her brows knitting into an expression of hurt. 'If I'm not being a help, maybe I should just leave.'

'Maybe you should.'

Hannah regretted the words the instant they were out of her mouth. Karen meant well. Everyone who had come to the house had meant well. Josh's disappearance had touched all their lives to a certain degree. They were only trying to cope, only thought they were trying to help *her* cope. The problem was, there was no coping. She could handle a city ER, deal with the stress of juggling that career with her family life, but there were no coping skills for this. She couldn't handle it and she couldn't see beyond it. The well-meaning hands reaching out to her seemed only to trap her in this nightmare.

Karen had her coat in hand and was halfway to the hall. Hannah blew out a breath and rushed after her, the need to smooth over bad feelings overruling deeper needs.

Megan watched her go, turning all these new puzzle pieces over in her head – the tension between Hannah and Paul chief among them. The situation was acting like a pressure cooker. Megan supposed even a good relationship would be strained under the circumstances, but she would have expected the husband and wife to turn to each other for support. That wasn't happening here. The pressure was crushing down on Hannah and Paul, and their relationship seemed to be cracking like an eggshell. The page from Josh's notebook rose in her memory – angry storm clouds and scowling people. *Dad is mad. Mom is sad. I feel bad. . . .*

Her instinct was to blame Paul Kirkwood entirely. He had an aura that left a bad taste in her mouth. Selfish, self-important – like her brother Mick, she realized. But it wasn't just that similarity she disliked. She had come here to tell him they had their first real lead and he hadn't wanted to take the time to listen. He wanted to be out in the field, where the television cameras could capture the grieving father in action.

A tug on the leg of her slacks pulled Megan's mind back to the present. She looked down in surprise to see Lily Kirkwood staring up at her with huge deep blue eyes and a shy smile.

'Hi!' Lily chirped.

'Hi there.' Megan smiled, at a complete loss what to do. She knew nothing about babies. Or children, for that matter. She had once been a child, of course, but she hadn't been very good at it. Always shy, feeling out of place, in the way, unwanted; the daughter of a woman who had been a dismal failure at mothering.

Megan's own awkwardness around children never failed to make her wonder just how much of her mother's lack of skill had been passed on to her. Not that it would matter. When she looked to the future, she saw her career, not a family. That was what she wanted. That was what she was good at.

Her heart gave a traitorous thump as Josh Kirkwood's baby sister stretched her arms up. 'Lily up!'

'Lily, sweetheart, come to Mama.'

Hannah scooped the baby up and pressed a fierce kiss against her cheek, hugging her tight, then turned to Megan. 'I'm sorry about . . .' She shook her head. 'I'm sorry, I'm sorry. The first words out of everyone's mouth these days.'

'Sorry, Mama,' Lily murmured, tucking her head beneath her mother's chin.

'Why don't I pour us both a cup of coffee?' Megan offered. The pot was still on the table, along with an assortment of clean mugs sitting in a cluster, waiting for the endless parade of cops and friends and neighbors.

'That sounds great.' Hannah sank down on the chair McCaskill had vacated earlier, her cheek pressed against the top of Lily's head. Lily traced a miniature forefinger around the D of Duke on her mother's sweatshirt.

'Would you like something to eat? We have every kind of sweet roll and doughnut and muffin known to man.' She gestured to the countertops that were lined with pans and plates and baskets heaped with baked goods. 'All of them homemade except the Danish from Myrna Tolefsrud, who has sciatica on account of Mr Tolefsrud's wild polka dancing at the Sons of Norway lodge.' She repeated the stories she had taken in by rote. 'Of course, according to Myrna's sister-in-law, LaMae Gilquist, Myrna has always been a poor cook and lazy to boot.'

Megan smiled as she chose a tray of cinnamon rolls with thick creamy frosting and brought it to the table. 'There's a lot to be said for small-town life, isn't there?'

'Usually,' Hannah murmured.

'Chief Holt and I are encouraged about the lead. We're pursuing it very enthusiastically.' Megan dug a roll out of the pan, plopped it on a paper plate, and set the plate in front of Hannah – directly on top of the newspaper article about herself.

Lily twisted around on her mother's lap and attacked the treat with both hands, ripping off a chunk and plucking out the raisins to be set aside in a little pile.

'I know,' Hannah said. 'I'm sure Paul knows, too. He's just –' *What*? Ten years of marriage and he was more a stranger to her now than he had ever been. She didn't know what or who Paul was anymore. 'You're not exactly catching us at our best.'

'In this line of work, I seldom catch anyone at their best.'

'Me, neither,' Hannah admitted quietly, her mouth twisting at the irony. 'I'm not used to being on the other side of it. The victim. This might sound stupid, but I don't know how to behave. I don't know what's expected of me.'

Megan licked frosting off her finger, her eyes on Hannah's. 'No, that's not stupid. I know exactly what you mean.'

'I've always been the one people turned to. The strong one. The one who knew how to get things done. Now I don't know what to do. I don't know how to let people take care of me. And I don't think they know what to do, either. They come here out of duty and then they sit around and look at me out the corner of their eye like they've just figured out I'm human and they don't like it.'

'Don't worry about them,' Megan said. 'It doesn't matter what they think or what they want. Concentrate on getting through this any way you can. Make yourself eat; you need what strength you can get. Make yourself sleep. Prescribe something for yourself if you need to.'

Hannah dutifully put a scrap of the demolished sweet roll in her mouth and chewed without tasting. Lily looked up at her, annoyed. Megan dug another roll out of the pan, put it on another plate, and slid it across the table. Without asking. Like a friend, Hannah thought. What an odd time to make a friend.

'What I need,' she said, 'is to *do* something. I know I have to be here, but there has to be something I can *do*.'

Megan nodded. 'Okay. The volunteers at the command post are labeling fliers to be mailed out across the country. Thousands of them. I'll send someone over with a stack for you to work on. In the meantime, how about thinking on this lead? Do you know anyone with a van that even vaguely matches the description? Have you seen one parked someplace that struck you as strange? Near the school or the hospital or the lake.'

'I don't pay attention to cars. The only van I can think of is an old clunker Paul used to have when he was going through his manly-hunter phase.'

'When was this?' Megan asked, tensing automatically.

Hannah shrugged. 'Four or five years ago. When we first moved out from the Cities. He had an old white van to haul his hunting buddies and their dogs, but he sold it. Hunting was too disorderly for Paul.'

'Do you know who he sold it to? Someone you know?'

'I don't remember. It didn't concern me.' Her eyes widened as the import struck.

Mitch had steered his questions on Wednesday night in the same direction. And she had pushed aside the possibility then that someone who had been in their home, eaten from their table, been taken into their trust, could turn on them so viciously. But even as her heart rejected the idea, her mind began scanning the names and faces of everyone she knew, everyone she didn't quite like, everyone on the fringe of their circle of acquaintance.

'We can't rule it out,' Megan said. 'We can't afford to rule out anything at this point.'

Hannah pulled her baby close, ignoring the sticky fingers and a face smeared with frosting and cinnamon. She stared unseeing across the room, rocking Lily. Her thoughts were on Josh – where he might be, what he might be going through. Horrors enough at the hands of a stranger, but how unspeakably terrible to suffer at the hands of someone he had known and trusted. It happened all the time. She read it in the paper, saw it on television, had been in a position to try to mend such damage to other people's children.

'My God,' she whispered. 'What is this world coming to?'

'If we knew that,' Megan murmured, 'maybe we could stop it before it got there.'

They sat in silence. Lily's eyes roamed the kitchen and she squirmed a little, wrenching her head out from under her mother's chin. She looked up into the beautiful face that had the answers to all of her questions and asked in a small voice, 'Mama, where Josh?'

8:22 a.m. 12°

Megan tracked Paul Kirkwood down at a parking area on the edge of Lyon State Park, seven miles west of town. The main search party was gathered – officers from the sheriff's department, officers from the Minneapolis Police Department canine unit with a trio of barking German shepherds, volunteers from all walks of life, so many people that the lot was full and cars were hanging off the shoulder a quarter mile up and down the main road. Four TV station vans had parked where they wanted, blocking in cars. Their satellite dishes telescoped up from their roofs, shooting signals to Minneapolis and St Paul and Rochester.

Megan parked behind the KTTC van and headed for the crowd. Russ Steiger shouted out instructions, posing for the cameras with his fists propped on his narrow hips and his feet spread wide, mirrored sunglasses hiding his squinty eyes. Paul stood fifteen feet away, looking grave, the cold wind ruffling his brown hair. Megan slipped in beside him, hoping the newspeople would be too enraptured with the sheriff to notice her.

'Mr Kirkwood, can I have a word?' she asked quietly, turning her back to the cameras.

Paul frowned. 'What now?'

'I'd like to ask you a couple of questions about the van you used to have for hunting.'

'What about it?'

'For starters, why didn't you mention it to me this morning?'

'I sold it years ago,' he said irritably. 'What could it possibly have to do with Josh?'

'Maybe nothing, but we want to check every possible avenue.'

She caught hold of his coat sleeve and moved away from the crowd and the ears tuned like microphones to catch any squeak of information.

Paul reluctantly followed her out of the line of cameras behind a Park Service truck.

'Hannah told me you sold the van several years ago,' Megan said. 'Who was the buyer? Would he have seen or met Josh at your house?'

'I don't know,' Paul snapped. 'It was years ago. I put an ad in the paper and someone answered it.'

'You don't have any record of who?'

'No. He was just some guy. He paid cash, took the van, and left. It was a piece of junk. I was happy to get rid of it.'

'What about the title? You didn't go with him to transfer the title?'

He gave her a look. 'Surely, you're not that naïve, Agent O'Malley.'

'No,' Megan said evenly. 'I'm not naïve. But you don't strike me as the kind of man who would ignore the rules.'

'Jesus Christ.' He stepped back from her and lifted his arms out in a gesture that invited the world to share his disbelief. 'I can't believe you!' His raised voice drew the attention of a number of people clustered near Steiger. '*My* son has been kidnapped and you have the gall to stand here and treat *me* like a criminal?'

Megan could see people turning their way. Tension closed bony fingers on the back of her neck. The last thing she needed was to attract more attention from the press. DePalma would yank her off this assignment and bury her so deep in the bowels of headquarters, she wouldn't be able to find her way out to University Avenue.

'Mr Kirkwood, I'm not accusing you of anything.' She used the same low, even tone she would have used with a jumper on a ledge. 'I apologize if it sounded that way.'

'I'll tell you how it sounds,' Paul said, his temper humming in his voice. 'It sounds to me like you don't know how to find my son and you're doing whatever you can to cover your ass! That's how it sounds!'

He stormed away from her, away from the hundred or so people who had gathered to watch the show, away from the cameras and the reporters. They set their sights on Megan and zeroed in.

'Agent O'Malley, do you have any comment on Mr Kirkwood's accusations?'

'Agent O'Malley, does the BCA consider Mr Kirkwood a suspect?'

'Agent O'Malley, do you have a comment on the article in the *Tribune*?'

Megan ground her teeth on a hundred nasty retorts. Diplomacy. Low-key, unobtrusive diplomacy. Those were her instructions from DePalma. That was bureau policy. She had sworn she could handle it. She had promised herself she could control her temper and take anything the press or anyone else dished out to her. She pulled in a deep breath and faced the cameras without flinching.

'Mr Kirkwood is understandably distraught. My only comment is that the BCA is doing all it can in cooperation with the Deer Lake Police

Department and the Park County sheriff's office to find Josh Kirkwood and bring his abductor to justice.'

Ignoring the volley of questions, she moved through the crowd, headed back to her car.

'Did I say you'd be here a month, O'Malley?' Steiger murmured with a nasty smile as she strode past him. 'That might have been optimistic.'

14

'What the hell were you thinking?' Mitch slammed the door shut behind him and Leo's 1993 Women of the Big Ten calendar jumped on its peg, sending Miss Michigan rocking back on her lovely haunches.

Megan didn't bother to play dumb and she refused to play meek. Temper snapping, she shot up out of the decrepit chair she had barely settled her fanny on. 'I was thinking of doing my job.'

'By going after Paul Kirkwood –'

'By following up on all possible leads,' she qualified, rounding the desk.

'Why the hell didn't you check with me first?'

'I don't have to check with you. You're not my boss –'

'Jesus Christ, don't you think the man's going through enough?' he snapped, leaning over her, his dark eyes blazing with fury.

Megan met his glare head-on. 'I think he's going through hell and I'm doing everything I can to get him out of it.'

'By grilling him in front of the press?'

'That's bullshit! He's the one who made a big scene, not me. I was asking for information he should have given me an hour before. Information that could very well prove pertinent to his son's disappearance. Don't you find it just a little odd that he would be annoyed with me for that?'

Mitch went still, pulling all his anger and energy inward, smoothing his face into a blank mask. He stared down at Megan. 'Just what the hell is that supposed to mean?' he asked, his voice a razor-edged whisper. 'Are you saying you think Paul Kirkwood kidnapped his own son?'

'No.'

She blew out a breath and swept back the tendrils of hair that had escaped her ponytail. Control. If he could have it, she could, too. Besides that, she was running low on adrenaline. As always happened on a big case, it would ebb and flow in an erratic tide, following the radical ups and downs of the investigation. She stepped back from him and leaned a hip against the desk as she dug a prescription bottle of ergotamine out of

145

her briefcase, fished out one tablet, and washed it down with Pepsi to ward off the headache that was sinking its talons into her forehead.

'I'm saying I went to him this morning with a lead and he blew me off,' she said. 'I'm saying he committed a rather peculiar sin of omission by not telling me he had once owned and sold a van that meets the general description of the one we're looking for, and when I called him on it, he went off. Don't you find that all just a little strange, Chief?'

'You don't know the kind of pressure he's under.'

'And you do?'

'Yes,' Mitch returned too sharply. The tone revealed too much when his instincts told him to reveal nothing.

He kicked himself mentally for the tactical blunder and turned away. Hands jammed at his waist, he prowled the small office, restless, edgy.

For the first time he noticed all of Leo's certificates and commendations still tacked up on his ego wall, and Wally the Walleye preserved for all eternity on a walnut plaque above the file cabinets, cigar butt sticking out of his ugly fish mouth. Poor old Leo had left no one behind to collect the souvenirs of his life. The malodorous aroma of his cheap cigars lingered in the air, lurking darkly beneath the choking sweet perfume of air freshener. Sitting on the front edge of the desk was the only physical sign of Megan taking over the office, a shiny brass nameplate – AGENT MEGAN O'MALLEY, BCA.

Megan watched him carefully, reading the set of his broad shoulders, the angle of his head. He wanted to dismiss her, but he was on her turf. He wanted to walk out, but he wouldn't. Even before she asked the question, she knew what his answer would be.

'Would you care to enlighten me, Chief?'

'We aren't here to talk about me,' he said, the words short and terse.

'Aren't we?' Megan advanced on him, hands on her hips, unconsciously mimicking his stance. They faced each other like a pair of gunslingers, and the tension in the air was as thick as the smell of old Dutch Masters cigars.

He glared at her, his face a rigid mask of hard planes and sharp angles. Pride and anger and something like panic squeezed into a knot in his chest. He wanted to push it away. He wanted to push *her* away, out of his way, away from the dark territory that was his past. Like a cornered wolf, he wanted to lash out, but the need to control that rage overruled. So he stood there with every muscle as rigid as the walls he had built to protect himself.

'You're on thin ice, O'Malley,' he said in a deadly whisper. 'I suggest you back off.'

'Not if what's going on here is you projecting your feelings onto Paul Kirkwood,' Megan said, stubbornly taking another step out onto that proverbial thin ice, knowing that if it cracked, she would be sucked into the vortex of the rage whirling beneath his surface. 'If that's what's going on, then we'd damn well better talk about it. An investigation is no place for that kind of involvement, and you know it.'

An investigation was no place for the kind of emotions that were stirring inside her now, either. She wanted to break his iron fist of control. She wanted him to let go. She wanted him to confide in her – not for the good of the case, but because in a corner of her heart she seldom acknowledged and never indulged, she wanted to get closer to him. Dangerous stuff all the way around. Dangerous and seductive.

The heat between them intensified by one degree and then another. Then he turned away abruptly, snapping the thread of tension.

As he fought to regulate his breathing and his temper, Mitch found himself staring at a snapshot of Leo at the annual Park County Peace Officers Association barbecue – red-faced, wearing a stained chef's apron over his considerable bulk and a cap with a plastic trout head sticking out one side and its tail sticking out the other. Beer in hand, cigar clamped between his teeth, he stood beside a pig roasting on a spit.

Life had sure as hell been simpler with Leo around. Leo had been a grunt-work old-fashioned cop not interested in new theories of criminology or psychology or personnel dynamics. He had never wanted to spill his guts to Leo. He didn't want to unlock the door to the old pain, didn't want to show any sign of vulnerability, especially not here, on the job. Here, more than anywhere, he needed to keep the emotions closed up tight in their little box in his chest.

'Look,' he said in a low voice, 'I think you could have been more diplomatic, that's all. If you want to track down Paul's van, fine. Do it through the DMV. I'll handle any questioning.'

'I've already called the DMV. They're checking,' Megan said, the adrenaline receding sharply, leaving her feeling drained. 'Or, rather, they're trying to. Their computer is down.

'I just wanted an explanation from him,' she confessed. 'I realize people react differently to this kind of stress, but . . . I get the feeling he doesn't want to talk to me – or look me in the eye, for that matter. My gut feeling is he's holding something back, and I want it.'

'It may have nothing to do with Josh,' Mitch said irritably. 'Maybe he doesn't like women cops. Maybe he feels guilty because he wasn't there for Josh that night. That kind of guilt can tear a man up inside. Maybe you look just like the girl who turned him down for the senior prom way back when.'

'Where was he that night?' Megan demanded, unwilling to give in. 'Why wasn't he there?'

'He was working.'

'Hannah called him repeatedly and he didn't answer the phone.'

'He was working in a conference room down the hall.'

She gave him a look of astounded disbelief. 'And he returns to his office and ignores the message light on his machine? Who does that? And while we're at it, who can corroborate it?'

'I don't know,' Mitch conceded. 'Those are valid questions, but I'll be the one to ask them.'

'Because you're the boss?' Megan said archly.

The muscles in his jaw tightened. A sculpture in granite couldn't have looked more forbidding. 'I told you not to rock my boat, O'Malley,' he said softly. 'This is my town and my investigation. We'll do it my way. There's only one top dog around here, and it's me. Is that clear?'

'And I'm supposed to come to heel and sit like a good little bitch?'

'Your analogy, not mine,' he said. 'This case is giving the press enough fodder as it is. I don't need Paul going off like a rocket in front of them.'

'We're agreed on that much. I don't need any more airtime, either, thanks anyway,' she said dryly. 'DePalma has already left three messages for me to call him so he can chew me out over the *StarTribune* article.'

'And you ignored them?' he mocked. 'Who does that?'

Megan narrowed her eyes. 'He isn't calling to tell me my child is missing. He's calling to sink his teeth into my throat and shake me like a dead rat – something I'd like to see someone do to that hack Henry Forster, now that I think of it.'

'Maybe we can set it up as a media event,' Natalie suggested, letting herself into the office. Her face was screwed into an expression of supreme displeasure as she looked up at Mitch. 'I like that irony, don't you? We can add Paige Price and her "inside informant" to the list of headline acts. Someone gave her the scoop on the notes.'

'No,' Mitch said, as if that would make it so. The bottom dropped out of his stomach as Natalie refused to retract the information.

'*TV* 7 just did a live report from the steps of the court-house. Paige Price read the world the messages you've found. She said the notes came from a laser printer and were printed on common twenty-pound bond paper.'

'Shit.' Mitch rubbed a hand over his face, imagining how Hannah would feel hearing those lines read aloud on television, imagining Paul's rage. Imagining every nut in the state cranking up their laser printers. Imagining wrapping his fingers around Paige Price's throat and squeezing.

'Jesus fucking Christ,' he snarled, his temper sparking like a live wire. He turned to Natalie. 'Call Hannah and tell her I'm on the way and tell her why. Radio Steiger. Tell him I need Paul ASAP and to get him away from the search with as little hoopla as possible.'

He rattled off the orders like a field general, a man who was used to giving orders and having them obeyed without question. The top dog, Megan thought. The alpha wolf.

His assistant nodded, sifting through the sheaf of pink message slips she carried, sorting them by priority. 'Just so you know, Professor Priest and his students are setting up in that vacant store next door to the command post – used to be Big D Appliance. It looks like all the volunteers are going to move in there, too. There's too many of them to all fit into the fire hall.'

'Go take a look at their setup,' Mitch ordered Megan as her phone rang.

She scowled at his back as he left the room. 'Bossy son of a bitch,' she muttered.

The answering machine spun out its request to leave a message and Bruce DePalma growled out an order to return his call *immediately*. Megan winced and reached for her parka.

10:02 a.m. 16°

'With the scanner we're able to create a high-grade computer image of Josh that can be transmitted electronically to computers all over the country and printed off from those computers onto more fliers,' Christopher Priest explained, raising his voice to be heard above the din of voices and the clank of chairs and tables being set down and shoved into place. In the background a radio was tuned to a local country station blasting out Wynonna Judd.

The student at the terminal was one of five in down coats and stocking caps clacking away on keyboards. Megan watched as Josh's image came up on the screen in full color. The bright smile, the unruly hair, the Cub Scout uniform – everything about the picture hit her like a fist in the solar plexus every time she saw it. He looked like such a happy little boy. He had so much life ahead of him.

If they could find him. Soon. She felt the seconds ticking by one after another, and resisted the urge to glance at her watch.

She looked away from the screen, taking in the makeshift volunteer center. The room was being transformed before her eyes. Tables and chairs and office equipment were being hauled in through both the front and back doors, creating a wind tunnel of frigid air through the building. The volunteers took positions at the tables the instant the legs hit the floor, piling all available surfaces with fliers and envelopes, staplers and stamps and boxes of rubber bands.

They came from all walks of life, from all over the state. Some men, many women. Middle-aged, elderly, college aged. They had already papered over the big front windows of the store with bright yellow Missing posters and with posters that had been drawn by Josh's third-grade classmates calling for Josh to come home, as if the power of their collective plea might be enough to bring him back. Nearly every storefront in town wore similar window dressing.

'We can also communicate with the National Center for Missing and Exploited Children and with Missing Children Minnesota,' the professor went on. He was bundled into a black down parka that seemed to be swallowing him whole. It crept up around his ears, and he jammed his hands in his pockets and jerked it back down. 'We can connect with a number of missing children's networks and foundations around the country. It's amazing how many there are. Tragic is the word I ought to use, I suppose. It seems for every child that disappears, a foundation springs up in his name.'

'Let's hope we don't need a Josh Kirkwood Foundation,' Megan murmured.

'Yes, let's hope,' he said on a sigh. He tore his eyes away from the computer screen and blinked at her behind the lenses of his oversize glasses. 'Can I offer you a cup of coffee, Agent O'Malley? Hot cider, hot tea? We don't have a shortage of volunteers or food.'

'Cider would be great, thanks.'

She followed him to a long table at the back of the main room, where all the edible donations had been laid out, and gratefully accepted the cup of steaming spiced cider. The heat radiated out through the cup and through her gloves to fingers that felt brittle with cold. She looked across the room bustling with volunteers, people who were giving their time, their talents, their hearts, and their money to bring Josh home. A fund had already been established for reward money, and donations were pouring in from all over the Upper Midwest, from individuals, civic groups, businesses. At last report they had collected in excess of $50,000.

One table of volunteers was dedicating their time to stamping the latest reward information on reams of fliers. Another table addressed and stuffed envelopes, another sorted the packets by zip code and bagged them for delivery to the post office. The fliers would go to law enforcement organizations, civic organizations, businesses, schools, to be distributed and posted in windows, on bulletin boards, stapled to light poles, tucked under windshield wipers all across the country.

Megan knew too well that their efforts could all be for nothing, that no matter how many people helped, hoped, prayed, Josh's fate was ultimately in the hands of one twisted person, and finding him would make wandering through a maze blindfolded seem simple by comparison. Still, it helped to know people cared.

'Seeing a community rally together this way helps to renew my faith in humanity a little,' she confessed.

Priest watched the crowd, his face lacking the animation he had shown while explaining the computer setup. 'Deer Lake is a nice town full of nice people. Everyone knows and loves Hannah. She gives so much to the community.'

'What about Paul? Does everyone know and love him, too?'

He shrugged. 'Everyone goes to the doctor, not that many people seek out accountants. Paul is less visible. But, then, I suppose most people would be less visible next to Hannah.'

Paul was the more visible of the two now, Megan thought, missing the hint of color that stained the professor's cheeks when he mentioned Hannah's name. Paul was shoving his face in front of a camera every chance he got, while Hannah was sentenced to house arrest.

'I believe people come together this way as a defense.'

Megan sipped her cider and glanced at the man who had joined them. He was a match for the professor in height – no taller than five nine – and in build, being slim almost to the point of slight. There the similarities ended. The newcomer's hair was blond and fashionably cut. His features were attractive. *Pretty* was the word that came to mind. Finely sculpted, almost effeminate with big dark eyes that seemed drowsy. He was dressed in gray wool trousers and an obviously expensive navy wool topcoat over a dark sweater.

'An instinctive herd-mentality response,' he said. 'Strength and safety in numbers. Band together to fight off a predator.'

'You sound like an expert,' Megan said.

'I can't say I've had a lot of direct experience with this kind of situation, but psychology is my department, so to speak. Dr Garrett Wright,' he said, offering his hand. 'I teach at Harris.'

'Megan O'Malley, BCA.'

'I'd say it's a pleasure, but that seems inappropriate,' he said, sliding his hands into his coat pockets.

Megan conceded the point with a tip of her head. 'Are you here to offer your services, Doctor? We could use some ideas about the mind of the person who took Josh.'

Wright frowned and rocked back on the heels of his black oxfords. 'Actually, I came to ask Chris for the keys to his file cabinets. We've got students working on a joint project together. In fact,' he said, turning to Priest, 'I should probably get the key to your office if you're going over to Gustavus Adolphus tomorrow.'

Setting aside his cider, Priest dug in his jacket pocket for a ring bristling with keys and set about the task of freeing the ones his colleague needed.

'I wish I could be of some help,' Wright said to Megan. 'Hannah and Paul are neighbors of mine. I hate to see them go through something like this. My wife has been helping Hannah out. I guess she's the official delegate from our household.' He shook his head. 'I've studied socially deviant behavior, but I don't have any degree in criminology. My area of expertise is learning and perception. Although, I suppose it's safe to assume you're dealing with a loner, a sociopath. If what they're reporting on the news about the notes he left behind is true, you may be looking at someone delusional – delusions of grandeur, delusions specifically regarding religion.'

'Everyone is buzzing about the notes,' Priest said, handing over a pair of small silver keys. His jacket crept up around his ears again. He tugged it down and took a sip of his drink, the steam from the cider fogging his glasses. 'A lot of the volunteers saw Paige Price's report on the television in the fire hall. Dramatic stuff. What do you make of it, Agent O'Malley?'

'It's not my job to speculate,' Megan said, congratulating herself for being a lady and not taking the opportunity to trash Paige Price. She would have given her last nickel to get her hands on the reporter and her inside informant. 'I have to deal in facts.'

'No intuition?' Wright asked.

Megan regarded him with a cool look, one brow sketching upward. 'Is that a sexist remark, Dr Wright?'

'Not in the least,' Priest returned on Wright's behalf. 'For all police officers profess to be pragmatic, I've read a lot about "gut instinct." What is that if not intuition?'

'You're interested in police work?'

'From a professional standpoint. With more and more law enforcement agencies moving into the computer age, the demand for new and better software increases. When I'm not teaching, I dabble at programming. It pays handsomely to keep abreast of new markets. In fact, we'll be using some of my programs here to sort information.'

'I see.'

'So, what *are* your gut feelings about the case?' Wright asked. 'I've heard theories on everything from radical fundamentalists to satanic cults. You must have an opinion.'

'Sure.' She tossed back the last drops of cider and set the cup aside, giving them a wry smile. 'But I know better than to state it in public. That's something else you should know about cops, Professor – we're a wary bunch.'

She wound her scarf around her neck. 'Thanks for showing me the setup. If you need anything, please check with Jim Geist next door. Thank you for your time and effort – and your students' as well.'

Priest shook off her gratitude. 'It's the least we can do.'

With one eye peeled for stray reporters, Megan slid behind the wheel of the Lumina and coaxed the engine to life. Mitch was off trying to smooth out the wake from the revelation of the note. The BCA agents who had been assigned to Megan were checking out hotline tips on vans; grunt work. Out in Lyon State Park, the ground search continued, but she would be of no real help there, just another pair of eyes, not to mention fair game for the press.

That left the list of Josh's activities. Activities that brought him into contact with any number of adults in the community, from scouting to the summer soccer program to serving as an altar boy at St Elysius. As she read the list she wondered which of these ordinary boyhood undertakings might have brought Josh to the attention of someone with the potential to hurt him. All of them, sad to say. The news was full of stories about children being abused by priests, coaches, Scout leaders, teachers. While those professions attracted people with a genuine love of children, they also attracted those with a sick obsession for children. There was no way of singling out the bad ones. Pedophiles seldom looked like monsters – quite often just the opposite was true.

Who do you trust? She remembered being taught to trust and obey that same list of people – her teachers, the priest, 'nice' people, 'good' people. But how could anyone make those distinctions anymore? What were children supposed to be taught today? There seemed to be no one left they could trust absolutely. Not even in Deer Lake, where everyone knew everyone and no one locked their doors at night.

ignorance is not innocence but SIN

Someone who knows the community, she thought. Or someone halfway to Mexico who just enjoyed the idea of screwing with their heads long-distance.

i had a little sorrow, born of a little SIN

Sin. Morality. Religion. Everything from radical fundamentalists to satanic cults. Or maybe a Catholic priest named Tom McCoy.

11:18 a.m. 19°

St Elysius was the one bastion of Rome in a town overrun with Lutherans. As such, it seemed only fitting that the church be of the grand old style, a mini-cathedral of native limestone and spires thrusting up to heaven, stained glass windows depicting the agony and triumph of Christ. It sat on the Dinkytown side of the lake, nearly out in the country, as if the Norwegians had thought it best to keep the papists out of sight.

Megan climbed the front steps, memories from childhood rushing through her head, old, unwelcome feelings churning in her stomach and bringing sweat to the palms of her hands. She and Mick had gone to parochial school. Mick had participated in every sport he could – as much to avoid having to take care of his little sister after school as out of a love for athletics. And Megan had been left to the care of Frances Clay, the joyless, washed-out woman who cleaned the church. She had spent endless hours in St Pat's, sitting on a hard, cold pew while Frances chased dust bunnies off the statues of the Holy Mother.

Half a dozen older women were mumbling the rosary as Megan stepped into the nave, the leader rattling through Our Father like an auctioneer. The interior of the church was every bit as lovely as the exterior. The walls were painted slate blue and decorated with intricate stencil and trim work in gilt, white, and rose. The flames of dozens of votive candles flickered patterns of light and shadow against the walls.

At the altar a tall, rail-thin man dressed in black moved around, arranging cloths and candelabra. Megan set her sights on him and marched down the center aisle, fighting the urge to genuflect. She had found neither refuge nor solace in the Church as a child, and so as an adult ignored it 363 days of the year, returning only on Christmas Eve and Easter – just in case.

The priest stood motionless as she drew near, his stare as dark and somber as his clothing. He looked sixty. Silver flecked the temples of his thin brown hair. He stood with his hands braced wide apart on the table, his mouth unsmiling. His face was so thin, he appeared to be anorexic. Hair prickled on the back of Megan's neck, and she said a little prayer for the parishioners of St Elysius for having the courage to face this grim man every Sunday. He looked like the sort who thought self-flagellation was an acceptable penance for farting in church.

She held up her identification as she mounted the steps. 'Agent O'Malley, BCA. I'd like to have a word with you about Josh Kirkwood, Father.'

The man frowned at her. 'The police have already been here.'

'I'm doing follow-up on initial interviews,' Megan said smoothly. 'I understand Josh had just begun serving as an altar boy here at St Elysius. We're trying to get a feel for Josh's routines, speak with any adults who might have noticed a change in his behavior recently or made note of anything he might have said regarding someone he was frightened of.'

'"Suffer the little children to come unto me, and do not hinder them; for to such belongs the kingdom of heaven."' The priest intoned the line from Matthew in a dramatic voice that made the rosary ladies falter in the middle of the Glory Be. The leader shot him a nasty look.

'We've been praying for Josh,' he said, lowering his volume to a hushed drone. 'I don't remember you being at the service last night.' His eyes narrowed just slightly, the perfect hint of censure tinted his words.

Megan bit her tongue on the reflex to beg forgiveness. Four hundred people had crammed into the church for the prayer service. She couldn't imagine he had memorized every face. Still, she said, 'No, I wasn't among the faithful in church. I was among the cops out in the cold, searching.'

'His fate is in the hands of God. We must have faith that God will bring him home.'

'I've been a cop for ten years, Father. I trust God about as far as I can throw him.'

He stepped back from her, looking as horrified as if her head had just spun around on her shoulders. Megan fully expected him to point a bony finger at her and scream, 'Heretic.' He drew in a breath that rattled in his throat ominously. The rosary ladies went silent and stared.

The merry mechanical music of a GameBoy cracked the tension. Heads turned in the direction of the sanctuary as a good-looking man in his thirties emerged, head bent over the game. Big shoulders tested the seams of a Notre Dame sweatshirt. His tan corduroy trousers were rumpled and he was wearing cowboy boots. The game ended with a series of bleeps and he made a fist and whispered, 'Yes! Twelve fifty-one!'

Megan thought it was probably the thick quality of the silence that made him bring his head up. He looked at the people assembled, blinking behind a pair of gold-rimmed spectacles. A blush rose in his lean cheeks, and he flicked the switch on the game.

'Am I interrupting something?' he whispered, his mildly confused gaze landing on Megan.

'Agent O'Malley, BCA,' she said automatically. 'I need a few minutes of Father McCoy's time.'

'Oh? Well, fine. I'm Father Tom McCoy.'

'But –' Megan shot a look at the thin man.

McCoy frowned. 'Albert, thank you for entertaining Ms O'Malley in my absence.' He took hold of Megan's arm gently but firmly and escorted her back whence he had come, his head bent down toward hers. 'Albert is very devout,' he whispered. 'In fact, he will gladly tell you he is more qualified for my job than I am.'

'I don't think he'll gladly tell me anything,' Megan confessed. 'I think he was about to douse me with holy water to see if I'd burn.'

McCoy directed her to a chair as he closed the door of his office. 'In another time Albert Fletcher would have been called a zealot. In the nineties with a shortage of priests we call him a deacon.'

'Is he all there?' she asked, tapping a finger to her temple.

'Oh, yes. He has an MBA from Northwestern. A very intelligent man, Albert.' Father Tom sank down into the high-backed chair behind his desk and swiveled it back and forth. 'Socially, he's not exactly the life of the party. He lost his wife three years ago. Some kind of mysterious stomach ailment no one could ever quite pin down. After she was gone, he became increasingly involved with the church.'

'Obsessed.'

McCoy gave her a look and shrugged. 'How do we draw the line between devotion and obsession? Albert functions well, keeps his house and yard immaculate, belongs to civic groups. He has a life; he just chooses to spend most of it here.'

He tossed his GameBoy onto the blotter and gave her a sheepish look. 'This is what keeps *me* sane when the world gets a little too heavy.' The smile faded. 'The treatment isn't holding up too well these days.'

'Josh Kirkwood.'

The priest shook his head. 'My heart breaks every time I think of him. Who knows what he's going through. And Hannah . . . This is killing her. She's tearing herself up trying to find some logic in it, but there's no understanding why things like this happen.'

'I thought you'd have all the answers.'

'Me? No. The Lord works in mysterious ways and I'm not privy to His motives. I'm just a shepherd; my job is keeping the flock together and herding them in the right direction.'

'Somebody's fallen off the path in a big way.'

'And you think that somebody is from St Elysius?'

'Not necessarily. I'm talking with everyone who had regular contact with Josh, looking for any scrap of information that might be helpful. Something Josh might have said, a change in his attitude, anything. Hannah tells me he had just started training as a server.'

The look in McCoy's blue eyes was sad and knowing. 'The altar boy and the priest. Is that what this is about, Agent O'Malley?' He shook his head slowly. 'I'm always amazed when one victim of stereotyping turns around and pigeonholes someone else.'

'I'm just doing my job, Father,' Megan replied evenly. 'It's not my place to draw conclusions, but it is my place to go on the basis of what evidence I have and pursue any and all leads. I'm sorry if that makes you feel discriminated against, but that's the way it is. If it makes you feel any better, I'll also be talking with Josh's teachers and coaches and his Scout leader. You're not a suspect.'

'I'm not? I'll bet I could find plenty of people in this town who have already decided otherwise.' He rose from his chair and walked back and forth behind the desk with his hands in his pockets. 'Can't really blame them, I guess. I mean, the papers are full of it, aren't they? This priest, that priest, a cardinal. It's deplorable. And the Church covers it up and pretends nothing is wrong, carrying on the fine tradition of corruption that's plagued us since the time of Peter.'

'Are you allowed to say that kind of thing?' Megan asked, amazed at his candor.

He flashed her a roguish grin. 'I'm a radical. Ask Albert Fletcher. He's spoken with the bishop about me.'

He seemed extremely pleased to be the object of controversy. Megan couldn't help but smile. She liked Tom McCoy. He was young and energetic and not afraid to say what he thought – a stark contrast to the priests she had grown up around. A stark contrast to Albert Fletcher. And she caught herself wondering why a man as charming and handsome as McCoy was would become a priest.

He read her thoughts too easily. 'It's a calling,' he said gently, easing back down into his chair, 'not a consolation prize for men who can't do anything else.'

'But sometimes it calls the wrong sort of people,' Megan said, steering back onto the topic and away from her embarrassment.

Father Tom's boyish face appeared to age before her eyes. 'No,' he said grimly. 'Those people are hearing a different voice.'

'The voice of evil? The devil?'

'I believe in it absolutely. You do, too, don't you, Agent O'Malley?'

She didn't answer right away. She sat for a minute, thinking about her Irish Catholic upbringing. Even with that stripped away her answer would be the same. She had seen too much on the streets to believe anything else. 'Yes, I do,' she said quietly. 'And as far as I'm concerned, child predators are about as evil as it gets. So is there anything you can think of that will help me nail this bastard's ass to a wall?'

He didn't bat an eye at her language. 'No. I wish I could. We had a prayer vigil here last night. I spent most of the time scoping out the crowd, thinking maybe I'd see someone who didn't fit in, thinking maybe he would come to see the kind of havoc he's wreaked on this community. Thinking maybe I'd see a sign, you know – glowing red eyes, 666 marked across his forehead – but I guess that happens only in the movies.'

'What about regarding Josh himself? Had you noticed any change in his behavior?'

'Well . . .' He took a moment to choose his words carefully. 'He'd been quieter lately. I think Hannah and Paul are having some trouble. Not that either of them has said anything; it's just a feeling I get. Josh is a sensitive boy. Kids pick up a lot more than adults realize. But I hadn't noticed anything overt. He takes his duties as a server very seriously.'

'You train the boys yourself?'

'We have girls now, too. The Church's effort to join the age of equality. Of course, they'll never consider women as priests, but –' He cut himself off from another radical tangent, giving Megan a sheepish look. He pushed his glasses up on his nose with a forefinger against the bridge. 'Anyway, to answer your question, Albert Fletcher and I both work with the kids. We do a kind of a good cop-bad cop routine. Albert drills the rules into them, then I give them a wink and let them know it's okay if they goof up every once in a while just as long as they don't sneeze on the hosts.'

Megan smiled at the joke, but her mind had turned toward Albert Fletcher. Albert Fletcher, the religious fanatic, the man who quoted the Bible in answer to her questions. She wondered if he could quote Robert Browning as well: *ignorance is not innocence but SIN.*

'Do you happen to know what kind of car Mr Fletcher drives?'

'A brown Toyota wagon. Is Albert *not* a suspect, too?' the priest asked dryly.

Megan rose from her chair, her expression sober. 'At this time, Father, everyone is *not* a suspect. What about you? What do you drive?'

'A red Ford 4X4 truck.' He grinned his rogue's grin and shrugged. 'Somebody's got to shake up the status quo. It might as well be me.'

She couldn't help but smile. If there had been any priests like Tom McCoy around when she was growing up, she might have actually paid attention in church instead of spending all her time doodling on the back of the missalette.

'Father Tom, can I have a word?'

Megan swung toward the door at the sound of Mitch's voice. He strode into the office, his coat hanging open, his hair windblown. He looked annoyed at finding she had beat him to St Elysius.

'Ah, Agent O'Malley,' he said, 'grilling the local clergy now?'

'Just asking Father to help me pray for patience in dealing with arrogant territorialism.'

Lacking a good comeback, he gave a snort and turned his attention to the priest. He played golf with Tom McCoy during good weather and liked him. There was always some gossip floating around town that the Father was in trouble with the diocese mucky-mucks for being too liberal, news Father Tom shrugged off with an indifference Mitch respected.

Tom McCoy met his gaze. 'You think I'm not a suspect, too?'

'Did Agent O'Malley lead you to believe otherwise?' Mitch asked.

'Father Tom and I were just having a routine chat,' Megan said coolly. 'Did I need your permission for that, Cujo?'

'Did you discuss the notes?'

'No.'

'What notes?' Father Tom asked. 'Has there been some kind of ransom demand?'

'I wish it were that simple,' Mitch said. 'Two notes have been found – one in Josh's duffel bag, one in a notebook of his. Both make a reference to sin.'

'And the natural correlation is to the Church,' the priest concluded.

'I'm looking for names of anyone in your parish you might think of as being mentally unstable, fanatical – particularly anyone with a connection to the Kirkwoods.'

'Our resident fanatic is Albert Fletcher, but Albert would no more commit a crime than he would denounce the Pope,' said Father Tom. 'And he was teaching Josh's class that night, if he needs an alibi. Mentally unstable – we've got a few of those, but I'm talking about people with problems, not psychotic monsters. Nor can I think of anyone who would have it in for Hannah or Paul.'

Mitch did his best to take the disappointment in stride. Cases like this were seldom made in one smooth move. A cop couldn't afford to take every setback and dead end hard; there would be too many of them. There had been too many today already. The search was going nowhere. Hannah and Paul had been predictably upset with the disclosure of the notes on television. The interviews of school employees were netting them nothing but paperwork. He had a leak in his department, every man on his force pulling overtime, and Megan O'Malley challenging his authority. The combination ate at the lock on his temper like a voracious virus.

'We've already discussed Josh's altar-boy training,' Megan told him. 'That looks like another dead end.'

'Then I guess we can let you get back to work, Father,' Mitch said. 'Give me a call if anything comes to mind.'

'I will,' Father Tom said, a grave expression tugging at his features. 'And in the meantime, we should all pray like hell.'

Megan preceded Mitch out the side door of the church and started down the steps to the neatly shoveled sidewalk. Snow was piled on the boulevard between the walk and the parking lot, rising up like a miniature mountain range through which passes had been cut at thirty-foot intervals. She aimed for the one nearest the Lumina.

'Did you expect me to sit in my office and do my nails all day?' she asked without bothering to look back at Mitch. 'But that wouldn't make me like Leo, either, would it?'

She paused on the sidewalk to pose with her chin on her mittened fist. 'Let's see. What would Leo do? I know,' she said brightly. 'We'll go on down to the Blue Goose Saloon and slam a few brewskis. Then we can sit around belching and farting and cursing our lack of clues.'

'Hey,' he barked, 'Leo was a good cop. Don't slam Leo. And I never said you shouldn't do your job.'

He started for his truck without waiting for a rebuttal. Megan hustled after him, tossing the tail of her scarf back over her shoulder.

'No, you said I shouldn't do it without asking first. So, in the interest of diplomacy, I'm asking where you want me to go next.'

His laugh cracked the cold air like a gunshot. He looked back at her over his shoulder. 'You're asking for it all right, O'Malley.'

'I've been hearing that for years.'

'Think it'll ever sink in?'

'I doubt it,' Megan said as they turned through the pass into the parking lot. She fished her keys out of her coat pocket while Mitch turned toward his truck. 'So where are you going?'

'Oh, I thought I'd stop off at the He-Man Woman Haters Club and then go bowling with the guys from the Moose Lodge.' He unlocked his door and pulled it open. 'Us guys are like that, you know.'

Megan cocked her head.

'I'm going to go hunt for the animal who took Josh Kirkwood,' he said. 'You, Agent O'Malley, can stay out of my way.'

15

Daylight was fading to black when Megan checked back in at the command center. She had spent the afternoon personally rechecking the other people on the list of adults with whom Josh had regular contact, dispensing sympathy and tissues and getting no answers to the questions that loomed larger with every tick of the clock.

Josh's teacher, Sara Richman, had two sons of her own. Despite the fact that she had been questioned twice already, she still couldn't speak or even think about what had happened without starting to cry. His Scout leader, Rob Phillips, was a clerk in the county attorney's office, a man who had been confined to a wheelchair for the last three years and for the rest of his life, thanks to a drunk driver. Phillips had taken vacation time from work to help at the volunteer center.

People were heading out of the fire hall – some to go home to their families, some to grab dinner and come back. Megan went in search of Jim Geist and found Dave Larkin in his place in the room where some of her agents and several of Mitch's men handled the hotline phones. There seemed to be a phone ringing constantly, punctuating the running underscore of mumbling voices. Cops and volunteers came in and left the room, bringing in fliers and food, taking out scrawled notes and fax messages.

Larkin wore a blue and white aloha shirt that accented his beach-bum image. A phone receiver was sandwiched between his shoulder and ear, and he was scribbling furiously on a legal pad. He glanced up at her and rolled his eyes.

'No, I'm sorry, Mr DePalma, I haven't seen Agent O'Malley. She's been out in the field all day working on a lead. Yes, sir, I understand it's important. I'll see that she gets the message.' He grimaced at Megan. 'She should call you at home? I understand. Yes, sir.'

He hung up the phone, stuck a finger in his ear, and wiggled it around, giving Megan a comic look of distress. 'Irish, you owe me *so big*.'

Megan slid into the chair beside him and leaned an elbow on the table. 'I'll promise you anything that isn't sex related.'

'Hell,' he grumbled. 'If I'd known that, I would have made you take the call.'

'You're such a pal. DePalma is the last person I want to talk to.'

'Rightly so. He sounded in a mood for some grilled agent.'

She sniffed. 'It's the reporters he ought to want roasted. If someone wants to run a spit through Henry Forster and Paige Price, I'll make the potato salad. So what are you doing here?' she asked. 'Did Jim go back to the hotel?'

'Yeah. I'm here on my own time,' he said, giving her a little smile. 'Told you you'd get volunteers.'

'And I appreciate it. Any word from the lab on the notes?'

'Nothing that hasn't already been on TV. We accelerated the reaction on the ninhydrin test with heat and humidification and ran it under the ultraviolet. If there were prints on the paper, they would have gone purple and fluoresced under illumination. We got zip. Sorry, kiddo.'

Megan sighed. 'Yeah, well, I didn't think we'd get that lucky. We're not dealing with your garden-variety idiot. This one would know enough to wear gloves. So what's the latest on the van?'

'I'd say every third person in the state knows someone weird who drives a light-colored utility van.' He pulled Geist's notes in front of him and flipped through the pages. 'First of all, the chief in New Prague checked the con with the yellow van. The van is now sporting an airbrushed mural of a desert sunset, and the con bowls Wednesday nights in a league. This week he scored a 220 high and won the beer frame twice.'

'Lucky dog,' she muttered without enthusiasm. 'Anything else turn up?'

'Jim organized the tips geographically. He met with Chief Holt this afternoon. They went over the list of local calls together, sorted a few out, then Jim sent a guy with one of Holt's men to check the rest.'

'Let me see the list.'

Larkin handed it over and leaned back in his chair, stretching his arms over his head. 'So after we nail this piece of dirt, you want to take a weekend and go skiing in Montana? I know a guy who has a friend who has a condo in Whitefish.'

Megan scanned the names and addresses of people in Park County whose neighbors had ratted on them. 'I don't ski.'

'That's even better. We can spend our time in the hot tub.'

'Maybe you should spend some time under a cold shower,' she suggested.

The name hit her with all the force of a line drive. She sat up straight in the chair as she took in the number of calls that had come in about this particular van and the fat red line drawn through them. 'What the hell is this?'

Larkin leaned over and glanced at the list. 'Holt said he already checked it out.'

'That son of a bitch,' Megan growled, shooting to her feet. She could feel her blood pressure climbing into the red zone. It pounded in her ears as her temper boiled. She stepped away from the chair and shoved it hard against the table. The noise cut through the bleating of telephones and low rumble of conversations and drew wide-eyed looks in her direction.

'Where are you going?' Larkin called as she stormed out.

'To kick some ass!'

He cupped his chin in his hand. 'I guess this rules out dinner and an evening of wild, unbridled sex.'

5:01 p.m. 23°

Mitch sat in his office with only the amber light of the lamp shining down on the reports and statements strewn across the desktop. He had sent Natalie home to help her two teenagers get ready for the torchlight parade. Valerie played flute in the high school band. Troy was riding on the senior class float. The town council had voted to go on with the Snowdaze activities, but every event would in some way now focus on Josh's abduction. The show of community unity would be both tremendous and tragic.

The day had beat Mitch down physically and mentally. The constant pressure, the sense of urgency, wore on nerves and patience. He had personally questioned much of the elementary school staff and walked the grounds again, trying to find something, anything, that would be a connection to or spark an idea as to the identity of the person who had planted Josh's notebook on the hood of his truck. All with reporters swarming after him like gnats. All for nothing. The parking lot was easily accessible and no one had seen anything. Planting the evidence had been a simple matter of driving up alongside the Explorer and reaching out the window. Slick, simple, diabolical. Infuriating. It made him feel like a chump, as if he'd been had in a shell game, played for a fool and beaten.

Somehow, he was going to have to rally in time to take his daughter to the parade. His mother-in-law had called to suggest she and Jurgen take Jessie, saying Jessie was, after all, staying with them for the weekend. Besides, she thought it might upset Jessie to go with him now, what with all this terrible business going on and policemen walking into the classrooms at school, frightening all the children.

Mitch had lost his temper. Joy tried his patience in the best of times, and this was hardly the best of times.

'Are you saying my daughter should be frightened of me?'

'No! Not at all! I'm just saying –'

'You're just saying what, Joy?'

'Well, that Kirkwood boy was taken right off the street.'

'Trust me, Joy, someone tries to take Jessie off the street while I'm standing there, I'll blow his fucking head off.'

'Well, you don't have to take that tone –'

'I get a little testy when you suggest my daughter isn't safe with me, Joy.'

'I never said that!'

But she thought it. She thought it all the time and she slipped those thoughts under his skin like poisoned slivers, so clever, so subtle. She had trusted him with her daughter and her daughter was dead. She had trusted him with her grandson and her grandson was dead. She blamed Mitch entirely and she kept that blame inside her, never saying a word outright, letting that blame grow and metastasize like a malignant tumor.

He knew because he did the same thing.

He rubbed his hands over his face. A part of him wished he could just go to sleep until the nightmare was over, but he got a nightmare either way. Awake, there was the case. Asleep, he dreamed of drowning in a sea of blood.

'Couldn't you just pick up those few things on your way home?'

'Allison, I've been on the job eighteen hours. I've got three hours to come home, sleep, eat, shower, and shave before I've got to be in court. The last thing I want to do is stop at the goddamn 7-Eleven. Can't you stop on the way to T-ball?'

'I hate that store on the way to the park. That's a rotten neighborhood.'

'For Christ's sake, you won't be in there five minutes. It's broad daylight. Those places get hit at night, when there's no one around.'

'I can't believe we have to have this argument at all. Why do we stay here? Every day it gets worse. I feel like a prisoner in my own home –'

'Jesus, don't start that now. Can we wait until I've slept thirteen or fourteen hours before we have this fight again?'

'All right. Fine. But I want to have a real discussion, Mitch. I mean it. I don't want to live this way.'

As his wife's last words echoed in his mind, he fingered the gold band that circled his finger.

There was no justice. No logic. There was no justice in Hannah Garrison losing her son to a faceless phantom whose only explanation was a cruel taunt. The joke was on the people who thought life should make sense.

And while Mitch stole these few moments for the futile exercise of punishing himself and shaking his fist at an unjust world, the clock ticked, each second adding to the sense of desperation inside him.

He needed to clear his mind and center himself, focus. Tightly gripping the arms of his chair, he tried to draw in a deep, calming breath the way the department shrink in Miami had tried to teach him. Focus the mind on a single thought and breathe slowly and deeply. More often than not, Mitch had focused on the idea of beating the ever-loving shit out of the psychologist, the pompous, condescending ass.

'If he's back here, he damn well *will* see me!'

The voice was unmistakably Megan's. Unmistakably furious. Punctuated by Noga's thundering footfalls.

163

'But Miss O – Agent, he said he didn't want to be disturbed.'

'Disturbed? How about dismembered?'

She was through the door before Mitch could do more than stand up. She stopped halfway into the room with her hands on her hips, her oversize coat falling back off her shoulders. The long gray scarf she could never quite seem to manage was slithering down over one shoulder, trailing nearly to the floor.

Noga appeared behind her. 'Sorry, Chief, I couldn't stop her.'

He had been able to stop Division I defensive linemen in college, but he couldn't stop Megan O'Malley. Somehow that made perfect sense to Mitch. He waved the patrolman off.

'My turn, Chief,' Megan snapped as the office door closed behind her. 'Why wasn't I told that Olie Swain drives an eighty-three white Chevy van? Why was I not informed that you spoke with Olie Swain about this van last night?'

'I don't answer to you, Agent O'Malley,' he said, tossing her own words back at her. 'You don't outrank me. You're not my boss.'

'No, you don't answer to anyone, do you?' she spat out angrily. 'You're Matt fucking Dillon and this is Dodge City. *Your* town. *Your* people. *Your* investigation. Well, it can be on *your* head when someone finds this kid's body in a Dumpster and it turns out Olie Swain did the job.'

Megan could almost feel him tense as he took that blow. Good. He needed to be hit over the head – figuratively if not literally.

'At least Steiger is up front. I knew he was an asshole the minute I laid eyes on him. You cooperate when it suits you, and when it doesn't, you pick up your toys and tell me to go home.'

'All right,' he said in that cutting, deceptively soft tone. 'Go home. I'm operating on a real lean mix here, Agent O'Malley. I'm in no mood to listen to you whine that I don't play fair.'

'In no mood –' Megan broke off, choking on her fury. For an instant she contemplated launching herself at him across the desk. She wanted to shake him until his teeth rattled. Instead, she glared at him.

'Your mood notwithstanding,' she continued sharply, 'I think we had better get a few things straight here. This is an investigation and I am a part of this investigation. Therefore I am entitled to know when someone I consider a suspect turns out to have a van matching the witness's description.'

'Nothing came of it,' Mitch snapped. 'Helen Black couldn't identify the van. Olie has an alibi –'

'Which no one has substantiated absolutely –'

'There was nothing inside the van –'

'You looked inside that van *without a warrant?*' Megan exclaimed, incredulous. 'God, of all the stupid –'

'I had his verbal consent –'

'Which doesn't mean shit!'

'If I'd seen anything, I could have had the van towed on a parking violation and we would have ended up with a warrant. I saw nothing whatsoever that could link Olie or the van to Josh's disappearance.'

'You can see fingerprints, Superman?'

Her sarcasm stung in ways she couldn't know. Anger was his automatic response against the pain. 'You couldn't have gotten a warrant on the van, Agent O'Malley,' he said, advancing on her. 'There's no way in hell you could have dusted it for prints or vacuumed it for fibers or sprayed it down with luminol, looking for traces of blood. We don't have *anything* on Olie Swain.'

'The fact remains,' she said, 'you know I consider the man a suspect. I should have been notified – if not last night, then at least this morning.'

'It didn't come up.' Mitch knew damn well he should have told her. He had known she would find out. She had hit too close to home with the Matt Dillon line. He wanted control of the game and the players. In a way she couldn't understand, Deer Lake *was* his town, his haven. He hated having it pointed out to him that his sense of control was just an illusion.

'We're working this investigation together, Chief,' Megan said. 'I'm not here for window dressing; I'm here to do a job and I don't appreciate being left out of the loop.'

That was the source of much of her anger: She had been excluded. Everyone had known about Olie and his van before her. The old-boy network had pulled another end-around and left her feeling like a fool, like an outcast. It wasn't the first time and it wouldn't be the last, but that didn't mean she had to like it or take it lying down.

He backed away from her slowly and turned away. The desk lamp hummed softly. The ringing of the telephones in the squad room barely penetrated the walls, the distant sound only adding to the sense of isolation.

'All right,' he conceded. 'I should have told you and I didn't. Now you know.'

It was as close to an apology as he was likely to give. Megan knew enough to take small victories when she could get them. She let some of her own tension go and looked around the office as if seeing it for the first time since she had come in.

'Why were you sitting here in the dark?'

'I was just . . . railing against fate,' he murmured. 'I prefer to do that in private, if you don't mind.'

'It doesn't do much good, does it?'

A statement of fact. A confession of sorts. Mitch heard the empathy. They were a lot alike, he supposed. As odd as that sounded. As cops, they had been through the same grind, seen too much, cared too deeply. She had his sense of justice, it just wasn't as tarnished as his. That truth made him feel old and battered.

He stared out the window behind his desk, through the open slats of the vertical blinds. The night looked as black as ink, cold, unwelcoming.

'You can't blame yourself, Mitch,' Megan said, easing closer to him without realizing they had shifted out of one quadrant of their relationship and into another. She hadn't called him Chief.

'Sure I can. For a lot of things.'

She took the final step, closing the distance between them, and looked up at him. They stood at the edge of the lamplight, near enough that it revealed lines of strain and old memories that etched deep into his face. He looked away, frowning, the scar on his chin shining silver in the pale light.

'For what?' she asked softly. 'Your wife?'

'I don't want to talk about it.' He turned toward her, his expression hard. 'I don't want to talk at all.'

He pulled her against him roughly, dropping his head down to touch his face against her cool, dark hair. It smelled faintly of jasmine. 'This is what I want from you.' He tipped her chin up and found her lips with his.

The heat of the kiss was searing. The kiss was rough and wild, pure raw sex that sparked a hot, elemental response. Megan kissed him back, trembling at the need it unleashed. The need to let go of her control and be swept away on this tide of fundamental need. She focused on the taste of him, the warm male scent of him, the contrast in their size and strength, the feel of the muscles in the small of his back, the erotic sensation of his tongue thrusting against hers.

A small sound of longing escaped her, and he responded to it instantly, hungrily. The arm he banded around her back tightened and lifted her against him. His other hand closed boldly over her breast and Megan gasped at the feel of his fingers kneading the sensitive globe, his thumb brushing across her nipple, teasing it through the fabric of her sweater.

'I want you,' he growled, dragging his mouth from hers to plant kisses against her cheekbone, her brow. 'I want to be inside you. Now.'

Megan shivered at the images his words evoked, at the sensations that rippled along her nerve endings. She could feel him against her belly, hard, ready to make good on his statement. And she wanted him. God, she ached with wanting him. She wanted to feel the full power of this desire unleashed, to know what it was like to let go completely of the control that ordered her life.

But they were in his office. He was the chief of police and she was an agent of the BCA. They would see each other in this office, conduct business in this office. And what happened when this fire between them died and they still came to this office every day?

'I – we can't,' she murmured, breathless, her body humming with the need to say yes.

'The hell we can't.' Mitch caught her chin in his hand and forced her to look at him. His gaze was hot, glittering with passion and the determination to lose himself in it. That was what he wanted – to sink into her and into some kind of white-hot oblivion where there was no guilt and no burden.

'It's sex.' He tightened his hand against her back, letting her feel him against her. 'We won't be wearing badges. Or maybe that's what you're afraid of?'

Pushing against his chest, Megan tried without success to back away from him. 'I told you, I'm not afraid of you.'

'But are you afraid to be a woman with me?'

She didn't answer him. She couldn't, Mitch thought. If she said yes, she admitted a vulnerability. If she said no, she committed herself to sleeping with him. She was too wary to box herself in that way. And not without good reason. He doubted he was the first cop to come on to her in her ten years on the job. He remembered the way it had been in Miami, the locker room bets on who would be the first to score with the new skirt on the squad. And he knew what it meant when it happened. The woman lost any respect she might have had from her fellow officers. Respect was everything to Megan. The job was everything to Megan. It would take more than simple lust to get her to cross that line, and Mitch reminded himself that he didn't want to give more.

Slowly, reluctantly, he let her go. 'It's probably just as well,' he muttered as he turned away to grab his parka off the coat tree.

Megan stood back, incredulous, as she watched him shrug into the heavy coat. He could kiss her like that, then calmly turn away and dismiss it as if it had been nothing. The idea made her want to kick him, but she didn't. And she swallowed back the scathing words that burned on the tip of her tongue. He had made an overture, she had declined. Simple.

'Where are you going?'

'I promised Jessie I'd take her out to McDonald's and to the torchlight parade.'

'Oh.'

Mitch glanced at her as he clipped his pager to his belt. Her dark hair had escaped its barrette altogether and fell like a wild horse's mane around her shoulders. Her eyes were wide and showing more than she would have allowed. She looked like the girl who never got asked to dance at the high school sock hop.

'You game for a Big Mac and some frozen Shriner clowns?' he asked, surprising himself.

Megan narrowed her eyes in suspicion. 'Why are you being nice to me?'

'Jeez, O'Malley. It's McDonald's, not Lutèce. Come or don't.'

'You're so gracious, I can hardly resist,' she said dryly, 'but I wouldn't want to intrude.'

He smiled a little at her rancor. 'Aw, tell the truth,' he said. 'You were on your way to Grace Lutheran Church for the annual Snowdaze lutefisk supper.'

167

Megan wrinkled her nose. 'Not in this lifetime. I make it a point never to eat anything that can take the finish off a table. Besides, I think lutefisk is one of those foods people used to have to eat because there wasn't anything else and it somehow became a tradition by mistake.'

'Yeah, no wonder Scandinavians are so morose. If I had to eat boiled cod soaked in lye solution, I'd look like Max von Sydow too.'

They shared a laugh that eased them back into the friends division of their relationship again.

'Big Mac?' Mitch asked, raising his brows.

She wanted to. But she really should go back to the office . . . call DePalma. A grim evening.

'Come on,' he said. 'I'll spring for the fries. What do you say, O'Malley?'

'Okay, let's go, Diamond Jim.' She twisted her scarf around her neck. 'You get the fries, I'll get the Tums.'

16

Day 3
6:16 p.m. 23°

Jessie was dubious about having an extra dinner partner. She gave Megan a long, hard look as they sat in their booth, waiting for Mitch to return with their supper. Megan said nothing, taking that time to size up Mitch's daughter. Jessie Holt was a darling little girl with big brown eyes and a button nose. Her long brown hair had been carefully combed back and plaited into a single thick braid that fell halfway down her back. Two Princess Jasmine barrettes had been added in odd places at odd angles that suggested they were Jessie's own touch.

'Are you my daddy's girlfriend?' she asked baldly, looking none too pleased with the prospect.

'Your dad and I work together,' Megan replied, neatly sidestepping the issue.

'Are you a cop, too?'

'Yep. I sure am.'

Jessie mulled this over, sitting back in the seat and crossing her arms. She wore a white turtleneck dotted with tiny colored hearts. Over that was a sweater knitted in bright blocks of primary colors. On the front of the sweater was an appliqué of the face of a girl with freckles and braided yarn hair. She took hold of one of the braids and tickled the end of her nose with it.

'I never saw a girl cop.'

'There aren't very many of us,' Megan confessed, leaning her elbows on the table. 'My dad was a cop, too. Do you think you might be a cop when you grow up?'

Jessie shook her head. 'I'm gonna be a beterinarian. And a princess.'

Megan contained the laugh that threatened. 'That sounds like a plan. What does a beterinarian do?'

'She helps aminals when they get sick and makes them better.'

'That's a good job. I like animals, too. I have two cats.'

Jessie's eyes widened. 'Really? I have a toy cat named Whiskers. My grandma says I can't get a real cat 'cause Grampa's 'lergic.'

'That's too bad.'

'I have a dog, though,' she added, scooting ahead on her seat. She laid her arms on the table in an imitation of Megan's pose. 'His name is Scotch – like butterscotch. He's older than me, but he's my dog. Daddy says so.'

'What Daddy says goes,' Mitch said, setting the heavily laden tray down on the table.

Jessie grinned. 'Goes where?' She scrambled into his lap as he sat down. She tipped her head back and looked at him upside down.

'Goes to Timbuktu!'

He made a goofy face, wrapped his arms around her, and pretended to tickle her. Jessie giggled and squirmed. They had obviously been through the routine many times before.

Megan felt she didn't belong. Mitch wanted to spend time with his daughter, had asked Megan along only as a courtesy. She kicked herself for accepting, and she kicked herself again for letting old memories sneak up on her. She was a grown woman and she had better things to do with her time than feel sorry for herself because she had a family that defined the word *dysfunctional*.

'Hey, O'Malley? You okay?'

'What?' She glanced back at Mitch, embarrassed to see concern in his eyes. 'Yeah, sure,' she mumbled, giving her attention over to the paper-wrapped burger in front of her. The smell of fried onions wafted up to tempt her. 'I was just . . . thinking about the case. Um . . . I should have gone over the background checks the guys ran on the hospital staff today. You know, maybe I'll pass on the parade.'

'Cut yourself some slack,' Mitch said. 'I realize the clock's ticking, but you can't work twenty-four hours a day. You go at it that hard, you burn up physically and mentally, then you're no good to anyone.'

Megan shrugged. 'I've put in only ten hours today. I can do a few more and still have a couple to spare.' She gave him her best poker face. 'I think better at night. There aren't so many distractions.'

Mitch frowned but said nothing.

Jessie took a gulp of her milk. 'Daddy, do you think – um – in the parade that there'll be those guys dressed up like pieces of cheese like last time? They were funny.'

'Probably, sweetheart,' he murmured, his eyes still on Megan.

Jessie launched into a detailed account of last year's torch-light parade. And Megan, glad for the distraction from Mitch's probing, concentrated on the little girl, knowing that by the time the story ended, the meal would be over and she would be able to escape. Mitch deserved some time alone with his daughter, and Megan wanted to retreat from this unfamiliar ground to the one thing she knew she could do well – her work.

Megan drove the deserted streets of Deer Lake, cursing the car's heater. It seemed a ridiculous time of year for a parade, and yet that seemed to be where everyone was. Megan wondered how many of the brass players in the high school bands would get their lips frozen to the mouthpieces of their horns.

Jessie's tale of last year's parade brought a smile to her lips. She could picture the floats she'd seen in the garage at the old fire hall. She could envision the clowns and the skiing wedges of cheddar from the BuckLand cheese factory slipping and falling in the street, tangling up with one another, the crowds on the sidewalks doubled over laughing.

How much laughing would there be tonight? Tonight, when a missing child was on everyone's mind, when every marcher wore a yellow ribbon and every float bore a banner that said BRING JOSH HOME.

Megan wished with all her heart they could bring Josh home. They had so little to go on. The hotline tips hadn't produced anything but dead ends and false hopes. Megan's mind kept going in the direction of Olie Swain. He was the closest thing they had to a suspect. Mitch had to think so, too, or he wouldn't have risked taking a look inside Olie's van.

She wished again he would have confided in her about the van. And about himself. She could have picked up the phone and uncovered his past with a couple of calls. If she had wanted, she could have called *TV 7* and gotten a copy of Paige Price's hatchet job on him. She could have reached out to someone on the force in Miami or tracked down the story through the archives of the *Miami Herald*. But she would do none of those things. It had to come from Mitch himself, and the reason for that scared the hell out of her. Deep inside, where logic meant nothing, she wanted him to trust her.

You're too stupid for words, O'Malley.

He wanted to take her to bed, not give her his heart.

She wanted to go with him. Her third day on the job and she wanted to have sex with the chief of police.

You're too stupid to live, O'Malley.

Lust. Chemistry. Animal attraction. The heightened emotions of a volatile situation. Physical needs too long ignored. The excuses bounced through her head, all of them true, none of them the truth. She wouldn't look for the heart of truth. She was too afraid of what she would find. A need that had never been fulfilled. A longing that had been with her forever. Foolish dreams.

There was no place in her life for a relationship, especially one with Mitch Holt with all the complications that would bring. She couldn't believe she was even toying with the idea. Fantasies of love and family and dark-haired little children had always been relegated to the deepest, darkest, most lonely hours of the night, where they could be dismissed as dreams when daylight and reality dawned. It confounded her that they would surface now, when she had neither the time nor the energy to deal with them. Her focus had to be on the case.

With the single-minded determination that had gotten her through her career, she turned her mind in that direction and pointed the car toward the hockey rink. She sat in the parking lot for a long while, staring at Olie's battered van, what-iffing, something anxious stirring inside her. A hunch, just forming, just out of reach, teased her like an itch she couldn't quite scratch. And in the back of her mind she could almost hear Josh's voice reading the line from his notebook: *Kids tease Olie but that's mean. He can't help how he looks.*

Inside the arena music sang out over the speaker system – Mariah Carey's 'Hero.' The seats were empty and dark. Lights shone down on the ice, where a single skater was going through a routine, moving and jumping in harmony with the flowing, lovely song. Megan made her way to the team bench, where she took a ringside seat at the red line.

The skater was a young woman, blond, petite but athletic in black leggings, a purple skating skirt, and a loose-fitting ivory sweater. She concentrated on the music, her footwork and arm movements. Every move was held out perfectly until it flowed into the next. Her jumps were graceful, powerful, with landings so smooth they seemed to defy physics. The music swelled and soared, then softened. The skater went into a final layback spin, looking like a ballerina on a music box.

Megan applauded, drawing the young woman's attention her way for the first time. The skater smiled and waved to acknowledge her tribute, then skated over with her hands on her hips.

'That was great!' Megan said.

She managed a shrug as she worked to even out her breathing. 'It still needs work, but thanks. Could you hand me that bottle of water?'

Megan picked a plastic bottle of mineral water up from the player's bench and handed it over. 'I'm Megan O'Malley with the Bureau of Criminal Apprehension.'

'Ciji Swensen.' She pulled a towel off the gate and blotted her lips and forehead, her dark blue eyes on Megan. 'I read about you in the paper. Are you here about the kidnapping? I feel so bad for Dr Garrison.'

'Do you know Josh?'

'Sure. I know just about everybody in town who can lace on a pair of skates. I'm an instructor with the Figure Skating Club.'

'Working overtime tonight?'

'Practice. The club does a little show every year for Snowdaze. This is one of my pieces. I knew everyone would be at the parade tonight, so I thought I'd take advantage of having the ice all to myself. It's a special number – for Josh, you know? The club voted to give the profits from the show to the volunteer center.'

'That's very generous.'

'Yeah, well, we had to do something. It makes me sick to think some pervert picked Josh up right outside this rink. For all I know, I could have been standing right here when it happened.'

'You were here that night?'

172

Ciji nodded as she took another swig of water. 'I had a class at seven.'

A male voice called out from the darkness at the far end of the rink. 'You want that music again, Ciji?'

'No, thanks, Olie,' she called back. 'I'm taking a break.'

Megan stared hard, just making out the shape of Olie Swain's head and shoulders as he moved in the shadows. 'Did you see Olie that night?'

'Yeah, sure.' She shrugged. 'Olie's always around here somewhere.'

'He resurfaced the ice before your class?'

She nodded. 'He did the ice right after the Squirts finished practice.'

'What time was that?'

'Five-fifteen, five-thirty.' Ciji's delicate brows pulled together in a look of concern. 'Look, I know there are people in town who are ready to blame Olie, but he's not a bad person. He's just odd. I mean, he's really kind of sweet, you know? I've never seen him behave inappropriately around the kids.'

'Did you see him later that night?'

'Sure. He did the ice again before seniors hockey at eight.'

Which left hours in which he could have done anything, including abduct Josh Kirkwood.

Ciji set her water on the ledge along the boards and wound the towel around her hands. 'You don't really think he did it, do you?'

'We're just trying to establish a chronology of the events Wednesday night,' Megan said smoothly, neither confirming nor denying. 'It's important that we know who was where when. You were here until what time?'

'Eight-fifteen. I always stay until the senior guys warm up.' She smiled a little. 'They like to flirt. They're a bunch of sweeties.'

'And you didn't see anything or anyone unusual?'

The smile disappeared. 'No. Like I told the officer who questioned me yesterday – I wish I could say otherwise. I wish I could be a hero for Josh, but I just didn't see anything.'

'Thanks anyway,' Megan said. 'I'll let you get back to work. It was nice meeting you.'

'Sure.' Ciji tossed her towel over the gate and gracefully skated backward toward center ice. 'I hope you can make it to the show Sunday!'

'I'll try,' Megan called, already moving out of the box and toward the end of the arena

Olie saw her coming. That lady cop who looked right at him. He didn't want to talk to her. He didn't want to talk to anybody. He knew what people were saying – that his van was like the one the cops were looking for. Well, Mitch Holt had already looked inside his van and hadn't found anything. So they could all just go hang themselves, those people who stared at him sideways and said things about him behind his back. He didn't care what they thought, anyway. All he wanted was to be left alone.

He grabbed his plastic liter bottle of Coke and his book on chaos theories and started toward the door to the locker rooms.

'Mr Swain? Can I have a word with you?'

'Talked to the chief,' he grumbled. 'Nothing else to say.'

Watch your manners, Leslie! Don't be rude, Leslie. Never turn your back to me while I'm talking, Leslie.

He winced at the strident voice in his head.

'This will take only a minute.'

If he went to his office, she would follow him. He didn't want that. He didn't like anyone going in there. He couldn't breathe when other people came into his space.

'I just have a couple of questions for you,' Megan said, catching up with him.

She could smell him five feet away. The rank onion smell of poor hygiene and overactive sweat glands wafted from him like cologne gone bad. He was wearing the same sweater and jacket he'd had on the first night. He stood facing her, a textbook clutched against his chest, his glass eye staring, his good eye darting all around her.

'Mr Swain, I know you did the ice here the night Josh disappeared. Right after his team finished practice, right?'

He nodded.

'And again just before the seniors team played?'

His head jerked again.

'Could you tell me where you were during the time in between?'

'Around.' He flinched at his own belligerence.

Don't take that tone with me, Leslie. You'll wish you hadn't, Mr Smartmouth. I'll make you wish you hadn't.

The lady cop was staring at him. He wanted to shove her away. He wanted to hit her in the face to make her stop staring, and hit her again while he screamed at her to leave him alone. But he couldn't do those things, and knowing he couldn't made him feel puny and weak and impotent. A runt. A freak. A mistake of nature. His hand tightened around the Coke bottle and he scowled, frowning so hard, his small mouth bent into the shape of a horseshoe.

'Can anyone back you up on that?' Megan asked. Her gaze flicked down to Olie's right hand covered by the same Ragg wool half-gloves. As he squeezed the bottle until it made a crackling sound, the fingerlets pulled back from his knuckles, revealing a glimpse of thin blue lines traced on each finger. Her heart kicked against her ribs.

'I didn't do anything,' Olie said angrily.

'I didn't say you did, Mr Swain,' Megan countered calmly. 'But you know, that van of yours looks a lot like the one our witness described. If you weren't driving it, who was? You have a buddy you might have loaned it to? You can tell me. You won't be in any trouble.'

'No,' he snapped, rocking back and forth on the sides of his ratty Nikes, squeezing the Coke bottle rhythmically.

'And you say you were here that whole evening, but you don't have anyone who can back you up on that?'

'I didn't do anything!' Olie shouted. 'Just leave me alone!' He hurled the Coke bottle into the trash barrel beside the door, then turned and ran down the dark hall.

'I don't know if I'll be able to do that, Mr Swain,' Megan murmured. Holding her breath, she leaned down into the trash barrel and came up holding the Coke bottle gingerly by the throat.

8:43 p.m. 20°

The torchlight parade included the usual Snowdaze traditions – King Frost and the Queen of the Snows with thermal underwear beneath her gown, the Happy Hookers ice fisherman drill team twirling their rods like parade rifles, the schnapps-soaked Shriners weaving precariously from curb to curb on their mini-snowmobiles. There were horse-drawn sleighs and dog sleds and a herd of Rotarians dressed as abominable snowmen. But as Mitch had suspected, the atmosphere was anything but festive. The spectators that lined the streets were all too conscious of the banners and posters of Josh and of the television cameras that had come to capture the small town's despair on videotape. When the contingent from the volunteer center silently marched past with candles burning, he could hear people around him crying.

Jessie clung to Mitch throughout, growing quieter and quieter until she put her head on his shoulder and asked to go home.

Mitch kissed the tip of her nose and hugged her. 'Sure, honey. We'll go see if Grandma will make us some hot chocolate to warm up our noses and toesies. Right?'

The giggle he had hoped for didn't materialize. She merely nodded and tightened her stranglehold around his neck.

'Mitch, can we have a word from you?'

Mitch wheeled on Paige Price, then herded her away from the crowd. 'Jesus Christ, Paige, do you never quit? Do you have any limits at all?'

Paige gave him the wounded look, though knowing he didn't buy it. If Garcia got any good shots of her, they could always use them later on, splice them into another piece. The cameraman backpedaled with her, tape running. 'This is hardly out of bounds, Chief Holt.'

'No, I guess this doesn't even begin to compare with giving away key evidence. My, you've had a busy day, Ms Price.' His voice sizzled with sarcasm. From the corner of his eye, he could see people looking at them, their attention drifting, away from Debbie Dutton's Little Sprites baton twirlers going by in snowsuits, twirling to the tinny sound of 'Winter Wonderland' blasting out of a boom box.

'I fail to see how the information on the notes could compromise the case,' Paige said.

'I'll enlighten you tomorrow, when we get a hundred and fifty laser-printed notes on twenty-pound bond in the mail claiming responsibility for the kidnapping. Maybe you and your cameraman here could go out on a hundred and fifty calls to check out the crackpots instead of spending time with the search and rescue squads or the few remaining officers who will be left to hunt for real clues.'

Jessie lifted her head, her lower lip trembling. 'Daddy, don't be ornery!' she whimpered, tears glittering in her eyes.

'It's okay, honey,' Mitch whispered. 'I'm not mad at you; I'm mad at this lady.' He tucked Jessie's head against his shoulder and backed Paige toward the renovated brick front of the Fine Line stationery store. 'Who's your source, Paige?'

'You know I can't divulge that information.'

'Oh, that's perfect,' he sneered. 'Your sources are sacrosanct, but confidential police information is fair game? There's something wrong with this picture, Paige.'

Giving her no chance to refute the statement, he jerked to the right and nearly hit Jessie's head against the lens of the video camera. He swatted the thing aside and leaned into the face of the cameraman. 'Get that fucking thing out of my face or you'll be wearing it for a hat!'

Jessie began to cry. Mitch tried to comfort her and glare at Paige simultaneously. 'I find out who leaked that information, I'll kick his ass into the middle of next week,' he said through clenched teeth. 'And then I'll get mean.'

Paige said nothing, feigning calm when everything inside her was trembling at the fury she saw in Mitch Holt's face. As Holt stalked away with his daughter in his arms, Garcia cradled his camera like a baby and leaned toward her conspiratorially.

'Shit, that guy has a temper. Remind me never to resist arrest around here.'

9:05 p.m. 19°

Joy Strauss clucked her disapproval as she hung Jessie's coat in the hall closet. 'This is just what I was afraid of,' she muttered just loud enough for Mitch to hear.

He glared at the back of his mother-in-law's head, in no mood for Joy's pecking. She was a slim, graceful woman who would have been attractive if not for the sour bend to her mouth. Her brown hair was threaded with silver and worn in a shoulder-length style that was ageless. She dressed in social matron wear and wore her pessimism like a strand of accent pearls.

'This kidnapping has just terrified her,' she continued. She shook her head as she closed the closet door. 'It's a wonder she's been able to sleep. Maniacs roaming loose, snatching children off the curbs.'

Mitch held Jessie close and gave Joy a warning look. 'It's one incident, Joy, not an epidemic,' he whispered. 'Jessie's just tired, aren't you, sweetheart?'

Jessie nodded.

Joy held her arms out. 'Well, come to Grandma, Jessie. We'll go up to bed.'

'I'll take her,' Mitch snapped. Joy sniffed, but didn't push her luck. Clucking her tongue, she moved off into the living room where *Washington Week* grumbled along on the television and Jurgen was engrossed in a book.

Mitch took Jessie to her room and helped her change into her nightgown. He rambled on about the Snowdaze activities that would take place over the weekend and how much fun she would have with her grandparents. Maybe Grandpa would take her to see the ice sculptures in the park or the human snow bowling. Maybe they would be able to go for a sleigh ride. Grandma had tickets to the figure skating show. Wouldn't that be fun?

Jessie contributed nothing to the conversation. She dutifully washed her face and brushed her teeth and climbed into the bed Mitch had turned down for her. He sat beside her and brushed a hand tenderly over her hair.

'Say your prayers, munchkin,' he murmured, pressing a kiss to her forehead.

Jessie turned her face up to him, her big brown eyes swimming with tears. In a tiny, trembling voice, she said, 'Daddy, I'm scared.'

Mitch held his breath. 'Scared of what, honey?'

'Scared that a maniac will get me, too!'

She crawled into his lap as the tears came in earnest. Mitch wrapped his arms around her and held her tight. 'Nobody's going to take you, sweetheart.'

'B-but s-somebody t-took J-Josh! G-Grandma s-says i-it h-happens e-every d-day!'

'Not here, it doesn't,' Mitch said, rocking her. 'Nobody's going to take you, honey. Remember how we talked all about how to be safe? Remember how we talked about stranger danger and how you should run away when you feel afraid of somebody?'

'B-but they t-took Josh and h-he's a b-big kid. I'm just little!'

Mitch's heart ripped. He pulled Jessie's head back against his chest and rocked her harder, blinking furiously at the heat stinging his eyes. 'Nobody's going to take you, baby. I won't let that happen.'

He would keep her safe.

The way he had kept her brother safe?

The thought was a knife. A stiletto driving deep, piercing flesh and bone and soul. He bit his lip until he tasted blood, squeezed his eyes shut until they burned. He held his daughter and knew she was his only child because he hadn't been able to keep her brother safe. And he knew that no matter how hard he tried, no matter how strongly he believed he deserved it, there were no guarantees he could keep Jessie safe, either.

Damn you, whoever you are. Damn you for taking Josh, for stealing this town's innocence. Damn you to hell and gone. I'll send you there myself if I ever get the chance.

He rocked Jessie and whispered to her until her tears ran out and she fell asleep. Then he tucked her under the covers with Oatmeal Bear and just sat there, watching her, drinking in the sight of her, loving her so much it was a physical ache. He sat there, unaware of time passing. He heard Jurgen and Joy come upstairs, knew Joy stopped and stood outside Jessie's door. He didn't acknowledge her and she finally turned away, shutting off the hall light as she went.

The house had been silent for a long while when he eased away from Jessie and slipped out of her room. He left the light burning on the bedside table in case she woke up afraid. He wished he could have taken her home with him, but Joy had asked for this weekend a month ago. Then there was the case. He had left standing orders to be called the instant anything happened regarding Josh. He didn't want to further upset Jessie by having his pager wake her.

The clock on the dash of the Explorer read 12:13. Around him the neighborhood was quiet and dark. The bars downtown would still be open, but he didn't want the noise. The Big Steer truck stop out on the interstate was open all night, but he didn't want the questions or the talk that would come from the patrons and the help. Across the alley his house sat empty, but he couldn't stand the idea of being alone.

He thought of Megan and almost laughed at himself. Of all the women . . .

Since Allison's death he had suffered an endless parade of eligible ladies. Nice women, gentle women, women who would have done anything to please him, and women who would have done anything to win his heart. He had turned them all away and sent them in search of worthier men. He had denied himself their company and their sympathy. When physical needs could no longer be ignored, he took himself to the Cities and found release with no strings attached. The one-night stands had become just another part of the cycle into which his life had settled.

It never occurred to him it was a pathetic excuse for a life. It was what he wanted and all he was ready for. It was safe and painless. And empty . . . and lonely . . . and he didn't want to suffer it tonight.

Without allowing himself to question the wisdom of it, he put the truck in gear and drove toward Ivy Street.

17

Megan dreamed of a world coated in the fine black soot of fingerprinting powder. It hung in the air like smog, and her lungs ached as she tried to breathe, as if she had an elephant standing on her chest. Every surface was covered with fingerprints. They floated in space like cinders in the wind. She woke with a start to find Friday sitting on her chest, staring down at her, his eyes liquid gold in the dim lamplight.

'God, you weigh a ton! Get off!' Megan groused, struggling to sit up.

The cat hopped onto a box of books and shot her a dirty look, then lifted his hind leg up behind his head in a yoga move and calmly began to groom his rear end.

Megan dismissed him and tried to dismiss the disorientation she felt waking up in what was essentially a strange place. She had to unpack her junk soon and make this apartment into a home, she thought, tightening the belt on her old blue plaid flannel robe. She couldn't stand the feeling of transience. Of course, she admitted, transient might well describe her state in Deer Lake if DePalma's fuse got any shorter.

If she could get a lead on the case, it would take some of the heat off, direct the press to something more important than the state's first female field agent. More important, if she could get a lead, they might be able to find Josh and bring him home.

Using her own ident kit, she had lifted Olie Swain's prints from the Coke bottle, transferred them to lift cards, and faxed them to Records at headquarters to be run through the MAFIN network. The automated system would search through its database for a match. If they got a hit, she would be notified immediately. She had also faxed the prints to the National Crime Information Center at FBI headquarters in Washington, D.C., to be run through their automated fingerprint identification system. They would do a search starting with the Upper Midwest and work their way out to the rest of the country.

Someone somewhere knew Olie Swain. Someone somewhere had sent him to prison.

In her mind's eye she saw again the fine blue lines on the backs of his fingers. A crude tattoo job. The kind cons gave other cons in the joint. She hadn't gotten a good enough look to swear, but it felt right. He smelled like a con in more ways than one.

The knock at the door was like another world crashing into her sphere of silence. Megan shot to her feet, automatically reaching for her gun on the end table. Out of habit she skirted around the door and flattened herself against the wall beside it. The knock sounded again. She waited, breath held deep in her lungs.

'Megan? It's Mitch.'

She blew out a breath, then undid the lock. 'Did you drop in on Leo after midnight?' she asked, pulling the door open.

'No,' he said softly.

He stepped inside, his hands stuffed into his jacket pockets, shoulders still hunched against the chill he had left outside. His gaze strayed to the slim black nine-millimeter pistol she set aside on the kitchen table, but he made no comment about it. Maybe all the women he visited in the dead of the night answered their doors with a fistful of firepower.

'I was driving by,' he murmured. 'Saw your light.'

Megan debated telling him about taking Olie's prints. She had railed against him for keeping information from her, but she didn't want to bring up the subject now. It was late. Besides, maybe nothing would come of it. Beyond that, he didn't look as if he wanted to talk business. He looked exhausted and lost. He wandered through the maze of boxes to the window that looked down on Ivy Street and just stood there, staring out at the night.

She followed the path he had taken, absently brushing her hand over Gannon as she passed the box he had picked for his bed. The gray cat raised his head and blinked at her, then turned his steady gaze on Mitch and made a throaty sound of contentment.

'Why'd you skip out tonight?' he asked as she leaned a shoulder against the window frame.

'You needed to be with Jessie. I didn't want to intrude . . .' She let the thought trail off. 'How was the parade?'

'Sad. They're all trying so hard . . . because they want to make a difference, because they're scared. They look to me to save them and they don't realize –' He looked at her, his whiskey-brown eyes bleary and bloodshot, the strain carved like knife lines into his face. 'I'm nobody's savior. I'm just a cop. And I'm tired of it.' He turned back toward the window but closed his eyes. 'I'm tired of it.'

Tired of the pain. Tired of the responsibility. Tired of the panic in his gut, the fear that he had no special powers to right all the wrongs, that he wasn't Superman, just Clark Kent with delusions of grandeur. He turned toward Megan, letting her read it all in his face.

The Megan of the slicked-back hair and gender-neutral wardrobe and the rules and regulations was not this woman who stood before him now. Her hair was loose around her shoulders. With nothing on her feet but a pair of baggy wool socks, she was short. Swallowed up inside an old plaid robe, she looked tiny, delicate. St Joan without her armor. She stood there, waiting, silent, patient.

'I'm not much of a hero,' he murmured. 'They ought to know that.'

'You're doing all you can,' Megan said. 'We all are.'

My best wasn't good enough. Again. The words he had spoken the day before in the garage of the old fire station came back to her, heavy with regret and self-loathing.

He turned his gaze out the window again. 'I keep thinking I should have been able to prevent this from happening, that I should have been able to see it coming, do something about it.' His mouth twisted with bitter black humor. 'A recurring theme in my life.'

Megan didn't ask. She wouldn't beg and she wouldn't drag it out of him. He would tell her because he needed to or wanted to, or they would stand there all night, saying nothing.

'I had a son,' he said at last. 'Kyle. He was six.'

Megan's breath caught on the lump in her throat.

'They were in the wrong place at the wrong time.' He shook his head at the irony. 'Why do we always say that? They weren't in the wrong place. My wife and son went to the store for milk and bread. The doper with the sawed-off shotgun was in the wrong place. But I sent them there, so what does that make me?'

A victim, Megan thought, though she knew his answer would be 'guilty'. No court would ever convict him, but he had convicted himself and for the rest of his life he would dole out the punishment. What a screwed-up world that a good man should have to pay again and again for something as small as a word or two, as simple as a decision of who should go to the store, while a killer would have no remorse, never feel a second's pain for the lives he had ruined.

'He just blew them away,' he whispered. 'Like they were nothing.'

He could still see them, bloody, lying on the dirty linoleum floor, their lives drained out of them. Their bodies bent at odd angles, like dolls that had been cast aside, their eyes wide open, staring the bleak, hopeless stares of the dead. Allison with one arm outstretched toward their son. Kyle, just out of reach, his too-big baseball uniform dyed maroon with his blood, a pack of baseball cards clutched in one hand. That bright small life crushed, wasted, discarded as carelessly as an empty can.

'I heard the call on the radio,' he said. 'Even before I saw Allison's car in the parking lot, I knew. I just knew.'

And the recriminations had started, as they started now. Relentless. Brutal. Inescapable. And the questions had started, as they started now, the rage building and building behind them. He worked so hard for right, for justice. He followed the rules. He had principles. He was a good man, a good cop, a straight arrow. He should have been rewarded, and instead, he had the most precious parts of his life torn out and blown apart.

'One hundred sixty-nine dollars,' he said, still staring out at the night.

'That's what the crook got out of the deal. That's what their lives were worth to him.'

He closed his eyes and a single tear slid down his cheek. He was a proud man, a tough man, but the pain and the confusion undid him. He was a cop. He believed in right and wrong, black and white, but his world had turned into a hazy place of smoke and mirrors. Megan could hear it in his voice – the desperation of a man trying to make sense of the senseless.

It must have been unbearable to have loved a partner, to have made a child and loved and hoped for that child, and lost them both. Better to have loved and lost, the saying went, but Megan didn't believe it. Better not to love at all than to have the heart torn out by the roots.

'I think of Hannah and Paul,' he murmured. 'I wouldn't wish this pain on anyone.'

Needing to offer him comfort, Megan slipped her arms inside his open coat, around his lean waist, and pressed her cheek to his chest. 'We'll find him. We will.'

Wishing he could absorb her certainty, he wrapped his arms around her and hugged her tight. He didn't think about her rule against cops. They weren't cops now. In his mind he pared away all but the basic truth – he was a man and she was a woman, and the electricity between them was hot and compelling, inviting them to shut out the rest of the world. He had no intention of resisting the temptation. Tonight that was all he wanted – to be a man with no past or tomorrow with a woman he could hold and a need he could lose himself in.

He slid a hand through her hair, the glossy strands sifting through his fingers. He lowered his mouth to hers, his kiss smothering any protest she might have made. The taste of her was sweet. The feel of her body in his arms regenerated his strength. Desire burned away the fatigue and the kiss burned hotter, wilder.

Megan hung on, her fingers pressing hard into the small of his back. She couldn't find the words to tell him no. All she could find inside herself was need. He bent her back over his arm, his mouth trailing heat down the side of her neck to the V of flesh exposed by her robe. Then he was sweeping her up into his arms.

He crossed the room in a matter of a few long strides, tumbling boxes en route, sending a cat scurrying for safer ground. His eyes never left hers. The expression he wore was fierce, determined, intense, as if he thought blinking or glancing away would snap the spell. In the bedroom he deposited her in the middle of the unmade bed and stepped back to shrug off his coat, never looking away. He pulled his sweater and T-shirt off over his head and flung them aside.

Megan sat up on her knees, drinking in the sight of him. His hair was tousled. The shadow of his beard darkened his jaw and accented the lean planes and angles of his face. He had the body of a warrior who had seen his share of battles. Trim, lean, ridged with muscle, scarred in places. Dark hair swirled across the planes of his chest and flat belly, arrowing into a line that disappeared beneath the low-riding waist of his jeans.

Her eyes on his, she undid the belt of her robe and let the garment fall open and fall back off her shoulders. There was no right. There was no wrong. There were no rules. There were no words. There was only this incredible sense of expectation and merging, aching souls.

Mitch reached out and ran the fingertips of one hand along her shoulder and down her arm. He traced the angle of her waist, the graceful flare of her hip. Her skin was the color of cream, the texture of silk. He kissed her slowly, erotically, his tongue probing deep into the warm, wet recesses of her mouth as his hand explored her. He wanted to devour her, to absorb the comfort of her soft warmth into his body – or better yet, be taken into hers. Lose himself. Feel the hard knot of loneliness and pain break apart and melt in the heat of their union.

They sank down on the bed, stretching against each other chest to chest, legs tangling. Megan arched into him, loving the feel of his hard body, the heat of his skin, the brush of his chest hair against her nipples. She gave herself over to sensation – touching him, tasting him, breathing in the warm musk of male need. She gave herself over to him, letting him take control. Surrendering . . . The word brought a shiver, but then his mouth was on her breast and thought was gone.

She tangled her hands in his hair, kneaded the muscles in his shoulders, ran the arch of her foot along the back of his leg, frowning at the fact that he still had his jeans on. Twisting beneath him, she reached for the button. Mitch allowed her, rising up on his knees as she tugged the zipper down over his erection.

Her hands were trembling as she pulled down jeans and briefs. Her whole body was trembling with the need to take him inside her. She curled her fingers around his shaft and stroked him gently. He closed his eyes and groaned.

'Come here,' he whispered, reaching for her.

Megan went to him, welcoming his kiss, pressing her body into his. She put her arms around his neck and let her head fall back as he trailed his mouth down her throat. His big hands stroked down her back to her buttocks and he lifted her and pulled her onto his lap as he sat back on his haunches. She reached between their bodies and guided him, held him steady as he lowered her.

Her breath left her in a slow hiss as he entered her. Her body tightened around him, on the brink of fulfillment. He lifted her again and slid her back down on him slowly, inch by inch.

Anticipation wound like a spring inside her, tighter and tighter, pounding for release. She began to move on him at her own pace, hands gripping his big shoulders, her head flung back. Faster and faster, until she was breathless, until the heat condensed to a slick gloss of sweat on her skin, until the anticipation exploded into a firestorm of sensation.

They held each other tight as they came back to earth, as their heartbeats slowed, as the real world took form around them. Mitch pulled the quilt up over them. The heat of passion had waned and the January night chilled them.

Gannon jumped up on the bed and curled into his spot behind Megan's knees. As if Mitch didn't exist at all. Megan could hardly remember the last time she'd had a man in her bed. Her relationships could be counted on one hand. All of them dismal failures. The rule of her love life was a catch-22: she didn't date cops, but no one understood cops except other cops, therefore . . . And beneath that excuse lay deeper reasons, intrinsic fears, demons that had followed her like shadows all her life. The fear that no one would ever love her, that she was inherently unlovable, tainted by the stain of her mother's sins. Fears that had no logic. Fears that existed in the darkest corner of her heart like toadstools.

Stupid to even think of them now. Mitch Holt didn't love her, he had needed her. They had needed each other to escape a lonely night, to escape a horrible case. It wasn't love. More like a favor between friends. Cast in that light, the beauty of their lovemaking faded, the comfort of lying there together lost its warmth.

He's not even single, she thought, staring at the ring on his left hand. She had just broken all her own rules for a man who was married to his past. *You sure know how to pick 'em, kiddo.*

Still, she couldn't find it in her to regret what they had just shared. Just as she couldn't stop herself from wanting something more. Just as she couldn't stop that need from scaring the hell out of her.

Mitch felt her shiver against him and pulled the covers up higher around her shoulders. She felt good in his arms. She fit against his side like a puzzle piece. Comfortable. Comforting. The sex had been incredible. Just thinking about it made him want her all over again.

He waited for the stab of guilt, that jagged dagger that had plunged into his heart after every sexual encounter he'd had since Allison's death. But it didn't come. He'd found an oasis for a little while, for a night. Dawn would arrive soon enough and they would be cops again, thrown back into the living nightmare of trying to find a kidnapper but with no real leads and no real suspects and no motive save a madman's. But until dawn, they had the night.

He turned onto his side, bracing himself up on one arm so he could look down at Megan. She stared back at him, her expression slightly wary, slightly defiant.

'If this is where you make the speech about what a big mistake we just made, you can save your breath,' she said.

'Because you already know it was a mistake?' he asked carefully.

Mistake was too small a word, too innocent. This was the kind of misstep that could end her career. Getting in too deep with Mitch Holt could leave her with nothing but a broken heart, and she'd had enough of those to last her.

'Are you saying you regret making love with me?' he said.

She stared up at him, at the lived-in, beat-up face and the eyes that looked as old as time. She thought of all the feelings he kept boxed inside – the rage, the pain, the self-doubt – that he allowed out only in small increments. She thought of his tenderness and his passion and the unabashed love he gave to his daughter. It would have been smart to say yes; the best defense was a good offense. She couldn't see a future for them. There was no point in prolonging the inevitable. She could end it now and come away with her pride battered but intact, but . . .

'No,' she whispered. 'I just don't think we should make a habit of it.'

She swung her legs over the side of the bed and grabbed her robe. Mitch leaned across and caught hold of one sleeve before she could slip into it. She met his gaze over her shoulder, her expression wary.

'Why not?' he challenged.

'Because.'

'That's not an answer for anyone over the age of seven.'

'The answer was implied,' Megan said. 'You shouldn't have to ask the question.'

She tugged her sleeve free of his grasp and walked away, pulling the robe around her and tying the belt tight. She went to her dresser and fingered the few items she had unpacked and set on top of it. The small gray china cat statue that had been a graduation gift from Frances Clay, the church cleaning lady who had looked after her when she was small. The jewelry box she had bought in a secondhand shop with her own money on her twelfth birthday. For a time she had pretended that her mother had given it to her, when in fact no one had given her anything.

'We're working together,' she said tightly. 'We shouldn't be sleeping together.'

She watched him in the mirror as he threw the covers back and climbed out of her bed. The automatic flush of desire frightened her. It frightened her that her body could so quickly become so attuned to his, that she could want him this badly, need him this much. Need. God, she couldn't let herself need him.

Their gazes met in the mirror. His expression was hard, predatory.

'This doesn't have anything to do with work,' he said, his voice a low rumble in his throat.

Slowly he turned her around to face him and tugged her belt loose. She sucked in a shallow breath as he slid his hands inside the robe and opened it, exposing her to his gaze, his touch. He cupped her breasts gently, brushing his thumbs across her nipples, and her breath caught again. Satisfaction and arousal flared in his gaze. His fingers skimmed down her sides and his hands settled on her hips. He lowered his mouth toward hers. 'And who said anything about sleeping?'

Journal entry
Day 4

Take a perfect family. Tear it all apart. We hold the pieces. We hold the power. As simple as nothing. Like pulling the linchpin on this small, stupid place. Like ringing the bell for Pavlov's dogs.

The police chase their tails. They search for evidence they won't find. They wait for signs from above. They bluster and threaten, but nothing will come of it. We watch and laugh. The volunteers pray and pin themselves with ribbons and pass out posters, thinking they can make a difference. Such fools. Only we can make a difference. We hold all the cards.

The game is growing dull. Time to up the ante.

18

Hannah sat on the window ledge, staring out at the trees as they transformed from shadows to vague shapes. The black of night was fading, shade by subtle shade. Another night gone. The start of another day without Josh. She couldn't imagine how she would live through it. She took no comfort in the knowledge that she would.

The line from the notes whispered through the back of her mind. The words crept over her skin like bony fingers. *ignorance is not innocence but SIN. i had a little sorrow, born of a little SIN.* Cold fear twisted inside her and she trembled with the longing for someone to take it away.

Paul lay sleeping, sprawled facedown in the center of the bed, his arms flung wide, claiming the entire mattress as his own. She wondered if he would go through his same routine when he woke to face the day. She wondered what had happened to the two of them. She closed her eyes and saw them each in separate rowboats on a sea that tossed them farther apart with each pulsing wave. In her mind's eye she reached out toward him mutely, but his back was to her and he didn't turn around.

Loneliness tightened like a fist in her chest, crushing her lungs, crushing her heart.

God, I'm not strong enough to get through this alone.. . . .

She pressed a hand to her mouth to hold back the cry of helplessness and need, and ached inside at the thought that she wouldn't even share this with her husband, with the father of her children.

Things had been so different when Josh was a baby. Paul had been different. He had been proud of her. She had never doubted his love. He had looked at life's opportunities with enthusiasm, eager to give his family the things he had missed out on growing up in a blue-collar neighborhood, where paychecks had to be stretched. He had looked at Josh and seen the chance to be the supportive, loving father he'd never had. He had looked at his wife and seen an equal, a partner, someone he could love and respect.

Now Hannah looked at him and saw a selfish, bitter man, jealous of her successes, resentful of his own anonymity. A man consumed by the need to acquire things and baffled that the things didn't give him the happiness he expected. She wondered what had become of the man she had married, wondered if he was as lost to her as Josh.

Oh, God, I didn't mean to think that! I don't believe he's gone. I won't believe it.

ignorance is not innocence but SIN. Loneliness, fear, guilt, hurtled through her. Panic closed her throat. She forced herself to her feet and paced the rectangle of pale light that fell from the window onto the carpet, forcing herself to think, to plan, forcing the wheels of her mind to turn. She was trembling like a drunk in the throes of DTs. It took every molecule of strength she had to keep from crumpling to the floor. Gritting her teeth, she fought against the need to double over. *One foot in front of the other, in front of the other, in front of the other . . . Step, step, step, turn. Step, step, step, turn . . .*

She paced the floor in an oversize Vikings jersey and wool socks, her legs and forearms bare. The cold seemed to seep through skin and tissue into her bones. It seemed to spill in through the window like moonlight.

So cold . . . Is Josh cold? Cold and alone. Ice cold. Stone cold . . .

'What are you doing?'

Hannah jerked around at the sound of Paul's voice. Her hands were like ice. She could see her palm prints on the window where her breath had steamed the glass around them.

'I couldn't sleep.'

Paul swung his legs over the edge of the bed and sat up with the comforter pulled across his lap. He looked thin and gray in the pale light of the room, older, harder, lines of anger and disappointment etched into his face beside his eyes and mouth. A sigh leaked out of his lungs as he flicked on the lamp and looked at the alarm clock on the nightstand.

'I have to do something today,' Hannah announced, surprising herself as much as him. The words echoed in her mind and hardened with resolve. She stood a little straighter. She wanted – needed – to get back something of herself. She was accustomed to taking action in the face of a crisis. Action at least provided the illusion of control. 'I have to get out of this house. If I have to sit here another day, I'll go crazy.'

'You can't leave,' Paul said. He tossed the covers back and rose, hitching up a baggy pair of striped pajama bottoms. He grabbed his black terry robe from the foot of the bed and thrust his arms into the sleeves. 'You have to be here in case they call.'

'You can answer a telephone as well as I can.'

'But I have to go out with the search party –'

'No, Paul, *I'm* going out.'

He gave a bitter laugh. 'What do you think you're going to do? You think you're going to save the day? Dr Garrison to the rescue. Her husband can't find their son, but she will?'

'Oh, Jesus, Paul!' she snapped, flinging her arms down to her sides.

'Why does everything have to be about you? I'm so sick of this jealous act of yours, I could scream. I'm sorry if you feel inadequate –'

'I never said I felt inadequate,' he barked, his eyes glowing with temper. 'I meant that you don't believe anyone can do anything as well as you.'

'That's absurd.' She turned her back on him. She pulled clothes out of her dresser drawers and tossed them into a tangled pile on top of her jewelry box, heedless of the bottles of perfume she overturned in the process. 'You've been out the last two days looking for Josh. Why can't you see that I need that chance, too? Why can't you –'

The rest of the question died as a wave of emotion surged through her.

'We used to share everything,' she whispered, her eyes on his reflection in the mirror. 'We used to be partners. As horrible as this is, at least we would have shared the burden. God, Paul, what's happened to us?'

She heard him sigh, but she didn't turn around and she didn't meet his gaze in the mirror, afraid that what she would see on his face would be impatience instead of regret.

'I'm sorry,' he murmured, stepping up behind her. 'I feel like I'm losing my mind. I feel helpless. You know what that does to me. I need to feel like I can make a difference.'

'So do I!' She swung around to face him, her expression a plea for understanding. She looked into his eyes, trying to find the man she had married, the man she had loved. 'I need that, too. Why can't you see that?'

Or don't you care? The question hung between them, unspoken, as the moment stretched taut. A dozen scenarios flashed through Hannah's mind – the rift between them healing, the Paul she used to know returning, the nightmare ending abruptly with her waking suddenly, the light going cold in his eyes as he told her he didn't care, the crevasse between them ripping as wide as a canyon. . . .

He looked away as Lily started to cry in her room down the hall. 'Yeah . . . Go ahead,' he said softly. 'I'll stay with Lily for a while.'

'She'll ask where Josh is,' Hannah murmured. 'It's been three days . . .'

She dragged a hand back through her tangled hair as the fears surged up inside her again. 'God, the things that go through my mind . . . Is he asking for us, is he cold, is he hurt?' The worst of the questions stuck like peanut butter to the roof of her mouth, gagging her, choking her. She was afraid to give them voice, and yet she needed to. 'Paul, what if he's –'

'Don't!' He pulled her roughly into his arms, his eyes still trained on the door, as if looking at her would turn the fears to reality. 'I don't want to think about it,' he whispered.

He was trembling. She pressed a hand over his heart and felt it race. *ignorance is not innocence but SIN*

'Go take your shower,' he murmured. 'I'll get Lily up.'

'Buy a chance! Give a dollar! Help bring Josh home!' Al Jackson's voice boomed across the park from the Senior Hockey League booth. He had found a rhythm and stuck with it, repeating the chant with the regularity of a metronome. The call was too reminiscent of a carnival barker luring the naïve to a rigged shell game.

Hannah's stomach churned. She looked out across the park, seeing a surreal version of the annual Snowdaze fair. Wooden booths draped in colorful festoons ringed and criss-crossed the park. Behind them, portable heaters rumbled, generating billowing clouds of steam in the cold air. Crowds had turned out in full winter regalia to play the games and watch the ice sculptors at work. But in addition to the usual causes – new band uniforms and computers for the public library and funds for the Legion Auxiliary summer beautification project – every game, every booth, was pledging money to the effort to find Josh.

Noble gestures. Overwhelming generosity. A touching show of support and love. Hannah repeated these phrases over and over, and still she couldn't shake her gut-level reaction – that she had escaped one nightmare and run headlong into another. There was something too Kafkaesque about watching people slide one by one down the hill from the courthouse into a stand of giant bowling pins, knowing they had each given a dollar to help bring her son home. It made her feel sick to think this festival had been twisted into so many acts of desperation and that she was queen for the day, the center of attention, the star attraction.

She had been led to the volunteer-center booth to be put on display like some freak. *See the grieving mother hand out posters! Watch the guilty woman pin yellow ribbons on the faithful!*

She could feel the gazes of the reporters on her. The second they spotted her, questions spewed out of them in an endless stream – questions about her feelings, questions of guilt and suspicion, requests for exclusive interviews. She had finally given them a statement and made a plea for Josh's return, but they weren't satisfied. Like a pack of hungry dogs that had been thrown a few meat scraps, they lingered and watched her, hopeful of more. She couldn't move or speak or wipe her nose without feeling their camera lenses zoom in on her.

The faces of some of the television people were familiar. She seldom had time to sit down and watch the news, but at six and ten it was always on in the background regardless of where she was. Minnesotans didn't miss their news; it was something of an inside joke among natives. Aside from the goings-on in the Cities, nothing much of consequence happened in the state as a rule, but everyone insisted on having the nonevents relayed to them at the end of the day.

Hannah could put names to several of the Twin Cities' reporters. Several of the stations themselves had set up booths to help raise money for the cause. Down the row from the volunteer-center booth, the channel eleven weatherman was offering his face as a target for cream pies. The *StarTribune* had teamed up with the policemen's association to fingerprint and photograph children for a dollar donation per child – a safety precaution most parents in Deer Lake had never thought about.

Noble gestures. Overwhelming generosity. A touching show of support and love.

A macabre drama, and she was the focal point.

It's your own fault, Hannah. You want to do something, to take charge like you always do.

But she couldn't find the strength to present herself as a leader. She felt drained, wilted. Dizziness swam through her head and she closed her eyes and leaned against the counter.

'Dr Garrison, are you all right?'

'I think she's going to faint!'

'Should we call a doctor?'

'She *is* a doctor!'

'Well, she can't treat herself. She'd have a fool for a patient.'

'That's lawyers –'

'What about lawyers?'

Fragments of conversation came to Hannah as if from a great distance down a long tunnel. The world swayed beneath her feet.

'Excuse me, ladies. I think maybe Dr Garrison needs to take a little break. Isn't that right, Hannah?'

She felt a strong hand close gently on her arm and willed her eyes to open. Father Tom came into focus. Her gaze locked onto the concern in his face.

'You need a little quiet time,' he said softly.

'Yes.'

The word barely made it out of her mouth when the ground seemed to dip. He caught her against his side and started across the square toward the volunteer center. Hannah did her best to move her feet. Reporters moved in on them, cameramen and photographers closing off the escape route.

'Please, folks.' Father Tom spoke sharply. 'Show a little decency. Can't you see she's had enough for one day?'

Apparently unwilling to risk the wrath of God, they stepped out of the way, but Hannah could hear the click of shutters and the whir of motor drives until they reached the curb.

'How're you doing?' Father Tom asked. 'Can you make it across the street?'

Hannah managed a nod, though she wasn't at all sure she wouldn't just collapse. Out of self-preservation she hooked an arm around Tom McCoy's waist and leaned into him, grateful for his solid strength.

'That's right,' he murmured. 'You just hang on, Hannah. I won't let you fall.'

He took her into the volunteer center, where volunteers ignored ringing telephones and blinking cursors on computer screens to stare. Hannah kept her head down, embarrassed to be seen this weak and more than a little uncomfortable being seen snuggled up to the town priest. But Father Tom ignored her feeble effort to put space between them. A determined look on his face, he guided her toward what had once been the stockroom, where chairs and tables had been set up for coffee breaks.

He eased her down onto a chair and shooed out the curious and concerned onlookers with the exception of Christopher Priest, who came bearing gifts of caffeine and sugar. The professor set a paper plate of brownies down on the table. Tom accepted the cup of coffee and pressed it into Hannah's hands.

'Drink up,' he ordered. 'You look like an ice sculpture. My truck is out back. I'll go warm it up, then I'm taking you home.'

Hannah murmured her thanks, trying to smile bravely. The compassion in his eyes let her abandon the effort. Compassion, not pity. An offer of the strength of his friendship. He brushed the back of his knuckles along her cheek absently, as if he did such things every day, but Hannah felt a tingle of electricity. She sat back, beating herself up mentally for her reaction. He was Father Tom, priest, confessor, erstwhile cowboy, absent-minded shepherd of the flock of St Elysius.

'You forgot your gloves again,' she murmured.

He pulled them out of his pockets and waved them at her, then headed for the back door. Hannah turned her attention to the coffee cup warming her hands, to put her mind on something mundane. She sipped the steaming brew, surprised that it had been lightened to her preference.

'I remembered you take milk,' the professor said, a twinkle of pride in his eyes. 'You sat across the table from me at the chamber of commerce dinner last year.'

'And you remembered that I take milk?' Hannah offered him a small smile.

He sat back against the edge of another table, his hands tucked into the pockets of a black down jacket that puffed out around him like an inflatable muscle suit. His head poked up above the collar on a skinny neck.

'I have a head for trivia,' he said. 'I haven't had a chance to tell you how sorry I am about Josh.'

'Thank you,' she murmured, glancing away. What an odd ritual, the manners dance of condolences. It seemed so useless for people to apologize over something in which they had no part; it seemed too civilized to thank them for it. This was just another aspect of her role of victim she couldn't reconcile herself to.

She could feel the professor's gaze on her, steady, studying as he studied everything that lived and breathed and couldn't be plugged into an electrical socket – as if he understood machines far better.

'I guess I'm not handling it very well,' she confessed.

'How do you think you should handle it?'

'I don't know. Better. Differently.'

He put his head on one side in a pose reminiscent of the android Data on *Star Trek: The Next Generation*. One of Josh's favorite TV shows. The reminder stabbed like a needle. 'It's curious,' he said, 'that people have come to a point where they almost feel they should be preprogrammed for everything that happens in their lives. Spontaneous reaction is a rule of nature; people can't control their responses any more than they can control the random events that trigger them. And yet they try. You shouldn't apologize, Hannah. Just let yourself react.'

A rueful smile turned her lips as she took another sip of coffee. 'Easier said than done. I feel like I've been cast in a play but I don't have a script.'

The professor pressed his lips together and hummed a note of consideration. Hannah envisioned his brain clicking and clacking like a computer as he processed the information.

'I should thank you while I have the chance,' she said, looking out through the open door into the former appliance showroom where people she didn't know were squinting at computer screens and stuffing envelopes with fliers. 'We really appreciate the time and talent you and your students have given. Everyone has tried so hard to be helpful.'

A hint of a blush tinted his pale cheeks as he waved off her gratitude. 'It's the least we can do.'

The back door opened and Father Tom made a dramatic entrance in a cloud of wind-driven exhaust fumes, his glasses completely fogged over. 'Come along, Doctor. If we hurry, we can still ditch those reporters.'

He tossed her a long, hideous scarf that had been knitted from every unappealing and uncoordinating color in the spectrum, and a black baseball cap with the words THE GOD SQUAD printed in bold white letters on the front.

'What's this?' Hannah asked.

From his coat pocket he pulled a pair of fake glasses with a big plastic nose and mustache attached. He flipped the bows open and shoved the glasses onto her face, then smiled at the effect. 'Your disguise.'

12:04 p.m. 20°

'I'm not much of a cook, but I can microwave leftovers with the best of them.'

'It smells wonderful,' Hannah said dutifully but without enthusiasm as he set the stoneware plate of beef stew down on the table in front of her. It looked like a cover shot for *Woman's Day* – thick chunks of meat and potatoes, bright orange disks of carrot, peas as green as spring grass, all in a thick, rich gravy. Too bad she couldn't find any desire to eat it.

'Don't even think about pushing it away,' Father Tom warned, sliding into the chair across from her. 'You'll eat it or I'll feed it to you. You need food, Hannah. You almost passed out.'

Reluctantly, she picked up her fork and speared a slice of carrot. Her hand was shaking as she raised it to her mouth. Tom watched her like a hawk while she chewed and swallowed. He twisted the cap off a bottle of Pete's Wicked Ale and slid it across the table to her.

'Improves the appetite,' he explained with a wink. 'Spoken like a true Irishman, eh?'

Hannah laughed softly. She tried a small bite of beef and washed it down with the ale. They sat in the kitchen of the rectory, a big old Victorian house that occupied the lot behind St Elysius. In times past, when clergy had been in more abundance, the house had served as home and hotel to a host of priests and ecclesiastics. It had served a stint as a halfway house for alcoholic priests in the fifties. Now the rambling place housed only Father Tom. He had closed off the whole second story to conserve heat.

The kitchen was sunny, with old glass-fronted cabinets and yellow wallpaper featuring teakettles. The small table was tucked into an alcove out of the flow of traffic – not that there was any. The house was empty except for the two of them.

'Thanks for rescuing me,' Hannah murmured, eyes downcast.

Tom buttered a chunk of homemade bread and handed it across to her. She was ashamed to need rescuing, he could see that plainly, just as she had been ashamed to cry on his shoulder. She was too brave for her own good. He ached painfully at the thought of her trying to get through this ordeal as the Hannah Garrison everyone in Deer Lake knew and loved – calm, stoic, confident, and wise enough to solve everyone's problems. The calm had been shattered, the confidence destroyed, all in a single blow. She was lost and he saw no sign of Paul helping her navigate.

What kind of man could be so blind that he could look at Hannah and not see a jewel?

'I know everyone is trying to help,' she said in a small, strained voice. 'They're being so wonderful, it's just that . . . It's all so . . . *wrong*.'

She raised her head and looked at him, pain and confusion swimming in her blue eyes. Her hair was still rumpled from wearing his cap. Curling strands of gold fell across her forehead and trailed down a cheek. She looked like an angel who had taken a long fall from her cloud.

'It's *wrong*,' she whispered. 'It's like we're on a train that's jumped the tracks and nobody can stop it. I want to make it stop.'

'I don't think we can, Hannah,' he confessed sadly. 'We can only hang on for the ride.'

He reached out to her across the table, offered his hand silently. For good reasons, just reasons, and reasons he wouldn't give voice even in the deepest, most private part of his mind. Reasons she could never know and would probably never suspect. So where was the harm? That question would open the floodgates on a hundred more for which he would find no answers, and so he silenced it. Nothing mattered at that moment but giving Hannah some comfort, some sign that she wasn't alone.

A single tear spilled over her lashes. Slowly she slid her hand across the table and took hold of his. Their palms fit against each other perfectly. Their fingers curled automatically. At the warmth of the contact and the feelings it stirred inside, Hannah's eyes widened slightly in surprise.

'I'd change it for you if I could, Hannah,' he whispered. 'If I could work a miracle, I'd do it in a heartbeat.'

Hannah thought she should thank him, but no words formed in her mouth. She couldn't seem to do anything but hold on to him and take in the quiet strength and conviction he offered. And she couldn't help but feel the sting of irony that the one man willing to share her burden and help her through this ordeal was not her husband but her priest.

She felt the intrusion seconds before Albert Fletcher cleared his throat. A sense of anger and disapproval tainted the moment like a layer of soot settling on her skin. She jerked her gaze to the basement door, cursing herself and Fletcher as she pulled her hand out of Father Tom's grasp. How long had Fletcher been standing there? He had no business spying on them or frowning at them as if he'd caught them doing something wrong. And she had no business feeling guilty . . . but she did.

'Jeez, Albert,' Tom said, pulling back the hand he had offered Hannah and pressing it against his chest. 'Give us heart attacks, why don't you? What the devil were you doing in the basement?'

The deacon regarded him with a somber look. He was dressed in his usual black garb — slacks, turtleneck, old quilted jacket — a habit that might have grown out of mourning his dead wife or out of his obsession with the church. He held a good-size cardboard box in his arms, a box with water stains and the white film of mildew. Its musty smell slipped beneath the robust aroma of the stew. 'I'm sorting through the storage room.'

'Back in the dungeon?' Tom shuddered in distaste. 'That stuff's been back there since the Resurrection. What would you want with any of that?'

'It's history. It deserves preservation.' The deacon shot a dark glance at Hannah. 'I'm sorry if I interrupted something.'

Tom pushed his chair back from the table and rose, working at containing his temper. God alone would be his judge. For all of Fletcher's pious posturings, he was not God or even a reasonable substitute.

'Dr Garrison needed a sanctuary. The last I heard, we were in the business of offering refuge and comfort.'

Fletcher looked through him. 'Of course, Father,' he murmured. 'If you'll excuse me . . .'

He nodded to Hannah and slipped out the back door, leaving behind a tension that hung in the air. Hannah dodged Tom's gaze and got up from the table. She pulled her coat off the back of her chair.

'I should get home,' she said quietly. 'Paul will be wondering.'

Tom sighed and pushed his glasses up. 'You didn't finish your lunch.'

'I'll eat when I get home. I promise. I've got plenty to pick from; the casseroles are multiplying geometrically.' She zipped her coat, then forced herself to push past her guilt and embarrassment and raised her eyes to his. 'Thanks, though. For the food . . . for the support . . . for everything.'

He started to say it was nothing, but it wasn't nothing. It was something more complicated than either of them needed and something so simple, it should have needed no explanation or apology. He shrugged his jacket on and dug his keys out of the pocket.

'Come on, Doc, I'll drive you home.'

They left her van downtown to avoid alerting the media to her plans. Hannah didn't ask him in. She didn't want to further ruin the day by having to listen to Paul snipe at him. But a heavy sense of loneliness pressed down on her as she climbed the steps and let herself in the mudroom. A BCA man sat at the kitchen table drinking Mountain Dew and reading *Guns & Ammo*. He gave her a nod. In the family room, the television was showing a figure skating competition to no one. The low murmur of voices drew her up the stairs and down the hall toward Lily's room.

'Paul? I'm home.'

Hannah pushed the door open and stopped. Karen Wright stood next to the crib with Lily perched on one hip. Karen was smiling at the baby, tickling her chin and cuddling her close. Paul stood beside her. Raising his eyes to meet Hannah's, he took a half step back, his face carefully blank.

Impervious to the sudden unease in the room, Lily beamed a smile and reached a hand out to Hannah. 'Hi, Mama!'

'Hi, sweetie,' she responded, her gaze skating past her daughter. 'Karen, I didn't expect you to come over again today. Is the neighbor brigade running low on recruits?'

Color flared across Karen's cheekbones. 'Oh, well, I, a – I hadn't planned to, then Garrett told me he had to go somewhere today, so I was alone, and I just thought –'

'Jesus, Hannah,' Paul grumbled. 'People are trying to be helpful. Do you have to give them the third degree?'

'I wasn't!'

He ignored her protest. 'Did you save the world while you were out?'

His sarcasm stung. Down the hall behind her the phone rang. 'I think I'll go change clothes.'

As she backed out into the hall, the BCA agent caught her attention. 'Dr Garrison? Please take the call in the family room.'

'Call?'

The phone chirped again and she hurried to the family room, unable to scrape together much hope. It was probably yet another reporter. Paige Price had been after her to do an in-depth interview. Heartless vampire.

Didn't these people realize what it was to hurt, to be afraid? Didn't they realize their morbid curiosity only made things worse?

She snatched up the receiver. 'Hannah Garrison.'

The static of a bad connection crackled over the line. Then came the voice, small and so soft she had to strain to hear it.

'Mom? I want to come home.'

19

They traced the call to a phone booth outside the Suds Your Duds laundry sixty-five miles away in the small, quiet town of St Peter, home of Gustavus Adolphus College and the state's maximum security institution for the mentally ill. The phone, its receiver dangling, was on the end of the building – a dreary little strip mall built in the sixties when blond brick and flat metal awnings were considered in good taste. Also occupying the shopping center was a small appliance repair service shop that was closed Saturday afternoons, a Vietnamese grocery where English was not even a second language, and the Fashionaire Beauty Salon, where the wash-and-set crowd got their beehives teased and their white hair dyed blue.

None of the patrons at the grocery wanted anything to do with cops. All the customers of the beauty salon wanted in on the action. Unfortunately, none of them had seen anything. Aside from being at the opposite end of the strip mall from the Suds Your Duds, the heat from the bonnet hair dryers and the mist from the rinse sinks combined to completely fog over the front windows of the shop. In the laundry two college students and three mothers of sticky-faced, wide-eyed toddlers answered all questions asked. But there were no windows looking out on that end of the building and there was no reason to go out into the cold to use the phone because there were two inside the laundry.

No one had seen Josh. No one had seen a light-colored van. For the cops, the wave of hope crashed and washed back out on yet another tide of disappointment.

'It could be a hoax,' Mitch said. 'Kids playing around. Hannah said she couldn't swear it was Josh's voice.'

He sat across from Megan at the fake woodgrain table in her room at the Super 8 Motel. The remains of a mostly uneaten Chinese takeout dinner cluttered the tabletop. The smell of congealing broccoli and beef almost masked the acrid stink of age-old cigarette smoke that permeated everything in the room. On the nightstand next to the bed, a cheap clock-radio glowed red: 9:57 P.M. Michael Bolton rasped out a song lamenting the demise of a love affair on the airwaves of the only station that would come in.

Megan flicked a chunk of almond chicken across her paper plate with her fork. 'I'd say I can't believe anyone would be that cruel, but then, that would sound stupid, wouldn't it?'

'I don't know,' he said quietly. 'Is it stupid to wish for small mercies? Crime is one thing, expecting ordinary people to be decent to each other is something else. If we can't even hope for that . . .'

'It gives me the creeps that that call came from here,' Megan admitted. 'I keep thinking about some of the people in that state hospital and my skin crawls. Sexual psychopaths, the criminally insane . . .'

'But they're *in* the hospital,' Mitch said. 'Not out. The county sheriff checked with the administration. They had no reports of anyone missing. They had no day passes issued to anyone we would have to worry about. That the call came from here and the hospital is here is just a coincidence. One thing we know for certain,' Mitch continued. 'Olie Swain didn't make the call. No less than fifty people can swear he was at the ice rink at the time the call came in.'

'That doesn't mean he's not involved,' Megan said stubbornly. 'It means he might not be in this thing alone. We've considered that option – that he *was* at the rink at the time of the kidnapping and someone else was driving his van.'

'Helen didn't ID the van,' he reminded her.

'Helen is confused and upset and couldn't tell a Ford from a Volkswagen if the fate of the nation depended upon it.'

The heater kicked in with an angry growl and blasted hot, dry air, recirculating the aroma of stale smoke.

'It could have been a tape recording,' Megan offered. They had been over this ground enough to wear a trench into it. All afternoon and half the evening, while the St Peter cops did a sweep of their city streets and the boys from the BCA mobile lab went over the phone booth with a fine-tooth comb, they had speculated and hoped and muttered threats they would never make good on. And still there was a need to chew that same bone with the hope of getting something out of it.

The choppers had been called out again. The original search area had been widened to include portions of Nicollet, Le Sueur, and Blue Earth counties. Search teams of county and municipal law enforcement agencies and local volunteers began a new ground search. Fliers with Josh's photo went up everywhere, in every store, on every light pole, on every bulletin board in every restaurant and bar.

The press had been there to record it all for the evening news. The frantic rush to grab the new lead. The desperate hope that limned every face of every cop and edged every question asked. A fresh lead brought a fresh rush, like speed in the bloodstream. It sent expectations soaring up from the depths of despair. It deepened the cold, it amplified the ticking of the clock that marked the hours a child had been gone from his family. And in the end it left them lost, struggling and wondering.

'Hannah said it was a bad connection. McCaskill told me it could have been a tape,' Megan said. 'The boys in the sound lab will be able to tell. They're the best.'

'And if it was a tape,' Mitch mumbled, 'the question is, why?'

They both knew the answer. Neither of them would say it. If the perp used a tape of Josh's voice, it was likely because he couldn't use Josh himself. Mitch dug a roll of Maalox tablets out of his shirt pocket and thumbed off three.

'Why call at all if not to make a ransom demand?' Megan asked.

The threat of a migraine had settled in behind her right eye like a hot coal, stubbornly defying the Cafergot she'd taken half an hour earlier. She needed something stronger, but anything stronger would knock her out, and she needed to think. She rubbed her forehead and stared down at the mess on her plate until it blurred into a mosaic of earth-toned colors.

'If this was the perp calling and all he did was play a tape of Josh asking to come home . . . That's taunting. That's just pure cruelty. And it's personal. He's jerking Hannah and Paul around for kicks. That seems personal.'

Mitch shrugged. 'Or it's power. Part of his game – like leaving that notebook on the hood of my truck. He's the kind of guy who pulls the wings and legs off flies and thinks it's funny.'

'A game,' Megan whispered. She didn't want to think that was the mentality of the person they were dealing with, because if it was, things were likely to get worse. 'Why would anyone pick on Hannah and Paul? They don't seem to have an enemy in the world.'

'What difference does that make?' Mitch snapped, too tired to keep the bitterness from his voice. 'You think bad things don't happen to good people?'

Megan winced. 'That's not what I meant.'

She thought of reaching out to touch his hand. A simple gesture that was against her nature. She never reached out. If she did, she could be pushed away. It was smarter to keep feelings buried deeply. She had let her guard down last night, but last night was over. The new day brought a fresh vow: no cops, no chiefs of police.

'We should call it a night,' she said, pushing to her feet.

Mitch watched as she fluttered around the table like a hummingbird, gathering the dirty plates and plastic silverware. The woman who burned like fire in his arms last night had transformed at dawn. All the passion, all the softness, had been zipped back up inside this woman with the slicked-back hair and unsmiling mouth. This woman of the baggy corduroy slacks and baggier sweater, who hid her femininity like a guilty secret.

He watched her as she stuffed the garbage into a wastebasket the size of a shoebox, her movements jerky and quick, her body language snapping that she didn't want his scrutiny. She was the first woman he'd slept with in two years who hadn't wanted to cling to him when it was over. He almost smiled at the irony. He had spent the last two years ducking the attentions of women who wanted more from him than he had to give. Megan wanted nothing from him, and his strongest urge at the moment was to pull her into his arms and make love to her. A curious puzzle, but for once he had no desire to take it apart and figure out the mystery.

'. . . and I thought, if nothing goes down tonight,' she rattled on, 'I'd go up to St Paul tomorrow. I should look in on my dad and I could stop at headquarters and see if I can't grease some wheels with the sound guys. Ken Kutsatsu likes to work Sundays. If he's in, maybe I can talk him into listening to our tape. And I could see if they've turned anything up on the notebook, though I'm not too hopeful. I also thought I'd try to see Jayne Millard – she does our suspect profiles. Maybe she can give us an edge somewhere.'

'You talk about your father,' Mitch said casually, rising from his chair, slowly twisting sideways to stretch the tightness out of his back. 'You never mention your mother. Is she around?'

Wrong question. Her face closed down defensively. 'I wouldn't know. She left when I was six. I never saw her again.'

She threw the pronouncement between them like a gauntlet, as if she dared him to make something of it. Mitch frowned. 'I didn't mean to pry. I just . . .'

Just what? *Wanted to know more about you. Wanted to know what makes you tick. Wanted to get close to you on a level I have no business thinking about.* Even as he told himself that, another part of his mind was busy fitting this new piece into the Megan O'Malley puzzle. He could picture her too easily – small and alone, too serious, trying not to draw any attention to herself; a little girl with big green eyes and long dark hair, trailing after her father the cop. The way Jessie trailed him.

'You and your dad must be close.'

She smiled. Not the warm smile of pride and affection; the brittle smile at a bad joke. 'It's late. Let's call it a day.'

He caught her arm as she tried to walk past him. 'I'm sorry if I said the wrong thing.'

'You didn't,' she lied, knowing the truth would be far too complicated and too messy to deal with tonight. 'I'm tired, that's all.' In a cool voice, she added, 'I believe your room is across the hall, Chief.'

She tried to pull away, but Mitch held on, annoyed with her for trying to give him the brushoff, annoyed with himself for wanting to break down her defenses. If he had any sense, he would take their one night of great sex and let the rest go. He didn't need the headache of a relationship, especially now. And he didn't need a woman with a chip on her shoulder the size of New Zealand.

But he didn't let her go.

'I know where my room is,' he murmured. 'I'd rather stay here.'

'And I'd rather you didn't.'

He narrowed his eyes in speculation. 'Do you mean that, or is this more of the tough-cookie act?'

'It's not an act,' she snapped, glaring at him, praying he wouldn't see the lie through the defiance.

'You can't pretend we haven't already crossed the line, Megan,' he said softly.

'Maybe it would be best if we did.'

'Why? What are you so afraid of?'

The answer came readily, but she refused to give it to him. She was too good at protecting herself to make that mistake.

This time he let her go when she stepped back from him, though she felt his narrow gaze on her as tangibly as his touch.

'Look . . .' Glancing down at her sweater, she scraped at a spot of dried garlic sauce with her thumb. 'It just complicates things, that's all. I mean, I can't be effective at my job if you don't respect me –'

'I respect your authority on the job –'

She strolled around behind the table with her hands on her hips, casually putting distance and furniture between them. 'Really? You've had a funny way of showing it.'

'I don't treat you any differently than I treat any of my men,' he said, stalking her.

'You try to get Noogie to go to bed with you? That's an . . . *adventuresome* lifestyle for a small-town cop.'

'Goddammit, don't be flip,' he growled, rounding the table. 'You know what I mean.'

Megan stepped away from him. 'Sure I do. Just like I know that if I have an affair with you, when it's over, everything will be awkward and there'll be resentment to deal with and my reputation will be damaged –'

'You're making some pretty ugly assumptions about my character.'

She stopped and held her ground, looking him in the eye, jaded and tough because that was how she had survived. 'I can't afford not to.'

'And why is that?' he asked, his mouth twisting with derision. 'Is the job that important to you – that you don't trust anyone, that you give your whole life to it? Jesus, what kind of life is that?'

'It's all I have.'

The instant the words were out, she wanted them back. She bit her tongue, but it was too late. They were out there, hanging in the air to be absorbed and digested by Mitch Holt. She felt as if she had torn a chunk out of her soul and tossed it to him, and she knew she could never get it back.

God, how stupid. How could you be so careless, O'Malley?

Appalled at her blunder, she turned her back to him and hoped he would have the good grace to simply leave. She didn't want his pity or his ridicule. She wanted him gone. She wanted to turn the world around and start this damned week over. Pain cut through her head like the blade of an ax, sharp enough to bring tears to her eyes. The last thing she would do was cry in front of him. And so she held her breath against the need to cry and held her muscles stiff against the aching weariness that pulled at her.

Mitch stared at the back of her head, at the uncompromising, rigid set of her slender shoulders. He called himself a bastard for picking a fight with her. The job came with its own kit for building walls of isolationism. He knew. He had walls of his own and he'd seen plenty of other cops put them up brick by brick. He understood the protection they afforded. He of all people should have respected them, but he didn't want walls between him and Megan. He wanted what they had found last night – mind-numbing passion . . . the comfort of holding each other.

She tensed even more as he settled his hands on her shoulders. He stood close behind her, bent his head down close to hers, close enough that he could catch just the faintest hint of perfume on her skin. The scent was so soft, so thin, it seemed almost imagined, as if she put on just enough that only she would know, as if it were only for that secret self she kept so carefully locked inside – the soft Megan, the feminine Megan, the Megan who liked pink walls and flowered sheets and little china statues of cats.

He let his hands slide down from her shoulders and slipped his arms around her. She held herself as straight as a post, unforgiving, unyielding, unwilling to surrender any more of her pride.

'The job is the job,' he murmured, his lips brushing the side of her neck. 'What goes on between us in bed has nothing to do with it. It's a rotten night, a rotten case, a rotten motel – why can't we at least have this? Hmm? Why can't we give each other a little pleasure?' He flattened his hands against her belly, his fingertips massaging subtly, awakening the fire inside her.

'Just go,' Megan said. She didn't want his tenderness. Anything else she could have fought off, but she had no defense against tenderness. God help her, she couldn't defend against something she'd craved all her life.

'Go,' she said on a trembling breath.

'No,' he murmured, tracing the tip of his tongue behind her ear.

She called on anger to save her. 'Go!' she shouted. 'Get out!'

'No.' He pulled her so close against him she couldn't hurt him and she couldn't escape him. 'Not now. Not like this.'

'Damn you,' she mumbled against his chest, her voice breaking as the tears fought for release and the frustration choked her. She struggled against him, tried to kick him, but her heart wasn't in it.

He tipped her chin up so she had no real choice but to look at him. 'Look me in the eye and tell me you don't want this,' he said darkly, his breath coming harder as desire pooled warm and heavy in his groin.

Megan glared at him, hating the way her body was heating and humming with awareness pressed to his. 'I don't want this,' she said defiantly.

203

His nostrils flared. Amber fire flashed in his eyes. 'Liar,' he said, but he let her go.

Megan stood at the foot of the bed for a long while after the door clicked shut, knowing what he'd said was too true for comfort.

Day 5
12:11 p.m. 16°

'Mick says he'll make a hundred thou this year.'

'Good for Mick.' *And did you ask your loving son why he never sends you a dime of it when he knows you eat beans and wieners twice a week because your pension check doesn't stretch and your daughter – who pays half your bills – is just a cop and doesn't get paid shit compared to a hotshot investment broker from L.A.?*

Megan didn't ask the question. She knew better. They had played out that scenario more than once. It didn't ease her own resentment. It only got Neil's blood pressure up. Yet it never ceased to amaze her that the child her father still doted on and bragged about could care so little, while she, the unwanted reminder of the faithless Maureen, the child who could have grown up alone in an alley somewhere for all Neil O'Malley cared, was the one who remained behind, chained to memories she hated by a man who had never loved her.

As if it would take her mind away from the memories, she looked around the tiny kitchen with the garish turquoise walls and the checked curtain that was stiff with the starch of age and airborne grease. She hated this room with its cheap, chipped white tin cupboards and enormous old dingy cast-iron sink. She hated the smell of lard and cigarettes, hated the gray linoleum and the chrome-legged table and chairs where her father sat. It was an ugly place, stripped bare of life and warmth – not unlike her father himself in some ways.

Not that Neil O'Malley was physically ugly. His features were sharp – had once been handsome – and his eyes were a brilliant blue. But time and bitterness had stolen their sheen as they had stolen the color from his hair and the vigor from his body. The man she remembered as a small block of muscle in a cop's blue uniform had shrunk and sagged. His right hand quaked as he raised his drink to his lips.

Megan stirred the thick roux in the Dutch oven on the old gas stove. Lamb stew. The same thing she always made when she came to visit on Sundays – not because she liked it, but because Neil would grouse about anything else. God forbid she should do something to displease him. She sniffed at that. She had never in her life done anything that *pleased* him.

'Have you talked to Mick lately?' she asked. *Of course not. Mick doesn't call you, even though he knows what it would mean to you. He hasn't visited since the year the NCAA basketball tournament finals were held in the Metrodome and he managed to weasel a ticket out of a wealthy client from L.A.*

'Aw, no.' Neil waved it off as if her question were nothing more than a cloud of bad gas. 'He's busy, you know. He damn near runs that outfit he works for. Probably would if it weren't for the goddamn Jews –'

'You want a refill on that beer, Pop?' She had no desire to hear for the millionth time his anti-Semitic diatribe or his anti-Black diatribe or his anti-English diatribe.

He lifted the bottle of nonalcoholic brew and grimaced at it while he hacked up a rattling glob of phlegm. 'Christ, no. This stuff tastes like shit. Why don't you bring me something decent to drink?'

'Because your doctor doesn't want you drinking at all.'

'Fuck him. He's a fucking fascist. He's not even American, y'know.' He pulled a cigarette from the pack of Kents on the table and shook it at her. 'That's half of what's wrong with this country. They let in too many goddamn foreigners.'

'And where did *your* father come from?' The sarcasm slipped out against her better judgment, but she couldn't help herself. If she held it all in, she figured she would die of something akin to uremic poisoning.

'Don't get smart with me,' Neil warned. 'My da was Irish and proud of it. He'd'a stayed in Connemara if it weren't for the goddamn Brits.'

He lit the cigarette, sucked in a lungful of smoke, and went through the ritual choking and hacking. Megan shook her head in disgust. His arteries were in worse shape than the seventy-year-old water pipes in the house – clogged with the crud of sixty-some years of fat, cholesterol, tar, and nicotine. It was a pure wonder a drop of blood made it to his brain – which, she supposed, could explain a lot. He had already suffered one small stroke, and his doctor warned that the big one was imminent if Neil didn't change his lifestyle. The doctor could have saved his breath on the antismoking speech as well. Despite the warning signs of lung disease, Neil went on with his habit as if he thought the congestion and shortness of breath were merely incidental to his smoking.

'You shouldn't smoke, either,' Megan grumbled, hefting the stew pot off the stove and carrying it to the table.

'And you, girlie, should mind your own goddamn business.'

She made a rude noise. 'Don't I wish.'

She stared down at the stew she had dished herself and pushed the plate away. She hated lamb. Her father chewed vigorously and sopped up a puddle of gravy with a chunk of butter-coated bread.

'So, have you heard about the big case I'm working, Pop? That child abduction down in Deer Lake?'

'World's full of perverts.'

'It's a tough one. Hardly any leads at all. We've been working practically around the clock – my guys from the bureau, the sheriff's department, the police department. The chief is an ex-detective from the Miami PD. We've even got a team of computer experts from Harris College working on it.'

'Worthless boxes of wire,' he grumbled, forking up another cube of lamb. 'They can't match good old-fashioned police work. Footwork – that's how cases get solved. And not by a bunch of college-boy pricks-up-their-butts detectives, either.'

'I'm the agent in charge, you know,' she went on doggedly. 'There was an article in the *Tribune*. You might have read it.'

Good for you, honey. I'm so proud of you. . . . Yeah, right.

Neil looked down at his plate, spit out a piece of gristle, gave a muffled snort, and shook his head. 'Worthless rag. I take the *Pioneer Press*. Always have.'

'God, would it kill you to say something nice to me just once?' she snapped, knowing it wasn't worth the effort. 'Would it be so hard? I'd settle for anything, you know – "congratulations," "good stew," "nice shoes." Even a noncommittal hum would do,' she said sarcastically. 'Anything to keep me from wondering why in hell I bother to come here. Do you think you could manage that just once, Pop?'

Neil's face flushed an unhealthy shade of maroon. He shook his fork at her, flinging little specks of gravy onto the table. 'You watch that smart mouth, girlie. You're just like –'

She cut him off with a violent wave of her hand. 'Don't you dare. Don't you *dare*! I'm *nothing* like her. She had the good sense to leave you twenty-six years ago!'

Her father's mouth tightened into a knot as he stared at his plate.

With angry tears stinging her eyes, Megan shoved her chair back from the table and went to stare out the window at Mrs Gristman's backyard, where her ancient poodle, Claude, had dotted the snow with little piles of shit. The neighborhood was drab and ugly, like everything about this house was drab and ugly. She wished she could stop coming back here, but she wouldn't. Because he was her father, her responsibility. She wouldn't shirk her duty to him the way he had done to her.

Unbidden, unwanted, an image of Mitch came to her. Mitch and Jessie, teasing and tickling over a Happy Meal at McDonald's.

She sniffed and wiped her nose on the back of her hand. She said nothing as she pulled her coat off the hook by the back door, giving Neil a chance to redeem himself. He didn't. He never would.

'Don't forget to take your medication,' she said tightly. 'I'll get back when I can . . . for all you care.'

20

Day 6
7:00 a.m. –18° windchill factor: –55°

Monday morning dawned rudely with a blast of air sweeping down from the Arctic and bringing a temperature of eighteen degrees below zero. A howling wind out of the northwest chased the windchill factor to a brutal minus fifty-five. Megan's spirits dropped in direct correlation. She lay in her bed at the Sheraton, dreading her meeting with DePalma, listening to the radio disc jockeys delight in telling Twin Citians that exposed skin could freeze in as little as sixty seconds.

Sunday had been a bust all the way around. Preliminary tests on the tape of the phone call had been inconclusive. No usable prints had been lifted from the notebook. Dinner with Jayne Millard, the agent who worked up suspect profiles, had netted Megan nothing but commiseration for having so little to go on and congratulations for breaking the glass ceiling that had heretofore kept women out of the field.

She lay in bed, staring at her reflection in the mirror above the dresser, thinking about the way some people perceived her as a heroine and others as a troublemaker. She felt curiously removed from the issue, as if the Megan O'Malley those people were looking at were nothing more than a hologram. She didn't want to be their champion or their demon. She wanted to do her job. She wanted to find Josh.

Hung over from fatigue and muscle relaxants, she dragged herself out of bed and into the shower. She dressed for her meeting with DePalma in the one change of clothes she'd thrown into the car – a pair of slim charcoal trousers and a soft black turtleneck that emphasized her pallor and the dark circles under her eyes. She thought she looked like a zombie or a coffeehouse refugee, but there was no hope for better.

She fantasized about an FBI assignment in Tampa as she zipped her parka, clamped on earmuffs, and wound her scarf around her head and neck. Florida shimmered in her mind like a distant mirage that was swept away the instant she stepped outdoors and the wind hit her like a brick in the forehead. No less than a dozen cars in the parking lot had their hoods open – the northland symbol of surrender – waiting for service trucks to show up and jump dead batteries. Two minutes later, Megan popped the hood on the Lumina and stomped back inside the hotel, muttering her cold weather mantra. 'I *hate* winter.'

9:00 a.m. -18° windchill factor: -55°

DePalma paced behind his desk with his hands on his hips and his head ducked down between his shoulders. He looked like Nixon doing Ed Sullivan.

'We've never had so many calls from the press,' he said, wagging his head.

'I'm a curiosity,' Megan pointed out. She stood on the opposite side of the desk. He hadn't asked her to sit. Bad sign. 'They'll get over it. Pretend I'm no big deal. *I* shouldn't be a big deal. Their focus should be Josh, not me.'

'You made it difficult for them to ignore you, interrogating the father in front of them.'

'I asked him a few questions. He lost his temper, that's all −'

DePalma wheeled on her, incredulous. 'That's all? Megan, the man has lost his son −'

'He deliberately withheld information from me! The man is holding something back. What am I supposed to do − act like a lady and shut my mouth or act like a cop and do my job?'

'You don't do that kind of a job with the press within shouting distance, and you damn well know it!'

Megan clamped her mouth shut. There was no weaseling out of this. She'd blown it with Paul Kirkwood. She wanted to say Paul Kirkwood had blown it for her, but life didn't work that way. Take no shit, make no excuses. She should have seen the potential for trouble, but she'd let her temper get the better of her. A good agent didn't do that.

'Yes, sir,' she murmured.

DePalma sighed as he slid into his high-backed chair. 'Whether you like it or not, you've got a great big magnifying glass on you and this case, Agent O'Malley. Watch your step and watch your mouth. You're a good cop, but no one's ever accused you of being overly diplomatic.'

'Yes, sir.'

'And for God's sake, don't bring up that sexual harassment business from last fall. The superintendent about had a stroke −'

'That's unfair,' Megan charged. 'I did *not* bring that up. It had nothing to do with me. Henry Forster opened that can of worms on his own −'

DePalma waved off her protest. 'It doesn't matter. We're all under scrutiny. If you can't handle the pressure or your own temper, I won't have a choice; I'll yank you in.'

He let that hang for a moment as he slipped on a pair of half glasses and glanced at the top page of a mountain of paperwork neatly stacked beside the spotless blotter. Megan drew a breath to ask permission to leave, and he looked up at her, the expression on his bloodhound face softening.

'Do you have anything at all?'

'Puzzle pieces. Nothing fits yet.'

His dark eyes strayed to the photograph of his sons. 'Make them fit. Make this case, Megan. Make it stick.'

11:13 a.m. -20° windchill factor: -48°

The weight of DePalma's ultimatums pressed down on Megan as she slipped into the law enforcement center via a little-used side door. The press were starved for any scrap of news on the phone call and she had none to give them. After her dressing-down, she wished fervently she could become invisible to media people, but she knew the only successful vanishing act around here was Josh Kirkwood's and it was her job to make him reappear.

The lingering aroma of cigars and air freshener hit her like an invisible wall when she let herself into her office. She made a mental note to buy an air-filtering gizmo.

The message light on her answering machine was flashing like a strobe. She hit the playback button, then unwound the scarf from her head. Paige Price wanted to do an interview.

'When pigs fly,' Megan muttered, prying off her earmuffs.

Henry Forster wanted a comment on the recorded phone call.

'Yeah, I'll give you a comment, you myopic old sack of shit,' she growled, unzipping her parka.

'Agent O'Malley, this is Stuart Fielding at NCIC. Please call me back ASAP. I've got a hit on your fingerprints.'

Olie Swain's prints.

'Jesus, Mary, and Joseph,' she whispered, her heart kicking into high gear.

She flung the parka in the general direction of the coat rack as she dove into her broken chair and grabbed the telephone receiver. Her whole body trembling, she punched in the number for FBI headquarters in Washington. Even her voice shook as she went through the usual rigmarole with receptionists. Finally, Stuart Fielding himself came on the line.

'Sorry it took so long for the search, but we couldn't get a match on the name or the prints in your geographical region. We had to enlarge the parameters of the search repeatedly. Finally got a hit in Washington State. Are you ready?'

'You can't know how ready. Shoot.'

'According to AFIS and the criminal history database, your guy is Leslie Olin Sewek. Born October 31, 1956. Served five years out of ten in the state facility at Walla Walla and was paroled on his birthday in 1989.'

'What was he in for?' Megan held her breath.

'He was convicted on two counts of child molestation. I'll fax you his rap sheet.'

Megan was vaguely aware of thanking Fielding and hanging up the phone. Her eyes burned as she stared at the notes she'd taken.

> *Olie Swain: AKA – Leslie Olin Sewek*
> *5 of 10 – Walla Walla*
> *Child molest*

Olie Swain had a light-colored van.
Olie Swain had access to Josh.
Olie Swain was a convicted pedophile.
'Gotcha, you son of a bitch.'

After receiving the fax she bolted out of her office and charged down the hall, weaving around officers and secretaries and citizens who had come in for reasons unknown. Heads snapped her way as she cut through the squad room and down the hall to Mitch's office. Natalie whirled around from her file cabinets, clearly affronted that anyone would have the temerity to barge into her stronghold.

'I have to see the chief.'

'He's with the sheriff –'

Megan didn't even slow down. She burst into the inner office, eyes bright, color high on her cheekbones. Not sparing Russ Steiger a glance, she marched up to Mitch's desk, tossed down the curled tube of thermal paper that was the faxed pages of Olie's rap sheet, and slammed a small hand down beside it.

'Your harmless Mr Swain is a convicted pedophile from the state of Washington.'

Mitch stared at her, stunned, dread coiling in his gut. 'What?'

'Leslie Olin Sewek, a.k.a. Lonnie O. Swain, a.k.a. Olie Swain, was sentenced to a state penitentiary in 1984 for forced sex with a nine-year-old boy.'

'Jesus, no.'

Mitch sat perfectly still in his chair. He'd had no way of knowing Olie Swain was anything other than a strange little man who worked at the ice rink. And still he felt responsible. This was his town. It was his job to protect the people of Deer Lake. And all this time a child predator had been living right under his nose and he hadn't suspected a thing. A pedophile had been working in proximity with children, and he had allowed it.

'How the hell did you get his prints?'

Megan had the grace to look sheepish, though she turned her back on

Steiger's scrutiny. 'An opportunity presented itself,' she fudged. 'I had to run him as a nonsuspect, but at least we got him.

'We can't arrest him for our case on the basis of his record alone,' she went on, 'but there is a bench warrant outstanding in the state of Washington for parole violation. I've already called Judge Witt about a search warrant for the house and vehicle. The rap sheet combined with the witness description of the van and the opportunity Olie had to take Josh gives us probable cause for a search. When we bring him in this time, we can let him have it with both barrels.'

She paced in front of his desk, her focus on her plan. 'But I was thinking we might want to hold off,' she said.

'What the hell for?' Steiger demanded, pushing to his feet from the visitor's chair. 'Let's go in and rattle the little shit's cage.'

'"Let's"? As in "let *us*"?' Megan sneered. 'Olie Swain lives within the city limits of Deer Lake. This is a police matter; it's out of your jurisdiction, Steiger.'

'Forget that.' Steiger glared at her. 'This is a multijurisdictional investigation. I'm in on nailing this creep —'

'Well, then, how about *we* prove he did it?' Megan interrupted. 'We can set up a surveillance and see if he leads us to Josh. We know Josh isn't at his place. He must have him stashed somewhere. And then there's the question of whether or not he acted alone. We know he didn't make that call from St Peter or leave the notebook on Mitch's truck. He might lead us to the person who did.'

Steiger looked at her as if she'd proposed they all put lampshades on their heads and dance the hokey-pokey. 'How the hell are we supposed to do a surveillance on somebody in a town this size? I take a dump at seven o'clock, everybody in Deer Lake knows it by five after.'

'That probably doesn't have anything to do with the size of the town,' Megan said derisively.

'The house across the street from Olie's place is vacant,' Mitch said as he rose from his chair to pace. 'Arlan and Ramona Neiderhauser spend the winter in a trailer park in Brownsville, Texas. I can get us into the house.'

'And what happens when Olie leaves his place?' Steiger challenged. 'There's no way in hell you can tail somebody through Deer Lake without getting made.'

'We do the surveillance at night. Use unmarked cars. Stay well back, leave the lights off. If he makes us, we're screwed, but if he doesn't, he might lead us to Josh.'

Steiger snorted. 'He's a little worm. I say if we roust him, he'll turn over and give us what we want.'

'And what if he doesn't?' Mitch demanded. 'What if he's got an accomplice? We drag Olie in, the partner panics, and Josh is dead.'

He punched his intercom button. 'Natalie? Will you please get me Arlan Neiderhauser on the line?' Turning back to the sheriff, he said, 'We have to give this a shot, Russ. If it doesn't work, we'll still have the warrants.'

'Damn waste of time, that's what it is,' Steiger grumbled.

'It's a shot at getting Josh back alive and nailing his abductors red-handed.' Mitch checked his watch and did some quick figuring in his head. 'Olie's at work from three until eleven. I'll put a man outside the rink right now, just in case. Let's pick our teams and meet in the war room at eight.'

Steiger left the office snarling. Megan blew out a breath as he slammed the door shut behind him. 'The loose cannon rumbles.'

'Fuck him.'

'I'll pass, thanks,' Megan drawled.

Mitch dismissed Steiger and the remark as he came around the desk. 'Good police work, Agent O'Malley. I'm in town two years and I don't get Olie Swain for anything; you're here five days and you prove he's a child molester. Hell, I even ran a check on him. Nothing. Nada. Zippo.'

Megan frowned at the self-recrimination in his voice. 'He had a valid driver's license in his assumed name and no record. You did your job. I just went a step further – and I may not have except that I saw Olie Friday night and I caught a glimpse of what I thought was maybe a crude tattoo job across his knuckles. I played a hunch that he got it in the joint. It paid off. I got lucky.'

'Luck had nothing to do with it,' Mitch murmured. 'You're a good cop.'

The sentiment was hardly intimate, but Megan felt a warm rush of pleasure just the same. The fact that he said it almost grudgingly, that he clearly didn't like being one-upped, made the compliment sweeter.

'Thanks, Chief,' she said, trying to sound unaffected.

Mitch didn't miss her embarrassment. The fact that she tried to mask her pride with indifference touched him.

'Why didn't you tell me you had his prints?' he asked.

Megan shrugged, not meeting his eyes. 'It didn't come up,' she said, unwittingly using the same line he had given her about Olie's van. 'I was just playing a hunch. I didn't know anything would come of it.' She lifted the glass Mickey Mouse paperweight from his desk and rolled it between her hands like a snowball. 'Technically, I suppose I went over your head. Does that mean you get to punch me out now?'

He sat back against the edge of the desk. 'I can't be too pissed off since the hunch paid out big-time,' he said. 'That doesn't mean I have to be happy about it.'

She set the paperweight back down with Mickey standing on his head. A frown curved her mouth. 'Happy's got nothing to do with this case, Chief.'

They hadn't spoken since Sunday evening, when she had called to let him know the lab had nothing for them yet. Neither of them had said a word about Saturday night. It was in his eyes as he looked at her now –

remembered hunger and heat. She could feel it just beneath her skin. An unnecessary complication, but there was no going back, and she knew she wouldn't have changed it if she had the chance. Not smart, but there it was.

'How'd it go with DePalma?' he asked.

Megan held her arms out at her sides. 'I still have all my limbs.'

'And your job?'

She gave him a wry smile. 'For the moment. Let's just say if this stakeout pays off, Josh won't be the only one getting saved. So, I'd better get back at it. I thought I'd run by the hospital and talk to the receptionist who called the rink the night Josh disappeared. See if she might be able to do a voice ID of the man she spoke with. If she could ID Olie's voice, then we'd know he took the call and that he knew Hannah would be late. Makes a stronger case for opportunity.'

'Good. I'll reach out to the authorities in his old stomping grounds, see if they can give us anything to go on. And I'll call the county attorney and apprise him of the situation.'

'Great.'

'Megan.' He said her name just to say it, then kicked himself for being a sap. The job was the job, he'd said. What went on between them in bed couldn't enter into it – nor should he have wanted it to. 'I'm glad DePalma didn't do any damage.'

'Nothing wounded but my pride,' she murmured. 'I'm out of here, Chief. Catch you later.'

1:07 p.m. -21° windchill factor: -48°

'I'm sorry. I just couldn't – s-s-s-ah-ah-ah-chew!' Carol Hiatt buried her nose in a handful of tissues and closed her eyes for a moment of weary surrender to the virus that was sweeping through the hospital staff.

'Bless you,' Megan said.

The receptionist blew her nose loudly and tossed the tissues into a brimming wastebasket. 'This bug is the worst,' she confided in a raspy voice. The virus had rendered her hair a wilted mop of dyed-black waves atop a long, oval face. Her ski-slope nose was an angry shade of red. She sniffed and groaned. 'I wouldn't be here myself, but the rest of the staff is sicker than I am.'

Megan nodded, trying to impart sympathy. Behind her, in the waiting area, a baby and a toddler were crying a discordant duet while a third child pounded out an atonal piece on a Fisher-Price xylophone. *Geraldo* was on the television – adult children of cross-dressing clergymen.

'I'm sorry,' Carol said again. 'I went through all this with that other officer on Friday. I know I made the call, but it was just nuts here that night. I can't tell you who answered the phone at the rink.'

'He didn't identify himself?'

'I don't know any men who identify themselves over the phone. They all just start talking like they think you ought to know who they are, like they think you were just sitting around waiting for them to call,' she said with weary disgust. She swiped a fresh tissue under her nose and crunched it into the shape of a carnation.

Megan drew a fat black line through the word *receptionist* in her notebook. 'You don't think it might come back to you if you heard his voice?'

'I wish I could say yes,' Carol said. She pulled another fistful of tissues out of the box beside the phone as her eyes filled and emotional distress tightened her features. 'I think the world of Hannah. She's the best person I know. And to think that anyone would just take a little boy and do God knows what to him —'

Carol Hiatt raised a face twisted with anguish. 'I'm sorry. I have a little boy of my own — Brian. He's best friends with Josh. They play on the same hockey team. He was there that night at the rink. It could have been him — It's so hard —'

Megan reached across the counter and touched the woman's shoulder. 'It's okay,' she said softly. 'I know you'd help if you could. This was a long shot; don't worry about it.'

'*Please* find Josh,' the woman whispered. Her plea struck Megan as the voice of every person in Deer Lake. They were all hurting, all stunned. They left their porch lights burning at night with signs on their front doors that said LIGHTS ON FOR JOSH. Because it wasn't only Josh who had been stolen, it was a part of their small-town innocence and trust.

Leslie Olin Sewek had a hell of a lot to answer for.

'We're doing all we can,' Megan said.

Walking away from the desk, she spotted the arrow on the wall pointing the way to the cafeteria. She followed it. Maybe caffeine would chase away her headache.

The cafeteria proved to be nothing more than a room with tables and chairs and a row of vending machines. A couple of maintenance guys sat at a far corner table throwing dice and drinking coffee. They didn't even look up when she came in.

Megan fed two quarters into the pop machine and punched the Mountain Dew button. Christopher Priest wandered in as the can rumbled down out of the belly of the machine. The black turtleneck clung to his narrow chest and crept up his forearms. His thin, bony hands looked a foot long sticking out of the too-short sleeves.

'Agent O'Malley.' His eyes brightened with surprise behind the big lenses of his glasses. The corners of his wide, lipless mouth flicked upward. 'What brings you here? Not that virus going around, I hope.'

'No. I'm fine. What about yourself, Professor?'

'I have a student here.' He fed change into the coffee machine and ordered himself a cup of sludge with cream and sugar.

Megan popped the top of her Mountain Dew, fished a Cafergot out of her purse, and washed it down with a long swallow, all the while absently watching Priest's attention to neatness and detail as he retrieved his cup and took it to a table. He gingerly wiped the overflow off the side of the cup with a paper napkin, which he folded neatly and placed squarely on the table just to the left of the cup.

'Oh, yeah,' she said, sliding down sideways onto the chair to the professor's left. 'The kid who was in that car accident the same night Josh was abducted.'

'Yes.' He sipped his coffee, his eyes straight ahead as the steam fogged over his glasses. 'Precisely.'

'How's he doing?'

'Not very well, actually. He seems to have developed some complications. They may have to transfer him to a larger hospital in the Cities.'

'That's too bad.'

'Mmm . . .' He stared off across the room at a particularly colorful poster for the Heimlich maneuver. 'Mike was running an errand for me,' he said so softly he might have been talking to himself. 'For the project concerning perceptions and learning.'

'The one Dr Wright mentioned the other day.'

'Yes. Mike keeps saying the road was completely bare and then he hit that curve.' He took another sip of coffee, blotted his lips with the napkin. 'Life is funny, isn't it?'

'Yeah, it's a laugh riot from where I stand.'

He ignored her sarcasm. His curiosity seemed wholly analytical; the question he posed was posed to the world at large. 'Is it fate or is it random? What brought Mike Chamberlain to that corner at that moment? What put Josh Kirkwood on that curb alone that night? What put you and me here at the same time?'

'Sounds like questions for the philosophy department.'

'Not necessarily. Computer science deals in logic, cause and effect, patterns of thinking.'

'Well, Professor,' Megan announced as she finished her soda and tossed the can into the recycling bin, 'if you and your computer come up with a logical explanation for the shit that happens in this world, I'd like to be the first to know.'

21

Arlan and Ramona Neiderhauser's home smelled strongly of mothballs. The smell wafted up Mitch's nostrils and burned his sinus linings. Sitting in a straight chair he had hauled up from the dining room, he stared through binoculars out the bedroom window at Olie's dark hovel across the street. Lights were on in Oscar Rudd's house, the illumination spilling out onto the junker Saabs parked in his side yard.

Megan stood beside the window, leaning a shoulder against the wall, peeking out from behind the curtain. They both wore their coats – to be ready to run out and to ward off the stale, cold air of the house. The Neiderhausers left their thermostat turned up just enough to keep the pipes from freezing. Outside, the temperature was inching downward, threatening to shatter a record low that hadn't been broken in thirty years. The cold was so extreme that ice crystals had begun to form in the air, creating a phenomenon called snow fog, a weird, thin fog that hung above the ground like a special effect from a horror movie.

Despite the cold, Steiger had opted to remain on the street in an unmarked car. BCA, police, and sheriff's department personnel had been dispatched to strategic locations around town so that no matter which way Olie went, he would be followed. The mobile lab waited at the old fire hall, ready to roll out at a moment's notice to execute the search warrants.

'God, I hate this weather,' Megan said, her voice lowered to the hushed tone darkened bedrooms seemed to require. 'Do you know it's going to be warmer at the North Pole tonight than it will be here?'

'You want to move to the North Pole?'

'I want to move to Grand Cayman.'

'The steel-drum music would drive you to suicide inside a month,'

'At least I'd die warm.'

Mitch switched hands on the binoculars and stuck his right one in his jacket pocket to snuggle up to a chemical hand-warmer packet. 'You know Olie's got something like five computers in there?'

'Where'd he get the money for five computers?'

'He told me they were castoffs from businesses upgrading their systems. The warden at Walla Walla told me Olie tested high for intelligence. He's always studying something.'

'Little boys, for instance.'

'Yeah, but Olie's parole officer seemed surprised when I told him what was going down here. He didn't think Olie would get violent.'

Megan dropped the curtain and gave Mitch a look. 'He was behind bars for forced sex with a child. That's not violent?'

'Force can be coercion. Violence has varying degrees.'

'Yeah, well, I read the sheet on this guy. It looked to me like he showed classic signs of escalation – window-peeping, then exposing himself, then fondling, then rape. What'd the boys in Washington have to say for their parole follow-up?'

Mitch shrugged. 'Olie's not the first con who skipped.'

Megan checked her watch. Nine o'clock. Olie wasn't supposed to get off at the rink until eleven, but they needed to be in place just in case. Her gaze swept the small, cluttered bedroom, lingering on the bed, where they had tossed their two-way radios on the white chenille spread. Walkie-talkies, cops loitering with guns strapped under their armpits and binoculars trained on the house across the street. If this wasn't the most excitement this room had ever seen, Arlan and Ramona were one fun couple.

Mitch's cellular phone bleeped. He set the binoculars down and snapped the phone open. 'Chief Holt.'

The tremulous little voice swept Mitch from one tension to another. 'Jessie? Honey, what are you doing up this late?'

There was a sniffle and a hitched breath. 'Are y-you gonna c-come and g-get me tonight?'

Mitch's heart crashed. Jessie. He'd forgotten her. There had been calls to make and a meeting with the county attorney. He'd had to pick his team and organize equipment and set up the surveillance points. And in the midst of all that he had forgotten his daughter.

'I'm sorry, honey,' he murmured. 'No, I can't make it tonight. You'll have to stay with Grandpa and Grandma. It's really important that I work tonight.'

'Y-you always s-say that!' Jessie wailed. 'I don't like you when you're a cop!'

'Please don't say that, sweetheart.' Did the plea sound as plaintive to Megan's ears as it did to his? He hated letting Jessie down. He hated it even more when she blamed his job, because that brought back memories of Allison and the arguments they'd had, the appeals she'd made that had fallen on deaf ears. Guilt wadded into a sour lump in his throat. 'I promise we'll have a night together soon, honey. This is just so important. I'm trying to find Josh so he can be with his mom and dad. You know, he hasn't seen them in almost a week.'

The line was silent while Jessie mulled this over. 'He must miss them,' she said softly. 'He must be sad. I miss you, too, Daddy.' She sounded too old to be five, too disillusioned to be a little girl.

'I miss you, too, baby,' he whispered.

Joy came on the line, her voice like a razor in his ear. 'I'm sorry we bothered you, Mitch,' she said with more rancor than contrition. 'Jessie was just so upset, we couldn't get her to settle down. I've told her she shouldn't count on you —'

'Look, Joy.' Mitch struggled hard to hold on to his temper. This wasn't the time or place. 'I'm in the middle of something here and I have to keep this line open. I'm sorry I forgot to call you. I hope it isn't an inconvenience for Jessie to stay tonight. We'll discuss whether or not Jessie can count on me at a later time.'

He broke the connection before she had a chance to cluck her tongue at him. He could see her pacing back and forth in front of their picture window — *I wonder where your daddy is . . . Funny he hasn't called . . .* — working Jessie into a state. Why the hell had he come here of all places after Allison and Kyle had been killed?

To punish himself for life.

Megan stood in silence along the wall, watching him through her lashes. The moment should have been private, but she couldn't just ignore his pain.

'My old man worked second shift so he wouldn't have to spend time with me,' she said. 'He never once said he missed me.'

Mitch looked up at her. Moonlight filtered in through the lace curtain and illuminated her face. The vulnerability she usually guarded so zealously with her pride was the most intimate thing she'd given him yet.

'Jessie's very lucky to have you,' she murmured.

Noga's voice came over the two-way and the moment shattered like glass. 'Chief! I got him going out a side door. He's headed your way on foot. Out.'

Mitch grabbed the radio. 'Roger, Noogie. All units — he's moving on foot toward home. Be ready.'

Megan crouched at the window. It was impossible to see the path Olie had tramped down between the ice arena and his converted garage home, but he had to round the side of the building to get in. She stared at the corner of the little asphalt-shingled building until her eyes burned and her lungs ached from holding her breath. Finally, Olie Swain appeared with a backpack dangling by one strap from his left hand. He fumbled with his keys, dropped them on the sidewalk, and bent to pick them up. As he straightened, the *TV 7 News* van pulled up in the street.

'No!' Megan shouted, springing to her feet.

'Shit!' Mitch overturned his chair as he grabbed his two-way and bolted for the stairs.

They burst out the front door and into the bitter cold night, one behind the other. Mitch ran ahead, the two-way jammed against his face.

'We're screwed!' he barked into the unit. 'And the son of a bitch who tipped the press had better eat his gun before I get my hands on him!'

Olie stood, frozen, horrified. The book bag dropped from his fingers and fell with a muffled thud at his feet. The side door of the *TV 7* van rolled open like the belly of the Trojan horse, and a mob spilled out. A man with a big video camera on his shoulder. Another with a brilliant white light on a long pole. Leading the charge was a woman he had seen on the news and around the ice arena in the past week. She was probably beautiful, he thought, but bearing down on him, she looked like one of his worst nightmares.

They found you, Leslie. You thought you could hide, but they found you. You're so stupid, Leslie.

Cold sweat ran down his body like rain.

The woman thrust a microphone in his face. The light on the pole blinded him. Questions came at him like a hail of bullets.

'Mr Swain, do you have any comment on the abduction of Josh Kirkwood? Is it true you were convicted of child molestation in Washington? Are you cooperating with the police in this investigation? Was the chief of police here aware of your history of crimes against children?'

They know. They know. They know. The voice chanted inside his head, louder and louder and louder. Until it was screaming. Until he thought his skull would split wide open and his brain would boil out of it.

Mitch Holt came running and put a shoulder into the back of the cameraman, sending him sprawling. The video camera crashed against the side of the house and fell into a snowbank.

Olie's bladder let go and warm urine gushed into his pants, freezing almost immediately on the fabric. He turned and bolted, running nowhere, running because instinct dictated it. His feet churned in the snow of the vacant lot. Beneath the drifts, dead weeds pulled at his boots like fingers reaching up from hell. The cold air sliced at his lungs, each ragged breath like a thousand knives. He flailed his arms like a struggling swimmer, trying to plunge onward. The world seemed to jerk up and down around him, a blur of stars and sky and snow and naked trees. He could hear nothing but the voice in his mind and the pounding of his pulse in his ears.

They know. They know. They know.

Then something hit him hard in the back and he went down with a strangled cry.

Mitch came down on Olie with a knee in the small of his back. He yanked the handcuffs off his belt and snapped one around Olie's right hand.

'Leslie Olin Sewek,' he said between gulps of frigid air. 'You're under arrest. You have the right to remain silent. Anything you say may be used against you in court. You have the right to an attorney. If you can't afford an attorney, the state will provide one free of charge.'

He twisted Olie's left arm up behind his back with enough force to make him cry out and slapped on the other cuff. 'Do you understand what I just told you?'

Coughing hard against the ache of cold in his lungs, he pushed himself to his feet and yanked Olie up with him.

'It wasn't me,' Olie whimpered. Tears ran down his face. Blood dribbled from a cut on his lip and froze on his quivering chin. 'I didn't do anything.'

Mitch jerked him around and leaned down into his ugly pug face. 'You've done plenty, Olie, but, by God, if you've done anything to Josh Kirkwood, you'll wish you'd never been born.'

Olie hung his head and sobbed. A mob had gathered behind his house at the edge of the vacant lot – cops, TV people. They all knew. They knew all about him. They knew his past and they would crush his future with the weight of it.

You'll wish you'd never been born, Leslie.

What none of them knew was that he had wished that already. Every day of his life.

Steiger pulled up in an unmarked Crown Victoria with a blue beacon held on the roof by a seventeen-pound magnet. Cops and *TV* 7 personnel scattered as the car roared up the walk alongside Olie's house, narrowly missing the fenders of two of Oscar Rudd's decrepit Saabs. Steiger climbed out, shouting orders.

'Get him in the car! I'll take him downtown.' He flashed a stern look at the small crowd, unaware that the video camera had been dispensed with. 'Move back, folks. This is police business.'

Paige stepped forward, microphone in hand. If they got the audio, they could run it with still shots they had on file and claim technical difficulties on the video. She already had the scoop; that was all that really mattered. 'Sheriff, do you believe this is the man who abducted Josh Kirkwood?'

'We'll be questioning Mr Swain in connection with this case as well as on charges pending in the state of Washington. That's all I can say at the moment.'

'How did you zero in on this suspect?'

He looked at her down his aquiline nose. His hair gleamed like a fresh oil slick in the moonlight. 'Good old-fashioned police work.'

Mitch steered Olie to the passenger side of the Crown Vic and handed him over to Noga. 'Put him in your car.'

Noogie looked from his chief to Steiger and back. 'But, Chief –'

'Put him in the goddamn car and drive him to the station,' Mitch ordered. 'If Steiger gives you any lip, shoot him.'

Noga's brows rose. 'Yessir.'

'I'll follow you downtown,' Megan told the patrolman. She put a hand on Mitch's arm. 'Nice collar, Chief. You nailed his ass.'

'Yeah?' he muttered, cutting a glance at Paige on the other side of the car. 'Well, you ain't seen nothin' yet.'

Megan refrained from comment and turned back to Noga. The patrolman clamped a huge gloved hand on the back of Olie's neck and ushered him past Steiger's car and toward the street where green and white cruisers sat in a haphazard cluster with lights flashing like carnival rides. Catching sight of Noga and Swain, Steiger abandoned Paige and hustled after his erstwhile prisoner.

'Hey, Noga! Load him into this car!'

'That's okay, Sheriff,' Noogie called. 'We can take him. Thanks anyway!'

Down the street, neighbors were peering out their front windows. Oscar Rudd came out of his kitchen door wearing trousers with red suspenders hanging down in big loops, and dress shoes with no socks. Only a grungy thermal undershirt covered his chest and enormous belly. More white hair sprouted out of his ears than covered his head.

'Hey!' he shouted at Steiger. 'Get that car off the lawn! And don't you back into my Saabs! They're collector's items!'

Mitch ignored the small circus and went straight for Paige. She held her microphone up in front of her like a cross to ward off vampires.

'Chief Holt, do you have any comment?'

He snatched the mike out of her hand and hurled it twenty feet into a snowdrift, then grabbed the zipper tab of her ski jacket and yanked it down.

'Is that it, Ms Price?' he snarled. 'No body mike? No tape recorder stuck in your bra?'

'N-no,' she stammered, stumbling back.

He stayed in her face, matching her step for step. The cameraman attempted to come to her rescue. 'Hey, pal, that was an expensive piece of equipment you trashed back there. You'll be lucky if the station doesn't sue.'

Mitch turned to him. His voice was eerily soft. '*I'll* be lucky? *I'll* be lucky.' He leaned down toward the cameraman until they were nose to nose. 'Let *me* tell *you* something, *pal*. I don't care about your fucking camera. You and the ice bitch here have interfered with a police investigation. That's a crime, junior. And if Josh Kirkwood dies because you blew this for us, you're an accessory to murder in my book.'

He wheeled back around on Paige. 'How would you like to report on that, Paige?' He swung an arm in her direction and bellowed out a cutting imitation of an emcee. 'Live from the women's correctional facility in Shakopee – it's Pai-ai-ge Price!'

Paige was shaking with fear and anger. She hated him for scaring her and she hated him for making her feel responsible. 'I'm just doing my job,' she said defensively. 'I didn't make Leslie Sewek into a child molester. I didn't abduct Josh Kirk-wood and I won't be responsible for anything that happens to him.'

Mitch shook his head in disgust and amazement. His lungs hurt from sucking in too much subzero oxygen during his sprint after Olie. His bare hands suddenly ached with cold, but he made no move to dig his gloves out of his pockets or to zip his coat. For the most part, he felt numb, stunned by the lost opportunity. Olie might have led them to Josh. The woman before him had stolen that chance and didn't even have the grace to apologize.

'You just don't get it, do you, Paige?' he murmured. 'This isn't about you. You're nobody. You're nothing. Your job, your ratings, your station – don't mean shit. This is about a little boy who should be home listening to a bedtime story. It's about a mother whose child has been torn away from her and a father who has lost his son. It's real life . . . and it could be real death, thanks to you.'

He turned and headed for the lone green-and-white that waited for him with the motor running, exhaust billowing in white clouds from the tailpipe. Paige watched him go, feeling a twinge of conscience for the first time in a long time. She thought she had eradicated it years before, removed it like an unsightly mole from her perfect chin. A conscience was excess weight. While she knew she had colleagues who carried it without complaint, she had always felt the run to the top would be easier without it. Now . . .

She shook the sensation off as she turned to Garcia. 'Did you get all that?' Paige asked.

The cameraman pulled a microcassette recorder from the breast pocket of his parka and clicked it off.

Paige glanced at the illuminated dial of her watch. 'Let's go. If I hurry, I can still have a story ready by ten.'

10:27 p.m. -30° windchill factor: -62°

'Would you like to have a lawyer present at this questioning, Mr Sewek?'

Olie flinched at the name as if it were a hand reaching out of his past to slap him. The voice in his head shrieked *Leslie! Leslie! Leslie!* like a record with a needle stuck in the groove. He didn't look up at the woman' cop who sat across from him. He could feel her eyes on him, burning with accusation. He could feel it pouring over his skin like acid.

'Mr Sewek? Are you aware of what I'm asking you?'

'It wasn't me,' he mumbled.

His vision blurred as he stared at his hands on the table. He picked at the ratty edges of his fingerless gloves, keeping them carefully pulled over the reminder of his stay in Walla Walla. He could still remember the crushing weight of the biker who had sat on him while a man called Needles dug the letters into the backs of his fingers. He could still remember the harsh laughter as he begged them to stop. The tattoo was the least of what they'd done to him during his five years. Not once had his pleas been answered with mercy, only sadism.

'. . . there is a warrant outstanding for your arrest for violation of parole . . .'

They could send him back. The thought sent agony rushing through him like an arrow.

'We know what you did to that boy back in Washington, Olie,' Mitch Holt said. He paced back and forth behind the woman, his hands on his hips. 'What we want to know is what you've done with Josh Kirkwood.'

'Nothing.'

'Come on, Olie, don't jerk us around. You've got the record, you had opportunity, you have the van –'

'It wasn't me!' Olie shouted, raising his face to glare at Mitch Holt.

Cops never believed him. They always looked at him like something they had to scrape off their shoe. A piece of dog shit. An ugly bug, squashed and oozing. In Mitch Holt's face Olie saw the same combination of disbelief and disgust he had seen so many times before. Even though he had seen it again and again over the course of his miserable life, he still felt a little piece of him break inside.

He had never meant to hurt anyone.

His lips curled back, quivering, and a strange whine crept up the back of his throat as he gritted his teeth against the urge to cry. He clamped a hand on top of his head and wiped it across his brush-bristle hair, down the port wine stain and over his glass eye. He felt as if his body were being steamed inside his heavy winter clothes. His pants and long underwear clung to him where he'd wet himself. The smell of urine burned his nose.

'Did you have an accomplice?'

'Is Josh all right?'

'Cooperation will make all the difference when it comes to indictments.'

'Is he safe?'

'Did you molest him?'

'Is he alive?'

The questions came in a relentless barrage. And between each one the voice shrieked, *Answer me, Leslie! Answer me! Answer me!*

'Stop it!' he cried, slapping his hands over his ears. 'Stop it! Stop it!'

Mitch banged his fists down on the table and leaned across it. 'You think this is bad, Olie? You want us to stop asking you questions? How do you think Josh's parents are feeling? They haven't seen their little boy in a week. They don't know whether he's alive or dead. Can you even imagine how much they hurt? How bad do you think they want this to stop?'

Olie didn't answer. He stared down at the imitation walnut grain of the table, his head and shoulders shaking. Mitch fought the impulse to grab him by the throat and shake him until his eyes popped out.

'Mr Sewek,' Megan said in a voice like polished marble, 'you are aware of the fact that even as we speak, a team of crime-scene experts is conducting a thorough search of your house and vehicle.'

'You're going down for the kidnap, Olie,' Mitch said tightly. 'And if we don't find Josh alive – if we don't find Josh at all – you'll go down for murder. You'll never ever see the light of day again.'

'You can only help your situation by cooperating, Mr Sewek.'

Olie put his head in his hands. 'I didn't hurt him.'

There was a knock at the door and Dave Larkin stuck his head in. His trademark beach-bum smile was nowhere in sight. 'Agent O'Malley?'

The formality was almost as alarming as his bland expression. Megan rose and slipped out the door into a narrow hall bleached by harsh fluorescent lights. Phones rang incessantly in the squad room down the hall, where the level of activity belied the hour. Paige Price might have scooped the competition, but everybody wanted a piece of the action before the end of the ten o'clock reports.

'Is he talking?' Larkin asked.

'No. What's going on at the house?'

'Jeez, that place is unbelievable. You wouldn't believe the stuff he's got crammed in there. He must have a thousand books and five or six computers –'

'Laser printer?'

'Dot matrix. But we came across something else I knew you'd want to see right away.'

He reached into an inside pocket of his thick down coat and pulled out a plastic bag of snapshots. Megan felt the color drain out of her face as she pulled the photographs from the bag and went through them one by one. There was no way of telling when or where they had been taken. She couldn't identify any of the subjects – all of them little boys in various stages of undress.

Her hands were trembling as she slipped the evidence back into the bag.

'They were in a manila envelope under his mattress,' Larkin said. 'Flash those and let's hear what tune he sings.'

Megan nodded and turned back toward the door.

'Hey, Irish?'

She glanced at him over her shoulder.

'Nail his ass good.'

Olie still had his head in his hands when she strode into the interview room. Mitch looked at her expectantly. Without a word she tossed the bag of photographs down on the table.

Olie peered down at them through his fingers and felt the bottom fall out of his stomach.

'What the hell have you got to say for yourself now, Mr Sewek?'

Olie squeezed his eyes shut. He whispered, 'I want a lawyer.'

Steiger had a ringside seat of the interrogation. The trouble was, he wanted to be *in* the ring, not sitting on the other side of a two-way mirror. Holt and O'Malley had shut him out. It wasn't his case. It wasn't his collar. It was fine for him to spend the last week tramping around in the snow, freezing his balls off for the cause, but they didn't want him in the room for the questioning.

Mr Hotshot Miami Detective Holt would grab all the glory for himself – what he could wrest away from that pissy little BCA bitch. First female field agent. Big fucking deal. She was nothing but a publicity stunt, the bureau trying to get equal rights advocates off their backs. Holt treated her as if she was a real cop, but he was probably drilling her after hours. Steiger smiled to himself as he thought of how the shit would fly if that kind of news hit the airwaves.

Propping his boots up on the window ledge, he checked his watch and sighed. Twelve-fifteen. The interrogation was fruitless. Swain, or Sewek, or whatever the little turd's name was didn't have anything to say without a lawyer or with one. Ken Carey, the public defender, advised him unnecessarily to keep his mouth shut. Finally, Holt threw up his hands and called the thing to a halt. Olie would be held pending charges on the possession of child pornography, suspicion of the abduction, and on the Washington State warrant. Noga was called in to usher Olie to a cell. The room was vacated, the lights flipped off, end of show.

Steiger stood and stretched, switching on the lights in his theater. He wondered if any reporters were left out in the cold, waiting for a word from someone important.

The door swung open and Holt stepped inside, closing it quietly behind him.

'I thought he would have rolled,' Steiger said. 'I thought the pictures would have kicked him over. How bad were they? I couldn't see them from here. Were they just naked kids or was there sex involved?'

Mitch narrowed his eyes. 'Yeah, that would be a juicy little detail for Paige, wouldn't it? What would she give you for a tidbit like that, Russ?'

'I don't know what the hell you're talking about.' Steiger reached for the coat he had tossed over the back of a chair.

'Leslie Olin Sewek,' Mitch said carefully. 'Only three people knew that name. Only one of us gave it to Paige Price.'

'Well, it wasn't me.'

'Would you care to look me in the eye when you say that?'

'Are you calling me a liar?' The sheriff didn't wait long enough for an answer. 'I don't have to take this from you,' he snapped, and started for the door.

Mitch caught him by the shoulder. 'You were against the surveillance so you called Paige and gave it to her.' He shook his head, his expression sour with disgust. 'Jesus, you're worse than she is. You're sworn to uphold the law, not break it. You're supposed to protect and serve the people of this county, not sell them to the highest bidder.'

The rage pushed harder, squeezed into his veins. He hit Steiger in the chest with the heel of his hand. 'You jeopardized the investigation. You jeopardized Josh —'

Steiger gave a hard laugh. 'You don't believe he's alive any more than I do. The kid is dead and —'

The kid is dead.

Instantly Mitch saw the convenience store, the bodies, the blood, the baseball cards in his son's limp hand. He heard the voices of the paramedics.

'Hey, Estefan, let's get 'em bagged and downtown.'

'What's the hurry? The kid is dead.'

In a heartbeat the walls shattered. The rage poured out. Blinding, wild, burning. His vision misting red, Mitch lowered a shoulder and slammed it into the sheriff's sternum, running him backward like a blocking dummy. Steiger's breath left him with a *whoosh* as his back hit the wall.

'His name is Kyle!' Mitch yelled point-blank into Steiger's face. The sound of his own voice rang in his ears — the fury, the volume, the name. *Kyle . . . oh, sweet heaven.*

Weakness washed through him and he fell back a step, shaking his head, as if the realization had hit him physically and dazed him. Steiger was staring at him, waiting, wary.

'Josh,' Mitch said quietly. 'His name is Josh, and you'd better believe he's alive, because we're all the hope he's got.'

22

Day 7
Projected daytime high: -25° windchill factors: -60° – -70°

News of Olie Swain's arrest and his secret life swept through Deer Lake like the howling northwest wind. With the help of every television station, radio station, and major newspaper in the state, there was scarcely a person in town who wasn't able to shake their head and bemoan the state of affairs over breakfast. The stories emphasized Olie's past history – 'The Making of a Child Predator' – and sensationalized his flight from Washington and the subsequent years spent hiding out in Deer Lake. Much was made of his chameleon ability to hide his true self and live an outwardly quiet life. More was made of the shock and horror of the citizenry at discovering that not only had they had a monster living in their midst, they had let him into close contact with their children.

Mitch and the county attorney held a press conference in a vain attempt to stem the flow of wild gossip. By afternoon there were stories all over town about Olie Swain molesting boys in the furnace room at the hockey rink and exposing himself to children in the city parks and peering in people's windows in the dead of night. There were rumors that horrific stuff had been discovered in the search of his house and van, and rumors that Josh Kirkwood had been found alive, half dead, dead, decapitated, mutilated, cannibalized.

By evening most of the townspeople had been whipped into a frenzy by a tangled mix of truth and fiction. The only thing that kept them from marching to the city jail to demand the head of Leslie Olin Sewek was an inbred Minnesotan aversion to creating a spectacle and a windchill factor of sixty-two degrees below zero.

The brutal cold had virtually brought the state to a standstill. The governor himself had ordered all schools and state offices closed. In Deer Lake, as in most towns around the state, every function, meeting, class, and gathering that could be canceled was canceled due to the dangerous conditions. Still, a group of nearly a hundred people made it to the volunteer center, where Paige Price and the crew from *TV 7 News* were doing a live special report on the case.

7:00 p.m. -29° windchill factor: -62°

'Tonight no police, no one from the sheriff's department.' Because Mitch Holt had forbidden any of his people to talk to her and Steiger had thought it best to lay low for a day or two. 'Tonight we talk with the citizens of Deer Lake, the small town rocked by the abduction of eight-year-old Josh Kirkwood and by the discovery of a monster in its midst.'

She moved between a computer desk and a long table stacked with bright yellow fliers. The people seated at the table in the Josh Kirkwood Volunteer Center gazed up at her. She had chosen slim dark slacks and a cashmere sweater set in a muted shade of violet that brought out her too-blue eyes. A look that was dressy enough to show respect, casual enough to make her seem almost one of the crowd. Her blond hair had been deliberately mussed and carefully sprayed into place, her makeup downplayed.

'Tonight we will listen to the people of Deer Lake, to the volunteers who have given their time, their money, their hearts to the effort to find Josh Kirkwood and bring his kidnapper to justice. We'll speak with a psychologist about the impact this crime has had on the community and about the minds of men who prey on children. And we'll talk with Josh's father, Paul Kirkwood, and get his reaction to the arrest of Leslie Olin Sewek.'

7:04 p.m. -29° windchill factor: -62°

'It isn't bad enough that she blew the surveillance,' Megan said in disgust when the show broke for a lottery commercial featuring a hibernating cartoon bear. 'By the time Paige and her cohorts are finished, there won't be an impartial juror left in the state.'

They watched the broadcast on the small color TV that perched on an old oak credenza in the office of assistant county attorney Ellen North. Mitch sat with his back to the set, refusing to look at Paige in her hour of glory. The show was on at Ellen's request. Her boss, Rudy Stovich, may have been the one telling the press they would prosecute the case to the full extent of the law, but most of the work of that task would fall on Ellen's shoulders.

Stovich was more politician than prosecutor. In Mitch's opinion, he was a bumbling idiot in the courtroom, something he could get away with in a rural county, where there wasn't much crime to speak of and not that many attorneys to pick from. The good ones were drawn to the Twin Cities, where there was more action, more money, and more courtrooms. The people of Park County were damn lucky to have Ellen North.

She sat behind her desk, eating a turkey sandwich. Her blond hair was swept back neatly into a tortoiseshell clip. She was thirty-five, a transplant from the judicial system of Hennepin County – or, as Ellen sometimes referred to it, the Magnificent Minneapolis Maze of Justice – where she had a reputation as a tough prosecutor. Tired of the workload, the bureaucracy, the game-playing, and the increasing sense of futility as crime rates in the Cities soared, she had sought the relative peace and sanity of Deer Lake.

'You can bet Sewek will ask for a change of venue,' she said, wiping her fingertips on a paper napkin. 'And you can bet he'll get it – provided we come up with enough evidence to charge him. Has anything turned up in the search? Possessions of Josh's? Anything in the van – hair, fibers, blood?'

'They sprayed the interior of the van with luminol and found some bloodstains in the carpet in the back,' Megan said. 'But at this point we don't even know if the blood is human, let alone Josh Kirkwood's. Trace evidence findings won't be in for a couple of days. We found nothing in the house that can link Olie directly to this crime.

'Early word on the photographs dug up last night is that they're more than five years old. They came from a Kodak instant camera Kodak had to stop making film for in the mid-eighties due to the verdict of a lawsuit brought against them by Polaroid. Which would mean Olie probably brought them with him when he moved here. So far no one has found anything in his books. No one has been able to access the files in his computers; he has all kinds of traps set up in the programming to prevent it.'

'And he's not talking.' Ellen looked to Mitch. 'Can your witness ID the van?'

He shook his head. 'Not absolutely.'

'Which is as good as nothing.' She sipped a can of raspberry-flavored seltzer and shook her head. 'We have to hope the lab boys come up with something fast. The public may be ready to convict him, but we don't even have enough to charge him. Unless Paige Price is the judge, we're nowhere with this.'

At the mention of Paige's name, Mitch scowled. 'Where do we stand in bringing obstruction charges for that stunt she pulled last night?'

Ellen made a face that discouraged hope. 'It's been tried once or twice in recent years, but it would be almost impossible to make it stick in this case. We would have to prove absolutely that harm came to Josh as a result of the interference. Media people can wrap themselves in the First Amendment and get away with almost anything. If you could prove collusion between Paige and Steiger, you'd have something, but that's almost impossible unless one of them was stupid enough to tape the conversation or hold it in front of a witness.'

'So we've got nothing,' Mitch said. The injustice ate at him.

'And Paige Price has the scoop of the week. Again.'

Paige slid into a chair beside a heavyset woman with an unsmiling, unpainted mouth and brown hair that had been smashed flat by a stocking cap.

'Mrs Favre, you told me you had suspicions about the man you knew as Olie Swain long ago. How did you feel when this information about his prior record surfaced?'

'I was furious,' the woman said loudly, grabbing hold of the mike and pulling it toward her as if she meant to devour it. 'You bet I was. I told the police there was something wrong with him. My boy come home from hockey more than once and told me how Olie was weird and all and acted strange around them boys. And the police didn't do nothing. I talked to Mitch Holt myself and he didn't do nothing. He wouldn't listen to me and now look what's happened. It makes me sick.'

Paige took the microphone back and turned to face the camera. 'Deer Lake police deny having any prior knowledge of Olie Swain's past life as pedophile Leslie Olin Sewek. City personnel in charge of the Gordie Knutson Memorial Arena also deny any knowledge of Mr Swain's past. They did not check into Olie Swain's background for a criminal record before hiring him to work as a maintenance man at the ice rink where Deer Lake's children play hockey and practice figure skating.'

She rose and walked away from the table, past a computer desk where a Harris College student sat before a color terminal filled with Josh's image. The camera zoomed in on the computer screen, then backed off and swung back to Paige.

'It is important that we make it clear Leslie Olin Sewek has not been formally charged with the abduction of Josh Kirkwood. He is being held in the Deer Lake community jail because of a warrant issued on parole violations in the state of Washington. As of late this afternoon the only evidence gathered implicating Sewek in any crime at all was a packet of sexually explicit photographs involving young boys. Photographs he allegedly brought with him when he came to Minnesota after leaving a Washington State correctional facility.

'Authorities in Columbia County, Washington, are all too familiar with Leslie Sewek. As is the case with the majority of child molesters, Leslie Sewek's record is a long one that began when he himself was little more than a boy. Here with us tonight to talk about the mind of the child predator is Dr Garrett Wright, head of the psychology department at Harris College.' She slid into the vacant chair beside Wright and regarded him with grave interest. 'Dr Wright, what can you tell us about the pattern of behavior in men like Leslie Sewek?'

Garrett Wright didn't look convinced this was a good idea. 'First of all, Ms Price, I want to make it clear that criminal behavior is not my area of expertise. I have, however, studied deviant behavior, and if I can shed some light on the situation and in any way help people deal with it, I will.'

'You're a resident of Deer Lake, aren't you, Doctor?'

'Yes. In fact, Hannah and Paul are neighbors of mine. Like most of the people in town, my wife and I are eager to help any way we can. Community support and involvement are very important to all concerned. . . .'

Paige listened with one ear, impatient to get to the juicier stuff, the questions that would keep viewers glued to their sets. Wright might be visually interesting – almost as pretty as she was, and very scholarly in a button-down shirt and blue blazer – but talk of community support was not what she'd had in mind when she had personally coerced him into appearing on the show. She could almost hear the viewing public yawning.

Worse, she could picture the network people yawning. When the news of Leslie Sewek's past record had hit the wires, the networks and tabloid shows had scrambled to get people to Deer Lake. Josh Kirkwood's case was made for television news. And if Paige could pull it off, it was a case that would catapult her to bigger and better things.

'Obviously,' Garrett Wright went on, 'it helps the victims to cope, but it also helps the rest of us to cope, to feel as if we're taking proactive measures against what is essentially an alien threat to our community – crime.'

'And about the crime,' Paige interjected smoothly. 'There is a fairly consistent story behind men who become child molesters, like Leslie Sewek, isn't there, Doctor?'

'Yes, there seems to be. First of all, pedophiles tend to come from abusive home situations themselves and have strong unmet needs for personal warmth.'

'Are you saying we should feel sorry for someone like Leslie Sewek?' Paige asked with perfect indignity. Inwardly, she smiled as the crowd behind her grumbled angrily.

Garrett Wright held up a hand to ward off rebuttal. 'I'm merely stating facts, Ms Price. This is the common background among child molesters; it isn't an excuse to break the laws of society. Nor am I saying this is Leslie Sewek's background. I know nothing about the man. And as you pointed out, we don't know that Leslie Sewek has broken any laws here. We can't say with any certainty that the person who kidnapped Josh Kirkwood is a pedophile. We could be dealing with a very different sort of mind altogether, and frankly, one far more dangerous than the quote *average* unquote pedophile,' he argued. The camera zoomed in on his expression of profound concern.

Paige's inward smile stretched wider. 'Such as, Dr Wright?'

Garrett Wright's disapproval was almost a tangible thing. He gave her a long, cool look. 'You're playing a dangerous game, Ms Price. I didn't come here to play Name That Psycho. That kind of conjecture on my part would be inappropriate, to say nothing of ghoulish –'

'I didn't mean to suggest such a thing,' Paige interrupted, the internal smile going brittle. *Damn*. 'Perhaps you could give us a better understanding of that quote average unquote pedophile?'

Wright relaxed marginally. 'Pedophiles often relate better to children than to adults and in most cases they seek to control the child rather than to harm the child,' he went on before Paige could jump in with another inflammatory question. 'They may truly believe they love children and will often seek employment that will put them in contact with or proximity to children.'

'A fact that brings us directly back to Deer Lake and the case of Leslie Olin Sewek,' Paige said, abandoning Garrett Wright for her special guest star. 'With the shadow of Josh Kirkwood's abduction hanging over this town, the discovery of a convicted child predator at the very ice arena from which Josh disappeared has frightened and outraged the citizens of this quiet community. Certainly no one in Deer Lake has more reason to feel anger at this revelation than Paul Kirkwood, Josh Kirkwood's father.'

Paul sat in one of two director's chairs at the front of the room. His brown hair was perfectly combed, the knot of a silk tie perfectly centered above the crew neck of a navy wool sweater he wore over his pinpoint oxford shirt. His deep-set eyes had naturally dark sockets that were emphasized by the camera, intensifying his haunted, angry expression. A great face for television.

Paige slid into the other director's chair. 'Paul,' she said softly, reaching out to touch his arm. 'Again, all our hearts go out to you and your wife, Dr Hannah Garrison. I understand Hannah is too distraught to join us tonight.'

Paul frowned. Hannah had refused to come to the center despite her repeated complaints of not being able to help in the search effort. She found the idea of this program repulsive, exploitative, and mercenary, in no way useful in finding Josh.

The Sunday papers had been splashed with color photographs of her collapsing in the volunteer-center booth and being escorted away by Father Tom McCoy. They painted her a heroine – valiant and courageous, trying to be strong in the face of incredible adversity. The brave, compassionate Dr Garrison, who had helped so many people. They made little mention of the fact that this whole situation was her fault, that her career had destroyed their marriage, torn their family apart, and driven him into the arms of another woman. Instead, they said that Josh had been abducted while Dr Garrison was fighting to save the life of an accident victim, turning it all around to make her the object of admiration and pity.

'She's home with our daughter,' he said flatly.

Paige looked directly into the camera. 'Dr Garrison, our prayers are with you.'

The television in the family room was on. Hannah could hear it – mumbled voices, changes in pitch, tone, and volume – but she couldn't make out what anyone was saying. She didn't want to. She hated that *TV 7 News* was running the interview, hated that her neighbors and friends would watch it, hated that people she didn't even know would be asked to voice their feelings about the terrible act that was tearing her life apart. She hated that Paul had agreed to be a part of it. That he could so callously discount her feelings was further evidence of the widening rift between them.

There had been a time when he would have found the program as invasive and self-serving as she did. Tonight he had fussed over what to wear and spent an hour in the bathroom getting ready. The thought that she didn't know him anymore whispered through her mind at regular intervals.

She stood in the center of Josh's room because she was too wired to sit. Olie Swain had been arrested but not charged. No official word had come of a confession or clues to Josh's fate. Nothing. Silence. She felt poised on the brink of a high precipice, every muscle, every fiber of her being held taut as she waited to fall one way or the other. The anticipation had built and built until she was certain she would explode from the pressure. But there was no explosion, there was no relief.

She paced the room, her arms wrapped around herself. Even with the thick sweater and turtleneck she wore she felt thin. She was losing weight and, as a doctor, she knew that wasn't good. That professional, practical, intelligent part of her mind told her to eat, to sleep, to get some exercise, but that part seemed to be disconnected from the rest. Emotion ruled. Erratic, irrational emotion.

She tried to think of what it had been like – what *she* had been like – when she had been the calm, rational head of the ER. Cool under fire. A leader. The person everyone looked to in a time of crisis. She tried to remember the afternoon before Josh had been taken. The patients she had treated. The people she had offered comfort and explanations. The precision of the trauma team as she had orchestrated the attempt to save the life of Ida Bergen.

A week had passed. It seemed a lifetime ago.

Squeals of delight came from the living room, where Lily had charmed the BCA agent on duty into playing with her. Hannah swung the bedroom door shut. Here, in Josh's room, she wanted to hear nothing but the silence that waited for his voice. She breathed in the waxy scent of crayons and felt as if one had been driven through her heart. On the small desk lay the photo album she had brought in one of the first days, as if having Josh's picture in there might help conjure him up. She stood over it and looked down at the photographs, each one raising a memory.

The three of them at the beach on the Carolina shore the summer they had gone to visit her parents. The year before Lily was born. Josh riding on his father's shoulders, his arms banded across Paul's forehead, Paul's baseball cap drooping sideways on Josh's head. Josh standing beside a sand castle in a white T-shirt and baggy shorts, his arms spread wide, a bright grin displaying gaps where baby teeth had fallen out. His hair was a tangle of sandy-brown curls, tossed by the same wind that bent the slender stems of spartina and panic grass on the dunes. The ocean was a belt of blue trimmed in lacy white.

The three of them standing together on a jetty. All of them laughing. Hannah wore a filmy summer dress in blue and white. The long skirt whirled around her legs like a matador's cape. Josh was standing on a piling. Paul was hugging him tightly from behind with one arm; his other arm was draped around Hannah's shoulders. Holding them all together. A family. So close, so happy. So distant from here. So far removed from what they had become.

The last picture on the page was of herself and Josh. On a sailboat at sunset. Him sleeping on her lap, her arms cradling him against her. Her eyes were closed as she bent over him. Her hair was blowing over her shoulder. She held him safe while the sea rolled and the wind snapped the sails. Safe and loved.

She could close her eyes and feel the weight of him in her arms. His small body warm against hers. His hair smelled of salt water. His eyelashes curled against his cheek, impossibly long and thick. And she could feel her love for him swell in her chest. Her child. A beautiful little person created and nurtured in love. And she could feel, as she had at that moment, all the hope she had held for him, all the dreams she had dreamed. Perfect dreams. Wonderful dreams.

Dreams that had been snatched away. Josh was gone. Her arms were empty. All she had left were photographs and memories.

A soft knock sounded against the door, startling her. She jerked around as yet another volunteer from the missing children group poked her head into the room. Another stranger from another town she'd never heard of.

'I brought you some hot chocolate,' the woman said softly, using the excuse to let herself into the room.

Hannah put her around forty, medium height with curvy hips and no breasts. Her hair was a mop of chestnut curls, and rumpled bangs tumbled over the tops of rimless glasses. Terry something. The names went in one ear and out the other. Hannah made no effort to remember them. They came to offer support, sympathy or empathy, and friendship, but she didn't want to have anything in common with them. Theirs was a club she had no desire to join.

'Your husband is on television,' Terry Whoever said as she set the mug of cocoa down on the nightstand. 'I thought you might want to know.'

Hannah shook her head. Terry made no comment. She stood with her back against the wall beside the door, her hands tucked into the pockets of tan corduroy slacks. Waiting. Hannah told herself again that she didn't want to reach out to this woman, but the warning couldn't penetrate the need to fill the silence.

'They asked me to go on,' she said, staring out the window at the cold black night. 'I don't want anything to do with it. I won't put what I feel on display for an audience.'

The woman didn't chastise her. She didn't say anything, as if she somehow knew there was more. The words tumbled out like a guilty secret.

'People expect me to. I know they do. They expect me to be at the rallies and the prayer vigils and on television. But I don't want to be weak in front of them, and I know I can't be strong. I can't be who they want me to be. Not now.' And the guilt from that was another weight added to the burden already crushing her.

'That's all right,' Terry said in an unflappable tone. 'Don't worry about what anyone else wants from you. You don't have to go on television if it feels wrong for you. We each do what we have to to get through the nightmare. Maybe it helps your husband to go on television.'

'I wouldn't know.'

Again the silence.

'We're not communicating very well these days.'

'It's hard. You do the best you can. Hang on to the pieces of your relationship and worry about putting them back together later. What's important now is just getting through it.'

Hannah's gaze strayed to the photo album on the desk, the smiling images of her son. She would have done anything, given anything, to have him back safe. She thought of Olie Swain sitting in a jail cell, thought of the secrets he had yet to reveal, and the unbearable sense of anticipation filled her again. What did he know? What would he tell? And when he told his secrets, would it be over?

'It's not knowing,' she whispered. She pressed the heels of her hands against her eyes to hold back the tears, but they came anyway. 'God, I can't stand not knowing! I can't stand it!'

Sobbing, she threw herself against the wall and slammed her fist against it again and again, oblivious to the pain. And when the burst of adrenaline was spent, she just stood there pressed against the carefully painted mural of boys playing baseball, and cried. She didn't move when she felt a hand rest on her shoulder.

'I know,' Terry murmured. 'My son was abducted when he was twelve, on his way home from the movies. We lived in Idaho then, in a town a lot like this one, a quiet, safe place. Not so safe, it turned out. I thought the not knowing would kill me. And there were times I wished it had,' she confessed softly.

Gently, she pulled Hannah away from the wall and led her to the bunk beds, where they sat down side by side. Hannah wiped her face on the sleeve of her sweater and struggled to pull herself together, embarrassed that she had come apart in front of this stranger. But Terry acted as if this were the most normal of scenes, as if she hadn't even noticed the outburst.

'He would have been sixteen this year,' she said. 'He would have been learning to drive, going on dates, playing on the basketball team at school. But the man who took him away from us took him away forever. They found his body in a landfill, thrown away like so much garbage.' Her voice strained and she went silent for a moment, waiting for the pain to ease.

'After they found him there was . . . relief. At least it was over. But when we didn't know at least we had some hope that he was alive and that we might get him back.' She turned to Hannah, her eyes bright with tears that wouldn't fall. 'Hold on to that hope with both hands, Hannah. It's better than nothing.'

She's gone through this, Hannah thought. *She knows what I'm feeling, what I'm thinking, what I'm fearing.* The bond was there. That she didn't want it didn't matter; it was there. They shared a common nightmare and this woman was offering what wisdom she had won from the ordeal. It didn't matter that Hannah didn't want to join this club; she was already a member.

She reached across the bedspread, took Terry Whoever's hand in hers and squeezed it tight.

7:42 p.m. -30° windchill factor: -62°

'. . . and I'm outraged that this sick, perverted animal was not only let out of his cage, but was allowed to work in the same building with my son and the sons and daughters of everyone in this community!'

Applause from the people in the volunteer center made Paul Kirkwood pause. He stared directly at the camera, head up, chin jutting forward, the light in his eyes fanatical. The look seemed to pierce the television screen and travel through the bars of the cell right into Olie's chest. He knew that look, that tone of voice. *You make me sick! You're nothing but a little freak!*

Spawn of the devil, that's what you are! I'll beat some good into you! And the other, shriller voice joined in harmony. *I told you, Leslie! You're good for nothing! Don't you cry or we'll give you something to cry about!*

He huddled into the corner of his bunk, curling up like a frightened animal as the voices ranted on. He had been locked in his own cell in the city jail, a luxurious place as jails went. Mainly empty. The newness of the facility lingered. The walls were white, the hard gray floors polished. Only the vaguest aroma of urine cut through the strong scent of pine cleaners. No smoking was allowed.

In the next cell was the proud owner of the small portable television. A stringy, narrow-eyed character named Boog Newton who was doing three months for repeatedly drinking himself into a stupor and climbing behind the wheel of his four-by-four. In his latest escapade, he had backed into the plate glass display window of the Loon's Call Book and Gift Shop. As the only semipermanent resident in the place, he was allowed amenities.

Boog sat on his bunk with his elbows on his knees, picking his nose, absorbed by Paul Kirkwood's passionate sermon on the failings of the system and the injustices against decent people.

'. . . I'm sick of turning on the evening news and having to listen to how another child has been raped or murdered or abducted. We have to *do something*. We have to put a stop to this madness!'

The broadcast broke for a commercial on a wave of applause. Boog rose and swaggered over to the wall of iron bars that separated the cells. His face was pitted with acne scars, his mouth twisted into a perpetual sneer.

'Hey, dumbshit, they're talking about you,' he said, leaning against the bars.

Olie stood and began to pace back and forth along the far side of his cage, back and forth, back and forth, head down, counting the steps in an attempt to shut the man out. He didn't like men. Had never liked men. Men only ever wanted to hurt him.

'Hey, you know what I'd do if I was a judge? I'd put a bag over your ugly head, give the father of that kid a steel pipe, and lock you in a room together. Let him beat the shit out of you. Let him bash your head in. Let him ream you a new asshole with that pipe.'

Olie paced, his hands in his pockets, his breath coming faster and faster.

'Hey, you know what I think they oughta do with freaks like you? I think they oughta cut your pecker off and shove it up your ass. No. They oughta put you in a cell with some nine-hundred-pound no-neck biker and let him put it to you all night every night for the rest of your life. See how you like it.'

Olie already knew. He knew what they did to child molesters in the joint. He remembered every excruciating moment, every pain, the sickening fear. He knew what it was to be tortured. Sweat burst out of his pores, sour with the knowledge that it would all happen again. Whether they kept him there or sent him back to Washington, it would all happen again.

'Hey, you're sick, you know that? That's sick, touching little boys and shit like that. What'd you do to that Kirkwood kid? Kill him? They oughta kill you –'

'It wasn't me!' Olie screamed. His whole face was flushed. His good eye bugged out, rolling wildly. He launched himself across the small space and slammed into the bars, pinching Boog's fingers. 'It wasn't me! It wasn't me!'

Boog jerked back, stumbling, shaking his stinging fingers. 'Hey, you're nuts! You're fucking crazy!'

A shout rang from the end of the hall as the jailer came running.

Olie sank to the floor like a marionette whose strings had been cut, sobbing, 'It wasn't me.'

23

'Grandma says you put the bad guy in jail and now it'll be easier to breathe,' Jessie said as she worked at tying a long, bedraggled red ribbon around Scotch's throat.

The old dog suffered the indignity with good grace, groaning a little and rolling his eyes up at Mitch, who sat on the couch studying the photocopied pages of Josh's notebook, looking for some mention of Olie beyond the one page – *Kids tease Olie but that's mean. He can't help how he looks.* The living room floor was littered with Barbie dolls and their paraphernalia. The television in the oak entertainment center across the room was tuned to a news magazine. As Jane Pauley dished out the headlines, images of the latest L.A. earthquake and a scandal-embroiled figure skater flashed across the screen.

Jessie looked up at Mitch from her seat on the floor. 'Why did Grandma say that?'

The first few answers that came to mind were not flattering to Joy Strauss. Mitch bit his tongue and counted to ten. 'She meant she feels safer now,' he said, turning over a page of carefully drawn spaceships and laying it facedown with the other pages on the coffee table.

And it meant Joy had been given a new needle to stick him with.

'I can't believe someone like him can just be allowed to walk the streets of Deer Lake.'

'He wasn't exactly wearing a sign, Joy. He didn't have a big P for pedophile branded on his forehead. How was I supposed to know?'

'Well, Alice Marshton says police departments have networks that keep track of this kind of person. Alice reads a lot of mysteries and she says –'

'This is real life, Joy, not an Agatha Christie novel.'

'You don't have to be so huffy. I was just saying what Alice told me.'

She was just saying what more than a few people in town were saying – that they blamed him for Josh Kirkwood's disappearance. He understood that they felt the need to blame somebody. Pointing the finger at a real live person was less frightening than believing they had no defense against what had happened. But that didn't make it any easier to take the abuse. Natalie had fielded angry phone calls all day; the tape on his home answering machine was full of messages from irate citizens.

He continued to let the machine take the brunt of the fury. He had no desire to play whipping boy tonight. He wanted some quiet time with Jessie – even if he had to divide his attention between his daughter and the stack of paperwork he had brought home with him. Joy had clucked about him taking Jessie home on such a cold night, insisting she would catch a virus. Mitch had reminded her they were only going across the alley and told her it was too cold for germs, refraining from yet another futile attempt at explaining how viruses are actually spread. Since he had never worked in the kitchen of the hospital like her friend Ione, Joy had no faith in his medical knowledge.

Finished with the bow, Jessie picked up a brush and began to groom Scotch's back. The Labrador made a sound of contentment and rolled onto his side, offering his belly for this treatment. 'Grandma said that man did all kinds of bad things to little kids that only God knows about,' Jessie said. 'But if God's the only one that knows, then how does Grandma know?'

'She doesn't. She only thinks she knows. No one has proven that man did anything.' Mitch felt amazed and vaguely ashamed of himself for defending Olie Swain just to take sides against his mother-in-law.

He turned to another page, this one full of Josh's thoughts about being made co-captain of his hockey team. *Its real cool. I'm real proud, but my Mom says not to brag. Just do a good job. No body likes a bragger.* The next page expressed his displeasure with having to go to religion class in the form of mad faces and thumbs-down signs, God with a long beard and halo, and a devil's scowling face.

'Then how come that man's in jail?'

'Jessie . . .' he said, trying not to grit his teeth. He leaned ahead to brush a hand over his daughter's head. 'Honey, Daddy's really tired from this case. Can we talk about something else?'

Guilt nipped him immediately. He had always made a point of being as honest and up front with Jessie as he could. It seemed to him that deflecting a child's questions caused more problems than it cured, but he didn't have the energy for answers tonight. Now that Olie was behind bars, the stress and long hours were hitting with a vengeance. And the worry for Josh's well-being had intensified with the discovery of the bloodstains in the van. They could do nothing but wait for the lab results. Unfortunately, Jessie's idea of changing the subject was not quite what Mitch had in mind.

A page of Josh's drawings caught her eye, and she abandoned Scotch to scoot over to the coffee table on her knees. 'Who made these pictures for you?'

'These are pictures Josh made.' He ran a fingertip along the crooked line of a forgotten game of tic-tac-toe.

'Can I color them for you?'

'No, honey, this is evidence. Why don't you make me a picture from one of your coloring books?'

Jessie ignored the suggestion. She picked up one of the pages Mitch had already set aside and studied it.

'Did you find Josh?'

Mitch sighed and speared his fingers back through his hair, lifting it into thick spikes. 'Not yet, sweetheart.'

'He must be sad,' she said quietly, carefully laying the drawing down. It showed a boy with freckles and a big hairy dog. *Me and Gizmo.*

'Come here, sweetie,' Mitch whispered, opening his arms in invitation. Jessie scrambled around the end of the table and climbed up on his lap. Mitch wrapped his arms around her and pulled her close. 'Are you still worried about someone taking you away?'

'A little bit,' she mumbled against his chest.

He wanted to tell her not to worry, that he wouldn't let anything happen to her, that nothing bad would happen to her if she followed all the rules. But he couldn't make any of those promises and he hated the sense of impotence and inadequacy that reality gave him. He wished the world were a place where little girls had nothing to worry about except playing with their dolls and dressing their dogs up in red satin bows, but that wasn't the case. Not even in Deer Lake.

He rocked his daughter slowly. 'You know, it's not your job to worry, Jess. Worrying is *my* job.'

She tipped her head back and looked up at him. 'What about Grandma? She worries about everything.'

'Yeah, well, Grandma is in a league of her own. But when it comes to you and me, I get to do all the worrying, okay?'

'Okay,' she said, trying to smile.

Mitch held a hand out in front of her, palm up. 'Here. You crunch up your worry like a piece of paper and give it to me.'

Jessie giggled and made a show of pretending to squish her worries into a ball. She plopped the invisible burden in Mitch's hand. He closed a fist over it and stuffed it into the breast pocket of his denim shirt. Scotch watched the proceedings with his head cocked and his ears up.

The doorbell rang and the dog lurched to his feet with a booming bark, tail wagging.

'That'll be Megan,' Mitch said, rising with Jessie in his arms.

Jessie stuck her lower lip out. 'How come she's coming over? You said I could stay up late 'cause there's no school tomorrow and we'd have fun.'

'We've had lots of fun, haven't we?' Mitch said. 'But you can't stay up as late as me, so who will keep me company when you go to bed?'

'Scotch.'

Mitch growled and tickled her, then sent her into a fit of squealing giggles by swinging her up over his shoulder legs first. He opened the door with a smile and backed into the living room, calling, 'Welcome to the monkey house!'

Megan's reluctance couldn't withstand the windchill factor of minus sixty-something. She stepped into the foyer of Mitch's house, closing the door behind her, instantly feeling like an intruder. Mitch was giving Jessie a wild ride around the living room on his shoulders while a big yellow dog gave chase with a Barbie doll in his mouth. No one seemed to notice her standing there swaddled in wool and goose down with a quart of chocolate chip ice cream clutched between her mittens. She wondered if they would notice if she simply backed out the door and went home.

Before she could take a step, however, Mitch came to a halt in front of her and nailed her to the spot with a knowing gaze. With one finger he tugged the scarf down from her face.

'Take your coat off and stay awhile, O'Malley,' he said softly.

She gave him a wry smile as she unwound her scarf and draped it over a coat tree. She looked up at the little girl perched on his shoulder. 'Hi, Jessie, how are you?'

'I don't have kindergarten tomorrow 'cause it's too cold for brass monkeys. That's what my grandpa says.'

'That's pretty cold,' Megan agreed, amusement tugging hard at the corners of her mouth.

'So I get to stay up past my bedtime and have fun,' Jessie said in a cautionary tone, as if it just might be too much for Megan to deal with.

Mitch rolled his eyes. 'Yeah, you get to stay up long enough to have some of this ice cream Megan brought us. Wasn't that nice of her?'

'I like cookies better.'

'Jessie . . .' Mitch gave her a stern look as he set her down.

Across the room the phone on the end table rang, the answering machine picked up.

'Mitch? Mitch, can you hear me?' The woman's voice was nearly frantic. 'It's Joy. I can see your lights on.' She turned away from the receiver and spoke to her husband somewhere in the background. 'Jurgen, he's not answering! Maybe you should go over. They could have carbon monoxide poisoning!'

Forcing a weary smile, Mitch heaved a sigh. 'I'd better take this.' He looked to his daughter. 'Jessie, please take Megan into the kitchen and help her get out bowls for the ice cream.'

Resigning herself to her fate with a much-put-upon look, Jessie headed for the kitchen. Megan followed dutifully. The dog trotted past them both, the doll in his mouth smiling with one arm raised, as if waving.

'That's my dog, Scotch,' Jessie said. 'I put that bow on him. I can tie my own shoes and ribbons and stuff. Kimberly Johnson in my class can't tie anything. She has to wear shoes with Velcro and she picks her nose, too.'

'Yuck.'

'And she eats it,' Jessie went on, digging the ice cream scoop out of a drawer crammed with spatulas and plastic spoons. 'And she's mean. She bit my friend Ashley once and had to have time-out in the corner all through recess and didn't get to have any of Kevin Neilsen's birthday treats at milk break. And she said she didn't care 'cause they weren't really Tootsie Rolls, they were cat poop.' She gave Megan a look. 'That wasn't true.'

'Sounds like a tough customer.'

Jessie shrugged, dismissing the subject. She pulled a chair across the linoleum and climbed up on it to get bowls out of a cupboard. Megan set about the task of opening the carton and dishing out the treat.

'I can eat two scoops,' Jessie said, peering over the edge of the tile-topped kitchen table. 'Daddy can eat about ten. Scotch can't have any 'cause he's too fat.'

Megan's gaze skated around the kitchen, taking in the crayon and fingerpaint masterpieces taped on the wall and refrigerator. They tugged at a vulnerable corner of her heart – their naïveté, their unabashed enthusiasm and attention to odd detail. And the fact that Mitch displayed them so proudly. She could almost picture him, the hard-ass cop fumbling with Scotch tape, cursing under his breath as he tried for the third time to get the latest work of art straight on the wall. She couldn't help but compare this kitchen to the one on Butler Street in St Paul that smelled of grease and cigarettes and bitter memories. A cardboard box under her bed had acted as treasure chest for the things she and no one else had taken pride in.

'You're quite the artist,' she said to Jessie. 'You made all these pictures for your dad to put up?'

Jessie went to one that was taped at her eye level. 'This is my daddy and this is me and this is Scotch,' she explained. Mitch was depicted in an abstract arrangement of geometric shapes like a man made out of building blocks. There was a badge as big as a dinner plate on his chest. Scotch was roughly the size of a Shetland pony with teeth like a bear trap. A long pink tongue hung out of his mouth.

'I used to have a mommy,' Jessie said as she came back to the table and rested her arms on top of it. 'But she went to heaven.'

The statement was matter-of-fact, but it struck a chord in Megan. She slid down onto a chair and leaned against the table, her gaze steady on Mitch's pretty dark-eyed daughter with her crooked barrettes and purple sweatshirt.

'I know,' she said quietly. 'That's hard. I lost my mom when I was little, too.'

Jessie's eyes widened a little at this unexpected common ground. 'Did she go to heaven?'

'No,' Megan murmured. 'She just went away.'

'Because you were naughty?' Jessie ventured timidly.

'I used to think that sometimes,' Megan admitted. 'But I think she just

243

didn't love my dad anymore and I think she didn't want to be a mom, and so she just left.'

The moment stretched between them. The refrigerator hummed. Mitch's daughter regarded her with somber brown eyes.

'That's like diborce,' Jessie said. 'My friend Janet's mom and dad got a diborce, but he still wants to be her dad on Saturdays. It's hard to be a little kid.'

'Sometimes,' Megan said, amazed with herself. She didn't talk about her past, ever, with anyone. It was over, long gone, didn't matter anymore. Yet here she was having a heart-to-heart with a five-year-old and it felt . . . *right*, which scared the hell out of her. What was she doing? What was she thinking?

You've been working too hard, O'Malley.

Mitch stood in the dining room with his feet rooted to the floor. He hadn't intended to eavesdrop, had meant only to take a peek in through the door to see how Megan and Jessie were getting along. Jessie was very protective of him and jealous of their time together. He wanted to see if she behaved herself without him right there to enforce her manners. He sure as hell hadn't counted on overhearing a confession from Megan about her well-guarded past.

He remembered the way she had told him about her mother. Defiantly. Resentfully. Sticking out that chip on her shoulder as if it were a shield. The woman confiding in his daughter over bowls of chocolate chip ice cream was none of those things. She was a woman who had once been a little girl afraid she had done something to drive her own mother away. That truth struck a tender spot inside him.

Damn. He had decided he could manage the passion that sparked between them. He could understand it, control it to a certain extent. But he hadn't bargained for anything more. Didn't want anything deeper.

Keep it light, Holt. It's just sex, not marriage. She's married to the badge. Lucky you.

He leaned in the kitchen doorway, smiling a pained smile.

'Joy wanted to be certain I was aware Channel Four is doing a special segment on Deer Lake and our 'troubles' on the ten o'clock news. They're going to give safety tips. I guess she thought maybe I could learn something.'

Megan bit her lip against a threatening smile.

'Yeah,' he drawled, picking up a bowl and spooning up a small mountain of ice cream. 'That anchorman Shelby might know something about law enforcement I failed to pick up in fifteen years on the job.'

'She's just trying to help,' Megan offered.

He swallowed hard and bared his teeth. 'If only.'

They ate their ice cream and played an exciting round of Candy Land, Mitch and Megan putting off their plan to go over statements until Jessie was in bed. Jessie struggled valiantly to remain awake until the news came on and protested when Mitch declared it time for her to go to bed. Tired and out of sorts, she cried a little as he carried her up to her room, but was asleep almost the instant her head hit the pillow.

When Mitch came back downstairs, Megan was prowling around his living room restlessly. Scotch lay on his back in the middle of the floor, waiting for a belly-scratching, wagging his tail hopefully every time she stepped past him.

'You've got a nice house,' she said, leaning a hip against his leather recliner.

'Thanks.'

Mitch looked around the room, seeing it as a stranger would. The walls were blank sheets of eggshell white that blended with a Berber carpet the color of oatmeal. Bland and lifeless, rescued from complete dreariness by a brick fireplace and flanking glass-doored bookcases. The furniture was stuff he had picked out himself. He hadn't been able to bring himself to keep anything he had shared with Allison. Those pieces evoked memories that brought him pain. He had replaced them with uninteresting, overstuffed pieces in neutral colors that evoked nothing. His one indulgence had been the caramel-colored leather chair.

'I guess I should hang up pictures or something,' he mumbled awkwardly. 'I'm not good at that kind of thing.'

Megan refrained from offering to help with his decorating. The idea was too domestic. Domestic and presumptuous. Like she wanted to stake a claim. They would have what they would have until it was over. That was all. They were colleagues first, lovers second. A long way from picking out wallpaper patterns.

'Jessie's asleep?'

'Like a rock. She was worn out, poor kid.'

Mitch went to the fire and tossed another log on the blaze. He poked at the glowing embers in the grate, then stood there with one hand braced against the thick mantelpiece, gazing down into the flames. 'Her grandmother, the panic queen, has her all wound up over Josh's abduction. And God knows I haven't been paying much attention to her since all this started.'

'You've been a little busy.'

'The story of my life.'

'Well, now we've got Olie . . .'

'But we don't have Josh.'

'Maybe we'll get something from the lab we can use as leverage against him.'

Mitch didn't want to think about the bloodstains found in the van. More than anything about this case, he dreaded the thought of having to tell Hannah and Paul their son was dead. He didn't want them to know that pain, and truth to tell, he didn't want it reawakened within himself. And he didn't want to think that he had failed Hannah and Paul as he had failed Allison and Kyle. The chain went on and on, around and around in an endless loop, like a wheel in a hamster cage.

'Have you talked to Hannah about taking blood samples from her and Paul?'

Mitch pushed himself away from the fireplace. Across the room, Scotch was in an armchair watching *Letterman*. 'I'll do it tomorrow.'

'The lab needs them to make comparisons.'

'I know. I'll do it.'

'If you don't want to —'

'I said I'll do it.' He wheeled around with his hands raised in surrender.

'Fine.' Megan mimicked his gesture, backing away from him. She stared down at the stacks of papers strewn over the oak coffee table. Statements from people associated with the ice rink, statements from neighbors of the ice rink, neighbors of Olie's, curling tubes of fax paper with information provided by the authorities in Washington State and NCIC in Washington, D.C. And amid the standard forms with their standard questions, the pages from Josh's think pad.

'Have you found any more references to Olie?' she asked. She already knew the answer, had already been over her own copy of the notebook half a dozen times. There were plenty of drawings of creatures from outer space, only one of Olie, and beside it the note that wrenched her heart when she thought of Olie Swain betraying Josh. *Kids tease Olie but that's mean. He can't help how he looks.*

'No.'

'And I've gone over these statements until my brain went dyslexic, and I still can't see anything we can give to the county attorney. Nothing but suspicion and conjecture and downright ugly meanness. Some of Olie's neighbors could stand a lesson in charity.'

They could have learned a thing or two from Josh. The irony was too bitter to contemplate.

'I don't like the way it feels,' Mitch said, prowling the room with his hands in his pockets, his head down, brow furrowed. 'If the kidnapper took Josh's notebook two months ago and planned out this whole deal like a mastermind . . . that just doesn't feel like Olie. It feels . . . sinister. Olie's pathetic, not sinister.'

'So his partner is sinister,' Megan offered.

'That's the other thing that doesn't feel right. Olie is a loner. Always has been. Suddenly he's got a partner?' He shook his head.

'He's a convicted pedophile with means and a van that has bloodstains in the carpet,' Megan argued. 'If you've got a better suspect than that, I'd like to hear about it.'

'I don't,' Mitch admitted. 'I'm not saying he's innocent. I'm saying it doesn't feel right.'

'What part of this case feels right? The whole thing stinks like a slaughterhouse in a heat wave. His house was full of computer equipment —'

'But not the printer –'

'I've got a couple of guys checking print shops that offer the use of laser printers, all you have to do is take in your diskette.'

'Christ, you think he just walked into Insty Prints and ran off a bunch of psycho notes?'

Megan shrugged. 'It's a long shot, but I'll take any odds I can get.'

Mitch said nothing. He stopped in front of the fireplace again and stared into the flames, turning the questions and facts and theories over and over in his head.

Megan watched him. His doubts irritated already sore spots. 'Is it Olie you object to, or the fact that I made him?'

He shot her a narrow look over his shoulder. 'Don't be a bitch. I already congratulated you, Agent O'Malley. I'd just feel better if we could turn up some hard evidence – or better yet, if he'd give us Josh.'

'Well,' Megan said on a long sigh, 'that makes two of us.'

The phone rang yet again and the answering machine picked up. Mitch glared at it from across the room. 'That makes fifteen thousand of us – fourteen thousand nine hundred ninety-eight of whom have called here tonight.'

Bone-weary, he shuffled toward the couch, stopping when he came toe to toe with Megan. She was giving him that skeptical what-do-you-think-you're-doing look that had probably backed off more aggressive males than he could shake a stick at. It didn't faze Mitch. It was part of the act, like the tough talk, like the tomboy clothes. He wasn't scared off by an act.

'What do you say we drop this for tonight?' he suggested. 'I don't know about you, but my brain feels like fried eggplant. Let's just be people for a while.'

Megan glanced away and blew out a breath, shoving her hands into the hip pockets of her jeans. 'Yeah, sure, fine.' Of course, that would pretty much kill their conversation, since she didn't have anything to talk about except work. *Now is when you show off your amazing social skills, O'Malley. You're such a well-rounded individual.*

Mitch watched her shoulders sag and her gaze drop to her wool socks. She was so sure of herself as a cop, so unsure of herself as a woman. Everything male in him wanted to confirm her femininity for her. The impulse brought a welcome rush of energy, and he let it carry him.

'Come here.' He towed her around the end of the coffee table to the couch. He sank down into the cushions, pulling her down with him. 'We need to do something mindless.'

Megan struggled unsuccessfully to push herself back to her feet, unable to break his hold around her waist. 'Sleep is mindless,' she said. 'I should go home and get some.'

Mitch ignored her logic, nuzzling her braid aside to kiss the back of her neck. 'Let's make out,' he whispered, his voice low and silky. 'Like when we were in high school. You know how you'd come home with a date after the basketball game and your folks were asleep and you'd sit out on the couch and make out and hope nobody caught you.'

Megan stiffened a little against him. 'I didn't date much in high school.'

Didn't date at all was more like it. She had been painfully shy with boys, too aware that she had no breasts to speak of and too aware of the blood that ran in her veins. She didn't want to be her mother's daughter, didn't want to give her father any more reason to dislike her than he already had. There had been one boy in her honors English class, studious and serious as she was. Cute behind his thick glasses. They had traded a few kisses, done a little groping. Then he got contact lenses and suddenly became sought after by popular girls, and Megan was forgotten.

Mitch kissed her neck again, nibbled at her earlobe, his tongue caressing the tender bud of flesh. 'Ah, well then, let me teach you. Learn from the master makeout artist.'

Leaning back without letting her go, he switched off the lamp on the end table, leaving the room illuminated by the fire and the television. He turned her to face him and kissed her lightly on the mouth. 'See, the idea,' he murmured between kisses, 'is for you to pretend you shouldn't let me do anything, even though what we both really want is to get naked and screw our brains out.'

Megan laughed softly, twisting out of reach as he tried to brush a hand against her breast. 'So, did you ever get lucky?'

'I don't kiss and tell. Maybe I'll get lucky tonight.'

'I don't think so.' She gave him a teasing look from beneath her lashes as she scooted back toward the opposite end of the couch. 'You'll ruin my reputation.'

She didn't let herself think about the truth in that statement. They both needed this time together, away from the burdens of the case. Time to be people instead of cops. Time to feel something good, something life-affirming.

Mitch followed her, moving over the cushions on his knees. A wicked grin curved his mouth.

'Oh, come on, Megan,' he whispered, trailing a fingertip down the short slope of her nose to the perfect bow of her mouth. 'Just a kiss, that's all. I promise.'

Megan smiled, surprised at the way her body was responding to the game. Her heart was beating a little too fast. Her skin was warm and tingling with anticipation. Silly. They had already been to bed together. There were few secrets left between them physically. Still she felt excited at the prospect of a little heavy petting.

Their lips met tentatively, experimentally, as if this experience were new. Nothing to be rushed. Something to be savored. Breaths mingling. Mouths softly touching. The slightest increase of pressure. The angle shifting by small degrees. The anticipation warming and thickening. He slid his arms around her shoulders and drew her closer. The kiss deepened just a shade, and then another. The tip of his tongue skimmed the seam of her lips, asking for a little more, probed gently at the corner of her mouth, asking again. She opened her mouth and moaned softly as he took full possession.

Megan caught hold of his hand as he raised it but didn't try to stop him as he filled his palm with the weight of her breast. His fingers kneaded her gently, her fingers closed over his, and he made a low sound of arousal in his throat as she increased the pressure. He found her nipple with his thumb and rubbed it slowly through the soft layers of her clothing. Then the buttons surrendered one by one.

'God, you're pretty,' he whispered, exposing her, touching her reverently.

Megan let herself drift on the sea of sensation . . . until she felt his hand on the button of her jeans. And again they went through the game of mock protest and persuasion.

The button gave way. The zipper inched down. She raised her hips. He eased her jeans down, expecting to see a pair of lacy underpants to tease him. What he found was black silk that seemed to go on and on. Brows tugging together in confusion, he looked up at her.

'Long underwear,' Megan whispered, embarrassed. 'It's thirty below outside!'

Mitch chuckled wickedly, peeling the black silk down. 'Yeah, well, it's a hell of a lot warmer in here. Especially down here,' he said, sliding his fingers into the thatch of dark curls. 'Especially in here,' he murmured, easing two fingers deep between her legs.

'Oh – Mitch –' Megan reached for him, tried to pull him down to her. She wanted him close, wanted him losing his control, finding fulfillment at the same time, not watching her at her most vulnerable.

'Trust me,' he whispered.

Trust me. Trust wasn't something she offered easily. There were good reasons not to trust. Logical, practical reasons. But she didn't feel logical or practical. When he touched her, she felt like a woman, not a cop. It frightened her to let go of that identity, but there was Mitch, whispering, coaxing . . . *Trust me* . . . touching the heart of her need . . . stroking the most feminine part of her . . . caressing . . . loving . . . *Trust me* . . .

Megan's eyes drifted shut. Her breath caught. She lay back as the last of her restraint slipped from her mental grasp. Overpowered by sensation and passion and need. Her hips moved in perfect rhythm with his hand. Her breath came in short, shallow puffs. The excitement swelled and burst inside her, hot, dizzying, intoxicating.

'I love to watch your face when you come,' Mitch murmured. 'You concentrate so hard.'

Megan felt a blush spread across her cheeks and tried to deflect his attention from her embarrassment by rolling on top of him. 'Your turn, Chief,' she said.

The smile that teased her lips as she rose over him was sparkling with wicked mischief. Slowly she unbuttoned his denim shirt and bared his chest. Her small hands massaged the muscles, traced the ridges, brushed across the mat of dark hair. Mitch watched her intently, pleasure and tortured need twisting together inside him like vines. He sucked in a breath as she bent her head and took his nipple into her mouth. The feel of her lips, her tongue, her teeth, fueled the fire burning in his groin.

'Megan –'

She pressed a finger against his lips. 'Shh . . . Let me do this for you, Mitch.'

She trailed her kisses across his belly. Long, hot, open-mouthed kisses. Kisses that followed the descent of his jeans.

'Megan –'

'Shh . . . Trust me.'

He groaned as she took him into the silky heat of her mouth. Thought and control burned away, leaving nothing but feeling so intense, he couldn't breathe. Feeling – the stroke of her tongue, the caress of her lips, the touch of her hand, the slight abrasion of her teeth. Feeling – a fire burning hotter and hotter, rushing toward explosion.

He pulled her up into his arms and rolled her beneath him, driving into her, filling her in one powerful thrust. She was hot and tight around him, as wet as her mouth. Her thighs tightened against his sides. Her fingertips dug into the muscles of his back. He moved in and out of her faster, harder, reaching, straining. She gasped his name as her climax gripped her, gripped him, and he came in a hot rush.

Feeling – trust, excitement, a bond that went beyond the physical. Feelings he hadn't known, hadn't allowed himself in two years of one-night stands.

He didn't want to think or talk or ponder the implications. He wanted to pull the cotton throw down from the back of the couch and cover their cooling bodies, capture the heat in a cocoon and hold it around them. Preserve the moment and put off deciphering the meaning.

Still, the doubts were there, as inescapable as ghosts. He shuffled through the excuses and the rationalizations like a deck of dog-eared playing cards. This was just sex. An affair and nothing more. He wasn't ready for more. She didn't want more. He liked his life the way it was – simple, ordered, controllable. He didn't want to commit himself to taking responsibility for another person.

Not that Megan needed anyone to take responsibility for her. Not that she would allow it. Christ, she was the most independent woman he knew. On the outside . . . On the inside she was an abandoned little girl, a woman uncertain of her own appeal and wary of everyone.

Tenderly, he brushed a hand over her hair, brushed a kiss against her forehead.

Megan shifted sideways, wedging herself between Mitch and the back of the couch. She lay her hand on his chest, over his heart, wishing fleetingly she could have access to what was *in* his heart. A pointless wish

– a fact that was only emphasized when he covered her hand with his and the gold of his wedding band caught the dying light of the fire.

The hurt was sharp and surprising, and foolish. He wasn't ready to let go of his past. That wasn't any of her business. She hadn't asked him for a future. She wouldn't. She hadn't asked for this affair; it had just happened. He was attracted to her, not enchanted by her. She had never enchanted anyone that she knew of. So what. Big deal. She had better things to do with her time.

'I should go,' she whispered. 'It's late.'

'Five more minutes,' he murmured, tightening his arm around her shoulders. 'I just want to hold you. Five more minutes.'

She should have said no. But then, she should have said no all along, she thought wearily.

Five more minutes . . .

8 3:00 a.m. -35° windchill factor: -69°

The phone on the end table rang, jolting Megan awake. Disoriented, her brain scrambled to sort the facts into place. Mitch. Mitch's house. Mitch's dog lying on his back on the living room rug, watching an infomercial for spray-on hair.

Mitch sat up, groggy, running a hand over his face. The phone rang again and the answering machine kicked on and gave the usual song and dance. At the tone, instead of a voice came a long silence, then whispered words. 'Blind and naked ignorance. Blind and naked ignorance. Blind –'

Mitch grabbed the receiver. 'Who the hell is this?'

Silence. Then the line went dead.

'Damn crank,' he muttered without conviction, turning back toward Megan.

Her fingers fumbled at the task of buttoning her blouse. 'Yeah, right. Just a crank.'

'He didn't really say anything.'

'And Olie Swain is in jail.'

'Right.'

So why were they both spooked? Mitch had a feeling in his gut that usually came from lingering nightmares. The hair on the back of his neck prickled. Instinctive responses he tried to rationalize away.

When the phone rang again, he jerked as if a hundred volts had gone through him. Megan grabbed his shoulder.

'Let the machine get it.'

'Yeah, I know.'

The voice that came over the line was breathless with panic, the words tripping over each other on the way out of the speaker's mouth. 'Chief, it's Dennis Harding – Sergeant Harding. We need you down to the jail right away. Something's happened – Jesus, it's awful –'

251

Mitch grabbed the receiver. 'Harding, it's me. What's going on?'
'It's – it's Olie Swain. Oh, my God. Oh, sweet Jesus. He's dead.'

Journal entry
Day 8

Blind and naked ignorance
Delivers brawling judgments, unashamed

The police are fools. They stepped on a slug and called
him a villain, and the desperate rushed blindly to embrace
their ignorance. And the doctor is no god. Just another
helpless woman. The illusion of power gone. We
are the kings.

24

The corpse of Olie Swain, a.k.a. Leslie Sewek, lay crumpled on the floor near the back wall of the cell, an empty husk drained of life. Blood pooled on the gray linoleum, as thick and dark as oil. The stench of violent death was thick and cloying, a rancid perfume that invaded the nostrils and crawled down the throat. Blood and bowel content. The sharp scent of vomit from witnesses unaccustomed to horror.

Only sheer stubbornness and an iron will kept the contents of Megan's stomach in place. The smell always got to her; the rest she had hardened herself to long ago. Mitch's face was unreadable, nearly expressionless. She imagined he had seen worse. He had been a detective in a town notorious for drug wars and violent street crime. He had seen his own wife and son lying dead. Nothing could be worse than that.

'Hey! I want outta here!' Boog Newton called, his voice strained with a fear he was trying unsuccessfully to cover with bravado. 'I don't have to stay next to no dead guy. That's cruel and unusual.'

Mitch shot him a dangerous look. 'Shut up.'

Boog scuttled to the far side of his bunk and sat with one foot up on the thin mattress. One skinny arm hugged his knee as he rocked nervously. His other hand inched up the side of his face like a crab, making for his right nostril.

Mitch gave Olie one last long look.

Blind and naked ignorance . . . blind and naked ignorance . . . blind and naked ignorance . . . Blind . . . Blind . . . Blind . . .

'What do we do?' Harding asked weakly. He remained outside the cell, hands gripping the bars, his face the color of old paste.

'Call the coroner,' Mitch ordered, stepping out of the cell. 'Get somebody up here with a camera. We process it like a crime scene.'

'But, Chief, nobody could have —'

'Just do it!' he bellowed.

Harding bolted backward, tripping over his own feet, then turned and hustled out of the cell area. Mitch let himself into Boog Newton's cell. Newton's small eyes darted from Mitch to Megan to Olie to Mitch.

'What happened, Boog?' Mitch's voice was silky and low as he moved toward the cot.

'How should I know?' Boog blurted, jerking his finger out of his nose. 'It was dark. I didn't see nothin'.'

He arched a brow. 'A man in the cell next to yours just killed himself and you don't know anything? You must be a sound sleeper.'

Boog scratched nervously at a scab on his chin, his eyes on his blank television. His pallor was waxy, shiny with the kind of sweat that comes with nausea. 'He maybe made some sounds,' he offered weakly. 'I didn't know what he was doin'. Pervert child molester. I didn't wanna know what he was doin'. I thought he was gettin' off or somethin'.'

'He was getting dead, Einstein!' Mitch exploded, suddenly looming over Newton like an avenging god or the devil himself. 'Our only lead in this fucking case and now he's dead!'

'Jesus, it's not my fault!' Boog whined, covering his head with his arms, cowering like a whipped dog.

'No, nothing's ever anybody's fault,' Mitch sneered. 'I am so fucking tired of that excuse!'

The fury rolled through him like a storm, clouding his vision and his judgment. He made no attempt to stop it. He kicked the foot of Newton's cot hard, again and again, the clang and rattle of boot connecting with metal reverberating off the block walls. 'Goddammit, goddammit, GODDAMMIT!!'

'Mitch!' Megan snapped, rushing into the cell. He wheeled on her as she grabbed hold of his arm, his expression fierce, wild with rage. 'Mitch, come on,' she said, her gaze steady on his. 'Chill out. We've got work to do.'

He could see Boog Newton tucked into a ball on his cot, frightened eyes peering at him over his bony knees. *You lost it, Holt. You lost it.*

He'd lost it with good reason. His gaze tracked slowly away from Newton through the bars into the next cell, where Olie Swain lay on the floor in a pool of blood. Their only lead. Their only suspect. He might have led them to Josh, but Paige had blown the stakeout. He might have cut a deal and handed them Josh or cut a deal and handed them his accomplice, but now there would be no deals. Everything he knew was gone, like a slate wiped clean.

Mitch told himself none of this would have happened in the old days, when his instincts were as sharp as razors. He had lost his edge. In the last two years he had purposely let the instincts rust. He had lulled himself into thinking he wouldn't need them here. A chief didn't need instincts; he needed diplomacy. Nothing ever happened in Deer Lake. Nothing at all . . .

The harsh fluorescent light glared down on Olie Swain, on the birthmark dark against his ashen skin, on the empty socket that had held his glass eye. A fragment of the eye lay in the puddle of blood near his left hand — a sharp wedge of brown iris and black pupil staring up at the

255

ceiling. He had smashed the porcelain ellipse and used one of the shards to dig open the veins in his wrists, draining his life's blood onto the floor of the Deer Lake city jail. On the wall above his corpse, smeared in red, were the words NOT ME.

4:32 a.m. –32° windchill factor: –64°

The Park County coroner was a balding, pear-shaped man named Stuart Oglethorpe, director of the Olgethorpe Funeral Home. He was in his fifties and wore thick black horn-rimmed glasses and a sour frown that made Mitch suspect he could never get the smell of embalming fluid out of his nose. He examined Olie briefly, touching his body gingerly with gloved hands, grumbling about the empty eye socket and the bloody mess.

It was common knowledge that the only reason Stuart Oglethorpe had run for the job of county coroner was so his funeral home could get first crack at the corpses. If the body was already in his embalming room, the grieving family was likely to leave it there and purchase a casket and order a memorial service. Stuart could then route the flower orders to his cousin Wilmer at the Blooming Bud greenhouse.

No one was going to order flowers for Olie Swain. Unless some long-lost relative from Washington claimed him, he would be buried at the county's expense. No Cadillac casket, no frills, no memorial service. Stuart had been roused from his warm bed to go out into thirty-two-below-zero cold with no hope of big profit. Stuart was not a happy man.

'Well, he killed himself. Any fool can plainly see that.'

'Yeah, but we need *your* signature on the report, Stuart,' Mitch said. 'And he'll have to be transported to Hennepin County for an autopsy ASAP.'

'Autopsy! What the heck for?' Oglethorpe groused. Once the body hit the slab at Hennepin County Medical Center, he had no hope in hell of getting it back. Park County would give it to the cut-rate Quaam brothers in Tatonka.

'It's standard procedure when a prisoner takes his own life, Mr Oglethorpe,' Megan explained. 'It leaves no room for doubt or speculation as to the circumstances of the death.'

Oglethorpe scowled at her. 'Who's she?'

'Agent O'Malley, BCA.'

He snorted in response.

'Charmed, I'm sure,' Megan muttered under her breath. She turned to the officers preparing to load Olie into a body bag and cart him away. 'Watch the blood, guys. He was low man on the totem pole in prison for five years; he's a definite AIDS risk.'

'Oh, jeez,' Harding groaned. 'And I didn't think this could get any worse.'

She gave him a wry look. 'Welcome to the club.'

10:00 a.m. -27° windchill factor: -55°

The press room at the old fire hall had been jammed since nine forty-five.

There was no question that missing children and child predators had become the hot topic. But Megan saw the intense coverage as a medium for creating an unwarranted panic that crimes of this nature were increasing at epidemic rates. According to statistics from the National Center for Missing and Exploited Children, the rate of stranger abductions of children remained remarkably constant from year to year – not a statistic to be regarded lightly, but not an epidemic. Many more children were killed with handguns every week.

She watched the camera and sound people jockey for position as reporters did the same. The pecking order had changed dramatically with the local press pushed back by the Cities press, pushed back by the tabloid people, pushed back by the network people. Any space left over at the very back of the room was taken by people from the volunteer center. She caught a glimpse of the disgruntled Mrs Favre from Paige Price's prime time special. Almost hidden behind her was Christopher Priest. Rob Phillips, head of the volunteer center, had been granted a ringside seat because of his wheelchair.

At ten on the dot Mitch stepped behind the podium. He had showered and shaved and dressed in a dark brown suit, a conservative white shirt, and a tie without cartoon characters. What color the wind had whipped into his cheeks was leeched out by the blinding sun-guns.

'At approximately three A.M. Leslie Olin Sewek, a.k.a. Olie Swain, was found in his cell at the city jail, dead due to self-inflicted injuries,' he announced without preamble.

The shock wave that went through the crowd had all the power of a sonic boom. There were gasps and exclamations. Camera shutters clicked at a furious rate, motor drives whined. Then came the questions in a gust that rivaled the wind outside.

'How do you know the wounds were self-inflicted?'

'Wasn't he being watched?'

'What kind of weapon did he use?'

'Did he leave any notes admitting his guilt in the kidnapping?'

'Did he give any indication to the whereabouts of Josh?'

'Mr Sewek was not considered a suicide risk,' Mitch went on. 'He exhibited no signs that would have led us to believe he was a danger to himself. I'm not at liberty to divulge the exact details of his death other than to say he did not have access to anything that would be deemed a conventional weapon. His body has been transferred to Hennepin County Medical Center for a routine autopsy. We are confident the medical examiner's findings will support those of my office and of the Park County coroner.'

'Did he leave a note, Chief?' called a reporter from *20/20*.

Mitch thought of the two words scrawled in blood on the wall above Olie's body. NOT ME. 'He left no note explaining his actions or his state of mind. He left no message about Josh.'

'Have you established that he was indeed the kidnapper?'

'We're still waiting for lab reports from the BCA.'

'And when will those be in?'

At Mitch's invitation, Megan stepped up to the podium. She had dressed carefully and conservatively in charcoal wool slacks and turtleneck with an unstructured tweed blazer. The antique cameo pin on the lapel was her only ornamentation. She looked out on the crowd with cool professionalism.

'The tests on Mr Sewek's van have been given priority status. I expect to hear back on several of them today.'

'What kind of tests?'

'What was found? Blood?'

'Articles of clothing?'

'It would be premature for me to reveal the nature of the tests without being able to elaborate on the findings or their significance to the case.'

Paige Price, who had somehow managed to procure a seat directly behind the *48 Hours* people, rose with pen and pad in hand, as if she might actually take notes. 'Agent O'Malley,' she said coolly. 'Can you tell us your whereabouts when you received word of Leslie Sewek's demise?'

A cold finger of dread traced down Megan's back. Her hands tightened on the podium. 'I fail to see the relevance of that question, Ms Price,' she replied coldly, then dismissed the woman by turning her attention toward a reporter for the *NBC Nightly News*.

'Agent O'Malley –' he began.

'I believe your answer may be relevant to the people of Deer Lake,' Paige interrupted with just the perfect hint of drama. Inside she was grinning like the Cheshire cat. She had the attention of the other reporters – the network people and those from the syndicated shows, people who could smell a story the way sharks smell blood in the water. She could see the wheels turning in their minds – *How does she know something we don't?* The anticipation was as delicious as fine chocolate on her tongue. God bless Russ Steiger.

'Isn't it true that when the call came at three A.M. announcing Leslie Sewek's death you were at the home of Chief Holt?'

Somewhere beyond the pounding of Megan's pulse in her ears, the crowd's reaction sounded like bees swarming. Her fingers were white. Her knees felt like Jell-O. She didn't dare chance a look at Mitch or solicit support from him. She was on her own, as she had always been. The phrase *swinging in the breeze* came to mind. God, if DePalma got wind of this . . . *When* DePalma got wind of this . . .

She stared hard at Paige. Mercenary bitch. Ms Blond Ambition, digging for any scrap that could set her apart from the pack. The idea made Megan sick and furious. She had worked damned hard to get where she was. Too damned hard to have her dreams punctured by Paige Price's spike heels.

'Ms Price,' she said evenly, 'don't you believe you've done enough damage to this investigation as it is without now trying to divert the focus of this press conference away from the case and the fate of Josh Kirkwood and onto yourself?'

'I'm not diverting the focus onto myself, Agent O'Malley, I'm diverting it onto you.'

'That's not how I see it,' Megan challenged. 'I see you drawing the attention of your peers by implying some imagined impropriety to which only you are privy. Maybe you think this will get you a big job on *Hard Copy*, but I'll tell you, it doesn't cut much ice with me.' She dismissed the reporter again. 'Does anyone have a question *germane* to the case?'

'Why won't you answer my question, Agent O'Malley?' Paige pressed. 'What are you afraid of?'

Eyes blazing, Megan turned back to her adversary. 'I'm afraid I'm going to lose my temper, Ms Price, because your line of questioning is not only irrelevant but the answer is none of your damn business.'

She regretted the words the instant they were out of her mouth. She had just as much as admitted her guilt. It didn't matter that what she said was true, that it was nobody's business. She had given just enough answer to pique imaginations. God, what a nightmare. She felt as if she had stepped into a tar pit and was being sucked in deeper with every move she made in an attempt to extricate herself. Now there would be no graceful way out. She couldn't tell the truth and she doubted anyone would swallow an edited version. *We were discussing the case and we just fell asleep. Honest.* Right. She felt like a teenager who had been caught coming home after curfew. The analogy nearly made her laugh out loud as she recalled Mitch's words of the night before – *Let's make out. Like when we were in high school . . .*

Paige put on her righteous-crusader-for-the-First-Amendment face, internally vowing to wring Garcia's neck if he didn't get a long shot of it. 'At three A.M., while your prime suspect in an unsolved child abduction was committing suicide, you were reportedly in the home of Chief Holt with all the lights off. If your priority is not with the case, the public has a right to know, Agent O'Malley.'

'No, Ms Price,' Megan retorted, her voice trembling with cold rage. 'The public has a right to know that I and all the other cops on this case have been working virtually around the clock in the attempt to find Josh, to get just one good lead on the piece of human garbage who stole him. They have a right to know that no one could have known what Olie Swain had done before he came here, that what happened to Josh was an isolated act of senseless violence and not the first sign of anarchy. They have a right to know that your job hinges on your ratings and your ratings hinge on sensationalism and exploitation. They do not have a right to follow me after I've spent eighteen hours on the job. They do not have a right to know what flavor of ice cream I like or what brand of tampons I use.

'Am I making myself clear, Ms Price? Or do we need to discuss how you came to find out about the stakeout on Olie Swain's house the other night? Perhaps you, in your patriotic, open-minded spirit, can see that the public has a right to know how it came to pass that you and your news crew interfered with an investigation and ultimately ruined our chances of possibly finding Josh Kirkwood that night.'

Momentum, fickle bitch that she is, swung heavily away from Paige. She felt it go. She felt the jealous admiration of her fellow journalists cool like a hot iron in the snow. She felt the eyes of volunteers bore into her back, felt their sense of betrayal and their anger. She would lose their trust, which meant she might lose potential sources. Worse than that, she would lose viewers, which meant she would lose leverage in her contract negotiations. She took her seat, her gaze on Megan O'Malley, burning with hate.

'DePalma is going to skin me alive and make a desk set out of my hide,' Megan muttered. She paced the length of an antique fire truck, shaking, not from the biting cold of the old garage, but from shock.

The press conference was over, but the trouble had just begun. The match had just been touched to the fuse – and the fuse was attached to the dynamite that would blow her out of Deer Lake. 'Dammit, I knew something like this would happen! I knew better!'

'Megan, you didn't do anything wrong,' Mitch said. He sat on the running board of the old truck, freezing his balls. He was too drained to care. 'You said so yourself in there. You made your point very sharply.'

Megan stared at him in disbelief. 'You think that's going to make a difference? You think that pack of jackals in there is going to say "Oh, yeah, she's right, it's none of our business who she sleeps with"? What turnip truck did you fall off?'

'I'm saying there are more important things to focus on here. For them and for you.'

'What the hell is that supposed to mean? You think I care more about my career than I care about finding Josh?'

Mitch rose. 'I don't hear you ranting about the fact that our only suspect is dead. You took that in stride. But somebody takes a poke at you and it's the end of life as we know it.'

Beyond words, Megan could only gape at him. Then she looked away, rubbing a hand across her forehead, muttering to herself. 'I guess I should have expected this. A man is a man is a man.'

'What do you mean by that?'

'I mean, you don't get it,' she snapped, wheeling back around on him.

Every muscle in her body was rigid with anger, her hands balled into white-knuckled fists at her sides. 'My authority and integrity have been compromised. Once this hits the airwaves, my credibility is suspect and my effectiveness on the job suffers. Provided I still have a job. The Vatican likes scandalous publicity more than the BCA does.' Phantom images of DePalma's angry face floated through her head. Nixon as the grim reaper, the face of doom.

'Do you know how I got this job, Mitch?' she demanded. 'I got this job by working twice as hard and being three times better than any man in line for it. I fought tooth and nail for it, because I believe in what we do.

'There is *nothing* I want more than to find Josh Kirkwood. I have given over all that I am, all that I know, every ounce of will and determination I have to find Josh and stick his abductor's head on a pike. And now I'm very probably going to be denied the satisfaction and this investigation is very probably going to lose one damn good cop because I was stupid, because I broke my own cardinal rule and slept with a cop.'

'Stupid?' he said in a deadly quiet voice. 'That's what you think about us?'

'What *us*?' Megan asked sharply. She would have liked to believe they had something special, but she had no faith in that being true. She wanted to think he was holding out the chance to her now, but she wouldn't trust him. Love didn't happen this fast. Love didn't happen at all for her. Life had taught her that lesson a long time ago.

'There is no us,' she said bitterly. 'We had sex. You never made any promises to me. My God, you never even bothered to take off your wedding ring when you took me to bed!'

Instantly, Mitch's gaze dropped to his left hand and to the thick gold band he wore out of habit. He wore it to punish himself. He wore it to protect himself from women who might want more than he was willing to give. And it worked like a charm, didn't it?

Megan stood there in front of him with her feet braced apart, shoulders squared, ready to take a blow – physical or metaphorical. So tough on the outside, so alone on the inside. She had more than made her priorities clear: the job, the job, and then the job. But there was still hurt in her eyes and behind the pride that kept her chin up. He had coerced her into breaking her rules, gave her sex, offered her nothing, and now she would pay the price.

What does that make you, Holt? King of the shitheels.

He blew out a long breath. 'Megan, I'm s –'

'Save it.' She didn't want to hear the word. Bad enough to see it written all over his face. 'We both should have known better.' She told herself it wasn't Mitch who was hurting her, that it was the injustice of a double standard that would punish her for attempting to have a private life.

'You won't have to worry, of course.' She forced a sharp, unpleasant

261

smile. 'Everybody knows boys will be boys. And I'm used to going through my professional life with an ax hanging over my head. So, hey, this is nothing new.'

'Megan . . .'

He reached a hand out to touch her cheek. She slapped it away.

'Goddamn you, Mitch Holt, don't you dare pity me!' she said through her teeth. She had no defense against tenderness. She backed away from him, jaw set, her mouth pressed into an uncompromising line. 'I'm a big girl. I can take care of myself. Hell, I've been doing it my whole life. Why stop now?'

Chin up, she walked past him, wondering if there was any hope of getting her coat from the press room without being seen.

'Where are you going?'

Megan stopped a foot from the door, but she didn't turn around. She didn't need a man in her life. She didn't need anyone. To be a good cop – that was all she had ever really wanted. She ignored the hollow ring of those words inside her.

'I'm going to work,' she told him. 'While I still have a job.'

25

Olie Swain had no known associates. He had no friends. He was, as they were so fond of saying on the nightly news, a loner. He did his job and kept to himself. According to the ink stamp on the inside covers, he bought most of his books at The Pack Rat, a secondhand shop near Harris College.

The store was empty except for a clerk who would have looked perfect selling love beads out of the back of a Volkswagen van with a psychedelic paint job. Tall and lean as a stick of beef jerky, he parted his rusty blond hair in the middle and pulled it back into a bushy ponytail. What passed for a beard on his chin more resembled the thin wad of loose hair Megan periodically cleaned out of her hairbrush. He wore a tie-dyed T-shirt with a rumpled plaid flannel shirt open over it. Baggy jeans clung precariously to his skinny hips, held in place by a length of clothesline cord. His name was Todd Childs and he was a psych major at Harris who had been spending some of his free time working in the volunteer center.

Megan let her gaze roam around the store as they chatted about the case. Housed in an old creamery building, the place was jam-packed to the rafters, a treasure trove of outdated textbooks and clothes, 'decorative' pieces that cycled between trendy kitsch and unwanted junk, pennants and pompoms and other assorted memorabilia from Harris. Behind the counter, an ancient electric heater that looked like a fire hazard groaned in its effort to supplement the clanking furnace.

Todd tapped a forefinger to the thin gold rim of his glasses. 'Observation is the key to insight,' he said slowly. He propped his bony elbows on the counter and leaned across it to stare into Megan's eyes. His pupils were dilated to the size of dimes and the scent of burning hemp clung to his clothes. 'For instance, I'd have to say you're very tense.'

'Comes with the territory,' Megan said.

'Yeah . . .' He nodded in slow motion. 'Seeking justice in an unjust world. Trying to plug the dam with chewing gum. Most cops are control freaks, you know. That's not meant to be an insult; it's just an observation.'

'And what did you observe about Olie?'

'He was weird. He never wanted to talk to anybody. Came in, bought books, left.' Todd stood back and sucked down half a Marlboro Light 100. 'We were in the same class a couple of times,' he said on a cloud of smoke. 'He never spoke to the other students. Never.'

'He was actually taking courses at Harris?'

'Just auditing. I don't think he could spring for tuition. He was way into computers, you know. I think he felt more comfortable with machines than people. Some folks do. He sure didn't strike me as the kind of guy who likes to fuck with people's heads. You know, with that note business and that phone call and everything.' He shook his head, inhaled a quarter of the cigarette, and blew the smoke out through his nostrils. 'I don't see it, unless he had a multiple personality disorder, and that's pretty unlikely.'

'I guess he was leading a secret life,' Megan said, pulling her mittens on.

Todd gave her a dreamy look. 'Don't we all? Isn't that what everyone does – build camouflage walls around our inner selves?'

'I guess,' she conceded, clamping on her earmuffs. 'But most of us don't have inner selves who molest children.' She tapped the business card she had left on the counter. 'If you think of anything that might help, please give me a call.'

'Sure thing.'

'Oh, and Todd?' She gave him a look as she tossed the end of her scarf over her shoulder. 'Don't smoke dope on the job. You never know when a cop might come in.'

From The Pack Rat, Megan hurried next door to a small turquoise clapboard house that had been converted into a coffee place called The Leaf and Bean. The tiny front porch was crowded with snow-crusted bicycles apparently waiting out the winter. Inside, she took a seat at a tiny white-draped table near the front window and ordered latte and a chocolate chip cookie from a girl dressed like Morticia Addams. What few other customers there were sat back by the old wooden counter in what had probably once been a dining room, perusing the newspapers and chatting quietly. An alternative rock station was playing on the radio behind the counter, filling the emptiness with Shawn Colvin's spare, evocative lyrics to 'Steady On'.

The walls of the place were chalk white and hung with old black-and-white photographs in plain black frames. The windows were curtainless, allowing cold bright sunlight to pour in. Megan left her sunglasses on, to discourage eye contact and to block the light. She sipped her latte and nibbled absently on her cookie as she stared down at her notebook.

She needed to find a thread that would tie the random bits of information together, but there didn't seem to be one. All she had were theories. Olie had acted alone. Olie had an accomplice. Who? He had no friends. Olie had computers no one could get into, but his printer was dot matrix and the note found in Josh's gear bag and in the back of his notebook had come from a laser printer. Olie had photographs of naked boys, but they were years old, from his life in another place.

For someone who knew so much, she knew very little.

ignorance is not innocence but SIN
i had a little sorrow, born of a little SIN
Blind and naked ignorance . . . blind
and naked ignorance . . .

Mind games. Mitch had said Olie didn't seem the type for mind games. Olie had been lying in his own blood when the call had come to Mitch's house.

Blind and naked ignorance

She had looked up the quotation in *Bartlett's*. It was from Tennyson's *Idylls of the King. Blind and naked ignorance delivers brawling judgments unashamed.*

Someone's way of telling them they had the wrong man? Or was it Olie's partner, unaware that at the very moment he called to torment them his cohort was slitting his wrists with the shards of his porcelain eye?

The theories swirled through her mind, making her head ache. And in a separate swarm were the fears for what would happen to her career if someone decided to make an issue of her involvement with Mitch. At best, she would lose face with the men she worked with. Worst ranged from losing her field post to ending up as a security guard at a shopping mall someplace. No. Worst would be not being able to close this case, she decided as she looked down at her copy of Josh's photograph.

He smiled up at her, so full of life and enthusiasm and bright-eyed innocence. For just a second she let her guard down and wondered how he was, what he must be thinking, how frightened he must be . . . provided he was still alive. She had to think he was. Believing kept everyone going.

And beneath all the other thoughts was the acute awareness of every passing second.

'We're doing the best we can, Josh,' she whispered. 'Hang in there, scout.'

Tucking the photograph back into her folder, she forced her gaze to focus again on the notes she had made. *Olie – computers. Olie – audit courses – Harris College. Instructors?*

Christopher Priest was head of the department. Maybe he would have an idea what Olie kept locked away inside his machines. Maybe he would have an idea of how to get at it.

She paid her tab and went back out into the deep freeze with her file folder and notebook clutched against her as if they might afford some protection from the wind. The Lumina started grudgingly and the fan belt shrieked like a banshee all the way back to the station.

The only good thing about the extreme cold was that it discouraged the press from hanging around outside the station doors. Having been banned from the hallways of the law enforcement center, they congregated in the main entry to the City Center building or sat in their cars in the parking lot with the motors running. Megan pulled into the slot designated for Agent L. Kozlowski behind the building and ducked in the door before any of the vultures could alight from their perches.

Her message light was blinking when she let herself into her office, but the call was from Dave Larkin, not DePalma. She hoped the silence meant the dirt from the press conference had yet to hit headquarters. She debated the wisdom of beating them to the punch, calling DePalma herself and giving him the laundered version of what had gone on – she and Mitch had been discussing the case; exhausted from the hours they had been putting in, they fell asleep sitting in front of his fireplace; then came the call . . .

Calls. Plural. *Blind and naked ignorance.* The voice played through her mind as she hung up her coat. Whispery. Low. Eerie. In her mind's eye she saw the message scrawled in blood on the white wall of Olie's cell – NOT ME. What if he were innocent? What if they had wasted all this time chasing down a red herring while the real kidnapper sat back and watched them, laughing?

The what-ifs spun around and around in her head. She needed to put her thoughts back on track methodically, one by one. They had followed their leads. Olie had the record, he had the opportunity. His van matched the witness description. His van had traces of blood in the carpet.

'Larkin,' she murmured.

Snatching up the receiver, she punched in the number and prayed he would be at his desk. He picked up on the sixth ring.

'Larkin.'

'Dave, it's Megan. What have you got for me?'

'Condolences on the passing of your suspect. Man, Irish, talk about bad breaks.'

'Yeah, if it weren't for bad luck, we'd have no luck at all,' she said. 'Have you heard anything else from this end?' she fished.

'Like what?'

'Nothing. Never mind. Did you get the reports on the blood?'

'Yeah. I personally went over there and hounded them. I figured I'd get back to you quicker than they would.'

'Thanks. You're a pal, Dave. What'd they find?'

'It wasn't human.'

Megan let out the breath she'd been holding. 'God, I don't know if I should be relieved or disappointed.'

'I know. I'm sorry, kiddo. I wish I could give you something to go on, but this blood ain't it. It probably came from some poor Bambi and it was probably in that rug for years. There were no sporting rifles or shotguns, no guns of any sort found in your guy's house. I'll fax you the report, and the minute I hear anything on the trace evidence, I'll call you.'

'Thanks, Dave. I appreciate it.'

'Don't mention it. And chin up, Irish. When you crack this thing, dinner's on me.'

Megan didn't bother to tell him he would be dining alone. No cops. Never again.

She wondered what would happen to the easy camaraderie she shared with Dave Larkin when Paige Price's story hit the grapevine. She had kept his amorous advances at bay with her rule of not dating cops. He enjoyed kidding around about the subject, but he had always respected her boundaries. How would he feel when he found out she'd been sleeping with Mitch? Would he try to understand or would his ego inflate between them like an air bag?

She cursed herself for the hundredth time. She had compromised so much, and for what? A few hours of intimacy with a man she barely knew.

Other reasons whispered through her mind. Excuses and half-formed wishes. The physical attraction was stronger than anything she had ever known; she hadn't known how to fight it. He had been persistent, persuasive. She had felt a connection with him that awakened within her the desire for things she had never had – closeness, companionship . . . love.

She closed her eyes and shook her head. She was tough enough to break the testosterone barrier and make detective on the Minneapolis force. She was strong enough to fight for her right to this field post with the BCA. She had taken down characters as bad as any cop ever had to face. And all of that was forgotten in a heartbeat for a little scrap of tenderness and the chance to feel that she mattered to a man as a woman.

The fax machine behind her beeped. Megan swung around on her desk chair, expecting to see the lab report on the bloodstains. Instead, the cover sheet was from the DMV regarding the routine trace on Olie's van. Using the manufacturer's vehicle identification number, they had traced the van's life history in the state of Minnesota from first owner to last. According to the report, the title had been transferred in September 1991 to Lonnie O. Swain. The previous recorded change of ownership had occurred in April 1989. The lucky owner: Paul Kirkwood.

Goose bumps rippled down Megan's body. The van Paul Kirkwood hadn't wanted to tell her about was Olie Swain's van.

2:14 p.m.

'The council members are really upset here, Mitch. They can't understand how something like this could happen. I mean, how did he get hold of a knife? You don't give those guys table knives with their suppers, do you?'

Mitch stared across his desk at Mayor Don Gillen, trying to manufacture patience from stress and stomach acid. 'He didn't have a knife, Don. He didn't have a weapon of any kind. He cracked his glass eye and slit his wrists with the pieces, and if you can find me anyone on the town council who could have foreseen that happening, I will gladly pin my badge to their chest and retire from law enforcement.'

'Jeez,' Gillen muttered, horrified. His blue eyes blinked behind his gold retro spectacles. In addition to his position as mayor, he held an administrative position with the Deer Lake Community Schools. Pushing fifty, he still tended to dress like a yuppie on the cutting edge of fashion, flashy ties and suspenders being his trademarks. 'Jeez, Mitch, that's ghoulish.'

Mitch spread his hands. 'I'd rather you didn't tell anyone but the council members.'

'Yeah, sure.' Gillen shook his head as he rose from the visitor's chair. 'So, you think it's nearly over?' he asked hopefully. 'That Olie did it and killed himself because he felt guilty or couldn't face going back to prison?'

'Honestly, I don't know, Don,' Mitch said, rising. 'I just don't know.'

Gillen started to say something, but cut himself off as a sharp knock sounded against the door. Megan stuck her head in the office without waiting for an invitation.

'Excuse me, Chief,' she said, glancing quickly past the mayor. 'I'm sorry to interrupt, but I have something here that's extremely urgent. I need to speak with you immediately.'

She let herself in, a tube of fax paper clutched in one hand, her face taut and pale except for the brightness in her eyes. Mitch's instincts came up like radar. She had something concrete. He could feel it.

'Yes, come in, Agent O'Malley,' he said, moving out from behind his desk. 'You've met our mayor, Don Gillen?'

Megan offered the mayor a cursory nod, too aware of the cautious look Gillen passed from her to Mitch. The word about the two of them was apparently out around town, but at the moment she didn't give a damn.

'Please keep me up to date, Mitch,' Gillen said. 'I'll do what I can with the council.'

'Thanks, Don.'

Gillen slipped out, pulling the door shut behind him. Megan waited a full ten seconds, her heart pounding in her chest, her breath coming as hard as if she had sprinted down the hall from her office. Mitch stood in front of his desk with his hands on his hips, his expression inscrutable, careful.

'Last Friday I requested a report from the DMV on the van Paul Kirkwood used to own – the one that conveniently slipped his mind,' she began. 'Their computers were down. They didn't get back to me; turns out they lost my request. In the meantime, we requested a check on Olie

268

Swain's van – the results of which I am holding in my hand. Three guesses as to where he got it.'

'Not Paul,' Mitch said, nerves coiling like snakes in his belly.

Megan handed him the fax as if presenting him with a diploma. 'Give the man a cigar. Nailed it in one.'

Mitch uncurled the paper and stared at it. 'I can't believe he wouldn't remember selling his van to Olie.'

'There are a number of things I find difficult to believe about Kirkwood. He's at the volunteer center. I called and asked him to come over for a little chat. I thought you might like to be present.'

Paul sold his van to Olie, tried to conceal that fact even before Olie was officially considered a suspect. The implications were too ugly. Mitch didn't want to even consider it, let alone broach the subject with Paul. But he held the proof in his hand, as damning as a smoking gun.

'I think it would be better if I spoke with him,' he muttered.

'You thought that last week,' Megan said tightly. 'I don't remember it happening.'

His head snapped up and he stared at her, his eyes as hard and bright as amber beneath the ledge of his brows. 'Other things took precedence. Are you suggesting I deliberately avoided talking to him?'

'I'm not suggesting anything,' she said, poker-faced. 'All I'm saying is: It didn't happen. Now I've called him over here and I fully intend to make sure the questions get asked.'

The silence stretched between them as they stood there, squaring off, combatants in a turf war. Mitch felt as if she had taken her toe and drawn a line on the carpet between them. And he felt a vague sense of loss, whether it was smart or not.

He stepped across the line, knowing Megan never would. Neither would she back away. She held her ground defiantly, raising her chin, her gaze steady on his.

'Megan,' he said, lifting a hand to brush his knuckles against her cheek.

She turned her face away. 'Don't make this any harder than it has to be, Mitch,' she murmured. 'Please.'

'We don't have to be enemies.'

'We're not,' Megan insisted. She forced herself to take a step sideways. His tenderness was always her undoing. That had to stop if she was to salvage anything from this situation.

'Look,' she said on a sigh. 'I'm feeling cornered and put upon. I'm not blaming you for what happened. I'm just not being a good sport, that's all.'

'I'll talk to DePalma if you want, tell him nothing happened. It's none of their damn business, anyway.'

She smiled sadly. 'Thanks, but it won't make any difference. He isn't going to be interested in what did or didn't happen between us if they've decided I've become a public relations problem. If that happens, they'll call me in to headquarters and I'll be relieved of my field post, the official reason being I'm not making progress on the case, even though everyone will understand it was my lack of circumspection.'

'But you're a hell of a cop,' Mitch said, handing her the DMV fax. 'Circumspection never sent a crook to jail.'

Megan shrugged, trying not to let his compliment mean too much. 'Swap you,' she said, handing him the second tube of thermal paper.

'What's this?'

'The blood analysis from the van. It's not human. We struck out.'

'Thank God . . . I guess.'

'Yeah.'

Natalie buzzed through on the intercom. 'Chief, Paul Kirkwood is here to see you.'

Megan arched a brow. 'He must have misunderstood my request,' she said sardonically.

Mitch went around behind his desk and punched the button. 'Send him in, Natalie.'

Paul stormed into the office, ready to go off on a diatribe about 'that BCA bitch,' but he stopped dead in his tracks as his gaze landed on Megan O'Malley. She stood beside Mitch Holt's desk with her arms crossed over her chest. The look she wore was one he recognized from his childhood back in the old St Paul neighborhood – a touch of defiance, a hint of temper, a hefty dose of plain old toughness. Had they been kids, she might have been telling him she could kick his butt all the way down the block.

He drew himself up and passed his gaze on to Holt, who sat behind his desk with his shirtsleeves rolled up and his elbows on the blotter, relaxed, a little rumpled.

'I thought you were alone,' Paul said.

'Anything you have to say about the case, you can say in front of Agent O'Malley,' Mitch said. 'Take off your coat and have a seat, Paul.'

Ignoring the offer, Paul began to pace along the front of the desk. 'Yes, I hear the two of you are like this.' He held up crossed fingers. 'It's nice to know something is being accomplished with all your overtime.'

'I think you have some more important things to think about here besides idle gossip, Mr Kirkwood,' Megan said pointedly. 'Your failing memory, for instance.'

'My what?'

'Paul, have a seat,' Mitch suggested again, the buddy, the pal. 'We need to clear up a little something about that van you used to have.'

'That again?' He flopped his arms against the loose sides of his black wool topcoat. 'I don't believe this. You people manage to kill the one suspect we had –'

'Olie killed himself,' Mitch corrected him calmly.

'Or we'd be able to ask *him* these questions,' Megan added.

Paul came to an abrupt halt and stared at her. He looked a little thinner – his nose seemed sharper, his eyes set deeper – but instead of looking haggard, he seemed energized, as if he were drawing on the tension of the situation for adrenaline. She couldn't help but think of Hannah, who was looking more like a death camp prisoner every day.

'Just what is that supposed to mean?' he asked.

'Paul, why didn't you tell us you sold that van to Olie Swain?' Mitch asked in a tone that was almost matter-of-fact.

Incredulous, Paul jerked around to stare at him. 'I didn't! I said I don't remember who bought it, but it wasn't *him*. Christ, I think I'd remember if I sold it to *him*.'

'Funny,' Megan muttered, 'that's just what I said – "You think he'd remember selling it to Olie" –'

'I didn't!'

Mitch held the fax up and uncurled it like a scroll. 'That's not what the DMV says, Paul.'

'I don't give a shit what the DMV says! I did *not* sell that van to Olie Swain!' Unable to restrain his agitation, he resumed his pacing. 'And what would it matter if I had? That was what – four or five years ago –'

'September 1991,' Megan supplied helpfully.

'Of course it wouldn't matter,' Mitch said. 'What matters is that it appears you lied to us about it, Paul. *That* matters a lot.'

Paul slammed his fists down on the desktop, fury forcing a vein to bulge out in his neck. 'I did *not* lie to you! How dare you accuse *me*! My son is still missing –'

'And we're examining every lead, every single scrap of anything remotely resembling evidence, Paul,' Mitch said quietly. 'We're doing our jobs.'

'And what were you doing last night when your only suspect was slitting his wrists?' Paul snapped, his face red and twisted.

Mitch rose slowly, his expression stony. He came around the desk, clamped a hand on Paul's shoulder, and assisted him into the visitor's chair. 'Have a seat, Paul.'

He leaned back against the desk then, half sitting, the pose deceptively casual. 'Let's get a few things straight here, Paul. First of all, we're doing everything we can do to get Josh back. *No one* is exempt from scrutiny. Do you understand what I'm saying here, Paul? *No one*. That's the rule. That's the way these investigations are done. Absolutely no stone is left unturned. If that hurts your feelings, I'm sorry, but you have to understand that everything we do, we do for Josh.'

'We're not saying you're a suspect, Mr Kirkwood,' Megan interjected. 'We ran a routine trace on Olie Swain's vehicle. Believe me when I say I was not expecting to see your name as the last owner listed before Olie.'

'If you can set your emotions aside for a second here, Paul, imagine how this looks to us,' Mitch said. 'You claim you can't remember who bought your van, then it turns up in the hands of the man suspected of kidnapping your son. You'd better be glad I know you, Paul' – he leaned ahead to point a finger in Paul's face – 'because, I'm telling you, if I were just another cop, we would be having this conversation down the hall with a lawyer present.'

Paul shifted in his chair, his expression half scowl, half pout, like a petulant student trying to act tough in the principal's office. 'I didn't sell the van to Olie Swain.' His voice trembled slightly. 'The guy who bought it from me must have resold it without changing the title.'

Mitch sat back with a sigh and picked up the DMV fax. 'Do you remember what time of year it was when you sold it?'

'I don't know. Spring, I think. April or May.'

'Title was changed in September,' Mitch said, handing the document to Megan. She gave him a look that did not go unnoticed by Paul.

'Ask Hannah,' he said belligerently. 'Hannah remembers everything.'

'You wouldn't have any paperwork on the sale in your tax records?' she asked. 'You being an accountant and all . . .'

'Probably. I would have looked by now, but I've been busy with the search and, frankly, I couldn't – can't – see what bearing this has on anything.'

'Look it up,' Mitch suggested, the good guy again. 'It'll tie up the loose end.'

'Fine.' Paul crossed his legs and shifted his body so that his focal point was away from Mitch and Megan.

Wise to that ploy, Megan strolled behind him directly into his line of vision. 'Mr Kirkwood, I still have a couple of questions about the night Josh disappeared.'

'I was working,' Paul said wearily, rubbing his forehead.

'In the conference room at your office,' Megan finished. 'And you never checked your answering machine?'

'No,' he whispered as Josh's voice played inside his head – *Dad, can you come and get me from hockey? Mom's late and I wanna go home.* A tremor went through him. 'Not until . . . after . . .'

'After what?'

Dad, can you come and get me from hockey? Mom's late and I wanna go home.

He sniffed and ducked his head, shielding his eyes with his hand. 'The next day.'

'Do you still have the tape?'

Dad, can you come and get me from hockey? Mom's late and I wanna go home.

'A – no,' he lied. 'I . . . I couldn't keep it. I couldn't listen –'

Dad, can you come and get me from hockey? Mom's late and I wanna go home.

He shuddered. 'I just want him back,' he whispered through the tears. 'I just want him back.'

Megan blew out a long breath as Mitch sent her a warning look. 'I'm sorry to put you through this, Mr Kirkwood,' she said quietly. 'I don't enjoy it.'

Mitch offered Paul a box of Kleenex and a pat on the shoulder. 'I know it's hell, Paul. We wouldn't ask if we didn't have to.'

'Chief?' Natalie's voice came over the intercom. 'Noogie's on line one and I think you're going to want to hear what he has to say.'

He went around the desk again, picked up the receiver, and punched the blinking light. 'Noogie, what's up?'

'I'm at St Elysius, Chief. I think you better come out. I picked up a radio call to the sheriff's department. A woman out here on Ryan's Bay is reporting her dog found a kid's jacket. They think it might be Josh Kirkwood's.'

26

Ryan's Bay was the rather grandiose name for what was essentially a big wet spot in an area of sloughs west of Dinkytown, windswept and bleak in winter's grip. The land had been annexed into the Deer Lake municipality in the seventies, but there was no city sewer or water service and the residents of the Ryan's Bay area thought of themselves as being independent from the town, which explained why Ruth Cooper had called the sheriff's department when her Labrador came charging out of a stand of cattail stalks with a child's jacket in his mouth. Steiger himself was on the scene wearing a shearling coat with the collar turned up, a big fur trapper's hat warming his greasy head. He appeared to be the star attraction in what was already a media circus.

'So much for preserving the scene,' Megan muttered as Mitch pulled his Explorer in alongside the KSTP news van, blocking the van in.

Newspeople, civilians, sheriff's deputies, and loose dogs trampled the snow as they milled around. Mitch cut the engine and started to turn toward Paul in the back seat, but Paul was already out the door and hustling toward the center of the storm. Reporters turned and stepped back for him. Cameras swung in his direction. Mitch jumped out of the truck and sprinted after him, hoping in vain that he might be able to prevent the very scene into which Paul Kirkwood plunged himself.

Steiger was holding up the bright-colored ski jacket like a trophy. A strangled cry wrenching from his throat, Paul launched himself at the sheriff, grabbing the jacket and sending Steiger staggering backward. Paul fell to his knees in the trampled snow. Clutching the coat in both hands, he buried his face in it, sobbing.

'Oh my God, Josh! Josh! Oh God! No!'

Mitch shoved his way through the ranks of press that had closed in, his temper spiking. As he broke into the center of the circle, he turned on them, shouting, 'Get out of here!' He batted down the lens of a video camera zooming in on Paul. 'Jesus, don't you people have any compassion at all? Get out of here!'

Behind him he could hear the awful sound of Paul Kirkwood crying.

274

There was nothing in the human experience with which to compare a parent's grief. It was a dismemberment of a living soul, so excruciating it went beyond all known adjectives. That wasn't a thing for people to witness on the six o'clock news.

Father McCoy was on one knee beside Paul, a hand on Paul's shoulder, his head bent as he tried to keep his words of comfort from being swept away by the cutting wind. Steiger stood six feet in front of them, looking disgruntled and at a loss, spiritual matters beyond him.

Mitch flashed the sheriff a twisted smile. 'Thanks for alerting my office, Russ.'

Steiger sniffed and spit a glob of mucus in the snow.

'Move it back, people!' Megan called, flashing her ID as Noogie and two other officers herded the crowd back up onto Old Cedar Road. 'You're on a possible crime scene! We've got to ask you to move back!'

'Leave me alone!' Paul shouted suddenly. He shoved at Father Tom as he pushed himself to his feet, sending the priest sprawling in the snow. 'I don't want anything from you! Get the hell away from me!'

'Hey, Paul.' Mitch took hold of his arm and steered him toward the sloughs, away from the watchful eyes of the press. 'Come on. We need to take a minute and think about what this means.'

'He's dead,' Paul said thickly. He held the jacket out in front of him, staring at it as if his son had just vanished from inside of it. 'He's dead. He's dead —'

Mitch pushed the coat down. 'We don't know that. We've got his jacket, not him. This jacket is described on every poster and report about Josh. The kidnapper would have been smart to dump it right off the bat.'

Beyond reason, Paul had started to cry again, a soft, eerie keening. 'He's dead. He's dead. He's dead.'

'Houston!' Mitch called, motioning one of his officers over from the crowd-control detail.

The burly, bearded cop shambled over, snow screeching beneath his heavy-duty Arctic boots. The moisture from his breath had frozen white in his thick facial hair. What was visible of his face was red from the cold and the wind.

'I need you to take Mr Kirkwood home,' Mitch said. 'Explain what happened to Dr Garrison and stay with them until I get there.'

'You bet.' Houston draped a beefy arm across Paul's shoulders. 'Come on, Mr Kirkwood. Let's get you home. It's too darn cold to stand around out here.'

Before they could take a step, Mitch took hold of Josh's jacket and tried to extricate it gently from Paul's grip. 'Come on, Paul,' he said quietly. 'This is evidence now. We need to send it up to the crime lab.'

Reluctantly, Paul let go. Hands over his face, he walked away with Houston.

'He's in a lot of pain,' Father Tom said, dusting the snow off the seat of his parka.

'How about you, Father?' Megan asked. 'Are you all right?'

His glasses were askew. He straightened them and tugged down on the earflaps of his hunting cap. 'I'm all right. I should have known better. Paul isn't one of my bigger fans. But when Noogie came into St E's to use the phone and told us what was going on, I felt it was my duty to be here.'

'Us?' Mitch said, looking off toward the church. It was perhaps a quarter mile away to the southeast, its spires thrusting up above the naked trees.

'Albert and I were going over some church accounts,' the priest said. 'If you're concerned about discretion, I think the cat's already out of the bag.'

Mitch said nothing. He took a good long look at the area. The 'bay' itself was frozen and adrift with snow that piled up against the thick stands of skeletal blond cattail stalks. A winter-white desert with dunes that shifted beneath the frigid breath of the wind. It had to be a haven for mosquitoes in the warmer months, but people had still chosen to build homes around the edge of it. The half-dozen houses that ringed the northwest side of the bay ranged from a winterized cottage to a pricey custom cedar shake job with elaborate decks that would have looked at home on Nantucket. They sat back from the shore on large, well-spaced lots of three to five acres that were thick with evergreen and hardwood trees.

Beyond them to the west, beyond the rolling open farmland and copses of trees, the horizon was milky with airborne snow. The sky was awash with brilliant paintbox shades of fuchsia and tangerine as the sun began its descent. There were no houses on the southeast shore, only a huge thicket of scrubby brush and thin young trees like a stand of giant toothpicks. The nearest homes in that direction ran south on the block behind St Elysius, small, neat boxes with ribbons of smoke curling up from their chimneys.

Mitch completed the circle, drawing his gaze up to Old Cedar Road, lined with cars and vans and people stamping their feet to keep the feeling in them. Albert Fletcher stood at the end of the line, a tall figure in a somber black coat, a black hood drawn tight around his thin face.

'Did the two of you ride over with Noogie?' Mitch asked.

'I did.' Father Tom raised his brows as he, too, spotted the deacon. 'Albert must have come on his own. I didn't think he was interested in coming out. He told me he wasn't feeling well, thought he had a cold coming on. . . .'

'Apparently he's feeling better,' Megan said, hunching her back against a gust of wind.

'Hmm . . . I'd better get going,' the priest said. 'I'm sure Paul won't be happy to see me, but I think Hannah is going to need a shoulder to cry on.'

He trudged off across the snow and climbed the bank to where Albert Fletcher was standing. The two men left together.

Mitch turned his attention to the small jacket he held and the name that was written inside the collar with indelible laundry marker. He held it out for Megan's inspection and she took it from him, sighing heavily. 'This doesn't leave any room for doubt, does it?'

Steiger came over with a woman who held a big black Lab on a leash. The dog danced along beside her, barely able to contain his excitement. 'Mitch, this is Ruth Cooper. Her dog found the jacket.'

Mitch nodded. 'Mrs Cooper.'

Megan shot the sheriff a look, then introduced herself. 'Mrs Cooper, I'm Agent O'Malley with the BCA.'

'Oh, yes. How do you do? Caleb, sit,' the woman said, tugging on the leash. Caleb had the lean, muscular body of a young dog, and he wiggled and shivered from his head to the tip of his tail as he cast a hopeful look up at his mistress.

Beneath her thick cream knit stocking cap and inside a puffy cream and mauve ski jacket, Ruth Cooper was a small, rounded woman in her sixties. Her pert nose was showing the effects of too much time out in the extreme cold by turning the shade of red worn by deer hunters in the fall. She shifted her weight back and forth from one snowmobile boot to the other as she told her story.

'I was walking with Caleb,' she began, and the dog wagged his tail enthusiastically at the sound of his name. 'He can go off his leash, but we don't trust him not to run off on an adventure, so either Stan or me goes out with him – even in this weather. And Stan, he can't go out in this now, you know; he's got that awful flu bug going around. I told him to get the shot this fall, but he's so stubborn. Anyway, we were walking around the bay, and Caleb, he likes to go out into the reeds and scare up birds, so off he goes, and he comes running back with this.' She grabbed one sleeve of Josh's coat and held it up. 'I knew right away. I just knew. That poor little tyke.'

'Mrs Cooper,' Mitch said. 'You walk Caleb out here every day?'

'Oh, yes. He needs to get out and Stan and me don't care for kennels – not with a big dog like Caleb. We're out here every day. That's our place over there – the tan Cape Cod house. Would you like to come in for coffee? It's awfully cold out here.'

'Maybe in a few minutes, Mrs Cooper,' Mitch said. 'I'm sorry to keep you out in the cold like this, but we'll need to see exactly where Caleb dug this up.'

Ruth and Caleb led the way with Steiger right beside them.

Noogie walked beside Mitch, talking in a low voice. 'Chief, I was on the search team out here Friday. We were all over this ground and no one found so much as a gum wrapper. We had a dog from Search and Rescue, too. That jacket wasn't out here.'

Mitch frowned. 'When was the last time you saw Caleb go out into this general area, Mrs Cooper?'

'We were in this same spot yesterday afternoon.' She stopped along the edge of the slough and pointed.

'Did you see anyone here between then and this afternoon?' Megan asked, idly unzipping a pocket on the jacket to check the contents – a wad of tissue, a Bubble Yum wrapper.

'I see people out here from time to time. We got this nice path, you know, for snowmobiles or walkers or cross-country skiing. Some of these fitness people are just crazy. They'll go out in all weather for their jogging or whatever,' she said. 'There was a man out here early this morning. I was in my kitchen heating up water for Stan's Theraflu, and I looked out and saw him walking on the path.'

'Did you get a good look at him?' Mitch asked.

'He came right up to the house, but he was all bundled up, you know,' she said. 'He'd lost his dog. Wanted to know had I seen him. A big hairy thing – the dog, not the man. I told him no and he asked would I keep an eye out. I said sure. You know, I just love dogs. I'd sure look out for one lost in this awful cold.' Caleb wagged his tail and bowed at her feet.

'My men searched this area already,' Steiger said to Mitch. He had his hands rammed into his coat pockets and looked as stiff as a carved totem pole from the cold. 'There's nothing else here to see. I say we take Ruth up on that coffee.'

'I just want to have a quick look,' Mitch said, and started down the bank.

'His son's dog, he said,' Ruth went on. 'The dog's name was something kind of old. Grimsby? Gatsby? Gizmo. That was it. Gizmo.'

A cold blade of dread went through Mitch. He froze halfway down the bank. Gizmo. In his mind's eye he could see the drawing from Josh's notebook – a boy and his dog. A hairy mutt named Gizmo.

'Mitch.'

Megan's tone turned his head in her direction. He looked up at her. Her eyes were wide, her face as colorless as the snow. In her gloved hand she held a strip of paper. The wind made it flutter like a ribbon.

He charged up the bank and caught the end of it between his fingers. He realized he hadn't known what cold was until he read the words and his blood ran like ice water in his veins.

> *my specter around me night and day*
> *like a wild beast guards my way*
> *my emanation far within*
> *weeps incessantly for my SIN*

4:55 p.m. -27° windchill factor: -45°

What the hell does it mean?' Steiger stalked around the table, his hands on his lean hips.

Megan sat on the table with her feet on the seat of a chair and her elbows on her knees. This was the conference room where she had first seen Mitch, dancing in long red underwear, one week ago to the day. He leaned back against the wall directly in front of her now, his arms crossed, his expression hard and worn. His face was carved with lines of strain and shadowed with fatigue, lean and tough.

The room had changed as well. They called it the war room now. A map of Park County and one of the state of Minnesota covered the cork bulletin board, red pins poked into them marking search territories. The long wall held a time line of the investigation on a sheet of white paper three feet wide and twelve feet long. Everything that had happened since Josh's last sighting was noted on the time line, scribbled tributaries branching out from the main red artery, notes in red ink and blue ink and black ink. On the white message board at the end of the room, Mitch had added the verse from the latest note in his bold, slanted handwriting.

This was where they came to brainstorm. Away from the noise and activity of the command post. The war room had no phone, no volunteers underfoot, no press peering in. In this room they could sit and stare at the latest of the messages and listen to the clock tick as they struggled to decipher the meaning. All they knew with certainty was that the quote was from William Blake's 'My Specter'.

'He could be saying he has a split personality,' Megan offered, earning a derisive snort from the sheriff. 'Or an accomplice.'

'Olie Swain,' he grunted. 'He was guilty as sin. You saw those pictures he had –'

'They were old,' Mitch argued. 'He had a clean record here –'

The sheriff rolled his eyes as they crossed paths in their pacing. 'Once a chicken hawk, always a chicken hawk. You think he lived here all that time without putting it to some kid?'

'We never had a report –'

'Big deal. Shit like that goes on and nobody hears about it. Kids are greedy. Olie offers some kid ten bucks for a little touchy-feely, maybe the kid thinks it's no big deal – he takes the cash and keeps his mouth shut. Olie did it.'

'Then swore in his life's blood it wasn't him,' Megan pointed out, more to needle Steiger than because she believed it.

He scowled at her. 'You fell for that?' He shook his head, malicious glee tightening the corners of his mouth. 'Well, I guess we all know how you made detective.'

'What the hell is that supposed to mean?' Mitch growled, straightening away from the wall.

'It means he's a jerk,' Megan said smoothly. She steered the conversation back on track before Steiger could offer a rebuttal. 'He could be saying he feels guilty for what he's done, but I don't believe it. He hasn't done anything remorseful; all he's done is taunt us. I think he's standing back, laughing his head off, while we run around like the Keystone Kops.'

'Goddamn head games,' Mitch muttered. Head games from a mind as twisted as a corkscrew. Warped enough to plant a piece of evidence, then calmly walk up to a house and strike up a conversation with the woman inside, casually dropping clues into the conversation, then walking away.

'I agree. We know Olie didn't have anything to do with the call made Saturday from St Peter. He didn't plant the notebook. He couldn't have planted the jacket. That call last night didn't come from Olie, either.'

'What call?' Steiger demanded.

Megan ignored him. 'It might have been a crank, but it fits too well.'

The sheriff stepped into her line of vision, a scowl pulling his features into a sour mask. 'What call?'

'I got a call last night,' Mitch said, pointing to the message board. 'He just said the same thing over and over – "blind and naked ignorance". I wrote it off as a crank.'

'Blind and naked?' Steiger sniffed. 'Maybe someone was looking in your windows.'

'And maybe you should keep your mind on the case and your comments to yourself, Russ.'

Megan slipped down off the table as her beeper went off. Unclipping the pager from her belt, she hit the display button and frowned. 'I have to make a call,' she mumbled, meeting Mitch's eyes with her best poker face. 'Chief, are you about ready to go have that chat with the Kirkwoods?'

Mitch nodded. He didn't like the look of strain on her face. The call would be to DePalma. As much as he kept telling himself she was blowing things out of proportion, he still couldn't help but tense. He didn't want her off the case. He didn't want her punished for something he had been as much a part of as she – more, if you got right down to it. Megan had her rule against cops; he was the one who had coerced her into breaking it.

'Five minutes,' he said. 'I'll stop by your office.'

He watched her slip out the door, forgetting Steiger's presence for a moment. A moment was all the sheriff allowed.

'So, how is she?' Steiger asked, swaggering across the room, his arms crossed over his chest, a smirk twisting his thin lips. 'She doesn't look like she'd be much of a fuck, but then, maybe she can do better things with that mouth than shoot it off.'

Mitch's response was pure reaction. He swung a hard right that caught Steiger square in the nose. The resounding *crack!* of breaking bone went through the room like a gunshot. Steiger's head snapped around and he went down on one knee, blood gushing through the hands he pressed to his face.

'Jethus! Chou bloke my nothe!' he exclaimed. The blood ran thick and red between his fingers, dripping in rivulets down the backs of his hands and falling in droplets to stain the carpet.

Shaking his hand to relieve the stinging, Mitch leaned down over him, his eyes glittering and feral. 'You got by easy, Russ,' he snarled. 'That was for siccing Paige Price on Megan, leaking information, and being a son of a bitch in general. One lousy broken nose for all of that? Hell, you weren't that good-looking to begin with.

'But let me give you a little advance warning here, Russ,' he continued, lifting a finger to emphasize his point. 'If I turn on the ten o'clock news tonight and hear Paige reciting William Blake, I'm going to come out to that tin can you live in, stick a gun up your ass, and blow your brains out. Do you understand what I'm saying here, Russ?'

'Fluck chou,' Steiger blubbered, fumbling in his hip pocket for a handkerchief.

'Well said, Sheriff,' Mitch drawled as he straightened and started for the door. 'A master of articulation, as usual. Too bad you're not half as good a cop.'

She twisted the facts,' Megan said into the receiver. Elbows on her blotter, she leaned her forehead heavily against one hand. 'What am I saying? She didn't even *have* the facts! Bruce –'

'Don't call me Bruce when I'm angry with you,' DePalma snapped.

'Yes, sir,' she said on a sigh. She felt as if some unseen hands were stabbing darning needles into her eyes. 'She fabricated that story out of thin air –'

'You weren't at Chief Holt's house at three in the morning?'

'There is a very simple, innocent explanation – which, I might add, Paige Price did not bother to try to get from me before jumping me at the press conference.'

'So you're saying this is all a misunderstanding that has been blown out of proportion?'

'Yes.'

'That's become a recurring theme in your life, Agent O'Malley.' The tone was sharp enough to make her wince. 'We've already had this discussion about the gender issue. The last thing this bureau needs is to be dragged into a sex scandal.'

'Yes, sir.'

'Do you have any idea the kind of feeding frenzy that could go on here? We finally give a woman a field post and the first thing she does is seduce the chief of police?'

She nearly came out of her chair. 'I did *not* seduce –'

'I'm not saying you did, but that doesn't mean the press will be as kind. What *did* go on?'

Megan swallowed hard and crossed her fingers. 'Chief Holt and I were discussing the case over coffee –'

'In the dark?'

'He had a fire going and the television was on. The two combined provided more than adequate light.'

'Go on.'

'As you know, we've been putting in hellish hours on this case. We were both exhausted. We simply fell asleep.'

During the lengthy silence that ensued, Megan felt beads of sweat pop out on her forehead like bullets. She wasn't a liar by nature and she detested the need for it now. What she did after hours should have been nobody's business. Had she been a man, she doubted anyone would have cared enough to follow her around. Had she been a man, she thought sourly, she probably would have been *expected* to have seduced someone by now.

Seduced. The word left a bad taste in her mouth. It sounded so cheap. Regardless of what became of her relationship with Mitch, she didn't want to think of what they had shared in those terms.

'My sixteen-year-old comes up with better stories than that,' DePalma said at last.

'It's the truth.' *Part of it, anyway.*

DePalma heaved a sigh that sounded like gale-force winds over the telephone. 'Megan, I like you. You're a good cop. I want this job to work for you, but you're putting the bureau in an untenable position. We name you our first woman in the field and we get accused of tokenism. Every time you turn around you stick your foot in something new – fighting with Kirkwood, sleeping with Holt –'

'I *told you* –'

'Save your breath. It doesn't matter if you did or you didn't. People will believe what they want.'

'Including you.'

'And now your only suspect turns up dead in jail –'

'Are you accusing me of murdering him, too?'

'It looks bad.'

'God forbid crime should be anything but tidy –'

'That kind of smart remark is exactly what gets you in trouble, Megan. You've got to learn to curb that Irish tongue of yours before it gets you fired.'

Which meant she wasn't fired yet. She would have breathed a sigh of relief, but she knew damn well she was still on a high wire juggling bowling balls. One more misstep and it was all over.

'I don't want it to come to that, Megan. God knows what kind of mess we'll have on our hands if we have to pull you in. But we've got a mess already, so don't think that will stop it from happening.'

'No, sir.'

'Where are you with the case?'

Down a rabbit hole with a madman. She kept that thought to herself and explained without embellishment or false hope where they stood. In police work it didn't pay to promise more than you could deliver.

DePalma asked questions at intervals.

'Can this Cooper woman identify the man who came to her house?'

'She's not sure. He was bundled up pretty well against the cold. I've got her with the composite artist right now.'

'Was there blood on the jacket?'

'Not that I could see. It's gone to the lab.'

'What do you think about the note? Do you think he's saying he killed the boy?'

'I don't know.'

'Have you considered the possibility that Swain's accomplice might have been someone from his past in Washington?'

'According to everything we've got on him,' Megan said, 'he was a loner there as well. The closest thing he had to a friend was the cousin whose identity he was carrying around, and the nicest thing he has to say is that Olie was a freak. Of course, I'd be a little cranky too if my cousin stole my driver's license and assumed my identity in another state, then committed a heinous crime that garnered national attention.'

DePalma ignored her sarcasm. 'Maybe you need some help,' he suggested.

Megan felt the fine hair on the back of her neck rise. 'What do you mean?'

'You're not getting anywhere. Maybe you need someone to come in with a fresh perspective.'

'I can handle the case, Bruce,' she said tightly.

'Of course you can. I just believe that when things are at a standstill, a person coming in fresh can shake something loose.'

Like me, Megan thought sourly. The game plan was painfully clear. DePalma would send out another agent to quietly usurp her authority, and when the reins had changed hands, she would be called back quietly to headquarters. No muss, no fuss, all neat and tidy, just the way the brass liked things.

'I think it would be a mistake.' She struggled to hang on to some semblance of cool. 'Anyone coming in cold would have to wade through all the statements, reinterview witnesses, get to know the family – and frankly, they don't need any more upheaval in their lives.'

'I'll bear that in mind. In the meantime, Megan, you need to make something good happen. Do you understand what I'm saying?'

'Perfectly.'

They said their goodbyes and she hung up the phone, making a nasty face at it. 'And don't call me Megan when I'm angry with you,' she jeered.

'Yes, ma'am,' Mitch replied as he stuck his head in the door.

Megan looked up at him, too weary and too worried to even try to smile. 'I'm not angry with you.'

He ambled into her office with his coat thrown over his shoulder.

'What'd you do to your hand?'

A frown curved his mouth as he glanced at the swollen knuckles. 'I felt a need to hit something.'

283

'Like what – a brick wall?'

'Steiger's face.'

She raised her brows in amazement. 'Damn, Chief, I would have paid money to see that.'

He shrugged. 'Better not to have witnesses,' he said. 'Steiger's been leaking information to Paige Price. I expressed my displeasure.'

The rage of injustice only made her temples pound harder. 'She's screwing Steiger for information and she has the gall to stand up at a press conference and point a finger at me. I wouldn't mind hitting something myself.'

'Lay a finger on her and she'll have more than your job,' Mitch pointed out, running a finger along the ridge of her brass nameplate. He picked it up and read the inscription on the back: TAKE NO SHIT, MAKE NO EXCUSES. 'What did DePalma have to say?'

'What did he say or what did he mean? Officially, they won't comment on hearsay about an agent. They will express their full confidence in me in the most lukewarm terms they can think of. Officially, they may send in another agent "to assist me with the investigation". If that happens, he'll end up with my job and I'll end up at a desk in the bowels of headquarters doing paperwork on petty fraud schemes.'

Scowling, Mitch stalked her around the end of the desk as she turned for the coat rack. 'I wish you'd let me talk to him.'

She shook her head. 'I don't want you fighting my battles for me.'

'It's called supporting a friend, Megan.'

She turned and tipped her head back to meet his gaze. He was standing too close again, trying to intimidate her, calling her attention to the fact that he was bigger and stronger and capable of dominating her – or protecting her. A part of her found the idea tempting, but she wouldn't give in to that part.

'It's called giving false information, which I already did,' she said. 'I won't have you lie on my account, and that's that.'

Her answer brooked no disagreement. Mitch said nothing as he watched her shrug into her monstrous down-filled coat. So damned stubborn. So damned independent. He wanted her to lean on him, he realized with no small amount of wonder. He wanted to help her. He wanted to defend her honor. Old-fashioned notions, and she was no old-fashioned woman. Notions that hinted at commitment – something they both claimed not to want.

'We'll work it out,' he murmured, not certain what aspect of this tangled mess he meant.

What? Megan wanted to ask. The job situation? Their personal situation? She chose the former, knowing that was where their focus needed to be, knowing that damn clock would not stop ticking.

'That means one thing,' she said, her expression grim. 'We find Josh.'

27

Hannah stood at the window, staring out at the lake. The final rays of sunlight streaked the far horizon like angry red lines of infection radiating from a wound. Funny how such a hot color was an indication of such a cold sky. As she stood there, she could feel the cold seeping in through the glass, seeping into her body. She wished it would numb her, but it didn't; it simply made her shiver.

Across the lake, lights winked on. The helicopters had been called in again. She could see one in the distance, hanging over Dinkytown like a vulture. In her memory she recalled the thumping of the rotors and how she had lain awake listening to their eerie passing back and forth over the town. Beyond Dinkytown, out toward the flaming horizon, lay Ryan's Bay. On Ryan's Bay a dog had discovered Josh's jacket, discarded like a piece of litter.

She could see the jacket in her mind's eye – bright blue with splashes of green and yellow. She knew the size and the brand name. She knew the pockets where he stashed small treasures and Kleenex and mittens. She knew the smell of it and the feel of it, and all those memories hovered in her mind, intangible and untouchable. Only the second sign of Josh to surface in a week, and she had not been allowed to see it or touch it. The jacket had been whisked off to St Paul to be studied and analyzed.

'I would have liked to just hold it,' she said quietly. She tried to imagine it in her hands, raising it to her face, brushing it against her cheek.

'I'm sorry, Hannah,' Megan said gently. 'We felt it was essential to get it to the lab as soon as possible.'

'Of course. I understand,' she murmured. But she didn't, not outside that logical, practical square of brain that answered by rote.

'You'll get fingerprints off it?' Paul said. He sat by the fire-place in faded black sweatpants and a heavy gray sweatshirt with a University of Minnesota logo. His hair was still damp from the shower he had taken to warm himself. Lily sat on his lap, trying unsuccessfully to interest him in her stuffed Barney.

Megan and Mitch exchanged a look.

'No,' Mitch said. 'It's virtually impossible for nylon to hold finger-prints.'

'What then?'

'Do you really want to make them say it?' Hannah said sharply. 'What do you think they'll be looking for, Paul? Blood. Blood and semen and any other grisly leftover from whatever this animal has done to Josh. Isn't that right, Agent O'Malley?'

Megan said nothing. The question was rhetorical. Hannah neither needed nor wanted an answer. She stood with her back to the window, defiance and anger a thin mask over the raw terror that consumed her.

'The woman whose dog found the jacket may have seen the man who planted it,' Mitch said. 'In fact, she may have had a conversation with him.'

'May have?' Hannah said, puzzled.

Mitch told them the story of Ruth Cooper and the man who had come to her door after she'd seen him through her kitchen window. When he came to the part about the dog's name. Hannah turned ashen and took hold of the wing chair for support.

Paul came to attention. He rose slowly, setting Lily down on the floor. She toddled over to Mitch and offered him her dinosaur. Father Tom rose from the couch and scooped her up, tickling her into giggles as he carried her to the bedroom upstairs.

'So, she can identify this man,' Paul said.

'She's working with a composite artist,' Megan explained. 'It's not as easy as we'd like it to be. The man was bundled up to be out in the weather. But she thinks she might be able to pick him out if she sees him again.'

'Might? Maybe?' Pulling a poker from the stand of brass tools, Paul turned his attention to the fire, stabbing at the glowing logs, sending a shower of sparks up the chimney.

'It's better than nothing.'

'It *is* nothing!' He wheeled around, poker in hand, his lean face twisted with bitter rage. 'You've got nothing! My son is lying dead someplace and you've got nothing! You can't even manage to keep the one suspect you had alive!'

Hannah glared at him. 'Stop it!'

He paid no attention to her, his anger directed for the moment at Mitch and Megan. 'You're too busy fucking each other to worry about my son –'

'Paul, for God's sake!'

'What's the matter, Hannah?' he demanded, rounding on her, his fingers tightening on the grip of the poker. 'Did I offend your sensibilities?'

'You offended everyone.'

'I don't care. They screwed up and my son has to pay the price —'

'He's my son, too —'

'Really? Is that why you left him on the street to be kidnapped and murdered?' he shouted, flinging the poker sideways. It hit the wall with a resounding crack and fell to the floor.

Hannah could barely draw the breath to respond. He could have run the poker through her and not hurt her as badly. 'You bastard!' she said, her voice a trembling whisper.

'Paul!' Mitch barked, clamping a hand down on his shoulder, his anger making the grip punishing. 'Let's go into your study,' he said through his teeth.

Grimacing, Paul twisted away from him. 'So you can lecture me again on how I should give my wife my support?' he sneered. 'I don't think so. I'm not interested in anything you have to say.'

'Tough.' Mitch grabbed him again and steered him off in the direction of his office.

Hannah didn't watch them go. Struggling to keep hold of her control, she crossed the room, picked up the fireplace poker, and put it back in its stand. Her hands were shaking so badly, she couldn't remember them ever having been steady enough to hold a scalpel.

'Well,' she said, wiping her palms on her jeans, 'that was ugly.'

'Hannah —' Megan started to say.

'The worst part of it is, it's true. It's my fault.'

'No. You were late. That shouldn't have cost you Josh.'

'But it did.'

'Because of the man who chose to take him. You had no control over his decision.'

'No,' she murmured. 'And now I have control of nothing. Because of that one moment in time, my life is flying apart. If I had made it out of the hospital before Kathleen rounded that corner to call me back in, Josh would be here. I would be picking him up from hockey today. Josh would be complaining about having to go to religion class at seven.

'One moment. A handful of seconds. A heartbeat.' Staring at the fire, she snapped her fingers. 'That much time and that car accident would never have happened. I wouldn't have been called back into the ER, and Josh wouldn't have been left all alone, and we wouldn't be standing here now, feeling awkward because my husband blames me . . .'

She let the thoughts trail off. There was no going back in time, only forward into uncertainty. Drained, she sank down into a chair and curled her legs beneath her. The muffled sound of angry voices came from behind the closed door of Paul's study.

Hannah picked at a dried scab of blue paint on the knee of her jeans. 'I'd like to go back and find that moment when Paul changed, too,' she whispered. 'He used to be so different. We used to be so happy.'

Megan didn't know how to respond. She had never been much for

287

sharing confidences with other women. Her lack of skill with relationships gave her no expertise to draw upon for sage wisdom. She turned to the one thing she knew. 'When did you start to notice a change in him?'

'Oh, I don't know.' Hannah shrugged. 'It was so subtle. In little ways, years ago, I suppose. A year or so after we moved here.'

After she had begun to establish herself at the hospital and in the community. Moving here had been Paul's idea, and she often wondered what he had imagined in his heart of hearts. She wondered if he had seen himself as becoming the fixture in the community she had become, becoming someone well known and well liked and well respected. In their early days together he had confided he wanted to be somebody, somebody other than the bookworm son of a blue-collar family. Had he thought he would become someone different here, someone outgoing and gregarious, when he didn't have those qualities in him? She hated to think it was jealousy that had driven this wedge between them and poisoned the love they had shared. It seemed such a pointless emotion, nothing that belonged between people who had pledged to respect and support each other.

'And he's been withdrawing more recently?' Megan asked.

'He resents the time I spend at the hospital since I was promoted to head of the ER.'

'What about his schedule? He was working that night.'

'It's nearly tax season. He'll be putting in a lot of nights.'

'Does he normally ignore his answering machine when you call him at the office at night?'

Hannah sat up a little straighter, her eyes narrowing, something in her chest tightening. 'Why are you asking me these questions?'

Megan gave her what she hoped was a convincing sheepish look. 'I'm a cop; it's what I do best.'

'You can't possibly think Paul had something to do with this.'

'No, no, of course not. It's just routine,' Megan lied. 'We need to know where everyone was – you know, before the lawyers get ahold of the case. They're fanatics for detail. Mother Teresa would need an alibi if she were here. When we catch this guy, his lawyer will probably try to pin it on someone else. He'll try to prove his client was somewhere else at six o'clock this morning. If he's sleazy enough, he'll ask where you were at six o'clock this morning, and where Paul was.'

Hannah blinked at her, her face carefully blank. 'I don't know where Paul was. He was gone when I woke up. He said he went out on his own, just driving around town, looking . . . . I'm sure that's what he did,' she said, sounding as if she were trying to convince herself as much as Megan.

'I'm sure you're right,' Megan agreed. She was filing everything about this scene in her memory – the facts, Hannah's tone of voice, her expression, the tension that hovered around her like static electricity. 'I didn't mean to imply otherwise. I just want you to understand how this works, why we have to ask some of these questions. What I really wanted to ask was if any names had come to you – people who might have a grudge against you or Paul. A dissatisfied patient, a disgruntled client, that sort of person.'

'You've already interviewed everyone we know,' Hannah said. 'I honestly can't think of any patients who would have felt driven to such horrible lengths. Most of what we see in a small hospital like ours are cases that are either easily curable or instantly fatal. Most critical cases – accident victims and so on – are flown directly to HCMC. Patients with serious illnesses are referred to larger hospitals as well.'

'But you must lose a few here.'

'A few.' Her mouth curved in sad memory. 'I remember when I worked in the Cities we used to call little rural hospitals like Deer Lake tag 'em and bag 'em joints. We do the best we can, but we don't have the equipment or the staff of a large hospital. People here understand that.'

'Maybe,' Megan murmured, making a mental note to stop by Deer Lake Community Hospital to feel out the staff in the ER herself.

'As far as Paul's clients go, there are a few who squawk every year about what they have to pay in taxes, but that's hardly his fault.'

'No big catastrophic audits; people sent to prison, that kind of thing?'

'No.' Hannah pushed herself up out of the chair, the nervous restlessness never allowing her more than a few minutes of stillness, regardless of fatigue. 'I'm going to make some tea. Would you like some? It's so cold –'

And Josh was out there somewhere without his coat.

Outside the big picture window, night had fallen, cold and black as an anvil.

'Do you think he's alive?' she whispered, staring out at the darkness into which Josh had disappeared eight long days before.

Megan rose to stand beside her. A little over a week ago everyone in town would have said Hannah had it all – the career, the family, the house on the lake. Half the town had looked on her as an icon of modern womanhood. Now she was just a woman, shattered and vulnerable, clinging to a thread of hope as thin as a hair.

'He's alive until someone proves to me he isn't,' Megan said. 'That's what I believe. That's what you need to believe, too.'

The door to Paul's office swung open. He stormed out and left the house through the door that led to the garage. Mitch emerged from the study, his face grim and drawn with lines of fatigue.

'I don't know how to get through to him,' he muttered as he walked into the family room.

'Neither do I,' Hannah confessed. 'Should we start a support group?'

Mitch mustered half a smile for her stab at humor. He took her hands in his and gave them a squeeze. Her fingers were as cold as death. 'I'm sorry, Hannah. I'm so sorry for all of this. I wish there were something more I could do.'

'I know you guys are doing all you can. It's not your fault.'

'It's not yours, either.' He pulled her into his arms and gave her a hug. 'Hang in there, honey.'

Hannah walked them to the door and saw them out into the frigid night. On her way back through the family room she stopped for a moment and listened to the silence. Their 'watcher,' as she referred to the agent assigned to the house, had gone for dinner when Mitch and Megan had arrived, and had yet to return. She had asked for and received a reprieve from the tag team companions sent from the neighborhood and the far-flung reaches of the missing children's organization. The house was quiet, calm, the tension gone.

She wondered where Paul was, wondered how long she would have until he returned and the hostilities resumed. She wondered how long the rift between them would take to heal. A week, a month, a year. She wondered if they would have Josh back before it happened. She wondered if she really wanted it to heal.

In her mind she saw his jacket lying tangled in the reeds at Ryan's Bay.

As the fear and dread and guilt began another cycle inside her, she went up the stairs and down the hall to Lily's room. Lily would give her comfort and love, unconditional, non-judgmental, no questions asked.

The sound of a low, soft voice inside the room brought Hannah up short in the hall. The door was ajar, soft light spilling out onto the carpet like a moonbeam. She peered in through the crack and saw Father Tom sitting in the old white wicker rocking chair, Lily on his lap, his arms looped around her to hold the storybook he was reading.

Any stranger would have imagined they were father and daughter. Tom in his sweatshirt and rumpled corduroy trousers, the lamplight striking a starburst off the gold frames of his glasses. Lily in a purple fleece sleeper, her cheeks pink, her big eyes heavy-lidded; drowsy and content to listen to the adventures of Winnie-the-Pooh and his pals.

Something stirred inside Hannah, something she didn't dare name, something that came with an aftertaste of disappointment and shame.

She slipped into the room before the feeling could drive her back. Tom was a friend and she needed a friend, that was all there was to it – no complications, nothing to engender regret. He finished the story and closed the book, and both he and Lily looked up at her expectantly.

'Hi, Mama,' Lily said sweetly, tilting her head and waving.

'Hi, Lily-bug. Everyone's gone.' She bent down to take her daughter into her arms. Lily snuggled into her mother's embrace, laying her head on Hannah's shoulder.

'Paul, too?' Tom said, raising his brows. He stood up and made a halfhearted attempt to brush the wrinkles out of his pants.

'I don't know where he went.' Hannah turned away, not wanting to see the sympathy in his eyes, tired of people feeling sorry for her.

'I heard the fight,' he said softly. 'I'm sure he didn't mean it. He's just lashing out. Of course, that doesn't make it hurt any less, I know –'

She shook her head. 'It doesn't matter.'

'It *does*,' Tom insisted. 'He should be able to see this isn't your fault, or if not that, forgive you at least.'

'Why should Paul forgive me when I can't forgive myself?'

'Hannah . . .'

'It's true,' she said, restlessly walking around the cozy bedroom with its soft pink walls and Beatrix Potter details. 'I've relived that night a thousand times. If only I'd done this. If only I hadn't done that. It always comes down to the same thing: I'm Josh's mother. He relied on me and I let him down. I don't know if anyone should pardon me from that sin.'

'God forgives you.'

The statement was so guileless, it struck Hannah as being almost childlike in its faith. She turned to him, wishing he could answer her questions, knowing he couldn't.

'Then why does He keep punishing me this way?' she asked, pain swelling inside her. 'What have I done to deserve this? What has Josh done or Paul? I don't understand.'

'I don't know,' he whispered hoarsely. He didn't understand it any better than she did, and that was his sin, he supposed – one of many – not trusting that God knew best. How could this be best for anyone? Why should Hannah suffer when she gave so much to so many people? He couldn't understand or accept it or keep himself from feeling anger toward the God to whom he had devoted his own life. He felt betrayed as Hannah felt betrayed. And he felt guilty because of it, and angry because of the guilt, and rebellious because of the limitations put on him by his station, and frightened by what he thought that might drive him to. The emotions spiraled down and down.

'It hurts *so much*!' Hannah said in a tortured whisper. She squeezed her eyes closed and hugged Lily tight, rocking her back and forth.

Without hesitation, Tom put his arms around her and drew her close. She was in pain; he would comfort her. If there were consequences to pay later, he would pay them. He coaxed Hannah's head to his shoulder and stroked her hair and shushed her.

'I know it hurts, honey,' he whispered. 'I wish there was something I could do to stop it. I'd do anything to help you. I'd give anything to take this all away.'

Hannah let herself cry on his shoulder. She took the comfort he offered. It felt so good to be held. He was solid and strong and warm. Tender. Feeling what she felt. Wanting to take her pain away. All the things her husband should have been and wasn't.

She slipped one arm around his waist and squeezed him tight as another flood of tears came – not for Josh, but for herself and for the torn fabric of the life that had once seemed so perfect. A dream, shattered and swept away. She wondered if it had ever been real.

Tom murmured to her. He touched her hair, her cheek, as careful as if she were made of spun sugar. His lips brushed against her temple. She raised her face and felt the warmth of his breath. She opened her eyes and met his gaze and saw the reflection of the tumult of her own emotions – need, longing, pain, guilt.

The moment caught and held, stretched between what they wanted and who they were, between what was right and what was required. Revelation and fear held them breathless.

It was Lily who broke the spell. Protesting being sandwiched between adults, she pushed at her mother's shoulder in irritation and said, 'Mama, down!'

Tom stepped back, Hannah dropped her gaze to the floor.

'It's bedtime, Lily,' she said softly, turning around to place her daughter in her crib.

Lily frowned at her. 'No.'

'Yes.'

'Where Josh?' she demanded, standing up at the railing. 'Me want Josh.'

Hannah brushed Lily's fine gold hair back and bent to kiss her forehead. 'Me, too, sweetheart.'

Tom stepped around to the end of the crib, curling his hands around the corner posts, too aware that he preferred the feel of Hannah in his arms. He couldn't bring himself to admit that was a mistake. Instead of trying, he changed the subject.

'Can I make a suggestion?' he said. 'Do an interview.'

Hannah looked up at him, puzzled. 'What?'

'I know everyone is clamoring for an exclusive with you, and I know you don't want to do it, but I think it would be good for you. Pick the show with the biggest ratings and go on. Tell America what you told me – how you feel, how difficult it is to deal with the guilt, what you believe you did wrong, what you would change if you could have that night back.'

Hannah shot him a look. 'I thought confession was sacrosanct.'

'Think of it as penance if you want. The point is that maybe by doing this you'll make someone else think twice. You can't have that night back, but you might be able to prevent someone else from having to go through this hell.'

Hannah looked down at her daughter, who now lay curled on her side on flannel sheets printed with images of Peter Rabbit and Jemima Puddle-Duck. She would give her own life to protect this precious little one. Such was the bond between mother and child. If she could help another mother, save another child, would that serve as payment for the mistakes she had made?

'I'll think about it.' She looked up at Father Tom, at his strong, handsome face and his kind blue eyes. Her heart beat a little too hard. 'Thank you. I – a –'

The words didn't form, which was probably just as well. Better for him not to know what she was feeling; it would only make things difficult, and she didn't want to lose his friendship.

'Thanks.'

He nodded and moved away from the crib, sliding his hands into his pockets. 'I should go. And you should try to rest.'

'I'll try.'

'Promise?' he asked, raising his brows at her as she walked him to the bedroom door.

Her mouth curved. 'I promise to try.'

'I'll take what I can get. You stay here with Lily; I can find my own way out. You know where to find me if you need me.'

She nodded and he turned away before he could say something they would both regret. She didn't have to know the depth of his feelings; only that he cared and was there for her. The rest couldn't matter.

Outside, the night was so cold it seemed that anything touched would shatter. Like a heart. He dismissed the analogy as foolhardy and tried to concentrate on something priestly as he coaxed his truck to start. Lines from the Lord's Prayer scrolled through his head. *Lead us not into temptation . . . deliver us from evil . . .*

'I'm in love with Hannah Garrison,' he murmured. 'A madman stole her child.'

He looked up through the windshield. Heaven was black and silver with the light of a broken moon. A sea of stars so far away. A feeling of abandonment yawned inside him.

'Someone up there's not doing their job.'

6:24 p.m. –28° windchill factor: –50°

Paul's lungs hurt from the cold. His legs ached from struggling through the deep snow and his toes hurt as if each one had been struck with a hammer. The only part of him that was warm was the glowing coal of his anger in his chest. He stepped over a fallen limb and leaned against the trunk of a cedar tree at the edge of the woods that ran behind the houses of Lakeside. To the east and north lay Quarry Hills Park, wooded and pretty with its groomed cross-country ski trails. One of his badges of honor, one of his deserved rewards: living with the lake out his front door and the park out his back door. One of the signs that he had made something of himself.

And Mitch Holt and Megan O'Malley wanted to treat him like a criminal.

How could they look at him as if he were a suspect when he had thrown himself into the effort to get Josh back? He had gone on the searches, made appeals on television. What more could he do?

This was all the fault of that little bitch from the BCA. She was the one who was so hung up on that damned old van. She was the one who kept trying to poke holes in his explanation of why he hadn't checked his messages that night and called Hannah back. And they both, of course, felt sorry for Hannah. Poor Hannah, who gives so much of herself. Poor Hannah, the mother who lost her son.

The stinging in his fingers brought Paul's attention back to the here and now. He had trudged through the woods because the street in front of his house was lined with the cars and vans of reporters. He had plenty to say to them, but not just then. Now he had other needs. A need to be held by a real woman, someone who understood him and would do anything to please him.

He crossed the Wrights' backyard and went in the back door of the garage. Garrett's Saab was gone. Karen's Honda sat alone, as it did most evenings. Garrett Wright was married to his work, not his wife. Home was the place he came to shower and change clothes. Karen's place in his life was largely ornamental – someone to take to faculty dinners. Any other interest he had once had in her as a woman had dwindled away. According to Karen, they rarely had sex, and when they did, it was more duty than desire on Garrett's part.

They had no children. Karen wasn't able to conceive by the usual means and Garrett wasn't willing to go through the endless marathon of tests and procedures involved with the *in vitro* process. Having children wasn't important to him. Karen talked of adoption, but that process was daunting as well and she didn't know if she had the strength or endurance to tackle it alone. And so they went on, just the two of them, in a shell of a marriage with which Garrett seemed perfectly content and to which Karen clung because she didn't have the courage to break free.

Paul seldom thought of Garrett Wright in anything but abstract terms. Even though they were neighbors, they barely knew each other. To Paul, Garrett Wright lived in an alternate universe. He was a shadowy figure who buried himself in his psychology texts and his research at Harris and gave what free time he had to a bunch of juvenile delinquents called the Sci-Fi Cowboys. He and Garrett Wright existed on two different planes that intersected in only one place – Karen.

Using the spare key that was always left under an old coffee can full of nails on the workbench, he let himself into the laundry room. He took off his heavy boots and brushed the snow from the legs of his sweatpants.

'Garrett?'

Karen opened the door to the kitchen, her dark eyes going wide at the sight of him. She stood there in her stocking feet, a green checked dish towel in one hand, purple leggings clinging to her legs. A shapeless ivory V-neck sweater reached down to her knees. Her ash-blond hair hung as limp as silk, the bangs soft above her doe eyes. Small and soft and feminine, full of comfort and concern for him. The first rustlings of desire whispered through him.

'Are you expecting him?' he asked.

'No. He just left to go back to work. I thought he might have forgotten something.' Self-conscious, she tucked a strand of hair behind her ear and brushed her fingers through her bangs. 'I thought you'd be with Hannah tonight. I heard about the jacket. I'm so sorry, Paul.'

He slipped off his old black parka and tossed it on the dryer, his eyes on hers. 'I don't want to talk about it.'

'All right.'

He took the towel from her hand and looped it around the back of her neck, pulling her closer with it. 'I'm sick of it,' he said, winding the checked cloth into his fists. The anger burned in his chest. 'I'm sick of the questions and the accusations and the waiting and everyone looking at Hannah and saying "Poor brave Hannah." It's all her fault. And that little bitch is trying to blame me.'

'Hannah blames you?' Karen asked, puzzled. She had to strain back against the towel to look up at him.

'Agent O'Malley,' he sneered. 'She's too busy screwing Holt to do her job right.'

'How could anyone blame *you?*'

Dad, can you come and get me from hockey? Mom's late and I wanna go home.

'I don't know,' he whispered as his throat tightened and tears burned his eyes. 'It wasn't my fault.'

'Of course it wasn't.'

'It wasn't my fault,' he murmured, squeezing his eyes shut and dropping his head. He wound the towel tighter. 'It wasn't my fault.'

Karen flattened herself against him to escape the pain. She slipped her small hands beneath his sweatshirt and stroked the lean muscles of his back. 'It wasn't your fault, sweetheart.'

Dad, can you come and get me from hockey? Mom's late and I wanna go home.

The voice haunted his mind. It overlaid images of the afternoon: O'Malley questioning him – *you never checked your answering machine?* The jacket in his hands – He's dead. He's dead. He's dead. . . .

The towel fell from his hands to the floor.

'. . . not my fault,' he whimpered, trembling.

Karen pressed a finger to his lips. 'Shh. Come with me.'

She led him through the kitchen and down the dark hall to the guest bedroom. They never made love in the bed she shared with Garrett. They seldom met there in her house; the risk of discovery was too great. But he made no move to stop her as she undressed him like a child, and he made no move to stop her as she undressed herself. This was what he had come for, but he made no advances. It wasn't his fault. He deserved to be comforted.

He lay on the clean peach sheets in the soft glow of the bedside lamp and allowed her to arouse him with her lips and her hands and her body. She teased with her mouth, caressed with her fingers, rubbed her small breasts against him, opened herself, and took him inside her. She moved on him slowly, murmuring to him, stroking his chest, stoking a fire of physical need that gradually burned through the haze of numbness.

Grabbing her by the shoulders, he pulled her to him and rolled her beneath him. He deserved this. He needed it. Release for his body and for the anger smoldering inside him – anger with Hannah, with O'Malley, anger at the injustices that had been heaped on his life. He let it all pour out as he pumped himself in and out of another man's wife. Deeper, harder, until the thrusts were more punishment than passion.

And then in a burst it was over. The strength was gone. The power drained away. He collapsed beside Karen and stared at the ceiling, oblivious to her curling against him, oblivious to her tears, oblivious to time passing. Oblivious to everything but the insidious weakness that crawled through him.

'I wish you could stay,' Karen whispered.

'I can't.'

'I know. But I wish you could.' She raised her head and gazed at him. 'I wish I could give you all the love and support you need. I wish I could give you a son.'

'Karen . . .'

'I do,' she insisted, rubbing the palm of her hand over his heart. 'I'd have your baby, Paul. I think about it all the time. I think about it when I'm in your house, when I'm holding Lily. I pretend she's mine – ours. I think about it every time we're together, every time you climax inside me. I'd have your baby, Paul. I'd do anything for you.'

This was just another of life's cruel ironies, he thought as he watched her bend her head and press kisses to his chest. He had the wife he had always thought he wanted – the independent, capable Dr Garrison – and now he wanted the kind of woman he had grown up loathing – Karen, born to serve, subjugating her needs to his, willing to be anything he wanted just to please him.

He checked the clock on the nightstand and sighed. 'I have to go.'

He washed up in the guest bath while she changed the sheets. As always, there would be no evidence of their stolen time together, not so much as a scent of sex in the linens. They dressed in silence and walked in silence back down the dark hall to the kitchen, where a single light burned over the sink.

'I heard they're going to resume the ground search tomorrow,' Karen said, leaning a hip against the oak cupboards. 'Will you go out?'

Paul took a glass from the drainer beside the sink and filled it. 'I guess,' he said, staring at his reflection in the window.

He took a sip from the glass and dumped the rest of the water. He rinsed the glass and put it back in the drainer; blotted his mouth with the green checked towel, refolded it, and laid it back on the counter.

From beyond the laundry room came the sound of the door to the garage opening and closing. Paul's nerves jangled. Guilt gripped its fist inside of him. The kitchen door swung open and Garrett Wright walked in, tucking his gloves into the pockets of his navy wool topcoat.

'Paul!' he said, his dark eyes widening. 'This is a surprise.' He set his briefcase on the oak kitchen table and unbuttoned his coat. Karen took up her rightful place beside him, leaning up to brush a passionless kiss to his cheek. They made a pretty couple, both blond and fair with dark eyes and carefully sculpted features. The kind of couple that could have passed for brother and sister.

'I stopped by to ask Karen if she would be willing to do some extra duty at the volunteer center tomorrow,' he said. 'We're resuming the ground search, regardless of the cold.'

'Yes, I heard. I didn't see your car out front.'

'I walked.'

Garrett's pale brows rose in unison. 'Cold night for a walk.'

'I thought it might clear my head.'

'Yes, well,' he said, making a good show of being concerned, 'you've got a lot on your mind these days. How are you holding up?'

'I'm getting by,' Paul said, trying not to sound grudging. On the occasions of his conversations with Garrett Wright he had always felt like a bug under a microscope. As if he were a potential candidate for psychoanalysis, as if Wright was, even as they spoke, analyzing his words and gestures and expressions or lack of them.

'I know you've been very active in the search,' Garrett said, slipping off his coat. The dutiful wife, Karen took it from him without a word and went to hang it in the front hall closet. 'That's a healthy way of dealing with the situation, even if there are a lot of frustrations. How's Hannah doing?'

'As well as she can,' Paul said stiffly.

'I haven't seen her on the news – except in the paper last Sunday. She collapsed, didn't she?' Garrett shook his head. Frowning gravely, he slipped his hands into the pockets of his dark pleated pants and rocked back on his heels. 'The loss of a child is a terrible strain on the parents.'

'I'm well aware of that,' Paul said tightly.

Garrett gave a little jolt of realization, his dark eyes widening with contrition. 'I'm sorry. I didn't mean to sound patronizing, Paul. I just wanted to say if either of you feel a need to talk to someone, I can recommend a friend of mine in Edina. He specializes in family therapy.'

'I've got better things to do,' Paul said, his jaw rigid.

'Please don't take offense, Paul.' Wright reached a hand out toward him. 'I only meant to help.'

'If you want to help, then show up at Ryan's Bay tomorrow morning. That's the kind of help we need, not some overpriced shrink in Edina.' He turned his attention to Karen. 'I'll see you tomorrow at the center.'

Karen nodded, her gaze on the floor. 'I'll be there.'

She stood there, holding her breath until she heard the door to the garage open and close.

'That wasn't very sensitive of you, Garrett,' she admonished her husband softly.

'Really? I think it was extremely generous of me, all things considered.'

He went to the sink and ran a finger down the side of the water-dotted glass in the drainer. He picked up the neatly folded green checked towel, dried the glass, and refolded the towel.

'You should be more careful where you leave things,' he said, holding up the towel.

The towel Paul had taken from her. The towel with which he had drawn her to him, his fists wrapping tighter and tighter into the cloth.

The towel he had dropped on the floor in the laundry room.

Karen said nothing. Garrett set the towel aside on the counter and walked away.

28

Mitch stared at the message board on the war room wall until the messages from the kidnapper began to swirl together. Elbows on the table, he put his face in his hands and tried to rub the weariness from his eyes. A futile effort. The fatigue went far deeper. It beat at him relentlessly, a cold, black club that struck again and again to loosen his hold on his logic, his objectivity. It stung his temper, made him feel mean and dangerous. It cracked the hard protective shell of control and allowed guilt and uncertainty to seep in like a toxic ooze.

Guilt. He'd seen the look on Hannah's face when Paul had hurled his accusation at her with the same violence that had sent the fireplace poker hurtling into the wall. A burst of pain, but beneath it guilt. She blamed herself as much as Paul blamed her. He knew exactly how that felt – the constant, pointless self-punishment, the pain that became so familiar that in a perverse way you almost didn't want to let it go.

'You should probably put something on those knuckles,' Megan said quietly. 'God knows what kind of cooties might be running around in Steiger's bodily fluids. I'm on my way to the hospital. Wanna ride along?'

Mitch jerked his hands from his face and slapped them palms-down on the tabletop. He didn't know how long she had been standing there, leaning against the door frame, while he wrestled with his inner demons. She came into the conference room with her eyelids at half mast as she rubbed at the tension in the back of her neck.

'I'm fine,' he said, glancing at the hand he had skinned breaking Steiger's nose. 'I've had my tetanus shot.'

'I was thinking more along the lines of rabies or maybe hoof-and-mouth disease,' she said dryly, perching a hip on the tabletop across from him.

'Why are you going to the hospital?'

'Trolling for suspects. I know we've questioned everyone down there, but I want to dig a little more. Hannah doesn't think any of her patients or their families could have been driven to something like stealing Josh, but I think it's worth checking out again. Hannah might not be aware of any animosity toward her, but I'm willing to bet the nursing staff will come up with a name or two. Everybody is hated by somebody.'

'Cynic.'

'Realist,' Megan corrected him. 'I've been on the job long enough to know that people are basically selfish, bitter, and vindictive, if not out and out nuts.'

'And then there's our guy.' Mitch rose from his chair, his eyes on the message board. His gaze passed over each line, the hair on the back of his neck prickling. 'Evil.'

Evil. The thing all of them had feared from the beginning. A kidnapping for ransom was about greed; greed could be dealt with, greed could be tricked. Mental illness was dangerous and unpredictable, but sickos usually screwed up somewhere along the line. Evil was cold and calculating. Evil played games with unknown rules and hidden agendas. Evil planted evidence, then calmly walked to a neighbor's house and asked for help finding his victim's dog.

The composite drawing of Ruth Cooper's early morning visitor was pinned to the cork bulletin board. A man of indeterminate age with a lean face that seemed almost devoid of features. The eyes were hidden behind a pair of high-tech sport sunglasses. The hair might have been any color beneath the dark cap. Not even his ears were visible. The hood of a black parka created a tunnel around his face, making him seem like a specter from another dimension.

'It's not exactly a photograph, is it?' Megan said dejectedly.

'No, but at least Mrs Cooper thinks she might be able to ID him if she sees him again. She thinks she'll remember his voice.'

The rage rose inside him at the thought of the overconfidence, the contempt, the cruelty of the act this man had played out to flaunt his power and his cunning mind. Mitch's hands curled into fists at his sides. 'Arrogant son of a bitch,' he muttered. 'You'll take a wrong step somewhere, and when you do, I will take you down hard.'

'If we're lucky, his partner might trip him up for us,' Megan said, slipping down off the table. 'I'm arranging to have Christopher Priest take a look at Olie's computers and see if he can get into the files. Olie was auditing computer courses at Harris. I figure if anyone has a chance at getting past his booby traps it's Priest. In the meantime, there's still Paul to deal with.'

Before Mitch could react, she hurried on. 'You can't deny his connection to the van,' she said, ticking her points off one by one on her fingers. 'You can't deny that he tried to hide it from us. His alibi for the night Josh disappeared holds as much water as a two-dollar sieve. No one knows where he was at six o'clock this morning while Ruth Cooper was meeting our mystery man. He told the agent on duty he was going out to drive around, looking for Josh. The timing seems a little coincidental, don't you think?'

'What's his motive?' Mitch demanded. 'Why would he do something to his own son?'

'It happens,' Megan insisted. 'You know it does. What about that case up on the Iron Range last year? What that man had done to his own daughter was unspeakable, and he showed up for the search every day, made pleas through the media, took a second mortgage on his house to put up reward money. It happened there and it could happen here.

'This is not Utopia, Chief,' she continued, her patience wearing thin with his resistance, with the situation. 'It's just a town like any other town. The people are just like people everywhere – some are good and some are rotten. Even the Garden of Eden had a snake in it. Deal with it.'

The look he cut her way was dark and dangerous. 'You think I'm not dealing with it?' His voice was whisper-soft and stiletto-sharp.

'I think you don't want to.'

'Well, we know you do, don't we?' he said sardonically. 'All you care about is pulling your fanny out of the fire and getting a nice gold star on your evaluation sheet. Even if you have to tear up a few people on the way. The end justifies the means.'

'You can save that bullshit speech for Paige Price,' Megan snapped, jamming her hands at her waist. 'You know damn well I want to get Josh back. Don't you snipe at me for telling the truth. I think it's too easy for you to put yourself in Paul Kirkwood's place, and that could cost us.'

Mitch was in no mood to have his conscience or his cop instincts poked at. Tired and frustrated, he lashed out at her.

'In other words, Agent O'Malley, I should forget this man has lost his son and go straight for the jugular. I should get my priorities straight, like you. The job comes first. The job, the job, the fucking job!' he shouted in her face.

'The job is who I am,' Megan said, fierce pride sparking in her eyes. 'If you don't like it, tough shit.'

'It's who you are because it's all you'll allow,' Mitch snarled. 'God forbid you should take off the badge and be a woman for a while. You wouldn't know what to do.'

Megan jerked back as the blow landed with almost physical force. She *had* taken off the badge. She *had* been a woman. For him. Apparently, she hadn't done a very good job of it. The idea cut her to the quick.

'Oh, like you'd give me so much more?' she struck back, her tone dripping sarcasm. 'What will you give me, Chief? A roll on your sofa? Yeah, that's worth throwing my career away.'

His mouth twisted in a sneer. 'I don't recall you complaining when you had your legs wrapped around me.'

'Oh, no,' Megan admitted without flinching, holding the hurt deep inside a fist of control. 'It was great while it lasted. Now it's over. A big relief to you, I'm sure. Those relationships that drag on for more than three or four days can put a real crimp in your martyrdom.'

'Don't!' Mitch shouted, holding up a hand in warning. His left hand.

301

The hand that bore his wedding ring. The gold band caught the light, gleaming, giving the lie to the denial that hadn't even made it out of his mouth.

He turned away from her and blew out a long breath. Jesus, how had they gotten on to this? What did he care what Megan O'Malley would and would not allow in her life? They'd had sex. Big deal. He didn't want anything more from her and his reasons had nothing to do with penance for past sins. *This* was why he didn't want anything more from Megan O'Malley. She was bullheaded and opinionated and she provoked him and antagonized him. He couldn't control himself when he was around her, and he sure as hell couldn't control *her*.

Megan pulled the emotions back and locked them up where they belonged. *This* was why she couldn't fall for Mitch Holt. He had just proven the very rule he had coaxed her to break: no cops. Now that it was over between them, everything she had given him, every private aspect of herself she had shared, would be used against her. Now there would be this awkwardness between them. Every time they had to be in the same room together, every time they had to work together.

Work should have been her only focus all along. *You knew better, O'Malley. Whatever made you think you could have something more?* She swallowed down the knot of emotion in her throat and forced her mind back on track.

'We have to get Paul's fingerprints,' she said. 'He owned that van; he might still have a key. If his prints are in it now, after all this time, he'll have some explaining to do. You get him in here, Chief, or I will.'

Mitch marveled at the way she slid into her cop skin so easily and ignored the emotional blood they had just drawn. He could almost feel the cold from the walls of ice that went up around her to close him off, to protect herself and the feelings he had just raked his claws through. It irked him that she had that kind of control when he felt wild inside, when he wanted to scream at her and shake her. It irritated him that he felt the slightest twinge of remorse and regret, that he felt something when she seemed to have turned her feelings off.

'Don't boss me around, O'Malley,' he warned.

Megan arched a brow. 'What are you going to do about it? Tell the press you've seen me naked?' She walked away from him with her head up. 'Do your job, Chief, or I'll do it for you.'

Mitch said nothing as she walked out of the war room and closed the door. He paced the room, trying to hang on to his control, trying to put his focus where it belonged.

Snarling, he wheeled around and glared at the message board. He couldn't see Paul typing out those twisted missives. He knew parents lost their tempers or their minds and committed sins that could never be atoned for. Then he thought of Kyle and what it had felt like to see his son lying dead, to live every day with the thought of how old Kyle would have been and what he would have been doing had he lived. He thought of the way it hurt every time he saw little boys playing ball, chasing up and down the street on bikes with dogs in hot pursuit. He couldn't reconcile the idea of willfully harming a child, because he still hurt so badly from having his taken from him.

I think it's too easy for you to put yourself in Paul Kirkwood's place, and that could cost us.

Easy? No. *Easy* wasn't the right word at all.

He walked back to the table, where Josh's think pad lay. He needed a suspect. Someone who knew the Kirkwoods, knew the area, knew Josh.

He turned through the pages of doodling and games of hangman, his pride at being made co-captain of his hockey team, his sadness at the trouble between his parents. *Dad is mad. Mom is sad. I feel bad . . .* Marital problems didn't make Paul Kirkwood the kind of monster who could steal his own son and leave behind quotes on sin and ignorance.

Sin.

Mitch turned another page and stared hard at the drawings. Josh's interpretation of God and the devil, his opinions of religion class – mad faces and thumbs-down signs. *Sin.* In his mind's eye he could see Albert Fletcher, the St Elysius deacon, standing on the verge of Old Cedar Road with the hood of a black parka framing his lean face.

9:57 p.m. –30° windchill factor: –55°

'In a perfect world, Hannah would be a candidate for sainthood,' Kathleen Casey pronounced. She sat on the sagging couch in the nurses' lounge, running shoes propped up on a blond oak Scandinavian coffee table. Dressed in green surgical scrubs and a white lab coat with the business end of a stethoscope tucked into the breast pocket, she chewed thoughtfully on a plastic needle cap as she stared unseeing at the television across the room. 'All those in favor of making this a perfect world, say aye.'

Megan sank deeper into what had once been an over-stuffed leather armchair. Barely stuffed was a more appropriate description. They were the only people in the lounge. Beyond the open door, the small hospital was quiet. The occasional telephone ringing. The occasional page. A far cry from the city hospitals with their codes and crises. Megan entertained thoughts of finding an empty bed and crashing. Maybe one nice shot of Demerol and then eight or ten hours of oblivion. She rubbed at her forehead and sighed.

'How do her co-workers feel toward her?' she asked, underlining the word *co-workers* on her notepad.

'Like I told the last nine cops, she's a nurse's dream. I regularly pinch myself when we're working together.' Her small bright hazel eyes showed her years of a different experience. 'Sixteen years in this business. I cut my teeth on arrogant residents and chiefs of staff who swore they couldn't have a God complex because they *were* God. If those guys are in heaven when I get there, I want my visa revoked at the gate.'

'How does she get along with the other doctors?'

'Great – with the exception of our Chad Everett wannabe. Dr Craig Lomax. He was miffed when Hannah was named head of ER. It has somehow escaped his attention that he's a lousy doctor.'

'How miffed?'

'Enough to punish us all with his sulking. Enough to challenge Hannah's authority.' She took a sip of her caffeine-free Pepsi, then replaced the needle cap between her teeth and bit down. 'If you're asking me was he pissed enough to take Josh, the answer is no. He's obnoxious, not insane. Besides, he was on duty that night.'

'What about patients?' Megan asked. 'Anyone you can think of who didn't handle the outcome of a case well? Someone who would have blamed her.'

Kathleen ran a hand back through her thick hedge of red hair as she thought. 'This isn't like the city, you know. People in small towns don't sue for malpractice. They trust their doctors and have enough common sense to know everything doesn't always work out for the best and it isn't always somebody's fault.'

Megan persisted. 'What about relatives of people who didn't make it? A parent who lost a child, maybe.'

'Let's see. . . . The Muellers lost a baby to SIDS last fall. Brought him in DOA. Hannah worked on him forever, but there was nothing she could do.'

'Were they angry?'

'Not with Hannah. She went above and beyond the call.' She thought some more, scanning a mental list and discarding names. 'I can't think of anyone who would do this kind of thing. Hannah is an excellent doctor. She can calm people down faster than a handful of Valium. And she knows the limitations of our hospital. She doesn't hesitate to send a patient on to a better-equipped facility if she thinks it's warranted.' She pulled her feet off the coffee table and tucked them beneath her on the couch. Tugging the needle cap from between her teeth, she used it like a pointer. 'I remember the time she personally drove Doris Fletcher to the Mayo Clinic for tests because her husband refused to take her.'

'Fletcher?' Megan sat up straight. 'Any relation to Albert Fletcher?'

Kathleen rolled her eyes. 'Deer Lake's own Deacon of Doom. The world's going to hell on a sled. Women are the root of all evil. Sackcloth and ashes as a fashion statement. *That* Albert Fletcher? Yes. Poor Doris had the misfortune to marry him before he became a zealot.'

'And he wouldn't take her to a hospital for tests?' Megan asked, incredulous.

The nurse rolled her eyes. 'He thought they should have waited for the Lord to heal her. Meanwhile the Lord is throwing His hands up in heaven, saying "I gave you the Mayo Clinic, for crying out loud! What more do you want!" Poor Doris.'

'How did Fletcher react to Dr Garrison taking his wife for those tests against his will?'

'He was pissed. Albert isn't big on women asserting themselves. He thinks we should all still be paying because Eve screwed up.'

'What did his wife die of?' Megan asked.

'Her whole gastrointestinal system went haywire, then her kidneys failed,' she explained. 'It was sad. No one ever came up with a concrete diagnosis. I said Albert was feeding her arsenic, but nobody listens to nurses.'

When Megan didn't laugh, Kathleen gave her a look. 'I was joking. About the arsenic. That was a joke.'

'Could he have killed her?' Megan asked, straight-faced.

The nurse's eyes widened. Her pale brows shot up toward her hairline. 'The deacon break a commandment? The sky would turn black and the earth would shake.'

'Was there an autopsy?'

Kathleen sobered. She turned the needle cap over and over in her small hands. 'No,' she said softly. 'Mayo pressed for it. They couldn't stand the idea of a disease they had no research funding for. But Albert refused on religious grounds.'

Megan stared at her notes. Messages about sin. A personal vendetta. If Fletcher had somehow managed to poison his wife and get away with it, he might still be inclined to punish Hannah for interfering. If he were crazy enough, twisted enough. He had been teaching religion classes the night Josh disappeared, but if they were looking at tag-team lunatics, then all alibis were irrelevant.

'You don't really think he took Josh, do you?' Kathleen asked in a quiet voice. 'I'd rather believe Olie did it and now he's roasting in hell.'

Megan heaved herself up out of the armchair. 'I imagine he's roasting, but I think he's probably saving a spot for somebody. It's my job to find out who.'

The question that nagged her as she drove across town was whether or not it would still be her job by the end of the week.

She cursed office politics to hell and gone. She had come here to do a job, plain and simple. But there was nothing plain or simple about the situation into which they had all been thrust – herself, Mitch, Hannah, Paul, everyone in Deer Lake, all the people from outside the community who had come to help. One act of evil had changed all their lives. The taking of Josh had set into motion a chain of actions and reactions. Their lives had been wrested from their control and now hinged on a madman's next move.

She wondered if he knew that, whoever he was. As she stared out the windshield into the bleak shadows of the cold night, she wondered if he was thinking even now about his next move and how it would affect the unwilling players of his sick game.

Power. That was what this was all about. The power to play God. The power to break people until they begged for mercy. The rush of showing how much smarter he was than everyone else.

'It's easy to win the game when you're the only one who knows the rules,' Megan muttered. 'Give us a clue, jerk. Just one lousy clue. Then we'll see what's what.'

Soon. It had to happen soon. She could feel her time running out. DePalma's ultimatum hung over her head like an anvil – *make something good happen.*

She turned onto Simley Street a block west of St E's, killed the headlights, and let the Lumina roll for half a block before pulling in along the curb. There was no life on Simley Street at ten o'clock. Residents of the neat, boxy houses were all glued to the news – with the notable exception of Albert Fletcher. There was no light in the living room window of 606 Simley. There was no light in any window of the story-and-a-half house.

Where would a sixty-year-old Catholic deacon be at ten-fifteen on a Wednesday night? Out tripping the light fantastic with some hot widow? The image made Megan grimace.

She crossed the street and made her way down the sidewalk with a purposeful stride, as if she had every reason to be there. The trick of fitting in where you don't belong – pretend you do. She headed up the driveway of 606 and slipped around the side of the garage, taking herself out of sight of any neighbors who happened to glance out their front windows.

The snow screeched like Styrofoam beneath her boots. Even the fabric shell of her parka was stiff from the cold. Every move she made sounded like someone crumpling newspaper. She cursed herself for staying in this godforsaken deep-freeze as she fumbled in her coat pocket for a small flashlight. Mittens did not lend themselves to skills involving dexterity – one reason the number of burglaries always fell off dramatically during cold spells.

The side door of the garage was locked. Shielding the light with one hand, Megan held it up to the window and peered in, holding her breath so as not to fog the glass in the window. The only car in the garage was a sedan of indeterminate make encased in canvas sheeting, like an old couch hiding beneath a slipcover. The near stall was empty. The place was immaculate. Not so much as a grease spot on the floor.

She turned and followed the walk toward the back porch steps. She wanted to peek in the windows, but all shades were drawn. Even the basement windows were covered. The foundation of the house had been wrapped with thick, cloudy plastic, then banked with snow for insulation.

Swearing, Megan knelt down directly beneath a first-floor window and dug the snow away with her hand. She pulled off one mitten, dipped in her coat pocket for a penknife, and used it to pry loose a few of the staples from the lath that held the plastic in place. Tugging the plastic down, she shone the flashlight into the basement. What she could see of it was swept as clean as a dance floor. No stacks of old paint cans. No piles of newspapers. No boxes of discarded clothing. No dungeon. No chamber of horrors in evidence. No little boy.

Half disappointed, half relieved, Megan sat back on her haunches and shut off the flashlight. At the same instant, headlights beamed up the driveway.

'Shit!'

She scrambled to stuff the flashlight and penknife back into her pocket, managing to stick herself in the palm with the blade in the process. Biting down on the desire to yelp, she used her good hand to scoop the snow back up against the window. The garage door began its automatic ascent. She packed the snow as best she could, slapping at it with both hands. Her eyes kept darting to the garage. Fletcher drove in without seeing her, but if he came out the side and headed for his back door, her ass was fried.

The car engine rumbled, then quit. Crouching, Megan ran up the back steps, jumped down off the stoop, and ducked around the far side of the house, running headlong into a man.

Her scream was smothered by a big gloved hand. An arm banded around her with punishing strength, pulling her hard against a man's body. Twisting around, he pinned her between himself and the side of the house. Megan lashed out with the toe of her boot, connecting with his shin. He grunted in pain, but only leaned into her harder.

'Be still!' he ordered in a harsh whisper.

A familiar whisper.

Megan stared up inside the tunnel of his hood. Even in the shadows it was impossible not to recognize Mitch's face. He slid his hand away from her mouth.

Megan didn't say a word, but struggled instead to breathe in soundless pants. The cold air felt like fists pounding her lungs, and she brought a hand up to cup around her mouth as a filter. Fletcher's car door slammed. His footsteps crunched up the packed snow toward the back door. Chances were good that he would walk up his steps and into his house as he had done a million times without noticing anything out of the ordinary, like a footprint in the snow where there should not have been one. People were creatures of habit and routine, for the most part unobservant – unless they felt they had to be on guard.

He hesitated. She could picture him standing in the spot where she had dug the snow away from the basement window. *Come on, Albert. Move. Move. Please.* He moved on slowly. Up the steps slowly. Megan held her breath. Was he wondering? Was he looking off the south side of the stoop? Could he make out footprints in the shadows?

The rattle of keys. The turn of a lock. The heavy door thumped shut and the storm door sighed as it settled back against the frame.

Megan let out an echoing sigh. The adrenaline rush passed, leaving her trembling. She looked up at Mitch and whispered, 'What the hell are you doing here?'

'What the hell are *you* doing here?' he demanded.

'Do you think we could have this argument inside a building?' she muttered. 'I'm freezing my butt off.'

10:55 p.m. –30° windchill factor: –55°

There wasn't much action at the Blue Goose Saloon, a hole-in-the-wall bar with blessedly poor lighting to keep the patrons from noticing the moth-eaten condition of the dead animals mounted on the walls. The bartender, a portly woman with mouse-brown curls that fit her head like a stocking cap, stood behind the bar, smoking a cigarette, and drying beer mugs with a dingy towel. She stared up at a *Cheers* rerun on the portable television, small dark eyes tucked into the fleshy folds of her face like raisins in bread dough. Her only customer at the bar was an old man with bad teeth who drank schnapps and carried on an animated conversation with himself about the sorry state of politics in Minnesota now that Hubert Humphrey was gone.

Mitch had chosen the last booth in the line before the pool-room and sat so he could see the entrance and the front window that looked out on the street. Old habits. He ordered coffee and a shot of Jack Daniel's on the side. The Jack went down in a single gulp. He sipped at the coffee while Megan told him about her conversation with Kathleen Casey, the mysterious demise of Doris Fletcher, and her husband's enmity toward Hannah Garrison for interfering.

Megan dumped her whiskey into the coffee and added fake cream. The drink was hot and potent and warmed her from the inside out, taking the edge off her shivering. She checked her hand, squinting in the dim light. The penknife had lanced her palm with a short cut now decorated with drying blood and mitten fuzz. It would need a Band-Aid but nothing more.

'Why wait three years to get revenge?' Mitch asked.

'I don't know. Maybe it took that long for the plan to ferment – or for his mind to snap.'

'He was teaching class at St E's the night Josh disappeared.'

'Enter the ever-popular accomplice.'

On the television above the bar Cliff Claven did a manic dance as someone zapped him with jolts of electricity. The bar-tender's cigarette bobbed on her lip as she chuckled with malicious glee. Another shiver went through Megan and she took a long sip of her drink.

'You were at Fletcher's, too, Chief,' she pointed out. 'Why are you playing devil's advocate with me?'

'Because I like it.'

308

'Your natural perverse tendencies aside, I have to assume you had a reason for being there.'

He gave a lazy shrug. 'Just sniffing around. Fletcher's obsessed with the church. Three of the notes mention sin. Josh didn't like religion class.'

'Who could blame him with Fletcher for an instructor?' Megan said, shuddering. 'Albert Fletcher would have given Vincent Price the creeps.'

'I went back over the statement he gave Noogie the night Josh disappeared,' Mitch said. He chose a peanut from the basket that sat on the table, cracked it with one hand, and tossed the nuts into his mouth. 'There's nothing in it to draw suspicion.'

On the surface there was nothing about Albert Fletcher that would have drawn notice. He was a retired professional, a respected member of the community. Not what most people would consider the profile of a child predator, but there were just as many pieces that fit. Fletcher's duties with the church put him in proximity with children. His authority at St E's translated into trust in the eyes of children and adults alike. He would hardly have been the first to abuse that trust.

'Did he know Olie?'

'I can't imagine they ran in the same circles, but we'll check it out. I'll talk to him myself in the morning.' He wished he could have run Fletcher in to the station that night, but that wasn't how things were done. He couldn't go after the man with nothing more than a hunch and some three-year-old rumors. No one had mentioned him in connection with Josh other than in his position with the church. No one had reported anything suspicious going on at Fletcher's house. Mitch had assigned a man to keep an eye on the residence through the night, just the same.

He dug out his wallet and tossed some ones on the table. Megan followed suit. The bartender waddled out from behind her post to scoop up her booty as they headed for the door.

'You folks come again,' she called in a voice that sounded like Louie Armstrong with a bad head cold.

As they stepped out onto the sidewalk, the cold nearly took Megan's breath away. Not even the warmth of the whiskey in her belly could keep her teeth from chattering.

'Jesus, Mary, and J-Joseph,' she stuttered, digging her car keys out of her pocket. 'If it weren't for Josh, I think I'd be *hoping* to get fired. Humans weren't meant to live like this.'

'Get tough or die, O'Malley,' Mitch drawled without sympathy.

'If I get any tougher, bullets will bounce off me,' she tossed back as she slid behind the wheel of the Lumina.

She began the ritual of coaxing the car to start, her gaze on Mitch as he climbed into the Explorer. The streets of Deer Lake were deserted, the Blue Goose the only business open. Watching him drive away gave her an empty feeling inside, as if she were the only human left on the planet.

There were worse things than being alone. But as she sat there alone in the cold, dark night with a child missing and her future hanging by a thread, she had a hard time thinking what they were.

Journal entry
Day 8

They found the jacket today. They don't know what to think. They don't know which way to turn. We can smell their panic. Taste it. It makes us laugh. They are as predictable as rats in a maze. They don't know which way to turn, so they turn on each other and they grasp at anything, hoping for a clue. They deserve whatever fate befalls them. The wrath of God. The wrath of colleagues, of neighbors, of strangers. Wrath rains down on the heads of the guilty and the fools.

Should we give them something and see where it leads them? All scenarios have been mapped out, far beyond the immediate moment. If we give them A, will it lead them to B? If it leads them to C, what then? On to D or E? We can't be surprised. We have planned for all contingencies, all possibilities. Ultimately, we are invincible and they will know that. The game is ours. The suffering is theirs. Deserving victims of the perfect crime.

29

The ground search resumed in the gray light of a sunless morning. The governor had volunteered cold-weather gear from the National Guard, and a pair of military trucks sat in the alley behind the old fire hall to dispense Arctic mittens and thermal ski masks to any volunteer in need.

With the discovery of Josh's jacket, the panic level around town had soared. More volunteers than ever crowded the briefing room in the fire hall, anxious, desperate to help. They flocked to the focal point of the search with the zeal of the mob storming Dr Frankenstein's gates. They were angry and terrified and tired of the waiting. They wanted their town and their lives back, and they wanted to believe determination alone could win the day.

Mitch sat in his Explorer and watched the search teams and search dogs disperse. Most cases had a feel to them, a rhythm that picked up as things progressed and clues came in and leads were followed and evidence built. This one had no rhythm, and the only feeling he got was bad. The deeper they went into this maze the more lost and disoriented they became.

Maybe there were two kidnappers. Maybe Olie had been one of them. Maybe not. Maybe Paul was involved, but how and why? Maybe Albert Fletcher was a suspect. Maybe he was insane. Had he known Olie, or was the accomplice someone they hadn't even considered? Was there an accomplice at all?

A stocky sergeant from the Minneapolis K-9 squad directed his German shepherd into the stand of cattails. The dog loped up onto the bank, tail wagging, nose to the snow. Uniformed officers herded volunteers out of the dog's path. Mitch's heart picked up a beat. The dog seemed to have a scent. He trotted south, away from the houses, along the snowmobile trail and up onto Mill Road, which ran east into town and west to farm country. He stood there, looking toward town, looking toward the field across the road where ash-blond cornstalks stood unharvested, row upon row, in testament to the wet fall and early winter.

The scent was gone. Like every other scrap of hope they had been given, this one was snatched away. Mitch put the truck in gear and headed for Albert Fletcher's house, less than a half-mile away.

By daylight the Fletcher home was an uninspired square, one-and-a-half stories high, painted a somber shade of gray. No remnants of the Christmas season decorated the door or the eaves. Albert apparently refrained from garish displays. Mitch recalled hearing something about a brouhaha in St E's over decorating during Advent. The ladies' guilds were for it, the deacon was against it. Mitch hadn't paid much attention. His Sunday mornings were spent beside his daughter and his in-laws at Cross of Christ Lutheran, where he spent every sermon doing math in his head as an act of rebellion.

He rang the doorbell and waited for the sound of footsteps. None came. No light escaped through the drawn shades. He hit the bell again and bounced on the balls of his feet in an attempt to shake off the cold. Earmuffs clamped his head like a vise. The hood of his parka stemmed the flow of body heat out the top of his head.

No one came to the door. Of course, Albert was the only known resident of the house. Mrs Fletcher was dead and the deacon had never been linked romantically with anyone. Despite the fact that he had had a successful career as comptroller of BuckLand Cheese and was probably comfortably well off, the ladies apparently did not consider him a catch.

Doris wasting away might have had something to do with that, Mitch thought as he made his way along the neatly shoveled path to the garage. As far as he had been able to discern, no one had suspected Albert at the time of his wife's illness and subsequent death.

The garage was immaculate from what he could see through the window. The doors were locked. The only car in residence sat beneath a dust-laden canvas cover. It looked as if it hadn't been moved or touched in years. Garden tools were lined up neatly along the wall. Peg-Board above the workbench displayed a neat array of Joe Handyman stuff – wrenches, screwdrivers, hammers.

Clutching the chemical hand-warmer packets in his coat pockets, Mitch headed around the back of the house to check the basement window.

His temper boiled at the memory of how close Megan had come to getting caught snooping around here the night before. What if Fletcher was insane? What if he had found her there alone?

Mitch looked down at the foundation of the house, at the thick plastic sheeting that obscured the basement windows.

The staples had been replaced.

At the church Mitch found Father Tom kneeling with two dozen women, chanting the decades of the rosary. A wall of votives flickered and saturated the air with the thick vanilla scent of melting wax. On the wall beside the tiers of candles, the catechism classes had taped handmade posters. Carefully printed messages in colored marker on newsprint paper

– Jesus, please keep Josh safe. Lord, please bring Josh home. Crayon drawings of angels and children and policemen.

All eyes turned to Mitch as he hesitated beside the priest's pew. They looked to Mitch for some kind of deliverance, for some news he couldn't give. Father Tom rose and slipped out the end of the pew. The leader of the prayer dragged the rest of them on with her droning monotone.

'Hail Mary, full of grace. The Lord is with thee . . .'

'Is there some news?' Father Tom whispered, his voice as taut as a guy wire. He let out a breath as Mitch shook his head.

'I need to ask you a couple of questions.'

'Let's go in my office.'

Father Tom led the way, genuflecting hastily at the foot of the altar before moving on. In the office he motioned Mitch to a chair and shut the door. He looked as priestly as Mitch had ever seen him, with a clerical collar standing up stiffly above the crew neck of his black sweater. Comb tracks suggested he had even made an attempt to style his unruly hair into submission, though sandy sprigs sprung up defiantly at the crown of his head like wheat stubble. The pope gazed down on him from an oil painting on the wall behind him, looking more skeptical than benevolent, as if the collar didn't fool him in the least.

'What's the occasion?' Mitch needled, pointing at his throat. 'Is the bishop coming to town?'

Tom McCoy gave him a sheepish look. 'One of those little deals we make with God. I'll try to be a better priest if He'll give Josh back to us.'

Mitch sensed an underlying motive but didn't press. He knew Father Tom well enough to golf with him, not well enough to act as confessor to a man rungs above him on the spiritual ladder.

'Unfortunately for all concerned, I don't think God kidnapped him,' he said. 'How was Hannah when you left last night?'

The priest frowned down at the Game Boy on his blotter. 'She's doing the best she can. She feels helpless; that's unfamiliar territory for her.'

'Paul isn't exactly helping.'

Father Tom's jaw tightened. 'No. He isn't,' he said shortly. He drew in a slow breath and raised his head, his gaze glancing off Mitch's left shoulder. 'I suggested she take up one of the news magazines on their request for an interview. I think it might help her if she can present her story in a way that could benefit other mothers, help prevent this kind of thing from happening to someone else. That's the role she's most familiar with – helping others.'

'Maybe,' Mitch murmured, thinking of his own role as helper/ protector and how he had retreated from it after his crisis.

'You said you had some questions?'

'Is Albert Fletcher around?'

Father Tom's brows pulled together. He tucked his chin and sat back in his swivel chair. 'Not at the moment. I think he's at the rectory. Why?'

Mitch gave him his deadpan detective face. 'I need to talk to him about a couple of things.'

'Is this about Josh?'

'Why would you ask that?'

Father Tom gave a laugh that held no amusement. 'I believe we already had this little chat. Albert had Josh for server instruction and religion class. Doesn't that automatically make him a suspect?'

Mitch let the defensive tone slide. 'Fletcher was teaching classes the night Josh disappeared. Why? Do you think he could have done it?'

'Albert is the most devout man I know,' Tom said. 'I'm sure he secretly thinks I'm doomed to perdition because I had cable installed at the rectory. No.' He shook his head. 'Albert would never blatantly break the law – secular or holy.'

'How long have you known him?'

'About three years.'

'Were you around during his wife's illness?'

'No. She died, I believe it was January ninety-one. I came here that March. I got the impression he must have been close to her by the way he turned to the church for solace afterward. The way he immersed himself, he must have had a big void to fill.'

Or he had already been in love with the church and wanted Doris out of the way so he could pursue his obsession with full zeal. Mitch kept that theory to himself.

'He had a funny way of showing his affection for her,' he said. 'It seems to be fairly common knowledge that he didn't want her to seek treatment for her illness. He claimed he wanted to heal her through prayer, and he wasn't too pleased when Hannah intervened.'

A frown curved Father Tom's mouth. 'Mitch, you're not suggesting –'

'I'm not suggesting anything,' Mitch said, getting out of his chair, hands raised in denial. 'I'm fishing, that's all. I'll throw back a lot of chubs before I catch anything for the frying pan. Thanks for your time, Father.'

He started for the door, then turned back. 'Would Fletcher have made a good priest?'

'No,' Father Tom answered without hesitation. 'There's more to this job than memorizing scripture and church dogma.'

'What's he lacking?'

The priest thought about that for a moment. 'Compassion,' he said softly.

Mitch had never been a fan of old Victorian houses with their heavy dark woodwork and cavernous rooms. The St Elysius rectory was no exception. It was big enough to house the entire University of Notre Dame football team, whose photograph hung prominently on the wall of the den above the evil cable box.

He wandered through the rooms of the first floor, calling for Albert Fletcher and receiving no answer. The smell of coffee and toast lingered in the kitchen. A box of Frosted Flakes sat on the table. Beside it squatted a half-empty coffee mug, a souvenir from Cheyenne, Wyoming. The *Star Tribune* had been left open to a story about the plight of the Los Angeles quake victims and the reprise of the old fake-priest scam – con men impersonating clergy and collecting cash donations intended for those left homeless.

'Mr Fletcher?' Mitch called.

The basement door opened and Albert Fletcher emerged from the gloom. Gaunt and pale, he looked as if he had been held captive down there. His black shirt hung on shoulders as thin and sharp as a wire hanger. A black turtleneck showed above the button-down collar – a reverse image of Father Tom's clerical collar. The dark eyes that met Mitch's were bright with something like fever, but opaque, hiding the source of their glow. They were set in a face that was long and sober, the skin like ash-white tissue paper stretched taut over prominent bones, the mouth an unyielding line that seemed incapable of bending upward. Mitch tried to superimpose this face over the featureless composite drawing of Ruth Cooper's visitor. Maybe. With a hood ... with sunglasses.

'Mr Fletcher?' Mitch held out his hand. 'Mitch Holt, chief of police. How are you today?'

Fletcher turned away to close the basement door behind him, ignoring the pleasantry as if pleasantry were against his personal beliefs.

'I need to ask you a couple of questions, if you don't mind,' Mitch continued, sliding his hands into his pants pockets.

'I've already spoken with several policemen.'

'It's standard procedure to follow up interviews,' Mitch explained. 'New questions come up. People remember things after the first cop is gone. We don't want to miss anything.'

He leaned back against the work island and crossed his ankles. 'You can have a seat, if you'd be more comfortable.'

Apparently comfort was also a sin. Fletcher made no move to find himself a chair. He folded his long, bony hands in front of him, displaying the evidence of his trip to the basement. The deacon looked down at the dirt-streaked backs of his hands, and frowned. 'I've been going through some church artifacts in the storage room. They've been down there a long time.'

Mitch called up a phony smile as he straightened. 'Must be quite a basement under a big old place like this. Mind if I take a look? These old Victorian houses fascinate me.'

Fletcher hesitated just a second before opening the door. Then he descended once more into the bowels of the St Elysius rectory. Mitch followed, quelling a grimace at the scent of mold.

The basement was exactly what he'd expected – a chambered cave of old brick and cracked cement. Rafters hung with festoons of cobwebs. Bare bulbs gave off inadequate light. The chamber beneath the kitchen held the water heater, the furnace, the electrical circuit box, and an ancient chest-type freezer. In the next section was junk – old bicycles, a hundred battered folding chairs, a stack of collapsible tables, row upon row of green-painted window screens, a squadron of rusty little wire carts loaded with croquet equipment, a forest of bamboo fishing rods.

The room Fletcher led him to was crammed with statuary from the days when church icons came complete with human hair and everyone in the Holy Family looked amazingly Anglo-Saxon. The moldering relics stared unseeing into the gloom, their limbs and faces chipped and cracked. An old altar and baptismal font gave testimony to the rise and fall in popularity of cheap blond wood veneer. A jerry-rigged rack hung down from an exposed water pipe and displayed the fashion in clerical vestments through the years, the damp rotting the garments on their hangers. Floor-to-ceiling shelves lined three walls of the room. The shelves and all available flat surfaces were stacked with boxes of old church records and curling photographs. Decaying books gave off a musty sweet aroma.

Albert Fletcher looked oddly at home among the forgotten castoffs of the faithful of generations past. 'I've been making an inventory,' he explained, 'and moving the old books and records out to properly preserve them.'

Mitch arched a brow. 'That on top of your duties as deacon and teacher? I know you were Josh Kirkwood's instructor for religion class, as well as being in charge of the altar boys. You're very generous with your time.'

'My life belongs to the church.' Fletcher folded his hands in front of him again, as if he wanted to be ready at any moment to fall to his knees in prayer. 'Everything else is secondary.'

'That's admirable, I'm sure,' Mitch murmured. 'I was wondering, Mr Fletcher, if, as his instructor, you might have noticed any changes in Josh's behavior over the last few weeks?'

Fletcher blinked, the glow went dark, like a light switching off inside him. 'No,' he said, his thin mouth pinching closed into a tight hyphen.

'Had he been unusually quiet or had he mentioned any problem, anyone who might have been bothering him?'

'The children come to me for instruction, Chief Holt. They go to Father McCoy for confession.'

Mitch nodded. Pretending interest, he touched a tarnished chalice, brushed a finger over an old brass collection plate. 'Well, do you have any personal observations about Josh? Do you think he's a nice kid, a troublemaker, what?'

'He is generally well behaved,' Fletcher said grudgingly. 'Although children these days seem to have no grasp of respect or discipline.'

'He's Dr Garrison's son, you know.' Mitch fingered the dusty brass plate on the old baptismal font that read GIVEN IN MEMORY OF NORMAN PATTERSON 1962. 'You know Dr Garrison, don't you?'

'I'm aware of who she is.'

'Wasn't she your wife's doctor?' Mitch asked, watching Fletcher's reaction through his lashes.

The eyes narrowed slightly. 'Doris saw her on occasion.'

'I was of the understanding Dr Garrison actually drove your wife to the Mayo Clinic once to see that she had tests run. Above and beyond the call of duty, don't you think?'

Fletcher offered no reply. Mitch could feel anger vibrating out from the rigid body.

'Dr Garrison is a remarkable woman,' he continued. 'She's dedicated her life to saving lives and helping people. It's a tragedy that someone so good has to go through something like this.'

The mouth tightened into a sour knot. 'It's not our place to question God.'

'We're looking for a madman, Mr Fletcher. I'd hate to think he's doing God's work.'

Albert Fletcher made no comment. He didn't even bother to feign sympathy or offer the platitudes people unaffected by a tragedy mouth out of a sense of decency. He stood rigid before a statue of Mary, the Holy Mother reaching a hand out over his head as if she couldn't decide whether to give him her blessing or a karate chop. Mitch would have rooted for the latter. For a man so devout, Albert Fletcher seemed awfully short on the more popular Christian virtues. Father Tom had said he lacked compassion. Mitch wondered if he lacked a soul as well.

'Terrible what happened with Olie Swain, isn't it?' Mitch said. 'He might have been able to end this whole nightmare for us if he hadn't killed himself. Did you know Olie?'

'No.'

'Well, I guess we have to hope he finds some peace in the next world, huh?'

'Suicide is a mortal sin,' Fletcher informed him piously, the knuckles of his clasped hands bone-white from the tension of his grip. 'He damned his own soul to hell.'

'Let's hope he deserved it, then,' Mitch said tightly. 'Thank you for the tour. It's been . . . enlightening.'

He made his way out of the storage room and back to the stairs. Fletcher followed like the shadow of doom. Mitch turned back toward him, one hand on the stair railing.

'One last thing,' he said. 'We had a report of a prowler in your neighborhood last night. I was wondering if you had seen anything suspicious.'

'No,' Fletcher said flatly. 'I was out until after ten, and when I got home, I went straight to bed.'

'After ten, huh?' Mitch forced a conspiratorial smile. 'Kind of late for such a cold night. Seeing someone special?'

'The Holy Mother,' Fletcher said, deadpan. 'I was praying.'

As he walked back to his truck, Mitch wondered why Fletcher's admission left him feeling queasy instead of comforted.

11:00 a.m. –20° windchill factor: –46°

ignorance is not innocence but SIN
i had a little sorrow, born of a little SIN
my emanation far within
weeps incessantly for my SIN

The messages burned in the back of Megan's mind as she walked up and down the time line Mitch had taped to the long wall of the war room. At the end of the room the messages from the original notes had been copied in red ink against the white board. Urgent red. Bloodred.

She stared at the time line, looking for a key, looking for something they had missed the first few hundred times they had looked at it. Looking for anything that should have given them a name. It was there somewhere. She wanted to believe they were close, they weren't just seeing something they needed to see, something just around the corner, teasing them, taunting them, waiting for them to pick up the one key piece of information that would unlock all the doors and lead them to Josh.

Ignorance and *sin*. The words suggested feelings of superiority and piety. Albert Fletcher had a grudge against Hannah. A grudge three years old. *Revenge is a dish best served cold.* That was not among the quotes on the message board, but it could have applied.

There was Paul Kirkwood with his violent temper and his secrets. He hadn't told them about the van. What else might he be hiding? He played the martyr for the television cameras, then turned on his own wife in rage and contempt. Could he have turned on his own son? Why? What could possibly have driven him to do such a thing? To have taken Josh and then put on the elaborate show of the grieving father would take a soul as black and cold as obsidian. But Megan knew it happened. She had read files of other cases, cases with details that had made her physically ill, where parents had harmed their own offspring in the most hideous ways, then covered their tracks with grief.

Kirkwood would have to come in today to give them his fingerprints so they could check them against prints found in the van. Megan's stomach rolled at the thought of the stink he would make. If he chose to play the persecuted innocent for the press, the heat from the resulting furor would be enough to melt badges and fry careers – namely hers.

Ignorance and *sin*. The words throbbing in her mind, she walked slowly backward along the time line, from that day's date back, reading the notations, the most significant details in red, the peripheral events in blue. The discovery of the jacket. Olie's suicide. Olie's arrest and interrogation.

The phone call to Hannah. The discovery of the duffel bag. The first report of Josh missing.

She stood at the far end of the line. Day one. Ground zero.

5:30 – Josh leaves GKM Arena after hockey practice.

5:45 – Hospital calls GKM to notify Hannah will be late.

5:45 – Beth Hiatt picks up Brian Hiatt at GKM. Brian last to see Josh.

6:00–7:00 – During this time period Helen Black sees boy getting into light-colored van in front of GKM Arena.

7:00 – Josh no-show at St E's religion class taught by A. Fletcher.

7:00 – Hannah calls Paul at work. NA. Leaves message.

7:45 – Hannah reports Josh missing.

8:30 – Olie Swain questioned at GKM. Did not take call from hospital regarding Hannah being late.

8:45 – Josh's duffel bag found on grounds of GKM with note: a child vanishes, ignorance is not innocence but SIN.

They had reduced the crime down to a timetable. What they didn't have was the itinerary of the criminal. What time, what day was it when he first decided to take Josh Kirkwood? What did he do that day? Whom did he see, talk to? Who could have stopped him? If the guy ahead of him at the convenience store had decided to buy fifty lottery tickets and held up the line for another ten minutes, would Josh still be with them today?

Timing is everything.

And ignorance is not innocence but sin.

Tension gripped Megan by the temples like a pair of ice tongs. Tighter and tighter.

'I'll see it,' she muttered. 'I'll see it and I'll nail your ass.'

A sharp rap on the door preceded Natalie's appearance. She stepped into the room with a sheaf of files and papers in her left arm and a steaming coffee mug in her right hand. Behind her big red-framed glasses, her dark eyes were bleary and bloodshot, reminding Megan she wasn't the only one losing sleep over this case.

'Girl, you need coffee,' Natalie announced, plunking the mug down on the table.

Megan lifted it and breathed in the aroma as if it were smelling salts. 'I'd take it intravenously if I could. Thanks, Nat.'

Natalie waved off the gratitude with a cranky snort, a trio of colorful wooden bead bracelets clacking together on her arm. A matching necklace that looked like Tinkertoys on a rope rode the slope of her bosom. She looked like a fashion ad for larger women in a rich mocha tunic over a matching calf-length broomstick skirt. Megan felt like the Before photo. She had dozed off at dawn, overslept, and jumped into the first clothes that had come to hand as she stumbled out of bed – a pair of gold corduroy pants with diagonal wrinkles from having been thrown haphazardly over the back of a chair and a hunter green sweater Gannon had used for a bed. She picked off a cat hair and flicked it away.

'The way my phone's been ringing off the hook, I figure you need all the friends you can get,' Natalie said, sitting in one of the chrome-and-plastic chairs. 'The tabloid shows have offered me big bucks if I could give them evidence you and the chief been doing the wild thing in his office.'

Megan closed her eyes and groaned, sinking down onto the next chair.

'I told them they could take their dirty money and give it to the volunteer center. It's none of my business what goes on with folks behind their own closed doors and it's none of theirs, either.'

'Amen.'

'Personally, I'd like to see Mitch find someone who could make him happy. God knows, we've all been trying to find that someone for him ever since he moved here. Poor man's had more blind dates than Stevie Wonder.'

She gave another snort as Megan managed a weary chuckle.

'I appreciate the support,' Megan said, 'but I don't think I'm that someone. We're at each other's throats half the time.'

'And the other half you're at something else altogether. Sounds like love to me,' she said as matter-of-factly as if she'd been diagnosing a common cold.

Megan didn't want to think the situation was so transparent. It wasn't that simple. It was never as simple as loving someone. They had to love you back.

'Well,' she said, 'the way things are going with the case, I won't be here long enough to unpack my bags.'

Natalie shook her head. 'I pray to God and then I swear at Him and then I pray some more. I want a miracle and I want it now,' she said, thumping her fist on the table.

'I'd settle for a clue,' Megan admitted. 'Is Mitch in yet?'

'No, but Professor Priest is here looking for you. Should I send him this way?'

Megan glanced around the war room with the time line and the messages written out and the chalkboard for brainstorming with names and motives and question marks. It wasn't the place to bring a citizen, but the urge was strong. Maybe what they needed was someone with a computer brain like Christopher Priest's to walk in cold and analyze the whole mess. Someone to walk in cold . . . like a new agent.

'No,' she said, shrugging off the thought and pushing herself to her feet. 'I'll see him in my office. Thanks, Natalie.'

'Anything for the cause. And don't you scratch Mitch off your dance card yet, girl. He's a good man . . . and you're okay,' she said, the twinkle in her eyes betraying her grudging admission. 'You'll do.'

The professor listened, wide-eyed and attentive, as Megan laid out the situation with Olie's computer booby traps. He had shrugged off his black down jacket to reveal a blue Shetland wool sweater he must have inadvertently tossed in the dryer. The sleeves hit two-thirds of the way down his forearms, showing too much of the white oxford shirt beneath it.

Megan felt a certain amount of frustration at the thought that the case might not be solved by sweat and grunt police work, but by a pencil-necked computer nerd. But solved was solved, and Megan would take Josh back any way she could get him. If she had to resort to psychics and séances, she would pay for the crystal balls out of her own pocket.

'I understand Olie was auditing computer courses at Harris,' she said. 'We're hoping you might be able to get past these traps he'd set up. If we can find out what information he kept on those computers, we might find a clue as to his involvement in Josh's kidnapping.'

'I'll be glad to help in any way I can, Agent O'Malley,' the professor said, his eyebrows lifting into a little tent of concern. 'I have to say, I have a hard time believing Olie was involved. He certainly never gave me any indication . . . I mean, he worked hard in class, never bothered anyone . . . I never would have imagined . . .'

'Yeah, well, John Wayne Gacy dressed up as a clown and visited sick kids in hospitals.'

'"Who knows what evil lurks in the hearts of men?"' the professor quoted, murmuring the words almost to himself.

'If we knew by looking, the prisons would be overflowing and the streets would be safe,' Megan said. 'Do you have any idea what Olie was doing with all those machines?'

'He liked to tinker with them. Upgrade the boards, augment the memories, then write his own programs to perform various functions. He had an old Tandy model when he first approached me about auditing classes. It wasn't good for much besides word processing. I told him where he might be able to get a better machine for little or nothing. I guess he turned that into his hobby.'

'If we're lucky, his hobby might lead us to Josh. We might even find out if he had an accomplice, but we have to get into the computers first.'

'As I said, I'll help any way I can, Agent O'Malley,' Priest reiterated, rising from his chair, tugging on the bottom of his too-small sweater that had crept up to his waistband. 'I can't make any promises, but I'll do the best I can.'

'Thank you, Professor. We'll set you up in a room here. A computer expert from the BCA will be working with you. That's standard procedure when someone from outside the agency is called in.'

'I understand. I don't have a problem with that.'

'Good.'

Megan reached out to shake his hand, but the contact was never made. Her office door swung open and Mitch leaned in.

'Paul's coming in,' he announced in a voice as hard as rock. 'And he's bringing an entourage.'

30

The circus set up in the City Center lobby. A ring made of television lights and cameras. An audience of shocked and angry people from the volunteer center, print media reporters, reporters from competing television stations, their eyes glowing with jealousy. As ringmaster: Paige Price, resplendent in a cardinal-red hacking jacket over a short black shift and black hose.

The main attraction at the City Center circus was, of course, Paul Kirkwood. He had been livid when Mitch had cornered him at Ryan's Bay and informed him he had to come in to be fingerprinted. He was still livid. This was all the fault of that bitch O'Malley. By God, he would make her pay. She and Mitch could both pay as far as Paul was concerned – for the humiliation, for the suspicion. He should have been the object of sympathy and concern and compassion. Instead, he was being fingerprinted.

He put on his best martyr's expression and gave it the perfect hint of indignation and outrage. He had considered going home first to shower and change into better clothes, but Paige had pointed out the potential for impact if he came in straight from the search in his jeans and Sorels and heavy sweater. His hair was mussed from his cap, his nose still red from the cold.

A *TV* 7 technician did a light check on Paige's face. Another minion sidled up to her with a compact mirror so she could check her makeup. She nodded her readiness. The countdown came from a disembodied voice just beyond the ring of light.

'Three . . . two . . . you're live.'

'This is Paige Price coming to you live from the Deer Lake City Center with Paul Kirkwood, whose son Josh was abducted outside an ice arena here in Deer Lake eight days ago. As the search for Josh and his abductor drags on, law enforcement authorities working on the case have suddenly turned their focus on Josh's father. Today Paul Kirkwood was ordered by Deer Lake Chief of Police Mitchell Holt to submit to having his fingerprints taken.' She turned to Paul, microphone in hand, grave expression in place. 'Mr Kirkwood, can we get a reaction from you on this latest development?'

'It's an outrage,' Paul replied, his voice shaking with the strength of his fury. 'The BCA and the police have botched this case from the beginning. The only real suspect they had committed suicide while in their custody. They're desperate to appear as though they're making progress on the case when all they're doing is grasping at straws. But to turn the focus on me is absolutely unconscionable.'

Tears welled up in his eyes, sparkling like diamonds under the lights. 'Josh is my son. I love him. I would never, *never* do anything to harm him. We did everything together. Camping, sports. He used to come to my office sometimes and I'd give him a calculator and he would pretend h-he was j-just like m-me.'

Giving Paul a chance to compose himself or make a spectacle of himself, whichever way he wanted to play it, Paige turned once again to face the camera. She let a single tear slide down her cheek, her big too-blue eyes like a pair of shimmering lakes. 'This is certainly an unexpected and, if I might editorialize for a moment, a most callous turn taken by the BCA-led investigation into the disappearance of Josh Kirkwood. From the first terrible moments of this investigation we've seen Paul Kirkwood at the forefront of the search to find his missing child.'

She turned back to Paul, who was managing to look noble and long-suffering at once. 'Mr Kirkwood, do you have any explanation for their interest in you as a suspect?'

He shook his head sadly, wearily. 'I once owned the van that belonged to Olie Swain. Years ago. Agent O'Malley has decided those intervening years mean nothing.'

'Agent Megan O'Malley with the BCA?'

'Yes.'

'And Chief Holt is going along with her theory that you are somehow involved in Josh's kidnapping because of this vague past connection to the van?'

'I don't understand it. I've done everything I can to aid in the investigation. How they can turn on me like this, I – I just don't understand. I've known Mitch Holt since he moved here. I can't believe he could think I was involved.'

Mitch and Megan and Sergeant Noga stood on the periphery of the mob at the mouth of the hall to the law enforcement center, unnoticed at first with all the jockeying for position by rival camera crews, their attention on Paul and Paige. Then at the mention of Mitch's name, one person turned and glared at him, then another. Then a camera swung around in his face and a microphone was thrust out in front of him.

'Chief Holt, do you have any comment on the situation with Paul Kirkwood?'

Before Mitch could do more than think of an obscenity he couldn't voice, the whole media tide swung toward them, babbling questions, thumbing their noses at Paige Price. Mitch made no attempt to answer or to placate them. A ferocious scowl tightening his features, he waded through them, his eyes on Paul. Megan tailed him. Noogie fell in behind her, guarding them from the rear.

Paige's face lit up. She couldn't have written a more perfect scenario. She stepped in front of Paul to intercept Mitch.

'Chief Holt, do you have anything to say about this apparent lack of compassion for this poor grieving father?'

He wanted to smack the poor grieving Paul upside the head for pulling this stunt. The play for sympathy had nothing to do with Paul's grief and everything to do with his petty vindictiveness. Mitch turned his glare on Paige, then looked over her shoulder at the mayor and half the town council standing in the hallway to the city offices.

'As I explained to Mr Kirkwood quite thoroughly this morning,' he answered, 'this procedure is necessary for the purpose of identifying all prints found in the van. He once owned the van, therefore, we're taking his fingerprints for comparison. Mr Kirkwood is under neither arrest nor suspicion.'

He turned back to Paul, his face ruddy with anger. 'If you'll come with me, Paul, we can have this over in a matter of minutes with a minimum amount of fuss.'

Paul's expression would have looked more fitting on a pouting ten-year-old. Noogie turned around to clear the path, and they started for the law enforcement center. The shouted questions of reporters echoed and amplified, filling up the atrium with a tower of sound.

Megan wasn't quick enough in her attempt to fall in line. Paige cut her off, clearly annoyed at having her exclusive interview disappear down the hall with a police escort.

'Agent O'Malley, what do you have to say about the BCA's role in this drama?' she asked, a gleam of vengeance in her eyes. 'Do you consider Paul Kirkwood a suspect?'

Megan frowned as a spotlight hit her in the face. 'No comment.'

'Is it true you're responsible for focusing this attention on Paul Kirkwood?'

Megan's stomach churned as she imagined DePalma watching this, his blood pressure hopping higher into the danger zone with every second. 'A connection was found between Mr Kirkwood and the van owned by Olie Swain,' Megan replied, measuring her words carefully. 'What we're doing now is simply standard procedure and is in no way an indictment or a persecution of Mr Kirkwood. We're simply doing our jobs.'

Paige moved in a little closer. Her eyes narrowed with what looked to Megan like malicious glee, though viewers would probably mistake it for sharp journalistic instincts. 'Your job is pulling the focus of your investigation off legitimate leads and placing it on Josh's father?'

'We're following *all* leads, Ms Price.'

'By "we," you mean yourself and Chief Holt, with whom you've been linked −'

'By "we," I mean the agencies involved −'

'And this attention on Paul Kirkwood is not in retaliation for his criticism of your handling of the case?'

'I'm with the BCA,' Megan snapped. 'Not the Gestapo.'

'Mr Kirkwood has been openly critical of your conduct −'

'*My* conduct?'

A red haze filmed Megan's vision. How dare Paige Price prostitute herself for inside information, then turn around and point a pious finger at someone else?

'We're doing everything we can to find Josh. Perhaps you could ask Sheriff Steiger to elaborate on the details the next time you're in bed with him.'

Paige fell back a step, gasping, her face flushing as red as her jacket. Megan gave her a *gotcha, bitch* smile, then turned on her heel to push her way through the mob.

She ignored the hands that grabbed at her. The shouted questions ran together in a cacophony of babble. She had nothing to say to any of them. These parasites offered little in the search for Josh or the effort to capture the predator who had taken him. As far as she was concerned, they were nothing but carrion feeders, getting in the way and clouding the focus of the case with their endless dust storms of manufactured controversy.

Let them feed on each other, she thought, striding purposefully down the hall of the law enforcement center. Her gaze was focused straight ahead, her mind moving beyond, to the booking room where Paul Kirkwood was grudgingly giving up his fingerprints.

9:23 p.m. −23° windchill factor: −50°

The reaction to Paul's theatrics was immediate and overwhelming. Phones in the police department and city hall offices rang off the hook all afternoon. Paul would have been dismayed, however, to learn that not all of the callers were expressing their displeasure with 'this disgraceful turn of events,' as one of his supporters called it. While some sympathies ran in Paul's favor, there were those who thought he'd done it all along. And on the gossip grapevine, which thrived even in these frigid temperatures, the rumor that his arrest was imminent quickly gained momentum and strength.

On the more visible pro-Paul front, outraged citizens called their council members, council members called the mayor, the mayor called on Mitch in person. Mitch, still furious with Paul, offered no apology. He got paid to do a job and he did it. If people wanted control of who fell under suspicion, they would have to find someone else to wear the badge.

At the moment, that didn't seem like such a bad idea, he thought.

To get away from ringing telephones, Mitch sat in the war room, but reminders of the case shouted at him from the walls and the tables that were piled with copies of reports and statements and files on hopeful tips that had hit dead ends. Where the clock on the wall ticked the seconds away loudly: 9:23.

He had spent the past four hours personally checking out a possible sighting of Josh in the small town of Jordan, seventy-five miles away. Another dead end. Another adrenaline rush and crash. He had returned to a desk stacked with statements from Deer Lake citizens pointing the finger of blame at neighbors, at cops, at teachers, at Father Tom, at Paul. He returned to a telephone that refused to stop ringing with calls from more people casting more blame.

This was an ugly case full of ugly possibilities, the ugliest being that Paul was indeed somehow involved.

Logic made a case against Paul that he had not been able to argue away without leaving behind the metallic aftertaste of lies. Logic dictated they take Paul's fingerprints, and Paul had protested too much.

Logic also made a case against Albert Fletcher. The man also made the hair on the back of Mitch's neck stand up. He didn't like the deacon, got that old corkscrew feeling in his gut when he thought of Fletcher. He would have bet his badge Fletcher was guilty of something. Trouble was, he didn't know what and couldn't prove anything. So far the most suspicious thing his men had to report on the deacon was a trip to a dry cleaner's in Tatonka even though there were two in Deer Lake. Not exactly a smoking gun.

Mitch stared at the blackboard. Chalk circles wreathed names and questions – scattered clouds from various brain-storming sessions. Suspicions and conjecture. Theories about the darker minds and motives in Deer Lake. His haven. His purgatory. He felt as if he had been living in a fog of bland niceness for the past two years, oblivious to the abscesses beneath the placid surface of the town. Willingly blind to it. Willfully shutting off his cop instincts.

He resented Megan for going after him every time he turned around, pushing him to see things he didn't want to see, to consider things he didn't want to consider. But she was right in doing it. He might have come here with the idea of hiding to lick his wounds, but he couldn't hide from this. He couldn't look at Deer Lake and see a haven. He had to think like a cop.

He stared hard at the chalkboard, at the thick white circle around Albert Fletcher's name.

Fletcher had been teaching class at the time of the kidnapping. If he was involved, he had to have had an accomplice. No connection had been made between him and Olie Swain.

No solid connection had been made between Olie and the crime. Olie's van was a near-perfect fit to the one Helen Black had seen the night of the abduction, but the lab had turned up nothing useful in the van Olie had purchased from Paul. . . .

The message board mocked him.

ignorance is not innocence but SIN
i had a little sorrow, born of a little SIN
my emanation far within
weeps incessantly for my SIN

'Give me something to go on, you son of a bitch,' Mitch muttered. 'Then we'll see who's ignorant.'

'I keep thinking maybe he's already given us something and we're just not seeing it.'

Megan stood just inside the door, looking rumpled and ragged. Of course, her day had been the equal of his. Possibly worse. She looked in need of someone to lean on, but she wasn't likely to accept an offer from him. He could all but see the chip on her shoulder, and he knew he'd put it there.

'Hear anything from DePalma?' he asked after she sat two chairs down from him.

Megan shook her head. 'I would like to think no news is good news, but I'm not that naïve. Aside from fingering Paul, I revealed Paige's secret life as a mercenary slut on live TV. I'll hear something. No good deed goes unpunished.'

Mitch gave her a crooked smile. 'As a diplomat, you make a great street cop.'

Her mouth tugged up on one corner. 'Thanks.' She drew an aimless pattern on the tabletop with her thumb. 'There seem to be more than a few people around town willing to believe Paul could have done it.'

'They want to believe someone did it,' Mitch said. 'They would rather believe it was one of their own than some faceless evil. They would rather believe it was Paul, because then the evil would all be contained nice and neat within one family. Then they can go back to thinking they're all safe because the rotten apple was in someone else's barrel.'

'That or they really believe he did it.'

Mitch sighed. As badly as she felt pressured, Megan knew the pressure was, in many different respects, worse for him. He had family and friends taking sides in the case, looking for him to tie it all up in a nice neat yellow bow like the ones the residents of Deer Lake had tied around tree trunks and light poles in a show of hope. He had the past she had thrown in his face last night.

'We'll see what the lab has to say about his prints,' he mumbled, staring once more at the time line taped to the wall.

'The lack of his prints in the van won't clear him,' she reminded him, winning herself a scowl. 'Logic dictates he would have been wearing gloves.'

'Logic dictates,' Mitch repeated. Logic dictated many things. It seemed few people took heed – including him. Logic dictated he steer clear of Megan, yet he made no real effort to do so. 'I think logic clocked out a while ago. We should do the same. How about a pizza?'

The easy camaraderie in his offer surprised her. Mitch made a face at the wary look she was giving him. 'Truce, okay? It's late. It's been another pisser of a day.'

'Do I have to take off my badge?' she said, her voice cool.

He winced. 'Okay, I was a jerk last night,' he admitted, sliding into the chair between them. 'This case hasn't done much for my temper. We both said some things we wouldn't have if the world were a sane place.' He gave her his shrewd, hard-bargain look. 'I'll spring for extra cheese.'

'See each other after hours?' Megan made her eyes wide with false shock. 'What will the public think?'

'Screw 'em,' Mitch growled. 'If we don't crack this case, they'll throw us both out in the street anyway.'

'No,' she said. 'You'll survive failure; people forgive that all the time. But heaven help you if the bad guy turns out to be someone they really like. That kind of truth pisses them off every time.'

She stared at the door that seemed a mile away. The idea of a cold apartment full of boxes served as no incentive.

'Come on, Megan,' he cajoled. 'It's just a pizza.'

Temptation curled its tentacles around Megan and pulled. It was just a pizza. And then it would be just a touch, just a kiss, just a night, just sex.

'Thanks anyway,' she murmured. 'I think I'll just go home and lose consciousness.'

But she just stood there. Wanting.

'Megan . . .'

He said her name in a low voice, a quiet, intimate tone that struck a chord of longing inside her. The beam of his whiskey-amber gaze caught her and held her in place as he rose from his chair. Then his arms were around her.

Mistake. Weakness. The words stabbed her hard, but her lips parted and met his. Her lashes fluttered down and heat enveloped her, enveloped them both. The kiss was long, yet impatient; gentle and urgent; aggressive and questioning and comforting. She wanted to touch him, to feel his need for her, to imagine it was the kind of need that transcended the physical. But it wasn't.

'What are you doing?' she asked as she pulled back, the demand lacking the sting she had intended.

'Changing your mind,' Mitch told her. 'If I'm lucky.'

Megan stepped out of his arms. She pressed her hands together and brought her fingertips to her lips as if in prayer. She tried to focus on the granite-gray carpet, but her gaze strayed back to Mitch, standing now with his hands on his hips and one leg cocked – not in any attempt to disguise his state of arousal, but daring her to look. The aura of the dangerous male glowed around him – rough, slightly rumpled, impatient, big, and masculine – as if the day had rubbed away the polish of manners and civilization.

'No,' she whispered, everything inside her protesting the denial. 'My job is hanging by a thread.'

'And the people with the ax will cut it regardless of what we do.'

'Oh, thanks for the vote of confidence,' Megan said, her voice sharp with sarcasm and hurt.

'It's got nothing to do with what I want or what I think, or what you want or what you think,' he argued. 'They'll do whatever is best for them. You know that as well as I do.'

'So if they're going to punish me, I might as well be guilty of something?' she said bitterly.

He gave a shrug, as if to say 'why not?' his face hard, impassive.

'I don't think so,' she said softly. As foolish as it was to want to love him, she couldn't think of loving him as an act of spite or a consolation prize.

She turned slowly and went to the door, holding her breath against a hope she wouldn't name. Mitch said nothing. She forced her chin up and gave him a last look as she gripped the doorknob. 'I won't go to bed with you just because it's convenient. I've got my faults, but a lack of self-respect isn't one of them.'

Day 10
1:02 a.m. -24° windchill factor: -41°

Hannah sat in the wing chair in a corner of her bedroom. She was wide awake. Again. In the nine long nights that had passed since Josh had disappeared, she had forgotten what it was like to sleep deeply and peacefully. She had written herself a prescription for Valium but hadn't been able to bring herself to have it filled. Maybe she didn't want the sympathy of the pharmacist, or maybe it was symbolic of a weakness she didn't want to display. Maybe she didn't want – didn't deserve – the relief of sleep. Or maybe she was afraid she would give in to the pressure and the despair and succumb to the temptation to take too many.

Paul had been asked to submit to fingerprinting.

He had come home from the police station outraged, his temper out of control. Hannah had witnessed the *TV* 7 live report, by turns shocked, angered, sickened, and frightened. Shocked because she'd had no warning; Paul had told her nothing. Angered that he would be so thoughtless. Sickened by the possibilities that pried open in her mind. Frightened because she couldn't make them go away.

She stared at their empty bed, while in the theater of her mind she replayed the scene. She could see herself standing in the family room, arms crossed, jaw clenched, gaze hard on Paul as he stormed in. She could see the agent of the day at the kitchen table, fielding yet another of the calls that had come without cease since the *TV* 7 broadcast. Friends and relatives expressing their concern, offering their support, probing for oily secrets. She could see Paul's mouth moving and realized she wasn't hearing him above the roar of her blood in her ears.

'. . . that little bitch,' he snapped, jerking off his coat. He threw it on the love seat and toed off the heavy boots he should have left at the door. The laces were matted with snow that melted and ran like beads of sweat down into the carpet. 'The only part of her job she can handle is fucking Mitch Holt.'

Hannah ignored the remark. 'I'd like to speak with you privately,' she said tightly.

Paul stared at her, perturbed that she had interrupted his tirade. 'I suppose you like her,' he accused. 'You progressive women have to stick together.'

'I don't even know who you're talking about,' she snapped.

'Thanks for paying attention, Hannah,' he sneered. 'It's so nice to have the support of my wife.'

'If you want my support, you might consider letting me know what's going on.' Her gaze darted to the agent at the table and back to Paul, who seemed oblivious to the third party. The phone rang yet again, the sound piercing her brain like a skewer. 'You were asked to give your fingerprints and you didn't bother to let me know. How do you think that made me feel?'

'*You?*' Paul said, incredulous. 'How do you think it made *me* feel?'

'I'm sure I wouldn't know. You certainly didn't share it with me. It was just a fluke that I saw that sideshow at City Center. Did you think it was more important to get Paige Price on your side than me?'

'I shouldn't have to *get you* on my side. You should *be* on my side!'

His raised voice drew a look from the agent.

'If you want to continue this conversation,' Hannah said, 'I'll be in our room.'

She strode across the room and up the steps. She felt as if they were living in a fishbowl; she didn't need a live audience for the disintegration of her marriage.

Paul caught hold of her arm from behind and jerked her to a stop. 'Don't you walk away from me!' he snarled. 'I've about had it with your attitude.'

'*My* attitude!' Hannah gaped at him. '*I'm* not the one who was fingerprinted today!'

'You think I wanted that?'

She stared at him, at the hand that gripped her arm so hard his knuckles had gone white, at the lean face that was red and twisted with rage. She didn't know this man, didn't trust him, didn't know what to believe about him.

She pulled away from his grasp and rubbed at the soreness in her arm. 'I don't know what to think,' she whispered, shivering.

He blinked at her, color draining from his face. 'Jesus, Hannah. You can't think I had anything to do with it.'

Guilt came on a tide of exhaustion. It wasn't that she believed he had, it was that she wasn't sure he hadn't. The technicality would be lost on Paul. Truthfully, it was all but lost on her. How could she think Paul would hurt their son, take their son away, put her through this hell? How could she think it? What kind of wife was she? What kind of person?

'No,' she said in a small voice. 'I just don't know what to think, Paul. We used to share everything. Now we can't even talk without going for each other's throats. You can't imagine how I felt seeing you on television, hearing about the van and the fingerprints. All of it was like a scene from a bad soap opera. Why didn't you tell me?'

He dodged her plaintive look by staring into Lily's empty room. Karen Wright had offered to take the baby for the evening. Hannah had been too much in shock after seeing Paul on television to protest.

'There wasn't time,' he explained. 'I was out on the search and Mitch Holt came and . . .'

He was lying. The thought was instantaneous. Hannah felt ashamed for thinking it, but she couldn't push it aside. It was written all over her face.

'And you wonder why I didn't confide in you?' He shook his head. 'I'm out of here.'

'Paul –'

'I'll be at my office,' he snapped, turning away. 'You might want to alert the police so they can set up a surveillance.'

He hadn't returned. He hadn't called. She hadn't tried to call him for fear he wouldn't answer. The way he hadn't answered the night Josh disappeared.

A tremor shook her and she curled herself more tightly into the chair, wrapping her arms around her knees. She didn't want the doubts and questions that ate away at the corners of her mind like mice. She didn't want to think about the interview she would do tonight with Katie Couric. All she wanted was to close her eyes and make it all go away.

Instead, she closed her eyes and saw Josh.

He was alive. Expressionless. Standing in a gray, formless void. He didn't speak. He showed no sign of recognizing or even seeing her. He simply stood there as her perspective shifted around him, circling slowly, taking in everything about him. There was a bruise on his right check. He wore striped pajamas she had never seen before. Even though she couldn't see through the sleeves, she knew he wore a gauze bandage on his left arm at the inner elbow. Just as she knew his mind was filled with the same gray fog that surrounded him, with the exception of one thought – *Mom*.

Hannah's heart raced out of control. She wanted to touch him, but couldn't move her arms from her sides. She tried to call out to him, but no sound came out of her mouth. She willed him to look at her, but he looked through her, as if she were not there. Frustration built and built inside her like steam in a kettle until she screamed, and screamed and screamed.

She jerked in the chair, her eyes snapping open, her heart galloping. The nightshirt and leggings she wore were soaked with sweat. She thought she'd slept a matter of minutes. The clock on Paul's nightstand told her she had dozed more than an hour. It was two-forty.

The bed was still empty.

The phone rang and she dove for it, knocking the base to the floor. 'Paul? Paul?'

Silence answered her, heavy and dark.

She sank down to sit on the floor, leaning back against the bed. 'Paul?' she tried again.

The voice came, low and eerie, a whisper like smoke. 'A lie is the handle which fits them all. A lie is the handle which fits them all. A lie is the handle which fits them all.'

31

Sin has many tools, but a lie is the handle which fits them all came from Oliver Wendell Holmes, they found out.

They had looked the phrase up in an old dog-eared book of quotations in Paul's home office, an immaculate room that should have been featured in a home decorating magazine. Megan's gaze had roamed. Not a book, not a pen out of place. Not a speck of dust. Not a picture hanging crooked on the wall. Compulsively, fanatically neat. Not Hannah's doing; Hannah wasn't certain Paul had a book of quotations. Anyone keeping a room that clean had to know every title on the shelves.

Serial killers were often compulsively neat. Megan knew that from her behavioral science courses at the FBI academy. No one considered Paul Kirkwood a potential serial killer; still, she filed his compulsive tendencies away in the back of her mind. That and the fact that he had been out of the house when the call had come. The watch commander had sent a unit to the Omni Complex, and the officers had awakened Paul from what he claimed was a sound sleep on the sofa in his office and escorted him back home.

Megan saw the apprehension in Hannah's eyes when Paul came into the kitchen. She felt the tension that lay between them like a sheet of ice. God, wasn't the loss of Josh enough? Did they have to lose their marriage, too? On the other hand, didn't Hannah deserve better than Paul? Weak and petulant and self-absorbed, he got Megan's back up, and had almost from the moment she'd met him. But had he called his wife in the dead of night and taunted her with hints of lies?

If he had, he was a damn good actor. News of the call had shaken him. With fear or abject guilt?

The call had come from somewhere in Deer Lake. There hadn't been sufficient time to trap it to get more than the exchange. It could have come from anywhere – a house across the street or across town or across the lake where Albert Fletcher lived in the shadow of St Elysius. It could have come from Paul's office. It could have come from any pay phone in town.

The possibilities buzzed like flies in Megan's brain. She hadn't been sleeping long or well when the call had come. Thoughts of the curt message DePalma had left on her answering machine for her to call him ASAP had kept her mind from winding down. And now that she was back home from the Kirkwoods' house, it was too late to go back to bed and too early to go in to the office.

She sat at the round oak table she had rescued from a flea market and stripped herself, another of her faux heirlooms. A tremor rattled through her body. Caffeine overload. Between the coffee and the drugs to stave off a monster migraine, she felt as if her body were running on rocket fuel. Her heart was pumping too fast and she felt dizzy. She had been abusing her body and abusing her medications, taking too much of some and ignoring others because they knocked her out and she couldn't afford to be groggy or unconscious.

She would be paying for her sins soon. She just had to hang in there a while longer. Just until they could make the pieces fit. Just until they saw the one thing they had been missing.

Sin has many tools, but a lie is the handle which fits them all.

Whose lie? Whose sin? What was there that they couldn't see?

Pain squeezed her temples like a giant forceps. Trying to will it away, she pushed herself to her feet and went into the bathroom. She fumbled with the cap on the prescription bottle of Propranolol, finally tipping a pill into her trembling hand. She washed it down with water and stood there for a moment after, scowling at herself in the mirror.

'One more strike and you're out, O'Malley,' she mumbled.

The pain dug into her temples like a pair of spurs.

A little voice in the back of her head whispered she was out already.

7:15 a.m. -19° windchill factor: -38°

She avoided her office, having no burning desire to return DePalma's call of the night before. She stopped first at the command center to see if anything useful had come in over the hotline. Lots of calls pro- and con-Paul. One call from a woman who claimed Josh had been abducted by aliens. A dozen or more from people who wanted to chastise Megan personally for picking on Paige Price. A whole lot of nothing. She left the center with a promise to return at eight to brief her people on the latest developments and make assignments for the day.

At the station her first stop was the war room. Mitch had been there ahead of her. The Oliver Wendell Holmes line had been added to the list on the message board. The call to Hannah had been noted on the line, and Paul's noticeable absence had been starred.

Megan walked backward along the line, looking for a sign that Paul was at the heart of the mystery. Paul had lied to them. Paul had been evasive. He had a secret, of that she was certain, but was his secret dark enough, evil enough to drive him to harm his own son?

Albert Fletcher appeared on the time line only once – on the night of Josh's abduction, when he had been teaching the class Josh should have attended. The line was for facts only, no conjecture, no suspicions, which served only to magnify their lack of solid leads. Their crook might be any one of fifteen thousand people in Deer Lake – if he was from Deer Lake at all. He might be someone she had passed on the street. He might be sitting at the coffee shop down the block. All they knew with any certainty was that someone had happened upon Josh at a moment when he was absolutely vulnerable. That truth pointed to Olie Swain, and Olie Swain was gone forever.

Her next stop was to see that Olie's computers had been set up for Christopher Priest. Not only had they already been set up, Priest was already inspecting them. The machines had been lined up on a long table in a small gray room that held nothing else but a pair of chrome-and-plastic chairs. The disk drives hummed quietly. The monitors glowed in varying shades and combinations of black and white and green. Priest was bent over one, frowning at the message on the screen. He looked up as Megan entered the room and pushed his oversize glasses up on his nose.

'You're early, Professor. I wasn't expecting you until eight-thirty.'

'I just stopped in to see if we're set up.' The sleeves of his blue turtleneck crept halfway to his elbows. 'I'd like to get an early start if possible.'

'I'll see if the computer guy from headquarters is around,' Megan said. 'He must be here somewhere if the machines are on. You didn't turn them on, did you?'

'No.' The professor crossed his arms like a little boy who had been told not to touch anything in the toy store.

'Good. Actually, you shouldn't even be in here without him,' she pointed out, her gaze scanning the screens in the fruitless hope of detecting whether or not they had been tampered with. What she knew about computers was limited to writing reports and calling up information from headquarters. 'Procedure,' she added as a diplomatic afterthought.

Priest looked at her blankly.

'Why don't you have a seat in the break room, help yourself to a cup of coffee while I see if I can find him?' Megan suggested, holding the door open.

'I hope he's here,' he said, reluctantly backing away from the table. 'I have a faculty meeting at one. I would like to be finished . . .'

He let the thought hang, sliding the computers a longing glance.

'He's probably waiting in my office,' Megan said, standing firm, doorknob in hand. They couldn't afford a kink in the chain of evidence. If Olie's machines yielded some relevant link to an accomplice, their means of obtaining that tidbit had to be squeaky clean in order to stand up to a judge's scrutiny. If that connection ended up getting thrown out because a judge decided they hadn't played by the rules, everything they found as a direct result of that link would go as well. Fruit of the poisoned tree, the lawyers called it. Cops called it bullshit nitpicking, for all the good it did them.

Priest slipped past her into the hall. 'I *am* trustworthy, Agent O'Malley,' he said, giving her a hurt look. 'I've worked with the police before.'

'Then you know it's nothing personal.' She gave him a pained smile as she locked the door behind him. 'I'm just covering my backside.'

And she felt a little bit of a draft. Christopher Priest might have been a model of virtue, teacher, volunteer, role model for rehabilitating juvenile delinquents; but he had known Olie Swain. A defense attorney would gnaw on that bone all day long if he found out Priest had been in the room with the computers all by his lonesome.

She made her way through the labyrinth of halls, oblivious to the people she passed. Her vision was changing subtly, blurring a bit at the edges, her perception of light and dark becoming sharper. Warning signs. If she could just hold it off until afternoon, until this, until that. The bargains were old and timeworn. She would leave early and sleep all night. She would eat regular meals and avoid stress. Lies she told herself every time the talons of pain began to dig in.

Her hand was trembling so badly, she could barely insert the key in the lock of her office door. As it turned out, she didn't need to. The door was open, the office occupied.

A man rose from her visitor's chair with a copy of *Law and Order* in one hand and a half-eaten glazed doughnut in the other. He looked about thirty, though he had the kind of face that would appear boyish long after thirty had passed him by. His eyes were wide, bright, and brown, and his nose was too short. His hair – a mop of brown curls – put Megan in mind of a cocker spaniel. She scowled at him for invading her territory.

'Megan O'Malley,' she said, tossing her briefcase on her desk. She went on glaring at him as she hung her coat on the rack. 'In case you were wondering whose office you'd barged into.'

Spaniel Boy gave her a look of exaggerated sheepishness, fumbling with the magazine and the half-eaten doughnut, dumping them on her desk. He brushed his hand off on the leg of his navy chinos, leaving behind flakes of sugar glazing, then offered the hand to Megan.

'Marty Wilhelm.'

Megan ignored the show of manners. The message light on her phone was blinking like an angry red eye. 'I assume you know you're all set up in the small room down by Evidence. The professor is chomping at the bit to get started.'

'Ah . . . huh?'

'The professor. The computers,' Megan said flatly. 'Out the door.

Hang a left. I'd say you need a key, but that didn't stop you from coming in here.'

A crooked, embarrassed smile quirked his lips. 'I think you have me confused with someone else.'

'That depends on who you are.'

'*Agent* Marty Wilhelm. Headquarters was supposed to notify you. Actually' – he lifted a finger to emphasize the point, still grinning – 'Bruce DePalma said he would speak to you personally.'

Megan's gaze shot to the blinking message light. A chill swept over her. She forced her eyes back to Marty with his puppy-dog enthusiasm and regimental-striped tie.

'I'm sorry,' she said, amazed that she sounded perfectly normal when all internal systems were going haywire. 'I'm afraid you have me at a loss. I haven't spoken with Bruce today.'

'Oh, gee. This is awkward.' He cleared his throat and patted his chest, then raised both hands with fingers spread. 'I'm your replacement. You've been temporarily suspended from active duty. You're off the case.'

The internal alarm went off, too late to do any good. Marty Wilhelm. The Marty Wilhelm who had reportedly been in the running for this field post before affirmative action bumped him out. The Marty Wilhelm who was engaged to the daughter of Hank Welsh from Special Operations. The Marty Wilhelm who had evidently been standing in the wings, waiting for her to screw up.

Megan's first impulse was to pull her Glock 9-mil and blow that silly fucking smirk off his face. Smarmy little weasel, playing dumb, stringing her along. She could imagine the only thing that would have made him happier was to have had an audience. It was a wonder he hadn't waited for her in the squad room so he could have made a fool of her in front of other cops.

'I'll need to see some ID,' she said, biting down hard on her temper.

Marty's brows shot up. But he dug his ID out and handed it over. Megan glanced at it, then dropped it like a hot rock on her desk – *Spaniel Boy's* desk. Her knees shook a little and she sat down on Leo Kozlowski's broken chair.

'I'll need to make a couple of phone calls,' she announced.

Marty eased back down into the visitor's chair and made a magnanimous gesture toward the phone.

'And you will kindly get the hell out of this office while I do so,' she said through her teeth.

'Now, Megan,' he began in a practiced patronizing tone. 'You're really not in any position to order me around.'

'No,' she said, 'but I am in a position to generate headlines the likes of "Disgruntled Agent Goes on Shooting Spree." You wouldn't want to be listed first in a story like that, would you, Marty?'

His chuckle was forced and more than a little tense. He stood again and backed toward the door. 'I'll just see if I can't straighten out this confusion about the computers and the professor.'

'You do that.'

'I'll stop back.'

'Take your time.'

He slipped out the door and closed it quietly. The sound was magnified in Megan's mind. The door slamming on her career, shutting her out.

You blew it, O'Malley. You're screwed. They were waiting like wolves for you to stumble and now they're going to chew you up and spit you out. Way to go.

The self-recriminations were like lashes from a whip. What was the matter with her? This was the job she'd been waiting for, and she'd ruined it – by compromising herself with Mitch Holt. And how many times had she warned herself to curb her tongue, to restrain her temper, just to turn around and blow up on live TV.

Stupid. Careless.

She tried to gather her composure. She wouldn't give up without a fight. She wouldn't be reduced to the kind of bawling, begging woman she despised.

She reached for the telephone, her hand shaking like a palsy victim's as the migraine expanded in her head like a balloon. As she pressed the receiver to her ear, the dial tone sliced through her brain. Groaning, head swimming, she dropped the receiver and threw up in the wastebasket.

7:42 a.m. -19° windchill factor: -38°

'I saw Josh.'

Father Tom slid into the pew beside Hannah. She had called him at the crack of dawn and asked to see him before morning Mass. The sun had been up barely an hour, sending pale fingers of light through the stained glass windows. Cubes and ovals of soft color flickered shyly on the drab flat carpet that ran down the center aisle. Tom had rolled out of bed and pulled on pants and a T-shirt and sweater. He hadn't bothered to shave. Absently, he combed his hair with his fingers, as unconcerned with his own appearance as he was concerned with Hannah's.

She was pale and wan, her eyes fever-bright. He wondered when she had last eaten a meal or slept for more than an hour or two. Her golden hair was dull and she had swept it back into a careless ponytail. A bulky black cotton sweater disguised her thinness, but he could see the bones of her wrists and hands as she gripped them together in her lap, as delicate as ivory carvings, the skin almost translucent over them. He offered her his hand and she immediately took hold with both of hers.

'What do you mean, you saw him?' he asked carefully.

'Last night. It was like a dream, but not. Like a – a – vision. I know that sounds crazy,' she added hastily, 'but that's what it was. It was so real,

339

so three-dimensional. He was wearing pajamas I'd never seen before and he had a bandage —' She broke off, frustrated, impatient with herself. 'I sound like a lunatic, but it happened and it was so *real*. You don't believe me, do you?'

'Of course I believe you, Hannah,' he whispered. 'I don't know what to make of it, but I believe you saw something. What do you think it was?'

A vision. An out-of-body experience. A psychic something-or-other. No matter what she called it, it sounded like the desperate ravings of a desperate woman. 'I don't know,' she said, sighing, shoulders slumping.

Father Tom measured his words carefully, knowing he was treading a fine line through sensitive territory. 'You're under tremendous stress, Hannah. You want to see Josh more than you want to breathe. It wouldn't be unusual for you to dream about him, for the dream to seem real —'

'It wasn't a dream,' she said stubbornly.

'What does Paul think?'

'I didn't tell him.'

She pulled her hands back and rested them on her thighs, staring at the rings Paul had placed on her finger to symbolize their love and their union. Was she betraying him with her doubt? Had he betrayed them all? The questions twisted in her stomach like battling snakes, venomous, hideous, creatures over which she had no control. She turned her gaze to the soaring arched ceiling of the church, to the intricate and towering glass mosaic window of Jesus with a lamb in his arms. She stared at the ornately carved crucifix, Christ looking down at the high altar from his place on the cross. Empty, the church seemed a cavernous, cold place, and she felt small and powerless.

'The police asked him to give his fingerprints yesterday,' she murmured in the hushed tone of confession.

'I know.'

'They're not saying it, but they think he's involved.'

'What do you think?' Father Tom asked gently.

She was silent as the snakes wrestled inside her. 'I don't know.'

She closed her eyes and let out a shuddering breath. 'I shouldn't doubt him. He's my husband. He's the one person I should trust. I used to think we were the luckiest people on earth,' she murmured. 'We used to love each other. Trust. Respect. We made a family. We had priorities. Now I wonder if any of that was real or was it just a passing moment. I feel like maybe our lives were set to run on the same plane for just that time and now we've gone in such different directions, we can't even communicate. And I feel so cheated and so stupid. And I don't know what to do.'

She sounded so lost. As capable and intelligent as she was, Hannah was ill-prepared to face this kind of catastrophe in her life. She had lived the kind of life most people dreamed of. She came from a loving family, had been given advantages, had achieved and excelled, married a handsome man and started a nice family. She had never developed the tools to deal with pain and adversity. To him now, she looked stunned and defenseless, and he caught himself cursing God for being so cruel.

'Oh, Hannah,' he murmured. He didn't try to stop himself from brushing a lock of hair back from her cheek. He was well-schooled in the art of compassion, but if he had ever held any wisdom, it deserted him with this woman. There was nothing he could offer her that was more than empty words . . . except himself.

She turned to him, put her head on his shoulder. Her tears soaked into his sweater. Her muffled words tore at him.

'I just don't understand! I'm trying so hard!'

To deal with something that should never have touched her life.

Tom folded his arms around her and held her protectively, tenderly. He looked around his empty church at the votives – small tongues of flame in cobalt glass, symbols of hope that flickered out and died unanswered. The fear that yawned inside him made him tighten his arms around Hannah, and Hannah's arms stole around him, her fingers curling into the soft wool of his sweater. He rubbed a hand up and down her back, up into the fine hair at the base of her skull. He breathed in the clean, sweet scent of her, and ached with a longing he had never known. A longing to connect with the kind of love men and women had shared since the dawn of time.

He didn't ask why. Why Hannah. Why now. The questions and recriminations could wait. The need could not. He held her tight, held his breath, prayed for time to stand still for just a moment, because he knew this couldn't last. He brushed a kiss to her temple, and tasted her tears, salty and warm.

'Sinners!'

The charge came like thunder from heaven. But the bellow was not from God; it was from Albert Fletcher. The deacon descended on them from behind the screen that hid the door to the sacristy. He flew down the steps, a wraith in black, his eyes wild, his mouth tearing open, a large stoneware bowl in his hands. At the same time, the doors of the narthex at the back of the church were pulled open. The morning faithful wandered in to be struck dumb by the bizarre tableau in front of them.

Father Tom surged to his feet. Hannah twisted around to face Fletcher. He bore down on her, a madman shrieking like something from a nightmare.

'Sinners burn!' he screamed as he flung the contents of the bowl.

The holy water hit Hannah like a wall and splashed Father Tom. An elderly woman at the back of the church let out a shriek.

'Albert!' Tom yelled.

'The wages of sin is death!'

He was beyond hearing, certainly beyond listening to anything Father Tom had to say.

'Wicked daughter of Eve!'

Fletcher hurled the stoneware bowl at Hannah. She screamed, trying to dive out of the way and ward off the blow at the same time. Tom lunged in front of her, grunting as the missile glanced off his right hip. It clattered down onto the seat of the pew in front of him and bounced onto the floor, shattering with a loud *crack!* Ignoring the pain, Tom launched himself into the aisle, grabbing for Fletcher. The deacon jumped back, just out of reach.

'The wages of sin is death!' he screamed again, backing up the steps toward the altar.

'Albert, stop it!' Tom demanded, moving toward him aggressively. 'Listen to me! You're out of control. You don't know what you're doing. You don't know what you saw. Now, calm down and we'll discuss it.'

Fletcher moved continually backward, up another step, onto the level of the altar. His narrowed eyes never left Father Tom.

'"Beware of false prophets who come in sheep's clothing but inwardly are ravening wolves,"' he quoted in a low monotone. He backed into the altar, his hands behind him, fingers searching. His face was waxy white and filmed with sweat, the muscles drawn against the bone as tight as a drumhead, twitching spasmodically.

Father Tom eased up onto the last step, reaching out slowly. Should he have seen this coming? Should he have done something sooner to prevent it? He had always thought of Albert Fletcher as obsessive, not insane. There were worse obsessions than God. But madness was madness. He reached out with the intention of pulling his parishioner back across that line.

'You don't understand, Albert,' he said quietly. 'Come with me and give me a chance to explain.'

'False prophet! Son of Satan!' He swung his arm and caught Father Tom hard in the side of the head with the heavy base end of a fat brass candlestick.

Stunned, Tom fell to his knees on the steps and couldn't stop himself from veering backward, sideways, down. He had no control of arms or legs. What senses hadn't been knocked out entirely were a hopeless jumble in his pounding head. He tried to speak but couldn't, tried to point as people rushed up to surround him, gaping at him in astonishment. Albert Fletcher fled out a side door.

32

'Lonnie, Pat, check the garage. Noogie, you're with me; we'll take the house.'

They stood beside a pair of squad cars in front of Albert Fletcher's house, the cold pressing in on them, penetrating the layers of Thinsulate and Thermax and goose down and wool as if they were gossamer chiffon. None of the neighbors seemed curious enough about the presence of police to step outside into the cold. Mitch caught the flick of a drape in the rambler across the street. A wrinkled face peered out at them from the window of the Cape Cod next door to Fletcher's house.

'Don't look like he's home,' Dietz said, rubbing his gloved hands against each other. The black fake-fur hat perched on his head looked like some synthetic creature trying to mate with his wig.

'He just assaulted a priest,' Mitch drawled. 'I don't think he'd be inclined to roll out the welcome mat.'

Assault with what intent? he wondered. With what motive? Father Tom had explained as much as he could in the Deer Lake Community Hospital ER while Dr Lomax poked at the gash in the side of his head and made grave doctor faces. Fletcher had seen him with his arms around Hannah and misunderstood the embrace.

An innocent hug hardly seemed enough to catapult a man over the edge of sanity.

Mitch had looked to Hannah for confirmation as she paced the width of the small white room. She was shaking – with cold or with shock or both. Shaking hard.

'I don't know what he was thinking,' she muttered, eyes downcast. 'The whole world has gone insane.'

Amen, Mitch thought as he started up the walk to Fletcher's front door. Noogie went around to the back in case Fletcher was home and would try to make a break for it. Wherever the deacon had gone, he had gone on foot. His Toyota sat in the parking lot beside St E's.

Mitch had assigned half a dozen officers to search the neighborhood on foot and in cruisers. Every other cop in town and the county was on the lookout. He doubted Fletcher had come home, but that might depend on just how far Albert had gone off the deep end. In any event, they had a search warrant. If they didn't get Fletcher, they would at least get a look around.

He pulled open the storm door and knocked hard on the inner door. 'Mr Fletcher?' he called. 'Police! We have a search warrant!'

He waited a slow ten count. Megan would have his hide for doing this without her, but she hadn't been in her office when the call came in, and he couldn't wait. He raised the two-way radio and buzzed Noga.

'Do your thing, Noogie.'

'Ten-four, Chief.'

Mitch figured he was too damn old to be busting exterior doors in with any part of his anatomy. They had a battering ram in the trunk of Dietz's cruiser, but they had something bigger and better in Noga. After the demise of his college football career due to a bum knee, Noga was always happy to crash into something or someone.

The sharp *crack!* of splintering wood cut through the crisp morning air. Seconds later, Noga pulled the front door open from the inside. 'Whatever you're selling, I don't want any.'

Mitch stepped into the small foyer. 'Really? I'm running a two-for-one special on excessive force this month. Anyone giving me shit gets his ass busted twice.'

Noga's thick eyebrows reared up like a pair of woolly caterpillars. He stepped back into the living room, waving Mitch inside. 'You want the upstairs or the downstairs?'

'Up. Be sure to check the basement.'

Mitch took the stairs slowly, knowing he was vulnerable if Fletcher was perched up there waiting for him with a candle-stick or an Uzi. There was no predicting what Fletcher might feel driven to do. There was no telling what he might already have done. He may have lost his marbles years ago, but managed to keep a lid on his madness until now. Until he had seen Hannah in the arms of his priest.

The wages of sin is death. Wicked daughter of Eve.

Had he hated her all this time for interfering with his wife's treatment, for trying to cure the illness that had eventually killed Doris Fletcher? Had he killed Doris himself?

'Mr Fletcher? Police! We have a search warrant!'

There was an arrest warrant as well, though Mitch doubted Father Tom would press charges. It gave them access to him for the time being. The fact that Fletcher had run off with the weapon had been enough for Judge Witt to issue the search warrant.

A floorboard creaked a protest as Mitch stepped up into the narrow hall. A window straight ahead let in butter-yellow morning light through a double layer of sheer white curtains that obscured the view to and from the street. On either side of the hall, matching white six-panel doors led into what would be architecturally matching bedrooms.

He tried the door on the left first, letting himself into the room cautiously, but the room was vacant in more ways than one. It had been stripped of whatever life it might have held when Doris Fletcher was alive. Mitch felt instinctively the stark monastic quality of the furnishing and decoration was post-wife. The bed was a narrow bunk covered with an army surplus wool blanket made up so tight, he could have bounced dimes off it. The nightstand held a lamp and a worn black Bible. The only other piece of furniture was a chest of drawers, the top bare of the usual personal debris. The only decorations on the stark white walls were a crucifix and a sepia-toned print of Jesus festooned with old palm fronds.

The room across the hall was locked, a situation that was dealt with with the bottom of Mitch's boot. The door swung back on its hinges, banging against the wall. Downstairs, Noogie responded to the sound with a shout, but Mitch was too stunned to answer him.

Blackout shades blocked all light and all vision from the outside world, but the room was aglow with the flames of candles, their waxy scent thick in the air. A single row of sconces lined the walls, the shadows of their flames dancing. Candles in glass holders – some clear, some red, some blue – sat in clusters on side tables. Their light was sufficient to show the room for what it was – Albert Fletcher's personal chapel.

The walls of the room were painted the same shade of slate as the walls of St E's, and someone had gone to great pains to imitate the intricate stencil patterns that adorned the church. Even the ceiling was painted to simulate the arches and frescoes. Crude renderings of angels and saints looked down from gray clouds, their faces weirdly distorted, grotesque.

At one end of the room stood an altar draped with a white brocade antependium and rich lace runners. On it were arranged all the accoutrements of a Catholic Mass – the thick cloth-bound missal, the golden chalice, a pair of candelabra mounted with more fat white candles. On the wall above the altar hung a huge old crucifix with a painted effigy of Christ as gaunt as a greyhound, dying in agony, blood running from the gory wounds in his hands and the gash in his side.

Artifacts. The word struck Mitch as he took it all in. These were not homemade imitations, they were the genuine articles. He could envision Albert Fletcher sneaking them up here from the basement of the St Elysius rectory in the dark of night; cleaning them, his long, bony fingers stroking over them lovingly as he stared at them with the light of fanaticism in his eyes. The candlesticks, the crucifixes, the plaques of the stations of the cross, the statuary.

Perched on mismatched pedestals around the perimeter of the room were old statues of the Holy Mother and various saints whose names he could only guess at. Their sightless eyes stared out from faces that were chipped and cracked. Their human hair was ratty and thin, looking chewed off in places and plucked out in others. They stared over a congregation that was equally unanimated – four small pews of mannequins.

345

Mitch's skin crawled as he looked at them. Heads and torsos, some with arms, some without. None with legs. The males were dressed in shirts and ties and old castoff suit coats. The females were swaddled in black cloth, sheer black draped over their heads. They all sat at perpetual attention, staring blankly at the altar, the light from the candles flickering over their plastic faces.

And to the side of the altar stood yet another of their silent rank. The mannequin of a boy dressed in a black cassock and dingy white surplice. An altar boy.

A rumble of thunder announced Noogie's ascent up the stairs. He pounded down the hall and came to a dead stop in the doorway of the room, his service revolver pointed at the ceiling.

'Holy sh – shoot.' He stared, wide-eyed, his jaw hanging halfway to his chest. 'Man,' he whispered. 'I've never seen anything like this. This is creepy.'

'Did you find anything downstairs?' Mitch asked as he bent and ran a hand over the well-worn velvet padded kneeler before the altar.

'Nothing.' Noga remained in the doorway, his gaze skating nervously over the faces of the mannequins.

Mitch rose. 'It's not a real church, Noogie. You don't have to whisper.'

The big officer's gaze fixed on the statue of the Virgin Mary with half its face missing. He swallowed hard and a shudder rippled down him. 'It's weird,' he said, his tone still hushed. 'Downstairs it's like no one lives here. I mean, there's no stuff – no newspapers lying around, no mail, no knick-knacks, no pictures on the wall, no mirrors.' His eyes went wide again. 'You know, vampires don't keep mirrors.'

'I don't think he's a vampire, Noogie,' Mitch said, opening the closet door at the back of the chapel. 'Crosses ward them off.'

'Oh, yeah.'

In the closet hung a row of priest's vestments, old and frayed but clean and pressed. Some were still in the plastic bags from Mueller's Dry Cleaning in Tatonka. Black cassocks and red ones, white surplices and mantles in royal purple and cardinal red and rich ivory with elaborate embroidery.

'Mitch!' Lonnie Dietz hollered below. 'Mitch!'

'Up here!' Mitch bellowed.

The run up the stairs winded Dietz. His face was ashen, setting off the bright red of his nose. His hat had tumbled off and his wig was askew, looking like a small, frightened animal clinging to his head. He stopped on the landing as Mitch wedged himself past Noogie into the hall.

'I think you better come out here,' Dietz said. 'We think we just found Mrs Fletcher.'

Pat Stevens lifted the dust cover on the mummified remains of Doris Fletcher sitting behind the wheel of her 1982 Chevy Caprice. She was

346

dressed in an old cotton house shift that had rotted away in places where fluids had leaked from the body during one phase of decomposition. Mitch had no idea what she had looked like in life, whether she had been thin or heavy, pretty or homely. In death she looked like something that had been freeze-dried until all fluid evaporated and the tissue and skin shrunk down tight against bone like leather – which was precisely what had happened. Hideous didn't begin to describe her sitting there shriveled inside her dress.

That she had died in the winter had saved her from being ravaged by insects and rot. By the time warm weather had arrived, she had already been partially petrified. Timing had also prevented the neighbors from detecting her fate with their noses. Had Albert Fletcher locked his wife's dead body in a Chevy Caprice in July in Minnesota, he would not have been able to keep the secret three days, let alone three years. But Doris Fletcher had been obliging in death, if not in life.

'How do you suppose he got her here?' Lonnie pondered nervously as he paced back and forth alongside the car. Noogie stood back against the wall of the garage, mouth hanging open in a trance, his winter-white breath the only indication he had survived the shock.

'Religious nut like him, why wouldn't he give her a decent Christian burial?' Pat Stevens asked.

'Apparently, he didn't believe she deserved one,' Mitch said.

He read the note pinned to the front of Doris Fletcher's dress.

> *Wicked daughter of Eve: Be sure*
> *your sin will find you out.*

9:41 a.m. -19° windchill factor: -38°

The press buzzards, circling town with their ears tuned to their police scanners, picked up the radio calls and made it to Albert Fletcher's house ahead of the coroner. They clustered in the driveway, moving like a school of fish – drifting in unison, then scattering as their ranks were broken by cops, quickly drawing back into their group.

Mitch swore at them under his breath as he tried to direct his men and the BCA evidence techs between the garage and the house. The photographers and video people were the worst, trying to blend in with the official personnel in order to sneak shots of the body and the chapel.

The scene was trouble enough without gawkers. A three-year-old mummified corpse presented a whole array of logistical problems. The BCA people argued among themselves as to how to handle the situation. Noticeably absent from the discussion was Megan.

Mitch couldn't believe she hadn't beaten a path to the scene the second the call had gone out. She should have been right there in the thick of it as the crime scene unit took Fletcher's house apart board by board; taking

347

notes, making a mental picture, processing the information through her cop's brain to formulate fresh theories.

He turned away from the bickering agents and headed for the side door of the garage. He jerked the door open and nearly ran head-on into a puppy-faced reporter with bright eyes and a stupid-looking grin on his face.

'You'll have to wait outside,' Mitch snarled. 'Law enforcement personnel only in here.'

'Chief Holt!' The grin stretched wider and he offered Mitch his gloved hand. 'I've had a call in to you since nine o'clock. That secretary of yours is a real guard dog.'

'Natalie is my administrative assistant,' Mitch said coldly, ignoring the proffered hand. 'She runs my office, and if she hears you call her a guard dog, she'll rip your head off and shout down the hole. Now, if you'll excuse me, I have work to do.'

Puppy Boy didn't seem to know whether he should be amused or contrite. Mitch scowled at him and backed him into the driveway. Whatever else this guy might have been, he was tenacious. He hustled alongside Mitch as he headed to the house.

'You'll have to wait for the press conference like everyone else,' Mitch snapped.

'But, Chief, you don't seem to understand. I'm not with the press. I'm with the BCA.' He dug an ID out of his coat pocket and held it up. 'Agent Marty Wilhelm, BCA.'

Mitch stopped in his tracks, unease creeping along his nerve endings. 'I haven't seen you on this case before.'

Puppy Boy gave him a lopsided grin that seemed wholly inappropriate considering the circumstances. 'I was just assigned.'

Mitch kept his expression carefully blank. *Agent?* Megan had told him DePalma was considering sending another field agent to assist her. She said she would take it as a sign of her imminent demise.

'Well, *Agent* Wilhelm,' he said softly, tightly. 'Where is Agent O'Malley? She's the one you should be dogging, not me.'

Marty Wilhelm stuffed his ID back in his coat pocket. 'I wouldn't know. She's been relieved of this assignment.'

2:20 p.m. −16° windchill factor: −32°

You get yanked off the job. You get sued for slander. You get kicked in the head with a migraine. You've just about topped your day of days here, O'Malley. And the night is young.

Megan supposed it was still afternoon, but time had ceased to mean anything to her and the living room shades were down, making the room dark. But not dark enough. Death wouldn't be dark enough to ease the pain in her eyes, or quiet enough to keep sound from piercing her brain.

The refrigerator kicked on with a thump and a whine, and she whimpered and tried to curl into a tighter ball.

She still had her coat on, though her boots had come off – one by the door and one somewhere along the path between the still-unpacked boxes. The confounded gray scarf tried to choke her as she changed positions. She jerked at it with a trembling hand and wrestled it off to fling it on the floor. Her hair was still tied back. She could feel each individual strand as if some unseen hand were pulling relentlessly on her ponytail, but she couldn't concentrate hard enough to get the rubber band undone.

The pain was unrelenting, a constant high-pitched drill boring into her head, an ax splitting her skull. God, she *wished* someone would split her skull with an ax and put her out of her misery.

She should have been injecting herself with Imitrex, but she couldn't move from the couch. If she had been able to get herself upright, she didn't think she would even know where the bathroom was. She had pulled one of the few empty boxes in the apartment within puking range. Any port in a storm.

Gannon and Friday had taken up their posts on a stereo speaker box across the room, and watched her intently. They were old hands at the vigil. They never came too close or made a sound. As if they were perfectly attuned to her suffering, they lay across the room and watched her, ever diligent. Friday's white-tipped tail hung down the side of the box, the last inch twitching slowly back and forth, back and forth, like a pendulum.

Megan stared at it for a while, then closed her eyes and saw it still. Back and forth, back and forth. The rhythm made her dizzy, nauseated, but she couldn't erase it from her mind. Right, left, right left. Then it picked up words: *Paige Price, Paige Price, right left, right left, Paige Price, Paige Price.*

DePalma's voice came in, crackling with anger. 'How could you be so stupid? How could you say that in front of twenty goddamn news cameras?'

Paige Price, Paige Price, Paige Price . . .

'. . . five-million-dollar slander suit . . .'

Paige Price, Paige Price . . .

'. . . against you and the bureau . . .'

Paige Price, Paige Price . . .

'. . . I don't care if she's the whore of Babylon . . .'

Paige Price.

'. . . you're off the case . . .'

Off the case.

Oh, God, she couldn't believe it. Couldn't stand it. Off the case. The words brought a wash of shame. Worse than that – far worse – was the fist of panic that tightened in her chest. She couldn't be off the case. She wanted it so badly. To find Josh. To catch the monster who had taken him and tormented them all. She wanted to be there to slap the cuffs on him and look him in the eye and say, 'I got you, you son of a bitch.' She wanted it for herself and for Josh and for Hannah. But she was off the case and the truth of that shook her to the core.

The pain burst inside her head like a brilliant white light bulb, and she pressed her face into the couch cushion and cried.

Another wave of pain obliterated all thought. Helpless to do anything else, Megan gave herself over to it. Somewhere in the distance she could hear the beat of helicopter rotors, the sound like bird's wings thumping against her eardrums. The search went on without her. The case went on without her.

The phone rang and the machine picked up. Henry Forster wanted to talk to her about Paige. *When hell freezes over.* Which may be imminent, she thought, shivering, pulling her coat tighter around her.

The phone chirped again, making her whimper, and again the machine picked up. 'Megan? It's Mitch. I just heard you got yanked. Um – I thought you might be home, but I guess not. I'll try to get you on the radio. If you get this message first, call me. We've got a situation with Fletcher.' There was a beat of silence. 'I'm sorry. I know how much the job means to you.'

The apology sounded awkward and sincere, as if he didn't make many, but the ones he made counted. He was sorry. He was giving his condolences, one cop to another. *Tough luck, you're off the case. It's been nice knowing you, O'Malley.* She would become a memory, someone who had barged into his life for a week, shared a bed with him for a couple of nights, and moved on.

She couldn't expect him to feel anything deeper than physical attraction to her. She knew nothing of love or relationships, or being a woman – as Mitch had pointed out so bluntly. He had been in love enough to marry, enough to have a family, enough to still mourn the loss of that woman. She'd never had anything that came close. She only had the job and it was going down in flames.

How could she have been so stupid?

The phone seemed to ring incessantly. The press had gotten wind of the debacle. Paige, the bitch, had probably broken the news herself in a live exclusive from the steps of City Center.

Megan wondered about the 'situation' with Albert Fletcher. What situation? She couldn't remember. It hurt to try. A dozen different half-remembered conversations tumbled together in her mind, all the voices talking at once in a dissonant chorus that made her ears ring and her head swim.

Please stop. Please stop.

The telephone shrilled again.

Please stop.

Tears ran down her face. Dizzy, wishing she would pass out, she slid down off the couch and crawled on her hands and knees to unplug the phone. She made it back to her barf box in time to be sick, but she couldn't muster the strength or coordination to get herself back on the couch. Beyond caring, she curled into a ball on the floor and lay there, waiting for the pain to end.

4:27 p.m. –20° windchill factor: –38°

No one had seen a sign of Fletcher. He had vanished. As Josh had vanished. As Megan had vanished.

She didn't answer her telephone. She didn't answer her car radio. It seemed she had walked out of the station and disappeared off the face of the earth.

Mitch prowled the streets of town looking for any glimpse of Albert Fletcher, directing the search for their fugitive from the radio of the Explorer. The radio crackled. Positions of units. Complaints about the cold. Frustration at another dead end. A chopper passed by overhead, sweeping slowly over the rooftops of Deer Lake for a glimpse of the demented deacon.

Wicked daughter of Eve: Be sure your sin will find you out.

Megan had run into Fletcher at St E's. He had been less than charmed by her. If Fletcher knew where Megan lived . . . She wouldn't have thought twice about taking him on.

He caught sight of her white Lumina parked at a cockeyed angle to the curb in front of her apartment house. The driver's door was ajar. Visions of her being pulled from the car pushed him into a trot up the sidewalk to the big Victorian house. He took the stairs two at a time to the third floor. No sound came from her apartment. No light leaked out under the door.

'Megan?' he called, pounding on the heavy old door. 'Megan, it's Mitch! Let me in!'

Nothing.

If her car is here and she isn't, then where the hell is she?

'Megan?' He knocked again, tried the knob, found it locked. 'Shit,' he muttered, stepping back. 'You're too damn old for this, Holt.'

He took a deep breath and did it anyway. Thank God she hadn't thrown the deadbolt. The door gave up on the third kick and swung inward.

'Megan?' Mitch called, his gaze scanning the dark apartment.

The shades were drawn. What sun they had had in the morning had retreated behind a thick shroud of gray in the afternoon, leaving the apartment dimmer than twilight. The room was cold, as if the heat had been off for some time. His heart thumping, Mitch eased his Smith & Wesson out of his parka and pointed it at the ceiling. He moved slowly, silently, through the maze of boxes, walking on the balls of his feet, ready to jump.

His toe kicked a boot that had been abandoned. 'Megan?'

Megan thought it was a hallucination. The banging, the voice. She was fading in and out of consciousness, in and out of reality. She wasn't certain the pounding wasn't inside her head – the pain. The pain took on dimensions beyond physical feeling. It became sound and light, an entity unlike any other, beyond description.

'Megan?'

But it never called her name. She was sure of that. The word ripped through her brain and she whimpered and tried to press her hands over her ears.

'Megan? Jesus!'

Mitch dodged a stack of boxes and dropped to his knees on the floor beside her. His hands shook violently as he reached for her.

'Honey, what happened? Who hurt you? Was it Fletcher?'

Megan tried to turn away from him. But he grabbed her shoulder and pulled her onto her back. The lamp at the end of the couch went on and she cried out.

'What is it?' Mitch demanded, leaning over her, pulling her hands aside as she tried to cover her eyes. 'Where are you hurt, honey?'

'Migraine,' she whispered. She squeezed her eyes shut tight. 'Turn off the fucking light and go away.'

The light went out, allowing her to breathe again. Weakness trembling through her, she turned onto her side again and pulled her knees up to her chest.

Mitch had never seen anyone in this much agony who wasn't bleeding profusely from a bullet hole or knife wound. He would never have imagined a headache severe enough to knock someone to the ground.

'Should I take you to the hospital?'

'No.'

'What can I do, honey?' he murmured, bending close.

'Stop calling me honey and go away.' Her pride didn't want him to see her like this – weak, vulnerable.

'The hell I'll leave,' Mitch growled.

He scooped her up in his arms and stood. Megan curled against his chest, clenching a handful of his parka, willing herself to not throw up as he carried her out of the living room and down the hall.

He eased her down onto the bed and she sat there shaking, doubled over. He took off her coat, her cardigan and her shoulder holster, her turtleneck and her bra. Then he dressed her in an oversize flannel shirt that lay across the foot of the bed. She lay down and he set about stripping off her slacks and the .380 A.M.T. Back-Up she wore in a custom-made holster around her right ankle.

'Do you have medication to take?' he asked.

'In the medicine cabinet,' she whispered, trying to burrow into her pillow. 'Imitrex. Don't talk so loud.'

He left and returned with the needle cartridge, then argued that he should take her to the hospital when she coached him on how to administer the injection.

'Megan, I can't give you a shot; I'm a cop, not a doctor.'

'You're a wimp. Shut up and do it.'

'What if I screw up?'

'It's subcutaneous; you can't screw up,' she said, swallowing back the nausea. 'I'd do it myself, but my hands are shaking.'

Scowling ferociously, he pressed the cartridge against her bare arm, depressed the trigger button and counted to ten. Megan looked up at him from beneath half-lowered lids. He tossed the used cartridge in the wastebasket and gazed down at her.

'You're being nice to me again,' she muttered.

'Yeah, well, don't get used to it.' The words held no sting and the only thing in his touch as he brushed her hair back from her face was tenderness.

'Don't worry, I know better,' she whispered.

Mitch didn't know whether she was referring to her job or their relationship. He wasn't certain what they had could be called a relationship, but now was not the time to discuss it.

'You scared the hell out of me,' he said softly. 'I thought our nut case *du jour* had gotten ahold of you.'

'Who?' Megan asked, thoughts tipping and tumbling in her mind again.

'Fletcher flipped out and cracked Father Tom's head open with a candlestick. But then, you probably know how that feels.'

'Piece o' cake,' she mumbled. 'Did you get him?'

'We will.' Mitch decided to save the rest of the Fletcher story for later. She was in no condition to hear about the case, especially when she had been taken off it. 'Don't worry about it, O'Malley. You'll give yourself a headache.'

Megan thought she smiled a little, but she wasn't sure. Her brain kept shorting out as pain flashed like fire behind her eyes.

'You need to rest,' Mitch told her. 'Is there anything more I can do?'

Strange that she should be stricken with shyness, she thought. What she wanted to ask wasn't intimate in the least. Just a service. But she felt so vulnerable. . . .

'Let my hair down?' She turned her face away from him, giving him access to her ponytail, at the same time avoiding his eyes.

Funny it should seem such a personal thing, Mitch thought as he slipped the bedraggled velvet bow from her dark hair and undid the rubber band. He had done the same for Jessie more times than he could count. Maybe that was part of it – that she seemed as defenseless as a child. That he was taking the role of protector. She had to hate it. She was so fiercely independent, so proud, and pain had reduced her to asking for help with something as simple as taking her hair down. An ironic cycle – that her vulnerability brought out a strength in him that ultimately made him vulnerable as well.

He sifted his fingers through the mahogany silk, spreading it out on the flower-sprigged pillow. His touch as light as a whisper, he massaged the back of her head and the tightly corded muscles in the back of her neck. Tears seeped between her lashes and she cried softly, but she didn't tell him to stop.

'You know, I never did this for Leo,' he said quietly, bending to kiss her cheek. 'Try to get some sleep, sweetheart – can I call you sweetheart?'

'No.'

'Okay, hard case. I'll be in the next room if you need me.'

If you need me . . . Megan said nothing as he pulled the covers up around her shoulders, straightened, and turned to go. To leave her alone. Just her and her pain alone in a room that would never be home because she had blown her chance. Already it seemed colder, emptier, as if the place somehow knew she would be leaving.

. . . if you need me . . .

'Mitch?' She hated the weakness in her voice, the echoes from a long, lonely past, but God help her, she didn't want to be alone with those ghosts tonight.

He hunkered down beside the bed and squinted at her in the dusky light. She closed her eyes against the tears, ashamed to have him see them. 'Hold me. Please.'

Mitch tightened his lips against the sudden wave of emotion. He touched a fingertip to the tip of her nose and forced words around the rock in his throat.

'Jeez, O'Malley,' he said teasingly. 'I thought you'd never ask.'

He toed off his boots and settled in behind her, the old bed creaking and groaning beneath their combined weight. He tucked her back against him spoon-style. He slipped her hand into his, and kissed her hair so softly she might not have felt it. And he listened to her breathing as she surrendered at last to sleep.

33

'Hannah, beyond fear, what are you feeling throughout this ordeal?'

Hannah breathed deeply, thought carefully, the same steps she had taken for each of the previous questions. She tried to block out the presence of the cameras and lights and focus completely on the concerned face of the woman seated across from her. That was how she thought of Katie Couric – as a woman, as a mother, not as a celebrity or a reporter.

'Confusion. Frustration,' she said. 'I can't understand why this happened to us. I can't begin to comprehend it, and that's frustrating.'

'Do you feel this is some kind of personal attack or vendetta?'

Hannah looked down at her hands in her lap and the handkerchief she had twisted into a knot. 'I don't want to think anyone I know could be capable of this kind of cruelty.'

Couric leaned ahead slightly in the small rose damask armchair. The NBC news crew had taken over the better part of the top floor of the Fontaine. An elegantly restored Victorian hotel in downtown Deer Lake, the Fontaine was furnished with antiques and reproductions. The crew had chosen the Rose Suite for the interview, partly for its size, partly for its beauty.

'Hannah, you were involved in an incident this morning at St Elysius Catholic Church,' Katie Couric said carefully. 'Father Tom McCoy was attacked by Albert Fletcher, the man who taught Josh in catechism and supervised him as an altar boy. Later this morning the police made a bizarre discovery at Mr Fletcher's home – finding what they believe to be the body of his wife, who passed away several years ago. The authorities are now conducting an extensive manhunt for Albert Fletcher. Do you think he could have been involved with Josh's disappearance?'

'I was so stunned when it happened – the attack,' Hannah replied. 'I'm still stunned. I would never have thought he could be violent, or we would never have trusted him with our son. That's part of the frustration. I saw this town as being safe. I saw the people in our lives as good people. Now all of that is shattered and it makes me angry and it makes me feel like I was naïve.'

'Does it make you more angry that you've been singled out when, as a physician, you've done so much for the people in Deer Lake?'

Deep breath, deep thought. She had been raised to do service for and give to people with no expectations for personal gain. The answer that came automatically brought guilt, but it was the honest answer and she gave it in a strained whisper. 'Yes.'

Paul watched the interview on a portable television in his office and seethed with a jealousy he would never admit. Local stations weren't good enough for Hannah. She had to hold out for a network interview. She was probably breaking hearts across America with her tear-filled blue eyes and quiet voice. The camera loved her. She looked like an actress with her wavy golden hair pulled back loosely. Darryl Hannah as Hannah Garrison, devastated mother.

He poured himself a shot of scotch from the bottle he had taken out of his partner's office and sipped at it, grimacing. They said scotch was an acquired taste. Paul had every intention of acquiring it as quickly as possible. The burden of his life these days was just too much to deal with. Hannah was certainly no help. Christ, she had all but accused him of taking Josh! After everything he had done to aid in the search. So much for faith. So much for trust. So much for undying love.

So much for undying love.

He had called Karen to come and console him and she had told him no. Paul had gotten the impression Garrett had been within earshot, but the rejection still stung. He took another face-twisting swallow of scotch and scowled at the television screen.

Katie Couric was managing to look grave and perky at once. She tilted her head and squinted. 'Different people react differently to this kind of trauma. Some find strength they never knew they had. Some find that while someone vital is gone from their lives, their relationships with the people around them deepen. Others find it difficult and painful to maintain those relationships. How would you say Josh's abduction has affected your personal relationships, Hannah? How has it affected your marriage?'

Hannah was silent for a moment. Her mouth pulled down at the corners. 'It's been a terrible strain.'

'Do you think your husband blames you for that night?'

The blue eyes filled with glittering tears. 'Yes.'

Couric's eyes glistened as well. Her voice softened. 'You blame yourself, don't you?'

'Yes.' The camera held the close-up as Hannah fought for control. 'I made a mistake that seemed so small –'

'But did you make a mistake at all, Hannah? You had someone call the rink to let them know you'd be late. What could you have done differently?'

'I could have had a back-up plan in place, an arrangement with someone I know and trust to pick Josh up if I couldn't. I could have coached Josh more on how to be safe. I could have helped the youth hockey program organize a formal plan to make sure all the children got home safely. I didn't do any of those things and now my son is gone. It never occurred to me I would need to take any of those measures. I was naïve. I could never have imagined the price I would have to pay for that.

'That's what I want other people to get out of this interview: that it took only one mistake at the wrong moment to change our lives forever. I don't want anyone else to have to go through what we're going through. If something I say can prevent that from happening, then I'll say it.'

'And yesterday, when your husband was asked to submit to being fingerprinted by the Deer Lake police, what did you think about that? Is there any question in your mind about your husband's involvement?'

Hannah lowered her eyes. 'I can't believe Paul would do anything to harm our son.'

She said it stiffly, as if it were a rule she had been forced to adopt whether she believed it or not. The bitch. Paul took another hit of scotch and fought the urge to belch it back up.

'Hannah, your husband has charged the law enforcement agencies involved with mishandling the case. Do you share his point of view?'

'No. I know they've done everything in their power. Some of the questions they've had to ask have been difficult, sometimes painful, but I've known Mitch Holt since the day he moved here with his daughter, and I know everything he's done on this case has been with one objective: to find Josh and bring his kidnapper to justice.'

'Thank you, Hannah,' Mitch murmured.

He sat on Megan's couch, watching the nineteen-inch color set with rabbit ears that sat on a box across the living room. Beside him, the black and white cat lay like a lion, watching the television, too. The little gray cat was curled in his lap, asleep.

He had been on the phone every fifteen minutes, keeping in contact with his men. There was still no sign of Fletcher, and with the exception of patrol cars, the ground search was being pulled in because of the extreme cold. If the deacon was hiding where searchers could find him without a warrant, they wouldn't need to worry about his going anywhere – he would be as stiff and cold as old Doris by morning. Hourly calls to their state patrol kept Mitch informed of the lack of progress on their end of things. If Fletcher had somehow managed to escape Deer Lake in a car, no one had seen him on the Minnesota highways.

Not being out in the field beating the bushes for Fletcher himself ate at him. He knew he wouldn't be able to do anything more than what was already being done. But the inactivity went against his street-cop nature.

357

And now that the old instincts had been reawakened, he could feel that old restless edginess coming back to life.

He had left Megan sleeping deeply, and he hoped for her sake she would sleep through the night. It still shook him to think of the pain she had been in . . . and the way it had affected him. He had wanted to care for her, to soothe her, to protect her. He wanted to fight for her, for her job – the thing that meant so much to her, more than him, more than anything. Those individual components added up to something he didn't feel prepared for.

He stared down at his hand on the back of the gray cat, at the ring. He could still hear the bitter hurt in Megan's voice – '*My God, you didn't even bother to take off your wedding ring when you took me to bed!*' And he could still feel the guilt, and knew that in a twisted way he had welcomed it.

God, was that really what he had reduced himself to? Emotional purgatory. And he had dragged Megan there with him. Whatever she wanted out of their relationship, she didn't deserve that.

Allison was gone. Forever. He might have prevented her death, but he couldn't resurrect her from it. How long did he go on paying? How long did he *want* to pay?

Life could change so quickly. In a snap. In the blink of an eye. In a heartbeat.

. . . it took only one mistake at the wrong moment to change our lives forever. Hannah's words echoed what he had known since that day in Miami, when he had been too tired to stop for milk on his way home. One second, one offhand decision, and the world spun off its axis like a top gone berserk.

So was it better to live a half-life and never again run the risk of that kind of pain, or better to grab what came along and live it to its fullest for as long as the fates allowed? He knew which was safer, which hurt less yet punished him more.

He looked at Hannah on the television screen, doing her best to be strong, to atone in her own way for the imagined mistake that had cost her so much. The pain had painted dark circles beneath her eyes and carved hollows beneath her elegant cheekbones. The stress had fractured her marriage. If she could, would she choose to avoid it all by never having had Josh in her life? Mitch thought he knew what her answer would be. He knew *he* wouldn't have traded his time with Allison and Kyle for anything. Not even peace.

'How's she doing?'

Still pale, Megan stood in the doorway, rubbing her eyes, her hair a mess. The flannel shirt hung to her knees.

'She's doing okay, considering,' he said. He dumped Gannon on the floor as he rose from the couch. 'How about *you*? How are you feeling?'

She gave a small shrug. 'A little woozy. I'll be okay. It's nothing new.'

Mitch tipped her face up, staring down at her with intense scrutiny. 'It's new to me. How often does this happen?'

Megan turned her face away. Now that the worst had passed, she wanted to forget how helpless she had felt and how badly she had wanted his compassion. If she could have suffered through the migraine alone, it would have been easier to slip out of town and out of his life. Now there was the sticky aftermath of compassion and embarrassment to deal with. Emotional loose ends that would not be easily tied off.

'It depends,' she said. She sank down into a corner of the couch, her eyes on the television, where an ad genius had somehow managed to connect pizza with an old lady putting on lipstick in the rest room of an airplane. 'Every time I lose my job or get sued for five million dollars.'

She winced inwardly at his expression. He squatted down beside the arm of the couch, his gaze that same one that had looked too deep inside her before. She refused to meet it. The feelings were far too close to the surface and she was too tired to be anything other than transparent.

'Megan, I wish —'

'Don't bother; it doesn't do any good.'

He leaned toward her. 'Why won't you let me help or at least sympathize?'

'Because you can't fix it,' she said wearily. 'There's nothing you can do to change DePalma's mind. You can't change the fact that Paige Price is a mercenary whore, or that I said so on television. You can't fix it and I don't want sympathy.'

His temper simmering, Mitch rose. 'No, you wouldn't. You don't need sympathy. You don't need anyone — isn't that right?'

Megan stubbornly stared past him at the television. He wanted to shake her. He wanted her to need him and say so. She had asked him to hold her when she was in so much pain she couldn't see straight, but that Megan and this one were two different people — a pair of nesting dolls, one hiding inside the other, rarely coming out into plain sight.

He could have kicked himself for caring. Hadn't he told himself he liked his life just the way it was — simple, controllable, safe . . . empty?

On the television Hannah's interview was about to resume. Mitch dropped down on the couch a foot to Megan's right, forcing Friday to vacate his spot. The cat gave him a dirty look and stalked away to leap onto a box marked STUFF I DON'T USE.

Katie Couric leaned forward in her chair, eyes luminous with sympathy. 'Hannah,' she said very softly. 'Do you think Josh is alive?'

The camera zoomed in on Hannah's face. 'I know he is.'

'How do you know?'

She took her time answering, obviously considering both the question and the implication of her answer. When she spoke, her voice was clear and sure. 'Because he's my son.'

'She wasn't that certain the other night,' Megan commented, nibbling at her cuticles. 'She asked me twice if I believe Josh is alive. Asked as if she needed my reassurance. What's this about?'

'It's a coping mechanism,' Mitch murmured. 'She'll believe what she has to believe.'

Megan felt there was something more to it, but she couldn't say what. Not that her opinion would have mattered. Marty the Spaniel Boy was in charge now. He wouldn't listen to her if she told him the world was round. It couldn't make any difference in the case, anyway. Hannah could believe or not. Neither sentiment would help them find Josh or his abductor.

'If you knew Josh was listening right now, what would you say to him?' Katie Couric asked Hannah.

The screen was a tight shot of Hannah's face, the camera allowing no nuance of expression to go unrecorded. America saw everything – the anger, the confusion, the pain. Cornflower-blue eyes shimmering with tears. Mouth trembling against the need to cry. 'I love you. I want you to know that, Josh, and believe it. I love you so much. . . .'

The close-up of Hannah faded into a shot of Josh. The school picture. Josh in his Cub Scout uniform. The gap-toothed grin. The bright eyes and unruly hair. The photo faded away and suddenly Josh was alive on the screen, thanks to videotape. Playing the part of a shepherd in a Christmas pageant, posing with Lily in front of the family tree. Linda Ronstadt's clear, sweet soprano voice sang out as the images shifted and changed. 'Somewhere Out There,' the words poignant with longing, bright with hope.

Megan bit her lip hard. Damn, damn, damn. She could have made it through the interview – she had interviewed Hannah herself – but this was dirty pool. The song could just as well have been Josh himself calling out from the twilight into which he had disappeared ten days before. The video transformed him into a living boy, full of energy and idiosyncrasies and tenderness for his baby sister. His innocent face coupled with the childlike trust in the lyrics of the song swept the case far out of the realm of work and made it achingly, painfully personal.

The case that had been snatched away from her.

Never, never let it get personal, O'Malley.

Too late. The tough dictate couldn't override the emotions. Pandora's box had been pried open. She could only fight to keep all the feelings from flooding out of it. She blinked hard and clenched a fistful of the shirttail that covered her thighs. Maybe if she squeezed hard enough, she could keep from crying.

Then Mitch's hand settled on top of hers, enfolded it within his, tightened with a silent message of understanding and empathy.

Damn you, O'Malley. How can you be so stupid? Why do you have to give in? You ought to be tougher than this by now.

She took a shaky breath, her jaw rigid as she fought to keep her lower lip from trembling. 'Dammit,' she said between her teeth. 'I wanted to get that son of a bitch.'

'I know,' Mitch murmured.

'He's close. I can feel it. I want him so bad it hurts.'

But it didn't matter how badly she wanted it or how deeply Mitch sympathized. She was off the case. DePalma expected her to drop the ball and run back to headquarters so the superintendent could chew her out in person and then she could sit in a room with a pack of lawyers and endure their company while they made plans to do battle with Paige Price and her legal Dobermans. Just like that she was supposed to drop the life she had begun in Deer Lake. Forget about the people; they were only names on reports. Forget about the apartment; she hadn't been in it long enough to call it home. Forget about Mitch Holt; he was just another cop, and she knew better than to get involved with a cop. Forget about Josh; he was Spaniel Boy's responsibility now.

Josh looked out at her from the television screen, wide eyes and freckles, a gap in his grin where a tooth had been. What little control Megan had left snapped in the face of the frustration and fury. She shot up off the couch. Swearing, crying, she swung at a stack of paperbacks perched on top of a box, sending the books hurtling across the room. The cats scrambled down from their perches and streaked down the hall to hide. Megan turned and swung at another target. She turned again and swung her fist, connecting solidly with Mitch's chest.

'Dammit! Goddammit!' she shouted.

Mitch caught her by the upper arms and she fell against him. Her shoulders shook with the effort to hold back the tears.

'Cry, dammit,' Mitch ordered, wrapping his arms around her. 'You're entitled. Let go and cry. I won't tell anybody.'

When the tears came, Mitch pressed his cheek against the top of her head and whispered to her and apologized for things that were beyond his control.

Everything was beyond their control. And all of it had been put in motion by a madman. In one moment, with one action, so many lives had been changed, and none of them could do a damn thing about it. She would lose her job, her home, her chance to belong . . . but she had this moment, and she didn't want to let it go.

She looked at Mitch, at the lines time and pain had etched into his face, at the eyes that had seen too much. She couldn't have him forever, but they could have this night. She could lose herself in his embrace, block out the ugly world with the haze of passion.

He slid his fingers into her hair, his thumb rubbing the tender spot on her forehead where the pain had been centered.

'You should go back to bed,' he whispered.

Megan felt her heart beat against him, felt the tempered strength and gentleness in his hands, saw the longing and regret in his eyes. She loved him. As pointless as that might have been. She had to leave. He hadn't asked her not to. He hadn't asked for anything, had promised nothing, had loved someone else so deeply . . . and no one had ever loved her. But

361

she could keep those secrets in her heart, keep her love held tight and safe. This might be the last night they had.

'Will you take me?' she said softly, her eyes locked on his.

'Megan –'

She pressed two fingers against his lips, silencing his concern. Mitch looked down at her, so fragile, so pale, her incredible strength bowing beneath the weight of the world. He was falling in love with her. For all the future there was in that. In a day or two she would be gone to try to salvage the career that meant everything to her. He would be left to the life he had built here – orderly, empty, carefully blank. The life he wanted, safe and plain.

But they could have this night together.

He took her hand and kissed it softly. She turned and led him down the hall to her room, leaving the television on to mumble to itself.

She had left the bedside lamp on to cast a shadowy amber glow over the tangled sheets. It lit her from behind as she unbuttoned the flannel shirt and let it fall back off her shoulders and drop to the floor. It cast an aura around her dark hair and gave her skin an alabaster glow. She stood before him willing to bare herself if not her soul, willing to take as much of him as he would give her. She deserved more than a night. She deserved more than life had given her, more than *he* had given her.

His hands shook as he slipped the wedding band off and set it aside on the dresser.

Megan's heart caught and stumbled. The possibilities raced through her mind, foolish thoughts and hopeless wishes. She pushed them all aside to grasp the one truth she could manage: They would have the night with no shadows of past loves or past sins.

Taking his hand, she raised it to her trembling lips and kissed the band of pale skin the ring had covered. Then she was in his arms and his lips were on hers.

Megan pushed Mitch's shirt back off his shoulders and he flung it aside, impatient for the feel of her naked against him. He lowered her to the bed, dragging his mouth down her neck to her breasts. She arched beneath him, inviting him, begging him to take the tight bud of her nipple between his lips, crying out as he sucked strongly at the tender point. He swept a hand down her side, over her hip, pulling her leg around him, bringing the moist heat of her womanhood against the quivering muscles of his belly.

A deep animal groan rumbled at the base of his throat as she reached down and took his erection into her hands. He closed his hand over hers and tightened her grip, bent his head down and caught her earlobe between his teeth.

'That's how tight you are when I'm inside you,' he said, sending arousal singing through her.

Mitch watched her face as he entered her. Panic seized him at the knowledge that in a handful of days and nights he had fallen in love; at the knowledge that this would all be gone in a day, in a heartbeat.

Then the need overran the fear. He thrust into her fully, deeply, the tight wet heat of her gripping him, squeezing all thought from his mind. They moved together, straining together toward a fulfillment that obliterated the bounds between the physical and the emotional and the spiritual. They reached it, one and then the other. Breathless, shaking, holding tight.

I love you . . . The words were on her lips. She held them back.

I love you . . . He held the thought within his heart, afraid to give it away.

Then it was over and they were silent and still, and old doubts crept back from the corners of their banishment. The boundaries settled back in place, the guards went up again. Hearts in armor, beating separate and lonely into the night.

8:55 p.m. -25° windchill factor: -47°

Hannah sat in the dark in her room. *Her* room. How quickly the mind made those little alterations. Paul hadn't slept in this bed for two nights and already her brain had omitted plural references. She didn't want to think about what that meant for their future. She didn't want to deal with the feelings of guilt and loss and failure associated with the marriage she would once have called perfect. She had all she could do to shoulder the weight of the guilt and loss and sense of failure associated with Josh.

It would have been so nice to walk off the set of the interview and have the man she had married put his arms around her and reassure her and take her home. To know that she had his love and support. Instead, she had driven herself home. Kathleen Casey, who had volunteered to sit with Lily, was on the couch in the family room with McCaskill, the BCA agent, watching *The X Files* and eating popcorn. Paul was gone.

Paul is gone. The Paul she had loved and married. She didn't know the man who had lied to her, hidden things from her, blamed her for the act of a madman. She didn't know the man who had all but courted the media, the man who had been asked to submit his fingerprints to the police. She didn't know who he was or what he might be capable of doing.

Unwilling to consider the possibilities, she forced herself out of the chair and began to undress. She concentrated on each menial task, unbuttoning buttons, folding, putting away. She chose her well-worn Duke sweatshirt and pulled it on over her head, shaking her hair back out of her eyes. The telephone on the nightstand rang as she reached for her sweatpants.

Hannah stared at it. Memories of the last call she had taken in this room rushed through her, pebbling her skin and filming it with perspiration.

363

She couldn't just let it ring. She didn't want to pick it up. McCaskill and Kathleen would be wondering why she didn't answer it.

With a trembling hand she lifted the receiver.

'Hello?'

'Hannah? This is Garrett Wright. I saw the interview. I just wanted to tell you I thought you were very brave.'

'Uh – well –,' she stammered. It wasn't a faceless stranger tormenting her or Albert Fletcher spouting lunacy. It wasn't Josh. Just a neighbor. Karen's husband. He taught at Harris. 'It was just something I had to do.'

'I understand. Still . . . Well, for what it's worth, I think you did the right thing. Listen, if you need any help getting through this, I have a friend in Edina who specializes in family therapy. I mentioned him to Paul when he was here the other night, but I'm afraid he didn't want to hear it. I thought I'd let you know. You can take his name and call him or not, but I thought you should have the option.'

'Thank you,' Hannah murmured absently, sinking down on the bed.

She copied the name and number down on the notepad automatically, her mind busy wondering what Paul had been doing at the Wrights' house and why he wouldn't have mentioned it to her. But then, a visit to a neighbor's house was the least of his secrets. She didn't want to know what the worst might be.

The thought lingered and echoed in her mind as she hung up the phone, and a terrible sense of loneliness and fear yawned wide inside her, threatening to swallow her whole. That was the hardest part of all of this – the feeling that no matter how the people around her wanted to help, on the most fundamental level she was alone. The one person who should have been closest was drifting farther and farther away.

She stared at nothing. When the phone rang again, she picked it up without hesitation and murmured a flat greeting. The voice that answered her was a low and gentle drawl, as welcome to her raw nerves as the kiss of silk on a sunburn.

'Hannah? It's Tom – Father Tom. I thought you might need to talk.'

'Yeah,' she whispered with a trembling smile. 'I'd like that.'

Journal entry
Day 10

As Shakespeare said:
All the world's a stage,
And all the men and women merely players:
They have their exits and their entrances . . .

And we are the directors, the puppet masters pulling their hidden strings.

And so, from hour to hour we ripe and ripe,
And then from hour to hour we rot and rot,
And thereby hangs a tale

Time for a new act and another fine twist in the plot.

We are brilliant.

34

On Saturday the temperature rose and the sky fell. A ceiling of fat clouds the color of lead hung low above the rolling wooded countryside, sifting down a fine powder of snow. In the wake of the deep freeze and the dark moods it had inspired, the radio weathermen had fled the state, leaving the storm predictions to the weekend deejays.

Megan listened with one ear. Blizzard? Maybe if it hit fast enough it could prevent her from driving to St Paul. If she spent enough time driving around town looking for Albert Fletcher . . . If this old piece-of-shit car would conk out . . . A dozen different scenarios flashed through her mind, like a kid desperate to cut school. If she could just have today . . . But DePalma wanted her out of Deer Lake. He would never have called her in on a Saturday unless he was desperate himself. The lawyers wouldn't be there; the hell if the bureau would pay them time and a half. This was a simple case of snatching her out of town before she could do any more damage.

She would have to go if she was to salvage anything of her career. Go and kiss ass and repent and do penance. The idea stuck in her throat like a fur ball. She was a damn good cop. That should have counted for something, but it wouldn't.

She rubbed her mitten at the sore spot above her right eye. The headache lingered, threatening, then retreating in an exhausting fencing match with her tattered stamina. She should have stayed in bed, but she didn't want to be there alone. She had been driving around since dawn, her brain chewing on the mess she had made of her life. *Should have taken that FBI post, O'Malley.* She could have been in Memphis now, a thousand miles away from the cold and snow, a thousand miles away from a broken heart.

That heart still wished things could have worked out. Her head knew better. What could she offer Mitch? She wasn't wife material, didn't know anything about raising a five-year-old girl. All she really knew was being a cop. Thanks to her own reckless temper, that would be taken from her, too. Panic tightened in her chest.

Thinking she was asleep, Mitch had slipped out early. He had a manhunt to oversee. According to the snatches of information Megan was picking up on the police radio, there had still been no solid sign of Albert Fletcher. Citizens had been calling in sightings, but none had turned into anything. Deer Lake was crawling with police cruisers and county cruisers and state patrol cruisers. The choppers circled overhead like buzzards.

Megan shook her head in amazement. She had pegged Fletcher as weird right off, but she hadn't envisioned anything like what Mitch had finally described to her last night. No doubt about it, the deacon was a few beads short of a rosary. Crazy enough to kidnap Josh to be his own private altar boy? Yes, but he had to have had help. He'd been lecturing on sin and damnation at St E's that night. She tried to picture him and Olie as compadres, but couldn't manage it. Fletcher was a loner. He never would have been able to hide his ghoulish secrets otherwise.

She drove slowly through the campus of Harris College, keeping her eyes open for the deacon. She wondered if Mitch had sent any men there. With classes resuming Monday, the buildings had probably been opened but would still be largely unoccupied. Fletcher could have found himself a nice hiding spot out of the elements.

Harris was the kind of college they didn't build anymore. Many of the classroom and administrative buildings were of native limestone and looked as if they dated back to the origin of the school in the late 1800s. Handsome and substantial, they sat back from the winding drive, the grounds around them studded with ancient oak and maple and pine.

The road wound past dormitories, their parking lots a third full, students tracking back and forth to the buildings to carry in the laundry they had done over the break and the books they had probably neglected. Goalposts sticking up out of the snow marked an athletic field that backed onto a vacant pasture, and suddenly Megan found herself in the farm country that ran on and on to the west.

She turned onto Old Cedar Road and headed south. If she remembered correctly, this eventually ran past Ryan's Bay and served as a back way into Dinkytown. She pulled over to the side of the road and put the car in park, letting the engine rumble on as she stared out the window at the bleak landscape. The naked hardwood trees like blackened matchsticks in the distance; the snow robbing the contours from the land, making everything look flat and one-dimensional; the sky hanging low above it all like slabs of slate. In a field beside the road, a pair of shaggy paint horses pawed listlessly at the dirty blond stubble of cornstalks. Up ahead, at a bend in the road, a rooster pheasant cautiously made his way out from under the low branches of a spruce tree to peck for gravel on the verge. A brown house sat back from the road on a rise, shades pulled, garage closed, looking vacant. The name on the mailbox at the end of the drive was Lexvold.

Lexvold. It rang a dim bell. Maybe she had seen it on a report. The paperwork on the Kirkwood case would put any blizzard to shame. They had interviewed dozens of people, taken countless statements of non-clues from citizens who wanted to be helpful or at least involved. Like ripples in a pond, the crime had touched them all.

Megan put the car in drive and eased back onto the road. The temperature might have climbed to twenty-two degrees, but the Lumina's heater was good to only about twenty-five, if it was any good at all. She needed something hot to drink, which would delay her even more in leaving for St Paul. Then, if she drank enough, she would have to stop to go to the bathroom, stalling a little longer.

She was thinking of hot chocolate at The Leaf and Bean, when her gaze caught on the angry black skid marks that criss-crossed on the road ahead. Checking the rearview mirror, she pulled off on the shoulder again and sat with her foot on the brake.

Skid marks. Lexvold. Old Cedar Road. Car accident.

The scene blurred as her mind tried to shake loose what she needed.

The college kid. A patch of ice. A patch of ice the officer at the scene had felt was manufactured.

She slammed the transmission into park and climbed out of the car. She trudged back up to the curve and stood there with her hands tucked into the pockets of her parka, her shoulders hunched against the wind. To the north and east lay the Harris campus. To the south, farmland gave way to the sloughs of Ryan's Bay. Old Cedar Road intersected with Mill Road. To the east on Mill the spires of St E's punctuated the sky above the treetops. She turned and looked up the hill at the brown house and attached garage.

She remembered Dietz in his Moe Howard wig sitting at the end of their booth in Grandma's Attic. . . . *looks to me like someone snaked a garden hose down the driveway* . . .

'So where's the hose?' Megan murmured.

That kind of prank was usually borne of opportunity. If the Lexvolds didn't have a hose out, there was no opportunity. If there was no opportunity, that meant someone brought a hose to the party, which meant premeditation. Premeditation meant motive. What motive?

She turned back toward the road, an empty ribbon of asphalt. The only sounds were the wind and the hoarse cluck of the rooster pheasant, hiding now beneath the spruce trees, annoyed with Megan for interrupting his snack. Up at the drive into Harris, a red Dodge Shadow pulled onto the road and roared toward her, whizzing past with a pair of young men with wispy grunge-look goatees. Students taking the back way off campus. Like that kid the night of the accident.

The accident that had kept Hannah Garrison late at the hospital.

Megan pictured the time line taped to the wall of the war room. Everything started with Josh's disappearance. But what if the thing they had missed, the thing that had been there all along that they hadn't been able to see, had happened earlier? What if the accident hadn't been an accident at all?

Adrenaline surged through her as the possibilities clicked fast-forward through her brain. Students used the back road to the college. Anyone living around there would know that. Albert Fletcher, whose house was no more than a mile away. Olie Swain, who had audited courses at Harris. Christopher Priest, who had sent his student on an errand that night.

Priest. Megan tried to shake off the idea. The funny little professor with the bad fashion sense and limp-fish handshake? He was as unlikely a suspect as Elvis. He had no motive. He openly admired Hannah, had gone out of his way to help with the case. . . . Had installed himself in a position where he would be privy to all incoming news of the case, maybe even have access to confidential police information. He had known Olie Swain, had taught him. He was probably at this very moment communing with Olie's computers down at the station, ostensibly searching for clues. And she had put him there. *ignorance is not innocence but SIN.*

Sin. Religion. Priest. *Christopher Priest.*

'Oh, Jesus,' she muttered.

In her mind's eye she could see him bending over the glowing screen of a terminal in the room where Olie's equipment had been set up. She couldn't have put a possible suspect in a position to tamper with evidence. Her stomach rolled and twisted at the thought. She had wanted so badly to crack this case. It was the one that could make or break her career, but the stakes were so much higher than that and she knew it. She would have sold her soul for a nickel to nail the bastard who had taken Josh. If Christopher Priest was dirty and she had put him in that office with those machines . . .

The sound of a car rolling up snapped her back to the moment. A gunmetal-blue Saab had come to a halt in front of her. The passenger's window buzzed down. As the driver hunched down to see her, the fur collar of his navy wool topcoat crept up around his ears.

'Agent O'Malley! Are you having car trouble?' Garrett Wright asked.

'Uh – no. No, I'm fine.'

'Kind of a cold day to be standing out in the wind. Are you sure you don't need some help? I've got a cellular phone –'

'No, thanks.' Megan forced a polite smile as she leaned down into the window of the car. 'I'm just checking something out. Thanks for stopping, though.'

'Still looking for Albert Fletcher?' He shook his head, frowning. 'Who would have guessed . . .'

'No one.'

In the beat of silence his dark eyes went bright with the kind of embarrassed curiosity that fueled the fires of coffee-shop gossip every-where. 'So . . . is Paige Price really sleeping with the sheriff?'

'No comment,' Megan replied, forcing a wan smile, straightening away from the Saab. 'You'd better move it along, Dr Wright. We wouldn't want you to cause an accident.'

'No, we wouldn't want that. Good luck finding Fletcher.'

He gave her a salute as the window hissed upward, and the Saab rolled on. The purr of the motor faded into the distance, leaving her standing there listening to the wind in the pines, staring at the only visible evidence of the accident that had claimed two lives outright and possibly altered the lives of an entire community.

ignorance is not innocence but SIN.

10:28 a.m. 22° windchill factor: 10°

'Where's Mitch?'

Megan burst into Natalie's office. Mitch's assistant stood behind her desk, the telephone receiver pressed to her ear. She gave Megan a scowl and picked up a copy of the *Star-Tribune* from her desk, holding it up to display Henry Forster's headline – *O'Malley Strikes Out: BCA's First Female Field Agent Told to Hit the Road.*

'I'm sorry, *Mr DePalma*,' she said pointedly into the receiver. 'I've got to put you on hold.'

She punched the hold button and arched a thinly plucked brow. 'Well, if it isn't the elusive Agent O'Malley. People in high places are looking for you, girl.'

'Screw 'em,' Megan snapped. 'I've got more important things to do.'

Natalie gave her a long, measuring look, pursing her lips. 'He's in the war room.'

'Thanks.' Megan pointed to the blinking red light on the telephone console. 'I'm not here.'

'I never heard of you,' Natalie said, shaking her head.

Megan blew out a breath and turned for the door. 'Natalie, you're the best.'

'Damn straight.'

'He has to be somewhere.' Marty Wilhelm stated the obvious. He strolled up and down the time line with his hands in the pockets of his teal blue Dockers. 'He hasn't been outside all this time. I'm guessing he's holed up wherever he has Josh stashed. We should check at the courthouse and see if he owns any other property in the area – a cabin or something.'

Mitch gave the agent an irritated look. 'Been there. Done that. He doesn't.'

Puppy Boy went on, undaunted. 'They haven't found anything useful in Olie Swain's computers – no mention of Josh or Fletcher. We should get Fletcher's phone records –'

'At the command post,' Mitch snapped. 'Stevens and Gedney are going over them.'

He'd been on the manhunt himself since the crack of dawn, had come in to the station only at Wilhelm's request for a brainstorming session. So far the storm had been more of a light drizzle.

'Look, Marty, I've got to tell you, having you jump in here midstream is a real pain in the ass.'

Marty grinned that innocent-boy grin Mitch was growing to hate. 'I'm doing all I can to get up to speed, Chief. By rights, this case should have been mine from the start. It isn't my fault that didn't happen. I guess I just don't look as fetching in a short skirt.'

The veneer of tolerance peeled away like dead skin. A dangerous look tightening his features, Mitch rose from his chair and advanced on Marty Wilhelm one slow step at a time until they were close enough to dance. Wilhelm's bright eyes widened.

'Agent O'Malley is a damn good cop,' Mitch said softly. 'Now, Marty, for all I know, you can't find your dick in a dark room. But I'll find it for you if I hear you make another remark like that one. Are we clear on that, Marty?'

His face pale, he held his hands up in surrender as he backed away. The trademark grin quivered and twisted. 'Hey, Chief, I'm sorry. I didn't know this was a serious thing with you and Megan. I thought it was just –'

The words strangled in his throat at Mitch's glare. This *thing* between him and Megan was nobody's damned business, whatever it was. God knew, he'd bent his brain into a knot thinking about it in the predawn while she lay beside him. It seemed so much simpler in the night, when she wasn't afraid to need him and he couldn't think beyond the next caress. Then morning came, and the world and their lives were just as screwed up as ever.

A knock at the door brought Mitch back to the moment. Megan made her entrance, parka hanging off one shoulder, dark hair escaping her ponytail. The bright color along her cheekbones might have come from the great outdoors, but he suspected it had more to do with the energy radiating around her. He could sense her tension across the room and knew the source of it. He had felt that same rush himself more than once when he'd been onto something.

'What have you got?' he asked, moving toward her.

'I need to talk to you.' She made a beeline toward him, not so much as glancing in the direction of her replacement.

'Agent O'Malley,' Marty Wilhelm said sardonically, 'aren't you supposed to be in St Paul right now?'

Megan cut him a nasty glare and looked back up at Mitch. 'I had an idea about that accident out on Old Cedar Road the night Josh disappeared.'

'Bruce DePalma called me looking for you,' Wilhelm went on.

Megan turned her shoulder to him. 'What if it wasn't an accident at all? What if it was set to happen as a means of keeping Hannah at the hospital?'

Mitch frowned. 'It wouldn't change anything, except to make the crime even more diabolical. We already know it wasn't a random act.'

'I realize that, but think about it – think about the location. It's a mile or so to Fletcher's and St Elysius.'

Marty perked up at Fletcher's name. 'What? How does Fletcher tie in?'

'He could have slipped out of the church, made the icy patch on the road, and gotten back in time for his classes,' Mitch speculated. 'Causing the accident that kept Hannah at the hospital and still providing himself with an alibi. It works, but he still had to have an accomplice.'

'It's probably a long shot,' Megan said, 'but I was thinking if we could find a witness who saw someone hanging around the Lexvold place that day, we might get a link we don't have now.'

'*We?*' Wilhelm's voice made her cringe as sure as fingernails on a chalkboard. 'Agent O'Malley, might I remind you, you're *off* this case.'

'I don't need reminding,' Megan said, still refusing to look at him.

He gave an incredulous half-laugh. 'I beg to differ.'

He snatched a copy of the *Star Tribune* off the table and displayed it in front of him. 'You're on temporary suspension from active duty. That takes you off this case, out of this room, and all the way to St Paul.'

She tilted her chin up, glaring at him. 'I'm taking care of some loose ends.'

'You're off the case,' he repeated, throwing the paper down, then thrusting a forefinger in front of her face like an exclamation point.

Megan wanted to grab his hand and bite him. Instead, she clenched her jaw and her fists. 'I don't take orders from you, Wilhelm. Don't try to push me around. Better men than you have tried and regretted it.'

A beeper went off like an alarm, shrill and piercing. They all flinched automatically in response, looking down at the little boxes on their waistbands. Wilhelm stepped back and unclipped his from his belt.

'If this is DePalma,' he said, moving toward the door, 'I'll tell him you're on your way, Megan, because you are *off this case.*'

Megan held her tongue until he was out the door and had closed it behind him. 'The hell I am, Spaniel Boy.'

'Megan, you're going to get yourself fired,' Mitch said.

'I've already been fired.'

'You've lost the field post, not your career. You jerk DePalma around this way and he'll have your badge.'

Megan stared down at the toes of her boots. She had been over all of this in her mind again and again. She had told herself her career was all she had, that she had to do everything she could to protect it – don't get involved with a case or with a cop. But she *was* involved and she couldn't walk away from this case for the sake of her career. A little boy's life was at stake.

'I'm not walking away from this until it's done. We're too close and it's too important. Now, you've got to get Christopher Priest away from Olie's computers.'

'Why?'

'Because everything we just said about Albert Fletcher could apply to him, too.'

'Megan, get a grip. He's been nothing but helpful on this case from day one.'

She nodded. 'And most arsonists return to the scene of the crime to watch the firemen. Listen to me, Mitch. I know it sounds crazy on the surface, but it could fit. The kid behind the wheel of that car was a student of his,' she reminded him, refusing to back down. 'Priest told me he had sent him out to run an errand. He had to know the kid would take Old Cedar Road.'

'What possible motive would Priest have for taking Josh?'

'I don't know,' she admitted, wishing she had more to go on than the uneasy feeling in her gut. 'Maybe it's not about motive. We've said all along he's playing games with us. Taking Josh was the opening move. Then came the taunts, the messages, the notebook, his conversation with Ruth Cooper. Maybe it's just about winning, outsmarting everyone.'

'And yesterday it was a personal vendetta against Hannah and Paul. And the day before that Paul did it —'

'What's that supposed to mean?'

'It means you'll beat your head against a wall until the wall moves.'

'I'm doing my job,' she insisted.

'And the rest of us aren't?' he said, spreading his hands.

Megan scowled at him. 'I never said that.'

'You've been taken off the case, Megan.'

'And you think I should just back down and drop it?'

'I think you should have a little faith that someone besides you can do the job,' he said, ticking his thoughts off on his fingers one by one. 'I think you should realize DePalma's got you by the short hairs. I think you should take a look in the mirror and see what you're doing to yourself. Yesterday you couldn't even stand up!'

He reached out to touch her, to touch her forehead, where pain was gathering in a tightening knot.

She stepped back from him. 'I'm fine now. I sure as hell don't need you —'

'That's what it comes down to, isn't it?' Mitch snapped, dropping his hand. 'You don't need anybody. Mighty Megan O'Malley taking on the whole fucking male-dominated world!'

'Yeah, well,' she jeered, 'it's an ugly job, but somebody's got to do it.' She gave a bitter attempt at laughter. 'Like you want me to need you.'

Megan stared up at him, wary and defiant. She had spent her whole life learning not to trust emotions, not to be vulnerable, not to put her heart in someone else's hands because she got it back when they found out she wasn't what was really wanted.

'I can take care of myself,' she said, chin up, eyes glittering. 'I've been doing it my whole life.'

And she would go on doing it, Mitch thought. She was afraid to need and he had spent the last two years afraid of being needed. Where did that leave them? Squaring off in the war room. How apropos.

'Fine,' he said, focusing past her head to the slick white board where the kidnapper's messages mocked them in bright-colored marker. 'Then go do it. I don't have time for this bullshit game of yours, knocking the chip off your shoulder so you can pick it up and put it right back. I've got better things to do with my time. I've got a legitimate suspect at large.'

'Yes, and since he's *your* suspect, he's the only suspect,' Megan sneered. 'Good luck finding him with your head up your ass.' She ignored the dangerous glint in his eyes. She felt something dangerous herself.

'You're a great one to talk about playing games,' she lashed out. 'I told you from the first I didn't want to get involved with a cop, but you pushed and pushed, and now that you've had what you wanted, the game's over. How nice and neat for you. You don't even have to bother foisting me off on some other guy. I'll just be gone and you can have your town back and put your ring back on and go back to –'

He jerked a finger up in front of her face, cutting her off. 'Don't,' he said, his voice nearly a whisper, and yet stronger, more frightening than a shout, vibrating with emotion, sharper than steel. 'Don't you dare. I loved my wife. You don't even know what that means.'

No, she didn't know what that meant. Nor did she stand a chance of finding out, Megan thought as he turned and stormed out of the room. He left her standing there, slamming the door shut on her, on them. She stood there, the sudden silence pounding in her ears; angry, hurtful words echoing in her head – her words, his; the aftertaste of heartbreak bitter in her mouth.

35

Christopher Priest was not at the station. Megan stuck her head into the little room assigned to Olie's computers, to find a brush-cut, bow-tied pencil neck from headquarters who had obviously been told not to share with her. He offered no explanation for the professor's absence and gave no indication as to whether or not Olie's machines had turned up anything of interest.

The carrion feeders were waiting for her as she tried to slip out a service entrance to the City Center. The mob lunged at her with microphones, hand-held tape recorders, cameras.

'Agent O'Malley, do you have a comment on your firing?'

'Not one you can print,' she snarled, shouldering her way through the crowd.

'Do you have any comment on the lawsuit?'

'Do you have any proof Paige Price is sleeping with Sheriff Steiger?'

From behind the mirrored lenses of her sunglasses, she shot a glare at Henry Forster. His beetle brows were drawn together in a furry V as he stared back at her through the smudged lenses of his crooked glasses. The wind had blown his comb-over into a spike that stood straight up from his liver-spotted head like a horn.

'You're the hotshot investigative reporter,' she snapped. 'Dig up your own dirt.'

They trailed her halfway across the parking lot, then gave up, disheartened by the lack of usable sound bites. Vultures. Megan scowled at them as she wheeled the Lumina out onto Main Street.

No one at the volunteer center had seen Christopher Priest since Friday. Classes began again at Harris on Monday. She might try his office there, suggested one of Priest's student volunteers, while other members of the volunteer staff shot her looks from the corners of their eyes. A copy of the *StarTribune* lay on the end of a table, where fliers were being stuffed into envelopes, Henry Forster's headline jumping off the page – *O'Malley Strikes Out.*

'I haven't finished swinging yet, Henry,' she muttered. She climbed

375

back into her car and for the second time that day headed through the snow toward Harris.

Priest's office, she was told by a perky young woman in the administration building, was on the fourth floor of Cray Hall. Megan trooped across the Harris grounds. She tried not to breathe too deeply; the fresh air seemed to knife right up behind her eyes. Brain freeze – like swallowing too much ice cream.

'Just let me get through today, God,' she mumbled as she climbed the stairs of Cray Hall. 'Just let me get a good lead and then you can nail me. Just one solid lead. Don't let me go down in flames here.'

One lead that might come from a man no one would ever suspect – or want to suspect. Professor Priest. Quiet, unassuming, more enamored of machines than of people. Fascinated and bewildered by the vagaries of fate and human nature. *Is it fate or is it random? What brought Mike Chamberlain to that corner at that moment? What put Josh Kirkwood on that curb alone that night?*

Had he been toying with her that day at the hospital? Trying to plant clues in her mind without her ever suspecting? Or was she grasping at straws, so desperate for an end to the case that she was beginning to see suspects every time she turned around? Megan's gut told her no, and her gut was seldom wrong. Unlike her mouth, which blurted out the wrong thing at the wrong moment with regularity. Or her heart . . .

The fourth floor of Cray Hall was a warren of offices and narrow halls the color of mustard. The building was old, the kind of place that would feel dank and clammy year-round. The sharp clack of her boot heels against the old brown flooring carried down the hall like the report of gunshots.

The door to Priest's office stood open, but it was not Christopher Priest who looked up at her from behind a mountain of books and papers on the desk. Todd Childs, the clerk from The Pack Rat, looked up at her with surprise in his sleepy, drug-dilated eyes.

'Hey, it's Dirty Harriet!' he said with a grin. A strand of rust hair fell in his face and he swept it back. Behind him, Garrett Wright looked up from browsing through a file cabinet.

'We seem destined to cross paths, Agent O'Malley,' Wright said, smoothing a hand over his trendy silk tie as he came around the desk. 'What brings you to the hallowed halls of Harris?'

'I'm looking for Professor Priest,' Megan said. She glanced around the office. 'This *is* his office, isn't it?'

'Yes. I think I told you – Chris and I are conducting a joint project dealing with learning and perception. It involves a computer program designed by his students,' he explained. Slipping his hands into the pockets of his dark pleated trousers, he rocked back on his heels. 'It's fascinating stuff. We're gearing up for the next phase of testing. Todd and I are going through some of the data we compiled last semester.'

'It's way cool,' Todd said. 'How individuals perceive the world around them. How different personality types perceive and learn. The human psyche is a fascinating creature.'

'Is Priest around?' Megan asked, her interest in learning and perception limited to the case.

'I'm sorry, no,' Wright said. 'He told me he had to go to St Peter. Is this about the case?'

'I just wanted to ask him a few questions,' Megan said, her face carefully blank. St Peter. The call from Josh had come from St Peter. 'I'm fuzzy on a couple of things I thought he might be able to help me with.'

'Ah ... excuse me,' Wright said, hesitant and a little awkward, 'but didn't I read something in the *StarTribune* about you being taken off this case?'

Megan flashed him a phony smile and lied. 'Can't believe everything you read, Dr Wright.'

He didn't believe her, but he gave a shrug as if it made no difference to him. 'Oh, well ... He told me he would be home about two-thirty. I'm sure he'll be eager to help. He's been so involved with the case, he hardly talks about anything else.'

How involved was what Megan wanted to ask, but if Priest was in fact the man at the heart of the mystery, she doubted he shared that information with his college colleagues. *What did you do over winter break, Chris? Oh, I kidnapped a little boy and held an entire community hostage to the whims of my madness. How about you?*

'I've wanted to take a more active role myself,' Wright continued, rocking back on his heels again. 'I feel so bad for Hannah and Paul. Such a perfect family,' he said with a tight little smile. 'I haven't been able to contribute much to the effort, I'm afraid. The media grabbed me because I teach psychology. I keep telling them I don't have any degrees in criminal behavioral studies. They don't seem to grasp that.'

'Yeah, well, they're that way,' Megan said, backing toward the door.

'They don't see the big picture,' Todd said, wagging his shaggy head sadly.

Megan forced a polite smile and directed it at Wright. 'Thanks for your help, Dr Wright.'

'Any time. Do you know where Chris lives?'

'I can find it.'

He nodded, smiling. 'Right. You're the detective.'

'For the moment,' Megan muttered to herself as she retraced her route to the stairs.

Outside, the snow had begun to fall, fine white flakes sifting down like flour from the sky. Pretty. Clean. The Harris campus looked like a postcard setting. Winter wonderland. In the parklike square across the street, a group of young women were on their backs making snow angels, their laughter clear and pure as it rose into the naked branches of the trees.

Megan walked to her car and sat behind the wheel for a few moments with her eyes closed and her forehead pressed against the cold window. She turned off the incessant crackling of the police radio and tuned the car radio to a light rock station that always promised the latest weather updates.

Mariah Carey told her to look within herself and find strength. 'Hero.' Good advice, but what happened when the strength ran out, or time ran out, or the villain was too damn smart? What happened to heroes then? And what happened to the people who counted on them? Like Josh.

Mariah blasted out the final note, turning it into a dozen notes with vocal gymnastics.

'It's going to take a hero to make it through this weather,' the deejay said. 'A word of advice for travelers – don't. We're looking at eight to ten inches of the white stuff in the metro area before it's all over tomorrow. Outlying areas are already reporting poor driving conditions. So bundle up and keep your dial on KS95, where it's always ninety-five and sunny.'

The Beach Boys launched into 'Kokomo'. Megan cut them off with a twist of her wrist, put the car in gear, and headed for Deer Lake Community Hospital.

Mike Chamberlain wasn't able to add any pieces to the puzzle. While his injuries incurred in the car accident hadn't been critical, he had developed a serious bacterial infection that was threatening his life. He had been transferred to Hennepin County Medical Center, where he was in surgical intensive care with no visitors but family members allowed.

Megan took the news with resignation. He probably couldn't have helped. If he had played a part in this drama, he was an unwitting pawn. If the accident was indeed the first move in this madman's game . . .

She drove through town with her headlights on and wipers slapping ineffectually at the windshield. Main Street looked like a ski run for automobiles, tire tracks cutting through the heavy snow in a series of trails that told tales of control problems and fender benders. A team of city workers struggled to bring down the Snowdaze banner that spanned the street, the painted oilcloth billowing and snapping like a sail in the wind.

As she drove out of the business district toward the lake, she encountered more snowmobiles than cars. Yards that should have been overrun with children building snowmen and forts were mostly empty. With Albert Fletcher at large, the children of Deer Lake were being held captive in their homes by fear of abduction.

Gossip down at the Scandia House Cafe had it that he might have poisoned poor Doris and that he had always taken an unnatural interest in the altar boys at St E's. Some of the regulars nodded over their coffee and said they had always thought he was 'a little funny'. They were all angry and wary and afraid, and they all grew quiet when they realized the person sitting at the front table eavesdropping on their conversations was 'that BCA woman'.

Megan didn't blame them. Josh's abduction had cracked the placid surface of their quiet town and revealed a nest of worms. Betrayals and secrets, twisted minds and black hearts, all tangled together so no one could decipher the knot. Olie Swain had been transformed from a harmless loser to a wolf loose among the lambs. Albert Fletcher had metamorphosed from deacon to demon, Paul Kirkwood from victim to suspect. She wondered what they would say if she told them she was on her way to question the mild-mannered professor who had worked with juvenile offenders. Christopher Priest was a source of pride for Deer Lake. Would they turn on him or on *her?*

She thought she knew the answer. One more reason not to stay here, she told herself as she drove past the beautiful old Fontaine, past the courthouse, taking a left at the stoplight to drive past City Center. It was just a town, like a million other towns. If the bureau let her go, she could move to a better climate and find a town as nice as this. Her father could come with her or rot. He could live with Mick in L.A. and gush over him in person, and she could be free to start a new life. Alone.

Christopher Priest's home was on Stone Quarry Trail, a fraction of a mile north of the Kirkwood house, but not so easily reached. Especially not on a day when the country roads were fast becoming covered with pristine blankets of new wet snow. Megan navigated with the extreme caution of a city dweller, letting the Lumina creep along what she hoped was the center of the road. There was no other traffic. Woods crowded the shoulders of the road, the naked branches of the trees reaching overhead, nearly lacing together to form a bower. The occasional mailbox marked a driveway. Two to be exact. In the gathering gloom, with the snow coming down, the houses were hidden, crouching like giant forest creatures behind the cover of the woods.

The road simply ended. A yellow and black dead end sign stated the obvious at a point where the road crews had given up and let nature alone. The thick tangle of trees and brush belonged to the back reaches of Quarry Hills Park, the same park that ran behind Hannah and Paul's house. The park where Josh and his buddies had explored and played, never imagining that any of them would ever be in any kind of danger.

A simple black mailbox marked Christopher Priest's driveway, a signpost for a road no one had been down recently. The drive was narrow and thick with fresh snow. Priest hadn't made it back from St Peter yet. If Garrett Wright knew what he was talking about, Priest would be at least another forty-five minutes – probably more with the weather – which would give her plenty of time to look around.

Not trusting the Lumina to make it up the driveway, let alone back out, Megan abandoned it at the end of Stone Quarry Trail and started up the drive on foot. The trees created a false calm, cutting the wind to innocuous puffs of air. They diminished what little light the day offered as well, giving the impression of a weird kind of twilight, a gray shadow kingdom with a small, dark castle at its heart.

The house sat in a clearing, like something from one of the Grimms' grimmer fairy tales. A shingle-sided Victorian painted the color of slate and ashes, a small turret squatted at one corner. The windows were dark, staring blankly at her through the falling snow. To the east of the house stood a double garage and south of it an old shed, both painted to match the house. Megan trudged up the steps onto the porch. She stamped the snow off her boots and knocked on the old glass-paned front door. With Priest gone, there should have been no one to answer. According to the background check they'd run on him, he was unmarried and had no children or roommates – unless he was keeping Josh locked up in the turret. No lights went on. No faces peeked out from behind the drapes.

She made the rounds of the first-floor windows, peering in to see no living creatures, only old furniture and books and computer equipment, everything as neat and tidy as if no one lived there. All doors were locked. Not that she would have dared go inside without a warrant or a damn compelling reason. She had no intention of tainting any future bust by breaking rules.

Crouching down in the snow along the south side of the foundation, she put her face up against a basement window as cold as a block of ice and strained her eyes to see into the gloom with the aid of her pocket flashlight. Nothing of interest. No sign of Josh.

The shoveled walkways to the garage and shed were filling in with several inches of fresh snow. Megan waded through it, cursing. The side door to the garage was unlocked and let her into a space that was disgustingly neat and clean.

Like Fletcher's garage, she thought. God knew he was a more likely suspect than the professor. She was probably just grasping at straws, desperate as she was to make something happen. The note Fletcher had left pinned to his wife's corpse scrolled through her head – *Wicked daughter of Eve: Be sure your sin will find you out.* Sin was a theme in the messages. Being fixated on his religion gave Fletcher an automatic preoccupation with sin. The question that nagged her was the deacon's sudden trip over the lunacy line. If he was that close to breaking, could he have orchestrated a game a chess master would envy? They had been manipulated from the word go, led one way then another. Clues had been planted to taunt them. Could Fletcher have managed all that, then flipped out over something as trivial as Father Tom putting his arm around Hannah?

Megan backed out of the garage, closing the door behind her. The shed was an older building, maybe fifteen feet deep and thirty feet long. It had probably housed farm equipment at one time. What it housed now was a mystery that made Megan hesitate at the end door. Her cop sense tickled the back of her neck. Logic tried to argue. There was no one here. She would have seen their tire tracks on the road or the driveway.

Unless they had come on foot.

Stepping to one side of the door, she tugged off her right mitten and unzipped her parka. The Glock slid out of her shoulder holster and filled her hand with its familiar weight and shape. Security. Protection. She snicked the safety off. Albert Fletcher had to be hiding somewhere. Christopher Priest's shed was as good a place as any.

Heart thudding slow and hard, she moved along the length of the shed. Her left hand traced over the big front doors. Her right hand held her gun, business end to the sky. Despite the temperature, perspiration filmed her skin beneath the layers of clothes.

At the far end of the building she saw the tracks. Footprints in the snow that came out of the woods of Quarry Hills Park and led across Christopher Priest's backyard to the door on the end of the shed. Her pulse picked up a beat. She stood to one side of the door and knocked with her left hand.

'Police! Come out with your hands up!'

No one answered. The only sounds were the wind singing through the treetops and the creak of old buildings. Her pulse throbbed in her ears, pounded inside her forehead. She blinked to clear her vision as it blurred around the edges.

She pushed the door open, staying to the side.

'Police! Come out with your hands up!'

Silence.

Megan scanned the yard. Electrical wires ran from the utility pole to the house and to the garage. None ran to the shed, meaning no interior lights. Only a fool would go into a dark building alone after a suspect. The dark diminished the advantage the gun gave her. The best thing she could do would be to go back to the car and radio for backup, then sit and wait. If it was Fletcher in the shed and he decided to run, he couldn't get far on foot. If it wasn't Fletcher, they had a trespasser to deal with, and she would rather turn it over to a local.

She flexed her numbing fingers on the handle of the Glock, took a deep breath, and stepped quickly past the open door and around the corner of the shed. Thirty feet and she would be clear of it.

She only made it fifteen.

He hit her from the side. Bursting out through the front doors of the shed, he struck a blow that sent Megan sprawling headlong in the snow. The gun flew out of her hand.

Training and instinct spurred her. Move! Move! *Move!* She lunged ahead in the snow like a beached swimmer, arms swinging, legs kicking, gasping for air as she scrambled frantically toward the gun.

He was behind her. She could feel his presence like an ominous weight in the air. She imagined she could feel his shadow fall across her, a black apparition, the shadow of evil, as cold and heavy as steel.

One more lunge. Eyes straight ahead, staring at her fingertips as they scraped across the textured handle of the Glock. His weight came down on her. She gasped and twisted her body, rolling out from under him.

His image flashed on her brain like quick snapshots. Black clothing, ski mask, eyes, and a mouth. He dove toward her, swinging a short black club. Megan caught the shattering blow on her left forearm. She scuttled backward, fighting to get her feet under her, to get some balance, to swing her gun hand into position. He rushed her, swinging the club again and again, hitting her shoulder, hitting her a glancing blow off the side of her head, hitting her bare right hand so hard that the pain roared up her arm and exploded in her brain, dimming her consciousness.

The Glock fell into the snow. Her arm dropped to her side, useless. She stumbled back another step, trying to turn, to run. One thought dragged through her mind – *Oh, shit. I'm dead.*

36

Father Tom's head throbbed in time to his footsteps as he made his way down the center aisle of the church, cassock swishing around the ankles of his black jeans. Every third step coincided with a booming bass note from the pipe organ.

Several people, including Dr Lomax, who had tended his head, and Hannah – who had hovered over him in the emergency room – had advised him to skip the Mass that night. He could have called in help from the archdiocese. They would have sent a retired priest or a rookie from one of the large city parishes, where priests actually had assistants. But he had been stubborn in his refusal. He took another step as Iris Mulroony hit that blasted bass note and thought maybe *foolhardy* was a better word.

He had a concussion. His ears were still ringing with the sound of the brass candlestick bashing the side of his head. Double vision came and went like a camera lens that wouldn't hold its focus. Dizziness buzzed around his head like a swarm of gnats. But he was conducting Mass. He wouldn't stay home and be perceived as hiding out – not only from Albert Fletcher, but from those members of his parish who had jumped at the chance to spread barbed gossip about the circumstances surrounding the incident. He hadn't done anything wrong. Hannah hadn't done anything wrong. She had needed the support and comfort of a friend. The day offering compassion became wrong was the day he gave up on the world.

Guilt nipped its sharp little teeth into his conscience. He had wanted to offer Hannah more than his friendship. He wanted to offer his heart. Was that so wrong, or was it just against the rules?

He took his position behind the altar. Iris mashed down on the keys for a final note he felt in his chest. The small Saturday-night crowd doubled briefly before his eyes.

'The peace of God be with you all.'

'And also with you.'

'*Heretic!*'

The shout echoed over the crowd. Tom looked up at the balcony, where Albert Fletcher stood on the railing, crucifix in hand, ready to jump.

5:07 p.m. 23° windchill factor: 12°

Mitch winced at a knot in his shoulder as he settled in behind the wheel of the Explorer. He had spent the better part of the day beating the bushes for Albert Fletcher with Marty Wilhelm dancing around him like a hyperactive border collie and the press swarming along behind them.

'Chief Holt, do you have any comments on the firing of Agent O'Malley?'

'Chief Holt, your truck was allegedly parked outside Megan O'Malley's apartment all night. What do you have to say about that?'

'That it's none of your goddamn business.'

He supposed that remark would warrant more calls from the city council, but he didn't care. His personal life shouldn't have been an issue. The issue here was Josh. He couldn't believe anyone was bothering to zero in on irrelevant details.

Irrelevant. Good word for what had gone on between him and Megan. *Finished* was another.

Life had been so much simpler when good old Leo had the office down the hall. He had been safe in his emotional cocoon, insulated by the scar tissue of old pain.

He wondered how long it would take to seal himself back into a life that consisted of work and Jessie and fending off the matchmakers. Emotional purgatory. The life that hurt less and punished him more.

He looked at himself in the rearview mirror, his eyes narrowed with contempt at what he saw. Oh, well, he would go home to Jessie, who was too young to realize what a jerk her father was. He could choke down some supper with her before he took her back over to the Strausses so he could spend the rest of the night looking for Fletcher.

They had covered better than half the town in a house-to-house search. They'd been in basements and potting sheds and back-alley Dumpsters and found not a trace of the man. The choppers had hovered over town like birds of prey until the weather set them down. The most exciting report they turned in was that of a nude hot-tub party going on in the backyard of a Dinkytown frat house.

Mitch found himself giving some thought to Wilhelm's theory of Albert and an unknown accomplice splitting town. The deacon could have been a hundred miles away before they'd even gotten the roadblocks up outside of town Friday – and he could have had Josh with him.

The radio blasted out a staccato burst of garbled static as he reached to turn the ignition.

'All units: 415 in progress at St Elysius Church. Repeat – disturbance in progress at St Elysius Catholic Church: Possible 10–56A. Repeat – possible attempted suicide. Be advised: suspect is Albert Fletcher. Chief, if you're listening, they need you.'

'We have a treat for you, clever girl.'

The voice was soft, a whisper, disembodied, unrecognizable. Megan opened her eyes and saw nothing. Blackness. The irrational thought that she might be dead went through her like a lightning bolt. No. Her heart wouldn't race if she were dead. Her head wouldn't pound. She wouldn't feel pain. Then light as faint as shadows slipped beneath the blindfold. She looked down. Her lap. A small wedge of concrete floor on either side of her. She was sitting on a chair. Correction – she was tied to a chair. Her arms were tied to the arms of the chair, her ankles bound to the legs. She didn't think she would have been able to sit on her own. She felt woozy, as if her soul and her body were attached by only the thinnest of threads. Drugs. He had given her something. *They* had given her something.

We have a treat for you, he had said. Odd, but it didn't feel as if there were more than one other person in the room. Her captor was standing close to her, behind her, but she didn't sense anyone else.

'Clever girl,' he whispered again, tracing his fingertips around her throat. She swallowed, and he chuckled to himself, a sound that was little more than a breath. 'You think we're going to kill you? Perhaps.'

He tightened his hands slowly, fingertips pressing on her larynx until she coughed. He allowed her half a breath, then pressed harder. Her head swam and what vision she had went dim. Panic spurred her to struggle. She jerked and choked. When he released the pressure, she sucked in a wheezing breath, and another and another, while he laughed his breathy laugh.

'We could kill you,' he murmured, his mouth brushing against her ear. 'You wouldn't be the first by a long, long way.'

'Did you kill Josh?' she mumbled. Her mouth felt as if it were coated with rubber cement. Saliva pooled beneath a tongue that felt bloated. Effects of the drug or the choking.

'What do you think?' The voice floated around her like a cloud. 'Do you think he's dead? Do you think he's alive?'

Megan struggled to focus, to use anger to keep herself lucid. 'I . . . think . . . you're a lunatic.'

He struck her right hand and pain shot along her nerve pathways, the shock of it taking her breath away. He struck her again, hitting her fingertips with what felt like the narrow edge of a steel ruler. The pain ripped through her and tore up out of her throat in a scream that trailed off into shuddering sobs.

'Respect.' The voice seemed to come from the center of her forehead. 'You ought to respect us. We're so far superior to you. We've fooled you all along, so easily. It's a game, you see,' he said. 'We've calculated all the moves, all the options, all the possibilities. We can't lose.'

A game. A chess match with living pieces. Megan shivered. Her coat had been taken. And her sweater. Finally she realized she was clad only in the black silk long underwear Mitch had chuckled at. The .380 A.M.T. Back-Up she wore in her ankle holster must have been discovered and taken. Not that she could have used it if she had wanted to.

'Did you kill Josh?' she murmured.

Her tormentor let the question hang. Megan didn't know if two minutes passed or twenty. The drug had warped her perception of time. For all she knew, days had gone by since she had driven out to Christopher Priest's house. She could still be there, but she had vague memories of riding in a vehicle of some sort. The smell of exhaust, the rumble of an engine, the feeling of movement.

The dizziness swirled around her. Nausea crawled up the back of her throat and she swallowed it down.

'The game isn't over yet,' he whispered. Winding a hand into her ponytail, he pulled her head back slowly. Megan opened her eyes wider, tried to see more of the room, but all she could see was a strip of gray the color of concrete. Basement. 'We can't lose. Do you understand me? You can't defeat us. We're very good at this game.'

Megan was in no position to argue, and antagonism seemed unwise after her last attempt. Killing her would be a simple chore. She wouldn't be the first, he had said. Not by a long way. Fear skittered through her – for herself and for Josh, wherever he was. They had known almost from the first they weren't dealing with the average criminal, but she had never imagined this – a multiple murderer who would play with the lives of people like a cat with a mouse.

He let go of her hair abruptly and her head fell forward, the motion bringing another wave of nausea. A shoe scuffed against the floor. A single black boot came into view beside her right leg, then vanished. The chair tipped back and spun around – or she imagined it did. She imagined parts of her flying out away from her body and snapping back in place like something from a weird cartoon. Her consciousness swam in a thick black morass and white noise pressed in on her eardrums like a clamp tightening around her head. She couldn't tell if she was awake or in a nightmare, didn't know if there was a difference.

Then everything went still, the sudden absence of movement and sound as disorienting as the assault of sound and movement. She was floating on nothing in a black void. Then came a lighted image, just a glimpse, so brief it registered in the subconscious and came forward into the conscious mind one detail at a time: a face, a boy, brown hair, striped pajamas.

'Josh?'

Another glimpse. Freckles, a bruised cheek, blank eyes.

'Josh!' She tried to move but couldn't, tried to reach out to him but seemed to have no control over her body at all.

The image flashed again. He stood like a statue, like a mannequin, his arms outstretched toward her, his face expressionless.

'Josh!' she screamed, but he didn't seem to hear her at all.

The blackness fell again like a curtain. She drifted on it. So tired, but her heart was pounding out of control and the pain came at her from all directions – *bam! bam! bam! bam!* – hitting her everywhere at once like a dozen rods wielded by twelve angry men.

The voice vibrated against the top of her head.

'You wonder who we are, clever girl?' he whispered. 'You wonder why we play this game?'

He settled his hands on her shoulders and sensuously stroked the aching, knotted muscles. A shudder of revulsion rippled through her, provoking his laughter.

'We play the game because we can,' he said, sliding his hands down over her breasts. 'Because no one can catch us. Because no one ever suspected. Because we're brilliant and invincible.'

He squeezed a breast in each hand until she whimpered.

'You came too close, clever girl. Now you get to play, too.'

Megan tried to think who or what she had come close to. Names and faces floated through her mind, but she could grasp none of them.

'What will I do?' she asked as she tipped forward again.

He leaned so close she could smell the mouthwash on his breath. When he spoke, his lips brushed her cheek. 'You're going to be our next move.'

5:15 p.m. 23° windchill factor: 12°

Albert Fletcher stood on the balcony rail, his left arm wrapped around a column. In his right hand he clutched an ornate bronze crucifix, which he brandished high over his head as he shouted at the people below him.

'Beware false prophets who come in sheep's clothing! They are ravening wolves!'

The congregation had been ushered out of the church, replaced by police and sheriff's deputies. Father Tom remained behind the altar, his gaze fast on Fletcher, as if it would hold him in place. He prayed it would. Guilt twisted like a knife in his belly. This situation was his fault. Right or wrong, his feelings for Hannah had been the trigger.

'Albert,' he said, the microphone clipped to his vestments picking up his voice clearly. 'Albert, you have to listen. You're making a big mistake.'

'Wicked spawn of hell!'

'No, Albert. I'm a priest,' he said quietly, hoping he was punching the button that would make Fletcher listen instead of push him over the edge.

'I'm *your* priest. You have to listen to me. That's what you've been taught, isn't it?'

Fletcher shook his crucifix angrily; the railing shook with him. 'I know where Satan's throne is!'

'Satan's throne is in hell, Albert,' Tom said. 'This is the house of the Lord.'

'I will cast you out, demon!' Fletcher's left foot slipped on the railing. Everyone in the church held their breath until he regained his balance.

In the silence Mitch could hear the nerve-tightening sound of wood cracking. Crouched low in the shadows at the head of the stairs, he had a clear view of Fletcher, and through the spindly carved balusters of the railing he could see the vast open space beyond the balcony. Slowly he straightened and moved out into the light.

'Mr Fletcher? It's Chief Holt,' he said, his voice low and even.

Fletcher's head snapped around. The railing wobbled. Mitch's body tensed, ready to spring forward. The deacon's eyes were wild, bright with madness.

'You're right, you know,' Mitch said. 'We're onto Father Tom. We're going to arrest him. We'll need you to help us.'

Fletcher stared at him, pulling the crucifix down to clutch it against his body. 'Beware false prophets,' he muttered. 'Beware false prophets. Shapen in iniquity. Conceived in sin.'

'You know about sin, don't you, Albert?' Mitch said, inching toward the railing. 'You can tell us all about it. But we'll need you to come to the station. You can be our witness.'

'Witness,' Fletcher mumbled. He thrust the crucifix skyward again and shouted, 'Witness! Witness the wrath of God!'

The railing groaned. Mitch was moving even as the sickening sound of wood breaking cracked in his ears. He lunged for Fletcher as the balcony railing gave way, catching hold of the deacon's left hand. Momentum yanked him toward the edge. His shoulder slammed into the support column and he wrapped his free arm around it, gritting his teeth against the pain, against the strain of holding Fletcher's weight. A fraction of a second later, the hold was broken and the deacon's fate was sealed.

'*No!*' Tom shouted.

He saw Fletcher's body dropping from twenty feet up. He ran as hard as he could, but his cassock caught at his legs, pulled at him, slowed him down. He could see the cops rushing in. They were all too late.

Fletcher landed like a rag doll tossed out a window, his body shattering as it fell across the pews. Someone called out to God. Someone else shouted an expletive. Father Tom fell to his knees, his hands trembling as he reached out to cradle Fletcher's fractured skull. Paramedics rushed in with a stretcher. Too late. He passed a hand over the man's face, closing the sightless eyes, and he murmured a prayer for the soul of Albert Fletcher . . . and one for his own.

37

The drug was fading. The fog in her brain was thinning, letting the pain come through like a hot desert sun, searing, unbearable. Megan tried to focus on the questions that floated through her head like wisps of angel hair. He said she had come close. To what? She tried to think back. He had caught her at Priest's house. Was that coincidence? Had she simply stumbled into the wrong place at the wrong time and flushed Albert Fletcher out of hiding?

You don't believe in coincidence, O'Malley. Nor did she believe the disembodied voice belonged to the deacon. There had been no spouting of Bible verse, no promise for damnation. The voice was cool, controlled, frighteningly so. A voice without a soul.

Did it belong to the professor? He had gone to St Peter. He couldn't have known she would go to his house. He couldn't have been lying in wait for her.

Unless someone had warned him.

Only two people had known she was asking after him – Garrett Wright and Todd Childs.

Todd Childs, the psych major who worked at The Pack Rat. He had known Olie Swain, had been in computer classes with him – and with Priest. He had helped out at the volunteer center – with Priest. He was working on a project with Priest. She had no doubt he knew all about chemical substances. He would have known what to give her.

'It's almost showtime.'

The words were whispered against her lips, an obscene kiss. Megan recoiled, earning a breathy chuckle. He had been silent so long, she had begun to think he'd left. She looked down, tilting her head to the side as much as she dared. A portion of the anonymous black boot came into view.

'Why Josh?' she murmured, her mouth as dry as powder. 'Why his family?'

'Why not?' he replied, sending a chill straight through her. 'Such a perfect little family.' The softly spoken words were venomous with contempt.

Megan stared down at the boot as he rocked back on his heels, the action flipping a switch of recognition. She'd seen him do that half a dozen times. Just a habit, a quirk, a minor detail she filed away in the back of her mind like eye color or a mole. The words were familiar, too. *I feel so bad for Hannah and Paul. Such a perfect family . . .*

Garrett Wright.

He had seen her standing along the road where Mike Chamberlain had lost control of his car. The helpful Dr Wright, offering roadside assistance with a benign smile, later offering all he knew about his colleague's whereabouts.

Hannah and Paul's neighbor. A man who molded the impressionable minds of the students at Harris College. Respected. Above suspicion. A man the media had chosen as an expert witness. For once they had struck pay dirt. The irony was that they might never know it.

8:41 p.m. 22° windchill factor: 10°

Mitch drove away from City Center for the second time that night. The rush of adrenaline that had pumped through him as he'd sped across town to St E's was long spent. He had hit rock bottom with the death of Albert Fletcher. If Fletcher had taken Josh, they weren't going to hear it from him now. Fletcher couldn't tell them where Josh was, whether Josh was alive or not.

He wanted to hit something, hard. Or be touched by something soft. The first night he had gone to Megan, she had reached out to him and taken away his pain. She didn't think she needed anyone. Had it ever occurred to her that someone might need her? Someone like him. A beat-up, broken-up, bad-tempered cop.

He pulled the Explorer in along the curb in front of the big Victorian on Ivy Street and sat there listening to the wipers thump back and forth. The snow was coming down fast and furious. With predictions that the storm would continue through the night, city crews had made no attempt to clear the side streets. People had parked haphazardly. The cars wore blankets of snow four inches thick. Except Megan's car, which was nowhere in sight.

There were no lights on in the third-floor windows. The black cat sat in the front window, visible against the backdrop of pale curtains, keeping watch for his mistress. She must have gone to St Paul after all. Mitch didn't know whether to be relieved or disappointed. He didn't know what the hell he was doing here. What was he going to do – tell her Fletcher was on a slab down at Oglethorpe's Funeral Home and ask her did she want to go to bed with him for old times' sake because he was feeling battered and lost? She'd pull that Glock and plug him right between the eyes.

The cellular phone nestled in his coat pocket trilled. Mitch dug it out, swearing under his breath. 'What now?'

The silence was broken by a thin, shaky breath. The hair on the back of his neck rose.

'M-Mitch?'

His heart jammed at the base of his throat. 'Megan? Honey, what's wrong?'

'G-get the sonofabi –' A strangled cry choked off the sentence.

'Megan!' Mitch shouted, gripping the steering wheel hard with his free hand. 'Megan!'

The voice that came on the line was not Megan's. Whisper-soft, it skated like a razor along his nerve endings. 'We have a present for you, Chief. Come to the southwest entrance of Quarry Hills Park in thirty minutes. Come alone. Not one minute sooner, or Agent O'Malley will die. Do you understand?'

'Yes.' Mitch bit the word off. 'What do you want?'

The eerie, breathless chuckle went down his spine like a bony finger. He tightened his grip on the phone and swallowed at the tightness in his throat.

'To win the game,' the voice murmured. The line went dead.

Megan did her best to brace herself as she heard him set the phone down. He would punish her. She knew that. He was a control freak and she had broken a little piece of that control. If she was lucky, he would rage and shout and she would at least be able to testify she had heard his voice clearly and distinctly. If she was unlucky, he would kill her.

'We thought you were a clever girl.' He didn't raise his voice even a fraction, but the anger was there, humming like a power line. 'We thought you were a clever girl, but you're just another stupid bitch!'

The blow caught her in the side of the head. Not the club, but the back of his hand. So hard that the chair rocked sideways. Color burst behind her eyelids and the taste of blood bloomed fresh and thick in her mouth. Before that explosion subsided, he brought his fist down on her battered hand. The tears were instantaneous. As much as Megan hated them, as much as she hated to have him see them streaming out from under the blindfold, there was nothing she could do to stop them. Still, she bit her lip and held her breath against the need to sob aloud.

This was what he wanted as much as anything: to humiliate her, to prove his own superiority in every way. He had calculated every move, every possibility, but he hadn't counted on her defying him. She could only hope it rattled him enough that he would make a mistake, that the mistake would give Mitch an opportunity to nail him.

She wanted that opportunity herself. The chance to beat him at his game. The chance to beat him physically, the son of a bitch. She wanted to take that little baton of his and bash his head in, beat him until he told her where Josh was and then beat him some more.

He used it on her with expertise, knowing just the spots to hit and the perfect amount of force to cause pain but not to make her lose consciousness. Her right knee, her left shoulder, her left calf, her right hand. Again and again he hit the hand, until the slightest touch made her scream.

When his fury was spent, she could no longer distinguish one pain from the next. The pain had taken on proportions larger than she was, suffocating her, deafening her, breaking her. The only thing she clung to was the burning coal of hatred in her chest and the knowledge that he was the key to finding Josh.

The bindings around her arms and ankles abruptly loosened and the chair tipped forward, dumping her to the cold floor. His voice seemed to be in both ears at once.

'Rise and shine, bitch.'

Megan made no effort to move. The baton cracked against her back, her ribs, her buttocks, and she fought to make her body move. She couldn't get her feet beneath her, couldn't tell which way was up or which way to go to escape the beating. He grabbed her by the hair and hauled her up, slamming her sideways into a wall.

'We could make you *so* sorry, little bitch,' he whispered. He closed his teeth on her ear and bit her through the blindfold until she cried out. 'If only we had more time to play. But we have a date with your loverboy.'

38

Mitch settled back in the trees to wait. From his vantage point he had a clear view of the southwest entrance – as clear a view as the snow allowed. He had come in from the west, from the Lakeside neighborhood, no more than six blocks from the Kirkwood house. Noogie had dropped him off and gone on in the Explorer to wait until the designated time, and Mitch had set out through the thick woods that edged the park, wading through snow that was nearly knee-deep, skidding downhill, tripping on hidden roots and fallen branches.

He crouched against the thick, rough trunk of an oak tree, fighting to catch his breath. The drive that ran a bent horseshoe circuit between the east and west entrances of the park was no more than thirty feet away, with the parking area less than fifty yards to the south. Mercury-vapor lights were spaced out along the parking lot and farther apart along the drive. Snow danced like thick swarms of fireflies beneath their light.

He checked his watch. Twelve minutes to spare. Twelve minutes to wait and sweat and wonder what the bastard might have done to Megan. Twelve minutes to worry that his hasty instructions to Dietz and Stevens hadn't been clear enough, that someone would somehow screw up and get Megan killed. There hadn't been time to formulate much of a plan, and he was only too conscious of the fact that the officers he had to work with had no experience with hostage situations. They didn't dare risk radio communications for fear of being overheard on a scanner – by their bad guy or a citizen or a reporter.

Twelve minutes to wonder who the bastard was. Was it Priest? Had Megan's hunch paid off? Damn her for going off half-cocked with no backup. She knew better. But there hadn't been anyone to go with her. She'd been relieved of duty. And when she had told him her latest theory, he had discounted it and blown her off.

He couldn't believe it was Priest. He'd been around the man for two years and never felt a bad vibration.

And you thought Olie was harmless, and that nothing bad would happen in broad daylight at the 7-Eleven.

393

He closed his eyes. Oh, Jesus, not again, not Megan, not right before his eyes. Not because he'd been wrong or stupid or too stubborn to see the truth. He couldn't have another person die because of him. Especially not Megan, who had badgered and bullied him from the start to open his eyes and see something besides the bland haven he had created for himself. Not Megan, who had been abandoned and neglected and harassed, and deserved so much better from life.

The pickup turned in the drive at 9:05, ten minutes ahead of schedule. A late model GMC 4X4, jacked up on heavy tires and sporting the latest in roll bars and a bug guard that read ROY'S TOY. It rolled past the parking area and crept along through the fresh snow. Crouching low behind the cover of the trees, Mitch plowed his way north, rushing to come even with the truck before the driver got out, hoping this was their man and not some horny teenagers looking for a spot to make out.

The heavy snow sucked at his boots, costing him precious seconds. He lunged ahead, breath sucking in and hissing out through his teeth, his eyes on the pickup as it appeared and disappeared on the other side of the trees. The brake lights went off and he fell against a walnut tree. He slid his hand inside his open parka and cased his Smith & Wesson out of the holster, never looking away from the truck.

The driver's door opened. A black-clad figure slid out from behind the wheel, featureless, anonymous, a ski mask hiding the face. Dark Man. He took a long look around, scouting for any sign of betrayal. Mitch willed himself invisible, pressing hard against the trunk of the tree, holding his breath as the faceless eyes passed over his section of woods. The air seeped out of his lungs as Dark Man went around to the other side of the truck and let his passenger out.

He marched her a dozen paces back toward the parking area. Mitch strained to make her out, an impossibility in the poor conditions. It could have been ayone about the right height with dark hair. It could have been a decoy. This could all have been a trick. Megan could have been in a basement somewhere, her fate hinging on whether or not he screwed up here.

He fought the panic. *Think like a cop. See like a cop. What do you see?*

She was leaning heavily against Dark Man, as if unable to walk on her own. Bending over slightly, the gait off-rhythm, a limp. She was in pain. If this was a trick being set up ten minutes ahead of schedule, there would be no reason for the decoy to put on a show. It *was* Megan, and she was hurt badly. Jesus, what had that animal done to her?

Megan hobbled away from the truck, leaning hard against her captor, not by choice but necessity and because she thought any hardship she caused him was a small point in her favor. Her hands were bound behind her, the blindfold still in place. She wore no coat, only the thin silk underwear and a sheet for a wrap. The cold bit into her, exacerbating her pain instead of numbing it. She couldn't straighten her right knee. It felt swollen and every step brought a small explosion of pain. She wasn't sure it would hold her weight, but she exaggerated the limp, stumbling into Wright and causing him an awkward step. In punishment he squeezed her hand, wringing a sound of agony from her.

'Play your part, little bitch' – he brought the nose of a pistol up under her cheekbone – 'or I'll blow your brains out.'

Her role in his game was Humiliation. He had outsmarted them. He had snatched Josh away from under everyone's noses, laid out his little clues and red herrings, and fooled them all. She was to be his grand gesture, the ultimate insult. He had taken her and beaten her and wrapped her in a sheet of evidence he believed would do them no good at all because he believed he was invincible.

That would ultimately be his undoing, Megan thought. He believed his own delusions of grandeur. God only knew what he had gotten away with over the years, but he wouldn't get away with this. Not as long as she was alive.

He faced her the way they had come in, arranging the sheet around her to his satisfaction like an oversize shawl, the ends fluttering and snapping in the wind. He had draped it around her before taking her out to get in the truck. A bedsheet. White with red flecks. She knew what it was: bloodstains. Evidence, he told her. He would hand them this evidence wrapped around a cop and still no one would touch him.

Think again, you bastard.

She felt him lean close, his breath warm and minty on her face. 'It's been lovely,' he murmured, and touched his lips to hers.

Megan spat at him and won herself a backhand across the mouth with the butt of the gun. As she staggered, the taste of blood bubbled up in her mouth like a warm spring. She spat it out, concentrating not on this newest pain, but on the thought that Mitch would be coming. He had to have risked coming in early. It meant catching their monster. But it could also mean her life. Would he take that chance?

Come on, Mitch. Be here. Be here.

She counted the footsteps as Wright moved away from her. Two, three ... Had he holstered the gun? She inched herself around, her limited gaze on the ground, searching for footprints to tell her she was pointed toward the truck. Bending her head down to her shoulder, she tried to dislodge the blindfold and gained another fraction of an inch of vision in her right eye. Enough to see his legs.

If she rushed him – if she could – would it delay him enough for Mitch to arrive? Or would she die for nothing? The thoughts and questions shot through her mind, all of them boiling down to a simple truth: She didn't want to die like this – in disgrace, with so much left undone and unsaid.

Mitch held himself rigid. He wanted to nail the son of a bitch now, tackle him and beat him senseless for striking Megan. But he would wait. Let him get in the truck and drive out. Count on Dietz and Stevens to stop him at the east entrance. Dietz and Stevens, whose biggest busts had been drunks and petty drug dealers. This asshole was the key to finding Josh. If they had him in their sights and let him get away . . . He was halfway back to the truck. Once he was in the truck, he could be gone.

In a heartbeat the decision was taken away from him. Megan turned and flung herself at the man. He wheeled and caught her head-on, and together they tumbled into the snow.

Mitch launched himself down the hill, fear and fury driving his legs, bellowing out of his lungs. 'Freeze! Police!'

Megan's breath left her in a rush. She gasped for more as she struggled to free herself from Wright's grip, from the damned sheet, struggled to get her legs under her. The blindfold came off, but Wright's grip never loosened. He pushed to his feet, dragging her up in a headlock and bringing his gun up hard into her temple. He half dragged her, half pushed her toward the truck, snarling in her ear.

'Tell him I'll kill you! Tell him I'll kill you!'

'Tell him yourself, asshole,' she snapped. 'Kill me and you're a dead man right here.'

'Bitch!'

He jerked her sideways, his forearm tightening against her windpipe.

'Drop the gun!' Mitch shouted.

He came to a halt ten feet from them, the Smith & Wesson in position, cocked and ready, his finger itching to take the slack out of the trigger and blow the bastard's head open like a rotten watermelon. But he couldn't chance a shot; Megan was too close, too good a shield. The nose of a black nine-millimeter was biting into her temple. Mitch knew if he did the wrong thing, made the wrong decision, she would be dead. Sweat dripped into his eyes and he blinked it away. The image of Allison dead and Megan dead alternated in his mind like freeze-frame shots. Allison lying on the gray linoleum, her blood spreading out in a pool. Megan lying crumpled in the snow, her blood soaking it like cherry syrup on shaved ice.

'Drop it!' he bellowed. 'You're under arrest!'

Wright pulled Megan another half-foot toward the open door of the truck. The engine was rumbling, waiting.

'You'll never get out of here in that truck,' Mitch yelled. 'I've got unmarked cars waiting on both entrances.'

'Tell him he doesn't play fair,' Wright whispered.

Megan cut him a glare out the corner of her eye. 'Fuck you.'

She let her legs buckle abruptly. Her dead weight jerked Wright off balance, giving Mitch the opportunity to charge. Wright shoved Megan into Mitch, sending them staggering backward in the snow. Firing blindly in their direction, he vaulted into the cab of the truck.

Mitch rolled Megan beneath him, shielding her, flinching as the bullets struck within inches.

'It's Garrett Wright!' Megan shouted.

Mitch raised himself up on his hands and knees over her. 'Are you hit?'

'No! Go nail the son of a bitch!'

He lunged to his feet as the truck lurched into motion, tires spinning in the fresh snow. The back end fishtailed, swinging toward Mitch, who grabbed the side panel just as his feet were knocked out from under him. His hands slipped as he struggled for a better hold, and the Smith & Wesson clattered into the bed of the truck. Then the pickup slid the other way, dragging him in its wake.

As it straightened out, Mitch heaved himself up and over the side, rolling into the bed with a grunt of pain. Instantly, he spotted his gun and dove for it. Scrambling into a crouch, he lurched toward the cab, then grabbed hold of the roll bar.

'Stop the truck, Wright!' he shouted, pounding the back window with his gun hand. 'You're under arrest!'

Wright responded by jerking the steering wheel, throwing Mitch sideways. They slid into a curve off-balance, rocking violently, the right side wheels coming up off the ground. Mitch was thrown back in the other direction. He grabbed again for the roll bar, brought the Smith & Wesson up, and fired through the back window. The bullet cut cleanly through it but shattered the windshield into an intricate spiderweb of cracks.

'Stop the truck!' He smashed the bullet hole with the butt of the pistol, cracking the safety glass and bending it in.

Wright twisted around and fired over his shoulder, the bullet sailing wide as Mitch ducked sideways, aligning himself directly behind his man. Still holding the roll bar with his left hand, he reached in through the broken window with his right and jammed his gun up behind Wright's ear.

'Stop the goddamn truck! You're under arrest!'

Wright twisted the wheel sharply to the left and gunned the engine. The pickup roared off the path and into space as it sailed off an embankment. Shouting a curse, Mitch dropped to his knees. He jammed his gun inside his coat and grabbed hold of the roll bar with both hands.

The truck landed bucking, then skidded sideways and slammed into the trunk of a tree. Mitch bounced around the bed like a ball in a game of bumper pool. A wedge of snow-flecked sky flashed across his vision as he was thrown, then solid white, then color burst behind his eyelids when he landed.

He was on his feet and drawing the gun out before his vision cleared. He ran for the truck, trying to spot Garrett Wright, wondering if the crash might have knocked him out. Gunshots answered the question for him – three quick rounds that sent him diving for cover behind a fat spruce tree.

He crouched there for a moment, trying to catch his breath, trying to catch a glimpse of Wright from between the branches, but it was too dark. Staying low, he crept ahead from spruce tree to hardwood, moving toward the truck. It had come to rest in a small oasis of trees. To the south and east was nothing but open ground. To the west was a fifty-yard sprint to the thick woods that blanketed the hillside. If Wright was going to run, west would be his only option.

Mitch darted behind another tree, his eyes on the truck.

'Give it up, Wright!'

Silence. The wind. The groaning of the trees.

Taking a deep breath, he ran low for the passenger side of the truck. No shots. Nothing but the hiss of the pickup's wounded radiator. Slowly, Mitch straightened. The cab was empty. Through the windows he could see Garrett Wright running, no more than thirty feet from the edge of the woods.

'Damn, you're too old for this, Holt,' he muttered, gathering his strength. Then he pushed away from the pickup and ran. He expected Wright to fire on him as he crossed the open ground, but no shots came. He charged up the bank, plunging into the trees and brush, leading with his gun.

A flash of movement among the tree trunks to the north sent Mitch in that direction. A bullet chipped a tree a foot to his left at the instant the sound of the shot reached him. He dropped to his belly and waited, scuttling sideways, ignoring the sharp broken branches that poked at him through the snow. His hand caught hold of something soft and warm. He jerked back instantly, thinking it was something alive, but it was a black knit ski mask.

'Wright!' he shouted. 'Give it up! You can't win!'

A game. A goddamn game. That was what he called destroying people's lives. The hell if he would win this one.

Another shot zinged toward him. Mitch zigged right and ran on, returning fire. He caught another glimpse of Wright, a darker shape among the shadows, then he was gone again, leaving Mitch swearing.

The muscles in his legs and back were burning. The cold night air came into his lungs like needles. The toe of his boot hit something and he went down hard. As he stood, a bullet cut through the left sleeve of his parka, nicking his arm and spinning him sideways.

'Shit! Shit! Shit!' He ducked behind a tree. The wound stung like hell, but it wasn't debilitating and it wasn't his gun hand.

Carefully, he eased his head around the tree trunk. No sign of Wright. An aura of light limned the crest of the hill. Beyond the last of the trees lay the Lakeside neighborhood. Hannah and Paul's neighborhood. Garrett Wright's neighborhood. Garrett Wright, who taught psychology and worked with the Sci-Fi Cowboys and drove a Saab. Who would ever have looked at him and wondered if a madman lurked beneath the neatly pressed surface?

Another flash of movement cut through the falling snow. Mitch gave chase, keeping his eye on Wright's back as he hit the cross–country ski trail that ran along the lip of the hill. Mitch hit the path seconds after him.

'Wright! Stop! You're under arrest!'

His quarry ducked left and disappeared into a stand of snow-laden spruce trees. Praying he wouldn't be running into a bullet, Mitch bolted after him. On the other side of the trees the houses of Lakeside stood on their oversize lots, lights glowing softly in windows. He narrowed his eyes, scanning the yards for Garrett Wright. A shadow moved along the next house to the north. Just a shape along the back wall of the garage, running through an open back door.

'Freeze, dammit!' Mitch shouted, charging through the drifts, never taking his eyes off the door as it swung shut two seconds before he reached it.

He lowered a shoulder and hit the door running. It burst open with an explosive *crack!,* the wood frame splintering. Mitch's momentum carried him straight into Garrett Wright. They went down hard, skidding across the concrete floor, Wright grunting as his breath left him.

'You're under arrest, you son of a bitch,' Mitch snarled, rising up above him, his lungs working like a pair of bellows. He held the Smith & Wesson half an inch from Wright's pale face, the barrel quivering like a rattlesnake tail. 'Game's over, Garrett. You lose.'

39

'What's going on?' Karen Wright stood in the doorway that led from the garage to her kitchen, her expression pale and horrified.

'It's a mistake,' her husband said. He lay facedown on the concrete floor of the garage, his hands cuffed behind his back. He twisted his head around to glare up at Mitch, who stood with the Smith & Wesson still trained on him.

'Yeah,' Mitch snarled. 'It's a mistake – and *you* made it.'

Karen's big doe eyes brimmed with tears. She twisted her hands in the bottom of her baggy pink sweater. 'I don't understand! Garrett hasn't done anything! He doesn't even speed!'

Mitch spared her a glance. He had read many cases where a woman had lived with a man for years, oblivious to the fact that he led a secret life as a rapist or murderer or child predator. That was undoubtedly the case with Karen Wright. She had been working at the volunteer center, mailing out fliers in the effort to find Josh, while her husband had been playing his sick game. Still, she would have to be questioned to see just what she knew and what she didn't, to see if she could corroborate or destroy her husband's story. Mitch couldn't imagine she would hold up very well. She didn't look very resilient.

'Garrett, what's this about?' she cried. 'I don't understand!'

'I'm sorry, ma'am,' Mitch said. 'If you could just wait inside –'

'Garrett!' she sobbed.

The big garage door was up, a huge open window to the street, letting in the wind and the snow, affording a view of the cruisers coming up the block with Mitch's Explorer right behind them. The vehicles turned in the drive. There were no lights or sirens. Mitch had given specific orders for silence when he had called the dispatcher on his cellular phone. No mention of a code or a crime, just a specific request for Noogie, Dietz, and Stevens, and one other patrol car to report to 91 Lakeshore Drive.

Wright's own house. Mitch supposed he had thought to take the Saab in the garage and escape, but there would be no escape. Tonight, justice got the win.

Megan sat in the Explorer and watched as Noogie escorted Garrett Wright to a police car. She stared at the face of the man who had beaten her, tormented her, tormented them all. No more than four feet away, he turned and looked right at her. No emotion registered on the face that was cast half in shadow, half in the grainy light that shone down from above the garage door. He simply stared at her. Then Noogie clamped a big hand on his shoulder and stuffed him down into the car.

Megan shivered. She couldn't seem to stop shaking, and it wasn't from cold. Noogie had bundled her up in wool blankets and left the motor running and the heater blasting. She had refused to let him call an ambulance. She had no intention of being whisked off to the emergency room without knowing that Mitch had caught Garrett Wright ... without knowing that Garrett Wright hadn't shot him.

Dietz and Stevens came out of the garage, one at either elbow of Karen Wright, holding her upright as she sobbed. Wright's eerie whisper floated through Megan's head – *we . . . we . . . we . . .* Never *I*, always the plural. But she couldn't picture Karen as the other half of the team. There had been too much contempt for women in that disembodied voice. *You're just another stupid bitch!*

She jerked at the memory of the blow that had followed.

'Dammit, Megan, you belong in the hospital!'

Mitch had pulled open the passenger door and was scowling at her. But it wasn't anger she saw in his eyes.

'I had to know,' she whispered. 'I had to see that you got him.'

Something twisted hard in his chest as he looked at her. Her right eye was blackening. Her lower lip was split and swollen. That son of a bitch had pounded her, yet she sat there with her chin up and defiance shining behind the tears in her eyes.

'I got him,' he whispered. Stroking a hand over her hair, he leaned into the truck and coaxed her head to his shoulder. '*We* got him.'

He shuddered at the thought that the outcome could have been very different. She could have been killed. He could have lost her. But she was here and alive. Relief left him feeling a little shaky.

They were both blinking furiously as he pulled back. He sniffed hard. A crooked smile canted his mouth.

'You're a hell of a cop, Megan O'Malley,' he murmured. 'Now let's get you to a hospital.'

11:47 p.m. 17° windchill factor: 0°

'Did he tell you where Josh is?' Hannah asked.

Mitch had told her to sit, but she couldn't. She prowled the family room, her arms crossed tight. Her pulse was racing off the chart. She probably should have been lying down, but she needed to move and to keep on moving until Mitch gave her the answer she needed. And then

401

she would sprint out the door and run to Josh. Conversely, Paul sat at the end of the couch, bent over with his head in his hands, seemingly unable to move or speak.

The call had come nearly two hours before – Mitch telling her Garrett Wright had been arrested and that he would come by the house himself to explain. She had asked him to notify Paul at his office, then waited, stunned and numb.

Mitch looked at his boots and heaved a sigh. 'No. So far he isn't talking.'

Mitch had asked him to show a little compassion, tell them if Josh was alive at least, but Garrett Wright held no compassion. He met Mitch's gaze straight-on, nothing showing behind his cold, dark eyes, his fine features blank, devoid of emotion.

'Garrett Wright,' Hannah muttered. 'You're certain . . .'

'There's no doubt in my mind,' Mitch said. 'He's been toying with us all along, teasing us with clues. He meant to use Megan – Agent O'Malley – to make his point tonight, to show us all how superior he is, but he danced a little too close to the flame this time. I chased him down myself, Hannah. He's our man – one of them, anyway. Whether Olie Swain was connected, or someone else, we don't know yet.'

Mitch refrained from telling them a Harris College student named Todd Childs had been brought in for questioning. Nothing had come of it yet. Nor did he make any mention of the fact that he had issued a bulletin for Christopher Priest to be brought in. The professor hadn't returned from St Peter, if that was where he had gone. The St Peter police were checking motels to see if he was among the motorists stranded by the storm.

'My God, *Garrett Wright*.' Hannah shook her head. It seemed inconceivable. He was their neighbor. Karen's husband. A teacher at Harris. He had called her just last night and given her the name of a family counselor. '*Why?*'

'I can't answer that, honey,' Mitch murmured. 'I wish I could.'

'Why would he hurt us?' she said as if Mitch hadn't spoken.

'Because he's a lunatic!' Paul shouted, vaulting up from the couch. 'He's insane!'

And he was trapped in a nightmare. This couldn't possibly be happening. Garrett Wright arrested. No. It couldn't be Garrett. He couldn't stand for it to be Garrett.

'Anybody who would do this kind of thing has to be insane!' he insisted. He turned away from the fireplace, where a photo of Josh stared out at him from a cherry frame on the mantel. On the VCR shelf in the entertainment center sat a stack of Josh's video games. Everywhere he turned were reminders. Inside his head, Josh's voice echoed and echoed. *Dad, can you come and get me from hockey? Dad, can you come and get me from hockey? Dad, can you –*

'I can't believe this,' he muttered. He stared at the carpet, afraid to look anywhere else. He couldn't stand the reminders of Josh. He couldn't look at Mitch Holt. He especially couldn't look at Hannah. He couldn't think about Garrett Wright. Guilt and panic and self-pity clogged his throat. 'I can't believe this is happening to me.'

No one heard him.

Hannah's attention was on Mitch. He looked as if he had run to hell and back, hair disheveled, coat open and hanging crooked on his shoulders. One sleeve was torn at the biceps, bleeding goose down. The strain of the night sharpened the angles of his face, darkening the shadows, deepening the lines. The worst of it was in his eyes – regret, sympathy, empathy.

'You think Josh is dead, don't you?' she said softly.

Mitch sank down into a wing chair. They had all prayed for this case to end, but no one had wanted it to end like this, with no sign of Josh, with one of their own neighbors in custody, with Megan in the hospital.

'It doesn't look good, honey,' he answered. Hannah knelt at his feet and looked up at him. 'There were bloodstains on the sheet. We have to think the blood came from Josh. We'll need both you and Paul to submit to blood tests so the lab can try to get a match on the DNA.'

'He's not dead,' Hannah whispered almost to herself. She rose slowly, touching the fingers of her right hand to her left inner elbow. 'They drew blood,' she murmured. 'I saw a bandage on his arm.'

'Hannah . . .'

Paul wheeled around. 'Jesus Christ, Hannah, give it up! He's dead!'

She met his outburst with steely determination, strength rising up from somewhere deep inside. In a far, detached corner of her mind, she thought it was odd that she should find the strength now in the face of such devastating news. She had imagined this moment in her nightmares, had envisioned herself breaking into a million pieces. But she wasn't breaking. She wasn't giving up on Josh and she was all through putting up with Paul.

'He's not dead, and I'm sick of you telling me he is!' she said, glaring at the man who had once been husband and lover and friend. 'You're the one who's dead – at least the part of you I used to love. I don't know who you are anymore, but I know I'm sick of your lies and your accusations. I'm sick of you blaming me for losing Josh, when all you seem to want to do is bury him and hope the cameras get your good side at the funeral!'

Paul splayed a hand across his chest as if she had plunged a knife into his heart. 'How can you say that?'

'Because it's the truth!'

'I don't have to listen to this.' He looked away from her, away from the contempt in her eyes.

'No,' Hannah said, picking up his coat off the back of the sofa. She flung it at him, her mouth trembling with fury and with the effort to hold the angry tears at bay. 'You don't have to listen to me anymore. And I don't have to put up with your moods and your wounded male ego and your stupid petty jealousy. I'm through with it! I'm through with you.'

She tried to draw in an even breath. She wouldn't cry in front of him. She would shed her tears in private for what they had lost. He stood there, staring down at the coat in his hands. The man she had married would have fought back. The man she had married would have said he loved her. Too bad for both of them that man no longer existed.

'You don't live here anymore, Paul,' she murmured. 'Why don't you leave now. I'm sure there are still reporters around eager to get a sound bite from the grieving father.'

Paul took a step back, her words hitting him with the force of a physical blow. *I've lost everything. I can't believe this is happening to me.*

Josh's words whispered in the back of his mind – *Dad, can you come and get me?* The guilt nearly choked him. He fought to contain it, to hide it. He could feel their eyes on him – Hannah's, Mitch Holt's. Could they see it? Could they smell it on him like the stink of sweat? He was losing everything – his son, his marriage, everything. And for the rest of his life he would have to live with the secret – that while he had been cheating on his wife, his mistress's husband had abducted Josh.

Nausea and weakness shuddered through him. 'I have to get out of here,' he muttered:

Hannah watched him go, listened to the door close and the muffled sound of a car starting. She could see Mitch sitting there in the wing chair, his face averted, as if he were pretending he wasn't there at all.

'I'm sorry you had to see that,' she said.

He stood, at a loss, out of energy. 'This has been rough on both of you. You need some time –'

'No,' she said quietly, firmly. She reached up and tucked a strand of hair behind her ear. 'No, that's not what we need.'

Mitch didn't try to argue.

'What happens now?' she asked.

'We're conducting an extensive search for the place Wright took Megan. We figure it can't be more than seventy-five miles away. Probably less. We're checking to see if he owns any other property, see if he owns a van. As soon as his lawyer gets here, he'll be questioned. In the meantime, we bust our asses to build a case that'll put him away for the rest of his life.'

Hannah nodded. 'And Josh?'

'We'll do everything we can to find him.' Him or his body. He didn't say it, but Hannah could read it in his eyes.

'Tell me you won't give up on him, Mitch,' she said. 'You know what it is to lose a child. Promise me you won't give up on Josh.'

Mitch slipped his arms around her and held her for a moment. He did know what it was to lose a child, and, practical or not, he couldn't make Hannah face that pain if there was even just a sliver of hope.

'I promise,' he whispered hoarsely. 'He's alive until someone proves to me otherwise.'

'He's alive,' Hannah said with quiet resolve. 'He's alive and I'm not giving up until I find him.'

Mitch promised to call her if anything developed, to keep her as well informed as he could. She saw him to the door and watched him back his truck out of the driveway and head south, taillights glowing, the only color in a black and white night. The snow was still falling, driven by a wind that cut to the bone.

Hannah stepped back into the house, rubbing the chill from her arms, though she knew it went much deeper. It gripped the core of her as she stood in the family room and realized her family no longer existed. The house felt huge and empty. She felt alone, and she shivered at the thought that she would be alone from then on.

Except for Lily.

Lily lay on her side in her crib, curled around Josh's old teddy bear, her thumb just out of her mouth. Hannah looked down on her daughter. The thinnest edge of a night-light touched Lily's face, so sweet, so innocent, so precious, framed in golden ringlets. Long lashes against a plump cheek flushed with sleep. Her mouth a rosebud just opening.

'My baby,' Hannah whispered, reaching out to brush her fingertips over Lily.

She could still remember what it had felt like to carry this precious life within her. She could still remember what it had felt like to carry Josh. Every moment of joy, of fear, of wonder at the miracle that would be her first child. Their excitement − hers and Paul's − at the news that they would be parents. The nights they had lain in bed and talked in quiet voices, planning the future, Paul's hand on her belly.

It broke her heart to think that they would never lie together that way again, that she would never plan a future because she knew how bitterly the present could turn on her. She felt as if she'd been robbed. Robbed of her son, of her marriage, of her belief that the world was a place full of wonderful promise.

'There's nothing left but us, Lily-bug,' she whispered.

Lily's wide eyes blinked open. The baby sat up, rubbing a small fist against her cheek. She looked up at Hannah, frowning at her mother's tears.

'No no cryin', Mama,' she murmured, raising her arms in a silent plea to be picked up.

Hannah scooped her up and held her close, sobbing for all she had lost, for the uncertainty of the future. Pain and fear raked through her, and all she could do was hold her child and pray for hope. It seemed so little to ask when she had lost so much.

Her strength waning, she sank down into the old white wicker rocker. Lily stood on her lap and tried to wipe her tears away with her hands.

'No no cryin', Mama,' she said.

'Sometimes Mama needs to cry, sweetie.' Hannah kissed her daughter's fingertips. 'Sometimes we all need to cry.'

Lily sat down to ponder this. Silence filled the room, while outside the wind howled a hostile counterpoint. Hannah slipped her arms around her little girl and pulled her close.

'Where Josh, Mama?' Lily murmured, her thumb inching toward her mouth.

'I don't know, honey,' Hannah answered quietly, her gaze on the empty crib and the ragged panda bear that had been her son's. She had bought it for him the day her doctor told her she was carrying him. He had slept with it near him every night of his life. Every night but the last eleven.

'Let's think he's somewhere warm,' she whispered, breathing deep of Lily's sweet, powdery scent, rocking her gently. 'That he's not afraid. That he misses us, but he knows we'll bring him home just as soon as we can. That he knows we love him. That he knows we'll find him . . . because we will . . . I promise.'

She closed her eyes and held her breath and held her baby. She prayed for hope and for the strength to make good on the promise and for the belief that somehow, somewhere, prayers were heard and answered.

40

She could see the boy's face, a pale oval with freckles like a sprinkling of nutmeg over cream. He stared through her, his eyes wide and blue and blank. Then he was gone, like a light switching off to leave her in total darkness.

We have a treat for you, clever girl . . . clever bitch . . . A voice with no body, as smooth and sinister as a snake. She trembled and felt herself tipping, twirling in the black void. Powerless. Vulnerable. Waiting. Then pain struck from one direction, then another, then another.

Megan jerked awake. The surgical scrubs Kathleen Casey had procured for her clung to her body like wet tissue paper. She took stock of her surroundings item by item, forcing herself to calm, to pull back her control inch by inch, to shake the disorientation and the fear. She was safe. Garrett Wright was behind bars.

She wondered if they had found Josh.

The calendar on the wall across the room said it was Monday, January 24. Tom Brokaw was talking to himself on the wall-mounted television.

She remembered Mitch bringing her to the hospital. Everything after that blurred together like images whirling inside a kaleidoscope. A little man with an Indian accent and an enormous nose, calmly giving orders and asking questions. Nurses murmuring to her as they moved around her bed on air cushion shoes. Needles. Pain. Visions of Harrison Ford looking down on her.

She supposed that had been Mitch checking up on her.

She had slept through Sunday and most of that day, knocked out by exhaustion and drugs. Now she felt groggy and fuzzy-headed. The pain cut through whatever it was they were giving her. Fine lines of it were drawn directly from her injuries to her brain. Her right knee. Her left forearm. Her kidneys. Her right hand – the hand that had helped fill out a thousand police reports. The hand that had held a pistol steady enough to win her half a dozen awards for marksmanship. The hand that was now encased in a temporary cast.

Dr Baskir, he of the nose and accent, had been in earlier in the day,

407

during one of her brief periods of lucidity. Humming and muttering to her various body parts, he had checked her vital signs and her sore spots. Many, many contusions, he told her back. He told her knee it would want physical therapy. He addressed her hand last. 'Poor, poor darling little bones.'

With a grave expression of sympathy, he told Megan he couldn't promise she would regain full mobility of the hand. He spoke in a near whisper, as if he didn't want the darling little bones to hear the bad news. He had done what he could as a temporary fix, but now that the weather had finally cleared, they would transfer her to Hennepin County Medical Center, where an orthopedic surgeon would begin the painstaking process of repairing the extensive damage to the delicate structure.

Fear cut through her like a machete as his words replayed in her head. A cop needed two good hands. A cop was all she had ever wanted to be. The job was her life. Now her life stretched before her with the possibility of her never being able to hold that job again.

Fighting the tears that threatened, she looked around the private hospital room. Flowers and balloons decorated the cabinets. Kathleen had read the cards to her. They were from the Deer Lake force, the bureau, her old buddies in the Minneapolis police department. With the exception of a beautiful miniature rosebush from Hannah, they were from cops. Nearly everyone she knew was a cop. What would happen if she ceased to be one?

She felt as if she were attached to her world by a single thin tether, like an astronaut walking in space, and the line was in danger of being severed. And she was absolutely powerless to stop it.

In an attempt to push away the fear, she pressed the volume button on the television remote control. Her right hand was immobilized in a sling against her. The left had hosted an IV catheter for eighteen hours, but that was gone now. Maybe she could teach herself to become left-handed, she mused as she punched the channel button, surfing through the stations as the six o'clock local news came on.

She flipped past *TV* 7, home of Paige Anything-for-a-Story Price, and settled back on Channel Eleven. A shot of Minnesotans digging out after the weekend storm gave way to the file photo of Josh in his Cub Scout uniform.

'. . . but our top story tonight comes from Deer Lake, Minnesota, where, over the weekend, authorities apprehended a suspect in the abduction of eight-year-old Josh Kirkwood.'

Videotape of a press conference filled the screen. The press room in the old fire hall, standing room only. Mitch stood at the podium, looking grave and tired. Marty Wilhelm stood to his right, looking stupid. Steiger sat at the table, frowning, his nose a triangle of adhesive tape. Mitch read a prepared statement, stating only the barest of facts about the harrowing events of Saturday, refusing to answer most questions pertaining to details of evidence, refusing even to confirm Wright's name, on the basis that releasing any information could possibly endanger the integrity of the ongoing investigation.

'Josh Kirkwood is still missing and all law enforcement agencies involved are still actively searching for him,' he said.

'Isn't it true that evidence recovered Saturday night included a bloodstained sheet?'

'No comment.'

'Is it true the suspect in custody is a faculty member at Harris College?'

'No comment.'

'So much for protecting the integrity of the investigation,' Megan muttered. The media weasels would dig and hunt and bribe and trick their way into getting what they needed for their headlines and damn the consequences.

'Is it true you personally chased the suspect on foot half a mile through the woods?'

Mitch gave the woman offscreen a long look. Camera shutters clicked and motor drives whirred. When he spoke it was in the low, measured voice he used when his patience was wearing thin. 'You've all tried to make me out to be some kind of hero in this. I'm no hero. I was doing my job, and if I'd done it better, there wouldn't have been a chase. If there's a hero in this, it's Agent O'Malley. She risked her life, and nearly lost it, in the attempt to bring Josh Kirkwood's kidnapper to justice. She's your hero.'

'Oh, Mitch . . .'

'It's the truth.'

He stood in the doorway, tie askew, hair mussed, looking tough and tired, his shoulders sagging a little. Jessie stood beside him, a plush tiger-striped stuffed cat under one arm.

Natalie herded them into the room. 'Don't you keep me standing out here in the hall, where any stray nurse wandering by could poke my big behind with a needle.'

Megan sniffed and mustered a smile. 'Hey, look who dragged a cat in. Hi, Jessie. Thanks for coming to see me.'

'I brought you Whiskers,' Jessie said, presenting the stuffed toy as Mitch hoisted her up and stood her on one of the lower side rails of the bed. 'So you don't get so lonesome for your real cats.'

The toy looked well loved. The ears lined with pink satin were a little worn around the edges. The long white whiskers were a little bent. Megan's eyes instantly brimmed with tears at the thought that Jessie would give her such a treasured possession. She rubbed her fingertips over the soft gray fur.

'Thank you, Jessie,' she whispered.

'Me and Daddy are taking good care of Gannon and Friday,' Jessie said, her attention on the toy as she stroked it. 'They like me.'

'I bet they do.'

'And they like to play with string.' She looked at Megan from under her lashes. 'Daddy said maybe I could still visit them after you're better.'

'I'm sure they'd like that.' Megan's heart sank at the knowledge that Jessie wouldn't be able to visit her cats at the house on Ivy Street because they wouldn't be in the house on Ivy Street much longer.

'Daddy said you aren't going to heaven like my mommy did,' Jessie said solemnly. 'I'm glad.'

'Me, too.' The words barely squeaked out of Megan's mouth. She had never allowed herself to become attached to anyone because she knew it would hurt. It hurt to feel the emptiness and the longing for something she couldn't have, and it hurt to know the relationship would end. It hurt now, the longing to pull Jessie close and hug her.

'I brought cookies,' Natalie announced. She pulled an enormous Tupperware tub out of her tote bag like a magician pulling a moose head out of a hat, and plunked it down on the bedside table. 'Chocolate chunk. You need fattening up.' She turned an eagle eye on Megan. 'You hurry up and get out of here, *Agent* O'Malley. That puppy-faced boy the bureau sent down here is like to drive me crazy.'

'I think you'll probably have to get used to him,' Megan said with a rueful smile.

Natalie gave a harrumph. 'We'll see about that,' she muttered ominously. Fishing several cookies out of the tub, she gave Jessie a nudge and wink. 'Come on, Miss Muffet, let's go see if we can scare up some milk and spoil your supper.'

'Catch you later, Megan!' Jessie beamed as she leaned over the railing to give Megan an awkward high-five, then scrambled down and scampered out of the room with Natalie right behind her.

Megan looked down at Whiskers, rubbing her thumb over one tatty ear. 'She's pretty special.'

'I think so,' Mitch said. 'But I suppose I'm biased.'

Gently, he hooked a knuckle under her chin and tipped her face up. 'How do you feel?'

'Like a sadistic psychopath beat me head to toe with a baton.'

'That son of a bitch. I'd like to take a club after him.'

'Get in line,' Megan said. She turned away from him and eased her legs over the side of the bed to slip her bare feet into a pair of hospital slippers.

'Are you allowed out of bed?' Mitch asked with some alarm. He rounded the foot of the bed and hovered beside her, ready to catch her if she collapsed.

Megan did her best to ignore his concern. Shooting him a look of annoyance, she hobbled toward the window, leaning heavily on a single crutch tucked under her left arm. 'As long as I promise not to run up and down the halls shouting obscenities.' She had never dreamed so many parts of her could hurt simultaneously, but she would get through it, tough it out, because she had to. 'I need to stand awhile. Lividity was setting in.' She propped herself up against the window well.

Night had fallen outside. Black over a blanket of pristine white. The snow lay in drifts over the hospital lawn, sculpted into elegant lines by the wind. She could feel Mitch standing behind her, his warmth, his energy, tempting her to lean back into him. She could see his faint reflection along with her own in the window, dark shadows with haunted eyes.

'But, life's not *all* bad,' she said with cynical humor. 'I'm getting a commendation from the bureau. I'm losing my field post, but I'm getting a commendation. Beats the hell out of a pink slip, I suppose. And Paige is dropping the lawsuit in light of the photos old Henry Forster snapped of her sneaking in and out of Steiger's trailer. Lucky for me she was too greedy for details about the arrest to keep her panties on.'

'Greed is a great motivator.'

'That's a fact,' she murmured. 'I wish that's all this case was about – greed. At least that's something everyone can comprehend. Garrett Wright's motive . . . How can anyone understand a game as twisted as the one he's been playing?'

Mitch offered no answer. She knew he didn't have one any more than she did.

'Is he talking yet?' she asked softly.

'No.'

'You haven't found the place he took me.'

'Not yet. It could take some time.'

'And Josh . . .'

'We'll find him,' Mitch declared as if there weren't hundreds of cases that went unsolved forever. 'We'll go on looking until we do.'

'I saw his face,' Megan said slowly. 'In between beatings. I saw him, but I don't know if I was conscious or if I was hallucinating. I don't know if what I saw was real. I wish I knew, but I don't.'

It made her head hurt to try to separate the real from the surreal. Knowing that Wright was a psychologist, an expert in learning and perception, only complicated the issue. Could he have somehow planted that image in her mind? Possibly, but that didn't explain the conversation she had had with Hannah earlier in the day.

Hannah had come in to deliver the rosebush herself. Pale and thin, looking as if she belonged in a bed instead of standing beside one, she presented Megan with the plant and with her thanks for all she'd done.

'I got myself caught and beat up,' Megan admitted. 'I don't feel like I deserve thanks.'

'Because of you, Garrett Wright is behind bars,' Hannah said simply.

Megan didn't ask her how she felt about the fact that her neighbor, someone she had trusted, had been the one to put her through this hell. Enough people would ask that question over and over, poking at the open wound in Hannah's soul.

'I have to ask,' Hannah murmured, trying to hide the tremor in her voice. Her gaze darted from Megan's to the square of bed covers she continually smoothed with her fingers. She started to speak, stopped, took a breath, and tried again. 'Did he say . . . anything . . . about Josh?'

'No,' Megan whispered, wishing with all her heart she could offer something more, some concrete evidence that Josh was alive. But all she had was a vision that might well have been drug induced. She looked up at Hannah, at the dark rings around her eyes and the emotions she couldn't hide and made her decision. Slim hope was better than no hope at all.

'I did . . . see . . . something . . .' she started, choosing her words as carefully as picking her way through a mine field. 'He drugged me, you know, so I can't say if what I saw was real. In some ways it seemed like it was. In other ways . . . I just can't say.'

'What did you see?' Hannah asked carefully, her expression guarded. Megan could feel her tension level rise. Her fingers left the sheet and wrapped around the bed rail.

'I thought I saw Josh. It might have been a projection of some kind. It might have been something Wright planted in my mind. I don't know. But I thought I saw him standing across the room, just looking at me. He didn't say anything. He just stood there. I remember his eyes and his freckles.' She looked back into her own memory for details, for some hint of reality. 'He had a bruise on his cheek and he was wearing –'

'Striped pajamas.'

Hannah finished the thought for her. Megan looked up at her, stunned, a chill running through her. 'How did you know that?'

She breathed deeply and stood back from the bed. 'Because I saw him, too.'

'How?' Megan whispered, nearly dumbstruck with astonishment. Was this the reason Hannah had sounded so confident on TV about Josh being alive?

'In my mind I saw him one night, and he looked so real that it couldn't have been just a dream. What you've told me confirmed what I already believed. Josh is alive. I'll get my son back.'

Megan wanted to believe it, too. That they would find Josh safe and sound and bring him home to live happily ever after. She stood there now in her room, staring out at the night, wishing, and knowing wishes wouldn't get them anywhere.

'I asked him, you know,' she said to Mitch. 'If he killed Josh. He wouldn't say. He told me the game wasn't over yet. He told me they had considered every possibility, that they couldn't lose.'

Mitch's eyes narrowed. 'He's sitting in a jail cell, booked on charges of kidnapping, depriving parental rights, assaulting an officer, attempted murder, auto theft, and fleeing arrest. Ruth Cooper ID'd him in a lineup as being the man she saw on Ryan's Bay last Wednesday, and she ID'd his voice. We've got him dead to rights. I'd say he's a big-time loser.'

'No sign of a record on him?'

'No.'

Meaning if Garrett Wright had committed murder, as he had told her, no one had ever pinned anything on him. The thought only deepened the hollow feeling in Megan's stomach. She tried to ease it with the thought that now every stone of Wright's past would be turned over. A vision of squirming maggots filled her head and she blinked to clear it away.

'Any connection to an accomplice yet?'

'Olie looks like a good bet. He sat in on some of Wright's classes. He had the van, the opportunity, the history. Wright might have had some kind of hold on him psychologically.'

'What about Priest?'

'Volunteered to take a polygraph and passed it with flying colors. Todd Childs claims he was with a friend most of Saturday. Says he was at the movies the night Josh disappeared.' He blew out a breath, his broad shoulders sagging under the weight of it all. 'I've been talking to Karen Wright, trying to find out if she might know something without realizing it, but she hasn't been any help. She's so distraught, she can hardly function.'

'Yeah, well, that's a pretty ugly surprise – to find out you're married to a monster. Seems to be an ongoing theme since I came here – ugly surprises. Do you think that's a sign?'

She tried to smile, but it hurt too much that she didn't belong there – and it just plain hurt, tugging at the stitches in her lip. She looked down at the cast on her hand and felt that lifeline stretching thin. There was no promise she would belong anywhere. She turned a whiter shade of pale.

'I think you should lie down,' Mitch said gruffly.

'Don't boss me around,' she shot back with a fraction of her usual fire.

'What are you going to do about it, O'Malley? Hit me with your crutch?' The mock irritation did a poor job of covering his concern.

'Don't tempt me. I'm cranky.'

'Get back in that bed or I'll put you there myself.' He pointed the way for her. 'Natalie is right, we need you better and back on the job. That Tom Hanks impersonator they sent down here is driving me nuts.'

Megan gave him a look. 'Like I didn't?'

'At least you're a good cop,' he grumbled. 'And I can kiss you when you make me mad.'

'Marty might like that, too. Have you asked him?'

'Very funny. Come on, now, Megan, I'm not kidding. Get back in bed.'

Megan ignored the dictate, turning her attention back out the window. Talk of work only made her more keenly aware of her tenuous position. The fear swelled inside her like a balloon. She told herself to handle it as she had handled most everything else in her life – alone. Mitch didn't want her burden. He had made it clear what he wanted from her – a brief affair, no strings attached, no complications. She was one big complication now.

413

Still, the pressure of an uncertain future built inside her, trembling like a clenched fist, and she couldn't seem to keep the words from leaking out.

'I might not be coming back to the job,' she said in a small voice. 'Here or anywhere. Maybe never.'

She watched his reflection in the glass as he moved a little closer. He ran a hand over her hair and settled it on her shoulder.

'Hey, I thought you were a tough cookie,' he said. 'It ain't over till it's over, O'Malley.' She turned wary eyes on his reflection. 'I know about your hand, honey.'

'Don't call me honey.'

He slipped his arms around her with infinite care. He held his breath as he waited for her to lean back against him.

Megan held her breath against the need to let him hold her, waited for the need to pass. It wasn't smart to need that way. She'd known that all her life. *Stand on your own two feet, O'Malley. Hang on to your heart.* The trouble was, she didn't feel strong enough to stand alone, and her heart was already gone. She had nothing left to lose but her pride, and that was tattered and threadbare.

The tears came despite all efforts to fight them off. She didn't have the strength for shields and armor, the defenses that had guarded a too-tender soul for so long. She could feel everything she'd ever wanted, ever loved, sliding through her grasp, leaving her alone, with nothing, with no one. She'd been alone so much and it hurt so badly.

The words, like the tears, came grudgingly. 'I'm ... so ... scared!'

She turned and pressed her face against his chest and cried. Mitch held her and whispered to her. He lay his cheek on top of her head and squeezed his eyes shut.

'It's all right,' he whispered. 'I'm here for you, Megan. You won't be alone.'

He tipped her face up and looked into eyes that were wary and wide, that had seen too much disappointment. His hand cradled a face so fragile, so pretty, it took his breath away. At that instant he didn't see the black eye or the battered lip. The feeling that swelled in his chest scared the hell out of him.

'I'm saying I love you, Megan.' He swallowed hard and said it again. 'I love you.'

'No,' she said, stepping back from him. 'No, you don't.'

Mitch scowled at her. 'Yes, I do.'

'No.' She shook her head, hobbling toward the bed, the rubber tip of her crutch squeaking against the polished floor. 'You don't love me. You feel sorry for me.'

'Don't tell me what I feel, O'Malley,' he growled. 'I know when I'm in love with somebody. I'm in love with you. Don't ask me why. You're the most stubborn, confounding woman I've ever known. That's how I know I'm in love with you.' He lifted a finger to emphasize his point. 'If I weren't in love with you, I'd want to wring your neck.'

'What a romantic,' Megan said dryly, covering her emotions with sarcasm. 'It's a wonder women aren't hurling themselves at your feet.'

'No, I have to pick a woman who'd rather hurl something at my head.'

'Lucky you I'm crippled,' she grumbled, struggling to get herself up onto the bed.

Mitch made a sound of boiling frustration between his teeth and came to her aid. 'Let me help you.'

'I don't want your help.'

'Tough.' He put his hands around her waist and lifted her like a doll. 'Dammit, Megan, it's not going to kill you to say you need me or to let me know when something hurts you.'

'*You* hurt me,' she said. 'Don't tell me you love me when you don't. I'm not what you need or want and you know it! I don't know anything about being in love. All I know is how to be a cop and how to be alone. So why don't you just get out!'

He heaved a sigh. 'Aw, Megan . . .'

She narrowed her eyes at the look on his face. 'Don't you dare pity me, Mitch Holt. And don't argue. Just leave.'

'I don't pity you,' he said quietly, stepping closer and closer. 'I love you. And God knows I've wanted you from the minute I laid eyes on you.'

'So, you had me. You should be happy.'

'I'm going to have to knock that chip off your shoulder every damn day, aren't I?' he murmured half to himself. 'I can't say I would have asked for this. You punch my buttons. You make me mad. You make me feel. Maybe that's not what I thought I wanted, but I need it. To feel again.'

He brushed a knuckle against her cheek. 'I almost lost you, Megan. I'm not going to walk away from you. Our lives can change so fast. In the blink of an eye, in a heartbeat. It's stupid to let a chance go by because we're too proud or too scared. That chance may never come again.'

A chance at love. It hung in this moment between them, a pale, shimmering promise. A chance Megan had longed for in silence all her life. It terrified her now to think it might be a mirage, that it might vanish if she reached for it. But what if she didn't? What would she have then?

'Come on, O'Malley,' Mitch goaded. 'What are you – chicken?'

'I'm not scared of you, Holt,' she returned. Her breath hitched in her throat and she scowled.

'So prove it,' he challenged her, stepping closer, sliding his fingers into her hair, cupping the back of her head. 'Tell me you love me.'

Megan met his gaze, his tough-cop look, his eyes that looked a hundred years old. Eyes that had seen too much. She raised a hand and traced a fingertip over the scar on his chin.

'Break my heart and I'll kick your ass, Chief.'

415

A crooked smile broke across Mitch's face. 'I guess that's close enough.'

He leaned down and pressed a kiss to her unbruised cheek, breathed in the scent of her hair and the faintest breath of perfume that clung to her skin.

'So I know you've got a rule against dating cops, O'Malley,' he murmured in her ear. 'But do you think you could marry one?'

Megan lay her head against his chest and listened to his heart beat in time with hers. 'Maybe,' she whispered, smiling. 'As long as the cop is you.'

41

Day 13
10:04 p.m. 16°

Boog Newton sat with his feet on his bunk and his back against the wall, picking his nose, his eyes fixed on his little television. He never missed the news. A lot of it seemed like bullshit to him, but he never missed it anyway. That was tradition. The fact that Paige Price made him horny as hell was just a bonus.

The top story of the night was the press conference on that kidnapping deal. Boog felt a personal connection to the case after what had gone on with that Olie character. He listened closely as Chief Holt told the reporters practically nothing.

'Digging for gold, Boog?' Browning, the jailer, sauntered past the cells. He was making rounds every fifteen minutes instead of every couple of hours the way he used to, which had to cut into his magazine reading in a big way.

'Take off, pork,' Boog sneered, flicking a big fat booger at Browning's beer gut.

'Jeez!' The jailer jumped back as if he'd been shot. His face twisted with disgust. 'Look at that! God!' He ducked out the door. Boog snickered and turned back to his news. The guy in the next cell was watching, too. He was creepy, sitting there all day, never saying anything, his expression never changing. Boog had caught him looking at him different times, staring at him as if he were a bug under a microscope.

'Hey, that's you they're talking about, ain't it? You're the one took that Kirkwood kid. That's sick,' Boog declared, sticking out his bony chin. 'You're sick.'

Garrett Wright said nothing.

'Hey, you know what happened to the last guy they brought in here? They said he done it. They put him right in that cell you're sitting in. You know what he did? He took his glass eyeball right out of his head and killed himself with it. I figure he was nuts. Anybody who'd do that has to be nuts.' He pressed his lips together and scratched at his greasy hair, figuring some more. 'You must be nuts, too,' he deduced.

The corners of Wright's mouth flicked up. 'I teach psychology at Harris College.'

Boog made a rude noise, eloquently expressing his opinion of teachers. On the television they were showing cops and lab guys from the BCA trooping in and out of a fancy house in Lakeside – Wright's house. A pretty woman with dishwater-blond hair stood by the front door, bawling her eyes out.

'Hey.' Boog shot another look Wright's way. 'What'd you do with the kid? Did you kill him or what?'

Garrett Wright smiled to himself. 'Or what.'

Day 14
Midnight 12°

Hannah woke sharply from a troubled sleep. Sleeping alone triggered some internal alarm system that was oversensitive and went off at the slightest hint of sound or movement. She lay in the middle of the big bed and stared up at the skylight and the black rectangle of January night, listening, waiting, every muscle tense. Nothing. No sound, no movement. The house was still. The night was silent. Even the wind, which had been relentless for days, as cold and sharp as an ice pick, held its breath as one day passed and a new one began with the tick of the clock: 12:01.

A new day. Another day to face. Another twenty-four hours to wander through, trying to function, looking like a normal person, appearing as her former self, an impostor. Nothing about her life or herself was normal anymore. She would get through this day and the next and the one after that because she had to for herself, for Lily . . . and for Josh.

He's somewhere warm . . . he's not afraid . . . he knows I love him. . . .

She came out of bed before the sound even registered in her conscious mind. Her bare feet hit the carpet. She grabbed the old velour robe Paul had discarded. Doorbell. At midnight – ten past now. Her heart pounded. Possibilities flashed through her head: Paul looking for forgiveness, Mitch coming with news – good? Bad?

She hit the switch for the front porch light with one hand while the other clutched the robe together over her breast-bone, over her heart. The bell sounded again. She pressed her eye to the peephole.

'Oh, my God.'

The words came out in a strangled whisper. Josh stood on the front step, waiting.

In the next instant Hannah was on her knees on the cold cement. She pulled her son into her arms. She held him against her body as tight as she could, crying, thanking God, kissing Josh's cheek, kissing his hair, saying his name over and over. She didn't feel the cold or the scrape of the concrete step against her knees. She felt only relief and joy and her son's small body pressing into hers. The relief was so enormous, she was terrified it was a dream. But if it was a dream, she knew she wouldn't let go. She would stay on this step and clutch him to her, feel his warmth, breathe in the scent of him.

'Oh, Josh. Oh, my God,' she whispered, the words trembling on her lips, mixing with the salty taste of tears. 'I love you. I love you so much. I love you. I love you.'

She stroked a trembling hand over his tousled brown curls and down the back of the striped pajamas he wore. The same pajamas she had seen him in. The same pajamas Megan O'Malley had seen him in, though she had not been sure whether what she had seen had been real or imagined. There were so many questions yet unanswered. They flashed through Hannah's mind. If Garrett Wright had taken Josh, then who had brought him home?

She opened her eyes and looked beyond her front step into moon-silvered night. No one. No cars. No shadows except those of the trees against the pristine snow. The town lay sleeping, unaware, quiet.

Josh squirmed a little in her arms, and Hannah pulled herself back to the moment. Such a perfect moment, the one she had held as a brilliant and fragile hope in her heart. She had her son back. She would have to call Mitch – and Paul . . . and Father Tom. She would call the hospital and leave a message for Megan. Josh would have to be taken to the hospital to be examined. The press would descend again . . .

'Honey, who brought you home?' she asked. 'Do you know?'

She leaned back to look at him. He simply shook his head, then tightened his arms around her neck and put his head down on her shoulder.

Hannah didn't press him. For this moment she wanted to think of nothing but Josh. No questions of how or why or who. Only Josh mattered. And he was home and safe.

'Let's go inside, okay?' she said softly, fresh tears squeezing between her lashes as Josh nodded against her shoulder.

Hannah rose with her arms around him, barely noticing his weight as she carried him into the family room. Doctor's instincts and mother's instincts prompted a quick evaluation of his physical condition. The small bruise on his cheek – the bruise she had seen in her dream – was fading. He was thinner and pale, but whole, and he wanted to be held. Hannah complied readily. She wanted him with her, next to her, physically connected to her. She held him on her lap as she sat on the love seat and used the portable phone to call Mitch, then Paul's office. Mitch promised to be over in a matter of minutes. Paul's machine picked up. Jealously channeling all her emotions to Josh's return, she didn't bother to feel irritation toward Paul for not being there; she simply left the message and hung up.

'It doesn't matter, sweetie.' She kissed the top of Josh's head, hugging him tight again as another wave of relief washed through her. 'All that matters is that you're home, you're safe.'

She blinked away more tears as she looked down at him. He was asleep. His head lolled forward as he breathed deeply and evenly. His thick, long lashes curled against his cheek. *My angel. My baby.* The thoughts were as familiar as his face, thoughts she had recited in her mind since before his birth and countless nights after it, when she had slipped into his room to watch him sleep. *My angel, my baby . . . so perfect.*

A sliver of pain pierced her joy. *Perfect.* Josh had always been a happy child, a joy to her. Who would he be now? What had he gone through? The possibilities had tormented her every hour he had been away. Now they gathered at the edge of her relief like a pack of hyenas. She chased them back as she carefully eased out from under her son and lay him down on the love seat. He was in one piece, whole and clean. She kissed his forehead as she tucked an afghan around him and breathed in the scent of shampoo. She wanted to push his sleeve up to see if there was a bandage on the inside of his elbow, but she didn't want to wake him. And she wanted him to have these few moments of peace before having to face an examination and answer questions.

She let her hand rest on his instead, her fingertips on his wrist. His pulse was regular and normal. She didn't count the beats, but concentrated on what they represented – life. He was alive. He was with her. The piece of her heart that had been missing was returned and it beat in tandem with his.

'Has he said anything about Wright?' Mitch asked quietly. He sat in a wing chair with his forearms braced against his knees, his parka open. After Hannah's call he had literally rolled out of bed and into a pair of jeans and a sweatshirt. His hair stuck up in all directions. He wished Megan could have been here to help him ask these questions, to close the case she had fought so hard to solve.

'No.' Hannah sat on the floor in front of the love seat where Josh lay sleeping beneath the folds of the red afghan. She touched him constantly in small ways, stroking his hair, rubbing his back, petting his hand, as if breaking physical contact would shatter the spell and he would disappear again. 'He hasn't said anything. I asked him if he knew who brought him home. He shook his head no.'

'He's in shock. It may take him a while . . .'

He let the thought trail off, not wanting to follow it. Of the paths it might take, most of them led to more unhappiness, and he wanted to spare Hannah for the moment. Still, duty dictated. Procedure had to be followed, questions had to be asked. Even now, in the dead of night, he had men knocking on doors down the block looking for anyone who might have glanced out a window and seen anything out of the ordinary.

'We'll have to take him in to the hospital tonight –'

'I know.'

'And I'll have to try to get him to answer some questions. If he can tell us anything about Wright –'

Hannah's fingers stilled on Josh's hand; she looked up at Mitch. 'What will this mean? Garrett Wright is in jail and now Josh comes home. What will that do to the case against him?'

'I don't know. A lot depends on Josh, on what he can tell us. But even if he can't tell us anything useful, we've still got the lineup ID, and we'll have DNA and trace evidence from the sheet. If Wright thinks this gets him off the hook, he can think again. We caught him, honey,' he said, his gaze unwavering, his voice quiet but strong with conviction. 'We nailed Garrett Wright cold, he's as guilty as sin, and we'll keep looking until we find his accomplice. Then we'll nail him, too.'

He rose from the chair and offered Hannah a hand up. 'That's a promise. Garrett Wright's next game will be in a court of law. I predict Lady Justice will kick his butt.'

'I hope so.'

Mitch gave her fingers a reassuring squeeze. 'I know so. But I don't want you worrying about it. The only thing you should think about tonight is that Josh is home. That's all that matters.'

'That's the only thing that really matters at all,' she agreed, looking down at her sleeping child.

He could have been lost forever, vanished into a shadow world, as many children were every year, never to be seen again, leaving behind only questions and heartbreak for the people who loved them. For reasons known only to the dark mind of his abductor, Josh had been allowed to cross back out of the shadows. That was all that counted. The truth, justice, revenge, were distant and abstract thoughts for Hannah. Their world had been shattered, their lives irrevocably altered, but Josh was home. That was all that really mattered.

Josh was home. Their lives could begin again.

Epilogue

Journal entry
Day 13

They think they've beaten us at our own game.
Poor simple minds.
Every chess master knows in the quest for victory
he will concede minor defeats.

They may have won the round, but
the game is far from over.

They think they've beaten us.
We smile and say,
Welcome to the Next Level.

Dear Readers:

I hope you found *Night Sins* as compelling to read as it was for me to write. Sadly for all of us, child abductions have been in the forefront of the national news. Even where I live, in a place not unlike Deer Lake, tragic cases have turned our attention to ugly truths and raised questions in our minds about what it would be like to have to live through such a nightmare. At the same time I was watching these cases unfold, a dear friend of mine was dealing with a devastating illness. Being on the outside looking in at these heart-wrenching situations left me feeling helpless and wondering endlessly why bad things happen to good people. For a writer, questions are best explored in one way – through a story.

So began *Night Sins*, with questions such as: What would it be like to be a cop on a case with few clues and much pressure for a resolution? What would it do to the parents in a relationship already on shaky ground to be put under the kind of pressure a tragedy like this brings? What kind of mind does it take to commit a crime of such callous evil? How far will that evil go?

One of the great benefits of writing fiction is the ability to control the outcome of the story. In real life, happy endings are not guaranteed. The bad guys don't always get caught. Loose ends are not always tied up. Justice is not always done. Children don't always come home. I was able to bring Josh home at the end of *Night Sins*, although, as in real life, some questions remain unanswered, an intentional act on my part. So the pursuit of justice is not over for the people of Deer Lake. As in real life, the apprehension of the criminal at the end of *Night Sins* is only half the story. Exacting justice is the job of the courts. The challenge of prosecuting this case will fall on the shoulders of Assistant County Attorney Ellen North in *Guilty As Sin*, where I get to explore a whole new set of questions. How far will the game go? Will justice triumph? And for Ellen North, as she finds herself in a dangerous maze full of shadows and mirrors and players with hidden agendas, the most essential question of all: Who can you trust?

I hope you will all look forward to searching for the answers to those questions in *Guilty As Sin*.

GUILTY AS SIN

To the Divas,
for support in times of crisis and madness.

Acknowledgments

My heartfelt thanks first and foremost to legal assistant, sister writer, and friend Nancy Koester for acting as my guide into the court system. Your generosity in sharing your expertise and answering my myriad questions was greatly appreciated. Thanks also to attorney Charles Lee, assistant county attorney Steve Betcher, Judge Robert King, and everyone in the Goodhue County Attorney's office for allowing me a glimpse into your world and for answering my questions. My hand to God, the people in the Park County courthouse are pure figments of my imagination, but feel free to fantasize.

Justice has but one form, evil has many.

Moses Ben Jacob Meir Ibn Ezra

Prologue

'Time to die, birthday bitch.'

Birthday. Thirty-six. The birthday Ellen had been dreading. Suddenly thirty-six seemed far too young.

She flung herself up the stairs, stumbling as one heel caught an edge. She grabbed for the handrail, her fingers scraping the rough plaster of the wall, breaking a nail, skinning her knuckles.

The stairwell was barely lit, drawing in the ragged edges of illumination that fell from the lights in the halls above and below. Security lights. They offered nothing in the way of security. In the back of her mind she heard a low, smoky voice, '*Your boss needs to have a word with someone about security. This is a highly volatile case. Anything might happen.*'

She reached the third floor and turned down the hall, heading east. If she could make it down the east stairs – If she could make it to the walkway between the buildings – He wouldn't dare try to take her in the walkway with the sheriff's department mere feet away.

'We've got you now, bitch!'

There were telephones in the offices she ran past. The offices were locked. Her self-appointed assassin was jogging behind her, laughing. The sound went through her like a spear, like the sure knowledge that he would kill her. Pursuit may not have been his plan, but it had become a part of the game.

The game. The insanity of it was as terrifying as the prospect of death. Beat the system. Wreck lives. End lives. Nothing personal. Just a game.

She ran past Judge Grabko's courtroom and ducked around the corner that led back toward the southeast stairwell. Scaffolding filled the stairwell, cutting off her escape route. The scaffolding for the renovators. Christ, she was going to die because of the stupid plaster frieze.

'Checkmate, clever bitch.'

The northeast stairs looked a mile away. Midway stood the iron gates that blocked the skyway between the courthouse and the jail. She lunged for the fire alarm on the wall, grabbing the glass tube that would break and summon help.

The tube snapped. Nothing. No sound. No alarm.

'Oh, God, no!' She clawed at the useless panel. The goddamn renovations. New alarms going in. State of the art.

'Come along, Ellen. Be a good bitch and let me kill you.'

She grabbed the handle of the door to the fire hose and yanked.

'You have to die, bitch. We have to win the game.'

His hand closed on her arm.

Her fingers closed on the handle of the ax.

Journal Entry

They think they've beaten us at our own game.
Poor simple minds.
Every chess master knows in the quest for victory
he will concede minor defeats.

They may have won the round, but
the game is far from over.

They think they've beaten us.
We smile and say,
Welcome to the Next Level.

1

Monday, January 24, 1994

'He said it was a game,' she murmured, her voice whisper-soft, and tight with pain.

She lay in a hospital bed, the deep purple bruises on her face a stark contrast to the bleached white of the sheets and the ash white of her skin. Her right eye was nearly swollen shut, the flesh the color of an overripe plum. Bruises circled her throat like a purple satin band where she had been choked. A fine line of stitches mended a split in her lip.

The pain triggered flashes of memory – sudden, violent, blaring. A memory of pain so sharp, so intense, it took on qualities of sound and taste, the smell of fear, the presence of evil.

'Clever girl. You think we're going to kill you? Perhaps.'

Her throat being closed by hands she couldn't see. The instinct to survive surging. Fear of death riding the crest of the wave.

'We could kill you.' The voice a silky murmur. 'You wouldn't be the first. . . .'

The air caught like a pair of fists in her lungs, then slowly seeped out between her teeth.

Assistant County Attorney Ellen North waited for the moment to pass. She sat on a high stool beside the bed, a legal pad and small cassette recorder on the bedside tray to her right. She had met Megan O'Malley only days before. Her impression of the field agent for the Minnesota Bureau of Criminal Apprehension had consisted of a handful of adjectives: tough, gutsy, capable, determined, a small woman with fierce green eyes and a big chip on her shoulder. The first woman to break the male ranks of BCA field agents. Her first day on the job in the Deer Lake regional office had been day one of the Kirkwood kidnapping. Twelve days ago. Twelve days that had taken the previously innocent, quiet, rural college town into the depths of a nightmare.

In her efforts to crack the case, the chip had been effectively knocked off Megan's shoulder and smashed, and Megan along with it. She had come too close to unraveling the puzzle. Beneath the covers, her damaged right knee was elevated. Her right hand was encased in a cast. According to her doctor, the hand was badly smashed, and he despaired of the 'poor darling little bones' recovering, even with the meticulous attention of a specialist.

Megan's transfer from Deer Lake Community Hospital to the Hennepin County Medical Center in Minneapolis was scheduled for Tuesday, weather permitting. She would have been transported the night of her ordeal, but Minnesota had been clutched in the grip of a January storm. Two days later Deer Lake was just beginning to dig out from under ten inches of new snow.

'He said it was a game,' Megan started again. 'Taking Josh. Taking me. Fooling everyone. *We* fooled you all along, he said . . . *We*, always *we* ...'

'Did you at any time hear another person in the room?'

'No.' She tried to swallow and her face tightened against a new wave of pain.

'*We've calculated all the moves, all the options, all the possibilities. . . . We can't lose. Do you understand me? You can't defeat us. We're very good at this game. . . . brilliant and invincible.*'

Eight-year-old Josh Kirkwood had disappeared from outside the Gordie Knutson Memorial Ice Arena after hockey practice on an otherwise normal Wednesday night. No useful physical evidence left behind. The only witness a woman casually glancing out her window half a block away and seeing nothing to cause alarm: a little boy being picked up from hockey practice; no sign of fear or force. The only trace of him left behind had been his duffel bag with a note tucked inside.

a child has vanished
ignorance is not innocence but SIN

A game. And she had been used as a pawn. The idea brought Megan a rush of useless emotions – anger, outrage, a hated sense of vulnerability. The only satisfaction was in the fact that they had spoiled his little coup de grâce and now Garrett Wright was sitting in a cell in the Deer Lake city jail.

Garrett Wright. Professor of psychology at Harris College. The man the media had pulled in as an 'expert witness' to attempt to explain the twisted workings of the mind that had perpetrated this crime. The Kirkwoods' neighbor. A respected member of the community. A volunteer counselor of juvenile offenders. A man above reproach.

But though Wright had been apprehended, there was still no sign or word of Josh.

'You were blindfolded?'

'Yes.'

'You didn't actually see Garrett Wright.'

'I saw his feet. He has this habit of rocking back on his heels. I noticed it the first time I met him. He was doing it that night. I could see his boots when he stood close enough.'

'That's not exactly a fingerprint.'

Megan scowled at the assistant county attorney, her temper cutting through the haze of drugs and pain. Goddamn lawyers. Garrett Wright had drugged her, terrorized her, abused her, humiliated her. He may well have ended the career that was everything to her. A decade in law enforcement, a degree in criminology, a certificate from the FBI academy – she was a damn good cop, yet Ellen North could sit here, every blond hair in place, and calmly question her as if she were just another civilian as blind as Lady Justice herself.

'It was him, the son of a bitch. He knew where I was going. He knew I was that close to finding him out. He caught me, beat the shit out of me, wrapped me in a sheet of evidence proving he stole Josh –'

'We don't know yet what the bedsheet will prove,' Ellen interjected. 'We don't know whose blood is on it. The lab has a rush on it, but DNA tests take weeks. The blood could be Josh's or not. We have the blood samples from his parents. If the DNA analysis shows the blood on the sheet could be from a child of Paul Kirkwood and Dr Hannah Garrison, we've got something we can use. We might just as easily have a red herring. It would make more sense for the kidnapper to try to throw us *off* his trail –'

'It makes *his* kind of sense,' Megan argued. 'He believes he can get away with anything, but he underestimated us. We got him dead to fucking rights. Whose side are you on?'

'You know what side I'm on, Megan. I want to see Wright punished as much as you –'

'You can't even come close.'

She couldn't argue the point. The bitter hate that laced Megan's tone was indisputable. The emotion Wright had forged and hammered within her with every blow was something deeper than Ellen could even imagine. It was a victim's private rage compounded by the humiliation of a proud cop. Ellen knew that her own personal, moral hunger for justice was a pale appetite in comparison.

'I want him convicted,' she clarified. 'But the case against him has to be airtight. I don't want his attorney to see even a hairline crack. The stronger our case, the better our chances of squeezing the truth out of him. It could mean getting Josh back.'

Or finding out the whereabouts of his body.

She left that line unspoken. Everyone involved in the case knew the chances of finding Josh Kirkwood alive. Wright and his accomplice, whoever that accomplice might be, could not afford to let go the one person who could identify them absolutely as the kidnappers.

'If we can present Wright and his attorney with a strong enough case. If we can threaten them with a murder charge and make them believe we can make it stick even though we have no body, then Wright might give us Josh. We can force his hand if we're careful and clever enough.'

'We thought you were a clever girl, but you're just another stupid bitch!' A disembodied voice. Never rising above a whisper, but taut and humming with fury.

434

She trembled. Blind. Powerless. Vulnerable. Waiting. Then the pain struck from one direction, then another, then another.

A cry of pain, of weakness, of fear started in the heart of her, and Megan struggled to choke it off in her throat.

'Are you all right?' Ellen asked with quiet concern. 'Should I call for a nurse?'

'No.'

'Maybe we should quit for now. I could come back in half an hour –'

'No.'

Ellen said nothing, giving her a chance to change her mind, though she didn't expect that to happen. Megan O'Malley hadn't got where she was in the bureau by backing off. The BCA was the top law-enforcement agency in the upper Midwest. One of the best in the country. And Megan was one of the best of the best. A good cop with the tenacity and fire of a pit bull.

Ellen was counting on that fire. She had a meeting with the county attorney in an hour. She needed Megan's statement and time to fit it into the game plan she was formulating in her head.

She wanted her ducks in a row when she sat down across the table from her boss. Rudy Stovich could be unpredictable, but he could also be herded. In her two years in Park County, Ellen had honed her shepherding skills to the point that they had become instinctive, reflexive. She didn't know that she even *wanted* the Wright case, and still she was aligning her strategy.

'Will you be handling the prosecution?' Megan asked, working hard to even out her breathing. A fine sheen of sweat glazed her forehead.

'I'll certainly be a part of it. The county attorney hasn't made his final decision yet.'

'Well, hell, why rush? It's only been two days since we made the collar. Initial appearance is what – all of hours away?'

'The bond hearing is tomorrow morning.'

'Will he charge it out or wimp out and go for a grand jury?'

'That remains to be seen.'

The media loved to make much of grand jury proceedings. As if the word 'grand' somehow implied 'better' or 'more important.' A grand jury hearing was a prosecutor's showcase – they got to present their evidence with no interference from the defense, no cross-examination of their witnesses. There was no need to prove anything beyond a reasonable doubt; all they had to show was probable cause that the defendant committed the crime. The grand jury had its uses. In the state of Minnesota only a grand jury could hand down first-degree-murder indictments. But, as yet, they weren't dealing with murder, and the thought of handing the fate of this indictment into the hands of two dozen citizens made Ellen's palms sweat.

The members of a grand jury could do whatever they wanted. They didn't have to listen to the prosecutor's argument. If they didn't want to believe Garrett Wright was capable of evil, he would walk. She could only hope that the ego appeal of doing a solo act in front of a grand jury didn't override Rudy's common sense.

Stovich had survived more than a decade as Park County attorney not so much by his legal wits as by his political wiles. More comfortable with civil law than with criminal law, he handpicked the few felony trials he prosecuted, choosing them for their political value. His courtroom style was dated and clumsy, with all the finesse of a vaudeville player. But Rudy's constituents seldom saw him in a courtroom, and as a glad-handing, ass-kissing backwoods politician he was without peer.

'Is Wright talking?' Megan asked quietly.

'He isn't saying anything we want to hear. He insists his arrest was a mistake.'

'Yeah, right. *His* mistake. Who's his lawyer?'

'Dennis Enberg, a local attorney.'

'Is he just a lawyer or is he an asshole lawyer?'

'Denny's okay,' Ellen said, flicking off the tape recorder. She'd been in the system too long to take affront. The distinction was one she had made herself from time to time. And, having come from a family of attorneys, she was long since immune to lawyer jokes and slurs.

She slid down off the stool and reached for her briefcase. Megan was slipping away from consciousness. Exhaustion and medication were going to end the interview whether she was finished asking questions or not.

'He's your basic ham-and-egger,' Ellen continued. 'He does the misdemeanor prosecutions for the city of Tatonka, gets pressed into service as a public defender here from time to time, has a decent practice of his own. You know how the system works in these rural counties.'

'Yeah. *Mayberry RFD*. So what're you doing here, counselor?'

She shrugged into her heavy wool coat and worked the thick leather buttons into their moorings. 'Me? I'm just here to do justice.'

'Amen to that.'

Ellen had spent her entire twelve-year career in the service of one county or another. Much to the consternation of her parents, who had wanted her to follow their footsteps into the lucrative life of tax law. Hennepin County, which encompassed the city of Minneapolis and its wealthy western suburbs where she had grown up, had swallowed up the first decade of her life after Mitchell Law in St Paul. She had immersed herself in the hectic pace, eager to put away as many bad guys as she could. Veterans of the overloaded Hennepin County court system had taken in her enthusiasm with the knowing skepticism of the war weary and speculated on her burnout date.

In ten years her tenacity had only toughened, but her enthusiasm had tarnished badly, coated with the verdigris of cynicism. She still remembered clearly the day she had stopped herself in the hall of the Hennepin County courthouse, chilled to the bone by the realization that she had become so inured to all of it that she was beginning to grow numb to the sight of victims and corpses and perpetrators. Not a pleasant epiphany. She hadn't become a prosecutor to foster an immunity to human suffering. She hadn't stayed in the system because she wanted to reach a point where cases were little more than docket numbers and sentencing guidelines. She had become an attorney out of genetic predisposition, environmental conditioning, and a genuine desire to fight for justice.

The solution seemed to be to get away from the city, go somewhere more sane, where gangs and major crime were an aberration. A place where she could feel she was making a difference and not just trying to stick her thumb in a badly leaking dam.

Deer Lake had fit the bill perfectly. A town of fifteen thousand, it was near enough to Minneapolis to be convenient, and just far enough away for the town to maintain its rural character. Harris College provided an influx of youth and the sophistication of an academic community. A growing segment of white-collar Twin Cities commuters provided a healthy tax base. Crime, while on the increase, was generally petty. Burglaries, minor drug deals, workers from the BuckLand Cheese factory beating each other senseless after too many beers at the American Legion hall. People here were still shockable. And they had been shocked to the core by the abduction of Josh Kirkwood.

Briefcase clutched in one gloved hand, the low heels of her leather boots clicking against the hard polished floor, Ellen walked down the corridor of Deer Lake Community Hospital. Most of the activity in the hundred-bed facility seemed to center on the combination nurses' station/reception desk in the main lobby, where people with appointments were complaining about the long wait and people without appointments tried to appear sicker than they really were in hopes of getting worked in faster.

A clutch of reporters loitering at the periphery of the sick zone perked up at the sight of Ellen and scooted toward her, pencils and pads at the ready. Two women and four men, an assortment of expensive wool topcoats and scruffy ski jackets, spray-starched coifs and greased-back ponytails. A photographer angled a camera at her, and she turned her head as the flash went off.

'Ms North, do you have any comment on the condition of Agent O'Malley?'

'Ms North, is there any truth to the rumor Garrett Wright sexually assaulted Agent O'Malley?'

The second question drew a peeved look from Ellen. 'I've heard no such rumor,' she said crisply, not even breaking stride.

The key to handling the media in full frenzy: keep moving. If you stopped, they would swarm and devour you and you would be regurgitated as a headline or a sound bite with film at ten. Ellen knew better than to allow herself to be trapped. She had learned those lessons the hard way, having been thrown to the hyenas on occasion as the sacrificial junior assistant on a case.

The lack of a juicy answer seemed only to sharpen the reporters' hunger. Two cut around to her left. Two scuttled backward in front of her. The one on her right hopped along sideways, the end of a dirty untied shoelace clacking against the floor with every stride.

'What kind of bail will the county attorney request?'

'Can you give us a rundown of the charges being filed?'

'The county attorney will be giving a press conference at the courthouse later this afternoon,' Ellen said. 'I suggest you save your questions until then.'

She pushed through the hospital's front door, bracing herself automatically for the cold. A pale wash of sunlight filtered weakly down on the pristine snow. On the far side of the parking lot a tractor rumbled along, plowing the stuff into a minor mountain range.

She headed across the lot for her Bonneville, well aware that hers were not the only pair of shoes squeaking over the packed snow. Looking down from the corner of her eye, she saw the loose lace flapping alongside a battered Nike running shoe.

'I meant it,' she said, fishing her keys out of her coat pocket. 'I don't have anything for you.'

' "No comment" don't feed the bulldog.'

She cut him a glance. He had to be fresh out of high school, so wet behind the ears he shouldn't have been allowed to go out in the cold without a snowsuit. His face was finely sculpted. Black hair with a suspicious red cast swung down across his narrow brown eyes. He swept it back impatiently. *Young Keanu Reeves. God spare me.* Not much taller than her own five feet seven inches, he had the build of an alley cat, lean, agile, with the restless energy to match. It seemed to vibrate in the air around him as if someone had plugged him into a high-voltage generator.

'Then I'm afraid your dog will go hungry, Mr – ?'

'Slater. Adam Slater. *Grand Forks Herald.*'

Ellen pulled open the car door and hefted her briefcase across into the passenger's seat. 'The Grand Forks paper sent their own reporter all the way down here?'

'I'm ambitious,' he proclaimed, bouncing up and down on the balls of his feet as if he had to keep himself ready to bolt and run at a second's notice. Cub reporter trying to race ahead of the ravenous pack.

'Are you old enough to have a job?' Ellen asked, cranky with his enthusiasm.

'You used to be ambitious, too,' he said as she climbed behind the wheel of the car.

She looked up at him, suspicious that he might know anything at all about her.

'I have some contacts in Hennepin County.'

Contacts. He looked as if his contacts would have been the guys who stole the midterm from the algebra teacher's desk.

'They say you used to be good when you were there.' *Way back when.*

'I'm still good, Mr Slater,' Ellen declared, twisting the key in the ignition. 'I'm good in any zip code.'

'Yes, ma'am,' he chirped, saluting her with his reporter's note-book.

'Ma'am,' she grumbled as she put the car in gear and headed out of the lot. Her gaze strayed to the rearview mirror as she broke for traffic on the street. Mr Ambition from Grand Forks was bouncing his way back to the hospital entrance. 'See if you ever have an affair with an older woman, you little twerp. *Used to be good.* I haven't lost it yet.'

She wasn't entirely sure whether she meant her skills in the courtroom or her allure as a woman. As the reporter loped out of view, her gaze refocused on her reflection. Her face was more interesting than beautiful. Oval with a graceful forehead. Gray eyes – a little narrow. Nose – a little plain. Mouth – nothing to inspire erotic fantasies, but it was okay. She scrutinized for any sign of age, not liking the depth of the laugh lines that fanned out beside her eyes when she squinted. How long before she had to stop calling them laugh lines and start calling them crow's-feet?

A birthday was looming large on the horizon like a big black cloud, like the *Hindenburg.* Thirty-six. A shudder went down her back. She pretended it was from the cold and goosed the Bonneville's heater a notch. Thirty-six was just a number. A number closer to forty than thirty, but just a number, an arbitrary marking of the passing of time. She had more important things to worry about – like a lost boy and bringing his kidnapper to justice.

2

The Park County courthouse was a small monument in native limestone with Doric columns and Greek pediments out front. It dated to the late 1800s, when labor was cheap and time of little consequence. The interior boasted soaring ceilings that most likely raised heating bills, and ornate plaster moldings and medallions that undoubtedly required endowments from historical preservationists to maintain. A restoration was under way on the third floor, scaffolding set against the northeast wall like giant Tinkertoys.

The courtrooms on the third floor were the kind of rooms that called to mind Henry Clay and Clarence Darrow. Between the judges' benches, the jury boxes, and the pews for spectators, a sizable forest of oak trees had fallen for the cause. The wooden floors were worn pale in spots from the pacing of generations of lawyers.

He was well familiar with courthouses like this one, though he had never been anywhere near Deer Lake, Minnesota. Nor would he ever care to venture back here once his mission was accomplished. Damned cold place.

It was a safe bet the Park County courthouse was seldom as busy as it was today. The halls were bustling, not with staff, but with reporters and cameramen and newspaper photographers jockeying for position in front of a podium bristling with microphones. He leaned over the second-floor railing and looked down through the dark lenses of a pair of mirrored military-issue sunglasses.

The kidnapping of Josh Kirkwood had garnered national attention. The arrest of Dr Garrett Wright had only turned up the fever pitch another hundred degrees. All the major networks were represented, their correspondents instantly recognizable. The syndicated tabloid news shows were here in force, as well, their people skirting the periphery like hyenas looking to snatch a juicy tidbit from the big network lions. Forced to scramble for camera angles were the local newspeople. They had been thrown into the big pond and clearly didn't care to swim with the big fish, but there it was. The story was bigger than small-town sensibilities and small-town manners. It was as big as America and as intimate as family.

Good juxtaposition of images. He committed the line to memory.

The scene below was not unlike a movie set waiting for the arrival of the stars. Lights, cameras, grips, technicians, makeup people dabbing the shine off foreheads and noses.

' "All the world's a stage," ' he mumbled with cynical humor, his voice raspy from too many cigars and too little sleep the night before. The price of schmoozing. You oiled the wheels with good whiskey and smooth talk, easy smiles and expensive cigars – all to be chased the following morning with a handful of aspirin and a gallon of strong coffee.

He turned slowly for a casual glance at the reporters waiting outside the door to the county attorney's offices thirty feet down the hall. No one paid him any mind. He wore no press pass, had not been asked for any ID. He could have been anyone. He could have been a sniper; there were no metal detectors at the doors of the Park County courthouse. Another detail to file away for future reference. The case was the focus of everyone here to the exclusion of all else. Elvis could have been sweeping the floors and no one would have so much as glanced twice.

He counted this tunnel vision as being both potentially useful and a blessing to him personally. He could live without the interference as he got himself in where he wanted to be. Inside. The bird's-eye view. The catbird seat. Into the inner workings of the small-town justice system taking on a big-time case.

The door to the county attorney's offices opened and the reporters started shouting questions, sending up a racket like a pack of baying fox-hounds. He straightened from the railing and propped himself up against a marble pillar, careful to remain in its shadow, his hands stuffed into the pockets of the black parka he had bought after getting off the plane in Minneapolis.

A uniformed sheriff's deputy cleared a path, leading the way for the man he recognized as Rudy Stovich. Tall, rawboned, with a face like Mr Potato Head and kinky wire-gray hair that was slicked down into a marcel look with a quart of something greasy. Stovich had been featured in one of many news clippings about the case, scowling at the camera, piously promising to prosecute the villains to the fullest extent of the law. It would be interesting to hear what he had to say now that it appeared the villain was not some slimy ex-con from the wrong side of town and the lower end of the evolutionary ladder, but a psychology professor from their own exclusive college.

Garrett Wright was the twist that made the story unique, the hook that made it bankable instead of clichéd.

Stovich stepped into the hall, waving off the shouted questions, mugging an expression of exaggerated impatience. A woman fell into step beside him. Cool, composed, blond hair the shade of polished gold, features that were more interesting than striking. Ellen North, rumored to have her ambitious eye on the county attorney's corner office. She walked past the reporters without making eye contact, a queen oblivious to the presence of the unwashed masses. Classy, self-possessed, not rattled by the attention of the press. Intriguing.

He stayed where he was as the mob passed by and headed down the steps for the first floor. Show time.

No director could have choreographed the scene more perfectly. Just as Stovich and his entourage reached the first floor, the main doors of the courthouse swung open and State Attorney General William Glendenning and his cadre made their grand entrance. They came into the building on a gust of cold air, stamping the snow from their shoes, their cheeks and noses polished cherry-red with cold. Stovich and Glendenning shook hands as flashes went off in blinding starbursts.

Glendenning opened the proceedings. A seasoned politician, he looked good before the lights – solid, conservative, trustworthy. A pair of rimless spectacles gave him a certain resemblance to Franklin Roosevelt – more emphasis on trust and old-fashioned values. He spoke with a strong, confident voice. Platitudes and promises of justice, assurances of his trust in the system and his trust in Rudy Stovich and his staff. He sounded impressive while he actually said very little; a handy trick in an election year.

Stovich followed, stony-faced and serious, his old photo-gray glasses cockeyed, his suit looking like something he had pulled out of a laundry basket. His necktie was too short. He told everyone he was deeply troubled by the events that had rocked his community. He was just a country lawyer who had never imagined he would have to deal with a case of this nature – which was why he was passing the buck to Assistant County Attorney Ellen North. She had the kind of courtroom experience it would take. She was young and sharp and relentless in her pursuit of justice.

'Slick move, Rudy,' he mumbled, leaning once again on the railing. 'Slick as snot, you old country fox.'

Dumping the case on her was calculated damage control. He painted himself as a man concerned for justice above all else, willing to admit there was someone better suited to achieve that end – and a woman, no less, scoring a point for him with the growing faction of enlightened young professionals in his constituency. At the same time, he distanced himself from the prosecution, deflected the blows of public criticism, and kept his bulbous nose clean. If Ellen North won, Rudy would look like a wise and humble genius. If she lost, it would be entirely her fault.

Whether Stovich had a genuine respect for his assistant or was in fact throwing her to the wolves was another twist with possibilities. One thing was perfectly clear as Ellen North stepped up to the podium: she wasn't afraid of the job or the press.

Her statement was brief and to the point: she intended to prosecute this case aggressively and win justice for the victims. She would do all that was in her power to try to find the answer to the ultimate question in this situation: the whereabouts of Josh Kirkwood. She refused to take questions from the press, deftly maneuvering her boss back into the spotlight. Ever grateful for a press opportunity in an election year, Stovich grabbed the chance, pulling Glendenning into the limelight with him. Photos with the head honcho of the state's justice system always made for nice campaign posters.

Ellen North snagged a deputy for protection and made her break for the stairs. He watched as several reporters broke away from the pack to pursue her. She stopped them with a look and a sharp 'No comment,' never slowing her step.

'Mmm – mmm, Ms North,' he growled under his breath as she mounted the steps, the hem of her deep-green skirt swirling around her calves. 'I do believe I am in lust.'

She came down the hall, the low heels of her boots smacking sharply against the polished floor, all business and no distractions; her mind occupied by things other than the notion that someone might be watching her from the shadows.

He didn't look like the kind of man who could steal a child and plunge a community into a vortex of fear. Ellen had met Garrett Wright at a number of civic functions over the past two years. He had seemed pleasant enough, not the type to draw attention to himself. He would have melted into a crowd if not for the almost pretty quality of his face – a fine, alabaster oval with a slim nose and a prim mouth.

He took his seat with as much dignity as he could, considering the rattling of the hardware the police had used to accessorize the blaze-orange city-jail jumpsuit. 'Ms North,' he said with a spare smile. 'I would say it's a pleasure to see you again, but considering the circumstances . . .'

He shrugged, lifting his shackled hands by way of further explanation, then settled them gently on the tabletop. Smooth, pale hands with no scrapes, no contusions, no obvious signs of having struck a woman repeatedly. Ellen wondered if he had put his hands before her knowing she would look. She raised her gaze to his. His eyes were a deep, fathomless brown, large, almost drowsy looking behind lashes most women would have killed for.

'This isn't a social call, Dr Wright,' she said crisply. 'Pleasure doesn't enter into it.'

'Ms North will be handling the prosecution,' Dennis Enberg explained. He turned to Ellen. 'I hear Rudy put on a good show at the press conference.'

'I'm surprised you weren't there.'

The attorney shrugged it off. 'Not my style. It was Rudy's circus. No place for a pissing contest.'

In her two-year acquaintance with Dennis Enberg, she would have said it was exactly his style to crash the county attorney's party if he thought it would do him good. She had certainly never known him to demur for the sake of manners. It struck Ellen as a tactical error. Had she been Wright's attorney, she would certainly have done her best to steal Rudy's thunder, if only to make the obvious perfunctory statement of her client's innocence.

'Denny, you know Cameron Reed,' she said, nodding to the young man sitting to her left at the fake wood-grain table.

The men half rose from their chairs to shake hands – Enberg, thirty-seven and pudgy with brown hair in serious retreat from his forehead, and Cameron Reed, twenty-eight and fit beyond reason, his hair a shock of rich copper that came with a full accompaniment of freckles. Two years out of Mitchell Law, he was sharp and eager, a true anomaly in the Park County office. How he had ended up in Park County was beyond Ellen – though that thought always brought her up short. No one would have expected *her* to be here, either.

'Dr Wright, your bond hearing is set for ten o'clock tomorrow morning,' she began. 'I want you to be aware of the fact that the State intends to serve you at that time with a complaint charging you with a long list of felonies regarding the kidnapping of Josh Kirkwood and the kidnapping and assault of BCA agent Megan O'Malley.'

She glanced up at Wright over the rims of a pair of reading glasses that were more prop than prescription. He seemed almost impassive, returning her gaze with his steady dark eyes. No one spoke, and for a few seconds Ellen had the strange sensation that Cameron and Enberg had somehow been frozen out of the moment.

'Is that supposed to induce me to confess to crimes I didn't commit?' he asked quietly.

'It's a statement of fact, Dr Wright. I want you to be fully aware of my intent to prosecute.'

Enberg's brows drew together. 'I heard rumors of a grand jury.'

'I don't need a grand jury. Of course, if Josh Kirkwood isn't returned, I may well convene a grand jury to consider murder charges based on the evidence we have.'

'Murder!' The exclamation propelled Enberg half a foot off the seat of his chair. 'Jesus, Ellen! Isn't that a little premature?'

'Even as we speak, the state crime lab is conducting tests on the bloody sheet your client wrapped around Agent O'Malley. Evidence – he said so himself.'

'So says a woman who was, by her own admission, drugged and beaten senseless –'

'The lab has confirmed that in addition to Agent O'Malley's blood, there is blood on the sheet type AB negative. Josh Kirkwood's blood type.'

'And a billion other people's!'

'Clear evidence of grievous bodily harm,' she continued. 'From this evidence we might deduce that the reason the police aren't finding Josh is that Josh is dead.'

'Oh, for –' Enberg sputtered, at a loss for a suitable diatribe. The red in his face pushed out to the rims of his ears. Seemingly unable to contain his temper to the confines of a chair, he rose and began to pace along the end of the table.

Ellen had seen this act before and, frankly, he had been more convincing. It seemed forced this time, as if he was having trouble working up outrage. He paced along the end of the table, behind an empty chair rather than behind Garrett Wright, which would have been symbolic of his support for his client.

'I didn't kill Josh Kirkwood,' Garrett Wright said softly.

Ellen found herself holding her breath, waiting, expectation building inside her. The weight of his silence hinted at an announcement. God, was he going to confess after all? For a heartbeat she had the insane thought he was going to smile; then in a blink the expression was gone and she thought she must have imagined it.

'I'm an innocent man, Ms North,' he said. 'I keep telling you that. What would possibly motivate me to kidnap a neighbor's child? I admire Hannah Garrison tremendously. My wife and I consider Hannah and Paul friends. And as for kidnapping Megan O'Malley, that seems more like the work of a madman. Do I strike you as being insane?'

'That's not for me to determine.'

'I don't believe this,' he muttered. 'I'm a professor at one of the most highly respected small colleges in the country. For anyone to believe I could have done any of these things . . . It doesn't make sense.'

'It makes his kind of sense.' In her mind's eye Ellen could see Megan's face, bruised and battered, the fire of hatred burning in her eyes. *'It was him, the son of a bitch . . . We got him dead to fucking rights.'*

'My job is applying the law to what you did, Dr Wright, not making sense of it. I leave that unenviable and unproductive task to sociologists.'

'I did nothing.'

'How strange, then, that Chief Holt apprehended you fleeing the scene.'

Wright tipped his head back and blew a sigh at the acoustic tile in the ceiling. 'I keep telling you, it was a mistake. I had just got home. I parked my car in the garage and started for the house. I heard what I thought might be gunshots and stepped out the back door to see. I saw a man running toward me from the neighbor's yard. Understandably frightened, I stepped back into the garage with the intent of going into the house to call the police. Then the door flew open and Mitch Holt tackled me.'

Cameron leaned forward, his forearms braced on the table, his blue eyes bright. 'You thought you heard gunshots in your backyard, so you stepped outside? That seems odd, Dr Wright. I think that would be the last thing I'd do. Weren't you afraid of being shot?'

'People don't get shot in Deer Lake,' Wright scoffed. 'I thought it was probably some kids fooling around in Quarry Hills Park, shooting at rabbits or something.'

'At night, during a blizzard?'

The muscles around his mouth tightened ever so slightly as he regarded Cameron Reed.

'The man Mitch Holt chased through the woods was dressed in black,' Ellen said. 'When apprehended, you were dressed in black, breathing hard, perspiring even.'

'If Mitch Holt burst into your garage and tackled you, you'd be breathing hard and sweating, too,' Dennis said, jumping back into the fray with halfhearted sarcasm. He dropped back down into his chair and crossed his arms. 'Mitch Holt never saw the face of the man he was chasing. Agent O'Malley never saw the face of the man who tortured her. I'm told the suspect was wearing a ski mask. My client was not wearing a ski mask when he was tackled.'

'But a ski mask was found in the woods along the trail,' Ellen reminded him.

'What about the gun?' Enberg challenged. 'The paraffin test taken Saturday night revealed no traces of gunpowder on my client's hands.'

'People generally wear gloves in the winter,' Cameron offered with his own twist of sarcasm.

Denny shrugged dramatically. 'So where are they?'

'Disposed of during the chase, like the hat,' Ellen said. 'They'll be found.'

'Until they are, and until you can prove they were on my client's hands, they don't exist.'

'You can pretend they don't exist, Dennis,' she said. 'The same way you can pretend your client is innocent. Your denial won't change the fact that he's as guilty as sin and, barring new developments, will be going away for the rest of his life with no hope of ever setting foot outside the walls of a prison.'

She turned her attention back to Garrett Wright as she gathered her notes. 'As for your story, Doctor, I've seen sieves with fewer holes. I suggest you do some hard thinking tonight. Though I won't make promises, I think it's safe to say the county attorney's office would view this situation in a kinder light if you were to tell the truth.'

'Is it really the truth you want, Ms North?' he asked quietly. 'Or is it another conviction for your record? It's no secret you're a very ambitious lady.'

'It's always news to me.' Ellen snapped her briefcase shut and rose, giving him a look as cold as steel. 'What I want, Dr Wright, is justice. And make no mistake – I'll get it.'

Denny Enberg watched the pair of prosecutors leave, a sick heaviness resting like a stone in the pit of his stomach. Whether it was the prospect of losing the forthcoming battle or the idea of fighting this fight at all that made him nauseous, he didn't know. He wasn't sure he *wanted* to know.

He could feel the weight of his client's gaze on him and felt compelled to dredge up some scrap of wit.

'You always know where Ellen stands on a case,' he said, busying himself scooping his notes together. 'Just to the right of your jugular.'

'Do *you* think I'm guilty, Dennis?' Wright asked.

Color touched Enberg's cheekbones. 'I'm your attorney, Garrett. I told you up front, the only thing I ask is that you don't lie to me. You agreed. If you tell me you're innocent, you're innocent. I'll do everything I can to make the court believe it, too.'

The jailer came in then, granite-faced, and led Garrett Wright through the door to the cell block. Denny watched him go, listened to the rattle of the leg irons, that weight in his gut growing heavier and heavier.

He always stated his Big Rule to his clients with a bluff sense of worldly wisdom, as if to tell them they might as well not even try to keep the truth from him because he could smell a lie like stink on shit. Most of them fell for it. Most of them were doofus losers who wouldn't have needed his help if they'd had two brain cells to rub together. But the Big Rule had a big catch-22, and he knew it.

If Garrett Wright was guilty, then he was guilty of horrible things, and lying would surely be the least of them.

'That's a pretty lame story,' Cameron said as he and Ellen walked toward the security door at the end of the hall. 'You might think a professor could come up with something more compelling.'

'Maybe that's his angle. It's so weak we're supposed to believe it couldn't be anything but the truth.'

The door swung open. Nodding to the officer, they took a right and started down the stairs. Cameron glanced at his watch and grimaced.

'Oh, man, I'm late. I've got to run,' he said. 'I told Fred Nelson I'd meet with him at four-thirty. He wants to talk dispo on that trucker from Canada. Will you need me later?'

'I don't think so. Phoebe is typing up the complaint even as we speak.'

Ellen watched him bolt down the stairs two at a time with the grace of Baryshnikov. She followed, all but dragging her feet, the weight of the day bearing down on her.

Rudy had handed the case to her – or dumped it on her. She still wasn't sure which, still wasn't sure who had manipulated whom in that meeting. The self-preservationist in her told her she didn't want within five miles of this case. It had the smell of bad meat, looked to be rife with booby traps, and the media would scrutinize her every move. Harris College students with picket signs had already begun protesting Wright's arrest on the sidewalk in front of the courthouse. But her sense of justice told her that if Josh Kirkwood and his parents and Megan O'Malley were to get any justice at all, she would have to be the one to prosecute the case. That was a fact that had nothing to do with ego. She was, flat out, the best of the five prosecutors in the Park County attorney's office.

And so, she would clean up the tag-end stuff she had on her schedule, shift newer cases to Quentin Adler, and hope he could bungle his way through them without completely screwing up. And she would concentrate on putting Dr Garrett Wright in prison.

No reporters were waiting to ambush her in the lobby of the law-enforcement center. Mitch Holt had banished them from his wing of Deer Lake's City Center. The lovely new brick building housed the city jail and police department in one-half of its two-story V-shape and the city government offices in the other.

The atrium at the apex of the V would be lousy with reporters. That was the scene of their last great spectacle related to the case: a live interview with an outraged Paul Kirkwood. Josh's father had been livid at Mitch's request that he come in to be fingerprinted, even though the request had been more than reasonable. It would have been within Mitch's power to haul Kirkwood in as a suspect at that point. Paul had failed to inform the police that he had once owned the van belonging to suspect and convicted pedophile Olie Swain, had in fact denied knowledge of any such van after a witness had come forward to say she may have seen Josh getting into a vehicle of that description on the night of his disappearance.

That still bothered Ellen, like a sliver she couldn't quite get at just beneath her skin. Why lie about the van? Why deny he had sold it to Olie Swain when the proof was right there in the DMV records?

Unfortunately, Olie wasn't around to help solve the mystery. Facing certain prison time on parole violations, to say nothing of the possible charges regarding Josh's disappearance, Swain had committed suicide while in custody. The BCA had gone over his van with every tool they had and had found nothing. Not a hair, not a thread from a mitten, not a thing belonging to Josh. Olie had sworn his innocence to the very end, scrawling it on the wall of his cell in blood.

Cutting through the squad room of the police department, where desks were piled with paperwork and phones rang without cease, Ellen headed for Holt's office. The door to his outer office stood open, but Ellen still paused in the hall and rapped her knuckles on the door frame before sticking her head in. Mitch's administrative assistant, Natalie Bryant, swung around from her filing cabinets with a scowl on her round mahogany face and thunder in the dark eyes behind her red-framed glasses, ready to take a bite out of the interloper. The look relaxed upon recognition to show the same kind of weariness Ellen was feeling.

'Girl, tell me you're going to crack that man like the cockroach he is I'd pay money to see it,' she said, propping a fist on one well-rounded hip.

'I'll do my best,' Ellen promised.

'I'd like to do my best all over his head.'

'Is Mitch in?'

'He figured you'd drop by. Go on in.'

'Thanks.'

Deer Lake's police chief sat behind his desk looking the way Ellen imagined Harrison Ford would look after a week-long bender: brown eyes bloodshot and underlined with dark circles, lean cheeks shadowed with stubble. He had jerked loose the knot in his tie and combed his hair with his fingers, leaving tufts standing up here and there.

'Well, it's official,' she said. 'I have been duly appointed to slay the dragon.'

'Good.'

His response held more confidence than she could muster at the moment. Ellen glanced around the office. There was no ego wall laden with the plaques and commendations he had garnered in his years as a cop, though she knew there were many. He had been a top detective with the Miami force for a dozen years, coming to Deer Lake after the death of his wife and young son in a convenience-store holdup. He had chosen Deer Lake as a sanctuary in a truer sense than she had.

'I've had my little tête-à-tête with Wright and his lawyer. Basically told him to confess or else. For all the good that will do.'

'Oh, for the days of rubber truncheons . . .'

'Yeah,' she drawled. 'Human rights can be such a drag.'

'He doesn't qualify as human in my book.' He brightened with sarcastic false hope. 'Hey, a loophole! That might be all the defense I'd need.'

'I'm going to try to talk to Wright's wife tonight,' Ellen said. 'She's still at the Fontaine?'

'Yeah. The BCA guys were still going over the house today. We've got Karen under twenty-four-hour surveillance, in case she was involved. I don't think she had a clue what her husband was doing. She's not the brightest bulb in the chandelier, to begin with. Now she's so distraught, she can barely function. I didn't get anywhere with her, but you might have better luck woman-to-woman.'

'Let's hope.'

She could hear the phone ringing in the outer office, but no calls were being put through to Mitch. Natalie was running interference for him. The last two weeks had been hell on him. As Deer Lake's chief and the only detective on the thirty-man force, he had shouldered the burden of the search for Josh and an investigation that ran virtually around the clock. His professional and personal lives had been under constant scrutiny by the press.

'I spoke with Megan this afternoon,' she said as he rose and came around the end of the desk to see her to the door. 'She's got a rough road ahead of her.'

'Yeah.' He tried to put on a game expression, but it hung a little crooked, letting the worry peek through. 'But she's a tough cookie. She'll gut it out.'

'And you'll be there to help her.'

'If I have anything to say about it.'

'She's lucky to have you. You're a good guy, Mitch.'

449

'Yeah, that's me. Last of the good guys.'

'Don't say that. I'd like to think there's a couple left out there for us single women. It's that hope that keeps us shaving our legs, you know.'

The press had either lost her or given up on her for the afternoon. Deadlines beckoned them if Ellen North did not. He had no deadlines except the statute of limitations of his anonymity.

He stood just outside a back door to Deer Lake's City Center, freezing his ass and cursing Minnesota's stringent antismoking laws. In the time it took to smoke a cigarette, he had already lost the feeling in his smaller toes.

She came out of the building through a side door, muttering to herself, head bent as she pulled her keys out of her handbag. He tossed his cigarette butt at a snowbank.

'Ms North? May I have a word?'

Ellen jerked her head up at the sound of the voice – a honey-and-smoke drawl from the Deep South. Damned reporters. Lurking everywhere but under the bushes – and they would have been there, too, if the bushes hadn't been buried under three feet of snow. This one came toward her with a long, purposeful stride, the collar of his black coat turned up high, hands jammed into his pockets.

'No – that's your word,' she snapped. 'I said all I have to say at the press conference. If you didn't get your sound bite then, that's too bad.'

She kept walking, frowning as he stayed just in front of her, walking backward. 'You're lucky I believe in handgun control,' she said. 'Don't you know any better than to sneak up on a woman in a dark parking lot?'

He grinned at her, a wicked pirate's grin that flashed white in an angular face shadowed by a day's growth of beard. 'Don't you know any better than to assume a stranger coming at you in a dark parking lot is a reporter?'

The question cut through Ellen like a knife. What sun there had been earlier in the day was gone, swept away by a bank of clouds and the onset of evening. Though there was a police force inside the building she had just left, there wasn't another soul in the parking lot. She thought of Josh Kirkwood, his parents, everyone in Deer Lake who had made the assumption they were safe here. Even after everything that had happened in the last two weeks, she still felt personally immune. How stupid. How naive.

An image of Megan flashed through her mind. Megan, her face a palette of bruises and stitches. Megan hadn't seen her attacker. '*We fooled you all along, he said . . . We, always we . . .*'

Even in the faint wash of light from the streetlamps he had to see the color drain from her face. Her gaze darted toward her car, then back to the building, judging distances as her step slowed to a standstill.

'I'm no rapist,' he assured her with a certain amount of amusement.

'I'd be a fool to take your word for that, wouldn't I?'

'Yes, ma'am,' he conceded with a tip of his head.

'*Ma'am*,' Ellen snarled under her breath, trying to muster up some anger to counteract the sudden burst of fear. She took a slow step back toward the building. 'Now I *do* wish I had a gun.'

'If I were after you for nefarious purposes,' he said as he advanced on her, 'would I be so careless as to approach you here?'

He pulled a gloved hand from his pocket and gestured gracefully to the parking lot, like a magician drawing attention to his stage.

'If I wanted to harm you,' he said, stepping closer, 'I would be smart enough to follow you home, find a way to slip into your house or garage, catch you where there would be little chance of witnesses or interference.' He let those images take firm root in her mind. 'That's what I would do if I were the sort of rascal who preys on women.' He smiled again. 'Which I am not.'

'Who *are* you and what *do* you want?' Ellen demanded, unnerved by the fact that a part of her brain catalogued his manner as charming. No, not charming. Seductive. Disturbing.

'Jay Butler Brooks. I'm a writer – true crime. I can show you my driver's license if you'd like,' he offered, but made no move to reach for it, only took another step toward her, never letting her get enough distance between them to diffuse the electric quality of the tension.

'I'd like for you to back off,' Ellen said. She started to hold up a hand, a gesture meant to stop him in his tracks – or a foolish invitation for him to grab hold of her arm. Pulling the gesture back, she hefted her briefcase in her right hand, weighing its potential as a weapon or a shield. 'If you think I'm getting close enough to you to look at a DMV photo, you must be out of your mind.'

'Well, I have been so accused once or twice, but it never did stick. Now my Uncle Hooter, he's a different story. I could tell you some tales about him. Over dinner, perhaps?'

'Perhaps not.'

He gave her a crestfallen look that was ruined by the sense that he was more amused than affronted. 'After I waited for you out here in the cold?'

'After you stalked me and skulked around in the shadows?' she corrected him, moving another step backward. 'After you've done your best to frighten me?'

'I frighten you, Ms North? You don't strike me as the sort of woman who would be easily frightened. That's certainly not the impression you gave at the press conference.'

'I thought you said you aren't a reporter.'

'No one at the courthouse ever asked,' he confessed. 'They assumed the same way you assumed. Forgive my pointing it out at this particular moment, but assumptions can be very dangerous things. Your boss needs to have a word with someone about security. This is a highly volatile case you've got here. Anything might happen. The possibilities are virtually endless. I'd be happy to discuss them with you. Over drinks,' he suggested. 'You look like you could do with one.'

'If you want to see me, call my office.'

'Oh, I want to see you, Ms North,' he murmured, his voice an almost tangible caress. 'I'm not big on appointments, though. Preparation time eliminates spontaneity.'

'That's the whole point.'

'I prefer to catch people . . . off balance,' he admitted. 'They reveal more of their true selves.'

'I have no intention of revealing anything to you.' She stopped her retreat as a group of people emerged from the main doors of City Center. 'I should have you arrested.'

He arched a brow. 'On what charge, Ms North? Attempting to hold a conversation? Surely y'all are not so inhospitable as your weather here in Minnesota, are you?'

She gave him no answer. The voices of the people who had come out of the building rose and fell, only the odd word breaking clear as they made their way down the sidewalk. She turned and fell into step with the others as they passed.

Jay watched her walk away, head up, chin out, once again projecting an image of cool control. She didn't like being caught off guard. He would have bet money she was a list maker, a rule follower, the kind of woman who dotted all her *i*'s and crossed all her *t*'s, then double-checked them for good measure. She liked boundaries. She liked control. She had no intention of revealing anything to him.

'But you already have, Ms Ellen North,' he said, hunching up his shoulders as the wind bit a little harder and spit a sweep of fine white snow across the parking lot. 'You already have.'

3

The Fontaine Hotel sat kitty-corner from the City Center, on the opposite side of the park that made up the old-fashioned town square. In ordinary times Ellen would have enjoyed a brisk walk around the park ending in the warmth of the Fontaine's beautiful restored Victorian lobby. But these were not ordinary times. She parked her car in the lot beside the hotel and sat with the heater and fan running full blast, as if the trembling in her arms and legs had anything to do with the cold.

She liked to think of herself as strong, smart, savvy, able to handle herself in any situation. In a matter of moments, in the course of a few sentences, a lone man had managed to summarily unnerve her. Without ever laying a hand on her, without ever making a verbal threat, he had shown her just how vulnerable she really was.

Jay Butler Brooks. She had seen his face on the cover of *People* as she'd stood in the checkout line at the supermarket. She had seen his name on book covers, remembered glancing through an article about him in a recent issue of *Newsweek*.

He was one of the current pack of lawyers-turned-authors. But instead of making his fame with courtroom fiction, Brooks had chosen to capitalize on actual crime. His books sold millions, and Hollywood snapped them up like Godiva chocolates.

The story had left a bad taste in Ellen's mouth. She looked at the business of turning true crimes into entertainment as twisted and sleazy, vulgar voyeurism that only helped blur the lines between reality and fantasy, and further inured Americans to violence. But money talked, and it talked big. Jay Butler Brooks was worth more than most third-world countries.

'*I prefer to catch people . . . off balance . . .*'

The remembered timbre of his voice rippled through her. Dark, warm, husky. *Seductive.* The word whispered through her mind against her will, against logic. He had said nothing seductive. There had been nothing sexual about the encounter. Still, the word hung in her mind like a shadow. *Seductive. Dangerous.*

'*If I wanted to harm you, I would be smart enough to follow you home . . .*'

Reporters came out of the mahogany woodwork the instant she set foot in the Fontaine's elegant lobby. Ellen shouldered her way past them without comment and breathed a sigh of relief at the sight of a uniformed police officer guarding the doors to the elevator. He nodded to her as she stepped into the car and halted those who would have followed her, demanding that they produce room keys. As a number of them scrambled to reach into their pockets, the doors closed.

Wright's wife had been given a room on the second floor to discourage any notions of flinging herself out a window. The woman who answered the door to room 214 was not Karen Wright. Teresa McGuire's pixie face peeked out from behind the safety chain, eyes narrowed with suspicion, mouth tightened into a knot. The victim-witness coordinator for Park County, she had drawn baby-sitting detail because there were no women on either the Deer Lake or Park County forces.

'Ellen! Thank God,' she whispered, closing the door enough to slide the chain free. 'I thought you were Paige Price. Would you believe yesterday she actually thought she could talk her way past me just because she once interviewed a friend of mine for a story on victims' rights? That bitch. I wouldn't watch Channel Seven if you held a gun to my head.'

'I hear she's been reassigned to cover that sewage-plant disaster in Minot, North Dakota,' Ellen said softly, setting her briefcase on a side table. 'She blew it big time getting into bed with the sheriff for her inside information.'

A shudder of revulsion jiggled through Teresa's small, plump body. 'That is so gross! Paige Price and Russ Steiger. *Anybody* and Russ Steiger. Do you think he ever changes the oil in that hair?'

'I try not to wonder. How's Mrs Wright holding up?'

Teresa shot a look toward the bedroom that was separated from the entrance by a partial wall. 'She's not, poor thing. She keeps saying it has to be a mistake. She's been sedated. I don't know how much good she'll be to you.'

Ellen shrugged out of her coat and hung it in the closet. 'We have to keep trying to get through to her. She could be the key to this whole thing.'

Karen Wright sat in a flowered chintz chair, staring at the print that hung in an ornate gilt frame above the bed: a mother cat watching her plump, fluffy kittens cavort with a ball of yarn. She had curled herself into the chair, pulling her feet up onto the seat and wrapping her arms around her knees. A variation on the fetal position. She was a lovely woman with delicate features and ash-blond hair that hung like silk in a classic bob. The only sign that she had spent the past several days in tears was the red that rimmed her big doe eyes and tinted the end of her upturned nose. Somehow the color managed to coordinate with the rose-colored leggings and soft gray sweater she wore.

'Karen? I'm Ellen North, with the county attorney's office.' Ellen pulled out the chair from the writing desk and sat. 'I'd like to talk with you for a few minutes if that's all right.'

'It was a mistake,' Karen said without looking away from the print. 'Garrett's never even had a parking ticket.'

'We have a good deal of evidence against him, Karen,' Ellen said gently. 'By law you can't be compelled to testify against your husband, but if you know anything at all that could be helpful in finding Josh, you would tell us, wouldn't you?'

Karen nibbled at a cuticle and dodged Ellen's gaze.

'Do you know any reason he would single out the Kirkwoods, any reason he would take Josh?'

The silence stretched into a moment, two.

'This must be especially hard for you. You must feel betrayed, maybe even guilty in a way.'

The feelings had to be there somewhere, deep inside. She had been stuffing missing-child fliers into envelopes at the Josh Kirkwood Volunteer Center, had gone to the Kirkwoods' house to baby-sit Josh's little sister, while her husband had been holding them all in the grip of fear. Had he fooled her that completely or had she known all along?

'Karen, you have to be aware that you could be considered an accessory,' Ellen said. 'People are having a hard time believing you didn't know what Garrett was doing.'

Not a flicker of response. Karen combed a strand of hair behind her ear. Slowly, a smile spread across her mouth. 'Lily's so sweet,' she murmured. 'I don't mind watching her. Garrett and I don't have any children.' Tears glittered in her big dark eyes. 'I suppose Hannah won't let me watch her anymore.'

She put her head down on her knees and sobbed softly, as if the prospect of not being able to baby-sit was too much for her but the idea that her husband was some kind of sociopathic monster made no impact on her whatsoever. Ellen didn't know whether to feel sympathy or horror. Frustration took up the slack.

'Karen, you have to listen to me.' Leaning forward, she reached out and took a firm hold of the woman's wrist. 'Josh is still out there somewhere. If you have any idea where Garrett may have taken him, you have to tell us. Think of Hannah and Lily. Think how much they must miss Josh.'

'And Paul . . . .,' Karen murmured, lifting her head a fraction. Her gaze fixed on the fringed lamp that sat on the night table. 'He has such a nice family,' she said wistfully.

'Yes, Josh has a very nice family and they miss him very much. You have to help them if you can, Karen. Please.'

Ellen held her breath as she watched the play of emotions in Karen Wright's eyes. Confusion, pain, fear. Was she afraid of her husband? Had he somehow brainwashed her? He was a professor of psychology; he had to know how to manipulate minds.

'He can't hurt you, Karen. It can only help everyone for you to tell us what you know.'

Karen slowly pulled her arm from Ellen's grasp and unfolded herself from the chintz chair. Hugging herself, she wandered the room, ending up in front of the antique ash dresser, staring at her own reflection in the oval mirror above it. Slowly, she picked up a brush and started on her hair with gentle strokes.

'A terrible mistake,' she whispered. 'Garrett would never . . . He wouldn't do that to me.'

Ellen pushed herself to her feet and headed for the door.

'I'll leave you my card, Karen,' she said, placing it on the dresser as she passed. 'You can call any time of the day or night. Any time you think of something that might be helpful or if you just want to talk.'

'No. It's just a mistake,' Karen mumbled to herself, stroking the brush through her hair.

He watched Ellen North emerge from the Fontaine Hotel, wondered what she'd got. Karen was there, being watched by a hundred eyes. He wanted to go to her, talk to her, but that wasn't possible. She would never betray him. He consoled himself with that thought even as fear rose inside him like a tide of acid.

Life had betrayed him again and again, tricked him into thinking he wanted one thing when he needed something else. The job, the house, the car, the trophy bride. Every time he grabbed a prize, he found he wanted something else. The hunger never abated, it simply changed its guise.

He wanted someone to blame for that, but he could never see where the blame should lie. When he was younger, he had blamed his parents. His father, a man who settled for less than his family deserved, and his mother, a woman who stood in her husband's shadow. Lately, he had thrown the blame at Hannah's feet. Her career came first, before her family, before him. She had never been any man's shadow. Her shadow fell across him. And he hated her for it.

Ironically, no one else blamed Hannah for anything. Throughout this ordeal they had painted her as a victim, as a valiant figure struggling to cope. Poor Hannah, the mother whose child had been taken. Poor Hannah, she helped so many people, she didn't deserve all this pain.

Poor Hannah, who had left their son standing outside the skating rink while she'd tended someone else's needs at the hospital. Poor Hannah, who'd sat at home waiting for the phone to ring while he had gone out and beat the bushes with the search teams and made pleas on television.

No one ever said 'poor Paul'. Thanks to that BCA bitch O'Malley, they had turned to him with suspicious eyes because of that damned van. They had tried to tie him to Olie Swain, had tried to blame everything on him when he had done everything he could to play the hero.

A victim, that was what he really was. A victim of circumstance. A victim of fate. He didn't even have a home to go to tonight.

'*. . . I don't know who you are anymore, but I know I'm sick of your lies and* your accusations. *I'm sick of you blaming me for losing Josh, when all you seem to want to do is bury him and hope the cameras get your good side at the funeral!'*

'I don't have to listen to this.' He looked away from her, away from the contempt in her eyes.

'No,' Hannah said, picking up his coat off the back of the sofa. She flung it at him, her mouth trembling with fury and with the effort to hold the tears at bay. *'You don't have to listen to me anymore. And I don't have to put up with your moods and your wounded male ego and your stupid petty jealousy. I'm through with it! I'm through with you.... You don't live here anymore, Paul.'*

The scene played through his mind. Saturday night. Mitch Holt had come to give them the news of Garrett Wright's arrest.

Hannah would divorce him. And everyone would look at her and say, 'Poor Hannah.' No one would look at what had been taken from him. No one would say, 'Poor Paul' . . . except Karen. No one understood him except Karen.

A yawn pulled at Ellen's mouth and she gave in to it, stretching, rustling the thick down comforter that covered her legs and drawing a one-eyed look from the big golden retriever sprawled across the foot of her bed.

'I know it's late, Harry,' Ellen said, shoving her reading glasses up on her nose. She resettled herself against the mountain of pillows and among the piles of law books and fought off another yawn. The cube shaped clock radio on the cherry bedside stand pronounced it to be 12:25 A.M. 'I'm working to put away the guy who took Josh.'

The dog whined a little, as if he, too, had absorbed the hours of news coverage about the abduction.

Ellen let *Minnesota Rules of Court – State and Federal* fall shut in her lap as an image of Garrett Wright rose in her mind. The image he had given her in the interview room – pale, drawn, delicate: a victim, not a monster.

Although there were people ready to pin the blame for these crimes on anyone, there were a great many people in Deer Lake who would *not* want to pin the blame on Garrett Wright. People who had trusted him, respected him, looked up to him. The students from Harris. The people who backed the juvenile offenders' program he had helped establish. There would be people who wouldn't want to believe, because, if a man like Garrett Wright could be guilty of something so ugly, then who could they trust?

Who can you trust? The question brought a chill with it. A memory of old cynicism and hard-won wisdom. *Trust no one.*

She didn't want to believe that anymore. She had done her time on cases of smoke and mirrors, where nothing was as it seemed, where enemies came with smiles and stroked with one hand while the other plunged the knife in deep.

'Long ago and far away,' she murmured, magic words to ward off the memories.

She could see Wright against a dark background. Staring at her with eyes that were bottomless black holes, soulless, staring into her, through her. The corners of his mouth turned up in a smile that made her blood run cold. He knew something she didn't. The game plan. The big picture. He looked inside her and laughed at something she couldn't see.

Then his image blurred into another. '*I frighten you, Ms North? You don't strike me as the sort of woman who would be easily frightened.*' He stepped closer, leaned closer. She tried to back away and found herself held to the spot, unable to move. She could feel the energy around him. *Seductive.* The word wrapped itself around her like curling fingers of smoke. '*... assumptions can be very dangerous things . . .*'

Ellen jerked awake with a cry that brought Harry's head up. Her heart was pounding, her glasses askew. She pulled them off and set them aside with a trembling hand as she tried to jump-start her brain. A sound. A sound had snapped her to consciousness. A bang or a thump, she wasn't sure.

Holding her breath, she strained to listen. Nothing. But in the back of her mind that dark voice whispered. '*If I were after you . . . I would . . . follow you home, find a way to slip into your house or garage . . . catch you where there would be little chance of witnesses or interference.*'

The killer-blue eyes stared up at her from the pages of the *Newsweek* she had dug out of the recycling bin. She picked up the magazine and glared at his image. It was an artsy shot full of shadows. He stared at the camera, looking tough, his hands curled around the bars of a wrought-iron fence. His hair was brown, cropped short with a hint of a cowlick in front. His face was masculine, angular, with a slim, straight nose and a stubborn chin. In contrast his mouth was full, sculpted, almost feminine, far too sexy. The kind of mouth that hinted at dark, sensual, secret talents.

The headline read 'Crime Boss' in bold black letters. The caption – 'Crime pays big time for Jay Butler Brooks.'

Ellen scowled at the photograph. 'I should have had you arrested.'

Disgusted with herself, she tossed the magazine aside and crawled out from under the covers and the books. Trying to ignore the uneasiness that curled through her midsection, she picked up the half-empty glass of white wine from the table and padded barefoot across the plush ivory carpet. Her doors were locked. Her alarm system was on the bed, watching her.

Sipping absently at the wine, she pulled aside the thick swag of ivory lace at the window and looked out at the night. The new snow sparkled like a carpet of white diamonds beneath the light of a crescent moon. Beautiful. Peaceful. No hint of the storm that had slapped Minnesota over the weekend. No evidence of the violence that had put Megan O'Malley in the hospital. No sign of Josh Kirkwood. Just another quiet night in the Lakeside subdivision. The Kirkwoods' neighborhood. Garrett Wright's neighborhood.

Her house was less than two blocks away from theirs. She could see a wedge of lake from her living room, was within walking distance of Quarry Hills Park, where Mitch and Megan and Garrett Wright had played out a life-and-death drama Saturday night. Ellen had been sitting in front of her fireplace sharing cappuccino and conversation with a friend, oblivious to what was happening a stone's throw from her own home.

Harry raised his head abruptly, a growl rumbling low in his throat. The dog jumped down off the bed and stood at attention at the door that led into the darkened hall. Ellen stood in the center of the room, pulse rate jumping, trying to recall in detail the actual act of locking the doors. She had come in from the garage into the kitchen. She always locked the dead bolt as she came in for the night. It was habit. She had gone out the front door for the mail, come back in, turned that dead bolt as her gaze scanned the words YOU MAY HAVE ALREADY WON TEN MILLION DOLLARS.

The doors were locked. There were no odd sounds emanating from the nether regions of the living room. With that knowledge bolstering her courage, she stepped past the dog and into the hall. Harry gave a little whine of embarrassment and trailed after her, bumping up against her legs as she paused on the short flight of steps that led down to the living room.

Faint silver light filtered in around the edges of the blinds. The comfortable sofas and chairs were indistinct hulks in the dark. Nothing moved. No one spoke. Beneath the warm flannel of her pajamas Ellen's skin pebbled with goose bumps. The fine hairs on the back of her neck rose as another low growl rumbled in Harry's throat.

The telephone trilled its high-pitched birdcall. The sound ripped through the room like a shotgun blast. Harry gallumphed in a clumsy circle, his booming bark all but rattling the framed photographs on the walls. The phone rang again.

The last call she had got in the middle of the night had been Mitch telling her Olie Swain was dead. Maybe Wright had been struck down with remorse and killed himself too, but she doubted it. She had told Karen Wright to call any time of day or night. Maybe Wright's wife had found her way out of the fog of denial.

'Ellen North,' she answered, her voice automatically taking on the same tone she used at the office.

Silence.

'Hello?'

The silence seemed to grow thicker, heavier with expectation.

'Karen? Is that you?'

No response. The caller remained on the line, silent, waiting. Another minute ticked past on the nightstand clock.

'Karen, if it's you, don't be afraid to talk to me. I'm here to listen.'

Still nothing except the creepy certainty that someone was on the other end of the line. The hope that that someone was Karen Wright evaporated. Ellen waited as another minute slipped past.

459

'Look,' she said crisply, 'if you're not even going to bother to talk dirty to me, hang up and free the line for someone who knows how to make an obscene phone call.'

Not a sound.

Ellen slammed the receiver down, telling herself it was a tactical move rather than nerves, a lie that was made painfully clear by the way she jumped as the phone rang again. She stared at it as it rang a second and third time, then gave herself a mental kick and picked it up.

'Ellen North.'

'Ellen, it's Mitch. Josh is home.'

Journal Entry
January 25, 1994

They think they have us
Guilty as sin
Caught in the act
Dead to rights

Dead wrong.

4

'Josh, did the man hurt you?'

Josh didn't answer. He looked away at the poster on the wall instead. The poster was of a man on a gray horse jumping a fence. It was bright and colorful. Josh thought he might like to ride a horse like that someday. He closed his eyes and pretended to dream he was riding the gray horse on the moon.

Dr Robert Ulrich bit back a sigh, flicked a glance at Mitch, then turned to Hannah. 'I can't find any signs that he's been sexually abused.'

Hannah stood beside the examination table where Josh sat wearing a thin blue-print cotton gown. He looked so small, so defenseless. The harsh fluorescent lighting gave his skin a ghostly pallor. She kept one hand on his arm to reassure him – and herself. A doctor herself, she knew better than to interfere with the proceedings, but she couldn't bring herself to sit in the chair three feet away. She hadn't broken contact with him since she had opened the front door of the house and found him standing on the step two hours ago.

She had been trying to sleep – something she didn't do very well anymore. The bed seemed too big, the house too quiet, too empty. She had told Paul to leave Saturday night, but he had been lost to her long before that. The happy partnership they had once shared seemed a distant memory. Lately all they had between them was tension and bitterness. The man she had married ten years ago had been sweet and gentle, full of hope and enthusiasm. The man she had faced two nights ago was angry and petty and jealous, discontented and emotionally abusive. She didn't know him anymore. She didn't want to.

And so she had lain alone in their big bed, staring up at the skylight and the black swatch of January night, wondering what she would do. How would she cope, who would she be. That was a big question: who would she be? She certainly wasn't the same woman she had been two weeks before. She felt like a stranger to herself. The only thing clear was that she *would* cope, somehow. She had to for herself and for Lily . . . and for Josh, for the day he came home.

Then there he was, standing on the front step.

Afraid the spell might break, she hadn't let go of him since that moment. Her fingers stroked the soft skin of her son's forearm, assuring her he was real and alive.

'Hannah? Are you listening to me?'

She blinked and focused on Bob Ulrich's square face. He was closer to fifty than forty. He had been a friend to her from the day she had come to interview for a staff position at Deer Lake Community Hospital. He had been influential in the board's recent decision to name her head of the ER. He had delivered Lily and removed Josh's tonsils. He had come to the hospital tonight at her request to examine Josh. He looked at her now with concern.

'Yes,' Hannah said. 'I'm sorry, Bob.'

'Do you want to sit? You look a little woozy.'

'No.'

Mitch contradicted her without saying a word, sliding a stool up behind her and pressing her onto it with a hand on her shoulder. Her blue eyes were glassy, her hair a mass of golden waves hastily tied back. The past weeks had taken a toll on her physically. Naturally slender, she now looked thin to the point of anorexic. She had stood beside the table for the entire exam, holding Josh's hand, staring at his face, leaning over to kiss his forehead. She didn't seem to be aware of the tears streaming down her cheeks. Mitch pulled a clean handkerchief out of his hip pocket, pressed it into her free hand, and wondered where the hell Paul was.

He should have been here for this, for Josh, for Hannah. Hannah had tried to call him at his office, which was where he had been spending his nights, and had got his machine. Mitch had sent a squad car to the office complex. Nearly two hours later there was still no sign of Paul. And God knew, tomorrow, when Paul would be the center of attention for the press, he would blame the police department for not rushing him to his son's side.

Josh had been absolutely silent throughout the whole ordeal, not uttering a sound of fear or discomfort. He answered no questions.

Mitch hoped the last would be a temporary condition. This was already a case with too many questions and not enough answers. While Josh's reappearance was cause for celebration, it added to the Q column. With Garrett Wright sitting in a jail cell, who had brought Josh home? Did Wright have an accomplice? What few clues they had pointed to Olie Swain. Olie had audited some of Wright's classes at Harris. Olie had the van that fit the witness description. But the van had yielded them nothing, and Olie Swain was dead.

'There's no sign of penetration,' Dr Ulrich said quietly, keeping one eye on Josh, who seemed to be asleep sitting up. 'No redness, no tearing.'

'We'll see what the slides show,' Mitch said.

'I'm guessing they'll be clean.'

The doctor had conducted the standard rape kit, searching Josh literally from head to toe for any sign of a sexual assault. Oral and rectal swabs taken would be tested for seminal fluid. Mitch had overseen the exam as a matter of duty, watching like a hawk to be certain Ulrich didn't skip anything, well aware the doctor had little in the way of practical experience with this kind of procedure. Just another of the challenges of law enforcement outside the realm of a city, where rape was not an uncommon crime. Deer Lake Community Hospital didn't even own a Wood's lamp – a fluorescent lamp used to scan the skin surface for signs of seminal fluid. Not that a Wood's lamp would have done them much good in Josh's case. The boy appeared scrubbed clean, and the scent of soap and shampoo clung to him. Any evidence they may have got had literally gone down a drain.

'What about his arm? You think they drugged him?'

'There's certainly been a needle in that vein,' Ulrich said, gently pulling Josh's left arm toward him for a second look at the fine marks and faint bruising on the skin of his inner elbow. 'We'll have to wait for the lab results on the blood tests.'

'They took blood,' Hannah murmured, stroking a hand over her son's tousled sandy-brown curls. 'I told you, Mitch. I saw it.'

He gave her a poker face that told her he was politely refraining from comment. He probably thought she'd finally cracked. She couldn't blame him. She had never put much stock in the ravings of people who claimed they saw things in dreams. If she had been asked to diagnose a woman in her own situation, she would have probably said the stress was too much, that her mind was trying to compensate. But she knew in her heart what she had seen in that dream Friday night: Josh standing alone, thinking of her, wearing a pair of striped pajamas she had never seen before. The same striped pajamas he had been wearing tonight, which Mitch Holt had bagged to send to the BCA lab.

Mitch leaned down to Josh's eye level. 'Josh, can you tell me if someone took blood from your arm?'

Eyes closed, Josh turned to his mother, reaching for her. Hannah slid off the stool and gathered him close. 'He's exhausted,' she said impatiently. 'And cold. Why is it so damn cold in this hospital?'

'You're right, Hannah,' Ulrich said calmly. 'It's after two. We've done all we need to for tonight. Let's get you and Josh settled into a room.'

Hannah's head came up as alarm flooded through her. 'You're keeping him here?'

'I think it's wisest, considering the circumstances. For observation,' he added, trying to take the edge off her panic. 'Someone is watching Lily, right?'

'Well, yes, but –'

'Josh has been through a lot. Let's just keep an eye on him for a day or so. All right, Dr Garrison?'

He added the last bit to remind her who she was, Hannah thought. Dr Hannah Garrison knew how things were done. She knew what logic dictated. She knew how to keep her composure and her objectivity. She was strong and levelheaded, cool under fire. But she had ceased to be Dr Hannah Garrison. Now she was Josh's mom, terrified of what her child must have gone through, sick at heart, racked by guilt.

'How's that sound, Josh?' Ulrich asked. 'You get to sleep in one of those cool electric hospital beds with the remote controls, and your mom will be right there in the room with you. What do you think about that?'

Josh pushed his face into his mother's shoulder and hugged her tighter. He didn't want to think at all.

Ellen paced the confines of the waiting room like an expectant aunt.

Marty Wilhelm, the agent the BCA had sent down from St Paul to replace Megan, sat on the couch, flicking through cable channels with the remote, seemingly mesmerized by the changing colors and images. He looked young and stupid. Tom Hanks without the brain. Too cute, with a short nose and a mop of curly brown hair.

Ellen had taken an instant dislike to him, then chastised herself for it. It wasn't Wilhelm's fault that Paige Price had decided to play dirty and turn the media's attentions on Megan and Mitch's budding relationship. Nor was it Marty's fault Megan had a hot Irish temper and a tongue that was too sharp and too quick for prudence. That Megan had become a public-relations problem which had outweighed her value as a cop had nothing to do with Marty.

All those issues considered, she still disliked him.

He glanced up at her with eyes as brown and vacuous as a spaniel's and said for the ninth time, 'It's taking them long enough.'

She gave him the same look she had given thick-headed boys in high school and kept on pacing.

The only other person in the waiting area, Father Tom McCoy, rose from a square armchair that was too low for him and stretched a kink out of his back. Having grown up Episcopalian, Ellen knew him only in passing and by reputation. Barry Fitzgerald he was not. Tom McCoy was tall and handsome with an athlete's build and kind blue eyes behind a pair of gold-rimmed glasses. He had come to the hospital wearing faded blue jeans and a flannel shirt that gave him more resemblance to a lumberjack than a priest.

He gave Ellen a questioning look as he fished some change out of his pocket. 'Coffee?'

'No, thanks, Father. I've had too much already.'

'Me, too,' he admitted. 'What I really need is a drink, but I don't think the cafeteria has a machine that dispenses good Irish whiskey.'

As McCoy walked away, Wilhelm cocked his head. 'He's not like any priest I ever knew. Where's his collar?'

Ellen gave him The Look again. 'Father Tom is a nonconformist.'

'So I gathered. What did you think of his deacon – Albert Fletcher?'

'I didn't know Albert Fletcher. Obviously, he was a very disturbed individual.'

Fletcher had fallen under suspicion regarding the kidnapping because of his ties to Josh through the Church as Josh's instructor for religion class and as an altar boy. Obsessed with the Church, Fletcher had crossed the line from zealot to madman, unnoticed until he'd attacked Father Tom and Hannah early Friday morning as they'd sat talking in St Elysius Catholic Church. He had given Father Tom a concussion with a brass candlestick. Later that morning the mummified remains of Fletcher's long-dead wife had been discovered in his garage. The incident had sparked a man-hunt that had ended in tragedy during Saturday evening Mass, where Fletcher, ranting and wild-eyed, had fallen to his death from the balcony railing. Whether or not there would be further investigation into Doris Fletcher's demise had yet to be determined.

So much that was bad had happened in so little time. Kidnapping, suicide, madness, scandal. It seemed as if a hidden seam in the fabric of life had given way, allowing evil to pour into Deer Lake from some dark underworld. And if they didn't figure out how to close it up, it would continue on, poisoning everything and everyone it touched. The thought gave Ellen a chill.

The hospital was quiet, the halls dimly lit. Word of Josh's return had gone out on a need-to-know basis. What staff were on duty at this time of night hovered around the main desk, talking in low tones and casting worried glances down the hall toward the examination room Hannah and Josh had disappeared into with Mitch and Dr Ulrich.

Reaching for the can of warm soda she had set on an end table, Ellen froze midgesture as the examination-room door swung open and Mitch emerged. She hustled to meet him.

'Did he name Wright?' she asked.

Crossing his arms over his chest, Mitch propped a shoulder against the wall. 'He didn't name anybody. He isn't talking.'

'At all?'

'Not a word.'

Ellen's sinking feeling was the sure-thing conviction sliding away. An instinctive response that had nothing to do with her sense of compassion. They were separate entities – the lawyer in her and the woman. The lawyer thought in terms of evidence; the woman thought about a small boy who had been through God-only-knew what hell in the past two weeks.

'How is he?'

'Physically, he seems pretty good. No signs of sexual abuse.'

'Thank God.'

'He may have been drugged or had blood taken from him. His blood had to get on that sheet some way, and he had no injuries to speak of. We'll know more when the lab results are in.'

'We'll know what?' Wilhelm demanded, rushing up, his proper paisley necktie flipped over his shoulder.

Mitch frowned at him. 'We'll meet in my office at seven and I'll go over it all with both of you.'

'What about questioning the boy?' Wilhelm blurted, looking as if he had come all the way to the North Pole only to find out Santa wouldn't grant him an audience.

'It'll wait.'

'But the mother —'

'Is an emotional wreck,' Mitch snapped. 'She didn't see anyone, didn't see a car. All she knows is she has her little boy back. You can talk to her in the morning.'

Wilhelm's dark eyes shone bright with temper even though his trademark boyish grin still stretched across his face. 'Now look, Chief, you can't shut me out of this. I have the power —'

'You don't have jack shit here, Marty,' Mitch said. 'Do you understand me? I don't care if the BCA sent you down here with a golden crown and scepter. You try to push me on this and I'll squash you like a bug. Nobody sees Hannah or Josh until they've had some rest.'

'But —'

Marty's protest was cut off as the emergency-room doors to the street swept back and Paul Kirkwood stormed into the lobby with a pair of uniformed officers at his heels. His brown hair was windblown back from his lean, angular face. Cold and excitement rouged his cheeks. His deepset eyes fixed on Mitch as he strode down the hallway.

'I want to see my son.'

'Hannah and Josh are being settled in a room.'

'Hannah?' he said peevishly. 'What's wrong with her?'

'Nothing having Josh back won't cure. She's just a little rattled, that's all.'

'And what about me? You think I'm not rattled?'

'I don't know what you are, Paul,' Mitch said wearily. 'Other than late, that is. Where the hell have you been?' His gaze strayed to the officers who stood behind Josh's father.

'We caught him coming back to his office, Chief.'

'Caught me? Am I under arrest here?' Paul's voice was sharp with indignation. 'Should I be calling my attorney?'

'Of course not, Mr Kirkwood,' Ellen intervened, trying to break the mounting tension between the men. 'We wanted to make you aware Josh had been returned, that's all. We also thought you might want to be with your son during the physical examination.'

'I was out driving around.' Paul's mouth turned in a petulant curve. 'I haven't been having a lot of success sleeping lately. How is Josh? What did that animal do to him?'

'He's fine,' Mitch said, then amended the overstatement for the sake of his conscience. 'He seems fine, physically. I'll walk with you to his room, fill you in.'

As they started down the hall, Wilhelm started after them. Ellen snagged him by the shirtsleeve and held him back. The BCA agent wheeled on her.

'I'd like to hear a better explanation of where he was tonight.'

'So would I. We'll hear it in the morning.'

'What if he's involved? What if he's the one who took Josh home? He could skip.'

'Don't be stupid,' Ellen said impatiently. 'If he wanted to skip, do you think he would drop off the son he kidnapped, then drive around town for two hours, then go back to his office, *then* run?'

Wilhelm wagged a finger in her face. 'He owned that van.'

'That van that yielded us nothing.'

'I think we should take Mr Kirkwood downtown and discuss his whereabouts tonight.'

'Then you feel free to express that opinion to Chief Holt. Push him far enough, and you'll be able to question Dr Ulrich while he tries to set the broken bones in your face. Personally, I've seen enough of this hospital for one night.'

Wright's bond hearing was less than eight hours away. Garrett Wright, who would be charged with the abduction of Josh Kirkwood. Josh Kirkwood, who had been returned home safe while Garrett Wright sat in a cell in the city jail.

Hannah refused the offer of a patient's gown to sleep in. She ignored the cot that had been set up for her next to Josh's bed. She pulled her boots off and climbed onto the bed with her son.

Josh played with the control switch, slowly raising and lowering the head of the bed, the foot of the bed, bending it in two in the middle. The ride was not unlike the one Hannah's emotions had been on for the past two weeks. The ride they were still on now. The idea that Josh was back safe was a giddy high. The fear of what had been done to him mentally was a crashing, black low. The feelings chased each other inside her, around and around, up and down as the bed went up and down.

She slipped her arm around Josh and settled her hand over the control. 'That's enough, sweetheart. You're making me seasick,' she murmured. She smiled softly as one of his sandy-brown curls tickled her nose. 'Remember the time we went out on Grandpa's boat and Uncle Tim got seasick after he teased us about being landlubbers?'

She waited for him to roll over and grin at her, eyes bright, giggles bubbling just behind his smile. He would laugh and tell her the whole story, complete with sound effects, and she would feel the most incredible swelling, brilliant, warm rush of love and relief and joy. But he didn't roll over and he didn't laugh. He didn't move. He didn't speak. He just went still. The rush of love was an ache. The joy was tangled in anguish.

The door swung open and Paul stepped into the room looking anxious and hesitant at once. Hannah bit down on the questions she wanted to snap at him. Where had he been? Why hadn't he been here for Josh?

468

How like him to leave the worst moments for her to deal with, then walk in after the fact. And what a sad commentary on their relationship that in this moment that should have been so happy for them both, the first thing she wanted to do was attack him.

He rushed into the room, his gaze fixed on their son.

'Oh, God,' he whispered, struggling visibly with a knot of emotions – disbelief, joy, uncertainty. 'Josh.'

Josh sat up and stared at him, unsmiling.

'I tried to call you,' Hannah said softly. 'I tried your office –'

'I was out,' Paul said shortly, not taking his eyes off his son. He mustered a smile, reaching out slowly. 'Josh, son –'

Josh hurled the bed control at him and flung himself at Hannah.

'Josh!' Hannah cried. Her expression of surprise was directed at Paul.

'Josh, it's me, Dad,' Paul said, confusion furrowing his brow.

He sat on the edge of the bed, reaching out again to touch his son's shoulder. The gesture was batted away. Josh's legs kicked out as if he were trying to run.

'I don't understand this,' Paul said. 'Josh, what's the matter? Don't you know me?'

His only answer was a frightened squeal as Paul tried once more to turn Josh toward him. The boy surged against Hannah, pushing her backward.

'Paul, don't try to touch him!' she snapped. 'Can't you see you're only making it worse?'

'But I haven't done anything!' Paul stepped back from the bed just the same. 'He's my son, for God's sake! I want to see him!'

'No!' Josh's shout was muffled against his mother's body. 'No! No! No!'

'Hush, sweetheart,' Hannah murmured against the top of his head. Panic rose inside her.

'What's going on in here?' Dr Ulrich demanded as he strode in from the hall.

'I wish I knew,' Paul muttered.

'What did you do that upset him?'

'Nothing! He's my son!'

Ulrich raised a hand. 'Just calm down, Paul. I'm not accusing you of anything,' he said quietly, turning his back to Josh and Hannah, working his way between them and Paul. 'But I think it would be a good idea if you go now and come back in the morning, after Josh has had some time to rest and get his bearings.'

'You're throwing me out?' Paul yelled, incredulous. 'I don't believe this! After everything I've done to try to get my son back. After everything I've gone through –'

'This isn't about you, Paul,' Ulrich said, his voice low. 'I'm sure this is upsetting to you, but you know we have to put Josh first. We have to realize it's going to take some time to sort out what happened to him and how he feels about it. Let's you and I go down to the cafeteria and have a talk.'

Paul knew a brush-off when he heard one. Ulrich was slowly backing him toward the door, away from Josh and Hannah. Shutting him out. Wasn't that the story of his life? Everything went to Hannah – the glory, the pity . . . their son.

'Jesus, Hannah,' he said, 'you could help a little here.'

'What am I supposed to do?' She looked at him as if he were a stranger, someone to be wary of, someone to keep at bay. Anger burned inside him.

'Some support would be nice!'

'No! No!' Josh mumbled, kicking at the covers.

Dr Ulrich took another step. 'Come on, Paul. Why don't you go down to the cafeteria and get a cup of coffee? I'll join you in a few minutes and fill you in on the examination.'

'He doesn't have any reason to be afraid of me!'

'Paul, for God's sake, *please*,' Hannah pleaded.

'Fine,' he muttered. 'Hell of a homecoming.'

Tom McCoy watched from down the hall as Paul Kirkwood stormed into and out of his son's hospital room. His training dictated he try to intervene and smooth things over between family members. His training didn't apply anymore. Not here. Not between Hannah and Paul.

He had tried. Paul resented his attempts, considered it interference rather than help. In the process, Tom's feelings toward Paul had become something less than Christian. It was difficult for him to find understanding in his heart for a man who had married a jewel and treated her like dirt. Paul Kirkwood had so much and was so blind to it – two beautiful children, a comfortable home, a stable career. Hannah.

Therein lay the heart of the problem. Hannah.

Glad for the shadows in the hall, Tom leaned back against the wall and stared up at heaven. He couldn't see it, of course. There was too much in the way – physically and metaphorically.

Hannah had turned to him, the one person she thought she could trust absolutely – her priest. And her priest had committed a cardinal sin. He couldn't for the life of him admit that what he had done was wrong. He hadn't broken any vows. He had kept silent. Locked tight in his heart was the fact that he had fallen in love with Hannah Garrison.

'I could use a little help here, Lord,' he murmured. But as he looked up, all he could see was a faint brown stain in the ceiling where a water pipe had once sprung a leak.

With a weary sigh he walked down the hall to Josh's room and cracked the door open a few inches. A lamp on the far side of the bed washed the room in soft topaz. Josh lay curled on his side with his thumb in his mouth, asleep. Hannah lay behind him, his small body tucked back against hers, her arm around him. She looked like an angel who had tumbled to earth, tendrils of wavy golden hair escaping their band to fall against her cheek.

The picture brought a bittersweet ache. He started to turn away from it, then Hannah opened her eyes and looked right at him. And he could no more walk away than he could stop his heart from beating.

'I just wanted to check on you two before I left,' he whispered, slipping into the room. 'It looks like Josh is out cold.'

'The wonders of modern sedatives,' Hannah murmured, raising herself on her elbow.

'How are you doing?'

'I've got Josh back. That's all that matters.'

'Paul didn't stay.'

Careful not to disturb Josh, she sat up and tucked her legs beneath her. 'Josh didn't want him here. He acted as if . . . as if he were afraid.'

The words had the bitter taste of blasphemy, as if she were somehow betraying Paul by speaking them, even though they were nothing less than the truth.

'God, I hate Garrett Wright for what he's done to us,' she admitted. 'He did more than take our child. Whatever problems Paul and I had before all this, at least we trusted each other. When Josh reacted to him tonight, I looked at Paul like I'd never seen him before, like I actually believed he could have . . . I don't,' she whispered, even as the doubts scrolled through her mind – the lies about the van, the times he had been gone, his answering machine at the office picking up when he should have been there.

Father Tom sat on the edge of the bed, reaching out to take her hand. She grabbed hold and hung on tighter than she meant to, wishing with all her heart he would put his arms around her and just hold her for a while. The longing that rose in her soul was for comfort and friendship and compassion. Things Tom McCoy would offer freely with no strings attached. He would never suspect her feelings had grown deeper; she would never tell him. She wouldn't risk losing what they had by asking for more than he could give her.

'Don't add more guilt to the burden, Hannah,' he said softly.

She jerked her head up and looked at him, her pulse quickening at the absurd idea that he had somehow read her thoughts.

'You can't control a reaction like that. Who knows why Josh reacted badly to his father? He's frightened and confused. We don't know what he's been through. We don't know what Wright might have planted in his mind. Josh responded and you reacted to that. You're allowed; you're his mother.'

'And Paul is his father. He would no more hurt Josh than he would –'
Hurt me. Which he had done again and again; hurt her in ways that didn't leave obvious bruises or scars. 'He wouldn't hurt Josh.'

'I'm sure he wouldn't.'

Tom raised his other hand and brushed a stray tear from beneath her eye. His fingertips threaded into the golden silk of her hair, and she turned her face to rest her cheek against the cool of his palm for just a moment. She held her breath, as if she could hold the moment within it.

'Get some sleep,' he whispered, fighting the urge to lean down and press a kiss to her forehead or her lips. Her hand was still in his. He gave it a squeeze. She answered it back. 'We'll talk tomorrow.'

'Thanks for coming tonight. You've gone above and beyond the call through all of this.'

'No,' he said. 'You deserve a lot more than what you've been given.' And he wished like hell he could have been the man to give it to her, but he couldn't be – or so he was told. And so he turned and walked away.

And Hannah lay back down beside her child, listening to the rhythm of his breathing and wishing for things that could never be.

472

5

There was no way of containing the news that Josh Kirkwood had been returned. The hospital staff told friends, who told other friends who worked nights and stopped into the Big Steer truck stop out on the interstate for coffee and pie. The Big Steer served as restaurant to the Super 8 motel, where four out of five rooms were occupied by reporters.

They were lying in wait like a pack of wolves when Ellen pulled into the City Center lot at five to seven. She promised to give them something later and hurried into the building, hanging a left into the law-enforcement center.

They met in a conference room that had been dubbed The War Room in the first hours of the investigation into Josh's kidnapping. A time line was taped to one long wall to keep track of everything that had happened pertaining to the case. From a fat red main artery, numerous tributaries branched out in various colors of ink. The notes that had been left by the kidnapper to taunt them were emblazoned across a white melamine message board in Mitch Holt's bold, slanted handwriting. A large cork bulletin board was covered with a map of Minnesota and one of the five-county area. The maps were bristling with pins that marked search areas.

Ellen poured herself a cup of coffee and took a seat at the table next to Cameron. Wilhelm sat across from her, nursing the same lack-of-sleep hangover she was fighting. Sheriff Steiger had claimed the chair at the head of the table, a minor power play in an ongoing pissing contest with Mitch. Steiger was fifty, lean and tough with a narrow face and a complexion like old leather. Adhesive tape across his nose suggested he had lost a battle in the war for supremacy. The looks the two traded were stony.

As much as she disliked Steiger for the sexist jerk he was, Ellen took no pleasure in the seething enmity between the two men. A successful investigation, an investigation that would lead to a conviction, required teamwork and open lines of communication between all team members.

Mitch paced along the time line as he filled them in on Josh's exam and what had transpired later in Josh's room.

'So Paul Kirkwood is still a suspect,' Wilhelm declared.

'Suspect is too strong a word,' Mitch said. 'Josh's reaction could have been caused by any number of reasons other than guilt on Paul's part. It could have been that Paul shares some physical characteristics with Wright. Or maybe it was the way Paul approached him or something in the tone of his voice.'

'We have to tread lightly here,' Ellen cautioned. 'Mr Kirkwood is already hypersensitive to the attention he's gotten. He feels victimized by the crime and by the police. If we mishandle this and he's completely innocent, we're going to be looking at lawsuits.'

'I'm seeing him this morning,' Mitch said. 'I'll be the soul of diplomacy.'

'I want in on that,' Wilhelm said.

'Any progress on finding the location Wright held Megan?' Ellen asked.

'We know it wasn't his own house,' Wilhelm said, trying unsuccessfully to stifle a yawn. 'We know it wasn't Christopher Priest's house, even though the initial attack took place in Priest's yard. Wright drove her somewhere.'

'We're doing a records search in a fifty-mile radius,' Steiger interjected. 'Trying to find out if Wright owns any other property in the area.'

'He could own it under another name or under a dummy business name,' Cameron suggested bleakly. 'Or the house could belong to his accomplice, whoever that might be.'

'Well, we know now it couldn't have been Olie Swain,' Mitch said. 'And Karen Wright was locked up tight in the Fontaine last night.'

Wilhelm raised his eyebrows. 'But Paul Kirkwood was out driving around town in the middle of the night.'

'Maybe we should be looking for connections between Kirkwood and Wright,' Cameron said, uncapping a fountain pen and jotting a note on his legal pad.

Mitch looked unhappy at the suggestion. 'What motive could cause Paul to conspire with Garrett Wright to steal his own son? That's just fucking bizarre.'

'World's full of perverts and kooks, Holt,' Steiger commented, chewing on a toothpick. 'You ought to know that.'

The tension in the room thickened like the air before a lightning strike.

'What about that student of Wright's?' Ellen prompted, steering the conversation back on track. 'Todd Childs?'

'We're checking him out, too,' Steiger grumbled. 'Goddamn pothead.'

'And Priest?'

'Him too.'

'Priest passed a polygraph,' Mitch reminded them. 'He was in St Peter Saturday. We've confirmed he spent the night in a motel because of the storm. It looks like Wright sent Megan to Priest's place knowing the professor wouldn't be home. The isolated location made it the perfect spot for an attack.'

'What about the third professor involved with the Sci-Fi Cowboys?' Cameron asked.

'Phil Pickard,' Mitch said. 'He's on a year-long sabbatical in France.'

'Wright claims he was working in the Cray building at Harris at the time Josh was abducted,' Ellen said. 'If we could find someone who saw him leave the building before Josh was taken –'

'Trouble is, there was hardly anyone on campus because of winter break,' Mitch said. 'And there's the possibility that the accomplice picked Josh up. Wright may well have been right where he says he was.'

'Agent Wilhelm, I'm assuming you've got someone digging into Wright's past?' Ellen said.

He nodded and rubbed his eyes like a sleepy child.

'And we can hope to hear from the evidence techs as soon as they find anything in the stuff they confiscated from Wright's home?'

'Yes.'

Ellen checked her watch and rose, fighting off a yawn herself. 'I want to be the first to know.'

'What about Stovich?' Steiger scowled at the prospect of having to report to a mere woman or a second-in-command or both.

She looked him square in the eye. 'This is my case, Sheriff. Report to me,' she said, snapping the latches on her briefcase. 'Thanks, gentlemen. We're out of here. We've got a bond hearing to prepare for.'

The pack had grown to a mob. Ellen made them follow her all the way to the courthouse and gave them their sound bite on the front steps with the grand façade of justice looming up behind her.

'We're overjoyed at Josh's return. This is the conclusion everyone was praying for.'

'How will this affect the prosecution's case against Garrett Wright?'

'Not at all. The evidence against Dr Wright is more than sufficient. All this shows us is that he wasn't acting alone, a suspicion we harbored all along.'

'Is Josh talking?'

'Did he identify Wright?'

Ellen gave them a ghost of a smile. 'We're very confident about our case.'

She turned and walked away from them with Cameron falling in step beside her. They pushed through the main doors and turned up the steps to the second floor. The reporters didn't hesitate to follow, storming into the building like a human tornado, all noise and motion. Ellen couldn't help but think about what Brooks had said to her about the lack of security. *This is a highly volatile case you've got here. Anything might happen. . . .* She made a mental note to talk to Rudy about it. There was no sense taking unnecessary risks.

She kept her poise as the reporters' questions filled up the cavernous hallway and resounded off the high ceiling, drowning out the noise of the third-floor renovations. She let them draw their own conclusions from her cool silence, let them think she had this case in her pocket, when those same questions rattled around inside her like a pair of dice. Would Josh pick Wright out of a photo lineup? Would they get him to talk about what had happened? Or had he been so traumatized he would lock the secrets inside his mind forever?

'You're a cool one, Ms North,' Cameron said with a smile as they entered the sanctuary of the outer office.

Ellen gave him a wry look. 'Never let 'em see you sweat, Mr Reed.'

She breathed a sigh of relief. This was her turf, her second home, this warren of scarred wooden desks and ancient filing cabinets that smelled of 3-In-1 Oil. Portraits of county attorneys past hung high on the dingy beige walls that were waiting for the renovators. Bulletin boards sported notices and dictates from higher offices and court-related cartoons. Telephones rang ceaselessly, ignored by the people arriving for work in favor of unwrapping the layers of outerwear from their bodies. Someone had started the first pot of coffee – Phoebe, by the exotic scent of it.

The secretary who served as Ellen's assistant shunned the ordinary in most respects, a tendency immediately obvious in her choice of clothes. The standard office look for Phoebe was Holly Hobby meets Buddy Holly – cotton peasant dresses with Doc Marten shoes and black-rimmed nerd glasses. Somehow Phoebe managed to make the look work. Rudy had raised his eyebrows at her more than once, but her work was exemplary, and Ellen was her staunchest advocate.

'What's our treat this morning?' she asked, grabbing her mug off the shelf above the pot.

'Cinnamon Praline,' Phoebe said, her voice muffled by the thick llama-wool poncho she was struggling out from under. She emerged with her long kinky hair a wild black cloud around her head. A tiny, breastless thing, she had dressed in filmy layers today – a tunic the color of eggplant over a skirt the color of dirt over a pair of black tights with army boots. She tossed the poncho over her chair, her brown eyes bright with excitement and fixed on Ellen. 'Is it true? Is Josh back?'

'He showed up at home around midnight.'

'That's so great!' she said, tears of joy welling up. Her emotions never ran far from the surface; only the sheer weight of the boots kept her feet on the floor. 'Is he all right?'

Ellen weighed her words as she warmed her hands with her coffee mug and let the scent of cinnamon tease her nose. ' "All right" might be a stretch, but he seems in good shape physically.'

'Poor little kid.' Phoebe dug a tissue from somewhere among the layers of her outfit and rubbed it under her reddening nose. 'Imagine how scared he must have been.'

'It could have been worse,' Ellen said.

It could have been unspeakable. Other cases from other places went through her mind as she let herself into her office. Horrible tales of bodies found in pieces cast into drainage ditches or discarded in the woods like so much garbage for scavengers to feed on. They were so very lucky to have Josh back, talking or not. Not even the lingering feeling that it was all part of Wright's twisted game could dampen Ellen's sense of relief.

She tried to hit her office light switch with an elbow, missed, and moved on. Setting her briefcase on the floor beside her desk, she took a sip from her coffee and reached to set the mug on the cork coaster beside her blotter. The mug hit a neat stack of reports instead. Surprised, she pulled back.

She was fanatic about her desk. Her first year in Deer Lake, Phoebe had given her a plaque for Christmas that read *Persons Moving Objects On This Desk Will Be Prosecuted To The Full Extent Of The Law*. It resided in its usual spot at the front edge of the blotter. The stacks of papers and files were neat, but not quite where she had left them. All pens were in their tooled leather cup, but the cup was six inches out of place.

Must have been someone new on the cleaning staff, she rationalized as she moved the reports and unearthed the coaster. But as she shrugged out of her coat and hung it on the rack in the corner, that smoky drawl whispered in the back of her mind – '*assumptions can be very dangerous things. Your boss needs to have a word with someone about security . . .*'

A shiver skittered like a bony fingertip down the back of her neck.

'Things have taken quite an interesting turn, haven't they, Ms North?'

Ellen wheeled around. He stood just inside the door. The light coming through the window was gray and grainy. It suited him, playing on the angles of his face. He hadn't bothered to shave, looked, in fact, as if he had yet to go to bed.

'How did you get in here?'

A smile quirked one corner of a mouth that would have looked perfect on a high-priced hooker and was somehow sexier on him. 'The door was open.'

Ellen went on the offensive.

'See this?' she asked, curling her hand into a fist and raising it. 'Around here it's customary to make one of these and strike it against a door or door frame prior to entering another person's home or office. We call it *knocking*.'

'I'll try to remember that,' Brooks commented, strolling away from her.

He started on a slow circuit of the cramped room, absorbing the details of it – the framed diplomas, the well-tended plant on the credenza, the small CD player and neat rack of CDs nestled in among the law tomes in the bookcase. Everything neat and tidy, like Ellen North herself. Not a hair out of place, literally. Her hair was swept back flawlessly into a slick, no-nonsense twist his fingers itched to pull loose.

'Can I help you, Mr Brooks?' Her tone was acid with sarcasm.

'I came to make an appointment.'

'I have an assistant for that. And before you bypassed her desk, you

477

walked past our receptionist, who could also have taken care of you. You actually could have saved yourself a trip – we do have telephones.'

'They're ringing off their hooks today.' He watched her from the corner of his eye as he circled around behind her desk.

She clearly didn't like him trespassing. She stood with her arms crossed over the front of her smart charcoal suit, her lips pressed into a thin line, her gray eyes narrowed slightly. He could tell she was building up a fine head of steam, and yet she kept it contained inside the pretty, polished exterior.

'I understand the boy showed up last night.'

'His name is Josh.'

'Reappeared like magic, I'm told.'

'Told by whom?'

He chose not to answer. Looking away from her, he noticed the crystal candy dish on the upper right-hand corner of the desk, filled with polite little after-dinner mints in pastel colors. He fished out a green one and met her eyes again as he placed it on his tongue.

'The bond hearing is this morning?'

Ellen had to force her gaze away from his mouth, but jerking it upward was a mistake, because there were his eyes – watchful, unblinking . . . amused.

Picking up her briefcase, she skirted around him. 'Yes, the bond hearing is this morning. I'm very busy. If you'd care to make an appointment, stop and do so on your way out.'

Jay ignored the dismissal. He surrendered the space behind the desk and sauntered back to the bookcase, scanning the titles of her CD collection. Quiet, orderly music: Mozart, Vivaldi. New Age artists: Philip Aaberg, William Ackerman. Background music. Nothing that could distract her from her work. Nothing that could hint at the woman behind that cool control. The lack of clues only served to intrigue him further.

'You can call me Jay,' he offered.

'I can also call security and have you thrown out.'

The threat bounced off. 'Think he'll make bail?'

'Not if I have anything to say about it.'

She settled herself in her chair and slipped on a pair of scholarly-looking reading glasses. If her intent was to hide or tone down her femininity, she failed miserably. The spectacles were more a counterpoint to her looks than a cover. He could imagine leaning across that neat desk and sliding them off her face or kissing her and watching her surprise as they fogged up.

He had the most devilish urge to rattle her, but he would keep it in check. At least for the moment. He was already pushing his luck with her, though he could have argued that was a vital part of the process. He wanted to know more about her; she wasn't the kind of woman who offered those insights freely. On the other hand, it would be essential for him to have her cooperation if he decided to make this case his next bestseller.

It had all the ingredients – a fascinating criminal, sympathetic victims, a setting that would draw readers in; a crime with complications, twists, the extras, the side stories that elevated it above the level of news story. Most of all, it had captured his attention as nothing had in a long time. He didn't know yet what approach he would take or even if he would do it. All he really knew at this point was that he wanted to know more, that he needed the distraction – badly.

He eased himself down into the visitor's chair. 'He stays in the can, it shortens your prep time for the probable-cause hearing.'

'I'm not concerned.'

Picking up a purple glass paperweight from atop a stack of reports, he curled his hand around it as if it were a baseball and he was fixing to throw a slider. The slider was a great pitch. His personal favorite. It looked as if it were going one way, then exploded in another.

'You could set a reachable bail,' he suggested. 'Buy yourself a little time.'

Her eyebrows rose above the rims of her glasses. 'And release a kidnapper, a man who brutally assaulted a police officer? You must be insane.'

'He *allegedly* committed those crimes. What happened to the presumption of innocence?'

'It's for jurors and fools. And if you quote me on that, I'll sue your ass eight ways from Sunday. I'm not about to let Garrett Wright out of jail.'

'What's he gonna do if he gets out?' Jay needled. 'Steal another kid? I don't think so. He's smarter than that . . . if he's your man at all.'

'He's our man.'

'So who brought Josh home?'

Ellen bit down on her reply. He was baiting her and she was sitting here and taking it. Here, in her own office. What the hell was he doing here, anyway? Pumping her for information as if he had a personal stake in the case, as if *he* were Wright's attorney. Denny Enberg should have been sitting in that chair making that same argument. She glanced at the message slips to see if any of them bore the name of Wright's attorney. None did.

'Other than dispensing unsolicited advice, do you have a purpose for bothering me, Mr Brooks?'

The pirate grin stretched across his mouth. 'I bother you, Ms North? Why is that?'

'It could have something to do with the fact that you're an extremely annoying person.'

He splayed a hand across his chest. 'Who, me? *Time* magazine said I'm loved by millions.'

'So is McDonald's, but you won't find me eating there. I'm a woman of discriminating taste.'

The grin curled into a smile that was nothing short of feral. He came out of the chair and leaned across the desk, planting his hands on her blotter.

'I can see that you are, Ms North,' he said in a voice like black velvet. 'A woman of incomparable style and taste. Sharp-tongued. Sharp-witted. Makes me wonder what you're doing in a nowhere place, in a nothing job like this.'

Ellen resisted the urge to grab her letter opener and stab him with it. For all the satisfaction it would have brought, she had to prepare for court and didn't have time to deal with the mess. She met his gaze with a cool look as she rose slowly from her chair to take away his dramatic height advantage.

'I don't have to justify my life to you. Nor do I have to put up with you, Mr Brooks. If you're here because you want to do a book about this case, I have no intention of cooperating. I'm asking you to leave. I suggest you do so, or I *will* call security, and won't that do wonders for your image as a beloved personality – front-page photos of you being physically removed from these offices.'

Instead of the expected show of bad temper, he stood back and regarded her with a look that suggested he was proud of her. Ellen wanted to throw something at him.

'I look forward to watching you in court, Ms North. I'll make that appointment on my way out.'

As he strolled out, it seemed as if all the energy in the room went with him. Feeling limp, Ellen sank back down onto her chair.

Phoebe burst into the office, eyes as big as saucers, her cheeks glowing. She shut the door and pressed back against it.

'Ohmygod!' she gasped. 'I'm in *love!*'

'Again?'

She swept into a chair, perching on the edge of it. 'Do you know who was just in here?'

'Jay Butler Brooks.'

'Jay Butler Brooks! He is *such* a babe! He was number seventeen on *People* magazine's list of the twenty most intriguing people of the year.' She brought herself up short, out of breath, her brows drawing together as the obvious dawned on her belatedly. 'What was he doing in here?'

'Annoying me,' Ellen groused, digging through her briefcase for the complaint forms against Wright. 'You forgot "pain in the butt" in your tribute.'

'I'm not even going to try to turn that into a sexual reference,' Phoebe said. 'Suffice it to say, I would sit still and let him annoy me all day long if I could just look at him.'

'Phoebe, you amaze me,' Ellen complained, scanning the pages of the document. 'You're an intelligent, articulate, educated woman panting after a man who –'

480

' – is a total hot babe. Intelligence and hormones are not mutually exclusive, Ellen. You should remember that.'

'What's that supposed to mean?'

Phoebe refrained from comment, trooping to the door in her clunky boots. 'He made an appointment to see you later. Is he interested in the case? Is he going to write a book?'

'I don't know and I don't want to know,' Ellen said stubbornly. 'Cancel the appointment. I'm sure I have something more important to do at that time.'

'I don't think you'll want to cancel,' her secretary warned.

'And why is that?'

'He's bringing the state attorney general with him.'

Surely, no bond hearing in the history of Park County, Minnesota, had ever attracted so much attention. The courtroom was full, observers packed on the benches like sardines in a tin. Jay stayed at the back of the mob, timing his entrance so attention would be focused away from him. Wearing a baseball cap pulled low over his shades, he slipped in and took a spot on the aisle. The reporters leaped to their feet, craning their necks for a better look at Garrett Wright as he made his entrance with his attorney.

Wright and his lawyer were flanked by a deputy and the Park County sheriff himself – Russ Steiger.

Another politician in search of a photo op. No sheriff would ever have lowered himself to escorting prisoners, unless he hoped to gain something from the visibility of the case. Wright wasn't even Steiger's bust. According to the *Minneapolis Star Tribune*, Steiger's bust was a 36C who went by the name of Paige Price and didn't mind playing a little horizontal hokeypokey to get her story for the Channel-Seven news.

Ellen North and her associate Reed had already taken their seats at the prosecution's table. She didn't look up as Wright entered the courtroom, as if she couldn't be bothered to give him the least consideration. She kept her attention on the papers she was idly reviewing, glancing up only when the judge emerged from his chambers.

Everyone in the room rose on command as the Honorable Victor Franken took the bench. Franken was small and bald and misshapen, with an unhealthy yellow cast to his skin. He looked like a hundred-year-old hand puppet in his long black robe, like Yoda from *Star Wars*. He banged his gavel and banged it again, looking secretly pleased at the way people jumped reflexively at the sound.

'This is *The State versus Dr Garrett Wright*,' he croaked, his voice rusted by age. 'Who am I dealing with here?' He squinted at the defense as if he hadn't just spent half an hour in chambers with the lawyers involved and grumbled, 'Dennis Enberg,' then turned his wizened countenance on the prosecution. 'Ellen North. Who's that with you?' he barked, and pulled his pince-nez off the withered red nub of his nose, then rubbed them against his robe.

'Assistant County Attorney Cameron Reed, Your Honor,' Reed said loudly, rising halfway from his chair.

Franken waved Ellen's associate back to his seat. 'Let's have it, Miss North.'

Wright and his lawyer were officially served with the complaint. Jay smiled to himself. *Good move, Ms North.* Having the complaint presented now meant it had to be read aloud into the record. The clerk of the court, a matronly sort who likely had a brood of children of her own, read the charges, one after another after another. Kidnapping, denying parental rights, kidnapping a police officer and causing great bodily harm, attempted homicide, assault, assault, assault – enough counts and variations of assault to sound as if Wright had attacked half the town.

While she did her best to keep the emotion from her voice, the clerk couldn't seem to keep her throat from tightening or her eyes from shooting daggers at the defendant as she read the bit about the bloodstained sheet that had been wrapped around Megan O'Malley – bloodstains that matched Josh Kirkwood's blood type.

Round one went to the prosecution. The members of the media soaked it all in – the allegations stacked one on top of another, Mitch Holt's report of the events that had taken place Saturday night, up to and including the chase and Wright's apprehension.

The defense was allowed to make no rebuttal. Enberg sat scratching the arm of his wool jacket, looking as if he were fighting a losing battle with acid indigestion.

When the clerk finished reading, Franken fixed the accused with a baleful glare. 'Dr Wright, do you understand the charges being made against you?'

'Yes,' Wright said softly.

'Don't mumble!'

'Yes, Your Honor!'

'I want you to know that, in the eyes of the court, you are innocent until the State proves your guilt beyond a reasonable doubt.' The glare seemed to suggest otherwise, but, then, it could have been cataracts or constipation causing the judge's sour expression. 'You will have the opportunity to plead guilty or not guilty. You'll have the right to a trial. If there's a trial, you will have the right to hear the State's evidence, to cross-examine the State's witnesses, and to present witnesses of your own. You may testify on your own behalf or remain silent. You already have a lawyer, so we don't need to talk about that.

'Did you get all that?' Franken shouted.

'Yes, Your Honor.'

Ellen rose. Jay leaned to the right for a better look down the aisle. Even through the bars of the gate that kept the spectators at bay, he caught a nice glimpse of leg. She never cast a glance at the gallery, giving the impression that they meant nothing to her. Her only interest was her job – to bring the hobnailed boot of justice down squarely on Garrett Wright's head.

'Based on the complaint and the statements of the officers involved, Your Honor, the State requests the defendant be booked and a date set for the omnibus hearing.'

'The purpose of the omnibus hearing, Dr Wright,' Franken explained, 'is to hear all issues that can be determined before trial – evidentiary issues, pretrial motions – and determine whether or not there is probable cause to bind you over for trial.'

Franken drew a wheezing breath to replenish his withered lungs and fell into a coughing fit, nearly disappearing behind the bench as he hunched over. Everyone in the room seemed to hold a breath, waiting for his tuft of cotton-white hair to vanish as he crumpled to the floor in a small, dead heap. The bailiff peered around the edge of the massive bench. Franken popped up again, like a moldy jack-in-the-box, and made an impatient gesture at his clerk.

'Omnibus hearing on Tuesday, February first?' she suggested.

'Let's see about the bail.'

'Your Honor, in view of the seriousness of the charges,' Ellen said, 'the State requests bail in the amount of one million dollars.'

A gasp went up from the gallery. Pens scrambled frantically across paper. The murmur of voices into minicassette recorders was like the low hum of an engine. Franken banged his gavel.

Enberg hopped up from his chair. 'Your Honor, that's outrageous! My client is a professor at one of the top private colleges in the country. He works with juvenile offenders. He is a well-respected member of this community –'

'Who happens to be charged with heinous crimes,' Franken said.

'He has ties to the community, and the charges are ludicrous –'

'And he was apprehended after a lengthy chase. Save it for the hearing, Dennis,' Franken ordered. 'He's a flight risk. I'm setting bail in the amount of five hundred thousand dollars, cash. Omnibus hearing on the – the –' He shook a crooked finger at his clerk. 'Whatever Renee said.'

'Tuesday, February first.'

'The defendant shall be booked, photographed, and fingerprinted,' Franken stated. 'And he shall undergo a physical exam for scratches, bruises, et cetera, and surrender samples of blood and hair for analysis and comparison with evidence.'

He cracked the gavel again, signaling the end of the proceedings. The reporters jumped up and scrambled over one another to get to the door or to get to the lawyers or Paul Kirkwood, who had positioned himself directly behind the prosecutors. Jay eased out of his seat and took a position at the back of the pack.

'He should rot in jail,' Kirkwood said. 'After what he put my son through. After what he put us all through.'

483

'If Garrett Wright is guilty, then who returned Josh?'

'Has your son identified Garrett Wright as his kidnapper?'

'Is there any truth to the rumor the police are still considering you a suspect?'

Kirkwood's face flushed. His eyes were bright with temper. 'I had *nothing* to do with my son's disappearance. I am one hundred percent innocent. Any accusation to the contrary is just another example of the incompetence of the Deer Lake police department.'

'Let's break it up, folks!' the white-haired bailiff called. 'We've got business to conduct in this courtroom!'

As the circus moved out into the hall, Jay took a seat, keeping his head down as he jotted notes and avoided recognition. As much as he enjoyed his fame and fortune, there was something to be said for anonymity. Particularly now.

The case had drawn him here. He wanted to be able to take it all in without the interference discovery would bring. Unfortunately, he wasn't going to be able to get the kind of access he wanted without using his name like a pray bar.

He took one last look at Ellen North, who sat in conference with her associate at the prosecution's table. He speculated as to what he might get there besides a hot tongue and a cold shoulder. A challenge, some insight, a kick in the ego.

He knew what he wanted. And he could guaran-goddamn-tee it she wouldn't give it to him without a fight.

6

'The goddamn lawyers strike again.'

'I can't believe that bitch asked for a million dollars' bail. A million dollars! Shit!'

'*Ms North* was only doing her job,' Christopher Priest said. He stood at the front of the classroom, a small man with big glasses and bad taste in clothes. His students sometimes teased him about perpetuating the stereotypical image of computer people as nerds, but their comments and suggestions went unheeded. There were certain advantages to the image. Unfounded assumptions could be useful things.

'*Her job,*' Tyrell Mann jeered. Even his posture was disrespectful. He sprawled back in his chair with his long arms crossed over the front of his Chicago Bulls starter jacket. 'Her job is to fuckin' pin this on somebody. Fuckin' cops would'a nailed a brother for it, but there ain't hardly no niggers in this fuckin' hick town.'

'That's not logical, Tyrell,' Priest said, unaffected by the bravado or the language.

He had helped found the Sci-Fi Cowboys. Even though there had been encouragement to expand the program, they kept it at a manageable level – ten young men from Minneapolis inner-city schools, teenagers whose brushes with the law ran the gamut from gang activity to grandtheft auto. The point of the program was to bring the boys' positive qualities of intelligence to the surface, to interest them in science and engineering through innovative projects with computers and robotics.

The boys had requested this emergency meeting – a logistical headache that required a dozen phone calls to schools to get permission for the boys to leave in the middle of the day, and to probation officers to find one willing to drive them down to Deer Lake. At least the van simplified matters somewhat. Fund-raising and contributions had helped pay for a used Ford van four years ago.

'Think,' Priest said. 'If the authorities were looking for a scapegoat, would they choose a man like Dr Wright?'

'Hell no, but that loser they dragged in from the hockey rink offed himself –'

J. R. Andersen leaned forward in his seat. His rap sheet included charges for raiding bank accounts electronically. 'Professor, are you saying it *is* logical to believe Dr Wright did it?'

The others in the group reacted in an explosion of sound. Priest waited for the fury to die down.

'Of course not. I'm asking you to look at the system without emotion coloring your perceptions. The police apprehended someone they believe to be involved in the crime.' He held up a finger to ward off the automatic protests. 'You are all well aware that the next step in the process belongs to the county attorney's office. It's Ms North's job –'

'Fuckin' bitch.'

'Tyrell . . .'

Tyrell unfolded his long arms and spread them wide. 'A *million?*'

'A lesson in bargaining. Always ask for more than you think you can get. The judge cut that number in half.'

'Five hundred large. Where we supposed to raise that kind of green?'

'I'm sure Dr Wright will appreciate your intentions,' Priest said. 'But no one expects you guys to raise that kind of money.'

'I could get it,' J. R. offered with a twisted grin, cracking his knuckles with dramatic flair.

The professor ignored the inference. Crime was never rewarded within the group in any way, not even as a joke. 'If you want to show your support, there are things you can do. You've got brains. Use them.'

'Our name,' J. R. said, his gaze sharp on the professor. 'We're a media draw.'

'Very good, J. R.'

'We could start a defense fund for the Doc.'

'And the news crews will hear about it and make a big deal about us –'

'And the money will come rolling in.'

A knock at the door drew Priest's attention away from the conversation.

'Professor?' Ellen North inched the door open. 'I'm sorry to disturb you. I was told you didn't have a class this hour.'

'I don't.' He stepped into the hall and closed the door behind him. 'The Cowboys called an emergency meeting. They were understandably upset over Dr Wright's arrest, then they heard the news reports of this morning's bail hearing . . .'

He offered a little shrug that sent his shrunken wool sweater crawling up his midriff. 'You have to understand, they're not very trusting of the system.'

Ellen reserved comment. From her perspective the system wasn't the problem with juvenile offenders, but she hadn't come to Harris College for a philosophical argument.

She wanted to meet and speak with Wright's friends and colleagues herself, face-to-face to look for some hint of doubt or unease in them. It seemed impossible that Wright could be so twisted without giving someone close to him a clue.

But wasn't that what everyone in Deer Lake wanted to think? That a monster had to look like a monster and walk like a monster and talk like a monster so they could see the monster coming? If evil came in plain clothes and a pretty face, then evil could be anyone anywhere.

'I wanted to ask you a couple of questions about the night Josh Kirkwood disappeared,' she said. 'It won't take long, but if you'd rather I come back —'

'I heard he's been returned unharmed.' Priest raised a bony hand to rub his chin. 'A fascinating turn of events. Obviously, Dr Wright didn't return the child — not that I believe Garrett took Josh in the first place.'

'We believe otherwise, Professor.'

He put his head a little on one side and looked at her as if he were an android attempting to decipher the illogical workings of the human mind. 'Do you truly believe, or are you following a path of least resistance?'

'Believe me, prosecuting a well-respected member of the community is hardly a path of least resistance.'

'However, he *is* the bird in the hand, so to speak.'

'Just because there's still one in the bush doesn't mean this one isn't guilty,' Ellen pointed out. Priest just blinked at her, frowning the way he probably frowned at students who couldn't grasp the latest computer language.

'I want to clarify a couple of points about that night,' she said. 'You told the police you were here working.'

'In the computer center, yes. Garrett and I have a group of students working together on a project involving learning and perception. One of those students was here with me.'

'Mike Chamberlain,' Ellen said. 'Whom you sent on an errand around five o'clock — an errand he never accomplished because he was involved in a car accident.'

'That's correct.'

'The accident that kept Hannah Garrison at the hospital when she would have been picking Josh up from the hockey rink.'

Priest looked down at his loafers. 'Yes,' he said softly. 'If I hadn't sent Mike out at that precise moment, perhaps none of this would have happened. You can't imagine how that makes me feel. I think the world of Hannah. It was such a relief to hear she'd got Josh back — unharmed.'

The professor's cheeks colored as he spoke of Hannah Garrison. Interesting. And a little odd. He didn't seem the sort for romantic crushes. Or perhaps the shy glance at his shoes was something else altogether.

Megan O'Malley didn't believe that car accident had been an accident at all, but rather the first move in the kidnappers' game. Was the involvement of Priest's student in that car wreck accidental, or was that all part of the plan as well? If one professor could be involved, why not two?

'After Mike Chamberlain left, you were here alone?'

Priest's eyes narrowed a fraction. His skinny shoulders pulled back. 'I

487

thought I was past needing an alibi, Ms North. I voluntarily took a lie detector test on Sunday.'

'I'm aware of that, Professor,' Ellen said without apology. 'Did you see Dr Wright here that evening?'

'No. I wish I could say I did, but I was in the machine room in the computer center, and Garrett was in his office.'

'So he claims.'

'Only the guilty live their lives with alibis in mind.'

'You and Dr Wright are friends. You work together, founded the Sci-Fi Cowboys together. You don't happen to jointly own any property, do you? A cabin, maybe?'

'We're friends and colleagues, Ms North, not husband and wife.'

The door behind him opened, and a tall youth with angry dark eyes glared out over the professor's head. 'You got a problem here, Professor?'

'No, Tyrell. There's no problem,' Priest said evenly.

Tyrell kept his gaze fixed hard on Ellen. 'Hey, you that bitch lawyer.'

'Tyrell . . .'

Priest turned and attempted to contain the trouble to the classroom, an effort as futile as trying to shove the cork back in a champagne bottle. The door swung wide and two more members of the Sci-Fi Cowboys stared out, arrogant and indignant and big enough to pick their mentor up and set him aside like a child.

'Dr Wright is innocent!'

'He's gonna kick your ass in court!'

'Guys! Please go back to your seats!' Priest ordered. They stared past him as if he were invisible, their attention on the woman who was, in their minds, an enemy.

Ellen held her ground. She had tried enough hardened criminals of sixteen and seventeen to know the rules. Show no fear. Show no emotion. With hormones at high tide, the kids had enough emotion for everyone – all of it negative, ready to boil up into violence.

'Dr Wright will have his chance to prove his innocence in court.'

'Yeah, right.'

'Court didn't give me a chance. Court screwed my ass.'

Priest frowned at her.

'You've got your hands full, Professor,' Ellen said. 'I'll let you go. If anything occurs to you that may be of help to the case, please call me or Chief Holt.'

'When hell freezes over, bitch!' the one called Tyrell shouted as she turned and walked away.

The neighborhood to the south of the Harris College campus had once been a town in its own right. Harrisburg had competed with Deer Lake for commerce and population during the latter part of the nineteenth century. But Deer Lake had won the railroad and the title of county seat, and Harrisburg had lost its identity. At some point, what was left of it had been annexed by the Deer Lake municipality, and someone had slapped it with the nickname Dinkytown.

The old buildings on the main drag housed businesses that targeted the college crowd. The buildings were shabby, but the signs were trendy and artsy. The Clip Joint Hair and Tanning salon, the Tome Bookstore, the Leaning Tower of Pizza, Green World – a nature and New Age shop – the Leaf and Bean Coffee House, a mix of bars, restaurants and tiny art galleries.

Ellen headed for an old creamery building on the north end. The Pack Rat was a secondhand shop crammed with a boggling array of junk. Racks of 'vintage' clothes from the sixties and seventies crowded the front of the room. A hand-lettered sign above them read *Blast From the Past!* Ellen scowled at the thought that anything she might have worn in high school was now considered nostalgic.

She worked her way back through the haphazard displays of outdated textbooks and Harris mementos that alumni had undoubtedly trucked out of their basements and attics to make room for more timely junk. The clerk behind the counter was a large girl with a shock of purple hair, black eye shadow, and a ruby stud in the side of her nose. She was engaged in animated conversation with a tall young man as slender as a rope, stoop-shouldered and rusty-haired. He wore the scraggly chin whiskers that passed for a beard with the grunge crowd and sucked on a cigarette with serious purpose. The pair of them caught sight of Ellen simultaneously and gave her the kind of look that suggested they were more interested in making small talk than money.

'I'm looking for Todd Childs,' Ellen said.

'I'm Todd.' He tapped the ash off his cigarette into a tin ashtray with a plastic hula dancer perched on the rim.

'Ellen North. I'm with the county attorney's office. I'd like to have a few minutes of your time if I could.'

He took a last deep drag, crushed the cigarette out, and blew the smoke out his nostrils on a sigh of disgust. 'I was just leaving. I've got a class in half an hour.'

'It won't take long.'

She watched his face as he weighed the merits of denying her. He exchanged a look with Vampira behind the counter. Behind his round-rimmed glasses his pupils were dilated, large ink-black spots rimmed by thin lines of color. Steiger called him a pothead. The scent that underscored the cigarette smoke on him was unmistakable. But smoking a little grass was a long way from being an accessory to the kind of crimes Garrett Wright had committed.

'Clock's ticking,' she said with a phony smile.

Todd heaved another sigh. 'All right, fine. Let's go back in the office.'

He led the way through the maze to a room the size of a broom closet, where he took a seat between piles of junk on the desk. The only chair was a dirty green beanbag. Ellen gave it a dubious glance and leaned a shoulder against the door frame.

Wright's student jumped on the offensive. 'The charges against Dr Wright are so bogus.'

'The police caught him fleeing the scene.'

He shook his head, fishing in the pocket of his flannel shirt for another Marlboro. 'No way. It was some kind of frame job or something.'

'You know Dr Wright that well?'

'I'm a psych major,' he said, cigarette bobbing on his lip. 'I've spent the last two years of my life immersed in the workings of the human mind.'

'So are you the next Sigmund Freud or the next Carl Jung?'

He kept his eyes on her as he lit up and took the first drag. 'Freud was a pervert. Garrett Wright is not.'

'I admire your loyalty, Todd, but I'm afraid it's misplaced.'

He shook his head, his stubbornness manifesting itself in the set of his mouth, a tight hyphen encircled by the ratty goatee. 'He would have to be a total sociopath to do what you say he did. No way. We would have known.'

'Isn't that part of sociopathic behavior? The ability to fool the people around you into thinking you're perfectly normal?'

The cigarette came up in a hand that wasn't quite steady. He took another puff and looked away.

'You realize there's a strong possibility you'll be called to testify at the hearing next week,' Ellen said.

'Oh, man . . .'

'You were with Dr Wright Saturday morning when Agent O'Malley came to his office. You were a part of the conversation when Dr Wright and Agent O'Malley were discussing her driving out to Christopher Priest's home. You told the police you left Dr Wright's office around one-fifteen and didn't see Dr Wright again that day. You'll have to say that in court.'

He banded one arm around his skinny midsection as if he had suddenly developed a stomachache. 'Fuck.'

'The truth is the truth, Todd,' Ellen murmured, caught between sympathy and suspicion. Was he reluctant because Wright was his mentor or because Wright was his partner in crime and he now saw the whole thing unraveling around them? 'Think of it this way – you won't actually be testifying *against* Dr Wright. It's not as if you saw him commit a crime . . . is it, Todd?'

His answer was a long time coming. He stared at the wall, at a Magic Eye calendar that looked as if someone had squirted out ketchup and mustard in no discernible pattern. Ellen wondered if he saw the hidden picture. She didn't. Only the guilty knew the secret. Only the guilty could see the pattern through the chaos.

'No,' he said at last.

'I'll let you get to that class.' She straightened from the door and started to turn, then looked back at him. 'Can you tell me where you were last night around midnight?'

'In bed. Alone.' He tossed his half-finished cigarette into an abandoned coffee cup. 'Where were you?'

She faked a smile. 'One of the perks of the job – I get to ask all the questions.'

The scent of smoke lingered on her coat. Ellen sniffed at a lapel and frowned as she wound her way through the outer office to Phoebe's desk.

'Shouldn't your generation be smart enough not to smoke cigarettes?' she complained.

'Yes, but we're largely without focus and grounded in the disillusion-ment of the times, so . . .' She shrugged, screwing her pixie face into a look of apology.

'Be sure Todd Childs gets a subpoena. And please call Mitch and tell him if he brings Childs in for questioning again, I want to watch.'

'Gotcha.' Like a kaleidoscope image, Phoebe's features rearranged themselves again, blooming into a look of excitement. 'You've got a full house,' she said, hooking a thumb in the direction of Ellen's office.

Realization dawned with a sick thud in her stomach. Appointment time. 'Oh, God,' she groaned. 'I must have led a very wicked past life.'

'I'd like to lead a wicked present life,' Phoebe said. 'You could pass that information along to Mr Gorgeous Blue Eyes if you'd like.'

Ellen shook her head and let herself into her office. The room seemed much too small for the size of the egos present. She had the wild feeling that if she opened the window to alleviate the pressure, she would be sucked out and dumped in the snow two stories down.

'Sorry I'm late,' she said, setting her briefcase down and shrugging out of her coat. 'I've got a lot of legwork to do before the hearing next week.'

'You couldn't make Reed do it?' Rudy groused.

'I'm lead prosecutor. I'd damn well better know who I'm dealing with.'

Brooks smiled at her, the kind of secret, knowing smile lovers share. Ellen scowled at him and took her seat behind the desk.

'We understand perfectly, Ellen,' Bill Glendenning said magnani-mously.

The state attorney general sat in one visitor's chair. The eyes behind the spectacles could easily have been mistaken for kind, but she knew better. Bill Glendenning was a shrewd man with a taste for power. She admired and respected him but was careful to temper that admiration with common sense. He was at the top of the food chain; he hadn't got there by being benevolent.

Rudy hovered behind him, too wired to sit down even if there had been a chair available for him. Unable to contain his excitement at having Glendenning in the offices two days running, he paced, his face glowing with zeal or a fever. He pulled a rumpled handkerchief out of his pants pocket and dabbed at his forehead.

'I'm sure I don't need to tell you, Ellen, we have a very unusual situation in this case,' Glendenning said in a fatherly voice.

'No, you don't need to tell me.' She resented the Ward Cleaver act, but she was careful to keep that resentment out of her reply. Instead, she rose from her chair to counteract the idea that she was a child to be lectured. Keeping every move casual, she stepped around the end of her desk and leaned a hip against it, standing with her arms crossed loosely.

'The abduction itself was an aberration,' Glendenning went on. 'Things like that don't happen in Deer Lake – or so we all like to think. The fact that it *did* happen here has drawn the focus of the nation. They see it as a metaphor for our times. Isn't that so, Jay?'

Jay blinked at the sound of his name, breaking the trance he had fallen into staring at Ellen North's legs. The lady had a fine set of pegs on her – infinitely more worthy of his attention than Bill Glendenning's pointless pontificating. The attorney general was in this for himself, pure and simple. He was well aware that Jay's name was currently white-hot, and like any politician, Bill Glendenning would gladly bask in the warmth if he could. He wanted a piece of the action, all of the credit, and as much publicity as he could grab. *A metaphor for our times.*

'That's a fact, sir.' Jay nodded.

'It's a story bigger than Deer Lake, bigger than all of us,' Glendenning went on, shamelessly plagiarizing the words Jay had dazzled him with two nights ago over whiskey and cigars. 'Ellen, you understand that, which is part of the reason Rudy entrusted you with this case.'

Rudy beamed at the mention of his name, an expression that crashed in the next instant.

'I was taught to put cases on even ground,' Ellen said. 'I won't approach this case any differently because of the circumstances or because the man who stands accused is someone no one would have suspected.'

Impatience flashed behind Glendenning's Roosevelt glasses.

'I'm doing my job,' Ellen went on calmly. 'My job is to put away Garrett Wright. I can't afford to lose my focus on that end or be distracted by a bigger picture. I can't stop people from taking an interest in this case or dissecting it as a "metaphor for our times," but I can't let that become a part of my agenda.'

Rudy was turning burgundy from his throat up. He stood behind Glendenning, his eyes bugging out as if he were being choked. 'But, Ellen –'

'Is absolutely right,' Jay drawled, smiling inwardly at the reactions. Ellen's look was wary. Glendenning scrambled to regroup. Behind him, Rudy Stovich pretended a coughing fit. 'Lady Justice is blind, not looking to get her good side in front of the camera.'

'My point exactly,' Glendenning said, leaning over toward Jay like a buddy on a bar stool. 'This is precisely why Ellen is the one to try this case.'

'That's why I chose her,' Rudy interjected, hooking a finger inside his collar and tugging at the figurative noose around his neck. 'I knew from the start she was the one for the job.'

Ellen checked her watch instead of rolling her eyes. 'Forgive my bluntness, but I have to be in court soon. What does any of this have to do with Mr Brooks?'

His blue eyes twinkled with suppressed amusement. One corner of his mouth kicked up. He sat with his legs stretched out in front of him and crossed at the ankles. He had made concessions for this meeting. The jeans and denim shirt had been traded in for a button-down blue oxford and khakis. The parka had been replaced by a navy blazer tailored to emphasize the set of his shoulders. But he still hadn't shaved, and his silk tie was loose at the throat. All in all, he looked as if he had been rolled by thugs on his way home from a Chi-O mixer.

'As I'm sure you are well aware, Ellen,' Glendenning said, 'Mr Brooks is a fixture in the ranks of true crime best-sellers. His abilities as an author speak for themselves.'

'I'm sure they do,' Ellen said dryly.

'*Justifiable Homicide*,' Rudy spouted, trying to wedge himself back into the conversation. 'That's a personal favorite of mine.'

Glendenning shot him a quelling look over his shoulder. 'We're all familiar with Mr Brooks's work —'

'Actually, I'm not,' Ellen lied. 'As a prosecutor, I find the growing mania for true crime disturbing and tawdry.' She offered a smile of false apology to Jay. 'No offense intended, Mr Brooks.'

He rubbed a hand across his mouth to hide his grin. 'None taken, Ms North.'

Bill Glendenning's jaw tightened to the quality of granite. Behind him, Rudy looked horrified.

'Jay has taken an interest in this case,' Glendenning said. 'As a story that will touch the hearts and minds of people everywhere. He has expressed a particular interest in presenting it from our point of view.'

Ellen stared at Jay Butler Brooks, disgust twisting inside her. He was sitting beside the state attorney general. Bill and Jay, best pals. Jay Butler Brooks, current darling of the media, a man with money, a man with clout in the publishing world and in Hollywood; a man people would trust just because they had read about him in *People* and *Vanity Fair* and had come to the ridiculous conclusion that they knew him. Bill Glendenning, who would gladly use the publicity such an association would bring to help catapult himself into the governor's office.

Slowly, she retreated back behind the desk on the excuse of sticking papers into her briefcase. ' "Our point of view." What exactly is that supposed to mean?'

Brooks pushed himself up in his chair and leaned forward, his forearms on his thighs. Ellen could feel his gaze sharpen on her, but she refused to raise her eyes to meet his.

'A small-town justice system takes on a big-time case,' he said. 'The last bastion of decency in America assaulted by the poisonous evil of our modern society. This case has captured the attention and imagination of millions. I know it certainly intrigues me.'

Ellen bit back a dozen scathing remarks. The case intrigued him, and if it intrigued him enough, he would capitalize on it. Suddenly the reporters that had been feeding off this tragedy seemed like small fish. The shark had just come into the waters.

News was one thing. That Jay Butler Brooks would twist this into entertainment and make a fortune off it was reprehensible beyond words. She wanted to tell him so, but there he sat with his good friend the attorney general and her immediate boss hovering behind them – the nerd boy allowed to tag along with the cool guys because of his potential usefulness.

'What does this have to do with me?' she asked tightly.

'Oh, I am particularly intrigued by your role in all this, Ms North,' he said. 'Prosecuting attorney Ellen North leading the charge for justice.'

She jerked her head up and stared at him while every internal alarm system she had went off. His slow smile should have come complete with canary feathers sticking out the corners of his mouth.

'I'm just doing my job, Mr Brooks. I'm not Joan of Arc.'

'That's all a matter of perspective.'

'Nevertheless, I'm not comfortable with the analogy.'

'Ellen, you're too modest,' Glendenning said.

She was tempted to remind him that Joan had been burned at the stake, but there was the chance he already knew it. The implications of that made her vaguely queasy.

'Jay has expressed an interest in following the case from the perspective of the prosecution,' Glendenning said again. 'I've assured him you'll be accommodating.'

'Excuse me?' Ellen gaped at Bill Glendenning. 'I'll be accommodating in what way?'

'Now, Ellen,' he said, returning to that patronizing tone that set her teeth on edge, 'we're not suggesting anything unethical. Jay won't be privy to anything sensitive. He simply wants a chance to watch you work. He doesn't need our blessing to do that, but he asked for it anyway, as a courtesy.'

As a courtesy that would get him into the good graces of the state attorney general, which would damn well guarantee him access. No, he didn't need permission to watch the case from afar, but stroking Glendenning would grease wheels no reporter could even venture near, and it put Ellen in the untenable position of having to act the gracious hostess or run the risk of angering the powers that held the strings on her job.

The complexity and diabolical qualities of this move hit a nerve inside her and ground on it like a stiletto heel. Her temper flared and she clenched her jaw against the need to let it go. She shut her briefcase slowly, deliberately, the click of each lock as loud as a gunshot in the silence of the room.

She leveled a gaze on Jay Butler Brooks that had turned better men to ashes. 'No, you obviously don't need my permission, Mr Brooks. And it's a good thing because I'd throw you out of here in a heartbeat.

'I'm due in court,' she announced with a cursory nod to Glendenning and Stovich. 'If you gentlemen will excuse me.'

She expected a reprimand, but none came as she walked out of the office. Or perhaps it was that she simply couldn't hear above the roar of her blood pressure in her ears.

Phoebe jumped up from her desk, wide-eyed, abandoning Quentin Adler in midcomplaint.

'Phoebe!' he wailed.

She made a face at the grating sound but ignored him, her attention on Ellen. 'What did they want?'

'To make my life a living hell,' Ellen snarled.

The phrase attracted Quentin like a bell for Pavlov's dogs. A career grunt in the Park County system, Quentin was a man whose ambition overreached his abilities – a truth that left him with a perpetually bitter taste in his mouth. Fifty-something, he held himself stiffly erect, discouraged from relaxation and respiration by a super-control girdle that seemed to push all his fat up into his florid face. His latest affectation to battle the aging process was a dye job and permanent that left him looking as if he had a head covered with pubic hair – a transformation that coincided with rumors of a fling between Quentin and Janis Nerhaugen, a secretary in the county assessor's office.

'Ellen, I have to speak with you about these cases you've dumped on me,' he said.

'I can't talk, Quentin. I've got to be in court. If you don't want them, talk to Rudy.'

'But, Ellen –'

Phoebe butted in front of him, pulling a handful of pink message slips out of a patch pocket on her tunic. 'I've got messages for you. Every reporter in the western hemisphere wants an interview, and Garrett Wright has fired his attorney.'

'There's a big surprise,' Ellen muttered. Denny Enberg's heart hadn't been in the case from the start. She wondered if Wright had truly fired him or if he had withdrawn and allowed Wright to call it what he wanted so as not to prejudice his case in the eyes of the press. She would call on Denny later to find out what she could, although she didn't expect to learn much. What went on between a client and his attorney was privileged; a severed relationship didn't change that. 'Any word on who's taking his place?'

'Not yet.' Phoebe lowered her voice conspiratorially. 'He has a really volatile aura.'

'Who? Denny?'

'Jay Butler Brooks. It suggests inner turbulence and raw sexuality.'

'Ellen, this is important,' Quentin wailed.

'Tell that to Judge Franken when he cites me for contempt,' Ellen said, handing the slips back to Phoebe. 'His aura suggests intolerance. I'm out of here.'

7

'Miss Bottoms,' Judge Franken wheezed. 'Do you understand the charges against you?'

Ellen had a suspicion much of life was a mystery to Loretta Bottoms. The woman stood gaping at the judge like a beached bass. An exotic dancer whose stage name was Lotta Bottom, Loretta had been working the circuit of strip clubs along the interstate between Des Moines and Minneapolis. She claimed to have been 'working her way back home' when she was arrested for soliciting at the Big Steer truck stop on the outskirts of Deer Lake.

She stood before the court in a zebra-stripe knit dress that redefined the limitations of spandex. Built like an hourglass, tilting over on four-inch heels, breasts heaved up into her décolletage like a pair of huge cling peaches. Franken was mesmerized by the sight. When he spoke, he addressed her breasts. Ellen figured he had as much chance of getting an intelligent answer from them as from any other part of Loretta.

'Miss Bottoms, have you discussed the charges with your attorney?' the judge asked.

'Yeah.'

'And?'

'And what?' Loretta sank a long red fingernail into her mare's nest of bleached hair to scratch her head. 'I don't get it.'

Beside her, her attorney, Fred Nelson, rolled his eyes and banged a fist against the side of his head as if trying to dislodge the rocks that would explain his having taken on Loretta as a client.

'Loretta' – he spoke to her as if she were a thickheaded child who had asked 'why' ten times too many – 'we've heard the police report. The officer tells us he caught you in the men's room of the Big Steer truck stop performing a sex act with a twenty-dollar bill in your hand.'

Loretta jammed her hands on ample hips. 'I wasn't performing a sex act with a twenty-dollar bill. His name was Tater.'

The spectators burst out laughing. Ellen bit the inside of her lip.

Judge Franken banged his gavel. His whole misshapen little head turned maroon – a sign that his temper had been worn down to the nub and his blood pressure was soaring in direct proportion.

'How do you plead, Miss Bottoms?' the judge demanded.

497

'Well, Freddy here tells me I gotta plead guilty, but I don't see why. It's nobody's business whose dick I had in my mouth.'

Franken smashed his gavel down to quell the new wave of mirth. 'We've been through this three times, Miss Bottoms,' he croaked, trembling with frustration. 'You don't have to plead guilty if you don't want to. You can plead not guilty, but then you'll have to come back from Des Moines to stand trial. Do you want to stand trial?'

'Well, I don't really, but –'

'Then do you want to plead guilty?'

'No.'

Fred Nelson squeezed his eyes shut. 'Your Honor, I have been over this with my client. We discussed the possibility of Ms Bottoms entering a plea of not guilty, the court setting a date for trial and bail in the vicinity of two hundred fifty dollars cash. Then Miss Bottoms can go home and give this matter some more thought.'

Two hundred fifty dollars was a usual fine for soliciting, and no one had any hope of or interest in Loretta Bottoms returning to Park County to stand trial. Ellen and Fred had hashed out the agreement in the judge's chambers. The county would get its money out of Loretta in the form of the forfeited cash bail when she failed to appear, and Loretta would be out of everyone's hair. It seemed a sweet deal to everyone but Loretta. The proceedings had already dragged on half an hour longer than they should have because they couldn't state the deal outright in front of God and the court reporter, and the need for discretion had confused Loretta. Franken was sinking down farther behind the bench. In another minute only his wrinkled forehead would be visible.

'Is that what you want to do, Miss Bottoms?' he asked through his teeth.

Loretta batted her false eyelashes. 'What?'

No one held back their groans, including Franken. His was the loudest. His head popped up, and he groaned again, louder, a look of surprise widening his tiny eyes. Then he disappeared from view altogether, a dull thump the only clue he was behind the bench.

For a moment no one moved or spoke as everybody waited for the judge to pop back up like a puppet. But the moment stretched into another. Ellen looked to the bailiff, who started for the bench. Renee, the clerk, beat him to it, disappearing behind the bench herself. In the next second her scream split the air like an ax blade.

'He's dead!'

Ellen bolted from her chair and around the bench, where the clerk was on her knees, sobbing hysterically and pulling at Franken's robes.

'He's dead! Oh, my God, he's dead!'

'Call an ambulance!' Ellen shouted, and the bailiff dashed into the judge's chambers. As Ellen called out for someone to help with CPR, she was already tipping the judge's head back and feeling for a pulse.

'Has he got a pulse?' someone asked.

'No.'

'Then let's have at it, Ms North.'

The voice registered with a jolt. She jerked her head up, and saw Brooks positioning his hands over the judge's sternum.

'As much as I'd rather have you putting those lovely lips against mine,' Brooks murmured, 'I think the judge here has a more urgent need.'

'He was a good judge,' Ellen murmured as she stared out the window of Franken's chambers.

The view overlooked the park and a sidewalk crowded with protesting college students. The imitation gas streetlamps were winking on. Life was continuing. The world was still turning.

The last hour was a blur of paramedics and people rushing in and out of the courtroom. Reporters loitering in the rotunda had stormed the courtroom for this latest twist in the tale, and a near riot had ensued when someone had recognized Brooks. The bedlam had culminated with a deputy clearing the room and the ears of the sound technicians with a shrieking bullhorn. The silence now seemed both welcome and odd.

'He was tough and fair,' Ellen said, her thoughts returning to Victor Franken. She wanted to remember him as she had known him for the past two years, not as a crumpled husk on the floor of his courtroom, the black robes he had prized so highly torn open to reveal the thin, sunken chest of a very old man. 'He had common sense and a sense of humor.'

'Did you know him well?' Jay asked softly.

He watched her from his seat on the end of Franken's massive oak desk. They were the only people left in the room that had been the judge's office and sanctuary. Bookcases towered on all sides of the room, the shelves filled to capacity. The furniture looked so old it might have set roots into the floor. The ferns that sat in massive pots all around the room were the size of bushel baskets. With the green-shaded desk lamp the only light on, the atmosphere was almost forestlike.

Ellen lifted a shoulder. 'I know he lost his wife years ago. He lived alone. He liked to garden.' She fingered the frond of a fern that filled the window ledge. 'The bench was his life. And now he's gone. Just like that.'

She brushed a tear from her cheek, not embarrassed to have shed it in front of a stranger. A good man had just vanished from existence. There was no shame in mourning that. Still, she drew in a deep breath and composed herself, turning to Jay with a dignified facade.

'Thank you for helping.'

He shook it off, frowning. 'I don't need thanks. Jesus, my being there turned the whole thing into a damn circus. I'm sorry that happened.'

'So am I,' Ellen said. 'He deserved a more dignified passing, although I heard him say it more than once – he wanted to die on the bench.' She shrugged again and reached for some cynicism to insulate herself. 'He got his wish and you got some publicity. Not a bad deal if you look at it that way.'

'I didn't come here for publicity.'

'No. You came here for a story.'

He pushed himself away from the desk and crossed the room slowly, his gaze assessing, scrutinizing. The sensation it evoked was disturbing, but Ellen refused to let herself move away from it, from him. The rule she had applied with the Sci-Fi Cowboys came back to her – show no fear. Jay Butler Brooks posed no physical threat to her, but he was a threat in other ways, a clear and present danger on other levels – professional, ideological . . .

She knew she was leaving one out as he stopped just a hair's breadth too close. His eyes were silver in the colorless light from the narrow window.

'Are you all right?' he asked softly.

Her hair had come loose from its twist as she'd worked to revive the judge. Strands fell along her cheeks, making him wonder how she would look with it all down. Younger, softer, vulnerable – traits that didn't complement her professional image. But the image was slipping now. Her studious glasses were gone, along with the jacket of her charcoal suit. The top button of her proper white blouse was open, giving him a glimpse of the tender hollow where throat met collarbone. The armor was coming undone. She couldn't seem to decide who she should be in this moment – Ellen North the consummate professional, or Ellen North the woman.

An opportune chance for him. The reason he had hung around as the paramedics packed their things and zipped the black bag on old Franken, he told himself. So he could take advantage of her when she was off balance. So he might be able to catch a glimpse of something she never would have shown him otherwise.

What a guy you are, Brooks. Prince of the jerks.

'I'm fine,' she announced, though she clearly was not. The hand she raised to comb the loose strands behind her left ear was trembling.

'Looks to me like you could use a drink. I know I could,' he admitted. 'I never had a judge drop dead on me before – though I admit I wished it a few times.'

'That's right. You used to practice before fame and fortune came calling.'

He shrugged, ignoring the sting of her words. 'I did my time as a lowly associate, chased an ambulance or two, tried a little of this, a little of that. "Little" being the operative word, according to my ex-wife. She had to be the first lawyer's wife in history who actually wanted her husband to put in eighty-hour weeks.'

Even now he could hear Christine's criticism. It had worn a trench into the back of his mind like water running over stone; the years only made it deeper. '*Why can't you work harder? Why haven't you made junior partner? Why won't you join the family firm? You'll never amount to anything the way you bounce around.'*

'Well, you got her in the end,' Ellen said. *'Justifiable Homicide* – an overworked young attorney is framed for the brutal murder of his scheming ex-wife. The book's dedication: "To Christine, who, I am pleased to say, will never get a dime of the royalties." A charming sentiment.'

'And well deserved, I assure you.' A wry smile twisted across his mouth. 'I thought you were unfamiliar with my work, Ms North.'

'I lied,' Ellen said without remorse. 'I read the article in *Newsweek.*'

'And what did you think?'

'I think I made my opinion clear earlier. I don't like what you do.'

'I present actual, terrifying events to my readers in a way that can bring them to a deeper understanding of what happened, why it happened, how the justice system worked – or failed to work in some cases,' he said. 'I give them insight. I give them closure. What's wrong with that?'

'You're a mercenary profiteer who's no better than a vampire. A hack looking to steal the lives and pain of victims to compensate for a lack of any real imagination. You feed off people's fears and morbid curiosities and contribute to the nation's unhealthy obsession with sensationalism,' Ellen countered. 'Don't try to put a noble face on it. You're in the entertainment business – those were your own words.'

'Everything I say can and will be used against me,' he said dryly.

'Do you deny it?'

'No. I'm not a journalist. People get their news from a paper or on TV. They don't fork over twenty bucks in the bookstore for a hardback version of *Time*. People read true crime to escape – same reason people read anything.'

'And you don't find that just the least bit twisted? Escaping into someone else's real-life tragedy?'

'No more so than picking up a Stephen King novel or an Agatha Christie mystery. To that reader my book is just a story, something to get lost in and ponder; all the more interesting because it really happened.'

Ellen moved away from him then, shaking her head in disgust. 'Fine. You go talk to Hannah Garrison about what she's been through and what she's going through, and be sure to tell her it's just a story. That'll be such a comfort to her.'

Jay pursued her across the dusky room to the desk, automatically reacting to her righteous indignation. He was contrary by nature, born to take the opposite side just for the sake of a good argument. It wasn't anger that rushed to the fore – it was excitement, adrenaline.

'Hey, I can't change what's happened to make a story a story. It's there, it's happened, it's history.'

'So you might as well make a buck off it?' She pulled her jacket off the back of Franken's chair and slipped it on.

'If I don't, someone else will.'

'Oh, well, that makes it all right.'

'I didn't invent the game, counselor –'

'No, but you're hell-bent on winning it, aren't you? Going straight to the top, dragging Glendenning into it. Of all the dirty –'

'Not dirty,' Jay clarified, wagging a finger in her face. 'That's hardball and it's the way I play this game. I go after what I want and I get it.'

The declaration hung in the air between them, a challenge that took on deeper nuances as Ellen stared up at him. He was standing too close again. She was leaning toward him. The scant few inches of air between them seemed to thicken, and a dormant sixth sense came to life inside her, rising to the surface like air bubbles in water. Awareness, not of an adversary in a duel of wits, but of something much more fundamental.

'I go after what I want, Ellen North,' he whispered again, sliding a hand beneath her chin. His thumb brushed across the bow of her lower lip. 'And I get it,' he breathed. 'Remember that.'

'That you're ruthless?' Ellen murmured, telling herself to brand it into her mind.

'Determined.'

'Dangerous' was the word she settled on. Dangerous to her in ways she had never anticipated a man could be.

'Damn, I like the way you fight, counselor,' he said softly. 'How about that drink?'

The invitation in his expression was far more intimate than an offered glass of brandy. That he could slide so easily from contention to seduction, as if it didn't matter what she thought of him, disturbed her.

'Just because we disagree doesn't mean we can't be civil,' he said. 'I like you, Ellen. You're smart, sharp, not afraid to say what you mean.' He chuckled. 'I thought ol' Rudy was gonna have a stroke in your office. And you just stood there, cool as well water. What do you say we go find a nice quiet bar with a fireplace and argue the evening away?' He served the suggestion with the kind of smile that could have charmed nuns from their habits.

This was why he was a celebrity, Ellen decided, instead of just a name on a dust jacket. The very air around him vibrated with sex appeal.

'I don't think so, Mr Brooks. It would be too much like fraternizing with the enemy,' she said, stepping away from him, slipping her glasses on – shielding herself against his charm.

'I'm not the enemy. I'm just an observer.'

'You may not be *the* enemy, but you're an enemy just the same. I can't differentiate between who you are and what you are, Mr Brooks.' She stared him straight in the face. 'Maybe your conscience will let you exploit what's happened in this town – or maybe you don't have a conscience. Either way, I won't condone it and I don't want to be a part of it.'

With that she walked out on him for the second time that day.

Jay sat back against the judge's desk and gave a low whistle. He had had doors slammed in his face before. That was nothing new. It went with the territory. Sometimes people were willing to work on a story with him and sometimes they weren't. If he wanted the story badly enough and the front door closed, he went to the back. If the back door closed, he went in a window. If he couldn't get in through a window, he went in through the basement. If he wanted the story bad enough, he would get it. He didn't need Ellen North's cooperation. He could write this story from a dozen different angles.

But he wanted Ellen North's cooperation. Hell, he wanted Ellen North.

He knew better than to get involved with a source. Crossing that line was like walking into a nest of vipers – an invitation for disaster. He would compromise his credibility, color his perception of the story.

As tough as he played this game, he played it by rules. He had already broken one – getting involved with a live case. That was just asking for trouble. Of course, as Uncle Hooter always said, he may not have looked for trouble, but when it came calling, he was never out of earshot.

This case had grabbed him and hung on. He wanted inside of it, wanted to know why it had happened and what it had done to the people whose lives it had touched. He wanted to watch it all unfold – the trial, the strategy behind prosecution and defense, the reactions of the public as sides were taken. Something important was happening here. This wasn't just another crime; it was a crossroads, a crisis point for small-town America. He felt a need to capture that.

And to distance himself from another crisis, he admitted in a shadowed corner of his mind – one he had turned away from before it could suck him in. *This* case was his focus. The trick was to get inside and yet maintain emotional distance. A tough call when a part of him wanted no distance at all between himself and the prosecuting attorney.

But then, it appeared Ellen North would maintain that distance for him. She was as unimpressed with his bag of tricks as a skeptic who had caught sight of the mirrors in a magic show. She didn't give a damn about the bankability of his name, would not have cared a lick that his latest work had been at the top of every best-seller list in the country for three solid months or that Tom Cruise had signed on for the lead in the movie version of *Justice for None*. She didn't care who he was, she cared *what* he was, and she had made up her mind on that score right out of the box.

The hell of it was, she was probably right.

The hell of it was, he wanted her anyway.

8

Mitch slid in behind the wheel of his Emplorer, bone-weary. The better part of the day had been spent overseeing the search for the missing gloves Garrett Wright had cast off during the chase the night of his arrest. Mitch's men and the evidence techs from the BCA had spent two days combing the ground the chase had covered through the woods of Quarry Hills Park, along the cross-country ski trail that ran the rim of the park behind the Lakeside neighborhood, and into the yards of the homes that backed onto the park.

Seven inches of fresh snow had fallen to cover the tracks from the chase, and every step taken by an officer or agent had the potential to further bury evidence that would not be seen again until April. They had gone over the ground with shovels and rakes, dug with garden tools in the areas too small for anything else. And still, in the end, it was dumb luck that did the trick. Lonnie Dietz had plunked down on a fallen log, tired and frustrated, and while he'd stared down at a crevice in the dead tree, something had caught his eye. A small slip of white – the size tag sewn inside the cuff of a black leather glove.

The gloves had been sent to the BCA lab in St Paul. Then there had been the ever-present press to deal with, the mob of reporters already in a frenzy from the bond hearing. And constantly in the back of Mitch's mind were thoughts of Megan.

She had been transferred to Hennepin County Medical Center in Minneapolis that morning and had gone into surgery for her hand at three. He wanted to be there with her, but the case took precedence. Megan knew that. She had been the first to say it. She was a cop, she understood the priorities. She was a victim as well, which gave her an added motivation to want to see the investigation completed.

She was also alone and afraid. The prognosis for her regaining full use of her hand was not good. If she couldn't use her right hand, she couldn't handle a gun, she couldn't defend herself, she couldn't return to the kind of duty that had been her whole life. All she had ever wanted was to be a good cop.

And all Mitch wanted at the moment was to be able to hold her. He didn't relish the thought of an hour's drive to the Cities, and guilt nipped him at the thought of leaving his daughter with her grandparents for yet another evening, but he started the engine and focused on Megan. The last thing he had expected to find in this nightmare of Josh Kirkwood's abduction was love, and he would never have expected love to come packaged in a tough Irish cop with a chip on her shoulder the size of Gibraltar, but there it was.

He eased the truck out of his parking spot, fighting the urge to gun the engine and send the reporters who had followed him out scrambling for their lives. He waved them off when he would rather have given them the finger, and pulled out onto Oslo Street. He was half a block from the interstate when his cellular phone trilled in his coat pocket.

'Jesus, now what?' he muttered, pulling up to the curb.

Leaving the engine running, he dug the phone out and unfolded it, telling himself it might be Megan or it might be Jessie calling to see where her daddy was.

'Mitch Holt.'

The silence made him think the caller had given up while he had fumbled with his gloves and the pocket flap trying to get to the damn phone, but he hung on, an eerie sensation scratching through him.

'Hello? Who's there?'

The truck engine grumbled to itself. Outside, the shabby little neighborhood that backed onto the interstate was quiet in the twilight. People were in their homes having supper and watching the news as night began to settle down around them. It was the time of night Josh had disappeared.

As the thought shot a chill through him, the voice came over the phone. A whisper.

'Ignorance is not innocence but sin. Ignorance is not innocence but sin. Ignorance is not innocence but sin.'

The line went dead.

Mitch sat perfectly still, his heart banging like a fist against his ribs. *Ignorance is not innocence but sin.* The message in the note that had been left behind at the scene of Josh's abduction. Common knowledge, he told himself. The press had splashed it all over. And yet he couldn't shake the sick sensation of dread. His muscles quivered with it. It steamed from his pores even though the temperature in the cab of the truck was below freezing. The number of his cellular phone was *not* common knowledge.

A minute passed. Then five. The phone rang again and the uneasiness pressed down on him like an anvil.

'Mitch Holt.'

'Chief, it's Natalie. We just got a call from the sheriff. He's in Campion. They've got a child missing . . . and a note.'

Josh sat on the family-room floor, cross-legged, staring at the flames in the fireplace. A giant sketch pad and a new box of markers lay on the floor beside him, untouched. *Aladdin* was running in the VCR, but the cartoon didn't interest him. His baby sister, Lily, however, was delighted and toddled around the room, singing along, dancing with a stuffed Barney the Dinosaur.

Josh didn't care about cartoons anymore. He didn't want to play. He didn't want to talk. He stared at the fire and imagined he was a fireman on Mars, where it was hot all the time and there were no kids.

Hannah stepped down into the family room from the kitchen, rubbing lotion into her hands. The supper dishes were done, such as they were – glasses for soda and plates for pizza from the Leaning Tower of Pizza. Josh's favorite. Nutrition be damned tonight. She had called out for a medium pepperoni and mushroom and offered brownies for dessert. She hadn't made them, either, selecting instead the best from the pans friends and neighbors and absolute strangers had sent over during the course of Josh's absence.

She had brought her son home today. Against Bob Ulrich's wishes. Against the advice of the advocate from Park County Social Services. They had wanted to continue observation, as if Josh were a freak in a sideshow. But he had checked out all right physically, and Hannah had argued that his unwillingness to talk to anyone was no reason to keep him in a hospital bed. It was time to go home, where things were familiar and safe. She was a doctor herself; if Josh exhibited signs of physical problems, she would be the first to notice.

And so they had come home, where reporters blocked the driveway and well-meaning friends crowded the house. Home, where everything looked familiar but nothing would ever be the same again.

Hannah put the thought out of her head. She had sent the friends home, and the police had chased the reporters off the lawn. She had ordered pizza and built a fire and put one of Josh's favorite movies in the VCR. She had made things as normal as she could, considering the circumstances.

Lily danced up to her, all smiles and rosy cheeks, and offered her Barney. Hannah scooped up her daughter instead and hugged her close. 'Mama, Josh!' Lily announced, pointing at her brother.

'Yep, Josh is home. We missed him, didn't we, Lily-bug?'

'Josh! Josh! Josh!' Lily sang, euphoric over her brother's return. At eighteen months, she worshiped Josh. He had always been wonderful with her, sweet, gentle, loving. He read her bedtime stories and played with her.

He hadn't spoken a word to her since coming home. He ignored her efforts to engage him in play. He looked through her as if she weren't there. Fortunately, Lily was too excited to notice her brother wasn't returning her affections. It would have broken Hannah's heart if there had been any pieces left intact.

She settled on the couch with the baby in her lap as the movie rolled to a close. Lily twisted around, blond curls bouncing. 'More!'

'Let's ask Josh,' Hannah said, her eyes on her son. 'Josh, honey, do you want to run the movie again?'

He didn't answer, didn't look at her. He sat as he had for the last hour, staring into the fire. He hadn't touched the sketch pad or markers.

The advocate had said to keep them handy, to encourage Josh to draw in the hopes that he would vent his experiences with his kidnappers through his artwork. So far, the only mark on the pad was the one the advocate herself had made, trying to draw Josh into a game of tic-tac-toe. Josh was keeping his experiences locked up tight, and his emotions along with them. Aside from his violent reaction to his father, he had reacted to nothing and no one.

'More, more, Mama!' Lily insisted.

'Not tonight, sweetheart,' Hannah murmured. 'It's time to watch something quiet so we can all settle down for bedtime.'

Lily protested by taking Barney and moving to the love seat. 'Where Daddy?'

'Daddy's staying somewhere else tonight,' Hannah answered, watching Josh for a reaction at mention of his father. There was none.

She was angry with Paul for not being there, even though she really didn't want him. He had upset Josh before; she didn't want a repeat performance. Nor did she want the tensions between her and Paul to be telegraphed to the children.

Still, a foolish part of her wanted Paul to assert his rights as a father, to make some kind of stand to keep their marriage from disintegrating. She wanted to see the man she had married, the man she had loved, but he was lost. It seemed he had been an aberration, that for the first part of their marriage Paul had been at his peak and for reasons she couldn't understand had slowly fallen backward until she could no longer reach him, could hardly recognize who he was. It frightened her that she had thought she had known him so well, but now she didn't seem to know him at all.

Sighing, she flipped through the television channels, looking for something without sex, violence, or reality involved, settling on an independent station out of Minneapolis that was running *The Parent Trap* for the millionth time. Hayley Mills in a madcap adventure as twin sisters. Classic fluff from the sixties, when the world had still clung to its last shreds of innocence.

The nineties intruded immediately in the form of a news bulletin. A grim-faced anchorwoman with a helmet of spray-starched red hair filled half the screen while the photograph of a little boy popped up in one corner under a red banner that proclaimed him missing.

'Oh, my God,' Hannah murmured.

'Authorities in the small Park County town of Campion tonight are launching a massive search for eight-year-old Dustin Holloman, abducted from a city park where he was playing with friends after school this afternoon. The abduction bears marked similarities to the case of Josh Kirkwood of Deer Lake, also in Park County. Josh, abducted January twelfth, was returned to his family unharmed late last night. The family of Dustin Holloman can only hope for a similar outcome.

'Dustin is eight years old with blond hair and blue eyes. He was last seen wearing blue jeans and a black-and-yellow ski jacket with an orange stocking cap. Anyone who thinks they may have information about Dustin is asked to immediately call the Park County sheriff's office.'

Josh turned slowly and looked at the television screen as it filled with the smiling, slightly blurry image of Dustin Holloman and the hot-line phone numbers. He rose and moved to stand directly in front of the set in the cherry entertainment center, staring without expression at the boy who had been proclaimed missing.

'Josh,' Hannah murmured, coming out of her seat, reaching for him. She dropped to her knees on the floor beside him.

He stared at the little boy's photograph and lifted a finger to point at him.

'Uh-oh,' he said softly. 'He's a Goner.'

9

'Will you disclose the contents of the note?'

'How does this affect the case against Dr Wright?'

'Do you believe this is the work of the same kidnapper?' 'Do you still believe Wright had an accomplice, or do you think you've got the wrong man sitting in jail?'

'When will you release the contents of the note?'

'How does this change your strategy?'

The questions echoed through Ellen's head, swam through it, whirled around it. The faces of the reporters did the same. Some were familiar, some famous, many obscure. All of them wanted the same thing. The scoop, the hot quote, the exclusive tidbit. After two weeks of covering Josh Kirkwood's abduction, they came to Dustin Holloman's as ravenous as ever, driven by ambition to grab whatever details they could.

'*I'm ambitious*,' Adam Slater had proclaimed yesterday outside the hospital. She had spotted him in the sea of faces, out on the edge, on the fringe of the mob, his young eyes bright as he soaked it all in.

Ambitious. Or maybe 'desperate' was the word. Desperate for answers. Desperate for some clue as to why the fabric of this quiet rural county was unraveling. That was what Ellen felt – a sharp, choking sense of desperation, the kind of panic that threatened to swell up and swallow her whole. It was just as strong now, as she pulled into her driveway, as it had been when she had driven away from the reporters in Campion.

Campion was a farming community of two thousand. A simple, quiet place that made Deer Lake, a half-hour drive away, seem like a teeming metropolis. A town too small and too dull to need its own police department, it contracted with the county for the use of deputies to keep things in order. The people of Campion had watched the evening news when Josh Kirkwood had been taken and reflected that the world beyond them was an increasingly dangerous place. Thank God they lived in Campion, where everyone was safe. Until tonight.

News that a child had been taken had the town reeling, stunned and confused. It was déjà vu for the volunteers who flocked over from Deer Lake. Having been through it all before, they organized search teams quickly and set up a command post in the Sons of Norway hall because it was the only place in town big enough. But, as had been the case two weeks before, there was little for the investigation to go on.

'Witnesses?' Ellen hurried toward Mitch, turning her coat collar up against the bite of the wind.

'None,' he answered, half shouting to be heard above the pounding of helicopter blades.

State patrol choppers had already begun their search, sweeping back and forth over the town in an ever-widening grid while helicopters from the Twin Cities television stations hovered over the crime scene like vultures. Campion Civic Park had been turned into a surrealistic circus ground, the barren trees and deep snow cover illuminated by portable floodlights and the colored beacons of police vehicles. Yellow crime-scene tape had been wound around saplings and fluttered in the sharp wind like banners around a used-car lot.

'The boy's older brother was supposed to be watching him,' Mitch said as Ellen fell in step beside him. 'They were all skating on the outdoor rink over there. The older boys got a hockey game going and the younger kids got pushed out. Apparently Dustin wandered away.'

He pulled a gloved hand out of his parka pocket and pushed back a lacework of small branches for Ellen to pass. 'Don't worry about where you're stepping,' he said bitterly. 'The trail the boy took has already been tramped over by sixty or seventy sets of boots.'

They skidded down a short slope Ellen could easily envision as a favorite sledding spot for smaller kids. At the bottom, the woods of the park thinned out to brush. Beyond the brush, cop cars sat, strobes twirling, tossing disks of colored light across a winding back street where the nearest house was three hundred yards away. Directly across the street from the park, the tumbledown remnants of what had once been farm buildings crouched, gray and bleak, open doorways and empty windows gaping like wounds black with rot.

Ellen's stomach clenched at the thought of being eight years old, standing in this forlorn spot, knowing you were about to be taken by a stranger.

If the kidnapper had been a stranger. They would have to question the Hollomans and the Kirkwoods, looking for any mutual acquaintances. Josh had not been taken by a stranger. Provided Garrett Wright was the man who had taken him.

She blew out a steamy breath as the doubts surfaced. She believed Wright was guilty, and even she was having second thoughts now. The press would have a field day casting doubt and muddying the waters of the potential jury pool.

'*He said it was a game.*' Megan's words came back to her, bringing a chill that had nothing to do with the falling temperature. If this was all a game to him, then taking Dustin Holloman was a brilliant and ruthless move. In addition to raising questions in the press, the search for the second missing child would take priority and consume hours of manpower from two law-enforcement agencies already investigating the Kirkwood kidnapping – the BCA and the Park County sheriff's department. The Deer Lake police would be involved because of the possible connection to their own case. They would be forced to widen the investigation because of the involvement of a whole new group of people – the Hollomans and their friends and associates and enemies. In one move their adversary had taken their team and scattered it all over the board.

'This is where they took off,' Mitch said, flashing his badge at the deputies who stood wary watch around a naked sapling on the boulevard.

Ellen let him herd her through the group to the center, foreboding pressing down on her like a great weight.

Tied around a branch of the tree was a bright-purple scarf. Crocheted by someone who loved Dustin. He had probably got it for Christmas and had probably wished it were a Power Ranger toy instead. It fluttered on the branch, an oversize ribbon marking a terrible trail. And pinned to the scarf was the note.

> *but sad as angels for the good man's SIN,*
> *weep to record and blush to give it in.*

Ellen shuddered. She couldn't get the sight of that scarf out of her mind. A small symbol of a small child snatched into a madman's game for a purpose known only to him.

He said it was a game.

But with what rules and what goal and what motivation? And what players? Virtually everyone in Deer Lake who had ever had a conversation with Garrett Wright had been questioned. His acquaintances were well-respected professional people, baffled by the turn of events that had landed him in jail. His students had rallied to support him. The faculty at Harris had nothing but respect for him. No one had uncovered or hinted at Garrett Wright being anything other than what he appeared. No secret taste for child pornography. No ties to the criminal underworld. No hidden life of satanic worship.

As his wife had said, Garrett Wright didn't so much as speed in his perfectly sensible Saab, let alone hang out with criminal types. There were precious few people on the list of Wright's known associates who looked even remotely like an accessory to kidnapping and assault.

But someone had brought Josh Kirkwood home and someone had taken Dustin Holloman away.

And she was too damn tired to try to figure it out tonight.

As Ellen reached toward the remote control for the garage door, something hit the driver's side window with all the force of a rock. Bolting sideways, a little shriek of surprise ripping up her throat, she twisted around wide-eyed to see Jay Butler Brooks looking in at her.

'You gonna sit here all night or put the car away and invite me in for coffee? I'm freezing my ass out here.'

Ellen answered him with a scathing look. It was late, she was tired, and she still had work to do before she could lapse into unconsciousness for a few hours. But as she drove the Bonneville into her garage, he sauntered in beside her as if he had every right to be there.

'Glendenning can't force me to be "accommodating" in my own home,' Ellen said, hefting her briefcase out of the car. 'As much as I may feel like one from time to time, I'm not a slave.'

'I'll take that for you,' Jay offered, reaching for the attaché. It was old leather that had taken a beating no live cow could have endured. The size of a small building, it looked as if she had packed it with granite blocks.

'No, you won't,' she said, and headed for the door that led directly into the house.

Jay hopped up on the stoop beside her and held the storm door while she dug for her keys. 'Ellen, I'd like to talk to you.'

'And I'd like to go to bed.'

He leaned ahead, into her line of vision, and gave her a slow, sexy smile, glittering with humor. 'Can we talk afterward?'

Ellen told herself disgust was what made her fumble with her keys and drop them, not the mental image of Jay Butler Brooks in her bed wearing nothing but a sheet and that smile.

'I'm in no mood for sophomoric humor, and I've had my quota of arguments for the day,' she said, letting herself into the mudroom, where Harry lay curled up on his cedar-stuffed cushion. He boomed a bark of greeting and hopped to attention, his toenails tapping out Morse code on the vinyl flooring. Ellen gave the dog an absent pat, still scowling at the man who seemed bent on invading her life. 'Why don't you go back to wherever you came from?'

'I came from Campion,' Jay said, smoothly stepping inside before she could close the door on him.

'You'd make a great Fuller Brush salesman,' Ellen muttered, toeing off her boots and setting them on the mat beside the door.

'Been there. Done that.' He pulled off his gloves and stuffed them into his coat pockets. 'My respectable old southern family ran out of respectable old southern money long before I went to college.'

He offered his hand to Harry. The golden retriever sniffed him, then slurped his big pink dog tongue along the back of Jay's knuckles. Ellen gave her pet a look that branded him a traitor and headed for the kitchen.

'So your morbid curiosity drove you to Campion,' she said to Jay. 'I'm not surprised. The plot grows thicker for you. Did you get a good, close look at the boy's mother? I would suggest Kathy Bates to play her in the movie. I thought there was a strong resemblance – but, then, she was bawling her eyes out, so it's hard to say.'

'I didn't go near the woman.' Jay stopped in the doorway between the kitchen and dining room. 'It makes me sick to think another child is going to suffer. I'm not a ghoul, Ellen, and I resent the insinuation.'

She hefted her briefcase onto a cherrywood table with graceful Queen

Anne legs, setting it down with a solid thud. 'Tough. I didn't ask you to come here. I didn't ask you into my home. And, frankly, I'm in no mood to play hostess.'

'I came to see how you were doing,' he said. 'You've had a hell of a day.'

He took in the dining room in a single look – mottled soft gold walls decorated with brass sconces and primitive portraits of eighteenth-century people. Tasteful, simple, classy. The back wall was taken up by a bay window, the center section of which was a door that probably opened onto a deck or patio. Opposite the window, a railing ran some eight or ten feet, providing a graceful spot to look down on the living room below.

'See how you've misjudged me?' He shuffled down the carpeted steps to the living room. With a flick of a switch the brass table lamps filled the room with muted light. 'I came here out of concern for you. I mean, we shared a bonding experience of sorts this afternoon, you and I. Trying to raise someone from the dead is a pretty intimate experience.'

'Yeah, we're practically blood brother and sister,' Ellen said dryly. She slipped her coat off and hung it on the back of a chair, her wary attention on the man who was intruding not only in her house but in her case. He prowled her living room like a restless cat, running a hand over the furniture as if marking the territory.

'And aside from your great concern for me,' she said, descending the stairs, 'you had no intention of coming here to try for a little inside information on the kidnapping of Dustin Holloman?'

'I can get that information from other sources. Better sources, if you want the truth.' He flipped a brass-framed switch beside the fireplace, and flames instantly leaped to life around a stack of fake logs. Neat, clean, no muss, no fuss. He turned his back to the fire, pressing his hands against the screen to absorb the warmth that was real even if the logs were not.

Ellen stood across the room from him, beside a sturdy overstuffed chair. She obviously hadn't made it home before being called to the crisis in Campion. She was still in the charcoal suit she had worn at Wright's bond hearing and Judge Franken's demise. Her hair had come down, pure, straight silk that fell artlessly to brush the tops of her shoulders. Her veneer of makeup and manners had long since worn off. She looked exhausted and short-tempered and utterly unapproachable.

But even as he saw this, he could remember the way she had looked going into the command post in the Campion Sons of Norway hall – shaken, afraid. Their bad guy had thrown them a wicked curveball, and no one had been ready for it.

'The judge on your case dies on you, another child is kidnapped while your bad guy sits in jail,' he said, coming toward her slowly. 'That's a lot to deal with.'

'Yes, and now I have to deal with you,' Ellen said, crossing her arms.

'Wondering if you're committing my every word to memory or if you've got a tape recorder in your pocket.'

'You're damned suspicious.'

'I wouldn't trust you any farther than I could throw you.'

'After I came to check up on you and convince myself of your well-being?'

'Uh-huh,' she said with no conviction.

'You can frisk me if you'd like,' he offered in that dark, sexy tone. 'But I'll warn you right now – that's *not* a tape recorder in my pocket.'

'I'll take your word for it. So now you've seen that I'm still in one piece.' She held her arms out from her sides to display the fact. 'You've done your Good Samaritan deed for the decade. You're dismissed.'

Ignoring the suggestion that he had worn out his welcome, Jay sat down on the fat arm of the overstuffed chair. He could be as deliberately obtuse as a post. It was a skill that had served him well as an attorney and more so as a writer. Persistence was the name of the game when it came to getting information.

'Do you think it's part of Wright's plan?' he asked. 'A diversionary tactic? I should have thought bringing back the Kirkwood kid accomplished that.'

'But it didn't spread out the defense,' Ellen mumbled more to herself than to Jay.

'I don't follow.'

'A football analogy. I had a law professor who used to play for the Vikings.'

'Ah. I'm a baseball man myself.'

'The offensive team shows a formation that causes the defensive team to spread themselves all over the field, inevitably creating holes for the offense to slip through.'

'Involving a whole new set of victims in another town forces the investigation to broaden instead of focusing tightly on Wright and Wright's secret pal,' Jay deduced. He gave Ellen a nod. 'Sharp thinking, counselor.'

'It's conjecture and speculation,' she said as she went to the door. 'For all I know, the kidnapping of Dustin Holloman is unrelated to the kidnapping of Josh Kirkwood.'

He thought of what he'd seen and felt in Campion tonight. The sharp metallic taste of fear, the sense that the place had somehow slipped into an alternate universe. Evil. It had been as much a presence as the police and the press. It seemed to permeate the night, dyeing it blacker, giving the wind a razor's edge. And fluttering brightly against it was a little boy's bright-purple scarf tied to the naked branch of a winter-dead tree.

He remembered thinking, *Jesus, Brooks, what have you walked into here?*

More than he had bargained for.

'I think we both know better,' he said to Ellen, slowly pushing himself away from the chair. 'The question is, how will it affect the prosecution of Wright?'

Ellen took a deep breath and let it out in a gust, leaning back against the wall, too worn-out to keep herself upright. 'Look, you're right, it's been a long day and I still have work to do, and there's no point in your staying because I'm not going to share anything with you –'

'Regarding the case or you?'

'Either.'

'I just can't win with you, can I?' He pretended frustration, his brows tugging together. But, as always, the wry amusement was there in his eyes.

Ellen steeled herself against the effect. 'Not on your best day.'

Jay weighed the wisdom of trying to press for something more but decided not to push his luck. He needed to win her over, not piss her off. He was already digging himself out of a hole after the Glendenning debacle, which he had to admit had been a major blunder on his part. Instead of smoothing the track for him, bringing in Glendenning had had the effect of throwing down a gauntlet. That's what he got for rushing into this thing, but he was in it now, a part of it. That had been the goal – to get inside.

'Good night, Mr Brooks,' she said, pulling the door open.

He shoved his hands into his coat pockets and hunched his shoulders against the mere idea of cold, casting a longing look back toward the fire. The retriever lumbered down the stairs and sauntered past him, wagging his tail but not pausing on his way to a warm spot in front of the hearth. The homeyness of the scene gave him a little unexpected kick in a spot he would have sworn was tougher.

'Well,' he drawled, moving toward the open door, 'at least the dog likes me.'

'Don't make too much of it,' Ellen advised. 'He drinks out of the toilet, too.'

He stopped in front of her. Close enough that when she looked into his eyes, she thought she saw something old and sad, like regret. *Foolish*, she told herself. He wasn't the kind of man to have regrets. He went after what he wanted and he got it, and she doubted he ever looked back.

'Good night, Ellen,' he murmured, his tone as intimate as if they had known each other for a lifetime. 'Get some rest. You've earned it.'

With his eyes on hers, he leaned down and kissed her cheek. Not a quick, impersonal peck, but a soft, warm, intimate pressing of his lips against her skin, seducing her to turn toward him and invite the kiss to her lips. The idea sent quicksilver tremors through her and triggered a flood of forbidden questions. What would it be like to feel that incredible mouth of his –

She slammed the mental door on the vision, bringing herself back to the moment, embarrassed that a simple kiss on the cheek could quicken her pulse and send her common sense spinning off its axis. The knowing look on Brooks's face was enough to make her want to slam the door on him.

'Sweet dreams, Ellen,' he whispered, and sauntered out into the night.

Ellen stood in the open doorway, hugging herself against the cold as she watched him cross the street and climb into a dark Jeep Cherokee. The engine roared to life and he was gone, though the uneasy restlessness he had awakened in her lingered.

He kept her off balance – charming one minute, concerned the next, then seductive, then mercenary. Even the article she had read about him had alluded to 'contradictions within him that were not easily reconciled'. She thought of Phoebe's assessment of his turbulent aura hinting at inner turmoil and raw sexuality. She wondered who he really was, and told herself she didn't need to know. All she needed to know was not to trust him.

Who can you trust?

Trust no one.

Trust no one. The idea made her feel hollow and ill. By nature she wanted to trust. She wanted to feel safe. She wanted to believe those things were still possible, but the evidence didn't back her up. Another child was missing, and she was suddenly surrounded by people she didn't dare turn her back on – Brooks, Rudy, Glendenning, Garrett Wright.

Judge Franken's death suddenly took on symbolic proportions. He was the last honorable man. He was justice, and his death was the death of an era.

'Good Lord, Ellen.' She chastised herself for being melodramatic, but the fear remained within her that her world had changed and there would be no going back.

To distract herself, she stepped out onto the porch in her stocking feet to dig her mail out of the box that hung beside the door. Bills, sweepstakes, a month-late Christmas card from her sister, Jill, more sweepstakes. Junk.

She reached in once more, her fingertips brushing something that had got jammed down into the bottom of the box. Making a face, she twisted her hand in the narrow confines, just catching hold of the corner of the paper. She pulled it out, expecting yet another sale flyer. What she got stopped her heart cold.

A crumpled slip of white paper with bold black print.

it ain't over till it's over

10

'He quotes Oliver Wendell Holmes, Robert Browning, William Blake, Thomas Campbell, and *Yogi Berra*?' Cameron said, settling into a chair at the long table with a raisin bagel in one hand and a cup of Phoebe's Kona blend in the other. 'It doesn't follow. Has to be a copycat.'

At eight in the morning the conference room was as cold as a meat locker. In a move of fiscal responsibility, the county commissioners had determined it unnecessary to keep the heat in the courthouse above fifty degrees at night. It took the building half the day to warm up. Everyone in the room had hands wrapped around a coffee mug.

'Or one of Wright's supporters,' Rudy offered. He had claimed the head of the table for his own. After spending two days in the wake of Bill Glendenning's powerful aura, he felt a rise in his own sense of power. He was in Glendenning's good graces, relatively safe on the sidelines of this case, and Victor Franken had finally croaked, obligingly vacating his seat on the bench. All may not have been right with the world, but Rudy Stovich didn't personally have a lot to complain about.

'It could have been one of Wright's students,' Mitch said, his lack of inflection subtly giving away his doubts. He had declined the offer of a chair, opting instead to slowly pace the length of the table. Operating on too little sleep and too much stress, he was fueling his system with high-test caffeine and sugar doughnuts. 'Ellen, you said you had a run-in yesterday with the Sci-Fi Cowboys. What's your feeling?'

'I don't know,' she said, picking at a blueberry muffin. She was exhausted. Two nights with a total of eight hours' sleep left her feeling heavy and slow, as if the air around her was as dense as water. 'Yesterday's mail was on top of it in the box, so I'd say the note had to be there before two o'clock yesterday afternoon.' She was repeating the theory she had told last night to one cop and then another and another. 'If it was one of the Cowboys, they had to have run straight to my house after I saw them.'

'My guys will be canvassing your neighbors this morning asking if they saw anyone around your house yesterday.'

And they would probably learn nothing. Her neighbors were professional people, with daytime jobs downtown or at Harris or in Minneapolis. There was always the chance someone had been home with the flu that was going around and had glanced out the window at the right moment, but she felt no hope for that. What she felt was a sense of disquiet that had been lingering since Monday.

Monday night kept coming back to her – waking suddenly, Harry growling, the silent phone call, then the call that Josh was home.

She recited it all for Mitch, step by step, half-embarrassed to be saying it at all. From an objective, rational perspective, nothing had happened. There had been no intruder in her home. The call had probably been a wrong number. But the timing of all that 'nothing' made her uneasy.

Mitch stopped his pacing and faced her, pressing his palms flat on the table. 'Is your home number listed?'

'Under my initials – E. E. North.'

'I got a call myself last night,' he confessed. 'On my cellular phone – a number only a few people have access to. The caller whispered, "Ignorance is not innocence, but sin." Right after he hung up, I got the word about the abduction in Campion.'

Rudy looked alarmed. 'Are you saying this lunatic is someone you know?'

'No.' Mitch shook his head, his mouth twisting. 'Our boy had the balls to call my mother-in-law and weasel the number out of her. I was just thinking, if he had to finagle Ellen's number out of someone, we'd have two people who might possibly be able to identify his voice.'

Cameron looked at Ellen with concern. 'Why didn't you say anything about this call yesterday?'

'I dismissed it as nerves. Josh came home. I've been busy with the case; I didn't think about it again – until I found the note. Even now I'm not sure it was anything. I mean, you're probably right – Yogi Berra is hardly Wright's style.'

'But it might be his partner's style,' Mitch argued. 'Or it might be his idea of a joke. I'm no expert, but that note sure looked like the others.'

'But the press made public the fact that the kidnapper's notes were on common twenty-pound bond and came out of a laser printer,' Cameron said, automatically playing devil's advocate. 'Any nut with access to a laser printer could have done it.'

'True, but the press didn't actually see the notes, the type font, the preference for lower-case letters.' He straightened away from the table, pulling his parka off the back of the chair where he had abandoned it earlier. 'We'll see what the lab boys have to say. In the meantime, we'll check with your neighbors,' he said to Ellen. 'One of them might have seen a kidnapper.'

He didn't look as if he believed that any more than she did, Ellen thought. Hope had become a scarce commodity. 'What's the latest word from Campion?'

' "Help," ' he answered, shrugging into his coat. 'They don't have a damn thing to go on. We've set up a multijurisdictional team of my people, guys from Steiger's office, and the BCA to work on connections.

So far, there aren't any. The Hollomans don't know the Kirkwoods, Hannah isn't their doctor, Paul isn't their accountant, the boys have never met. Dustin and Josh share some physical traits – light hair, blue eyes, same age. That would be more significant if this were a sexual–predator thing, but it doesn't appear to be. It's some kind of goddamn chess game.'

Rudy pushed his chair back and rose, hiking up his baggy suit pants by the belt. 'Be sure to keep us abreast of the developments, Mitch,' he said importantly.

'Yeah, I'll do that. If there are any. Ellen, I want you to call the department if you have any more odd happenings. It may be our boy or not. Wright has a lot of supporters. They may not all confine their anger to the picket line in front of the courthouse. You're a likely target.'

'Thanks for reminding me,' Ellen said sardonically, then remembered Megan. Megan, who was lying in a hospital bed because of this case. She could have as easily been dead. If the note had come from Wright's accomplice, then that could mean she had been singled out for inclusion in the game, as Megan had been singled out.

'Did anyone tell you Karen Wright went home yesterday?' Mitch asked, backing toward the door.

'Home – as in down the block from the Kirkwoods?' Cameron said, appalled.

'It's the only home she's got,' Mitch said. 'The BCA was through with the place, and the city council was making noise about the cost of putting her up at the Fontaine, so we took her home.'

'What about the accomplice?' Cameron asked. 'If Karen knows something, she could be in danger.'

'The BCA has a man on her. We should be so lucky that this creep is stupid enough to come calling.'

'I'm concerned with her mental health,' Ellen said. 'Is she staying alone?'

'She has friends looking in on her, and Teresa McGuire, the victim-witness coordinator, is checking on her and reporting back to my office. Still hoping she'll turn on Wright?'

'She might have an attack of conscience.'

'I wouldn't count on it, counselor. Denial is pretty tough armor.'

Cameron turned to Rudy as Mitch made his exit and Ellen stuck her head out the door to call for more coffee. 'Any word on who'll get the case with Franken gone?'

'None yet. They may delay the whole thing until a replacement is named,' Rudy said, then frowned, worrying suddenly that his connection to this case, as much as he had tried to minimize it, would somehow jeopardize his chances for appointment to Franken's seat.

'If that happens, we can count on Wright's lawyer raising a stink,' Ellen said.

She walked back along the length of the table slowly, her eyes scanning the mountains of paperwork the case had already generated – piles of statements, search warrants, arrest warrants, police reports. She and Cameron had commandeered this conference room for their own war room, where they could lay everything out and study it. A replica of the time line in the law-enforcement center was taped to one peeling dark-salmon wall.

Lying across a stack of news clippings was the morning *Star Tribune* opened to a photo of Jay Butler Brooks scowling at the camera. The headline read ' *"Crime Boss" Fights to Save Judge.'* Ellen tossed it onto the credenza. Behind it dusty, hot air from the vents blew straight up along the old window, where eighty percent of the heat escaped through the glass.

'By law Wright is entitled to that hearing without delay,' she said. 'I bet they'll divvy up Judge Franken's caseload between Witt and Grabko and float another judge in here to catch the overflow until the governor names a replacement.'

Rudy breathed a sigh of relief. 'Who *is* Wright's attorney now?'

Cameron shrugged.

Ellen shook her head. 'I'm going to see Dennis later. Maybe he'll know something we don't.'

'You can bet he knows something we don't,' Cameron said darkly. 'Rumor has it he had a long talk with his client after the bond hearing yesterday and that he left the jail looking sick.'

'He'd just lost a client and a chance for a lot of publicity,' Rudy pointed out.

Cameron reserved comment, his gaze steady on Ellen.

'I'll find out what I can,' she said. 'But how much can he tell me without committing a breach of ethics?'

'How much can he keep to himself without committing a breach of decency?'

'Let me know what you find out,' Rudy instructed. 'Where do we stand as far as ammunition for this hearing?'

'We've got the statements from Mitch and from Megan O'Malley regarding her abduction and that whole drama,' Cameron said. 'We won't have the DNA results back on the bloody sheet Wright wrapped around her that night, but we've already got the blood types – one of which is the same as O'Malley's and one of which is the same as Josh's.'

'Regarding O'Malley's situation,' Ellen said, 'as you know, Wright was apprehended fleeing the scene. To paraphrase Megan, we've got him dead to rights.'

'But what about the boy's case? So far, we've got a victim who's not talking.'

'We've got Ruth Cooper, the witness who identified Wright in the lineup as being the man she saw on Ryan's Bay the day Josh Kirkwood's jacket was found,' Cameron said.

Rudy made a rumbling sound in his throat that might have been discontent or phlegm. 'I was there. The lineup was wearing parkas and sunglasses. A good defense attorney is going to take it apart like Tinkertoys.'

'The visual may be iffy,' Ellen conceded, 'but you'll remember, Mrs Cooper also made a voice ID. The two together will be hard to discount.'

'We've also got Agent O'Malley's testimony as to what Wright confessed to her regarding Josh,' Cameron pointed out.

'He said, she said,' Rudy grumbled.

'She's a police officer.'

'She's a victim. Hardly an impartial hearsay witness.'

Ellen tipped her head. 'Maybe, maybe not. I think her credentials will carry her through.'

'Wright knows the Kirkwood family,' Cameron went on. 'And he has a flimsy alibi for the time Josh disappeared. He claims he was at his office working that night, but so far that's just his say-so.'

'So what's his motive?' Rudy asked.

'We don't have one, other than that he's playing some kind of sick game,' Ellen said. 'All we have to do for the moment is get him bound over. We don't need a motive until trial. We have to bear in mind that Wright wasn't even a suspect until Saturday night. The investigation is really just beginning.'

Rudy ambled to the window and looked down on the early shift of protestors gathering on the sidewalk.

'It sounds like you've got everything under control, Ellen,' he said, glancing at her from the corner of his eye.

Rumors had been churning for months that the yuppies of Park County were looking to root him out of office and replace him with Ellen North. When he moved into Franken's seat, the path would be clear for her. She and her backers likely saw this case as her chance to step into the limelight, but limelight wouldn't be the only thing she would step in. He pulled in a deep, cleansing breath and envisioned his judgeship, so close, he could feel his new black robes draping over him.

'You know, I'm just an old country lawyer at heart,' he said. 'When I came on this job, there was no such thing as a high-profile case. Folks around here didn't lock their doors. They let their kids run all over town without worrying about them. Deer Lake was the kind of town America is supposed to be all about.'

Ellen recognized the speech immediately. He had used it as his closing statement in a drug dealer's trial eighteen months ago. He heaved an exaggerated sigh and twisted his features into the expression of a sad clown.

'Do your best, Ellen,' he instructed. 'Always let your constituents know you did your best.'

'Rudy, I've told you a hundred times, I have no intention of running for your office.'

And for the hundred and first time he didn't listen. The irony was too much. Her ambition topped out right where she was. She had no political aspirations, had thought leaving Hennepin County had been a clear statement to that effect. Yet, in the place she had come to settle herself into a comfortable niche, she was constantly viewed with suspicious eyes as being an ambitious woman with her sights on bigger things.

'Yes, well . . .,' he said, sauntering away.

As he opened the door, Phoebe popped in, coffeepot in hand.

'Garrett Wright has a new attorney.' Her face glowed with the excitement of it all. She set the coffeepot on the table, unable to give the announcement adequate fanfare without using her hands. 'A *big* big shot,' she said, bracelets rattling. 'Anthony Costello.'

Cameron gave a low whistle. 'Wow. Where'd Wright get that kind of money? Costello's retainer is more than a professor at Harris makes in a year.'

'That was my question, too,' Phoebe said, sliding into the chair next to him, settling in for a round of juicy speculation.

'It doesn't matter who his lawyer is.' Rudy spouted false confidence like a fountain, the promise of his judgeship making him magnanimous. 'We've got the team to beat him. Isn't that right, Ellen? Ellen?'

Ellen jerked her head in Rudy's direction, feeling faint. 'Yes, of course.'

Her voice sounded far away to her, as if it had come from someone out in the hall. Her hands were curled over the back of a chair, fingertips digging into the upholstery.

'Wright can bring in his big-shot lawyer from the Cities. We've got Ellen,' Rudy declared as he marched off down the hall, thanking God he had dropped this hot potato in Ellen North's lap.

'Did you ever come up against Costello when you were with Hennepin County?' Cameron asked.

'A few times.'

She imagined if she was to look in a mirror, her reflection would be pale and wide-eyed, but neither Phoebe nor Cameron seemed to notice anything odd about her appearance or her manner. She pulled out the chair and slid into it. Her body seemed to be working independently of her mind, and thank God for that. In her mind she was floundering, scrambling, knocked off balance by a blind-side shot.

Tony Costello's was not a name she had ever expected to hear in these offices. He was big money, style and flash, one of the top defense attorneys in the Twin Cities and rapidly making a name for himself on a larger scale. Which was, of course, what he would be doing with Garrett Wright – soaking up publicity like a sponge, posing for the cameras and preaching his propaganda of justice for the common man.

That was why he had taken Garrett Wright's case, Ellen told herself. It had nothing to do with the fact that she was the prosecutor, and it certainly had nothing to do with the fact that they had once been lovers.

Garrett Wright couldn't have known anything about her past with

Tony Costello. It was just a coincidence that he had chosen the one defense attorney in the state who knew her better than any other, the one who had slipped under her guard and stabbed her in the back.

Even as she tried to placate herself, the tide of the uneasiness that had been with her since Monday night rose a little higher inside her.

'*We've calculated all the moves, all the options, all the possibilities*,' Garrett Wright had whispered to Megan. '*We can't lose*.'

'We can't lose,' Anthony Costello said, his voice clear and strong, his eyes on the network cameras. 'Dr Wright is an innocent man, wrongfully accused and wrongfully imprisoned.'

Shutters clicked. Motor drives whirred. Cameras loved his face – square, rugged, utterly masculine, perpetually tanned. His eyes were the color of espresso, set deep beneath the ledge of his brow. He had long ago perfected a piercing stare that could make witnesses crumble and jurors sway.

He stood on the front steps of the Campion Sons of Norway hall, the wind ruffling his jet-black hair. The cameras had to shoot up to get him, an angle that made him look taller than five feet ten and emphasized the solid squareness of his build and the excellent hand-tailored cut of his black wool topcoat. He would have preferred to make his first statements to the press regarding his new client in front of the Park County courthouse because he liked the symbolism of storming the halls of justice, but the press was in Campion covering the second child abduction, so he had gone with Plan B. It was the mark of a good defense attorney to be flexible, to be adaptable. He had to be able to shift on the run, think on his feet.

He had begun to formulate a strategy for the defense the moment he had accepted Garrett Wright as a client. He wanted to strike hard and fast at the media, grab their attention and keep it on him. The kidnapping of Dustin Holloman was a terrible tragedy, but Costello had also seen it immediately as the opportunity it was. Naturally, he felt sympathy for the family – in the way one might feel sympathy for fictional characters in a movie. He couldn't allow the feeling to become more personal than that. It was essential for him to put their tragedy in a perspective that would potentially be of some benefit to his client.

'My client sits in jail, his reputation suffering more with every passing hour, while a madman stalks the children of Park County,' he said. 'The investigation of the kidnapping in Deer Lake was mishandled from the start. As a result, there have been needless deaths, an innocent man has been incarcerated, and now another family has been torn apart.'

The reporters clamored for his attention, barking out questions, thrusting microphones up at him. He gave the answer he wanted to give, not caring whether the question had been asked.

'I'm here in Park County to see that justice will be done.' Sound bite extraordinaire. 'I'm here in Campion as an emissary for my client, to offer his deepest concern to the family of little Dustin Holloman. I know Dr Wright would want me to extend a personal plea to the kidnappers to return Dustin unharmed.'

He knew no such thing, of course. He had yet to speak directly to Garrett Wright. It was unlikely Wright had even heard about the kidnapping. For all Costello knew, Wright was a coldhearted son of a bitch who wouldn't have felt a second's pity if all the children in Campion were torn from their families and carted off to concentration camps. It didn't matter. As of this moment the press would look upon his client as a compassionate man with a deep, abiding respect for families, for the law, for America.

'Who do you blame for botching the Kirkwood investigation?'

He frowned in the general direction of the reporter who had shouted the question. 'I think there's blame enough to go around, don't you?'

Not having paid close attention to the case from the outset, he had spent six hours last night going over news clippings from both major dailies in Minneapolis and St Paul. He had watched videos of newscasts and interviews, absorbing as much as he could about the principal players, though he wasn't ready yet to single any one out for public castigation.

The female BCA agent was sleeping with the chief of police. A convicted pedophile had been working at the ice arena, then killed himself while in custody. A mummified cadaver had been found in the garage of a church deacon who had eluded capture for two days, then fell to his death before he could be apprehended. There were enough plot twists for a soap opera – which was exactly what had caught the attention of the networks and the tabloids. Immune to everyday crime, they sought the sensational, the kind of stuff writers were paid for in Hollywood. It was so much cheaper to get it from real life.

'But though there has been a gross miscarriage of justice,' Costello went on, 'I want it made clear that Dr Wright himself bears no grudges. He still has trust in our justice system and faith that the truth will out and he will be exonerated – just as we all must have faith that the kidnapper of Dustin Holloman and Josh Kirkwood will be found and punished; that justice will be swift and sure.'

On that glorious note, Costello stepped down from his impromptu podium and moved quickly through the crowd toward his waiting black Lincoln Town Car, his staff clearing the path for him. He had brought with him an associate, a legal assistant, and a personal assistant who was also his driver. Another of his associates had been sent ahead to Deer Lake for the purpose of leasing an office suite. It would be far inferior to his offices in the IDS tower in downtown Minneapolis, but it would serve the purpose. He believed it was important to establish a presence, like a show of muscle before a fight. It would also be easier to have a base of operations in the town rather than try to do everything long-distance. By the end of the day, the Deer Lake office would have a full complement of business machines and one of his secretaries would be hard at work.

'Excellent presentation, Mr Costello,' Dorman said. A fellow Purdue alumnus, Dorman was twenty-seven, sharp but not ambitious, more interested in being secure than in being famous; comfortable to learn at Costello's elbow, work like a dog, and take none of the credit – all of which made him ideal for his job.

Costello chose his people carefully, with just such things in mind. He accepted no associates with Ivy League educations because he had not been able to afford one himself, and he did not want any snotty, silver-spoon rich kids who felt they were socially superior to him. Nor did he want his office projecting an image of elitism. He was himself the product of a middle-class, blue-collar upbringing, and proud of it.

In choosing associates, he hired primarily family men, none of them taller than he was. Sensitive to society's current mania for political correctness, he had peppered his staff with an assortment of women and minorities. Levine, the legal assistant who sat in the front seat ahead of him, was an equal-opportunity triple score – a black, Jewish woman. He was careful to select female staff members who were neither unattractive nor beautiful.

Everything in the offices of Anthony Costello – from plants to personnel – had been selected by Costello to showcase Costello. That was the way image was made, and in today's world image was everything. Image was perceived as success. Success bred greater success. Success opened the doors of opportunity that led to fame. Opportunity had to be seized and wrung out for all it was worth.

Levine turned sideways in her seat and handed a neatly folded copy of the *St Paul Pioneer Press* back to him. 'Here's the article on the death of Judge Franken, Mr Costello.'

The story was situated directly below the continuation of the front-page piece concerning Garrett Wright's bond hearing, as if one event had led to the other. A photograph the size of a postage stamp portrayed Franken in his robes. He looked like an apple-head doll that had begun to rot. A second, much larger photo depicted the chaos in the courtroom where Franken had died – a group of people huddled over an indistinct form on the floor. The focus of the picture was on one familiar face that had turned to glare at the cameras. Jay Butler Brooks.

Costello hummed a note to himself. A Cheshire-cat smile creased the corners of his mouth.

'I've got a call in to the district assignments clerk,' Dorman said, 'to find out what kind of delay we can expect.'

'Don't be passive, Dorman,' Costello said. 'We won't *expect* a delay. We'll demand there be none.'

His associate's brows rose, a pair of beige hyphens barely discernible from his skin tone. 'We could use the extra time to prepare.'

'The prosecution would use the extra time to prepare,' Costello clarified. 'Wright was arrested Saturday night. Prior to his arrest, he had not been a suspect. I can guarantee you the county attorney's office is scrambling to put their case together. Should we allow them extra time to do that, Mr Dorman?'

'No, sir.'

'No, sir,' he echoed, his gaze drifting out the window, his memory drifting back in time. 'Hit 'em hard, hit 'em fast,' he murmured. 'We'll have this case dismissed before Ellen North can turn around.'

11

'But though there has been a gross miscarriage of justice, I want it made clear that Dr Wright himself bears no grudges. He still has trust in our justice system, and faith that the truth will out and he will be exonerated – just as we all must have faith that the kidnapper of Dustin Holloman and Josh Kirkwood will be found and punished; that justice will be swift and sure.'

Jay clicked off the nineteen-inch color television that sat on the carton it had come in. Costello vanished, but the smell of his game lingered like bad gas. Jay knew the game plan well enough. He had employed it himself in his brief life as a defense attorney. Costello would attack where and when he could, create opportunities if he had to. He would paint a glowing portrait of his client that would bear only a passing resemblance to the man and slam the opposition with every kind of accusation he could think of. It was a game of diversion that tied in quite neatly with the kidnappers', as it happened. Nice coincidence that they were all on the same team.

He took a last deep drag off his cigarette and threw the butt into the fireplace that was gray with the dust of ashes long since swept away.

His sudden pilgrimage to Deer Lake had left him without many options in the way of accommodations. There wasn't a hotel room to be had for miles; all of them were filled with reporters. Furnished apartments were the domain of Harris College students, who were just returning to classes after their winter break. Impatient and unconcerned with the cost, he had taken this house.

He needed to work, to immerse himself in a world that had no connection with the life he had so abruptly left in Alabama. It didn't matter what it cost him in terms of cash. He would have paid anything to make the fresh memories fade into oblivion. Lobotomy and alcoholism, while they would certainly have dulled the pain, were not viable alternatives. Work was the best thing he could find. Why he had chosen this particular case in which to lose himself was a question he chose to ignore.

'And you don't find that just the least bit twisted? Escaping into someone else's real-life tragedy?'

It's just a story. He repeated to himself the pat answer he had given

527

Ellen, knowing there was more. Still, he clung to the lie for his own sanity's sake.

The case was timely and fascinating. Writing about it was his job, and he was damn good at it. And so he had come to Deer Lake . . .

With such blind, desperate haste that he hadn't packed much more than a change of underwear.

Dismissing the temptation to self-analyze, he turned his attention to his surroundings. Overpriced by Deer Lake standards, the house had been on the market long enough that the owners had gratefully accepted three months' exorbitant rent and turned over the keys and the burden of heating the place.

As yet, he had been unsuccessful in warming it up. Even with the thermostat cranked into the seventies, the rooms seemed cold, as if furniture and family were required for the warmth to stay instead of sailing up through the roof to be swallowed greedily by the cold. He had set himself up entirely in the living room, because the huge stone fireplace at least *suggested* warmth. Unfortunately, the owners had seen fit to take all fireplace tools and accoutrements with them, including the grate. There wasn't so much as a stick of kindling or a kitchen match, let alone a neat stack of fake logs ready to glow with the flick of a switch.

He stood and tried to stretch the kinks out of his back that had set in from sleeping in a sleeping bag on the floor. His gaze did a slow scan of the room, automatically comparing it to Ellen's cozy living room. Here there was only emptiness and impermanence. Instead of overstuffed armchairs, he had badly strung lawn chairs that had been left in the garage. Instead of a cherrywood coffee table, he had a pair of eight-foot fold-down rent-all tables with fake wood-grain tops. Instead of folk art and potted plants, he had leased office equipment – a laser printer, copier, fax-and-answering machine. The tables were strewn with file folders and news clippings. His laptop computer sat open and ready, its screen blank, waiting for him to fill it with the words that would bring this story to life for the hundreds of thousands of people who read his books.

He turned away from it and went to the kitchen for a fresh cup of coffee – from the coffeemaker that sat beside the box it had come in. He had stocked the cupboards with paper plates and cups, the refrigerator with beer, the freezer with pizzas and frozen entrées. Since his divorce five years previous, he had left cuisine to restaurant chefs. Cooking a meal for himself only reminded him he had no one to share it with.

Not that he missed Christine. He occasionally mourned the loss of the girl she had once been – pretty, sweet, undemanding. The wife who had left him was another matter. In retrospect they had been mismatched from the first. Christine had a deep-seated need for stability; he was impetuous and reckless. The bright, hot love that had sprung up between them had quickly cooled and soured to frustration. Frustration fostered resentment. Resentment bred pain. With pain came disillusionment.

And hate. She must have hated me. She must still.

528

The thoughts he had been trying to hold at bay for the last week crept in. They were never far from the surface when he was tired. He cursed his ex-wife for coming back into his life for those few days last week, however accidental their meeting might have been. He had long been over Christine, but he didn't know that he would ever get over what she had done to him without his consent or knowledge.

In his mind's eye he saw the boy standing beside her with his thick shock of brown hair and sky-blue eyes.

She must have hated me. She must still.

Sipping at the coffee that was strong enough to take the finish off the kitchen cabinets, he wandered through the empty dining room and back to his base of operations.

With four bedrooms, three baths, and a living room with a two-story cathedral ceiling, the house was certainly more than he needed, but not more than he was accustomed to. His home on the outskirts of Eudora was twice this size, a reproduction plantation-era mansion that made the Brookses' ancestral home look like a tacky bungalow. He had built it to impress and to inspire jealousy and to flaunt his success in the faces of the people who had always pegged him as his generation's Bad Brooks, destined to dereliction and drunkenness. He lived in a fraction of it, and the ostentation of the place meant nothing to him on a personal level. He would have been just as satisfied living in a two-bedroom apartment.

He wasn't sure what that meant, considering he had never in his life felt satisfied. There had been a restlessness within him since boyhood and before. All his life his mother had taken great delight in complaining about what a restless baby he had been, so impatient to be born he had come two weeks early and hadn't bothered to wait for the doctor.

'You hit the ground running, boy,' Uncle Hooter had often said.

Unfortunately, in all his Johnnie Walker wisdom, Uncle Hooter had never given any indication of where or what he was supposed to be running to. *Trouble* had been the general consensus, and Jay had borne that out well enough. He had been a burden and a blight on the Brooks family name more times than he could count, and yet he always managed to come out smelling like a rose in the end, always twisting disaster into irony.

He was the Brooks who had broken windows and minor laws and major traditions. The one who had forsaken Auburn – the Brooks-family alma mater since Christ was an undergraduate – for a baseball scholarship at Purdue. He was the one who had turned his nose up at the venerable old Brooks-family law practice, the one whose wife had left him. But he was also the Brooks who had made a fortune and a name for himself, the Brooks who was courted by New York and Hollywood and had his face either on the cover or the inside of every known magazine in America. He was the black sheep whose exploits the family had criticized with relish, whose fame they accepted grudgingly, whose money they took without qualm.

There was a book in there somewhere, but he had no desire to write it. He preferred digging for skeletons in the closets of perfect strangers, trying to make some sense of the twists and snags in their lives. And so he had come to Deer Lake.

. . . you're a mercenary profiteer no better than a vampire . . . a hack looking to steal the lives and pain of real people to compensate for your own lack of a real imagination.

Ellen's words echoed sharply in his mind. He told himself they didn't matter, that what she thought couldn't matter to him because he couldn't allow himself to get involved with her. He was here for a purpose, and it wasn't having sex with Ellen North.

He stood at the big windows that rose to a peak in the main wall of the living room and stared out at the harsh white landscape. Ryan's Bay, the realtor had called it, though it wasn't a bay at all but an area of sloughs out on the edge of nothing, west of the part of Deer Lake known to locals as Dinkytown. Whatever water the 'bay' held lay secret beneath the dunes of snow, a frozen desert, bleak and uninviting. Blond weeds and cattail stalks rose through the drifts to flutter in the bitter wind.

The nearest house was a quarter mile off to the north, hidden by a thick stand of pine trees. To the east he could see the last Deer Lake neighborhood that straggled out to the edge of the marsh and farm fields, small square houses with smoke curling up from their chimneys into the winter-white sky. The spires of St Elysius Catholic Church rose above the rooftops, a pair of lances thrusting toward heaven. They seemed a long way from where he stood, though he reckoned it wasn't more than three quarters of a mile. There was a sense of isolation here that had little to do with distance.

Josh Kirkwood's jacket had been found out here, tucked in the weeds just off a trail used for snowmobiling and cross-country skiing. An older woman named Ruth Cooper had gone out with her dog to let him run, even though the windchill factor that day had clocked in at fifty degrees below zero. The Labrador had dragged the jacket up from the weeds, and Ryan's Bay had become the focus of the search and the media.

Jay could very clearly remember the news footage of Paul Kirkwood falling to his knees in the snow, his son's coat clutched in his hands while he sobbed. '*Oh my God, Josh! Josh! Oh God! No!*'

He could still hear the anguish, could feel it run through him like a pike. For a fleeting second he put himself in Paul Kirkwood's place and imagined the kind of wild, hot panic that would tear through him if all he had left of his own son was a jacket and a madman's twisted message.

The emotion hit him with physical force, punishing, crushing. Nine times sharper than the pain he had brought here with him. He pushed it away, cursing himself for a masochist. He didn't need to feel what these people felt, he only needed to capture it on paper.

With that squarely at the forefront of his mind, he abandoned his coffee, grabbed his coat, and headed for the door.

The accounting firm of Christianson and Kirkwood was housed in a new two-story square brick building that bore the grandiose name of The Omni Complex. According to the list of tenants in the foyer, the building also housed a real-estate agency, an insurance agency, and a pair of small law firms. Christianson and Kirkwood was located on the second floor.

Jay walked up, found the oak door with the appropriate stenciling job, and let himself into the outer office, which looked like a thousand other outer offices he had been in – white walls hung with pseudo-southwestern artwork, the requisite potted palm, nondescript furnishings of oak and oatmeal-colored upholstery. A secretary with flame-red hair looked up questioningly from her computer terminal and gave a little jolt of recognition.

'Is Mr Kirkwood in?' Jay asked, flashing a smile. 'Name's Jay Butler Brooks. I'd take a minute or two of his time if he's free.'

The secretary sucked in a little gasp of breath, her blue eyes round as silver dollars in her freckled face. Apparently rendered speechless, she popped up from her chair and disappeared into Paul Kirkwood's office. Jay eyed the small sofa that had likely been picked more for the decor than comfort, and stayed on his feet. His own face stared up at him from the cover of an outdated *People* magazine on the oak coffee table. *Crime Czar: Jay Butler Brooks Pens Arresting True Crime And Makes A Killing In The Process. People's* penchant for puns never failed to make him cringe.

'Mr Brooks.' A handsome smile turned Paul Kirkwood's mouth as he strode out of his office. 'It's a pleasure to meet you.'

Jay closed the distance between them. 'I have a regrettable habit of dropping in on people. I hope this isn't an inconvenient time.'

'No, not at all.' Kirkwood met Jay's handshake automatically, but his grip was uncertain. 'Come on into my office. Would you like coffee, Mr Brooks?'

'No thanks.' Jay said.

While Paul gave instructions for privacy to his secretary, Jay took a moment to survey the room, looking for clues about Josh's father. As in the outer office, the furnishings were oak with smooth rounded modern lines. A framed print of wood ducks hung on one dark-green wall. Another displayed diplomas and certificates. The office was neat and tidy – compulsively so. If not for the open file on the desk, he would have thought he had walked into a display in a furniture store. The only sign of Paul Kirkwood living here was the neatly folded green-plaid blanket on the sofa.

'I read in the paper about your performing CPR on Judge Franken,' Paul said as he entered the office and closed the door behind him. He was clean-shaven, his pin-striped white shirt neatly pressed, the crease in his brown trousers sharp. 'What a strange and unpleasant happening that must have been.'

'Imagine how the judge must have felt about it,' Jay said dryly. A framed photograph in the bookcase caught his eye: Josh in a too-big baseball uniform, Paul kneeling beside him with a proud and silly grin on his lean, handsome face. The image caught Jay unaware.

'Josh is quite the little athlete, huh?' he asked, nodding to the photo. 'Baseball, hockey. He was at hockey the night he was abducted, right?'

'Yes. He plays wing on his Squirts team. Hannah was supposed to pick him up that night, but she got hung up at the hospital . . .'

He spoke carefully, trying to keep the accusation out of his voice, but a hint of it remained like a phantom coffee stain that wouldn't come out of a shirt. The feeling had become dyed into the fabric of the answer.

'I'm sorry for your pain,' Jay said. 'I can only imagine the toll this all has taken on you and your wife. And then to have the perpetrator turn out to be someone you knew and trusted . . . Must have been one hell of a shock.'

'You don't know the half of it,' Paul muttered.

'Let me tell you what I'm doing here, Mr Kirkwood.'

Jay walked around behind the desk and glanced out the narrow window that overlooked the parking lot full of cars crusted in winter grime.

'What's gone on here, what's going to go on here in bringing this case to trial, has caught the interest of the nation,' he said, turning around. 'A crime like this one in a small town touches a lot of nerves. If a crime like this can happen here in Deer Lake, Minnesota, then it can happen anywhere. People want to feel they have some understanding of why that is and what they might do to prevent it.'

'You want to do a book about Josh's kidnapping.'

'Possibly. Probably. It's an intriguing story. Complicated. Compelling. I imagine it will prove to be only more so as the trial unfolds.'

'And you'd like to make some kind of deal?'

Jay looked up from his examination of the items meticulously arranged on the desk. There were dollar signs in Paul Kirkwood's deep-set hazel eyes.

'Deal?' Jay said, playing dumb.

Kirkwood shrugged. '*Inside Edition* offered me a hundred thousand.'

And you're waiting for me to up the ante, Jay thought. He had been through it all before. Sometimes victims threw him out of their houses, outraged at the very idea of a book about their ordeal, and sometimes they wanted him to compensate them for their suffering as if he had perpetrated the crime himself for the sole purpose of setting the scene for a book. And then there were the Paul Kirkwoods of the world. Paul Kirkwood had greed oozing out of his pores like sweat. *And Ellen thinks I'm the profiteer . . .*

'I don't do deals, Mr Kirkwood. What I write is not a biography. This story will involve many people. If I grant any one of them a portion of the book, then I run the risk of having the story slanted to reflect their view of things. Contrary to what some might believe, I have ethics and I do apply them.'

'And your "ethics" don't include sharing the millions you'll make on a book?' Paul scowled at him, a look that was more petulance than menace. 'I fail to see how you can publish a book about events in someone's life without compensating them.'

'It's like this, Mr Kirkwood: the crime, the trial, that's all a matter of public record. If you choose to talk to me, then I may include your point of view. If you choose not to, then I'm forced to form opinions based on the testimony of others and the records of the events that have taken place. It's your call.'

'It's *my life*,' Paul snapped.' I deserve –'

Jay narrowed his eyes.

'Josh is my son,' he said, scrambling to cover his mistake. 'He deserves something from this.'

Jay had made up his mind on that issue before he'd even climbed onto the plane to come to Minnesota. He would set up a trust for Josh, as he had for other victims whose stories he had told. A sizable chunk of the book advance and royalties would go into it. This was his standard procedure, a practice he kept absolutely out of the press, for the obvious reasons.

He chose to withhold this information from Paul Kirkwood as well. Paul had failed the test. *It's my life . . . I deserve . . . Inside Edition offered me . . .*

'Well, I'll tell you what, Mr Kirkwood,' he drawled, 'Josh sure as hell deserves better than what he's got.'

Letting that hang in the air, he crossed the room slowly and rested a hand on the doorknob.

'I'll leave my number with your secretary. You can think on it some and call me if you'd like – if you can find time between *Hard Copy* and *Oprah*.'

Paul watched him walk out, rage curling inside him. Bastard. He could pay lip service to ethics and the integrity of his story, but he wouldn't pay cash. He would rake in five million and still had the gall to sneer at the man whose suffering would be an integral part of what would make him that fortune.

I deserve . . . Paul refused to feel guilty for thinking it. He *did* deserve something. He was a victim, too.

Even as a part of him insisted on his entitlement, another part of him thought of Josh in the hospital, while another filled with images of that night two weeks ago. All of it twisted inside of him until he felt as if he were caught in a whirlpool sucking him down to drown in panic and remorse.

Josh's frantic cries of 'No!' echoed in his ears. He pressed his hands over them. Even with his eyes squeezed tight against the images, he could see his son kicking against the hospital bed, felt as if each kick were landing squarely in his belly.

A thin cry slipping between his lips, he sank down in the chair behind his desk and doubled over. Shudders racked his body. His mouth twisted open; the chaos in his brain thinned to a single thought – *my son, my son, my son, my son* . . .

Then came the guilt. A wall of it. It was the guilt that made him open the bottom drawer of his desk. It was the guilt that had made him keep the answering-machine tape from that fateful night. He kept the tape in a microcassette recorder he had bought for dictating letters but never used.

He placed the small black rectangle on the desk, pressed the play button. And Josh's voice spoke to him from the crossroads that had turned all their lives onto a dark path.

12

'*I'm here in Park County to see that justice will be done.*' Ellen chewed on Tony Costello's words as she drove all the way across town.

'As if the state outside the metro area is a lawless frontier,' Cameron complained. 'And he's Wyatt Earp, come to bring us justice.'

'It's all part of the show,' Ellen murmured, turning onto Lakeshore Drive.

'It doesn't bother you?'

'Of course it does. Using the Holloman kidnapping in a naked grab for publicity – it's too sleazy for words. But you can't let Tony Costello get to you any more than you let Denny Enberg or Fred Nelson get to you, Cameron. He's just another hired gun.'

'A hired gun in an Armani suit.'

'That's what success will buy you in the big city, Cam. If you're willing to pay the price.'

'I'm not interested in becoming the next Anthony Costello.'

'Glad to hear it. The world has more Tony Costellos that it needs.'

'He doesn't impress me.'

'Well, he should,' Ellen said, turning in at the Kirkwoods' drive. 'He's extremely good at what he does. Don't underestimate him and don't let him get under your skin.'

She turned the Bonneville off and sat for a moment, looking at the Kirkwoods' home, a cedar-sided multilevel that fit in gracefully with its wooded surroundings. Built on the last oversize lot on the street, it had an unrestricted view of the lake to the west. On the north and east the thick woods of Quarry Hills Park wrapped the property in a feeling of seclusion that must have cost a pretty penny. On the front yard a half-finished snow fort gave testimony to the normalcy of life in this home before a kidnapper destroyed it.

Her eyes lingered on the Wrights' house two doors down.

Ellen heaved a sigh. 'Okay, let's get it over with.'

Hannah answered the door, looking pale and thin. The smile she gave as she invited them in was brittle and quick.

'Hannah, this is my associate, Cameron Reed.' Ellen pulled her gloves off and stuffed them into her coat pockets.

'Yes, I believe we met last summer over a soccer injury,' Hannah said, shaking hands with Cameron.

He smiled warmly. 'I recovered fully, and you were right – the scar is a definite icebreaker at the gym.' The smile faded. 'I can't tell you how sorry I am for all you and your family have gone through, Dr Garrison.'

'Thank you,' Hannah replied automatically. 'Let me take your coats.'

'How's Josh doing?' Ellen asked.

The brittle smile came and went. 'It's good to have him home.'

'Has he said anything? Given any indication of who took him or where they took him?'

Hannah glanced into the family room. Ellen's gaze followed, searching. Josh was nowhere to be seen.

'No,' Hannah answered at last. 'He hasn't said a word about it. Come in. I've got coffee if you'd like.'

They followed her through the comfortable family room with its sturdy country-colonial furnishings and scattering of toddler's toys, and up the three steps into the spacious kitchen.

'I heard about that boy in Campion,' Hannah said as she went through the ritual of setting out mugs and pouring the coffee. 'I wouldn't have wished that hell on anyone. My heart goes out to the family.'

'It's all the more incentive for us to build a strong case,' Cameron explained. 'The more pressure we can bring to bear against our man, the more likely he may be willing to give us his accomplice.'

Hannah's eyes widened. Her hands were trembling as she set their coffee mugs down. 'You're not going to make a deal with him? After everything he's done?'

'No,' Ellen assured. 'No deals. He's going down for all of it. We're hoping Josh will be able to help us nail him. As I explained to you over the phone, Hannah, we want to have Josh take a look at what we call a photo lineup. If he picks our man out of that, we'll want to proceed with an actual lineup at the police station. We felt it would be less traumatic for him to start with the photographs. We don't want to upset Josh, but his ability to identify his abductor would certainly be key to our prosecution.'

'Will he have to testify in court?'

'That will depend on how much he remembers or is willing to tell,' Cameron said.

'If Josh is able to testify, we'll do everything we can to prepare him so he won't be frightened,' Ellen explained.

Hannah reached up to toy nervously with an earring. 'Couldn't he testify on videotape? I've seen that on television.'

'Possibly,' Ellen said. 'There is precedent. I'll talk with the judge when the time comes, but for now all we want is to have Josh look at photographs. Could you bring him in?'

As Hannah left the kitchen, Cameron opened his briefcase, pulled out a sheet of plastic pockets from a photo album, and placed it on the table.

'She's not holding up well,' he murmured.

'I'm sure we can't even imagine what it's been like,' Ellen said, keeping an eye peeled for Hannah's return. 'I heard their marriage is all but over.'

'Garrett Wright has a lot to answer for.'

Hannah herded Josh into the kitchen. Josh eyed them warily. He seemed like an impostor of the boy in the 'missing' posters, with his gaptoothed smile and Cub Scout uniform. The physical resemblance to that boy was there, but none of the sparkle, none of the joy. His eyes looked a hundred years old.

'Hi, Josh, my name is Ellen.' She leaned down to eye level with him.

'And this is my friend, Cameron. He likes to play soccer in the summer. Do you go out for soccer?'

Josh stared at her, silent. His mother ruffled his curly hair. 'Josh plays baseball in the summer. Don't you, honey?'

He looked from Ellen to Cameron, then turned and faced the refrigerator, losing himself in the photographs and school artwork stuck to it with magnets. Hannah knelt down beside him.

'Josh, Ellen and Cameron want you to take a look at some pictures they brought with them. They want to see if the man who took you away from us is one of the men in the photographs. Can you do that?'

He gave no answer, no reaction of any kind. She turned him gently by the shoulders toward the table.

'Just take a look at these, Josh,' Ellen instructed, sliding the sheet of photos toward him. 'Take your time and look at all the men. If you see the man who took you, all you have to do is point at him.'

Ellen held her breath as he bent his head over the pictures, looking at one face, then another. All were mug shots, some of criminals, some of Deer Lake police officers. Garrett Wright's occupied the upper right-hand pocket. Josh looked at them all, his gaze lingering on Wright's face, then moving on.

'All you have to do is point at him, Josh,' Ellen murmured. 'He's not going to hurt you. We'll make sure he'll never hurt you or any other kids ever again.'

His gaze slowly skated back up across the faces; then he turned away and went to the refrigerator to stare at a construction-paper snowman.

'Josh, are you sure you didn't see the man?' Hannah asked, a desperate edge to her voice. 'Maybe you should come back and look again. Come on —'

Ellen rose and gently caught hold of her arm before she could drag Josh back to the table.

'It's okay, Hannah. Maybe he just isn't ready to look yet. We'll try it again another day.'

'But —' Hannah's gaze darted from her son to the mug shot of Wright.

'It's all right,' Ellen said, wishing she felt as nonchalant as she sounded. 'When he's ready, he'll talk about it. He's just not ready yet.'

537

'What if he's never ready?' she whispered.

'We'll make the case,' Ellen promised. But as they drove away from the Kirkwood house, she wondered if it was a promise she would be able to keep.

Josh was the only witness who could identify Wright and his accomplice. Josh had seen the person who'd picked him up at the hockey rink. The witness, Helen Black, had glanced out her window that night and seen a boy who could only have been Josh willingly climbing into a van. He had to have seen who was driving it.

'Maybe the accomplice picked him up,' Cameron offered. 'Maybe he never saw Wright.'

'Maybe.'

He was silent for half a block as they drove past a Kwik Trip and a Vietnamese grocery. 'And if we don't have Josh take the stand, Costello will say he couldn't identify Wright because Wright didn't do it.'

'Then we jump all over Costello for being a heartless bastard,' Ellen countered. 'We say we're not putting Josh on the stand, because he's been traumatized and victimized enough. We don't want to put him through the ordeal of cross-examination, to say nothing of having to face Wright in the courtroom.'

He nodded as they turned onto Oslo and headed up the hill toward the courthouse. They passed the knot of protestors on the sidewalk and turned in at the entrance to the sheriff's-department lot, swinging around behind the building.

'Poor kid,' Cameron said. 'It's up to us to get him some justice.'

Ellen found a ghost of a smile for him as she palmed her keys. 'That's why they pay us the big bucks, Mr Reed.'

'Judge Rudy Stovich.' Rudy spoke the title aloud to test the sound of it. Sounded good.

He had occupied this corner office on the second floor of the Park County courthouse for a dozen years. The oak credenza was piled with file folders and law books he never consulted. His desk was awash with debris, the decorative scales of justice that sat on one corner tipped heavily with golf tees. A set of Ping clubs leaned into one dark corner of the room, resting up for the annual February trip to Phoenix. A trip he would gladly postpone in order to move himself into old Franken's chambers.

'Judge Rudy Stovich,' Manley Vanloon echoed. He plucked a filbert from the nut dish on the desk and cracked it with a tool disguised to look like an angry mallard. Fine slivers of shell rained down like flecks of tobacco onto the front of his tan wool sweater. He was built like a Buddha, all belly and a round, smiling face. His eyebrows tilted up above his tiny eyes. 'Maybe you should go by Rudolph. Sounds more dignified.'

Rudy swiveled his chair back and forth as if the motion would act as a centrifuge and separate the good decisions from the bad. 'Sounds pretentious. Folks like my country-lawyer image.'

'Good point.' Manley nibbled his filbert, his gaze speculative as he imagined his pal in judge's robes. He and Rudy had been buddies since snow was cold, backing each other in business ventures and political campaigns. 'How long before the governor makes up his mind?'

'Oh, he'll have to wait a decent interval after they bury old Franken. A week or so, I should think. By the way, the viewing is tomorrow at Oglethorpe's. Funeral Friday, three-thirty at Grace Lutheran.'

'Grace Lutheran? All this time I thought he was Methodist. He struck me as a Methodist.' He dusted the filbert-shell shrapnel off his cardigan and reached for a pecan. 'Dinner after the funeral? Friday's all-you-can-eat fish at the Scandia House.'

'Yeah, sure,' Rudy mumbled dreamily, imagining himself delivering a stirring eulogy before a congregation that would include judges and lawyers and politicians from all over the state. Franken had lived a long time, accumulating a long list of powerful friends and colleagues. The funeral seemed a fitting time for Rudy to impress them all with his eloquence and sincerity.

The intercom buzzed, and Alice Zymanski's voice snapped out of it like a bolt of lightning. 'Ellen is here to see you. I'm leaving.'

'Send her in.' Rudy forced himself to his feet, though it seemed too late in the day for manners. Once he was firmly ensconced in his judgeship, he was going to give up manners.

Ellen let herself in, manufacturing a smile for Manley Vanloon. Manley had amassed a small fortune in real estate during the agriculture depression of the seventies, buying out farms on the fringe of Deer Lake and developing the land into pricey subdivisions for the influx of yuppies from the Cities. He had then bought a trio of car dealerships and had made himself another fortune luring car buyers out of the Cities with his hayseed image, then cleaning their pockets for them.

'Hey there, Ellen.' Manley lifted himself out of his chair no more than he would to fart and settled back down to the business of digging his pecan out of the shell. 'How's that Bonneville running? Heck of a nice car.'

'Just fine, Manley.' She turned her attention to her boss. 'I just got a call from the assignments clerk. They're giving Garrett Wright to Judge Grabko. I thought you'd want to know.'

'Are you all right with that choice?'

She shrugged. 'We could do worse.'

'Will you recuse?'

And let Tony Costello throw a public fit about the prosecution delaying his client's right to a speedy trial, to say nothing of alluding to the maneuver as the tactics of someone with a weak case? He had already made noises on both those points at his four o'clock press conference in the courthouse rotunda.

Ellen had sent Phoebe to the press conference as her spy, refusing to show up herself and give Tony the golden opportunity of engaging her in some impromptu sparring. When he marched upstairs to the county attorney's offices afterward, with reporters in tow, she made the receptionist lie and tell him she was out, for the sole purpose of spoiling his big moment of confrontation.

That small victory had been sweet, but the fact that she was letting Costello affect her decision making irritated her in the extreme. *Strategy*, she told herself. She had to think in terms of strategy rather than in terms of being manipulated. Always put a positive spin on a negative possibility. Control was the name of the game.

'No, I won't recuse Grabko. He knows his stuff. He's fair. I've never had any big complaints about him other than that he tends toward pretension.'

Rudy shot an I-told-you-so look at Manley, who pursed his lips as if holding back a belch.

'I'm still amazed Wright got Costello to represent him,' Rudy said.

'I'd like to know how that happened,' Ellen said. 'Who called him in? Wright isn't allowed to make long-distance calls from jail. I doubt Denny Enberg would have been so gracious as to contact his own successor. Who does that leave?'

'Wright's wife.'

'Who is barely functioning. I saw her myself the other night. Unless that's all been an act, she could no more have had a coherent conversation with Tony Costello than my golden retriever. That leaves Wright's accomplice.'

'Which could mean Costello has been in contact with the kidnapper of that Campion boy,' Rudy surmised.

'And fat chance we'll get him to tell us anything.'

Rudy made a serious, contemplative sound, arranging his features in an expression he thought would look judicial. 'Yes, well, do what you can, Ellen. I'm confident you can handle Costello.'

Ellen took the platitude for what it was worth, which was nothing. She left Rudy to his scheming for Franken's seat on the bench and headed back to her own office. The staff was clearing out for the day. Sig Iverson and Quentin Adler were headed out the door, heads bent toward each other as they discussed some point of law or gossip. Phoebe was pulling on her llama poncho over her daisy-print dress and thermal leggings. Her head popped up through the opening and she pulled her mass of kinky hair free.

'I put a stack of messages on your desk,' she said, straightening her glasses. 'Mr Costello called again. Mitch called to say no news is bad news and that he's going to Minneapolis tonight.'

To check on Megan. The thought warmed Ellen and left her feeling a little empty at once. She leaned a shoulder against her office door and rested her hand on the knob. 'Thanks, Phoebe. See you tomorrow.'

The secretary frowned at her. 'Don't stay too late. You look tired.'

'I'm fine.'

Phoebe didn't buy it, but she let it drop. Ellen let herself into her office and picked up the stack of pink slips. She noted the fact that there wasn't one from Jay Butler Brooks and told herself she was glad. Still, she caught herself thinking of the moment just before he had left her house last night, when he had stood a little too close to her and held her gaze with his a little too long.

'You can't avoid me forever.'

She wheeled around, half expecting to see Brooks standing there, but the timbre of the voice registered a split second before her eyes focused on the man standing inside the door. The light from the outer office cast him in relief, giving him a menacing darkness that seemed fitting. Tony Costello was a shadow from her past coming back to haunt her. She reached around and flicked on the desk lamp to break the spell.

'Avoiding you, Tony? As usual, your ego is working overtime. It never occurred to you that I'm a busy woman with more important things on my agenda than playing an obliging role in your media drama.'

'Contrary as ever, aren't you?' he said pleasantly, closing the door behind him. 'I was afraid living in the boondocks might have mellowed you.'

Ellen settled into her chair, slipping her glasses on and pretending attention to the message slips she had yet to set down. 'It has.' She glanced up at him over the rims of the glasses. 'If you had sneaked up on me like that when I was working in Hennepin County, I would have broken your nose. I've let my self-defense skills slide completely.'

'Lucky for me.'

He smiled what she knew he considered to be the most charming smile in his arsenal. She remembered it well – square, white against his dark complexion. A smile he had splurged on to the tune of fifteen thousand dollars, mortgaging the house his parents had left him to pay for porcelain caps. He considered it a business investment.

He looked as fit and perfectly groomed as a show horse. The suit today was just a shade bluer than navy, tailored to show off the build he honed in a private gym with a personal trainer. He casually undid the buttons of the double-breasted coat and settled himself easily into her visitor's chair.

'What can I do for you, Tony?' she asked with just enough indifference to irritate him.

He ignored the bait, his gaze steady on hers. 'It's been a long time.'

'Not long enough.'

The hurt appeared genuine but, then, so had his feelings for her, once upon a time.

'You still blame me for what happened with Fitzpatrick,' he said. 'I was hoping time might have given you some perspective.'

'My perspective on criminal tampering with a case isn't liable to change in this lifetime.'

He shook his head, frowning. 'How could you believe I would do that, Ellen? Ethics aside, how could you believe I would turn on you that way after everything we'd been to each other?'

'Ethics aside.' She gave a harsh laugh and rose again, anger humming in her muscles as she paced the small confines behind her desk. 'Someone feeds Fitzpatrick's side information, virtually off my desk. The case blows up, and the next thing I see is you and Fitzpatrick's attorney palling around —'

'We were having dinner. That's not against the law.'

'It's certainly not against *your* law.'

'Oh, Jesus, Ellen,' he growled, pushing to his feet. 'It was a business dinner —'

'I'm sure it was.' Ellen advanced toward him. 'Did he slide your thirty pieces of silver to you under the table, or did he have the waiter bring it on a platter?'

'There were plenty of people in your own office who had access to that information. Fitzpatrick could have paid off any one of them.'

'Yeah, but you know, Tony, none of them was suddenly driving a Porsche or hanging out at Goodfellows with Gregory Eagleton —'

'And, of course, it never occurred to you that your case blew up because Fitzpatrick was innocent,' he shot back. 'It never occurred to you that the girl was lying, pressing criminal charges after Fitzpatrick refused to meet her blackmail demands.'

The argument touched a nerve that sent a red mist across Ellen's vision. He didn't deny her charges; he diverted attention, tried to shed the blame onto someone else. Pointing the spotlight on the victim crossed the line. She stepped toe to toe with him and thrust a righteous finger at him. 'Art Fitzpatrick raped that girl because he believed his money and his position entitled him to do as he damn well pleased. And the thing that makes me sickest is that he was right. He bought his way out of a conviction, and you sold yourself into his good graces.'

'Then prove it!' he shouted.

He didn't deny it. He never had.

They had been over this ground so many times, they had worn it to dust. Ellen knew she couldn't prove a thing against him. All she'd had were puzzle pieces and a gut feeling that drilled into the core of her. No hard evidence. Nothing she could take to the county attorney or to the bar association. At the time she had racked her brain trying to come up with a way to punish him, to publicly burn him at the stake, to get him disbarred, to send him to jail. But in the end there had been only the realization that any such effort would blow up in her face. She would be the one publicly humiliated, scorned, and professionally ruined. She was the prosecutor who had been foolish enough to get involved with an ambitious defense attorney.

She had gone into the affair cautious, convinced she was smart enough to handle it. She had come away from it with her self-esteem battered.

He had drawn her in, charmed her into believing he had integrity. And just as soon as all her shields were down, he had betrayed her.

Nearly three years had passed and she still wanted to cut his heart out. Not because she had loved him, but because he had used her, made a fool of her, mocked the system she prized so highly.

She turned away from him and rubbed her hands over her face, trying to clear away the lingering haze of emotion. She didn't want to feel any of it. She especially didn't want to feel it in front of him. Control. Hadn't she just been preaching that word? Hadn't she told Cameron not to let Costello get under his skin? And here she was, going off like a bomb the first time he set foot in her office.

'I cared about you, Ellen,' he murmured.

'Well, it's all in the past tense, isn't it?' she said, sliding down onto her chair. 'Ancient history.'

Tony took his seat in the visitor's chair. Like boxers retiring to their respective corners, she thought. The tension dissipated to a tolerable level.

'I certainly never meant to drive you from the city,' he said.

'Don't flatter yourself, Tony,' she returned. 'You were just a symptom of a much bigger problem. I left Hennepin County because I was fed up to my eyeteeth with all the bullshit game playing. Obviously, you're not content to contaminate just the metropolitan judicial districts. You've decided to take your show on the road.'

'I'm representing Garrett Wright.'

'So I heard.' Ellen fixed her gaze hard on his face. 'And how did that happen?'

'It's a fascinating case.'

'High profile, you mean. What I want to know is *how* you came to be Garrett Wright's attorney. Who contacted you? Or did you come sniffing?'

'Are you accusing me of soliciting a client?' he asked with a healthy show of affront.

'No, you would never be that crass. So who called you? I know it wasn't Wright himself or Dennis Enberg.'

'You also know I won't discuss this with you,' he said, poker-faced. 'It's privileged.'

Ellen leaned toward him, her arms braced on the desktop. 'You think so? If Garrett Wright's accomplice contacted you — if you can reveal to us the identity of the kidnapper of the Holloman boy and do not — I will sink my teeth into charges of obstruction and shake you like a dead rat.'

Costello smiled like a lover, his dark eyes glowing. 'Ah, you're still my Ellen at heart — or should I say at my throat?'

'I never belonged to you, Tony,' she said coldly. 'I just slept with you. Trust me, it wasn't that big a deal.'

'Ouch.' He winced. 'Hitting below the belt. How unlike you.'

543

'What can I say? You bring out the mean in me. You'll find out the hard way if you're aiding and abetting a kidnapper.'

'You're going on the assumption my client is guilty,' he said soberly. 'I presume him to be innocent, therefore can have no knowledge of an accomplice. I certainly have no knowledge of the Holloman kidnapping.'

'God help you if you're lying to me, Tony,' Ellen said tightly. 'A child's life could be at stake.'

'I know what's at stake, Ellen. I *always* know what's at stake.'

He opened his Louis Vuitton calfskin briefcase on the chair beside him and withdrew a sheaf of documents. 'Demand for Discovery. Since you have virtually nothing on which to base your case, I expect disclosure to happen quickly.'

'We've got more than enough for the hearing,' she said. 'Your little "rush to justice" ploy is only going to cramp your efforts, Tony, not mine. Send one of your minions around tomorrow afternoon for the papers.'

'I'll stop by myself,' he said, slipping into his topcoat. 'Judge Grabko will be hearing my motion to reduce bail. Admirable the way the district is striving to keep the wheels of justice turning, isn't it?'

'I suppose you're trying to take credit for the work of our assignments clerk.' Ellen strove to sound bored. 'As if anyone in this district could care less who you are.'

Costello narrowed his eyes. He looked cruel, and she knew he had the potential for it.

'I think you could care less, Ellen,' he said in a low voice. 'Let's hope for the sake of the case you don't let your vindictiveness cloud your judgment. I don't want anyone saying it wasn't a fair fight.'

She wanted to pick up her paperweight and hurl it at him, but it was out of reach, and restraint dictated a cooler response. 'Why don't you take your ego out for a nice big dinner, Tony? The energy it consumes must be tremendous.'

His mouth twisted into a thin smile. 'As a matter of fact, I am on my way to dinner. I'd ask you to join us, but . . .'

'I have other plans.'

He tipped his head. 'Until tomorrow . . .'

He stepped into the dim light of the hall, turning back to look at her. 'You know, Ellen,' he said softly, 'aside from the circumstances, it really is good to see you again.'

Ellen said nothing. When he was gone, she raked her hands back through her hair and blew out a sigh as tension rushed out of her muscles. A logical assessment of their conversation told her it hadn't been a total bust. She had scored some points, held her own. Beyond logic, she felt naked and vulnerable.

He had found a way to hurt her before, when she had thought she was invulnerable. She had chosen to walk away, but here he was again, invading her life. No logical argument could take the edge off her uneasiness.

And at the heart of that disquiet was not Tony Costello, but Garrett Wright.

Why had he chosen Costello? How could he have known the one man she would least want to face in court or out? Who had contacted Costello for him?

Who was the other part of *us*?

'*As a matter of fact, I am on my way to dinner. I'd ask you to join us . . .*'

Possibilities sprang up like mushrooms in her head. He could have been talking about members of his staff, but he might have been referring to the person who had contacted him on Garrett Wright's behalf.

Grabbing her coat and briefcase, she hustled out of her office. The purveyors of justice had closed shop for the night, and the dimly lit halls echoed with the hollow, lonely sound of a single pair of heels. She hurried down the stairs, cut across the rotunda, and made for the side door closest to the parking lot. She braced herself for the cold as she pushed through the door, then stood on the step.

She scanned the parking lot, looking for Costello, hoping to catch a glimpse of him driving away. But she didn't see anyone. Mumbling a curse under her breath, she started toward her car. She hoped he had gone back to his office first. If she could pick him up there and follow him to the restaurant –

'Ms North?'

The dark form seemed to fly out of the shadows like a wraith. Ellen bolted sideways, broke a heel, turned her ankle. Stumbling, she dropped her briefcase. Adam Slater stood stock-still, wide-eyed, watching her flounder. The wind blew his hair into his eyes and he swept it back impatiently.

'Jeez, Ms North, I didn't mean to scare you. I'm really sorry.'

Ellen scowled at him. She picked up the amputated heel of her shoe and stuffed it into her coat pocket.

'Mr Slater,' she said, trying to hold her patience. 'There really isn't a need to rush at a subject when you are the only reporter in the vicinity.'

His lean face contorted into a variety of sheepish looks. 'I'm really sorry. It's just that I wanted to catch you before you – well – got away.'

'Why aren't you in Campion with the rest of the horde?'

'There's nothing much going on there. I mean, the search, but they haven't found the kid or anything. A bunch of people came back here for Anthony Costello's press conference, but then they went back to Campion for the prayer vigil. I thought I'd hang around, see if I could get a comment from you.'

'It's better than nothing, huh?'

'Yeah – I mean – it's something. I mean, what's your take on Dr Wright bringing in a hired gun like Costello?' He pulled his notebook out of his coat pocket and stood with pen poised.

Ellen's breath rolled out in a transparent cloud and billowed up into the darkness. The sodium-vapor lights around the parking lot were on. One shone down on her Bonneville, spotlighting it as the only car for twenty yards in any direction. The sense of urgency deflated inside her.

'Garrett Wright is entitled to counsel,' she answered by rote. 'Mr Costello is very good at what he does.'

'Do you think it means Wright's guilty? That he feels like he's going to need a better lawyer than he could find in Deer Lake to get him off?'

'I'm not privy to his thoughts. I wish I were. That would make my job easier.' She bent and hefted her briefcase, balancing herself on her right toe to compensate for the missing heel. 'I believe Garrett Wright is guilty. I will do everything in my power to prove that and to convict him. It makes no difference to me who his lawyer is.'

'Costello doesn't intimidate you?'

'Not in the least.'

'Even though he beat you about every two out of three times when you went up against him as a prosecutor in Hennepin County?'

'Where did you hear that?'

He shrugged. 'My source in the system.'

'Cases are individual,' Ellen said, hobbling toward her car. 'I'm confident in our case against Garrett Wright. I will also do everything I can to aid in the capture and prosecution of his accomplice.'

'Got any clues as to who that might be?' Adam Slater asked, shuffling beside her. 'Got any clues about motive?'

'I'm not at liberty to comment.'

'I won't use your name,' he promised. 'I'll call you "a highly placed source in the county attorney's office."'

'There are only five attorneys on staff, Mr Slater. That wouldn't exactly ensure my anonymity.'

He rebounded with the undaunted resilience of youth and bounced on to the next question. 'There's been no word on motive. What do you think this is all about? Crime is always about something – sex, power, money, drugs. Or in the existential, cosmic view, is it really just about good and evil?'

Ellen looked at him, at the avid light in his eyes as he waited for her answer, for a juicy, sensational tidbit his readers back in Grand Forks could scarf up with their breakfast cereal. She had seen degrees of good and evil all around throughout this ordeal: shades and shadows of darkness, small bright spots of hope for humankind. If Brooks was right about nothing else, he was right about one thing – that the drama being played out around them was, in many ways, a metaphor for the times. But Ellen had no desire to wax philosophical with a reporter who grew up on *Brady Bunch* reruns and was too young to remember the Beatles.

'I'm not an existentialist, Mr Slater,' she said. 'I'm a realist. I realistically believe I can win this case. I won't be spooked by an attorney who spends more on suits than I make in a year or by the preposterous notion that we're up against a malevolent entity whose evil genius is larger than all of us struggling against it. When you come right down to it, Garrett Wright is just another criminal. I won't give him any more credit than he deserves.'

It made for a good sound bite, she thought as she drove out of the parking lot. Too bad she didn't quite believe it.

13

Hannah prowled the quiet house alone, soft music from the stereo her only company. Lily was asleep in her crib. Josh had fallen asleep on the couch watching *Back to the Future*.

Hannah had kept the VCR loaded since the night before. She didn't want Josh watching the news. She told herself she was afraid it might upset him, but the truth was that his reaction to the news bulletin about the Holloman kidnapping had upset *her*. She had tried to talk about it with him, but after his initial chilling comment he'd had nothing more to say.

'Josh, do you know who might have taken that boy away from his family?'

He shrugged, indifferent, and turned his attention to his box of markers, taking out each one and subjecting it to intense scrutiny.

'Honey, that little boy's family will be worried sick about him, just like we were worried about you. And he's probably scared, too, the way you must have been. If you could help find him, you would, wouldn't you?'

He pulled a purple marker from the box and held it at arm's length, slowly swooping it through the air as if he were pretending it was an airplane.

He had retreated once more into his imagination. Hannah was at a loss as to how to draw him out or even if she should try. Perhaps it was better to let him come to terms with it on his own, to simply offer him love and support and patience. Then she would think of Dustin Holloman's mother, knowing every fear the woman was experiencing, and she would think she should force the issue, that she should call Mitch and tell him what Josh had said, that she should have told Ellen North, that she should immediately drag Josh back to the child psychiatrist he had seen earlier in the day and relinquish her responsibility.

The arguments tumbled around and around in her mind, in her conscience. Ultimately, she felt she would do nothing, and she felt selfish and weak and wrong because of it. But in her heart she wanted first and foremost to protect Josh, to keep him safe with her, hoping all the ugliness would just go away.

She looked down at him, sleeping soundly, and every molecule of her being hurt. She had failed to protect him once. She didn't want to fail him again, but she was flying blind and she felt so alone. She felt as if she had been taken from the world she knew, where she was certain of her

548

role and her skills, and thrust into an alien world, where she didn't understand the language or the customs.

Until Josh's abduction, she had never faced real adversity in her personal life. She had never acquired the skills necessary to cope. Even now, as she acquired them unwillingly, she wielded them clumsily, uncertainly. She felt out of balance and knew what was missing was her husband's support. She and Paul had been a team for a long time before that balance had begun to shift. To be without him was to suddenly become an amputee.

Beyond the kitchen the door from the garage to the mudroom opened and closed. Hannah whirled around, automatically putting herself between the unseen intruder and her son. Then the kitchen door swung open and Paul stepped in.

'You could have called first,' Hannah said angrily as she stepped up into the kitchen.

'It's still my house,' Paul answered defensively.

Hannah drew breath for another attack, then stopped herself short. It had become habit – the thrust and parry of verbal warfare. They didn't even bother with greetings anymore. They had shared a decade of their lives, brought two children into the world, and had reduced themselves to this.

'You frightened me,' she admitted.

'I'm sorry.' He offered the apology grudgingly. 'I guess I should have known better. I didn't think you'd get used to having me gone so quickly.'

'It isn't that.'

He arched a sardonic brow. 'Oh, so you've decided maybe there's some reason to be afraid of me after all?'

'Oh, Christ.' She pressed the heels of her hands against her closed eyes. 'I'm trying to be civil, Paul. Can't you at least meet me halfway?'

'You're the one who threw me out.'

'You deserved it. There. Are you happy now? Have we been ugly enough to each other?'

He looked away, staring at the refrigerator and the notes and photos and drawings that cluttered the front of it. Evidence of their life as a family.

'I came to see Josh,' he said quietly.

'He's asleep.'

'I can't frighten him then, can I?'

Hannah bit her lip on a retort. She wasn't sure what he wanted her to make of it or what she *should* make of it. She didn't want to think Josh had any reason to be afraid of his father. Logic told her there was no reason, that Garrett Wright was the man to blame. Garrett Wright was in jail.

And another child had been taken.

And it was Paul who had caused Josh to react so violently.

'He fell asleep on the couch,' she said, and turned and walked down into the family room.

Paul followed her, hands in his pockets, feet seeming to drag across the Berber rug. He looked down at their son over the back of the sofa, some nameless emotion tightening his features.

'How's he doing?'

'I don't know.'

'Is he talking?'

She hesitated for a split second, wanting to confide, but realizing she didn't want to confide in Paul. 'No. Not really.'

'When will he see the psychiatrist again?'

'Tomorrow. Ellen North and Cameron Reed from the county attorney's office came by today with a photo lineup for him to look at to see if he would pick out Garrett Wright.'

Anticipation sharpened his expression. 'And?'

'And nothing. He looked at it and walked away. He seems to be blocking the whole thing out. Dr Freeman says it could be a long time before he faces it. The trauma was too much for him. He was probably told not to talk about it. Threatened. God only knows.'

'God and Garrett Wright.'

Paul bent down and touched Josh's hair. One stray lock curled around his forefinger, and his eyes filled with tears. Hannah stood where she was, knowing that not long ago she would have gone to him and put her arms around him and shared his pain. That she would no longer do so brought a profound sadness. How could their love have gone so completely? What could they have done to stop it from leaving?

'I wish we could go back,' Paul whispered. 'I wish . . . I wish . . .'

The chant was as familiar as her own heartbeat. Hannah couldn't count the empty wishes, the unanswered prayers. The most important one had come true – to get Josh back – but it had brought on a whole new set of needs and longings and questions she wasn't sure she wanted answers for.

'*I wish we could go back . . .*' to the time in their lives that seemed like a distant fairy tale. Once upon a time they had been so happy. Now there was only bitterness and pain. Happily ever after was as far beyond their reach as the stars.

'I'll carry him to bed,' Paul murmured.

Hannah started to say no, worried that Josh might awaken at the movement and panic at the sight of his father. But she held her breath instead and asked God for this one small favor. Whatever had gone wrong between the two of them, she didn't want to see Paul hurt that way. She didn't want to believe he deserved it.

She followed them up the short flight of stairs and stood in the doorway to Josh's room as Paul settled him into the lower bunk and tucked the covers around him. He kissed his fingertips and pressed them softly against Josh's cheek, then went across the hall and looked in on Lily.

'She asks about you,' Hannah admitted.

'What do you tell her?'

'That you're staying somewhere else for a while.'

'But it isn't just for a while, is it, Hannah?' he said with more accusation than hope. 'You don't need me.'

'I don't need *this*,' she said sharply as they stepped down into the family room. 'The constant sniping, the snide remarks, the feeling that I have to walk on eggshells around your ego. I would give anything for us to be able to set all that aside for Josh's sake, but you can't seem to manage that –'

'*Me?*' Paul thumped a fist against his chest. 'Yeah, *I'm* to blame. Bullshit. *You're* the one who –'

'Stop right there!' Hannah demanded. 'I will not listen to this again. Do you understand me, Paul? I'm tired of you blaming me. I blame myself enough for both of us. I'm doing the best I can. I can't speak for you; I don't know what you're doing. I don't even know who you are anymore. You're not the man I married. You're no one I want to be with.'

'Well, that's fine,' he sneered. 'I'm out of here.'

And so the vicious circle completed itself again, Hannah thought as the doors slammed. They had danced the dance so many times, just the thought of it made her dizzy. Exhausted, she sank down onto a wing chair and reached for the portable phone on the end table. She needed an anchor, a friend, someone she could feel safe loving even if he could never love her back.

The phone on the other end rang once, twice.

'God Squad. Free deliverance.'

A smile trembled across Hannah's mouth.

'We've got a special on penance tonight – three rosaries for the price of two.'

'What about shoulders to cry on?' she asked.

The silence was warm and full. 'Buy one, get one free,' Father Tom said softly.

'Can I put it on my tab?'

'Anytime, Hannah,' he whispered. 'Anytime.'

Paul picked his way along the edge of the woods that bordered Quarry Hills Park. The moonlight was intermittent, blinking on and off as dark clouds scraped across its path like chunks of soot in the night sky. He knew the way well enough. The path meant for cross-country skiers had been trampled by countless boots in the last few days as the police had combed the hillside for evidence. Tattered ribbons of yellow plastic crime-scene tape clung to tree trunks like synthetic kudzu.

He tried to ignore it and not think about the reason it was there. He needed a break from the nightmare. He needed comfort. He needed love. He deserved something better than Hannah's running him down.

She should have been able to see the strain he was under. If she had been a true wife to him, he would have been sleeping in his own bed tonight. Instead, he wanted to seek out another man's wife.

That the man was sitting in jail tonight, accused of stealing Josh, brought on a complex matrix of emotions. None of them made him turn back.

The kitchen light was on in the Wrights' house. From the woods his views of the interior were abstract – a rectangle of kitchen, a square of bathroom wall and ceiling, a triangle of bedroom through the inverted V created between the tied-back curtains.

Karen was home. He had called her from a pay phone and hung up when she'd answered, afraid that her telephone might be bugged. There were no cars in her driveway, no evidence of visitors.

Caution and cowardice and guilt held him there at the edge of the woods. Need finally drove him forward.

He tracked across the backyard to the door that led into the garage and let himself in as he had many times before. Garrett's Saab had been impounded by the police and taken away, leaving Karen's Honda to take up only a fraction of the floor space. This was where Mitch Holt had arrested Garrett Wright. For a second Paul could almost hear the sounds of the scuffle, the low pitch of Holt's voice as he recited the Miranda warning.

Paul barely knew Garrett Wright. They were neighbors, but not the sort who shared summer evenings and backyard barbecues. Wright held himself apart, superior. He gave his life to his work at the college and regarded the people around him as if they were specimens to be studied and picked apart. It brought a certain bitter pleasure to think of him sitting in jail. How superior was he now?

'Paul?'

Karen stood behind the storm door looking fragile and startled. Her fine ash-blond hair framed her face. A pink rose bloomed across the front of her oversize ivory sweater. Feminine. Delicate. Everything he wanted in a woman.

'Paul, what are you doing here?'

'I needed to see you,' he said, pulling the door open. 'Can I come in?'

'You shouldn't.' But she stepped back into the laundry room anyway.

'I had to see how you're doing. I haven't seen you since Garrett –'

'That was a mistake.' She shook her head, not quite looking at him. 'Garrett should never have been arrested. He's never been arrested.'

'He took Josh, Karen.'

'That's a mistake,' she mumbled, twisting a finger into her hair. 'He would never . . . hurt me like that.'

'He doesn't love you, Karen. Garrett doesn't love you. I love you. Remember that.'

'I don't like what's happening.' The words came on a trembling whine. 'I think you should leave, Paul.'

'But I need to see you,' he said urgently. 'You can't imagine what I've been going through, wondering about you – wondering if you're all right, wondering if the police have been interrogating you. I've been worried sick.'

He lifted a hand to touch her cheek. 'I've missed you,' he whispered. Soft. She was so soft. Need ached through him. He needed comfort. He deserved comfort. 'Every night I lay awake, wishing you were with me. I think about us being together – really together. It can happen now. Hannah and I are finished. Garrett will go to jail.'

'I don't think so,' she murmured.

'Yes. You don't love him, anyway, Karen. He can't give you what you need. You love me. Say you love me, Karen.'

She hitched a breath, tears spilling over her lashes. 'I love you, Paul.'

He lowered his mouth to kiss her, but she turned her face away. She pushed at him, her small hands spread across the front of his coat.

'Karen?' he whispered, confused, crushed. 'I *need* you.'

She shook her head, tears tumbling down her cheeks, her lower lip trembling. 'I'm so sorry. It was all a mistake.' She slowly sank down along the front of the dryer to sit on the floor. She wrapped her arms around her legs, rested her cheek on her knees and cried softly. '... a terrible mistake.'

I made a mistake. The line blinked on and off in Denny Enberg's head like a neon sign. On and off, on and off, the relentless beat like Chinese water torture.

'You should be happy, Denny,' he mumbled, pouring himself another shot of Cuervo. 'You're out of it. You're off the hook.'

He had never expected to be put on the hook in the first place. Deer Lake was not a place of intrigue. His clients were generally ordinary, their cases unremarkable. He lived a quiet, decent life, dull by many standards. There was his law practice, his hunting and fishing, his wife Vicki. She worked nights as an LPN at the rest home and was taking classes at Harris to become an elementary-school teacher. They talked about adopting a baby but had decided to wait until Vicki finished school.

The Cuervo went down like liquid smoke. Edges were beginning to blur and soften as he looked around his office. The Manly Man Cave, Vicki called it. The place where he was allowed to hang his hunting trophies and keep his guns and play poker with his buddies once a month. The walls were knotty pine, the floor covered in flat, hard carpet the color of dirt. His inner sanctum. He allowed no clients back here. His secretary left the vacuum cleaner at the door every Friday. He used it once a month.

The building that housed his modest practice sat on the edge of a strip-mall parking lot and had once been a laundromat and dry cleaner's. Now the other half was occupied by a dentist who gave him a deal for referring clients who had ruined their teeth in car accidents and barroom brawls. The kind of clients he handled best – uncomplicated.

I made a mistake.

'Let it go, Denny,' he croaked, staring across the room at the ten-point buck that hung above his gun rack. 'You can't win 'em all.'

That was what he had told Ellen North when she had stopped by trolling for information. *'I wasn't aggressive enough. I let my client down. He fired me. It happens.'*

The case could have made him some money, made him a name, but it was gone now, and good riddance. He didn't need the pressure, didn't want the secrets.

'You seem distracted, Denny,' Ellen said.

'Yeah, well, it was a big case. I could have used the business it would have brought me. But what the hell. Who needs the headache?'

'Your heart didn't seem to be in it.'

'No? Yeah, well . . . Vicki didn't like the idea of my defending Wright.'

'She thinks he's guilty?'

'Trick question.'

'Withdrawn,' she said with a nod.

'Anyway, the crank calls were getting annoying.'

'What calls?'

He shrugged. *'The usual "You scum lawyer" variety. Some people believe he's guilty. Now Costello can worry about it. I'm out.'*

She started to leave, turning back toward him at the door, her expression pensive. *'You know I would never ask you to compromise your ethics, Denny. But I trust you to do what's right. If Garrett Wright is the monster we think he is, he has to be stopped. His accomplice has to be stopped. If you could do something to stop them, I know you would. You would do the right thing. Wouldn't you, Denny?'*

Do the right thing.

I made a mistake.

He tipped the Cuervo over his glass and drained the bottle.

Josh sat up in his bed and looked at the glowing dial of the clock on his nightstand. Twelve A.M. His mom had left a night-light on for him even though he was much too grown-up to have one. He was old now in ways Mom would never understand, in ways he could never explain.

He crawled out from under the covers and went to the window that looked out on the lake. In the moonlight it looked as if it could have been a white desert or the surface of a faraway planet. The ice-fishing huts clustered in an area down the shoreline could have been a village of alien life-forms.

He left his room and went down the hall to check on his mother. The door to her room stood open. She was asleep in bed, though he knew from experience the slightest sound might wake her. He wouldn't make a sound. He could be like a ghost, could move all around, be anywhere and no one would see him or hear. The quiet was in his mind, and he could make it as big as he was and put it all around him like a giant bubble.

He backed away from the door, went down the hall to the bathroom, where a window looked out on the backyard. He climbed up on the clothes hamper and parted the curtains. The snow was silver, the woods beyond like black lace with the here-and-gone moon shining between the bare branches of the winter-dead trees. There was a mystical, magical quality to the scene that called to him. The feeling frightened him a little, but pulled at him like a pair of big invisible hands. He wanted to be out there, alone, where no one would watch him as if they expected him to explode, and no one would ask him questions he wasn't supposed to answer.

In the mudroom he pulled on his snow boots and put on, over the new purple Vikings sweat suit Natalie Bryant had bought him, the new winter jacket his mom had bought him. People had bought him a lot of presents, like it was Christmas or something. Only when his mom gave them to him, she seemed sad and anxious instead of happy.

Josh knew he was the cause of those feelings. He wished he could fix her broken heart. He wished he could make the world right again, but he couldn't.

What's done is done, but it isn't over.

He didn't like to think about that, but it was in his head, put there by someone he didn't dare go against. The Taker. The Taker said he wasn't supposed to tell, or bad things would happen, and so he didn't talk, even though bad things seemed to be happening anyway. Josh stayed inside his mind, even though it was a lonely place. It was the safest place to be.

As quiet as a mouse, he let himself outside.

The call came at 2:02 A.M., jolting Ellen from a restless sleep. She sat bolt upright in bed, scattering the files and documents she had fallen asleep reading. The fat three-ring binder that was her bible for the Wright case tumbled to the floor with a thud. She stared at the phone, her mind rationalizing as it had Monday night. The call was probably work related. A cop in need of a warrant. There were other cases ongoing in Park County besides the Holloman kidnapping. Or maybe it was about the Holloman case. Maybe it was Karen Wright, calling to confess her husband's sins.

Still, she couldn't bring herself to pick up the receiver. Harry raised his massive head from the mattress and made a disgruntled sound at having his sleep disturbed.

'Ellen North,' she answered. Silence hung heavy on the end of the line. 'Hello?'

When the voice came, it was whisper soft, androgynous, a disembodied spirit that sent chills rushing over her skin like ice water.

' "The first thing we do, let's kill all the lawyers." '

The phone went dead, but the words floated and echoed and wrapped bony fingers around her throat. Ellen pulled the covers up high and sat shivering, wondering, waiting, while the night held its breath around her.

Journal Entry
January 26, 1994

They're running in circles, chasing their tails.
We play the shell game with lightning-quick minds.
Where is Dustin? Where is Evil?
Who is evil?
Who is not?

14

'Denny Enberg is dead.'

'Wh-what?' Ellen had been literally on her way out the door. Her coat was half-buttoned. Her gloves dropped out of her hand. '. . . looks like suicide,' Mitch said. '. . . In his office . . . sometime last night . . .'

The sentences came to her fragmented, as if the phone connection were bad.

The first thing we do, let's kill all the lawyers . . .

'Oh, my God,' she whispered, nausea rolling like a ball in her stomach, stirring her meager breakfast of toast and tea.

Even after reporting her crank call and being assured the night commander would send a patrol car past her house, she had slept poorly. Dreams of evil and fear had chased her up from the depths of unconsciousness and trapped her in an exhausting limbo.

'Hell of a way to start the day,' Mitch growled. 'Denny was a decent guy for a lawyer.'

Ellen tried to gulp a breath, dimly aware that she was hyperventilating. Clammy sweat slicked a film over her skin. 'Preserve the scene,' she said desperately.

'What?'

'Preserve the scene. I'll be right there. I think he may have been murdered.'

A steady stream of foot traffic flowed between the Donut Hut on the corner and Denny Enberg's office on the fringe of the Southtown Shopping Center. The press, swarming like flies, drifted back and forth, impatient for the news being denied them by closed doors and burly cops. Several recognized Ellen's car and rushed toward her as she turned into the parking lot. She pretended not to see them, letting them fend for life and limb as she roared past them and into the inner circle of green-and-white police vehicles. She flung her door open as she slammed the transmission into park and hurried toward the building as if she might still be able to prevent what had already happened.

The outer office was crowded. Denny's wife Vicki and his secretary huddled together on the small sofa, holding each other and sobbing, their grief intertwining in a wrenching duet. The air was thick with cigarette smoke and the sour tang of sweat from overdressed bodies and overstressed nerves.

Ellen grabbed hold of a dark-green parka sleeve, not bothering to focus on the face above it. 'Where's Mitch?'

'In the back. You don't want to go there.'

'It's my job,' she snapped, walking away. But it was something else that sent her down the short hall toward Denny's private office. *The first thing we do, let's kill all the lawyers. . . .*

The smell hit her like a rolling wave a dozen feet from the open door. Violent death. A putrid miasma of blood, bladder and bowel content. Thick, choking, cloying, underscored by the sharp, acidic scent of vomit. Ellen tried to breathe through her mouth. Fighting the urge to gag, she stepped into the office and looked for Mitch.

The room was hot and too crowded. Dead animals stared down from the paneled walls with unblinking glass eyes – a deer, a gigantic walleye with nasty teeth sporting the lure that had been his undoing in some northern lake, an assortment of game birds frozen in midflight for all eternity. A radio was playing country music while portable cop radios crackled with static and mumbled messages. The voices of the men present to investigate and gawk ran together in an indecipherable murmur.

Marty Wilhelm's mouth was drawn into a knot, his pallor a sickly pearl-gray. A uniformed officer sat on the low black vinyl sofa with his head down between his knees and a puddle of puke between his boots. Ellen wheeled away from the sight, bile rising in her throat. Mitch caught sight of her.

'Here,' he said, thrusting a small jar of Mentholatum at her. 'Are you sure you want in on this, Ellen? He used a shotgun. It's pretty gruesome.'

'I've seen it before,' she said gamely, smearing menthol beneath her nostrils.

'Yeah, but it probably wasn't someone you saw at the courthouse every day.'

'I'll be fine.'

'You'll be on the floor,' he muttered. 'You're as white as chalk.'

'Who found him?'

'His wife. She got home from work about seven-fifteen this morning. No sign of Denny, no sign that he'd ever come home last night. She tried to call him here and got no answer. It worried her, so she came on down.'

'Chief Holt says you have reason to believe Enberg may have been murdered.' Wilhelm leaned into the conversation, close enough to let everyone know he was one of the spectators who had lost his breakfast at the sight. Ellen swallowed hard and scooped out another finger of Mentholatum.

'I got a call last night,' she said, focusing on Mitch. 'A voice I couldn't recognize.'

'Male or female?'

'I'm not sure. Male, I think.'

'What did he say?'

'He quoted Shakespeare. "The first thing we do, let's kill all the lawyers." '

It echoed inside her head, the disembodied voice, the eerie silkiness of the delivery.

'What time was this?' Mitch asked.

'A little after two. I called it in, but what could anyone do?' she said. 'I thought it might be a threat directed at me. Your watch commander sent a patrol around. I never imagined – It never occurred to me –'

'You couldn't possibly have known, Ellen,' Mitch reassured her. 'You still can't know.'

'It has all the earmarks of a suicide,' Wilhelm said. 'There are no signs of forced entry, no signs of a struggle. The gun came from his own rack. He rigged the trigger with string.'

'I saw him just last night,' Ellen said. 'He was distracted, a little down, maybe, not suicidal.'

'He had just lost a client in a high-profile case,' Wilhelm said.

'But his heart was never in the case,' she insisted. 'I think he was as relieved as he was disappointed. He told me he'd been getting crank calls.'

'Threatening?' Wilhelm asked.

'He described them as the "You scum lawyer" variety.'

'People pissed off because he was defending Wright,' Mitch said. 'So why would any of them kill him after he'd been booted off the case?'

Wilhelm shook his head. 'They wouldn't. What would be the point?'

'You're right,' Ellen said, 'but he could have misinterpreted. For all we know, he got the same call I got.'

'I can't base an investigation on something that vague, Ms North.'

Mitch ignored the agent's play at power. 'So you think what? That Wright canned him for doing a half-assed job and the accomplice whacked him to keep him from talking about things that might have been attorney-client related?'

'An attorney can't reveal that kind of information,' Wilhelm argued. 'It's unethical. He'd get his ass disbarred.'

Mitch shot him an impatient look. 'You've never heard of anonymous tips? Jesus, Wilhelm, what were you – hatched yesterday?'

The BCA agent turned pink with temper. 'Wright fired Enberg Tuesday. Why wait a full twenty-four hours to off him? It doesn't follow, and the evidence doesn't bear it out.'

'Because it's a game to them,' Mitch growled. 'Wright and his pal like to fuck with people's minds. Wright might have confessed anything to Enberg before he fired him, just for the pleasure of knowing the man would wear a hole in his conscience trying to decide what to do about it. Like pulling the wings off flies, the sick son of a bitch.'

559

The idea shot ice through Ellen's veins. But she did her best to pull together the remnants of the tough shell she had developed working in the city, and shed there two years ago.

'Let's get this over with,' she muttered.

Mitch tipped his head in deference. 'If you say so.'

He steered her in the direction of Denny Enberg's desk. *Be calm, be detached*, she recited, calling up old skills that were rusty with disuse. That was the key, not to think of the body as a human being who had a wife sitting out in the reception area. It was just a body, evidence in a crime, not a man she had spoken with just last night in this very room.

'You know I would never ask you to compromise your ethics, Denny. But I trust you to do what's right. If Garrett Wright is the monster we think he is, he has to be stopped. His accomplice has to be stopped. If you could do something to stop them, I know you would. You would do the right thing. Wouldn't you, Denny?'

They would never know. Denny Enberg's conscience was gone, along with most of his head. His body was sprawled in his desk chair, the shotgun used to kill him resting between his spread legs, barrel up. Brain matter, bone fragments, and blood had exploded up and back from the body, sticking to the knotty-pine paneling and acoustic ceiling tile in a grisly spray.

Stuart Oglethorpe, Park County coroner and director of the Oglethorpe Funeral Home, stared at what remained of Denny Enberg.

'Well, he killed himself,' he announced with disgust.

'Maybe.'

Oglethorpe glared up at Mitch through his thick black horn-rimmed glasses. 'What? It's plain and simple!'

'Nothing is simple.'

Wilhelm blew out a breath. 'Look, Chief, he's sitting in his desk chair, there's no sign of a struggle. Do you think he just watched the killer walk in and obligingly opened his mouth for the gun barrel?'

Mitch turned away from him, only half listening. 'There's no suicide note,' he mumbled. He pulled a pencil out of the crowded cup beside the bloodstained blotter and tapped it against the empty bottle of Cuervo. 'He'd been drinking,' he muttered. 'We don't know how much.'

'That bottle was half-full when I was here,' Ellen said.

'What time was that?'

'Seven, seven-thirty.'

'And there's only one glass sitting here,' Mitch said. 'That's a lot of tequila. The toxicologist can tell us how much. If he drank enough to pass out, that would explain the lack of a struggle.'

'What about the string on the trigger?' Wilhelm countered. 'The gun was rigged –'

Mitch scowled at him. 'For Christ's sake, Wilhelm, if you wanted a murder to look like a suicide, wouldn't you be smart enough to trick out the goddamn gun?' He held up a hand and rolled his eyes. 'Don't answer

560

that.' Turning to Oglethorpe, he said, 'As soon as the scene has been processed, we'll get him bagged and you can transport him up to HCMC. The sooner they get tissue samples to the lab, the better.'

'An autopsy?' The coroner groaned. Once a body was transported to the Hennepin County Medical Center, there was no guarantee of its coming back to the Oglethorpe Funeral Home for preparation for the world beyond, and therefore no guarantee of profit.

'I'll call for the mobile lab.' Wilhelm's tone indicated that he considered it too much trouble.

'Call for a new attitude while you're at it,' Mitch ordered. 'If you think crimes should be committed in an orderly fashion, one at a fucking time to fit into your schedule, you're in the wrong job, *Agent* Wilhelm.'

The exchange barely registered in Ellen's mind. Her attention was drawn by Denny Enberg's hand, frozen by rigor mortis on the arm of his chair. Broad across the palm, with short, blunt-tipped fingers. The plain gold band on his ring finger gleamed.

Just an ordinary man with a decent law practice and a wife who worked nights. A nice, quiet, ordinary life that had been taken from him by force. If what she suspected was true, he had been used as a pawn, toyed with and destroyed as if he were nothing more than a playing piece in the game.

'I'll talk with his secretary myself,' Mitch said, steering her toward the door. 'See if he had any late-night appointments scheduled. I wouldn't expect a killer to leave his name, but we might be able to narrow down the time frame. We could even get lucky and find ourselves a witness. He didn't mention anyone to you, did he, Ellen?'

'No. I didn't see anything out of the ordinary, either. My mind was on the case. But humor me and check to see what Todd Childs and Christopher Priest were doing last night, will you?'

'They're on my list.'

'And Paul Kirkwood,' Wilhelm said.

Mitch's jaw tightened.

'We can't ignore him, Mitch,' Ellen murmured with apology in her eyes.

'Yeah, I know,' he said with crackling sarcasm. 'He *is* from the BCA.'

'She meant Kirkwood,' Marty grumbled.

Ellen checked her watch as she stepped into the hall. 'I've got to get out of here. I've got a meeting at ten, and if I don't shower and change out of these clothes, Judge Grabko is liable to hold me in contempt.'

She looked up at Mitch with gratitude. 'Thanks for listening to me, Chief. I'm afraid if it had been left up to Agent Wilhelm and our esteemed coroner, Denny would be on an embalming table this afternoon.'

'I think Wilhelm got a little more than he bargained for with this field post. He comes here in the middle of a kidnapping. Before his first week is up there's another, and now a potential homicide. Before this thing is over, he's going to wish he could give the job back to Megan.'

'How's she doing?'

He glanced away, his jaw tightening. 'As well as can be expected. Unfortunately, no one is expecting much – except Megan herself. She's too damn stubborn for her own good.'

'She's a fighter.'

'Yeah. I'm just worried about what happens if she can't win this fight.'

The cruelty of Wright's game just kept spreading outward like an ink stain, blacking out Megan's career, Josh's innocence, Dustin Holloman's future, Denny Enberg's life. It had touched Ellen's own life as simply and easily as a phone call.

The first thing we do, let's kill all the lawyers . . . .

'We'll get a trace on your home phone,' Mitch said, backing down the hall as someone called to him from Denny's office. 'I'll talk to you later.'

Ellen nodded and waved him off. For a moment she was all alone, halfway between the death scene and the mourners. She would have to stop on her way out and offer her condolences to Denny's wife, then fight her way through the media mob to get to her car.

All she wanted was a nice, quiet, well-ordered life . . . like Dennis Enberg . . . like the Kirkwoods and the Hollomans.

Suddenly she needed to breathe air that didn't stink of death, to let the cold air clear her head. She turned right, went down the short hall, and let herself out on the back side of the building.

A stiff wind slapped her face. She opened her mouth and gulped it in. Leaning back against the building, she let herself mourn for the loss of a life and the loss of something less tangible – peace and safety, the sense of immunity people here had wrapped around themselves like a warm woolen blanket.

She had left Minneapolis, but she hadn't run from it, no matter what Tony Costello believed. She had chosen to go, had chosen this town and the life she led here. If she had to fight for it, she would fight with everything she had.

Ellen took a final deep breath and walked back inside to face a colleague's widow and the voyeurs who would report this latest tragedy to the world.

15

Gorman Grabko had an extensive collection of bow ties. As a second-year law student he had been impressed with the idea that every memorable man created his own image. That year he had begun wearing bow ties. He had been wearing them for thirty-three years. Always discreet and tasteful. Never the clip-on variety.

Today he had chosen a dignified gray-on-gray stripe that complemented the steel color in the close-cropped salt-and-pepper beard he wore to hide the ancient craters of rampant teenage acne. The hair on the sides of his square head was darker, with flags of silver at the temples. There was no hair on top of his head. Baldness had been a distinguishing trait of the Grabko men for centuries. He wore it as proudly as his judge's robes and the dark Brooks Brothers suit beneath them.

Grabko was well aware there were judges in the rural districts who paid little attention to style. He had accepted it as his mission to uphold standards. He had degrees from Northwestern, had taught at Drake Law, was a patron of the arts, and aspired to someday sit on the state supreme court.

He hoped that day would not be too far in the future, though it was difficult for a judge to distinguish himself in a place like Park County. For the most part, crimes here were petty, trials simple, the attorneys uninspired. The chance to hear a case the likes of *The State versus Dr Garrett Wright* was a rare occasion. Gorman Grabko had prepared himself accordingly.

He sat behind his immaculate desk with the air of a benevolent monarch, smiling warmly at Anthony Costello.

'Mr Costello, it's a pleasure and an honor,' he said. 'It isn't every day we get an attorney of your reputation in the Park County courthouse – is it, Ellen?'

Ellen made a small motion with her lips. No one could have called it a smile. She wanted to tell Grabko he should be thankful – but, then, that wasn't the comment he wanted to hear. The question was rhetorical, at any rate. The judge continued without waiting for her opinion, essentially shutting her out of their little male-bonding ritual. Or maybe it was less a guy thing than it was a celebrity thing. She could have got a better handle on it if Cameron had been there, but he had a competency hearing in Judge Witt's courtroom that morning, and so she was on her own.

'You're a Purdue man, I'm told,' Grabko said.

Costello grinned. 'I hope as a Northwestern alumnus, you won't hold that against me.'

Grabko beamed, obviously flattered that Costello knew anything about him. 'Both fine Big Ten schools. You've certainly done yours proud. You've made quite a name for yourself. I keep abreast of the goings-on in the metropolitan courts,' Grabko said importantly, as if he had been appointed to do so by some higher power and wasn't motivated by simple envy.

'I keep busy.'

Ellen struggled not to gag on Costello's false modesty. 'Dr Wright was lucky you could squeeze him in between murder trials.'

'Yes, things do get hectic in the Cities.' Costello cut her a look. 'But, then, you knew all about that once upon a time, didn't you, Ellen? It's understandable it could become overwhelming for some people.'

He made it sound as if she had cracked under the pressure and been shuttled out to the country to live in shame and secret. Grabko put his head a little on one side and looked at her with a glimmer of suspicion. Ellen narrowed her eyes at Costello.

' "Sickening" is a better word, though some people don't seem to mind wading through sewage. But we shouldn't take up Judge Grabko's time reminiscing,' she said with a saccharine smile. 'He has a very full schedule.'

'I'm concerned about the timetable with your just arriving on the case, Mr Costello,' Grabko said. 'Can I assume you'll want the omnibus hearing postponed?'

'No, Your Honor. The defense will be fully ready to proceed. Eager to proceed, in fact. Every day these changes hang over Dr Wright's head is another day his character is unnecessarily blackened.'

Costello hit Grabko full-beam with his game face – tough, direct, intense. 'Your Honor, my first duty to my client is to rectify the injustice done him earlier in the week when the late Judge Franken set bail well beyond his reach.'

'The man was apprehended running from the scene of a crime,' Ellen jumped in.

'Allegedly.'

'He brutally beat an agent of the BCA –'

'Allegedly.'

'And did his best to escape. He's an obvious flight risk –'

Costello stood abruptly, taking Grabko's gaze with him. He walked toward the windows where milky light drained in through fat venetian blinds.

'Dr Wright is entitled to the presumption of innocence,' he said. 'He is, in fact, an innocent man. Under the statutes of this state he is entitled to a reasonable bail. Half a million dollars in cash is hardly reasonable.'

Grabko stroked his beard.

'Neither is kidnapping an eight-year-old child or torturing a woman –'

Costello wheeled around. 'Oh, come on, Ellen. You can't possibly believe Garrett Wright did any of that. He's a respected professor –'

'I know *exactly* what Garrett Wright is, *Mr* Costello.' Ellen came to her feet, advancing toward him with her hands planted on the hips of her narrow tobacco-brown skirt. 'He is a man who stands accused of multiple felonies and did his best to elude capture.'

'I don't argue that the *assailant* fled the scene. I argue that my client was not the assailant.'

'Funny, then, how he was the one taken into custody.'

'He was, obviously, the man captured, but he was not the perpetrator of the crimes.'

'The evidence suggests otherwise.'

'We'll see about that, counselor,' Costello said calmly. 'If it goes that far.'

Ellen crossed her arms and stood there as Tony slid back into his chair and crossed his legs, carefully straightening the jacket of his pin-striped suit to avoid wrinkles. He looked too cool, like a cardsharp with an ace up his sleeve. She weighed the idea of calling his bluff. Her silence lasted long enough to force his hand.

He looked at Grabko. 'Your Honor, I'm going to state right up front, we plan to file a motion to dismiss on the grounds of unlawful arrest. The Fourth Amendment prohibits police, absent exigent circumstances or consent, from making a warrantless entry into a suspect's home in order to make a felony arrest – Payton versus New York.'

'Oh, please,' Ellen sneered, positioning herself at the side of Grabko's desk. 'The man was fleeing arrest, armed and dangerous – you don't consider those exigent circumstances? The situation meets all criteria.' She ticked them off one by one on her fingers. 'A grave offense was involved, the suspect was believed to be armed, there was obvious likelihood of escape; not only was there reason to believe he was on the premises, Mitch Holt virtually followed him through the door!'

'Virtually, but not actually.' Costello directed his attention to the judge, choosing not to waste his energy or his argument on Ellen. It was Grabko he needed to sway. 'The truth of the situation is that the suspect Chief Holt was pursuing was wearing a ski mask. He never saw the man's face, had no reason to assume the man he was chasing was Dr Wright. By his own admission, Chief Holt lost sight of his suspect numerous times during the chase, including just before he burst into Dr Wright's garage.

'It is our contention that Chief Holt in fact lost sight of his suspect for too long a period of time to continue pursuit into Dr Wright's garage without benefit of a warrant.'

Ellen made no effort to contain the sarcastic laugh. 'That is the most preposterous load of –'

'Ellen, that's enough,' Judge Grabko said firmly.

She pressed her lips together and took her seat.

'The decision will be mine to make,' Grabko said. 'File your paperwork, Mr Costello. Your argument has merit. It's worth consideration.'

'But, Your Honor –'

'You'll get your chance, Ms North,' Grabko said, jotting a note to himself. 'It sounds to me as if the arrest skirts some boundaries. Convince me otherwise. At any rate, it's an issue for the omnibus hearing, and I believe we're here to discuss the matter of bail.'

With one point scored, Costello drew in a refreshing breath and leaned forward, his you're-my-pal look firmly in place. 'Your Honor, considering Dr Wright's ties to the community, his lack of a record, and what can only be called flimsy evidence against him, we request bail be reduced.'

Grabko turned to Ellen, eyebrows raised.

'I believe Judge Franken was more than fair and reasonable, considering the weight of the charges.'

The judge sat back and swiveled in his chair, tugging at a white spot in his beard. 'Wouldn't you say, Ellen,' he began in his law-professor voice, 'that bail in the amount of half a million dollars, cash, is, for all intents and purposes, denial of bail?'

Ellen said nothing. Of course it was denial of bail. She thought of Josh Kirkwood, who had barely spoken a word since his return. She thought of Megan, battered, broken, haunted, her career likely ended by Garrett Wright's vicious brutality. She thought of Dennis, the smell of his death sneaking down the back of her throat. She thought of Wright himself, imagined she could feel his gaze probing into her as she had that day in the interview room.

'It seems extreme to me,' the judge went on. 'I'm familiar with Dr Wright's reputation and with his juvenile-offenders program, and from what I know of the man, I have difficulty seeing him as a flight risk at this point.'

'But, Your Honor, that's just the point, don't you see?' she pleaded. 'The college professor isn't the man we're dealing with here. We're dealing with a side of Garrett Wright that might be capable of anything. The man is evil.'

Costello rolled his eyes. 'Isn't that a little melodramatic, Ellen?'

'You wouldn't think so if you'd been in your predecessor's office this morning.'

He had the gall to let amusement tint his surprise. 'You're blaming my client for Enberg's death? That would be quite a trick, considering he was in jail at the time.'

Grabko frowned at her and brushed a thumb along his jaw. 'One hundred thousand dollars, cash or bond.'

'Mr Brooks, what angle are you planning to take on this story?'

Jay frowned at the reporters that had clustered around him. They had gathered in the courtroom to catch the latest twist of the case. Anthony Costello was going to ask for bail to be reduced. But the stars of the show had yet to come onstage, and the press had grown as restless as toddlers in church. One group was circled around Paul Kirkwood, who had positioned himself in the first row behind the prosecution bench. With a writer's ability to eavesdrop and carry on a conversation at the same time, Jay picked up the gist of Paul's statement – justice, victim's rights, the American way.

'I don't know that there'll be a book,' Jay said, shaking his head. 'I'm just here as an observer. Y'all are the ones working this case.'

He might as well have told them he had come to declare himself dictator and absolute ruler of the state of Minnesota. They heard what they wanted to hear and ignored the rest.

'Will you be working with the family, or are you interested in Dr Wright's story?'

'No comment, fellas.' He flashed them a grin. 'Now, listen, y'all got me talking like a lawyer. That's more work than I want to do.'

Their eyes lit up like Christmas bulbs, and he knew he had made a grave mistake. A blond with a microphone leaned toward him.

'As a former defense attorney, Mr Brooks, what is your opinion of the firing of Dennis Enberg, who allegedly committed suicide early this morning, and the arrival of his replacement, Anthony Costello?'

A man had blown his head clean off, and Blondie slid it into the scheme of things as if it were just another point of minor interest in her story. The idea disgusted him. The disgust amused him in a twisted sort of way. Ellen would have said he was no better than this woman, with her hunger for a story. He had come here for what was, on the surface, the same reason. In truth, he had deeper reasons, but they may in fact have been worse.

Self-loathing twisted his mouth into a bitter smile. 'Ma'am, I haven't been an attorney in a very long time,' he said. 'And, hell, if I'd been any good at it, I'd probably still be doing it, wouldn't I? I can't see where my opinion on any of this is worth a hill of beans.'

'And yet you don't hesitate to take sides in your books.' She refused to be brushed off with 'Aw, shucks' and a famous grin. 'Your critics – prominent defense attorneys among them – say you have a sharp eye for the law and that your analysis of trials is akin to laser surgery.'

At the front of the courtroom the door to the judge's chambers swung open, and instantly the attention of everyone in the room swung forward. Ellen emerged first, looking furious. Jay could tell she was fighting to keep her expression blank, but her whole body looked as tight as a clenched fist, and her eyes glittered with the same kind of fire she had directed at him a time or two.

Costello strolled out behind her, relaxed, confident. He looked directly at the members of the press. The conquering hero. The champion for the common man – provided the common man could come up with the bucks.

The judge, the Honorable Gorman Grabko, climbed to his perch and seated himself. Prim was the first adjective that came to mind. He looked like the kind of man who would use shoe trees and wax his bald spot. Hallway scuttlebutt indicated he was a stickler for form and that he tended to lean toward the defense, holding the prosecution to a higher standard. By the look of things, Ellen had fallen short.

A side door opened and Garrett Wright was led in by a pair of deputies and seated at the defense table.

It was over in a matter of minutes. The skirmish had been fought in chambers, as most of them were. This show was for the record and for the spectators who had gathered to watch the drama unfold.

Costello formally stated his request. Ellen argued against it. Grabko's mind was made up.

'Bail is set in the amount of one hundred thousand dollars, cash or bond,' the judge announced.

'This is an outrage!' Paul Kirkwood shouted, leaping up from his seat. His face flushed the color of dried blood, and a vein stood out prominently in the side of his neck. 'That animal stole my son and you're letting him out!'

A beefy deputy rushed up the aisle and grabbed hold of him. Paul put a shoulder into him and staggered him back a step toward the defense side of the room.

'You ruined our lives!' he screamed, thrusting an angry fist in Wright's direction.

Grabko smashed his gavel down. He had risen to his feet and called for more deputies. The courtroom rang with shouts and shrieks and the scuffling sounds of physical struggle. More deputies rushed in. Three of them grabbed hold of Paul Kirkwood and herded him toward the nearest exit.

He twisted around as they dragged him. 'I want justice! I want justice!'

The reporters rushed after him in a flock. The remaining deputies hustled Wright and Costello out a side door. Grabko shook his head, banged his gavel, and declared court adjourned for the morning. The room was empty in a matter of seconds, everyone running into the hall to catch the continuation of Paul's show. Everyone except Ellen.

She sat at the table with one arm banded across her middle and the other hand raised as a prop for her chin. She stared up at the empty bench as if she were trying to will the blindfold off the figure of Lady Justice. Jay hung back, his eyes on Ellen. He should have been out in the hall. Paul Kirkwood's penchant for theatrics intrigued him. There was something slightly off about those performances, something that struck Jay as calculated, disingenuous. But he couldn't seem to make himself turn away and walk out.

Instead, he opened the gate and let himself onto the business side of the bar. Because he wanted to hear Ellen's take on things, he told himself. That was all. Not because she looked small and forlorn, sitting there all alone. Not because it touched him in any way that she was taking the loss hard.

'It's only bail,' he said.

'Tell that to Paul Kirkwood,' Ellen murmured. 'Drive out to Lakeside and break that news to Josh's mother. Or maybe you want to call Megan O'Malley in the hospital and tell her?

'It's only bail.' She faked a nonchalant shrug as she turned in her chair to face him. 'Why shouldn't Garrett Wright be free to walk the streets, free to communicate with his accomplice, who may have committed murder last night? Who is, as we speak, doing God-knows-what to Dustin Holloman.'

He moved closer, his hands stuffed into the pockets of his rumpled slate-colored Dockers. He had shed his coat somewhere. A bright silk tie hung like a strip of modern art down the front of his worn denim shirt. The knot was jerked loose and the top button undone as if he just couldn't bear the symbolism of a noose around his neck and yet felt compelled to make a token show of formality.

'You lost the round, not the game,' he said, settling a hip on the corner of the heavy oak table. His thigh brushed against the back of her hand.

The contact had the quality of an electric shock. Ellen tried to cover the involuntary reaction by shifting positions, reaching up to brush at a stray hair that had come loose from her twist. 'It's not a game.'

'Of course it is. You've played it a thousand times. You know the rules. You know the strategies. You gave up some points. It's not the end of the world.'

Ellen glared at him, anger burning through the haze of defeat. 'A man gave up his life last night. How many points is that worth?' she asked bitterly, pushing to her feet. 'What's that worth to you? Another chapter? A page? A paragraph?'

'I didn't kill him and I can't bring him back. I can only try to put it in context. Isn't that what you want to do? Make sense of it, understand it?'

'Oh, I understand it. Now let *me* put it in a context *you* can understand. It's a game, all right, Mr Brooks. Dennis Enberg was a piece they didn't need anymore, and now he's dead and his replacement just drew the Get Out Of Jail card for his twisted bastard of a client, and I couldn't manage to stop any of that from happening!'

The rage and the pain boiled up inside her, boiled over the rim of her control. She turned her back to him and pressed her hands over her face, furious with herself. She had thought she had control of her emotions if nothing else in all this madness. She had vowed to fight this battle, but somehow she hadn't seen the possibility for this early defeat. She thought of Costello's threat to get the arrest thrown out and felt sick at the possibility. If she could lose this battle, she could lose that one. That vulnerability was terrifying and raw.

Jay watched her struggle to rein in her feelings. Her back was ramrod straight, her shoulders straining against the need to shake. Despite all the time she had spent working in the system, she had managed to hang on to a sense of right and a sense of honor. She fought hard and took her losses harder. Cynicism hadn't dulled the lance of justice for her as it had for so many. As it had for him. It seemed only to have made her more keenly aware of her place in the scheme of things.

'You didn't think it could happen here, did you?' he murmured, stepping behind her.

'It shouldn't be happening here,' she whispered. 'Children should be safe. Dennis Enberg should be alive. Garrett Wright and whatever other madman is playing this game with him should be stopped forever.'

'Is that why you left the city?' He was close enough that the scent of her perfume caught his nose and drew his head down. The nape of her neck was no more than a breath away – tempting, too tempting.

He wanted her and knew better than to give in to that seductive need. She was part of the story. The story was what he had come here for – to bury himself in it, to lose himself in it, to run away from his own pain and dissect someone else's.

The reminder brought a bitter taste of self-loathing. The anger made him cruel.

'Is that why you left, Ellen? Because you didn't want to fight this kind of fight? Is that what you ran from?'

She wheeled on him and he caught hold of her arms before she could slap him.

'I didn't run from anything.'

'You were on the short list of up-and-comers in Minneapolis,' he said, deliberately goading her. 'Then suddenly you're riding roughshod over drunks and losers in Mayberry.'

'I *walked* away. I wanted a saner life. I made a choice, and I certainly don't have to justify it to you.'

'There's sure as hell nothing sane about what's going on here now,' he growled.

Ellen didn't know if he meant the case or the heat building between them at that moment. He was too close, his hands too tight on her upper arms, his mouth just inches from hers.

'Let go of me,' she ordered, jerking out of his grasp.

The hall door swung open, and Henry Forster, a longtime reporter for the *Minneapolis Star Tribune*, stepped in. Through the perpetually smudged lenses of his thick bifocals, his gaze hit Ellen with full magnified force.

'Ellen, are we going to get a comment from you?' he barked. 'Or are we just supposed to draw our own conclusions?'

'I'm coming right now,' she said.

Not sparing Jay so much as a glance, she picked up her briefcase and walked out.

He followed at a distance, waiting for her to capture the full attention of the reporters before he slipped into the hall. The wait also gave him a moment to clear his brain. Damn, but he had got his balls in a vise this time.

This was what he got for sniffing around a live case. Ordinarily, he had sense enough to come in after the fact, after the strongest of the immediate emotions had faded away and the parties involved had gained perspective on the crime that had touched their lives. There was no perspective here. This case was as hot as a live wire . . . and just as dangerous.

Scuttlebutt had the body of Dennis Enberg being hauled away for a look-see by a medical examiner. Ellen had as much as said she believed the lawyer had been murdered, even though the official rumor was suicide.

Jay had heard the calls on the police scanner, had found his way to the Southtown Shopping Center and bided his time in the relative warmth of his vehicle until the reporters lost interest in the scene and split in search of quotable sources. A single uniformed cop had been left on guard duty in front of the building.

Jay had wandered up, bummed a cigarette, stayed to chat as if he had nothing better to do with his time. The cop, young and unaccustomed to the sight of gruesome death, had eventually let the details of the scene come rolling out. His hands shook so violently, he could barely bring his cigarette to his lips.

'Man, I mean, you see things like that in the movies, but this was *real*,' the kid mumbled. Far across the way, half a dozen cars were parked in front of Snyder's Drug Store. People came to buy cold tablets and headache remedies, ignorant of the fact that a hundred yards from them a man had had his brain splattered all over the wall of his office.

'It's a tough sight to stomach,' Jay said. 'Truth to tell, I've seen many a strong man toss his cookies right there and then. And there's no shame in it, if you ask me. Sight like that oughta make any decent person sick.'

'Well . . . it did me,' the kid admitted. He looked at Jay out the corner of his eye. 'I suppose you've seen a lot. I read *Twist of Fate*. That was grisly.'

'True enough. Never ceases to amaze me the violence people will do to one another.'

'Yeah . . .' He sucked his Winston down to the filter, the ash glowing red as he tossed the butt. The look in his eyes was faraway, deep inside, where people keep their darkest fears and seldom look at them. 'I can't imagine sticking a shotgun in somebody's mouth and pulling the trigger.'

Murder. As if this case hadn't been sinister enough to begin with.

Jay now shot a sweeping glance across the crowd gathered for Ellen's impromptu press conference. The old warhorse with the beetle brows and bad comb-over who had walked in on them shouted down his colleagues.

'Ms North, what is your reaction to Garrett Wright's release pending payment of bond?'

'It goes without saying, I'm extremely disappointed.' She was all cool control once again, as if those moments of discomposure in the courtroom had never happened. 'However, Judge Grabko listened to both sides and made his decision, and we'll live with it. That's the way our system works.'

Which was essentially saying it hadn't worked this time.

'Will Dr Wright return to his home in the Lakeside neighborhood – virtually yards away from the Kirkwood home?'

'I don't know,' Ellen said. 'I hope not, for the family's sake.'

'What about rumors that Dennis Enberg's body was transported to the Hennepin County Medical Center for an autopsy?'

'Mr Enberg died a violent and unexpected death. The city and county agencies are obligated to investigate that death to determine beyond question whether or not it was self-inflicted.'

'Was there a suicide note?'

'No comment.'

'With Garrett Wright in jail at the time, you can't possibly suspect involvement on his part in either Mr Enberg's death or the kidnapping of Dustin Holloman, can you?'

'I have no comment regarding ongoing investigations.'

The stone wall had gone up. She had made her point about Wright's release; the rest would be for show. The tough lady prosecutor showing the world this small defeat didn't faze her. None of these reporters had seen her tears or heard the self-castigation in her voice.

Jay had. And that mattered to him in a way that was patently unwise.

He pulled his gaze off her and continued to scan the crowd. Courthouse personnel hung around the fringes of the media group, curious to see their allegedly ambitious assistant county attorney in action. Until the first kidnapping, press conferences had likely been a rarity here.

A flash of rusty-red hair caught his eye. He moved slowly down the hall, skirting the crowd, like a hunter easing up on wary prey.

Todd Childs had focused his attention on Ellen, his gaze flat and cold behind retro-look glasses. He stood half-hidden by a marble column, wearing a long olive-drab wool coat that looked as if it had been fending off moths in someone's attic for years. A student of Wright's at Harris, Childs had been mentioned in the news reports following the O'Malley incident on Saturday. One of the local TV stations had included a shot of him and a comment as to Dr Wright's innocence in their follow-up story on Sunday.

Jay eased up beside him, tipping his head conspiratorially. 'She's a cool one, isn't she?' he murmured.

'She's a bitch,' Childs said between clenched teeth. He jerked his gaze away from Ellen, looking at Jay as if he felt he had been tricked into responding. 'You a reporter?'

'Me? Naw. Just interested. How about you?'

He scratched his scruffy goatee and sniffed. 'Yeah . . . I'm interested. Dr Wright is sort of a mentor of mine. The man is fucking brilliant.'

'Yeah, but is he guilty?'

Childs glared down at him, pale skin tightening over his bony face. Even though the light in this part of the hall was poor, his pupils were black pinpoints, suggesting he had indulged in some substance other than the dope he smoked, the smell of which had become as ingrained in his ratty coat as the scent of mothballs.

'The man is fucking brilliant,' he said again, enunciating each word crisply. 'The case against him is bullshit.' He cut a nasty glance toward Ellen. 'She'll wish she'd never started this.'

He backed away from the pillar and turned toward the steps at the far end of the hall. The sudden mix of voices talking all at once told Jay the press conference was over. He didn't look for Ellen but fell in step behind Todd Childs. Keeping his head down, he hustled down the first set of stairs, coming even with Childs on the second-floor landing.

'So are you involved with the protest out front?' he asked as they made their way toward the ground floor.

'Yeah.' Childs shot him a sideways look. 'You ask a lot of questions. Who are you?'

'James Butler,' he lied without hesitation. 'I'm doing some independent consulting work with the county auditor's office. You might have guessed, I'm not from around here. I just sort of dropped in on all of this – like tuning into the middle of a movie, you know?'

'Yeah, well, you know what they say, man,' Childs muttered as he flipped down his clip-on shades. 'Truth is stranger than fiction.'

He pushed through one of the heavy main doors and cut diagonally down the steps, his bushy hair bouncing like a foxtail down the center of his back. Jay watched from the door, his sixth sense stirring restlessly.

'Hey!' a voice sounded beside him. 'You're Jay Butler Brooks! Adam Slater, *Grand Forks Herald*. Could I ask you a couple of questions?'

'Yeah, sure,' Jay mumbled resignedly. His eyes remained on Todd Childs, who approached the small crowd of student protestors now celebrating his mentor's release . . . and walked right past them as if they weren't there.

16

The news of Garrett Wright's release on bond swept through Deer Lake and on to Campion like a blizzard wind. Telephones at the courthouse and law-enforcement center were jammed with irate calls from the faction of the population who believed Wright was guilty. In Campion the search for Dustin Holloman went on unrewarded, and the reporters lost interest in shooting still more footage of grim-faced volunteers trudging through the snow. Word that Anthony Costello would be giving a formal statement in front of the Park County courthouse about Wright's release sent them packing.

The sidewalk in front of the courthouse took on the carnival atmosphere of a political campaign riding the tide of victory. The Harris College students who had been protesting Dr Wright's incarceration took up new celebratory chants. The Sci-Fi Cowboys, freed by a teacher in-service day in the metropolitan school system, had set up a vendor's cart on the sidewalk and were selling T-shirts to raise money for Wright's defense fund. A boom box blasted out rap music with strong themes of injustice and oppression. Deer Lake natives watched the festivities with wary eyes from the front window of the Scandia House Cafe. In typical rural Minnesota fashion, all overt displays of emotion were considered suspicious.

Ellen looked down on the goings-on from the window of the conference room. Momentum was swinging Wright's way. Just days ago she had held the control. Now her handhold was being pried away one finger at a time.

'Do you think they have a permit to sell those T-shirts?' Cameron asked.

'They do,' Phoebe said, holding her glasses on her button nose as she looked down. 'I checked. And we can't stop Mr Costello from speaking on the steps of the courthouse, either.'

'He would only use it against us if we tried,' Ellen muttered.

She turned away from the window and faced her team. Mitch had seated himself at one end of the table. Steiger positioned himself at the opposite end, standing with one dirty boot planted on the seat of the chair. Wilhelm sat halfway between them, looking shell-shocked, glassy-eyed. The idiot grin he had worn to Deer Lake a week ago had slipped badly in the last few days. Between developments in the Kirkwood case, the Holloman kidnapping, and Denny Enberg's death, the hours had been hellish, the pressure immense, the leads nonexistent.

'I'm familiar with Costello's tactics,' Ellen said. 'He believes the best defense is a good offense. He'll do everything he can to make us look bad.'

'You mean he'll throw as much shit as he can at the wall and hope some of it sticks,' the sheriff said bluntly.

'I'm sure he wouldn't put it quite that way, but that's the gist of it. He plays big-league hardball.'

'He's an out-of-town stiff,' Steiger snorted. 'Just because he's from the Cities, we're all supposed to crap our pants at the sight of him. He's just another shyster lawyer.'

Cameron rolled his eyes. Phoebe gave the sheriff a look that suggested he smelled as if he had already seen Costello and fulfilled his statement.

'This shyster is like having a great white shark land in our lake, Sheriff,' Ellen said. 'Do *not* underestimate him.'

'He's got his own private investigator,' Mitch interjected. 'Raymond York. The guy was sniffing around St Elysius today. Father Tom called to complain.'

Steiger scowled at him. 'So?'

'So this PI will be working full-time to find anything that might get Wright off the hook, while the rest of us are trying to work this case, find Dustin Holloman, figure out whether or not Denny Enberg killed himself, and deal with our everyday, garden-variety mopes.'

'The Holloman case and Denny's death complicate our situation,' Ellen admitted. 'But if we go on the assumption they're tied to Josh Kirkwood's case, that it's Wright's accomplice carrying on the game, then we're still focused on nailing Wright.'

'That could be a dangerous assumption if it's wrong,' Wilhelm stated.

'But it's not wrong,' Mitch said. 'We know the kidnappings are related. The thing we can't be sure of is Enberg. The autopsy is scheduled for Monday. If we're lucky, we'll get the word on fingerprints Monday, as well.'

'Did Denny's secretary know anything about any late-night appointments?' Ellen asked.

He shook his head. 'She said it was a light day. Three appointments with clients and a couple of reporters dropping by for comments. He didn't have anything scheduled after five, told her he was going to stay late and do some paperwork. I've got guys talking to the clients, trying to get a handle on his state of mind. Barb, the secretary, said he was down about the Wright case, but that he didn't want to talk to her about it.'

'No witnesses from around the shopping center?' Cameron asked, tapping the end of his fountain pen against his legal pad, impatient for a break.

'None yet, but we haven't been able to track down the night staff from the Donut Hut. They're gone to Mankato for the day – skiing.'

'Well, we know one thing,' Wilhelm said. 'Wright didn't kill him. He was still sitting in jail at the time.'

'Grabko remedied that situation,' Mitch muttered.

'It may actually work to our advantage to have Wright out on bail,' Cameron offered. 'If we can put him under surveillance, he could lead us to the accomplice, to Dustin Holloman, tie the whole mess up in a nice, neat bow.'

'Somehow I don't think he'll be that obliging,' Mitch said. 'But I've already assigned a plainclothes detail to him, in case there's a God after all.'

'I've assigned an agent to the surveillance team, too,' Marty Wilhelm said without enthusiasm.

'I'm assuming nothing has turned up from the search of Wright's home?' Ellen asked.

He shook his head. 'Nothing at all out of the ordinary. You might think he's an innocent man.'

Mitch gave him a look that could have frozen fire. 'I *don't* think he's an innocent man, Agent Wilhelm. Neither does your predecessor. And you had damn well better not think he's innocent either.'

'Hey, I've got an ongoing situation in Campion –'

'Garrett Wright is an ongoing situation,' Ellen stated sharply, pulling Wilhelm's attention back to her. 'We've got a probable-cause hearing in less than a week and a judge who has "Innocent Until Proven Guilty" embroidered on his underwear. I need every scrap of ammunition I can get to nail Wright. Costello fired his first shot today – he's going to try to get the arrest thrown out.'

'Fuck him!' Mitch jumped to his feet. 'That was a righteous bust!'

Ellen held up a hand. 'I said he would try. He won't succeed if we have anything to say about it. I don't believe he'll convince Grabko, but in the meantime he'll be feeding his theories to the press, tainting the jury pool.'

'Goddamn weasel,' Steiger muttered.

Ellen turned to Wilhelm again. 'Tell me you've got someone working with the computer equipment you confiscated from Wright's home.'

'Yes, but they're not going to find anything. We all know that.'

'The notes from Josh's and Dustin Holloman's kidnappings were computer generated and printed on a laser printer. Garrett Wright owns a laser printer.'

'But the thing doesn't have a memory. There's no way to tell if the notes came from *that* printer,' Wilhelm argued. 'And so far we haven't found a computer diskette labelled "Terroristic Threats and Creepy Poetry." Wright isn't stupid enough to have hung on to anything incriminating.'

Mitch glared at him. 'Well, you would know more about stupidity than the rest of us, Wilhelm, but I know this – guys like Wright get cocky. And when they get cocky, they get careless.'

'He told Megan they had done this sort of thing before,' Ellen said. 'He told her they had committed murder. If that's true, then he has to have left a trail somewhere. And if he's proud of his accomplishments, I can't believe he hasn't kept some sort of souvenirs. No luck on the search for another property in the area?'

Steiger shook his head. 'Not in Wright's name. Not in his wife's name. Nothing for Priest or Childs.'

She looked to Wilhelm. 'You haven't found anything in his background?'

Wilhelm dug through a messy file folder on the table in front of him and tugged out a typed report. 'He was a Boy Scout.'

Cameron took the papers. 'Any merit badges for cruel and unusual behavior?'

'I've read the report,' Wilhelm said. 'There's nothing out of the ordinary. His parents split up when he was a kid. He was raised by his mother, an office manager for a shoe factory in Mishawaka, Indiana. National Honor Society in high school, graduated with honors from Ball State, went on for his master's and doctorate at Ohio State,' he recited the history in a bored monotone, surreptitiously checking his watch. 'He came here from the University of Virginia and before that Penn State.'

'He gets around for someone in a profession where tenure is the big brass ring,' Cameron said.

'Have you checked with NCIC?' Ellen asked. 'They can scan their database for similar crimes in other parts of the country.'

'The man has no record, Ms North.'

'All that means is he's never been caught,' Mitch said. He began to pace. 'Jesus Christ, Wilhelm, if you don't want to do the job, fucking delegate. I'll call NCIC myself.'

Wilhelm scowled at the table, color splashing across his cheekbones. 'I'm doing my job, Chief Holt. I can't do everything at once.'

'I'm beginning to wonder if you can manage to walk and chew gum at the same time –'

'Time out!' Ellen shouted, rising from her chair. The men looked at her with surprise and annoyance for interrupting their argument. 'We've got a case to make. You guys tear each other's throats out on your own time.'

'This is pointless,' Steiger grumbled, waving a hand at them.

Before he could take his foot off the chair, a beeper went off. Everyone but Phoebe reached for a pager.

'It's mine,' Steiger said, reaching for the phone on the table.

Tension crackled like static in the air as he punched in the number and waited. No one spoke. Ellen knew that they were all thinking the same thing, that they were all thinking the worst and hoping for the best.

'Steiger,' the sheriff barked. A muscle ticked in his cheek, marking

577

time as he took in the news. Four seconds . . . five seconds . . . Air hissed out between his teeth, taking his color with it. 'Shit. Keep it quiet. Don't do anything. I'll be right there.'

He slammed the receiver down. 'That was Campion. They found the boy's boot with a note inside. "Evil comes to him who searches for it."'

The three cops grabbed their coats and headed for the door, grim-faced and silent.

'I'll be there as soon as I can,' Ellen promised.

Cameron closed the door behind them and clamped his hands on top of his head. 'Shit. Shit, shit, shit.'

Phoebe shoved her glasses up into her hair and covered her eyes with her fingers.

Ellen sank back down on her chair. 'Look at the timing,' she said, her gaze catching Cameron's. 'Just as Costello is about to start his press conference with Garrett Wright standing beside him, a clue is found in an identical case twenty miles away.'

'You think Costello knows?'

Tony had shown his colors before, but could he be that cold, that ruthless? Could he know the name of the person who held the fate of Dustin Holloman and not tell them?

'I don't know,' she whispered.

'That poor little boy,' Phoebe squeaked behind her hands.

'The best thing we can do for him is our jobs,' Ellen said, fighting to push away the mental fatigue and uncertainty. 'Cameron, I want you to write the best damn brief in history on exigent circumstances and probable cause regarding the Fourth Amendment. We're not letting Wright weasel out of this on a technicality.'

'You got it.'

'I also want you to ride herd on Agent Wilhelm. Keep after him about digging into Wright's background. He should have a man on it fulltime. If they can't catch Wright's accomplice, then his past is our way in.'

'I'll make some phone calls.' He slid into his chair and started making notes.

'Phoebe, it's your job to run interference.' Ellen caught one of the girl's wrists and gently pulled her hand away from her damp face. 'Are you listening to me?'

'Y-yes.'

'I know you're used to giving the defense attorneys free access to files and information. We've always had an open-door policy. You're going to slam that door shut in Tony Costello's face. If he wants something from this office, he has to request it in writing. Make this as inconvenient for him as possible. I'm never in when he calls. He never gets in to see me without an appointment. Understand?'

Phoebe nodded, bouncing her glasses down out of her hair. She shoved them into place, sniffed, and sat up straighter, putting on her bravest face to accept her duty.

'Now, turn that television up,' Ellen ordered, nodding to the portable set they had perched on a file cabinet. The Channel-Eleven news camera was homing in on Costello's handsome face. 'In the words of Sheriff Steiger, let's see what shit he's throwing at the wall now.'

'An innocent man is free,' Costello began. A cheer went up from the students gathered on the sidewalk behind the press. 'Upon reviewing the circumstances and the facts of this case, Judge Grabko has seen fit to grant Dr Wright bail and reverse the earlier injustice imposed by the prosecution and the late Judge Franken.'

The afternoon was growing dark with the promise of night and more snow. Portable lights had been set on the steps of the courthouse to illuminate the players in this melodrama. The cameraman was positioned down the steps, shooting upwards. The effect was dramatic, with the pillars of the courthouse as a backdrop. Costello looked powerful, his shoulders filling the screen in close-ups, his face as masculine and classic as a Roman sculpture. Garrett Wright stood beside him like a pale shadow, the contrast in their builds and coloring giving him an image of delicacy and refinement.

Hannah stared at him as the camera pulled in close on his face. She watched the press conference on the kitchen television that sat tucked back into a corner on the counter. The ingredients for lasagna were scattered around it. In the family room Lily was dancing to a tune from the talking candlestick in *Beauty and the Beast*.

Josh ignored the video, sitting on a stool in front of the picture window, staring out at the lake. He had taken to carrying his backpack around the house with him, as if he felt a need to keep essential items with him in case he was taken away again. The backpack sat on the floor beside his stool, purple and teal and plump with who-knew-what.

'Dr Garrett Wright is an innocent man,' Costello said. 'The presumption of innocence is his constitutional right.'

'And what about *our* rights?' Hannah murmured, glaring at the television.

Ellen North had called to break the news about the reduced bail. Not only had the new judge reduced the amount of the bail, he had given Wright the option of securing a bond, which meant he had to come up with only ten percent of the actual amount. For ten thousand dollars Garrett Wright could walk out of jail. No amount of money could free Josh from the prison in which Wright had locked his mind.

'The investigation of Josh Kirkwood's kidnapping was mishandled from the first,' Costello went on, 'and right up to the arrest of Dr Wright – who had never been considered a suspect. He had never been questioned. He had, in fact, offered assistance and had been consulted for his expertise. He was *never* a suspect.'

'How do you explain Dr Wright's capture?' shouted a reporter offscreen.

Costello fixed him with an eagle eye. 'Dr Wright was not *captured*. He was *attacked*. In his own garage, on his own property. That's the truth of this situation. The Deer Lake police department was desperate to make an arrest. Chief Holt lost sight of his suspect during the chase Saturday night, and he grabbed the first person he could. He couldn't let that opportunity slip by when he had already had one suspect die in custody. He needed to arrest somebody and Dr Wright was handy. But the fact of the matter is, there is a more viable suspect who remains at large. The kidnapping of Dustin Holloman has proved that.'

'What about the theory of an accomplice?'

Costello looked disgusted. 'Dr Wright doesn't have *accomplices*. Dr Wright has colleagues and students and friends.'

Another cheer went up from the assembled fans.

Fury boiled up inside Hannah, and she stabbed the power button on the set. Costello froze midword; then the tube seemed to suck his image inside it, leaving only blankness.

She knew the attorney was only doing his job. She knew it was up to the prosecution to prove Garrett Wright's guilt. But it made her sick and angry to see Wright portrayed as a victim. Josh was the victim. Their family had been victimized, their lives torn apart.

She didn't for a second believe Costello's contention that Garrett Wright had simply been in the wrong place at the wrong time. Costello was paid to make his client look innocent. Hannah had known Mitch Holt since the day he and his daughter had moved to Deer Lake, two years before. Mitch couldn't be bought. If Mitch said Garrett Wright was the man, Garrett Wright was the man. On the night of the arrest Mitch had come to the house, wounded and exhausted, and explained every detail of the chase and capture.

She replayed the scene in her mind as she went through the motions of preparing supper for her children, her hands shaking so badly she spilled tomato sauce on the counter. It splashed across the tile like blood, the color of violence and rage. For a long moment she just stood there staring at it. She thought of Megan O'Malley, beaten, the lifeblood of her career rushing out of her. She thought of that night Mitch had come, the night she'd told Paul it was over between them. The last lifeblood of their marriage had been drained from them. She thought of Josh and the blood that had been drawn from his arm.

Hannah didn't know if any of them could ever get back what they had lost. And yet Garrett Wright could make a down payment and buy back his freedom. If he wanted, he could come home to the house down the block. He could resume his residence in Lakeside with no regard for the lives he had wrecked at the end of the street. It seemed he could wipe the slate of his conscience clean as easily as she wiped away the spilled sauce on the counter. No consequences. Clean up the mess and forget about it.

He won't get away with it.

Ellen had assured her the county attorney's office was working diligently to bring the case to trial and to convict Garrett Wright. Mitch had told her all the law-enforcement agencies involved in the Dustin Holloman case were focused on capturing Wright's accomplice. She had to trust the system. She believed in it, believed it worked more often than not. She had to believe in justice.

He won't get away with it.

She slid the lasagna into the oven, wiped her hands on a dish towel, and walked down into the family room. The movie was still rolling, but no one seemed to be watching it. Lily was singing a tune of her own composition and her own language, and wiggling around the cherry trunk that served as a coffee table. She had pulled a pair of huge pink play sunglasses out of the toy box and wore them at a jaunty angle. Hannah grabbed a discarded baseball cap and plunked it sideways on her daughter's head, finding a smile that had become too rare in the last weeks.

'Hey, Lily-bug, are you doing the diaper dance?' she asked, squatting down and wiggling her own behind, sending Lily into a giggling frenzy.

Hannah laughed, amazed at how good that felt. Then her gaze strayed to Josh and the laughter died. He hadn't moved from the window, his expression hadn't changed. He didn't seem to be with them. His emotional isolation took on magical physical properties – an invisible force field around him that didn't allow him to see or hear or reach out to the people who loved him.

The idea came with a swift needle stab of pain. A force field was something Josh would have created a story around . . . before. He was fascinated by science fiction, loved to make up his own tales after watching *Star Trek: The Next Generation*. Since fall he had carried a notebook with him everywhere – his 'Think Pad' he called it – to draw pictures of rocket ships and race cars. He had filled the pages with his thoughts and ideas.

The notebook was gone now, given over to the state crime lab. The kidnapper had used it as one of his taunts, placing it on the hood of Mitch Holt's truck. Another piece of Josh's childhood gone.

Even as she thought it, Hannah's gaze caught on the sketch pad the county child advocate had given Josh. It lay on the floor, pushed aside, unused, blank. She shivered at the thought that Josh's mind might be that blank. There was no way of knowing as long as he chose not to share his feelings. He had spent another fifty minutes with the psychiatrist that afternoon staring at the woman's aquarium, watching the fish swim back and forth. His only comment had come at the end of the session. He had turned to Dr Freeman and said, 'They're trapped, aren't they? They can see out, but they can never get out.'

As he sat staring out the window, Hannah couldn't help but wonder if he felt the same way.

On impulse, she turned away from him and went back through the kitchen to Paul's immaculate home office. He had yet to clean out the room, though she supposed that day would come when he would box up his half of their marriage and take it all away.

Hannah found what she was looking for on a shelf in the closet, where Paul kept supplies – a brand-new blue spiral notebook. From the organizer on the desk she chose the most exotic-looking pen she could find – a fat red one with a fancy blue clip and a removable cap. She left the office and went into the laundry room, where one cupboard drawer held gift wrap, tape and string and sheets of stickers. Digging through the mess, she found an assortment of stickers she knew would appeal to Josh and used them to decorate the cover of the notebook. With a laundry marker she carefully wrote *Josh's New Think Pad* across the center of the cover, then at the very bottom printed *To Josh From Mom*, and finished the line with a heart.

He was still sitting by the window when she returned to the living room. Lily had lost all interest in the movie and was busy dragging toys out of the toy box.

'Josh, honey,' Hannah said, laying a hand on his shoulder, 'I've got something for you. Will you come sit with me on the couch so I can give it to you?'

He looked up at her, away from the window and the dark view of the lake, then gathered up his backpack and went to the couch. He sat back in a corner, the pack on his lap, his arms around it as if it were a favorite old teddy bear. Hannah took the opportunity to close the drapes, though she left the stool he had been using. Sitting next to him, she resisted the urge to pull him close. Dr Freeman had impressed upon her the need to give Josh a little breathing room, even though what she wanted most to do was hold him twenty-four hours a day.

'Remember your Think Pad and how it got lost?' she asked.

Josh nodded, though his attention seemed to be caught on the baseball cap Lily had discarded on the floor.

'I remember how you used to draw and write in it all the time. All the neat pictures you used to do with spaceships and everything. And I got to thinking you probably still miss it. I mean, that sketch pad you got is pretty cool, but it's sort of big, isn't it? You can't really carry it around. It won't fit in your backpack. And so . . . ta-da!' She held out the new notebook in front of him. 'Josh's New Think Pad.'

Hannah held her breath as he looked at it. He made no move to take it at first, but his gaze traveled the cover from top to bottom, taking in the stickers of the starship *Enterprise* and football helmets and Batman. Slowly he uncurled one arm from around his backpack and reached out with his forefinger. He touched one sticker and then the next. He traced beneath the title, then dragged his fingertip down to the bottom of the page. *To Josh From Mom*. He opened his hand and stroked the line, his expression wistful and sad.

'Go ahead, honey,' Hannah whispered around the lump in her throat. 'It's yours. Just for you. You can write down whatever you want in it – stories or secrets or dreams. You don't ever have to share it with anyone if you don't want to. But if you want to share it with me, you know I'll listen. Anything you want to tell me, you can, and it'll be all right. We can work out anything because we love each other. Right?'

His eyes filled with tears as he looked at the notebook, and he nodded slowly, reluctantly. Hannah wished she could have known what part of her statement made him hesitate. Was it that he didn't believe he could tell her or that he didn't believe they could work it out? She had no way of knowing. All she could do was offer him support and reassurance, and hope to God the promises she made him weren't empty.

As he took the notebook from her, she pulled him close and kissed the top of his head.

'We *will* work it out, Josh. However long it takes. It doesn't matter,' she whispered. 'I'm just so happy to have you home, to be able to tell you how much I love you.' She pulled back from him a little and made a goofy face at him. 'And get mushy all over you.'

A tiny smile of embarrassment hooked one corner of his mouth and he rolled his eyes. Like the old Josh. Like the boy who loved to kid with her and laugh. 'It's okay, Mom,' he said in a small voice.

'It better be,' Hannah joked. ' 'Cause, you know, even when you're a grown-up and the star quarterback in the Super Bowl, I'll still be your mom and I'll still get mushy.'

Josh wrinkled his nose and turned his attention back to the notebook. He ran his finger over the stickers one by one, naming each one in his head. He recognized them all from Before, when he had been a regular kid, when life had been simple and his biggest secret had been kissing Molly Higgins on the cheek. He wished he could go back to Before. He didn't like secrets, didn't like the way they made him feel inside. But he had to keep them now. There could be no telling. He had been warned.

So he chose not to think about the secrets at all. He would think about other things, like his new pen and how it looked like something astronauts might use, and his new Think Pad. Blank pages just for him, not for sharing with strangers or anyone. Blank pages that were like part of his imagination – space for thinking and storing thoughts away. He liked that idea – taking thoughts out of his head and storing them away where he didn't have to think them anymore.

He slipped the notebook into his backpack and carried it to his room.

17

Ellen pulled her glasses off and rubbed her hands over her face, unconcerned about her makeup. Her makeup was long gone. There was no one around the office to see her anyway. Even the cleaning people had come and gone. Ellen had done the reverse – she had gone to Campion and come back.

At Campion she had run the gauntlet of reporters and stood in the windswept parking lot of the Grain and Ag Services on the edge of town, where Dustin Holloman's boot had been found in the cab of an employee's pickup.

'Doesn't this confirm Dr Wright's innocence?'

'Will you try to delay next week's hearing?'

'Is it true Garrett Wright was never a suspect before his arrest?'

'Is it true Wright plans to sue for malicious prosecution?'

'Is the owner of the pickup being questioned? Is he a suspect?'

The questions came at her like lances. The reporters swarmed around her, their eyes bright and feral.

The parking lot was a rough sea of ice, rutted and polished by truck tires. Under the sodium-vapor security lights it took on a pearly glow. The buildings and huge metal bins of the grain elevator made an austere backdrop, Shaker-plain and simply functional, unlit, unwelcoming. Clouds had taken the daylight early and snow had begun to fall. Small, sharp flakes hurled down from heaven on a frigid, unforgiving wind.

The BCA mobile crime lab was parked at a cockeyed angle twenty feet away from the lone pickup truck. Evidence technicians swarmed around the truck, working in the brilliant light of portable halogen lamps.

'They're taking their time,' Mitch said. 'They don't want to miss so much as a hair – which is all well and good, but the guy who owns the truck raises cattle and his dog rides around with him in the cab. They'll be here all night getting hair off the goddamn seat cover.'

Ellen squinted against the pelting snow and the glare of the lights. 'Who owns the truck?'

'Kent Hofschulte. He works in the office here.'

'Any connection to the Hollomans?'

'Casual acquaintance, I hear. You want details, you'll have to talk to Steiger.'

She stepped a little closer to the truck just as an evidence tech moved aside from the open driver's door. Dustin Holloman's boot sat on the bench seat of the truck, center stage under the halogen spotlight. A single winter boot, the purple-and-yellow nylon of the upper portion too bright in this bleak setting.

She had returned to the office because she had more cases than Garrett Wright's on her schedule. There were loose ends that needed tying, and then there were Quentin Adler's endless questions about the two cases she had handed over to him. But she had appetite for neither the work she needed to accomplish nor the turkey sandwich she had picked up at Subway for her supper. All systems were crashing due to lack of fuel, but the thought of food turned her stomach.

Out of practice. When she had worked in Minneapolis, she had got to the point where she could go from a murder scene to dinner and not think twice about it. The mind was an amazing machine, able to develop what defenses it needed. But it had been a long time since she had needed defenses.

'Call it a night,' she murmured, checking the clock. Nine-fifteen. Poor Harry wasn't seeing much of his mistress these days. At least he had Otto. Otto Norvold, her neighbor and fellow dog lover, who didn't mind seeing to Harry when Ellen had to put in a late night.

She sorted through the stack of files in front of her, taking those pertinent to Wright and two other cases she would have to deal with the next day – a burglary for which she expected the defendant to cop a plea, and a DUI she fully intended to put in jail for as long as she could. The files went into her briefcase; then she set about her daily ritual of arranging everything left on her desk in precise order. She had learned long ago that her office was the one place in her professional life where she could always be guaranteed order and control. She exercised the ritual with religious dedication and found it much more calming than the pointless raking of a Zen garden.

Satisfied with the task, she pushed her chair into its cubbyhole, dug in her coat pockets for her gloves. Her mind was already halfway out the building, wondering how much snow had fallen in the two hours since she had come back. Four to six inches was predicted. The road back from Campion had already begun to drift over in spots.

She dug her keys out of her purse, slung the bag over her shoulder, and started for the door just as the telephone rang.

'What now?' she muttered on a groan, fearing the worst behind the screen of annoyance.

'Ellen North,' she said into the receiver.

Nothing.

'Hello?'

It was Monday night all over again – the heavy sense of a presence on the other end of the line, a silence that seemed ominous. Her stomach churned as the line from last night's call played through the back of her mind. *'The first thing we do, let's kill all the lawyers.'*

'If you've got something to say, then say it,' she snapped. 'I've got better things to do with my time.'

A breath. Soft and long. It seemed to come out of the receiver and curl around her throat like a snake. 'Ellen . . .'

The whisper was little more than thought. Androgynous. As thin as gauze.

'Who is this?'

'Working late, Ellen?'

She slammed the receiver down. Mitch had set up a caller–ID tracer on her home telephone, but there was nothing on the office phones, and she questioned the legality of installing anything.

The call had come in on her direct line, a number that was not listed in any public directory. Did that mean the caller was someone she knew or someone who had been in her office without her knowledge? Business hours were long over. Had the caller caught her here by chance or was he aware hers was the only office light on in the building?

'The first thing we do, let's kill all the lawyers. . . .'

'Working late, Ellen?'

She cast a glance at her window. Even with the blinds drawn, the light would be visible from outside. Lifting the blinds away from the glass at one side, she tried to peer out, but there was nothing to see except the weird mix of night and swirling snow.

'Your boss needs to have a word with someone about security. This is a highly volatile case you've got here. Anything might happen. . . .'

'Ellen . . . you're a likely target. . . .'

'The first thing we do, let's kill all the lawyers. . . .'

The blinds clattered back against the window glass. Ellen grabbed up the receiver and punched the number for the sheriff's department in the adjacent building. For two years she had worked in this building without fear. She had never felt a need for a security guard, had never turned a hair walking the halls alone at night. That sense of calm was one of the things she had come here looking for. In Deer Lake she could walk her dog along the lake at night, she could leave her bedroom window open and go to sleep with a cool fall breeze caressing her face. Now she was calling for a sheriff's deputy to escort her to her car.

The deputy who appeared at the office door five minutes later was Ed Qualey. Pushing sixty, he was lean and sinewy with a pewter-gray flattop and piercing blue eyes. He had testified in court for Ellen from time to time. A good, solid cop.

'I hope I didn't pull you away from anything too important,' she said as they headed together down the dimly lit hall.

Qualey shook his head. 'Naw, accident reports is all. Nothing much more than fender benders going on around here tonight. I'm on light duty, anyway. Banged up a knee playing hockey. I guess all the action tonight was over in Campion, huh?'

'Mmm.'

'Well, I don't blame you for wanting a walk to your car. Everyone's a little edgy these days. A person just don't know what to expect anymore.'

'I used to have a motto,' Ellen said. ' "Expect the worse, hope for the best." '

Qualey frowned as they started down the stairs. 'We're sure getting more of the one than the other lately. You parked on the side?'

'Yes.'

They cut across the rotunda, the sound of their footfalls soaring up three stories. A sharp crack rang down one of the dark corridors, and Ellen flinched, then scolded herself. The building had a century's worth of creaks and groans.

'Too bad about Denny Enberg,' Qualey said. 'He was a decent sort for a defense attorney. Everyone says it looked like suicide.'

'Looked like. We'll see what the ME has to say.'

Qualey hummed a noncommittal note. It struck Ellen that people would have much preferred Dennis to have stuck a gun in his mouth and ended his own life, as terrible as that would have been. They would rather he had been so crushed by the weight of his problems that he saw no other way out, then the madness was contained to one man. Something to lament, but not contagious. The alternative was vulnerability, and no one wanted any part of that.

Ellen's Bonneville was the only car in the courthouse lot. Sixty yards in the other direction, adjacent to the sheriff's department and county jail, a dozen or so vehicles were clustered together like a herd of horses, snow mounting on their backs.

The wind swept in from the northwest, wrapping itself around the contours of the buildings, creating small powdery-white cyclones that skittered across the unplowed parking lot. The sidewalk had disappeared. Streetlights took on the hazy glow of tiny moons. The streets themselves were all but deserted. Residents had chosen to hole up for the evening, to wait for the ten o'clock news and the predictions for the morning commute to work and school.

'Thanks, Ed,' Ellen said, waving him off as they neared the car.

'No problem. Stay warm.' Hunching his shoulders, he started up the slight grade toward the sheriff's-department entrance.

Ellen hit the button on her remote that unlocked her car doors and brought the interior lights on. Her gaze swept the area, seeing it in a far more critical light than she had when she had parked here in Rudy's personal spot two hours ago. The spot that was close to the building, that had looked so handy, that shortened her walk through the weather, now struck her as a stupid choice. Better to have parked in the second row, away from the building – where shadows and shrubbery could offer cover – and under a security light.

Still, no deadly figure darted out of the darkness along the building. She had almost begun to relax as she rounded the trunk and came up along the driver's side of the Bonneville.

The momentary letdown made the instant burst of fear seem all the more extreme. A gasp caught in her throat as she jumped back, the deep, new snow grabbing at her boots like chilled quicksand.

Scratched into the paint of the driver's-side door in large, irregular letters, was a single ugly word – *BITCH*.

18

The weapon of choice was a switchblade knife, conveniently left behind – plunged to its hilt in the left front tire.

'There won't be no patching that,' Officer Dietz said. Lonnie Dietz was fifty, a decent officer with a bad Moe Howard toupee, which was covered tonight by a towering fake fur hat that made him look as if he had a pack of weasels nesting on his head. 'You got a spare?'

'Just that little doughnut thing,' Ellen said, hugging herself, her eyes on the knife.

The first thing we do, let's kill all the lawyers. . . .

'You have any ideas who might have done this, Ms North?' Officer Noga asked. Noogie Noga was roughly the size of a grizzly bear. A native of Samoa, he had come to Minnesota on a football scholarship and stayed even after a bum knee had ended his NFL hopes.

Ellen shrugged. 'Specifically? No. But I've been getting some odd phone calls.'

'Related to the Wright case?'

She nodded. 'I just got another one before I came down. That's why I had Ed here walk me down.'

'What did the caller say?' Noga asked, pencil poised against his notepad.

'For a long time there was nothing, then he said my name, asked if I was working late.'

The three cops looked at one another blankly, and frustration knotted in Ellen's chest. She couldn't blame them for thinking she was overreacting. Stated flatly, the call lost all its darker, disturbing qualities.

'The call that came last night after two in the morning said, "Let's kill all the lawyers," ' she added, hugging herself a little tighter. She felt as if she were being split in two, half of her the cool professional, the other half a panicking creature.

'Shi – oot,' Noga muttered as the import hit. Everyone on the job had heard the gruesome details of Dennis Enberg's death.

'But you don't have any idea who's making these calls?' Dietz asked.

'I can't recognize the voice. It's too soft, indistinct I'm not even sure if it's a man or a woman.'

'And no one's threatened you outright?' Qualey asked.

'There are plenty of people unhappy with me for prosecuting Garrett Wright, but none of them have made an overt threat to my face.'

She listed the names for Noga, the faces floating through her head like puzzle pieces. Wright was out on bail, but he would never risk such a foolish gesture himself, and she doubted Costello had let him out of his sight. Then there was Todd Childs, and Christopher Priest. Karen Wright. Paul Kirkwood, who blamed her for Grabko's decision on bail. The students who had taken up Wright's cause on the picket line in front of the courthouse.

Her confrontation with the Sci-Fi Cowboys came most vividly to mind. *'Hey, you that bitch lawyer . . .' Bitch lawyer . . . BITCH.* She could see Tyrell's angry face, eyes seething with hate.

She didn't want to blame the Cowboys out of hand. The whole point of the program was to show that these young men had the potential to be productive citizens. But she had worked in the system and knew too well the destruction and violence these kids were capable of. She had seen too many with no conscience and no respect for anyone or anything.

'The program has sure got a lot of press,' Qualey said.

Dietz sniffed and spit a gob into the snow. 'I don't care what anyone says. They're a bunch of city punks. Did you see them out here today with that damn rap music cranked up? We don't need their kind of trouble. If I want to fear for my life walking around town, I'll go up to Minneapolis and take a stroll down Lake Street after dark.'

'We'll check it out, Ms North,' Noga said. 'See what we can come up with on any of those people.'

He crouched down and snapped a couple of Polaroids of the damage, slipping the undeveloped photographs inside his parka.

Ellen stared at the word gouged on her car door. An angry scrawl written with a blade deadly enough to kill. The knife handle thrusting up from the tire was like a misplaced exclamation point. She shivered at the thought of what might have happened had she come out of the building alone and surprised the vandal at work.

'You'll have to have someone take care of that tire,' Dietz said. 'Won't happen tonight. You want a ride home?'

'I'll take her, officer.'

Ellen jerked around at the sound of the voice. Brooks stood behind her, his shoulders hunched, coat collar pulled up high. He squinted against the wind and the cold and her scrutiny.

'What are you doing here?'

The annoyance in her tone didn't stop Jay from asking himself the same question. He had notes to go over and sort, and phone calls to make to pry into the past lives of Garrett Wright and his disciple Todd Childs, and he sure as hell would rather have been in his rented house making use of the fireplace tools he had picked up that afternoon than standing out in a snowstorm. But here he was.

'I heard the call on the scanner,' he said. And a chill had gone through him. He tried to tell himself it was adrenaline, the excitement of a new lead, a fresh angle. Then he tried to put it off to the fact that he hadn't got warm since he'd stepped off the plane into the great white North. Then he thought of Ellen, fighting a battle because she believed in the cause, standing up beneath the burden of it with grace and courage. Ellen, alone, victimized for doing her job.

Not that she wanted him there.

She looked at him askance. 'And you didn't have anything better to do than check out a simple vandalism?'

He cast a pointed look at the knife handle jutting up from her tire. 'Doesn't look so simple to me, counselor.'

Her pique couldn't quite hide the glimmer of fear in her eyes as her glance stayed on the knife. Her lack of a snappy comeback told the rest of the truth. She was scared, plain and simple. She could more than hold her own in a verbal sword fight, but when the hardware was the real deal, that was a whole different ball game.

Noga looked from Ellen to Jay and back. 'Ms North?'

Ellen's knees had gone wobbly as she stared at the knife. *'The first thing we do, let's kill all the lawyers. . . .'* Dennis Enberg's body, his head shattered like a rotten melon. . . *'The first thing we do, let's kill all the lawyers. . . .'* Garrett Wright walking free . . . Dustin Holloman's little boot left to taunt them . . . *BITCH . . . BITCH . . . 'The first thing we do, let's kill all the lawyers. . . .'*

'Come on,' Brooks said, stepping close enough to slide an arm around her shoulders buddy-style. 'Let's go get some hot coffee in you.'

'That sounds good,' Ellen heard herself say, the professional still attempting to function, still pretending she could handle all of this madness at once.

'We'll finish up here, Ms North,' Noga said. 'We'll call you as soon as we have anything.' He turned to Jay with a shy smile and stuck out his hand. 'It's a pleasure, Mr Brooks. I really enjoy your work.'

'Well, thank you, Officer Noga. I'll tell you what, it's always gratifying to hear that from people in law enforcement.'

What Ellen thought of as his public face beamed with a big old country-boy grin. She imagined she could actually feel the level of energy in and around him increase by a thousand volts. It was a wonder the snow didn't melt beneath his feet. Amazing.

Dietz jumped in, thrusting out his report notebook. 'Would you mind an autograph? *Twist of Fate* was my favorite.'

'Thank you. Hear that, Ellen?' he said as he scribbled his name across the paper. 'These gentlemen actually enjoy what I do.'

'There's no accounting for tastes,' she grumbled.

'Come along, Ms North,' Brooks said, resting a big gloved hand on her shoulder. 'I know just the place to warm you up.' He gave her a roguish look as they waded through the snow toward his Cherokee. 'Note what a gentleman I'm being. I could have said I'm just the man for the job.'

'You just did.'

'And, true as it might be, I am much too well brought up to take advantage of a vulnerable woman.'

'Yeah, right.' Ellen stiffened against another attack of shakes. She needed to focus. She focused on Brooks, tried to stir up irritation to warm her and center her thoughts. 'I'd bet my last dime you would take advantage of your own mother if it meant getting the story you want.'

'That wounds me, Ellen. Here I am, rescuing you in your hour of need and you impugn my motives.'

'You've made your motives very clear,' she said as he handed her up into the passenger side of the truck. 'And I quote, "I'm here for a story. I go after what I want and I get it." '

'Excellent memory. People must have hated you in law school.' He stamped back around the hood of the truck and climbed in on the driver's side. 'You know, where I come from, folks at least pretend gratitude, even if they are truly unappreciative.'

'I didn't need rescuing,' Ellen said. 'I'm perfectly capable of taking care of myself.'

'Oh, you fend off knife-wielding maniacs every day, do you?'

'I didn't have to fend off anyone.'

'Yeah, well, the night is young,' he growled.

He put the Cherokee in gear and did a slow U-turn to get out of the lot. The truck's heater was on full blast. The wipers beat furiously at the snow hurtling down. The street was a broad ribbon of white corrugated with tire tracks.

A nice night to curl up by the fire with a good book and a cup of hot chocolate, Ellen thought as she looked out the window, wishing she could do just that, knowing that she would have been doing just that if not for Garrett Wright and his faceless partner. Instead, she would have another night of preparation for the battle with Costello. Another night of trying to piece together the facts to come up with some kind of theory as to why a man like Garrett Wright would steal a child and hold a community in the grip of fear. Another night of sifting through the growing haystack of information, searching for a clue as to who Wright's accomplice might be . . . as to who her tormentor might be.

Were they one and the same? Had they killed Denny Enberg? Would they try to kill her?

BITCH.

'*The first thing we do, let's kill all the lawyers.*'

She felt as if she were fighting battles on all fronts at once, as if she were surrounded. She put her back to the door and faced her unlikely rescuer.

'Where are we going?'

'Someplace quiet, out of the way, homey. Your place, actually.' He glanced at her, studying her in the gloom of the instrument panel. 'I'd take you to my place, but guests tend to be put off by a total lack of furniture.'

'Where are you staying?'

'I rented a house out on Ryan's Bay.'

'Ryan's Bay? That's where Josh's jacket was found.'

'A macabre coincidence,' he assured her. 'Honest.'

'I'm sure you're probably guilty of many things, Mr Brooks. But I think we're safe in eliminating you from the list of possible accomplices.'

'You have a list?'

'Figure of speech.'

'Mmmm. You have theories,' he murmured. 'I have a couple of my own.'

He gunned the engine, plowing up the incline of her driveway.

'Thank you for the ride,' Ellen said politely, her gaze fixed on the dark house, fear swelling inside her at the thought of going in alone. But she let herself out of the truck before Brooks made it around the hood.

'I'm not helpless,' she insisted as he pulled her keys out of her hand. She twisted away from him when he would have taken her briefcase from her.

'No, you're not helpless. You're a damn target,' he grumbled, stomping through the snow to the front door. 'Your buddy Enberg is lying on a slab tonight, shorter by a head; somebody uses your car for an Etch-A-Sketch and leaves you a switchblade. If you think I'm letting you walk into this house alone, you are dead wrong – pardon the expression.'

'And who appointed you to the role of guardian?' Ellen demanded, walking into the foyer and toeing off her boots.

'Nobody. I do as I please.'

'Well, it doesn't please me.'

'Nothing much about this case pleases me.' He stepped out of his boots and took off his parka.

Ellen stood off to the side, watching as he turned on lights and lit the fireplace.

'Lucky you,' she said, 'you can walk away from it. It's just another story. The world's full of them, I'm sad to say.'

'I'm not going anywhere.'

'Why not?'

'Because what doesn't please me personally makes for a hell of a book.'

'Why this case of all cases?'

He stared into the fire, his face an inscrutable mask, no hint of the engaging rascal who charmed his way past barriers with a wink and a grin.

'I have my reasons,' he said darkly.

'Which are –?'

'None of your business.'

'Oh, fine. You can butt into other people's lives, novelize their suffering, sell it for a profit, but your life is off-limits?'

'That's right,' he said, coming toward her. 'Though I may indeed be

593

guilty of many things, none of them is criminal. Therefore, my private life remains just that − private.'

'What a convenient double standard.'

He ignored the gibe and curled a hand around her arm. 'Come over here by the fire. You need to warm up. Christ, you're shaking like a hairless dog in a meat freezer.'

He led her across the room, hooked a footstool with one stockinged foot, and dragged it into place in front of the fire.

'Sit.' He pressed her down with a hand on her shoulder. 'Do you have any liquor?'

'In the hutch in the dining room. I'll get it.'

'You'll sit,' he barked, his expression promising dire consequences.

Ellen shrugged off his hand. 'You know, I really don't need you barging into my house, bossing me around, Brooks. This day has been rotten enough as it is. I didn't ask to have you −'

The telephone on the table behind her rang. She wheeled around to stare at it, and what little bravado she had left vaporized, leaving cold, hard fear behind. She hated it. The sanctity of her home had been violated, by such a simple act as a phone call.

'Reach out and touch someone.'

'The first thing we do, let's kill all the lawyers. . . .'

'Ellen?' Jay stepped into her line of vision, bending down a little to look into her eyes. 'Ellen,' he asked gently, 'aren't you going to get that?'

The machine clicked on before she could answer. A woman's voice, pleasant but concerned.

'Ellen, honey, it's Mom. We just wanted to see how you're doing. We heard about the reduced bail. Daddy says not to take it too hard; the game isn't over yet. Call when you get in, sweetheart. We want to get together with you for your birthday.'

Her parents wanted to know how she was. She was tired and heartbroken and too damn scared to answer her own phone.

'It's s-so wrong!' she whispered. She closed her eyes and fought against tears. She couldn't afford to cry. The game wasn't over.

He said it was a game.

A game − with lives and minds and futures and careers at stake. A game with no rules and no boundaries, faceless players and hidden agendas.

Jay watched her struggle. She cared too much, fought too hard, took it all to heart. While he had stopped believing in anything, walked away from fights, let nothing touch his heart . . . except the sight of this woman crying.

If you had any sense, you'd walk away from this, Brooks.

Instead, he reached for her, gathered her close, guided her head to his shoulder. She resisted each movement, holding herself as stiff as a board. He dropped his head down, let his cheek brush her temple.

'It's okay,' he whispered. 'Any port in a storm, counselor. You just go on and cry. I promise, it's off the record.'

The tears came in a hard torrent, soaking into his shirt. She curled her fists against his chest but didn't try to push him away. Jay wrapped his arms around her slender shoulders, feeling for the first time in forever an urge to protect, as ironic as that was. He wanted to protect her while she was doing her best to protect herself from him. She didn't trust him, had every reason *not* to trust him.

You're a damn fool, Brooks.

He was an observer, just passing through her life. That was how he liked it – sliding like a shadow from one vignette to another, watching, absorbing, interpreting, moving on, never letting it touch him too deeply, never letting his heart get involved. That was smartest, safest, easiest. That was why he shied away from live cases, preferring to trail in after the physical and emotional firestorms had passed. Like a scavenger.

Yet here he was, with his arms around the prosecuting attorney, a part of his mind gravitating down the hall where there had to be a bedroom.

A fool and a scoundrel.

But the recriminations didn't make him let go. They didn't stop him from breathing in the soft scent of her or turning his head and touching the tender skin of her temple with his lips. The warmth that swelled within, the hunger for this contact, were only partly sexual, making him wonder dimly who was finding more comfort in the embrace. He felt as if he'd been starved of human contact and knew that the abstinence was an act of both self-denial and self-preservation.

Ah, what a sorry soul you are, Brooks. . . .

Sorry and alone.

The need overtook the inner voice. He kissed her cheek, damp with tears. He kissed her mouth, soft and trembling. His lips moved slowly, sensuously, over hers. Gentle, hesitant, needing more than he dared take. Needing the fresh taste of her like air, like water. Her mouth opened beneath his and he caught her breath and gave it back. Slowly he skimmed the soft inner swell of her lower lip with the tip of his tongue, then ventured deeper into the satin warmth of her mouth. With one hand he cradled her head, his fingers threading through the silk of her hair. He framed her face with the other, fingertips skimming the line of her cheek, the pad of his thumb probing the very corner of her mouth. A soft sound of desire escaped her and the need leaped inside him like a flame.

Need. Hot, bright need. It took Ellen by surprise, but she grabbed it with desperation and hung on. The alternative was fear and weakness. This was a surging sense of life; vital, fragile and strong at once. She felt as if she were absorbing everything about the moment – the feel of his mouth, full against hers, hot and wet; the taste of him dark and erotic; the feel of his tongue against hers, searching, stroking, imitating the rhythm of sex. He pulled her close, closer, his hand sliding down the small of her back, pressing her hips forward into his, letting her feel his arousal, *his* heat, *his* need.

The insanity of what she was doing struck her and she turned her face away.

'I can't do this,' she said, breathless. 'I can't get involved with you. My God . . .' She shook her head, stunned that she had let him kiss her, touch her. Stunned at what the kiss had made her feel. 'This is a really bad idea. I think –'

'That's your problem, sugar,' he said in a low, dangerous tone. 'You think too damn much.'

Cupping her chin in his hand, he turned her back toward him and lowered his mouth to hers again. But the moment was gone, the kiss still and passionless. He opened his eyes and found Ellen's wary gray ones staring up at him.

Her breath caught in her throat at the emotion in his face. Just a fleeting glimpse, there and gone. Pain and longing. Every time she thought she had him pegged, he turned colors on her. It was easiest and best to think of him as a mercenary, but he had layers and shadows, dimensions that tempted her to look deeper. She couldn't afford to get pulled into something. She was already up to her neck in one mire.

'I'll get us that drink,' he muttered, his voice lower, rougher than it had been.

He turned away, walked up the steps to the dining room, and pulled a full bottle of Glenlivet from the liquor cabinet. She watched his movements, studied the dark look on his face, wondering what it was about, what *he* was about. Which Jay Butler Brooks was the real man? The charmer? The mercenary? The man with the haunted face?

Don't go down that road, Ellen . . .

The warning came as she mounted the steps. He splashed the Scotch into a pair of short, thick tumblers.

'I – I have to check on Harry,' she said awkwardly, stepping past him.

She hurried through the kitchen to the laundry room, where she was greeted enthusiastically by the big retriever. She let him out into the fenced backyard where he spent most of his days and stood for a moment in the open doorway, breathing in the crisp night air to clear her head. The snow was still coming down.

Harry did his business, then made a mad dash around the yard, excited by the fresh powder. Ellen left him to play, knowing they would both regret it later when he came in wet and aromatic and would have to be banished from his usual spot on the bed.

When she came back to the living room, she took her coat off and hung it in the closet. Jay stood with his back to the fire, watching her, tumbler of Scotch in one hand, the other stuffed into his pants pocket. Too aware of his gaze, Ellen picked up her glass from the coffee table and sipped at it. The liquor seared a smooth path to her stomach.

'It's been quite a day,' she said, settling herself into the corner of the couch. She pulled her legs beneath her, careful to keep her skirt around her knees.

'Why didn't you take that call?' he asked. Though the tone was casual, those cool blue eyes focused on her like a pair of lasers.

She weighed her answer. Her impulse was to keep the calls a secret, to protect herself from yet another avalanche of publicity. Of course, Brooks would have no desire to inform the press. He was here for his own purposes. She had to think he would guard the confidence jealously. And if she didn't give it to him, he would dig for it.

'Cranks,' she said with an air of dismissal. 'I've had a couple of calls. My nerves are just a little too frayed right now to take another one.'

A half truth, Jay decided. Better than a lie. Less than trust. He couldn't have expected more.

'Enberg's secretary told me he'd got some nasty calls,' he said. 'Think they're related?'

'It wouldn't follow. We were on opposite sides.'

'That all depends on your point of view. From where I stand, ol' Denny looked like he'd just as soon throw the game.'

'The first thing we do, let's kill all the lawyers. . . .'

Ellen looked away from him, into the fire, curling her fingers tighter around her glass. Dennis had got calls, and now Dennis was dead. She was getting calls and . . . In the flames of the fire she could see the switchblade protruding from the tire of her car and the word scratched into the paint. *Bitch.*

'Rumor has it you think Enberg had some help with that shotgun,' Brooks said, his eyes narrowed as he watched her for a reaction.

'Where did you hear that?'

'Around.'

'If there's a leak on this case —'

'No one fed it to me,' he said. 'I don't have a mole in your office, if that's what you're worried about. This is a small town, Ellen. People like to talk. I know how to listen.'

'I'm not paranoid,' she said defensively. 'Corruption makes no geographical distinctions. A week ago Sheriff Steiger was trading information for sex.'

The pirate's grin made a return even as he feigned shock. 'Are you suggesting something tawdry, Ms North?'

'In your dreams.'

'Mmm . . . I should say so,' he drawled, his gaze caressing her bare calf.

He moved away from the fire, prowling, his eyes locked on her. Once again playing the rogue, the sexual tomcat, master at seduction.

'The point is,' she began.

'The point is, I don't pay for information — cash or favors,' he said, easing himself down beside her. His hard, muscular thigh brushed her bare foot. 'And so far, the only one who's made any noise about it is Paul Kirkwood.'

'Paul asked you for money?' Ellen said, surprised. 'Well — for Josh, I suppose,' she rationalized.

597

He shook his head. 'I get the impression Paul thinks about Paul first and the rest of the world can queue up behind him, including his son.'

'He's under a lot of pressure,' she said with forced neutrality.

He made a dubious sound and pulled a cigarette out of the pack in his shirt pocket. Ellen took it from his fingers and, ignoring his frown, set it out of his reach on the end table.

'He was a suspect for a while, you know,' she pointed out.

'But he isn't anymore.'

'There's no evidence against him.' Even as she said it, she was recalling the night Josh had been returned. Paul nowhere to be found for hours, showing up at the hospital in a snit. The story Mitch later relayed of Josh reacting violently to his father's appearance in his room.

'There was that bit about the van,' Brooks offered.

'That went nowhere.'

Wilhelm was supposed to be looking for connections between Paul and Wright. He had turned his suspicion on Kirkwood days ago but hadn't said a word about it since. Ellen had to wonder if he had followed up or if the other cases had taken all his attention.

'What about Todd Childs?' Jay asked carefully, watching her through his lashes.

Ellen gave a little shrug. 'What about him? We'll be serving him with a subpoena calling him to testify at the hearing. He isn't happy about it, but life is hard.'

'Maybe he decided to take it out on you.'

'It's hard to imagine his getting up the energy for that kind of rage.'

'*She's a bitch.*' Jay could hear Todd Childs's voice, see the venom in his eyes as he watched Ellen talk to the press. 'Rage can be chemically induced. I'd hazard a guess he'd know all about that. I had me a little chat with Todd this morning.' He took another sip of his drink and looked at her sideways. 'Just long enough to give me the willies.'

'Oh, great,' she groaned. 'That's what I need – you tampering with my witnesses.'

She swung her feet down off the couch and sat with her elbows planted on her thighs and her face in her hands.

'I wasn't tampering,' he said. 'I can have a conversation with anyone I choose. I'm a private citizen.'

'With an in to the state attorney general and a truck parked in my driveway.'

She had to fight the urge to get up and peek out her front window for signs of reporters staking out her house. The unwanted, unwarranted publicity that Mitch and Megan's relationship had drawn was fresh in her mind. It had indirectly cost Megan her field post, and she and Mitch were on the same side. Ellen shuddered to think what the ramifications of having Jay Butler Brooks in her home might be. He was looking for inside information. She was the lead prosecutor on the case.

She turned and looked at him. 'I don't need any more complications in my life.'

Complications. The case. His involvement in it. The attraction that sparked between them whether she liked it or not. It struck him as funny, in a bitter, twisted sort of way, that he had come here to escape the complications of his own life and had become a complication in someone else's. And Ellen had come to Deer Lake to escape the complications of her life in Minneapolis and now found herself in the center of a madman's web.

He stared at Ellen. Backlit by the fire, her hair was burnished gold. The barriers were down. He could have turned the moment to his advantage. Instead, he tossed back the last of his Scotch and set the glass aside.

'No,' he said. 'You need a break. In the case and *from* the case. So tell me about your mother.'

'My mother?'

'You know, the woman who gave you birth. The woman who called to see how you're doing.'

Suspicion lowered her brows. 'Why?'

He dropped his head back against the couch and rolled his eyes. 'I reckon she called because she loves you, but that's just speculation on my part. If you're asking why I asked, it's called making conversation. Or if you're intent on casting me as a bastard, call it looking for background.'

That was the problem with him, Ellen thought – there was no telling which definition suited.

'My mother is an attorney,' she said. 'My father, too. And my sister, Jill. Tax law.'

'Ah, a nest of lawyers,' he said with a warm, teasing smile. 'And you're the white sheep.'

The term brought pleasant surprise. Her father called her the white sheep, always with a gleam of pride in his eyes.

'My father says I inherited the recessive North gene for justice. His grandfather was a circuit court judge back in frontier times. They called him Noose North.'

Jay laughed. Ellen let herself relax marginally, glad for the diversion. Whatever his motive, she had to be grateful. She needed the downtime, a chance to lower her shields for a moment or two. She turned toward him, once more tucking herself into the corner of the couch.

'Anyway, they have a nice practice in Edina – the suburb where I grew up.'

'And you're close.'

'Yeah,' she said, smiling to herself.

Glancing up, she caught a glimpse of something sad in Brooks's eyes. He covered it in a blink.

'You come from a family of lawyers, too,' she said.

He leaned toward her in confession. 'I'm the black sheep.'

'Big surprise. You were an attorney, though,' she pointed out. 'Why not with the family firm?'

'I go my own way. Make my own rules. I was too much of a rebel for an old southern law firm, as contradictory as that may sound to a Yankee.'

'Your opinion or theirs?'

He narrowed his eyes at her, not liking the probing quality of her gaze. 'We were talking about you.'

'And now we're talking about you. Do you have a problem with that, Mr Brooks?'

'Oooh, trick question.' He grinned and tipped his head. 'I can't wait to see you handle a cross-examination. You know what I thought when I first laid eyes on you? I said to myself, *Jay, that little gal looks sharp as a tack and cool as tungsten steel. What the hell do you think she's doing here?*'

'Asked and answered.'

'You seemed evasive.'

'Not so. There simply isn't anything more to tell.'

'Then your leaving Minneapolis had nothing to do with the rape trial of Art Fitzpatrick?'

The shields came up again. 'What would make you ask that?'

'It was the last trial of any real consequence you were involved with up there.'

'A number of victims of other crimes might beg to differ with you. I tried any number of cases after Fitzpatrick.'

'But none so high profile. A prominent businessman accused of an ugly crime. It was common knowledge you took the loss hard.'

'A rapist went free. Of course I was unhappy. And, in point of fact, I was not the lead prosecutor on Fitzpatrick. That was Steve Larsen's case. I was his second. May I ask why and how you've been digging up this information?' Just what did he know about the Fitzpatrick case? Did he know about her relationship with Costello? About Costello's link to Fitzpatrick?

'It's part of my job,' he explained. 'I know you think I'm just as lazy as a poor boy's sigh, too unimaginative and slothful to create plots of my own; that I just waltz into the middle of a story and save up the news clippings. But the fact is, I do my homework, Ellen, same as any good journalist.'

'Then why aren't you doing homework on Wright? Why dig into my boring past when you could be revealing this man for the monster he is? You could actually be doing someone some good.'

'You don't want me tampering with the case – unless it's on behalf of the prosecution. Is that it?'

'Associate you with my office and run the risk of having my conviction thrown out on appeal? No, thanks. I would just like to think that maybe you wanted something more out of this than money.'

'Such as?'

'Justice.'

'That's your quest, counselor. I'm just an observer.'

'And that excuse is supposed to absolve you of all responsibility, humanity, compassion, emotion? How can you look at Josh, at his parents, and not feel something?'

He felt plenty. Pity, compassion, sympathy . . . lucky, confused. He had come here to escape his own tearing sense of loss. Had come deliberately to study people who had lost more, thereby consoling and punishing himself at once.

'You don't know what I feel,' he said quietly.

'And you won't tell me.'

'Not tonight.' He drew in a deep breath, mustered a weary smile, and pushed himself to his feet. 'I think you've had enough intrigue and twisted drama to last you. What you need is a good night's sleep.'

He offered her a hand up from the couch. She gave it a dubious look.

'Is that an overture, Mr Brooks?' she asked dryly, accepting the gesture just the same.

'Hell, no.' He pulled her close, bending his head down so that his gaze met hers full force. 'I'm being damned gallant. When you go to bed with me, sweetheart, the last thing you'll be getting is sleep.'

Remarkably, Ellen caught herself smiling at his audacity.

'You're incorrigible, Mr Brooks,' she murmured. 'Among other things.'

She walked with him to the door, where he dealt with laces on his boots and zippers on his parka.

'I don't see how people live in this state,' he complained. 'It's too much damn work.'

'Winter is nature's way of weeding out the faint of heart,' Ellen said. 'Thanks again for driving me home.'

'You ought to have a cop sitting out front,' he cautioned.

She shook her head. 'With all that's been going on, there's no manpower for baby-sitting detail. There's a patrol car prowling the neighborhood, and I've got a trace on my phone. And I've got Harry. If someone tries to break in, he'll knock them down and lick their face until help arrives.'

'I could stay all night,' he offered with a leer.

'I don't think so.'

'Like I said before,' he murmured, hooking a finger under her chin, 'you think too much.'

Ellen caught her breath, expecting him to kiss her. Half hoping he would. But he turned and walked out. And she was left alone to call herself a fool.

19

By Friday morning Mother Nature had dumped six inches of new snow on southern Minnesota, and a blast of air had come sweeping down from Saskatchewan to stir it into a ground-scudding cloud that limited visibility to a fraction of a mile. The temperature, which had been teetering on the brink of tolerance, went over the edge and into a long, hard fall, taking spirits with it. School was canceled. Roads outside of Deer Lake were closed. In Campion the search for Dustin Holloman had to be called off because of the danger to the volunteers. No one spoke of the danger to Dustin.

The hope was that his kidnapper was keeping him safe and warm, that he would eventually be found or returned unharmed, as Josh had been. The hope was that they would get lucky. The idea that they were all relying on the kindness and benevolence of a psychopath sat like a mace in the center of Mitch's chest. There was no way of knowing what the next move in the game would be. No way of knowing when their luck would run out.

The pressure had snipped his temper down to the short hairs, so that even at nine o'clock in the morning his daily quota of patience was nearly spent.

Ignoring the proffered chair, he paced the width of Christopher Priest's small office, a room crowded with file cabinets and bookcases. Short towers of text and reference books and stacks of student papers were neatly aligned across the surface of the scarred old desk. A personal computer sat whirring softly to itself, green cursor blinking impatiently beside a prompt sign on the screen.

'So the Sci-Fi Cowboys spent the night in Deer Lake?' he asked.

Priest watched him with owl eyes and an impassive expression. 'Yes. The Minneapolis schools were off yesterday and today for in-service. We had arranged for the boys to spend the weekend in Deer Lake doing fund-raising activities for Garrett's defense.'

'And they stayed where?'

'At the youth hostel here on campus.'

'Supervised?'

'I was with them most of the evening. We had a celebratory dinner with Garrett and his attorney,' he said with just a hint of smugness, his gaze sliding toward Ellen.

'What time did you finish?' she asked.

'Things started breaking up around eight.'

'And what about the rest of the evening? Can you account for the whereabouts of all the boys?'

A hint of angry color stained his cheeks. He tugged at the too-short sleeves of his black turtleneck. 'They're not prisoners, Ms North. A bond of trust is essential to the success of our program.'

'Yeah, well, maybe that trust isn't always deserved,' Mitch grumbled.

Priest gave a little sniff of affront. 'Just what is this about, Chief?'

'Last night someone defaced Ms North's car with a switchblade.'

'And you automatically assume that *someone* is one of the Cowboys? That's patently unfair and discriminatory.'

'Not at all, Professor,' Mitch said, bracing his hands on the back of the chair he had declined. 'With all due respect to your program – and you know I've been a fan in the past – your kids are A-students in this kind of shit. They have records. They have motive. They are, therefore, *logical* suspects. You, of all people, should be able to grasp that.'

'The Cowboys aren't the only people in town unhappy with Ms North,' Priest pointed out.

'No, they're not,' Mitch conceded. 'And my office will follow all possible avenues. Which brings me to my next question – where were you last night around nine?'

Priest's jaw dropped, a show of spontaneous emotion that looked genuine. 'You can't possibly think I would be involved in something so – so –'

'Juvenile?'

His face flushed and he shot up from his chair. 'After all the hours my students and I put in at the volunteer center – After I've bent over backward to help with the investigation – I took a polygraph, for heaven's sake! I can't tell you how angry this makes me.'

Mitch straightened, shoving the chair into the front of Priest's old oak desk with a rattle and a thump. 'Welcome to the club, Professor. I've been working this case around the clock from day one and it just keeps getting worse. I can no longer afford to be polite. I can't afford to worry about whether or not it offends people to be questioned. I don't have time to step around egos. Here's the bottom line: Garrett Wright stands accused. You are a friend and colleague of Garrett Wright. That makes you fair game.'

'Chief Holt is simply doing his job, Professor,' Ellen said, working to show a little diplomacy, though her own temper was slipping. She'd had to begin the day arranging to have her car towed from the courthouse lot to Manley Vanloon's garage for repairs and repainting. Stooping to what she felt was an abuse of her position, she had called Manley himself and asked him to have one of his service mechanics deliver a loaner to her house before answering all of the calls from the hardworking people who needed jump-starts for frozen batteries.

'I understand your protective attitude toward the Sci-Fi Cowboys,' she said. 'But the fact remains, their very existence makes them logical suspects in the vandalism.'

Priest regarded her with the thinnest hint of a frown touching his wide, lipless mouth. 'Is it standard procedure for victims to attend police interrogations of suspects?'

'This isn't an interrogation, Professor,' she said, 'although Mitch or one of his men will need to talk with all the boys, just as they will be talking with other possible suspects. What I've come for is to request that you turn over to my office a list of names and addresses for all the Sci-Fi Cowboys past and present.'

'For what purpose?' he asked tightly. 'So the police can harass everyone who ever knew Garrett? This is an outrage!'

'As part of the ongoing background check,' Ellen answered, rising. 'We need to speak with as many people who have worked closely with Dr Wright as we can. It's nothing extraordinary, Professor. I was surprised Agent Wilhelm hadn't already made the request.'

'It's an invasion of privacy.'

'No, it's not.'

She leveled a steely look at the little man with his shrunken sweater and oversize eyeglasses and moral outrage cracking his usual emotionless façade. Two weeks ago she had thought he was a generous, compassionate man of foresight; a helpful citizen who had thrown himself into the efforts at the Josh Kirkwood volunteer center and volunteered to aid the police with his computer skills. Today she harbored suspicions that he might be protecting a criminal or worse – that he was himself a player in Garrett Wright's twisted game.

Megan had suspected Priest. Olie Swain, the convicted pedophile who had committed suicide in jail, had audited Priest's computer courses. Their association may have gone deeper. Megan had been investigating the possibility when she was attacked – in the front yard of Priest's secluded country home. There may well have been more to that than mere coincidence. Every way Ellen turned, reality was mutating into something ugly.

'It's called doing a thorough job,' she said. 'And if it weren't for the fact that it's touching you directly, you'd be glad for it.'

She picked up her briefcase and nodded to him. 'Thank you for your time, Professor. If you could put that list together today and fax it to my office, I would appreciate it. If you choose to be stubborn, I can get a warrant, but I really don't think you want to play that game. The publicity could only hurt the Cowboys. I know you don't want that.'

'No, I don't,' he said, blowing out a breath. His arms fell to his sides, bony shoulders slumping in defeat. He looked from Ellen to Mitch, the uncharacteristic emotions draining from his face, leaving the slate blank. 'I don't want that at all. I'm sorry if I overreacted, but this program means a great deal to me. And having tried to help with the investigation into Josh's disappearance, then having this kind of scrutiny turned on me and the Cowboys . . . I don't know,' he muttered, shaking his head. 'I feel a certain sense of betrayal.'

'I understand, Professor,' Ellen said. 'I think we both do.'

The closest Mitch came to acknowledgment or apology was a twist of his mouth. As he turned toward the door, a pair of lanky teenagers stepped in.

'Hey, it's Lady Justice!' Tyrell Mann said with a big grin splitting his face. He strutted past Ellen. 'Our man Costello kicked your pretty behind yesterday, Lady Justice.'

Ellen borrowed an attitude from Brooks. 'It's only bail.'

'Give it up, Goldie,' Tyrell sneered, leaning over her. 'You haven't got a prayer.'

She held her ground, staring him square in the face, meeting the belligerence burning in his eyes full on. 'We'll see. You know what they say − it ain't over till it's over.'

She watched for a flicker of recognition or wariness, but there was nothing. His lip curled derisively. 'You ain't got shit on the Doc.'

Mitch stepped in, planting a hand on Tyrell's chest and moving him back. 'You'll show the lady respect.'

Tyrell glared at him. 'Who the fuck are you?'

'Tyrell,' Priest said, stepping between them, 'this is Chief of Police Holt.'

'A cop.' Contempt twisted Tyrell's features. 'I should'a guessed.'

The other boy stepped forward with the plastic smile of a salesman, sticking his hand out. 'J. R. Andersen, Chief. Tyrell's cranky. You'll have to excuse him.'

'No, I won't,' Mitch said flatly. 'But I don't have time for this now. We'll have a little chat later today, Tyrell.'

'The hell −'

'We will.' He turned to Priest. 'I'll set something up for this afternoon. Someone will call you.'

Priest looked resigned and unhappy. 'Can we at least do it here in my office?'

'Do what?' Andersen asked.

Mitch nodded and ushered Ellen out into the hall, closing the door behind them.

'I hate to come down on them,' he said as they made their way toward the stairs. 'It *is* a good program, but the potential for trouble is there, too. I mean, if you think about it, what's worse − below-average kids with no consciences or smart kids with no consciences? And don't try to tell me Tyrell there has a consciences lurking under all that hostility. He's a stick of dynamite with a short fuse.'

The question was, had Garrett Wright provided the spark that had ignited an act of violence against her? Ellen turned the possibilities over in her mind as they walked. Priest's office was located on the fourth floor of Cray Hall, a dank old mausoleum of a building, each level a maze of narrow hallways and cracker-box offices. Not even the mustard-colored walls could save the place from cheerlessness.

'There's no denying Tyrell blames me for Garrett Wright's predicament,' Ellen said. 'But the professor had a point – the Cowboys aren't the only ones in Wright's corner.'

'We know Wright himself has an alibi for last night,' Mitch said. 'After dinner he was with Costello in Costello's office until nearly ten-thirty. Then Costello drove him home.'

'Home – to Lakeside?'

Mitch answered her look of shock with one of sympathy. 'It's part of the show, I suppose. If he's an innocent man, why shouldn't he feel free to live in his own home?'

'Because it shows a callous disregard for the feelings of the Kirkwoods,' she said angrily. 'But, hey, who cares about them? Not Tony Costello, I can guarantee you that.'

Not only was Wright's return to his home an affront to the Kirkwoods, it completely screwed any chance they might have had to turn Karen Wright.

'Wright isn't paying him a five-figure fee to be sensitive,' Mitch said.

'If Wright *is* paying him that kind of money, I'd like to know where it's coming from. Pity we don't have just cause to seize his bank records.' She stopped on the landing, her eyes brightening as the proverbial lightbulb flashed on above her head. 'But we *should* be able to seize his current month's records from the phone company. If we can get our hands on those, we'll be able to see if any of the strange calls that happened during Josh's abduction came from Wright's house – which, of course, they won't have because he would never be that careless – but we may be able to find out whether or not Karen Wright was the one who called in Costello. If she didn't, that strengthens my suspicion that Costello was contacted by the accomplice. If I can find a way around Costello's argument of privilege and nail his ass with charges of complicity . . . Oooh, that would be *sooo* sweet.'

Mitch arched a brow as they started down the last flight of steps. 'Remind me never to get on your bad side.

'We haven't been able to locate Todd Childs,' he said. 'He isn't answering his phone, doesn't appear to be home, and he isn't scheduled to work at the Pack Rat until Monday. No one seems to know where the hell he might have gone in weather like this, but no one's seen him since yesterday afternoon.'

And since then, Dustin Holloman's boot had been discovered and someone had carved up her car.

On the first floor they crossed another empty hall and went into the foyer, where double doors flanked with sidelights afforded a view of the

606

horrendous weather. Snow blew across the campus like bleached-white sheets torn free from a clothesline. Even through the doors the sound of the wind was an ominous roar. Small trees bent away from it like cowering stick figures. Across the street someone in a cardinal-red parka rushed along, being blown south like a scrap of bright wrapping paper.

'Goddamn this weather,' Mitch grumbled. 'I don't mind winter, but this is ridiculous.'

'It certainly doesn't seem to be playing on our side.'

Ellen set her briefcase at her feet and set about the task of wrapping her thick wool scarf around her head and neck. 'Let me know as soon as you've talked to Childs,' she said. 'We've got him on the list to testify at the omnibus hearing. We'll look like idiots if it turns out he's involved.'

'I've got someone on it.'

'What about the employees from the Donut Hut? Any word on what they might have seen the night Denny died?'

'They're stuck in Mankato, but we're not sure where they're staying.' He clamped a pair of earmuffs on his head and flipped up the thick hood of his parka. 'I spoke with Vicki Enberg. She says Dennis told her he wished he'd never got involved with the case, but he wouldn't say whether or not Wright had confessed anything to him. She doesn't believe he killed himself, but we have to consider the source there.'

'Do *you* believe he killed himself?' Ellen asked.

Mitch looked out at the desolate snowscape. 'To tell you the truth, counselor, I don't know what the hell to believe anymore.'

'I don't believe it's necessary, Ellen,' Rudy said, moving restlessly behind his desk. He shoved aside a stack of paperwork and rummaged through a pile of newspaper clippings – all identical, featuring a photograph of him angrily pledging to pursue justice in the case he had dumped on Ellen. 'The sheriff's department is right next door.'

'Which does no good if the trouble is *in* the courthouse,' Ellen insisted. 'This is a highly volatile situation, Rudy, and it's getting personal. We're going to be putting in a lot of hours on this in the next few days before the pretrial. I don't want to have to fear for my life while I'm at it. I mean, my car can be repainted, but next time this jerk might decide to carve *me* up.'

Scowling, he pulled a scrap of a page from under a yellow legal pad and discovered a long-forgotten grocery list. 'No one can get in the building at night without a key.'

'Big deal. So they come in during the day and hide in a broom closet until night. Or they jimmy a lock or they get in through a window. Then what?'

He crumpled the grocery list, tossed it at the waste basket, and missed. Grumbling, he bent to retrieve it, and his eyes widened as his gaze caught on something he had discarded earlier. 'Ha!' he huffed, unwadding the ball of paper.

Ellen watched him with a mix of disgust and disbelief. 'You know, I'm sorry to trouble your mind with this, Rudy, but I would prefer not to end up like Dennis Enberg.'

'He committed suicide.'

'I don't think so, and if you would pay attention to something other than taking Judge Franken's seat on the bench before it even has a chance to cool, you wouldn't think so either.'

'Ellen! I don't know what you're taking about. How could you suggest such a thing? Judge Franken isn't even in the ground yet. The funeral is today. This is part of his eulogy I'm holding.'

Meaning tomorrow, after the eulogy had been delivered in front of a crowd of court cronies and minor muck-a-mucks, and the judge was put in permanent cold storage, it would be all right to angle openly for the appointment.

'Fine,' she said. 'You're a choirboy, Rudy. Now can I have my security guard?'

'It's not that simple. I can't just hire someone. I'll have to talk to the county commissioners.'

'Oh, great. Maybe they'll approve the funding sometime before the year of the flood. Can't you just arrange something with Steiger?'

'Maybe, but they've got their hands full, you know. I don't know that Russ has a man to spare.'

Ellen blew out a breath. 'All right. I can't wait to hear what the press has to say about this. Park County can't protect its children, can't even protect its own attorneys. . . . I suppose you'll want me to make a statement. Tell the press it's out of your hands. Make the usual "If it were up to me" noises.'

Behind the lenses of his crooked glasses, Rudy's eyes sharpened and narrowed. 'They know about your car?' he asked.

'The phones are ringing off their hooks,' she said, poker-faced. She had yet to check her own messages, had no idea how many calls might have come in from the press. Rudy didn't seem to notice that she hadn't answered his question. The prospect of bad publicity had snagged his full attention.

'What about these weird calls you've had? Do they know about that?'

'We've managed to keep that quiet so far, but you know how it is. This is a small town.'

Rudy pursed his lips and ran a broad hand over his slicked-down hair, his hand coming away from the gesture as greasy as if he had palmed a bucket of fried chicken wings. Without thinking, he used the leg of his suit for a napkin. He strolled back and forth in front of the window. Outside, the weather and the release of Garrett Wright on bail had combined to keep the protestors off the streets.

'You think it's one of those science-fiction kids?' he asked.

'I have no idea. It could be.'

'Could be. But you think it is, don't you?'

608

'I don't know.'

He frowned a little, wondering what good it would do him if he did get that kind of admission from her. The program was popular and politically correct and had brought Deer Lake a lot of good publicity. Sig Iverson, whom Rudy had chosen to succeed him as county attorney, had already associated himself with Christopher Priest the past fall, acting as chaperon on a couple of Sci-Fi Cowboy trips to science fairs and competitions. If Ellen took a stand against the group and they in fact turned out to be rotten troublemakers, she would get an edge on Sig. In the meantime, if Rudy took no action and she ended up getting attacked, it would definitely reflect badly on him.

'I'll see what I can do,' he said at last. 'Twist Russ's arm a little. I'll take care of it. We don't want you getting hurt, Ellen. You know I think of the people in this office as family. I certainly don't want any harm to come to one of my office daughters.'

Ellen forced a smile, thinking he probably would have sold his 'daughter' to gypsies by now if not for the bad press. 'Thanks, Rudy.'

'Are you going to the funeral?' His attention had already returned to his eulogy notes.

'Of course.' She didn't have the time to spare, but she felt a certain obligation, having been one of the people who had worked to revive the judge. She wondered if Brooks would feel any obligation or if he would attend in search of color commentary for his book.

'Where are we at with the case?' Rudy asked.

'Nothing new. We're at the mercy of the crime lab waiting for any info on evidence. The DNA testing of the bloody sheet won't be completed for another month.'

'But it matched Josh Kirkwood for type.'

'Yes. And since we have only to show cause, I think we're safe. Figuratively speaking, Costello would shred that sheet to rags in front of a jury, but by the time we get that far, he'll have to fight the DNA experts.'

If we get that far.

'We have plenty to get him bound over for trial,' she stated, as much to counteract her own insidious doubts as to convince her boss.

She would have liked to talk through the problems with him, as she had with her old boss in Hennepin County; to strategize, theorize, play devil's advocate. But Rudy had never been a confidant. The best she could do was find a sounding board in Cameron and trust her own instincts.

She pushed the sleeve of her blazer up with one finger and checked her watch. 'I've got to get upstairs. Good luck with the eulogy.'

Ellen headed to her office, where the phones were still ringing almost without cease. Word would have spread by now about the vandalism of her car. She had officially become a target.

Phoebe stood up from her desk, her fresh-scrubbed face bright with panic.

'I'm sorry, Ellen,' she said, clutching her hands against the bodice of her prison-gray jumper.

'Sorry?'

Quentin Adler butted into the conversation from the side. 'Ellen, I need to talk to you about this burglary case.'

'In a minute, Quentin.'

'I tried to stop him, but he frightens me,' Phoebe squeaked. 'He's a Leo, you know. I can't relate to Leos.'

'What?'

'You know,' Quentin complained, color mottling his fleshy face. 'That burglary you dumped on me – Herman Horstman. I can't find the deposition you took from his girlfriend, and now she's suddenly gone to Mexico and –'

'Mr Costello,' Phoebe admitted, squeezing her eyes shut as if bracing herself for a blow. 'He's in your office. I'm *really* sorry!'

'– and I'd like to know how a little tramp like that gets the money to fly to Cancún, but that's neither here nor there. I need that deposition, Ellen.'

'Quentin,' Ellen said sharply. 'Take a number and wait.'

She reached around him and plucked Phoebe by a sleeve.

'Tony Costello is in my office? Alone?'

'I'm *really* sorry!' Phoebe mewed. 'I *tried*. It's just that the phone won't stop ringing and – and – I heard you were a-a-t-t-acked a-a-and he fr-frightens me!'

'Oh, Phoebe, don't cry!' Ellen pleaded.

Phoebe sat back against the edge of her desk and covered her face with her hands. 'I-I-I-I'm t-t-ry-y-ying!'

'Ellen, I have to say I resent your attitude,' Quentin pouted. 'You dumped this case on me –'

Ellen wheeled on him, barely resisting the urge to grab hold of his lapels. 'Quentin, I am not your mother, I am not your secretary. I gave you my files on the case. If you can't find something, deal with it. Now, please excuse me while I go eviscerate Mr Costello.'

She stormed into the room and slammed the door.

'How dare you!' she snapped. 'How dare you come here and bully my secretary and walk into my private office without an invitation! I ought to call security and have you thrown out of the building!'

'You do that, Ellen,' he said. 'That will only add credence to my story when I relate to the press how you've attempted to shut me out. How you don't answer my phone calls and refuse to schedule me for appointments. I've left no fewer than five messages this morning alone.'

'Oh, pardon me that my life doesn't revolve around you, Tony. You think I should just drop everything and answer to you because I was once foolish enough to become involved with you?'

He stepped closer, but she refused to back away.

'No,' he said quietly. 'I think you're shutting me out to punish me, and if that's true, then maybe you should remove yourself from this case and give it to someone with no emotional baggage.'

'You'd like that, wouldn't you?' Ellen said with a humorless laugh. 'I'm far and away the best prosecutor in this office and you know it. You think I'll hand this case over so you can maul a lesser attorney in court? Get real.'

On that shot she walked away from him, taking her place behind her desk. She did a quick scan of the room, looking for anything out of place, any indication that he had taken advantage of his time alone.

'You realize you're laying the groundwork for an appeal.' He sat once again, control firmly in hand. He seemed almost casual, though she knew he was equally dangerous in this mood as when he was in full fury – if not more so.

Ellen arched a brow. 'Already planning the appeal? That bodes ill for your client. I'm not concerned, at any rate. I haven't done anything unethical. If you try to drag the past into it, the spotlight will end up on you, Tony. I don't think you'd like to be the star of that particular show.'

He leaned back, a smile cutting across his handsome mouth. 'You've still got it, Ellen. Hard as nails and twice as sharp when you have to be. I used to love debating with you. Passion at the touch of a button.'

That many of their debates had taken place in bed or ended up in bed was a point he undoubtedly wanted to make. But she wouldn't give him the satisfaction.

'Let's stick to the subject,' she said, resting her arms on her blotter. 'You, of all people, have no business coming into my office without my permission.'

'You don't really think I came here to steal something, do you?' He had the gall to look amused. *Poor, paranoid Ellen.* 'In the first place, I know you would never leave anything of real value to a case lying around. I know how you operate – you've got every scrap of pertinent information tucked away in your neat little three-ring binder in your briefcase, which you never let out of your sight. Secondly, I don't need to steal from you to make my case. My client is innocent.'

'Save it for the judge.'

'With whom we have an appointment in five minutes,' he said, consulting his platinum Rolex.

'What?'

He tipped his head. 'I *tried* to call you, Ellen. I need to see Grabko, and I certainly don't want to be accused of trying to have an ex parte conversation with him.'

'I have a meeting with someone else in five minutes.'

'Not anymore,' he said. 'Rule number one in the laws of courtroom survival: don't piss off the judge.'

'And what's so pressing that we have to attend to it right now?'

'I'm going to petition the court for the release of Josh Kirkwood's medical records,' he said smoothly.

'What? Why?'

'Because I have reason to believe the child has been physically abused – by his father.'

20

'Of all the dirty, sleazy, underhanded, back-alley tricks, this absolutely takes the prize!' Ellen ranted, too furious for circumspection. She paced a track behind Judge Grabko's visitor's chairs, her red wool blazer open, hands jammed on her hips.

Costello sat with his legs crossed, a long-suffering expression directed at the judge. 'It's a legitimate request, Your Honor. My client is entitled to present facts that exonerate him, including evidence pointing to other suspects.'

'Legitimate?' Ellen repeated. 'It's utter bull!' She turned toward Grabko. 'Your Honor, Mr Costello isn't preparing a defense here. He's preparing to mount a smear campaign against Josh Kirkwood's parents in order to divert attention away from his client and the hard evidence against him. An act so low I can't believe even Mr Costello isn't disgusted by the mere concept.'

Judge Grabko fingered his plaid bow tie, a frown bending the line on his forehead. 'Have a seat, Ellen. We'll discuss the issue like rational adults.'

She forced herself to comply, bristling inwardly at Grabko's patronizing attitude. He seemed bent on treating her like a second-year law student, and she knew the show was for Costello's benefit. But she also knew she had to rein in her temper. She couldn't let Tony get her back up.

She settled in the chair, straightened her jacket, crossed her legs, and picked a fleck of lint off the leg of her black slacks, flicking it subtly in Tony's direction.

'Your Honor,' she said with forced calm. 'Josh Kirkwood's medical records have no bearing on his abduction.'

'They do if Paul Kirkwood is guilty of the crime,' Costello said. 'In that event, they go to motive. During their investigation and questioning of potential defense witnesses, my associates have had several incidents mentioned to them. Seeing the child with bruises, injuries, a broken arm at one point –'

'He's an eight-year-old boy,' Ellen interjected. 'They fall off bikes and out of trees. They play rough sports –'

'They fall victim to abusive parents. Paul Kirkwood is known to have a volatile temper, to be subject to mood swings –'

'Paul Kirkwood isn't on trial here –'

'Perhaps he should be.'

'Perhaps he would be if he had been the one chased down and apprehended by the police,' Ellen said derisively. 'What possible motive could Paul have for stealing his own child, then playing twisted mind games with the police? But let's say for argument's sake Paul kidnapped his own child and led police on a bizarre hunt – why would he then turn around and bring Josh home? None of this follows any known form of logic, and you know it.'

Costello arched a thick brow. 'The infamous accomplice was *your* theory,' he said. 'But we're getting off the point here, Your Honor.' He dismissed Ellen, giving Grabko his full attention. 'The boy's medical records –'

'Fall under doctor-patient privilege,' Ellen argued. 'They are private and beyond the scope of this hearing.'

'That will be for me to determine, Ms North,' Grabko chastened.

Elbows on the arms of his chair, he steepled his long fingers in front of him and looked from one attorney to the other. A Vivaldi concerto played softly in the background. The judge shut his eyes for a moment and breathed deeply, letting the purity of the music cleanse his mind.

'Ellen,' he said in his law-professor voice, 'would you deny a defendant the right to present a defense on the grounds that that defense implicated another suspect?'

The letter of the law. All emotion pared away. No bias.

'No, Your Honor, of course not. It's part of the adversarial system.'

'You simply object to having Paul Kirkwood singled out as that other suspect?'

Justice was supposed to be blind, impartial, unsentimental.

'The police investigated the possibility of Mr Kirkwood's involvement and dismissed it,' she said. 'There was no real evidence against him –'

'If we could get those records –' Costello began.

'The family has been through hell as it is, Your Honor.'

Costello cut her a look from the corner of his eye. 'We can subpoena the records.'

'It is within your rights to try, Mr Costello,' Grabko said. 'However, the family also has the right to seek a protective order to prevent you from doing so.'

He pursed his lips and let his eyes drift shut once again as the second movement of the concerto built to a finish. Ellen held her breath, waiting, muscles tensed. It hadn't occurred to her that Grabko's tendency toward pretension included a tendency toward theatrics. This was his big case, his time to shine, to get his name in the papers. *The distinguished Judge Gorman Grabko.*

Vivaldi soared from a shelf loaded with scholarly treatments of the gentlemanly art of fly-fishing.

'The court will request the records,' Grabko said at last. 'I will review them privately to determine relevance to the case, and we'll go from there.'

Costello smiled. 'Thank you, Your Honor.'

They emerged from Grabko's chambers half an hour later, walking into the empty courtroom, where Ellen had a DUI sentencing scheduled for two o'clock. The buzz of conversation from the hall penetrated in a dim way. Lawyers hanging around, chewing the fat with county welfare advocates, cutting deals with prosecutors while they waited for their cases to be called in Judge Witt's court.

Intermingled with the usual crowd were reporters, lying in wait like cheetahs ready to jump up and run down their prey. There had been more than a few in the hall when she and Costello had come up. By now they would be thick all down the corridor. Between her own headline potential as a victim of vandalism, and Costello's sensational bomb, they had to be drooling in anticipation.

In no hurry to throw herself into the fray, she paused in front of the bench and leaned back against it, crossing her arms over her chest. 'Your media puppets await.'

Costello looked amused. 'What makes you think I asked them here?'

'I haven't been innocent in a very long time, Tony. Whenever two or more reporters are gathered, you'll give them a show. And they'll eat this up – your casting the blame on the family. The stuff tabloids are made of. It's disgusting.'

'It's a valid argument,' he said, bracing a hand beside her shoulder. 'You know as well as I do Kirkwood has inconsistencies in his story.'

'It's a big leap from "Can you prove you were getting a burger at the Hardee's drive-through while your son was being abducted?" to "Isn't it true you abducted your own son?" ' Ellen pointed out. At the same time she dismissed the little voice of truth that reminded her she had never been very comfortable with Paul's excuses herself. 'Your client was caught red-handed.'

'He has an alibi for the night Josh Kirkwood was abducted.'

'Which is about as phony as your tan. He has no witnesses to corroborate –'

'I'll have to correct you there, Ellen.' A nasty, anticipatory gleam in his dark eyes, he took his briefcase to a counsel table, popped it open, and extracted a sheaf of documents. 'Disclosure pursuant to rule 9.02. Happy reading.'

Ellen scanned the first page, where one of Tony's assistants had typed an elaborate explanation of the fact that they as yet had no written or recorded statements from witnesses. What a joke. Tony would never take a written statement prior to trial for the express reason that he would be compelled by law to turn it over to the prosecution. The second page stated Wright's alibi for the time of Josh's abduction. As he had stated repeatedly, it said he was in his office in the Cray building, at Harris. What he had never said before was that he was working in the company of a student – Todd Childs.

Ellen's heart picked up a beat. She turned the pages to the witness list, and a chill of apprehension pebbled the skin of her arms and ran down her back. At the top of the list was Todd Childs, 966 Tenth Street NW, Apartment B.

'When did you speak with Todd Childs?' she asked carefully.

'Does it matter?'

'It matters that he has already stated to the police he wasn't with Dr Wright that evening.'

'He'll swear under oath that he was.'

'He's lying.'

'Prove it.'

'I intend to,' she said, anger shuddering through her. 'You might have taken notice of his name on *my* witness list.'

He raised his brows in mock innocence. 'Was it? Things have been so hectic this week. . . . Has he been served?'

'I'm sure you'll be stunned to hear we've been unable to locate him. You wouldn't happen to know where he's staying, would you?'

Costello deflected the pointed question with a humorless laugh.

'Ellen, your paranoia is reaching new heights if you believe I'm hiding a witness from you.'

She took the verbal shot and pressed on, immune to his attempts to hurt her. 'How is it you've spoken to him while the cops can't even find him?'

'That might have something to do with the caliber of cops you're working with.'

'You underestimate them, Tony. And I think you underestimate me, which is fine. It'll be all the more gratifying when I kick your ass next week.'

'You're overestimating your case, Ellen,' he said. 'And you're grasping at straws going after Wright's phone records. You can't believe you'll find anything linking Dr Wright to the kidnapping, which means you're really looking for something else. I'm surprised Judge Grabko didn't call you on it.'

'Actually, I don't expect to find anything at all,' she admitted coolly. 'I don't expect to find your phone number listed under calls placed on the twenty-fifth, for instance. Which will mean that Karen Wright didn't call you on behalf of her husband. And if Karen Wright didn't call you, then who did?'

'So we're back to *that* conspiracy theory. You know, maybe you need help for this, Ellen. Although I'm sure our mutual friend Mr Brooks will find your psychological quirks an interesting added facet for his book.'

'Mutual friend?' she asked, the cool disinterest in her tone completely at odds with what she was feeling. 'I've barely met the man,' she lied. 'How do you know him?'

What did he know? Did he know about Jay's connection to the attorney general? He had a private investigator working the case. Did he know Brooks had taken her home last night? Would he try to make an issue of it?

'I met him years ago, actually,' he answered casually. 'We were both at Purdue, though we were several years apart. Small world, isn't it?'

Ellen felt the floor dip beneath her feet. Brooks knew Costello. They had gone to the same college. He had never said one word.

'Ellen? Are you all right?' Costello asked. 'You look a little pale.'

'Don't worry about it, Tony.' She spurred herself to move, to turn away, to duck her head. 'It's nothing the truth won't cure.'

She hefted her briefcase onto the other counsel table and stuffed the disclosure into the appropriate file folder. 'You don't have to concern yourself about my mental state – unless, of course, I'm right and your client's accomplice called you in on this case, thereby making you an accessory in the Holloman kidnapping.'

She clicked the locks closed and gave her adversary a final, challenging stare. 'As an officer of the court, I'm sure I don't have to remind you of your obligation to report Todd Childs's whereabouts to the police – should you *happen* to see him. Who knows? Maybe we can kill two birds with one stone – serve our witness and nail an accomplice all in one shot. Wouldn't that be nice and neat?'

'Only two birds?' he questioned. 'I thought you were after my head, too.'

'Oh, I am, Tony,' she said with a nasty smile. 'You'll be my bonus dead duck.'

He stepped close enough that she could smell the expensive aftershave he wore and lowered his head as if to share a secret.

'It's so nice to know you still think of me as special,' he murmured.

God, she hated that he thought he could manipulate her with memories and sex appeal. '*Special* isn't how I think of you, Tony. You're at the wrong end of the adjective spectrum altogether.'

'Does that mean you won't have dinner with me for old time's sake after all this is said and done?' he asked, his tone still intimate, his expression hungry and amused.

'I'd rather have my limbs gnawed off.'

He had the nerve to laugh and the gall to hold the door for her as they left the courtroom.

They were mobbed as soon as they stepped into the hall, a dozen voices shouting questions at once. Bodies pressed in on them, hands thrusting forward with microphones and tape recorders. Ellen found herself trapped at Costello's side, her shoulder brushing against his arm. As she was jostled, she had to steady herself with a hand against the small of his back. She hated to touch him.

'Our mutual friend Mr Brooks . . .'

'Ms North, is it true you've been threatened?'

'We were both at Purdue . . .'

'Ms North, are there any suspects in the vandalism?'

'Small world, isn't it?'

'Mr Costello, does Dr Wright have any comment on possible involvement of the Sci-Fi Cowboys in the attack on Ms North?'

'Mr Costello, is it true you're pushing for the investigation to turn toward Paul Kirkwood?'

'My client is innocent,' Costello shouted, fixing his eagle glare just to the left of a portable sun gun. 'The police have been negligent in pursuing leads that might take their investigation in a direction they don't want to consider. My investigators have pursued *all* leads. I can guarantee you that when the hearing begins next week, Dr Garrett Wright will not be the only one on trial.'

The statement had the effect of pouring gasoline on a fire. The noise level rose to a deafening din. Wanting nothing more than to escape, Ellen positioned her briefcase to use as shield and battering ram and started against the current of the crowd.

'Ms North, do you have any comment?'

'Ms North, can we get a statement?'

She lowered her head and pushed forward, slamming the briefcase into someone's knees. Down the hall the door to Judge Witt's courtroom opened, and the old bailiff, Randolph Grimm, barged into the hall, shouting for quiet, his face as red as a cherry tomato.

'Keep it down out here! Court is in session! Don't you people have any respect?'

Without waiting for an answer, he raised his cane and smacked it against the wall, the sound ringing out like a gunshot. People ducked and gasped and swung toward him. Cameramen wheeled with tape running.

Ellen took advantage of the diversion to make her escape, rounding a jungle gym of scaffolding and riding a service elevator down to the second floor.

Costello was going to turn the spotlight on Paul. Theoretically, the ploy would have no bearing on the probable-cause hearing. Grabko had to base his decision whether or not to bind Wright over for trial on the evidence presented, and Tony had no real evidence against Paul Kirkwood. But there wouldn't be a potential juror in the district who wouldn't have picked up on a story as sensational as this.

'You have to get it to a jury first, Ellen,' she muttered as the elevator landed and the doors pulled open.

Phoebe stood outside the county clerk's office with a ream of paperwork clutched to her meager bosom and a shy smile on her face, absorbed in conversation with the boy wonder of the *Grand Forks Herald*.

Adam Slater's eyes widened as he caught sight of Ellen. He swung away from Phoebe, digging a notepad out of the hip pocket of his baggy jeans.

'Hey, Ms North, can I ask you a couple of questions about last night?'

'I'm surprised you aren't upstairs with the rest of the pack.'

Slater shook his head. 'Can't get anywhere that way. Everyone will have the same story. If I want to make my mark, I've got to get something fresh. You know, like they say in baseball – hit 'em where they ain't.'

'Charming analogy,' Ellen said, 'but I don't want you swinging your bat around my secretary. Is that understood, Mr Slater?'

His smile went flat. Beside him, Phoebe stood with her jaw dropped and her cheeks tinting.

'I have no comment for your story,' Ellen went on. 'You'll have to use someone else to make your mark. Phoebe, let's go. We've got work to do.'

She started toward the office but turned back when Phoebe didn't fall in step behind her.

The girl had ducked her head in abject embarrassment. 'God, I'm really sorry, Adam. I didn't –'

Phoebe,' Ellen said sharply.

'Man, this sucks,' Slater complained, flopping his arms at his sides. 'We were just talking.'

Phoebe kept her head down as she walked beside Ellen. Neither spoke. In the outer offices phones rang, and Kevin O'Neal, the county SWAT commander, stood talking and laughing with Sig Iverson and Quentin Alder.

'Hey, Ellen,' O'Neal called as he caught sight of her. 'The ATF caught your pals the Berger boys down in Tennessee.'

'Was there gunplay?' she asked with sadistic hope.

'Gave up without a fight and with a van full of stolen cigarettes. ATF wants to keep them on the federal beef. What do you want to do about extradiction?'

Ellen shook her head. 'Good riddance. Save the county some money.'

She turned around just as Phoebe was slinking behind her desk.

'I'd like to speak with you in my office.'

The girl didn't answer but followed Ellen as if going to her death.

'How do you know Adam Slater?' Ellen asked as soon as they were in the office.

'I met him at the Leaf and Bean last night,' she said quietly, still hugging her papers. 'We drank coffee and listened to music. Thursday is open-mike night.'

'Did you know he was a reporter?'

'Yes. He said so. We didn't talk about the case, Ellen. I know better.'

'I know you wouldn't mean to say anything, Phoebe, but he's a reporter. They have ways of wheedling information out of people. Believe me, I know.'

'*Our mutual friend Mr Brooks . . .*'

'I was very up-front with him about it,' Phoebe said. 'I told him right off I couldn't say anything about the case, and he was fine with that. Maybe he just wanted to have coffee with me. Maybe he just likes me as a human being. Our psyches are very in tune.'

Ellen rolled her eyes. 'Oh, please, Phoebe. He's a reporter looking to make a name for himself. He'll do anything to get what he wants. That's what reporters do – they screw people over for their own glorification.'

'*I'm here for a story . . . I go after what I want and I get it.*'

'Well, I'm sorry, I'm not as cynical and paranoid as you are.' Tears beaded on Phoebe's lashes. 'And I'm sorry you don't trust me, Ellen.'

'It's not you I don't trust,' Ellen said softly. She let out a pent-up breath, trying without success to force the tension out of her shoulders. 'It's the rest of the world I don't trust – Adam Slater included.'

God, what a tangled mess. She took her secretary to task for talking to a cub reporter from a nothing newspaper in nowhere, North Dakota, while Jay Butler Brooks, renowned rogue and writer, old college buddy of her arch-nemesis, had been making himself at home in *her* home, drinking her liquor . . . kissing her, touching her, reaching past her barriers.

Who do you trust?

Phoebe? Adam Slater? Costello? Brooks?

Trust no one.

'*Rumor has it you think Enberg had some help with that shotgun.*'

'*Where did you hear that?*'

'*Around.*'

'*If there's a leak on this case –*'

'*No one fed it to me. I don't have a mole in your office, if that's what you're worried about. . . .*'

'*I'm not paranoid.*'

If she *was* paranoid, it didn't mean they *weren't* out to get her.

She stood at her window and looked out. Deer Lake was a ghost town, windswept and deserted; a place from a science-fiction movie, where all had been abandoned in an unknown moment for unknown reasons. 'Abandoned' – it was a good word for what she was feeling. Abandoned by the security and trust and safety she had embraced here.

'We can't take chances,' she said, turning back toward Phoebe. 'Look what happened with Paige Price and Steiger, and that whole mess. This case is too important. We can't risk a mistake. Josh and Megan are counting on us.'

'And Dustin Holloman,' Phoebe added in a small voice. She gnawed her lower lip for a moment, a moment of silence for the victims, then swiped a tear from her cheek. 'I'm s-sorry. I-I w-w-w-ouldn't –'

Ellen held up a hand. 'I know you wouldn't, Phoebe. Just be careful. Please.'

She nodded and sniffled and pushed her glasses up on her nose.

'Cameron and Mitch and Agent Wilhelm are waiting for you in the conference room.'

Ellen briefed them on the meeting in Grabko's chambers. Mitch reacted with anger, Cameron with disgust. Marty Wilhelm looked troubled and confused.

'Is abuse a possibility?' he asked.

'Absolutely not,' Mitch said. 'I've known Hannah and Paul since I moved here. There's no way.'

'But Costello is right,' Wilhelm argued. 'Paul Kirkwood has a temper. We've seen it.'

'Hannah would never allow him to hurt Josh. She wouldn't put up with that kind of shit for a minute.'

'Then what's she doing married to the jerk? She doesn't strike me as the kind of woman who would put up with any of Paul Kirkwood's lesser qualities, but there she is. There might be a lot we don't know about their marriage.'

'He's changed,' Mitch said. 'People do.'

Cameron arched a brow. 'The question may be – How much? Has he gone off the deep end? We know the marriage is all but over. Paul isn't living at the house. We know Josh reacted very badly when Paul showed up to see him in he hospital.'

'And you think it's because he's a child abuser and Hannah knows it but has failed to report it,' Mitch stated flatly.

'Stranger things have been proved true.'

His face set in stubborn lines, Mitch turned his scowl from Cameron to Wilhelm and back. 'Use your heads. We're saying Wright's accomplice nabbed Dustin Holloman. Nothing in that case points to Paul.'

'Maybe there are three of them,' Wilhelm suggested.

'Yeah,' Mitch said. 'Maybe Deer Lake has a whole underground community of psychotic child abusers and they're all trying to draw suspicion off their pal Wright.'

'There's no point in fighting about this among ourselves,' Ellen said. 'Costello is forcing the issue. If he's looking at Paul, then we'd better make at least a token show of looking at Paul or we'll end up with egg on our faces.'

'There was the van –' Wilhelm started.

'All together now.' Mitch raised his arms like a symphony conductor. 'The van that yielded us nothing.'

'Mitch is right,' Ellen said. 'Don't waste time on the van. Talk to people around Paul. Talk to his secretary. Talk to his partner.'

'He won't be any help pinning down Paul's movements in any way,' Cameron said. 'I know Dave Christianson from my health club. He's been working strictly from home for the past three months. His wife is having a difficult pregnancy with twins.'

'Okay, so we talk again with the secretary,' Wilhelm said. 'And the security guard at his office complex. Neighbors. See what we can tie him to. Maybe he's not in with Wright. Maybe he's trying to frame Wright.'

Mitch slapped his hands down on the table. 'Jesus Christ, Costello would love this. We're here to discuss new evidence against his client and instead we're tripping over conspiracy theories. This isn't a case we're on, it's a fucking Oliver Stone movie.'

'Evidence?' Ellen asked, sitting up straighter. 'What evidence?'

Wilhelm pushed a curled tube of fax paper across the table to her. 'I pulled some strings and got a friend in the lab to release a preliminary report on some more of our physical evidence – the gloves, the ski mask, and the sheet that was wrapped around Agent O'Malley the night she was attacked.'

'And?'

'The glove has bloodstains that look to match Agent O'Malley for type. We already know about the blood types on the sheet. Now we're looking at hairs recovered from the sheet. Four distinct types. One unidentified. One consistent with Agent O'Malley. One consistent with Josh. And one consistent with Garrett Wright.'

'We finally catch a break,' Ellen said, a sense of relief seeping through her.

'Regarding the stocking cap,' Wilhelm went on, 'they found two distinct types of hair – one consistent with Wright, and one matching the unidentified hair found on the sheet.

'The question now,' he said, 'is, who does that other hair belong to? And if we got a sample from Paul Kirkwood, would we get a match?'

622

21

Father Tom sat in a pew toward the back of the church. On the left-hand side of the aisle – opposite where his one-time deacon, Albert Fletcher, had fallen to his death six days ago. Albert, devout servant of the Lord, his faith turning into fanaticism into madness; his madness leading him to his death, here, in this place he had loved. Tom couldn't decide if it was poetic or ironic. It was sad, he knew that. And it struck him as cruel, as many things did these days.

He sat alone. The weather had kept the faithful few away from morning Mass. He had gone through the motions for his own sake, hoping he would feel something, some kind of deep, binding affirmation that he still belonged in the vestments. But all he felt was hollow desperation, as if he were truly, totally, spiritually alone, abandoned by the same God who had allowed Josh to be taken and Hannah to suffer and Albert to die.

He had considered confessing his feelings, but he already knew the empty platitudes that would be handed him in response. He was being tested. He needed to reflect, to pray. He needed to keep his faith. A pat on the head and a hundred Hail Marys. At most, they would send him on retreat for a week or a month to one of the secluded spots where the Church tucked away its embarrassments – the alcoholic priests, the burnouts, the mentally fragile, the sexually suspect. Time to reflect among the casualties, but not too long, because the archdiocese was woefully short of priests and better to have one in place who had lost his faith than not to have one at all. At least he could go through the motions.

The politics of the Church disgusted him, and always had. He had come to the priesthood for better reasons, nobler reasons. Reasons that were drifting away from him.

He tipped his head back and looked up at the soaring ceiling with its delicate gilt arches and ethereal frescoes. St E's had been built in the era when minicathedrals were still affordable and parishioners tithed to the Church instead of to their IRAs. The exterior was of native limestone. Twin spires thrust heavenward like lances of the soldiers of God. The windows were stained-glass works of art, jewel-tone mosaics depicting the life of Christ. Inside, the walls were painted slate blue and trimmed with lacework stencils in gilt and white and rose. The pews were oak, the kneelers padded with worn velvet. It was the kind of place meant to inspire awe and offer comfort. A place of ritual and wonderful mysteries. Miracles.

He could have used one about now.

Along the south wall a rack of cobalt-glass votives cradled the flames of three dozen prayers, filling the air with the buttery scent of melting wax. On the wall beside the tiers of candles, the handmade posters put up by the catechism classes praying for Josh's safety had been replaced with prayers for Dustin Holloman. Prayers children should never have to make, fears their lives should never have known.

In the silence he could hear the memory of his father's voice as he read the Billings newspaper three days after the fact, because that was as fast as the mail could get it to them on their small ranch near Red Lodge, Montana. Every morning Bob McCoy would come in from chores and read the paper while he had his breakfast, and shake his head and say, 'The world's going to hell on a sled.'

Tom thought he could hear the runners screeching. But the thump that resounded in the church brought him back to reality, such as it was. Someone had come in the main doors at the back, the main doors that needed oil in their hinges. He turned in the pew, squinting to recognize the man walking toward him from the dark shadows beneath the balcony.

'I'm looking for Father Tom McCoy.'

'I'm Father Tom,' he said, rising.

'Jay Butler Brooks.'

'Ah, the crime writer,' he said, offering his hand.

Jay clasped the priest's hand in his and gave it a pump. 'You're familiar with my work, Father?'

'Only by reputation. My reading taste runs more toward fiction. I get enough reality on a daily basis. What can I do for you, Mr Brooks?'

'I'd like a moment of your time, if I might. I wasn't interrupting anything, was I?'

Tom McCoy cast an ironic glance around the deserted church, but the emotion that twitched the corners of his mouth seemed self-deprecating. He looked nothing like any priest Jay had ever seen or imagined. He was too young, too handsome, built like an athlete, and dressed like a slacker in creased black jeans and a faded green sweatshirt from the University of Notre Dame. The clerical collar seemed at odds with the cowboy boots. A man of contradictions. A kindred spirit.

'We're not exactly having a rush on salvation today,' he said.

'With weather like this I reckon folks figure they'll take their chances,' Jay reasoned. 'What's another day or two in purgatory, give or take?'

'You know about purgatory, Mr Brooks? Are you Catholic?'

'No, sir. I was born a Baptist and later converted to cynicism, but I do know all about purgatory.' Weariness crept into his voice against his will. 'Y'all haven't cornered the market on hell or its suburbs.'

624

Father Tom tipped his head in concession. 'No, I suppose not. Did you want to go into my office?'

Jay shook his head. His gaze scanned the grand interior of the church, taking in the windows, the statuary, the cast bas-relief plaques that hung at regular intervals along the wall. 'This is fine. Quite a place you've got here.'

The altar was traditional, draped in linen, set with brass candelabra, a gleaming chalice, a huge old book with marker ribbons trailing from between its pages. According to the newspaper articles from one week ago, the demented deacon had given Father McCoy a concussion with one of the brass candlesticks from that altar. Jay wondered if it was sitting up there now, absolved of guilt, or if the police had taken it away as evidence.

From the huge crucifix that hung behind the altar, the delicately carved face of Christ glowered down at him as if in disapproval of his thoughts.

Father Tom moved farther down the pew. Jay sat beside him, his parka rustling like newspaper. He had unzipped it as a concession to being indoors, but the cold seemed to have sunk into him bone-deep in the ten minutes it had taken him to get there, navigating the Cherokee along unplowed roads and through three-foot drifts. At any rate, the church didn't seem as warm as the interior of the truck. The thermostat probably went up only for parishioners. No sense heating the barn when the flock was gone.

'You're here to do a book,' Father Tom said flatly.

'You disapprove.'

'It's not my place to approve or disapprove.'

A smile cracked Jay's face. 'Well, I've never known that to stop anybody.'

'Hannah and Josh have been through enough,' McCoy said without apology. 'I don't want to see them hurt any more than they already have been.'

Jay arched a brow at the omission. 'And Paul?'

The priest glanced away. 'Paul has made it clear he doesn't want anything from me or the Church.'

'Can you blame him?'

'Not for that.'

His candor was surprising, but, then, nothing much about Tom McCoy seemed ordinary. Depending on who you asked around town, Father McCoy was a rebel, refreshing, an affront to the traditions of the Church. He did not define himself by uniform or convention. His parishioners either loved him or tolerated him. Behind the lenses of his gold-rimmed glasses, his blue eyes were honest.

'I'm not interested in exploiting victims, Father.'

'You'll record their suffering, dissect their lives, package their story as entertainment, and make a whole lot of money. What do you call that?'

'The way of the world. Stuff happens. People want to know about it. Their knowing doesn't change what happened. Nothing can. What I'm after is the truth. Reasons. Motives. I want to know where ordinary people find the strength to deal with extraordinary tragedy. I want to know what the rest of us can learn from them.'

'And make a lot of money.'

'And make a lot of money,' he admitted. 'The poor might be rich in the kingdom of God, but I'll take mine now, thanks.'

'Hannah isn't ordinary,' Father Tom said. His expression softened slightly, tellingly. 'Ask anyone. She's stronger than she knows. Kind. Good. I can't begin to tell you what she's meant to this community as a doctor, as a role model.'

'It must have been difficult to see her go through this,' Jay offered, watching closely for the true reaction. Anger. There and gone. Quickly veiled by something more acceptable. But there was no priestly wisdom forthcoming, no magic motto meant as a blanket banality for all-purpose suffering.

'It's been hell,' McCoy said frankly. 'I've been a priest for more than a decade, Mr Brooks. I have yet to understand why bad things happen to good people.'

'God's will?' Jay ventured.

'I certainly hope not. What purpose is served punishing the faithful and the innocent? I'd call that sadism, wouldn't you?'

Jay leaned back and crossed his arms, regarding Tom McCoy with a quizzical scrutiny. 'Are you sure you're a priest?'

He gave a humorless laugh and looked away. The word 'no' reverberated in the air around him. 'After the last couple of weeks, I don't think any of us can be sure of anything.'

The answer struck a chord. Truth. The kind nobody really wanted to hear.

'But you must see this all the time,' McCoy said. 'It's your job – going from one set of victims to another. Does it get to you, or are you immune?'

'Not immune; careful. I keep my distance. Don't let it get personal. I'm there to ask questions, look for answers, patch it all together and move on.' Even as he rattled off his stock answer, he could see Ellen in his mind's eye. He could feel her in his arms, feel her fear, her tears soaking into his shirt. Some distance.

'It's not about me,' he said. That was a lie, too.

He might have called coming to Deer Lake running away, but he couldn't escape the fact that immersing himself in this particular case was certainly about him, about his own sense of loss. It was about punishing and comforting himself with perspective, which made him both selfish and opportunistic. Why couldn't he have just jumped on a plane to Barbados after seeing Christine? He could have been soaking up sun and rum instead of freezing his ass and digging up unwanted emotions out of the deepest corners of his soul.

'I'm just recording the story,' he stated, as if that could make it so.

'Nothing personal,' Father Tom said. His gaze had narrowed, focusing deeper than the surface excuses and public facade. 'Do you have children?'

Depends on who you ask, he thought, but he kept that answer to himself. Confession was for the regulars of St Elysius, not smart-mouth mercenary hacks from out of town.

McCoy interpreted the silence as a no. 'Have you met Hannah and Josh?'

'Not yet.'

'Why is that? The story is about their lives.'

'There are other people involved. I've been busy getting background, getting to know the players.'

'Really?'

'If you're waiting for me to say it didn't seem right to approach her, you'll be waiting a long time, Father,' he said, wondering just how many strikes God would list against him for lying to a priest.

He had been avoiding Hannah Garrison on the excuse that the story was about more than her son. It was about the court system and the cops and Garrett Wright and Dennis Enberg. But at its heart it was about a little boy. An eight-year-old boy who had had his whole life pulled up by the roots.

He had chosen this story specifically for the parallels, to force himself to examine the pain and to probe the questions while maintaining his usual safe distance . . . and he had shied away from the heart of it. Josh. Josh, who was eight years old, freckle-faced, gap-toothed. Who liked to play hockey and Little League. He remembered the picture in Paul's office – Josh in his baseball uniform with Paul, the proud father, beside him. The fist of longing tightened.

What the hell are you doing here, Brooks?

Father Tom rose to his feet. 'Let's take a ride, Mr Brooks. There's someone I think you should meet.'

They drove down Lakeshore, past Garrett Wright's home with a few intrepid reporters parked out front, on to the Kirkwood house, and turned in the driveway. Jay had parked in front of this house once before only to back off and drive away. Nothing had changed in the few days in between. The snow fort in the front yard was still half-finished. He wondered if Josh would ever finish it or if what he had gone through had so changed him that something as simple and childish as a snow fort would forevermore seem unimportant.

Father Tom stepped out of the Cherokee. Jay gave a cursory glance at his minicassette recorder lying on the console between the seats and left it.

They walked up the driveway together, Jay quietly absorbing the feel of the place, the detail. The house was the last one on the block. It looked comfortable, the kind of place to raise a family. From the front step the view of the street and the rest of the neighborhood was limited, cut off by the attached garage that jutted out in front of the house itself. The view was of the lake and the trees that lined the banks. Through the lacework of leafless branches and across the frozen expanse, the buildings of Harris College were just visible.

It was on this step that Josh Kirkwood had been left four nights ago. Alone. Dressed in a pair of striped pajamas. His mother had seen no one, no car. Garrett Wright's house was just down the block, but as yet no evidence had been found to suggest Josh had ever been inside it. Karen Wright had been under guard that night at the Fontaine Hotel.

Who had brought him back? Todd Childs? Christopher Priest? Or was Wright's accomplice someone so anonymous he or she was able to move around town freely, unknown, unseen, unsuspected? And what was the connection to Wright? Or was the connection to the people who lived in this house?

Hannah Garrison opened the door, a smile lighting her face when she saw Father Tom.

'You forgot your gloves again,' she chided. 'If you don't end up with frostbite, it'll be a miracle.'

'Well, that would certainly improve my stock with the bishop.'

Hannah had been the less visible one during the ordeal, staying in the background while her husband joined the search teams and played to the press. But Jay had watched her one television interview enough times that he had already memorized the sound of her voice, the cadence of her speech, the cornflower-blue of her eyes. He knew she blamed herself because she hadn't been there to pick Josh up that night. He had seen the pain in her face, heard the confusion in her voice. She'd had the perfect life and suddenly it was broken all around her.

And he wanted to write a book about it.

'Jay Butler Brooks, ma'am,' he said, offering his hand.

The pretty, fragile smile went brittle, and her gaze cut to her friend, Father Tom.

'I thought it was important' was all he said.

'I'm not a reporter, ma'am,' Jay said.

Hannah lifted her chin, her gaze cool. 'I know what you are, Mr Brooks. Come in,' she said. She directed them, not into the family room where the television was on and toys were scattered across the floor, but into a formal dining room with furniture that likely hadn't been used since Christmas. She was distancing him from her real home, from her children. Jay accepted the subtle slight as part of the big picture, part of the whole story, part of who Hannah Garrison was.

She took the seat at the head of the table. Even though she looked as if she had been ill – thin, pale, with dark circles beneath her eyes – her bearing was regal. Her wavy golden hair was pulled back from her face, accenting the kind of bone structure that made fashion models wealthy, but she wore no makeup, no jewelry. Her sweatshirt was a well-worn relic from her alma mater, Duke University. She could have made a gunnysack look chic.

'My husband told me he'd spoken with you,' she said.

'Why does that make me think I've already got a strike against me?'

'Certainly you have in Paul's eyes. I make my own judgments.'

Jay nodded. 'That's fair. I've been told you're a remarkable woman, Dr Garrison.'

She moved one long, elegant hand in a dismissive gesture. 'By circumstance, that's all. Which is why you're here, isn't it?'

'I won't lie to you about that, Dr Garrison. I'm a writer. You've got a hell of a story here. I'd like the chance to tell it.'

'And if I decline, you'll tell it anyway?'

'Probably. I'd like to be able to include your perspective, but it's up to you whether or not you want to participate.'

'Well, that was simple. My answer is no. Living this nightmare once is quite enough. I don't have any desire to go through it again in retelling the tale to you or in thinking thousands of people will live it vicariously reading your book.'

'Not even if it might help someone to understand –'

'Understand what? No part of this is understandable. I know. I've spent every night, every day, trying to understand. All I've got for the effort is more questions.'

'There will be a considerable amount of money for Josh,' Jay said. He found it very telling that Hannah herself hadn't spoken a word about payment when it had been virtually the first thought in her husband's head.

She gave him a frosty look. 'I won't prostitute my son or myself, Mr Brooks. We don't need your money. All I want is to get away from this nightmare, for us to distance ourselves from it emotionally and get on with our lives. Any money associated with what happened would only be like dragging the experience with us. It would be like blood money.'

She stood and smoothed her hands along the baggy hem of her sweatshirt. 'No. That's my answer. Would you like coffee?'

Subject dismissed, on to obligatory hostess duties. Jay had the feeling that if he had come here a month ago, Hannah would have been softer, gentler, less blunt, more elaborate in her guise of good manners. The ordeal had pared away the unnecessary in her, cut away the crap of social ceremony, leaving only the honest, the essential. Like many people he had interviewed, people who had gone through harrowing experiences, Hannah had seen how much of life is just bullshit, just meaningless ritual made important to give humankind some pretense of being better than the rest of the animals on the planet.

In another part of the house a telephone rang. She excused herself to answer it.

'The trust fund will be set up,' he said to Father Tom. 'They can do what they want with the money. Give it away for all I care.'

The priest gave a lazy shrug. 'It doesn't matter to you. You've absolved yourself, done your part, paid your fee.'

'I can't win for losing around here,' Jay grumbled. 'If I kept every nickel for myself, I'd be a greedy son of a bitch. If I give it away, I'm trying to buy a conscience.'

'Are you?'

He barked a laugh and looked away. What the hell would he want with a conscience? It was just excess baggage, another rock around his neck to drag him down. If he had a conscience, he would have to believe that it was all his own fault that Christine had kept his son from him all these years, that it wasn't just virulent spite on her part. He hurt enough as it was. To think it was his own doing that had taken eight years of his son's life away from him, denied him even knowledge of the boy, would be too much.

A mop of sandy-brown hair and a pair of big blue eyes suddenly appeared in the doorway to the family room. The eyes were somber with a steady stare.

'Hi, Josh,' Father Tom said in a casual voice. 'Would you like to join us?'

The boy eased the rest of his body into view but kept one hand on the doorjamb. The other clutched the handle of a bulging nylon backpack. He was dressed in baggy blue jeans and a Blackhawks hockey jersey several sizes too big. He made no move to come forward.

Jay turned sideways on his chair and rested his forearms on his thighs. 'Hey, there, Josh,' he said quietly. 'My name's Jay. Your dad tells me you're quite the baseball player.'

Josh's expression didn't flicker. There was no relaxation at the mention of his father, no response at all. He had a face made for a mischievous grin. Jay remembered the smile from the photograph in Paul's office – shining eyes and shy pride – and the photograph from the 'missing' posters – a gap-toothed grin and a Cub Scout uniform.

Slowly Josh crossed the hall and came into the dining room, skirting all the way around the room, his eyes on Jay. When he was even with Father Tom, he stopped and dug a spiral notebook out of the backpack, opened it, and tore out a page.

'I guess hockey is the sport now,' Jay went on, making conversation to break the tension that filled the room, hoping he might strike the right chord and draw the boy out. 'We don't play much hockey where I come from. We don't have any winter to speak of.'

Josh paid no attention to him as he knelt on the floor and carefully folded the sheet of paper in half and in half again. When he was finished, he stood, hooked his backpack over one shoulder, and walked a straight line across the area rug, as if he were on a tightrope. When he reached the table, he held the paper out for Father Tom.

'For me?' he asked, accepting the gift.

Josh nodded. 'But don't open it now.'

'All right.' He slid the note into an inner pocket. 'I'll save it for later.'

The boy nodded again, scooted behind Father Tom, and scurried along the edge of the room again to the doorway, watching Jay with those big, somber eyes.

Hannah came back, pausing to touch her son's head. Josh ducked out from under the caress and disappeared into the family room.

'I'm sorry for the interruption,' she said. 'Did you decide about the coffee?'

Jay rose. 'No, thank you, ma'am. I've got to be going.' He dug a card out of one of the many pockets on his parka and handed it to her. 'In case you change your mind.'

'I won't,' she said firmly, but tempered it with an apologetic look.

She was a far cry from her husband. Their marriage would be a story in itself, he supposed. Which of them had changed for better or worse? How long would they have hung on if Josh's abduction hadn't pulled them apart?

'It was a pleasure meeting you, Hannah,' he said. 'Father Tom is right. You're an extraordinary person. Whether you care to think it or not.'

A deep sadness darkened her eyes. 'But that's just my point, Mr Brooks – I don't want to be a heroine. I just want our lives back.'

It didn't look as if she would get that any time soon, he thought with pity when he stepped out through the front door and a photographer shot his picture from the window of a Toyota parked on the street.

'She doesn't deserve what's happened to her,' Father Tom said once inside the Cherokee.

Wasn't it the role of priests to listen to their faithful ponder the cruelties of the world? Jay thought. Tom McCoy seemed to have more questions than answers, a burden that appeared to be weighing on him heavily.

'In my experience, Father,' Jay said, 'life is scattershot with random acts of cruelty. Trying to make sense of it either keeps us human or makes us crazy.'

Father Tom said nothing but slipped Josh's note out of his coat pocket and unfolded it.

The drawing was simple: a sad face with blank dark eyes, set in the center of an inked-in black square. The caption broke his heart. *When I was lost.*

Josh wasn't the only one who had been lost in this ordeal. Lost lives, lost love, lost trust . . . lost faith. Tom had tried to make sense of it, had prayed for some comfort, but all he felt was fear as the faith that had anchored his life slipped farther and farther away, and all he wanted to hold on to was another man's wife.

When I was lost . . .

He folded the page and tucked it back into his coat pocket.

The funeral dragged on interminably. Victor Franken had accumulated scores of acquaintances in his seventy-nine years, none of whom was shy about using his death as an excuse to show off their skills as orators. The weather had prevented those from any distance outstate from coming, which the locals interpreted as meaning more time at the pulpit for themselves.

Ellen sat toward the back of Grace Lutheran, fanning herself with her program, wondering if all the hot air was coming from the furnace or if it was simply a by-product of this many lawyers in one place.

The narthex was crowded with reporters, lying in wait to jump people for comments on their way out. Franken's relatives sat in the front pews, including the great-grandson from L.A., who had opened the ceremonies with an interpretive liturgical dance that made the locals squirm in their seats. Minnesotans rarely interpreted anything with their bodies, and never clad in a black unitard.

Life in Deer Lake had taken on all the weirder qualities of a Fellini film, with Rudy Stovich as the sad clown. He stood at the pulpit, his voice rising and falling as dramatically as his expressions.

Mike Lumkin, an attorney from Tatonka, leaned into Ellen and whispered, 'If he's like this on the bench, I'm going into real estate.'

'Cross your fingers,' she whispered back. 'Maybe he'll be discovered by television. He could be the next Wapner.'

'Who'll play Rusty?'

'Manley Vanloon.'

'Sounds like an episode of *Hee-Haw*,' he said with a grimace. 'Hey, we need to talk dispo on Tilman. What do you think about time served?'

'I think you're dreaming. Time served and eighty hours of community service.'

His eyes bugged out. 'Eighty?'

'Ninety?'

'Sixty.'

'A hundred.'

'Eighty sounds good,' he said reasonably, and sat back as Rudy launched into the last leg of his tribute.

Ellen stifled a sigh. She tried to block everything around her from her mind in order to give Judge Franken her own personal tribute. Brief and to the point. He was a good man, a good judge, he would be missed.

The burial had to be postponed until a good thaw. After the final prayer, and three verses of 'Abide with Me,' everyone trooped to the church basement for cake and Jell-O from the Lutheran ladies' auxiliary and conversation that centered not on Judge Franken but on Garrett Wright and the kidnappings. Ellen made one obligatory round of the room and escaped through a little-used side door that let out onto the parking lot.

By the time she made it back to the courthouse, those who had remained behind to conduct business were closing down for the night and for the weekend. Coats were going on, computers and typewriters turning off, pumps going into tote bags while feet were sliding into snow boots.

Quentin Adler stood with briefcase in hand, talking at Martha, their receptionist. 'I would have gone to pay my respects, but I'm up to my ears in work,' he stated importantly. 'You know, Rudy asked me to take on some of Ellen's cases.'

Ellen rolled her eyes and ducked behind him, heading to Phoebe's desk. Her secretary sat with her wooly poncho across her lap, her expression that of a third-grader who was being made to stay late after school.

'Do I have any messages?' Ellen asked, pretending not to notice the pout.

'Your mail is on your desk. Someone sent you roses. Pete Ecklund wants to cut a deal on Zimmerman. A gazillion reporters called. Agent Wilhelm says toxicology shows traces of Triazolam in Josh Kirkwood's bloodstream,' she recited, thrusting the slips up at Ellen. 'Do I have to stay?'

'Got a hot date?' Ellen raised her brows, trying for girlish camaraderie.

'Not anymore.'

'No, you don't have to stay.' Ellen dropped her gaze to the note from Wilhelm and tried not to feel like an evil stepmother. 'But we could use your help tomorrow afternoon.'

Ignoring the hefty sigh, she went into her office. *Triazolam.* She went directly to the bookcase and pulled a reference book that listed virtually every drug, legal and otherwise, known to mankind. Triazolam, better known as Halcion. A central nervous system depressant once commonly prescribed as a sleeping pill, also commonly used in psych wards. She scanned the list of side effects that included memory loss and hallucinations. *When withdrawn suddenly, there may be bizarre personality changes (psychosis) and paranoia.*

That might have been one explanation for Josh's behavior, she thought. A strong enough dose could have kept Josh in a hypnotic state during his captivity, during which time Wright could have planted anything in his mind – including threats. Taking him abruptly off the drug might have set off a mild psychosis.

She dialed Wilhelm's number and noticed for the first time the bouquet of red roses in an all-purpose green office vase. Brooks was her first thought. The bastard thought he could ease past her guard with flowers and that damned smile. He and Costello had probably had a good chuckle, strategizing about her over drinks. Sandwiching the receiver

633

between her shoulder and ear, she plucked the note card out from between the thorny stems and tore it open.

'Agent Wilhelm.'

'Ellen North here. Thanks for calling about the tox report,' she said. 'It might answer some questions for us.'

'I've got people looking into prescriptions for Halcion filled locally,' he said. 'We might get lucky. Then again, it might have been filled in Minneapolis where there must be a couple hundred pharmacies.'

'Gotta start somewhere,' Ellen said. 'Have you got a report on O'Malley's blood tests? She believed Wright injected her with something while she was unconscious. If we could get a line on both drugs . . .'

The rustle of paper sounded like static over the phone. 'Hang on.'

Ellen opened the note card. A folded piece of paper dropped out. The card itself was blank. Odd. Ellen set the card aside and opened the folded paper.

evil comes to SHE who searches for it
search S for SIN
see where we've been

Ellen dropped the note and shot up out of her chair, jumping back from the desk. The telephone receiver clattered down over the drawer fronts and dangled.

'Ms North? Are you there? Ms North? Hello?'

search S for Sin . . . see where we've been . . .

'Oh, God,' she whispered, looking wildly around her office. Her sanctuary. The one place in her professional life she felt she had absolute control. Her gaze landed on the filing cabinets.

search S for Sin . . .

Shaking, she jerked the drawer open and flipped through the files. One stood out – cleaner, stiffer, unworn. The word 'sin' in bold caps on the tab.

He'd been in her office. The son of a bitch had been in her office.

She lay the file atop the others in the open cabinet and turned the cover back. Staring up at her from the small square of a Polaroid snapshot, blank-eyed and expressionless, was Josh Kirkwood.

22

The day had seemed to last forever, and yet night fell too soon. The contradiction, Hannah thought, was just a reflection of her own inner turmoil. She had been gone from the hospital longer than two weeks. She couldn't imagine leaving Josh and Lily, and yet she missed her work terribly. She missed the place and the people, her patients, her co-workers, her friends, the normalcy of routine, the drudgery of paperwork. Most of all, she missed who she was at work. The strength of mind and will she wore in that role seemed to have come off with the white lab coat and the fake brass name tag.

She would never have said she defined herself by her job. It wasn't who she was, it was what she did. But without the frame of reference it provided, she felt lost. And with the feeling of loss came guilt. She wasn't only a doctor; she was a mother. Her children needed her. Why could she not define herself in those terms?

The curse of the nineties woman, she thought, struggling for a sense of humor. A futile struggle. The day had held little to laugh about and was only going to get worse.

The weather had forced her to cancel Josh's appointment with Dr Freeman. A friend from the hospital had called and told her Dr Lomax was beginning to make noises to the administration about officially naming him temporary director of the ER – a condition he would then fight to make permanent. Director of the ER – the promotion that had passed over his head and landed squarely on Hannah's shoulders just a month ago. She worried that they might actually listen to him, then raked herself over the mental coals for letting anything but Josh's situation take precedence in her mind.

Ellen North had called to tell her they had another piece of physical evidence against Wright, but that Garrett Wright's attorney wanted access to Josh's medical records, a ploy meant to divert attention away from Wright and onto Paul.

And Jay Butler Brooks wanted to write a book about it all.

Hell of a day.

Costello's charge occupied her mind like a big black rat chewing at her nerves. The implication was that Paul had abused Josh – a charge that she had rejected out of hand. Paul would never intentionally hurt his children. He didn't even believe in spanking. And yet how many times lately had she been struck by the horrible sensation that he had become a stranger? He had lied to her, lied to the police, evaded questions and twisted non answers into self-righteous outrage.

She remembered too well how Megan O'Malley had questioned her about Paul after Josh's jacket had been found on Ryan's Bay.

'When did you start to notice a change in him? . . . he's been withdrawing more recently? . . . Does he normally ignore his answering machine when you call him at the office at night?'

'Why are you asking me these questions? You can't possibly think Paul had something to do with this.'

'It's just routine. . . . Mother Teresa would need an alibi if she were here. When we catch this guy, his lawyer will probably try to pin it on someone else. . . . If he's sleazy enough, he'll ask where you were . . . and where Paul was.'

'I don't know where Paul was. He was gone when I woke up. He said he went out on his own, just driving around town, looking . . .'

She didn't know where he had been that morning or why he hadn't called her back the night Josh went missing or why he had lied to police about once owning a light-colored van. She didn't know why Josh had recoiled from him that night in the hospital.

Another tide of guilt rose into her throat. It wasn't that she believed Paul was capable of any of it, it was that she couldn't be sure he wasn't.

She knew that he was coming to dinner. That he would be there in a matter of minutes.

She had managed to prepare the meal, even though her attention had been fractured. The salad had been tossed. The scent of rosemary chicken and roasting potatoes filled the air.

In the family room Lily was stacking blocks in a precarious tower. Josh had built himself a fort with chairs and footstools and couch cushions, creating a space he could go into and shut everyone else out. Hannah had herded him out of his bedroom every day to prevent him from doing just that – shutting her out, shutting himself in with the memories he refused to share. The fort reminded her he could keep the rest of the world out without walls, with only his silence.

He had spent the better part of the day in his new burrow, with his backpack and his new Think Pad. Hannah had been relieved to see him making use of the notebook. Perhaps memories and feelings would start flowing onto the pages, then spill over and out of him, and he would begin to talk about what he had been through.

Ellen had asked about him, whether or not he seemed to be opening up. Hannah knew it would help the case against Garrett Wright, but there was no pushing Josh, as tempting as it might have been. Dr Freeman said Josh had to come to it in his own time, that trying to force him to talk about what had happened could trigger a trauma from which he might not recover for months or years. He needed time.

The probable-cause hearing began on Tuesday.

She stepped down from the kitchen into the family room. 'Josh, time to get cleaned up for supper. Dad will be here any minute.'

Josh peered up at her from under the couch-cushion roof of his little hut. He had said nothing one way or the other about Paul's intended visit.

Paul had called midmorning. He wanted to see the children, especially Josh. He had always been so proud of Josh, so pleased to have a son. His own father had never taken much interest in his bookish younger son, preferring the company of Paul's older brothers. To have Josh reject him had to hurt unbearably.

'Come on,' she said, lifting the cushion.

Josh slapped his Think Pad shut and clutched it to his chest. Hannah leaned down, brushing a hand over his sandy curls.

'Dad's really looking forward to seeing you,' she said. 'He misses you and Lily.'

Josh said nothing. He had yet even to ask why his father was no longer living in the house. His lack of curiosity unnerved her.

Beyond the kitchen a door opened and closed. Paul coming in from the garage. Josh's eyes widened and he bolted like a deer, jumping out of his fort and running for the hall that led to the bathroom and bedrooms. Lily smashed her blocks down and dashed in a mad circle around the living room, squealing, 'Daddy! Daddy!'

'I forgot the ice cream,' Paul announced as he stepped into the kitchen. The tone was challenging, defensive. In truth, he hadn't forgotten at all. After Costello's announcement had been splashed all over the news, he hadn't been able to bring himself to go into a store. People would stare at him, think God-knew-what. They would forget all about him putting in hours on the search, making pleas on television. They would think back to the day Mitch Holt had told him to come in to be fingerprinted. They would remember O'Malley ragging about that goddamn van.

Lily scrambled up the steps into the kitchen, her little face wreathed in smiles. 'Daddy! Daddy!'

She flung herself at his legs and Paul scooped her up, perching her in the crook of his arm. 'Well, at least someone is glad to see me.'

'Don't worry about dessert,' Hannah said. 'People are still bringing food to the house. We've got enough brownies to last into the next millennium.'

Lily looped her arms around his neck and lay her head down on his shoulder. 'Daddy home. Home, home. *My* Daddy!'

Paul brushed an absent kiss across her forehead and set her down on the kitchen floor.

'Where's Josh?' He unbuttoned his long wool topcoat and went to hang it in his office.

'He's getting washed up,' she answered, carrying the salad bowl to the table, stepping around Lily, who had seated herself in the middle of the floor, lower lip trembling threateningly.

'Has he said anything?'

'No.'

'What the hell is that psychiatrist doing? Besides charging us a hundred fifty bucks an hour.'

Hannah's eyes flashed impatience as she turned toward the stove. 'She's a psychiatrist, not a plumber. She can't just Roto-Rooter out his memory. It's going to take time.'

She bent down to reach for Lily. The baby twisted away from her and began to sob.

'Da-a-d-dy!'

'Meanwhile, Anthony Costello is going to make me out to be some kind of child abuser. Did you hear about that?'

Hannah bit back the remark that burned on the tip of her tongue. Once again Paul had managed to make this about him. What would people think of *him*? How would this inconvenient delay in Josh's recovery affect *him*?

'Yes, I heard. Ellen North called.'

'Sure,' Paul sneered. 'She can't manage to stop it from happening, but she can handle calling around to dispense the bad news. You know, it really pisses me off that the county attorney isn't handling this himself. What is it with him? We're not important enough for him to bother with? Have we finally stumbled onto someone who doesn't worship the great Dr Garrison as a goddess?'

'Stop right there, Paul. Just drop it,' she said sharply. 'You're here to see the children. We're going to be a family tonight. I don't care what it takes, we're going to at least pretend we haven't grown to hate each other. No sniping. No snide remarks. No poor put-upon Paul.

'Do you understand me? Have I made that clear enough? We're going to be a family tonight,' she declared. 'Now, pick up your daughter and pay some attention to her while I go get Josh.'

She turned away from him and her heart stopped. Josh stood at the foot of the steps. Face scrubbed, hair damp, blue eyes wide and somber, backpack clutched to his chest.

Lily let out another wail. Paul abandoned her, turning toward his son instead, a brittle grin stretching across his face like a crack in a plaster wall.

'Hey, Josh. How ya doin', slugger?'

As Paul descended the steps, Josh backpedaled. Hannah watched them, frozen at the kitchen counter. Lily's plaintive squalling stabbed into her brain like an ice pick, but she couldn't bring herself to tend to her daughter. Her gaze was riveted on the scene before her.

'I've missed you, son,' Paul said in a wheedling voice. 'Won't you let your ol' dad give you a hug?'

Josh shook his head, taking another step back, his arms tightening around his backpack.

'Paul, don't push it,' Hannah said with gentle desperation. For all the good it would do. Already she knew he wouldn't listen, that he would try too hard and ruin his chance and whatever fragile hope she had held for a normal family evening.

He moved toward Josh, bending over, reaching out. 'Josh, come here.'

'No.'

'Josh, please –'

'No.'

'Dammit, Josh, I'm your father! Come here!'

He lunged for Josh's arm. Josh twisted out of reach, dropped to the floor, and scooted inside his furniture fort, dragging his backpack with him. Hannah launched herself into the family room, grabbing Paul's arm, holding him back from pursuit. He looked at her, his face a contorted mask of hurt and disbelief.

'He's my son,' he said in a tortured whisper. 'Why is he doing this to me?'

Hannah closed her eyes and put her head on his shoulder, hugging him because it had once been a natural thing to do, apologizing for reasons she didn't fully understand. In the background Lily cried as if her world had come to an end, and Hannah wondered in that moment if it hadn't.

But the moment passed and the doorbell rang, and she pulled herself away from the man who had been her husband. She felt Josh's eyes on her as she crossed the family room, watching her from under the cover of his couch-cushion roof.

Mitch stood on the front step looking tired and apologetic. His brows drew together as he met her gaze, and Hannah could only assume that she looked like hell. 'Hannah? Honey, what's wrong? Has something happened?'

She forced what would have to pass for a smile. 'Oh, it's just another fun-filled evening at the Kirkwood house. What can I do for you, Mitch?'

'I'm looking for Paul. Is he around?'

'What now?' Paul loomed up behind Hannah, bracing a hand against the door frame, silently barring Mitch's entry. 'Have you decided to take up Costello's cause?'

Mitch let the shot bounce off. 'We need to have a little talk. Would you mind coming down to my office?'

'Now? Yes, I'd mind that very much. If you have something to say to me, say it here.'

Mitch looked from Paul to Hannah and back. 'All right. It's about Dennis Enberg. I need to know what you were doing in his office Wednesday night and whether he was dead or alive when you got there.'

'The clerk at the Blooming Bud says it was a mail order,' Wilhelm said, flipping through his pocket notepad. 'No name, no return address, just an order for a dozen red roses, instructions for the note card to be included, and cash – including a tip for the delivery person.'

'And the clerk didn't think that was strange?' Cameron asked.

'She thought it was romantic. A secret admirer.'

'So did I,' Phoebe admitted in a tiny voice. She gave Ellen a guilty glance. 'I thought they were from – Well, you know Jay Butler Brooks sends out very strong sexual vibes, and your horoscope is predicting a magnetism thing, and . . .'

She trailed off, Wilhelm looking at her as if she had just hopped off the spaceship.

'It's not your fault, Phoebe,' Ellen said. 'You didn't do anything wrong. What I want to know is when that son of a bitch was in my office.'

No stranger could have wandered in during the day without drawing notice, which meant he had somehow managed to slip in during the night. So much for Rudy's argument that they didn't need better security. The idea that it might have been days ago somehow disturbed her. It added to the sense of vulnerability, suggested a certain omnipotence in their adversary. He could reach out and touch whoever he wanted, whenever he wanted, wherever they were.

'Have you noticed anything missing?' Wilhelm asked.

'No.'

'He could have been looking for files about the case.'

'I keep my notes with me. Obviously, we don't keep any physical evidence here. Anything left in these offices regarding the case, Wright's attorney has legal access to. What would be the point in stealing it?'

She shook her head. 'It's just another part of the game. Another taunt.'

Wilhelm slipped his notepad into his shirt pocket and zipped his parka. 'We'll see what we can find. We've bagged the card and the note. The fingerprint guys should be done in an hour or so.'

Leaving their grimy black dust behind, marking every surface, making sure Ellen wouldn't forget anytime soon that her sanctuary had been invaded.

'So now you're going to try to blame me for Enberg's killing himself?' Paul ranted in the dining room. 'Or do you think maybe *I* killed him for no earthly reason?'

Mitch jammed his hands at the waist of his trousers. 'I'm not saying either of those things, Paul. If you'd spare the histrionics for five minutes, we could get this over with.'

'You come into my house, accuse me of God-knows-what – I think I have a right to be upset!'

'Fine, but you know your children are in the next room, Paul. Do you have the right to upset and frighten them, too? Is that what you want? Haven't they been through enough?'

'Haven't we all?'

'Two clerks at the Donut Hut both say they saw a Celica that matches yours to a T.'

Paul looked dumbstruck. 'Doughnut helpers. Doughnut people come forward days after the fact and you beat a path to my door.'

'They've been out of town.' Mitch advanced, forefinger drawn to thrust at Paul. 'We just located them this afternoon. They saw what they saw. I don't care if they sell doughnuts or donkey dicks. They both saw a car at the side lot of Enberg's office that sounds remarkably like yours. Now, I'm asking you nicely here, Paul. I'm giving you a chance to tell me your side. Quit jerking me around before you piss me off and I haul your ass down to the station.

'Start talking, Paul,' Mitch ordered. 'And don't try to tell me you weren't there if you were. The fingerprints will be back Monday.'

Paul slumped down onto the chair at the head of the table. 'I went to see him . . . on a personal matter. He was drunk. I left.'

'You went to consult the lawyer who had once represented the man who stole your son. Interesting choice of attorneys.'

'He was my attorney first.'

And now that attorney was dead.

Hannah heard it all as she stood in the hallway, and hours later, with the clock ticking off the minutes to midnight, she still felt wrung out. She wished there was something mundane to occupy her, but the ruined dinner had been disposed of, the remnants of the frozen pizza thrown out. Lily's toys were in the trunk, Josh's videos neatly stacked.

The children were tucked in bed. Lily had gone down with a fight, overtired and out of sorts. Hannah tiptoed into her room. The night-light cast a soft pink glow that just touched her daughter's face. She was sleeping hard, sweat dampening her golden curls, a frown furrowing her little brow.

What impact would all this have on her? Hannah wondered. She was just a baby. Would she remember any of it? Would all of it linger in the dim reaches of her memory, haunting her forever?

Josh was out, too, sleeping flat on his back, utterly still. He had always been as active in his sleep as he was awake, kicking off his covers, sleeping in all known positions all over the bed, dragging stuffed animals with him, dropping them off the top bunk to the floor between bedtime and morning. Since his return he had slept only on the lower bunk with just a favorite old stuffed monkey snuggled next to him.

Hannah slipped into his room and sat down on the floor at the foot of the bed, where she could watch him sleep, where she could be near him physically if in no other way. She had spent so much time in this room when he had been gone because it helped her feel spiritually closer to him, and now that he was home, she felt a distance between them that couldn't be bridged.

She wanted to gather him close and by the will of her love alone drive out the darkness that had settled over him like soot. But she only sat there, feeling helpless and alone. For someone who had always taken charge of her life, it was like being cast adrift in the ocean.

She thought of all the other times she had done this – sat with him in the dark, watching over him, dreaming for him. Before he was born, when the discomfort of pregnancy had kept her awake, she had spent long quiet hours in the night sitting, her hand on her belly, thinking of the future. How she would love him, teach him, protect him. What a sweet young man he would grow to be, with her sense of duty and Paul's sensitivity, and a solid foundation of love and stability.

She looked around the room, cataloguing the familiar. A friend had painted murals depicting different sports on each wall. The small desk between the windows was stacked with books and action figures and the photo albums she had brought in here when Josh was missing, as if concentrating on the memories of the happy times might conjure him up like a spirit from another dimension.

His backpack leaned against the nightstand, flap rolled back so it could accommodate his new Think Pad along with everything else he had packed inside. Hannah inched toward it, one eye on Josh. She wouldn't touch it, wouldn't give in to the overwhelming desire to see what he had put into the notebook she had given him. She had promised it was his, that he wouldn't have to share it with anyone until he was ready. All she wanted was to peek into the bag, to see if she could get some idea of what he had been carrying with him. Maybe if she knew what he carried with him to feel secure, she could do something to give him that security, give him some kind of assurance.

The illumination from the night-light was too faint to see well. She shifted onto her knees and tilted her head to a better angle, but all she could make out was the Think Pad and pen, one of the walkie-talkies he had got for Christmas, and a scrap of bright knit fabric tucked behind it. A stocking cap or mitten the blaze-orange of a hunter's garb.

Odd. There hadn't been any gear like that in the house since Paul had come out of his manly-hunter phase two years ago. They had got rid of all the equipment and clothing at a rummage sale to benefit the conservation club. But Josh was carrying a piece around with him. Carrying it as if it were a long-treasured possession he couldn't bear to do without.

The peculiarity of it jarred her. She had taken pains to make everything in the house seem as normal, as familiar, to Josh as possible. Then to find something out of time, out of place . . . She sneaked another peek at Josh. He sighed in his sleep and turned his face away from her.

Ignoring her conscience, she reached for the backpack. It could be important that she know . . . It could break Josh's trust in her if he woke up and saw her.

If she could just tip it, get a better look . . .

The walkie-talkie shifted. Josh stirred, mumbled, turned onto his side, curling into a fetal position beneath the covers. Hannah held her breath and counted to ten, then pulled the bag a little closer to the night-light.

The rib pattern of the knit came into focus, and a wedge of a patch that had been sewn in place – an insignia of some sort, a brand name or a club name arching over the silhouette of a deer. She could make out only some of the letters: PION.

Campion.

Fear snaked through her, coiling in her throat, squeezing her heart. *Campion.*

'Oh, my God.'

Her mind formed the words, but she didn't know if she spoke them aloud. With a shaking hand, she reached into the pack and caught hold of the fabric between her fingers. A stocking cap. Small and nubby with wear. She pulled it from the bag while revulsion roiled inside of her. The shaking traveled up her arms, into her chest, until her whole body was jerking, as if giant unseen hands had her by the shoulders. She wanted to drop the cap, to throw it out of the house as if it were a carcass crawling with maggots. Instead, she held it to the light and read the patch.

Campion Sportsmen.

She twisted the cap inside out.

Printed in block letters on the laundry tag was a single name. DUSTIN.

Journal Entry
Friday, January 28, 1994

We have thought out a cunningly conceived plot.
Deep and dark.
Black and brilliant.
They cannot outmaneuver us.
Because their minds are so small.
We despise them.

23

Josh sat, body drawn into a tight ball, arms wrapped tight around his knees, back pressed up against a corner post of his bed. He kept his head down, peeking up only occasionally. There were too many people in his room. He didn't want any of them to be there. His room was *his* space, not theirs. His things were *his* things; he didn't want them touched by outsiders.

His mom stood near the door, crying. Josh hated that. He hated hearing her cry and he hated knowing that it was all his fault. He had hardly ever seen his mom cry or get hysterical like other kids' moms sometimes did – until lately. Since Dad had started getting more angry and they fought all the time. But she cried only in private then. This was different. This was because of him.

She never should have gone into his backpack. He never thought she would. Mom was big on respecting people's privacy. It hurt him that she had looked. It hurt him more that he couldn't answer her questions. He couldn't tell her about the Taker, or bad things would happen. Worse things than what were already happening. The idea scared him so much he wanted to cry himself, but he didn't dare do that either.

'Josh? Can you tell us anything at all about how that stocking cap got into your backpack?'

Chief Holt sat on the edge of the bed, looking at him with a really serious face. Josh glanced up at him; then his gaze darted to the humongous police officer standing by the dresser. Handcuffs glinted on his thick black belt. Maybe the cops would arrest him and throw him in jail. Maybe they thought that other kid was a Goner because of him. Fear lumped in his throat and he tried to swallow it down.

'Have you ever seen this boy, Josh?' The other cop in regular clothes held out a flyer with a picture of the Goner. Josh put his hands over his face and peeked out through the narrow cracks between his fingers. This cop looked kind of like Tom Hanks, only he didn't seem like he would be funny at all. He looked impatient.

'Did someone give you the hat, Josh?'

'Did you find it someplace?'

'It's really important for you to tell us.'

'You could save that little boy's life.'

They didn't understand. They didn't know about the Taker or what it was like to be a Goner. There were so many things they didn't know about at all. Josh squeezed his eyes shut tight. In his mind he opened the door to his secret place and went inside, where no one could touch him or frighten him or ask him questions he had been told not to answer.

Wilhelm turned away from the bed, flapping his arms at his sides in frustration. Mitch rose slowly, as worn out as an old, old man.

'Isn't there *something* we can do?' Wilhelm whispered urgently. 'Hypnosis? Sodium pentothal?'

'Yeah, Marty,' Mitch muttered. 'I'm certain it's okay to drug small children in order to coerce answers out of them.'

He turned to Hannah. She was shaking, and her eyes were red-rimmed and wild. It would not have surprised him at all to have her fall apart, but she held herself together, toughing it out when she had to have precious little strength left. She pushed past him and went to Josh, pulling him into her arms and rocking him, probably as much to comfort herself as to comfort her son.

At least they had managed to keep the press away, Mitch thought. For now. Because Hannah had called him at home, he had been able to order radio silence and gather his people through less trackable means. It wouldn't last, of course. By the time they left the house, there would probably be reporters camped on the lawn. But for the moment that burden was off.

Another burden absent was Paul. No one had called him. He would have argued that he had a right to be there, and he probably did, but he was a complication no one needed. Especially not Hannah, and especially not after his performance earlier in the evening. She needed an emotional anchor, someone to calm her, and to that end they had called Father Tom. He stood in the bedroom doorway looking like a vagrant – unshaven, his brown hair sticking up in spots.

'If you've got any clout with the Man Upstairs, Father, we could use a break here,' Mitch said.

'If I had any clout, we wouldn't be here.' His gaze on Hannah and Josh, he crossed the small bedroom and bent down to touch Hannah's shoulder and murmur something in her ear.

'What do you think?' Ellen North asked, backing into the hall.

Mitch followed her. He could feel Wilhelm at his heels and wished Megan were here instead.

'Hannah says Josh hasn't been out of her sight any waking moment since he came back. No one could have given the thing to him without her seeing. And Josh hasn't let the backpack out of *his* sight, so . . .'

'Someone came into the house in the dead of night and planted it in Josh's backpack? Without Hannah's knowing?' she said. 'That seems pretty far-fetched.'

'If you've got another explanation, let's hear it.'

'Wright is back home just down the block,' Wilhelm said.

'He'd never risk coming near this house,' Mitch insisted. 'But we'll need a list of everyone else who has been here in the last few days.'

'The key is the boy,' Wihelm said. 'He's got the answers to all our questions locked up in his head. I say we try hypnosis.'

Mitch looked to Ellen. 'Would anything he revealed under hypnosis be admissible in court?'

'It would be a fight. Even if we got it in, the defense would tear into it big-time. In general, the testimony of small children isn't considered very reliable. Children are highly suggestible, susceptible to having ideas planted in their minds – conscious and subconscious. But if Josh could reveal something that would put you on track to finding Dustin Holloman, or tell us who the accomplice is, or point us toward more solid evidence, that would certainly be worthwhile, whether it was admissible or not.'

Mitch weighed the pros and cons. 'I'll talk to Hannah about it.'

'Did you find anything else in the backpack?' Ellen asked.

'It's in the dining room.'

The pack lay open, the items pulled from it strewn across the cherry table like the entrails of a gutted animal. Sadness settled in Ellen's chest as she looked at the things Josh had packed, as if he were afraid he might be taken again and this time wanted pieces of his life with him. There were several small, obviously cherished toys, and a Cub Scout pocket knife. A flashlight to ward off darkness. A walkie-talkie to call home. A child-size travel toothbrush with a Teenage Mutant Ninja Turtle on the handle. A snapshot of him with his mother and baby sister at the baby's baptism – Josh in a miniature blue suit, his hair slicked into place, a proud grin on his face as he held the baby.

'Poor kid,' Wilhelm mumbled, running a finger along the seam of an old grass-stained baseball.

'Like his life isn't bad enough right now,' Mitch growled, 'we have to come into his house and violate what little privacy he has.'

Ellen stared down at a spiral notebook. *Josh's New Think Pad. To Josh From Mom.* A carefully drawn heart punctuated the sentiment. Mitch was right. It felt as if they were reaching dirty hands into Josh's childhood and soiling it forever. These things were his private possessions, pieces of his boyhood. And they would rub the glow of innocence from them and call them evidence.

She pulled a slim Cross pen from her purse and used it to lift the cover of the notebook. The action was old habit, meant to keep her fingerprints off potential evidence, but in her mind she also thought of it as prevention against tainting the book in a more intimate way. This had been a special gift from a mother to her son. No one else should have touched it, ever.

She knew what she wanted to find: the names of Josh's abductors, drawings of the place they had held him. What she found were small, strange pictures of black squares and sad faces and thin, wavy lines. On one page he had written *When I was a Goner*, and beneath the words the tiniest pinpoints of ink made eyes and a mouth. There were no admissions, no revelations, just the fractured thoughts of a damaged child.

'I don't see any point in holding this stuff,' she said. 'Dust what you can for prints, for all the good that'll do us.'

The front door opened and closed, bringing in a gust of cold air and animosity. Sheriff Steiger's voice grated like sandpaper over asphalt.

'Where the fuck is Holt?'

'Chief's in the dining room, Sheriff.'

Mitch made a sound between his teeth.

Ellen drew her coat around her. 'I'm gone. Call me if you need me.'

Steiger nearly bowled her over on his way into the room, his craggy face set in furious lines. Ellen dodged him, wanting no part of the jurisdictional skirmish that was about to take place. The Holloman case belonged to Park County, not City of Deer Lake. Mitch had pulled an end-around on Steiger, calling Wilhelm instead on the argument that the BCA was overseeing all the investigations. Russ Steiger wouldn't see it that way.

'Heading out, Ms North?' Noga asked, reaching to open the door for her. The big man winced as voices barked in the dining room like the report of machine-gun fire.

Ellen shook her head. 'Yep, the testosterone level in there is getting a little deep for me. Good night, Noogie.'

She stepped out into the cold, digging the keys to her loaner out of her coat pocket. The Manley Vanloon Pace Car, she called it. Never one to miss an opportunity to capitalize, Manley had given her a great, big rolling advertisement: an enormous white Cadillac with painted flames arching back from the tires. The front doors were emblazoned with the slogan 'Vanloon Motors: Steal a Hot Deal from "Crazy" Vanloon.' The embarrassment was almost enough to turn her into a pedestrian.

In her peripheral vision she could see someone had blocked the Cadillac in the driveway. She stopped in her tracks when she saw who it was.

'Another long night, counselor,' Brooks said, easing out of the Cherokee. 'Another long *cold* night. I'll say this for your weather – it's sure as hell conducive to long nights warming the sheets with a partner. Never thought I'd look at sex as a survivalist tactic. Does that take the fun out of it?'

'I wouldn't know.' Ellen marched to the Cadillac.

'We could find out,' he drawled. The hood of his parka framed his face, giving Ellen the impression of a wolf staring at her from inside its lair. His interest in her was self-serving, an idea that was degrading enough when applied to her professional capacity. That he would use her sexually as well touched every red button she had.

'I'd sooner die of hypothermia, but I'd rather not do it here, so will you kindly get your truck the hell out of my way?'

He leaned back in surprise, as if her verbal punch had hit him squarely in the mouth.

'What are you doing here, anyway?' she demanded. 'You didn't pick this up on any scanner.'

'I followed Steiger. We were having a drink down at the Blue Goose.'

'How cozy. If you want to get into bed with somebody, I hear he's not averse to getting screwed for a little information.'

'He's not my type, thanks.'

'Well, I've got news for you, Brooks. Neither am I. Did your friend Costello tell you differently?'

'Costello? What the hell does he have to do with us?'

'You tell me. No.' She held up a hand to forestall the answer. 'I've been lied to and manipulated enough lately.'

'I haven't lied to you.'

'Semantics. You haven't told me the truth, not that I give a damn what you do. Move the truck. I'm going home.'

She slid behind the wheel of the Cadillac and slammed the door shut, hoping she would catch some of his fingers. But he went back to his truck unmaimed and backed it out into the street. Headlights coming from the south heralded the arrival of the first media scavengers. In a matter of moments the street would be clogged with them. The noise would wake the neighbors. They would come out on their steps to investigate and watch for glimpses of themselves on the morning television news.

The windows in the Wright house were dark. Was he sleeping, oblivious to the latest turmoil, or was he sitting in the dark, smiling?

'You'll make a mistake eventually,' Ellen murmured. 'All I have to do is get you to trial.'

As she turned the corner onto her street, the headlights behind her followed. Brooks. Visions of vehicular homicide flashed through her head. She could nail Brooks and destroy this god-awful car in one stroke. She was tired, depressed, disillusioned – the perfect time for a confrontation.

Get it over and done with. Get him out of your life before you can screw up again.

She said nothing as she let him in. Harry trotted into the kitchen to greet them, took one look at her face, and beat it back to the bedroom.

'Don't take your coat off, you won't be staying,' Ellen said, shrugging out of hers.

'Do I get to hear the charges against me, or are we skipping straight to sentencing?'

He leaned back against the wall, at ease, as if it would make no difference what she accused him of. He likely didn't care, she thought. He'd made his purpose clear up front. It wasn't as if he hadn't warned her. She was the one who had fooled herself, fooled herself into thinking she wouldn't make the same mistake twice, fooled herself into believing she was too smart, too savvy – the same way she had with Costello.

'You went to Purdue on a baseball scholarship,' she began, reciting the information she had confirmed in the *Newsweek* article.

'That's not considered a crime in most states, even if I couldn't hit a high inside fastball.'

Ellen ignored his attempt at humor. 'You stayed on at Purdue Law.'

'Much to the dismay of my family. They could hardly show their faces at the Auburn alumni functions.'

'Tony Costello went to school at Purdue.'

He didn't so much as blink. 'Small world, isn't it?'

'You show up in town with an interest in this case. Then suddenly Wright fires his attorney and brings in Costello, an attorney he can't possibly afford on a professor's salary.'

His eyes widened then, the amusement in them stoking the fires of Ellen's temper.

'Are you implying *I* brought Costello in?' he asked. 'To what end?'

'You came here for a story. Maybe you had a particular ending in mind. Maybe you get off on manipulating people. Maybe you're no better than Wright, and it's all a game to you.'

'Well, aren't I the criminal mastermind!'

Ellen glared at him, advancing on him, her body rigid with rage. 'Don't you dare be amused at me. I don't give a shit what your game is. All you need to know is I'm not playing anymore. No more view inside the prosecutor's office. Take that to Bill Glendenning if you want, but I don't think he'll be quite so starstruck after he considers the ramifications of involving you in this. He wants to run for governor. People in Minnesota won't take kindly to the idea that he traded a child's justice to bask in the glow of a dubious celebrity.'

Brooks winced. 'Ouch. That's a mean tongue you got there, sugar. You ought to have it registered as a dangerous weapon.'

His gaze drifted to her mouth, and she realized that this time *she* was the one who had stepped too close. If he straightened away from the wall, they would be touching. But she refused to back away.

'What would you say if I told you I don't know Costello from a sack of pig feed?' he asked.

'I'd say I have no reason to believe anything you tell me.'

'Hmm . . . We're having a little problem with trust here, Ellen.'

'You can't have trouble with something that doesn't exist,' she said. 'I don't trust you, and I sure as hell don't trust Costello.'

Curiosity sharpened his gaze. 'And why is that? What'd he ever do to win your animosity?'

'He's a shark. He'll do whatever he has to do to win a case or anything else he happens to want.'

'And did he want you?' he asked. 'Is that what this is really all about, Ellen? Costello fucked you over figuratively *and* literally –'

'Get out of my house,' she ordered. 'I've said what I had to say. You know where the door is. Find it. Use it.'

He caught her by the arm as she started to turn away. In one dizzying move Ellen found her back to the wall and Brooks leaning in on her, his face inches from hers.

'I don't think so, counselor,' he said. 'Not until I've had a chance to defend myself.'

'This isn't a trial. You don't have any rights here. I don't have to listen to you. I don't have to deal with you.'

'You damn well *will* listen to me,' he growled. 'I've been accused of a lot of things in my life. Hell, I've been guilty of most of them. But I don't know Costello more than to nod and say hello. I met him once at an alumni dinner. He tried to sell me on doing a book about a case he was involved with. I declined. I have no interest in making Anthony Costello's career for him. I didn't come here looking to renew the acquaintance, and I sure as hell didn't bring him in.'

'And you want me to believe it's just a coincidence you're both here?'

'Believe what you want. I've had my say. I came here to watch this thing unfold; to get a story, not make one.'

'Well, you're getting your money's worth, aren't you?' Ellen whispered bitterly.

'And then some.'

He held her gaze with his, his expression taut, intense. *Dangerous*. The word came back to her again and again when she thought of him. He was a threat. Professionally. Sexually.

'You're a story all by yourself, Ellen.' He brought one hand down from the wall beside her head and traced his thumb across her chin and down the column of her throat. 'I want to know more about you. I want to know everything. Hell, I just plain want you.'

The admission triggered an automatic quickening in her body, one that brought a flash of embarrassment and shame. Nothing had changed. She still didn't trust him. He had nothing to gain by admitting collusion with Costello, plenty to lose. He had everything to gain by seducing her.

'I'd take you right here, right now,' he whispered, settling his thumb in the V of her collarbone, his fingertips subtly kneading the tender area just above her breast. 'If you'd let me.'

She found her voice with great difficulty. The words came out thready. 'I won't.'

'No.' The look that came into his eyes was weary. 'No. You're too smart, too careful, too neat and tidy. No room on the agenda for a wild card like me. I'm not some instant fire you can turn on and off with a switch. You get too close to me, you might end up getting burned. God forbid you should take a chance, make a mistake.'

'This isn't about just me.'

'Isn't it? If it weren't for this case, would we be in your bed right now?'

he asked, his mouth too close to hers, his eyes too blue. 'Would I be inside you right now, Ellen?'

Her mouth had gone dry. 'If it weren't for this case, you wouldn't be here.'

That was the bottom line. She drew it unerringly. He couldn't argue. The truthfulness of it did nothing to assuage the ache of desire inside him. The foolishness of wanting this particular woman did nothing to change the fact that he did. It wasn't just sex; sex could be easily had. Women had always come willingly to his bed. But that wasn't his need. His need was for *this* woman, who was all the things he had never been – dedicated, good, the champion for justice sacrificing her own needs in her duty to others. He had spent his whole life shrugging off obligation, pursuing his own ends, justifying all means. He could put whatever face on it he liked, but in the end he was exactly what she had called him from the start – a mercenary, and a damn good one, worth millions. That it had ultimately cost him his family, his soul, was not self-sacrifice, but irony.

'No,' he said at last. 'But I'm here now. Will you try to redeem me, Ellen?'

Would there be any point in trying? She didn't ask, afraid of what his answer might be. The look that had come into his face was a little stark, a little haunted, as if he were afraid of the answer himself. The look touched her in a way she couldn't afford to allow. Not now. Not when so much was riding on her shoulders. And after the trial was over, he would be gone, mission accomplished, on to someone else's tragedy.

'If you want redemption, talk to a priest,' she said quietly. 'You're not my responsibility, and I'm not fool enough to think you should be.'

'No. You're nobody's fool.' He backed away from her and turned to the cherry hutch where she kept her meager supply of liquor. He helped himself to two fingers of Scotch, tossing it back in a single shot. 'And I'm nobody's front man. I came here for my own reasons. I came here looking for answers.'

She had the distinct feeling that the questions had little to do with Josh Kirkwood or Garrett Wright. That perhaps they were far more personal than professional. 'And are you finding them?'

He smiled sadly as he twisted the cap back onto the bottle of Glenlivet. 'No. The questions only get harder. Joke's on me.'

She followed him to the door, wrestling with the need to ask for the truth and the wisdom of letting it go. In the end she said nothing, and he seemed to know why better than she did.

'You're right. Stick to the straight and narrow, counselor,' he said. 'You're better off. I'm no good for anybody. That's a known fact.'

He leaned down and kissed her good night, a tender kiss that tasted of longing and Scotch, and walked out into the night.

The streets of Deer Lake were absent of life. Even stray dogs had more sense than to be out roaming in the middle of the night when the temperature was dipping to minus twenty and the windchill factor was doubly cold. A night for fools and cops. The patrols stayed on the roads to rescue the idiots who ran into ditches. The detectives came out for the latest clue in the ever-twisting case.

Jay sat at the corner of Lakeshore Drive with the motor running, debating a return to the Kirkwood house. But the press had descended, and he knew that any opportunity he might have had to catch a fresh insight was gone. He found he had no hunger for it now, at any rate. The adrenaline rush that had come with the call to Steiger at the Blue Goose was spent. All he felt now was a restlessness and an emptiness that would make him avoid going to the house on Ryan's Bay.

He drove away from Lakeside, took a right on Oslo, and headed to Dinkytown, where the businesses looked abandoned, the buildings decayed. A night clerk stared out the window of a garishly lit convenience store, an oasis beckoning no one.

Lights still glowed in a few dorm windows on the Harris campus, but the class buildings stood dark. Even in the dead of night, Harris College gave the impression of tradition and money. The buildings were solid, substantial, erected in an era when college meant more than a means to higher earning. The grounds were parklike, studded with tall hardwood and pine trees.

Garrett Wright claimed he had been working here in Cray Hall the night Josh had been taken, as did Christopher Priest. If they were partners in this madness, then why would they not have given each other alibis? It could have been part of the game, Jay supposed. It could have been a small bit of truth to help Priest fool the polygraph.

Curiouser and curiouser, this case, he thought as he left the campus the back way, driving slowly south on Old Cedar Road. The secrets and sins that lay beneath the surface of seemingly ordinary lives had always fascinated him. The things no one suspected were going on behind façades of normalcy in picture-book settings like Deer Lake.

Jay let the Cherokee roll to a stop in the middle of the deserted road, lit his last cigarette, and sat staring out the passenger window. A chunk of moon glowed down on the winterscape, giving the snow a silver cast, turning the bare trees to silhouettes of black against a starry sky of midnight blue. The land that ran west of the college was farmland and woodland, rolling hills and fields where stubbled cornstalks poked up through occasional thin spots in the snow. A setting of apparent peace.

Running south, the road eventually skirted the eastern edge of Ryan's Bay, where Josh's jacket had been found nine days ago. According to Agent O'Malley's theory, this was where the game had been put in motion, along this strip of lonely county road. It was here that the car accident had taken place, the accident that had kept Hannah Garrison late at the hospital. Christopher Priest had sent a student on an errand. The student had taken the back way off campus, as students often did. His car had hit an unexpected – and, O'Malley speculated, a *manufactured* – patch of ice that sent him into the path of an oncoming vehicle. The elderly female driver of the other car had been killed instantly; a passenger in her car had died of a heart attack upon arrival at Deer Lake Community Hospital. Two other passengers had been transported by helicopter to Hennepin County Medical Center in Minneapolis, where the student now lay in critical condition, having developed a bacterial infection that was threatening to take his life.

So many lives touched or taken by this game. And if O'Malley was right, it had started here, in this quiet, pretty spot on the far edge of town. Like a stone dropped into the lake, the effects had rippled outward in ever-widening circles.

Cause and effect. The chain reaction of events. He wondered how much the master of this game had foreseen, how much he had known going in and how much had been twisted serendipity. He couldn't have known that Ellen North would get the case, or that the story would have been seized on by a writer from Eudora, Alabama, as an escape and an act of self-examination. Yet he had chosen an attorney who had ties, however oblique, to them both – Anthony Costello.

The sense of being watched by brilliant dark eyes from a darker dimension sent a current of uneasiness down his spine.

He was no longer an observer, but a player. Another one caught in the web of this crime.

'It's your job – going from one set of victims to another. Does it get to you, or are you immune?'

'Not immune; careful. I keep my distance. Don't let it get personal.'

A chill tightened his shoulders, and he reached to turn up the heater only to find it cranked to high already. Damn cold place. And here he sat like a damn fool in a truck in the middle of nowhere. He would sure as hell rather have been in bed . . . with Ellen, who thought he was not only involved in this case, but playing some sinister role. Ellen, who didn't trust or respect him. Who shouldered the weight of winning justice for a child, for a family, for a cop, for a town.

'You're just a regular damn prince, Brooks,' he muttered.

He reached for another cigarette, finding the pack empty. Putting off the inevitable reality of a sleepless night and more introspection, he swung the Cherokee around and headed back through the Harris campus, taking the shortest route to the Tom Thumb. The clerk, a thick-bodied kid with volcanic patches of acne pebbling his red face, sold him a carton of Marlboros and made the usual tired, obligatory comment about the cold. Fresh out of small talk, Jay grunted an answer and pushed out the door.

A lone car rolling south held him up at the edge of the Tom Thumb lot. Directly across the street squatted the Pack Rat secondhand shop where Todd Childs worked part-time when he wasn't concocting alibis for his mentor. No one had seen him since before Ellen's car had been vandalized. Rumor had him stashed in a Twin Cities hotel courtesy of the

Costello team, who had leaked the information about his pending testimony. But it seemed just as possible that Childs was tucked away in a farmhouse somewhere, guarding Dustin Holloman and carrying out the legwork of Wright's demented scheme while Wright himself sat at home playing innocent.

Jay eased the truck out into the street, angling across the northbound lane, something about the Pack Rat holding his attention. A reflection in the window. An odd glow coming from within. Light. A faint glow, like the beam of a flashlight.

Odd time of day to be browsing for bargains in a junk shop.

He turned the corner and doubled back down the alley, cutting the engine and the headlights on the truck as he rolled up behind the store. The security light was out, if there had ever been one, but enough illumination leached over the roof from the streetlight on the corner to set the scene. A set of crumbling concrete steps with a bent pipe railing led to the only back door. A Dumpster sat to one side of the steps. At the foot of the steps waited a dirty gray Crown Victoria from the late eighties. It sat, engine running, exhaust billowing from the tailpipe – ready for an escape that was now blocked by the Cherokee.

Who the hell robbed a secondhand shop? What was there to steal? There probably wasn't anything in the store worth more than ten bucks, and Jay couldn't imagine that there would be a lot of money in the till. Maybe the place had a safe. Employees would know. Like Todd Childs. Or maybe Childs had left something crucial in the building, something he couldn't risk coming back for in the light of day.

Jay called 911 on his cellular phone and reported a break-in in progress, then let himself out of the truck, pocketing the keys, careful not to let the door slam. Precious minutes would tick by before a patrol car could arrive. The perpetrator wouldn't escape by car, but if he could get out of the building, he could still run. If it was Childs, and if Childs was Wright's accomplice, this was the chance to nail him and possibly bring the case to a close.

And if you catch yourself a suspect, just think of the publicity angle, he thought sarcastically. That would be Ellen's first reaction – not that he had found some scrap of nobility within and helped them catch the bad guy, but that he wanted to help himself. Not that it should have mattered to him what she thought.

He made his way toward the building, the snow squeaking beneath his feet. He hoped that the rumble of the car's engine masked it, or that the midnight visitor was too intent on his task to hear. His lungs holding on to his breath, he eased up one step and then another.

The door burst open as Jay reached for it, hitting him hard, knocking him back and off balance. A black-clad figure followed, rushing him, swinging something short and black. It caught Jay on the side of the head and shorted out all thought. He felt himself falling backward, off the steps, arms flailing, colors bursting and swirling inside his head. He hit the rutted ice pack of the parking area hard.

He fought for orientation, struggled to discern up from down. A car door thumped shut and an engine roared. He managed to turn himself onto his hands and knees as the Crown Vic's headlights blazed on, blinding him. The car roared, tires whining on the ice as it rocketed backward. The sickening crunch of metal on metal told Jay the Cherokee wouldn't be spared any more than he had been. Then there was no time to think of anything as the car lurched forward, charging him.

He lunged sideways, his feet slipping out from under him, his left elbow cracking hard on the cement steps. He caught hold of the steel-pipe post that thrust up crookedly from the top step and heaved himself up. The bumper of the Crown Victoria followed just behind, the metal grating over the concrete of the second step.

Engine and tires screaming, the car rocked backward once again, once again smashing into the Cherokee, pushing its nose sideways and opening enough space in the alley for the car to turn north.

The son of a bitch was going to run. If the cops didn't show in the next ten seconds, he would be gone.

Rage pushed Jay off the steps. He staggered drunkenly toward the mangled Cherokee, trying to run and struggling to keep himself upright. The passenger door was jammed shut, punched in like a second-rate boxer's face. He lost seconds as he stumbled around to the driver's side. The Crown Vic inched forward, toward the street and freedom, its back end sliding sideways as the tires spun to gain purchase on the slick surface.

Spewing curses, Jay stabbed the key at the ignition again and again, his vision blurred and swirling, doubling, tripling. Hit the bull's-eye. Cranked it over. The engine roared to life, a belt inside it screaming like a banshee at the wounds that had been inflicted. He threw the transmission in gear and stepped on the gas. The four-wheel drive grabbed hold and the truck shot forward, rear-ending the car but at the same time giving it the push it needed to reach the plowed street.

The car lunged west down the residential side street. Jay turned the Cherokee out of the alley, the wheel seeming to spin too far, too easily. The truck rocked sideways, then straightened, and he stomped on the gas. The brake lights of the Crown Vic flashed two blocks down as it turned south. Taking the same turn, the Cherokee sideswiped a station wagon, careened across the street, and nicked the front end of a Honda, the sound of glass shattering a high-pitched accompaniment to the crash of steel.

They made a right onto Mill Road. Jay spun the Cherokee's wheel hard, swinging the nose of the truck around just as the front wheels jumped the curb. The truck plowed through the deep snow on the boulevard, narrowly missed a tree, and bucked back down onto the road.

The paved road gave way to gravel. The streetlights ended, and the velvet-black of the country night enveloped them, only a wedge of moon and headlights brightening the dark. The road split between farm fields, rose and fell with the hills, then plunged down, curving into a valley dark with the winter skeletons of a thick hardwood forest.

With every turn the Cherokee's steering loosened more. With every curve and dip, Jay's battered brain swam wilder and wilder. Too fast, he thought. Out of control. The pop of gravel beneath the tires was like firecrackers snapping. The road was icy in patches, rutted and rough. He didn't know shit about driving in these conditions. The Crown Victoria was running away from him, putting more ground between them with every jog in the road.

It disappeared over a crest. Jay followed, foot too heavy on the gas. The Cherokee left the ground as the road dropped sharply down. There was no way to pull the truck down, to rein it in, to make the hard right-angle turn.

I'm fucked, he thought, gripping the steering wheel, bracing his body as best he could.

The truck plunged nose-first into a thicket, bounced up hard, throwing Jay around the cab like a rag doll. The headlights flashed at crazy angles as the Cherokee bucked and skidded down the slope, spraying up snow in blinding plumes, coming to a violent stop when it slammed sideways into a tree trunk.

Jay landed against the mangled passenger door, his head smacking hard against the cracked window. His mind drifted ever farther from his body, the connection between the two pulling as thin as hair. The truck's radiator hissed. The lights on the police scanner glowed red in the gloom of the cab. The radio crackled, picking up the transmission of the patrol car that had finally arrived on the scene at the Pack Rat.

The last conscious thought Jay had was *You blew it, hotshot*.

24

'Tell me what you remember.'

Jay closed his eyes and winced. Pain ran down his right side like a mallet playing xylophone on his ribs. Dr Baskir, a small man with an enormous nose and a lilting Indian accent, had examined him thoroughly upon his delivery to the Deer Lake Community Hospital, addressing his various bruised and battered body parts as if each possessed self-awareness. He told the ribs they were not broken and tried to verbally placate his muscles, announcing to Jay in a whispered aside that they were likely to be 'angry' for days to come. He had deftly stitched two gashes in the side of Jay's head, picking broken glass out of his hair with tweezers and muttering to the hard plates of bone in his skull.

The upshot was that he would live to tell about his adventure. The downside was that the cops would make him tell it over and over. Already he had related the details to the sheriff's deputy who had picked up the chase down Mill Road and arrived on the scene just moments after the crash. The patrolman who had taken the call to the Pack Rat had been next and another patrol officer who had been called in by the owner of one of the smashed cars on the route of the chase.

Now the unholy trinity of Steiger, Wilhelm, and Holt stood in a semi-circle around the end of the emergency-room examining table. All of them looked grim and surly, adjectives that likely applied to himself as well. He sat on the table in his bloodstained, rumpled khakis, his shirt gone, cut to shreds by overzealous volunteer ambulance people. Dr Baskir had swathed his ribs in a tight, unyielding bandage that kept him from inhaling more than a teaspoon of air at a time. His chin was split, his head felt as if someone had taken a ten-pound hammer to it, and he was fucking cold.

'I've told you twice,' he said through his teeth.

'You didn't recognize the guy coming out of the store?' Holt asked.

'He was wearing a ski mask. He hit me fast and kept on running. I don't know how tall he was. I don't know what he looked like.'

'You don't know shit, do you, hotshot?' Steiger snarled. The overtures to buddyhood they had made in the Blue Goose Saloon earlier in the evening were forgotten now that he had been deprived of sleep and glory.

658

'What did he hit you with?' Wilhelm asked.

'Some kind of club. Short. Black. Hurt like fucking hell.'

Holt traded looks with the BCA man. 'Sounds like what Wright used to work Megan over.'

'Sounds like. But it could have been just a flashlight.'

'Or some piece of junk from that rat hole,' Steiger groused. 'Who the fuck robs a place like that? What's the point?'

'Good question,' Mitch said. 'The owner says he never keeps more than fifty bucks in the place, and that goes home with him Friday nights. All his help knows that.'

'Maybe they weren't after money,' Ellen suggested.

She stood just inside the door, leaning against the jamb, hoping she looked relaxed instead of dead on her feet. The men made a little break in their circle, looking at her with a certain amount of annoyance. She returned the favor, in no mood for niceties. Her gaze landed on Brooks, and a sharp sliver of alarm wedged into her at the sight of him. She forced her attention to Mitch.

'If it was Childs, maybe he had something stashed there,' she said. 'If he's tangled up with Wright, it might be evidence.'

Wilhelm yawned hugely. 'We're tearing the place apart right now. There had better be something there. It's going to take forever to go through it all.'

'There's no guarantee he didn't take it with him,' Mitch said. 'And there's a good chance "it" doesn't have anything to do with this case.'

'Any word on the car?' Ellen asked.

'Childs drives an old Peugeot,' Mitch said. 'We got nothing on this Crown Vic —'

'Including the tag number,' Steiger complained.

'It was dirty,' Jay said. 'It was dark.'

'Yeah, yeah . . . Why should we assume it was Childs or that this break-in has one goddamn thing to do with the kidnappings? If you ask me, it's just another big huge waste of time, taking our attention off what we ought to be doing just because Truman Capote here decided to play Dirty Harry.'

Jay cocked a brow. 'There's an image for you.'

The sheriff gave him a look. 'My men have a description of the car. If they see it, they'll stop it. That's as far as we're taking it. I'm going home.'

Jay tried to sit up a little straighter, immediately regretting it. 'But shouldn't you do a house-to-house or garage-to-garage or whatever you want to call it? What if this *is* your guy? What if he's the one who took the Holloman kid?'

'Do we have any reason to think it is? Do we have any reason to think it isn't just some doped-up kid looking to score a few bucks?'

'But if it was Childs —'

Steiger turned his back and headed for the door. 'I'm going to bed. Nobody call me unless there's a major felony involved.'

659

'Man,' Wilhelm said to no one in particular. 'When the bean counters get a load of the overtime on this gig, they're going to eat me alive.'

Mitch glared at him. 'Tell them to sell tickets. They'll be back in the black in no time.'

'Very funny.'

As the agent disappeared into the hall, Mitch looked to Ellen. 'He thought I was joking?'

Shaking his head, he turned back to Jay. 'Bottom line here, Mr Brooks. You should have let us handle it. We're the cops, you're the writer,' he said in an exaggerated, patronizing tone. 'Remember that from here on out. We've got enough trouble without having civilians kill themselves trying to do our jobs for us. If that deputy hadn't caught sight of you, you'd be a Popsicle by now. And if there'd been anybody in those cars you hit, I'd be hauling your ass downtown. I don't give a damn who you are. As it stands, you'll be getting a hefty citation.'

'I'll pay the damages,' Jay muttered. Working to dredge up some humor, he cast a hopeful look at Ellen. 'Maybe I can sweet-talk my way out of that ticket.'

Mitch barked a laugh. 'Yeah, when pigs fly. Try it here, where there's a full medical staff to put the pieces back together.' He turned to Ellen. 'I'm out of here. There's nothing more we can do tonight. Wait and see what Wilhelm's guys come up with – but, you know, Steiger might be right for once in his miserable, brain-atrophied life – it could be nothing. I've got to get some sleep. I'm picking Megan up from HCMC at noon.'

Ellen nodded. When Mitch exited the room, she suddenly realized the folly of coming down here. What had she been thinking? She could have sent Cameron as her backup; she had already taken one call for the night. Or she could have waited until morning. Brooks hadn't offered them any revelation, no evidence, nothing but a writer's hunch that the man he had pursued had been their man.

'What do you have to say for yourself?' she demanded.

'I wish I'd taken the insurance on the rent-a-Jeep?'

She just stared at him.

'So,' he said, 'is this where you tell me you think I staged it all to boost interest in my book?'

'I don't think you'd go so far as to risk killing yourself. That would rather defeat the purpose, wouldn't it? Then again, the waiting room is SRO with reporters ready to tout you as a would-be hero.'

Jay gave a harsh laugh that ended in a hiss of pain and eased himself down off the table, gritting his teeth. It wasn't that she didn't think him capable of concocting the whole thing as a publicity stunt, or calculating enough to capitalize on a real brush with death. But had he ever given her reason to believe otherwise? Had he ever given himself reason to believe, for that matter?

'Believe me, counselor. I'm nobody's hero. I had no intention of

660

trying to catch the son of a bitch until he tried to kill me. *That* pissed me off.'

'What were you doing there in the first place?'

'I was just riding around, contemplating the meaning of life. Ironic that I ended up damn near getting my ticket punched, isn't it?'

'Don't be a smart-ass.'

'Oooh, that's a tall order, sugar. Might as well ask a cat to change his stripes.'

Ellen refused to be amused. How could he make wisecracks? He could as easily have been in a body bag right now, could have been killed in any number of ways, according to his story. And the evidence bore his story out.

'Do you have any idea how long it takes to freeze to death on a night like this?' she asked.

'No, but I'd say I'm well on my way there.' He opened and closed drawers in the table base in search of something to use as a shirt. 'Christ, don't they have heat in this place? What do y'all do up here – freeze the germs to death?'

'Make all the jokes you want, but I personally feel that enough people have been broken or killed in this goddamn game! There's nothing funny about it!'

She turned her back to him, cursing herself mentally for letting her control slip. This wasn't the time or the place. He wasn't the man to lose it for.

She needed to hang on, tough it out. The hearing would begin Tuesday. She couldn't afford to let the pressure get to her now.

'I have to go,' she whispered.

Jay watched her move toward the door, telling himself to let her go. Leave awkward enough alone. Then he reached out anyway and caught hold of her shoulder.

'Ellen, wait.'

She stopped but didn't turn. Over her shoulder he could see she had closed her eyes.

'You didn't have to come down here,' he said. He was glad she had; it had to be a sign of a crack in her armor, one that he might charm open to let himself in. 'You were worried about me?'

'It must be the sleep deprivation.'

'Must be.'

He stepped around in front of her, hooked a knuckle under her chin, and lifted her face. Her skin looked too pale, accented by harsh shadows of exhaustion and etched with fine lines of strain.

'Thanks anyway,' he whispered.

She let him settle his mouth against hers. It was just a kiss. Something both of them could easily walk away from, and would.

'Get some sleep,' he murmured. The pirate's smile showed. 'Will you dream about me?'

'Not if I have any sense left at all,' she said sadly, and walked out.

Paul sat in his borrowed car at the end of Lakeshore Drive. He wouldn't dare stay long for fear some cop car would come rolling up and hassle him, and then the press would descend again. Two weeks ago he had sought out the media. Now he found himself sneaking around, driving someone else's car so he wouldn't be recognized. He was being made to feel like a criminal.

There was no one he could turn to for support. His family in St Paul had never been anything but a burden and an embarrassment to him. He wasn't one of them – blue-collar, beer-drinking dullards. Collectively, they had the intellectual depth of a mud puddle. He had no real friends, he was finding out. The people who had called to offer their sympathy at the start of this ordeal now looked at him with a subtle reserve in their eyes. He saw it, sensed the emotional barriers they were erecting.

None of them had offered him the use of their car. None of them would have understood his sudden need for anonymity. A reporter had bartered with him for the use of this one – exclusive comments for occasional use of the dirty, nondescript sedan.

Karen was the person he wanted to go to. He had tried to call her tonight just to hear her voice as she answered the phone, but the number had been changed and the new one was unlisted. He couldn't go to the house because Garrett was there. Karen wouldn't come to him because she was frightened.

It wasn't that she didn't love him. He knew she did. He thought back to the last time they had made love, a week into the search for Josh. The day they found Josh's jacket out on Ryan's Bay. He had fought with Hannah that night. He had fought with Mitch Holt. Holt thought he should be more supportive of Hannah, that he shouldn't blame Hannah. Hannah, Hannah, Hannah. He had retaliated in his own way by going to Karen. Karen understood him. Karen loved him. Karen didn't blame him for anything.

They seldom met at her house, because the risk was too great. But he had gone there that night. She had taken him into the guest bedroom and they had made love on clean peach sheets. She did all the work of arousing him, teasing him, caressing him, riding him until he grabbed her and rolled her beneath him and fucked her until he couldn't see. She took everything he gave her and clung to him afterward.

'I wish you could stay.'

'I can't.'

'I know. But I wish you could.' She raised her head and gazed at him. *'I wish I could give you all the love and support you need. I wish I could give you a son. . . . I'd have your baby, Paul. I think about it all the time. I think about it when I'm in your house, when I'm holding Lily. I pretend she's mine – ours. I think about it every time we're together, every time you climax inside me. I'd have your baby, Paul. I'd do anything for you.'*

Of course, she couldn't do for him the thing he needed most now. She couldn't be with him, couldn't support him, couldn't take his mind off his worries – because of Garrett. It was the fault of that North bitch that Garrett Wright was out on bail. He should have stayed in jail until the trial. After the trial he would be out of the way permanently.

That part wouldn't change. It couldn't. It all had to work out for him, Paul thought. He deserved it.

25

The courthouse was officially closed Saturdays, which meant that not only would they have the office to themselves, but the press would be locked out of the building. Thank heaven for small favors, Ellen thought. They had been rabid last night, descending first on the Lakeside neighborhood after the discovery of Dustin Holloman's stocking cap, and then on the hospital after Brooks's wild chase. She hadn't thought they would let her out of the hospital intact, tearing at her verbally, sending up a racket more suited for a soccer stadium than for a hospital waiting room. And waiting for her out in the cold of the parking lot like a junkyard dog was Adam Slater.

'Willing to freeze my *cojones* for a comment,' he said with a grin, dancing from one battered Nike to the other.

'I have no comment.' Ellen barely broke stride as she stepped around him.

'Aw, come on, Ellen,' he whined. 'Just a sound bite for the folks back in Grand Forks. Just a quick line about the deviant brilliance of evil.'

'How about the twisted deviance of the media masquerading in the guise of public service?' she said. 'I have a job to do, Mr Slater, and I'm sick to death of having to trip over you people every time I turn around. I don't owe you a comment, and you may *not* call me Ellen.'

He hadn't liked that. No comment *and* she had chased him away from her secretary. He would no doubt make her look like the Bitch Queen of the North in the *Grand Forks Herald*. Big deal. She had been called worse things and survived. The personal opinions of reporters were the least of her worries.

She went into her office and spent an hour cleaning, wiping the fingerprint grime away and setting things back the way she wanted them, trying without success to erase the feeling of having been invaded.

How the hell had he got in here without her knowing it?

How could Dustin Holloman's stocking cap have ended up in Josh Kirkwood's backpack?

Phoebe arrived, her natural ebullience apparently still weighted down by Friday's incidents. Dark circles ringed her eyes. Even her springy mane seemed to be drooping, hanging down her back like a limp rope, bound midway by a strip of black ribbon. She dropped her black leather backpack into her chair and made a beeline to the coffeemaker.

Cameron showed last, bearing a container of chocolate-chip cookies in apology for being late.

'I swung by the law-enforcement center,' he said, depositing his briefcase on the conference table and shrugging out of his ski jacket. 'The stocking cap definitely belongs to Dustin Holloman. His parents identified it.'

'I know. I've already spoken with Steiger.'

Phoebe frowned down into her steaming mug of Irish-cream blend. 'It's just too creepy that Josh had it.'

'The cops are fuming,' Cameron said. 'They're going to look like total stooges in the press. The bad guy waltzed right past them into the Kirkwood house and planted that thing. Unbelievable.'

'We're not going to look so brilliant ourselves,' Ellen reminded him. 'Unless he has a tunnel running beneath the Lakeside neighborhood, Garrett Wright can't be the one who planted it.'

'The shell game continues.' He pulled three files out of his briefcase and laid them on the table. Pointing to each, he said, 'Wright's house phone, office phone, cellular phone. Let's see if we can find a winner in one of these.'

None of the records showed the strange, taunting calls that had been made to Hannah, to Mitch, to Ellen. There was no unusual recurring number. They found nothing, which, to Ellen's way of thinking, was *something*. None of the records showed a call to Tony Costello's office, which meant Karen Wright hadn't called him in. And if Karen Wright hadn't called him in, then that left one obvious choice.

Ellen knew Costello was capable of ruthless selfishness. What he had done on the Fitzpatrick case had proved the point well enough. But this was a step beyond. A child was still missing. It sickened her to think he might have knowledge of the crime and the criminal and not do anything about it.

Beyond appealing to him as a human being, she had no recourse. He had technically done nothing illegal. He would make the blanket of confidentiality stretch to cover his ass. Charges of aiding and abetting would be turned inside out and jumped through like circus hoops. If she brought the issue to the attention of the press, she had no doubt he would fight dirty to discredit her.

'But what if someone else brought it up?' she mused aloud, tapping her pen against her lower lip. 'What if we could get Wilhelm to turn the heat up on Costello?'

Cameron snickered, a nasty gleam coming into his eyes at the idea of duping Wilhelm into something. 'Yeah, ask Marty. He'll say anything – as long as he thinks it's his idea.'

'All he has to do is make some noise, talk about trying to get a warrant for Costello's phone records. It's about time Costello had the press snapping at his heels instead of wrapped around his little finger.' She turned to Phoebe. 'See if you can get hold of Agent Wilhelm. Ask him to stop in later.'

Phoebe nodded and slipped out of the room, a silent wraith in coffee-house black.

Cameron arched a brow. 'Is she in mourning or something?'

'Death of a budding romance. One of the lesser vultures had her in his sights. I cut him off at the knees and sent him crawling.'

'Wow. What a mom you'd make, Ellen.'

Ellen gave him a wry look. 'Is that a proposal?'

'Observation. You're lovely, but you frighten me.'

She managed a chuckle at his teasing. 'Thank you, Cameron. You're the little brother I never wanted.'

'Hey, my sisters all say the same thing!'

'Go figure.'

He sobered then, looking at her with concern. 'How are you doing after last night? Jeez, Ellen, you could have called me to go to the Kirkwoods'. After what happened here –'

'I wasn't sleeping anyway,' she said. 'Every time I closed my eyes, I saw that photograph of Josh.'

'Maybe the lab wizards will be able to pick something up from it. Find something in the background that might give us a clue to where he was held.'

The image was too clear in Ellen's mind. Josh in striped pajamas, his face as blank as the background. His skin color washed sickly white by the flash; a stark contrast to the darkness behind him. He appeared to be standing in a black void.

'Maybe,' she murmured without hope.

'So is Grabko going to find anything in those medical records?'

Ellen shook her head, grateful for the change in subject. They had business to do. Better to focus on what they had to do rather than on what they couldn't change or had no control over.

'Costello's blowing smoke,' she said, 'hoping the press will yell fire.'

'But he's planting doubt in Grabko's mind while he's at it.'

'Grabko has to rule on the evidence. This ought to tip the scales in our favor.' She tapped the copy of the fax with the preliminary lab analysis. 'Josh's blood was on that sheet. Josh's hair was on that sheet. Garrett Wright's hair was on that sheet. That's our first concrete piece of physical evidence that ties Wright to Josh.'

'Makes you wonder what the hell Wright was thinking, wrapping that sheet around O'Malley that night.'

'He was thinking he would escape. He was thinking he was invincible, that even if he gave us that evidence, it wouldn't make any difference because we wouldn't have him.'

It was a taunt, the same as that photograph of Josh. Had that file been

666

in her cabinet a day or a week? When had she last opened that particular drawer?

She slid her reading glasses down her nose and peered at her colleague over the rims. 'How's that brief coming? We *will* have Garrett Wright, won't we?'

He shot her a cocky grin as he pulled a document from his open briefcase. 'Anthony Costello should wish his high-priced associates could write a brief this good. He doesn't have a leg to stand on when it comes to arguing this arrest away on the basis of Fourth Amendment rights.'

Ellen plucked the brief from his fingers and looked it over. She felt as much confidence as she could that Grabko would rule in their favor. Cameron's arguments were dead-on, but beyond that the case was too big to throw out the arrest on a dubious technicality.

Costello had to know that as well. This was just another example of what Ellen called a 'kitchen sink' defense, where the lawyer threw in everything he could find – including the proverbial kitchen sink – in the attempt to muddy the waters and cloud the issues. And to divert the energies of the prosecution. Cameron had spent hours on this brief, constructing an argument against what was essentially a bluff on Costello's part. He could have been using that precious time helping to strengthen the case against Wright.

'Did you hear the toxicology reports came back on Josh's blood?' she asked. 'Traces of Triazolam, aka Halcion.'

'If we can put Wright at a pharmacy filling that prescription . . .'

'We'll be too lucky for words,' Ellen finished.

'Bet Todd Childs could get us some Halcion if we asked nice.'

'If we could find him.'

'Or someone who buys pharmaceutical goodies from him.'

'We need more manpower. Our resources are spread too thin as it is without sending guys out hunting for Childs's buyers. We don't even know that he deals drugs, just that he indulges. Have you got anything from Wilhelm's guy regarding Wright's background?'

Cameron rolled his eyes. 'Yeah, a lot of lame excuses. They faxed me the same information two days in a row.'

'Oh, great.'

'Mitch put in a request to NCIC for cases with a similar MO perpetrated in any of the areas Wright has lived since 1979, but nothing has come back yet. He requested info on unsolved murders in the same geographical areas as well.'

'Building a haystack to find our needle,' Ellen grumbled, thumbing through the thin file folder Cameron handed across to her.

'And the thing is, of course, we don't have time for it. Even if NCIC gets back to us before the hearing, all we'd have is conjecture and supposition. There won't be any time to investigate. We won't have anything admissible.'

'No, but we have to think beyond the hearing. Have you found anything on your own?'

'It's all in there, such as it is. I started at Harris and worked backward. Before coming here Wright taught briefly at the University of Virginia; before that, Penn State – where Christopher Priest also taught during the same period.' He bobbed his eyebrows. 'Neat coincidence, huh?'

Nerves prickled along Ellen's spine. 'I don't believe in coincidence. Where did you get that information?'

He looked sheepish. 'I read it in the *Pioneer Press*.'

'God,' she groaned, 'the press has better access to information on our suspect than we do.'

'They had a head start. A lot of what they've written on Wright is coming out of old pieces they did on the Sci-Fi Cowboys a couple of years ago. I looked them all up at the library and made copies. They're in there, too.'

Ellen flipped through the pages of typed notes to the clippings. One featured a photo of Christopher Priest and one of the Cowboys bent over a small robot that was supposed to scoop up balls and deposit them in a basket. Wright and three more boys stood in the background, their faces distorted by the poor quality of the copy.

'Priest sent over his list of Sci-Fi Cowboys past and present,' she said. 'Grudgingly, I might add.'

'You think there might be something there?'

'I don't know. I think he doesn't want the scrutiny. He may talk those kids up like they're National Honor Society material, but he knows darn well any one of them could have taken a knife to my car.' She stared at the article titled 'Juvenile Hall Meets Hallowed Halls.' 'Anyway, I called a couple of people I know in the Hennepin Country system to see if they might be able to help us track down some of the former members to get their take on Wright. And I got my hands on rap sheets on the present members. I want to know who we're dealing with.'

'Priest could make some big noise if he thinks we're stepping over right-to-privacy boundaries,' Cameron warned. 'He's connected, you know. The Sci-Fi Cowboys is a popular tax-deductible contribution with some major political players.'

'He's an inch away from being considered an accessory. I don't care if he's connected to the pope.'

'He passed a polygraph,' Cameron reminded her.

'Big deal. All that means is he's devoid of emotion when he has to be. It's not a stretch to imagine that. He could pass for an android most of the time.'

She turned back to the initial typed report listing Wright's former teaching positions, tapping a finger under 'Penn State.' 'Wright and Priest were at Penn State during the same time period. It makes sense to request the NCIC reports on unsolved kidnappings and murders in that geographical area first.'

'Done.'

'Good.'

'But if Wright's done this kind of thing in the past,' Cameron said, 'he's done a bang-up job covering his tracks. I haven't found a hint of trouble in his background. He grew up in Mishawaka, Indiana. His parents split when he was eleven. Father remarried and moved to Muncie. Wright and his sister stayed with the mother, who died of a brain embolism a few years ago.'

'Sister?' Ellen perked up. 'Where's the sister? Have you talked to her?'

'I've got nothing on her. She's probably married somewhere. Wright himself would be the only one to ask, and I can't see him giving us that information out of the goodness of his heart. I'd say the sister's a dead end, though she may come out of the woodwork now to star on *The Ricki Lake Show* – the siblings-of-evil-serial-criminals segment.'

'Slight change of topic,' Cameron said, waving a photocopy of Wright's official written alibi. 'Wright states he came home for a late lunch Saturday, the twenty-second, then returned to Harris around two thirty. They have a witness who claims to have seen Wright's Saab headed south on Lakeshore at that time.

'Now, we, of course, don't believe Wright was driving the car, because that was about the time O'Malley was attacked. But we also know Christopher Priest was in St Peter. So who do we think was driving the Saab? Childs? The wife?'

Ellen pulled her glasses off, pushed her chair back, and stood slowly, grimacing at the tension that had settled in her back.

'We know Priest stayed in St Peter Saturday night,' she said. 'Does he have anyone who can verify he was there Saturday afternoon?'

Cameron checked his notes. 'He had lunch with a professor friend from Gustavus Adolphus. Time unspecified. I'll double-check.'

'God, what a Gordian knot,' she murmured, turning toward the window. The park across the street was empty. Downtown looked windswept and deserted. Yellow ribbons that had been tied to every light pole as a symbol of hope for the return of Josh Kirkwood now fluttered for Dustin Holloman. The posters and pleas that had been plastered to the windows of stores and restaurants had been replaced with a fresh set.

'We have only to put doubt in Grabko's mind that it was Wright behind the wheel.' Cameron walked around the end of the table and settled a hip on the credenza. 'All we have to do is get him bound over for trial. It's up to the cops to catch the accomplice.'

'I know. I just can't shake the feeling that Costello's got a big fat rabbit to pull out of his hat.'

'Childs.'

A scowl knitted Ellen's brow. 'Grungy weasel. I can't wait to get him on cross and nail him for the lying little shit he is. Although I have to say, I'm hoping the police find him first – up to his ears in incriminating evidence.

'No,' she said. 'It's not just Childs. I know Costello. He's always cocky, but there's a certain quality to this. . . . I've been over his disclosure until I've got it memorized, and I don't see any red flags, but there's still . . . something.'

'You're working too hard,' Cameron pointed out. 'And they're working hard to make you crazy. Between vandalizing your car and that business last night, you've got good call to be jumpy. But we've got enough to hang Wright at the hearing. Costello can't change the evidence we've got.' He gave her a smile. 'Aren't you the one who said "Don't let him get to you"?'

'Was that me?' She forced a laugh. 'What was I thinking?'

That she knew Tony Costello, knew all his tricks, all his secrets. But now the ground had shifted beneath her feet – or Costello had pulled the rug out from under her. Again. *'Our mutual friend Mr Brooks . . . Small world, isn't it?'* In her mind's eye his image faded into Jay's, dark eyes turning translucent blue. *'Then your leaving Minneapolis had nothing to do with the rape trial of Art Fitzpatrick? . . . I do my homework, Ellen. . . .'*

Or he had it handed to him.

She told herself it shouldn't have mattered. She knew better than to trust either of them. She knew better than to let her guard down.

Then why did you go to the hospital last night, Ellen?

She raised a hand and brushed her fingers across her lips, the memory of his kiss stirring, warm and restless inside her.

'Let's get to work,' she said. 'I want plenty of rope in that figurative noose.'

They settled back into their chairs. Cameron pulled a cookie out of the tub and munched on it as he looked over their list of evidence.

'So, aside from the arrest itself, do you have any idea what Costello is going to challenge?'

'No,' Ellen admitted. 'And he'll wait till the eleventh hour to tell us, you can bet on that. Speculate, though. What do you think he'll try to get rid of?'

'The gloves. They weren't discovered for days. He'll argue they could have been planted. He'll argue they could belong to anybody, that we don't have proof they're Wright's.'

'Good points. So we don't enter the gloves as evidence at the hearing. We hang on to them for trial. By that time we should be able to prove they *are* his. If we're extra lucky, the snow will be gone by then and we'll find the gun to go with the gloves. Has anything turned up as to Wright having registered a handgun in this state?'

'Nada. Big surprise. I'm checking with Virginia, Pennsylvania, Ohio, and Indiana, but maniacal serial criminals tend to think themselves above such mundane formalities.'

Ellen conceded the futility of it. 'He'd never be so careless as to leave a paper trail. What else?'

He shrugged. 'We've got the ski mask, the bloody sheet, Mitch's testimony, Megan's testimony, Ruth Cooper's lineup ID –'

'Which happened BC – Before Costello.'

'So? Wright had an attorney. It went down by the book. No problem. We've got a hell of a lot more than Costello. His witness list consists of Childs, who we can turn inside out, the neighbor who saw Wright's Saab on Saturday, and Karen Wright. What's she going to say? All anyone's been able to get out of her so far is that her husband's arrest is just a big misunderstanding.'

'Good question. No one has ever claimed she's an alibi witness. If Wright was at work at the times the crimes were committed, as he claims, what *can* she say?'

'*That he called her on the telephone!*' they said in unison.

They both grabbed the phone records again.

The door swung open and Ellen glanced up, expecting to see Phoebe, her eyes widening instead on Megan O'Malley with Mitch standing right behind her.

'Megan!' she said with genuine surprise. 'It's good to see you up and around!'

'And more or less in one piece,' Megan said dryly.

She looked like hell. The bruises on her face had reached the putrid-fruit stage. The crescents beneath her vibrant green eyes were the color of eggplant. She limped in, leaning heavily on one crutch. Her right hand was encased in a rigid cast that extended to the very tips of her fingers.

Cameron moved to pull a chair out for her, but she waved it off. Mitch cut her an impatient look that she completely ignored.

'Finding any goodies?' she asked, scanning the papers strewn over the table.

Ellen closed the folder and rose, blocking her view. 'Just hunting for tidbits,' she said casually. 'You know, phone records, that kind of thing. Dry stuff. Are you all set to testify?'

Megan's mouth curved in a nearly feral smile. 'I can't wait.'

'We're not staying,' Mitch said, catching Ellen's body language. 'I just wanted to let you know I talked to Hannah about trying hypnosis with Josh. We talked to the psychiatrist and she's reluctant, but she agreed to try it.'

'When?'

'Tomorrow. Four o'clock. Her office in Edina. We'll videotape the session, just in case.'

'I want to be there.'

'I knew you would.'

'Have you found anything in Wright's background?' Megan asked. 'Any connection to Priest or Childs?'

'We're looking,' Ellen said. 'Priest and Wright taught at Penn State during the same period. We're checking into it. As far as Childs goes, nothing. We know he went to high school in Oconomowoc, Wisconsin, and that he's willing to perjure himself. We know he's nowhere to be found at the moment. We know someone broke into the Pack Rat last night – might have been Todd, might have been anybody. Wilhelm is supposed to be there right now. The evidence techs are going over the place. Of course, we don't know what they should be looking for, so how can we expect them to find it?'

Megan scowled. 'I wouldn't expect Wilhelm to find Waldo.'

'The thing is,' Cameron said, 'it could be just another diversion. One more stunt to make Wright look innocent.'

'But why target a place where Wright's phony alibi works?' Megan's gaze sharpened as the wheels of her mind began to spin. 'And why pull this stunt that late at night when it was just a fluke that anyone would happen by and see?'

'So,' Ellen speculated, 'maybe it *was* Childs and he sneaked in because he had something stashed there – drugs, for instance – which he grabbed and ran with. In which case your BCA pals are spending a lot of manpower on nothing.'

'That's the way it goes,' Megan said. 'Though I wouldn't want to be in your Marty's shoes when he has to explain that to headquarters.'

Phoebe came slinking back into the room. 'Agent Wilhelm is on his way over.'

'My cue to leave,' Megan said. 'If Wilhelm catches me here, he'll pop a cork and I'll end up hitting him with my crutch.'

Ellen walked her and Mitch to the door of the outer office, sympathy welling inside her at Megan's hobbling gait, and at the proud tilt of her chin.

'You know about the benefit for Wright tonight?' she asked Mitch.

He nodded. 'Got it covered. We'll keep an eye on Wright, see who approaches him. If Childs is there, we'll grab him.'

'Good. Thanks for stopping in. Mitch, I'll see you tomorrow. Let's keep our fingers crossed that Josh can clear everything up for us. In the meantime, we keep digging.'

'The key is Wright's past,' Megan insisted. 'I wish I could help with that hunt.'

Ellen gave her an apologetic look. 'You know I can't involve you, Megan. You're not the agent in charge anymore, you're a victim.'

Megan's eyes blazed with a hatred Ellen could only guess at. 'I know exactly what I am. And I have Garrett Wright to thank for it.'

'Ellen's hands are tied, Megan. You know that,' Mitch said.

He had stopped by her apartment that morning, fed her two cats, and turned the thermostat up so the place would feel more like a home than like a cold, drafty converted attic – which was essentially what it was. The third floor of a big old Victorian house on Ivy Street, it was probably the least accessible apartment in town. Two flights of stairs to climb with a bum knee and a crutch. He had to clench his jaw to keep from commenting yet again on her stubbornness.

Megan stood by the window in her pink living room, stroking the head of her little gray cat with her good hand, cradling the bad one against her. The set of her mouth was stubbornness personified.

'You're off the case, Megan,' he reminded her. He stepped around a pair of boxes she had yet to unpack. Josh had been kidnapped her first day on the job here.

'Officially,' she said grudgingly. 'But that doesn't mean I couldn't do a little background work off the record –'

'And risk getting the case turned on appeal? You're not thinking straight. Come here,' he said, turning her gently toward the old camelback sofa. 'You need to sit down or that knee is going to swell up like a water balloon.'

That she didn't put up a fight told him she was as near exhaustion as she looked. She eased herself down on the couch and sat quietly while he pulled a box of books over to prop up her leg.

'I just feel so damn helpless, Mitch,' she admitted as he carefully tucked a pillow beneath her damaged knee. She heard the little tremor in her voice and knew he had, as well.

'I know you do, honey. I know exactly.'

He had been in the same boat, hadn't he? she thought. On rougher seas than this. He had been a detective on the Miami force at the time his wife and son had been gunned down. She knew damn well he wouldn't have been allowed within a hundred yards of the investigation. And the guilt still weighed on him.

'It's so hard,' she whispered, sliding her good hand over his. 'We're cops. We're trained to think a certain way, to act, to go after the bad guys. To have that taken away when we need it most . . . It's hard.'

Mitch settled himself on the couch beside her, draping his right arm behind her shoulders. Friday, the black cat, hopped onto a stereo speaker box, curled his paws beneath him, and watched them across the gathering gloom of late afternoon.

'You still haven't told me what your surgeon had to say yesterday.'

Megan looked away. If she stared at her cat instead of at Mitch, it would be easier to lie, and that was what she wanted to do – lie, to Mitch, to herself.

'What does he know?' she muttered.

Mitch held back a sigh. Bad news. News that hurt her and frightened her, not that she would want to admit to either, or to concede defeat.

'Yeah.' He drew her over to lean against him. 'It's too soon for them to know anything for sure.'

'It is,' she said, her voice tightening. She settled her cheek into the hollow of his shoulder, and he could feel her chin quivering. 'They can't know yet.'

She didn't want to hear it yet. She wasn't ready to accept it, wouldn't

673

go down without a fight. As much as Mitch admired her courage, he knew it would only make it harder for her in the end. He already knew the prognosis. He had called her doctor, lied and told him he was Megan's brother Mick. The hospital would release information only to family, and Megan's family didn't give a rat's ass what happened to her.

The best thing the orthopedic surgeon had to say was that they hadn't had to amputate her hand. There would be more surgery and months of physical therapy, but it was unlikely she would ever regain full mobility.

Mitch would have sent Garrett Wright to the blackest pit of hell for what he'd done to Megan, to Josh, to Hannah, to Deer Lake. If he was lucky, he would get to help send him to prison. Justice and the law were seldom one and the same. He had learned that lesson the hard way a long time ago.

'We have to get him, Mitch,' Megan mumbled against his chest, where her tears soaked into his flannel shirt. 'He has to pay.'

'He'll pay, sweetheart.' Mitch wrapped his arms around her, hoping to God the promise didn't sound as hollow to Megan's ears as it did to his own.

She sniffed and raised her head, fighting to force one corner of her mouth up. 'Don't call me sweetheart.'

'I will if I want to,' Mitch growled, gladly falling into what had already become an old joke between them. 'What are you gonna do about it, O'Malley? Beat me up?'

'Yeah. With one hand in a cast.'

The smile sobered. Her gaze remained locked on his. 'What am I going to do, Mitch? Being a cop is all I've ever wanted.'

He brushed a tear from her check. 'But it's not all you've got, Megan. You've got me. You'll find a way around the obstacles. And I'll be there, hanging on to your good hand.'

'Jeez, Holt,' she whispered, leaning up to kiss him. 'You ought to write that down for Hallmark.'

26

The music wasn't half-bad – a fusion of blues and rock with lyrics by an English major. The band was a campus group that called themselves HarriSons. The lead singer was a rangy, raw-boned kid in ripped blue jeans and a sweaty T-shirt. He hugged an old red Stratocaster guitar and squeezed his eyes shut tight beneath the brim of a dirty baseball cap as he coaxed the music out of his soul.

Jay took a long pull on his three-dollar beer and did a slow scan of the place. Wright's followers had taken over the Pla-Mor Ballroom, a dance hall located just off campus. The Pla-Mor had apparently hit its peak in the forties and had not been changed a lick since. The dance floor had been sanded dull by decades of scuffing feet. The lights were kept low to serve the dual purpose of setting a mood and hiding the fact that huge scabs of plaster had flaked off the walls.

The place was likely cheap, and it was handy and served its purpose well enough. There were enough tables and chairs for 250 – all of them full. The place was SRO. It looked as if everyone in Deer Lake who believed in Wright's innocence had felt compelled to trudge out into the cold night to show their support. At five bucks a head admission, and with the jacked-up prices on the beer and setups and the Sci-Fi Cowboys' fifteen-dollar T-shirts, Wright's supporters would probably raise enough tonight to pay for a couple days' worth of Anthony Costello's time.

The man himself sat at the table of honor, his client beside him, the pair of them holding court like monarchs. Wright's wife and Costello's lackeys filled the rest of the chairs. A steady stream of students and what were probably faculty members offered words of friendship and support. Wright's expression was serene. Not the cocky, bullshit arrogance of his attorney, but a glassy calm, as if he knew something the rest of them didn't.

I want inside his mind, Jay thought, but knew he would have to wait. If Costello allowed the good doctor to say anything at all before the hearing, it would only be more propaganda. Still, the experience of an introduction was in itself useful, and so, as the band announced its break, he pushed himself out of the dark corner he had taken as his watch post and sauntered toward the table.

He spotted no fewer than three plainclothes cops. A squad car sat in the

675

parking lot. If the accomplice showed with Dustin Holloman in tow, they'd be on him like flies on roadkill. But if he showed up the same way everyone else showed up, looking ordinary, unassuming, offering Dr Wright nothing more than a handshake and a smile, would anyone be the wiser?

There was nothing to make Wright himself stand out in a crowd, no glowing eyes, no sign of the devil branded into his forehead. That was what frightened and fascinated people most – that monsters moved among them, unknown, unsuspected. They stood behind them in the line at the bank, bumped carts with them at the Piggly Wiggly. It was just that factor that kept readers returning to his work, Jay knew – the need to pull cases apart in the attempt to see the signs that should have been obvious to those involved. Too many times there was nothing there to see.

Costello spotted him before he reached the table, and a big, hungry smile stretched across the lawyer's face. He rose to offer the kind of hand-pumping, back-thumping greeting that struck Jay as too familiar. He endured it with a pained smile.

'Jay, I'm glad you could make it to our little soiree!' Costello said, the benevolent host although he'd had nothing to do with setting up the party. 'We heard you had a little adventure last night.'

'That's one word for it.' Jay discreetly rotated the sore right shoulder Costello had slapped. He had crawled out of the sack after noon feeling as if he had been trampled by a herd of Clydesdales. Only steady, low-dose self-medication of the Jack Daniel's variety had taken the edge off the aches.

'And of course the cops are trying to somehow associate that break-in with Dr Wright.' Costello made a grave face at the injustice. 'The level of incompetence here is unbelievable.'

The usual defense attorney shuck-and-jive. The cops are screwups, the prosecutors thickheaded plodders with no view of the big picture. Jay knew the drill. He had spouted the same trash talk himself once upon a time. He let it go in one ear and out the other as he turned to look at Garrett Wright – who was watching him with steady dark eyes and a placid half smile.

'Mr Brooks,' he said, rising, offering a hand that seemed nearly delicate. 'Anthony tells me you've taken an interest in the case with an eye toward doing a book.'

'Possibly. Depends on how it all shakes out in the end.'

The smile took on amusement. 'You mean it depends on my guilt? Quite a commentary on our society, isn't it? People don't want to read about innocence. They want twists, betrayal, blood.'

'That's nothing new, Dr Wright. People used to pay money to go to hangings – and they took their kids.'

'So they did,' he conceded with a tip of his head. 'Perhaps what mankind has been evolving toward all these centuries is simply a more streamlined, brilliant savagery.'

'That would certainly explain serial criminals, wouldn't it?' Jay said. 'You might just have a topic there for your next academic publish-or-perish project, Dr Wright.'

'No, no. Learning and perception are my areas of expertise. I don't pretend to be an expert on criminal behavior.'

Then again, maybe he didn't have to pretend. Jay reserved the comment, filing it away for future use in print. He let his gaze slide to Wright's wife, who sat beside him, pale almost to the point of appearing translucent. She flicked a nervous glance up at him, and a fleeting smile trembled across her mouth as she looked away. She looked distinctly unhappy when Christopher Priest slid into the chair beside her.

In an effort to look hip, the professor had dressed himself up in a black turtleneck a size too small. It clung to his bony shoulders like a diver's wet suit, the effect making his head look gigantic. He leaned ahead of Karen Wright to snag Garrett's attention.

'We've sold out of T-shirts. The boys are ecstatic.'

'They should be proud,' Costello interjected. He turned a shrewd eye back to Jay, shifting his position subtly to block Wright and the professor from view. 'You know, Jay, this story could be told from a number of perspectives. Dr Wright's innocence – the rallying of his friends, colleagues, students –'

'The brilliance of his attorney.' Jay forced a grin. 'Damned if this isn't sounding like a sales pitch, Tony.'

Costello didn't bother to feign contrition. 'I would be remiss if I failed to cultivate all possible venues to express my client's innocence.'

'Yeah, and we've all heard what happens to attorneys who don't defend their clients with vigor,' Jay said dryly, making a gun out of his thumb and forefinger and holding it to his temple.

Costello's face reddened. 'Dr Wright was still in jail at the time of Enberg's death. He would have to be something other than human to have been involved.'

Jay arched his brows, just for the pleasure of seeing Costello's blood pressure jump a notch. To his credit the attorney reined in his temper before it could do more than tighten his smile.

'Jay,' he said, slapping the sore shoulder again. 'You're wasting your talents. You'd give Lee Bailey a run for his money in cross-examination.'

'Yeah, but then that'd be work,' Jay drawled. 'I'd sooner watch. Leave the tough stuff to you and *Lee*.'

Ellen watched the exchange of grins and handshakes from just inside the door.

'What would you say if I told you I don't know Costello from a sack of pig feed?'

That you're a liar, Mr Brooks.

She had wanted to believe him and he had betrayed her. A sense of loss accompanied the anger as she watched them together.

It certainly had the look of best pals. A laugh, a grin, a slap on the back. Brooks and Costello, the law-school alums. A complementing pair of sharks – Costello the formal predator in a steel-gray Versace suit, Brooks the yuppie-turned-street person in creased Dockers and battered, unshaven face. And beside Costello, Garrett Wright, who turned and looked straight at her across the room. He smiled slowly, knowingly.

Ellen moved, seeking out the cover of a gaggle of tall college boys, cursing herself for giving in to the urge to come here. She and Cameron had worked until nine – Phoebe had begged off at eight, urgently needed in places unknown – then gone for a late dinner at Grandma's Attic. She should have gone home after Grandma's hot apple crisp. She should have, at this very minute, been deeply unconscious in her bed.

But the temptation had been too great – just to slip in for a few moments, to see for herself the kind of turnout, the mood and look of the crowd. The event had started at seven. The press would be long gone by nine, sound bites recorded, photos shot. She would be able to slip in, stay in the shadows, observe. By the time the money takers at the door spread the word of her presence, she would have seen enough and slipped back out. It seemed worth five dollars, even if that money was going to Wright's defense fund.

Now, in retrospect, it was a stupid idea. Wright himself had spotted her. She felt as if everyone in the room were turning to look at her. The tide of the crowd seemed to be running against her, taking her deeper into the midst of the enemy when she wanted nothing more than to make her way to the exit.

'Hey, what's *she* doing here?'

'Isn't that Ellen North?'

'She's got a lot of nerve.'

The comments came with barbed looks and pointed fingers. Ellen answered none of them, feigning calm as her heartbeat raced. She moved against the grain, her focus on the exit sign at the back of the room. She could have sent Cameron as her spy. She could have relied on the reports of Mitch's men. But no. She had to see for herself. She couldn't trust anyone else's perceptions. She had to sink herself into this thing up to her chin. Now she felt as if she were drowning in it.

A hand closed on her elbow. She tried to jerk free but the hold only tightened.

'What the hell are you doing here?' Brooks asked, his voice a low growl.

'I'd ask you the same question, but it was fairly self-evident.'

She tried once again to jerk herself free, but he was too close, moving with her – no – herding her. The course had changed without her consent. The exit was drifting off to the right. They were moving, instead, toward the dark hall where the coat check was located.

'You're drawing conclusions without facts, counselor,' he said as they passed the small oasis of light that was the coat check and moved to the edge of darkness.

Ellen put her back to the wall beside the emergency exit and gave him a furious look. 'And I'd be an idiot to accept your version of facts, Mr Brooks. Besides, I thought you didn't care what I believed or didn't believe.'

'And I thought you didn't care what I did or didn't do,' he shot back.

'I care that you lied to me. Beyond that, you can go to hell.'

'I didn't lie to you.'

'Ha! You tell me you don't know Tony Costello, that you don't have anything to do with his being on this case. Then I walk in and hail, hail, the gang's all here, the whole team rallied round the table, smiling, joking, slapping backs. Forgive me if I have a hard time believing a word that comes out of your handsome mouth, Brooks, but I wasn't born yesterday. Now, if you'll excuse me, I'd like to go. I've seen all I need to see.'

Ellen could see curious glances being directed at them, and she hoped she had been right in assuming the reporters had all come and gone. What a hell of a photo op this would be – the prosecuting attorney having a tête-à-tête with Jay Butler Brooks at a rally for the defendant.

One of Mitch's plainclothes guys stepped past the gawkers, his right hand inching discreetly beneath the tweed sport coat he wore.

'Is everything all right, Ms North?'

Brooks released her arm and stepped back into the shadows.

'Yes, thanks, Pat,' Ellen said, smoothing her coat sleeve. 'I was just leaving.'

'Would you like an escort out?'

'No, don't bother. I'm parked close by. I'll be fine. You've got better things to do here.'

She stepped past him and found a clear path to the front hall. The band had come back onstage from their break. The attention of the crowd turned toward them as the lead guitar took off on a wild, wailing riff.

Ellen berated herself mentally all the way to the main doors. *It doesn't matter what he does, what he says, what he thinks. You know better than to trust anyone. You don't have time to care.*

The people coming in from their cigarette breaks gave her a wide berth and sidelong glances.

Let them think what they want. What difference does it make if they believe in Wright? You know the truth.

Of course, she didn't. None of them knew the truth – except Josh, and he was keeping it locked tight within his mind. What part of the truth she did know she would wield like a club come Tuesday, and if Wright's believers came away with their illusions bruised and broken, it was nothing to her.

Ducking around a pair of incoming Harris students, she stepped outside

679

into the cold night. The parking lot in front of the dance hall was full. A green-and-white Deer Lake cruiser sat in the far corner, waiting for action that wasn't likely to happen. Ellen made her way to the east side of the old clapboard building. She had been lucky to get the spot on a residential street, pulling into the slot just as a Lincoln Town Car pulled out.

'Hey, lookee here, boys. It's Ms Bitch Lawyer.'

The voice brought her up short. A crucial mistake on her part, Ellen realized, as Tyrell Mann and his cohorts took advantage, moving away from the deeper shadows along the side of the building to step in front of her. A quick assessment of the situation told her she could be in trouble. They were out of view of the parking lot. To the east, a cedar privacy fence blocked the view into the neighboring house. The nearest house across the street was dark. The Manley Vanloon Pace Car sat at the near curb a dozen feet ahead. So close and so far. The music from the dance hall penetrated to the outside world, loud enough to mask the sounds of a struggle.

Tyrell's smile flashed bright in his dark face as he flicked away his cigarette. 'You got a fuckin' nerve coming here, lady.'

'I paid for the privilege,' Ellen said. 'That's all you should care about.'

'We care about the Doc. He's our man,' J. R. Andersen said.

'Yeah,' Speed Dawkins chimed in. 'He's our man. He's *the* man –'

'And you tryin' to throw his ass in jail,' Tyrell said, the smile gone.

The image of the switchblade that had been left in her tire came sharply into focus in Ellen's memory. She had spent part of the evening going over the file on the Sci-Fi Cowboys, with an eye to possible suspects in her vandalism. Andersen was a white-collar criminal, stealing money electronically. Dawkins had been in and out of drug-related trouble. Tyrell was a fairly recent addition to the group, a bright kid with a rap sheet that skirted the edges of some serious stuff – assault charges that had been bartered down, robbery charges that had been reduced because he wasn't the principal player and the county juvenile facility was bursting at its seams, a rape charge that had been dismissed.

At seventeen Tyrell was already a hard case. Vandalism wouldn't have been anything to him. Where he would draw the line was questionable. Ellen had seen too many kids just like him who made no distinctions at all, kids who wouldn't hesitate to pull a gun and shoot someone for their starter jacket or kick their head in for pocket money.

'I don't have to tell you how the system works, Tyrell,' she said. 'And I shouldn't have to tell you that your hassling me won't help Dr Wright's cause.'

'I don't want you tellin' me nothin', bitch.'

'I'm sure you don't, but you'd better listen.' In her coat pocket she singled out the biggest key on her ring to use as a defense weapon and curled her fist around the rest. 'You and your buddies fuck up here and you go to jail, and the Sci-Fi Cowboys will be no more. How do you think Dr Wright and Professor Priest and the rest of your backers would feel about that?'

She wanted him to see reason. He heard only challenge.

He took half a step closer. 'Is that a threat, Ms Bitch Lawyer?'

'It's a fact. You and I both know the only reason your ass isn't sitting on a Hennepin County cot right now is the Sci-Fi Cowboys. You want to trash that, Tyrell?'

'Naw. That's not what I fuckin' wanna trash.'

Ellen chanced a quick glance at the other two. Dawkins was watching Tyrell, ready to take his cue. Andersen stood back a little, his expression blank, his thoughts unreadable. In some ways he was more a wild card than Tyrell. His IQ was in the genius range, his probation officer's comments laced with hints of well-camouflaged sociopathic tendencies. He could intervene with charm or just as easily be the mastermind who came up with the foolproof way to dispose of her body.

'The dance is *inside* the building, boys.'

Ellen did her best to swallow her sigh of relief at the sound of Brooks's voice.

Impatience flashed in Tyrell's eyes. 'Who the fuck are you? The Lone Fuckin' Ranger?'

'More like the Lone Fuckin' Witness.' Jay stepped in front of Ellen, then backed her up to put some space between them and the angry-looking kid in the Bulls jacket. 'With the lone fuckin' cellular phone and my finger on the lone fuckin' speed-dial button for the cops. Do you understand what I'm fuckin' tellin' you, you fuckin' little shit?'

His voice rose with each angry word. He had come out here to confront Ellen. Now he found himself in the unlikely role of rescuer, holding his pocket cellular phone up as if it were a live grenade.

'Come on, Tyrell,' Andersen said, cuffing his buddy's shoulder. 'I'm freezing my dick off. Let's go in.'

He started toward the building. Dawkins hesitated. Tyrell stood his ground.

'Come on,' Andersen said impatiently. 'Before the professor blows a circuit.'

Tyrell thrust his chin out at Jay. 'Fuck you, man. We was just talkin' to the lady.'

The trio swaggered off together toward the yellow light of the parking lot. Ellen watched them go, slowly letting the air out of her lungs.

'Thanks,' she said to Brooks. 'He's a loose cannon in Wright's arsenal. I wasn't sure what he might do.'

'Yeah, well, I'd'a looked pretty damned stupid if he would have pulled a gun and gone off on me. The worst damage this phone can do is leak battery acid.' He held it out to her. 'You want to call this little encounter in?'

'They didn't break any laws. I just want to go home.' And double-bolt the doors, and sink into a hot bath and a big glass of brandy. 'Good night, Mr Brooks,' she said, starting for the Cadillac.

'Not so far, it isn't.' His footsteps crunched over the snow behind her. 'I came here for the same reason you did – to observe.'

'I think, then, that maybe you should look the word up in the dictionary. You seem to have observation confused with participation.'

'Costello is as much a part of this story as you are, Ellen. Of course I'm going to speak with him.'

'I don't want to hear about it.'

Ellen let herself in the car. She hit the power locks, even though Brooks had pulled up on the curb. She turned the key in the ignition, but the big engine made no sound at all, made no effort to start, made not even a grumbled refusal to start. The Manley Vanloon Pace Car had died.

'Hell and damnation!' Ellen swore, smacking her gloved fist on the steering wheel.

Fuming, she popped the hood, dug the pocket flashlight out of her purse, and climbed out of the car. The Cadillac's engine was the size of a small country, but parts were parts – or, in this case, parts were nowhere to be seen. The distributor was gone.

'Shit!'

'Ms North . . .' Jay clucked his tongue. 'Such language.'

Ellen shot him a scathing glare.

He held up his phone like a prize. 'Want to call a cab?'

'Don't be an ass.'

'Want to call a cop?'

What would be the point? The Pla-Mor was packed to the rafters with suspects. The possibility of anyone's coming forward as a witness was laughable. Although Tyrell and Andersen and Dawkins had been in the immediate vicinity, they wouldn't have been foolish enough to hang on to the distributor. The offense was too petty for the amount of time and energy it would consume.

'Come on.' Brooks pocketed the phone and pulled out his keys. 'I'll give you a ride.'

'I think you've already taken me for a ride,' she said dryly.

'I'll take you straight home. Scout's honor.'

He took her straight to *his* home.

Ellen gave him a speculative look across the cab of the GMC Jimmy he had talked Manley into renting him. 'You were never a Boy Scout, were you?'

He grinned. 'No, ma'am, I never was.'

'I could use that phone now,' she grumbled, 'to report my own kidnapping.'

'Or you could relax and enjoy my famous southern hospitality.'

'So far, "enjoyable" is not the word I would use regarding our association.'

'What word would you use?'

Unsettling. It came to her instantly, but she kept it to herself. She knew instinctively it would please him. He enjoyed knocking her off balance, used it to his own advantage – like now.

'It's time we had a talk,' he said. 'I figured it was best held in a place you can't have me thrown out of or walk away from.'

They turned off Old Cedar Road and drove into the development area around Ryan's Bay. The moon was waxing toward fullness, its light casting the bay in otherworldly shades of silver and white. Ellen had biked the trails out here many times in warm weather, had always felt a certain parklike comfort about the area. Now every time she went by that spot on the trail, she would think about Josh's little ski jacket planted among the reeds, a note tucked into one pocket.

' "My specter around me night and day like a wild beast guards my way. My emanation far within weeps incessantly for my sin." ' She murmured the lines from William Blake's poem, her gaze on the frozen reeds that thrust up from the drifts of snow. 'That was the note left in Josh's coat pocket.'

'I know,' Jay said softly.

'How? We didn't release that one to the press.'

'I'm not the press.'

He turned the Jimmy in at a driveway and hit the remote switch to raise one door on a three-car garage. The house was enormous by Deer Lake standards. And outrageously priced by Deer Lake standards – Ellen had seen the ads in the newspaper. She imagined he was paying a hefty price to rent it, but the money probably meant nothing to him. He had made a sizable fortune turning crime into entertainment. He would do so again with this case, and she would be part of the story.

He had the kind of money it would take to hire Tony Costello, the kind of money it had taken to bail Garrett Wright out of jail.

And she had wanted to trust him.

Without a word to Brooks, she left him in the gourmet kitchen and walked through the living room to the wall of glass that looked out on the frozen countryside. She could hear him pouring drinks, then, nearer, starting a fire in the stone fireplace. When he came to stand beside her, he had shed his parka.

'Whiskey and soda,' he said, handing her a paper cup.

He set his on the ledge and leaned his shoulder against the window frame. He had turned no lights on in the room, letting the fire and moonlight provide all they needed. Darkness seemed to bring out the moods in him. The Cheshire-cat grin and lazy, good ol' boy manner came off like a mask.

'I have a son,' he said without preamble.

He didn't look at Ellen to catch her reaction, concentrating his effort on controlling his own. He took a swallow of his whiskey and dug a cigarette out of his shirt pocket as the liquor slid like molten gold into his belly.

'The punch line is that I didn't know it, and he *doesn't* know it.' He lit the cigarette, took a deep pull on it, and blew the smoke up at the moon. 'He's eight. Just like Josh. His mother – my ex-wife – took him away from me before I even knew he existed. It's a hell of a strange thing, finding out after the fact that a part of you has been missing for the better part of a decade.'

'I take it she was pregnant when she left you,' Ellen said quietly.

'I figured that much out during the divorce war, but I never dreamed it was mine.' He gave a bitter half laugh. 'I was chasing ambulances back then, working like a dog, miserable as hell. Christine and I . . . well, it was pretty much over bar the shouting. She found herself a lawyer higher up on the food chain, a drone, the kind of guy who only wants a partnership and a new BMW every year. . . . I just assumed the baby was his. I didn't think she could have hated me so much. I was wrong.'

It surprised him, how close to the surface the sadness was. Must have been the whiskey – historically, it brought out the latent despondency in Brooks men. Uncle Hooter came to mind, sitting on the veranda on a warm summer night, sobbing at the memory of a dog he had lost as a boy.

As he let the silence drag on, Ellen watched his face, naked in the moonlight, battered and beard-shadowed, tight with a kind of pain that had nothing to do with his physical wounds.

'How did you find out?'

The tip of his cigarette glowed red as he inhaled. An odd dot of color among the shades of gray. 'Her grandfather lived in Eudora. She never came to visit, but they came back when he died. The funeral was ten days ago. I suppose she didn't think I'd be decent enough to pay my respects, but there I was, and there she was with her balding senior-partner husband . . . and my son.' He smiled in a way that made her heart ache. 'Damned if he isn't the spittin' image . . .'

'Did you ask her?'

'She said to me, "Carter Talcott is the only father he's ever known. He's a happy little boy. We have a nice life. Don't ruin that for him, Jay."' His chin quivered a little. He shook his head. 'Christ, what did she think I would do? Tell an eight-year-old boy right there the man he's called Daddy his whole life isn't? That I was such a bastard his mama saw fit to keep him a secret from me all these years? God.'

He took a last drag on his cigarette and carefully crushed the butt out against the cold windowpane.

'What did you do?'

'I came here,' he said simply. 'I'd been watching the case on the news, in the papers and all. I flew to Minneapolis that very night. Ran away. Came to see what real suffering was all about. Try to make some kind of sense of it, get some perspective.

684

'You know, my son is alive and – and he lives with people who love him. And I didn't even know I was missing him, so –' His Adam's apple bobbed in his throat as he broke off and swallowed. 'It's not like the Kirkwoods or the Hollomans, not like having him stolen by some maniac and taken to God-knows-what fate. It's not like Mitch Holt, who had his boy gunned down by some junkie. I don't have any call to complain just because I won't be the one taking my son to Little League.'

But he did, Ellen thought. He had every reason to hurt. That his tragedy wasn't on the same scale as the Kirkwoods' didn't make it any less a tragedy. And yet she could see him trying to grasp that line of reasoning, trying to minimize the pain. She caught a glimpse of vulnerability she would never have suspected lay beneath the layers of charm and cynicism. And she had a feeling it came as much of a surprise to him. Out of the blue. Blindsiding him. Sending him scrambling for familiar ground.

'You won't try to work something out?' she asked. 'Some kind of joint custody? Recognition as the boy's biological father, at the very least?'

He shook his head. 'He's happy. He's got a nice, normal life. What kind of son of a bitch would I be to come barging in and turn that all upside down?'

'But if you're his father –'

'Carter Talcott is his father. Me, I just provided the raw materials.'

He tossed back the last of his drink, crushed the cup in his hand, and turned to face her, his expression colder, tougher as he wrestled to regain control. 'I'm not looking for advice or sympathy,' he said tersely. 'You wanted to know why I came here, why I picked this story. There it is. It doesn't have a damn thing to do with Anthony Costello. I couldn't give a shit about the money I'll make. I came here to lose myself in someone else's misery.

'If you want to think I'm a bastard, go right ahead, because I surely am. Any number of people will gladly tell you so. I just want you to hate me for the right reasons, that's all. If I'm going to stand accused of something, I'd rather it be a sin I've actually committed.'

He walked away from her, across the room, tossed the empty cup into the fireplace and watched the flames swallow it up.

'Finish your drink,' he growled without looking up. 'I'll take you home.'

Ellen left the cup on the window ledge beside his crushed-out cigarette and moved slowly toward him. The house was cold, despite the fire, a kind of cold she associated with emptiness, with loneliness. Leaning back against the stone beside the fireplace, she took in the furnishings of his 'home' office machines and lawn chairs, an army cot and a thick down sleeping bag. A transient's home.

'I don't hate you,' she whispered. 'I hate this case. What it's doing to this town. What it's doing to me. It's reminded me of things I'd rather not believe about human nature – my own included.'

'You? But you're the heroine of the story.'

'No. I'm just doing my job, a job I walked away from two years ago because I couldn't stand what it was turning me into. Being a cynic wears you down, burns you out. I didn't want to stop caring about the people who needed justice. I thought if I came here, it wouldn't take so much out of me, that there'd be something left over for me. And now . . .'

'And now you have Garrett Wright and Tony Costello and a dead lawyer and a missing boy . . . and me.'

From some reserve she didn't know she had, she found a smile to match his. 'And you. Well, maybe you're not all bad. You're a diversion, at least,' she teased. 'Although I can ill afford to be diverted.'

'A diversion?' He tried the word on his tongue like a piece of strange fruit. The old devilish sparkle rekindled in his eyes. 'Mercy, Ms North, you make me feel like a gigolo.'

'You've been called worse things.'

'By you, no doubt.'

'No doubt.'

She hadn't realized he was so close, close enough to raise his hand and touch her cheek. Close enough to draw her to him with just a look, with just the longing in his pale eyes. He leaned down and kissed her, his lips warm and tasting of whiskey.

'My God, I want you, Ellen,' he whispered.

'I can't. The case −'

'This has nothing to do with the case.' Sliding a hand into her hair, he undid the clip that held it back. It fell free around her shoulders.

'This is just us,' he murmured, pressing a kiss to her temple. 'It's just . . . I need . . . to touch you. Let me touch you, Ellen.'

His vulnerability touched her. The yearning in his smoky voice touched her. The attraction that had sparked inside her from the first flared up as hot and bright as the flames of the fire. He was nothing she had been looking for. She wasn't a woman given to fits of passion. She didn't lower her guard. But even as his lips brushed her cheek, she could feel logic slipping away.

She made one last, halfhearted reach for it, drawing a breath for the voice of reason. Jay seemed to sense the words before she could form them. He touched a forefinger to her lips.

'Don't think,' he whispered. 'Not tonight. Please.'

Please. They could have this night, cross this line. There would be no going back. There would likely be regrets, but those were in the gray mists of the future, and they didn't outweigh the need to connect, to touch, to shut out the rest of the world for a few hours.

Ellen closed her eyes as he framed her face in his hands and kissed her again, deeper, slower. She let her mouth open beneath the pressure of his, allowed him access, shivered as he took it. He drew her away from the wall. Her coat fell to the floor. She slid her hands up the front of his shirt and brought them back down, parting the buttons from their moorings. Impatient for the feel of her hands on his skin, he slipped the shirt off and tossed it aside, pulled his dark T-shirt off over his head and flung it away. The firelight played over the ridges and planes of muscle in his chest. His shoulders were broad, in the way of a man who did physical work.

Ellen touched her fingertips to his belly, felt the muscles quiver beneath the tight bandage that bound his ribs.

'Will this be all right?' she asked. 'You won't hurt –?'

'That's not where I hurt,' he whispered. Curling his fingers around her wrist, he raised her hand and pressed it over his heart.

The honesty of the gesture surprised her. She spread her fingers and felt his heartbeat. He was just a man and he hurt and he wanted this time with her to escape that pain. She hurt in her own way, for her own reasons. She wanted the same escape. It was as simple and as complicated as that.

Leaning into him, she pressed a kiss where her hand had rested. Then Jay's mouth was on hers again, hotter, hungrier.

They sank to their knees together. His fingers stumbled down the line of buttons on her blouse. He pushed the blouse and her cardigan off her shoulders without completing the task, the need to see her, to taste her, too urgent.

She hadn't bothered with a bra. Her breasts were there for the taking, the color of cream, the texture of silk, a size that filled his palms perfectly. He cupped them together, rubbing his thumbs across the rosy buds at their center, the need snapping inside him like a whip as they hardened beneath his touch. Bending her back over his arm, he lowered his head to take one tightened peak between his lips.

The sensation was electric. A gasp caught in Ellen's throat. She clutched at his shoulders, then his head, raking her fingers through his short hair, pulling him tighter against her. The need for this act, for this man, burned within, wild, hot, too intense. She had never known what it was to let go of her self-control completely, but she felt it sliding away from her now. The feeling was terrifying and exhilarating at once.

He lifted his head and looked at her, his lower lip slick and shining, the pupils of his eyes huge, ringed with neon blue. He looked uncivilized, as if the same fire in her had seared away the thin veneer of manners he wore in public, revealing what she had sensed all along was at the core of him – something dangerous, untamed, raw.

He moved away from her for a moment, and the sudden absence of his body heat left her feeling cold. She pulled her blouse together over her breasts as she watched him snatch the thick down sleeping bag from the cot and spread it open in front of the fireplace. Then he offered her his hand.

She stood, passive, as he undressed her. He freed her arms from the blouse and sweater, caressing her shoulders, her back, her belly. He hooked his thumbs in the waistband of the leggings she wore and drew them slowly down her hips, kneeling at her feet to remove them. All thoughts of being cold vaporized as he reached up and inched her silk panties down, following their descent with his mouth.

He pressed a hot, openmouthed kiss to the soft spot below her navel as he slid his hands around to cup her buttocks, then dragged the kiss lower to the tender area just above the delta of dark-blond curls, then lower.

Ellen gasped at the touch of his lips, at the bold probing of his tongue. She tried to step back, but he held her easily, his fingers stroking, kneading, pulling her closer, tilting her hips into the shocking intimacy of his kiss. The intensity of the pleasure stunned her, scared her, swept her toward a towering precipice – and left her hanging there.

An involuntary whimper of frustration escaped her as Jay pulled her down to the floor with him and pulled her hard against him. He shared the taste of her own desire with her. She ran her hands along the taut muscles of his back, his arms, feeling his strength. His urgency seemed to feed her own.

When he rose on his knees to unfasten his trousers, she rose with him, pushed his hands away from his belt and unbuckled it herself. Her fingers trembled as she unbuttoned his khakis and eased the zipper down. She touched him through the fine silk of his boxers, savored the feel of his hardness beneath the whisper softness of the fabric.

Jay tolerated her delicate teasing with gritted teeth, holding on to his control until he could stand it no longer. He wanted her, needed more than the tentative feather touches she was giving him.

'Jesus, Ellen, touch me,' he rasped, closing her hand around his shaft, guiding it slowly up and down the length of him. 'Feel what you do to me . . . how much I want you.'

A sense of feminine power swelling inside her, Ellen followed his commands, savoring the feel of him in her hand. Hot, hard, thick, pulsing. She traced her fingertips over the tip of him and found a spot that made him suck his breath in through his teeth. With his hand still curved over hers, she reached down and cupped him, and a shudder rippled through his whole body.

He drew away just long enough to shuck his pants and fish a condom out of his wallet. He came back to her ready, eager, the muscles in his arms trembling as he braced himself over her.

She arched up to meet him. Her eyes drifted shut as he entered her. Her body tightened around him like a fist.

'Sweet heaven,' he groaned, fighting the instinctive urge to possess, to bury himself in a single stroke. 'Relax for me, sweetheart,' he whispered, slowly drawing her leg up along his thigh.

He slid a hand beneath her hip and lifted her into him, allowing himself to sink deeper, closer to oblivion. She caught her breath, then let go a sigh of pure sensual pleasure. Slowly, erotically, they moved together, without words, the glow of the fire gilding their bodies.

Ellen let go of the self-restraint that was so much a part of her, shivering inside at the idea of her own vulnerability.

Jay felt as if his soul were just an inch from hers, straining to connect in a way that was primal, more than physical, deeper than anything he'd known in a long time. More than he'd bargained for in coming to this place. He had meant to lose himself, now he wanted nothing more than to hold on to this moment, this night, this woman. The idea scared the hell out of him.

Then they were both beyond thought. There was only need and urgency, a rush to an explosion of bliss.

Ellen cried out as her climax came in wave upon wave. She held Jay tight as he came just after her. Even as the tension began to ease out of his body, she held him, suddenly afraid of what she would feel when she let go – alone.

Odd, when she had always felt comfortable with herself, self-sufficient, self-reliant, capable of sharing a relationship or going her own way. She had never defined herself in relation to her status with a man. It was the case, she supposed. She had been feeling the weight of it pressing down on her like a pile of stones. For just a while she had felt the burden lift. For the time she could lie here next to Brooks with his arms around her, she felt . . . safe.

Safe. With a man she barely knew and barely trusted.

At 4:06 A.M. an explosion rocked Dinkytown. The blast shattered windows up and down one block, including all the windows in the Pla-Mor Ballroom. At 4:08 Alvin Underbakke called 911 to report the incident and request the fire department come and put out the blaze that was engulfing a big white Cadillac across the street from his house.

27

'Where were you at four this morning?' Mitch asked, his hands braced on the back of the chair he should have been sitting in.

Tyrell Mann met his gaze with arrogance. 'Gettin' my beauty z's. Where'd you want me to be, Chief? What you tryin' to pin on my black ass?'

'Let's get something straight here, Tyrell,' he said. 'I don't give a shit what color your ass is, or any other part of you, and, frankly, I'm about ready to take that chip off your shoulder and put it where the sun don't shine. All I care about here is getting a straight answer. Where were you?'

'Like I said – asleep. We went to the party for the Doc, then crashed.'

'At the hostel on campus?'

'Whatever.'

Mitch straightened away from the chair and advanced toward him.

'Yeah, at the hostel,' Tyrell gave in. 'Why?'

'Someone blew up Ms North's car this morning.'

A nasty smile split Tyrell's features. 'Was the bitch in it?'

Mitch leaned down into his face. 'You know, Tyrell, it's that attitude that's going to land your ass in jail for the rest of your life one of these days. I thought you had to have some brains to get into the Cowboys.'

'I got brains enough to know I can have a lawyer here if I want one.'

'Why would you need a lawyer, Tyrell? You're not under arrest. Should you be?'

'Fuck you, Holt.'

Ellen watched the exchange from the hall, where a one-way mirror gave a thirty-inch view of the show. The chances of one Cowboy giving up another were nil. The chances of their being tripped up in their story was slim. No one was going to get anything out of Tyrell. Down the hall Agent Wilhelm and J. R. Andersen were going through the same song and dance. Andersen played innocent, false concern oozing out of him like sap.

If one of the Cowboys had torched the Cadillac, it was going to take an eyewitness to finger him, and people in Deer Lake were in their beds at four o'clock on a Sunday morning. No one had seen anything. No one had seen Tyrell Mann or J. R. Andersen or Speed Dawkins or Todd Childs or anyone else.

690

They were wasting their time. Again. Ellen wondered if Garrett Wright was home right now browsing the Sunday *Star Tribune*, smiling to himself.

She checked her watch and shook her head. They were due at the psychiatrist's at four. She needed to call Cameron to let him know to pick her up at the law-enforcement center. She wasn't looking forward to the hour-long drive. Cameron would no doubt have as many questions for her as the reporters who were stationed outside the building, waiting.

News of the car fire had come to her at Jay's house via her beeper. He had driven her to the scene, raising a few eyebrows among the cops hanging around. Luckily, by then the reporters had already come and gone. Unluckily, they had gone in search of her. Rumor that the charred wreck might have been hers had sent them off in full cry. By the time they found her, they were foaming at the mouth, rabid for answers. She offered them none. Brooks shucked off their interest in him with the explanation that the explosion had damn near rolled him out of bed.

That the only explosion either of them had paid any attention to was of a sexual nature was nobody's damn business, but the reporters would make it their business, and Ellen knew it. She had watched it happen to Mitch and Megan. And if they chose to do so with her and Brooks, how long would it be before they jumped onto the fact that Costello and Brooks were fellow Purdue alums or that Brooks had been seen slapping shoulders with Costello at the benefit? The media had the power to turn a trial into a circus, complete with sideshows. She didn't want to see that happen for the sake of Hannah and Josh. Or for her own sake, for that matter.

She pushed through the door into the squad room and headed for an empty desk. Christopher Priest rose from the chair where he had been left waiting, fury rouging his pale cheeks.

'This is an outrage, Ms North. How much longer are the boys going to be interrogated without the benefit of counsel?'

'They aren't being interrogated, Professor. They're being questioned.'

'I've called an attorney.'

'You have that right.'

'I've told you the boys didn't have anything to do with this. They were at the hostel. I checked on them.'

'So you said. At about four A.M. Quite a coincidence.'

His glare took on a sharpness Ellen felt like the blade of a razor, though he didn't raise his voice a decibel. 'I resent the implication. First you take me to task for not supervising them closely enough. Now you call me a liar when I *do* check up on them.'

'I didn't call you a liar, Professor,' she said calmly. 'I said it was an extraordinary coincidence. Just like Tyrell and Andersen and Dawkins being seen in the vicinity of my car last night, then the car's being disabled and subsequently blown to kingdom come.'

'They're easy scapegoats,' Priest began.

'No. Nothing about any of this is easy. I know you've got a vested interest in their innocence, Professor, but somebody has to be guilty, and it just might be your boys.' She picked up the telephone receiver but pressed the plunger down with her finger, eyeing Priest curiously. 'As long as we're standing here, Professor, can you tell me if you were with anyone last Saturday afternoon, after your lunch with your friend from Gustavus?'

The fury in his eyes was the strongest emotion she'd seen in him, yet he contained it.

'You're making enemies, Ms North,' he said quietly. 'You'll wish you hadn't.'

The Taker had warned him this would happen. Josh sat in the cushy blue chair in Dr Freeman's office, staring past her to the fish tank that was stuck into the wall. He had been told someone would try to get inside his mind and open all the doors. He had been told never to let that happen. He knew how to do that. It was stupid simple. He imagined his body as just a shell and drew his Self inward, like a ghost, into his mind, where he shut the doors and windows tight.

It didn't make him happy to do this. At first he had thought of this place in his mind as a special safe place, but he didn't like all the things the Taker had put there. They made him sad. They scared him. They made his tummy feel weird. But he had been warned and he was afraid to disobey. Too many bad things had happened already.

He didn't like the way any of the grown-ups around him were acting. It had been a relief to come to Dr Freeman's today. She was a pretty lady with dark-brown skin and a kind smile. She usually just talked to him, real easy-like. She asked him questions, but not the same way the cops had asked him questions. She never got that tone in her voice as if she wanted to shake him, or that tone that made him think she was almost afraid of him. She never seemed to mind when he didn't answer her. But then today she started talking about relaxing and asking him if he had ever played like he was hypnotized.

Bingo.

She wanted to hypnotize him. Just another trick to try to get him to say the things the Taker had warned him not to.

Josh gave Dr Freeman a look of huge disappointment, got up from the chair, and went to stare at the fish, trapped inside that tank the same way he had to stay trapped inside his mind.

Watching on the other side of a one-way mirror, Hannah pressed ice-cold hands to her cheeks and willed herself not to cry. Mitch gave her shoulder a sympathetic squeeze. Agent Wilhelm blew out a sigh of frustration. Ellen North exchanged looks with Cameron Reed.

'It's too soon, I suppose,' Ellen said.

Wilhelm grunted. 'It might be too late for Dustin Holloman.'

Rage twisted inside Hannah. It wrenched her out of Mitch's grasp and launched her at the BCA agent.

'Don't you dare blame Josh!' she snarled, hitting him before Mitch could pull her back. 'He's just a little boy! It's not his fault you can't do your job! It's not his fault the world is crawling with scum like Garrett Wright!'

Hannah clawed Mitch's arm to pry it away from her, the fury burning inside her. It terrified her, but she couldn't begin to suppress it. It was like acid in her chest, like blood pumping from an artery that had been severed.

'Let me go!' she shouted.

Ellen stepped forward, putting herself in front of Wilhelm. 'Hannah, please calm down,' she said quietly. 'We don't blame Josh –'

'I'm taking him home,' Hannah declared.

The decision was made without the usual mental weighing of pros and cons. It blurted out of her, this voice of instinct, now that the layers of education, domestication, socialization, had been slashed and torn apart.

She no longer cared what anyone thought. She knew she no longer bore any resemblance to the Woman of the Year image everyone in town had of her, and she didn't give a damn. All she cared about now was Josh, protecting him, fighting to get him the justice he deserved, fighting to protect him.

'I'm taking my son home,' she said again, looking over her shoulder at Mitch, who had brought them up in his Explorer.

'I'm sorry it didn't work out, Hannah, but we had to give it a try – for Josh's sake as well as our own.'

'No,' she murmured as his hold on her arm relaxed and she stepped away from him. 'None of this has been for Josh's benefit. Don't you realize that, Mitch? Nothing that happens now can change what Garrett Wright did to him or to our family. Nothing. Ever. The only thing we can hope for is revenge.'

She walked out of the room, heading toward Dr Freeman's office. At the door, she straightened her burgundy sweater and pushed her hair back over her shoulder. Then she knocked once and let herself in.

'Josh, we're going home,' she announced, holding out her hand to him.

Mitch shot a glare at Wilhelm, who stood frowning, rubbing the sore spot in the hollow of his shoulder.

'Are you taking sensitivity training from Steiger in your spare time?'

'We're *all* stressed out,' Wilhelm grumbled.

Ellen turned back to their window on the psychiatrist's office and watched through the smoky glass as Hannah knelt down to gather her son in her arms.

'Who can blame her?' she murmured to Cameron. 'She's right. We

693

didn't want this for Josh's sake; we wanted it to save our own hides. Sometimes I hate this job.'

'For all we know, Wright beat us to this hypnosis thing,' he said. 'The man's a psychology professor, specializing in learning and perception. He might have wrung this kid's mind out like a sponge and put in whatever he wanted.'

'There's a cheery thought,' Ellen mumbled. 'Think Dr Freeman would give us a group rate?'

The session over, Dr Freeman let herself into the room on their side of the glass. She offered no apologies and spared them none of her own feelings. She had felt it was too soon to try to pry into Josh's memories, and she had been right. He didn't trust her yet, and after this it would probably be some time before he would.

Mitch ushered Hannah and Josh out to his truck. Wilhelm climbed into his car alone and headed across town toward St Paul and a meeting with Bruce DePalma, his special agent in charge. Ellen crossed the parking lot with Cameron.

'Think we should check my car for bombs before we get in?' he asked, only half teasing.

'It wasn't a bomb. It was just a flaming rag stuffed into the gas tank.'

'Just.'

The end result was the same. The Cadillac was trashed. Poor Manley had been stunned, walking around and around the burned-out hulk – although he had perked up when the press had turned their attention on him, the prospect of more free advertising offsetting his grief. He had even gone so far as to offer Ellen another loaner – on camera. She had declined, saying instead that she would take her own car back as soon as his people could spray some primer over the damage to the driver's door.

The worst thing was not knowing whether she was a target of Wright's supporters or Wright's accomplice. Or both. And aside from scaring the shit out of her, whoever was responsible had managed to further disrupt her life and add to the already overwhelming burden of the case.

She had planned to visit her parents after the session with Dr Freeman. They lived just blocks away from Freeman's office, had called twice in the past week because they were concerned about her. But she had called them and canceled, not wanting to complicate Cameron's evening, and so he turned south on France Avenue and headed toward the freeway.

Maybe it was just as well, Ellen mused as they passed shopping centers and intersections that gave glimpses of quiet suburban neighborhoods. On the surface, a visit seemed to offer what she needed – support and sympathy. But what she was feeling couldn't be cured by going home. Just as it hadn't been cured by leaving the Cities two years ago – only put off for a time.

She fought it now as it rose to the surface like oil. The fear that what she had walked away from when she had left the Hennepin County system wasn't just politics or disillusionment, but the knowledge of a world and a system in decay, and the knowledge that she was as much a part of the problem as she was disgusted by it.

She thought of the many rape victims whose cases she had prosecuted over the years, the ordeal the system put them through, making them relive the crime over and over during the investigation and trial. It was no different now with Josh. He would be victimized all over again in the name of justice, and again in the name of therapy. His life had been violated, and he and his mother would be put through hell by the people who were supposed to protect them and help them in order to get a conviction. For the first time in two years she felt jaded and old in a way that had nothing to do with her upcoming birthday.

The feeling nagged her as they left the suburbs behind and the view softened to the rumpled white blankets of farm fields and valleys shaded gray with naked woods. And as they neared Deer Lake, another eerie restlessness crept in as she looked off at the countryside – the idea that their nemesis was out there somewhere right now, that if they just turned down the right road, they might drive night past the house where Dustin Holloman was waiting to be rescued.

Cameron took the exit at the Big Steer truck stop and rolled down the frontage road past Dealin' Swede's A-1 Auto and Manley's two biggest dealerships, where yellow ribbons had been tied to every car on the lots and the showroom windows had been painted with the slogan 'Bring Dustin Home.' Even the giant inflatable blue gorilla that hovered above the roof of the Pontiac place had been adorned with a yellow ribbon, fluttering gaily around its neck.

Driving through the streets of town, Ellen saw the same symbols over and over. The ribbons on the front doors meant to show support and perhaps to ward off the evil. The posters taped to store windows. The new banner the town council had had hoisted across Main Street – 'Protect our Children!'

The plea struck Ellen as personal. The citizenry turned instantly to the police they otherwise seldom thought about, expecting the crime to be solved, regardless of the lack of clues. They turned to the court system they likely knew nothing about, calling for justice at all costs. The pressure of their silent demands settled on her shoulders, turning the muscles to rock.

'Did you want to go back to the office?' Cameron asked. 'We could try to contact some more of Wright's old chums.'

'I'll pass for once,' Ellen said. 'I think we've suffered enough for one day. All I want to do is get some sleep.'

'Yeah, I don't suppose you got much last night.'

You don't know the half of it.

It seemed impossible that she had spent the night with Brooks. It seemed impossible that she had let her guard down that much. And with Jay Butler Brooks, of all men. But they had reached out to each other . . . and it had been incredible.

And it was incredibly complicated.

'Apparently, Manley thinks you're cursed,' Cameron said, pulling into Ellen's driveway beside the Bonneville. The driver's door wore a big splotch of gray primer where the word 'BITCH' had been.

'Can you blame him? Frankly, *I* was afraid to have my car at his garage. I don't want to be responsible for his business going up in flames.'

'*You're* not responsible,' Cameron reminded her. 'You're the victim.'

'Be that as it may, I'm dangerous to know.'

'Do you want me to come in with you?'

'No.' She nodded toward the gray sedan parked at the curb. 'Mitch gave me a guard. I'll be fine. Thanks for the ride.'

'Try to stay out of trouble for a few hours,' he said, offering her a gentle version of his teasing grin.

'I'm going to bed early. How much trouble could I get into?'

Visions of Jay's pirate smile rose in her memory as she drove the Bonneville into the garage.

'God, Ellen,' she mumbled as she hefted her briefcase out of the car. 'Of all the lousy times to develop a libido.'

'You won't hear me complaining.'

She whirled around. Brooks came out of the shadows of the garage. He hadn't bothered to shave, apparently hadn't bothered to run more than his fingers through his hair.

'Dammit!' Ellen complained. 'I'm not going to have to worry about Wright's accomplice getting me. You'll give me a heart attack first! What the hell are you doing in here?'

'I had my doubts about your surveillance team. Decided to test them for myself.' He reached out and took her briefcase from her. 'They failed.'

'I can see that. How did you get in? Everything was locked.'

He pulled a credit card from his coat pocket and held it up. 'Don't leave home without it. I parked on the next block, cut through the alley, hopped your fence —'

'And Harry?'

'Greeted me with tail wagging. He's not exactly Cujo.' He nodded toward the door that led directly from the garage to the backyard. 'You need a dead bolt there. I jimmied the lock with the credit card. Any two-bit burglar could do it.'

'There's a comforting thought.'

'Look on the bright side, sugar,' he said, following her into the house. 'At least I was the one to show you your security shortcomings. The only thing I'm after is some wild, hot sex.'

'Oh, is that all?'

'You weren't so blasé last night.' Wicked mischief lit his eyes as he planted a hand on either side of her and trapped her with her back against the wall. 'As I recall, you said something more along the lines of *all that, Jay?*'

'I was probably referring to the size of your ego.'

His grin deepened. 'You're blushing, counselor.'

'It's the sudden warmth.'

'Hear! Hear!'

He brushed his mouth across hers, his lips cold, his tongue warm, his gaze holding hers. Ellen's body responded to his as if they had spent years together instead of just a night. It was a frightening thought – that they could be so in tune, that she could be so easily won over, that her body could so eagerly shut out her mind.

She turned her face away. 'I need to let Harry in.'

She brought the dog in and gave him his supper. She could feel Jay watching her as she hung up her coat and turned up the thermostat. The quality of his gaze unnerved her – the intensity of it, the sense that he wasn't just watching her but observing her, studying her.

She drew a deep breath as she faced him. He had turned the fireplace on and stood with his back to it. In the deep shadows of the room he looked like the kind of man no sane person would cross paths with. In another time, in another place . . . they would never have met. That was the bottom line.

'I've been thinking,' she began, pacing nervously between the coffee table and the wing chair.

'Uh-oh.'

'Last night . . . last night was . . . incredible –'

'But . . .'

'It can't happen again.'

'Because?'

'Because everything. Because of the case. Because of who I am. Because of who you are.'

'Those are all the reasons we're together.'

'I know.' She shook her head. 'It can't work, Jay.'

'It worked pretty damn good last night,' he said, moving toward her. Ellen held her ground. 'You know what I mean. I've got priorities.'

'And I'm not one of them.'

'Would you want to be? You've got priorities of your own. I doubt I'm one of them.'

'Not so,' he said. 'I believe I made my interest in you clear from the first.'

'Your interest in me as a player,' Ellen clarified.

'You still don't trust me,' he charged.

'You know the position I'm in,' she said, stepping around the heart of the issue. 'You were an attorney, you should know better than to take it personally.'

'That's a little hard to do, all things considered,' he said with a sarcastic laugh. 'I thought we were past the cover-your-ass stage. You know, I've already seen yours from some very intimate angles.'

'Thank you for pointing that out,' Ellen said sharply, her temper fraying down to the nub. 'Would you care to see it again so you can describe it accurately in chapter nineteen?'

'Jesus Christ, you are so –' He broke off, clamping his teeth down on his temper, reining back the wrong words before they could make a bad situation worse. 'Dammit, Ellen, don't you know I wouldn't do anything to hurt you?'

'No, I don't know!' she shot back. 'I know you're the one who keeps warning me away and then pulling me back until I feel like a paddle ball. I know your stated purpose in coming to Deer Lake, and I've made it very clear that I hate it. I know you went to law school with Tony Costello, but you claim you don't know him. You pretend to be my friend, then get pissed off when I don't let you in on what you know damn well has to be confidential. You walk into my life out of the shadows like a stalker, then tell me you want to keep me safe. What the hell am I supposed to think about you?'

The question lay between them like a gauntlet. Ellen waited for him to take it up. Neither of them moved. He stood with his hands jammed at the waist of his jeans, eyes narrowed, mouth set in an uncompromising line.

'I've known you a week,' she murmured. 'A week. One of the worst damn weeks of my life. What am I supposed to think? That you're a hero? That I should trust you? Do you know what happened the last time I trusted a man who said he was my friend, who said he understood?

'He took that trust and used it, used me to buy himself some power. A rapist walked free.'

'Fitzpatrick?' Jay whispered.

'His victim was counting on my team. Art Fitzpatrick had destroyed her life, and he walked away from that like it was nothing, because I was stupid enough to trust the wrong man. Tuesday I get to stand across a courtroom from that man, knowing he'll stop at nothing to get what he wants.'

'Costello.'

He closed his eyes and muttered the name like a curse. The puzzle pieces he had been playing with for a week fell into place. He had known about the Fitzpatrick debacle, of course, but there had been no direct connection to Costello. Costello hadn't represented Fitzpatrick. But he sure as hell would have courted Fitzpatrick and his counsel for future reference. And he had gone through Ellen to do it. That son of a bitch.

'He'll do whatever he has to do to win a case or anything else he happens to want.'

'And did he want you? Is that what this is really all about, Ellen? Costello fucked you over figuratively and literally?'

The words exchanged in anger Friday night came back to him now. Costello had betrayed Ellen, and Costello was here, Wright's attorney of choice – a choice made after Ellen had been given the case, a choice made after Jay himself had come into the picture. Christ almighty, no wonder she was paranoid.

And what do you do, Brooks? Jerk her around like a goddamn rag doll.

He had played on her emotions, purposely kept her off balance in the attempt to get what he wanted – the story, the inside track . . . the woman; this woman who stood before him with her defenses worn thin, her pride held up like a shield.

'How's that for an extra twist to your plot, Mr Brooks?' she said bitterly. 'Maybe you'd rather write that story. Maybe you'd rather exploit those people, though I don't imagine sexually abusive corporate magnates sell as well as stolen children. You'd rather tap into that deeper vein of emotion, hit us where we'll all bleed. Well, congratulations, Jay, you managed to hit a double bull's-eye with me. You should be so proud.'

'Ellen –' he began, reaching out toward her.

She stepped back from him, holding her hands up in front of her, warning him away. 'I think you should leave. The night is young. You can go home and write this little fight scene down while it's fresh in your mind. You can call Costello up and compare notes about my sexual performance. There's just nothing like firsthand experience when it comes to research, is there?'

'Stop it.'

'Don't give me orders in my own home, Brooks. I'll call that officer in here and have him throw your ass in jail.'

She *would*, of that Jay had little doubt. Ellen didn't make a bluff she wouldn't back up.

'Ellen, I'm sorry,' he offered. 'I'm a son of a bitch. I admit it.'

'And you think that somehow gives you license to go on being a son of a bitch,' Ellen said, shaking her head in disbelief. 'As long as you warn people ahead of time, then they can't very well complain, can they? As long as you tell them up front you came to use them –'

'I didn't come here to use you.'

'Didn't you? Do you even know the difference anymore? You tell me last night didn't have anything to do with the case, but you turn around and use it against me in – in thinly veiled threats.'

'That's not true. You're twisting this out of proportion.'

'Am I? Let's see,' she said with cutting sarcasm. 'Last night we slept together. Today I go to witness the hypnosis of my victim. And here you are tonight, looking for a little pillow talk and getting ugly when I tell you no. What does that add up to?'

'So much bullshit,' he snarled, annoyed with her assessment of his character and angry because in his heart he knew she wasn't far wrong. He *did* want to know what had happened with Josh. He would have tried to get her to talk about it. But he didn't think of going to bed with her as part of the process, a sacrifice in the name of duty.

'God, you're no better than that reporter who was screwing Steiger,' she said with disgust.

'I do not prostitute myself for information.' Jay took a step toward her and then another, backing her up until a wing chair stopped her. 'I've said it before: what happens between us is between us. Maybe we met because of this case, but I sure as hell wasn't thinking about the case last night. I was thinking about how hot you were, how soft, how tight you were around me.'

With every word his voice dropped and softened. He leaned closer and closer until they were nearly belly to belly, thigh to thigh.

'What we had last night wasn't about the case,' he murmured. 'You know damn well it wasn't.'

She almost wished it had been. But there was no call for righteous indignation. She was a grown woman who had made a choice. He hadn't seduced her; he had needed her. And she had wanted him. And a part of her wanted him even now.

'You're a woman, Ellen. You're not this case. You can't just let it swallow you whole. Isn't that what you wanted away from?'

Yes. But where did she draw the line . . . and where did he? Where did the case end and their personal lives begin? Could the two even be separated or were they as hopelessly intertwined as everything else in this web?

'The choice doesn't seem to be mine to make this time,' she said sadly. 'I walked away from it once, but the evil came to me this time, to this place. Costello came here. You. The media. Hannah's turned to me. And Josh. And the people I work with. And the people I work for.' She forced half a smile, half a laugh. 'I'm surrounded.'

'I'm not the enemy, Ellen.'

No. He was one of those mythical creatures – sometimes good, sometimes bad, always shadowed and mysterious, his role unclear until the end of the story.

'You know what I'm dealing with,' she said. 'It's up to me to get justice for these people. This is the toughest case I've faced in my career. And I'm rusty. And it scares the hell out of me that this son of a bitch might just outsmart me and walk. And you – you just show up on my doorstep because you want to have sex.'

'I came over here because I was concerned about you, Ellen,' Jay said stubbornly. 'And I'm not leaving.'

The steel in his tone made her eyes widen. 'Excuse me?'

'Jesus, Ellen, someone blew up your damn car. You've been threatened. You've been singled out for attention from this lunatic and his pals and you've got Barney Fucking Fife parked in front of your house. If I can get in here without his knowing, your nemesis sure as hell can. I'm not leaving. I don't want to see you get hurt.'

He didn't want to see her get hurt, but he would hurt her himself. He would be a villain in one sense or another. He would write about this case, turn it into a diversion to be read and tossed aside and left on airplanes. He would reduce her to a character, and Hannah and Josh, and

700

Mitch and Megan. He would take what he wanted from this and leave. He had given her a part of himself, but he would still leave.

'Point taken,' she said. 'And I appreciate the thought. I'll have that dead bolt installed first thing tomorrow.'

'And tonight?'

'I'll take my chances.'

'No,' he argued. 'A chance is the last thing you're willing to take. It's smarter to walk away, play it safe. You got burned once, why risk it again?'

'I took a big chance last night.'

'And now you regret it.'

'No,' Ellen admitted. 'I just see the wisdom in not taking it again.'

Jay studied her face for a long moment – the honesty, the resolve, the regret for this moment if not for the night they had spent in each other's arms. He might have tried harder to change her mind. He might have seduced her, but then every rotten thought she had about him would have been true, and for the first time in a long time someone else's opinion mattered to him. For the first time in forever he caught himself wanting to be something he wasn't. Noble.

Life had become too damn complicated.

'Please, Jay,' Ellen murmured. 'It's not that I don't want to. I just can't. Not now. I'll have the officer come in and spend the night on the couch. Please go.'

'You'd rather have some fat ol' cop eating doughnuts on your sofa than have me in your bed? Christ.'

'No, but it's for the best.' She handed him his coat and started up the steps for the dining room. 'I wish things could be different, but the case is the case, and I am who I am, and you are who you are . . .'

'And I'm no damn good for you,' he said. 'Well, sugar, that isn't exactly headline news.'

'Maybe after this is all over . . .,' Ellen began, but she stopped herself. What was the point in saying it? They had shared a night and made no promises.

'Say good night, Ellen,' she ordered herself.

'Good night, Ellen,' he echoed, lowering his mouth to hers.

He kissed her slowly, deeply.

'If you decide to take that chance, counselor,' he whispered, 'you know where to find me.'

Then he slipped out the door.

Ellen stood at the storm door until the glass frosted over and the cold chilled the heat of need on her skin. But the heavy sense of yearning, of regret, remained as she took her briefcase to bed.

28

Monday morning brought an article in the *Pioneer Press* about the harassment of the Sci-Fi Cowboys; phone calls from the mayor, two state senators, and three congressmen; and the threat of a lawsuit. Rudy darkened Ellen's office door before her first cup of coffee could turn cold.

'They have no grounds for a lawsuit,' Ellen assured him, rubbing a smudge of fingerprint dust from the gooseneck of her lamp. 'Priest has his nose out of joint because his pets might turn out to be bad boys after all. Mitch had good cause to haul those kids in and question them.'

Rudy had somehow managed to tie his necktie over the top of one collar point. Green and yellow, it looked like an oversize garter snake trying to choke him.

'Ellen, that program has garnered national attention. Do you have any idea of the people who back it?'

People with money. People with clout on the local and state levels. People Rudy had sucked up to, or would, at some point in his career.

'I endorsed it myself.' Stopping by her window, he looked out, as if he expected an angry mob to be clamoring at the steps. He pulled a roll of Tums out of his pants pocket, thumbed off two, and popped them into his mouth.

'It's a fine program,' Ellen said. 'It wouldn't be your fault if it turned out to have some rotten apples in the barrel.'

'We can't have them suing the county attorney's office, for God's sake.'

'They're making noise, that's all.'

'Can't you make a statement of some kind? Placate them.'

Ellen bit down on a rebuke of his cowardice. 'Rudy, I have every reason to believe those kids torched that Cadillac. I will not placate them. And what if it turns out Priest is involved with Wright in the kidnappings?'

'He passed the polygraph. He was in St Peter when O'Malley was attacked —'

'We know Wright is the one who attacked Megan. That doesn't absolve Priest of guilt. He could be making this stink now for the sole purpose of getting us to back off so he can have room to maneuver.'

'Good grief.'

Ellen watched him stroke his hand back over his steel-wool hair. She could all but hear the oily wheels of his mind spinning as he tried to sort the dilemma into an order from which he could somehow benefit.

'Relax,' she said. 'The public will side with Priest. Sig Iverson will side with Priest. You can remain safely neutral. *I'm* the bad guy. You can't lose, Rudy. Unless, of course, Priest turns out to be a kidnapper and the Sci-Fi Cowboys fried that car.'

She almost laughed as his face contorted through a full range of expressions from relief to panic. He couldn't seem to decide which one to settle on.

'You can make the statement,' she said. Stepping up to him, she reached up and tugged his collar free of his tie. ' "No comment regarding ongoing investigations." You have confidence in my abilities – this said with a grave expression that might leave room for doubt. Same old non-committal song and dance. Fred Astaire couldn't do it any better than you, Rudy.'

He scowled at her askance as he tried to catch his reflection in the glass of a framed certificate hanging on the wall. 'You know that smart tongue won't do you any good when you run for office,' he said, snugging the knot in his tie.

'For the millionth time, I have no intention of running for office.'

He listened as well as he ever did.

'Where is Jay Butler Brooks?' he asked testily. 'I thought he'd be in the offices more. I want to sell him on an idea for a book.'

'Your life story?'

'Career of country lawyer,' he said, dead serious. 'I've faced some fascinating cases in my day. Like the time the Warneky brothers tipped a cow onto their hired man. It *seemed* like an accident, but –'

'You know, Rudy,' Ellen said, tapping a finger against her watch, 'I'm sure it's the stuff of a blockbuster, but I've got to be in Grabko's chambers in five minutes. He's ruling on Josh Kirkwood's medical records. I'll update you later.'

She hurried out of the office, pausing by Phoebe's desk only long enough to instruct her to lock up after Rudy. She took a back staircase to avoid reporters and had to squeeze her way around workmen's scaffolding, swearing under her breath as plaster dust rained down on her, dotting her navy-blue blazer like talcum powder. Brushing away the residue, she slipped past the law library and ducked behind a granite column to scope out the situation in the main hall.

Family court was in session. The hall in front of what had been Judge Franken's courtroom was clogged with kids and husbands and wives glaring at one another, county social workers and attorneys, all waiting their turn before the substitute judge the district had sent. Beyond them, milling around Judge Grabko's door and spilling out onto the rotunda balcony, were the esteemed members of the press, waiting to catch first word of Grabko's ruling.

Waiting to catch me, Ellen thought. They were steamed that the *Pioneer Press* had scooped them all on the interview with Christopher Priest, and they would take it out on her.

'I'll run interference if you give me an exclusive.'

Ellen jerked around. Adam Slater had slipped up behind her and stood close enough to touch. Dressed in grunge flannel and a letterman's jacket, he could have easily blended into the family-court crowd. His hair swung down into his eyes as he made a show of licking the tip of his pencil and poising it above his reporter's notebook.

'You just don't give up, do you?'

'It's a common misconception that Generation Xers have no focus. So are you really going after the Sci-Fi Cowboys? They're supposed to be the big success story. Bad boys turned good, snatched from the jaws of sociopathy and trained to use their powers for the good of mankind. That's what everyone believes – notable exception: you.'

'It's a wonderful program,' Ellen said by rote. 'I hope it turns out the boys had nothing to do with the explosion.'

'And the kidnappings?'

'No one ever said they were suspects in the kidnappings.' She shot a nervous glance toward Grabko's door and the crowd in front of it. The natives seemed to be growing restless, and there was no sign of Costello. He had either sneaked in early or was waiting to make his entrance. She was screwed either way. *Should have brought a deputy with me.*

'Routine background checks are being run on all of Dr Wright's close friends and associates,' she said. 'Now, I've got to be in judge's chambers, Mr Slater. I held up my end of the bargain. It's your turn.'

He scribbled a last line in his notebook, then tucked it into an inside coat pocket and slicked his hair back. 'No sweat, Ms North.'

He strutted off toward the family-court crowd, drawing a bead on Quentin Adler. 'Hey, Curly!' he bellowed, thrusting an accusatory finger in Quentin's face. 'You and me gotta have some words, man. You screwed me over!'

Quentin nearly gave himself a whiplash looking to one side and the other for a more likely target than himself. 'Me?' he squeaked, color crawling up his neck.

Slater jabbed him in the sternum with his finger. 'Those charges were, like, *so* bogus!'

His voice rang off the walls, drawing the attention of the bored reporters. He backed Quentin toward them as he ranted on, backed him towards the open area around the balcony, giving Ellen a route along the wall. She took it, head down, hustling toward the side door to Grabko's chambers. By the time anyone caught sight of her, she was able to throw out a handful of 'no comments' and duck into the outer office.

'It's all in the wrist, Mr Costello,' Grabko said, demonstrating his casting move in slow motion.

Costello stood beside him, looking like an ad for *GQ* in a pearl-gray suit that was worth a month of Ellen's salary. His shirt was as white as an angel's wings, his tie perfectly knotted. It was difficult to imagine he and Rudy Stovich belonged to the same species.

'As in so many aspects of life,' Grabko preached, 'success in fly-fishing is a matter of concentration, logic, and grace.'

'And me without my waders,' Ellen muttered, skewering Costello with a look. He gave her a smile that was all too generous.

With great care Grabko set his rod into a carved-walnut wall rack. 'Do you fish, Ellen?'

'Only in the metaphorical sense,' she said, sliding into a chair. 'Catch anything, Tony?' she asked under her breath as he settled into the chair beside her.

'That remains to be seen,' he murmured.

The judge sank down into the pillow softness of his leather chair, straightened his red-striped bow tie, and immediately began to pet his beard, stroking it like a cat. His gaze fell on Ellen with fatherly concern.

'I hear we're lucky to have you among the living, Ellen.'

'I don't believe it was an attempt on my life, Your Honor. Just a warning.'

'Dr Wright was disturbed to hear about it,' Costello said.

'That my car blew up or that I wasn't in it at the time?'

'You'd be surprised at his concern, Ellen.'

'Yes, I would be, seeing as how I have every intention of putting him behind bars for the rest of his life.'

'He's also concerned about the allegations against the Sci-Fi Cowboys. He doesn't want to see the program suffer because of its ties to him.'

'If the program suffers, it's because of the attitudes of the individuals involved,' Ellen said. 'I think Dr Wright and his colleagues may have overestimated a couple of their boys.'

'Do you have any evidence against the young men?' Grabko asked.

'Nothing solid at this point. The police and the BCA are working on it, but they're being spread thin these days. Thanks to your client and his friends,' she said, turning back to Costello.

He shook off the responsibility. 'My client is an innocent man. Our case will speak for itself.'

'Which brings us to the business of the day,' Grabko said. He tapped the cover of a red file folder sitting squarely on his blotter. 'Josh Kirkwood's medical records. I spent a good deal of time looking them over.'

Ellen pulled in a breath and held it.

'Parental child abuse is a horrible crime. One we seldom suspect in a family like the Kirkwoods'. A dangerous oversight on our part. Abuse knows no socioeconomic barriers.'

'Our point, exactly, Your Honor,' Costello said, leaning forward in his chair.

'However . . .' He drew the words out, savoring his moment. 'I found nothing in Josh Kirkwood's records that could be construed as out of the ordinary or as being relevant to the case.'

The breath sighed out of Ellen. 'Just as we expected all along.'

Costello gave a subtle shrug. You win some, you lose some. He had got what he wanted out of the play – media attention, the opportunity to sow the seeds of doubt.

'I suppose I shouldn't be surprised,' Costello said. 'Hannah Garrison is head of the ER at the hospital where Josh has been treated. Well respected, well liked, the kind of woman who might be able to persuade a fellow doctor or nurse to see an incident her way.'

'And convince them to falsify records?' Ellen said. After everything she had seen Hannah put through, she could have throttled Costello for taking his tack. 'Watch where you're stepping, Tony. You're about to put your handmade Italian loafer in a big hot pile.'

'I'm not trying to portray the mother as the villain,' he defended himself. 'The husband is emotionally abusive and manipulative. He coerced her or convinced her.'

'And maybe there's life on Uranus, but your speculation on that subject isn't admissible either,' Ellen said sharply. 'The issue at hand is the medical records. You're dead in the water, Tony. Let's move on.'

'Fine.' He reached into his briefcase and pulled out a document. 'Motion to dismiss.'

'And our argument against dismissal,' Ellen said, handing over Cameron's brief.

Grabko accepted the paperwork with the satisfied glow of a teacher taking extra-credit projects from his favorite students.

'And,' Costello said, pulling another rabbit from his hat, 'in the event we do proceed, motion to suppress the lineup ID.'

Ellen jerked around in her chair, gaping at him. 'What? On what grounds? That was a perfectly good by-the-book lineup!' She turned to Grabko. 'Your Honor, great pains were taken to ensure the fairness of that lineup.'

'You were there, Ellen?'

'No. Mr Stovich oversaw the process personally. But I've spoken with all parties involved.'

Costello handed the motion to Grabko. 'Then you should be aware of the fact that Dr Wright's attorney was barred from the room where Mrs Cooper filled out her written report.'

'Barred?' Ellen said, incredulous. 'I hardly think so. Dennis Enberg was present at the lineup. If he wasn't in the room when Mrs Cooper filled out the paperwork, it was his own choice.'

'That's not the way I hear it.'

'From who?'

'From my client –'

'Oh, there's a reliable source – a psychopathic child stealer.'

'And from Mrs Cooper herself. Her affidavit is attached, Your Honor.'

'I'd like a copy of that, if you don't mind,' Ellen snapped.

Costello permitted himself the tiniest of smiles. 'Of course, Ellen. You *did* specify your office wanted everything in writing and handled through the proper channels. I've sent your copies over via messenger.'

Fury burned in Ellen's cheeks. She glared at him and mouthed *You son of a bitch*. The smugness in his expression made her want to choke, particularly because she knew its origin. He had turned her own trick back on her. In the normal course of events around a rural courthouse, challenges were made over the phone or hashed out in person. Formalities were waived. She had imposed by-the-book standards on Costello to punish him, to slow him down, to irritate him. And here she sat. . . .

'And what kind of messenger did you send? A dog team via Winnipeg?' she said sarcastically. 'I should have been notified about this Friday at the latest.'

Manufacturing a look of abject innocence, Costello directed his explanation at Grabko. 'We weren't able to contact Mrs Cooper until Friday afternoon, Your Honor. With the time constraints –'

'Cheerfully accepted by you, Mr Costello,' Ellen pointed out.

He ignored her. 'We're doing the best we can, Your Honor. And we are thoroughly prepared for the hearing. We hoped you'd be lenient with regards to service of this motion, all things considered.'

The judge tugged at the white spot in his beard, looking grave. 'I can't disregard the motion, considering its gravity. And I do feel the circumstances can be considered good cause to make an exception to the general rule. Ellen, if you feel this upsets the balance, if you feel you need more time . . .'

'No, Your Honor,' she said tightly. 'We're ready. I just don't appreciate being ambushed – especially with something as groundless as this.'

'Why don't we let the judge decide the merits of the motion, Ellen?' Costello suggested in a patronizing tone.

Grabko perched a pair of reading glasses on his nose and turned to the affidavit. 'According to Mrs Cooper, Mr Enberg expressed an interest in coming into the room where she was filling out her report, but one of three officers present in the room turned him away, then followed him out.'

'I don't believe it,' Ellen challenged. 'What officer? Let's get him in here.'

Costello huffed a laugh. 'I'm sure he'll tell us the truth when he sees what's riding on his story. Every cop in town wants to see my client publicly hanged. Mrs Cooper is the only impartial witness to what happened.'

'Dennis Enberg would never have allowed himself to be barred from the room if he had wanted to be present,' Ellen argued.

'He's not here to tell us that, though, is he, Ellen?'

'Yeah, what a lucky stroke for you, Tony,' she said, her words dripping venom. 'Right about now Denny is on a stainless-steel table at Hennepin County Medical Center getting himself sawed in half by a medical examiner.'

'Ellen, please,' Grabko chastised her. 'I'll call the officer in, and I'll speak with Mr Stovich, but as Mr Enberg isn't able to speak for himself on the matter, I have to concur with Mr Costello – Mrs Cooper is the least biased of all involved parties.'

'But, Your Honor, Mrs Cooper never mentioned this when I spoke with her.'

'Did you ask her specifically?'

'I had no reason to ask such a question. We spoke at length about the lineup procedure –'

'And she had no reason to think anything was out of the ordinary,' Costello said. 'She isn't an attorney. She isn't a police officer. She had no way of knowing proper procedure. She trusted the police to conduct themselves properly, and they betrayed that trust.'

'I'm sure that's what you led her to believe,' Ellen sneered.

'That's enough, Ellen.' Grabko set the affidavit aside. 'I'll speak to all parties involved and come to a decision. Is there anything more we need to discuss today?'

Costello lifted his hands. 'Nothing further, Your Honor.'

'No, sir,' Ellen said grudgingly.

'Fine,' Grabko said, straightening the stack of documents. 'I'll see you both here tomorrow morning.'

'You really are a sleaze, Tony,' Ellen muttered as they left Grabko's chambers for the outer office. His secretary had vanished, leaving them alone.

'Why?' Costello pulled up short of the hall door and faced her, standing close enough for confidentiality. 'Because I'm doing my job? Because I don't believe my client is guilty?'

'You don't give a damn if he is. You play this system like a pickup soccer game. Nothing matters except that you win. You trick my witness into doing your dirty work for you. You call Josh Kirkwood's father a child abuser and impugn the reputation of his mother. If you publicly accuse Hannah Garrison of falsifying those medical records, I hope she sues your ass eight ways from Sunday.'

He made a pretense of being hurt. 'That's not a very charitable sentiment toward someone who is genuinely concerned for your safety, Ellen. You could have been killed in that car.'

'Is that your unbiased opinion, or do you know something the rest of us don't?'

'Yes, Ellen, I am not only trying to acquit a guilty monster, I am also in on the conspiracy to kill you. Christ, can't you take anything I say to you at face value?'

'The fact that you have at least two faces complicates the issue.'

708

He shook his head. 'You always took it too personally,' he said almost to himself. 'The job is the job, Ellen. Just because we stand on opposite sides of the courtroom doesn't mean we can't set it aside when we walk out the door.'

'Oh, that's rich coming from you, Tony,' she sneered. 'You're never off the job. As far as you're concerned, there are twenty-four billable hours to a day. No situation, no relationship, is exempt. Don't even try to argue with me on that score, and don't delude yourself into thinking you can win me over. I know just what lengths you'd go to.'

Their past hung between them, dense with complicated facts and feelings and fears that had never been proved true or false.

'Be careful, Ellen,' he said at last. 'While you're busy watching for me to strike, there's a real snake out there.'

'And his name is probably already in your Rolodex.'

'Your imagined accomplice?'

'Technically, I believe I would be correct in calling him *your* accomplice.'

'In your delusions of vengeance.' He buttoned his jacket and tugged it straight, preparing himself for the cameras. 'Nice try, siccing the BCA after me, getting Wilhelm to make noise about a warrant for my phone records. Sadly, it's just another example of how this investigation is being botched – which is what I'll have to point out to the press.'

'Point away, Tony,' Ellen said with a knife-edge smile. 'All the press needs is a suspicion of your involvement and they'll be digging like badgers. Who knows what they might turn up? I know I'll be standing right there to see what crawls out of your lair.'

She jerked the door open and stepped out into the hall, eager for once to upstage him in front of the cameras.

'I don't know how much help I can be to you, Mr Brooks,' Christopher Priest said without apology. His expression was as neutral as his voice, his face the blank oval of a mannequin's.

His office was exactly what Jay had imagined: a claustrophobic little cube crowded with books and file cabinets. A computer monitor on the desk displayed an endless repetition of starbursts. The room was filled with the stuff of academia – textbooks and reference books and student papers – but with none of the personal bric-a-brac that would have given a flavor of the man whose name was on the small placard outside the door. The desk was too neat, the office as devoid of personality as the professor himself.

'Some of my students and I were involved with the volunteer effort to find Josh,' he said, seating himself with prim precision. 'We set up computer stations at the volunteer center and went on-line to disperse and receive information through the various networks. That's the extent of my connection.'

Jay voiced his skepticism. 'That's a bit of an oversimplification, don't you think, Professor? You volunteered to help with the investigation, then one of the cops involved was attacked in your own front yard, then your best friend was arrested . . . You must be feeling like this whole thing is sucking you in like a tar pit.'

'It's been a little overwhelming, yes,' he conceded.

'And Dr Garrison is a friend of yours, right?'

'I know Hannah,' he admitted. 'I admire her. She's an extraordinary woman.'

Jay took in the hint of color that touched the professor's pale cheeks when he spoke of Hannah. 'Man, if I had all that buzzing around me, I'd be feeling downright dizzy. Now the cops are looking for that student – Todd Childs – and looking at the Sci-Fi Cowboys. You must feel almost as if *you're* under attack.'

Priest stared at him like an owl from behind his oversize glasses. 'I had nothing to do with any crime. Neither did the Cowboys.'

'Circumstances suggest otherwise where the boys are concerned.'

'Circumstances aren't always what they seem. The Sci-Fi Cowboys are a very select group of young men, Mr Brooks. Handpicked for their talents and potential.'

'Aren't most of their talents against the law?'

'*Academic* talents,' Priest specified, unamused. 'They are very bright young men who deserve a chance to prove they can be productive members of society.'

'And they're no doubt grateful for the opportunity,' Jay said. 'Giving a kid a gift like that inspires loyalty. Kids with the kind of backgrounds the Cowboys have might express that loyalty in, shall we say, *inappropriate* ways.'

'I stand behind the Cowboys,' Priest said flatly. 'I've said all I'm going to say about the subject to the police and to the press – and to you, Mr Brooks. If you came here hoping for an admission of guilt, there's no point in continuing this conversation.'

'No, no, not at all –'

'I know what you told the police about the encounter with Tyrell and the other two boys Saturday night,' he said in a strangely quiet voice, as if it were a lurid secret.

'I simply told them what happened, Professor. I'm not taking sides.'

'Aren't you?' His thin lips pressed together. 'You're not . . . aligning yourself with Ms North?'

'What would make you think I was?'

'The two of you had words at the benefit. You followed her out.'

And he had been watching from his post beside Garrett Wright's wife. The idea stirred a strange sense of violation.

'Ms North has a philosophical objection to my work,' Jay said with a well-rehearsed sardonic smile. 'She has managed to equate the writing and publishing of true crime with the Romans selling tickets to watch Christians being devoured by lions.'

Priest considered the response. 'An interesting correlation. The readers of your work are, of course, insulated from the immediate horror of the violence, but perhaps the two *do* share a common attraction.'

'Not for me.'

'Hmm, well, it's all in our perception, isn't it?' he said. 'And perception is dependent upon what? You can present the same set of facts and circumstances to five different people, and they may give you five different interpretations – which is why many seasoned courtroom attorneys will tell you there is nothing so unreliable as an eyewitness. The opinions we form are based on individual perceptions, something science has yet to fully understand.

'Fascinating, isn't it?' He gave his head a slight shake, as if humans were simply too much trouble, and cast an affectionate glance at his computer screen. 'The human mind can be infinitely logical and pragmatic, or stubbornly irrational. A hopelessly vacant mind can hold a kernel of brilliance. A brilliant mind can be fatally flawed.'

'Which would you say applies to our kidnapper?'

A slight smile touched the corners of his mouth. 'I wouldn't say. Human behavior is Dr Wright's specialty, not mine.'

'But you were working on a project together, right?'

'We *are* working on a joint project, dealing with, as it happens, learning and perception.'

'You've known each other a long time, you and Dr Wright?'

'We both taught at Penn State.'

'Yeah, but y'all knew each other before that, didn't you?'

'I don't know what you're talking about,' Priest said guardedly.

Jay feigned innocence. 'Well, gee, you know, I was just doing a little digging. Background work and all. Talking to an old colleague of yours from Penn State who mentioned you all grew up in the same town.'

'I grew up in Chicago.'

'Huh, well, you know, I'd read that,' he said, scratching his head. 'Strange thing for a friend to be wrong about, wouldn't you say?'

'Nevertheless,' Priest said impatiently, 'I might have visited Indiana as a boy, but I didn't grow up there.'

'So you *didn't* know Dr Wright?'

'We became friends at Penn State.'

'Good friends. The kind of friends who share things, stick up for each other, help each other out.'

'Is there a point to this line of questioning, Mr Brooks?'

Jay gave a shrug and a smile. 'I'm just trolling, Professor. Looking for background. I never know what I might find or where it might lead me. For instance, you might just up and say you'd do anything for Garrett Wright. Who knows where an answer like that might lead?'

'To a dead end.' Priest rose. 'I'm sorry to cut this short, but I have a class to prepare for, Mr Brooks.'

Jay checked his watch. According to the helpful young lady in the main office, Christopher Priest didn't have another class until evening.

'I guess I'll just have to check that background the hard way,' he said, pushing himself to his feet. 'Thank you for your time, Professor.'

He turned back at the door, catching Priest staring at him with that blank face. 'That student who was in the car accident the night Josh was abducted – was he working on that joint project with you and Dr Wright?'

'Yes, he was.'

'Hmm. I wonder what his perception of that coincidence would be.'

'I'm afraid we'll never know,' Priest said. 'I received word this morning he passed away.'

Jay sensed the news hit him harder than it had the professor. Death – delivered off the cuff, as an afterthought, with no more remorse than was socially required.

He stepped into the hall, his head buzzing. The car accident had set everything in motion; now the student who had been running an errand for Priest was dead. Todd Childs was a student of Wright's and Priest's. Olie Swain, the prime suspect until his jailhouse suicide, had audited classes of both men. Megan O'Malley had suspected Priest. She had been attacked in the yard of Priest's secluded country home.

Christopher Priest seemed as much a part of the story as Garrett Wright, and yet no one had anything on him. He was as clean as Teflon, visible in his efforts, first, to help in the effort to find Josh, and now, in his support of his colleague.

'*We are working on a joint project. . . .*'

He had passed a polygraph.

'*. . . it's all in our perception, isn't it?*'

Priest and Wright went back a long way. It wouldn't have been a stretch to imagine them as partners in more than a school project. A pair of sharp, calculating minds. Wright, handsome and charming; Priest, socially awkward with a crush on Hannah Garrison. Motive had been an elusive creature in this crime from the first. There had been no ransom demand. No one seemed to have it in for Hannah or Paul. The taunting, the planted evidence, suggested it was all about superiority, a game of wits. But taking Josh Kirkwood had also given Christopher Priest a chance to be close to Hannah, a chance to offer his help, to call attention to himself.

And damned if it wouldn't sell books, he thought. The twisted tale of the psychopathic professors. Brilliant minds fatally flawed.

But had Priest had opportunity to take Dustin Holloman, to plant those clues? It seemed unlikely he would take that kind of chance, knowing the police had their eyes on him. And then there was Todd Childs to consider. . . .

He turned down another hall. He could take a look at Wright's office as long as he was here, see if it offered any insights. The cops would already have taken the place apart hunting for evidence, but it was still important for him to have a sense of the places the people he wrote about inhabited. To be able to describe Garrett Wright's perfectly normal office would add to the unsettling idea that anyone could be warped beneath their ordinary facades. That kind of chill brought readers back again and again. Like Romans to the Colosseum.

The door to Wright's office stood slightly ajar. Jay brought himself up short at the sight. His escapade at the Pack Rat was still fresh in his mind – in the form of a dull headache that had nagged him since the accident. He moved cautiously along the wall, determined not to be taken by surprise this time.

Sidling up to the door, he gently eased it open another fraction of an inch, expecting to see Todd Childs.

The room was awash in paper. Books had been torn from their shelves and left on the floor. The place looked as if it had been tossed by goons, and in the middle of the mess stood Karen Wright. She looked utterly lost, fragile, overwhelmed by the state of the place. And he would take advantage of that, bastard that he was.

Not giving himself time to turn noble, Jay rapped his knuckles twice on the door frame and let himself into the office.

'Mrs Wright?'

She jerked around and looked up at him. 'I – I can't find anything,' she said meekly.

'Well, ma'am, it is a hell of a mess,' he said. 'What is it you're looking for?'

'Books. Garrett asked me to pick up some of his books. He'll be angry about this. He likes his office neat and orderly.'

'Do you have any idea who did this?'

'The police. They said they were looking for evidence.'

Looking for evidence and taking a little revenge, Jay reasoned. Garrett Wright stood accused of attacking and savagely beating one of their own. Cops didn't take a thing like that lightly.

'You should have seen our house when they finished,' she murmured as she began to set her husband's desk to rights. 'They even took up floorboards. All for nothing. I told them they wouldn't find anything, but they wouldn't listen to me.'

'They're stubborn that way.'

She picked up a coffee mug that had been knocked to the floor and held it to her chest like a treasured doll. 'You're that writer, aren't you? Garrett told me you're going to do a book about the case. He shouldn't be going to court. It's all a big mistake.'

'Is it?' Jay asked quietly, watching her carefully.

'He wouldn't take Josh.'

Her gaze was like a butterfly, lighting and flying away from point to point, all around the room. She might have been lying, or she might have been afraid. Or she might have been as cracked as Grandma's china, as

Teresa McGuire, the victim-witness coordinator, had suggested to him over coffee and cinnamon rolls at the Scandia House.

'Garrett wouldn't have,' Karen said, shaking her head. 'No. He wouldn't have ... He wouldn't do that to me.'

'Wouldn't do what?' he asked, trying to keep her attention focused on him.

'He doesn't like children,' she mumbled. 'He didn't like *being* a child.'

'Did you know him as a child?'

A thin smile trembled across her mouth, and she wandered off toward one of the gutted bookcases.

Jay moved with her to keep her face in view. 'I heard you helped out at the Kirkwoods' while Josh was missing. You helped take care of the baby.'

Karen might have been Wright's spy – willing or unwitting – filling him in firsthand about the havoc he was wreaking on the lives of Hannah and Paul.

'Lily,' Karen said. This time the smile was fuller, richer. 'She's so precious. I'd give anything for a little sweetheart like her.'

'You don't have any children of your own?'

The smile fell. 'Garrett and I can't have children.'

'I'm sorry,' he said automatically. 'That was good of you to help the Kirkwoods. Was that your idea?'

'Oh, I didn't mind at all. Hannah and Paul are friends.'

She used the present tense as if it were still true, as if she had no grasp of the magnitude of the charges against her husband. As if by saying it was all a mistake, everyone would accept her word and they would all continue their lives as if nothing had happened.

She set the coffee mug aside, picked several books up off the floor, and slid them into place in the bookcase.

'Garrett doesn't like messes,' she said with an odd light of amusement in her eyes.

'Well, he seems to have got himself smack in the middle of a big one.'

Karen Wright shook her head. 'Oh, no,' she said. 'It's all just a big mistake.'

29

'Barred from the room!' Mitch exploded. 'Bullshit!'

Cameron winced. Phoebe cowered. Ellen looked him in the eye.

'Were you present in the room when she filled out her statement?'

He raked a hand back through his hair as if trying to scratch loose a memory. 'Not right away. Stovich was bending my ear for a couple of minutes. When I did step into the room, no one said a goddamn thing to me. Everything was fine. If someone had tried to stop Dennis from going in, he would have squealed like a stuck pig.'

'That's what I said,' Ellen complained. 'And Grabko should know it, too. Costello has him dazzled. I've never seen so much preening and posturing in my life. While you were at the autopsy, Grabko was calling your officers in this afternoon to get their take on it, but my gut tells me we've already lost the round.'

'Fuck me,' Mitch grumbled. 'After all the trouble we went to, putting that lineup together. Jesus Christ.' He pulled in a deep breath and huffed it out. 'How bad does this hurt us?'

Ellen considered for a moment, turning her pencil over and over in her hands. 'For a hearing in front of a judge, not a lot. But I wanted Ruth Cooper on the stand in front of a jury,' she admitted. 'Costello would have taken apart the lineup ID because Wright was too bundled up for a dead-on no-doubt *that's him*. But her testimony combined with the voice ID would have made an impact.'

'Can you salvage anything?'

'She can testify that she saw a man on Ryan's Bay that morning, that he came to her house, that he spoke to her. Then Costello is going to get up on cross and ask her if that man is in the courtroom, if she can point him out to us, and she's going to have to say no.'

'Shit.'

They sat in silence for a moment, mourning the loss of their witness.

'So,' Ellen said, regrouping. 'What's the word from the ME?'

'Preliminary results of the autopsy show nothing to indicate murder,' Mitch said. 'Unless something strange turns up in the lab, he's going to sign it off as suicide.'

In her heart Ellen knew Dennis Enberg had been murdered. The shadowed voice that had haunted her since that night whispered in the back of her mind. '*The first thing we do, let's kill all the lawyers.*'

'He had a blood alcohol level of .30, so he was good and drunk.'

'Too drunk to rig up the gun?' she asked.

'There are too many factors we don't know. He could have tricked out the gun when he was at .10 then drunk some more to get up his nerve. Or he could have been passed out and been fed that gun by a killer. The killer could have bashed his head in and *then* pulled the trigger to make it look like suicide.'

'Any opinions from the BCA?' Cameron asked.

'I haven't heard from them directly. Wilhelm and Steiger are off chasing a lead on the Holloman kidnapping. The mother got a phone call, allegedly from the boy.'

A chill crawled down Ellen's spine. 'Just like what happened with Josh.'

'Apparently so. They traced the call to Rochester. They're down there now checking it out. I don't expect them back tonight.'

The inconvenience was too timely. Ellen had asked the three principal law-enforcement officers to meet to go over everything they had one last time before the hearing. She wanted to have the clearest possible picture as to the status of the case, the most up-to-the-minute information from the BCA on the analysis of the evidence. With Wilhelm gone she would have to track down the information by phone. A time-consuming process, and the clock was ticking. Four-forty.

Not for the first time, she felt as if their nemesis had a bird's-eye view of everything going on on their side of the case. He had been three steps ahead of them all the way, playing with them like a cat with a mouse.

'*We can't lose,*' Wright had told Megan. '*You can't defeat us. We're very good at this game. Brilliant and invincible.*'

What if they were?

'The report on the fingerprints in Enberg's office is about what you'd expect,' Mitch went on. 'The place was a mess. There were prints everywhere. God only knows the last time he cleaned the place.'

'Prints on the gun?'

'Denny's only.'

'What about time of death?' Cameron asked.

'The ME put it around one A.M., give or take an hour.'

'My mystery call came at two,' Ellen murmured.

'And the help at the Donut Hut put Paul Kirkwood at Enberg's office around nine-thirty,' Cameron said. 'That rules him out.'

'Unless he came back later,' Ellen offered.

Mitch shook his head. 'I don't figure Paul for this. What's his motive? Enberg was no longer representing Wright, and he was doing a half-assed job before he got canned. Why should Paul off him?'

'Why should Paul go to see him?' Ellen asked.

'It makes sense if Paul was Wright's accomplice,' Cameron suggested.

'We've had this conversation before,' Mitch said. 'It's too bizarre for words.'

'Well, Costello would buy half of it.' Ellen tossed her pencil down. 'He's already tipped his hand. He's going to do his best to divert attention to Paul. Grabko ruled against him on the medical records, but that isn't stopping him from making his case to the press.'

'Asshole lawyers,' Mitch muttered. He caught himself too late and gave Ellen a look. 'Present company excluded.'

She shrugged it off. 'What about the Sci-Fi Cowboys? Has anyone confirmed their whereabouts on the night Dennis died?'

'All present and accounted for, provided you can believe the people who gave them alibis. They were in Deer Lake as a group on Tuesday to meet with Priest and returned to the Cities that evening. They didn't come back until Thursday afternoon.'

'Any holes in their stories for Saturday night?' Cameron asked.

Mitch shook his head. 'Not yet. I'd bet my pension Tyrell Mann torched that Cadillac, but I don't have a witness and I don't have any evidence. In other words, at the moment we don't have shit. It's as simple as that.'

Ellen pulled her glasses off and rubbed her hands over her face. 'Nothing is simple where this case is concerned.'

'That's old news, counselor,' Mitch said. 'If anything new comes in, I'll call. I'll be at home if you need me. Jessie's making dinner for Megan, and I get to help.' A spark of happiness lit his bloodshot eyes. 'I'd better stop for antacid on the way. Kindergarteners aren't known for their culinary talents.'

Ellen followed him to the conference-room door. In the outer office Quentin was regaling someone with his harrowing tale of being accosted outside family court.

'. . . and just as security arrived,' he said, gesturing like a maestro, 'the guy steps back and says, "Hey, man, you're not who I thought. Sorry!" '

Ellen pulled her attention back to Mitch. 'How's Megan doing?'

'Chomping at the bit to testify. She doesn't like being on the sidelines, you know. She's a cop right down to her toenails.' A shadow of doubt crossed his face as he weighed the wisdom of telling her something. Then he set his jaw in a stubborn line and plunged in. 'I dumped Wright's background stuff on her to sort through.'

'Mitch —'

'I don't want to hear it, Ellen. We're just too shorthanded with everything that's been going on. And she's too damn sharp to waste,' he argued. 'I'll keep the paper trail clean.'

His expression softened. 'She needs it, Ellen. She needs to know she can still do the job.'

'Fine,' Ellen surrendered, too tired to fight, and too concerned for Megan's well-being. It wasn't as if Megan were being given access to physical evidence. The information she would be looking over was cut-

717

and-dried, facts that were years in the past. Anything she might find had already become a part of history and couldn't be tampered with. God knew they needed all the help they could get.

'Quentin's still reliving his narrow brush with excitement,' she announced back in the conference room.

'Polishing up the performance for his paramour,' Cameron suggested with a smirk. 'By the time he tells Jan, he'll have it sounding like a fight scene from *Die Hard*.'

'Our comic relief,' Ellen said, settling back into her chair.

Phoebe fluffed herself up like a little quail, tilting her chin to a proud angle. 'Well, I think it was really gallant and original of Adam, the way he helped you.'

Cameron pulled a face of mock horror. '*Adam?*'

Ellen frowned at her secretary. 'There was nothing noble about it. It was a business deal. And he enjoyed himself. He got to be annoying *and* got rewarded for it. And what's with the first-name basis?'

'Nothing.' Phoebe's gaze landed everywhere but Ellen's face. 'That's his name, that's all. What am I supposed to call him?'

'A distant memory,' Ellen suggested sharply. 'We've talked about this, Phoebe. He's a reporter. Being cute doesn't cancel that out.'

'You don't know him,' Phoebe said stiffly.

'Neither do you.'

'I'd never get to know anyone if I was as paranoid as you are. Just because *you* never trust anyone doesn't mean people aren't trustworthy.'

'That's an admirable attitude,' Ellen said impatiently. 'But you know something, Phoebe? This isn't Mister Rogers's neighborhood. This is a big case full of bad people out to get what they can and to hell with everyone else. So maybe you could do us a favor and grow up. You can make nice with anyone you want after it's over.'

Phoebe stood abruptly and gathered up her notebook and a messy stack of files. 'If you're through lecturing me, I'll go make those phone calls to the BCA now.'

Ellen pulled a typed list of names and numbers from one of the files and held it out.

'After you call the BCA, please call these probation officers and see if they've got anything for me.'

'You're so insensitive!' Phoebe charged. Dumping the files onto the table, she ran out of the room.

'I'm guessing it was something you said,' Cameron offered with a pained look. 'Are you going after her?'

'No, dammit. I'm not her mother. I'm her bitch-queen boss,' Ellen muttered glumly.

She had more important things to expend her energy on than her secretary's love life. What difference did it really make, anyway? Slater's paper didn't mean anything to anyone who didn't live in Grand Forks.

She put her head in her hands and groaned. 'Why didn't God make all secretaries postmenopausal?'

'Because then male bosses would never get any exercise chasing them around their desks?' Cameron offered.

A weak chuckle rippled out of her. Sobering, she raised her head and looked at her bright-eyed young associate.

'I've got a bad feeling, Cameron,' she confessed. 'The day before the hearing, and our boy pulls a stunt like that call to Dustin Holloman's mother. What do you think he might have in store for the main event?'

'I don't know,' he admitted quietly.

Ellen stared out the window at the ominous gray of the sky and felt foreboding thicken the air around her. 'I don't want to know.'

The old habits came back, like ghosts, unwanted, unwelcome, bringing with them an uneasy sense of déjà vu. In her days on the fast track, the night before a major court appearance became a time of ritual, almost superstition. Too wired to relax, too afraid there was something she had overlooked in her preparation, Ellen would spend the evening in her office, poring over and over the evidence, the questions she wanted answered, the strategy she intended to employ against her opponent.

In the two years since she had come to Deer Lake, there had been no nights like that. Until this one. In the usual course of Park County events, an omnibus hearing would last twenty minutes and there would be half a dozen scheduled for a morning – most of which would never take place because the defendant would plead out. Garrett Wright's hearing would be a whole different kind of circus. Because of the charges. Because of the defendant. Because of Costello. This would be a minitrial, complete with all the drama.

She shooed Cameron out the door at eight-thirty but flatly refused to go with him. She both needed and hated the need to fall back into the old rhythms. She both recognized and resented the edgy restlessness that hummed through her like an electric current.

It pushed her out of her chair and walked her up and down the length of the conference table, where she had spread out every document, every note they had. The heat in the building had been turned down into the refrigeration zone again, the county commissioners unwilling to bend the utility budget for the comfort of one attorney. She paced with her coat on, vaguely amazed that she couldn't see her breath.

They had enough. Megan's and Mitch's statements alone should have been enough to get Wright bound over for trial. In addition, they would have the testimony of the BCA criminalist as to the preliminary findings on the ski mask that had yielded Wright's hair, and the sheet Wright had wrapped around Megan, the sheet that had yielded strands of Josh's hair and more of Wright's hair, and bloodstains that were consistent with Josh Kirkwood's blood type. It should have all made for a prosecution slam dunk, but still the doubts crept in, eroded her confidence, choked her. Old, familiar feelings.

As Mitch had predicted, Wilhelm had not yet returned from Rochester. The call to Dustin Holloman's mother had been traced to a pay phone in a mall, where there had to have been a number of witnesses. The BCA and local cops had spent hours canvassing the stores and hallways, showing Dustin's photograph, asking people if they had seen anyone suspicious using the phones, asking if they might have seen anyone using a small tape recorder at the phones.

It would have been lunacy for the kidnapper to drag the boy himself into such a public place. Every newspaper and television station in the state had been flashing Dustin's picture since the night of his disappearance. Most likely the kidnapper had recorded Dustin's message and played the tape over the phone.

Still a risky proposition, Ellen thought as she made another slow circuit around the table. Brazen. Bold. He was feeling cocky, invincible. He had taken a careless chance just for the purpose of tying up the BCA. Or perhaps what he wanted was the public acknowledgment of his brilliance. But all it would take was one witness, one bored store clerk, one man sitting on a bench waiting for his wife, one teenager impatient to use the same phone, and they would have a description.

The prospect brought a small adrenaline rush – another old, familiar feeling. There had always been a high associated with cracking a big case; a tense excitement in watching the cops close in, knowing that the next part was her part.

It stirred within her now at the thought of Wilhelm bringing back a description, an artist's sketch, a videotape from a security camera. Who would they see? Todd Childs? Or someone they had never seen before?

Adam Slater's question about the Sci-Fi Cowboys came back to her as she stopped along the section of table where their file was laid out. None of the boys had been considered suspects in the kidnapping, but she now had firsthand knowledge of the lengths to which they would go to support their mentor. If they would commit vandalism, if they would commit arson, what else might they do? She had a good idea from their rap sheets – they had committed robbery, car theft, assault, drug deals, attempted rape. Would it be a stretch to include kidnapping?

Theoretically, perhaps not. Logistically, it wasn't realistic. The Cowboys were minors, living with parents, with guardians. They attended school, answered to probation officers. Slipping out of a dorm to set a car on fire was one thing, being able to commit to the kind of complicated scenario these kidnappings had followed would require total freedom of movement. Nor was it realistic to think Garrett Wright would put his trust and his future in the hands of someone so young.

Childs was a better bet. Childs, the psych major fascinated with the human mind.

Learning and perception was Wright's specialty.

What had they done to Josh's mind? What had they planted in his young mind to make him close himself off so completely?

As her own mind pondered the questions, Ellen paged slowly through the materials they had gathered on the Cowboys. The list of past members, the photocopies of old newspaper articles. One prominent headline announced the admittance of one of the first Cowboys into the University of Minnesota Medical School. Another had won a scholarship to MIT. Success story after success story.

She went down the list of names, many of which had been checked off or had notations beside them regarding the person's whereabouts. According to Wilhelm, the people he'd had checking into the past Cowboys were turning up nothing but young men who had become productive members of society and thanked Garrett Wright and his colleagues for it. Car thieves, vandals, burglars, gangbangers, all of whom Garrett Wright had helped turn around. Had any one of them ever seen Wright's other side? Had they ever looked into his eyes and had a moment of terrible revelation? Would they tell anyone if they had?

So far, the answer to that question was no.

Her gaze settled on an article she had reviewed before. The photo showed Christopher Priest and one of the boys in the foreground, the one who had gone on to MIT, working with a robot. Garrett Wright, with boys named James Johnston and Erik Evans, stood in the background. The article was dated May 17, 1990, the second year of the Cowboys' existence. The murkiness of the copy gave Wright a sinister look. Or perhaps it was that he hadn't realized the camera would catch him in its frame, and he had been showing his true face, the one that hid beneath the handsome mask.

The idea sent a finger of unease down Ellen's spine. Public sentiment was running higher and higher in Wright's favor. With every new exploit of Dustin Holloman's kidnapper, the public grew less patient with the prosecution – or persecution, as some saw it – of Garrett Wright, their local hero, their respected teacher.

'I'm beginning to feel like the only person in the movie who knows the charming count is a vampire,' she muttered.

Pulling the telephone toward her with one hand, she reached for the list of probation officers Phoebe hadn't called.

She made contact with two, both of whom had burned out and left the job within the last year, and scratched the names of two former Cowboys off her list of possible character assassins. Montel Jones, Sci-Fi Cowboy turned engineering student at the University of Minnesota, had died in a plane crash in 1993. James Johnston had breezed through his undergraduate work in three years and was currently going for his master's in counseling. His former probation officer told Ellen that Garrett Wright's program was the reason.

Darrell Munson, probation officer to two of the original Cowboys, had left not only the profession but the state, moving to Florida to run a diving school. His answering machine picked up with steel-drum music. Ellen left a message and hung up, feeling no sense of accomplishment at all.

But, then, what had she really expected? That one of Wright's former charges would suddenly blurt out a tale of bizarre abuse after all this time? Contacting the past Cowboys had never been more than an exercise in grasping at straws.

A knock on the outer-office door broke into her concentration. It might have been Wilhelm coming with news, or Deputy Qualey, her guard for the evening, or Cameron coming back because he'd had a brain-storm.

Brooks stood in the hall holding a picnic basket.

'Why am I not surprised?' Ellen muttered. 'Why would I actually believe you would stay away merely because I asked you to?'

'Can I assume that's a rhetorical question?' he asked, eyes sparkling with mischief.

'How did you get into the building?' she asked irritably. 'How did you get past the guard?'

'I bribed him with a chocolate cupcake and an autographed copy of *Justice for None*. Good thing I'm not a psycho killer, huh?' He stepped past her and set the picnic basket down on the receptionist's counter. 'I told him you and I were old friends from law school and I wanted to make sure you got supper – knowing how nervous you are the night before a big case and all.'

'He's supposed to call up –'

'I told him it was a surprise. Gave him a little wink, a little nudge. He's a nice fella – Ed. A little too nice.' He turned serious. 'He didn't check the basket. He didn't frisk me. He figured he knew me – which, of course, he doesn't – so I must be all right.'

'I don't know you, either,' she said quietly. 'Should I be in fear of my life?'

He took in the sight of her standing there swallowed up by her winter coat, her hair back in a haphazard knot that allowed thick strands to escape. Her eyes were bloodshot, the circles beneath them growing darker and deeper every day. This case was dragging on her, but she withstood it because it was her duty. He could have kicked himself for ever insinuating she was a coward, that she had been running away when she'd left Hennepin County.

'Actually, I think you know me pretty well,' he admitted. 'You sure as hell hit some nails on the head last night. I admit I'm a son of a bitch, but I'm contrite about it. Doesn't that just make you want to marry me?'

'Is that what you came here for?'

'No,' he murmured. 'I wanted to make sure you got supper. Knowing how nervous you must be the night before a big case and all.'

The admission was earnest, the apology sincere. Ellen's wariness melted.

'I'm surprised you wanted to bother,' she said.

'Why?' he asked, moving closer with just a shift of his weight. He caught a strand of her hair over his fingers and brushed it back behind her ear, his fingertips skimming the soft skin there. 'Because I didn't get what I wanted last night? I don't give up that easily.'

'I'm not sure if that's good news or bad news.'

'Then maybe I should sweeten the deal. It comes complete with cupcakes, fried chicken, and information.'

'Information?'

'Supper? It's a package deal, counselor. You gotta eat the chicken to get the scoop.'

Ellen's stomach made the decision for her. The egg-salad sandwich she'd pulled out of the vending machine in the cafeteria for supper had ended up in the trash, and lunch had been a hastily grabbed cup of peach yogurt hours before. The aromas escaping the basket were too much for her.

She led the way to her office, taking her place behind her desk. They spread the containers of food out on the blotter. Crispy fried chicken, coleslaw, french fries, buttery biscuits, the promised cupcakes.

'Are you sure you're not trying to kill me?' she said. 'This looks like death by cholesterol.'

'It's my Southern-fried Lawyer, Night Before a Big Case special. I'm from Alabama, you know. We have a strong belief in the powers of grease. Chow down.'

Ellen stabbed her plastic fork into a chicken breast and tore a succulent piece of white meat free. 'So what's this hot information?'

'I heard about the phone call to Dustin Holloman's mother,' Jay said, wandering to the bookcase to peruse the compact disks. 'I heard it came this afternoon around four-fifteen.'

'Yes. The BCA guys traced it to Rochester. Frankly, I'm surprised you didn't beat it down there with the thundering herd.'

'It's another snipe hunt.'

'Another chapter. "The Pathetic Desperation of the Futile Search." '

He ignored the gibe. 'I was over at Harris College having a little chat with Professor Priest at about two, two-thirty. He hustled me out, told me he had a class to prepare for.'

'He *is* a teacher.'

He selected a Philip Aaberg CD and loaded it into the player. New Age piano music with a subtle western edge drifted from the small speakers. 'So, according to the main office, he didn't have another class until seven tonight. Now, maybe he just doesn't appreciate my unique brand of southern charm, but that doesn't explain why he was driving out the campus gates when I was coming out of Cray Hall at two-fifty.'

'Why were you leaving the building after him if he threw you out of his office?'

'I made a detour past Garrett Wright's office, where the lovely but

723

loony Mrs Wright was trying to find some books her husband had asked her to stop for.'

Ellen stilled. 'What books?'

'She didn't say, but I can't imagine there was anything left that might have been incriminating in any way. The cops had tossed that place like a Caesar salad.'

'What *did* she have to say?'

'That her husband shouldn't be on trial, that this is all a big mistake. She said Garrett wouldn't steal a child, because he didn't like children, that he hadn't liked *being* a child. I asked her if she had known him as a child, but she didn't answer me that, either. That little gal is one blade shy of a sharp edge, if you ask me.'

Her appetite suddenly on hold, Ellen sat back in her chair. 'According to what we know, Karen and Wright met in college.'

'So he told her he had a rotten childhood. Confession is part of courtship, isn't it?'

'I wonder what else he might have confessed to her.'

'You'll never know, counselor. A wife can't be compelled to testify against her husband.'

'No. She's on Costello's list to testify on behalf of Wright. Of course, she's hardly a credible witness. Not that that will stop Tony from trying to get some mileage out of her,' she grumbled. 'So you're leaving Cray Hall and you see Priest driving away. He could have gone anywhere. He could have gone to the dry cleaner's. He could have gone home.'

'But he didn't.'

'You followed him?'

'All the way to the interstate. He turned south.'

Toward Rochester, an hour away. Ellen felt her pulse pick up a beat. If Priest was Wright's accomplice, would he have been so reckless as to leave an interview with a prominent crime writer in order to drive to the site of the next move in his sick game? Did he feel that invulnerable?

'Something else funny about my little visit,' he said. 'I talked to a professor at Penn State who used to know Priest and Wright, who told me they were all kids in good old Mishawaka. They were different ages, from different parts of town. He didn't know either of them back then, but he thought it was quite a remarkable coincidence that they had all ended up at Penn State. When I mentioned it to Priest, he flat out denied it. Said he grew up in Chicago.'

'Why would he lie about that? It's easy enough to check out through school records.'

'I don't know. Anyway, when I heard about the call to Mrs Holloman,' he went on, 'I got hold of Agent Wilhelm and told him. I figured you'd want to know, too, and I wasn't going to count on his getting back to you tonight.'

'Yeah, so what's in it for you?' she asked, her gaze sharp on him.

'Nothing.'

Ellen gave him a speculative look as she raised her fork. 'You're turning into a regular good guy, Brooks. You'd better look out, you'll ruin your reputation.'

She had said it before, Ellen thought, that for someone who claimed to be a mere observer, he had a hard time grasping the concept. More often than not his involvement had struck her as being self-serving, but what she saw in his face now, in the amber glow of her desk lamp, looked an awful lot like honesty. As if he cared. And it hurt him to care.

He had come to Deer Lake to lose himself in someone else's misery, he had said. But the misery of Dustin's parents and Josh's parents was too close a cousin to his own. He had a son. Had lost that son before he'd even known the child existed. Had found him and had him taken away again all in the space of a day. Ellen could feel the tug to reach out to him.

She reached for the telephone instead and punched in Mitch's home number. His machine picked up, but he answered himself as soon as Ellen began to leave her message. She told him everything Brooks had told her and added a couple of her own hunches, all to be relayed to Megan. Diversionary tactics aside, the case was revolving around Wright and his circle of acquaintances; revolving in what seemed to be a spiral into the past. He had done this before. *They* had done this before. Christopher Priest had been heading south at three o'clock. The call had come a little past four o'clock. If Megan could dig up just one key piece . . .

'I thought O'Malley was off the case,' Jay said carefully as Ellen hung up the receiver.

Regarding him with a poker face, she said nothing for a moment that stretched into another.

'You wanted me to trust you,' she said at last. 'I'm trusting you with this: Agent O'Malley is digging into Wright's background because Wilhelm wasn't getting the job done.'

Jay gave a low whistle. 'She's a little biased, don't you think?'

'I think she's a damn good cop, and there's nothing she can do to change Garrett Wright's past. Anything she comes up with will be established, corroborated fact.'

'Still, if Costello catches wind of this –'

'I'll know where he got it, won't I?'

'And you'll cut out my black heart with a grapefruit knife.'

'Worse. I'll let you answer to O'Malley. She won't bother with a knife.'

Unfamiliar pleasure coursed through Jay. It was about trust. Something Ellen had no reason to offer freely and every reason not to offer at all.

He rose from his chair and rounded her desk to kneel down beside her. Taking her hand, he raised it to his mouth.

'My lips are sealed,' he said, each word a caress against her fingertips.

She tried to draw her hand away, but he held it firm, and drew the end of her middle finger between his lips. Her breath shuddered at the subtle abrasion of his teeth along the pad of her fingertip, at the touch of his tongue, at the gentle sucking.

'Jay . . .'

He drew his lips down her palm, lingered at the delicate skin inside her wrist. 'You trust me, Ellen?' he whispered, drawing her up from her chair.

Apprehension and desire shivered inside her. 'There's so much at stake here, Jay.'

'I know,' he said, knowing she meant the case, knowing there was more.

'I've never been anyone's hero, Ellen,' he said. 'I've lived my life for myself and to hell with everyone else. I've never had any trouble justifying or rationalizing or outright lying when it suited my cause. And I look at you and I think: Brooks, you got no business touching her, 'cause she's better than you'll ever be. But I want you anyway.'

'And you always get what you want.'

'I used to think so,' he murmured. 'Now I stand back and look at what I've got and none of it means a damn thing to me. The money, the house, the spite I prized so dearly . . . I look at Hannah Garrison, see her fighting for her child . . . I look at you, see you fighting for justice . . . What have I ever fought for besides my own gain? What good have I ever been to anybody?'

He forced a smile that was sad and wry. 'Looks like you might redeem me after all.'

'No,' Ellen whispered. 'I don't want that responsibility. That's your choice. It has to be what you want.'

'What I want,' he echoed, pulling her closer. 'I want you.'

He kissed her slowly, deeply, and Ellen thought she could taste his yearning and the confusion that shrouded it. She kissed him back, her own emotions kindred spirits of his.

When he lifted his head a fraction, the need in his eyes took her breath away. The need to be touched by something good.

As tempted as she was, Ellen knew she couldn't fight that battle for him. She had her own war to wage, her own enemies all around.

'I need to prepare for tomorrow,' she murmured.

He kept his arms around her. 'You need a good night's sleep – preferably with me. You can prepare until your eyes bleed, but that won't make you any more ready. You can't give more than all you've got, Ellen. You've done the best you can.'

Her best. Her best hadn't measured up so far. She closed her eyes and saw Garrett Wright smile that knowing, omnipotent smile that made her think he already knew the outcome of his game.

'That's what scares me most,' she confessed in a whisper. 'What if my best isn't good enough?'

She moved away from him, feeling rumpled and wilted, trying in vain to smooth some of the wrinkles out of her blouse. Back in Hennepin

County she had kept a change of clothes in her office. But Hennepin County was miles away, literally and figuratively. She didn't have a change of clothes here. She didn't know that she had any of what she really needed. The sharp edge, the bright eye, the quick mind. She didn't know that she hadn't left it all in Minneapolis.

Watching her struggle, Jay remembered the blind panic that struck in the eleventh hour before a case went to court, the naked insecurities. He had never measured up to the standards of his family, and what if they were right? What if, behind all the bluff bravado, the swagger, the smile, there really was nothing of substance to call on when he needed it most?

The anxiety was one of the many things about being a trial lawyer that he never missed. There was no panic associated with what he did now, dealing with cases after the fact. It was safer. It hurt less. *Maybe you're the coward, Brooks. . . .*

Ellen hadn't wanted this case, but she had accepted the challenge – nor for personal gain or glory, but because she knew she was the county's best hope for justice.

Too good for you, Brooks . . .

He crossed the room to where she stood, staring out through the barely parted blinds. Slipping his arms around her from behind, he pressed a kiss to her hair and whispered, 'You'll win,' as if his own conviction was enough to make it so.

'I wish I could be sure of that,' Ellen said. But the one thing she knew with any certainty was that in this game, where the stakes were so high, there was no such thing as a sure thing. And she had the sick feeling that the other team was playing with a stacked deck.

At eleven-ten she trudged up the stairs to the third-floor law library. She had the dubious services of Deputy Qualey for another forty minutes. Time enough to pull the books she needed, for all the good they would do her. If Grabko had already made up his mind about the lineup ID, he would have found precedent to back himself. Anal-retentive bugger that he was, he would no doubt have scoured every obscure text of U.S. case law in existence to support his decision. Ellen had assigned Cameron the task of finding rulings to back their position. He had carted a stack of books home with him. But she wanted a solid familiarity with the cases cited in the general rule regarding violation of the right to counsel, and so she found herself in the darkened halls of the third floor.

She had thought of bringing Qualey up with her but had taken pity on him and his bum hockey knee. After Brooks had gone, she'd had her chat with Ed about security, and he had assured her he'd let no one else in. The third floor was vacant, the courtrooms and construction junk waiting out the night.

Logical assurances warred with creepy sensations. Chiding herself for being skittish, Ellen let herself into the library and flipped on the lights.

It was a room designed for function. Industrial-grade carpet the color of pea soup, no-frills oak bookcases varnished dark with age, mission-style library tables and straight chairs that had been in place long before the retro-mission decorating craze.

She prowled the stacks with purpose, pulling the books she needed and carrying them to a table. She had memorized the names of the cases, state and federal – *United States v. Wade, Gilbert v. California*, Minnesota: *State v. Cobb*, and *State v. Guevara*. She forced herself to look them up, to mark the pages. No sense getting all the way home only to discover she'd pulled the wrong book. Be thorough. Stay focused. Fight the nerves.

The first two cases were nearly thirty years old. *State v. Cobb* was dated 1979, not that it mattered if the ruling applied. *State v. Guevara* was the most recent, 1993, and the most pertinent, if memory served. That had been a child-abduction case as well, up in Dakota County on the southeast side of the metro area. A witness had picked Guevara out of a lineup, but Guevara's attorney had gotten the lineup thrown out. Unease crawled along Ellen's nerves as she remembered the trial had ended in an acquittal.

She was trying an entirely different case, the logical side of her brain argued. Guevara had been charged not only with kidnapping, but had been indicted by a grand jury on murder charges. The fact that the little girl had never been found had weighed more heavily with the jury than any other aspect of the case.

But that lineup might have tipped the scales the other way. . . .

Ellen turned the pages. Page after page of case law, stopping cold when she reached *State v. Guevara.*

Someone had been here before her and marked the page with a slip of white paper. She turned the book sideways and, heart pounding, read the message on the note.

it is a SIN to believe evil of others, but it is seldom a mistake

The clock on Josh's nightstand ticked one minute past midnight. Hannah sat cross-legged on the sleeping bag she had spread out on the floor across the room from Josh's bed. Anticipation wound like a watch spring inside her, tightening with every passing minute, building to she knew not what.

A battle, she thought. A battle for her son. Not simply for justice, but for Josh himself. He had been taken from her. She had played the role of victim, but no more. The longer she thought about it, the more clearly she could see it – the challenge of something evil, the role she needed to play. The struggle in the courtroom would begin in a matter of hours, but the battle would go on beyond the courthouse, beyond the reach of Ellen North or Anthony Costello. She could see that now.

Closing her eyes, she summoned the evil, a faceless entity. In her mind's eye she could see herself standing on a dark plain, the sky low and leaden. She could see Josh standing off to one side, just beyond her reach, his face completely without emotion, sightless. And she could feel the evil, cold and heavy.

'You can't have my son. I'll kill you if I have to.'

'I've already taken him. He's already mine.'

'I'll kill you.'

She raised her hand and a knife appeared in her grasp. She slashed downward through the oppressive air, slicing the blackness like a canvas that split open to reveal a wall of blood. The blood poured over her, knocking her off her feet, filling her mouth and nose, choking her, drowning her. She fought to come awake, but it dragged her down like an undertow, and then there was nothing.

Josh dreamed of a sea of blood. He was floating on it, like floating on an air cushion in the lake. Safe, but not safe. Safe because the Taker said so, and that scared him because he didn't want to trust the Taker anymore. He could feel his mother pulling at him, her hands reaching up from the sea to grasp at him. He wanted to go with her, but he was afraid that if he did, the Taker would drown them both. But if he stayed where he was, the Taker would always be with him, and the Taker scared him more and more. He could see the other Goner in his dream, being held above him by the Taker's hands, the hands tightening and tightening; the boy opening his mouth to scream but no sound coming out, his eyes going wider and wider with terror, a terror Josh could feel inside himself. He didn't like the feeling. It made him want to cry. It made him want to be sick. It made him want to turn to his mother, but she was beneath the blood sea.

In a panic, he turned within himself, using the Taker's trick to trick the Taker. He opened the door inside his mind, went into the smallest, most secret room, and vowed not to come out ever again.

it is a SIN to believe evil of others, but it is seldom a mistake

Ellen saw the note on the table before her, heard the message – an eerie whisper that seemed to surround her. She could feel his presence, feel his hands close around her throat.

Evil.

The hands tightened. She lunged up out of the chair and across the tabletop, sending books tumbling into the blood that covered the floor. She landed in it herself on her hands and knees and slipped and slid as she struggled to stand. She couldn't breathe, could feel her windpipe collapsing in on itself. Fighting, she staggered up and twisted around. Garrett Wright sat in the chair she had vacated, smiling. The hands around her throat were invisible.

'The first thing we do, let's kill all the lawyers.'

The line rang in her ears, louder and louder, until the words were indistinguishable.

Gasping for air, she jerked upright in bed and stared at the phone on the nightstand. Fear rose in her throat until she thought she would gag on it. But she forced herself to reach out and pick up the receiver.

'Ellen North,' she said, her mouth as dry as cotton.

The silence was a heartbeat, and then came the voice, gruff and unsteady.

'It's Steiger. We've found the Holloman boy. He's dead.'

Journal Entry
February 1, 1994

Our litany of sins is an old classic song
We started young and have lasted long
Infused with new blood, our game will go on

731

30

'Ms North, how will this affect the charges against Garrett Wright?'

'Ms North, are you ready to admit you're prosecuting the wrong man?'

'Ms North, are you holding to your accomplice theory?'

'Ms North, is it true your lineup witness recanted her identification of Wright?'

'Ms North!'

'Ms North!'

'Ms North!'

The frantic voices echoed in Ellen's brain, louder and louder and louder, like the voice in her nightmare, until all she heard was noise.

'Stop it!' she shouted, turning her face up into the punishing hot spray of the shower, trying to wash away the images, sharp and painful, in her memory. A child's body, the purple marks of strangulation a circlet of bruises around his small throat. A child's body with a slip of paper pinned to the striped pajamas he wore. A message that cut to the bone: *some rise by SIN, and some by virtue fall*. A child's body discarded like a blown tire along the side of the road, abandoned at the base of the sign that welcomed visitors to Campion, *A friendly place to live*.

The black humor, the twisted psychological intent of leaving the body when and where it was found, sickened Ellen almost as badly as the murder itself. The message was arrogance, disrespect for the police agencies involved; a callous disrespect for life, for decency, for small-town values. Just as the note in the book had been a nose-thumbing at the court system, a sneering disregard for the sanctity and security of the courthouse.

The total package of crimes that made up The Game was among the worst she had ever dealt with. With the discovery of Dustin Holloman's body, the situation, difficult enough to this point, had reached critical mass.

She could still hear the hysterical sobs of the Holloman family; the shaky voices of the cops. Even the coroner, the irascible Stuart Oglethorpe, had wept as Dustin's lifeless body was zipped into the too-big black bag and loaded into the hearse.

Ellen had held herself together as best she could, struggling to put a brave face over the emotions that ravaged her. She represented justice. If any entity needed to show strength in the face of evil, it was justice. The people looked to her, to the system, to make things right, to avenge the wrongs. She had to stand strong.

A blessed numbness had descended to insulate her. The miraculous self-protective properties of the human psyche at work. She had gone through all the motions, consulted with Steiger and Wilhelm as the evidence techs from the BCA mobile lab processed the scene under the harsh white glare of the portable halogen lights.

Individual faces in the surrounding crowd caught in her peripheral vision. Henry Forster from the *Star Tribune*. A correspondent from *Dateline*. Jay.

He had come there for the story. The cynic in her reminded her of that fact, but it couldn't discount the bleak expression on his face or the sound of his voice when several of the reporters had turned to him for opinions when they could get no answers from anyone else.

'It's a tragedy,' he said in a rough, low voice. 'There's nothing I can say to make it any less senseless.'

His words stayed with her as she prepared herself for the day, slicking her hair back into a twist, selecting her best black suit from the closet. Dustin Holloman's death was a tragedy that should never have happened anywhere, but most of all not here. This was a crime against the community of Park County, the murder of a collective innocence.

Ignorance is not innocence but sin.

Garrett Wright and his shadow may have viewed the innocence of this place as ignorance, but the sin was theirs, and they would be made to pay. They would damn well be made to pay. The vow burned in Ellen's mind, in her heart. *She* would see to it. She hadn't asked for this battle, hadn't wanted it to come here, but she would fight it with everything she had.

Not giving a damn if the reporters followed her, she drove across town to the new office complex on Ramsey Drive, where Costello had rented a suite for his stay here. The extravagance sickened her. This was what Tony Costello was all about – money, power, a staff of drones to do the work, an image polished to a diamond shine.

She marched past the secretary, homing in on Costello, who stood in the hall giving orders to one of his associates. Dorman's eyes widened at the sight of her. Costello's expression was guarded.

'Have you heard?' she demanded.

'About the Holloman boy?'

'He's dead.'

Costello reached for her arm. 'Let's go in my office.'

Ellen jerked away from his touch. 'Let's not. I'd rather your staff hear exactly what kind of a bastard they're working for – if they don't already know.'

Anger flashed in his dark eyes and he took another step toward her. 'Ellen, you're out of line –'

'*I'm* out of line? My God!' She shook her head in disbelief. 'You could have saved that child. You could have at least been a coward and called in anonymously. But if Wright's accomplice is nailed, then Wright is nailed, too, and you'll be damned if you'll lose a case over something as trivial as a child's life.'

She could see the secretary, wide-eyed and uncertain. Another associate, an African-American woman, stepped into the hall from an office, looking shocked. Costello's face was a stony mask.

'You'll be damned, all right,' Ellen snarled. 'I'm filing a complaint with the professional-relations board today. If I find one shred of evidence linking you to that boy's murderer, I will ruin you, Tony. You're as guilty of his death as if you put your hands around his throat and choked him yourself!'

She stormed out of the office, half expecting him to follow, but he didn't. She had taken him by surprise, knocked him back on his heels, and she could imagine what he was thinking. No time to appear in front of the press that waited in the hall. Better to say nothing, leave them wondering, leave her to deal with them, the coldhearted son of a bitch.

She pushed past the reporters, letting them draw their own conclusions as to why she would pay a visit to the opposition less than two hours before they were due in court.

By the time she arrived at the courthouse, the full flock of vultures had descended. The scene in Campion had been processed and abandoned, picked clean of details and metaphors, photographed from every possible angle. They perched themselves on the main steps of the courthouse, hovered around all the entrances. The only way into the building was to run the gauntlet, eyes forward, stride purposeful, mouth closed. They hurled their questions at her like stones and chased her into the building, demanding the answers she had refused them just hours before.

'Ms North, how will the discovery of Dustin Holloman's body affect the charges against Garrett Wright?'

'Ms North, are you ready to admit you're prosecuting the wrong man?'

'What were you doing at Anthony Costello's offices? Will there be some kind of deal?'

'Are you dropping the charges?'

'Ms North, are you holding to your accomplice theory?'

'Will you try to pin this on the Sci-Fi Cowboys?'

'Doesn't the Park County attorney's office have anything to say for itself?'

'Yes.' She tossed a glare over her shoulder without breaking stride. 'I have a hearing to prepare for and a suspect who's as guilty as sin. If you let this latest atrocity sway you from believing that, then you're just buying

734

into his sick game and you're as much accomplices as the person who dumped that child's body.'

If she had meant her words to silence or humiliate them, she would have been disappointed. As it was, the rise in volume as they all clamored to speak at once came as no great surprise. *Just like old times*, she thought as she stepped past the deputy who had been stationed outside the office door. *Only worse.*

The office was in a state of stunned chaos. Phones rang incessantly and seemed to go unanswered. One of the secretaries from Campion sat at her desk, weeping. Phoebe knelt on the floor beside the woman's chair, offering Kleenex and sympathy, her own eyes red-rimmed and brimming with tears. Rudy stood in the center of it all, looking like a captain on the deck of a sinking ship.

'This is an absolute nightmare,' he said half under his breath, glaring at Ellen as if the idea of dumping Dustin Holloman's body in plain sight mere hours before the probable-cause hearing had been her idea. 'Bill Glendenning called me at home to demand an explanation. He said from the position of his office, it appears you've lost all control of the situation, Ellen.'

You, not *we*, Ellen noted as she went into her office, Rudy following. He was ready to cut the ties and blame her in order to save his ass and his prospective judgeship. She wheeled on him.

'*I've* lost control? *I* never had control! I had a case to build and I've built it. I'm not omnipotent. If *I* were in control, none of this would ever have happened!'

'You know what I mean.'

'Yes, I certainly do.' She didn't care that Quentin Adler stood just behind him in the doorway, soaking up every word to be regurgitated later at the water cooler. 'You've really painted yourself into a corner this time, haven't you, Rudy? You dumped this case on me because you didn't have the guts to take it on yourself. Now what?' she demanded. 'God forbid you should look at the evidence we have against Garrett Wright and back me up.'

'I've backed you in this from the beginning, Ellen,' he said indignantly. 'I gave you my full confidence. I gave you free rein.'

He had given her ample rope and half hoped she would hang herself with it, but not before he could get himself clear of her kicking feet. He had never in all his scheming scenarios imagined anything as dire as this latest turn of events. If he washed his hands of her now, he would appear weak. If he backed her and she failed, she would take the brunt of the criticism, but the fallout would be on him. His decision-making abilities would be questioned. His qualifications as a judge would be questioned. He could almost feel the robes slipping from his grasp.

'Do I need to remind you Mitch Holt ran down Garrett Wright himself?' Ellen asked. 'He's guilty.'

'Not of killing that Holloman boy.'

'That's not the case we're hearing. But don't worry, Rudy, when that one comes in, I will be first in line. I want to nail that son of a bitch's hide to the wall and pick my teeth with his bones. Now, if you'll excuse me,' she said, backing him out into the hall, 'I've got a battle to wage.'

'All rise! Court is in session. The Honorable Judge Gorman Grabko presiding.'

The bailiff smashed the gavel down again as the noisy crowd surged to its feet. Jay watched as Gorman Grabko emerged from his chambers with a theatrical air of dignity, bald head polished to a high sheen, beard neatly trimmed. A gray-striped bow tie perched above the neck of his robes, properly discreet. He climbed up to his aerie on the bench and settled himself with quiet ceremony, arranging his stack of files and books just so before looking out on the assembled mob that filled his courtroom shoulder to shoulder.

Jay followed the judge's eyes, trying to imagine the scene from Grabko's point of view. Looking past the counsel tables into the gallery, he would see Paul Kirkwood sitting in the front row with a sour expression. Rudy Stovich right beside him, his greased gray hair rising off one side of his head like a loose asphalt shingle. He would see Mitch Holt in a suit and tie and Megan O'Malley wearing the ugly badges of her beating – bruises that had reached the pomegranate-and-puce stage, stitches crawling over her lower lip like a centipede.

The Harris College contingent had arrayed themselves on the other side of the aisle, behind the defense table. Christopher Priest and the assistant dean, a cadre of students – Todd Childs noticeably absent. Karen Wright, looking fragile and lovely in rose-petal pink. And the press all around.

From his lofty seat Grabko could literally look down on the lawyers – every judge's secret joy. At the prosecution table Ellen stood, her back rigid, her jaw rigid, her hands curled into fists at her sides. She was furious, almost to the point of shaking, Jay would have bet. And he had a sinking feeling her temper was directly attributable to the discussion that had gone on in chambers moments before, where Grabko would have announced to the lawyers his decisions on motions they had made prior to today.

Costello had filed two of note, had broadcast them to the press with a fanfare: a motion to dismiss and a motion to suppress the lineup identification. He stood at the defense table with his associate, smartly decked out in a tailored tobacco-brown suit, black hair gleaming almost blue under the lights, his expression allowing just a hint of overconfidence.

Christ, would Grabko have been so easily led? Would the news of the Holloman boy's death have swayed him as it had many of the reporters who had been on the scene in the pearl-gray hours before dawn? His decision on the dismissal had to be based on the evidence regarding the issue of the constitutionality of the arrest, but that didn't mean other factors couldn't influence him subconsciously or otherwise. If Grabko had been sufficiently starstruck by Costello, if he had already been leaning toward the defense . . .

Anxiety knotted in Jay's gut. He hadn't been able to get the morning's images out of his head. In the usual course of his job, he had seen hundreds of crime-scene photos, some grisly beyond imagining, but he had never actually been to a scene like this one.

He would never forget the sight of that small, lifeless body, would never forget the raw, nameless emotion that had cut through him, or the anguished keening of the boy's mother. There were no words to describe the kind of desperate tension that had thickened the cold air along that stretch of road leading into Campion. Acrid, volatile, like a toxic chemical cloud that could have ignited and exploded at the slightest spark.

And he knew it was all part of the master plan mapped out by Wright and his partner. A move meant to shock, meant to thumb their noses at their opponents in the game. *some rise by SIN, and some by virtue fall.* Who represented virtue more than the police, more than the prosecutor, more than a child? The goal was to get away with murder, to defeat the justice system and destroy the servants of that system in the process; and to destroy two innocent families in the bargain.

The pure evil of it was stunning.

And fewer and fewer people were willing to believe the defendant standing at the table was capable of embodying that evil. Evil was supposed to be ugly, instantly recognizable. Not a respected college professor who rehabilitated delinquents. Not an attractive, quiet man in a conservative blue suit.

'Be seated,' Grabko intoned. He perched a pair of half glasses on his nose and consulted a document, as if he had no idea what case was coming up before him. 'We are here on the matter of *The State versus Dr Garrett Wright.* This is the omnibus hearing. For those of you in the gallery unfamiliar with our system, the omnibus hearing is the equivalent of a probable-cause hearing, wherein the State bears the burden of proof to show that the defendant indeed may have committed the crimes of which he stands accused and should be bound over for trial.

'Counsel for the defense,' he announced, 'please state your names for the record.'

Costello and his minion rose in unison. 'Anthony Costello, Your Honor. Assisting me will be my associate, Mr Dorman.'

'Counsel for the prosecution.'

'Assistant County Attorney Ellen North, Your Honor.'

'Assistant County Attorney Cameron Reed, Your Honor.'

'Mr Costello,' Grabko said, turning his attention back to the defense. 'Regarding your previously filed motion to dismiss on the grounds that in the process of arresting Dr Wright the Deer Lake police force violated his rights under the Fourth Amendment of the United States Constitution: I have carefully considered your argument and weighed all factors involved, including Chief Holt's statement and the prosecution's argument.'

He paused for effect, stroking a hand down his beard, as if he were just now coming to his conclusion. Jay pulled in a breath and held it.

'I find your argument has merit. There was a certain delay between pursuit and apprehension, wherein Chief Holt lost sight of his suspect.'

A gasp went up in the gallery. In the front row Paul Kirkwood leaned forward to grasp the railing, as if preparing to vault over it.

'However,' Grabko said, 'the length of the delay is in dispute, and I am convinced the rule of exigent circumstances applied. Therefore, motion to dismiss is denied.'

Another wave of sound rolled through the courtroom. Grabko banged his gavel and frowned at the gallery. 'I will have order in this courtroom. This hearing is a legal proceeding, not a play. Those in the gallery will remain silent or be removed.'

Threat made, he resettled himself like a tom turkey that had had his feathers ruffled. He carefully set aside the documents concerning the first motion and took up another.

'With regards to the defense motion to suppress the lineup identification. Motion granted.'

Ellen rose from her chair as the gallery behind her defied fate and burst into a cacophony of sound. 'Your Honor,' she shouted over the noise as Grabko cracked his gavel down. 'Your Honor, I request the record show –'

'Ms North,' Grabko snapped, scowling at her over the rims of his glasses, 'you made your opinion of my ruling abundantly clear in chambers. Unless you would care to be served with a charge of contempt, I suggest you not make it again.'

Biting down on her temper, she did a mental count to ten. 'Yes, Your Honor.'

'You may call your first witness, Ms North.'

'The State calls Agent Megan O'Malley.'

Mitch gave Megan's good hand a squeeze. She rose from her seat on the aisle and made her way slowly through the gate and toward the witness stand, trying not to lean too heavily against her crutch, too aware of the eyes that followed her, scrutinizing, speculating. The bailiff hovered at her shoulder, as if he expected her to swoon. She backed him off with an icy glare and took her time climbing into the witness box.

Standing behind the table, Ellen assessed her witness as Megan was sworn in, noting with grim satisfaction that the BCA agent had taken no measures to cover the damage that had been done to her. She wore no makeup and had pulled her dark hair back off her neck, revealing the fading choke marks around her throat.

738

'Agent O'Malley,' Ellen began, 'please state for the record your occupation.'

'I am – was – the Deer Lake regional field agent for the Minnesota Bureau of Criminal Apprehension.'

'You say "was." Has your status with the bureau changed recently?'

'Yes,' Megan answered grudgingly. 'I'm currently on medical leave.'

'Due to injuries suffered on January twenty-second, 1994?'

'Yes.'

'Agent O'Malley, you were the agent in charge of the investigation of the abduction of Josh Kirkwood, were you not?'

'That's correct.'

'And were you investigating that crime on the twenty-second?'

'Yes, I was.'

'Would you please tell the court what happened on that morning?'

'Objection,' Costello said in a bored tone. 'Relevance.'

Ellen cut him a look. 'Goes to motive, Your Honor. We intend to establish a chronology of events that led to the vicious attack against Agent O'Malley.'

Grabko pursed his lips and nodded. 'Overruled.'

Ellen stepped out from behind the table and walked slowly toward the witness stand, pulling Grabko's attention away from Costello. 'Please continue, Agent O'Malley.'

'I had stopped my car on the side of Old Cedar Road, got out of the vehicle, and was examining a set of skid marks made on the road during an auto accident that had taken place on the night of Josh Kirkwood's abduction, directly prior to his abduction.'

'Why were you interested in the accident site?'

'I was suspicious of the cause and the timing of the accident. The resulting injuries to the drivers and passengers delayed Josh Kirkwood's mother, Dr Hannah Garrison, in leaving the hospital to pick him up from hockey practice. In the time between the accident and Dr Garrison's arrival at the ice arena, Josh was abducted.'

'And while you were examining these skid marks, were you approached by anyone?'

'Yes. Dr Garrett Wright stopped and expressed an interest in my purpose for being there. I simply said I was checking something out.'

'To the best of your knowledge, was Dr Wright aware of the accident that had taken place?'

'Yes, he was. The driver of the car that caused the accident was a student at Harris College who was involved in a project Dr Wright and Professor Christopher Priest were heading.'

'Did you see Dr Wright again later that day?'

'Yes. I went to Harris College looking for Professor Priest. The professor wasn't in his office, but I found Dr Wright there, along with a student.'

'How was Dr Wright dressed at that time?'

'He was wearing a shirt and tie and dark trousers.'

'You spoke to him then?'

'Yes. Dr Wright informed me that Priest had gone to St Peter and would likely return to his home around two-thirty P.M.'

'Was Dr Wright aware of your intention to go to his colleague's home?'

'He offered to give me directions.'

'Did you inform anyone else of your intention to go to Priest's home?'

'No.'

'And where is Professor Priest's home located?'

'10226 Stone Quarry Trail. Outside of town.'

'In a wooded, relatively isolated area, correct?'

'Yes.'

'When you arrived at that location, was Professor Priest at home?'

'No. The house was locked and dark. There was no car. I proceeded to walk around the property, the south end of which abuts Quarry Hills Park. As I neared the end of a storage shed on the southeast corner of the property, I saw a trail of footprints in the snow leading from the south – the park – into the shed. I found that suspicious, so I drew my weapon, announced myself as a law-enforcement officer, and demanded the person in the shed come out.'

'Did the person come out?'

'No.'

'What happened then?'

Megan blinked slowly, the scene flashing in broken frames behind her eyelids like a poorly spliced film.

A weird twilight quality to the afternoon. The sky leaden, snow falling thick and heavy. A forest of black, winter-dead trees surrounded the property.

'I decided to go back to my vehicle and radio for backup,' she said.

Her heart beat a little harder. She was moving past the shed. Thirty feet and she would be clear of it. She got no farther than fifteen.

'Someone burst out of the shed.'

The first blow struck with a power that sent her sprawling headlong. The gun flew out of her hand. She could see it, sailing away, falling, disappearing into the snow. She lunged toward it, kicking, flailing like a beached swimmer.

'I – I tried to get the gun. He came down on top of me.'

Black clothing, ski mask, eyes, and a mouth. A short black club swinging down at her.

'He . . . struck me,' she said, the tension building in her chest. 'With a baton – um – like a nightstick. Hard.'

Again and again. Hitting her shoulder. Hitting her a glancing blow off the side of her head. Striking her right hand as she held it up in defense, the blow so vicious that the pain roared up her arm and exploded in her brain.

The memory of the pain brought a wave of nausea. She pulled a slow, unsteady breath deep into her lungs.

'I lost consciousness,' she said quietly.

'When you regained consciousness, where were you?'

'Tied to a chair. I don't know the location.'

'Can you describe the surroundings?'

'I was blindfolded. I had only a small wedge of vision at the bottom of the blindfold.'

Ellen paused, resting a hand on the smooth old wood of the witness stand as gently as if it were Megan's hand. From this close she could see that Megan's ashen pallor had nothing to do with the quality of the lighting, and that despite the coolness of the room, a fine film of perspiration misted her forehead.

'Megan, I realize this is difficult for you,' she said, with genuine sympathy. 'But will you tell us what happened while you were held captive in this place?'

Megan swallowed hard. Control. She was a cop. She had testified a million times.

She had never been a victim.

She turned a narrow gaze on Garrett Wright, sitting so calm, beaming false innocence, and damned him to the vilest, blackest corner of hell.

'He . . . beat me . . . repeatedly,' she said, cursing the tears that filled her eyes. Damned if she would let them fall. 'He choked me. He talked about killing me – maybe he would, maybe he wouldn't. He talked about taking Josh. He called it a game.'

'And he made you a pawn in his game, didn't he?'

'He told me I would be their next move.' And the sense of helplessness and humiliation had nearly been worse than the pain.

'Agent O'Malley, even though you couldn't see your assailant's face, you came to a conclusion about his identity. How did you arrive at this conclusion?'

'Only two people knew I had gone to Priest's home, Garrett Wright being one of them. He had also seen me examining the skid marks at the accident site. If he was involved, he would have known I was onto something.

'I had met and spoken with Dr Wright on several occasions. I was familiar with his patterns of speech. I knew his height in relation to my own. I had also noticed he had a pronounced habit of rocking back on his heels. I could see a section of floor beside my chair. I saw his boots, saw him rocking back on his heels while he went on and on about how brilliant he was,' she said bitterly.

'And did he say anything specific that rang a bell with you?'

'Yes. I asked him why he had singled out Josh, why the Kirkwoods? With great contempt he said, "Why not? Such a perfect little family." When I had spoken with Dr Wright earlier in the day, he used the same phrase to describe the Kirkwoods – "such a perfect family." '

Ellen walked away from the stand, letting the testimony hang there, not only for Grabko, but for the press as well. Let them look at Megan, bruised and beaten; let them look at the well-dressed, well-groomed man who stood accused and begin to realize what a monster they had in their midst.

Slipping her reading glasses on, Ellen chose a report from the documents Cameron had spread out on the table.

'The injuries you suffered at the hands of this man were severe, weren't they?'

'Yes.'

'According to the medical report, marked people's exhibit C, you sustained a concussion, multiple severe contusions, bruised kidneys, cracked ribs, damage to your right knee. Nearly every bone in your right hand sustained multiple fractures – extensive damage that will require a number of operations if you're to have any hope of regaining mobility.'

She paused, looking up at Megan with sympathy, with apology. 'Agent O'Malley, considering the extent of the damage to your hand, can you realistically hope you'll ever be able to resume your full duties as a field agent for the Bureau of Criminal Apprehension?'

The question hit Megan like a brick to the solar plexus. The answer was one she had evaded and denied and lain awake nights contemplating. It scared the hell out of her. All she had ever wanted in life was to be a good cop. And if she couldn't be a cop, then what was she – *who* was she?

The tears blurred her vision, and she blinked furiously as she lifted her chin to a proud angle. 'It's not likely. No.'

Ellen glared at Costello. 'Your witness.'

He rose, his expression cool, unmoved, his brows drawing together as he consulted a newspaper clipping. 'I have to confess, I'm a little confused here, Agent O'Malley. You've told the court you were investigating aspects of the Kirkwood abduction on the twenty-second. Is that correct?'

'Yes.'

'But according to an article in the *Star Tribune*, dated Saturday, January twenty-second, you had already been officially relieved of your post, temporarily suspended from active duty. According to your special agent in charge, Bruce DePalma, you had been replaced in the Deer Lake region by Agent Martin Wilhelm the day before because of your mishandling of the investigation.'

'That's a lie,' Megan said sharply.

Costello arched a brow. 'You're calling your special agent in charge a liar?'

'No, Mr Costello,' she said plainly. 'I'm calling *you* a liar.'

Judge Grabko gave a little jolt in his seat, scowling ferociously.

'Agent O'Malley, I expect a certain decorum in my courtroom. Especially from those in law enforcement.'

Megan made no effort to apologize. If the pompous old fart wanted contrition, he'd damn well have to ask for it.

Costello pressed on, having no desire to break his rhythm. 'You'd been working the case for ten days with no satisfactory result. One suspect had died in custody –'

'Objection,' Ellen snapped, rising. 'There's no point to this attack. Agent O'Malley isn't on trial.'

'Your Honor, we feel Agent O'Malley's status with the BCA, as well as her mental state on the twenty-second, are very much factors here –'

'This is a hearing, Mr Costello' Ellen said, 'not a trial. You have the right to cross-examine the witnesses, not impeach them.'

Grabko smacked his gravel down. 'This is *my* courtroom, Ms North. I will oversee the implementation of the rules.'

'Yes, Your Honor,' she said tightly. 'Please do.'

'Objection overruled. Please continue, Mr Costello.'

Costello stepped out from behind the table and sauntered into the open area in front of the bench. 'Had you been directed by Special Agent in Charge DePalma to appear at BCA headquarters in St Paul on Saturday the twenty-second?'

'Yes,' Megan admitted grudgingly.

'And yet you were wandering around Deer Lake, looking at skid marks, asking questions – by your own admission, continuing an investigation that you no longer had any connection to. Is that correct?'

'No. I still felt a very strong connection to the case. Josh was still missing. I still had questions. I felt obligated to try to get answers. Appearing at headquarters did not outweigh the need to find a child in danger and apprehend the creep responsible.'

'So you defied direct orders from your superior?'

'Delayed.'

'Because you didn't want to let go of the case?'

'I may not have been agent in charge of the investigation any longer, but I was still a cop,' Megan said. 'I felt a moral obligation.'

'There was quite a lot of hoopla surrounding your assignment to the Deer Lake region, wasn't there?' Costello asked, changing lanes with the skill of a Grand Prix driver.

'I guess.'

'You're being modest. You were the first woman in the history of the BCA to hold a field post. Isn't that right?' he said with phony amazement.

'Yes.'

'There was a great deal of pressure on you to solve the Kirlwood case? More so than if you had been a man?'

'I wouldn't know,' Megan said, deadpan. 'I've never been a man.'

Snickers rattled through the gallery. Grabko bumped his gavel and glared at them.

'The press was scrutinizing, quite literally, your every move,' Costello went on. 'Headquarters was breathing down your neck. You were operating under tremendous stress. Is that a fair assessment?'

'Yes.'

'And you wanted very badly to solve the case? In fact, your very career was riding on it?'

'I wanted to solve the case. That was my job.'

'You were desperate?'

'Determined.'

Costello turned his profile to the gallery and smiled the charming, wide, white smile, shaking his head. 'You have a stubborn propensity for rationalization, Agent O'Malley.'

'Objection!' Ellen snapped.

'Sustained. Please confine yourself to questions, Mr Costello.'

He nodded slightly and moved back to the defense table. Dorman sat at attention like a trick poodle, holding out the proper statement, which Costello accepted and paged through.

'Agent O'Malley, at any time during the course of the investigation, was Dr Wright considered a suspect in the disappearance of Josh Kirkwood?'

'No. Not until he abducted and assaulted me and Chief Holt ran him down.'

A muscle ticked in Costello's jaw. His dark eyes flashed as he turned toward Grabko. The judge leaned over the witness stand, temper rouging his cheeks above his beard.

'Agent O'Malley, I'm quite certain you know better than to answer in such a manner. Do so again and you may be held in contempt.'

'Yes, Your Honor.' She tipped her head in a way that would seem deferential to Grabko but kept him from seeing her eyes.

'Isn't it true,' Costello went on, 'that in fact you had considered a number of other people as suspects, including Paul Kirkwood?'

'As dictated by standard operating procedures involving abductions, the immediate family was considered as part of the dual investigation.'

'You were a little more rigorous in your consideration of Paul Kirkwood than someone just going through the motions.'

Megan narrowed her eyes at him. 'I'm a good cop. I never "just go through the motions." '

'That's admirable. So you were dead serious when you brought Mr Kirkwood in to be fingerprinted?'

'Mr Kirkwood was fingerprinted for elimination purposes only.'

'You spoke with Dr Wright and his student on the twenty-second,' Costello said, switching tacks again. 'But you actually went to Harris College in search of Professor Christopher Priest. Is that right?'

'Yes.'

'Why?'

'I wanted to ask him some questions.'

'Did you consider *him* a suspect?'

'There was that possibility.'

'You gave Dr Wright the impression that you would be going out to Christopher Priest's residence later that day. Can you say whether or not

Dr Wright or Todd Childs might have spoken about that afterward with other people?'

'I couldn't say.'

'Is it possible your conversation might have been overheard by someone in the hall outside the office?'

'I couldn't say.'

'So you can't conclusively say that Dr Wright was only one of two people who knew you were going to Professor Priest's home?'

'To my knowledge, he was.'

'What time was it when you arrived at Priest's home?'

'Approximately one forty-five P.M.'

Costello arched a brow for his audience. 'But Dr Wright had specified Priest wouldn't be back until around two-thirty. Why did you get there so early?'

Megan cocked her head to a belligerent angle. 'I wanted to be there to welcome him home.'

'Agent O'Malley,' Grabko cautioned.

'You considered him a suspect,' Costello said.

'Asked and answered,' Ellen said wearily, rising. 'Your Honor, can we ask Mr Costello to cut to the chase here? It simply isn't relevant whether there was one suspect or a dozen. Dr Wright is the man who was apprehended.'

Grabko's face tightened as if he wanted to deny her but couldn't. 'Let's move on, Mr Costello.'

Costello didn't bat an eye. 'Agent O'Malley, did you see the face of the person who attacked you at the Priest residence?'

He hit her from the side, sent her sprawling. The gun flew out of her hand....

'No.'

'Did you see the face of the person who assaulted you while you were held at this undisclosed location?'

The pain came from all directions at once, striking her shoulder, her knee, her hand, again and again.

'Agent O'Malley?'

'I saw his feet.'

Costello looked indignant. 'And on the basis of *that* you would have us try a respected member of the community for heinous crimes?'

'No! I –'

'Did you recognize his voice?'

'You think we'll kill you, clever girl? You wouldn't be the first by a long, long way....' A whisper, soft, disembodied . . .

'No, but –'

Costello wheeled away from her. 'You didn't see him, couldn't recognize him, he never spoke his name,' he said, his voice growing louder with every syllable. He flung her written statement down onto the table and turned back toward her. 'Is there *anything* you can tell us, *former* Agent O'Malley, that should make us believe your conclusion that your

745

assailant was Dr Garrett Wright is anything more than the desperate grasping of a woman who'd bungled the case and had to do something to keep her career from going down the toilet?'

'Objection!' Ellen shouted.

Grabko pounded for order.

The sounds were blocked in Megan's mind by the white noise of fury. The fine thread on her control snapped, and the rage poured through her and out of her.

'I can tell you he's guilty!' she shouted, coming up out of her seat. 'I can tell you he's a sick son of bitch who thinks it's a game to steal children and ruin lives, and he deserves worse than anything this court will do to him!'

'Order!' Grabko screamed, pounding like a carpenter. The head snapped off his gavel and sailed at the defense table. 'Order!'

The bailiff started toward the witness stand, but jumped back at the sight of Megan's crutch.

Megan's focus was on Costello, who stood no more than a foot away, his face calm, his dark eyes bright, the barest hint of a smile tightening the corners of his mouth.

Oh, God, O'Malley, you played right into his hands. Way to go.

She had to appear just exactly as he had wanted to paint her – obsessed, biased, out of control. Desperate. The realization made her feel ill, dizzy. She sank weakly back into her chair and closed her eyes.

'No further questions,' Costello said, and walked calmly back toward his client.

31

'The State calls Chief of Police Mitch Holt,' Ellen said calmly, as if her first witness hadn't just been hustled out of the courtroom.

She didn't blame Megan for losing her poise. Considering what Wright had put her through, it was a wonder she hadn't pulled a gun and shot him – and Costello, too, while she was at it. The big question in Ellen's mind was what impact Megan's emotional testimony would have. The press might take her side – or not – but Grabko was clearly pissed off. This hearing was his show and Megan had upstaged him. Would he look at her testimony and see anything but red?

With luck Mitch would settle the judge and the gallery. He made an excellent witness – businesslike, his face set in the stony no-nonsense expression of a veteran detective. He took the stand and swore the oath, his gaze fixed on the defense table.

'Chief Holt, will you please tell the court about the events that occurred on the night of January twenty-second?' Ellen prompted.

'At approximately eight forty-five P.M. I received a call from Agent O'Malley,' Mitch said. 'She was in obvious distress. She wasn't allowed to say much. Then an unidentified male came on the line and instructed me to go alone to the southwest entrance of Quarry Hills Park at nine-fifteen.'

'Did he say why?'

'He said they had a present for me, that they wanted to win "the game." '

'And you went to the park as instructed?'

'Not as instructed. I immediately sent an unmarked car with two officers to the southeast entrance of the park, another to the southwest, and came into the park myself on foot from the west.'

'Where the park adjoins the Lakeside neighborhood?'

'Yes. I waited in the cover of the trees. At nine-oh-five a late-model GMC four-by-four truck entered the park, drove some distance along the road, and stopped. The driver got out, went to the passenger side and let the passenger out, then marched her approximately thirty feet back to the south.'

Megan, limping heavily, unquestionably badly injured. The fury he had felt then burned again like a coal.

'A struggle ensued between them,' he stated flatly. 'I ran out from the woods with my weapon drawn, announced myself as a police officer, and ordered them to freeze.'

'At this point, did you recognize either person?'

'Yes. I recognized Agent O'Malley. The assailant was wearing a ski mask.'

'Was he armed?'

'Yes. He had a nine-millimeter semiautomatic handgun.'

'And was he threatening Agent O'Malley?'

'Yes. At one point he had the gun pressed to her temple.' And Mitch had known a wrong move, a wrong decision, and she would be dead right there and then, before his eyes.

'I ordered him to drop the weapon, informed him he was under arrest,' he went on. 'Agent O'Malley knocked him off balance. He pushed her at me, fired several rounds, and jumped back into the truck, which was still running. I jumped into the back of the truck, fired a shot through the back window in order to break the glass, ordered him to stop the truck.'

'Did he?'

'No. He returned fire, then lost control of the vehicle.'

The truck roared off the path and into space, landed bucking, skidded sideways, sending up a spray of snow.

'I was thrown clear. The truck slammed into a tree.'

'You then pursued the suspect on foot?'

'Yes. He ran west, into the woods and up the hill toward Lakeside, occasionally stopping to fire at me.'

'Were you hit?'

'One shot cut through the sleeve of my coat and grazed my arm.'

'But you continued pursuit?'

'Yes. At one point he discarded his ski mask. I found it lying on the ground along the trail.'

'What did you do with it?'

'Left it where it was. The crime-scene unit later photographed it in place, then bagged it as evidence and sent it to the BCA lab to be processed.'

'Your Honor,' Ellen addressed Grabko as Cameron rose and presented several photographs to the clerk. 'The ski mask itself is still at the BCA lab, but the State would like to introduce the crime-scene photographs in its stead for the purpose of this hearing.'

'Mr Costello?' Grabko asked, arching a brow.

'No objections, Your Honor.'

Grabko nodded to his clerk. 'Receive the photographs into evidence.'

'Where did the suspect appear to be headed?' Ellen asked, turning back to Mitch.

'The Lakeside subdivision,' Mitch said. 'He ran up through the backyards of the houses on Lakeshore Drive.'

Running along the cross-country ski trail, darting in and out between the snow-

frosted spruce trees. The cold air like razors in his lungs. Thinking how insane it was to be chasing a college professor who drove a Saab and worked with juvenile offenders.

'I pursued the suspect through the yards, heading north. I saw him let himself into a garage through the back door, followed him in, took him down, and arrested him.'

'And is that man sitting in the courtroom?'

'Yes, he is.' He glared at the man whose game had shredded the fabric of life in Deer Lake irreparably. 'Dr Garrett Wright, the defendant.'

'Thank you, Chief Holt,' Ellen said with a nod. 'No further questions.'

Mitch watched Costello rise, wondering if he would play the same game he had played with Megan – moving closer and closer into her space until she lashed out at him. He would have liked the chance to lash out at Costello, himself. Preferably in a dark alley with no witnesses. It had killed him to sit impassively in the gallery watching Megan unravel. A female bailiff had escorted her from the stand into the jury room after her final outburst. He wanted only one thing more than he wanted to go to her, and that was to nail the lid on Garrett Wright's coffin.

'Chief Holt,' Costello began, standing at ease behind the defense table. 'You testify the suspect was wearing a ski mask when you first encountered him in the park. You did not see his face at that time?'

'No.'

'Did he speak to you?'

'No.'

'The truck he was driving was registered to whom?'

'Roy Stranberg, who was in Arizona at the time. The truck was stolen.'

'And were Dr Wright's fingerprints found in this truck?'

'No.'

'And when you were pursuing the suspect through the woods, did you see him discard the ski mask? Did you see his face?'

'No.'

'That's a fairly dense wood, isn't it, Chief Holt? A lot of trees?'

'That would be the definition of a wood, yes,' Mitch said dryly.

'You didn't have a clear and constant view of the suspect, did you?'

'Not constant, no, but the gunfire kept me apprised of his whereabouts.'

Another snicker ran through the gallery, but Costello jumped onto the opportunity.

'And when you apprehended Dr Wright, was he in possession of a weapon?'

'No.'

'According to the statements, Dr Wright's hands were later tested for gunpowder residue and the tests were negative – isn't that right?'

'Yes.'

Costello steepled his fingers and arranged his features in a contemplative mien. 'So you're running through the woods. It's dark. It's snowing.
You're dodging gunfire, dodging trees. You lost sight of your suspect
more than once, didn't you?'

'I saw him just fine when he went into that garage.'

'But you had lost sight of him prior to that?'

'For no more than seconds.'

'How many seconds?'

'I didn't time the instances.'

'Five seconds? Ten? Twenty?'

'Less than twenty. Less than fifteen.'

'But you have no way of knowing for certain?'

'No.'

'So it could be possible that the man you saw going into that garage
wasn't your suspect at all, isn't that right?'

'That would be unlikely.'

'But possible?'

'Remotely.'

'Prior to making the actual arrest, did you have any reason to believe
the suspect you were chasing was Dr Wright?'

'Agent O'Malley had told me it was Dr Wright.'

'I see,' Costello said with an exaggerated nod. He turned sideways,
cocking a hip against the table, absently twirling a pencil in his hands.
'Chief Holt, when you received that phone call from Agent O'Malley
and heard that she was in distress, in danger, what did that make you
feel?'

Mitch squinted at him, suspicious. 'I don't follow.'

'Were you in fear for her life?'

'Of course.'

'And when you saw her in Quarry Hills Park and she was obviously
badly wounded, did that make you angry?'

'Objection,' Ellen said, looking askance at Costello. 'Is there a point to
this?'

'A very sharp one, Your Honor.'

Grabko nodded. 'Proceed. Answer the question, Chief Holt.'

'Yes.'

'It made you angry. You were frightened for her. You wanted to get
the person responsible. You wanted that badly.'

'That's my job.'

'But your feelings went beyond a professional concern, didn't they?
Isn't it true you and Agent O'Malley are involved —'

'Objection!' Ellen surged to her feet. 'This is absolutely outside the
scope of this hearing! We're here to review facts and evidence, not the
personal lives of police officers!'

Grabko smacked his new gavel. 'I don't want to hear another lecture

750

from you, Ms North,' he snapped. 'Mr Costello, perhaps you'd better state your point for the court.'

Ellen tossed her pencil down and crossed her arms.

'Do you have a problem with my suggestion, Ms North?' Grabko asked coolly.

'Yes, I do, Your Honor. It gives Mr Costello the opportunity to present his case to the press, which is very likely the reason he went down this road in the first place.'

Grabko stuck his lower lip out like a pouting child. 'The outcome of this hearing will not be based on the opinions of the press, Ms North. The decision is mine and mine alone, to be made on the basis of the evidence presented. And so it is for me to decide the relevance of Mr Costello's line of questioning. If I feel it bears merit, I'll allow it. If not, it will be disregarded.'

'And will it be disregarded by every potential juror who reads the *Pioneer Press* or watches *KARE-Eleven News*?' Ellen argued. 'We may not have a jury seated, Your Honor, but we have a gallery who will act as jury *and* judge. If Mr Costello has to make this lame argument, please let him do it in sidebar.'

The judge's eyes scanned the eager faces in the gallery, every last one of them salivating at the idea of hearing something someone didn't want them to hear.

'Sidebar,' he declared unhappily.

They arrayed themselves at the side of the bench, Costello and Ellen shoulder to shoulder, flanked by their associates.

'Now, by all means, Mr Costello,' Ellen said under her breath with sharp-edged sweetness, 'enlighten us as to your big-city legal brilliance.'

Costello smiled. 'You'll have to forgive Ms North, Your Honor. It's understandable she wouldn't want this particular subject raised – the effect of personal relationships on motivation.'

The subtext cut to the quick. Ellen was stunned that even he would skate so close to such a dangerous edge. Turning back to the judge, she shifted her body just slightly and planted the heel of her pump on Costello's handmade Italian oxford, grinding down on his little toe.

'Your Honor, Chief Holt and Agent O'Malley were acting in their capacity as law-enforcement officers. They are here today testifying in that capacity,' Costello said through his teeth as he tried to surreptitiously wrench his foot out from under hers. 'But as Ms North well knows, Your Honor, emotions spill over from our personal lives into our professional. Particularly in a highly charged situation – which this obviously was. If those emotions affected Chief Holt's judgment, I think the court should know about it.'

'Will it make your client any less guilty?' Ellen asked.

'My client is an innocent man, victimized by circumstance and Agent O'Malley's desperate attempt to cling to her own professional life.'

Ellen narrowed her eyes at him. 'Your Honor, may I suggest the only

751

"desperate attempts" we're looking at here are Mr Costello's attempts to introduce a wholly inappropriate line of questioning.'

'No, you may not,' Grabko said. 'You will kindly stop trying to make my decisions for me, Ms North, and remember your place here in this courtroom.'

'My place?'

Cameron nudged her back a step in warning. 'Your Honor, I don't have as much experience in this type of proceeding as Ms North or Mr Costello,' he said, his freckled face shining with humility, 'but I thought the defense, if they are to present a case at all, are to bring hard evidence that is clearly exculpatory in nature, rather than speculative theory. Am I wrong about that?'

Grabko's expression softened somewhat at the opportunity to play law professor, and the tension diffused. 'You're correct, Mr Reed. However, statements can be exculpatory, can they not?'

'Uh, yes, Your Honor.'

'And, theoretically, even a statement from a prosecution witness can be considered such if given proper weight and light.'

And fertilized by the right defense attorney. Cameron's attempt at diplomatic steering had just been bent into a pretzel by Grabko's love of the sound of his own voice.

'Proceed with caution, Mr Costello,' Grabko went on. 'I want to hear a definite point made in the questioning, not counsel giving testimony in the guise of cross-examination.'

Costello nodded. 'Of course, Your Honor. Thank you, Your Honor.'

Ellen refused to give him the satisfaction of looking at him. Taking no chances, Cameron physically turned her back toward their table.

'Nice try, Opie,' she said under her breath.

He leaned his head toward hers as he took his seat. 'You're pissing him off, Ellen.'

'He's pissing me off.'

'Yeah, but his fate isn't in your hands.'

'In my dreams.'

Costello resumed his place behind the defense table, maintaining distance from the witness stand.

'Chief Holt, is it true you and Agent O'Malley are involved personally?'

Mitch's jaw hardened. 'I don't see how that's any of your damn business, Mr Costello.'

Grabko leaned toward the box. 'You'll answer the question, Chief Holt, and please refrain from using profanity in my courtroom.'

'Yes, Your Honor,' he responded grudgingly, glaring at Costello. 'Yes, we are.'

'So when you saw Agent O'Malley in danger, in pain, your reaction went beyond ordinary professional concern.'

'Yes.'

'You wanted to get the person responsible, and Agent O'Malley told you the person responsible was Dr Garret Wright.'

'Yes.'

'You believed the person you were pursuing was Dr Wright. Dr Wright lives on Lakeshore Drive. The chase took you in that direction, and when you saw someone going into Dr Wright's garage, you pursued, even though you admit you had lost sight of your suspect for an unknown period of time. Isn't that correct?'

'Seconds,' Mitch specified. 'A heartbeat. What are you getting at, Costello? Spit it out and spare us the theatrics.'

He wanted to punch the smug little smile off Costello's face, and he realized that the distance the attorney was keeping between them was aggravating him more than if the son of a bitch had been standing a foot away, as he had done with Megan.

'You wanted to see Agent O'Malley keep her position here as regional agent, didn't you?'

'Agent O'Malley is an excellent cop.'

'And your lover. And Agent O'Malley had decided, based on virtually no evidence, that Dr Wright was guilty. She told you Dr Wright was the one. You pursued Dr Wright.'

'I pursued the suspect,' Mitch corrected him, his blood boiling at the insinuation. 'I apprehended the suspect. I didn't give a damn if he was Dr Wright or Dr Spock.'

'It never occurred to you that the man you ultimately apprehended and the suspect you chased through the woods in the dead of night were not the same person?'

'Never.'

'Dr and Mrs Wright live at 93 Lakeshore Drive, is that correct?'

'Yes.'

'Can you tell me who lives just two houses north, at 97 Lakeshore Drive?'

'The Kirkwoods.'

'Paul Kirkwood?'

'Yes.'

'No further questions, Chief Holt.'

Ellen watched Costello as he settled into his chair.

'He's really going to do it, isn't he?' Cameron whispered. 'He's going to try to pin this on Josh's father.'

'He'll do whatever he has to,' she murmured. 'Garrett Wright and his shadow aren't the only ones playing a game here.'

She rose again just as Grabko started to dismiss the witness. 'Redirect, Your Honor?'

Impatience flashed in Grabko's eyes, but he grumbled a yes and sat back to pet his beard.

'Are the houses on Lakeshore Drive numbered on the back side, Chief?'

'Not that I'm aware of.'

'So when you followed the suspect into that garage, you didn't know if you were in 93 Lakeshore Drive or 95 or 91.'

'I had no idea. It didn't matter.'

'The suspect you chased through the woods was dressed in black, is that correct, Chief?'

'Yes. Black pants, black boots, black jacket.'

'And how was Dr Wright dressed when you apprehended him?'

'He was in black pants, black boots, and a black ski jacket.'

'Did he show signs of physical exertion?'

'Yes. He was breathing hard, perspiring.'

'And do you have any idea what the temperature was that evening?'

'About twenty degrees with a windchill factor of six degrees.'

'Not the kind of night the average person would break a sweat, was it?'

'Objection.'

'Withdrawn,' Ellen said, biting down on a sly smile. 'In regards to the tests for gunpowder performed on Dr Wright's hands: would the outcome of the tests be affected if he had been wearing gloves at the time he'd used the gun?'

'Yes.'

'No further questions, Chief Holt. Thank you.'

The final witness for the prosecution was a criminalist from BCA headquarters in St Paul. Norm Irlbeck had been on the scene the night of O'Malley's abduction, had been the one to collect the bloodstained sheet that had been draped around Megan. Ellen showed him photographs of the sheet taken at the scene and at headquarters.

'Is this the sheet, Mr Irlbeck?'

'Yes, it is.' He nodded a big, square head that sat like a block atop a big, square body. His voice was the deep, sonorous voice of authority that caught Grabko's attention and held it.

Ellen handed the photographs over to the clerk. 'The sheet is still undergoing some tests in the lab – is that correct?' she asked, coming back toward her witness.

'Yes. The DNA tests will take another four to five weeks to complete.'

'But there have been some conclusive preliminary findings, have there not?'

'Yes, there have been. Two distinct types of blood were found on the sheet. O positive, which is the blood type of Agent O'Malley, and AB negative, which is the blood type of Josh Kirkwood.'

'And the extensive DNA tests now being conducted will determine if indeed the AB-negative blood is in fact Josh Kirkwood's – correct?'

'Yes.'

'Hairs were also found on the sheet?'

'Yes. Hairs that were tested against samples and were found to be consistent in type with Agent O'Malley, Josh Kirkwood, and the defendant, Dr Garrett Wright. There were also hairs from an unidentified fourth person.'

'What about the ski mask found along the trail of pursuit, Mr Irlbeck? Were hairs also found on that?'

'Yes. Hairs that were consistent with the defendant and also hairs that matched those unidentified from the sheet.'

'Thank you, Mr Irlbeck. I have no further questions.'

'Mr Irlbeck,' Costello said before Ellen was even back to her seat. 'Is the analysis of hair an exact, reliable science?'

'No, it is not.'

'You can't make an absolutely positive identification as to whether a hair found on a sheet belongs to a particular person based strictly on the study of the hair itself.'

'No, sir.'

'Do you have any way of determining who last wore that ski mask?'

'No, sir.'

'And do you have any way of knowing precisely *how* any of the hairs came to be on that sheet?'

'No, I do not.'

'Could they have been deliberately placed on the sheet?'

'Possibly.'

'No further questions.'

'We have enough,' Cameron said, ignoring the chairs and sitting on the credenza. Phoebe handed him a white deli sack and placed Ellen's on the table without looking at her.

Ignoring her secretary's pique and the food, Ellen paced the length of the conference table. She was too nervous to eat. Their part of the hearing had gone well enough, even with Costello scoring a few points, but the afternoon would be Tony's show, and what little control she'd had in the morning would be taken from her.

'We've got more than enough,' Mitch said, pacing the lane on the other side of the table. 'Even if Grabko is tempted to buy into Costello's bullshit, there's more than enough weighing on Wright to push him into a trial. Grabko would never have the guts to cut him loose.'

But how much nerve would it take, Ellen wondered, with the press shouting out all the things Garrett Wright could not have done? He could not have brought Josh home. He couldn't have taken Dustin Holloman or killed Dustin Holloman. That was the public's focus now – the monster at large. Grabko's decision was to be based on law, but he was just a man, as susceptible to rumor and pressure as anyone.

'It's pretty clear which way he's leaning,' she said. 'I haven't seen a judge give that much leeway in a pretrial since *Perry Mason* went off the air. I'm sorry he let Costello put you through that, Megan.'

Megan sat at the end of the table, looking small and battered, as if the ordeal of the morning had caused her to pull in on herself. 'I'm the one who should apologize,' she mumbled, eyes down. 'I know better than to let some asshole lawyer punch my buttons.'

The tension in her voice, in the set of her jaw, hinted at a torrent of emotion building up behind the walls Megan erected around herself. Ellen had seen it happen before. Cops made lousy victims. They were, by nature, control freaks; victims were stripped of all control, all pride, all dignity.

'It's not your fault, Megan,' she said.

'He made me look like a raving lunatic who'd say anything, do anything, to get that arrest on my record.'

'Or like someone who was damn sure of her facts and set on convicting a guilty man,' Ellen countered. 'It's all in your perception. People see what they want.'

'We know what they want to see when they look at Wright,' Megan said. Nobody wanted to believe a man like Garrett Wright was capable of evil. And with the death of Dustin Holloman, the people of Park County would be even less willing to accept Wright as their devil.

'So we have to prove them wrong,' Ellen said, her gaze direct, her meaning clear.

Megan nodded. 'Yes, we do.'

32

'The defense calls Dr Garrett Wright to the stand,' Costello announced, setting the crowd buzzing, a noise that rose up to the high ceiling of the old courtroom like a swarm of yellow jackets.

It appeared to be a bold move, playing his ace first, offering up his client for direct scrutiny and cross-examination. That the defendant himself would be testifying at all was highly unusual for a probable-cause hearing, but, then, nothing about this case was ordinary. Jay sat back with his arms crossed, considering the strategy. If Wright was the sociopath Ellen painted him to be, then he was a consummate liar, an actor with a role he relished – the mild-mannered professor, well deserving of public sympathy.

Jay had to admit, he'd seen it before. A mind as cold as arctic ice; capable of charm, just as capable of murder. He had once sat opposite just such a man in a visitation booth in Angola Penitentiary one hell-hot Louisiana summer. A man who was pleasant, articulate on all the political issues of the day. Well-read, bright, with a sharp, sardonic wit. A man who had held three truck-stop waitresses hostage as sex slaves for three months, tortured them to death, then took up taxidermy and mounted their heads and breasts for his own private trophy room. D. Rodman Madsen, a sales rep for an irrigation-pump company, twice voted salesman of the year, and treasurer of the local Elks lodge. A killer behind the socially acceptable facade. No one who knew him had ever suspected.

Garrett Wright took the stand and quietly recited the oath. In his blue suit and regimental tie, he gave the appearance of the quintessential young professional – attractive, conservative, educated. Jay could all but hear the gears grinding in the minds around him, the sly speculation, the denial, the disbelief. Even the judge looked down on Garrett Wright with barely concealed incredulity, as if astonished to find such a man before him as the focus of a court proceeding.

Costello began by asking for Wright's litany of professional credits, the degrees, the résumé, then segued into his civic achievements before coming to the heart of the matter.

'Dr Wright, where were you on the evening of Wednesday, January twelfth, between five-thirty and seven-thirty P.M.?'

'I was working,' Wright said mildly. 'Researching documented case studies I thought might pertain to an ongoing study some of my students are involved in concerning learning and perception.'

'And where were you doing this research?'

'In a storeroom in the basement of the Cray building.'

'On the campus of Harris College?'

He gave a sheepish little smile. 'Yes. I'm afraid I have more books than my office can hold. I've more or less taken over a room in the basement as an auxiliary office.'

'Were you alone that evening?'

'No. Todd Childs, a student of mine, was with me until about eight-thirty.'

'And when did you first hear about the abduction of Josh Kirkwood?'

'Later that evening. On the ten o'clock news.'

'Do you know Josh?'

'As well as I know any of my neighbors' children – enough to recognize him, to say hello.'

'You know his parents?'

'Hannah and Paul, yes. They're acquaintances of mine and my wife. Casual friends.'

'Has there ever been any trouble between you?'

'No. None.'

'In fact, you spoke with Dr Garrison several times after her son was abducted, didn't you? To offer sympathy, to give advice.'

'Yes. In fact, I called her the night of the twenty-first to give her the name of a family therapist I know in Edina. It was clear the ordeal was taking a terrible toll on their marriage.'

'And the press called on you several times after Josh went missing, to act as a consultant, is that right?'

'Yes, although I told them repeatedly I have no expertise in the area of criminal behavior.'

'Prior to the night you were arrested, were you ever questioned by the police regarding Josh Kirkwood's disappearance?'

'Not as a suspect, no. They asked me some general questions – had I noticed any strangers in the neighborhood, had I noticed anything different about the Kirkwood household lately, that sort of thing.'

'And what did you tell them?'

'That I couldn't be of any real help to them. I spend most of my time at the college or in my office at home.'

'And where were you the afternoon of Saturday, January twenty-second?'

'Working. The new term began Monday. I was preparing.'

'Were you alone?'

'Todd Childs was with me until about one-fifteen. I was alone after that. I went home briefly for a late lunch, around one-thirty, returned to campus about an hour later. Otherwise I spent the afternoon and evening in the Cray building.'

'Arriving home at what time?'

'Around nine-fifteen that evening.'

'And will you please tell the court in your own words what occurred when you arrived home?'

'I had just parked my car in the garage and started for the door into the house when I heard what I thought might be gunshots behind the house. I stepped out the door, saw a man running toward me. I thought he might be a burglar or something, some kind of criminal. So I jumped back inside with the intention of going into the house to call 911. The door burst open, and the next thing I knew I was being tackled and told that I was under arrest.'

'You had no idea what was going on that afternoon and evening with regards to Agent O'Malley being kidnapped and assaulted?'

'Of course not. How could I know anything about that?'

'How, indeed,' Costello said, turning toward the gallery. 'Dr Wright, do you own a ski mask like the one we saw earlier in the prosecution photographs?'

'I did at one time. I used to be something of a fanatic about cross-country skiing. I used to ski three times a week, regardless of the cold, but I haven't done that the past couple of winters.'

'And do you have any idea what became of your ski mask?'

He shook his head. 'I don't know. I think my wife may have gotten rid of it at a garage sale.'

'Do you own a handgun?'

'No. I'm a strong proponent of gun control, as a matter of fact. I would never have a gun in my home.'

'And finally, for the record, Dr Wright, did you kidnap Josh Kirkwood?'

'Absolutely not.'

'Did you kidnap and assault Agent Megan O'Malley?'

'Absolutely not.'

'Thank you, Dr Wright. No further questions.'

Ellen rose before Costello was halfway back to his seat. She marched smartly around the end of the table to take command of the stage. She had watched Wright and Costello weave their web, drawing in Grabko, drawing in the press. They played their roles to the hilt. It was her job to make the audience forget their performances, to make them forget Garrett Wright's history of selfless duty to the community, to stick her fingers through the holes in his story and rip the fabric of his lies to shreds.

'Dr Wright, this storeroom you use in the basement of the Cray building is in the northwest corner of the building, is it not?'

'Yes, it is.'

'The first room at the bottom of the stairs?'

'Yes.'

'And just off the first-floor landing of those stairs is an exit that leads past some trash Dumpsters to a small faculty parking lot. Is that correct?'

'Yes, it is.'

'A very handy spot to have an auxiliary office,' she said. 'Easy to come and go quickly without being seen.'

'Objection.'

'I'll rephrase, Your Honor,' she offered, glad to make her point a second time. 'Did anyone see you exit the Cray building on the night of the twelfth?'

'I didn't see anyone.'

'You told us one of your students, Todd Childs, was with you that evening.'

'Yes, that's correct.'

'Todd Childs and no one else?'

'No one else.'

'Dr Wright, can you explain why, in his initial reports to the police, Mr Childs said nothing about being with you that evening?'

'Objection. Calls for speculation.'

'Sustained.'

'How about on the twenty-second? Can anyone back up your statement that you returned to the Cray building after your late lunch or that you then worked until past nine o'clock that night?'

'I was alone and unaware that I might need an alibi later,' he said dryly.

There was the barest hint of amusement in his eyes as he held Ellen's gaze for just a second. The kind of look that suggested he was only letting her play at control. The idea twisted inside her like a worm boring through her confidence. The image of Dustin Holloman flashed behind her eyelids. *some rise by SIN, and some by virtue fall . . .*

'And on the twenty-second,' she said, pressing on. 'After Todd Childs left your office, you didn't see anyone, not another living soul, all day and half the evening?'

'No, I didn't.'

Ellen crossed her arms and arched a brow as she paced slowly in front of the witness box. 'Doesn't that seem odd? As you stated, the new term was to begin the following Monday. Do you think you're the only teacher with an office in the Cray building who needed to prepare?'

'I can't speak for my colleagues,' Wright said calmly. 'Perhaps they were more well prepared than I. Or maybe the weather kept them from coming in to work. We were having a snowstorm.'

'Yes, we were,' she said, nodding. 'The weather was cold, nasty. Yet when Chief Holt arrested you, you were hot, perspiring. You were not wearing gloves. Can you explain that, Dr Wright?'

'I had just been subjected to a frightening experience, Ms North. I'd heard gunshots, saw a man rushing toward me, a man who then broke into my garage and attacked me. That seems just cause for a little perspiration.'

'And the gloves?'

'I'd forgotten them.'

'On such a bitterly cold night?'

'I was tired. It was late.'

'The windchill factor was six degrees.'

'Yes, I cursed myself all the way home.'

He gave her the look again. Intimate. Amused. Unnerving. Drawing her into a strange, shared moment that no one else seemed to see. Ellen turned her back to him and went to the prosecution table on the false pretense of consulting her notes.

'Dr Wright, Agent O'Malley testified that when she spoke with you in Professor Priest's office earlier in the afternoon, you were dressed in a shirt and tie and dark trousers. At the time Chief Holt arrested you, you were dressed head to toe in black. Why is that?'

'I changed clothes when I came home for lunch,' he answered, unperturbed. 'It was Saturday. I knew I was going to spend the rest of the day alone. I decided I might as well be comfortable.'

'So you dressed up like a ninja warrior?'

'Objection!' Costello shouted.

'Sustained.' Grabko frowned at her. 'Ms North, you know better.'

'Yes, Your Honor,' Ellen said blandly, turning away. 'No further questions.'

Murmurs raced through the gallery as she took her seat. Ellen knew what they were about. Why hadn't she confronted him? Why hadn't she hammered at him until he confessed – if there was anything for him to confess. The same questions courtroom newcomers always asked. The same ideas law professors beat out of their students early on. Garrett Wright would never confess on the stand. He would never admit to anything in a confrontation. He had his story, he had his act, and he would stick with them. She would end up looking a fool if she pressed him. There was no point asking questions if she knew the answers would be lies she couldn't break.

'The defense calls Annette Fabrino.'

The woman who took the stand had a softly rounded body and the face of a Raphael cherub. She looked out on the crowd like a deer caught in headlights, clearly unnerved at the prospect of testifying in front of an audience. Costello stepped close to the witness stand and attempted to put her at ease with a charming smile.

'I have just a couple of questions for you, Annette,' he said kindly. 'It won't take long at all. First of all, can you state for the record your home address?'

'Ninety-two Lakeshore Drive.'

'Just down the block from Dr Wright's home?'

'Yes.'

'On Saturday the twenty-second, did you look out your front window around two-thirty?'

'Yes, I did. My husband was supposed to have been home from a business trip around two, but he was late and he hadn't called. I was worried about his making it back at all because of the weather.'

'What did you see when you looked out?'

'I saw Dr Wright go by in his car, headed south.'

'Are you sure of the time?'

'Yes. I was checking my watch every few minutes.'

'Thank you, Annette.' Costello flashed the smile again and slipped his hands into his trouser pockets. 'That's all. Not so bad, was it?'

A rose blush bloomed across Annette Fabrino's round cheeks.

'Mrs Fabrino,' Ellen began as Costello walked away from his witness, 'your house is on the west side of the street, isn't it? The Tudor on the corner?'

'Yes.'

'And you state you saw Dr Wright's gray Saab going south. That means the driver was on the far side of the car from you.'

'Un – yes.'

'And it was snowing quite heavily that afternoon, wasn't it?'

She nodded. 'Oh, yes. It was really coming down. That was why I was nervous. I had heard the roads were getting bad.'

'So with the snow coming down and the driver on the opposite side of the car, when you say you saw Dr Wright drive past, did you actually get a good, clear look at his face?'

'Well . . .,' she faltered. 'Well, no. Just a glimpse, I guess.'

'You knew it was his car.'

'Yes. It's the only one like it in the neighborhood.'

'So it seems reasonable that you expected him to be the one driving,' Ellen said equably. 'But could you say with certainty it was?'

Annette Fabrino looked anything but certain. She glanced left to right across the courtroom, looking for reassurance from someone. She tried to settle her gaze on Costello. Ellen moved into her line of vision, not wanting to allow Costello a second to imply through his body language that his witness was betraying him.

'I thought it was him,' she said hesitantly.

'But could you swear it?'

'No.'

'No further questions,' Ellen said with a pleasant smile. 'Thank you for your cooperation, Mrs Fabrino.'

'The defense calls Todd Childs.'

The bailiff opened the door to the jury room and Todd Childs emerged. Costello had somehow managed the trick of secreting Childs into the courthouse over the lunch break. And that wasn't the only magic he had performed. He had taken Grunge Man and so transformed him Ellen had to stare for a long moment to be sure this was in fact Todd Childs. The ponytail had been clipped off at the nape, the flannel traded for a button-down oxford with a tie. Clean-shaven and clear-eyed, Todd Childs took the stand and the oath.

He was polite under direct examination. Yes, sir. No, sir. Not a hint of belligerence. Costello painted him as a candidate for the Young Republicans. Trustworthy, reliable, a scholarship student who earned pocket money as a tutor. The profile and the appearance bore no resemblance to the young man Ellen had spoken with at the Pack Rat. Costello had obviously been putting him up somewhere, having him groomed and coached, and was likely paying him for his trouble.

'Todd, were you with Dr Wright on the evening of the twelfth?'

'Yeah, I was.' He glanced down, pretending to pick lint off his new slacks. 'Downstairs in the Cray building. We were going through some data we compiled in the study last year, and looking for correlations in past studies.'

'In your statement to the police made on January twenty-fourth you said you were at the movies that night.'

Childs glanced up at Costello, over at Wright, and down again. 'I was mistaken. I went but it was the late show, not the early one.'

'What theater did you go to?'

'The mall in Burnsville.'

'Had you heard anything about the abduction of Josh Kirkwood?'

'No.'

'On Saturday, the twenty-second, Agent O'Malley stopped by Professor Priest's office while you were there, didn't she?'

'Yeah.'

'After she left, did Dr Wright seem upset or excited?'

'No.'

'Did he talk about going after her or going to Christopher Priest's home?'

'No.'

'Did he say anything about Josh Kirkwood's abduction?'

Todd bobbed his head down between his shoulders. 'Yeah. He said it was a shame, 'cause they were such a nice family.'

Costello turned around with a gracious gesture. 'Your witness, Ms North.'

Ellen walked toward the witness stand with her hands clasped in front of her, as if in prayer, her expression pensive. 'Todd, you've known Dr Wright for a long time haven't you? Ever since you began taking classes at Harris — isn't that right?'

He looked at her out the corner of his eye, suspicious. 'Yeah.'

'You declared your major early on. You always wanted to go into psychology.'

'Yeah.'

'And Dr Wright wasn't just a teacher for you, was he? He was your adviser, your mentor.'

'Yes.'

'Your friend?'

He gave her a hard look. 'I respect him very much.'

'That's admirable, Todd.'

'He's an admirable man.'

Ellen tipped her head. 'Very few admirable men stand accused of kidnapping and assault.'

'Your Honor!' Costello whined.

'Ms North, don't make me warn you again,' Grabko said coldly.

'I'm sorry, Your Honor,' she said, remorseless, her attention never leaving the witness. 'You respect and admire Dr Wright. How much? Enough to lie for him?'

'No!'

'Objection!'

'Sustained.'

'Where did you go to the movies that night, Todd?' she asked without slowing a beat.

'I said – Burnsville.'

She feigned puzzlement. 'Burnsville? You drove all the way to Burnsville to go to a late movie on a Wednesday night and that *slipped your mind* when you were talking to the police?'

'I told them I was at the movies.'

'I see. Then it was the fact that you had been with Dr Wright at the time of the kidnapping that *slipped your mind*? Or was it the fact that you claim to have been at the movies *in Burnsville* that slipped your mind, because there is no mention of Burnsville in your original statement.'

'It didn't seem important.'

'Until the police tried to check out your story at the Deer Lake theaters,' Ellen said sharply. 'You've got a 3.85 GPA at Harris, don't you, Todd?'

'Yes.'

'Then I should think it's safe to assume you know the meaning and the ramifications of perjury –'

Costello threw up his arms. 'Your Honor, this is badgering.'

'Change your tone, Ms North.'

'Yes, Your Honor,' she said automatically, never looking away from Childs. 'Todd, where have you been staying the last few days?'

'Objection.'

'Sustained.'

'Were you aware the Deer Lake police were looking –'

'Objection. Relevance,' Costello argued, getting to his feet.

'It's relevant to the credibility of the witness, Your Honor. If Mr Childs has been hiding out, avoiding –'

Grabko cracked his gavel, his cheeks tinting pink above his beard. 'Ms North, do not persist in this.'

She spread her hands. 'I'm sorry, Your Honor, but the witness has

764

given conflicting statements to the police and to this court. He is extremely biased toward the defendant and –'

'You've made your point, Ms North,' Grabko said.

She nodded her understanding and stepped back from the witness stand. 'No further questions.'

Childs climbed down from the box and was met on the other side of the gallery gate by Mitch Holt and a uniformed officer.

'What the fuck –?' he snapped, jerking his arm back from the officer's grasp.

Costello shot to his feet. 'Your Honor, this is an outrage!'

The crowd broke their silence as the scuffle in the aisle continued and reporters jumped up on their chairs for a better view. The bailiff hurried through the gate as Mitch and Officer Stevens took hold of Childs, and herded the lot of them toward the door, with Grabko destroying another gavel behind them.

The judge ordered the attorneys to the bench once again. Ellen took her place beside Costello, feeling the anger roll off him in waves as he accused her of turning the hearing into a circus sideshow.

'Really, Mr Costello,' she said calmly, 'don't you think you're being a little paranoid? The police have been looking for Todd Childs for days to question him on that break-in. Since they've had no luck and received no cooperation in finding him, I'm sure they felt they had to grab him when they could.'

'In front of the court?' he bellowed, his temper boiling up.

'I don't appreciate the theatrics either, Ms North,' Grabko said sternly. 'I'll be speaking with Chief Holt about this.'

'He should be taken off the case entirely,' Costello fumed. 'The conflict of interest is obvious.'

'The issue is not germane to this hearing, Mr Costello,' Ellen said.

'For the last time, Ms North,' Grabko said through his teeth, 'refrain from doing my job for me. Now, go back to your places and we will resume this hearing in a civilized manner. Call your next witness, Mr Costello.'

As they returned to their tables, the door at the back of the courtroom opened, and a neatly turned-out middle-aged man with slicked-back dark hair strode purposefully down the center aisle with a small manila envelope in one gloved hand. He leaned over the rail and handed the envelope to Dorman. Gravely murmured words were exchanged. Something bright and feral flashed in Costello's eyes as he turned back toward the court.

'The defense calls Karen Wright.'

Karen Wright settled herself in the witness chair. Ellen wondered if the thin veil of calm about her was drug induced. Her dark eyes were wide, unblinking. She fixed her gaze on Costello and waited for him to begin. He took his place at the corner of the stand, not wanting to obstruct anyone's view of her – pretty in pink, her ash-blond pageboy sleek and silky, her mouth slightly trembling.

'Karen, I want to thank you for testifying here today,' he began gently. 'I know this is difficult for you. This entire ordeal has been very hard on you, hasn't it?'

'You can't know.' She lifted a lace-edged handkerchief to catch a tear that had yet to fall. 'It's been terrible. All of it. I never would have thought –' She cut herself off and closed her eyes for a moment. 'It's terrible. I hate it.'

'Karen, how long have you and Dr Wright been married?'

A nostalgic little smile tugged at one corner of her mouth. 'It seems like forever. Sixteen years.'

'And in all that time, has Garrett ever been in trouble with the law?'

'No.' She shook her head, twisting her hankie in her lap. 'Garrett has never even had a traffic ticket. He's a very careful man. He shouldn't have been arrested. None of this should ever have happened.'

'Has he ever spoken ill of the Kirkwoods?'

'No. Never.'

'And you?'

'I considered them friends,' she said, dropping her gaze and her volume.

'In fact, you helped them out while Josh was missing, didn't you, Karen?'

'I sat with Lily.' A pair of tears skittered down her cheeks. 'Such a little sweetheart. I love babies,' she admitted. 'Garrett and I can't have children,' she added, dropping her gaze to her lap again, as if the fact carried shame with it.

'Karen, where were you the evening of the twelfth?' Costello asked abruptly, steering her away from potentially dangerous waters.

'At work. I do secretarial work part-time for Halvorsen's State Farm Insurance in the Omni Complex.'

'Do you often work in the evening?'

'I – no.' She closed her eyes again and drew in a hitching, shallow breath.

'Karen, *were* you working that night?'

A strange keening sound came up the back of her throat, and she began to rock herself forward and back. Even with her arms wrapped around herself, she was clearly shaking. The tears spilled over her lashes.

'It's not fair,' she whimpered. 'It's not fair . . .'

'Karen,' Costello murmured. 'Please answer the question. It's very important. You were at the Omni Complex that night. Were you working?'

She looked at him, her pretty face twisting with torment. Her eyes scanned the crowd, resting on someone in the gallery, then moving to her husband, who stared back at her blankly.

'I'm so sorry,' she whispered, dropping her gaze to her lap. 'I'm so, so sorry. Please don't . . .'

'Karen,' Costello prompted. 'You have to answer the question.'

She dropped her bomb with a voice so soft everyone in the courtroom was straining to hear.

'I stayed late because . . . I was having an affair with Paul Kirkwood.'

The admission hit Ellen like a sonic blast. Behind the bar the courtroom erupted, Paul Kirkwood's voice rising above the others.

'That's a lie! Goddamn you, Wright! You put her up to this! You'll pay, you son of a bitch!'

All Ellen could think was that someone had already paid – Josh.

'It is within counsel's rights to attempt to prove someone other than the defendant committed the crime,' Dorman recited. He stood at Costello's shoulder like an overeager valet.

Costello had settled himself into one of Grabko's visitor's chairs, legs crossed, suit coat arranged to minimize wrinkles, manila envelope in one hand. Ellen could feel his eyes on her, calm, sharp.

'It's a goddamn smear campaign and it's unconscionable!' she snapped, beyond circumspection, beyond anger. She may have drawn blood from some of his witnesses, but he had nicked a major artery and was waiting to see if Grabko would allow it to bleed out. She was too furious to sit, but she kept herself planted in the chair with Cameron standing guard behind her.

The judge glared at her in affront. 'Ms North, I won't have that kind of language in my chambers, particularly from a lady. This is a place of civil discussion.'

'There's nothing civil about what Mr Costello is attempting to do here, Your Honor. I don't care if he couches it with excerpts from Elizabeth Barrett Browning. It stinks to high heaven!'

Grabko had ordered them into his chambers before all hell could break loose in the courtroom. The dissonant clamor of the gallery as they adjourned from the room had been deafening. Ellen could only imagine what was going on out there now. A feeding frenzy. Paul Kirkwood pinned up against the gallery railing as the rabid mob tore chunks out of him. She wouldn't have minded tearing some chunks out of him herself if what Karen Wright claimed was true, but his infidelity was an issue of its own.

'Paul Kirkwood's sexual exploits are well outside the scope of this hearing,' she said, turning toward Costello. 'Although, if it's true, it gives your client motive beyond mere evil.'

'On the contrary,' he said coolly. 'It gives Paul Kirkwood motive.'

'Which is what?'

'We think the boy might have discovered his father's dirty little secret and Paul saw abducting the child as a way of killing two birds with one stone – shut the boy up and get his rival for Karen's affections out of the way.'

'Why stop there?' Ellen said sarcastically. 'Don't you think he might have been on the grassy knoll the day Kennedy was shot?'

'Ellen, facetiousness is not called for here,' Grabko chastened.

'Not unless it's in the guise of a defense,' she muttered, then winced as Cameron surreptitiously pinched her arm.

'Mrs Wright is prepared to testify she had a tryst with Paul Kirkwood in a vacant office in the Omni Complex the night Josh disappeared,' Costello said. 'That Paul was to meet her at six forty-five that evening and did not show up until seven. He wouldn't account for the time he had been gone, and he seemed extremely agitated.'

'So says the wife of your client,' Ellen said. 'It's absurd that she's even on the stand.'

Costello ignored her. 'Her testimony sets the stage, Your Honor. Paul Kirkwood has been under suspicion from the first. He's without an alibi for the time of the abduction, had a connection to the van owned by Olie Swain – who may well have been his accomplice. He repeatedly lied about the van. In her statement to the police the Ryan's Bay witness said the man who came to her house was looking for his son's dog and called it by name. Who's to say it wasn't Kirkwood himself?'

'Anyone with half a brain,' Ellen grumbled. 'If you'll recall, that witness identified your client in the lineup.'

'She identified a man in a parka and sunglasses.'

'She singled him out by his voice.'

'Paul Kirkwood wasn't in the lineup. She did the best she could. For all we know, Kirkwood disguised his voice. He was trying to pin this thing on Dr Wright –'

'Then why didn't he introduce himself as Garrett Wright?' Cameron asked. 'Why implicate himself in any way? It makes no sense.'

'And I say there's room for doubt,' Costello declared with an elegant shrug. 'The police went so far as to fingerprint him.'

'For elimination purposes!' Ellen argued.

He gave her a look. 'You know perfectly well the difference between what the police say and what they mean, Ellen.'

Ellen sniffed. 'Two days ago you thought they were too stupid to tie their own shoes; now you think their every action is fueled by an ulterior motive.'

'And there's still the matter of the actual arrest,' Cameron began.

'Easily explained if Kirkwood set out to frame Dr Wright,' Costello said. 'The hairs on the sheet, the hairs in the stocking cap – evidence easily planted. In fact, the criminalist stated there were unidentified hairs on both items. I suggest Mr Kirkwood be asked to surrender hair samples.' He turned to Ellen with exaggerated seriousness. 'For elimination purposes, of course.'

She curled her fingers around the arms of her chair and resisted the urge to take samples of Costello's hair with her bare hands. He undoubtedly would have been delighted to have her try. His goal from the first had been to make her look bad in front of Grabko, to get any edge he could any way he could. And she had let herself be drawn into his traps again and again. That truth made her want to tear her own hair out. She was supposed to have got over him, not just away from him and his kind. She was supposed to have changed her life and herself, not simply let the old Ellen go dormant to be reawakened.

'Your Honor,' she said with forced calm, 'Paul Kirkwood is not on trial here. He was investigated and eliminated as a possible suspect. There appears to be a direct connection between the abduction of Josh Kirkwood and the abduction and murder of Dustin Holloman. In fact, the Holloman case has been used to taunt the authorities in such a way as to make Wright look innocent. If Paul Kirkwood is the villain here, and trying to make Garrett Wright take the fall, it doesn't follow.

'We have to proceed with this case, make our judgments about this case, on the basis of the evidence we have. The evidence we have points clearly to Dr Wright and an accomplice who has yet to be apprehended.'

Grabko pursed his lips and dug a fingertip into his beard as if in pursuit of a tick. 'The Holloman case is outside the scope of this hearing,' he said. 'Paul Kirkwood is directly related to the case before us. Although I don't necessarily care for your method in bringing Mr Kirkwood's possible involvement to light, Mr Costello, this is a hearing and not a trial, and I am inclined to allow more leeway. After all, it is the truth we're after.'

'Absolutely, Your Honor,' Costello said gravely.

'We sometimes lose sight of that ultimate goal in our adversarial system,' Grabko pontificated, warming to his topic. 'Ambition crowds out purer motives. The rules of court are bent and corrupted. The truth is lost in a scramble to win.'

He paused, pleased with the ideals he had just brought out like shining jewels to show off to his small audience. It never occurred to him to look beyond his own brilliance to see which of the factions before him was guilty of the sins he had named.

'We'll hear what Mrs Wright has to say,' he said, snapping out of the afterglow.

Costello waited until everyone else was halfway out of their chairs to speak. 'Before we adjourn, Your Honor,' he said, lifting the envelope. 'My associate, Mr York, has brought in a piece of evidence I believe will add validity to our defense.' As smooth as a magician performing sleight of hand, he opened the envelope and produced a microcassette tape. 'This is a tape from Paul Kirkwood's office answering machine with messages from the night his son was abducted.'

'And how did you happen to come by that?' Ellen asked sharply.

Costello's expression was carefully blank. 'Apparently, someone dropped it through the mail slot at my office suite – anonymously.'

'I'll bet.'

'You've heard this tape, Mr Costello?' Grabko asked.

'No, sir. My assistant, Ms Levine, listened to it and deemed it important enough to send it straight over. I suggest we all listen,' he said, placing the cassette on Grabko's desk.

Ellen felt as if she'd been broadsided with a mallet. The hell he hadn't heard it. He would never have wasted a dramatic moment on a pig in a poke. Tony Costello knew exactly what was on that tape, and he was betting it would score him big points.

She shot to the front edge of her chair, bracing one hand against the desk, her fingertips inches from the tape. 'I have to object, Your Honor. There was nothing in counsel's disclosure about this tape. We have no idea where it came from or how it was obtained or who *allegedly* left it or what their motives might be.'

'Mr York has already managed to check with two of the parties who have messages on the tape, Your Honor,' Costello said. 'They confirm having made the calls on the night of the twelfth.'

'Let's have a listen,' Grabko said, reaching for the cassette. 'We can all hear the tape now, and, if there is any question as to its validity or admissibility, we'll deal with those issues later.'

Ever efficient, Mr Dorman produced a microcassette recorder from the pocket of his Brooks Brothers suit, popped his own cassette out of it, and handed the machine to Grabko.

The first thing they heard was background noise, the sound of an engine; then came the voice, and it pierced Ellen's heart like a needle.

'Dad, can you come and get me from hockey? Mom's late and I wanna go home.'

770

33

'*Dad, can you come and get me from hockey? Mon's late and I wanna go home.*'

His son's voice played through Paul's head over and over, as it had been doing for the last three weeks. An endless loop of innocence and accusation that raked through his brain like talons.

And layered over it, Mitch Holt's voice, low and tight.

'*What the hell were you thinking, Paul? Jesus Christ, Josh called you for help! You didn't so much as answer him. You pretend you never heard him. You hold on to the goddamn tape for three weeks and never say one fucking word! How do you explain that, Paul?*'

And layered over that, Ellen North's icy tone.

'*The defense is building a case against you, Mr Kirkwood. I'm not so sure that shouldn't be my job. You lied to the police. You withheld information –*'

'You blamed Hannah,' Holt said. '*And this time you dumped the guilt on her head. You son of a bitch. You never even had the guts to stand up and tell the truth.*'

The truth will set you free.

The truth would ruin him.

He couldn't believe this was happening to him. After all he had been through. After all he had suffered. Now this. Betrayal by the one person he thought had loved him. Karen.

It was incomprehensible to him to think that she could turn on him so completely. She loved him. She wanted to have his children. Her marriage to Wright was a sham – she had said so more than once. Garrett Wright couldn't give her what she needed, what she wanted. Garrett Wright loved his work, not his wife.

Paul shuddered at the memory of that moment in the courtroom. Every eye had turned on him, avid, accusatory. The press he had courted and played to from day one had turned on him. Damn them all. They had wanted Hannah for their heroine from the first. The grieving, guilt-ridden mother. Hannah, with her golden tresses and tragic blue eyes. Hannah, the dedicated doctor, the woman of the year. Hannah, Hannah, Hannah.

They would turn to her now with gushing sympathy, and he would be the sacrificial goat. They would never ask what had driven him from his home. They would never want to hear that Hannah wasn't any kind of wife, that she ignored her children in favor of her precious career, that she had done her best to emasculate him.

He had thought of trying to get to her before they could, but they had been all over him, swarming around him, their questions stinging his ears and stabbing his conscience. They had followed him to his car and followed his car as he tried to escape. He had finally turned out on the interstate and opened up the Celica's engine, leaving them behind as the speedometer swept toward ninety.

It was dark now. The press would have been to the house and gone long ago. Hannah had given them nothing in the past – a single interview, a photo op as the priest helped her into the volunteer center downtown. Paul had to think she would shun them again, even if it meant giving up a chance to publicly humiliate him. And the reporters would call her noble and long-suffering and paint her as the good woman betrayed. The idea turned his stomach.

The anger and anxiety churned inside him like acid, like a virus that raced through his system and pulsed just beneath his skin. It spread over his brain like a fungus and left him feeling feverish and bruised.

He drove down Lakeshore, driving through the neighborhood *he* had chosen for its prestige, toward the home *he* had wanted, with its lakefront view and park out the back door. This was the life he had coveted since his youth. Now it would end up being Hannah's. She would get the sympathy *and* the house. The irony was as bitter as bile.

Passing Wright's home, he fought the urge to drive his car in through their front door. He would have liked to have seen the look on Karen's face when he confronted her.

'*I love you, Paul. . . . I'd have your baby, Paul. . . . I'd do anything for you.*'

Except lie for him in court.

She could have given him an alibi. Instead she brought the whole world down on his head. Some love.

Women. Bitches, every last one of them. The bane of his existence. His mother, Hannah, O'Malley, Ellen North . . . Karen.

'*I stayed late because I was having an affair with Paul Kirkwood.*'

Was. Past tense.

'*I love you, Paul. . . . I'd have your baby, Paul. . . . I'd do anything for you. . . . I'm so sorry. . . . It was a mistake. . . .*'

A mistake.

God knew he'd made plenty of them, not the least of which had been keeping that damned tape.

'*We know the call came before six-fifteen, Paul. Were you there? Did you hear it? Where did you go when you left the office? Why can't we find anyone to corroborate that story? Why didn't you tell us about the call, Paul? How could you let Hannah take the blame?*'

Because it was her fault. All of it. If she had done her duty . . . if she had been there for her son . . . if she had been a decent wife . . .

Guilt was the last emotion Hannah wanted to feel. She had been drowning in it for weeks now. A mother's guilt compounded by a doctor's sense of failure because the patient she had stayed at the hospital for that night had been lost as well. But what came tonight was different, more futile, less deserved.

Could she have been a better wife, a better lover, more supportive, less critical? What had she done to make Paul hate her so? Why had he turned to Karen Wright?

The questions infuriated her. There were more important ones to ask. Had Paul been in his office when Josh had called him that night? Why had he lied and lied and lied – about the van, about so many things? Why was Josh so terrified of him? Why did he seem like such a stranger? Was he involved in all the horror that had taken place over the last three weeks? Perhaps it was because the possible answers to these questions frightened her so badly that she let the others creep into her mind and divert her attention. They made her angry with herself for thinking them, but they didn't make her husband out to be a monster.

'Do you think your husband abducted Josh?'

'Do you think he killed the Holloman boy?'

'He had access to a van –'

'Did you know about the affair'

'Damn you, Paul,' she whispered. Pulling her hands up out of the soapy water, she gathered up the dish towel and pressed her face into it.

She didn't know how much more she could stand. Dawn had brought the news of Dustin Holloman's murder, and with it fear and a terrible relief that it was someone else's child who had died and not hers. Josh seemed more withdrawn than ever, but he was still with her, physically. And as long as she had him with her, there was hope. And then had come the news from the courthouse. Not from Mitch or from Ellen North, but from the reporters who had come to the house demanding answers as if she owed them something for all the hell they had put her through.

'Can we get a reaction from you about your husband's illicit affair with the wife of the man on trial for abducting your son?'

If she had been shaky before, that had put her over the edge. And once again she had turned to Tom McCoy.

God, Hannah, you're not even calling him Father anymore. She remembered the pretense of title when they were speaking, because she didn't want to upset him or jeopardize their friendship. But in her heart she had grown beyond thinking of him as her priest. The need she felt for his company, for his support, for his comfort, was stronger than that.

And people think Paul is rotten for cheating on me. What would they think if they knew I'd fallen in love with a priest?

Of course, no one would ever know, most of all Tom himself. He was too good a friend to lose. When the news came from the courthouse, she had called him. He had come and chased the press away, and forced her to eat chicken soup, and read stories to the kids. He sat with her on the sleeping bag in Josh's room, watching Josh drift off to sleep, then shooed her out of the room because he knew she needed the break but would never take it.

A deep ache of yearning rolled through her, and she closed her eyes against it. Hadn't she endured enough without having to fall in love with a man she could never have?

The sound of the door opening from the garage into the laundry room tore her out of her self-pity. A wild, primal instinct swung her hand to the knife block on the counter. Dustin Holloman's killer was still at large. Who was to say he wouldn't come back for Josh? If Josh could identify him . . .

The kitchen door swung open and Paul cast a look at the knife in her hand.

'I suppose I can guess what you'd like to do with that,' he said.

The panic bottomed out, leaving a thick, sour anger in its wake. Hannah set the knife aside. 'It wouldn't be worth the trouble.'

He gave a bitter laugh. 'And the press wondered why I would cheat on you.'

Somehow the admission of guilt cut more coming from Paul's own mouth. The same mouth that had pledged love and fidelity. She had kissed that mouth in play and in passion, had loved its smile, worried at its frown. It had told her lies and tasted another woman.

She wanted to launch herself at him, to punish him. But when she opened her mouth to speak, the fight went out of her.

'I loved you,' she said quietly, knowing immediately that wasn't true. She had loved someone else, not this bitter, angry man. 'What happened, Paul? What happened to you?'

'Me?' he said, incredulous. 'Maybe if you'd paid attention to something other than your career the last few years, you wouldn't have to ask.'

Hannah shook her head. 'No, Paul, this isn't about my work. For once, it really is about you. You turned away from me. You turned to another woman. You made that choice. We had something wonderful and you threw it away.'

'Yeah, fine, blame me,' he said impatiently, starting past her.

'I will blame you,' she said sharply. 'I just wish I knew how much to blame you for.'

He wheeled around, brows lowered. 'What the hell is that supposed to mean?'

'It means Josh called you that night and you *did nothing*.'

'I wasn't in –'

'But no one can say where you were. Were you with *her*?' She swung an accusatory finger in the direction of the Wrights' house. 'When I was frantic, trying to find Josh, trying to call you, were you down the hall screwing Karen Wright? Where were you when Josh needed you?'

'It was your night to –'

'No! Don't you dare blame me. I was trying to save a life. You were fucking yours away – or worse. And you had the gall to dump all that guilt on me, as if you hadn't done anything wrong, as if you hadn't lied to me and to the police and done God knows what else!'

The implication struck Paul hard. *The defence is building a case against you, Mr Kirkwood. . . .*'

'I would never hurt Josh,' he insisted.

The doubt in her eyes was stark. 'Then why won't he let you near him?'

'You can't think I took him,' he said, stepping toward her, wanting to shake her. 'You can't think that!'

'Why can't I? You've lied about everthing else!'

'The defence is building a case against you, Mr Kirkwood . . .'

The press was on him. The prosecution was eyeing him. Now this. St Hannah casting judgment. And no one would blame her. She was golden; he was nothing, nobody. In that moment he hated her enough to want her dead.

His control snapped. There was no thought, only action, only fury. 'You bitch!'

Hannah saw the blow coming. The back of his hand caught her hard on the jaw, snapping her head to the side. The world blurred and tilted, and she staggered sideways, knocked off balance by the slap and by the idea of it. Never in her life had she been struck by anyone for any reason. As often as she had seen the aftermath of domestic violence in the ER, she had never in her darkest dreams imagined she would become a victim.

Paul advanced toward her, his eyes dark with rage, his mouth twisting.

'Paul, no!' Tom McCoy shouted, lunging up the steps to the kitchen.

Paul wheeled on him, arm drawn back. Tom blocked the punch and caught Paul square in the mouth with a right cross that dropped him to his knees. The action was automatic, instinctive. It stunned him to the core of his soul. He stared down at Paul, who sat back on his heels, his hands covering his mouth, blood leaking between his fingers.

'Why did you come here, Paul?' he asked. 'Haven't you done enough damage already?'

Paul glared up at him, wiping his mouth on his coat sleeve as he rose to his feet. 'I came to get my stuff.'

Tom shook his head. 'There's nothing here for you. Get out.'

'You can't throw me out of my own home.'

'This isn't your home,' Hannah said. The ache inside her rivaled the pain in her throbbing jaw. 'You just gave up your rights here. Get out before I call the police.'

He looked from her to Father Tom, eyeing the priest's sweater and jeans and stocking feet.

'Oh, I get it,' he said snidely.

'Don't say it, Paul,' Tom warned. 'At the moment I can't see that there'd be any sin in my beating the snot out of you.'

Silence descended. Paul picked the dish towel off the counter and blotted at his mouth.

'I'll have your things delivered to the office,' Hannah said.

She leaned against the refrigerator as he left, refusing to look at him. But in the corner of her eye she could see their Christmas photo, still held to the refrigerator door by magnets shaped like candy canes. The back door closed.

'Are you all right?' Tom asked, stepping closer, reaching out to her.

'No,' she whispered.

He took her in his arms as if it were the most natural thing in the world, cradled her head against his broad shoulder and stroked her hair with his hand. The love that welled inside him was the purest, the strongest he'd ever known in his life. He loved her in a way that meant he would do anything for her, be anything for her. He couldn't see how that could be wrong.

'I don't understand,' she murmured, her arms tight around him. 'We had a nice life. Why did it have to go so wrong?'

He couldn't share the answer that came to him – *So you could love me.* He didn't know if it was God's will or just his own.

He knew what the monsignor would tell him – that this was a test of his faith and his duty to the Church. The idea that God would use people that way, like pawns in a game, only made him want to rebel.

'I'm sorry, Hannah,' he murmured. 'I'd give anything to change it for you.'

'I just want to walk away from it. Take the children and go someplace new and clean and start over.'

'I know.'

'Would you go with me? I could use a friend when I get there,' Hannah said, pretending it was a joke.

But when she looked up at him, what she saw in his earnest blue eyes wasn't humor but truth. A truth that didn't need words. A truth that spoke to her battered heart. A truth he sealed with a kiss. A kiss so tender, so sweet. Full of the kind of promise she wanted to grab with both hands and use as a shield against an uncertain future.

Instead she put her head back on his shoulder, and they stood there for a long while, each wondering where they would go from here.

'So where do we go from here?' Cameron asked.

They had assembled in The War Room at the law-enforcement center, where the time line of all that had taken place in the last three weeks stretched the length of one wall.

'We've got to take a closer look at Kirkwood,' Wilhelm said. 'See if we can put him in the wrong place at the wrong time. Confiscate his phone records. Check –'

'What about the suspect we've got?' Mitch asked irritably. 'Garrett Wright is the man.'

'But the tape –'

'Doesn't prove shit.'

'How can you say that? The boy called –'

'And Paul was otherwise engaged.'

'But his mistress can't account for the time –'

'And why would he keep that tape?' Cameron asked.

'Guilt,' Mitch said simply.

'Yeah,' Steiger interjected around the toothpick he was chewing. 'The kind that comes with a sentence to the state hotel.'

'Don't be stupid,' Mitch snapped. 'If Paul *was* guilty of taking Josh, getting rid of that tape would have been his first priority. If he had taken the boy, he would never have gone up to Ruth Cooper's house and said he was looking for his own damned dog.'

'Unless he's nuts.'

Wilhelm was like a puppy with a new chew toy. 'And there's the connection to the van. And the kid's reaction. And –'

'And I've got a man standing before the court tomorrow,' Ellen said sharply. 'We've built a case against Garrett Wright. Mitch apprehended Garrett Wright. Agent O'Malley identified Garrett Wright. Our erstwhile witness identified Garrett Wright. What the hell are you doing to help me get Garrett Wright to trial?'

Wilhelm pouted, looked down at his coffee. 'Wright couldn't have taken the Holloman kid.'

'We're not dealing with Holloman,' Ellen reminded him. 'I'm sure you'd like to wrap all the crimes up in one neat package with one perp and move on, but that's not the way it works. We've focused on this game being played by Wright and an accomplice. Did you ever stop to think, Agent Wilhelm, that they *want* you to run off half-cocked after Paul Kirkwood?'

'We have to follow *all* leads, Ms North,' he said. 'I've asked Mr Stovich to get search warrants for Paul Kirkwood's home and office, and for a locker he rents at the U-Store-It on the south side of town. We'll execute the warrants tonight if we get them in time. In light of what's on that tape, I'd say we've looked the other way long enough where Paul Kirkwood is concerned.'

Ellen couldn't argue. As much as she hated having the investigation pulled in another direction, it seemed they had no real options. Costello had leaked word of the cassette tape to the press. The police had to act on it.

She looked to Cameron. 'Will you go with them?'

'Sure.'

Turning to Mitch, she asked, 'Did you get anywhere with Todd Childs?'

He scowled. 'Yeah, I got threatened with a lawsuit for false arrest.'

Ellen pretended surprise. 'Did Mr Childs get the impression he was under arrest?'

'A simple misunderstanding,' he said, straight-faced. 'He calmed down after we gave him a cup of decaf.'

'And got his prints off the cup?'

'They're being run in St Paul even as we speak. If we can put him at Enberg's office, that would give us a nice big lever to crack this thing open.'

'How soon will you know?'

'Couple of days.'

'The hearing will be over tomorrow morning,' Cameron said. 'Grabko could rule as soon as tomorrow afternoon.'

'We need a break, gentlemen,' Ellen said. 'And we need it tonight.'

Steiger pushed himself to his feet. He had shed the adhesive tape from his nose, but the bruising remained, streaking across his hard cheekbones like war paint. 'Grabko dismisses, you can always charge him again later. It's not like double jeopardy.'

Ellen stared at the sheriff. 'And if he hasn't packed up his little Saab and driven off into the sunset, we might actually get him to trial. I don't want to take that chance. I want him bound over. Tomorrow.'

'I've got men double-checking all hot-line tips that came into Campion,' Steiger said, moving toward the door, declaring the meeting over for himself. 'Don't get your hopes up.'

Seeing his chance to escape, Wilhelm hustled after him. 'A – yeah – Sheriff, I wanted to talk to you about those hot-line tips.'

Ellen watched their defection with a mix of anger and despair. If Wright's plan had been to divide and conquer, he was scoring points tonight. The revelation of Paul Kirkwood's answering-machine tape was acting like a wedge, splitting her team even more decisively than the kidnapping of Dustin Holloman had.

'Cameron, go offer them some suggestions,' she said with a meaningful look.

He grabbed his coat and hustled out.

Silence hung in the air for a moment before Ellen turned to Mitch. 'Well, do you want to jump on the bandwagon of people who think I should have asked the judge for a postponement right off the bat?'

'The Twenty-Twenty Hindsight Club?' He made a face. 'Why would I join them? The membership requirements are too low. Who's on your case?'

'Well, let's see,' she mused, tapping her chin with a forefinger. 'Not counting you? Everybody. Stovich, the state attorney general, the press, half the population of Deer Lake.'

'Pointless bullshit.'

'That's easy for you to say.'

'Are you forgetting the Olie Swain debacle?'

'Sorry. No.'

She blew out a sigh and rose with all the energy of a ninety-year-old arthritic. She stared at the time line, wishing something would jump out at her. Some heretofore overlooked minutia that would spark The Big Revelation and point to Todd Childs or Christopher Priest. Nothing. If anything, the words and lines and arrows became less coherent, a hopeless jumble of scribbling. The only name that leaped out at her was Paul Kirkwood.

Paul had owned Olie Swain's van. Olie Swain, the convicted child molester. The van had yielded them nothing. Paul had excuses instead of alibis. They had no hard evidence against him. Paul had searched tirelessly for his son in brutal subzero temperatures. His son, who wouldn't let him get within an arm's length.

'What do you really think about Paul?' she asked quietly.

Mitch's face was blank as he walked along the time line, his eyes resting on every notation that mentioned Paul. 'I've said it before – I think people would like for Paul to be the bad guy in all this. He's not well-known, he's not well liked. They'd rather think someone like him lost his marbles than believe a man like Garrett Wright is an evil genius.'

'I could see people thinking that when it was Josh missing,' Ellen said. 'They wanted to contain the malignancy to one family. But how does he tie in to Holloman? It doesn't make sense.'

'Depends on how you want to spin it, counselor. Who's framing who?'

'You're not beginning to have doubts, too, are you?'

He ran a hand back through his hair, leaving it standing up in tufts. The exhaustion dragged on his face, pulling at the lines time and trouble had dug in. 'In my gut I don't think Paul did it, but as Megan has pointed out to me more than once, I might be bringing too much of my own personal experience into it. Regardless, Wilhelm was right – we'll have to dig deeper into the possibility. I don't look forward to executing those search warrants, but it's got to be done.'

More time spent chasing wild geese, Ellen thought, while Garrett Wright sat back and smiled, and his accomplice slipped in and out of the shadows unseen, unsuspected.

'We need a loose thread we can pull on,' she said. 'How's Megan coming with Wright's background?'

'Nothing yet. It's slow going. If Wright's never been caught to this point, he probably hasn't left behind many bread crumbs.'

'We can't let him get away with this, Mitch.' She stopped at the time line entry for January 22. *Agent O'Malley assaulted and kidnapped. Suspect apprehended after foot chase: Garrett Wright.* It was all a game to him. 'That's what this is all about for him – beating the system, slipping out of the noose. He even spotted us evidence to make it interesting.'

The idea that he might win terrified her.

'On a related topic,' Mitch said, 'I've a got a witness who may have seen your mad bomber early Sunday morning.'

Ellen brightened. 'A witness? Who?'

'Wes Vogler. He's a trucker who lives over in that neighborhood. He was leaving for a run early Sunday morning, saw a black kid cut across the Pla-Mor parking lot. Didn't think much of it because a couple of black families have moved into the neighborhood recently. When he got back home today, heard about the explosion and the timing of it, he got suspicious, decided he should come in.'

'You think he saw Tyrell?'

'Maybe. Or he saw an opportunity to get some kid into trouble,' he said. 'Wes's neck is a little on the red side. He's none too excited about Deer Lake becoming "ethnically diverse."'

'Put together a photo lineup. If Vogler picks him out, we'll get Tyrell in for a live performance.'

'If we can find him. He seems to have made himself scarce. The Minneapolis cops are watching for him.'

Ellen frowned as she gathered up her things. 'I don't know if I should be relieved or in fear for my life.'

'The kid's a loose cannon, but he's not stupid,' Mitch said. 'After today he's got to know things are leaning Wright's way. What good would it do him to hurt you?'

'None,' Ellen admitted. 'But he might think it'd be fun, anyway.'

Megan O'Malley's apartment was the only one on the third floor. Jay knocked and waited. On the other side of the door something fell to the floor with a thud. The curse that accompanied it was short and raw.

'Who is it?'

'Jay Butler Brooks, ma'am.'

The door swung back as far as the safety chain would allow, and O'Malley glared out at him.

'I'll cut straight to the bottom line here, Brooks,' she said shortly. 'No comment. No comment. No fucking comment.'

'I'm not a reporter.'

'I know what you are. What do you want?'

'To make you a proposition.'

Her green eyes narrowed with suspicion.

'I know you're looking into Garrett Wright's background. I'd like to help.'

'I don't know what you're talking about,' she said flatly. 'I'm on medical leave.'

'Ellen North told me,' he confessed. 'She also told me you'd rip my heart out of my chest with your bare hands if I betrayed the secret.'

She stared at him for a minute, debating. 'It'd be hard right now,' she said, deadpan. 'I'd probably have to use a garden claw.'

She fumbled with the chain, then swung the door open, inviting him into the apartment. Packing boxes were stacked all around the main living area that comprised both living and dining room. Soft-pink walls and white woodwork. Antique furnishings and mismatched flea-market

780

finds. The old round oak table was piled and strewn with papers and photocopies of police reports. A black cat with a white bib and paws positioned himself in the center of it all.

'You'll have to forgive the mess,' Megan said, hobbling to her chair and easing herself down. Her right hand, in its pristine cast, was cradled gingerly against her midsection. 'Getting the shit beat out of me put me behind in my decorating schedule.'

'Some things take precedence,' Jay remarked, sliding into the chair across from her. The cat lowered its eyelids and ears to half-mast and stared at him.

'I hear you're doing a book.' O'Malley's expression was closed, giving away nothing, the eyes sharp with the same watchful caution he'd seen in many a cop over the years. 'You should know I have a deeply ingrained aversion to opportunists.'

'That's not why I'm here.'

She laughed. Fine lines etched by pain dug in at the corners of her mouth. 'You want in on the investigation, but it's got nothing to do with the book you'll make a few mil off? Let me save us both some time here, Mr Brooks. I know how the world works.'

'I have no doubt of that, Agent O'Malley. A woman doesn't get where you are in law enforcement on fresh-faced innocence.'

'No, most of us make it this far on sex.'

'Bullshit, ma'am,' he said with a polite smile. 'I know your service record. You're damn good at your job.'

'Yes, I am. What's that got to do with you – if you're not angling for a story?'

'You want to nail Garrett Wright.'

'Upside down to a cross. So?'

'So I can help you. I've got a house full of office machines. Fax computer with a modem, multiline phone. You're having to waste a lot of time, running things through Holt's office to maintain your cover. I eliminate the middle man. I'm your cover. I'm your legs. I'm your hands. I make a damn good living off my ability to do thorough research. I don't see how this is any different.'

'It's different in that you're a civilian and this is a live case,' she said. 'It's different in that your being in on it could bust the whole thing.'

'*Your* being in on it could bust the whole thing,' he pointed out. 'Costello is already making noises about conflict of interest regarding Mitch Holt. Imagine if he found out the woman hell-bent on sending his client to prison for the rest of his life was in any way still involved with the investigation. He'd take what's left of your career, cut it up into little bite-sized pieces, and wash it down with champagne.'

'Is that a threat, Mr Brooks?'

'No,' he said, never taking his eyes from hers. 'I'm merely pointing out that my involvement wouldn't be any more potentially dangerous than yours. Less so. After all, the machines are mine, I have no personal ties to the case. There's no law against my looking into someone's background, provided we're dealing with public record.'

She thought on that for a moment, watching him, reading him. 'Does Ellen know you're here?'

'No. She's got problems enough tonight,' he said, wishing he could solve all those problems for her.

'You never answered my question,' Megan said. 'If this isn't about your book, then what?'

He rose then, discomfort disguised as restless curiosity. He didn't want her looking too close, which could have been an indication of a lie, or of a truth that lived deeper than he wanted her to see. She suspected the latter. Jay Butler Brooks struck her as the kind of man who would look you straight in the face when he lied to you, his pretty blue eyes shining with sincerity. He had been a lawyer once, after all.

'When did you see your first murdered child?' he asked, glancing at her from the corner of his eyes as he leaned a hip against a stack of boxes.

'My second week in a uniform,' she said. 'A three-year-old killed by her alcoholic mother's alcoholic boyfriend.'

'I saw mine today.'

Dustin Holloman. He fingered the spines of some of her old textbooks, but she knew he wasn't seeing the titles. He was seeing a child's body, the same way she did whenever that three-year-old girl came to mind with sharp, grim detail, even a decade after the fact.

'I came to Deer Lake for my own reasons, Agent O'Malley. Selfish reasons, I readily admit. I thought I could maintain some emotional distance on this case, but I stood by the side of that road this morning and listened to that boy's mama cry. . . . I don't want to be the kind of man who can keep his distance from something like that.'

His voice had tightened, his emotion touching Megan.

'I want to help,' he said. 'I need to.' He looked up at her then with no mask, no pretense. 'You know what it is to need to prove yourself, even if you're the only one looking.'

'Yes,' Megan whispered, her gaze straying to the cast on her hand. 'Yeah, I do.'

'So what do you say? Am I in?'

It wasn't her natural inclination to trust at all, let alone to trust a man like Brooks. But she wanted Wright behind bars; he could help speed the process. They needed a break and they needed it fast. The key had to be buried somewhere in Garrett Wright's past, but with everything else that had been thrown at them in the last week, none of the agencies involved had been able to devote the time needed to the search. She was the only one really looking, and the injuries Wright had inflicted were holding her back, slowing her down. Brooks could be her legs, her hands, another brain working to decipher the puzzle.

Or he could be weaseling his way into a best-seller.

Garrett Wright stood on the brink of walking away from every evil thing he'd done.

'You're in,' she said at last. 'Don't make me regret it, Mr Brooks. I don't want to have to dig out that garden claw.'

They began executing the search warrants at nine forty-three, beginning, at Mitch's insistence, at the Kirkwood home. He did his best to smooth the process for Hannah, glad that Father Tom was close at hand to offer her support and comfort while the officers looked for any evidence that her husband was the one who had stolen her son and put her through hell.

As much as he loved what he did, there were times when he hated being a cop.

He expected the search of Paul's office to be punctuated by threats of legal action from Paul, but Paul was not in his current home-away-from-home. The blankets were neatly folded on one end of the couch with the pillow placed on top of them. The desk was immaculate. There was no sign that Paul had been there at all. There was no sign that Costello's PI, York, had let himself in and helped himself to evidence at some point during the last twenty-four hours. Not surprisingly, they found nothing.

By the time they reached the U-Store-It at the edge of the industrial park on the south side of town, it was past midnight. The night watchman, a grizzled old geezer named Davis who had bad teeth and beer breath, had to be roused from a deep, snoring sleep on the cot in the office. Grousing about the cold, he led them down the rows of storage units. Each was about the size of a one-car garage with bright-orange overhead doors and numbers stenciled on the cinder block with black spray paint. They stopped at number thirty-seven. Davis knelt down on the concrete apron, grumbling nonstop as he opened the padlock with the key from the office.

The locker was stacked with the usual castoffs of suburban life. Out-of-season lawn furniture and an old canoe. An outdated bedroom set and boxes of old baby clothes Hannah probably hadn't been able to bring herself to part with. The thing that set Paul Kirkwood's locker apart from most Mitch had seen was the fact that it was perfectly ordered. No teetering towers of haphazardly packed junk. Everything labeled and lined up, the neatness speaking to Paul's compulsive tendencies.

Davis declined the invitation to watch and shuffled back toward the office, lighting a cigarette. Cameron Reed stood at the door, the lone witness, hands in his coat pockets and shoulders hunched as the others went about their business. Mitch purposely avoided the more personal memorabilia and went instead to the dresser of the old bedroom set. So it was he who made the very discovery he had been praying they wouldn't find.

Tucked back into a bottom drawer, neatly folded and stored in a black plastic garbage bag, were a pair of boy's jeans and a blue sweater.

783

The clothes Josh Kirkwood had been wearing the night he'd disappeared.

34

As birthdays went, number thirty-six was off to a pisser of a start.

The thought was selfish on the surface, but Ellen knew that wasn't it at all. She had hoped for something better today for Josh, for Hannah, for Megan, for justice. She had hoped for an eleventh-hour gift in the form of evidence. And deep in a small, primitively superstitious part of her brain, she had held out the unspoken hope that they might get that gift because it was her birthday. She felt foolish admitting it even to herself.

The gift they received was from a higher power with an exceedingly black sense of humor. Evidence that clearly implicated Paul Kirkwood. At least in the eyes of the person who mattered most – Gorman Grabko.

'In light of the discoveries we've had since we adjourned yesterday, I don't see that I have a choice, Ellen,' the judge said, frowning at her gravely from behind his desk.

She refused to look at Costello, knowing too well what she would see in his face. Victory.

'But, Your Honor,' she said, 'we don't know how those clothes came to be in the Kirkwoods' storage locker –'

'The door was padlocked, Your Honor,' Costello said.

'Locks can be picked. Mr Costello should consult with his associate Mr York on that subject,' Ellen said bitingly. 'What we have here –'

'Is a mess, Ms North,' Grabko declared. 'The prosecution clearly was not thoroughly prepared to bring these charges before the court.'

'But, Your Honor, Chief Holt *apprehended* Garrett Wright. We have evidence –'

'What the prosecution has,' Costello said, going for the kill, 'are some half-baked notions unsupported by fact and not fully investigated. Ms North wanted a slam dunk on this case for reasons of her own and has proceeded in a fashion that skirts the bounds of ethics, persecuting an innocent man.'

The verbal knife slipped cleanly between her ribs. Ethics. Ambition. Costello had no respect for the first and lived and breathed the second. She was his mirror opposite in those aspects, and yet he neatly turned it all on her without batting an eye.

Her fingers curled on the arms of her chair, holding her down. 'That is a completely unfair, inaccurate assessment, Your Honor. My only interest in this case is justice.'

'And to that end, I see only one choice,' Grabko said, steepling his fingers before him. 'I must grant Mr Costello's motion to dismiss and hope that the county attorney's office and the law-enforcement agencies involved do a better job of untangling this case before it is brought before the court again.'

In her mind Ellen heard a gavel fall. Case dismissed. As simple as that, her nemesis had turned the tables on her. As simple as that, like a trick in a parlor game. And now she would have to walk into that courtroom packed with press and citizens and cops, and stand there while Garrett Wright was declared a free man. She would have to call Hannah Garrison before the press could get to her and tell her the man who had stolen her son would return to the house down the block a free man.

The failure was crushing. She could barely rise beneath the weight of it. But she forced her shoulders back and her chin up and started for the door. Cameron and Dorman went out first. Ellen would go next. Costello would come behind her and relish his own entrance like an overbearing stage actor.

Behind her she could hear the door close on Grabko's private bathroom, where the judge invariably retreated moments before taking the bench. Which left her alone with Costello. She turned toward him with her hand on the doorknob and simply looked at him in his tailored suit and smug satisfaction.

'Don't take it so hard, Ellen,' he said. 'You just didn't have enough to win the game this time.'

'You'll never get it, will you, Tony?' she said, shaking her head. 'This should never be about winning or losing. It should be about the truth.'

The light in his eyes hardened and glittered. 'No, *you'll* never get it, Ellen. It's always about winning. Always.'

Ellen singled out faces on her way in. Mitch, drawn and grim. Karen Wright, vacuous. Christopher Priest sitting beside her, expressionless. Noticeably absent was Paul, who had yet to be located after the search of his storage locker. Nor was Brooks among the information-hungry throng. His absence struck her harder than she should have let it. It shouldn't have mattered. She knew better than to allow herself the comfort of relying on someone, especially him.

Dismissing those thoughts, she took her place beside Cameron at the table.

It was over in a matter of moments. More moments than were strictly necessary, simply because Grabko liked to pontificate to a captive audience. Through the entire speech Ellen stood at the table, aware of every eye on her back. Her mind raced ahead, laying out the scenario for what would happen next. The press would champion Costello and she would be crucified. Rudy would lay the blame entirely at her feet in an effort to keep himself from being tainted. Garrett Wright would be painted as a martyr, and the people of Deer Lake would call for the head of Paul Kirkwood.

Worst-case scenario.

The hell of it was, as much as she had professed not to want it, she knew she would have taken the case again if she had it to do over.

Grabko pronounced the case dismissed and rapped his gavel dramatically. Behind the bar the gallery exploded into a deafening cacophony of sound. The doors to the hall burst open, and half the reporters poured out into the hall to array themselves for the inevitable impromptu press conference, while the other half pressed up against the railing in a mob, shouting questions.

'Ms North, will charges be brought against Paul Kirkwood?'

'Dr Wright, will you be filing suit against the county attorney's office?'

'Ms North, is there any truth to the rumors of your dismissal from the county attorney's office?'

Costello flashed them all his legal-eagle look and placated them with promises of answers out in the rotunda. Ellen refused to acknowledge them at all, keeping her back to them as she pretended to arrange the files in her briefcase. She could hear Cameron giving them the party line about an official statement coming from the office later in the day.

'Ms North?'

The voice was too close, too soft for any reporter. Ellen jerked her head up. Garrett Wright stood no more than a foot from her, his expression calm, almost apologetic. He offered her his hand.

'No hard feelings,' he said, the consummate gentleman. 'You were only doing your job.'

And I beat you. We beat you.

She could hear the words as clearly as if he had spoken them aloud. She could see them, deep in his eyes, in a moment just like the one they had shared in the interview room of the city jail. A moment no one else in the room had experienced. She could feel the reporters staring at them. She could hear the whir of motor drives on cameras, but she knew not one photograph would capture what was passing between them.

She ignored the offered handshake and stood a little straighter. 'I'm still doing my job, Dr Wright,' she said softly. 'You know what they say – it ain't over till it's over.'

'What does this mean?' Hannah asked, stunned, shaking. She sank weakly onto the couch, her knees buckling beneath her. She found herself holding the portable phone to her face with both hands because her fingertips had gone numb and she thought she might drop it.

'It means Wright is a free man – for the moment,' Ellen North said. 'But it isn't over as far as I'm concerned. I'll do everything in my power to get him to trial, Hannah. I promise you that.'

Hannah stared across the room to the corner where Josh had

sequestered himself for the morning. He faced the wall with his knees drawn up to his chest and his face hidden. Her son was locked in a mental prison, and the man who had put him there was walking free.

'You did that already, didn't you?' she said, the bitterness thinned by abject disappointment.

'I'm sorry, Hannah. What we had against him should have been enough, but with his accomplice still at large, and with the evidence that came to light yesterday . . .'

Ellen's voice trailed off. She was trying to be diplomatic, Hannah thought. The news was bad enough without emphasizing the fact that Paul was now wanted for questioning, that Josh's clothes had been found in the storage locker Paul rented because he had never been able to abide a cluttered basement.

Mitch had broken that news to her in the dead of night. *I don't know how to tell you this, Hannah. . . . We're not sure what it means. . . . The clothes could have been planted there for us to find. . . . We need to talk to Paul. . . . You don't know where he is?*

I don't know who *he is*, she thought. *I don't know what he's become. I don't know what he might be capable of. I don't know why Josh is afraid of him. I can't believe he struck me.*

'But Mitch caught Garrett Wright,' she said, talking more to herself than to Ellen.

'I know. Mitch knows. Costello blew enough smoke to cloud the issue for the judge. We just need a little more time, another piece of solid evidence against Wright or a break regarding his accomplice. It'll come, Hannah. Hang in there. And please let me know the minute Josh has something to say about what happened.'

Hannah held the phone in her lap for a long while after the connection had been broken. Her line to justice, she thought, cut off, and she and her children were left holding the frayed end of what should have been a lifeline to pull them past this ordeal.

Of the things she had to hope for, justice had seemed the most realistic, the most attainable. She could hope for Josh's recovery, but there was no guarantee how long that hope would have to last or that it wouldn't be crushed in the end. She had hoped for a mend in the tear of her relationship with Paul, but that would never happen. Their marriage was over. And so she had hoped for justice. There was a system in place to mete it out. There were people who cared fighting on her side. But the irony in the fight for justice was that not everyone played fair.

Lily scrambled up onto the couch beside her and reached for the phone. Holding it up with both hands, she began an animated conversation of gibberish punctuated by the word 'Daddy'.

Hannah thought of calling Tom but denied herself the comfort. On top of everything else, she didn't want the guilt that came with thinking she had corrupted him.

She knew there were people on the outside of her ordeal looking in who didn't believe she felt guilty enough for her initial sin of being late to pick up Josh that night because she hadn't thrown herself prostrate in front of the nation, sobbing and begging forgiveness. They didn't know anything. The pain was hers to bear. She wouldn't allow herself the luxury of begging for the sympathy of strangers. Her punishment was to cope, to care for her children, to deal with every individual rock in the avalanche that was raining down on their lives.

Like Garrett Wright going free.

Leaving Lily to her imaginary telephone conversation, Hannah went to her son and knelt down behind him. She put her arms around him and kissed the top of his head. He didn't move. He didn't speak.

'We won't let him beat us, Josh,' she whispered. 'I won't let him take you from me. I won't let you down again. I promise.'

Even the worst day in the history of mankind had only twenty-four hours. Ellen repeated that mantra all day long. All during her conversation with Hannah. All through Rudy's 'damage control' meeting. All through the brief but excruciating official press conference. This day had only twenty-four hours, and she would live through them to fight another day. Costello had roused the tiger within her. She wouldn't be happy until it tore his throat out, eviscerated Garrett Wright and his partner.

Rudy hadn't fired her. Wouldn't fire her. He needed her. He was too wily not to see that. He needed her now for a whipping boy, and he would need her later when this case went to trial. Whether or not he would put her in first chair or hide her as second to Sig Iverson's figurehead prosecutorial post remained to be seen, but he needed her either way. Ellen intended to make the most of that.

Tomorrow they would regroup. She would call her cops together for a strategy session. By tomorrow Todd Childs's prints could have matched up with prints found in Denny Enberg's office, and they would have the lever they needed to crack him open. By tomorrow they might have preliminary reports back from Dustin Holloman's autopsy, which was where Wilhelm and Steiger had spent the afternoon. If the ME came up with a few stray hairs, a skin scraping from under the boy's fingernails, a DNA fingerprint in the form of a drop of blood . . . they'd be back in business. If Megan could dig up just one anomaly in Garrett Wright's perfect past . . .

She grabbed the phone and dialed Megan's number again, getting the answering machine. O'Malley had been out all day. Mitch had said she'd found a better place to work, but he didn't have a number or the time to discuss it. Some of Harris College's rowdier students had used Garrett Wright's release as an excuse to run amok on campus and call it a victory celebration. Their celebration had spilled out into Dinkytown in the form of skirmishes, vandalism, and general mayhem. With an official victory party scheduled for eight o'clock and a promised appearance by the man himself, the police were bracing themselves for a night of trouble.

Ellen checked her watch. Nine-nineteen. The party was already well under way. She had given Phoebe orders to attend but suspected her once-loyal secretary was more likely to spend the evening giving Adam Slater an exclusive than paying attention to what was going on around her.

Their candidates for Accomplice of the Year would be there – Christopher Priest and Todd Childs. The Sci-Fi Cowboys would be there – would Tyrell Mann risk an appearance? Garrett Wright would be center stage with his wife beside him. Karen, drugged and distant, the secrets of her marriage locked inside her seemingly vacant mind.

Ellen would have bet Karen's affair with Paul was what had set the game in motion. It was Wright's motive for choosing Josh, for framing Paul. And Dustin Holloman had been nothing more than a pawn to make Wright look innocent.

But who had orchestrated the second half of the match? And why was Paul Kirkwood suddenly missing if he was guilty of nothing more than adultery?

The questions swarmed around Ellen's brain. She allowed herself a little groan as she rose from her chair and went to the window. Suppertime had come and gone without supper. The lack of fuel was dragging her mood down when she thought it couldn't sink any lower.

She was alone in the office. Beaten, hungry, freezing, old, and alone.

'Don't forget feeling sorry for yourself, Ellen,' she muttered as she stretched, then rubbed her hands together to ward off frostbite.

For once she *wished* Brooks would show up uninvited. But for all she knew, he had jumped sides now that Wright was off. The story of a 'good' man triumphing over a prosecutor out to get him would make a much better book than the tale of said prosecutor's failure to get a vicious monster to trial.

'I go after what I want, Ellen North. And I get it.'

Then in her mind's eye she saw his face the night before the hearing began, right here in her office.

'I've never been anyone's hero. . . .' Eyes shadowed with old pain, old uncertainty. *'Will you try to redeem me, Ellen?'*

That look lingered in her mind, until the practical side of her reared up. She was wasting time. She had a whole table of notes and statements to go over. Again. That was what she had wanted this quiet time for. Not for feeling old and alone and sorry for herself. Not for romanticizing about tarnished knights and wounded souls.

The phone rang and she flinched. She let it ring as she ticked off possible callers. It was her mother. It was Megan with the much-needed clue. It was Jay. It was some damned reporter who had wheedled her direct-line number out of Rudy. It was –

'Ellen North,' she said, grabbing up the receiver, forcing herself past the apprehension.

'Ellen, Darrell Munson. Sorry it took me so long to get back to you. I just got home from a dive trip off Key West.'

Munson. That name clicked slowly into place. Probation officer turned beach bum.

'Thanks for calling back,' she said without enthusiasm. The Sci-Fi Cowboys trail had led nowhere but to the Garrett Wright alumni fan club. She couldn't find much hope that this call would be any different from the rest, but she went through the motions, explaining to Munson the situation.

'That's pretty hard to believe,' he said, his voice going cold over the line. 'I knew Dr Wright fairly well. Had nothing but respect for the man. I'm not happy to hear you're looking to discredit him.'

'I'm doing my job, Mr Munson,' Ellen explained. 'The evidence is compelling or we wouldn't be proceeding. If Dr Wright is innocent, then he has nothing to worry about. He certainly wasn't anyone's first choice as a suspect.'

'Yeah, well . . .,' he said grudgingly. 'What was it you wanted from me?'

'I wanted to know if you kept track of the kids you had in the Sci-Fi Cowboys program. We're contacting past members as part of Wright's background check.'

'I had two the first year the program started; then I got out of Dodge and came down here.'

'Tim Dutton and Erik Evans.'

'Yeah. Sure, I know where Tim is. He sends me Christmas cards. He's an apprentice electrician up in New Hope. Erik, I lost track of. Last I knew he was at the U studying computers. Really bright kid. Very personable. A minister's son.'

'Doesn't sound like your average juvenile offender.'

'I don't suppose he was. He had some emotional problems, some problems at home. His mother was in and out of institutions. It all dated back to that business with the neighbor kid when Erik was ten. That kind of trauma would screw up anybody.'

'What trauma?'

'He saw a playmate hang himself.'

'Oh, no.'

'Yeah. It was a bad deal. The kid's mother blamed Erik. She was pretty vocal about it. It was all over the news at the time. I'm surprised you don't remember it. Slater was the kid's name.'

Ellen jerked her head up. 'Excuse me?'

'Slater. Adam Slater.'

A chill washed over her. *Adam Slater. Oh, my God.*

'Uh – uh – could you describe Erik Evans for me?'

'Last time I saw him, he was five four, five five, slim, blond.'

Blond. The part of her brain that specialized in denial grabbed hold of the detail.

'Thank you. Thank you, Mr Munson,' she stammered. 'You've been very helpful.'

She dropped the receiver before she could recradle it. Erik Evans. The kid in the newspaper photo standing beside Wright. Blond, smallish.

Kids grew. People dyed their hair.

She hurried to the conference room and homed in on the file lying among all the others. Her hands were shaking so badly, she could hardly pick through the reports and clippings. She dug front to back, back to front. The article was gone.

Adam Slater.

Reporter for an inconsequential paper. No one had bothered to check press credentials. There were too damned many reporters to sort through. Besides, all they were after was news. They were nuisances, irritations, nothing more.

Perhaps it was just coincidence that Adam Slater the reporter from Grand Forks shared a name with a child dead eleven years. A child who had been playmates with a future Sci-Fi Cowboy.

'You don't believe in coincidence, Ellen,' she muttered.

Adam Slater was romancing Phoebe, charming her, winning her over. Ellen had warned her he had an ulterior motive. God, she had never dreamed it could be this.

In her mind's eye she saw the note that marked the very page she needed in the book of Minnesota case law in the third-floor library. *it is a SIN to believe evil of others, but it is seldom a mistake*

Sin. So many of the notes had included references to sin.

Erik Evans was the son of a Methodist minister.

They had been turning over every rock they could find, hunting for Garrett Wright's accomplice, and he had been standing there the whole time, right beside them, taking it all in. He had been along the roadside in the predawn gray the morning Dustin Holloman's body had been found. If she was right, he was the one who had strangled the boy and propped him up against that signpost with a note pinned to his chest. *some rise by SIN, and some by virtue fall*

Erik Evans. Adam Slater. Garrett Wright's protégé.

She had to call Mitch. Slater was likely at the victory celebration, privately gloating. Probably with Phoebe. Oh, God, Phoebe. What if the party was over? What if she was with him? What if Adam Slater decided she wasn't useful anymore?

Dropping the papers she held, Ellen reached for the phone and stopped cold.

Lying across the base of the telephone was a single red rose, its stem entwined with the cord that should have been plugged into the wall jack.

'My sources tell me you've been asking too many questions, Ms

North.' He stood in the doorway to the conference room, his dyed hair drooping over one eye. 'I think it's time you stopped. Forever.'

35

'Light that and you're a dead man,' Megan said.

Jay paused, lighter halfway to the cigarette dangling from his mouth.

'Haven't I been abused enough?' she said. 'Did I survive that beating only to die of lung cancer contracted through secondhand smoke while trying to crack the case?'

Jay pulled the cigarette and set it on the table beside the pack. 'Do you realize tobacco is a substantial part of the southern economy?'

'Uh-huh,' Megan said without sympathy. '*Y'all* might try joining the age of enlightenment sometime in this century. Until that magic moment, you can take your filthy little death stick outside and kill yourself with it.'

They had already had this argument three times. Jay had lost each round. He knew he could have pulled rank on her – it *was* his house, after all – but every time he had ended up taking himself out onto the deck in the frigid fucking cold to stand at the front window glaring in at her. He blamed his ingrained southern manners but knew the truth was that he liked Megan, and she sure as hell *had* suffered enough.

'You could let me have my way just once,' he pouted.

'Quit your whining. I could hit you in the head with a hammer just once, too,' she said. Her eyes focused on the file spread out before her. 'Have you got any answers back yet on that AOL bulletin board?'

He hit a series of keys, calling up the proper screen on the computer. It had been his suggestion to go into America Online and hit the bulletin boards of alumni groups from the colleges where Garrett Wright had taught. They were hoping a former student might come forward with a nasty long-dead rumor or a memory of some peculiar incident that would give them a starting point.

'Only good stuff from UVA,' he said, scanning the replies to his innocuous question – *Were you ever a student of Dr Garrett Wright (psych) and how did you like him?* 'Salt of the earth. Prince of a guy.'

'He's a fucking madman,' Megan snapped, throwing down her highlighter. 'Can't *anybody* see that?'

Embarrassed at losing her cool yet again, she glanced at Brooks sideways and tried for humor. 'Gee, honey, maybe I need an Excedrin.'

He didn't smile. The look in his eyes was too astute for comfort.

'Maybe you need a break,' he said. 'You've been going hard for hours, Megan, and you know you're not up to it.'

The tenderness in his voice slipped around her guard. She'd never had any defence against tenderness. Looking away from him, she gathered together the threadbare scraps of her composure.

'I see him slipping away,' she said quietly. 'He said he would win, and I can't stand the thought of that happening. Don't tell me I need rest. I don't need anything more than I need that bastard's head on a pike.'

Jay heaved a sigh and ignored the craving for nicotine. He could see the pressure of this case squeezing Megan like a vise. She was a perfectionist, proud, a control freak like half the cops he'd known. Garrett Wright had broken her physically, and the post traumatic stress was breaking her mentally.

Garrett Wright, who was a free man tonight.

Ellen was likely taking the news only slightly better than Megan. Ellen, too conscientious, too focused on what she perceived as her responsibility – justice for all. She would take this defeat as a personal affront and dive back into the fight with single-minded determination.

He had wanted to be there for her after the news of the dismissal had come. But it had seemed even more important to stay here with O'Malley, to think harder, dig deeper.

He who skated across the surface of life, never getting involved, always standing back to observe from a distance.

Unbidden, his gaze strayed to the rug in front of the fireplace where he and Ellen had made such sweet, hot love Saturday night.

'I need a drink,' he growled, pushing himself up from his lawn chair. 'Want one?'

'As well as that would go with the narcotics I'm taking, I'll have to settle for a Coke,' Megan said. 'With ice, please,' she called as he disappeared into the kitchen.

She looked at the sea of paper she had spread out across the long table. Notes, faxes from the colleges Wright had taught for, faxes from half a dozen law-enforcement agencies local to those colleges, faxes from NCIC. And in it all, she had found nothing.

'We can't lose,' he whispered. 'You can't defeat us. We're very good at this game.'

An involuntary shiver rattled through her. The will it took to shut that black box of fear left her feeling weak.

Focus. She needed to focus. Concentration kept her on an almost even keel. She dug out her list of calls and ran down the names, awkwardly marking the ones she would call back in the morning. Contacts she'd made at law-enforcement conferences and in the agents' program at Quantico. Not for the first time since all this had begun, she wondered what kind of life she would be living if she had accepted the FBI field post in Memphis all those years ago. Memphis was a long way from Garrett Wright. But it was also a long way from Mitch and Jessie, and she wouldn't have given them up for anything. Not even for a climate without the word 'windchill' in it.

The NCIC request for unsolved child abductions, and abductions/murders, in the geographical areas where Priest had taught had yielded them little. Nothing that matched the macabre game that had played out here. It hadn't struck her until after the bad news of the dismissal had come from the courthouse that they might be looking on the wrong side of the win-lose column altogether. It didn't appear Wright wanted this case to go unsolved. It appeared he had every intention of framing Paul Kirkwood. If he framed Paul, who was to say he hadn't done the same thing before?

Maybe they didn't need information on *unsolved* crimes. Maybe they needed to look at cases that had been closed. Unfortunately, no one in law enforcement was as eager to share information on cases they believed to be tied up, neat and tidy, as they were to share information on cases they wanted to clean up. Megan knew it would take days of hounding to get anything.

Newspapers were the place to go. Newspaper-morgue librarians, and public-library reference-desk librarians. She had started calling immediately, requesting any stories found be faxed to Jay's machine ASAP. She had wheedled and begged, pleaded and lied and tossed around a rank she no longer held, then crossed her fingers and hoped that in the end the story of Josh and Dustin Holloman was enough to compel complete strangers in other states to do work they didn't really have to do.

Several faxes had rolled in late in the day. None of them were the piece they needed. Jay had put out the same request over a number of computer networks, using his name and his fame as a lure. Nothing had come of any of it yet.

Except to dispel her sense of powerlessness and uselessness. Garrett Wright had taken so much from her, but he hadn't taken the most important things that made her a good cop. Her mind. Her heart. Her determination. She could still do the job. She would just have to go about it differently, that was all.

'Christ,' Brooks muttered, staring at the computer screen. 'Everybody in the damn country has a story to tell. Here's a woman in Arkansas who claims her Welsh corgi was abducted by space aliens.'

'Sounds like a book to me,' Megan said, easing herself up out of her chair, moving carefully against the stiffness in her aching muscles. 'Have you attracted anyone besides lunatics?'

He scrolled down through the responses, skipping over states outside the regions they were searching and past stories of S-and-M queens and visitations from alternate dimensions. Megan watched over his shoulder, amazed and disappointed at once.

'You're a wacko magnet, Brooks. Is that the price of fame?'

'I don't mind paying the price,' he drawled. 'Just so long as I get reimbursed.'

He blew out a sigh and rubbed his eyes. 'I need a break. I gotta get out of here for a while.'

'Sure, go ahead,' Megan said. 'I'll hold the fort.'

'You sure you don't want a breather, too?' he asked, shrugging into his parka.

'I'm sure.' She gave him a sly smile as she slid down into his chair in front of the computer. 'Three's a crowd. Say hi to Ellen for me.'

She heard the kitchen door close, listened dimly to the muffled rumble of his truck's engine as she continued to go over the responses. His taillights were still visible heading east on Mill Road when she hit pay dirt.

She read through the scant few paragraphs regarding a crime that had been solved nearly ten years past. Her sixth sense – her cop sense – was humming on high voltage. Logic told her it was a long shot, but it was the first shot they'd had.

Sandwiching the telephone receiver between her shoulder and ear, she punched the number for the Pennsylvania state police. 'Mr Brooks, I think maybe we just caught a break.'

'We didn't think you'd dig that deep,' Slater said, stepping casually into the room, his hands in the pockets of his black ski jacket. 'The investigation isn't your job, after all.'

'My job is to prove my case,' Ellen said, using her peripheral vision to search out a usable weapon within reach.

He shook his head and smiled slowly. 'If you'd left the investigating to the cops, we might not have had to kill you.'

'Kill me and you'll be found out anyway.' She was amazed that she could sound so calm, so rational, when every alarm inside her was screaming. 'It won't take long for the cops to put two and two together. They'll follow the same trail I did.'

'I don't think so. They'll be more apt to follow the same trail they followed with Enberg.' Feigning sadness, he said, 'Poor guy, he just couldn't take the pressure.'

The scene from Denny's office flashed through Ellen's mind. The blood, the gore. Brain matter clinging to the wall behind his body. His head mostly gone, blown away. Nausea swirled in her stomach.

'No one will buy that,' she challenged, her fingers surreptitiously curling around the shaft of one of Cameron's fountain pens. She slipped her fists into the deep pockets of her heavy wool coat. 'I don't own a gun. I wouldn't have one.'

Slater took another step forward into the room. 'Don't be so literal. There are lots of ways a person can commit suicide. Hanging. Carbon monoxide. Pills. Razor blades.'

Ellen stepped back. If she could keep enough distance between them, get on opposite sides of the conference table . . . If she could just get to the outer hall . . .

'All I have to do is scream,' she said. 'There's a security guard –'

'Nice try, Ms North, but I happen to know Mr Stovich no longer saw the need, what with the charges against Dr Wright being dropped.' He flashed a quick grin and chuckled. 'According to my good friend Phoebe, ol' Rudy was pretty steamed about the way you blew the case.'

'You should be proud of yourself,' Ellen said, refusing the bait. 'Your efforts paid off. Keeping the cops busy running from one incident to another. Planting that evidence in Paul Kirkwood's storage locker. The credit is yours, not mine.'

He grinned again and tossed his hair back out of his eyes. 'Yeah. I done good.'

'You murdered an innocent child.'

'Nice touch, huh?'

'You don't feel anything?'

He shrugged, looking all of sixteen, innocent, oblivious to the consequences of his actions. 'Sure. It was a rush choking him.'

'Then why didn't you kill Josh?'

'Because that wasn't the plan.' He shook his head. 'You still don't get it. The game is more fun when you spot the other team points.'

'You're not worried about his talking?'

'No,' he said flatly, moving forward. 'And I'm tired of you talking. Let's get on with it, Ms North.'

Ellen had rounded the end of the table, putting it between them, but Slater was nearer the door. He stood quietly, without the bouncy energy she had come to associate with him. As if he had pulled that energy inward and held it at the core of him, burning hot and intense. His dark eyes were bright with it, watching her with predatory anticipation.

'If you think I'm just going to let you kill me, you're not as smart as I thought,' she said. 'I have every intention of fighting. Defense wounds will raise eyebrows.'

'There won't be any.'

She inched along the table, passing the stacks of files, the reports, the notes – none of which would have pointed to Slater. He was right. If it hadn't been for her own digging, if it hadn't been for her calling on old contacts in the world she'd left behind, no one would have looked at him twice. Christ, *she* hadn't looked at him twice. The only reason she had kept searching for information on the past Cowboys was that she had the connection and was desperate enough to play a long shot.

'When did Wright single you out?' she asked. 'Did he find out about the Slater boy when you came into the Cowboys?'

Pride and amusement glowed in his too-young face. 'He built the Cowboys around me,' he bragged. 'I'm the reason the Cowboys exist. Ain't that a kick in the head? The program exists because Garrett wanted me.'

The irony was as twisted as barbed wire. A program heralded

nationally for turning so many young lives around had come into being as a cover for the utter corruption of one.

'Is it just Wright?' Ellen asked, her fingers clenching and unclenching on the pen in her coat pocket. She stood directly across from him now. Equal distance to the door. He had fifteen years on her, but she would be running for her life. 'Or is Priest in on it, too?'

'I won't tell you everything, Ellen.'

'Why not? I'll be dead anyway.'

'True, but I don't want you to die satisfied. I want you to die wondering. That's just another point for my team.'

'What a waste,' she said, focusing on her anger instead of her fear. 'To take someone as bright and talented as you and turn you into a common criminal.'

'There's nothing common about me, Ms North.' His expression turned stony. 'Garrett searched a long time to find me – a child who understood the game, someone as superior as he is.'

'Superior?' Ellen arched a brow. 'He's nothing but a bully and a coward and a murderer.'

His eyes narrowed above reddening cheekbones. From his left jacket pocket he pulled a stun gun, a black plastic rectangle that didn't look any more menacing than a television remote control. 'No more talk, bitch.'

Ellen bolted for the door. Slater caught her at the end of the table, grabbing hold of her left arm and swinging the stun gun to her chest. She twisted away from him, and sixty thousand volts of electricity went dead against the thick wool sleeve of her coat. Screaming, she pulled the fountain pen from her pocket and stabbed with all the wild fury of the survival instinct.

Slater shrieked as the pen sank into his face through the hollow of his cheek and tore downward. The blood came in a gush as the soft tissue ripped open. Ellen wasted no time looking. She pushed off and lunged for the door, shouting for help, knowing the building was empty, knowing the sound would never reach the deputies in the building next door.

She could hear Slater coming behind her as she ran through the outer office. Chancing a glance over her shoulder, she slammed a thigh into the corner of Phoebe's desk. Black stars bursting in her head, she half sprawled across the desk, and her right hand hit the stapler. She closed her fingers around it and ran on.

'You fucking bitch!' Slater sobbed behind her.

He launched himself at her as she flung the door open, tackling her with his arms wrapped around her upper body. They landed on the floor, Ellen taking the brunt of it as she was sandwiched between the floor and her assailant. Her forehead hit hard. Her breath left her in a painful whoosh. But she pulled her feet beneath her and fought to buck Slater's weight off her.

They wrestled across the floor, Slater grabbing at her shoulder, trying to turn her onto her back beneath him. Ellen bit at his fingers, the blood dripping from his face into her eyes, into her hair, running down her cheek. She twisted suddenly beneath him and swung the stapler against his temple and cheekbone, snapping his head to the side, dazing him and giving her just enough opportunity to roll free.

She scrambled to her feet and started to run, realizing too late that she was pointed in the wrong direction – away from the sheriff's department. Now she would have to get to the first floor and double back.

Slater caught her at the stairs, grabbing the collar of her coat and a handful of hair, yanking her almost off her feet. The stun gun came up and Ellen blocked the hit with her shoulder. The gun gave an angry, crackling buzz. No defense wounds, he'd promised. If he'd nailed her the first time, there would have been none. The voltage would have dazed her senseless, and he could have quickly and easily slit her wrists for her.

Her left arm was wedged between their bodies. Ellen groped, latching on to Slater's testicles, squeezing as hard as she could. A howl pierced her eardrum and he shoved her away, doubling over, clutching himself. Ellen's shins hit the steps, then she fell up on her hands and knees. The stapler clattered free.

Up.

Shit. No options. Run now, figure it out later.

'Time to die, birthday bitch.'

Birthday. Thirty-six. The birthday Ellen had been dreading. Suddenly thirty-six seemed far too young.

She flung herself up the stairs, stumbling as one heel caught an edge. She grabbed for the handrail, her fingers scraping the rough plaster of the wall, breaking a nail, skinning her knuckles.

The stairwell was barely lit, drawing in the ragged edges of illumination that fell from the lights in the halls above and below. Security lights. They offered nothing in the way of security. In the back of her mind she heard a low, smoky voice, '*Your boss needs to have a word with someone about security. This is a highly volatile case. Anything might happen.*'

She reached the third floor and turned down the hall, heading east. If she could make it down the east stairs – If she could make it to the walkway between the buildings – He wouldn't dare try to take her in the walkway with the sheriff's department mere feet away.

'We've got you now, bitch!'

There were telephones in the offices she ran past. The offices were locked. Her self-appointed assassin was jogging behind her, laughing. The sound went through her like a spear, like the sure knowledge that he would kill her. Pursuit may not have been his plan, but it had become a part of the game.

The game. The insanity of it was as terrifying as the prospect of death. Beat the system. Wreck lives. End lives. Nothing personal. Just a game.

She ran past Judge Grabko's courtroom and ducked around the corner that led back toward the southeast stairwell. Scaffolding filled the stairwell, cutting off her escape route. The scaffolding for the renovators. Christ, she was going to die because of the stupid plaster frieze.

'Checkmate, clever bitch.'

The northeast stairs looked a mile away. Midway stood the iron gates that blocked the skyway between the courthouse and the jail. She lunged for the fire alarm on the wall, grabbing the glass tube that would break and summon help.

The tube snapped. Nothing. No sound. No alarm.

'Oh, God, no!' She clawed at the useless panel. The goddamn renovations. New alarms going in. State of the art.

'Come along, Ellen. Be a good bitch and let me kill you.'

She grabbed the handle of the door to the fire hose and yanked.

'You have to die, bitch. We have to win the game.'

His hand closed on her arm.

Her fingers closed on the handle of the ax.

He threw his body against the door and slammed it, snapping a bone in her wrist. Ellen screamed, the pain dropping her to her knees.

Sobbing, cradling her broken left wrist against her middle, she knelt at the feet of her killer. The workmen's tarps were spread all around, covered with plaster dust as thick and fine as flour, scattered with scabs of old plaster and empty Mountain Dew cans.

'Come along, Ellen,' Slater said, squatting down. 'Be a good bitch and let me kill you.'

He never noticed her right hand until it opened two inches from his face, throwing plaster dust into his eyes and into the gaping wound in his cheek.

Ellen stood and jerked the ax free. She whirled just as Slater lunged at her, grabbing her ankles, hitting her in the thigh. With the stun gun.

The current seared through her skirt, stormed along her nerve pathways. It hit the brain instantly, leaving behind stunned bewilderment. In a fraction of a second all control of arms and legs was gone. She fell like a stone, the ax sailing five feet away.

She lay on the tarp, eyes open as Slater bent down close.

'Some rise by sin, and some by virtue fall,' he murmured, his ravaged face inches from hers. 'Some by virtue die.'

The dispatcher, a round Nordic-looking girl with flyaway blond hair and an unflattering uniform, led Jay down the walkway between the sheriff's department and the courthouse, batting her lashes and offering her opinion that *he* should have starred in *Justifiable Homicide* instead of Tom Cruise.

He flashed her the smile, an absent, halfhearted gesture. 'Thank you, Mindy, but I'm more comfortable being a writer. I really didn't have anything to do with the movie.'

In fact, the story had been virtually unrecognizable by the time

Hollywood had finished with it. Jay had shrugged off that irksome little detail on the way to the bank. It didn't matter. It was just entertainment. He got paid either way.

A twinge hit his atrophied conscience. The people he wrote about were real, not fictional. They had lives that went on after the crimes that were his focus. They were people like Hannah Garrison and Megan and Ellen.

'Well, you should think about it,' Mindy bubbled on, unlocking the door to the courthouse. 'You're way better looking. He doesn't really have much of a chin, you know. Not that he isn't cute. He is. But you should have ranked lots higher than him in that *People* list, too. I don't know who makes that thing up. He's a Scientologist, too. Did you know that? That just spooks me. It's like a cult or something.' Her small eyes rounded suddenly. 'Ooh! You're not a Scientologist, are you?'

'No, ma'am. I belong to a snake-handling religion,' he drawled, straight-faced, lifting his hands as if each contained a fistful of writhing copperheads. 'Nothing more spiritual than takin' up snakes.'

Poor Mindy. The girl backed away, fighting a horrified grimace with her inbred Minnesota manners. Jay thanked her politely as she scooted back toward the sheriff's department.

As he headed through the deep gloom toward the stairs, he kept imagining the expression on Ellen's face as he shared the news that he was helping O'Malley hunt for leads on Wright's past. The image that came to mind was pride, which the cynic in him dismissed. He was a grown man, and he told himself he had long ago burned out his need for approval from 'respectable' people like his family, like Ellen.

He climbed the stairs to the second floor, shaking his head a little as he saw the door to the county attorney's offices standing open, light spilling out into the dark hall. He hadn't even bothered going by Ellen's house, despite the hour. She wouldn't go home to lick her wounds. She would go right back to the job and dig in harder than before.

He expected to find her in the conference room, bent over a pile of statements, glasses slipping down her nose. But the room was empty. Jay's nerves tightened as he took in the papers strewn across the floor. Papers painted with bright, thick splotches of blood.

Ellen lay flat on her stomach on the filthy tarp like a broken doll, her arms flung out to the sides at odd angles. She fought to make her brain work, tried in vain to will her arms to move. She had heard footfalls, knew someone else had come into the building. At the sound of Jay's voice calling her name, she tried to scream, but the sound was contained in her mind. Slater, straddling her on his knees, tightened his hand around her throat and squeezed until she couldn't breathe.

He had spent the last few minutes cutting a length of rope free from the scaffolding and fashioning a noose. All the while she lay helpless, unable to move, but able to watch him. At the first sound of another person in the building, he crouched over her and expertly slipped his fingers into position around her larynx.

She closed her twitching eyes and tried to direct her scattered mental powers to Brooks. *Please come looking, Jay. Please come upstairs. Please hurry.*

Footsteps sounded again below them. Hurrying. Breaking into a jog. Again in her mind she screamed, but no sound broke past the hold Slater had on her throat. What if Jay didn't come? What if he left the building, went back to the sheriff's department? Slater would have time to kill her and get away. Even if he had lost his chance to make it look like a suicide and clean up all evidence of himself after, he would still be able to kill her and escape.

She had to do something. Now.

The feeling was coming back into her arms. First, in the form of throbbing pain in her broken left wrist, then in small muscle spasms. If she could reestablish the connection between thought and movement . . .

Slowly her fingers curled into a fist, scraping chips and nuggets and chunks of old plaster into her palm. She would get only one chance. If she failed . . .

With all the concentration she could muster, she ordered her arm to move, to swing, ordered her fingers to open. Some of the debris fell short. Some hit the balusters of the railing and bounced back. The rest sailed into space and fell to the first floor. A meager effort to pin her life on. If Jay wasn't looking . . . Even if he noticed it, he might be too preoccupied to think it significant.

Slater, on the other hand, found it too significant. His hand tightened savagely on her throat. He bent down close and whispered hoarsely in her ear. 'You fucking bitch. You are dead. Now.'

His mouth closed on her ear, his teeth biting into the cartilage.

Ellen's mouth stretched open as she tried to gasp breath, succeeding only in dragging her tongue through the plaster dust. Her vision blurred with spiderweb lines of blackness. Her lungs burned with the desperate need for oxygen.

The instinct for survival shot adrenaline through her in a burst, jolting her body to action. Kicking, flailing, she swung an arm back, catching a finger in the torn flesh of his face and digging into the wound.

Plaster bits raining down to the floor of the rotunda caught Jay's eye as he hurried toward the stairs. Then came the cry – strangled, masculine. Above him – where the plaster had come from.

'Ellen!'

He shouted her name as he bolted for the stairs. If she was up there and not able to make any sound to call him, there was no time to spare. He didn't have the luxury of calling in cops.

He made the third-floor landing and ran toward the hall with no sense at all of what he might be rushing into – a knife, a bullet, a body. There were no thoughts at all for his own safety. His only thought was Ellen, that she was in danger, that she needed help.

'Ellen!'

Slater punched at her head, batted at her broken wrist, breaking her hold on his torn face. He pushed to his feet just as Jay came into view at the north end of the hall. Snatching up the fire ax, Slater rushed him.

Ellen struggled to her knees, gasping for air. In horror, she watched Slater bring the ax back and swing it like a baseball bat.

Jay dodged sideways, and the blade of the ax sang through the air. Too damned close. Before Slater could pull it back for another swing, before Jay could give any thought to his plan, he stepped in close and landed a left cross on Slater's jaw. Slater staggered sideways and dropped to one knee.

He came up swinging the ax backhanded. Jay ducked low and caught him hard in the ribs, knocking the wind from his lungs. He let his weapon go. The ax clattered to the floor, the handle spinning out of reach. Moving in quickly, Jay aimed a boot at Slater's chin as he doubled over. But Slater caught the kick and jerked Jay off his feet.

Jay landed hard on his back. Before his vision cleared, Slater was over him, the pale beam of the security light glinting off the blade of a hunting knife he had pulled from his coat.

Ellen staggered to her feet as Jay went down, fear and fury and pain coursing through her. Slater was the key to the evil that had contaminated her haven. He had killed Denny Enberg and Dustin Holloman. He would have killed her if not for Jay. And now he would kill Jay.

Jay managed to twist out of the way of the first knife strike, though the blade sliced the sleeve of his coat, releasing a mass of goose down that puffed up into the air between them. He wasn't as lucky the second time, or the third.

Slater stabbed viciously, his mouth open, the gaping wound sucking in and blowing out with his breath, blood and spittle spraying in a pink foam. The blade of the hunting knife stuck Jay's forearm as he tried to defend himself, tearing coat sleeve and muscle, hitting bone. He punched out with his other hand, barely connecting with Slater and leaving himself open to another assault.

The blade sank deep into the hollow of his right shoulder, and a white-hot burst of pain spread through his brain like a dark cloud, dimming his vision. He could feel the blood well up like water from a spring as his arm went dead.

Move, move, move!

Twisting, kicking, he got Slater off him and his feet beneath him. He scooted backward in a frantic retreat, with Slater in aggressive pursuit.

He hit the railing that overlooked the rotunda, saw Slater pulling the knife back, raising it high, the look in his eyes pure animal bloodlust, not human in any respect.

A hundred hard, clear truths cut across Jay's mind at the speed of light. He would never know his son. He had wasted too much time on spite. The only people who would mourn his passing would be the ones who made money off him. And what had begun with Ellen, what she had awakened in him, would die in this moment, unfulfilled.

Screaming, Slater pulled the blade another inch higher over his shoulder. Ellen hurled herself at him, hitting him in the side of the neck with the stun gun, shooting sixty thousand volts of electricity directly to his brain.

Eyes wide, he dropped to the floor, his body jerking and convulsing, then going utterly still.

Ellen stared at him, the horror of the last few moments hitting her. The strength that had carried her through vanished, and tremors shook her.

'It's all right,' Jay murmured, sliding his left arm around her and gathering her close. He pressed his face against the cool silk of her hair and kissed her. 'It's over, baby. It's over.'

An insidious numbness was creeping through him, creeping in on the edges of his mind. He felt that the energy that comprised his being was gathering into a softly glowing ball and slowly drifting out of the wounded shell of his body. He fought the sensation, as seductive as it was. All he wanted was to hold Ellen, shelter her.

'Oh, God, you're bleeding!' she whispered. She fumbled to press a hand against the gushing wound in his shoulder. His blood oozed out between her fingers and ran in rivulets down her hand.

'Don't worry,' he told her. 'I can't die a hero.' He gave her a pale shadow of his smile. 'It'd be too damned ironic.'

36

In his dream Josh saw blood. Rivers of it. Geysers of it. Smooth, oily pools of it. He was in it up to his chin. The undercurrent pulled at his feet. The hands of the Taker closed around his ankles and tried to pull him down. The Taker had chosen him. The Taker wanted him. It frightened him to disobey. He had gone into the smallest box of his mind to hide, and still the Taker had hold of him, pulling on him.

He had been told to obey. Bad things would happen. Terrible things. They had already started. Josh could see his whole world tearing apart, just the way the Taker had shown him. But still he clung to the sides of his box, holding on to what was left of his world.

If he could just hide long enough . . . If he could make himself even smaller inside the shell of his body. If he could get back inside the box . . .

His hands were slipping. He gulped a breath as the Taker pulled him under, through the blood.

Then, just as quickly, he was free. He broke the surface, soared, as if he had been thrown clear of a slingshot. Into the light. Into the air. He could breathe again. He was flying. And below him the blood drew into a smaller and smaller puddle, and then it was gone.

Josh's eyes snapped open. The room was dark, except for the nightlight and the numbers on his clock. He felt as if he had been sleeping for a long, long time. Days instead of hours. His mom was asleep in the sleeping bag on the floor. She looked so tired and worried. Her brow was frowning.

Because of me.

Because of the Taker.

There was so much she would never understand. So much he wished they could both forget and just start over, as if they hadn't even been alive until today.

Maybe they could do that, if he wished it hard enough, if he was good enough . . . if he could only find the courage.

37

The farmhouse sat on an isolated, wooded acreage just over the county line to the south in rural Tyler County. The nearest neighbors were Amish farmers who had no interest in the comings or goings of the 'English'. Ellen had to imagine they were taking notice this morning. Cars from the Tyler and Park county sheriff's departments, the Deer Lake PD, and the BCA filled the yard while news vans and reporters' vehicles clogged the road. Uniformed officers kept the press at bay while the detectives and evidence techs went about their work.

Parked in the machine shed was a rusting white 1984 Ford Econoline van. A match in age and condition to the van Paul Kirkwood had once owned and sold to Olie Swain. A match to the van a witness had seen at the hockey rink about the time Josh was abducted. A small toolbox behind the front seat held a roll of duct tape, folded squares of cloth – probably for administering ether – hypodermic needles and syringes for injectable sedatives. A kidnapper's tool kit.

Ellen backed away from the shed, shoulders hunched against the cold, and looked around the neat farmyard with its small buildings and perimeter of pine trees, boughs laden with the fresh snow that had fallen in the night. Great pains had been taken to make everything appear normal. The driveway was neatly plowed. A family of concrete deer stood posing in the yard near the bird feeder. Curtains hung at the windows. Christmas lights still hung from the eaves.

All part of the game.

Slater was under guard at the hospital, where he was being observed for any lingering effects from the electrical shock. He wasn't talking, but his name had provided the key they needed. Ellen, vaguely dopey from the pain medication Dr Lomax had given her before setting her wrist, had called Cameron from the hospital in the middle of the night and set him to work digging up information in Adam Slater's name. In short order they had a phone number, and from the phone number came an address.

Dawn had just lightened the gray of the eastern horizon. Ellen hadn't slept in any restful way, just in fits and starts in a hospital bed. Nightmares of the ordeal jolted her awake every time she drifted off. The feeling of Slater's hands tightening on her throat.

She had moved to Deer Lake to escape the violence and cynicism of the city, yet it was Deer Lake where she had been attacked, where she had been pushed to violence to save her own life and Jay's. A point for Wright's team. Just another ripple in the pond. Just another ramification of their game, along with broken trusts and a broken marriage, lost innocence and lost lives.

She thanked God Jay was not among the body count. Though he had lost enough blood to require a transfusion, the wounds themselves were not life threatening. Still, every time she closed her eyes, Ellen saw that horrible instant when Slater had pulled that bloody knife back for one final thrust, and everything inside her had clenched like a fist.

'You ready to go in, counselor?' Mitch asked, laying a hand on Ellen's shoulder.

She nodded and they moved toward the house. Cameron had argued that she was in no condition to go to the scene, but she wouldn't back down. She let him take the official role, but she needed to be there. It didn't matter that she hurt all over or that she could barely speak because of the bruising in her throat. She had accepted this case, and it would be her fight until the end.

Wilhelm unlocked the back door with a key from Slater's key ring, and they trooped in, holding their breath in anticipation of what they might find. The house was neat and tidy, with doilies on the end tables and a family photo of strangers hanging on the living-room wall.

Probably the family of one of their victims, Ellen suspected. Maybe even the real Adam Slater's family. She should have appreciated the twisted sense of humor, she supposed. If Slater hadn't taken the name of his first victim, he might never have been found out.

All part of the game.

'The game is more fun when you spot the other team points.'

One of the two bedrooms was decorated for a little boy, with shelves lined with an assortment of toys, each tagged with a name and date. Trophies from past games won. The notion sickened her. She stood in the hall, resisting the need to lean against the wall and risk ruining latent fingerprints. Leaning against Cameron, instead. He put a brotherly arm around her shoulders and stood silent, his face pale.

They all wore the same face, Ellen thought dimly. Mitch and Wilhelm and Jantzen, the Tyler County sheriff. Even Steiger wore it. Drawn, pale, grim, eyes hollow. There was a sheen of tears in Mitch's as he came out of the room.

'There's a red sneaker in there,' he said tightly. 'With the name Milo Wiskow. That's the case Megan dug up in Pennsylvania. All we have to do is find a connection between Wright and this house, and he goes away forever.'

End game.

They found what they needed in the basement, where Megan had been tied to an old wooden straight chair and tortured. The short black baton Wright had used to beat her hung on a pegboard above a small corner workbench, as if it were a common handyman's tool.

The basement was divided into three rooms, one of which was padlocked from the outside. Again, Wilhelm provided the key from Slater's ring, and they walked into the small chamber where the boys had been held.

The only furnishing was a cot. The only light a bulb in the ceiling with a switch outside the door. A video surveillance camera and stereo speakers hung high on the walls, their wiring connecting them to a system in the main workroom. From a pair of stools at the counter, Slater and Wright could watch their captive, speak to him, play the cassette tapes that were neatly stacked beside the tape deck.

Handling it gingerly with latex gloves, Mitch slipped a tape into the deck and hit the play button. Garrett Wright's voice came over the speakers, smooth and eerie.

'Hello, Josh. I am the Taker. I know what you think about. I know what you want. I can make you live or die. I can make your parents live or die. I can make your sister live or die. It's all up to you, Josh. You do what I say. You think what I tell you, remember what I tell you. I control your mind. I know everything you think.'

'Jesus,' Mitch muttered as he stopped the tape.

Mind control. Psychological terror of children. Having been in the cell where Wright had kept the boys, Ellen found it too easy to imagine how frightened they must have been, how lonely, wondering if anyone would come to save them, wondering if they would live or die, wondering if they might somehow unwittingly cause the deaths of the people they loved.

'I am the Taker. I know what you think about. I know what you want . . .'

She thought of Josh sitting in the psychiatrist's office as the doctor tried to coax answers from him. No wonder he wouldn't speak. Wright had buried the fear so deep inside his young mind, it could take years to extract it. He might never feel safe again.

'Bastard,' Steiger growled.

The shelves above the cassette deck housed a small library of audio- and videotapes. A sight that was horrible and welcome at once. Wright's training as an academician and a psychologist, as well as his own overconfidence, would do him in. He had apparently documented his games, his mind-control experiments . . . his crimes. Not even Tony Costello would be able to explain away videotape.

'He believed he'd never get caught,' Ellen said, her voice a whispery rasp. 'He thinks he's invincible.'

'He's dead fucking wrong,' Mitch growled. 'Let's go pick him up. We can sort through this stuff later. I want that son of a bitch in a cell.'

'Chief?' Wilhelm called from a desk ten feet away. 'I think you might want to take a look at this first.'

'What is it?'

'See for yourself.'

Wilhelm had pulled a three-ring binder from a row of similar binders and placed it on the blotter open to page one. Ellen stepped in beside Mitch and looked down at the childish handwriting.

Journal entry
August 27, 1968

They found the body today. Not nearly as soon as we expected. Obviously, we gave them too much credit. The police are not as smart as we are. No one is.

We stood on the sidewalk and watched. What a pitiful scene. Grown men in tears throwing up in the bushes. They wandered around and around that corner of the park, trampling the grass and breaking off bits of branches. They called to God, but God didn't answer. Nothing changed. No lightning bolts came down. No one was given knowledge of who or why. Ricky Meyers remained dead, his arms outflung, his sneakers toes up.

We stood on the sidewalk as the ambulance came with its lights flashing, and more police cars came, and the cars of people from around town. We stood in the crowd, but no one saw us, no one looked at us. They thought we were beneath their notice, unimportant, but we are really above them and beyond them and invisible to them. They are blind and stupid and trusting. They would never think to look at us.

We are twelve years old.

We.

'My money is on Priest,' Mitch said, hitting the blinker.

His Explorer led the procession of police vehicles turning onto Lakeshore Drive. A mob of press had already arrived and staked out Wright's lawn, making themselves useful for once, virtually trapping him in his own home. 'Megan had her eye on him. They may have known each other as boys; they taught together at Penn State. They founded the Cowboys together, and according to Slater, the Cowboys were formed around Wright's plan to develop him as a protégé.'

Ellen sat tense in the passenger's seat, anticipation tightening every muscle in her body. 'But if they were in on this game together,' she croaked, 'then why didn't they alibi each other for the night Josh went missing? Why have Todd Childs get up at the hearing and contradict the statement he gave the police?'

'You said he wanted to spot us points. Besides, they alibi each other, and those of us who believe one is guilty automatically believe the other is guilty.' He turned in at the Wrights' driveway and cut the engine. Reporters swarmed toward the truck. Ignoring them, he gave Ellen a hard look. His game face. 'Let's see if Dr Wright might be able to help us with the answers to those questions. He can provide the commentary when we play those videotapes.'

A whole other crop of questions assaulted them as they made their way to the front door, hurled by the news-hungry reporters like rice at a wedding. Steiger barked something out, grabbing the opportunity to look important.

Mitch hit the doorbell and waited, hit it again. 'Dr Garrett Wright,' he said in a loud voice, 'this is the police. Please come to the door. We need to speak with you.'

They waited a moment that stretched into another. Mitch lifted his two-way. 'Noogie? You got any action back there?'

Noga's deep voice came back. 'Nothing, Chief.'

Mitch knocked on the door again. 'Dr Wright, this is Chief Holt. We need to speak with you.'

'He has to be home,' Wilhelm muttered. 'He was at the victory celebration last night. We know he came back here.'

'But did he stay?' Mitch asked. 'If he caught wind of his boy wonder going down last night, he may just have split.'

Mitch hit the button on the radio again. 'Noogie? Take a peek in the garage. What have we got for vehicles?'

'Got a Saab and a Honda, Chief.'

'All present and accounted for,' Mitch said. He cast a look at Ellen. 'I say we go in. We've got probable cause.'

'And an audience,' Wilhelm said through his teeth.

'Then get them the hell off the yard, Marty,' Mitch ordered. 'Make yourself useful for once.'

As Wilhelm turned away, Mitch tried the doorknob. 'Locked.' He raised the radio again. 'Noogie? You got any company back there?'

'No, sir.'

'Then do your thing.'

'Ten-four.'

Noga was the force's official battering ram. The house door hadn't been made that Noga couldn't bust off its hinges with a shrug. In a matter of moments the front locks were tumbling and the big officer pulled the door open.

The house was quiet. Tastefully, expensively decorated in neutral tones and sleek, pale oak furnishings. Mitch scanned the rooms visible from the foyer.

'Dr Wright?' he called, sliding his Smith & Wesson nine-mil from his shoulder holster and holding it nose up. 'Police! Come out where we can see you!'

The silence hung around them.

'I guess we get to do this the hard way,' he muttered, turning toward Ellen and Cameron. 'Wait outside. I don't want any chance of this turning into a hostage situation. Noogie, back me up.'

Ellen laid a hand on his forearm. 'Be careful, Mitch. He doesn't have anything to lose now.'

They moved down the halls of the house, Mitch taking the lead, his back to one wall. Each closed door represented a potential nasty surprise. The tight quarters of an unfamiliar house were always a dangerous setting. They opened doors that led to a bathroom, to a guest room, to Karen Wright's hobby room. Not a sound. Not a thing out of place.

They could have easily left in the night, Mitch thought. With the charges dismissed, he had had no choice but to pull the surveillance team or risk charges of harassment. In the back of his mind he made a note to check with the twenty-four-hour car service that taxied people from Deer Lake to the airport in Bloomington. The Wrights could have been halfway to Rio by now.

He sidled up beside the last door on the upper level, reached over, and knocked. 'Wright, come out with your hands up! You're under arrest!'

Nothing. He turned the doorknob and pushed the door open, holding himself against the wall. No shots blasted out at them. And then he slipped inside the master bedroom and found out why Garrett Wright hadn't answered them.

Garrett Wright lay spread-eagled on the king-size bed, naked, his throat cut from ear to ear, a butcher knife buried to the hilt in his chest, his dead eyes gazing up at a heaven he would never know.

'He's not stiff yet,' Mitch said. 'He hasn't been dead more than a few hours.'

Ellen took a long look at the gaping wound that nearly severed Garrett Wright's head from his body, then turned away, taking in the room. 'There's no sign of a struggle.'

'Too bad. He should have had to look death in the face. He should have had to feel the fear his victims felt.'

'The cars are here and Karen Wright is missing,' Wilhelm said. 'Either she did it and walked away or the killer took her with him.'

'Paul Kirkwood publicly vowed revenge,' Cameron reminded them. 'He was having an affair with Karen.'

'Get out APBs on both of them,' Ellen said. Her gaze drew back to the man whose life had bled out of him.

A murderer. A man whose mind and heart had been as dark as the blood that soaked the ivory sheets around him. He had tormented, tortured, killed, and called it a game. Heartless and cruel. And even with his death, it continued. He had driven someone else to kill, and that person would touch other lives, and the effects would go on and on like a stream of oil bleeding into the ocean.

'I always wanted children,' Karen said, rocking the baby in her arms. 'Garrett and I couldn't have children. But Paul and I can. We can have Lily.'

Hannah stared at the woman who had invaded her home sometime in the hours before dawn. Karen Wright. Vapid, innocuous Karen. Always trying to help. Doe-eyed, pretty Karen. Her husband's mistress. Wife of the man who had kidnapped her son.

Hannah had awakened to the sound of a voice singing softly down the hall. A woman's voice coming from Lily's room. Groggy and confused, she'd crawled out of the sleeping bag in her leggings and baggy sweatshirt, her hair falling out of its loose braid and into her eyes.

She stood now in the hall between the bedrooms, still hoping this was yet another of the strange nightmares that had been plaguing her since the start of the ordeal; knowing it was not. Karen Wright stood in her daughter's room, holding Lily and a gun.

'How did you get in here?' Hannah demanded.

'With a key,' Karen said matter-of-factly, never taking her eyes off Lily. 'I have copies of all of Paul's keys.' She smiled dreamily. 'I can have the key to his heart now that Garrett won't come between us.'

She rose from the rocking chair, juggling Lily and the nine-millimeter gun, the load seeming too much for her. 'You're so sweet, aren't you, Lily?' she cooed. 'I've always pretended you were mine. I wanted Garrett to get you for me, but he only takes little boys. That's the way it's always been. He hated children.'

'You can't have her,' Hannah said flatly.

Karen's eyes narrowed, her mouth twisted on the bitterness. 'You don't deserve her. I do. I give and give and never get anything back. It's *my* turn. I told Garrett. He wouldn't listen. I told him I wanted Paul. I *love* Paul. Paul could give me a baby. But no. He had to make Paul look guilty. He had to ruin what *I* wanted. He made a very big mistake.'

Her arms tightened on the baby, and Lily squirmed and frowned. 'Down!'

'No, no, sweetheart,' Karen said with a sudden smile, stroking Lily's cheek with the barrel of the gun. 'You're going to be my little girl now. We have to go away and make a new life with your daddy. We'll be a happy family.'

'What about Garrett?' Hannah asked, inching forward to block the door. Damned if she was going to let a madwoman walk out of her house with her daughter. She would do whatever she had to do. She had pledged to keep her children safe. She was all through being a victim.

Karen's eyes glazed with tears. 'Garrett . . . wouldn't listen. He wouldn't let me be happy.' A single tear skimmed her cheek. 'I love Paul, and Garrett made me betray him. He shouldn't have done that.'

Lily twisted in her grasp, pushing against the arm that was banded around her middle. 'Lily down!' she demanded. She looked to Hannah. 'Mama, down!'

Anger flashing across her features, Karen gave the baby a shake. 'Stop it, Lily!' She turned Lily's head toward her with the barrel of the gun. '*I'm* your mommy now.'

Josh watched the scene from behind his mother. No one had noticed him. No one would. He could be like a ghost. The quiet was in his mind, and he could make it as big as he was and put it all around him like a giant bubble. He saw the gun. He heard the words. Karen was going to take Lily. Just as he had been taken. Just as that other boy had been taken. The other Goner was dead now, just as Josh had been warned. Now Lily, just as he had been warned. Bad things would happen if he told anyone the truth. But he hadn't told anyone and bad things were happening anyway.

The fear inside him struggled against the need to be free of it. He wanted to be free. He wanted his family to be free. He thought maybe if he wished hard enough . . . If he was good enough . . . If he could only find the courage . . .

'Does Paul know you're doing this?' Hannah asked, edging into the room. If she could get to the changing table, she could grab the baby powder, throw it in Karen's face, get Lily away from her before she could use the gun.

'Paul loves me,' Karen said, hefting Lily on her hip. 'I'm what he needs. I'm the kind of woman he deserves.'

'You're right about that,' Hannah said, laughing bitterly. Paul had brought this nightmare on them with his groundless discontent, with his myopic self-absorption. Karen Wright was exactly what he deserved.

'We'll be a happy family,' Karen said, jerking Lily against her as the baby tried to squirm out of her grasp. 'Lily, stop it!' she shrieked, raising the gun. 'Don't make me hurt you!'

As she brought the butt of the gun down toward Lily's head, Josh burst to life. Hurling himself into the room, flinging his body at Karen Wright's legs.

'Josh, no!' Hannah screamed.

Then everything was a blur of sound and motion as she jumped to grab Karen's gun.

'If it was Paul, Wright would have struggled,' Ellen said.

'Unless they drugged him first,' Wilhelm offered.

'Paul wouldn't have the guts to kill like that,' Mitch said. 'With a gun, maybe. With a knife, no way.'

'Karen got tired of his trying to control her the way he did his victims,' Ellen theorized. 'He used her to get to Paul. God only knows how he might have used her before.'

'The question is, Where did she go?' Cameron said. 'And was she alone?'

'Get on the phone to the cab company,' Ellen told him. 'I have a hard time believing Paul dropped by and picked her up after she essentially testified against him in court.'

'Tracks,' Noga said suddenly. He had been leaning against the wall, pale and wobbly. Straightening, he turned toward Mitch. 'There were tracks in the backyard.'

In the fresh snow.

'Let's go.' Mitch started for the door, tossing instructions over his shoulder to Wilhelm. 'Secure the scene and keep the press out.'

Ellen followed him out the kitchen door, through the garage where Wright had first been arrested, and to the backyard, where reporters were creeping around the perimeter of the property in the attempt to get an angle no one else had.

'Mitch, we'll need to make some kind of statement,' Ellen said. 'Get a photo of Karen to the TV people. If she's a possible killer, the public needs to know.'

'Do what you have to.'

He had just turned to follow Noga north along the footprints. North, toward the Kirkwood house, when the sound of gunshots cracked the crisp morning air.

They crashed into the dresser, sending a lamp tumbling; fell against the white wicker rocker and onto the floor, kicking and gouging. The gun flew free, spinning across the carpet. Hannah lunged for it but was pulled up short as Karen grabbed hold of her braid with a savage tug. Fingernails raked down her face. Karen's knee caught her in the stomach as Karen lunged forward. Too late.

Josh raised the black pistol with both hands and pointed it squarely at Karen Wright's forehead, just inches away, the barrel wobbling gently back and forth.

Karen went still. Lily lay on the floor near the crib, sobbing. Hannah struggled to sit up, to move back from Karen, her eyes on Josh.

'You're bad,' Josh said to Karen, his blue eyes flat. 'You can't take my sister. I won't let you.'

'Bad things will happen, Josh,' she said in an eerie tone. 'You know and I know. The Taker will punish you.'

'The Taker is dead,' he said.

Hannah's heart nearly stopped. She moved back from Karen and edged around toward Josh, holding out her hand. 'Josh, honey, give me the gun.'

'I have to stop them,' he said, tears swimming up. 'I'm the only one. It's my fault. They'll hurt you and Lily.'

'No, sweetheart,' she whispered as she crouched down beside him.

His small hands were tight on the stock of the pistol, knuckles white as he aimed the barrel at Karen Wright's face. 'She's a Taker, too. They have power. She'll take Lily. She'll hurt her. I have to stop them. It's up to me.'

'No, Josh,' Hannah said, inching closer. 'I won't let her take Lily. Give me the gun.'

He made no move to obey. Hannah eased her arms around him, waiting to hear the terrible sound of a shot. If she moved too quickly, if she tried to pull the gun away, it could go off. As much as she wanted justice, she didn't want it like this. She didn't want it weighing on Josh for the rest of his life.

Trying not to shake, she slipped her hands over his on the stock of the pistol. 'It's over, honey.'

His body was quivering in the circle of her arms. His eyes were locked, wide and staring, on Karen Wright as he struggled within himself.

'Give me the gun, Josh,' Hannah whispered. 'They don't have any power over us. Not anymore. It's over. They won't hurt anyone ever again. I promise. You're safe. I'll never let anyone hurt you again. I love you so much.'

If only love were enough to protect them, she thought. If only love were enough to heal the damage that had been done. She willed her love to be enough in this moment, enough to bring Josh back from the edge. If he crossed this line, even if he crossed it only in his mind, he would be lost.

I lost him once, God. Please don't make me lose him again. Please let us start over. Now.

Josh stared at Karen, felt the trigger in the curve of his finger. He wanted to be free. He wanted things the way they had been before. If he killed all the Takers . . .

'No, Josh, *please.*'

His mother's voice seemed to come from within his own mind. There were so many things she couldn't understand.

Please . . .

He wanted to be free.

He stared at Karen and felt . . . nothing.

'He's dead,' he whispered as realization dawned inside him. The connection was gone, broken in the night. He was free.

Free . . .

Pulling his hands away from the gun, he turned to his mother, put his head on her shoulder, and started to cry.

Hannah hugged him to her with one arm as she held the pistol trained on Karen. In another part of the house she heard a door open, and Mitch Holt's voice came like the voice of salvation.

38

'She wanted what she thought I had,' Hannah said softly.

She stood in the doorway to Josh's room, watching him sleep. The day had been a marathon. Police trooping through the house, wanting statements, asking questions, taking photographs. The press mounting a fresh full-scale campaign to get her to talk to them. Newspapers, magazines, tabloids. Television newsmagazines, talk shows, agents from Hollywood who wanted to put together movie deals. She had shut them all out and let in only one person – Tom McCoy.

'She wanted a happy family. We had that once,' she said wistfully. 'Once upon a time . . .'

The story of the Wrights' lives had unfolded throughout the day as the police and prosecutors examined the journals found in the farmhouse. A double life led from childhood on. Garrett – intelligent, sociopathic, controlling, manipulative. His sister, Caroline – a shadow, subservient, introverted. The children of a cold, bitter woman who valued appearances over substance; abandoned by their father, who had remarried and started a new family.

Garrett had taken control of Caroline, absorbed her into his life and into his psyche, until they seemed to become a single entity. She had managed to break free of him when she ran away from home at seventeen, only to have him find her again a year later. And the control, the manipulation, the whole twisted cycle started all over again. They lived as husband and wife, kept up a flawless front as the psychology professor and his demure, quiet spouse, while Garrett masterminded and played out his sick game.

'I keep wondering,' Hannah murmured, 'if Wright singled us out because he thought we had a perfect family, or because he knew we didn't.'

'Have you spoken with Paul?' Tom asked, propping a shoulder against the door frame, watching Hannah. In this light the bruise her husband had left on her jaw looked like a shadow.

'He contacted Mitch after the news broke. He'd checked into a hotel in Burnsville. He said he went there because he wanted time to think.' Mixed feelings wrestled within her like a pair of cobras. She didn't want Paul near her or the children, and yet she resented the fact that he had fled and left them to face the consequences of his mistakes. 'I didn't call him back. I don't have anything to say to him my lawyer can't say more diplomatically.'

This was where he was supposed to counsel her, Tom thought. If he was a good priest, he would tell her there was still hope, that wounds could heal, that what was broken in her marriage could be made whole through prayer and faith. But he didn't believe it was true, and he didn't see himself as a good priest. He didn't really see himself as a priest at all anymore.

'I'm sorry,' he said with sincerity.

'So am I,' Hannah whispered. Vignettes of her marriage flashed through her mind as she looked at Josh. The good times, when life had held such promise. 'It should have been forever.'

Instead the promise had been broken, and she was left to rage and mourn the jagged pieces.

Tom's hand closed around hers, offering comfort, offering strength. Bringing a thin veil of guilt to the complex mix of emotions she was already struggling with.

'I could use a glass of wine,' she said, turning away.

Evening was closing in outside. It only seemed like midnight. Exhausted from the ordeal of the day, both Josh and Lily had crashed late in the afternoon, but the night still stretched ahead. Long hours of quiet waiting to be filled with introspection and pointless longing.

She filled two glasses with chardonnay and carried them to the family room, where Tom was tending the fire. The light caught on the gold rims of his glasses, warmed the color of his strong, handsome face. He was in jeans and one of his lumberjack shirts. She saw no evidence of his clerical collar.

'What will you do?' he asked, setting the poker back in the stand. 'Will you stay?'

'No.' She waited for him to admonish her, to tell her she needed time, that she should wait and sort things out when the emotion had passed and she could think more clearly. But he said nothing. 'We have a lot of memories here, but even the good ones hurt. I think it's best if we make a break. Go somewhere new. Give Josh a fresh start.'

She settled into the corner of the couch nearest the fire and sipped her wine. 'You've been such a good friend through all this. I don't know how to thank you.'

'I don't need thanks,' he said, lowering himself to the edge of a chair that was close enough that their knees nearly touched.

'I know it's your job, but —'

'No. This isn't about my duty as a priest. Or maybe it is.' He drew in a deep breath. Anticipation and dread held it in his lungs a moment. 'I'm leaving the priesthood, Hannah.'

The look on her face was less than he had hoped for, but no different from what he had expected. Shock with an underlayer of fear.

'Oh, Tom, no.' She set her glass aside with a hand that trembled. 'Not because of – Please don't say I drove you to –' Her blue eyes shimmered like the lake in summer. 'I've got more guilt than I need already.'

'It's not for you to feel guilty, Hannah,' he said, leaning toward her, his forearms resting on his thighs, his face earnest. 'There is no guilt. I feel what I feel, and no rule can convince me what I feel is wrong.

'How can it be wrong to love someone? I've chewed on that question until there's nothing left. I don't see how it can ever be reconciled.' He smiled, a sad, fond smile. 'Monsignor Corelli always said my philosophy degree would get me in trouble. I think too much. You know, I've never been very good at toeing the company line.'

'But you're a wonderful priest,' Hannah insisted. 'You make people think, you make them question, you make them look deeper within. If we don't do those things, what are we?'

'Stagnant. Comfortable. Happy,' he conceded. 'Growth hurts. Growth precipitates change. Change is frightening. It would be easier for me to stay in the Church,' he admitted. 'Safer. It's what I know. There are parts of it I love. But if I have to be a hypocrite to do it . . . I can't live like that, Hannah.'

Still more of life's endless supply of irony, Hannah thought. He was a good priest, but he was too good a man to stay a priest. He couldn't go against his principles, even if his principles went against the Church.

'I shouldn't be dumping this on you tonight,' he said, glancing away. 'It's just that . . . I've made the decision, and you've made yours . . . I don't want to add to your burden, Hannah. I just wanted you to know.'

He went back to the fire and poked at the logs, kicking up sparks like a swarm of fireflies that shot up the chimney. He loved her. There had been a time, Hannah thought, that she would have said love would be the one thing to get her through an ordeal like the one they had just been through – her husband's love. But Paul didn't love her, and in all the madness the love she had found within her was for this man. This man who was supposed to be beyond her reach.

It seemed they deserved something better than to be pulled apart. But could they have something more? Something that wouldn't wither in the shadow of their past or be crushed by the burden of complicity.

'I need time,' she said, going to him. 'I think we both do. We've been through so much, so fast. I know I have to get away from it. I have to clear it all out, sort it into some kind of order. Can you understand that?'

'Yes.' He looked down at her, his eyes searching hers, his hands reaching up to frame her face, to touch her hair. 'As long as you don't clear me out when you're sorting through the rest of it. Don't throw away what we could have together because it would be easier, Hannah.'

There was nothing easy about any of it, she thought, closing her eyes against the bittersweet pain. The weight of her choices pressed down on her, a burden she couldn't bear at the moment. Time. They needed time.

Sliding her arms around his waist, she hugged him tight and whispered, 'I love you.'

He bent his head and kissed her cheek. She felt his gentle smile against her skin. 'Then I can wait as long as it takes. Just don't let it take forever.'

Ellen sat back in her desk chair and allowed herself a long, slow, heartfelt sigh. It felt like the first good breath she'd had all day. It was certainly the first moment's rest. Exhaustion felt like an anchor strapped to her shoulders. Pain throbbed through her body. Neither dimmed the sense of relief. It was over.

Garrett Wright had been passed on to a higher court for judgment. Karen Wright had been transported to the state psychiatric hospital for an evaluation she would almost certainly fail. Adam Slater was under twenty four-hour watch in the county jail. The BCA and FBI were working through the journals and contacting law-enforcement agencies in the other states where Wright had played his game, wrapping up cases that went back twenty-six years. Cases that had gone unsolved. Cases that had ended in convictions of innocent people, convictions that would now be overturned all these years after the fact.

The ripples were still going out from the rock in the pond. And they would go on and on and on. The surface would eventually smooth over, but underneath, the changes would remain. The people of Deer Lake would pretend to forget, but they would lock their doors and watch their children and never quite trust in the way they had. She would settle back into her old routine, but she would never feel the same kind of peace. And Brooks . . .

She had to think this had changed him as well. She didn't want to believe he could involve himself in the lives of the people who had been violated by these crimes and not be touched in some fundamental way. He had come here to stand on the edge of it and look in, but he had been drawn in time and again. He had saved her life. He couldn't be the same man who had come to Deer Lake two weeks ago, the mercenary looking to score off the suffering of others.

Or maybe he would go back to Alabama and write his book and make a lot of money and play himself in the movie version because everyone knew he was better looking than Tom Cruise. *People* would name him the Sexiest Man Alive, and she would never see him again except on the dust jackets of the books she wouldn't buy.

The events that had taken place, the revelations that had been made, were just what he had come looking for. Sensational, twisted, complex. Erik Evans' / Adam Slater's story alone was worthy of a book. What went wrong in a child's mind to turn him into a killer? She had to admit she was curious herself. She wanted to be able to comprehend what had happened, make some kind of sense of it.

Maybe she would end up picking up one of Brooks's works after all. Maybe there was some value in standing back from a crime and analyzing the why. Maybe there would be some comfort in isolating the madness of what had gone on. Then again, she'd been in the system too long to be naive. She knew too well there was no isolation of evil. It crept out and spread like a killing vine. Even to places like Deer Lake.

A knock at her door jolted her back to the moment. The excitement of the day had culminated with a press conference at six o'clock. Bill Glendenning had beat a path down from his lofty office in St Paul to personally commend her in front of the multitude of television cameras – with Rudy right by his side. The air of excitement had lingered, keeping people in the courthouse longer than usual as they hung around to rehash the fantastic details of the day and of Wright's lifetime exploits.

Cameron stuck his head in the door, eyebrows raised. 'You need a lift home?'

'No, thanks. I'm fine. I'm just winding down here before I have to fight my way through the media hordes. Did you find anything in Slater's phone records yet?'

He frowned. 'Sorry. Costello's number isn't there. Not on the house phone, not on the cellular phone. If we don't make that connection, he's off the hook.'

'And Tony Costello slips out of the grip of justice like the slimy eel he is.'

'If it's any consolation, I think it'll take him a long time to crawl out of the hole he's in,' he said, leaning a shoulder against the doorjamb. 'As it turns out, he was representing one of the country's more despicable career criminals.'

'And he got him off,' Ellen said soberly, knowing that was how Tony would look at it. Not as a shameful humiliation, but as a game won. The only difference between him and his client had been that Costello's games were sanctioned.

'I'll keep digging,' Cameron promised. 'How about you? Anything on Priest yet?'

'There's no mention of him by name in the journals. He claims the reason he lied about growing up in Mishawaka is that he had some emotional problems at the time and ended up quitting school. He falsified records to get into college, claiming he graduated from a good school in Chicago. He adamantly denies all knowledge of Wright's activities, but it's hard to believe he never suspected anything. At best, he had to have held a suspicion that might have prevented a lot of suffering if he had acted on it.

'The FBI has had him all afternoon. They confiscated all the records on the joint learning-and-perception project Wright's and Priest's students were working on, in case there might be something in that. They'll get the truth out of him eventually. And when they do, there'll be a line of attorneys waiting to prosecute.'

'You'll be filing perjury charges against Todd Childs?' he asked.

Ellen nodded. 'I'm betting he's the one who broke into the Pack Rat, too, though I don't know that we'll ever prove it. Childs knew we were looking for him, and Costello had told him to drop out of sight. Trouble was, he had product stashed at the store and knew it wouldn't be there long if he didn't get it.' She gave a shrug that pulled on muscles better left alone. 'That's my theory, anyway. We can worry about proving it another day.'

'In the meantime, you should go home and sleep for a day or two,' Cameron suggested. 'You'll need your rest. Rumor has it you'll be first in line for Rudy's job when he takes Franken's seat on the bench.'

'That's news to me. As usual.'

He laughed, though it didn't make him look quite as young as it had a week ago. 'I'll call you tomorrow.'

He started to back out the door, then leaned in again. 'I thought I'd stop by Phoebe's house and see how she's doing. She's really upset about the Slater thing. She's blaming herself for what happened to you. I'm worried about her. Any wisdom you want me to pass along?'

'Yeah. Tell her it's not a crime to trust someone, even if they don't deserve it,' Ellen said. She felt for sweet, gullible Phoebe. It would take her a long time to get over what had happened, even longer to shed the guilt. 'I don't blame her for what happened. Slater would have found a way to get what he wanted. I'm just glad he didn't hurt her physically.'

'Amen to that.'

Another victim in the game, Ellen thought sadly. Phoebe's trust and loyalty. She made a mental note to stop by Phoebe's house herself if she didn't show up for work in the morning.

She was trying to work up the energy to get out of her chair and put her coat on when Megan came to the door.

'I thought you'd be out celebrating,' Ellen said, motioning her to a chair.

'I'm waiting for Mitch. He's in with the Feebies and Priest,' she said. 'We'll celebrate later. What about you? All this wrapped up and the Minneapolis cops picked up your mad-bomber friend, too.'

'All I want is a long, hot soak and a bed,' Ellen confessed. 'It's a relief to have it over. There's a lot of satisfaction in knowing we've put an end to a long line of horrible crimes. But there's something in turning over that big rock and seeing what was under it that puts a damper on my appetite for festivities. The world's full of rocks, you know. I just want to finish the job and move on to the next one.'

Megan nodded, reflective. 'Well, I just wanted to thank you personally for letting me in on this. I know you took a risk.'

'It paid off. You're a good cop, Megan.'

She smiled with a kind of shy pride that was touching. 'Yeah, I am. And now I see that I can still be a good cop whether I can handle a gun or not. There can still be a place for me on the job. That means a lot to me. Thanks, Ellen. And thanks to your friend Brooks. If he hadn't offered to help, I'd still be on the phone calling directory assistance.'

'He did what?' Ellen asked stupidly.

'He offered me a deal. He knew I was looking into Wright's background —'

'And he wanted to use it.' Ellen's heart sank as her temper rose from the ashes of exhaustion.

'No,' Megan said. 'He wanted to help. He offered me the use of his computer, his fax, his phones. We worked together half of Tuesday night and all of yesterday. That was how we found that case in Pennsylvania. He didn't tell you this?'

'We got a little sidetracked with a homicidal maniac,' Ellen said, her mind spinning. 'Then, at the hospital, it was Mitch who told me about the Wiskow case.'

Because Brooks had been busy getting himself stitched back together.

He had offered to help. For the sake of the case, or for the sake of his book?

Megan rose carefully, pulling her crutch up under her left arm. 'You know, he's a pretty decent guy for someone who used to be a lawyer. No offense.'

'None taken,' Ellen murmured.

He had come to Deer Lake to watch, to observe from a distance, to soak it all in and sell it.

He had helped crack the case. He had saved her life . . . and stolen her heart. She hadn't wanted to admit that, but it was true. She hadn't wanted to believe it. Her life had been a whole lot simpler before he'd come into it, with his voice like smoke and eyes that saw through all her barriers. He had reached past those barriers and touched her, awakened something within her she had denied – need, the need to feel, the need to care too much.

He had come here for the case, and the case was over.

'Damn you, Brooks,' she whispered to the empty room. 'Now what?'

'I suggest a steak dinner and a long, slow night in bed,' he drawled, stepping in from the dark hall. 'Together. Sleeping.'

He looked much the way he had the first night she'd seen him, that wicked pirate's grin cutting across a two-day beard. His coat hung open, giving a glimpse of the sling that held his right arm against him.

Ellen ignored the idea that she had conjured him up out of her imagination and scowled at him instead. 'Is there a line out there?'

'No, ma'am. I'm the last.'

'What are you doing here?' she asked with concern. 'You should be in the hospital.'

He shook his head. 'Dr Baskir sent me on my way.'

'I have a hard time believing that.'

'All right,' he admitted with a sheepish look. 'Maybe I sorta talked my way out.'

'*That* I believe.'

He grinned again as he came around the end of the desk, perched a hip on one corner, and grabbed up her paperweight as if it were a baseball. 'My Uncle Hooter always said I could charm the skirt off a Sunday-school teacher.'

'A useful talent. Who did you charm to get in here?'

'My old friend Deputy Qualey. Did you know he once thwarted a burglar by throwing a live snake on him?'

'What was he doing with a live snake in the first place?'

'Don't know. Don't want to know. Sure as hell don't want to write a book about it.'

'No,' Ellen said. 'You've got enough to write about with this case. Twisted minds, sex, violence, corruption. Everybody's favorite stuff.'

'There isn't going to be any book,' Jay announced, watching her reaction. She met his gaze with wary surprise. 'I kind of lost my objectivity.'

And gained things he still wasn't sure he wanted – sympathy, nobility, a conscience. They felt like medals that had been pinned to his chest instead of his shirt.

'Megan told me what you did to help, Jay,' Ellen said. 'Thank you.'

'Yeah, well, don't let it get around. You'll ruin my reputation as a scheming opportunist.'

'Some people might catch on when no blockbuster best-seller comes out of this.'

'That's a chance I'll have to take. It's not that I think there's no value in telling the tales,' he qualified. 'It just won't be me telling them.'

'So you came all the way to Minnesota, froze your butt off, and nearly got killed all for nothing?'

'I wouldn't say that,' he said in a low voice, stepping close. 'I wouldn't say that at all. What I'll take from here is more valuable than any story.'

'You're leaving?' Ellen blurted, then scrambled to cover. 'I mean – well – I guess if there's no book to write . . .'

He had come here for a book. That was all. He had his life in Alabama. She had hers here. Their paths had crossed and now they would move on.

It just seemed so soon.

'I've got a son I'd like to meet,' Jay said quietly. 'Just meet him, get to know him. I've missed eight years of his life. I'm damned lucky I don't have to miss any more. I'm damned lucky I have a choice.'

Ellen found a smile for him. 'I'm glad you're making that choice, Jay. I hope it all works out.'

'Yeah,' he said, fragile hope building in his heart. It had been so long since he had allowed anything in there but cynicism.

'After that,' he said, setting the paperweight aside, 'I was thinking I might try my hand at fiction.'

'Really?'

'I'm thinking about a female protagonist,' he said, watching her carefully. 'The days and nights of a beautiful assistant county attorney.'

He straightened from the desk and stepped closer, his gaze holding hers. Ellen smiled slowly.

'Want to help with the research?' he whispered in a voice like smoke over satin as he leaned down to kiss her. 'I suggest we start with the nights. . . .'

Epilogue

She sat alone in the small white room, the only light coming from the moon through the barred window high on the wall. Truly alone for the first time in her life. Like a balloon cut free. From other rooms like hers she could hear the eerie keening and crying of faceless people. Night sounds. Sounds that gave her an odd sense of comfort.

Softly humming a lullaby to herself, she rocked her pillow in one arm while she wrote on the wall with a blue crayon.

Journal Entry
February 3, 1994

Goodbye to Garrett
Goodbye to we
Hello to me
Who will be my family?

Inside my mind
Inside my heart
Outside these walls
A new game to start

One day ...

A THIN
DARK LINE

This book is dedicated to the many victims who wait for justice, and to the law enforcement professionals who pursue that justice with dogged determination.

Author's Note

A Thin Dark Line takes place in a setting my longtime readers know is a favorite of mine – Louisiana's French Triangle. It is a place like no other in this country – ecologically, culturally, linguistically. I have done my best to bring some of the rich flavor of the region to you, in part with the occasional use of Cajun French, a patois as unique to Louisiana as gumbo. You will find a glossary for these words and phrases in the back of the book. My sources include *A Dictionary of the Cajun Language* by Rev. Msgr. Jules O. Daigle and *Conversational Cajun French* by Randall P. Whatley and Harry Jannise.

My sincere thanks and appreciation to Sheriff Charles A. Fuselier of St Martin Parish, Louisiana, for your generosity with both your time and your knowledge; for giving me the real tour of bayou country and a lesson in Lou'siana politics. The stories were great, the food was even better. *Merci!* Thanks also to Deputy Barry Reburn, my in-family consultant on police procedure. Any mistakes made or liberties taken in the name of fiction are my own.

Thanks to Kathryn Moe, Coldwell Banker Real Estate, Rochester, Minnesota, for unwittingly planting the seed of a gruesome idea when you offered to wait for the furnace inspection guy. Hope it doesn't give you nightmares. And thanks once again to Diva Dreyer for the trauma lingo.

Thank you, Rat Boy, wherever you are.

And finally, my most special thanks to Dan for never minding that I'm always on deadline.

Hide your heart under the bed and lock your secret drawer.
Wash the angels from your head, won't need them anymore.
Love is a demon and you're the one he's coming for.
Oh my Lord.

– 'Could I be Your Girl'
Jann Arden Richards

Prologue

'*Red is the color of violent death. Red is the color of strong feelings – love, passion, greed, anger, hatred.*

Emotions – better not to have them.

Luckier not to have them.

Love,

*   Passion,*

*   Greed,*

*   Anger,*

*   Hatred.*

The feelings pull one another in a circle. Faster, harder, blurring into violence. I had no power over it.

Love,

*   Passion,*

*   Greed,*

*   Anger,*

*   Hatred.*

The words pulsed in my head every time I plunged the knife into her body.

Hatred,

*   Anger,*

*   Greed,*

*   Passion,*

*   Love,*

The line between them is thin and red.'

1

Her body lay on the floor. Her slender arms outflung, palms up. Death. Cold and brutal, strangely intimate.

The people rose in unison as the judge emerged from his chambers. The Honorable Franklin Monahan. The figurehead of justice. The decision would be his.

Black pools of blood in the silver moonlight. Her life drained from her to puddle on the hard cypress floor.

Richard Kudrow, the defense attorney. Thin, gray, and stoop-shoul-dered, as if the fervor for justice had burned away all excess within him and had begun to consume muscle mass. Sharp eyes and the strength of his voice belied the image of frailty.

Her naked body inscribed with the point of a knife. A work of violent art.

Smith Pritchett, the district attorney. Sturdy and aristocratic. The gold of his cuff links catching the light as he raised his hands in supplication.

Cries for mercy smothered by the cold shadow of death.

Chaos and outrage rolled through the crowd in a wave of sound as Monahan pronounced his ruling. The small amethyst ring had not been listed on the search warrant of the defendant's home and was, therefore, beyond the scope of the warrant and not legally subject to seizure.

Pamela Bichon, thirty-seven, separated, mother of a nine-year-old girl. Brutally murdered. Eviscerated. Her naked body found in a vacant house on Pony Bayou, spikes driven through the palms of her hands into the wood floor; her sightless eyes staring up at nothing through the slits of a feather Mardi Gras mask.

Case dismissed.

The crowd spilled from the Partout Parish Courthouse, past the thick

Doric columns and down the broad steps, a buzzing swarm of humanity centering on the key figures of the drama that had played out in Judge Monahan's courtroom.

Smith Pritchett focused his narrow gaze on the navy blue Lincoln that awaited him at the curb and snapped off a staccato line of 'no comments' to the frenzied press. Richard Kudrow, however, stopped his descent dead center on the steps.

Trouble was the word that came immediately to Annie Broussard as the press began to circle the defense attorney and his client. Like every other deputy in the sheriff's office, she had hoped against hope that Kudrow would fail in his attempt to get the ring thrown out as evidence. They had all hoped Smith Pritchett would be the one crowing on the courthouse steps.

Sergeant Hooker's voice crackled over the portable radio. 'Savoy, Mullen, Prejean, Broussard, move in front of those goddamn reporters. Establish some distance between the crowd and Kudrow and Renard before this turns into a goddamn cluster fuck.'

Annie edged her way between bodies, her hand resting on the butt of her baton, her eyes on Marcus Renard as Kudrow began to speak. He stood beside his attorney, looking uncomfortable with the attention being focused on him. He wasn't a man to draw notice. Quiet, unassuming, an architect in the firm of Bowen & Briggs. Not ugly, not handsome. Thinning brown hair neatly combed and hazel eyes that seemed a little too big for their sockets. He stood with his shoulders stooped and his chest sunken, a younger shadow of his attorney. His mother stood on the step above him, a thin woman with a startled expression and a mouth as tight and straight as a hyphen.

'Some people will call this ruling a travesty of justice,' Kudrow said loudly. 'The only travesty of justice here has been perpetrated by the Partout Parish Sheriff's Department. Their *investigation* of my client has been nothing short of harassment. Two prior searches of Mr Renard's home produced nothing that might tie him to the murder of Pamela Bichon.'

'Are you suggesting the sheriff's department manipulated evidence?' a reporter called out.

'Mr Renard has been the victim of a narrow and fanatical investigation led by Detective Nick Fourcade. Y'all are aware of Fourcade's record with the New Orleans Police Department, of the reputation he brought with him to this parish. Detective Fourcade *allegedly* found that ring in my client's home. Draw your own conclusions.'

As she elbowed past a television cameraman, Annie could see Fourcade turning around, half a dozen steps down from Kudrow. The cameras focused on him hastily. His expression was a stone mask, his eyes hidden by a pair of mirrored sunglasses. A cigarette smoldered between his lips. His temper was a thing of legend. Rumors abounded throughout the department that he was not quite sane.

He said nothing in answer to Kudrow's insinuation, and yet the air between them seemed to thicken. Anticipation held the crowd's breath. Fourcade pulled the cigarette from his mouth and flung it down, exhaling smoke through his nostrils. Annie took a half step toward Kudrow, her fingers curling around the grip of her baton. In the next heartbeat Fourcade was bounding up the steps – straight at Renard, shouting, 'NO!'

'He'll kill him!' someone shrieked.

'Fourcade!' Hooker's voice boomed as the fat sergeant lunged after him, grabbing at and missing the back of his shirt.

'You killed her! You killed my baby girl!'

The anguished shouts tore from the throat of Hunter Davidson, Pamela Bichon's father, as he hurled himself down the steps at Renard, his eyes rolling, one arm swinging wildly, the other hand clutching a .45.

Fourcade knocked Renard aside with a beefy shoulder, grabbed Davidson's wrist, and shoved it skyward as the .45 barked out a shot and screams went up all around. Annie hit Davidson from the right side, her much smaller body colliding with his just as Fourcade threw his weight against the man from the left. Davidson's knees buckled and they all went down in a tangle of arms and legs, grunting and shouting, bouncing hard down the steps, Annie at the bottom of the heap. Her breath was pounded out of her as she hit the concrete steps with four hundred pounds of men on top of her.

'He killed her!' Hunter Davidson sobbed, his big body going limp. 'He butchered my girl!'

Annie wriggled out from under him and sat up, grimacing. All she could think was that no physical pain could compare with what this man must have been enduring.

Swiping back the strands of dark hair that had pulled loose from her ponytail, she gingerly brushed over the throbbing knot on the back of her head. Her fingertips came away sticky with blood.

'Take this,' Fourcade ordered in a low voice, thrusting Davidson's gun at Annie butt-first. Frowning, he leaned down over Davidson and put a hand on the man's shoulder even as Prejean snapped the cuffs on him. 'I'm sorry,' he murmured. 'I wish I coulda let you kill him.'

Annie pushed to her feet and tried to straighten the bulletproof vest she wore beneath her shirt. Hunter Davidson was a good man. An honest, hardworking planter who had put his daughter through college and walked her down the aisle the day she married Donnie Bichon. Her murder had shattered him, and the subsequent lack of justice had driven him to this desperate edge. And tonight Hunter Davidson would be the man sitting in jail while Marcus Renard slept in his own bed.

'Broussard!' Hooker snapped irritably, suddenly looming over her, porcine and ugly. 'Gimme that gun. Don't just stand there gawking. Get down to that cruiser and open the goddamn doors.'

'Yes, sir.' Not quite steady on her feet, she started around the back side of the crowd.

With the danger past, the press was in full cry again, more frenzied than before. Renard's entourage had been hustled off the steps. The focus was on Davidson now. Cameramen jostled one another for shots of the despondent father. Microphones were thrust at Smith Pritchett.

'Will you file charges, Mr Pritchett?'

'Will charges be filed, Mr Pritchett?'

'Mr Pritchett, what kind of charges will you file?'

Pritchett glared at them. 'That remains to be seen. Please back away and let the officers do their job.'

'Davidson couldn't get justice in court, so he sought to take it himself. Do you feel responsible, Mr Pritchett?'

'We did the best we could with the evidence we had.'

'Tainted evidence?'

'I didn't gather it,' he snapped, starting back up the steps toward the courthouse, his face as pink as a new sunburn.

Limping, Annie descended the last of the steps and opened the back door of the blue and white cruiser sitting at the curb. Fourcade escorted the sobbing Davidson to the car, with Savoy and Hooker just behind them, and Mullen and Prejean flanking them. The crowd rushed along behind them and beside them like guests at a wedding seeing off the happy couple.

'You gonna book him in, Fourcade?' Hooker asked as Davidson disappeared into the backseat.

'The hell,' Fourcade growled, slamming the door. 'He didn't commit the worst crime here today. Not even if he'd'a killed the son of a bitch. Book him yourself.'

The belligerence brought a rise of color to Hooker's face, but he said nothing as Fourcade crossed the street to a battered black Ford 4X4, climbed in, and drove off in the opposite direction of the parish jail.

The sheriff would chew his ass later, Annie thought as she headed for her own radio car. But then a breach in procedure was the least of Fourcade's worries, and, if anything Richard Kudrow had said was true, the least of his sins.

2

'He's guilty,' Nick declared. Ignoring the chair he had been offered, he prowled the cramped confines of the sheriff's office, adrenaline burning inside him like a blue gas flame.

'Then why don't we have squat on him, Nick?'

Sheriff August F. Noblier kept his seat behind his desk. Rawboned and rough-edged, he was working hard to affect an air of calm and rationality, even though the concepts seemed to bounce right off Fourcade. Gus Noblier had ruled Partout Parish off and on for fifteen of his fifty-three years – three consecutive terms, one election lost to the vote hauling and assorted skullduggery of Duwayne Kenner, then a fourth victory. He loved the job. He was good at the job. Only in the last six months – since hiring Fourcade – had he found a sudden yen for antacid tablets.

'We had the damn ring,' Fourcade snapped, slicking his black hair back with one hand.

'You knew it wasn't on the warrant. You had to know it'd get thrown out.'

'No. I thought for once maybe someone in the system would use some common sense. *Mais sa c'est fou!*'

'It's not crazy,' Gus insisted, translating the Cajun French automatically. 'We're talking about the rules, Nick. The rules are there for a reason. Sometimes we gotta bend 'em. Sometimes we gotta sneak around 'em. But we can't just pretend they're not there.'

'So what the hell were we supposed to do?' Fourcade asked with stinging sarcasm and an exaggerated shrug. 'Leave the ring at Renard's house, come back, and try to get another warrant? Can't use the 'plain view' argument to get the warrant. Hell, the ring wasn't in plain sight. So then what? Track down some of Pam Bichon's family and play Twenty Questions?'

He squeezed his eyes shut and pressed his fingertips against his forehead. 'I'm thinking of something of Pam's that might be missing. Can y'all guess what that something might be? *Mais non*, I can't just come right out and tell you. That would be *against the fucking rules!*'

'Goddammit, Nick!'

Frustration pushed Gus to his feet and flooded his face with unhealthy color. Even his scalp glowed pink through the steel gray of his crew cut.

He jammed his hands against his thick waist and glared at Fourcade leaning across his desk. At six-three he had a couple inches on the detective, but Fourcade was built like a light heavyweight boxer – all power and muscle and 3 percent body fat.

'And while we were all chasing our tails, trying to follow the rules,' Fourcade went on, 'you don't think Renard would be pitching that ring in the bayou?'

'You could have left Stokes there and come back. And why hadn't Renard pitched the ring already? We'd been to his house twice –'

'Third time's a charm.'

'He's smarter than that.'

Of all the things Nick had expected Gus Noblier to say to him, to insinuate, he hadn't anticipated this. He felt blindsided, then foolish, then told himself it didn't matter. But it did.

'You think I planted that ring?' he asked in a voice gone dangerously soft.

Gus blew a sigh between his lips. His narrow eyes glanced a look off Nick's chin and ricocheted elsewhere. 'I didn't say that.'

'You didn't have to. Hell, you don't think *I'm* smarter than that? You don't think if I knew what I was gonna find before I went there, I woulda had sense enough to list the ring on the goddamn warrant?'

The sheriff scowled, accentuating the sagging lines of his big face. 'I'm not the one who thinks you're a rogue cop, Nick. That's Kudrow's game, and he's got the press playing with him.'

'And I'm supposed to give a shit?'

'You, of all people. This case has folks spooked. They're seeing killers in every shadow and they want someone put away.'

'*Renard* –'

Gus held a hand up. 'Save your breath. We all want a conviction on this. I'm just telling you how it can look. I'm just telling you how this thing can be twisted. Kudrow plants enough doubt, we'll never get this creep. I'm telling you to mind your manners.'

Nick let out the breath he'd been holding and turned away from the cluttered desk, resuming his pacing with less energy. 'I'm a detective, not a damn community relations officer. I've got a job to do.'

'You can't just do it all over Marcus Renard. Not now.'

'So I'm supposed to do what? Have a gypsy conjure me up some more suspects? Cast suspicion on someone else, just to be fair? Buy into that bullshit theory this murder is the work of a serial killer everybody knows got his ticket punched for him four years ago?'

'You can't keep leaning on Renard, Nick. Not without some solid evidence or a witness or *something*. That's harassment, and he'll sue our asses eight ways from Sunday.'

'Oh, well, God forbid he should sue us,' Nick sneered. 'A murderer!'

'A citizen!' Gus yelled, thumping the desktop between stacks of paperwork. 'A citizen with rights and a damn good lawyer to make sure we respect them. This ain't some lowlife dirtbag you're dealing with here. He's an architect, for Christ's sake.'

'He's a killer.'

'Then you nail him and you nail him by the book. I've got enough trouble in this parish with half the people thinking the Bayou Strangler's been raised from the dead and half of them spoiling for a lynching – Renard's, yours, mine. This fire's burning hot enough, I don't need you throwing gasoline on it. You don't want to defy me on this, Nick. I'm telling you right now.'

'Telling me what?' Nick challenged. 'To back off? Or you want me off the case altogether, Gus?'

He waited impatiently for Noblier's reply. It frightened him a little, how much it mattered. The first murder he'd handled since leaving New Orleans and it had sucked him in, consumed his life, consumed *him*. The Bichon murder had taken precedence over everything else on his desk and in his head. Some would have called it an obsession. He didn't think he had crossed that line, but then again maybe he was in the middle of the deep woods seeing nothing but trees. It wouldn't have been the first time.

His hands had curled into fists at his sides. Holding on to the case. He couldn't make himself let go.

'Keep a low profile, for crying out loud,' Gus said with resignation as he lowered himself into his chair. 'Let Stokes take a bigger part of the case. Don't get in Renard's face.'

'He killed her, Gus. He wanted her and she didn't want him. So he stalked her. He terrorized her. He kidnapped her. He tortured her. He killed her.'

Gus cupped his hands together and held them up. 'This is our evidence, Nick. Everybody in the state of Lou'siana can know Marcus Renard did it, but if we don't get more than what we've got now, he's a free man.'

'*Merde*,' Nick muttered. 'Maybe I *shoulda* let Hunter Davidson shoot him.'

'Then it'd be Hunter Davidson going on trial for murder.'

'Pritchett's filing charges?'

'He doesn't have a choice.' Gus picked up an arrest report from his desk, glanced at it, and set it aside. 'Davidson tried to kill Renard in front of fifty witnesses. Let that be a lesson to you if you're fixing to kill someone.'

'Can I go?'

Gus gave him a long look. 'You're not fixing to kill someone, are you, Nick?'

'I got work to do.'

Fourcade's expression was inscrutable, his dark eyes unreadable. He slipped on his sunglasses. Gus's stomach called loudly for Mylanta. He jabbed a finger at his detective. 'You keep that coonass temper in check, Fourcade. It's already landed your butt in water hot enough to boil crawfish. Blaming the cops is in vogue these days. And your name is on the tip of everyone's tongue.'

Annie loitered in the open doorway to the briefing room, a leaking Baggie of melting ice cubes pressed to the knot on the back of her head. She had changed out of her torn, dirty uniform into the jeans and T-shirt she kept in her locker. She strained to make out the argument going on in the sheriff's office down the hall, but only the tone was conveyed. Impatient, angry.

The press had been speculating even before the evidentiary hearing that Fourcade would lose his job over the screwup on the warrant, but then the press liked to make noise and understood little of the intricacies of police work. They had written much about the public's frustration with the SO's failure to make an arrest, but they brushed off the frustration of the cops working the case. They all but called for a public hanging of the suspect based on nothing more than hearsay evidence, then spun around 180 degrees and pointed their fingers at the detective in charge of the case when he finally came up with something tangible.

No one had any evidence Fourcade had planted that ring in Renard's desk drawer. It didn't make sense that he would have planted evidence but not listed that evidence on the warrant. There was every possibility Renard had put the ring in that drawer himself, never imagining his house would be searched a third time. Perpetrators of sex-related homicides tended to keep souvenirs of their victims. Everything from pieces of jewelry to pieces of bodies. That was a fact.

Annie had attended the seminar on sexual predators at the academy in Lafayette three months before the Bichon murder. She took as many extra courses as she could in preparation for one day making detective. That was her goal – to work in plain clothes, dig deep into the mysteries of the crimes she now dealt with only at the outset of a case.

The crime-scene slides the class instructor had shown them had been horrific. Crimes of unspeakable cruelty and brutality. Victims tortured and mutilated in ways no sane person could ever have imagined in their worst nightmares. But then she no longer had to imagine. She had been the one to discover Pam Bichon's body.

She had been off duty the weekend the real estate agent was reported missing. On routine patrol Monday morning, Annie had found herself drawn to a vacant house out on Pony Bayou. The place had been for sale for months, though the renters had moved out only five or six weeks previous. A rusted Bayou Realty sign had fallen over on one side of the overgrown drive. Something she had read in Police magazine made Annie turn in the driveway – an article about how many female real estate agents each year are lured to remote properties, then raped or murdered.

Hidden in the brambles behind the dilapidated house sat a white Mustang convertible, top up. She recognized the car from the briefing, but ran it to be certain. The plates came back to Pamela K. Bichon, no wants, no warrants, reported missing two days previous. And in the dining room of the old house it was Pam Bichon she found . . . or what was left of her.

She still saw the scene too often when she closed her eyes. The nails in her hands. The mutilation. The blood. The mask. The flashbacks still awakened her in the night, the images entwining with a nightmare four years old, forcing her to rush to the surface of consciousness like a swimmer coming up from the depths, running out of air. The smell still burned in her nostrils from time to time, when she least expected it. The putrid miasma of violent death. Cloying, choking, thick with the scent of fear.

A chill ran through her now, twisting and coiling in the bottom of her stomach.

The Baggie dribbled ice water down the back of her neck, and she flinched and swore under her breath.

'Hey, Broussard.' Deputy Ossie Compton sucked in his stomach and sidled past her through the doorway to the break room. 'I heard you were a cold one. How come that ice is melting?'

Annie shot him a wry look. 'Must be all your hot air, Compton.'

He gave her a wink, his grin flashing white in his dark face. 'My hot charm, you mean.'

'Is that what you call it?' she teased. 'Here I thought it was gas.'

Laughter rolled behind her, Compton's included.

'You got him again, Annie,' Prejean said.

'I quit keeping score,' she said, glancing back down the hall toward the sheriff's office. 'It got to where it was just cruel.'

The shift would change in twenty minutes. Guys coming on for the evening wandered in to BS with the day shift before briefing. The Hunter Davidson incident was the hot topic of the day.

'Man, you shoulda seen Fourcade!' Savoy said with a big grin. 'He moves like a damn panther, him! Talk about!'

'Yeah. He was on Davidson like that.' Prejean snapped his fingers. 'And there's women screaming and the gun going off and nine kinds of hell all at once. It was a regular goddamn circus.'

'And where were you during all this, Broussard?' Chaz Stokes asked, turning his pale eyes on Annie.

Tension instantly rose inside her as she returned the detective's stare.

'At the bottom of the pile,' Sticks Mullen snickered, flashing a small mouth overcrowded with yellow teeth. 'Where a woman belongs.'

'Yeah, like you'd know.' She tossed her dripping ice bag into the trash. 'You read that in a book, Mullen?'

'You think he can read?' Prejean said with mock astonishment.

'*Penthouse*,' someone suggested.

'Naw,' Compton drawled, elbowing Savoy. 'He just looks at the pictures and milks his lizard.'

'Fuck you, Compton.' Mullen rose and headed for the candy machine, hitching up his pants on skinny hips and digging in his pocket for change.

'Jesus, don't fish it out here, Sticks!'

'Christ,' Stokes muttered in disgust.

He had the kind of looks that drew a woman's eye. Tall, trim, athletic. An interesting combination of features hinted at his mixed family background – short dark hair curled tight to his head, skin that was just a shade more brown than white. He had a slim nose and a Dudley Do-Right mouth framed by a neat mustache and goatee.

His face would have looked good on a recruiting poster with its square jaw and chin, the light turquoise eyes piercing out from beneath heavy black brows. But Stokes wasn't the type in any other respect. He cultivated a laid-back, free-spirit image advertised by his unconventional clothing, which today consisted of baggy gray janitor's pants and a square-bottomed shirt printed with bucking broncos, Indian tipis, and cacti. He pulled his black straw snap-brim down at an angle over one eye.

'You steal that off Chi Chi Rodriguez?' Annie asked.

'Come on, Broussard,' he murmured with a sly smile. 'You want me. You're always looking at me. Am I right or am I right?'

'You're full of shit and you're kind of hard to miss in that getup. So where were you during all the fun? You been working the Bichon case as much as Fourcade.'

He leaned a shoulder against the doorjamb, glancing out into the hall. 'Nick's the primary. I had to go to St. Martinville. They picked up my meth dealer on a DUI.'

'And that required your personal attention?'

'Hey, I've been working to nail that rat bastard for months.'

'If they had him in their jail, what's the big hurry?'

Stokes flashed his teeth. 'Hey, no time like the present. You know what I'm saying. The warrants came out of this parish. I want Billy Thibidoux on my résumé ASAP.'

'You left Fourcade swinging in the breeze so you could have Billy Thibidoux in your jacket. Yeah, I'd want to be your partner, Chaz,' Annie said with derision.

'Nicky's a big boy. He didn't need me. And you . . .' His eyes hardened a bit, even though the smile stayed firmly in place. 'I thought we'd already covered that ground, Broussard. You had your chance. But hey, I'm a generous guy. I'd be willing to give you another shot . . . out of uniform, so to speak.'

I'd rather mud wrestle alligators in the nude. But she kept the remark to herself, when she would have readily tossed it at any of her other co-workers. She knew from experience Chaz didn't take rejection well.

He reached out unexpectedly and pressed his thumb against the darkening bruise along the crown of her left cheekbone. 'You're gonna have a shiner, Broussard.' He dropped his hand as she pulled back. 'Looks good on you.'

'You're such a jerk,' she muttered, turning away, knowing she was the only one in the department who thought so. Chaz Stokes was everybody's pal . . . except hers.

The door to the sheriff's office swung open and Fourcade stormed out, his expression ominous, his tie jerked loose at the throat of his tan shirt. He dug a cigarette out of his breast pocket.

'We're fucked!' he snapped at Stokes, not slowing his stride.

'I heard.'

Annie watched them go down the hall. Stokes had worked the Bichon case when Pam was alive and claiming Renard was stalking her. He had missed the homicide call, but had worked the murder as Fourcade's partner. They weren't being held up to public scrutiny and ridicule as a team, however. It was Fourcade's name in the papers. Fourcade, who had come to Partout Parish with a checkered past. Fourcade, who had come up with the ring. Stokes wouldn't be raked over the coals after today's court ruling. He had assured that by making himself scarce.

'Billy Thibidoux, my ass,' she grumbled under her breath.

Annie stayed late to finish her report on the Davidson incident. When she came out of the building at 5:06, the parking lot behind the law enforcement center was deserted except for a pair of trustees washing the sheriff's new Suburban. The day-shift deputies had split for home or second jobs or stools in their favorite bars. The press had taken Smith Pritchett's brief official statement on Hunter Davidson's situation and gone off to meet their deadlines.

A sense of false peace held the moment. Any stranger walking through Bayou Breaux would have remarked on the lovely afternoon. Spring had arrived unusually early, filling the air with the perfume of sweet olive and wisteria. Window boxes on the second-floor galleries of the historic business district were bursting with color and overflowing greenery, ivy trailing down the wrought iron and wood railings. Store windows had been decorated for the upcoming Mardi Gras carnival. Down on the corner, old Tante Lucesse sat on a folding chair weaving a pine-needle basket and singing hymns for passersby.

But underlying the veneer of peace was something sinister. A raw nerve of disquiet. As the sun went down on Bayou Breaux, a killer sat somewhere in the gathering gloom. That knowledge tainted the shabby beauty here like a stain seeping across a tablecloth. Murder. Whether you believed Renard was the killer or not, a murderer was loose among them, free to do as he pleased.

It wasn't the first time, which made it impossible to discount as an aberration. Death had stalked this patch of South Louisiana before. The memories had barely gone stale. The death of Pam Bichon had dredged them to the surface, had awakened fear and stirred up doubt.

Six women in five different parishes had died over an eighteen-month period between 1992 and 1993, raped, strangled, and sexually mutilated.

Two of the victims had come from Bayou Breaux-Savannah Chandler and Annick Delahoussaye-Gerrard, whom Annie had known her entire life. The crimes had shocked the people of Louisiana's French Triangle into a state of near panic, and the conclusion of the case had shocked them even more.

The murders had stopped with the death of Stephen Danjermond, son of a wealthy New Orleans Garden District shipping family. The investigation had revealed a long history of sexual sadism and murder, hobbies Danjermond had practiced since his college days. Trophies from his victims had been discovered during a search of his home. At the time of his death Danjermond had been serving his first term as Partout Parish district attorney.

The story had put Bayou Breaux in the spotlight for a short time, but the glare had faded and the horror was put aside. The case was closed. The evil had been burned out. Life had returned to normal. Until Pam Bichon.

Her death was too close for comfort, too similar. All the old fears had bubbled to the surface, divided, and multiplied. People wondered if Danjermond had been the killer at all, their new panic clouding the memory of the evidence against him. Killed in a fire, he had never publicly confessed to his crimes. Other folks were eager to embrace Renard as the suspect in the Bichon killing – better a tangible evil than a nebulous one. But even with a target to point their fingers at, the underlying fear remained: a superstition, a half-conscious belief that the evil was indeed a phantom, that this place had been cursed.

Annie felt it herself – an edginess, a low-frequency hum that skimmed along her nerves at night, an instinct that heightened the awareness of every sound, a sense of vulnerability. Every woman in the parish felt it, perhaps more so this time than the last. The Bayou Strangler's victims had been women of questionable reputation. Pam Bichon had led a normal life, had a good job, came from a nice family . . . and a killer had chosen her. If it could happen to Pam Bichon . . .

Annie felt the uneasiness within her now, felt it press in around her as if the air had suddenly become more dense. The sense of being watched itched across the back of her neck. But when she turned around, it was no evil gargoyle staring at her. A small face with big sad eyes peered at her over the steering wheel of her Jeep. Josie Bichon.

'Hey, Josie,' she said, letting herself in on the passenger's side. 'Where y'at?'

The little girl laid her cheek against the steering wheel and shrugged. She was a beautiful child with straight brown hair that hung like a thick curtain to her waist and brown eyes too soulful for her years. In a denim jumper and floppy denim hat, the brim pinned up in front with a big silk sunflower, she could have been modeling for a GAP Kids fashion shoot.

'You here on your own?'

'No. I came with Grandma to see Grandpa. They wouldn't let me go in.'

'Sorry, Jose. They've got rules about letting kids into the jail.'

'Yeah. Everybody's got rules for everything when it comes to kids. I wish I could make a rule for once.' She reached out and tapped her finger against the plastic alligator that hung from the rearview mirror. The gator wore sunglasses, a red beret, and a leering grin designed to amuse, but Josie was in a place beyond amusement. 'Rule number one: No treating me like a baby, 'cause I'm not. Rule number two: No lying to me for my own good.'

'You heard about what happened in front of the court-house?' Annie asked gently.

'It was on the radio when we were having art class. Grandpa tried to shoot the man that killed my mom, and he was arrested. At first, Grandma tried to tell me he just tripped and fell down the courthouse steps. She lied to me.'

'I'm sure she didn't mean it to be a lie, Josie. Imagine how scared she must have been. She didn't want to scare you too.'

Josie gave her an expression that spoke eloquently of her feelings on the subject. From the moment her family had been notified of her mother's death, Josie had been fed half-truths, gently pushed aside while the adults whispered concerns and secrets. Her father and her grandparents and aunts and uncles had done their best to wrap her in an insulation of misinformation, never imagining that what they were doing only hurt her more. But Annie knew.

'Mama, Mama! We're home! Look what Uncle Sos got me at Disney World! It's Minnie Mouse!'

The kitchen door banged shut and she stopped in her tracks. The person sitting at the kitchen table wasn't her mother. Father Goetz rose from the chrome-legged chair, his face grave, and Enola Meyette, a fat woman who always smelled of sausage, came away from the sink drying her hands on a red checked towel.

'Allons, chérie,' Mrs Meyette said, holding out one dimpled hand. 'We go down the store. Get you a candy, oui?'

Annie had known right then something was terribly wrong. The memory still brought back the same sick twisting in her stomach she had felt that day as Enola Meyette led her from the kitchen. She could see herself clearly at nine, eyes wide with fear, a choke hold on her new stuffed Minnie Mouse, as she was pulled away from the truth Father Goetz had come to deliver: that while Annie was on her first-ever vacation trip with Tante Fanchon and Uncle Sos, Marie Broussard had taken her own life.

She remembered the gentle lies of well-meaning people, and the sense of isolation that grew with each of those lies. An isolation she had carried inside her for a long, long time.

Annie had taken it upon herself to answer Josie's questions when the sheriff's office had sent its representatives to break the news to Hunter

Davidson and his wife. And Josie, perhaps sensing a kindred spirit, had made an instant and yet-to-be-severed connection.

'You could have come to the sheriff's office and asked for me,' Annie said.

Josie tapped the alligator again and watched it swing. 'I didn't want to be with people. Not if I couldn't see Grandpa Hunt and ask him what really happened.'

'I was there.'

'Did he really try to kill that guy?'

Annie chose her words with care. 'He might have if Detective Fourcade hadn't seen the gun in time.'

'I wish he had shot him dead,' Josie declared.

'People can't take the law into their own hands, Jose.'

'Why? Because it's against the rules? That guy killed my mom. What about the rules he broke? He should have to pay for what he did.'

'That's what the courts are for.'

'But the judge let him go!' Josie cried, frustration and pain tangling in a knot in her throat. The same frustration and pain Annie had heard in Hunter Davidson's broken sobs.

'Just for now,' Annie said, hoping the promise wasn't really as empty as it felt to her. 'Just until we can get some better evidence against him.'

Tears welled up in Josie's eyes and spilled over. 'Then why can't you find it? You're a cop and you're my friend. You're supposed to understand! You said you'd help! You're supposed to make sure he gets punished! Instead, you put my grandpa in jail! I hate this!' She hit her hand against the steering wheel, blasting the horn. 'I hate everything!'

Josie scrambled from the driver's seat and dashed toward the law enforcement center. Annie hopped out of the Jeep and started after her. But she pulled herself up short as she caught sight of Belle Davidson and Thomas Watson, the Davidsons' attorney, coming out the side door.

Belle Davidson was a formidable woman in a demure sweater-and-pearls disguise. A steel magnolia of the first order. The woman's lips thinned as her gaze lit on Annie. She disconnected herself from Josie's embrace and started across the lot.

'You have an awful nerve, Deputy Broussard,' she declared. 'Throwing my husband in jail instead of my daughter's murderer, then playing up to my granddaughter as if you have a right to her devotion.'

'I'm sorry you feel that way, Mrs Davidson,' Annie said. 'But we couldn't let your husband shoot Marcus Renard.'

'He wouldn't have been driven to such desperation if not for the incompetence of you people in the sheriff's department. You let a guilty man run free all over town due to carelessness and oversight. By God, I've got half a mind to shoot him myself.'

'Belle!' the lawyer whined as he caught up with his client. 'I told you, you hadn't ought to say that in front of people!'

845

'Oh, for God's sake, Thomas. My daughter has been murdered. People would think it strange if I *didn't* say these things.'

'We're doing the best we can, Mrs Davidson,' Annie said.

'And what have you come up with? Nothing. You're a disgrace to your uniform – when you're wearing one.'

She gave Annie's faded T-shirt a sharply dubious look that had likely sent many a Junior Leaguer home in tears.

'I'm not working your daughter's case, ma'am. It's up to Detectives Fourcade and Stokes.'

Belle Davidson's expression only hardened. 'Don't make excuses, Deputy. We all have obligations in this life that go beyond boundaries. You found my daughter's body. You saw what –' She cut herself off, glancing down at Josie. When she turned back to Annie, her dark eyes glittered with tears. 'You *know*. How can you turn your back on that? How can you turn your back on that and still show your face to my granddaughter?'

'It's not Annie's fault, Grandma,' Josie said, though the gaze she lifted to Annie's face was tainted with disappointment.

'Don't say that, Josie,' Belle admonished softly as she slipped an arm around her granddaughter's shoulders and pulled her close. 'That's what's wrong with the world today. No one will take responsibility for anything.'

'I want justice, too, Mrs Davidson,' Annie said. 'But it has to happen within the system.'

'Deputy, the only thing we've gotten within the system so far is injustice.'

As they walked away, Josie looked back over her shoulder, her brown eyes huge and sad. For an instant Annie felt as if she were watching herself walking away into the painful haze of her past, the memory pulling out from the core of her like a string.

'*What happened, Tante Fanchon? Where's Mama?*'

'*Your maman, she's in heaven, ma 'tite fille.*'

'*But why?*'

'*It was an accident, chèrie. God, He looked away.*'

'*I don't understand.*'

'*Non, chère 'tite bête. Someday. When you get older . . .*'

But she had hurt right then, and promises of later had done nothing to soothe the pain.

3

We'll get him one way or another, Slick.'

Fourcade cast Chaz Stokes a glance out the corner of his eye as he raised his glass. 'There's plenty of people who think we already tried "another." '

'Fuck 'em,' Stokes declared, and tossed back a shot. He stacked the glass on the bar with the half dozen others they had accumulated. 'We know Renard's our man. We know what he did. The little motherfucker is wrong. You know it and I know it, my friend. Am I right or am I right?'

He clamped a hand on Fourcade's shoulder, a buddy gesture that was met with a stony look. Camaraderie was the rule in police work, but Fourcade didn't have the time or the energy to waste on it. His focus was, by necessity, on his caseload and himself – getting himself back on the straight and narrow path he had fallen from in New Orleans.

'The state ought to plug his dick into a socket and light him up like a goddamn Christmas tree,' Stokes muttered. 'Instead, the judge lets him walk on a fucking technicality, and Pritchett throws Davidson in the can. The world's a fucking loony bin, but I guess you already knew that.'

Par for the damn course, Nick thought, but he kept it to himself, choosing to treat Stokes's invitation to share as a rhetorical remark. He didn't talk about his days in the NOPD or the incident that had ultimately forced him out of New Orleans. As far as he had ever seen, the truth was of little interest to most people, anyway. They chose to form their opinions based on whatever sensational tidbit of a story took their fancy. The fact that he had been the one to find Pamela Bichon's small amethyst ring, for instance.

He wondered if anyone would have suspected Chaz Stokes of planting the ring, had Stokes been the one to discover it. Stokes had come to Bayou Breaux from somewhere in Crackerland, Mississippi, four years ago, a regular Joe with no past to speak of. If Stokes had found the ring, would the focus now be solely on the injustice of Renard walking free, or would the waters of public opinion have been muddied anyway? Lawyers had a way of stirring up the muck like catfish caught in the shallows, and Richard Kudrow was kingfish of that particular school of bottom feeders.

Nick had to think Kudrow would have cast aspersions on the evidence

847

regardless of who had recovered it. He didn't want to think that his finding it had tainted it, didn't want to think that his presence on the case would block Pam Bichon from getting justice.

Didn't want to think. Period.

Stokes poured another shot from the bottle of Wild Turkey. Nick tossed it back and lit another cigarette. The television hanging in one corner of the dimly lit lounge was showing a sitcom to a small, disinterested audience of businessmen who had come in from the hotel next door to bullshit over chunky glasses of Johnnie Walker and Cajun Chex mix served in plastic ashtrays.

There were no other customers, which was why Stokes had suggested this place over the usual cop hangouts. Nick would have sooner done his brooding in private. He didn't want questions. He didn't want commiseration. He didn't want to rehash the day's events. But Stokes was his partner on the Bichon case, and so Nick made this concession – to pound down a few together, as if they had something more in common than the job.

He shouldn't have been drinking at all. It was one of the vices he had tried to leave in New Orleans, but it and some others had trailed after him to Bayou Breaux like stray dogs. He should have been home working through the intricate and consuming moves of the Tai Chi, attempting to cleanse his mind, to focus the negative energy and burn it out. Instead, he sat here at Laveau's, stewing in it.

The whiskey simmered in his belly and in his veins, and he decided he was just about past caring where he was. Well on his way toward oblivion, he thought. And he'd be damn glad when he got there. It was the one place he might not see Pam Bichon lying dead on the floor.

'I still think about what he did to her,' Stokes murmured, fingers absently peeling away strips of the label from his beer bottle. 'Don't you?'

Day and night. During consciousness and what passed for sleep. The images stayed with him. The paleness of her skin. The wounds: gruesome, hideous, so at odds with what she had been like in life. The expression in her eyes as she stared up through the mask – stark, hopeless, filled with a kind of terror that couldn't be imagined by anyone who hadn't faced a brutal death.

And when the images came to him, so did the sense of violence that must have been thick in the air at the time of her death. It hit him like a wall of sound, intense, powerful, poisonous rage that left him feeling sick and shaken.

Rage was no stranger. It boiled inside him now.

'I think about what she went through,' Stokes said. 'What she must have felt when she realized . . . what he did to her with that knife. Christ.' He shook his head as if to shake loose the images taking root there. 'He's gotta pay for that, man, and without that ring we got shit for a bill. He's gonna walk, Nicky. He's gonna get away with murder.'

People did. Every day. Every day the line was crossed and souls disappeared into the depths of an alternate dimension. It was a matter of choice, a battle of wills. Most people never came close enough to the edge to have any knowledge of it. Too close to the edge and the force could pull you across like an undertow.

'He's probably sitting in his office thinking that right now,' Stokes went on. 'He's been working nights, you know. The rest of his firm can't stand to have him around. They know he's guilty, same as we do. Can't stand looking at him, knowing what he did. I'll bet he's sitting there right now, thinking about it.'

Right across the alley. The architectural firm of Bowen & Briggs was housed in a narrow painted brick building that faced the bayou; flanked by a shabby clapboard barbershop and an antiques store. The same building that housed Bayou Realty on the first floor. Bowen & Briggs was likely the only place on the block inhabited tonight.

'You know, man, somebody ought to do Renard,' Stokes whispered, cutting a wary glance at the bartender. He stood at the end of the bar, chuckling over the sitcom.

'Justice, you know,' Stokes said. 'An eye for an eye.'

'I shoulda let Davidson shoot him,' Nick muttered, and wondered again why he had not. Because there was still a part of him that believed the system was supposed to work. Or maybe he hadn't wanted to see Hunter Davidson sucked over to the dark side.

'He could have an accident,' Stokes suggested. 'It happens all the time. The swamp is a dangerous place. Just swallows people up sometimes, you know.'

Nick looked at him through the haze of smoke, trying to judge, trying to gauge. He didn't know Stokes well enough. Didn't know him at all beyond what they had shared on the job. All he had were impressions, a handful of adjectives, speculation hastily made because he didn't care to waste his time on such things. He preferred to concentrate on focal points; Stokes was part of the periphery of his life. Just another detective in a four-man department. They worked independently of one another most of the time.

Stokes's mouth twisted up on one corner. 'Wishful thinking, pard, wishful thinking. Idn' that what they do down in New Orleans? Pop the bad guys and dump 'em in the swamp?'

'Lake Pontchartrain, mostly.'

Stokes stared at him a moment, uncertain, then decided it was a joke. He laughed, drained his beer, and slid off the stool, reaching into his hip pocket for his wallet. 'I gotta split. Gotta meet with the DA on Thibidoux in the morning.' The grin flashed again. 'And I got a hot date tonight. Hot and sweet between the sheets. If I'm lyin', I'm dyin'.'

He dropped a ten on the bar and clamped a hand on Nick's shoulder one last time. 'Protect and serve, pard. Catch you later.'

Protect and serve, Nick thought. Pamela Bichon was dead. Her father

849

was sitting in jail, and the man who had killed her was free. Just who had they protected and what purpose had been served today?

'Pritchett's fit to kill somebody.'

'I'd suggest Renard,' Annie muttered, scowling at her menu.

'More apt to be your idol, Fourcade.'

She caught the sarcasm, the jealousy, and rolled her eyes at her dinner partner. She had known A.J. Doucet her whole life. He was one of Tante Fanchon and Uncle Sos's brood of actual nephews and nieces, related by blood rather than by serendipity, as she was. As children, they had chased each other around the big yard out at the Corners – the café/boat landing/convenience store Sos and Fanchon ran south of town. During their high school years, A.J. had taken on the often unappreciated role of protector. Since then he had gone from friend to lover and back as he proceeded through college and law school and into the Partout Parish District Attorney's Office.

They had yet to agree on a description for their current relationship. The attraction that had come and gone between them over the years seemed never to come or go for both of them at the same time.

'He's not my idol,' she said irritably. 'He happens to be the best detective we've got, that's all. I want to be a detective. Of course I watch him. And why should you care? You and I are not, I repeat, *not* an item, A.J.'

'You know how I feel about that too.'

Annie blew out a sigh. 'Can we skip this argument tonight? I've had a rotten day. You're supposed to be my best friend. Act like it.'

He leaned toward her across the small white-draped table, his brown eyes intense, the hurt in them cutting at her conscience. 'You know there's more there than that, Annie, and don't give me that "we're practically related" bullshit you've been wading in recently. You are no more related to me than you are related to the President of the United States.'

'Which I could be, for all I know,' she muttered, sitting back, retreating in the only way she could without making a scene.

As it was, they had become the object of speculation for another set of diners across the intimate width of Isabeau's. She suspected it was her blackening eye that had caught the other woman's attention. Out of uniform, she supposed she looked like an abused partner rather than an abused cop.

'It's not the cops Pritchett should be pissed at,' she said. 'Judge Monahan made the ruling. He could have let that ring in.'

'And left the door open for appeal? What would be the point of that?'

The waitress interrupted the discussion, bringing their drinks, her gaze cutting from Annie's battered face to A.J.

'She's gonna spit in your étouffée, you know,' Annie remarked.

'Why should she assume I gave you that shiner? I could be your high-priced, ass-kicking divorce lawyer.'

Annie sipped her wine, dismissing the subject. 'He's guilty, A.J.'

'Then bring us the evidence – obtained by legal means.'

'By the rules, like it's a game. Josie wasn't far wrong.'

'What about Josie?'

'She came to see me today. Or, rather, she came with her grandmother to see Hunter Davidson in jail.'

'The formidable Miss Belle.'

'They both tore into me.'

'What for? It's not your case.'

'Yeah, well . . .' she hedged, sensing that A.J. wouldn't understand the strong pull she was feeling. Everything in its place – that was A.J. Every aspect of life was supposed to fit into one of the neat little compartments he had set up, while everything in Annie's life seemed to be tossed into one big messy pile she was continually sorting through, trying to make sense of. 'I'm tied to it. I wish I could do more to help. I look at Josie and . . .'

A.J.'s expression softened with concern. He was too handsome for his own good. Curse of the Doucet men with their square jaws and high cheekbones and pretty mouths. Not for the first time, Annie wished things between them could have been as simple as he wanted.

'The case has been hell on everyone, honey,' he said. 'You've done more than your part already.'

Therein lay the problem, Annie thought as she picked at her dinner. What exactly was her part? Was she supposed to draw the boundary at duty and absolve herself of any further responsibility?

'We all have obligations in this life that go beyond boundaries.'

She had already gone above and beyond the call involving herself with Josie. But, even without Josie, she would have felt this case pulling at her, would have felt Pam Bichon pulling at her from that limbo inhabited by the restless souls of victims.

With all the controversy swirling around the case, Pam was being pushed out of view little by little. No one had helped her when she was alive and believed that Marcus Renard was stalking her, and now that she was dead, attention was being diverted elsewhere.

'Maybe there wouldn't be a case if Judge Edmonds had taken Pam seriously in the first place,' she said, setting her fork down and abandoning her meal. 'What's the point of having a stalking law if judges are just gonna blow off every complaint that comes their way as "boys will be boys" –'

'We've had this conversation,' A.J. reminded her. 'For Edmonds to have granted that restraining order, the law would have to be worded so that looking crossways at a woman would be considered criminal. What Pam Bichon brought before the court did not constitute stalking. Renard asked her out, he gave her presents –'

'He slashed her tires and cut her phone line and –'

'She had no proof the person doing those things was Marcus Renard. He asked her out, she turned him down, he was unhappy. There's a big leap from unhappy to psychotic.'

'So said Judge Edmonds, who probably still thinks it's okay for men to hit women over the head with mastodon bones and drag them into caves by their hair,' Annie said with disgust. 'But then that makes him about average around here, doesn't it?'

'Hey, objection!'

She broke her scowl with a look of contrition. 'It goes without saying, you're above average. I'm sorry I'm such poor company tonight. I'm gonna pass on the movie, go home, soak in the tub, go to bed.'

A.J. reached across the table and hooked a fingertip inside the simple gold bracelet she wore, caressing the tender skin of her inner wrist. 'Those aren't necessarily solitary pursuits,' he whispered, his eyes rich with a warm promise he had fulfilled from time to time in the past when the currents of their attraction had managed to cross paths.

Annie drew her hand back on the excuse of reaching for her pocketbook. 'Not tonight, Romeo. I have a concussion.'

They said their goodbyes in the tiny parking lot alongside the restaurant, Annie offering her cheek for A.J.'s good-night kiss when he aimed for her lips. Their parting only added to the restlessness she had been feeling all day, as if everything in the world were just a half beat out of sync. She sat behind the wheel of the Jeep, listening with one ear to the radio as A.J. drove out onto La Rue Dumas and turned south.

'You're on KJUN, all talk all the time. Home of the giant jackpot giveaway. This is your *Devil's Advocate*, Owen Onofrio. Our topic tonight: today's controversial decision in the Renard case. I've got Ron from Henderson on line one. Go ahead, Ron.'

'I think it's a disgrace that criminals have all the rights in the courts anymore. He had that woman's ring in his house. By God, that oughta be all she wrote right there. Strap him down and light him up!'

'But what if the detective planted the evidence? What happens when we can't trust the people sworn to protect us? Jennifer in Bayou Breaux on line two.'

'Well, I'm just scared sick by all of it. What's anyone supposed to think? I mean, the police are all over this Renard fella, but what if he *didn't* do it? I heard they have secret evidence that links this murder to those Bayou Strangler murders. I'm a woman lives alone. I work the late shift down at the lamp factory –'

Annie switched the radio off, not in the mood. She often listened to the talk station to get a feel for public opinion. But opinions on this case spanned the spectrum. Only the emotions were consistent: anger, fear, and uncertainty. People were nervous, easily spooked. Reports of prowlers and Peeping Toms had tripled. The waiting lists for home alarm systems were long. Gun shops in the parish were doing a brisk, grim business.

The feelings were no strangers to Annie. The lack of closure, of justice, was driving her crazy. That and her own minimal role in the drama. The fact that, even though she had been in it at the beginning, she had been relegated to bystander. She knew what role she wanted to play. She also knew no one would ever invite her into the game. She was just a deputy, and a *woman* deputy at that. There was no affirmative-action fast track in Partout Parish. A considerable span of rungs ran up the ladder from where she was to where she wanted to be.

She was supposed to wait her turn, earn her stripes, and meanwhile . . . Meanwhile the need that had pushed her to become a cop simmered and churned inside her . . . and Pam Bichon got lost in the shuffle . . . and a killer lay watching, waiting, free to slip away or kill again.

Night had crept in over the town and brought with it a damp chill. Sheer wisps of fog were floating up off the bayou and drifting through the streets like ghosts. Across the street from where Annie sat the black padded door to Laveau's swung open and Chaz Stokes stepped out, blue neon light washing down on him. He stood on the deserted sidewalk for a moment, smoking a cigarette, looking up one side of the street and down the other. He tossed the cigarette in the gutter, climbed into his Camaro, and drove away, turning down the side street that led to the bayou, leaving an empty space at the curb in front of a weathered black pickup. Fourcade's pickup.

It struck Annie as odd. Another piece out of place. No one hung out at Laveau's. The Voodoo Lounge was the usual spot for cops in Bayou Breaux. Laveau's was the mostly empty companion to the mostly empty Maison Dupré hotel next door.

Out of place. It was that thought that pushed her out of the Jeep. Even as she told herself that lie, she could clearly see A.J.'s accusatory face in her mind. He thought she had the hots for Fourcade, for all the good that would have done her. Fourcade treated her like a fixture. She could have been a lamp or a hat rack, with all the sexual allure of either. He didn't resent her, didn't harass her, didn't joke around with her. He had no interest in her whatsoever. And her only interest was in the case. She jaywalked across Dumas to the bar.

Laveau's was a cave of midnight blue walls and mahogany wood black with age. If it hadn't been for the television in the far corner, Annie would have thought she had gone blind walking into the place. The bartender flicked a glance at her and went back to pouring a round of Johnnie Walker for the only table of patrons – a quartet of men in rumpled business suits.

Fourcade sat at the end of the bar, shoulders hunched inside his battered leather jacket, his gaze on the stack of shot glasses before him. He blew a jet stream of smoke at them and watched it dissipate into the gloom. He didn't turn to look at her, but as she approached Annie had the distinct feeling that he was completely conscious of her presence.

She slipped between a pair of stools and leaned sideways against the bar. 'Tough break today,' she said, blinking at the sting of the smoke.

The big dark eyes were on her instantly, staring out from beneath a heavy sweep of brows. Clear, sharp, showing no foggy effects from the whiskey he had consumed, burning with a ferocious intensity that seemed to emanate from the very core of him. He still didn't turn to face her, presenting her with a profile that was hawkish. He wore his black hair slicked back, but a shock of it had tumbled down across his broad forehead.

'Broussard,' Annie said, feeling awkward. 'Deputy Broussard. Annie.' She brushed her bangs out of her eyes in a nervous gesture. 'I – ah – was on the courthouse steps. We took down Hunter Davidson. I was the one at the bottom of the pile.'

The gaze slid down from her face past the open front of her denim jacket and the thin white T-shirt beneath it to the flower-sprigged skirt that hit her mid-calf to the Keds she wore on her feet . . . and eased back up like a long caress.

'You out of uniform, Deputy.'

'I'm off duty.'

'Are you?'

Annie blinked at his response and at the smoke, not quite sure what to make of the first. 'I was the first officer on the scene at the Bichon homicide. I –'

'I know who you are. What you think, *chère*, that this little bit o' whiskey pickled my brain or something?' He arched a brow and chuckled, tapping his cigarette into a plastic ashtray bristling with butts. 'You grew up here, enrolled in the academy August 1993, got hired into the Lafayette PD, came to the SO here in '95. You were the second woman deputy on patrol in this parish – the first having lasted all of ten months. You got a good record, but you tend to be nosy. Me, I think that's maybe not such a bad thing if you gonna do the job, if you looking to move up, which you are.'

Astonished, Annie gaped at him. In the months Fourcade had been in the department she had never heard him volunteer a sentence of more than ten words. She had certainly never dreamed that he knew enough about her to do so. That he seemed to know quite a lot about her was unnerving – a reaction he read without effort.

'You were the first deputy on the scene. I needed to know if you were any good, or if you mighta screwed up, or if maybe you knew Pam Bichon. Maybe you had the same boyfriend. Maybe she sold you a house with snakes under the floors. Maybe she beat you out for head cheerleader back in high school.'

'You considered me a suspect?'

'Me, I consider ever'body a suspect 'til I can find out different.'

854

He took a long pull on his smoke and watched her as he exhaled. 'Does this bother you?' he asked, making a small gesture with the cigarette.

She tried without success not to blink. 'No.'

'Yes, it does,' he declared as he stubbed it out in the overflowing ashtray. 'Say so. Ain't nobody in this world gonna speak up for you, *chère*.'

'I'm not afraid to speak up.'

'No? You afraid of me?'

'If I were afraid of you, I wouldn't be standing here.'

His lips twisted in a faint smirk and he gave a very French shrug that said, *Maybe, maybe no*. Annie felt her temper spike a notch.

'Why should I be afraid of you?'

His expression darkened as he turned a shot glass on the bar. 'You don't listen to gossip?'

'I take it for what it's worth. Half-truths, if that.'

'And how you decide which half is true?' he asked. 'There is no justice in this world,' he said softly, staring into his whiskey. 'How's that for a truth, Deputy Broussard?'

'It's all in your perception, I suppose.'

' "One man's justice is another man's injustice . . . one man's wisdom another's folly." ' He sipped at the whiskey. 'Emerson. No reporter will sum up today's events as well . . . or with such truth.'

'What they say doesn't change the facts,' Annie said. 'You found Pam's ring in Renard's house.'

'You don't think I put it there?'

'If you had put it there, it would have been listed on the warrant.'

'*C'est vrai*. True enough, Annie.' He gave her a pensive look. 'Annie – that's short for something?'

'Antoinette.'

He sipped his whiskey. 'That's a beautiful name, why you don't use it?'

She shrugged. 'I – well – everyone calls me Annie.'

'Me, I'm not ever'body, 'Toinette,' he said quietly.

He seemed to have gotten closer or loomed larger. Annie thought she could feel the heat of him, smell the old leather of his jacket. She knew she could feel his gaze holding hers, and she told herself to back away. But she didn't.

'I came here to ask you about the case,' she said. 'Or did Noblier pull you off?'

'No.'

'I'd like to help if I can.' She blurted the words, forced the idea out before she could swallow it back. She held up one hand to stave off his reply and gestured nervously with the other. 'I mean, I know I'm just a deputy, and technically it isn't my case, and you're the detective, and Stokes won't want me involved, but –'

'You're a helluva salesman, 'Toinette,' Fourcade remarked. 'You telling me every reason to say no.'

'I found her,' Annie said simply. The image of Pam Bichon's body throbbed in her memory, a dead thing that was too alive, that would give her no rest. 'I saw what he did to her. I still see it. I feel . . . an obligation.'

'You feel it,' Fourcade whispered. 'Shadow of the dead.'

He raised his left hand, fingers spread, and reached out, not quite touching her. Slowly he passed his hand before her eyes, skimmed around the side of her head, just brushing his fingertips against her hair. A shiver rippled down her body.

'It's cold there, no?' he whispered.

'Where?' Annie murmured.

'In Shadowland.'

She started to draw a breath, to tell him he was full of shit, to defuse the prickly sensation that had come to life inside her and between them, but her lungs didn't seem to function. She was aware of a phone ringing somewhere, of the canned laughter coming from the television. But mostly she was aware of Fourcade and the pain that shone in his eyes and came from somewhere deep in his soul.

'You Fourcade?' the bartender called, holding up the telephone receiver. 'You got a call.'

He slid off his stool and moved down the bar. Air rushed into Annie's lungs as he walked away, as if his aura had been pressing down on her chest like an anvil. With an unsteady hand, she raised his glass to her lips and took a drink. She stared at Fourcade as he hunched over the bar and listened to the telephone receiver. He had to be drunk. Everyone knew he wasn't quite right at his most sober.

He hung up the phone and turned toward her.

'I gotta go.' He pulled a twenty out of his wallet and tossed it on the bar.

'Stay away from those shadows, 'Toinette,' he warned her softly, the voice of too much experience. With one hand he reached up and cradled her face, the pad of his thumb brushing the corner of her mouth. 'They'll suck the life outta you.'

4

Nick walked along the boulevard between the road and the bayou. Gloved hands in the pockets of his leather jacket. Shoulders hunched against the damp chill of the night. Fog skimmed off the water and floated past like clouds of perfume, redolent with the scents of rotting vegetation, dead fish, and spider lilies. Something broke the surface with a pop and a splash. A bass snatching a late dinner. Or someone with a heavy case of boredom, tossing rocks.

Pausing by the trunk of a live oak, he stared out past the branches hung with tattered scraps of Spanish moss and looked up and down the bank. There was no one, no foot traffic, no cars crossing the little drawbridge that spanned the bayou to the north. House lights glowed amber in windows beyond the east bank. The night air had gone heavy with a thick mist that was threatening to become rain. A rainy night did nothing to entice folks outdoors without a purpose.

And my purpose?

That remained unclear.

He was close to drunk. He had given himself the excuse of dulling the pain, but instead had only fueled it. The frustration, the injustice – they were like fire under his skin. They would consume him if he didn't do something to burn them out.

He closed his eyes, took a breath, and released it, attempting to find his center – that core of deep calm within that he had spent so much time and effort building. He had worked so hard to control the rage, and it was slipping through his grasp. He had worked so hard on the case, and it was crumbling around him. He felt the chill pass over him, through him. The shadow of the dead. He felt the need pull at him. And a part of him wanted very badly to go where it would lead him.

He wondered if Annie Broussard felt that same pull or if she would even recognize it. Probably not. She was too young. Younger than he had been at twenty-eight. Fresh, optimistic, untainted. He had seen the doubt in her eyes when he had spoken of the shadows. He had also seen the naked truth when she spoke of the obligation she felt to Pam Bichon.

The key to staying sane in homicide was keeping a distance. Don't let it get personal. Don't get involved. Don't take it home with you. Don't cross the line.

He had never been good at taking any of that advice. He lived the job. The line was always behind him.

Had the shadows drawn Pam Bichon? Had she seen Death's phantom coming, felt its cold breath on her shoulders? He knew the answer.

She had complained to friends about Renard's persistent, if subtle advances. Despite her rebuffs, he had begun sending her gifts. Then came the harassment. Small acts of vandalism against her car, her property. Items stolen from her office – photographs, a hairbrush, work papers, her keys.

Yes, Pam had seen the phantom coming, and no one had listened when she tried to tell them. No one had heard her fear any more than they had heard her tortured screams that night out on Pony Bayou.

'I still think about what he did to her,' Stokes said. *'Don't you?'*

All the time. The details had saturated his brain like blood.

With his back against the tree trunk, Nick lowered himself to sit on his heels and stared across the empty street at the building that housed Bowen & Briggs. A light burned on the second floor. A desk lamp. Renard worked at the third drafting table back and on the south side of the big room there. Bowen & Briggs designed both small commercial and residential buildings, with their commercial work coming out of New Iberia and St Martinville as well as Bayou Breaux.

Renard was a partner in the firm, though his name was not on the logo. He preferred designing residential buildings, especially single-family homes, and had a liking for historical styles. His social life was quiet. He had no long-term romantic involvement. He lived with his mother, who collected Mardi Gras masks and created costumes for Carnival revelers, and his autistic brother, Victor, the elder by four years. Their home was a modest, restored plantation house – less than five miles by car from the scene of Pam Bichon's murder. Nearer by boat.

According to the descriptions of the people who worked with and knew Marcus Renard, he was quiet, polite, ordinary, or a touch odd – depending on whom you asked. But other words came to Nick's mind. Meticulous, compulsive, obsessive, repressed, controlling, passive-aggressive.

Behind the mask of ordinariness, Marcus Renard was a very different man from the one his co-workers saw every day sitting at his drafting table. They couldn't see the core component Nick had sensed in him from their first meeting – rage. Deep, deep inside, beneath layers and layers of manners and mores and the guise of mild apathy. Rage, simmering, contained, hidden, buried.

It was rage that had driven those spikes through Pam Bichon's hands.

Rage was no stranger.

The light went out in the second-story window. Out of old habit, Nick checked his watch – 9:47 P.M. – and scanned the street in both directions – all clear. Renard's five-year-old maroon Volvo sat in the narrow parking area between the Bowen & Briggs building and the antiques shop next door, an area poorly lit by a seventy-five-watt yellow bug light over the side door.

Renard would emerge from that door, climb in his car, and go home to his mother and his brother and his hobby of designing and building elaborate dollhouses. He would sleep in his bed a free man tonight and dream the sinister, euphoric dreams of someone who had gotten away with murder.

He wasn't the first.

'*Protect and serve, pard. . . .*'

The rage built. . . .

'*Case dismissed.*'

. . . and burned hotter . . .

'*I still think about what he did to her. . . .*'

'*I saw what he did to her. . . . I still see it. . . .*'

'*Don't you?*'

Blood and moonlight, the flash of the knife, the smell of fear, the cries of agony, the ominous silence of death. The cold darkness as the phantom passed over.

The chill collided violently with the fire. The explosion pushed him to his feet.

'*He's gonna walk, Nicky. He's gonna get away with murder. . . .*'

Nick crossed the street, hugged the wall of the Bowen & Briggs building, out of sight from the elevated first-floor windows. Pulling a handkerchief from his pocket, he hopped silently onto the side stoop, doused the bug light with a twist of his wrist, and dropped down on the far side of the steps.

He heard the door open, heard Renard mutter something under his breath, heard the *click, click, click* of the light switch being tried. Footsteps on the concrete stoop. A heavy sigh. The door closed.

He waited, still, invisible, until Renard's loafers hit the blacktop and he had stepped past Nick on his way to the Volvo.

'It's not over, Renard,' he said.

The architect shied sideways. His face was waxy white, his eyes bulged like a pair of boiled eggs.

'You can't harass me this way, Fourcade,' he said, the tremor in his voice mocking his attempt at bravado. 'I have rights.'

'Is that a fact?' Nick stepped forward, his gloved hands hanging loose at his sides. 'What about Pam? She didn't have rights? You take her rights away, *tcheue poule*, and still you think you got rights?'

'I didn't do anything,' Renard said, glancing nervously toward the street, looking for salvation that was nowhere in sight. 'You don't have anything on me.'

Nick advanced another step. 'I got all I need on you, *pou*. I got the stink of you up my nose, you piece of shit.'

Renard lifted a fist in front of him, shaking so badly his car keys rattled. 'Leave me alone, Fourcade.'

'Or what?'

'You're drunk.'

'Yeah.' A grin cut across his face like a scimitar. 'I'm mean too. What you gonna do, call a cop?'

'Touch me and your career is over, Fourcade,' Renard threatened, backing toward the Volvo. 'Everybody knows about you. You got no business carrying a badge. You ought to be in jail.'

'And you oughta be in hell.'

'Based on what? Evidence you planted? That's nothing you haven't done before. You'll be the one in prison over this, not me.'

'That's what you think?' Nick murmured, advancing. 'You think you can stalk a woman, torture her, kill her, and just walk away?'

The nightmare images of murder. The false memories of screams.

'You got nothing on me, Fourcade, and you never will have.'

'Case dismissed.'

'You're nothing but a drunk and a bully, and if you touch me, Fourcade, I swear, I'll ruin you.'

'He's gonna walk, Nicky. He's gonna get away with murder. . . .'

A face from his past loomed up, an apparition floating beside Marcus Renard. A mocking face, a superior sneer.

'You'll never pin this on me, Detective. That's not the way the world works. She was just another whore. . . .'

'You killed her, you son of a bitch,' he muttered, not sure which demon he was talking to, the real or the imagined.

'You'll never prove it.'

'You can't touch me.'

'He's gonna get away with murder. . . .'

'The hell you say.'

The rage burned through the fine thread of control. Emotion and action became one, and restraint was nowhere to be found as his fist smashed into Marcus Renard's face.

Annie walked out of Quik Pik with a pint of chocolate chip ice cream in a bag and a little mouse chewing at her conscience. She could have picked up the treat at the Corners, but she'd had her fill of people for one day, and a prolonged grilling by Uncle Sos was too much to face. The politics of the Renard case had him in a lather. She knew for a fact he had bet fifty dollars on the outcome of the evidentiary hearing – and lost. That, coupled with his opinion of her current platonic relationship with A.J., would have him in rare form tonight.

'Why you don' marry dat boy, 'tite chatte? Andre, he's a good boy, him. What's a matter wit' you, turnin' you purty nose up? You all the time chasin' you don' know what, éspèsces de tête dure.'

Just the imagined haranguing was enough to amplify the thumping in her head. The whole idea of buying ice cream was to be nice to herself. She didn't want to think about A.J. or Renard or Pam Bichon or Fourcade.

860

She had heard the stories about Fourcade. The allegations of brutality, the rumors surrounding the unsolved case of a murdered teenage prostitute in the French Quarter, the unsubstantiated accusations of evidence tampering.

'Stay away from those shadows, 'Toinette. . . . They'll suck the life outta you.'

Good advice, but she couldn't take it if she wanted in on the case. They were a package deal, Fourcade and the murder. They seemed to go together a little too well. He was a scary son of a bitch.

She started the Jeep and turned toward the bayou, flicking the wipers on to cut the thick mist from the windshield. On the radio, Owen Onofrio was still prodding his listeners for reactions to the scene at the courthouse.

'Kent in Carencro, you're on line two.'

'I think that judge oughta be unpoached –'

'You mean impeached?'

As she slowed for a stop sign, her eyes automatically scanned for traffic . . . and hit on a black Ford pickup with a dent in the driver's-side rear panel. Fourcade's truck, parked in front of a shoe repair place that had gone out of business two years ago.

Annie doused her lights and sat there, double-parked, engine grumbling. This was not a residential street. There were no businesses open. A third of the places on this stretch of road were vacant . . . but the offices of Bowen & Briggs were located two blocks south.

She put the Jeep in gear and crept forward. She could see the building that housed Bayou Realty and Bowen & Briggs. There were no lights. There were no cars parked on the street. The sheriff had pulled the surveillance on Renard after the hearing, hoping the press would back off. Renard had been working evenings for the same reason. Fourcade was parked two blocks away.

' "*One man's justice is another man's injustice . . . one man's wisdom another's folly.*" '

Annie pulled to the curb in front of Robichaux Electric, cut the engine, and grabbed her big black flashlight from the debris on the floor behind the passenger's seat. Maybe Fourcade was taking it upon himself to continue the surveillance. But if that were the case, he wouldn't park two blocks away or leave his vehicle.

She pulled her Sig P–225 out of her duffel bag and stuck the gun in the waistband of her skirt, then climbed out of the Jeep. Keeping the flashlight off, she made her way down the sidewalk, her sneakers silent on the damp pavement.

'There is no justice in this world. How's that for a truth, Deputy Broussard?'

'Shit, shit, shit,' she chanted under her breath, her step quickening at the first sound from the direction of Bowen & Briggs. A scrape. A shoe on asphalt. A thump. A muffled cry.

'Shit!' Pulling the gun and flicking the switch on the flashlight, she broke into a run.

She could hear the sound of flesh striking flesh even before she entered the narrow parking lot. Instinct rushed her forward, overruling procedure. She should have called it in. She didn't have any backup. Her badge was in her pocketbook in the Jeep. Not one of those facts slowed her step.

'Sheriff's office, freeze!' she yelled, sweeping the bright halogen beam across the parking area.

Fourcade had Renard up against the side of a car, swinging at him with the rhythm of a boxer at a punching bag. A hard left turned Renard's face toward Annie, and she gasped at the blood that obscured his features. He lunged toward her, arms outstretched, blood and spittle spraying from his mouth in a froth as a wild animal sound tore from his throat and his eyes rolled white. Fourcade caught him in the stomach and knocked him back into the Volvo.

'Fourcade! Stop it!' Annie shouted, hurling herself against him, trying to knock him away from Renard. 'Stop it! You're killing him! Arrête! C'est assez!'

He shrugged her off like a mosquito and cracked Renard's jaw with a right.

'Stop it!'

Using the big flashlight like a baton, she swung it as hard as she could into his kidneys, once, twice. As she drew back for a third blow, Fourcade spun toward her, poised to strike.

Annie scuttled backward. She turned the full beam of the flashlight in Fourcade's face. 'Hold it!' she ordered. 'I've got a gun!'

'Get away!' he roared. His expression was feral, his eyes glazed, wild. One corner of his mouth curled in a snarl.

'It's Broussard,' she said. '*Deputy* Broussard. Step back, Fourcade! I mean it!'

He didn't move, but the look on his face slipped toward uncertainty. He glanced around with the kind of hesitancy that suggested he had just come to and didn't know where he was or how he had gotten there. Behind him, Renard dropped to his hands and knees on the blacktop, vomited, then collapsed.

'Jesus,' Annie muttered. 'Stay where you are.'

Squatting beside Renard, she stuck her gun back in her waistband and felt for the carotid artery in his neck, her fingers coming away sticky with blood. His pulse was strong. He was alive but unconscious, and probably glad for it. His face looked like raw hamburger, his nose was an indistinct mass. She wiped the blood from her hand on his shoulder, pulled the Sig again, and stood, her knees shaking.

'What the hell were you thinking?' she asked, turning toward Fourcade.

Nick stared down at Renard lying in his own puke as if seeing him for the first time. Thinking? He couldn't remember thinking. What he did remember didn't make sense. Echoes of voices from another place . . . taunts . . . The red haze was slowly dissipating, leaving him with a sick feeling.

'What were you gonna do?' Annie Broussard demanded. 'Kill him and dump him in the swamp? Did you think nobody would notice? Did you think nobody would suspect? My God, you're a *cop*! You're supposed to uphold the law, not take it into your own hands!'

She hissed a breath through her teeth. 'Looks like I believed the wrong half of those rumors about you, after all, Fourcade.'

'I – I came here to talk to him,' he muttered.

'Yeah? Well, you're a helluva conversationalist.'

Renard groaned, shifted positions, and settled back into oblivion. Nick closed his eyes, turned away, and rubbed his gloved hands over his face. The smell of Renard's blood in the leather gagged him.

'*C'est ein affaire à pus finir,*' he whispered. *It is a thing that has no end.*

'What are you talking about?' Broussard demanded.

Shadows and darkness, and the kind of rage that could swallow a man whole. But she knew of none of these things, and he didn't try to tell her.

'Go call an ambulance,' he said with resignation.

She looked to Renard and back, weighing the options.

'It's all right, 'Toinette. I promise not to kill him while you're gone.'

'Under the circumstances, you'll forgive me if I don't believe a word you say.' Annie glanced at Renard again. 'He's not going anywhere. You can come with me. And by the way,' she added, gesturing him toward the street with her gun, 'you're under arrest. You have the right to remain silent . . .'

5

You can't arrest Fourcade. He's a detective, for Christ's sake!' Gus ranted, pacing behind his desk.

The desk sergeant had called him in from a Rotary Club dinner where he had been ingesting calories in the liquid form, trying to dull the barbed comments of Rotarians unhappy with the day's court ruling. The civic leaders of Bayou Breaux had wanted Renard's indictment as something extra to celebrate for Mardi Gras. Even with half a pint of Amaretto in him, Gus felt as if his blood pressure just might cause his head to explode.

'What the hell were you thinking, Broussard?' he demanded.

Annie's jaw dropped. 'I was thinking he committed assault! I saw him with my own eyes!'

'Well, there's got to be more to this story than what *you* know.'

'I saw what I saw. Ask him yourself, Sheriff. He won't deny it. Renard looks like he put his face in a Waring blender.'

'Fuck a duck,' Gus muttered. 'I told him, I *told* him! Where's he at now?'

'Interview B.'

It had been a fight getting him in there. Not that Fourcade had resisted in any way. It was Rodrigue, the desk sergeant, and Degas and Pitre – deputies just hanging around. *'Arresting Fourcade? Naw. Must be some mistake. Quit screwing around, Broussard. What'd he do – pinch your ass? We don't arrest our own. Nick, he's part of the Brotherhood. Whatsa matter with you, Broussard – you on the rag or somethin'? He beat up Renard? Christ, we oughta get him a medal! Is Renard dead? Can we throw a party?'*

In the end, Fourcade had pushed past them through the doorway and let himself into Interview B.

The sheriff stalked past Annie and out the door. She hustled after him, a choke hold on her temper. If she'd hauled in a civilian, no one would have questioned her judgment or her perception of facts.

The door to the interview room was wide open. Rodrigue stood with one hand on the frame and one eye on his abandoned desk, grinning as he traded comments with someone inside the room, his mustache wriggling like a woolly caterpillar on his upper lip.

'Hey, Sheriff, we're thinking maybe Nick oughta get a ticker-tape parade.'

'Shut up,' Gus barked as he bulled his way past the desk sergeant and into the room where Degas and Pitre had sprawled into chairs. Coffee cups sat steaming on the small table. Fourcade sat on the far side, smoking a cigarette and looking detached.

Gus cut a scathing look at his deputies. 'Y'all don't have nothing better to do, then why are you on my payroll? Get outta here! You too!' he snapped at Annie. 'Go home.'

'Go home? But – but, Sheriff,' she stammered, 'I was there. I'm the –'

'So was he.' He pointed at Fourcade. 'I talked to you, now I'm gonna talk to him. You got a problem with that, Deputy?'

'No, sir,' Annie said tightly. She looked at Fourcade, wanting him to meet her eyes, wanting to see . . . what? Innocence? She knew he wasn't innocent. Apology? He didn't owe her anything. He took a drag on his cigarette and focused on the stream of smoke.

Gus planted his hands on the back of a vacant chair and leaned on it, waiting to hear the door close behind him. And when the door closed, he waited some more, wishing he would come to in his own cozy bed with his plump, snoring wife and realize this day had all been a bad dream and nothing more.

'What do you have to say for yourself, Detective?' he asked at last.

Nick stubbed out the butt in the ashtray Pitre had obligingly fetched him. What was he supposed to say? He had no explanation, only excuses.

'Nothing,' he said.

'Nothing. Nothing?' Noblier repeated, as if the word were foreign to his tongue. 'Look at me, Nick.'

He did so and wondered which was the better choice: to allow himself an emotional response to the disappointment he saw or to block it. Emotion was what unfailingly landed him in trouble. He had spent the last year of his life learning to hold it in an iron fist deep within him. Tonight it had broken free, and here he sat.

'I took a big chance bringing you on board here,' Gus said quietly. 'I did it because I knew your papa, and I owed him something from way back. And because I believed you about that business in New Orleans, and I thought you could do a good job here.

'This is how you pay me back?' he asked, voice rising. 'You screw up an investigation and beat the hell out of a suspect? You better have something more than nothing to say for yourself, or, by God, I'll throw your ass to the wolves!

'Why'd you go near Renard when I told you not to? Why'd you have to get in his face? Jesus Christ, do you have any idea what him and that anorexic lawyer of his are gonna do to this office? Tell me you had some kind of cause to go near him. What were you even doing in that part of town?'

'Drinking.'

'Oh, great! Good answer! You left my office in a flaming temper and went and threw alcohol on it!'

865

He shoved the chair into the table. 'Damage control,' he muttered. 'How the fuck do we spin this? I can say you were on surveillance.'

'You told the press you pulled the surveillance.'

'Fuck the press. I tell 'em what I want 'em to think. Renard is still a suspect. We got reason to watch him. That gives you cause to be there, and it shows I believe in your innocence on that evidence-tampering bullshit Kudrow's trying to stir up. So then what? Did he provoke you?'

'Does it matter?' Nick asked. 'Never mind that he's a murderer, and the goddamn court shoulda punched his ticket for him —'

'Yeah, the court should have, but it didn't. Then Hunter Davidson tried to and you stopped him. It looks like you just wanted the job all for yourself.'

'I know what it looks like.'

'It looks like assault, at the very least. Broussard thinks I should throw your ass in jail.'

Broussard. Nick pushed to his feet, the anger stirring anew. Broussard, who hadn't said ten words to him in the six months he'd been in Bayou Breaux. Who suddenly sought him out at Laveau's. Who appeared out of nowhere with a gun and the power to arrest him.

'Will you?' he asked.

'Not if I don't have to.'

'Renard'll press charges.'

'You bet your balls he will.' Gus rubbed a hand over his face and secretly wished he'd stayed in geology all those years ago. 'He's no shit-for-brains lowlife you can stick his head in a toilet and flush a confession outta him and won't nobody listen to him when he screams about it. Kudrow's been threatening a lawsuit all along. Harassment, he says. Unlawful arrest, he says. Well, I sure as hell know what he'll say about this.'

He dropped down onto a chair. 'All in all, I think I'm gonna wish you'd finished the job and fed Renard to the gators.'

What you hanging around for, Broussard?' Rodrigue asked. Blocky and nearly bald, he stood behind his desk shuffling papers with an air of false importance, as if he hadn't been kicked out of the interview room himself.

Annie gave the sergeant a defiant glare. 'I'm the arresting officer. I've got a suspect to book, a report to file, and evidence to log in.'

Rodrigue snorted. 'There ain't gonna be no arrest, darlin'. Fourcade, he didn't do nothing ever'body in this parish hasn't wanted to do.'

'Last time I looked, assault was against the law.'

'Dat wasn't no assault. Dat was justice. Oh, yeah.'

'Yeah,' Degas chimed in. 'And you interrupted it, Broussard. There's the crime. Why didn't you let him finish the job?'

Because that would have been murder, Annie thought. That Renard deserved killing didn't enter into it. The law was the law, and she was

866

sworn to uphold it, as were Fourcade and Rodrigue and Degas, and Gus Noblier.

'That's right,' Pitre said, swaggering toward her, pulling the handcuffs off his belt. 'Maybe we oughta be arresting you, Broussard. Obstruction of justice.'

'Interfering with an officer in the performance of his duty,' Degas added.

'I think a strip search is in order here,' Pitre suggested, reaching for her arm.

'Fuck you, Pitre,' she snapped, jerking away from him.

A salacious sneer lit his face. 'I'm up for it, sugar, if you think it'll help your case.'

'Go piss up a rope.'

'The sheriff told you to go home, Broussard,' Rodrigue said. 'You're disobeying an order. You wanna go on report?'

Annie shook her head in disbelief. He would condone brutality, and write her up for loitering. She looked at the door to the interview room, uncertain. Procedure dictated one course of action, her sheriff had ordered another. She would have given anything to know what was being said on the other side of that door, but no one was going to let her in either literally or figuratively. Gus had taken over, and Gus Noblier was absolute ruler of the Partout Parish Sheriff's Office, if not of Partout Parish itself.

'Fine,' she said grudgingly. 'I'll do the paperwork in the morning.'

She felt their eyes burning into her back all the way to the door, their hostility a tangible thing. The sensation made her feel ill. These were men she had known for two years, men she had joked with.

The mist had evolved into a steady, cold rain. Annie pulled her denim jacket up over her head and ran to the Jeep, where her ice cream had melted and was seeping through the carton into a milky puddle on the driver's side floor. A fitting end to her evening.

She sat behind the wheel, trying to imagine what would happen tomorrow, but nothing came. She had no frame of reference. She had never arrested a fellow officer.

'We don't arrest our own. Nick, he's part of the Brotherhood.'

The Brotherhood. The Code.

I broke the Code.

'Well, what the hell was I supposed to do?' she asked aloud.

The plastic alligator that hung from the mirror stared back at her with a mocking leer. Annie snapped at him with a forefinger and sat back as he danced on the end of his tether. She glanced at the paper bag she had tucked between the bucket seats. The bag her ice cream had come in. The bag she had used to collect Fourcade's bloody gloves. Each glove should have been bagged individually, but she'd made do with what she had on hand, slipping one glove in, then folding the bag and inserting the other in the top pocket created by the fold. Procedure dictated she log in the evidence, see to it that it was secured in the evidence room. Instinct kept her from running back into the station with the bag. She could still feel the burning gazes of Rodrigue and Degas and Pitre boring into her. She had broken the Code.

And yet, she had bent rules, had made concessions for Fourcade she wouldn't have made with a civilian. She should have called a unit to the scene, but she hadn't. The jurisdiction was City of Bayou Breaux, not Partout Parish, but it seemed like betrayal to turn Fourcade over to another department. She had called an ambulance for Renard, explained nothing to the paramedics, and hauled Fourcade to the station in her own vehicle. She hadn't even called in to dispatch to warn them, because she didn't want it on the radio.

She had made concessions to Fourcade because he was a cop, and still she was being made the heavy. Men she would have joked with last night suddenly looked at her as if she were a hostile and unwelcome stranger.

She started the Jeep and rolled out of the parking lot as two cars turned in. Deputies coming on for the midnight shift. The news of Fourcade's run-in would spread like hot oil in a skillet. Her world had suddenly turned 180 degrees. Everything simple had become complex. Everything familiar had become unfamiliar. Everything light had gone dark. She looked at the rain and remembered Fourcade's whispered word: *Shadowland*.

The streets were deserted, making the traffic lights seem an extravagance. The majority of Bayou Breaux's seven thousand residents were working-class people who went to bed at a decent hour weeknights and saved their hell-raising for the weekends. Commercial fishermen, oil workers, cane farmers. What industry there was in town supported those same professions.

The core of Bayou Breaux was old. A couple of the buildings on La Rue Dumas had been standing there since before the first Acadians got off the boats from *le grand dérangement* in the eighteenth century, when the British confiscated their property in Nova Scotia and kicked them out. Many more buildings dated to the nineteenth century – some clapboard, some brick with false fronts, some in good shape, some not. Annie drove past them, temporarily oblivious to their history.

A neon light for Dixie beer glowed red in the window of T-Neg's, the nightspot in what was still called the colored part of town. The modern rage for political correctness had yet to sift into the deeper recesses of South Louisiana. She hung a right at Canray's Garage, a tumbledown filling station that looked like something from a bleak postapocalyptic sci-fi movie, with junked cars and disemboweled engines abandoned all around. The houses down this street didn't look much better. Tatty one-story cottages rose off the ground on leaning brick pilings, the houses crammed shoulder to shoulder with yards the size of postage stamps.

The properties gradually became larger, the homes more respectable and more modern the farther west she drove. The old neighborhoods gave way to subdivisions on the southwest side of town, where contractors had lined cul-de-sacs with brick pseudo-Acadian and pseudo-Caribbean plantation cottages. A.J. lived out here.

But how could she go to him? He worked for the DA. The cops and the prosecutors may have technically been on the same big team for justice, but the reality was often more adversarial than congenial. If she went over the sheriff's head and crossed the line into the DA's camp, there would be hell to pay with Noblier, and the rest of the department would see it only as further proof that she had turned on them.

And if she went to A.J. as a friend, then what? Could she expect him to separate who they were from what they did when a possible felony charge hung in the balance?

Annie pulled a U-turn and headed for the hospital. Marcus Renard's beating was her case until someone told her differently. She had a victim's statement to take.

A pristine white statue of the Virgin Mary welcomed the afflicted to Our Lady of Mercy with open arms. Spotlights nestled in the hibiscus shrubs at the base of her pedestal illuminated her all night long, a beacon to the battered. The hospital itself had been built in the seventies, during the oil boom, when ready money and philanthropy were in abundant supply. A two-story brick L, it sprawled over a manicured lawn that was set back just far enough from the bayou to be both scenic and prudent in flood season.

Annie parked in the red zone in front of the ER entrance, flipping down her visor with the insignia of the sheriff's department clipped to it. Notebook in hand, she headed into the hospital, wondering if Renard would be in any condition to speak to her. If he died, would that make life easier or harder?

'We just got him moved into a room.' Nurse Jolie led her down a corridor that glowed like pearl under the soft night lighting. 'I voted for the boiler room – the boiler itself, to be precise. Do you know who beat him up? I wanna kiss that man all over.'

'He's in jail,' Annie lied.

Nurse Jolie arched a finely curved brow. 'What for?'

Annie bit back a sigh as they stopped before the door to room 118. 'Is he awake? Sedated? Can he talk?'

'He can talk through what's left of his teeth. Dr Van Allen used a local on his nose and jaw. He hasn't been given any painkillers.' A slyly sadistic smile turned the nurse's mouth. 'We don't want to mask the symptoms of a serious head trauma with narcotics.'

'Never piss off medical people,' Annie said, pretending to jot herself a note.

'Damn straight, girl.'

Jolie pushed open the door to Renard's room and held it. The room was set up as a double, but only one bed was occupied. Renard lay with the head of the bed tipped up slightly, the fluorescent light glaring down into his eyes, which were nearly swollen shut. His face looked like a mutant pomegranate. Just two hours after his beating and already the swelling and bruising made him unrecognizable. One eyebrow was stitched together. Another line of stitches ran up his chin and over his lower lip like a millipede. Cotton had been crammed up his nostrils, and what was left of his nose was swathed in bandaging and adhesive tape.

'Not a plug to be pulled,' the nurse said regretfully. She cut a glance at Annie. 'You couldn't have just hung back until Whoever put this asshole in a coma?'

'Timing has never been my strong suit,' Annie muttered with bitter irony.

'Too bad.'

Annie watched her glide away, heading back for the nurses' station.

'Mr Renard, I'm Deputy Broussard,' she said, uncapping her pen as she moved toward the bed. 'If it's at all possible, I'd like to get a statement from you as to what happened this evening.'

Marcus studied her through the slits left open in the swelling around his eyes. His angel of mercy. Beside the elevated hospital bed, she looked small. The denim jacket she wore swallowed her up. She was pretty in a tomboy-next-door kind of way, with a blackening bruise high on one cheek and her brown hair hanging in disarray. Her eyes were the color of café noir, slightly exotic in shape, their expression dead serious as she waited for him to speak.

'You were there,' he whispered, setting off a stabbing pain in his face. What little lidocaine the doctor had bothered to use was wearing off. The packing in his nose forced him to breathe through his mouth, and only added to the feeling that his head was twice its normal size. His sinuses were draining down the back of his throat, half choking him.

'I need to know what happened before I got there,' she said. 'What precipitated the fight?'

'Attack.'

'You're saying Detective Fourcade simply attacked you? No words were exchanged?'

'I came out . . . of the building,' he said haltingly. Tape bound his cracked ribs so tightly he wasn't able to take in more than a teaspoon of air at a time. 'He was there. Angry . . . about the ruling. Said it wasn't over. Hit me. Again . . . and again.'

'You didn't say anything to him?'

'He wants me dead.'

She glanced up at him from her notebook. 'He's hardly the only one, Mr Renard.'

'Not you,' Marcus said. 'You . . . saved me.'

'I was doing my job.'

'And Fourcade?'

'I don't speak for Detective Fourcade.'

'He tried . . . to kill me.'

'Did he state that he meant to kill you?'

'Look at me.'

'It's not my place to draw conclusions, Mr Renard.'

'But you did,' he insisted. 'I heard you say, 'You're killing him.' You saved me. Thank you.'

'I don't want your thanks,' Annie said bluntly.

'I didn't . . . kill Pam. I loved her . . . like a friend.'

'Friends don't stalk other friends.'

Marcus lifted a finger to admonish her. 'Conclusion . . .'

'That's not my case. I'm free to review the facts and come to any conclusion I like. Did you provoke Detective Fourcade in any way?'

'No. He was irrational . . . and drunk.'

He tried to moisten his lips, his tongue butting into the jagged edges of several chipped teeth and a blank space where a tooth had been. He shifted his gaze to a plastic water pitcher on his right.

'Could you please . . . pour me a drink . . . Annie?'

'Deputy Broussard,' Annie said, too sharply. His use of her name unnerved her. She wanted to deny his request, but he already had enough to file suit against the department. There was no sense exacerbating the situation over so simple a task.

She set her notebook on the bedside stand, poured half a glass of water, and handed it to him. The knuckles of his right hand were skinned raw and painted orange with iodine. This was the hand he would have held the knife in as he butchered a woman he claimed to love as a friend.

He tried to sip at the water, avoiding the mended split in his lip by pressing the glass against the left corner of his mouth. A stream dribbled down his chin onto his hospital gown. He should have had a straw, but the nurses hadn't left him one. Annie supposed he'd be lucky if they hadn't poisoned the water.

'Thank you, again . . . Deputy,' he said, attempting a smile that made him look more ghoulish. 'You're very kind.'

'Do you want to press charges?' Annie asked abruptly.

He made a choking sound that might have been a laugh. 'He tried to kill me. Yes . . . I want to press charges. He should be . . . in prison. You'll help me put him there . . . Deputy. You're my witness.'

The pen stilled in Annie's hand as the prospect went through her like a skewer. 'You know something, Renard? I wish I'd never turned down that street tonight.'

He tried to shake his head. 'You don't . . . want me dead . . . Annie. You saved me today. Twice.'

'I already wish I hadn't.'

'You don't . . . look for revenge. You look . . . for justice . . . for truth. I'm not . . . a bad man . . . Annie.'

'I'll feel better if a court decides that,' she said, closing her notebook. 'Someone from the department will get back to you.'

Marcus watched her walk away, then closed his eyes and conjured up her face in his mind's eye. Pretty, rectangular, a hint of a cleft in the chin, skin the color of fresh cream and new Georgia peaches. She believed in the good in people. She liked to help. He imagined her voice – soft, a little husky. He thought of what she might have said to him if she hadn't come in her capacity as deputy. Words of sympathy and comfort, meant to soothe his pain.

Annie Broussard. His angel of mercy.

6

The rain fell steadily, reducing the reach of the headlights, making the night close in like a tunnel. The sky seemed too low, the trees that grew thick seemed to hunch over the road. Jennifer Nolan's imagination ran wild with movie images of maniacs leaping out in front of her and cars suddenly looming up in the rearview mirror.

She hated working the late shift. But then, she hated being home at night, too. She had been raised to fear basically everything about the night: the dark, the sounds in the dark, the things that might lurk in the dark. She wished she had a roommate, but the last one had stolen her best jewelry and her television and run off with some no-account biker, and so she was living alone.

Headlights came up behind her, and Jennifer's breath caught. All anybody ever talked about anymore was murder and how women weren't safe to walk the streets. She'd heard that Bichon woman had been dismembered. That wasn't what had been reported on the news, but she'd heard it and knew it was probably true. Rumors leaked out – like the detail of the Mardi Gras mask. The police didn't want anyone to know that either, but everyone did.

Just imagining the terror that woman must have felt was enough to give Jennifer nightmares. She didn't even want to think about Mardi Gras, which was less than two weeks away, on account of that mask business. And now she had this car on her tail. For all she knew, this could have been what happened to Pam Bichon. She could have been forced off the road and herded up that driveway to her death.

The car swept up alongside her and her panic doubled. Then the car sailed on past, taillights glowing in the gloom. Relief ran through her like water. She hit the blinker and turned in at the trailer park.

She had her key in her hand as she went up the steps to the front door, the way she'd read in *Glamour*. Have the key ready to unlock the door quickly or to be used as a weapon if an attacker jumped up from the honeysuckle bush that struggled to live beside her stoop.

A lamp burned in the living room to give the impression someone was home all evening. After locking the door behind her, Jennifer hung her jacket on the coatrack and grabbed a towel off the kitchen counter to dab at her rain-wet red hair as she moved through the trailer, turning on more lights. She was careful not to step into a room until the light was on and she could see. She checked the spare bedroom, the bathroom. Her bedroom was at the end of the narrow hall. Nothing had been disturbed, no one was in the closet. A can of Aqua Net hair spray sat on the nightstand. She would use it like Mace if someone broke in during the night.

With the knowledge of safety, the tension began to subside, letting fatigue settle in. Too many nights with too little sleep, the hassle with her supervisor over the length of her coffee breaks, the past-due balance on her phone bill – each worry weighed down on her. Depressed, she brushed her teeth, took off her jeans, and climbed into bed in the T-shirt she'd worn all day. I'M WITH STUPID, it read, and an arrow pointed to the empty space in the bed beside her. She was with no one. Until 1:57 A.M.

Jennifer Nolan woke with a start. A gloved hand struck her hard across the face as she struggled to sit up and opened her mouth to scream. The back of her skull smacked against the headboard. She tried again to lurch forward, stopped this time by the feel of a blade at her throat. Her bladder released and tears welled in her eyes.

But even through the blur she could see her attacker. His image was illuminated by the green glow of the alarm clock and by the light that seeped in around the edges of the cheap miniblinds. He seemed huge as he loomed over her, the vision of doom. Terrified, she fixed on his face – a face half hidden by a feathered Mardi Gras mask.

7

Richard Kudrow was dying. The Crohn's disease that had besieged his intestinal tract for the last five years of his life had been joined in the last few months by a voracious cancer. Despite the efforts of medical science, his body was virtually devouring itself.

He had been told to quit his practice and devote his time to the hopeless task of treatment, but he didn't see the point. He knew his demise was inevitable. Work was all that kept him going. Anger and adrenaline fueled his weakened system. The focus on justice – an attainable goal – gave him a greater sense of purpose than the pursuit of a cure – an unattainable goal. In defying his doctors and his disease, he had already managed to live past all expectations.

His enemies said he was too damned mean to die. He figured the beating of Marcus Renard was going to give him another six or eight months' worth of fury to live on.

'My client was beat to within an inch of his life by your detective, Noblier. What kind of bullshit will you attempt to spread over that plain truth?'

Gus pressed his lips together. His eyes narrowed to the size of beads as he glared at Kudrow sitting across from him, gray and withering like a rotting pecan husk in his wrinkled brown suit.

'You're the bullshit expert, Kudrow. I'm supposed to swallow the rantings of your sociopathic homicidal pervert client?'

'He didn't break his own nose. He didn't break his own jaw. He did not break his own teeth out of his head. Ask your Deputy Broussard. Better yet, *I'll* ask your Deputy Broussard,' Kudrow said, pressing up out of the chair. 'I sure as hell don't trust you any farther than I could throw a grown hog.'

Gus rose with energy and thrust a finger at the lawyer. 'You stay the hell away from my people, Kudrow.'

Kudrow waved him off. 'Broussard is a material witness and Fourcade is a thug. He was a thug on the NOPD and you knew it when you hired him. That makes you culpable in the civil suit, Noblier, and, by virtue of the fact that you did not suspend Fourcade from the Bichon case after his obvious attempt to plant and manipulate evidence, you may well be guilty of collusion on the assault.'

Gus snorted. 'Collusion! You give yourself a hernia trying to drag that dead horse into court, you old goat. And you file as many goddamn civil suits as you want. You'll die poor before you get a dime out of my office. As for the rest, I don't remember anybody electing you district attorney.'

'Smith Pritchett will bring charges before you can digest the grease you ate for breakfast. He'll be all too happy to see Fourcade's ass in jail.'

'We'll see about that,' Gus grumbled. 'You don't know shit about what happened last night, and I am not obliged to talk with you about it.'

'It'll all be a matter of record.' Kudrow picked up his old briefcase, and the weight of it tilted him slightly sideways. 'It had damn well better be. Your deputy made an arrest last night. She took a statement from my client, asked if he wanted to press charges. If there isn't paperwork to go with those facts, there will be hell to pay, Noblier.'

Gus's features twisted as if he had just caught wind of day-old roadkill. 'Your client is delusional and a liar, and those are some of his better qualities,' he said, cutting past the lawyer to the front door of his office. 'Get out of here, Kudrow. I've got better things to do with my time than listen to you pass gas through your mouth all morning.'

Kudrow bared the teeth the toxins in his body had turned amber. Energy burned in his veins like rocket fuel and he envisioned it searing the cancer out of him. 'It's been a pleasure, as always, Sheriff. But not so much a pleasure as ruining you and your rogue, Fourcade, will be.'

'Why don't you just do the world a favor and drop dead,' Gus suggested.

'I'd never be that nice to you, Noblier. I plan to outlive your days in this office, if for no other reason than spite.'

'God should live that long, but you sure as hell won't, I'm glad to say.'

'We'll see who gets the last word.'

Gus slammed the door on Kudrow's back. 'Me, you rotting old turd,' he grumbled. He swung toward the side door to his secretary's office and bellowed, 'Get in here, Broussard!'

Annie's heart sank as she rose from the chair she'd been waiting in. She had listened with rapt attention to the angry voices that could be quite plainly heard through the door. The heat of the argument seemed to have physically enveloped her. She could feel sweat trickling down between her shoulder blades and moistening the armpits of her uniform.

Valerie Comb, Noblier's secretary, cut her a sideways look. A bottle blonde, she had been four years ahead of Annie in school, head basketball cheerleader and voted most likely to get pregnant on purpose, which she had done. Now divorced with three kids to feed, she placed her loyalties solidly in Noblier's corner.

Pulling in a deep breath, Annie let herself into the inner sanctum, and closed the door behind her. The sheriff stomped toward her with a bulldog glare and hands jammed at his belt line. Annie braced her feet slightly apart and locked her hands together behind her back.

'You took a statement from Marcus Renard last night?' he said in a tight voice.

'Yes, sir.'

'I told you to go home, didn't I, Broussard? Am I getting Alzheimer's or something? Did I just imagine I told you to go home?'

'No, sir.'

'Then what the hell were you doing down at Our Lady, taking a statement from Marcus Renard?'

'It had to be done, Sheriff,' she said. 'I was the officer on the scene. I knew Renard would be only too happy to charge the department with negligence, and –'

'Don't you preach procedure to me, Deputy,' he snapped. 'You don't think I know procedure? You think I don't know what I'm doing?'

'No, sir – I mean, yes, sir – I –'

'When I tell you to do something, I have a reason for it, Deputy Broussard.' He leaned toward her, his whole head as red as a radish out to the tips of his ears. 'Sometimes a situation needs to be sorted through before we proceed in the usual way. Do you understand what I'm saying here, Deputy?'

Annie held every muscle in her body stiff, too afraid that she knew exactly what he was saying. 'I saw Nick Fourcade beating the shit out of Marcus Renard, Sheriff.'

'I'm not saying you didn't. I'm saying you don't know the circumstances. I'm saying you didn't hear the call about a prowler in that part of town. I'm saying you weren't there when the offender resisted arrest.'

Annie stared at him for a long moment. 'You're saying I wasn't in the room last night when everyone was getting their story straight,' she said at last, knowing she was inviting Noblier's wrath. 'What Fourcade did last night was illegal. It was wrong.'

'And what Renard did to that Bichon girl wasn't?'

'Of course it was, but –'

'Let me tell you something here, Annie,' he said, suddenly quieter, gentler. He stepped back and sat on the edge of his desk. His expression was serious, frank, absent of the bluster he regularly blew at the world.

'The world isn't black and white, Annie. It's shades of gray. The world don't follow no procedure handbook. The law and justice are not always the same thing. I'm not saying I condone what Fourcade did. I'm saying I *understand* what Fourcade did. I'm saying we take care of our own in this department. That means you don't go off half-cocked and try to arrest a detective. That means you don't run and take a statement when I tell you to go home.'

'I can't change the fact that I was there, Sheriff, or that Renard knows I was there. How would it look if I *hadn't* taken his statement?'

'It might look like he was confused about the chain of events. It might look like we were giving him the night to recover before we troubled

877

him further. It might look like we were sorting out the jurisdictional questions here.'

Or it might have looked like they were ignoring the victim of a brutal beating, turning their heads the other way because the perpetrator was a cop. It might have looked like they were stalling for time until they could come up with a story.

Annie turned toward the wall that held a pictorial essay on the illustrious career of August F. Noblier. The sheriff in his younger, trimmer days grinning and shaking hands with Governor Edwards. An array of photographs through the years with lesser politicians and celebrities who had passed through Partout Parish during the years of Gus's reign. She had always respected him.

'You did what you did, and we'll deal with it, Deputy,' he said, as if *she* was the one who had broken the law. Annie wondered if he had given Fourcade a reprimand or a pat on the back. 'The point is, we could have dealt with the situation more cleanly if you'd stayed on the page with me. You know what I'm saying?'

Annie said nothing. It wouldn't have done any good to point out that she hadn't been given the opportunity to stay on the page, that the book had been slammed shut on her last night, that she had been cut loose and excluded from the proceedings like an outsider. She wasn't sure which was worse – being shut out or being included in a conspiracy.

'I don't want you talking to the press,' Noblier said, going around behind his desk to settle himself into his big leather executive's chair. 'And I don't want you talking to Richard Kudrow under any circumstances. You understand me?'

'Yes, sir.'

' "No comment." Can you manage that?'

'Yes, sir.'

'And, most of all, I don't want you talking to Marcus Renard. You got that?'

'Yes, sir.'

'You were off duty, which is why you didn't hear that 10–70 call that went out. You stumbled into a situation and contained it. Is that what happened?'

'Yes, sir,' she whispered, the sick feeling in the pit of her stomach swelling like bread dough.

Noblier stared at her in silence for a moment. 'How did Kudrow know you tried to arrest Fourcade? Has he already talked to you?'

'He left a message on my answering machine this morning while I was out running.'

'But you didn't talk to him?'

'No.'

'Did you tell Renard you arrested Fourcade?'

'No.'

'Did you Mirandize Fourcade in front of him?'

'Renard was unconscious.'

'Then Kudrow was bluffing, that ugly son of a bitch,' Gus muttered to himself. 'I hate that man. I don't care that he's dying. I wish he'd hurry up and get it over with. Have you filed an arrest report?'

'Not yet.'

'Nor will you. If you've started that paperwork, I want it shredded. Not thrown away. Shredded.'

'But Renard is going to press charges –'

'That doesn't mean we have to make it easy for him. Go ahead and write up his complaint, write up your preliminary report, but you did not arrest Fourcade. Get your sergeant's initials on the paperwork, then bring the file straight to me.

'I'm personally taking charge of the case,' he said, as if he were trying out the phrase for a future official statement. 'It's an unusual situation – allegations being made against one of my men. Requires my undivided attention to see to it justice is served.

'And don't look at me like that, Deputy,' he said, pointing an accusatory finger. 'We're not doing anything Richard Kudrow hasn't done time and again for the scum he represents.'

'Then we're no better than they are,' Annie murmured.

'The hell we're not,' Noblier growled, reaching for the telephone. 'We're the good guys, Annie. We work for Lady Justice. It's just that she can't always see what's what with that damned blindfold on. You're dismissed, Deputy.'

The women's locker room in the Partout Parish Sheriff's Department had originally been a janitor's closet. There had been no women on the job when the building was designed in the late sixties, and the blissful chauvinists on the planning committee hadn't foreseen the possibility. Their shortsightedness meant male officers had a locker room with showers and their own rest room, while female personnel got a broom closet that had been converted during the 1993 remodeling.

The only light was a bare bulb in the ceiling. Four battered metal lockers had been salvaged out of the old junior high school and transplanted along one wall. A cheap frameless mirror hung on the opposite wall above a tiny porcelain sink. When Annie had first come on the job, someone had drilled a peephole half a foot to the left of the mirror from the men's room on the other side. She now checked the wall periodically for new breaches of privacy, filling the holes with spackling compound she kept in her locker alongside her stash of candy bars.

She was the only female deputy who used the room with any regularity, and currently the only female patrol officer. There were two women who worked in the jail, and one female plainclothes juvenile officer, all of whom had come on before the broom closet had been converted and had adjusted to life without it. Annie thought of the room as her own and had tried to spruce it up a little by bringing in a plastic potted palm and a carpet remnant for the concrete floor. A poster from the International Association of Women Police brightened one wall.

Annie sat on her folding chair and faced the door. She couldn't bring herself to face the women in the poster. She was late for patrol, had missed the morning briefing. There was no doubt in her mind that every uniform in the place knew Noblier had called her into his office, and why. Sergeant Hooker had announced the first the minute she stepped into the building. The looks she had drawn from the rest of the men had hinted strongly at the second.

She looked at the file folder on her lap. She had gone so far as to type out the arrest report on Fourcade last night. It had given her a small sense of control to sit at her typewriter at home and put down in black and white what she had seen, what she had done. She had felt a sense of validation for just a little while there in the dead of night. Sheriff Noblier had smashed it flat beneath the weight of his authority this morning.

He wanted her to file a false report. She was supposed to lie, justify brutality, violate God knew how many laws.

'And no one sees anything wrong with that picture but me,' she muttered.

Anxiety simmered like acid in her stomach as she left the locker room and headed down the hall.

Hooker rolled an eye at her as she passed the sergeant's desk. 'See if you can't contain yourself to arresting *criminals* today, Broussard.'

Annie reserved comment as she signed herself out. 'I have to be in court at three o'clock.'

'Oh really? You testifying for us or against us?'

'Hypolite Grangnon – burglary,' she said flatly.

Hooker narrowed his little pig eyes at her. 'Sheriff wants those reports on his desk by noon.'

'Yes, sir.'

She should have gone straight to the report room and gotten it over with, but she needed air and space, some time on the road to clear her head, and a cup of coffee that didn't taste like boiled sweat socks. She let herself out of the building and sucked in air that smelled of damp earth and green grass.

The rain had subsided around five A.M. Annie had lain awake all night listening to it assault the roof over her head. Finally giving up on the idea of rest, she had forced herself to get out of bed and work out with the free weights and pull-up bar that gave her second bedroom such a decorative flair.

As she worked her aching muscles, she watched for dawn to break over the Atchafalaya basin. There were mornings when the sunrise boiled up over the swamp like a ball of flame and the sky turned shades of orange and pink so intense they seemed liquid. This morning had come in with rolling, angry slate-colored clouds that carried the threat of a storm with a bully's arrogance.

A storm would have suited her, she thought, except that a spring rainstorm would blow over and be forgotten, while the metaphorical storm in which she had landed herself would do neither.

'Deputy Broussard, might I have a moment of your time?'

Annie jerked around toward the source of the low, smooth voice. Richard Kudrow stood propped against the side of the building, holding the front of his old trench coat together like a flasher.

'I'm sorry. No. I don't have time,' she said quickly, stepping off the sidewalk and heading across the parking lot toward her cruiser. She cast a nervous glance over her shoulder at the building.

'You'll have to talk to me sooner or later,' the lawyer said, falling in step beside her.

'Then it'll have to be later, Mr Kudrow. I'm on duty.'

'Taxpayer time. Need I point out to you, Miss Broussard, that I myself pay mightily into August Noblier's fat coffers and am, therefore, technically, one of your employers?'

'I'm not interested in your technicalities.' She unlocked the car door with one hand while balancing her clipboard, files, and ticket books in the other arm. 'It's my sergeant who's gonna kick my butt if I don't get to work.'

'Your sergeant? Or Gus Noblier – for talking to me?'

'I don't know what you mean,' she lied. She added the car keys to the pile on her arm and started to pull the cruiser's door open.

'Can I hold something for you?' Kudrow offered gallantly, reaching toward her.

'No,' Annie snapped, twisting away.

The sudden movement sent the pile sliding off the clipboard. The keys, the ticket books, the files tumbled to the ground, the Renard file spilling its contents. Panicking, Annie dropped the clipboard and fell to the blacktop on her hands and knees, chanting expletives, scrambling to scrape the papers back into the folder before the wind could take them. Kudrow crouched down, reaching for the notebook that had blown open, its pages of details and observations and interview notes fluttering, as tantalizing to a lawyer as a glimpse of lacy underwear. Annie snatched it out of his hand, then saw his liver-spotted hand reach next for the arrest form she hadn't filed and hadn't shredded.

She lunged for it, cracking her elbow hard on the blacktop, crumpling the form in her fist as she grabbed it.

'I've got it. I've got it,' she stammered. Turning her face away from Kudrow, she closed her eyes and mouthed a silent thank-you to God. She clutched the mess of papers and folders and clipboard to her chest, rose awkwardly, and backed around the open door of the squad car.

Kudrow watched her with interest. 'Something I shouldn't see, Miss Broussard?'

Annie's fingers tightened on the crumpled arrest form. 'I have to go.'

'You were the officer on the scene last night. My client claims you saved his life. It took courage for you to stop Fourcade,' he said, bracing the car door open as Annie slid behind the wheel. 'It takes courage to do the right thing.'

'How would you know?' Annie grumbled. 'You're a lawyer.'

The gibe bounced off his jaundiced hide. She could feel the heat of his gaze on her face, though she refused to look at him. A faint, fetid scent of decay touched her nose, and she wondered if it was the bayou or Kudrow.

'The abuse of power, the abuse of office, the abuse of public trust – those are terrible things, Miss Broussard.'

'So are stalking and murder. It's *Deputy* Broussard.' She turned the key in the ignition and slammed the door shut.

Kudrow stepped back as the car rolled forward. He pulled his coat closed around him as the spring breeze swept across the parking lot. Disease had skewed his internal thermometer to where he was always either freezing or on fire. Today he was cold to the marrow, but his soul was burning up with purpose. If he could have been half a step quicker, he would have been holding an arrest report in his hand. An arrest report on Nick Fourcade, the thug who was *not* sitting in a jail cell this morning, thanks to August F. Noblier.

'I'll ruin you both,' he murmured as he watched the squad car turn onto the street. 'And there's the lady who's going to help me do it.'

8

As Annie had suspected, word of Renard's run-in with Fourcade had already hit the streets. Late-shift cops and nurses from Our Lady had carried what pieces of the tale they had to Madame Collette's diner, where the breakfast waitresses doled it out with announcements of the morning blue plate special. The smell of gossip and dissatisfaction was as thick in the air as the scent of bacon grease and coffee.

Annie endured a hail of barbed comments as she went to the counter for her coffee, only to be told by a hostile waitress the restaurant was 'out of coffee.' The patrons of Madame Collette's had passed judgment. The rest of Bayou Breaux would not be far behind.

They wanted someone to be guilty – in their minds if not in the courts, Annie thought. People felt betrayed, cheated by a system that seemed suddenly to favor the wrong side. They wanted to put this latest atrocity behind them and go on as if it hadn't happened. They were afraid they never would be able to do so. Afraid that maybe evil ran under the parish like an aquifer someone had tapped into by mistake, and no one knew how to plug the leak and send the force back underground.

At Po' Richard's, the woman at the drive-up window handed Annie her coffee and wished her a nice day, obviously out of the news loop. The brew was Po' Richard's usual: too black, too strong, and bitter with the taste of chicory. Annie dumped it into her spill-proof mug, added three fake creams, and headed out of town.

The radio crackled to life, reminding her that she was hardly the only person in the parish with trouble.

'All units in the vicinity: Y'all got a possible 261 out to the Country Estates trailer park. Over.'

Annie grabbed her mike as she punched the accelerator. 'One Able Charlie responding. I'm two minutes away. Out.'

When no response came back, she tried the mike again. The radio crackled back at her.

'10–1, One Able Charlie. You're breaking up. Must be something wrong with your radio. You're where? Out.'

'I'm responding to that 261 in Country Estates. Out.'

Nothing came back. Annie hung up the mike, annoyed with the glitch, but more concerned with the call: a sexual assault. She'd caught a handful of rape cases in her career. There was always an extra emotional element to deal with at a rape call. She wasn't just another cop. It wasn't just another call. She went in not only as an officer, but as a woman, able to provide the victim with the kind of support and sympathy no male officer could offer.

The Country Estates mobile-home park sat in exactly the middle of nowhere between Bayou Breaux and Luck, which qualified it as country. The place bore no resemblance to an estate. The name suggested a certain tidy gentility. Reality was a dozen rusting relic trailer houses that had been plunked down on a two-acre weed patch back in the early seventies.

Jennifer Nolan's trailer was at the back of the lot, a pink and once-white model with an OPERATION ID crime-watch sticker on the front door. Annie knocked on the storm door and announced herself as a deputy. The inside door cracked open two inches, then five.

If the face that stared out at her had ever been pretty, Annie doubted it ever would be again. Both lips were ballooning, both split open. The brown eyes were nearly swollen shut.

'Thank God, you're a woman,' Jennifer Nolan mumbled. Her red hair hung in frizzy strings. She had wrapped herself in a pink chenille robe that she clutched together over her heart as she shuffled painfully away from the door.

'Ms Nolan, have you called an ambulance?' Annie asked, following her into the small living room.

The trailer reeked of tobacco smoke and the kind of mildew that grows under old carpets. Jennifer Nolan lowered herself with great care to a boxy plaid sofa.

'No, no,' she mumbled. 'I don't want . . . Everyone will look.'

'Jennifer, you need medical attention.'

Annie squatted down in front of her, taking in the obvious signs of psychological shock. There was a good chance Jennifer Nolan wasn't fully aware of the extent of her injuries. She probably felt numb, stunned. The mental self-protection mechanisms of denial may have kicked in: How could this terrible thing have happened to her, it couldn't be real, it was just a terrible nightmare. Already her logic was skewed: She worried about the appearance of an ambulance, but not the cop car.

'Jennifer, I'm going to call an ambulance for you. Your neighbors won't know what it's coming here for. Our main concern is your well-being. Do you understand? We want to make sure you're taken care of.'

'Judas,' Sticks Mullen muttered, letting himself in without knocking. 'Looks like somebody already took care of her.'

Annie shot him a glare. 'Go call for an ambulance. My radio's out.'

She turned back to the victim, even though Mullen made no move to obey her. 'Jennifer? How long ago did this happen?'

The woman's gaze drifted around the room until it hit on the wall clock. 'In the night. I – I woke up and he – he was just there. On top of me. He – he – *hurt* me.'

'Did he rape you?'

Her face contorted, squeezing tears from her swollen eyes. 'I t-try to be s-so careful. Why – why did this happen?'

Annie skipped the question, not wanting to tell her that carefulness didn't always make a difference. 'When did he leave, Jennifer?'

She shook her head a little. Whether she couldn't or didn't want to recall was unclear.

'Was it dawn yet? Or was it still dark?'

'Dark.'

Meaning their rapist was long gone.

'Great,' Mullen muttered.

Annie took in Jennifer Nolan's appearance once again – the stringy hair, the bathrobe. 'Jennifer, did you bathe or take a shower after he left?'

The tears came harder. 'He – made me. An – and I *had* – to,' she said in an urgent whisper. 'I couldn't stand – the way I felt. I – felt him *all over me!*'

Mullen shook his head in disgust at the lost evidence. Annie gently rested a hand on Jennifer Nolan's forearm, careful to avoid touching the ligature marks that encircled the woman's wrist, just in case some fiber remained embedded in the skin.

'Jennifer, did you know the man who did this to you? Can you tell us what he looks like?'

'No. No,' she whispered, staring at Mullen's shoes. 'He – he was w– wearing a mask.'

'Like a ski mask?'

'No. No.'

She reached a trembling hand for a pack of Eve 100s and a white Bic lighter on the end table. Annie intercepted the cigarettes without a word and set them aside. It was probably too much to hope that Jennifer Nolan hadn't brushed her teeth or smoked a cigarette after the rapist had left the scene, but oral swabs would have to be taken nonetheless. Any trace left behind by the rapist could provide a key to identifying him.

'Horrible. Like f-from a nightmare,' the woman said, as spasms rocked her body. 'Feathers. Black feathers.'

'You mean an actual mask,' Annie said. 'From Mardi Gras.'

Chaz Stokes arrived on the scene eating a breakfast burrito. He was in one of his usual getups: baggy brown suit pants with a brown and yellow shirt that belonged in a fifties bowling alley. A crumpled black porkpie hat rode low over the rims of wraparound shades that were a testimony to the kind of night he'd had. The sun was nowhere in sight.

'She took a *bath*,' Mullen said, striding down off the rusty metal steps of the trailer. 'At least she didn't do the fucking laundry. We got a crime scene.'

Annie hustled after him. 'The rapist *made her* take a bath. Big difference, jerk. You of all people should be able to relate to a woman wanting to bathe after sex.'

'I don't need your mouth, Broussard,' Mullen snapped. 'I don't know what you're even doing in a uniform after last night.'

'Oh, pardon me for arresting someone who was breaking the law.'

'Nicky's a brother,' Stokes said, throwing the butt end of his breakfast into a patch of dead marigolds along the side of Jennifer Nolan's trailer. 'You turned on one of our own. What's the deal with that, Broussard? He come on to you or something? Everybody knows you think you're too good to do a cop.'

'Yeah, well, look what I've got to pick from,' Annie sneered. 'In case you're interested, there's a rape victim sitting just inside that open door, asshole. She says the guy was wearing a black feather Mardi Gras mask.'

Stokes winced. 'Jesus H., now we got us some kind of copycat.'

'Maybe.'

'What's that supposed to mean? Renard didn't do her and he did Pam Bichon. Or you got some other opinion on Bichon?'

Annie chewed back the temptation to point out no one had proven Renard guilty of anything. Stokes punched her buttons. He said black, she said white. Hell, she *believed* Renard was their killer.

'What are you?' Mullen said, curling his lip. 'Hot for Renard's shriveled little dick or something? You're all of a sudden his little cheerleader. Nick and Chaz say he did Bichon, he did Bichon.'

'Go start knocking on doors, Broussard,' Stokes ordered as the ambulance rolled into the trailer park. 'Leave the detecting to a real cop.'

'I can help process the scene,' Annie said as he popped the trunk of his Camaro.

The department wasn't large enough or busy enough to warrant a separate crime-scene unit. The detective who caught the call always brought the kits and supervised as officers on the scene pitched in to dust for prints and bag evidence.

Stokes's trunk was crammed with junk: a rusted toolbox, a length of nylon towrope, a dirty yellow rain slicker, two bags from McDonald's. Three bright-colored plastic bead necklaces from a past Mardi Gras celebration had become tangled around a jack handle. Stokes pulled out a latent fingerprints kit and a general evidence collection kit from the neater end of the junk pile.

Stokes cut Annie a sideways look. 'We don't need your kind of help.'

She walked away because she didn't have a choice. Stokes outranked her. The idea of him and Mullen processing the scene made her cringe. Stokes was a slacker, Mullen a moron. If they missed something, if they screwed up, the case could be blown. Of course, if Jennifer Nolan's description of events was accurate – not a guarantee with a badly shaken victim – there would be precious little evidence to collect.

Annie walked around the back side of the trailer, putting off the KOD duty. The attacker had come into Jennifer Nolan's trailer in the middle of the night, gaining entrance through the back door, which was not visible from any other trailer in the park. The chances of a neighbor having seen anything would be slim to none. The phone line had been cut clean. Nolan had made her call to 911 from the home of her nearest neighbor, an elderly woman named Vista Wallace, whom Nolan said was very hard-of-hearing.

Annie took a Polaroid of the torn screen door and the inside door that had been easily jimmied and left ajar. There would be no fingerprints. Nolan said her attacker had worn gloves. He had attacked her in her bed, tying her to the bed frame using strips of white cloth he had brought with him. There was no evidence of seminal fluid on the sheets, indicating that the rapist had either used a condom or hadn't ejaculated during the attack.

From her studies, Annie knew that contrary to popular belief, sexual dysfunction was fairly common among sex offenders. Rape was about power and anger, hurting and controlling a woman. Motivation that came out of rage against a particular woman in the rapist's past or against the entire gender, stemming from some past wrong. The attack on Jennifer Nolan had been premeditated, organized, indicating that it was primarily about power and control. The rapist had come prepared, wearing the mask, bringing with him something to jimmy the door and the white cloth ligatures to tie up his victim.

The Bayou Strangler's signature had been a white silk scarf around the throat of his victim. The bindings in this case would be close enough to generate a lot of gossip if word leaked out. Lack of semen could also be pointed out as a similarity. But in the Bayou Strangler cases the women had been violently brutalized and their bodies left exposed to the elements so that such evidence would most likely have broken down.

The primary difference between the Bayou Strangler cases and Jennifer Nolan's was that Jennifer Nolan was still alive. She had been attacked in her home, rather than taken to another location; raped, but not murdered or mutilated. Those were also the differences between Jennifer Nolan's case and Pam Bichon's, and yet the press was bound to draw correlations. The mask was going to be big as a shock factor.

Annie wondered if either the similarities or the differences in the cases had been intentional. If she wondered it, so would everyone else. The level of fear in Partout Parish was going to be pushed to heights that hadn't been seen in four years. It had been bad enough when Pam Bichon had been killed. But at least a great many people had focused on Renard as the killer. Marcus Renard had been in Our Lady of Mercy when Jennifer Nolan was attacked.

God, what a mess, Annie thought, her gaze on the ground. The sheriff's office had come under enough criticism for the Bichon case. Now they had a masked rapist running around loose, and while Jennifer Nolan was being attacked, the cops had been busy arresting each other.

That was how the press would paint it. And right smack in the middle of that painting would be Annie's own face.

The ground around the back side of the trailer was nothing but weedy gravel for several feet, then the 'estate' gave way to woods with a floor of soft rotted leaves. Annie worked her way from one end of the trailer to the other, looking for anything – a partial footprint, a cigarette butt, a discarded condom. What she found at the north end of the trailer was a fan-shaped black feather about one inch in length, caught in a tuft of grass and dandelions. She took a snapshot of the feather where it lay, then tore a blank sheet of paper from her pocket notebook, folded it around the feather, and slipped it in between the pages of the notebook for safekeeping.

Where had the rapist parked his vehicle? Why had he chosen this place? Why had he chosen Jennifer Nolan? She claimed to have no men in her life. She lived alone and worked the night shift at the True Light lamp factory in Bayou Breaux. The factory would seem the logical starting point to nose around for suspects.

Of course, Annie wasn't going to get the chance to interview anyone but the neighbors. The case belonged to Stokes now. If he wanted help, he sure as hell wouldn't come to her for it. Then again, maybe the rapist *was* a neighbor. A neighbor wouldn't have to worry about hiding his vehicle. A neighbor would be aware of Jennifer Nolan's schedule and the fact that she lived alone. Maybe that KOD duty wouldn't be so boring after all.

The ambulance was driving out of the trailer park as she came around the end of the Nolan home. A woman with a toddler on one hip and cigarette in hand stood in the doorway of a trailer two down the row. At another trailer, a heavyset old guy in his underwear had pulled back a curtain to stare out.

Annie bagged the feather and took it inside. She found Stokes in the bathroom picking pubic hairs out of the tub with a tweezers.

'I found this behind the trailer,' she said, setting the bag on the vanity. 'It looks like the kind of feather they use in masks and costumes. Maybe our bad guy was molting.'

Stokes arched a brow. '*Our?* You got nothing to do with this, Broussard. And what the hell am I supposed to do with a feather?'

'Send it to the lab. Compare it to the mask left on Pam Bichon –'

'Renard did Bichon. That's got nothing to do with this. This is a copycat.'

'Fine, then send it to the lab, get Jennifer Nolan to draw a sketch of the mask the rapist was wearing, and see if you can't track down a manufacturer. Maybe –'

'Maybe you don't know what the hell you're talking about, Broussard,' he said, straightening from the tub. He folded the pubic hairs in a piece of paper and set it on the back of the toilet. 'I told you before, I don't want you around. Get outta here. Go write some tickets. Practice

888

for your new job as a meter maid. That's all you're gonna be, sweetheart. If I'm lyin', I'm dyin'. You don't rat out a brother and stay on the job.'

'Is that a threat?'

He reached out with a forefinger and pressed it hard against the bruise on her cheek. His eyes looked as flat and cold as glass. 'I don't make threats, sugar.'

Annie gritted her teeth against the pain.

'Better get your story straight about what happened with Renard last night,' he said.

'I know exactly what happened.'

Stokes shook his head. 'You chicks just don't know shit about honor, do you?'

She pushed his hand away. 'I know it doesn't involve committing a felony. I'll go talk to those neighbors now.'

9

Nick stood in the pirogue, his gaze focused on a watery horizon, his mind concentrating completely on his slow, precise movements. *Balance . . . grace . . . calm . . . breathe . . . harmonize mind, body, spirit . . . sense the water beneath the boat – fluid, yielding . . . become as the water . . .*

Despite the cool of the day, sweat beaded on his forehead and soaked through his sleeveless gray sweatshirt. Biceps and triceps flexed and trembled as he moved. The strain came not from the Tai Chi form, but from within, from the battle to remain focused.

Move slowly . . . without force . . . without violence . . .

A scene from the night broke his concentration for a heartbeat. *Renard . . . blood . . . force . . . violence . . .* The sense of harmony he had been seeking pulled away from him and was gone. The pirogue jerked beneath his feet. He dropped to the seat of the boat and cradled his head in his hands.

He had built the boat himself from cypress and marine plywood, and painted it green and red like the old swampers had done years ago to identify themselves as serious fishermen and trappers. He had been glad to come back to the swamp. New Orleans was a discordant place. Looking back, he had always felt spiritually fractured there. This was where he had come from: the Atchafalaya – over a million acres of wilderness strung along the edges with a garland of small towns like Bayou Breaux and St. Martinville, and smaller towns like Jeanerette and Breaux Bridge, and places that seemed too small and inconsequential to have names, though they did.

He had passed his boyhood some miles removed from one of those places, on a house barge tethered to the bank of a nameless lake. He remembered his father as a swamper, fishing and trapping, before the oil boom hit and he took a job as a welder and moved the family to Lafayette. They had lived richer there, but not better. Armand Fourcade had confessed more than once he had left a part of his soul in the swamp. Only since coming back had Nick begun to realize what his father had meant. Here he could feel whole and centered. Sometimes.

This was not one of those times.

Reluctantly, he picked up his paddle and started the boat toward home. The sky was hanging low, dulling the color of the swamp, tinting everything a dingy gray: the fragile new lime green leaves of the tupelos that stood like sentinels in the water, the lacy greenery of the willows and hackberry trees that covered the islands, the few yellow-tops that had been tricked into opening by the warmth that had come too early in the season. This day was cool, but if the weather heated up again, the bright flowers would soon crowd the banks, and white-topped daisy fleabane and showy black-eyed Susans would grow down to the water's edge to blend in with the tangles of poison ivy and alligator weed and ratten vine.

The swamp was usually bursting with life in the spring. Today it seemed to be holding its breath. Waiting. Watching.

Just as Nick was waiting. He had set something in motion last night. Every action produces reaction; every challenge, a response. The thing hadn't ended with Gus sending him home. It had hardly begun.

He guided the pirogue through a channel studded with deadhead cypress stumps, and around the narrow point of an island that would double in size when the spring waters receded. His home sat on the bank two hundred yards west, an Acadian relic that had been poorly updated as modern conveniences became available to the people of rural South Louisiana.

He was remodeling the place himself, a room at a time, restoring its charm and replacing cheap fixes with quality. Mindless manual labor afforded an acceptable outlet for the restlessness he once would have tried to douse with liquor.

He spotted the city cruiser immediately. The car sat near his 4X4. A white uniformed officer stood beside the car with a stocky black man in a sharp suit and tie and an air of self-importance discernible even from a distance. Johnny Earl, the chief of the Bayou Breaux PD.

Nick guided the pirogue in alongside the dock and tied it off.

'Detective Fourcade,' Earl said, moving toward the dock, holding his gold shield out ahead of him. 'I'm Johnny Earl, chief of police in Bayou Breaux.'

'Chief,' Nick acknowledged. 'What can I do for you?'

'I think you know why we're here, Detective,' the chief said. 'According to a complaint made this morning by Marcus Renard, you committed a crime last night within the incorporated municipality of Bayou Breaux. Contrary to what Sheriff Noblier seems to think, that's a police matter. I assured DA Pritchett I would see to this myself, even though it pains me to have cause. You're under arrest for the assault of Marcus Renard – and this time it's for real. Cuff him, Tarleton.'

Annie took the stairs to the second floor of the courthouse, trying to imagine how she might escape having a private conversation with A.J. If she could slip into the courtroom just as the case against Hypolite Grangnon was called, then skip as soon as she had testified . . .

She'd had enough confrontations for one day. She hadn't been able to so much as fill her cruiser with gas without getting into it with somebody.

But the capper had been getting called to the Bayou Breaux Police Department.

The interview with Johnny Earl had seemed like the longest hour of her life. He had personally taken charge of the case and personally grilled her like a rack of ribs, trying to get her to admit to having arrested Fourcade at the scene of the incident. She stuck to the story the sheriff had force-fed her, telling herself the whole time that it wasn't that far from the truth. She hadn't heard any radio call about a prowler – because there hadn't been one. She hadn't really arrested Fourcade – because no one else in the department would let her.

Earl hadn't swallowed a word of it. He'd been a cop too long. But busting Noblier's chops over the cover-up was only secondary on his agenda. He had Fourcade in custody and would make as much political hay off that as possible. He didn't need her true confession to make the sheriff look bad, and he knew it. In fact, he might have been just as well off without it. This way he could allege the corruption in the sheriff's office was widespread, reaching into all echelons. He could count her as a co-conspirator.

Conspiracy, giving a false statement. What's next? To what new low can I aspire? Annie asked herself as she turned down the corridor that led past the old courtrooms. *Perjury.* Sooner or later she would be coming to this courthouse to testify against Fourcade.

The hall was clogged with loitering lawyers and social workers and people with vested interests in the cases being heard. The door to Judge Edmonds's courtroom swung open, nearly bowling over a public defender. A.J. stepped into the hall. His gaze immediately homed in on Annie.

'Deputy Broussard, may I see you in my office?' he said.

'B–but the Grangnon trial –'

'Is off. He copped a plea.'

'Swell,' she said without enthusiasm. 'Then I can get back on patrol.'

He leaned close. 'Don't make me drag you, Annie, and don't think I'm not mad enough to do it.'

The secretaries in the outer office of the DA's domain sat up like show dogs as A.J. stormed through, oblivious to their batting eyelashes. He tossed his briefcase into a chair as he entered his own office and slammed the door shut behind Annie.

'Why the hell didn't you call me?' he demanded.

'How the hell *could* I call you, A.J.?'

'You get in the middle of Fourcade trying to kill Renard, and you don't bother to mention that to me? Jesus, Annie, you could have been hurt!'

'I'm a cop. I could be hurt any day of the week.'

'You weren't even on duty!' he ranted, tossing his hands up. 'You told me you were going home! How did this happen?'

'A cruel twist of fate,' she said bitterly. 'I was in the wrong place at the wrong time.'

'That's not quite how Richard Kudrow put it when he dropped this little bomb on Pritchett this morning. He hailed you as a heroine, the only champion for justice in an otherwise morbidly corrupt department.'

'The department is not corrupt,' she said, hating the lie. What was a cover-up of police brutality if not corruption?

'Then why wasn't Fourcade in jail this morning? You arrested him, didn't you? Kudrow claims he saw the report, but there's no report on file at the sheriff's department. What's up with that? Did you arrest him or not?'

'And you wonder why I didn't call you,' Annie muttered, staring to the left of him. Better to look at his diploma from LSU than to lie to his face. 'I can do without this third-degree bullshit, thank you very much.'

'I want to know what happened,' he said, stepping into her field of vision, wise to all her argument strategies. 'I'm concerned about you, Annie. We're friends, right? You're the one who kept saying it last night – we're best friends.'

'Oh yeah, *best friend*,' she said sarcastically. 'Last night we were best friends. And now you're a DA and I'm a deputy, and you're pissed off because you looked bad in front of your boss this morning. That's it, isn't it?'

'Dammit, Annie, I'm serious!'

'So am I! You tell me that isn't true,' she demanded. 'You look me in the eye and tell me you're not trying to use our friendship to get information you couldn't get any other way. You look at me and tell me you would have accosted any other deputy in the hall in front of two dozen people and dragged him in here like a child.'

A.J. snapped his teeth together as he turned his face away. The disappointment that pressed down on Annie was almost as heavy as the inescapable sense of guilt. Hands clamped on top of her head, she walked past him to the window.

'You don't have any idea what I've fallen into,' she murmured, staring out at the parking lot.

'It's simple,' he said. The voice of reason, calm and charming as he came up behind her. 'If you caught Fourcade breaking the law, then he belongs in jail.'

'And I have to testify against him. Rat out another cop – a detective, no less.'

'The law is the law.'

'Right is right. Wrong is wrong,' she said, nodding her head with each beat as she turned to face him once more. 'I'm glad life is so easy for you, A.J.'

'Don't give me that. You believe in the law as much as I do. That's why you stopped Fourcade last night. It's for the courts to mete out

893

punishment, not Nick Fourcade. And you had damn well better testify against him!'

'Don't threaten me,' Annie said quietly. He took a step toward her, already contrite, but she held her hands up and backed away. 'Thanks for your compassion, A.J. You're a real friend, all right. I'm so glad I turned to you in my time of need. I'll look forward to getting your subpoena.'

'Annie, don't –' he started, but she waved him off as she pushed past him. 'Annie, I –'

She slammed the door on whatever he had been about to say. At the same time, the door to Smith Pritchett's corner office flew open and a quartet of angry men bulled their way into the hall, with Pritchett himself in the lead. The chief of police came close on his heels, followed by Kudrow and Noblier. Annie pressed her back against the door to let them pass, her heart tripping as Kudrow nodded to her.

'Deputy Broussard,' he said smoothly. 'Perhaps you should join us in –'

Noblier muscled the lawyer to the side. 'Butt out, Kudrow. I need a word with my deputy.'

'I'm sure you do,' Kudrow said with a chuckle. 'Need I remind you, witness tampering is a serious offense, Noblier?'

'You make me want to puke, lawyer,' Gus snarled. 'You get a murderer off and go after the cops. Somebody oughta turn you ass-end up and knock some decency into you.'

Kudrow shook his head, smile in place. 'You even preach brutality. How the press will prick up their ears when they hear about this.'

'His guts aren't the only thing that's cancerous in him,' Gus grumbled as Kudrow followed the others down the hall. 'That man's soul is black with rot.

'He pulled Pritchett's tail,' he said, seeming to talk to himself. 'That's my fault. I should have called Pritchett myself last night. Now he's got it into his head this is some kind of pissing contest. That man has an ego bigger than my granddaddy's dick.

'And Johnny Earl . . . I don't know who put the bug up his ass. The man is contrary. Doesn't understand the rhythms of life around here. That's what happens when the city council hires outsiders. They bring in Johnny Fucking Earl from Cleveland or some goddamn place where don't nobody know jack about life in this place. The man has an attitude. He thinks I'm some lazy, crooked, racist cracker out of a goddamn movie. Like I don't have blacks working in my department. Like I'm not friends with blacks. Like I didn't win thirty-three percent of the black vote in the last election.'

He turned his attention squarely on Annie with a ferocious scowl as he backed her toward Pritchett's empty office. 'I told you not to talk to Kudrow.'

'I didn't talk to him.'

'Then what's this bullshit he's spewing about an arrest report?' he whispered. 'And how come your sergeant told me he saw the two of you in the goddamn parking lot not twenty feet from the building?'

'I didn't tell him anything.'

'And that's exactly what you're gonna say at this press conference, Deputy. Nothing.'

Annie swallowed hard. 'Press conference?'

'Come on,' he ordered as he strode down the hall.

Pritchett opened the show with a statement about Marcus Renard's alleged attack. He announced Detective Nick Fourcade had been taken into custody by the Bayou Breaux PD. He promised to get to the bottom of the allegations and expressed outrage at the idea of anyone attempting to circumvent the justice system.

Kudrow, looking wan and tragic, quietly reminded everyone of Fourcade's checkered past, and asked that justice be served. 'I will state again my client's innocence. He has been proven guilty of nothing. In fact, while he lay in the hospital last night, put there by Detective Fourcade, the real criminal was at large and may well have committed a brutal rape.'

And then began the feeding frenzy.

The questions and comments of the reporters were pointed and barbed. They had been chasing the story of Renard in one form or another for better than three months with no solid conclusion as to his innocence or guilt. While they couldn't find sympathy for the officers who had endured the same frustration, they didn't hesitate to vent their own. They went after everybody, sided with no one, and homed in on the chance for fresh blood.

'Sheriff, is that true – that another woman was attacked last night?'

'No comment.'

'Deputy Broussard, is it true you formally arrested Detective Fourcade last night?'

Annie squinted into the blinding light of a portable sun gun as Gus nudged her forward. 'Ah – I can't comment.'

'But you *are* the officer who called in the ambulance. You *did* return to the sheriff's department with Detective Fourcade.'

'No comment.'

'Sheriff, if Renard was in the hospital while this other woman was being attacked, doesn't that prove his innocence?'

'No.'

'Then you're confirming the attack occurred?'

'Deputy Broussard, can you confirm taking a statement from Mr Renard at the hospital last night? And if so, why was Detective Fourcade not in custody this morning?'

'Ah – I –'

Gus leaned in front of her at the microphone. 'Detective Fourcade was responding to a report of a prowler in the area. Deputy Broussard was off duty and did not hear the call. She came across a situation she found questionable, contained it, and accompanied Detective Fourcade back to the sheriff's department. It's as simple as that.

'I immediately suspended Detective Fourcade with pay, pending further investigation. And that's where this case stands as far as I'm concerned. My department has nothing to hide, nothing to be ashamed of. If the district attorney wants to have the police investigate the matter, I welcome the scrutiny. I stand behind my people one hundred percent, and that's all I have to say on the matter.'

Pritchett stepped back up to the microphone, determined to have the last word, while Gus herded Annie away from the podium toward the door. Annie kept at Noblier's heels like a faithful dog and wondered if that made her some kind of hypocrite. She expected the sheriff to protect her but not Fourcade. *I didn't try to kill anyone. All I did was lie and file a false report.*

Disgusted with herself, with her boss, with the vultures trying to pick at her on the fly as she made her escape from the courthouse and went to her cruiser, she kept her mouth shut and her eyes forward. The mob split into factions then, some of them running back up the courthouse steps as Kudrow emerged, some trailing after Noblier as he drove away in his Suburban. Half a dozen tailed Annie to the law enforcement center and chased her across the parking lot to the officers' entrance to the building.

Hooker stood in the foyer, staring out at the show, arms crossed over his round belly. 'Where's the follow-up report on that cemetery vandalism?'

'I turned it in two days ago.'

'The hell you did.'

'I did!'

'Well, I don't have it, Broussard,' he stated. 'Do it again. Today.'

'Yes, sir,' Annie said, biting down on the urge to call him a liar. Hooker was an asshole, but fair in that he usually treated everyone with equal disrespect.

'Like it's not bad enough to have to do paperwork once,' she grumbled as she came up on the briefing room. 'I get to do mine twice.'

'Who you want to do twice, Broussard?' Mullen sneered. He and Prejean stood in the hall, drinking coffee. 'Your little pervert friend, Renard? I hear when he nails a woman, she stays nailed to the floor.' He snickered, flashing his bad teeth.

'Very funny, Mullen,' Annie said. 'And in such good taste. Maybe you could get a job doing stand-up comedy down at the funeral home.'

'I'm not the one gonna be looking for a job, Broussard,' he returned. 'We heard about you going over to the townies to suck Johnny Earl's dick.'

'I hate to spoil your sordid daydreams, but I didn't go over there because I wanted to, and the chief wasn't exactly happy when I left.'

Mullen smirked. 'Can't even get a blow job right?'

'You'll sure as hell never find out.'

Annie looked to Prejean, who was usually quick with a smile and a smart remark when she bested Mullen. He looked at her now as if he didn't know her. The snub hurt.

'That's okay, Prejean,' she said. 'It's not like I ever covered for you when your wife was working nights and you wanted a little extra time at lunch to, shall we say, satisfy your appetite.'

Prejean looked at his shoes. Annie shook her head and walked away. She needed ten minutes alone, just to sit down and regroup. Ten minutes to marshal her disappointment and corral the fear that was beginning to skitter around inside her. She had fallen into a deep hole and no one was reaching in to help her out. Instead, the men she had thought were her comrades stood around the rim, ready to kick dirt on her.

She headed for her locker room. But she knew before she even set foot inside that her sanctuary had been breached.

The smell hit her as she turned the doorknob – sickening, rotten. She flipped the light switch and barely managed to clamp her hand over her mouth before the scream could escape.

Hanging from a length of brown twine tied to the single bulb in the ceiling, the cord knotted together with its long, skinny tail, was a dead muskrat.

The muskrat had been skinned from the base of its tail to the base of its skull, the pelt left dangling down past its head. Annie stared at it, nausea rising up her esophagus. Air currents and the weight of its body twisted the rodent to and fro like a grotesque mobile. One hind leg was missing, suggesting the muskrat had met its untimely end in the steel jaws of a trap, as thousands did every year in South Louisiana.

Aware that her tormentor could have been watching through a fresh hole in the wall, Annie moved toward the muskrat, then stepped around it. She took in every detail – the knotted tail, the naked muscle, the piece of paper that had been stabbed to the corpse with a nail.

The note read: *Turncoat bitch.*

10

Broussard ratted you out,' Stokes said, curling his fingers through the wire mesh of the holding cell. 'Man, I can't believe she did this to you. I mean, it's one thing that she won't sleep with me. Some women are just masochists that way. But ratting out another cop . . . man, that's low.'

Stokes shouldn't have been allowed into the city jail holding cells. At least not as a visitor. Prisoners in holding had the right to see their attorneys, and that was all. But, as always, Stokes had known somebody and talked his way in.

'Goddamn, you think maybe she's a lesbian?' he asked, as the idea struck him.

An image of Annie Broussard came to Nick as he prowled his cell – her eyes widening, a hint of a blush spreading across her cheeks as he reached out and passed his hand too close to her.

'I don't care,' he said.

'Maybe you don't, but she's just taken on a whole new role in my fantasy life,' Stokes admitted. 'Damn, but I've always had a thing for lesbians. Pretty ones,' he qualified. 'Not the butch dykes. Don't you ever picture beautiful women naked together? Man, that gets my dick twitching.'

'She arrested me,' Nick stated flatly, impatient with Stokes. The man had no focus.

'Well, yeah, she'll be a bad lesbian in my fantasies. A black leather bitch with a whip. Man hater.'

'How'd she happen to be there?' Nick asked.

'Damn bad luck, that's for sure.'

Nick had mixed feelings about that. If Annie Broussard hadn't come along, he would have killed Renard. She had, in fact, saved him from himself, and for that he was thankful. But her motives troubled him.

'She thinks I should be held accountable.'

Maybe it was as simple as that. Maybe she was that idealistic. Having never been an idealist himself, he had a hard time accepting the prospect. In his experience, people were usually motivated by one thing: self-gain. They could couch their intentions in a million different guises, give no end of excuses, but most everything came down to one thought: *What's in it for me?* What was in it for Annie Broussard? Why had she suddenly popped up in his life?

'She's a pain in the ass,' Stokes said. 'Little Miss By-the-Book. I caught a rape case this morning out in that white-trash trailer park going toward Luck. She's out there butting into every damn thing. "You gonna send that nose hair to the lab?" ' he mocked in a high falsetto. ' "Maybe it's rapist nose hair. Maybe this guy did Bichon. Maybe he's the Bayou Strangler." '

'What made her think it was tied to Bichon?'

Chaz rolled his eyes. 'The guy wore a mask. Like that's an original idea. Christ,' he muttered. 'Whoever thought they should let broads on the job?'

He glanced over his shoulder, checking the door. The city jail was about a thousand years old and had no surveillance cameras in its holding cell areas. City cops had to listen in on conversations the old-fashioned way.

'Well, she's damn near the only one who thinks you should pay for this, man,' he muttered. 'Not even God himself would call you on it. An eye for an eye, you know what I mean?'

'I know what you mean. I'm supposed to be an avenging angel.'

'Hell, you should have been the Invisible Man. No one would have been the wiser if Broussard hadn't stuck her nose in it. Renard would be roasting in hell, case closed.'

'That's what you thought?' Nick said softly, stepping toward the chain-link that caged him in. 'When you called me at Laveau's – you thought I'd go over to Bowen and Briggs and kill him?'

'Jesus!' Stokes hissed. 'Keep your voice down!'

Nick leaned close to the wire mesh, slipping his fingers through just above Stokes's. 'Whatsa matter, *pard*?' he whispered. 'You worried about a conspiracy beef?'

Stokes jerked back, looking shocked, offended, hurt even. 'Conspiracy? Shit, man, we were drunk and talking trash. Even when I called you and told you he was over there, I never thought you'd really do it! I'm just saying I wouldn't blame you if you had. I mean, good riddance – am I right or am I right?'

'You're the one wanted to go to that particular bar.'

' 'Cause no one else hangs there, man! You can't think I was setting you up! Jesus, Nicky! We're brothers of the badge, man. I'm the closest thing to a friend you got. I don't know how you can even think it. It wounds me, Nicky. Truly.'

'*I'll* wound you, Chaz. I find out you fucked me over, you'll wish your mama and daddy never got past first base.'

Stokes stepped away from the cell. 'I don't believe what I'm hearing. Man oh man! Stop being so fuckin' paranoid. I'm not your enemy here.' He tapped his breastbone with one long forefinger. 'Hell, I called you a lawyer. The guys are gonna cover it. They all agreed –'

'I pay my own way.'

'You didn't do anything the rest of us hadn't had wet dreams about for the last three months.'

'What lawyer?'

'Wily Tallant from St Martinville.'

'That bastard –'

'– is slick as snot,' Stokes finished. 'Don't think of him as being on the other side of the fence. Think of him as the man who's gonna open the gate so you can get back on your own side. That ol' boy can make Lucifer look like the poor misunderstood neglected child of a dysfunctional family. By the time he's through, you'll probably end up with a commendation and the keys to the fucking city, which is what you deserve.'

He leaned toward the mesh again, slipping a hand inside his jacket and pulling out a cigarette like a magician. 'That's all I want, pard,' he said, passing the cigarette through the wire. 'I want everybody to get what they deserve.'

Annie stayed in the locker room for twenty minutes fighting to compose herself. Twenty minutes of staring at that skinned muskrat.

There was no way of knowing where it had come from or who had hung it, not without questioning people, looking for witnesses, making a fuss. Mullen was a sound bet, but she knew a half dozen deputies who did some trapping for extra income. Still, skinning would have been Mullen's touch. Annie had always pegged him for the sort of kid who had pulled the wings off flies.

Turncoat bitch.

Holding her breath against the sweet–putrid scent of decaying rodent, she cut the thing down with her pocketknife and grimaced as it hit the floor with a soft thud. She tore up the note, then pilfered a cardboard box from the garbage in the office supply room and used it for a coffin. She had no intention of taking the thing to Noblier and making a bad situation worse. And there was no leaving it. After she rewrote her final report on the cemetery vandalism and filed it, she grabbed the box and her duffel bag and left. She could toss the corpse in the woods after she got home, and Mother Nature would give it a proper disposal.

The drive home usually calmed her after a bad day. Today it only made her feel more alienated. Daylight was nearly gone, casting the world in the strange gray twilight of bad dreams. The woods looked forbidding, uninviting; the cane fields were vast, unpopulated seas of green. Lamps burned in the windows of the houses she passed; inside families were together, eating supper, watching television.

Always in times like this, she became acutely aware of her lack of a traditional family. This was when the memories crept up from childhood: her mother sitting in a rocking chair looking out at the swamp, a wraithlike woman, surreal, pale, detached, never quite in the present.

There had always been a distance between Marie Broussard and the world around her. Annie had been keenly aware of it and frightened by it, fearing that one day her mother would just slip away into another dimension and she would be left alone. Which was exactly what had happened.

She had had Uncle Sos and Tante Fanchon to look after her, and she couldn't have loved them more, but there was always, would always be, a place inside her where she felt like an orphan, disconnected, separate from the people around her . . . as her mother had been. The door to that place was wide open tonight.

'You're on the air with Owen Onofrio, KJUN, all talk all the time. Home of the giant jackpot giveaway. We're up over nine hundred dollars now. What lucky listener will pocket that check? It could happen any time, any day.

'On our agenda tonight: Murder suspect Marcus Renard was allegedly attacked and beaten last night by a Partout Parish sheriff's detective. What do you have to say about that, Kay on line one?'

'I say there ain't no justice, that's what I say. The world's gone crazy. They put that dead woman's daddy in jail, too, and everyone I know says he's a hero for trying to do what the courts wouldn't. Killers and rapists have more rights than decent people. It's crazy!'

Annie switched the radio off as she turned in at the Corners. There were three cars in the crushed shell lot. Uncle Sos's pickup, the night clerk's rusty Fiesta, and off to one side, a shiny maroon Grand Am that made her groan aloud. A.J.

She sat for a moment just staring at the place she had called home her whole life: a simple two-story wood-frame building with a corrugated tin roof. The wide front window acted as a billboard, with half a dozen various ads and messages for products and services. A red neon sign for Bud, a placard that read ICI ON PARLE FRANÇAIS, another sign handwritten in Magic Marker HOT BOUDIN & CRACKLINS.

The first floor of the building housed the business Sos Doucet had run for forty years. Originally a general store that served area swampers and their families who had come in by boat once or twice a month, it had evolved with the times and economic necessity into a landing for swamp tours, a café, and a convenience store that did its biggest business on the weekends when fishermen and hunters – 'sports,' Uncle Sos called them – stocked up to head out into the Atchafalaya basin. The tourists loved the rustic charm of the scarred old cypress floor and ancient, creaking ceiling fans. The locals were happier with the commercial refrigerators that kept their beer cold and handy, and the two-for-one movie rentals on Monday night.

The second-floor apartment had been home to Sos and Fanchon during the first years of their marriage. Prosperity had allowed them to build a little ranch-style brick house a hundred yards away, and in 1968 they had rented the apartment to Marie Broussard, who had shown up on the porch one day, pregnant and forlorn, as mysterious as any of the stray cats that had come to make their home at the Corners.

''Bout time you got home, *chère*!' Uncle Sos called, leaning out the screen door.

Annie climbed out of the Jeep with her duffel bag strapped over one shoulder and the muskrat box in her other hand.

'What you got in the box? Supper?'

'Not exactly.'

Sos came out onto the porch, barefoot, in jeans and a white shirt with the sleeves rolled halfway up his sinewy forearms. He wasn't a tall man, but even at sixtysomething his shoulders suggested power. His belly was as flat as an anvil, his skin perpetually tan, his face creased in places like fine old leather. People told him he resembled the actor Tommy Lee Jones, which always brought a sparkle to his eyes and the retort that, hell no, Tommy Lee Jones resembled *him*, the lucky son of a bitch.

'You got comp'ny, *chère*,' Sos said with a sly grin that nearly made his eyes disappear. 'Andre, he's here to see you.' He lowered his voice in conspiracy as she stepped up onto the porch. His face was aglow. 'Y'all had a little lovers' spat, no?'

'We're not lovers, Uncle Sos.'

'Bah!'

'Not that it's any of your business, by the way, for the hundredth time.'

He jerked his chin back and looked offended. 'How is that not my business?'

'I'm a grown-up,' she reminded him.

'Then you smart enough to marry dat boy, *mais* no?'

'Will you *ever* give up?'

'Mebbe,' he said, pulling open the screen door for her. 'Mebbe when you make me a grandpapa.'

A bouquet of red roses and baby's breath sat on the corner of the checkout counter, as out of place as a Ming vase. The night clerk, a crater-faced kid as skinny as a licorice whip, was running *Speed* on the VCR.

'Hey, Stevie,' Annie called.

'Hey, Annie,' he called back, never taking his eyes off the set. 'What's in the box?'

'Severed hand.'

'Cool.'

'Aren't you gonna say hello to Andre?' Sos said irritably. 'After he come all the way out here. After he sent you flowers and all.'

A.J. had the grace to look sheepish. He leaned back against a display counter of varnished alligator heads and other equally gruesome artifacts that titillated the tourists. He hadn't changed out of his suit, but had shed his tie and opened the collar of his shirt.

'I don't know,' Annie said. 'Should I have my lawyer present?'

'I was out of line,' he conceded.

'Try left field. On the warning track.'

'See, *chère*?' Sos smiled warmly, motioning her to close the distance. 'Andre, he knows when he's licked. He come to kiss and make up.'

Annie refused to be charmed. 'Yeah? Well, he can kiss my butt.'

Sos arched a brow at him. 'Hey, that's a start.'

'I'm tired,' Annie declared, turning back for the door. 'Good night.'

'Annie!' A.J. called. She could hear him coming behind her as she rounded the corner of the porch and started up the staircase to her apartment. 'You can't just keep running away from me.'

'I'm not running away. I'm trying to ignore you, which, I promise you, is preferable to the alternative. I'm not very happy with you at the moment –'

'I said I was sorry.'

'No, you said you were out of line. An admission of wrongdoing is not an apology.'

Two cats darted around her feet and onto the landing, meowing. A calico hopped up on the railing and leaned longingly toward the muskrat box. Annie held it out of reach as she opened the door. She hadn't intended to bring the thing into her apartment, but she couldn't very well dispose of it with A.J. breathing down her neck.

She set the box and her duffel on the small bench in the entry and proceeded past the telephone stand in the living room, where the light on her answering machine was blinking like an angry red eye. She could only imagine what was waiting for her on the tape. Reporters, relatives, and disgruntled strangers calling to express their opinions and/or try to wheedle information out of her. She walked past the machine and went into the kitchen, flipping on the lights.

A.J. followed, setting the vase of roses on the chrome-legged kitchen table.

'I'm sorry. I *am*,' he said. 'I shouldn't have jumped all over you about Fourcade, but I was worried for you, honey.'

'And it had nothing to do with you being caught flat-footed with Pritchett.'

He sighed through his nose. 'All right. I admit, the news caught me off guard, and, yes, I thought you should have told me because of our relationship. I would like to think that you would turn to me in that kind of situation.'

'So that you could turn to Smith Pritchett and spill it all, like a good lieutenant.'

Annie stood on the opposite side of the table, her lower back pressing against the edge of the counter at the sink.

'This is just another example of why this relationship thing isn't going to work out,' she said, her voice going a little rusty under pressure. 'Here I am and there you are and there's this – this – *stuff* between us.' She used her hands to illustrate her point. 'My job and your job, and when is it about the job and when is it about us. I don't want to deal with it, A.J. I'm sorry. I don't. Not now.'

Not now, when she suddenly found herself caught up in the storm Fourcade had created. She needed all her wits about her just to keep her head above water.

'I don't think this is the best time for us to have this conversation,' A.J. said softly, coming toward her, gentleness and affection on his face. 'It's been a rough day. You're tired, I'm tired. I just don't want us mad at each other. We're too good friends for that. Kiss and make up?' he whispered.

She let her eyes close as he settled his mouth against hers. She didn't try to stop her own lips from moving or her arms from sneaking around his waist. He pulled her closer, and it seemed as natural as breathing. His body was strong, warm. His size made her feel small and safe.

It would have been easy to go to bed with him, to find comfort and oblivion in passion. A.J. enjoyed the role of lover-protector. She knew exactly how good it felt to let him take that part. And she knew she couldn't go there tonight. Sex would solve nothing, complicate everything. Her life had gotten complicated enough.

A.J. felt her enthusiasm cool. He raised his head an inch or two. 'You know, you can hurt a guy making him stop like this.'

'That's a lie,' Annie said, appreciating his attempt at humor.

'Says who?'

'Says you. You told me that when I was a sophomore and Jason Benoit was trying to convince me I would cripple him for life if I didn't let him go all the way.'

'Yeah, well, *I* would've crippled him if he had.' He touched the tip of her nose with his forefinger. 'Friends again?'

'Always.'

'Who ever thought life could be so complicated?'

'Not you.'

'That's a fact.' He glanced at his watch. 'Well, I suppose I should go home and take a cold shower or page through the Victoria's Secret catalog or something.'

'No work?' Annie asked, following him to the door.

'Tons. You don't want to hear about it.'

'Why not?'

He turned and faced her, serious. 'Fourcade's bond hearing tomorrow.'

'Oh.'

'Told you so.' He started to open the door, then hesitated. 'You know, Annie, you're gonna have to decide whose side you're on in this thing.'

'I'm either for you or against you?'

'You know what I mean.'

'Yeah,' she admitted, 'but I don't want to talk about it tonight.'

A.J. accepted that with a nod. 'If you decide you do want to talk, and you want to talk to a friend . . . we'll work around the rest.'

Annie kept her doubts to herself. A.J. pulled the door open, and three cats darted into the entry and pounced on the muskrat box, growling.

'What *is* in that box?'

'Dead muskrat.'

'Jeez, Broussard, anybody ever tell you you've got a morbid sense of humor?'

'A million times, but I'm also in denial.'

He smiled and winked at her as he stepped out onto the landing. 'I'll see you around, kiddo. I'm glad we're friends again.'

'Me, too,' Annie murmured. 'And thanks for the flowers.'

'Ah – sorry.' He pulled a face. 'I didn't send them. Uncle Sos assumed . . .'

Annie held a hand up. ''Nough said. That's okay. I wouldn't expect you to.'

'But feel free to let me know who did, so I can go punch the guy in the nose.'

'Please. One assault a week is my limit.'

He leaned down and brushed a kiss to her cheek. 'Lock your door. There's bad guys running around out there.'

She shooed the cats out of the entry and went back into the apartment. The bouquet sat dead center on her kitchen table, looking almost as out of place there as it had in the store. Her apartment was a place for wildflowers in jelly jars, not the elegance of roses. She plucked the white envelope from its plastic stem and extracted the card.

Dear Ms Broussard,

I hope you don't think roses inappropriate, but you saved my life and I want to thank you properly.

Yours truly,
Marcus Renard

11

He wondered what she'd thought of the flowers. She should have seen them by now. She worked the day shift. He knew because the news reports about his beating identified her as 'an off-duty sheriff's deputy.' She had been on duty at the courthouse yesterday, and had helped save him from Davidson's attack. She had been on duty the morning Pam's body had been found. She had been the one to find it.

There was a thread of continuity running through all this, Marcus reflected as he gazed out the window of his workroom. He had been in love with Pam; Annie had discovered Pam's body. Pam's father had tried to kill him; Annie had stopped him. The detective in charge of Pam's case had tried to kill him; Annie had again come to his rescue. *Continuity.* In his drug-numbed mind he pictured the letters of the word unraveling and tying themselves into a perfect circle, a thin black line with no beginning and no ending. *Continuity.*

He moved his pencil over the paper with careful, featherlight strokes. Fourcade hadn't damaged his hands. There were bruises – defensive wounds – and his knuckles had been skinned when he fell to the ground, but nothing worse. His eyes were still nearly swollen shut. Cotton packing filled both nostrils, forcing him to breathe through his mouth, the air hissing in and out between his chipped teeth because his broken jaw had been wired shut. Stitches crisscrossed his face like seams in a crazy quilt. He looked like a gargoyle, like a monster.

The doctor had given him a prescription for painkillers and sent him home late in the day. None of his injuries were life-threatening or needed further monitoring, for which he was glad. He had no doubt the nurses at Our Lady of Mercy would have killed him if given ample opportunity.

The Percodan dulled the throbbing in his head and face, and took the bite out of the knifing pains in his side where Fourcade had cracked three of his ribs. It also seemed to blur the edges of all sensory perception. He felt insulated, as if he were existing inside a bubble. The volume of his mother's voice had been cut in half. Victor's incessant muttering had been reduced to a low hum.

They had both been right there when Richard Kudrow brought him home. Agitated and irritated by the interruption of their routines.

'Marcus, you had me worried sick,' his mother said as he made his way painfully up one step and then another onto the veranda.

Doll stood leaning against a pillar, as if she hadn't the strength to keep herself upright. As tall as both her sons, she still gave the impression of being a birdlike woman, fine boned, almost frail. She had a habit of fluttering one hand against her breastbone like a broken wing. Despite the fact that she was an excellent seamstress, she wore dowdy five-and-dime housedresses that swallowed her up and made her look older than her fiftysome years.

'I didn't know what to think when the hospital called. I was just terrified you might die. I barely slept for worrying on it. What would I do without you? How would I cope with Victor? I was nearly ill with worry.'

'I'm not dead, Mother,' Marcus pointed out.

He didn't ask why she hadn't come to the hospital to see him, because he didn't want to hear how she hated to drive, especially at night – on account of her undiagnosed night blindness. Never mind that she had hounded him to buy her a car years ago so that she wouldn't have to feel dependent upon him. She rarely took the thing out of the carriage shed they used as a garage. And he didn't want to hear how she was afraid to leave Victor, and how she disliked hospitals and believed them to be the breeding grounds for all fatal disease. The last would set Victor off into his germ litany.

His brother stood to one side of the door, his face turned away, but his eyes glancing back at Marcus, wary. Victor had a way of holding himself that was stiff and slightly cockeyed, as if gravity affected him differently from normal people.

'It's me, Victor,' Marcus said, knowing it was hopeless to attempt to put Victor at ease.

Victor had been in his teens before he figured out that putting on a hat didn't turn one person into another being. Voices coming from a telephone had baffled him into his twenties, and sometimes still did. For years he would never do anything more than breathe into the receiver because he couldn't see the person speaking to him, and, therefore, that person did not exist. Only crazy people responded to the voices of people who did not exist, and Victor was not crazy; therefore, he would not speak to faceless voices.

'Mask, no mask,' he mumbled. 'The mockingbird. *Mimus polyglottos*. Nine to eleven inches tall. No mask. Sound and sound alike. More common than similar shrikes. The common raven. *Corvus corax*. Very clever. Very shrewd. Like the crow, but not a crow. A mask, but no mask.'

'Victor, stop it!' Doll said, her voice scratching up toward shrillness. She sent Marcus a long-suffering look. 'He's been on his rantings all day long. I'd like to have lost my mind worrying about you, and here was Victor droning on and on and on. It was enough to make me see red.'

907

'Red, red, very red,' Victor said, shaking his head as if a bug had crawled into his ear.

'That lawyer of yours had better make the sheriff's department pay for the suffering they've caused this family,' Doll harped, following Marcus into the house. 'Those people are rotten to the core, every last one of them.'

'Annie Broussard saved my life,' Marcus pointed out. 'Twice.'

Doll made a sour face. 'Annie Broussard. I'm sure she's no better than any of the rest. I saw her on the television. She didn't have a thing to say about you. You blow everything out of proportion, Marcus. You always have.'

'I was there, Mother. I know what she did.'

'You just think she's pretty, that's all. I know how your mind works, Marcus. You are your father's son.'

It was meant to be an insult. Marcus didn't remember his father. Claude Renard had left them when Marcus was hardly more than a toddler. He had never come back, had severed all ties. There were times when Marcus envied him.

He closed his eyes now and let a wave of Percodan wash the memory from his battered brain. The miracles of modern chemistry.

He had gone straight to his bedroom and shut out his mother's incessant whining with a pill and two hours of unconsciousness. When he came to, the house was quiet. Everyone had settled back into their routines. His mother retreated to her room every night at nine to watch television preachers and work her word puzzles. She would be in bed by ten and would complain all the next morning that she had barely slept. According to Doll, she hadn't slept through a night in her life.

Victor went to bed at eight and rose at midnight to study his nature books or work on elaborate mathematical calculations. He would go to bed again at four a.m. and rise for the day precisely at eight. Routine was sacred to him. He equated routine with normalcy. The least deviation could set him off into a spell of upset, causing him to rock himself and mumble, or worse. Routine made him happy.

If only my own life were so simple. Marcus didn't like being the center of anyone's attention. He preferred to be left alone to do his work and to work at his hobbies.

His workroom was located just off his bedroom and had probably been a study or a nursery at one time in the house's history. He had claimed the small suite as his own the first time he had walked through the house with Pam. She had been his real estate agent when he had come to Bayou Breaux to interview with Bowen & Briggs – another strand in the thread of continuity.

The suite was on the first floor at the back of the house and you had to walk through one room to get to the other. A worktable held his latest project, a Queen Anne dollhouse with elaborate gingerbread and heart-shaped shingles on the roof. Houses he had designed and built over the years were displayed on deep custom-built shelves along one long wall. He entered them in competitions at fairs and sold all but the most special to him.

But it wasn't the dollhouse that claimed his attention tonight. Tonight he had risen from bed to sit at his drawing table. He worked to bring a mental image from his mind to the page.

Pam had been a lovely woman – small, feminine, her dark hair cut in a sleek, shoulder-length bob, her smile bright, her brown eyes sparkling with life. She had her nails done every Friday. She shopped at the most exclusive stores in Lafayette, and always looked as if she had just stepped from the pages of *Southern Living* or *Town and Country*.

Annie was pretty in her own way. She was taller than Pam, but by no more than an inch; sturdier than Pam, but still small. He pictured her, not in the slate blue sheriff's department uniform, but in the long, flowered skirt she had worn last night. He rid her of the sloppy denim jacket and put her instead in a white cotton camisole. Delicate, almost sheer, teasing him with the shadows of her small breasts.

In his mind's eye, he combed her hair back neatly and secured it at the nape of her slender neck with a white bow. She had a retroussé nose; a hint of a cleft gave her chin a certain stubborn quality. Her eyes were a deep, rich brown, like Pam's, but with a tantalizing tilt at the corners. He was fascinated with the shape of them – slightly exotic, slightly almond-shaped, like a cat's. Her mouth was nearly as intriguing. A very French mouth – the lower lip full, the upper lip a delicate cupid's bow. He had never seen her smile. Until he had, he would superimpose Pam's smile onto her face.

He set his pencil aside and assessed his work.

He had missed Pam these past three months, but he could feel the ache of that loneliness beginning to subside. In his drug-induced haze, he visualized having been parched all that time. Now a fresh source of wine was ebbing closer, tantalizing him. He tried to imagine the taste on his tongue. Desire stirred lazily in his blood, and he smiled.

Annie. His angel.

12

Bail hearings in Partout Parish were held Monday, Wednesday, and Friday mornings, a schedule carefully structured to produce revenue. Anyone bailed out on Friday had the weekend to break another law or two, for which they would have to be bailed out again come Monday. Wednesday was thrown in for good measure and civil liberties.

The presiding judge, as luck would have it, was old Monahan. Nick groaned inwardly as Monahan emerged from his chambers and took his seat on the bench. Cases were called. A mixed bag of petty offenses on this Friday morning: drunk and disorderly, shoplifting, possession with intent to distribute, burglary. The defendants, their eyes downcast like dogs that had been caught soiling the carpet, stood beside their lawyers. Some of the accused looked ashamed, some embarrassed, some were just used to playing the game.

The gallery of the courtroom filled steadily as the cases were dealt with in short order, one scumbag loser at a time. If these people going before him were losers, Nick thought, then what did that make him? Every person who came before the court claimed to have a good reason for what he or she had done. None was as good as his, but he doubted getting up and telling the court he had only done the job the court had shirked would win him any points with Monahan.

The esteemed members of the press filling the pews behind him were no doubt drooling for precisely that kind of dramatic statement. They waited restlessly through the preliminary goings-on, eager for the main event. Monahan seemed irritated by their presence, his mood more churlish than usual. He barked at the attorneys, snapped at the defendants, and set bail amounts at the high end of the spectrum.

Nick had exactly three thousand two hundred dollars in the bank.

'Don't piss off His Honor, Nick, my boy,' Wily Tallant murmured, leaning toward Nick. 'I do believe he's got an Irish headache today. Don't meet his eyes. If you can't look contrite, look contemplative.'

Nick looked away. Tallant was a sly, scheming bastard – good qualities in a defense attorney, but that didn't mean he had to like the man. He only had to listen to him.

The lawyer was nearly a head shorter than Nick, with a lean, European elegance about him. His thin, dark hair was slicked back neatly, accentuating the distinguished lines of his face. He wore black suits year-round and a Rolex that cost more than Nick made in four months. Wily's clients may have been scumbags, but they tended to be scumbags with money.

Nick scanned the crowd again. A number of cops had found their way into the balcony that had been the gallery for black spectators in the days of open segregation. He spotted a couple of sheriff's deputies, a couple of Bayou Breaux uniforms. Broussard was not among them. He thought she might have come. This was what she wanted: him facing the music.

In the balcony front row, Stokes touched the brim of the ball cap he wore low over a pair of Ray-Bans. Quinlan, another of the SO detectives, sat beside him, along with Z-Top McGee, a detective from the city squad they had worked with a time or two.

It struck Nick as odd that anyone other than Stokes had come. He had spent no time cultivating friendships here. More likely their attachment to him was through the job. The Brotherhood. He was one of them, and here but for the grace of God . . . Ultimately, their concern was for themselves, he decided. A comforting cynical thought.

He dropped his gaze to the main gallery seating, skimming the faces of the reporters who had hounded him from the outset of the Bichon case, and one who had hounded him longer than that – a face familiar from New Orleans. New Orleanians generally cared little what went on beyond the boundaries of the Big Easy. The Cajun parishes were a separate world. But this one had smelled Nick's blood in the water and had come hungry. Unexpected, but not surprising.

The surprises sat ahead of the New Orleans hack. Belle Davidson and, two rows in front of her, her erstwhile son-in-law, Donnie Bichon. What were they doing here? Hunter Davidson was not among the unfortunate waiting their turn before the judge. Pritchett would want to downplay that bail hearing. Pressing charges against a grieving father would be unpopular with his constituents. Pressing charges against 'a rogue cop' for the same crime was an altogether different matter.

'State of Lou'siana versus Nick Fourcade!'

Nick followed Tallant through the gate to the defense table. Pritchett had remained silent through the previous proceedings, letting ADA Doucet deal with the petty stuff, saving himself for the feature attraction. He rose from his chair and buttoned his suit coat, twitching his shoulders back and smoothing a hand over his silk tie. He looked like a little gamecock preening his feathers and scratching the dirt before a fight.

'Your Honor,' he intoned loudly. 'The charges here are extremely egregious: aggravated assault and attempted murder perpetrated by a member of the law enforcement community. We're dealing not only with a felony, but with a gross abuse of power and a betrayal of the public trust. It's an absolute disgrace. I –'

'Save your preaching for another pulpit, Mr Pritchett,' Judge Monahan barked as he snapped the cap off a bottle of Excedrin and dumped a pair of pills into his hand.

The judge glared at Nick, black eyebrows creeping down over piercing blue eyes.

'Detective Fourcade, I cannot begin to express my disgust at having you before my bench on this matter. You have managed to turn an ugly situation hideous, and I am not inclined to be forgiving. Could you possibly have anything to say for yourself?'

Wily leaned forward, his fingertips just resting on the defense table. 'Revon Tallant for the defense. Your Honor, my client wishes to enter a plea of not guilty at this time.' He enunciated each word as precisely as a poet. 'As usual, Mr Pritchett has jumped to all manner of extreme conclusions without having heard the facts of the situation. Detective Fourcade was simply going about the business of his job –'

'Beating the snot out of people?' Pritchett said.

'Apprehending a suspected burglar, who chose to resist arrest and fight.'

'Resist and fight? The man had to be hospitalized!' Pritchett shouted. 'He looks like he ran headlong into a steel beam!'

'I never said he was good at it.'

Laughter rippled through the gallery. Monahan banged his gavel. 'This is not a humorous matter!'

'I quite agree, Your Honor,' Pritchett said. 'We had ought to take a dim view of law enforcement officers crossing the line into vigilantism. A sheriff's deputy caught Detective Fourcade red-handed – in the literal sense. She will testify –'

'This isn't the trial, Mr Pritchett,' Monahan cut in. 'I am in no mood to listen to lawyers go on and on for the benefit of the press and the sheer love of the sound of their own voices. Get on with it!'

'Yes, Your Honor.' Pritchett swallowed his pride, his cheeks tinting pink. 'In view of the seriousness of the charges and the brutality of the crime, the state requests bail in the amount of one hundred thousand dollars.'

The words hit Nick like a ball bat.

Wily tossed his head back and rolled his big sloe eyes. 'Your Honor, Mr Pritchett's predilection for drama aside –'

'Your client is a law enforcement officer who stands accused of beating a man senseless, Mr Tallant,' Monahan said sharply. 'That's all the drama I need.' He consulted his clerk for his schedule, shaking the Excedrin tablets in his hand like a pair of dice. 'Preliminary hearing set for two weeks from yesterday. Bail in the amount of one hundred thousand dollars, cash or bond. Pay the clerk if you can. Next case!'

Nick and Tallant moved away from the defense table as the next defendant and his attorney came in. Nick stared at Pritchett across the room. The DA's small mouth was screwed into a self-satisfied smirk.

'I'll have Monahan recused from the case before the hearing,' Wily murmured, moving with Nick toward the side door, where a city cop waited to escort him back to jail. 'He's obviously too biased to hear the case. However, there's nothing I can do about Pritchett. That man wants your head on a pike, my boy. You made him look bad with that unfortunate evidentiary matter the other day. That's a felony in Smith Pritchett's book. Can you make bail?'

'Hell, Wily, I can barely pay you. I might get ten thousand if I hock everything I own,' Nick said absently, his attention suddenly on the gallery.

Donnie Bichon had risen from his seat and came forward, lifting a hand tentatively, like an uncertain schoolboy trying to attract the teacher's attention. He was a handsome kid – thirty-six going on twenty – with a short nose and ears that stuck out just enough to make him perpetually boyish. He had played third-string forward at Tulane and had a tendency to walk with his shoulders slightly hunched, as if he were ready to drive to the basket at any second. Everyone on the business side of the bar stopped what they were doing to look at him.

'Your Honor? May I approach the bench?'

Monahan glared at him. 'Who are you, sir?'

'Donnie Bichon, Your Honor. I'd like to pay Detective Fourcade's bail.'

Construction business must be doing better than I thought,' Nick said, moving around Donnie Bichon's office, rolling a toothpick between his teeth.

He had allowed the drama in the courtroom to unfold, not because he wanted Bichon's money, but because he wanted to know the motive behind the magnanimous gesture.

The press had gone wild. Headline frenzy. Monahan had ordered the courtroom cleared. Smith Pritchett had stormed from the room in a fit of temper at having his thunder stolen. After Donnie paid the clerk, they had all run the media gauntlet out of the courthouse and down the steps. Déjà vu all over again.

Nick had jumped into Wily's money green Infiniti and they had driven clear to New Iberia to shake the tail of reporters behind them. By the time they doubled back to Bayou Breaux on country roads, the press had gone off to write their stories. Nick had Wily drop him off at the house, where he grabbed the keys to his truck and left, skipping the shower and change of clothes he needed badly. He needed other things more. Answers.

The office gave the impression that Bichon Bayou Development was a solid company – sturdy oak furnishings, masculine colors, a small fortune in wildlife prints on the walls. Nick's investigation had told a different tale. Donnie had built the company on the back of Bayou Realty, Pam's business, and pissed away his opportunities to put it on solid financial ground. According to one source, the divorce would have cleanly severed the attachment between BBD and Pam's company, and Donnie would have been left to get business sense or die.

Nick traced a fingertip over the graceful line of a hand-carved wooden mallard coming in for a landing on the credenza. 'When I checked your company out, looked to me like you were in hock up to your ass, Donnie. You nearly went belly-up eighteen months ago. You hid land in Pam's company to keep from losing it. How is it you can write a check for a hundred thousand dollars?'

Donnie laughed as he dropped into the oxblood leather chair behind his desk. He had opened his collar and rolled up the sleeves of his pin-striped shirt. The young businessman at work.

'You're an ungrateful bastard, Fourcade,' he said, caught somewhere between amusement and irritation. 'I just bailed your ass out of jail and you don't like the smell of my money? Fuck you.'

'I believe I thanked you already. You paid for my release, Donnie, you didn't buy me.'

Donnie broke eye contact and straightened a stack of papers on his desk. 'The company's worth a lot on paper. Assets, you know. Land, equipment, houses built on spec. Bankers love assets more than cash. I have a nice line of credit.'

'Why'd you do it?'

'You're kidding, right? After what Renard did to Pam? And ol' Hunter and you are sitting in jail and he's out walking around? That's crazy. The courts are a goddamn circus nowadays. It's time somebody did the right thing.'

'Like kill Renard?'

'In my dreams. Perverted little prick. *He's* the criminal, not you. That was my statement. That deputy that hauled you in should have just minded her own damn business, let nature take its own course and finish this thing. Besides, I'm told I'm not out anything, unless you decide to skip town.'

'Why cash?' Nick asked. 'You pay a bail bondsman only ten percent for the bond.'

And get a fraction of the publicity, he thought. Donnie crossing the bar to write out a huge check had been a climactic moment. It hadn't been Donnie's first taste of the spotlight.

He had been right there soaking it up from the day Pam's body had been discovered. He had immediately offered a fifty-thousand-dollar reward for information leading to an arrest. He had cried like a baby at the funeral. Every newspaper in Louisiana had printed the close-up of Donnie with his face in his hands.

In the outer office, the telephone was ringing off the hook. Reporters looking for comments and interviews most likely. Every story that ran was free advertising for Bichon Bayou Development.

Donnie glanced away again. 'I wouldn't know anything about that. I never bailed anybody out of jail before. Christ, will you sit down? You're making me nervous.'

Nick ignored the request. He needed to move, and having Donnie nervous wasn't an altogether bad thing.

'Will you be able to go back to work on the case?'

'When hell freezes over. I'm on suspension. My involvement would taint the case because of my obvious bias against the chief suspect. At least, that's what a judge would say. I'm out, officially.'

'Then I'd better hope you have something else to keep you in Partout Parish, hadn't I? I sure as hell can't afford to lose a hundred grand.'

'Some folks would say you can afford to lose it now more than you could have when your wife was alive,' Nick said.

Donnie's face went tight. 'We've been down that road before, Detective, and I mightily resent you going down it again.'

'You know it's been a two-pronged investigation all along, Donnie. That's standard op. You bailing me outta jail won't change that.'

'You know where you can stick your two prongs, Fourcade.'

Shrugging, Nick went on. 'Me, I've had a lotta time on my hands in the last twenty-four hours. Time to let my mind wander, let it all turn over and over. It just seems . . . fortuitous . . . that Pam was killed before the divorce went through. Once the insurance company coughs up and you sell off Pam's half of the real estate company, you won't need that line of credit.'

Donnie surged to his feet. 'That's it, Fourcade! Get outta my office! I did you a good turn, and you come in here and abuse me! I should have left you to rot in jail! I didn't kill Pam. I couldn't possibly. I loved her.'

Nick made no move to leave. He pulled the toothpick from his mouth and held it like a cigarette. 'You had a funny way of showing it, Tulane: chasing anything in a skirt.'

'I've made mistakes,' Donnie admitted angrily. 'Maturity was never my strong suit. But I *did* love Pam, and I *do* love my daughter. I could never do anything to hurt Josie.'

The very thought seemed to distress him. He turned away from the school portrait of his daughter that sat on a corner of his desk.

'Is she living with you yet?' Nick asked quietly.

There had been rumors of a custody battle brewing within the divorce war. Something that seemed more like petty meanness on Donnie's part than genuine concern for his daughter's well-being. As in countless divorce cases, the child became a tool, a possession to be bickered over. Donnie liked his freedom too well for full-time fatherhood. Visitation would suit his lifestyle better than custody.

Nick had long ago discounted Josie as a motive for murder. It was the money angle that bothered him, and the land Donnie had hidden in Bayou Realty's assets. Even when he swore up and down Renard was their boy, the money issue kept tugging at him. It was a loose thread and he couldn't simply let a loose thread dangle. He would worry at it until it could be tied off one way or another. If it meant looking his gift horse in the mouth, then so be it. Donnie had decided on his own to bail him out. Nick felt no obligation.

'She's with Belle and Hunter,' Donnie said. 'Belle thought they could provide a more stable environment for the time being. Then Hunter goes off with a gun and tries to commit murder in broad daylight. Some stability. Of course, the press is making him out to be a celebrity. If he doesn't go to prison, they'll probably make a movie about him.'

The fight had run out of him. His shoulders slumped and he suddenly seemed older.

'Why are you dredging all this up again? You still believe Renard did it. I mean, I know some people are saying things after that rape the other night – all that Bayou Strangler bullshit and whatnot. But that's got nothing to do with this. You're the one found Pam's ring in Renard's house. You're the one put him in the hospital. Why are you dogging my ass? I'm the best friend you had today.'

'Habit,' Nick replied. 'Me, I tend to be suspicious by nature.'

'No shit. Well, I'm not guilty.'

'Ever'body's guilty of something.'

Donnie shook his head. 'You need help, Fourcade. You're clinically paranoid.'

A sardonic smile curved Nick's mouth as he tossed his toothpick in the trash and turned for the door. 'C'est vrai. That's true enough. Lucky for me, I'm one of the few people who can make a living off it.'

Nick left Bichon Bayou Development through the back door, made his way down two alleys, and cut across the backyard of a house where a teenage girl in a yellow bikini was stretched out on a shiny metallic blanket trying to absorb ultraviolet rays. With headphones and sun goggles, she was oblivious to his passing.

He had parked in the weedy side lot of a closed welding shop, the truck blending in with an array of abandoned junk. He climbed into the cab, rolled the windows down, and sat there, smoking a cigarette and thinking as the radio mumbled to itself.

'You're on KJUN with Dean Monroe. Our topic this afternoon: the release on bail of Partout Parish detective, Nick Fourcade, who stands accused of brutalizing murder suspect Marcus Renard. Montel in Maurice, speak your mind.'

'He done this kind of thing before and he got off. I thinks we all gots to be scared when cops can plant evidence and beat people up and just get off –'

Nick silenced the radio, thinking back to New Orleans. He had paid in ways worse than prison. He had lost his job, lost his credibility. He had crashed and burned and was still struggling to put the pieces back together. But he had more urgent things than the past to occupy his mind today.

Maybe Donnie Bichon was filled with regret for the demise of his marriage and the death of the woman he had once loved. Or maybe his remorse was about something else altogether. Except for the hideous brutality of the murder, Donnie had been an automatic suspect. Husbands always were. But Donnie seemed more the sort who would have choked his ex in a moment of blind fury, not the sort who could have planned a death like Pam's and carried it out. It took cold hate to pull off a murder like that.

'Renard did it,' Nick murmured. The trail, the logic led back to Renard. Renard had fixated on her, stalked her, killed her when she rejected him. Nick believed he'd done it in Baton Rouge shortly before moving here, but that woman's death had been ruled accidental and never investigated as a homicide.

Renard was their guy, he could feel it in the marrow of his bones. Still, there was something off about the whole damn deal.

Maybe it was the fact that no one had ever been able to prove Renard was the one stalking Pam. Hell, the word *stalking* never even appeared in the reports. That was how doubtful the cops and the courts had been. Renard had openly sent her flowers and small gifts. There was nothing menacing in that. Pam had thrown the gifts back at him in the Bowen & Briggs office one day, not long before her death.

No one had ever seen Renard going into Pam's office or her house out on Quail Drive when she wasn't there, and yet someone had stolen things from her desk and from her dresser. Someone had left a dead snake in her pencil drawer. Renard had access to the office building, but so did Donnie. No one had identified Renard as the prowler Pam had reported several times to 911 from her home, but someone had slipped into her garage and cut the tires on her Mustang. She had received so many hang-up and breather calls at home, she had taken an unlisted number. But there was not a single call listed in the phone company records from Renard's home or business number to Pam Bichon's.

Renard was meticulous, compulsively neat. Careful. Intelligent. He could have pulled it off. The flowers and candy could have been part of the game. Perhaps he had sensed all along she would never have him. Perhaps it was resentment that drove his fixation. Affection was the perfect cover for a deep-seated hatred.

Then again, perhaps Donnie had harassed Pam in a foolish and misguided attempt to get her back. Donnie had never been in favor of the divorce. He had argued it was not in Josie's best interest, but it was not in Donnie's best interest – financially. Pam had asked him to move out in February – a year ago, now. A trial separation. They went to a few counseling sessions. By the end of July it had been plain in Pam's mind that the marriage was over, and she filed the papers. Donnie had not taken the news well.

The harassment began the end of August.

Donnie could have pulled those tricks to scare her. He had the capacity for juvenile behavior. But again, there was no evidence. No witnesses. No phone records. A search of his home following the murder had turned up nothing. Donnie wasn't that smart.

'You need a break, Fourcade,' he muttered.

Like the snap of a hypnotist's fingers, the trance was shattered. He didn't need a break. He was off the case. He didn't want to let it go, and yet, he had thrown it away with both hands by going after Renard.

He had replayed that night in his head a hundred times. In his head, he made the right choices. He didn't accept Stokes's invitation to Laveau's. He didn't pour whiskey on his wounded pride. He didn't listen to Stokes's eye-for-an-eye nonsense. He didn't take that phone call, didn't go down that street.

And Annie Broussard didn't walk out of the blue and into his life. Where the hell had she come from? And why?

He didn't believe in coincidence, had never trusted Fate.

The possibilities rubbed back and forth in his mind and chafed his temper raw. He put the truck in gear, and rolled out of the parking lot.

The hell he was off this case.

13

Friday. Payday. Everyone was in a hurry to get to the bank, get to the bars, get home to start the weekend. Friday was a big speeding-ticket day. Friday nights were good for brawls and DUIs.

Annie preferred the tickets. With more people packing guns every day, brawls had become a little too unpredictable to be fun. Then there was the whole AIDS scare and the threats of lawsuits. The only cops she knew who still liked brawls were the boneheaded type who sweated testosterone, and short guys with big chips on their shoulders. Little guys always wanted to fight to prove their manhood. The Napoleon complex.

Just one more reason to be glad she didn't have a penis. The few skirmishes she had jumped into had been enough to win her a chipped tooth, two cracked ribs, and the respect of her fellow deputies. Men were that way. Being able to take a punch somehow made you a better person.

She wondered if any of them remembered those past brawls. It seemed not. When she had reported to the briefing room this morning, she had taken a seat at one of the long tables, and every deputy at the table got up and moved. Not a word was spoken, but the message was clear: They no longer considered her one of them. Because of Fourcade, a man who had befriended none of them and yet was lionized by them all for the mere fact that he had external genitalia. Men.

She had wanted to hear about the follow-up on the Jennifer Nolan rape, but the closest she was going to come to the case was rewriting her initial report, which Hooker had 'misplaced'. She had interviewed half a dozen of Nolan's neighbors yesterday, getting only one potentially useful piece of information: Nolan's former roommate had run off with a biker. Two of the doors she had knocked on had gone unanswered. She had passed all the information on to Stokes and doubted she would ever hear another word about it unless she read it in the paper.

She thought about the rape in fragments: the mask, the violence, the absence of seminal fluid, the ligatures, the fact that he made her bathe afterward. The fact that he hadn't spoken a single word during the ordeal. Verbal intimidation and degradation were standard fare in most rapes. She wondered which would be more terrifying: an attacker who threatened death or the ominous uncertainty of silence.

Careful. The word kept coming back to her. The rapist had been careful to leave no trace. He seemed to be perfectly aware of what the cops would need to nail him. That pointed to someone with experience and maybe a record. Someone should have been checking personnel records at the True Light lamp factory to see if any of Nolan's co-workers was an ex-con. But it wasn't her job, and it never would be if Chaz Stokes had anything to say about it.

Annie checked her watch again. Another half hour and she could head back to Bayou Breaux. She had pulled the cruiser off the road into the turnaround lot of a ramshackle vegetable stand that had blown down in the last big storm. The position was shaded by a sprawling live oak and gave her a view of two blacktop roads that converged a quarter mile south of the small town of Luck – a hot spot on Friday nights. Every rough character in the parish headed down to Skeeter Mouton's roadhouse on Friday night. Bikers, roughnecks, rednecks, and criminal types, all gathered for the popular low-society pursuits of beer, betting, and breaking heads.

A red Chevy pickup was coming fast out of town. Annie clocked it with the radar as it cruised past, the driver hanging a beer can out the window. Sixty-five in a forty zone and a DUI to boot. Jackpot. She hit the lights and siren and pulled him over half a mile down the road. The truck had a rebel-flag sunscreen in the back window and a bumper sticker that read USA Kicks Ass.

Nothing like a drunken redneck to make a day truly suck the big one.

'One Able Charlie,' she radioed in. 'I got a speeder on twelve, two miles south of Luck. Looks like he's drinking. Lou'siana tags Tango Whiskey Echo seven-three-three. Tango Whiskey Echo seven-three-three. Over.'

She waited a beat for the acknowledgment that didn't come, then tried again. Still no response. The silence was more than annoying; it was disturbing. The radio was her link to help. If a routine stop turned into trouble, Dispatch had her location and the tag number on the vehicle she had pulled over. If she didn't call them back in a timely fashion, they would send other units.

'10–1, One Able Charlie. We didn't catch that. You're breaking up again. Say again. Over.'

It was a simple thing to interrupt a radio transmission. All it took was one other deputy keying his mike when he heard her calling in and she was cut off. Cut off from communication, cut off from help.

Disgusted at the possibility, Annie grabbed her clipboard and ticket book and got out of the car.

'Step out of the vehicle, please,' she called as she approached the truck from the rear.

'I wadn' speedin',' the driver yelled, sticking his head out the open window. He had small mean eyes and a mouth that drew into a tight knot. The dirty red ball cap he wore was stitched with a yellow TriStar Chemical logo. 'You cops ain't got nothin' better to do than stop me?'

'Not at the moment. I'll need to see your license and registration.'

'This is bullshit, man.'

He swung open the door of the truck, and an empty Miller Genuine Draft can tumbled out onto the verge and rolled under the cab. He pretended not to notice as he stepped down with the extreme caution of a man who knows he has lost his equilibrium to booze. He wasn't any taller than Annie, a little pit bull of a man in jeans and a Bass Master T-shirt stretching tight over a hard beer belly. A *short*, drunken redneck.

'I don't pay taxes in this parish so y'all can harass me,' he grumbled. 'Goddamn gov'ment's tryin' to run my life. This here's supposed to be a free fuckin' country.'

'So it is as long as you're not drunk and driving sixty-five in a forty. I need your license.'

'I ain't drunk.' He pulled a big trucker's wallet on a chain out of his hip pocket and fumbled around to extract his license, which he held out in Annie's general direction. His fingers were stained dark with grease. A tattoo of a naked blue woman with bright red nipples reclined on his forearm. Classy.

Vernell Poncelet. Annie stuck the license under the clip on her board.

'I wadn' speedin',' he insisted. 'Them radar guns is always wrong. You can clock a goddamn tree doing sixty.'

Suddenly his squinty eyes widened in surprise. 'Hey! You're a woman!'

'Yep. I've been aware of that for some time now.'

Poncelet put his head on one side, studying her, until he started to tip over. He swung an arm to point at her and righted himself in the process.

'You're the one was on the news! I seen you! You turned in that cop what beat up that killer rapist!'

'Stay right here,' Annie said coolly, backing toward the squad. 'I need to run your name and tags.' And call for a backup. She had the feeling Vernell wasn't going down without a fight. Short guys.

'What kinda cop are you?' Poncelet shouted, staggering after her. 'You want killer rapists runnin' 'round loose? An' you're giving me a ticket? That's bullshit!'

Annie gave him the evil eye. 'Stand where you are!'

He kept coming, thrusting a finger at her as if he meant to run her through with it. 'I ain't takin' no fuckin' ticket from you!'

'The hell you're not.'

'You let a rapist run around loose. Maybe you wanna get lucky, huh? You fuckin' bitch –'

'That's it!' Annie tossed the clipboard on the hood of the cruiser and reached for the cuffs on her belt. 'Up against the truck! Now!'

'Fuck you!' Poncelet made a wobbly 180-degree turn and started back for his truck. 'Let a real cop stop me. I ain't takin' no shit from a broad.'

'Up against the truck, stubby, or this is gonna get so real it'll hurt.'

Annie stepped in behind him, slapped a cuff around his right wrist, and pulled his arm up behind his back. 'Up against the goddamn truck!'

She stepped into him, trying to turn him with pressure on his arm. Poncelet staggered, throwing her off balance, then swung around to take a punch at her. Their feet tangled in a clumsy dance and they went down in a heap on the side of the road, wrestling, grunting.

Poncelet swore in her face, his breath hot and acetous with beer gases bubbling up from his belly. He groped for a handhold to right himself, grabbing Annie's left breast. Annie kicked him in the shin and caught him in the mouth with her elbow. Poncelet got one knee under him and tried to surge to his feet, one hand swinging hard into Annie's nose.

'Son of a bitch!' she yelled as blood coursed down over her lips. She came to her feet and ran Poncelet headlong into the side of the truck.

'You picked the wrong day to fuck with me, shorty!' she snarled, closing the other cuff tight around his free wrist. 'You're under arrest for every stinkin' crime I can think of!'

'I want a real cop!' he bellowed. 'This is America. I got rights! I got the right to remain silent —'

'Then why don't you?' Annie barked, shoving him toward the cruiser.

'I ain't no crim'nal! I got rights!'

'You've got shit for brains, that's what you've got. Man, you have dug yourself a hole so deep, you're gonna need a ladder to see rock bottom.'

She pushed him into the backseat and slammed the door. Traffic passed by on the blacktop road to Mouton's. A kid with a goatee leaned out the window of a jacked-up GTO and gave her the finger. Annie flipped it back at him and climbed in behind the wheel of her car.

'You're a feminazi, that's what you are!' Poncelet shouted, kicking the back of the seat. 'You're a goddamn feminazi!'

Annie wiped the blood off her mouth with her shirtsleeve. 'Watch your mouth, Poncelet. You start quoting Rush Limbaugh to me, I'll take you out in the swamp and shoot you.'

She glanced at herself in the rearview mirror and swore as she pulled the radio mike. With the black eye from Wednesday and the bloody nose, she looked as if she'd gone five rounds with Mike Tyson.

'One Able Charlie. I'm bringing in a drunk. Thanks for nothing.'

Poncelet was still screaming when Annie escorted him to Booking. She had stopped listening, her own anger muting his words to an annoying roar in the background. What if Poncelet had hurt her? What if he had gotten hold of her gun? Would anyone have known the difference?

The Deputies' Association had voted to pay Fourcade's legal bills. She wondered if they'd also taken a vote on getting her killed. She hadn't been invited to the meeting.

The shift was changing — guys going in and out of the locker room, hanging around the briefing room. Time for bullshit and bad jokes over strong coffee. The relaxed smiles froze and vanished when Annie came down the hall.

'What?' she challenged no one in particular. 'Disappointed to see me in one piece?'

'Disappointed to see you at all,' Mullen muttered.

'Yeah? Well, now you know how the whole female population feels when they see you coming, Mullen. What did you think?' she demanded. 'That keying me out on the radio would make me disappear?'

'I don't know what you're talking about, Broussard. You're hysterical.'

'No, I'm pissed off. You got a problem with me, then be a man and bring it to me instead of pulling this adolescent bullshit –'

'You're the problem,' he charged. 'If you can't handle the job, then leave.'

'I can handle the job. I was *doing* my job –'

'What the hell's going on out here?' Hooker bellowed, stepping into the hall.

Too angry for circumspection, Annie turned toward the sergeant. 'Someone's covering my transmissions.'

'That's bullshit,' Mullen said.

'Musta been something wrong with your radio,' Hooker said. Annie wanted to kick him.

'Funny how I suddenly can't get a radio that works.'

'You got bad vibes, Broussard,' Mullen said. 'Maybe the wire in your bra is screwing up your reception.'

Hooker glared at him. 'Shut the fuck up, Mullen.'

'It's not the radio,' Annie said. 'It's the attitude. Y'all are acting like a bunch of spoiled little boys, like I ruined everybody's fun. Someone was breaking the law and I stopped him. That's my job. If y'all have a problem with that, then you don't belong in a uniform.'

'We know who doesn't belong here,' Mullen muttered.

The silence was absolute. Annie looked from one deputy to another, a lineup of stony faces and averted eyes. They may not all have felt as strongly as Mullen, but no one was standing up for her, either.

Finally, Hooker spoke. 'You got proof somebody did you wrong, Broussard, then file a grievance. Otherwise, quit your goddamn whining and go do your paperwork on that drunk.'

No one moved until Hooker had disappeared back into his office. Then Prejean and Savoy walked away, breaking the standoff. Mullen started down the hall, leaning toward Annie as he passed.

'Yeah, Broussard,' he murmured. 'Quit your whining or somebody'll give you something to whine about.'

'Don't threaten me, Mullen.'

He raised his brows in mock fear. 'What you gonna do? Arrest me?' The expression turned stony. 'You can't arrest us all.'

14

Late July: Pam makes it known around the office that she means to divorce Donnie. They have been separated since February. Renard begins to show an interest in her. Drops into the realty office to chat, to show his concern for her, etc.

August: Renard clearly has a crush. He sends Pam flowers and small gifts, asks her to lunch, asks her out for drinks. She goes with him only in a group, tells her partner she wants to be sure Renard doesn't get the wrong idea about their friendship, though she admits she thinks it's rather sweet the way he's trying to court her. She tries to stress to Renard they are just friends.

Late August: Pam begins to receive breather and hang-up calls at home.

September: Small items go missing from Pam's office and from her home. A paperweight, a small bottle of perfume, a small framed photo of herself and daughter Josie, a hairbrush. She can't pinpoint when the items were taken. Renard is hanging around, shows more concern than seems appropriate. Pam begins to feel uncomfortable around him. Breather and hang-up calls continue.

9/25: On leaving for work, Pam discovers her tires slashed (car parked in unlocked garage). Calls the sheriff's department. Responding deputy: Mullen. Pam expresses her concerns about Renard, but there is no evidence he committed the crime. Detective assigned to investigate alleged harassment: Stokes.

10/02 1:00 A.M.: Pam reports a prowler outside her home. No suspect apprehended. Renard interviewed regarding incident. Denies involvement. Expresses concern for Pam.

10/03: Renard comes to Pam's office, expresses concern for her in person.

10/09 1:45 A.M.: Pam again reports a prowler. No suspect apprehended.

10/10: On leaving house for school bus, Josie Bichon discovers the mutilated remains of a raccoon on the front step.

10/11: Renard comes to Pam's office again to express concern for her safety and *for Josie's safety. Unnerved, Pam tells him to leave. Clients waiting to meet with her confirm her level of upset.*

10/14: On arriving at her office, Pam finds a dead snake in her desk drawer. Later that day Renard approaches her yet again to express his concern for her. Says something to the effect that a single woman, like Pam, has much to fear, that any number of bad things might happen to her. Pam perceives this as a threat.

10/22: On returning home from work, Pam finds house has been vandalized: clothing cut up, bedding smeared with dog waste, photos of herself defaced. No suspect fingerprints recovered from scene. No witnesses. Pam calls Acadiana Security to have home system installed. Later realizes a spare set of house and office keys has gone-missing. Can't pinpoint when she last saw them.

10/24: Renard gives Pam an expensive necklace for her birthday. Pam, extremely angry, confronts Renard in his office with her suspicions, returns all small gifts he had given her during the months of August and September. In front of witnesses, Renard denies all charges of stalking.

10/24: Pam consults attorney Thomas Watson about a restraining order against Renard.

10/27: Watson petitions the court on Pam's behalf for a restraining order against Marcus Renard. Request denied for lack of sufficient cause. Judge Edwards refuses to 'blacken a man's reputation' with no more reason than 'a woman's unsubstantiated paranoia.'

10/31: Pam sees a prowler outside her house. Tries to call sheriff's department. House phones are dead. Calls on cellular. No suspect apprehended. Phone line had been cut. Back door of house smeared with human waste.

11/7: Pam Bichon reported missing.

Annie read through her notes. Laid out in this linear fashion, it seemed so simple, so obvious. A classic pattern of escalation. Attraction, attachment, pursuit, fixation, increasing hostility at rejection. Why hadn't anyone else seen it for what it was and stopped it?

Because a pattern was all they had. There was absolutely nothing to tie Renard to the stalking. His public reaction to Pam's accusations had been confusion, hurt. How could she think he would ever harm her? Not once in those months preceding Pam Bichon's murder had Renard expressed to any of his co-workers anger or hostility toward her. Quite the contrary. Pam had complained to friends about Renard. They offered support to her face and questioned her sanity behind her back. He seemed so harmless.

With the divorce looming and the settlement potentially affecting his business, Donnie Bichon had seemed a more likely candidate for villain. But Pam had insisted Renard was her stalker.

What a nightmare, Annie thought. To be so certain this man was a danger, but unable to convince anyone else.

Annie rose from her kitchen table to prowl the apartment. Half past nine. She'd been staring at those notes for an hour, cross-referencing newspaper articles, referring to photocopies of magazine articles and textbook passages on stalkers. She had kept track of the case all along – out of a sense of obligation, and to continue her self-education toward one day making detective. She had purchased a three-ring binder, storing all news clippings in one section, notes in another, personal observations in another. If not for the news clippings, it would have been a thin notebook. She had conducted no interviews. It wasn't her case. She was only a deputy.

Fourcade probably had two notebooks – murder books, the detectives called them. But Fourcade was off the case. Which left Chaz Stokes in charge. Stokes had been the detective assigned to check out the initial harassment charges. If he had been able to come up with anything at the time, maybe Pam would still be alive today.

Annie wandered restlessly into the living room. Out of old habit, she fell into a slow, measured pace along the length of her coffee table and back. The table consisted of a slab of glass balanced on the back of a five-foot-long taxidermied alligator, a relic Sos had once kept hung suspended from the ceiling of the store until one of the wires broke, and the gator swung down and knocked a tourist flat. Annie had taken the creature in like a stray dog and named it Alphonse.

She walked back and forth from one end of Alphonse to the other, pondering the current situation, ignoring the occasional ringing of the phone. She let the machine pick up – reporters and cranks. No one she wanted to deal with. No one who could solve her need to find justice for Pam Bichon.

She might have been able to talk Fourcade into letting her help with the investigation if it hadn't been for the incident with Renard. Now Stokes had the case and she would never ask Stokes. She would have struck out with him even if she hadn't arrested Fourcade. Stokes had never been able to get over the fact that she didn't find him irresistible. Nor would he let it go. He had taken her simple, polite 'No, thank you' first as a challenge, then as a personal insult. In the end, he had accused her of being a racist.

'It's because I'm black, isn't it?' he charged.

They were in the parking lot at the Voodoo Lounge. A hot summer night full of bugs and bats swooping to eat the bugs. Heat lightning sizzled across the southern sky out over the Gulf. The humidity made the air feel like velvet against the skin. They'd gone to the bar with others as a group, as they often did on Friday night. A bunch of cops looking to unwind a little. Stokes had too much to drink, mouthed off enough about her being frigid that Annie had walked out in disgust.

She gaped at his accusation.

'Go ahead. You might as well admit it. You don't want to be seen with the mulatto guy. You don't want to go to bed with a nigger. Say it!'

'You're an idiot!' she declared. 'Why can you not accept the fact that I'm simply not attracted to you? And *why* am I not attracted to you? Let me count the reasons: It could be that you have the maturity of a high school junior. It could be that you have an ego the size of Arkansas. Maybe it's because you have no interest in a conversation that doesn't center on you. It's got nothing to do with what kind of people are climbing around in your family tree.'

'Climbing? Like they're monkeys? You're calling my people monkeys?'

'No!'

He came toward her, his face hard with anger. Then a car drove in the lot and some people came out of the bar, and the tension of the moment snapped like a twig.

The scene was so vivid in Annie's memory that she could almost feel the heat of the night on her skin. She opened the French doors at the end of her living room and stepped out onto the little balcony, breathing in the cool damp air and the fecund smell of the swamp. There was just enough moonlight to silver the water and outline the eerie silhouettes of the cypress trees.

Funny, she'd never really thought about it, but she could relate in a small way to Pam Bichon's experience. She did know what it was like to deal with men who wouldn't take no for an answer. Stokes. A.J. Uncle Sos, for that matter. The difference between them and Renard was the difference between sanity and obsession.

'Men,' she said aloud to the white cat that jumped up on the balcony railing to beg for attention. 'Can't live with 'em, can't open pickle jars without 'em.'

The cat offered no opinion.

In all fairness, it wasn't just men, Annie knew. Stalkers came in both sexes. New studies were showing that these people were unable to shut off that focus. The impulse, the fixation, was always there. *Simple obsessionals*, the shrinks called them. Often these men and women seemed perfectly rational and normal. They were doctors, lawyers, car mechanics. Their level of schooling or intelligence didn't matter. But regarding the object of their fixation, their brains weren't wired right. Some moved on to what was known as *erotomania*, a condition in which the person imagined and actually believed there was an ongoing romantic relationship with the object of the fixation.

A simple obsessional or an erotomaniac – ahe wondered which description applied to Marcus Renard. She wondered how he could hide either so well from everyone around him.

927

Somewhere out in the swamp a bull alligator gave a hoarse roar. Then the shriek of a nutria split the air like a woman's scream. The sound razored along Annie's nerves. She closed her eyes and saw Pam Bichon lying on that floor, moonlight pouring in the window, spilling across her naked corpse. And deep inside her mind, Annie thought she could hear Pam's screams . . . and the screams of Jennifer Nolan . . . and the women who had died four years ago at the hands of the Bayou Strangler. Screams of the dead.

'*It's cold there, no?*'

'*Where?*'

'*In Shadowland.*'

Goosebumps racing over her flesh, Annie stepped back inside the apartment, closed the doors, and locked them.

'Nice place you got here, 'Toinette.'

Heart in her throat, she wheeled around. Fourcade stood just inside the front entry, leaning back against the wall, ankles crossed, hands in the pockets of his old leather jacket.

'What the hell are you doing here?'

'Not much of a lock you got on this door.' He shook his head in reproach as he straightened from the wall. 'You'd think a cop would know better. Especially a lady cop, no?'

He moved toward her with deceptive laziness. Even halfway across the room Annie could sense the tension in him. She sidestepped slowly, putting the coffee table between them. Her gun was in her duffel bag, which she had abandoned in the entry. Careless.

Her best hope was to get out. And then what? The store had closed at nine. Sos and Fanchon's house was a hundred yards away and they were out dancing just like every other Friday night of the year. Maybe she could get to the Jeep.

'What do you want?' she asked, edging toward the door. Her keys hung on a peg above the light switch. 'You want to beat *me* up, too? You haven't committed your daily quota of sins? You want to get rid of the witness? You should know enough to hire out that kind of job. You'll be the obvious suspect.'

He had the nerve to appear amused. 'You think I'm the devil now, don'tcha, 'Toinette?'

Annie broke for the door, grabbed for the keys with one hand, and knocked them to the floor. With the other hand, she grabbed the knob, twisted, pulled. The door didn't budge. Then Fourcade was on her, trapping her, hands planted against the door on either side of her head.

'Running out on me, 'Toinette?'

She could feel his breath on the back of her neck, laced with the scent of whiskey.

'That's not very hospitable, *chère*,' he murmured.

She was trembling. And he was enjoying it, the son of a bitch. She willed herself to control the shaking, forced herself to turn and face him.

He stood as close as a lover. 'We have so much to talk about. For instance, who sent you to Laveau's that night?'

Nick watched her face like a hawk. Her reaction was spontaneous – surprise or shock, a touch of confusion.

'What'd you think, 'Toinette? That I was too drunk to figure it out?'

'Figure what out? I don't know what you're talking about.'

His mouth twisted in derision. 'I'm in this department six months, you never say boo to me. All of a sudden you show up at Laveau's in a pretty skirt, batting your eyelashes. You want in on the Bichon case –'

'I *did* want in.'

'Then there you are on that street. Just happen to be passing by –'

'I *was* –'

'The hell you were!' he roared, enjoying the way she flinched. He wanted her frightened of him. She had reason to be frightened of him. 'You followed me!'

'I did not!'

'Who sent you?'

'No one!'

'You been talking to Kudrow. Did he set it up? I can't believe Renard would go for it. What if I came at him with a gun or a knife? He'd be stupid to take the chance just to ruin me. And he's not stupid.'

'No one –'

'On the other hand, maybe that was Kudrow's justice, heh? He has to know Renard is guilty. So Kudrow gets him off to save his own rep. Works it so I kill Renard. Renard is dead and I'm caged up with the red hats in Angola, twenty-five to life.'

He's insane, she thought. She'd seen what he was capable of. She cut a glance at the duffel bag sitting on the bench. Two feet away. The zipper was open. If she was fast . . . If she was lucky . . .

'I don't have a clue what you're talking about,' she said, keeping her mouth in motion to buy time. 'Kudrow's trying to jam me up with the department so I don't have anyone to turn to but his side. I wouldn't work for him if he paid in gold bullion.'

Fourcade didn't seem to hear her.

'Would he chance all that?' he mused to himself. 'That's the question. 'Course, he'd only have to pay off the blackmail 'til he's dead, and that won't be long . . .'

With all the power she could muster, Annie brought her right knee up into his groin, then dropped to the floor as Fourcade staggered back, doubled over, swearing.

'*Fils de putain! Merde!* Fuck! Fuck!'

Oh please oh please oh please. She plunged her hand into the duffel bag and groped for the Sig. Her fingertips grazed the holster.

'Lookin' for this?'

The Sig appeared before her eyes in the palm of Fourcade's hand, one finger hooked through the trigger guard. He had dropped to his knees behind her and now pulled her head back by a handful of hair and shoved his body into hers, pinning her against the bench.

'You fight dirty, 'Toinette,' he murmured. 'I like that in a woman.'

'Fuck you, Fourcade!'

'Mmm . . .' he purred, pressing against her, pressing his rough cheek against hers. 'Don't give me ideas, *'tite belle.*'

Slowly, he rose, his hand still tangled in her hair, drawing her up with him.

'You, you're not much of a hostess, 'Toinette,' he said, directing her toward the kitchen where the light was bright and cheery. 'You haven't even offered me a chair.'

'Sorry, I flunked home ec.'

'I'm sure you have other talents. A flair for decorating, I see.'

He took in the small kitchen with amazement. Someone had painted a dancing alligator on the door of the ancient refrigerator. Canisters in the likeness of stair-step doughboys lined one counter. The wall clock was a plastic black cat whose eyes and tail twitched back and forth with the passing seconds.

One chair was pulled out at the chrome-legged table. He sat her down. Snatching up the pen she had left on the tabletop, he backed up to the counter.

Annie stared at him. Some of the wildness had gone out of his eyes, though his gaze was no less intense. He stood with his arms crossed in front of him, her gun dangling from his big hand as if it were a toy.

'Now, where were we before you tried to kick my balls up to my back teeth?'

'Oh . . . somewhere between delusional and psychotic.'

'Was it Kudrow? He buy you and Stokes?'

'Stokes?'

'What? You thought you were getting all the pie? Stokes got me into that bar. Why go there? Nobody ever goes there. To be away from the grunts, he tells me. And Bowen & Briggs, that just happens to be right across the alley. How fucking handy. Then along comes little 'Toinette to keep an eye on me while ol' Chaz goes his merry way.'

'Why would I let Kudrow buy me?' she asked. A futile attempt at reason, she supposed. 'Yours isn't the only career taking a beating here, you know. I'll be mopping out jail cells before this is over. Kudrow doesn't have enough money to make up for that.'

Nick tipped his head to one side and considered. He hadn't eaten all day, but had fed on anger and frustration and suspicion, and washed it all down with a few belts of whiskey. And now something black and rotten surfaced in the brew and slipped out of his mouth in a whisper.

'Duval Marcotte.'

Son of a bitch. The pieces fit with oily ease. The similarity of the cases would appeal to Marcotte's sense of irony. And he sure as hell knew how to buy cops. The face of the New Orleans reporter at the courthouse came back to him. Shit. He should have seen it coming.

He pounced at Annie, making her bolt back in the chair. 'What'd he give you? What'd he promise you?'

'Duval Marcotte?' she said, incredulous. 'Are you out of your mind? Oh, Christ, look who I'm asking!'

He leaned down into her face, wagging the nose of the Sig like a finger. 'He'll take your soul, *chère*, or worse. You think *I'm* the devil? *He's* the devil!'

'Duval Marcotte is the devil,' Annie repeated. 'Duval Marcotte, the real estate magnate from New Orleans? The philanthropist?'

'That son of a bitch,' he muttered, pacing along the counter. 'I shoulda killed him when I had the chance.'

'I don't know Duval Marcotte, other than to see him on the news. Nobody bought me. I was in the wrong place at the wrong time. Believe me, I regret it.'

'I don't believe in coincidence.'

'Well, I'm sorry, but I don't have any other explanation!' she shouted. 'So shoot me or leave me the hell alone!'

Turning possibilities over in his mind, Nick reached back and scratched behind his ear with the nose of the gun.

'Jeez! Will you be careful with that thing!' she yelled. 'If you don't shoot me, I'd rather not be left to scrape your brains off my cupboards.'

'What? This gun?' He twirled it on his finger. 'It's not loaded. I figured it might be too tempting.'

Relief surged through Annie, and she rubbed her hands over her face. 'Why me?'

'That was my question.'

'I've told you all I know, which is exactly nothing. I would no more be in league with Chaz Stokes than I would be with someone like Marcotte. Stokes hates me. Besides, who sets up a frame that completely relies on the framee actually committing the crime? That's stupid. If someone wanted to set you up, why not just kill Renard and make it look like you're the guy? That's a piece of cake. So why don't you just take your elaborate conspiracy theories to Oliver Stone. Maybe he'll make a movie about you.'

Setting the empty gun aside, Nick leaned back against the counter. 'You got a mouth on you, *chère*.'

'Being terrorized brings out the bitch in me.'

He almost laughed. The urge to do so surprised him almost as much as Annie Broussard surprised him. He pressed his lips together and stared at her. She returned his stare, indignant, angry. If she was as innocent as she professed, then she had to think he was insane. That was all right. Perceived psychosis carried certain advantages.

'Tell me something,' she said. 'Did you go to Bowen and Briggs that night of your own accord?'

He thought of the phone call, but answered the real truth. 'Yes.'

'And you made your own decision to beat up Renard?'

He hesitated again, knowing the answer wasn't so simple, remembering the flashbacks that had burst in his head that night like fireworks. But in the end he could answer only one way. '*Oui*.'

'Then how is this anyone's fault but your own?'

Annie waited for his answer. He had never struck her as the kind of man who would shirk his responsibilities. Then again, she hadn't believed he was crazy either.

'Stokes didn't put you in that alley,' she said. 'Nobody held a gun to your head. You did what you did, and I was unlucky enough to catch you. Quit trying to blame everyone else. You made your own choices and now you have to live with the consequences.'

'*C'est vrai*,' he murmured. Just like that, the frenetic energy was shut off and he seemed to go still from deep within. 'Me, I did what I did. I lost control. I can't think of many people who deserved a beating more than Renard, and I feel no remorse for providing it – other than the impact it will have on my own life.'

'What you did was wrong.'

'In that force ultimately defeats itself. I disappointed myself that night,' he admitted. 'But the tendency is for every aspect of this existence to continue to be what it is, *mais oui?* Interfere with its natural state and the thing will resist. Fundamentally, I find it difficult to embrace a philosophy of nonaction. Therein lies the crux of my problem.'

He had taken a hard left turn on her once again. From raving maniac to philosopher in a span of moments.

'You pled not guilty,' she said. 'But you admit that you are.'

'Nothing is simple, *chérie*. I go down for a felony, I'm off the job forever. That's not an option.'

'The resistance of a being against interference to its natural state.'

He smiled unexpectedly, fleetingly, and for a heartbeat was extraordinarily handsome. 'You're a good student, *chère*.'

'Why do you do that?'

'What?'

'Call me *chère*, like you're a hundred years old.'

The smile this time was sad, wry. He came to her slowly and lifted her chin with his hand. 'Because I am, *jeune fille*, in ways that you will never be.'

He was too close, bending down so that she could see every year, every burden in those eyes. His thumb brushed across her lower lip. Unnerved, she turned her face away.

'So what's your beef with Duval Marcotte?' she asked, sliding out of the chair, walking toward the other end of the table.

'It's personal,' he said, taking her seat.

'You were quick enough to throw it out a while ago.'

'When I thought you might be involved.'

'So I've been absolved of guilt?'

'For the moment.' His attention caught on the papers spread out across the table. 'What's all this?'

'My notes on the Bichon homicide.' Slowly, she moved back toward him. 'Why do you think Marcotte might be involved? Is there some kind of connection to Bayou Real Estate?'

'There hasn't been to this point. It all seemed very straightforward,' Nick said as he took a quick inventory of what she had compiled. 'Why are you doing this?'

'Because I care about what happens. I want to see her killer punished, legally. I believed he would be – until Wednesday. As much as it pains me to admit this at the moment, I had faith in your abilities. Now, with Stokes in charge of the investigation, and attention being diverted elsewhere, I'm not so sure Pam will get justice.'

'You don't trust Stokes?'

'He likes things to be easy. I don't know if he has the talent to clear this case. I don't know if he would apply it if he did have it. Now you're telling me you think he set you up. Why would he do that?'

'Money. The great motivator.'

'And who involved with the case would want to see you go down besides Renard and Kudrow?'

He didn't answer, but the name had taken root in his mind like a noxious weed. Duval Marcotte. The man who had ruined him.

Annie moved toward the counter. 'I need some coffee,' she said, as calmly as if this man hadn't burst into her home and held a gun to her head. But her hands were trembling as she turned on the faucet. Breath held deep in her lungs, she reached for the tin coffee canister on the counter and carefully peeled the lid off. She flinched when Fourcade spoke again.

'So what you gonna do, 'Toinette?'

'What do you mean?'

'You want to see justice done, but you don't trust Stokes to do it. I go within spitting distance of Renard, I get tossed back in the can. So what you gonna do? You gonna see 'bout getting some justice?'

'What can I do?' she asked. A bead of sweat trickled down her temple. 'I'm just a deputy. They don't even let me talk on the radio these days.'

'You already been working the case on your own.'

'*Following* the case.'

'You wanted in on it. Bad enough to ask me. You wanna be a detective, *chère*. Show some initiative. You already got a knack for sticking your pretty nose in where it don't belong. Be bold.'

'Is this bold enough for you?' She turned with a five-inch-long, nine-millimeter Kurz Back-Up in hand, chambered a round with quick precision, and pointed it dead at Fourcade's chest.

'I keep this little sweetheart in the coffee tin. A trick I learned from *The*

Rockford Files. Call my bluff if you want, Fourcade. No one will be too surprised to hear I shot you dead when you broke into my house.'

She expected anger, annoyance at the very least. She didn't expect him to laugh out loud.

'Way to go, 'Toinette! Good girl! This is just the kinda thing I'm talking 'bout. Initiative. Creativity. Nerve.' He rose from his chair and moved toward her. 'You got a lotta sass.'

'Yeah, and I'm about to hit you in the chest with a load of it. Stand right there.'

For once, he listened, assuming a casual stance two feet in front of the gun barrel, one leg cocked, hands settled at the waist of his faded jeans. 'You're pissed at me.'

'That would be an understatement. Everybody in the department is treating me like a leper because of you. You broke the law and I'm getting punished for it. Then you come into my house and – and terrorize me. *Pissed* doesn't begin to cover it.'

'You're gonna have to get over it if you're gonna work with me,' he said bluntly.

'Work with you? I don't even want to be in the same room with you!'

'Ah, that . . .'

He moved quickly, knocking her gun hand to the side and up. The Kurz spat a round into the ceiling, and plaster dust rained down. In seconds Fourcade had the gun out of her hand and had her drawn up hard against him with one arm pulled up behind her back.

'. . . that would be untrue,' he finished.

He let her go abruptly and went back to the table, scanning her papers on the case. 'I can help you, 'Toinette. We want the same end, you and I.'

'Ten minutes ago you thought I was part of a conspiracy against you.'

He still didn't know that she wasn't, he reminded himself. But she wouldn't have gone to all the trouble of building a casebook on Pam Bichon's murder if she wasn't truly interested in seeing it solved.

'I want the case cleared,' he said. 'Marcus Renard belongs in hell. If you want to make that happen, if you want justice for Pam Bichon and her daughter, you'll come to me. I've got ten times what you've got lying here on this table – statements, complaints, photographs, lab reports, duplicates of everything that's on file at the sheriff's department.'

This was what she had wanted, Annie thought: To work with Fourcade, to have access to the case, to try – for Josie's sake and to silence the phantom screams in her own mind. But Fourcade was too volatile, too wired, too unpredictable. He was a criminal, and she was the one who had run him in.

'Why me?' she asked. 'You should hate me more than the rest of them do.'

'Only if you sold me out.'

'I didn't, but –'

'Then I can't hate you,' he said simply. 'If you didn't sell me out, then you acted on your principles and damned the consequences. I can't hate you for that. For that, I would respect you.'

'You're a very strange man, Fourcade.'

He touched a hand to his chest. 'Me, I'm one of a kind, 'Toinette. Ain'tcha glad?'

Annie didn't know whether to laugh or cry. Fourcade laid her weapon on the table and came toward her, serious again.

'I don't wanna let go of this case,' he said. 'I want Renard to go down for what he did. If I can't trust Stokes, then I can't work through him. That leaves you. You said you felt an obligation to Pam Bichon. You want to meet that obligation, you'll come to me. Until then . . .'

He started to lower his head. Annie's breath caught. Anticipation tightened her muscles. Her lips parted slightly, as if she meant to tell him no. Then he touched two fingers to his forehead in salute, turned, and walked out of her apartment and into the night.

'Holy shit,' she whispered.

She stood there as the minutes ticked past. Finally she went out onto the landing, but Fourcade was gone. No taillights, no fading purr of a truck engine. The only sounds were the night sounds of the swamp: the occasional call of nocturnal prey and predator, the slap of something that broke the surface of the water and dived beneath once more.

For a long time she stared out at the night. Thinking. Wondering. Tempted. Frightened. She thought of what Fourcade had said to her that night in the bar. *'Stay away from those shadows, 'Toinette. . . . They'll suck the life outta you.'*

He was a man full of shadows, strange shades of darkness and unexpected light. Deep stillness and wild energy. Brutal yet principled. She didn't know what to make of him. She had the distinct feeling that if she accepted his challenge, her life would be altered in a permanent way. Was that what she wanted?

She thought of Pam Bichon, alone with her killer, her screams for mercy tearing the fabric of the night, unheeded, unanswered. She wanted closure. She wanted justice. But at what price?

She felt as if she were standing on the edge of an alternate dimension, as if eyes from that other side were watching her, waiting in expectation for her next move.

Finally she went inside, never imagining that the eyes were real.

'I feel a sense of limbo, as if I'm holding my breath. It isn't over. I don't know that it will ever be over.

The actions of one person trigger the actions of another and another, like waves.

I know the wave will come to me again and sweep me away. I can see it in my mind: a tide of blood.

I see it in my dreams.

I taste it in my mouth.

I see the one it will take next.

The tide has already touched her.'

15

The call came at 12:31. Annie had double-checked the locks on her doors and gone to bed, but she wasn't sleeping. She picked up on the third ring because a call in the dead of night could have been something worse than a reporter. Sos and Fanchon could have been in an accident. One of their many relatives might have fallen ill. She answered with a simple hello. No one answered back.

'Ahhh . . . a breather, huh?' she said, leaning back against her pillows, instantly picturing Mullen on the other end of the line. 'You know, I'm surprised you guys didn't start in with calls two nights ago. We're talking simple, no-brain harassment. Right up your alley. I have to say, I was actually expecting the "you fucking bitch" variety. Big bad faceless man on the other end of the line. Oooh, how scary.'

She waited for an epithet, a curse. Nothing. She pictured the dumbfounded look on Mullen's face, and smiled.

'I'm docking you points for lack of imagination. But I suppose I'm not the first woman to tell you that.'

Nothing.

'Well, this is boring and I have to work tomorrow – but then, you already knew that, didn't you?'

Annie rolled her eyes as she hung up. A breather. Like that was supposed to scare her after what she'd been through tonight. She switched off the lamp, wishing she could turn off her brain as easily.

The pros and cons of Fourcade's offer were still bouncing in her head at five A.M. Exhaustion had pulled her under into sleep intermittently during the night, but there had been no rest in it, only dreams full of anxiety. She finally gave up and dragged herself out of bed, feeling worse than she had when she'd crawled between the sheets at midnight. She splashed cold water on her face, rinsed her mouth out, and pulled on her workout clothes.

Her brain refused to shut down as she went through her routine of stretching and warm-up. Maybe Fourcade's offer was all part of a revenge plot. If his compadres in the department hated her enough to get back at her, why wouldn't he?

'If you didn't sell me out, then you acted on your principles and damned the consequences. I can't hate you for that. For that, I would respect you.'

937

Damned if she didn't believe he meant it. Did that make her an astute judge of character or a fool?

She hooked her feet into the straps on the incline board and started her sit-ups. Fifty every morning. She hated every one.

Fourcade's ravings about Duval Marcotte, the New Orleans business magnate, should have been enough to put her off for good. She had never heard any scandal attached to Marcotte – which should have made her suspicious. Nearly everyone in power in New Orleans had his good name smeared on a regular basis. Nasty politics was a major league sport in the Big Easy. How was it Marcotte stayed so clean? Because he was as pure as Pat Boone . . . or as dark as the devil?

What difference did it make? What did she care about Duval Marcotte? He couldn't possibly have anything to do with the Bichon case . . . except there was that real estate connection.

Annie moved from the incline board to the chin-up bar. Twenty-five every morning. She hated them nearly as much as the sit-ups.

What if she went to Fourcade? He was on suspension, charged with multiple counts of assault. What kind of trouble could she get in with the sheriff or with Pritchett? She was a witness for the prosecution, for God's sake. Fourcade shouldn't have come within a mile of her and vice versa.

Maybe that was why he had made the offer. Maybe he thought he could win some points, get her to soften toward him. If he was helping her with the Bichon case, letting her investigate, maybe she wouldn't remember so clearly the events of that night outside Bowen & Briggs.

But Fourcade didn't seem the kind of man for subterfuge. He was blunt, tactless, straightforward. He was more complicated than French grammar, full of rules with irregularities and exceptions.

Annie let herself out of the apartment, jogged down the stairs and across the parking lot. A dirt path led up onto the levee and the restricted-use gravel levee road. She ran two miles every morning and despised every step. Her body wasn't built for speed, but if she listened to what her body wanted, she'd have a butt like a quarter horse. The workout was the price she paid for her candy bar habit. More than that, she knew that being in shape might one day save her life.

So what was the story with Stokes? Could someone have bought him or was Fourcade simply paranoid? If he was paranoid, that didn't mean someone *wasn't* out to get him. But a setup still didn't make sense to Annie. Stokes had taken Fourcade to Laveau's, true, but Stokes had left. How could he be certain Fourcade would find his way to Bowen & Briggs to confront Renard?

The phone call.

Fourcade had taken a call, then split. But if Stokes had meant to set up Fourcade, wouldn't he have had a witness lined up? Did she know he hadn't? Stokes himself could have been watching the whole thing play out with some civilian flunky by his side waiting to step into the role of witness for the prosecution. What sweet irony for him that Annie had stumbled into the scene. She and Fourcade could cancel each other out.

She dragged herself back up to her apartment, showered, and dressed in a fresh uniform, then dashed down to the store with a Milky Way in hand.

'Dat's no breakfast, you!' Tante Fanchon scolded. She straightened her slender frame from the task of wiping off the red checkered oilcloths that covered the tables in the café portion of the big room. 'You come sit down. I make you some sausage and eggs, *oui?*'

'No time. Sorry, Tante.' Annie filled her giant travel mug with coffee from the pot on the café counter. 'I'm on duty today.'

Fanchon waved her rag at her foster daughter. 'Bah! You all the time workin' so much. What kinda job for a purty young thing is dat?'

'I meet lots of eligible men,' Annie said with a grin. 'Of course, I have to throw most of them in jail.'

Fanchon shook her head and fought a smile. '*T'es trop grand pour tes culottes!*'

'I'm not too big for my pants,' Annie retorted, backing toward the door. 'That's why I run every morning.'

'Running.' Fanchon snorted, as if the word gave her a bad taste.

Annie turned the Jeep out of the lot onto the bayou road. She had the juggling act down – coffee mug clamped between her thighs, candy bar and steering wheel in her left hand while she shifted and turned on the radio with her right.

'You're on KJUN. All talk all the time. Home of the giant jackpot giveaway. Every caller's name is registered – including yours, Mary Margaret in Cade. What's on your mind?'

'I think gambling is a sin and your jackpot is gambling.'

'How's that, ma'am? There's no fee.'

'Yes, there is. There's the price of the long-distance call if a person don't live in Bayou Breaux. How can y'all sleep nights knowing people take the food out the mouths of their children so they can make those calls to sign up for your jackpot?'

Traffic picked up with every side-road intersection. People headed into Bayou Breaux to work or do their Saturday errands, or continued on up to Lafayette for a day in the city. Sports headed to the basin for a day of fishing. A big old boat of a Cadillac pulled out onto the blacktop ahead of her. Annie hit the clutch and the brake and reached for the shift, glancing down just enough for something odd to catch her eye. Her duffel bag, on the floor in front of the passenger seat, was moving, the near end rising up slightly.

She turned her head to look, and her heart vaulted into her throat. Slithering out from under the duffel, its body already edging past the gearshift toward her, was a mottled brown snake as thick as a garden hose. *Copperhead.*

'Jesus!'

939

She bolted sideways in her seat, jerking the wheel left. The Jeep swerved into the southbound lane, eliciting angry honks from oncoming traffic. Annie looked up and swore again as a ton truck bore down on her, horn blaring. A white-knuckle grip on the steering wheel, she hit the gas and gunned for the ditch.

The Jeep was airborne for what seemed like an eternity. Then the world was a jarred blur in every window. The impact bounced her off the seat and bounced the snake off the floor. Its thick, muscular body hit her across her thighs and fell back down.

Annie was barely aware of killing the engine. Her only thought was escape. She threw her shoulder against the door, tumbled out of the Jeep, and slammed the door shut behind her. Her heart was thumping like a trip-hammer. Her breath came in ragged, irregular jerks. She hugged the front fender to steady herself.

'Ohmygod, ohmygod, ohmygod.'

Up on the road, several cars had pulled to the shoulder. One driver had climbed out of his pickup.

'Please stay with your vehicles, folks! Move it along! I'll handle this.'

Annie raised her head and peered through the strands of hair that had fallen in her face. A deputy was coming toward her, his cruiser parked on the shoulder with the lights rolling.

'Miss?' he called. 'Are you all right, Miss? Should I call an ambulance?'

Annie straightened up so he could see her uniform. She recognized him instantly, even if he couldn't manage the same with her. York the Dork. He walked as if he had a permanent wedgie. A Hitler mustache perched above his prim little mouth. It twitched now as realization dawned.

'Deputy Broussard?'

'There's a copperhead in my Jeep. Somebody put a copperhead in my Jeep.'

While she probably wouldn't have died from a bite, the possibility was there. She certainly could have been killed in the accident, and she may not have been the only casualty. She wondered if her harasser had considered that when he'd been planting his little reptile friend, then wondered which answer would have upset her more.

'A copperhead!' the Dork chirped with a sniff. He peered into the Jeep. 'I don't see anything.'

'Why don't you climb in and crawl around on the floor? When it bites your ass we'll know it's real.'

'It was probably just a belt or something.'

'I know the difference between a snake and a belt.'

'Sure you weren't just looking in the mirror, putting your lipstick on, and lost control of the vehicle? You might as well tell the truth. It wouldn't be the first time I heard that story,' he said with a chortle. 'You gals and your makeup . . .'

Annie grabbed him by the shirtsleeve and hauled him around to face

940

her. 'Am I wearing lipstick? Do you see any lipstick on this mouth, you patronizing jerk? There's a snake in that Jeep and if you 'little lady' me again, I'll wrap it around your throat and choke you with it!'

'Hey, Broussard! You're assaulting an officer!'

The shout came from the road. Mullen. He had parked on the shoulder – a piece-of-crap Chevy truck with a bass boat dragging behind. Encased in tight jeans, his legs were skinny as an egret's. He compensated with a puffed-up green satin baseball jacket.

'She claims there's a copperhead in there,' York said, hooking a thumb at the Jeep.

'Yeah, like he doesn't already know that,' Annie snapped.

Mullen made a face at her. 'There you go again. Hysterical. Paranoid. Maybe you need to get your hormones adjusted, Broussard.'

'Fuck you.'

'Oooh, verbal abuse, assaulting an officer, reckless driving . . .' He swaggered around to the passenger side to look in the window. 'Maybe she's drunk, York. You better put her through the paces.'

'The hell you will.' Annie rounded the hood. 'Keying me out on the radio was bad enough, and I can take the crap at the station, but somebody other than me could have gotten killed with this stunt. If I can find one scrap of evidence linking you to this –'

'Don't threaten me, Broussard.'

'It's not a threat, it's a promise.'

He sniffed the air. 'I think I smell whiskey. You better run her in, York. The stress must be getting to you, Broussard. Drinking in the morning on your way to work. That's a shame.'

York looked apprehensive. 'I didn't smell anything.'

'Well, Christ,' Mullen snapped. 'She's seeing snakes and driving off the damn road. Tag the vehicle and take her in!'

Annie planted her hands on her hips. 'I'm not going anywhere until you get that snake out of my Jeep.'

'Resisting,' Mullen added to her list of sins.

'I think we'd better go in to the station to sort this out, Annie,' York said, straining to look apologetic.

He reached for her arm and she yanked it away. There was no out. York couldn't let her get back into her vehicle if there was a question of her sobriety, and she'd be damned if she was going to go through the drunk drill for them like a trick poodle.

'Uh – I think you better sit in the back,' he said as she reached for the passenger-side door on his cruiser.

Annie bit her tongue. At least she had driven Fourcade to the station in her own vehicle, calling as little attention to the situation as possible. No one was going to offer her the same courtesy.

'I need my duffel bag,' she said. 'My weapon is in it. And I want that Jeep locked up.'

She watched as he went back into the ditch and said something to

Mullen. York went around to the driver's side and pulled the keys, while Mullen opened the passenger's door, hauled her duffel out, then bent back into the vehicle. When he emerged again, he had hold of the writhing snake just behind its head. It looked nearly four feet in length, big enough, though copperheads in this part of the country regularly grew bigger. Mullen said something to York and they both laughed, then Mullen swung the snake around in a big loop and let it fly into a field of sugarcane.

'Just a king snake!' he shouted up at Annie as he came toward the car with her bag. 'Copperhead! You *must* be drunk, Broussard. You don't know one snake from the next.'

'I wouldn't say that,' Annie shot back. 'I know what kind of snake you are, Mullen.'

And she stewed on it all the way in to Bayou Breaux.

Hooker was in no mood for dealing with the aftermath of a practical joke, malicious or otherwise. He ranted and swore from the moment York escorted her into the building, directing his wrath at Annie.

'Every time I turn around, you're in the middle of a shit pile, Broussard. I've about had it up to my gonads with you.'

'Yes, sir.'

'You got some kind of brain disorder or something? Deputies are supposed to be out arresting crooks, not each other.'

'No, sir.'

'We never had this kind of trouble when it was just men around here. Throw a female into the mix and suddenly everybody's got some kind of hard-on.'

Annie refrained from pointing out that she'd been on the job here two years and had never had any trouble to speak of until now. They stood inside Hooker's office, which a maintenance person had painted chartreuse while Hooker was gone having angioplasty in January. The perpetrator of that joke had yet to come forward. The door stood wide open, allowing anyone within earshot to listen to the diatribe. Annie held on to the hope that this would be the last of the humiliation. She could weather the storm. Hooker would eventually run out of insults or have a stroke, and then she could go out on patrol.

'I've had it, Broussard. I'm tellin' you right now.'

From somewhere down the hall came another raised voice. 'What do you mean, *you can't find it?*' Annie recognized Smith Pritchett's nasal whine. Dispatch was down the hall. What would Pritchett want from them? What would Pritchett want badly enough to come in on a Saturday?

'Y'all are telling me you keep these 911 tapes for-frigging-ever, but you don't have the *one* tape from the night of Fourcade's arrest?'

A pulsing vein zigzagged across Pritchett's broad forehead like a lightning bolt. He stood in the hall outside the dispatch center in a lime green Izod shirt, khakis, and golf spikes, a nine iron in hand.

The woman on the other side of the counter crossed her arms. 'Yessir, that's what I'm tellin' you. Are you callin' me a liar?'

Pritchett stared at her, then wheeled on A.J. 'Where the hell is Noblier? I told you to call him.'

'He's on his way,' A.J. promised. Bad enough that Pritchett had sent him on this quest on Saturday morning – a surprise attack, he called it – now they could all have a knock-down-drag-out brawl besides. He bet his money on the dispatch supervisor. Even though Pritchett was armed, she had to outweigh him by eighty pounds.

He would have saved the news that the tape was missing, but Pritchett was like an overeager five-year-old at Christmas. He had called in on his cellular phone from the third tee. While Fourcade's lawyer had yet to submit a written account of his client's version of events, Noblier had stated the detective had been responding to a call of a possible prowler in the vicinity of Bowen & Briggs. A bald-faced lie, certainly. The 911 tapes would confirm it as such, and the dispatch center in the sheriff's office handled all 911 calls in the parish. But the 911 tape from that fateful night was suddenly nowhere to be found.

The door to the sheriff's office swung open, and Gus came into the hall in jeans and cowboy boots and a denim shirt, the pungent aroma of horses hanging on him like bad cologne. 'Don't get your shorts in a knot, Smith. We'll find the damn tape. This is a busy place. Things get mislaid.'

'Mislaid, my ass.' Pritchett shook the nine iron at the sheriff. 'There's no tape because there's no damn call on the tape referring to a prowler in the vicinity of Bowen and Briggs.'

'Are you calling me a liar? After all the years I've backed you? You are a small, ungrateful man, Smith Pritchett. You don't believe me, you talk to my deputies on patrol that night. Ask them if they heard the call.'

Pritchett rolled his eyes and started down the hall toward the sheriff, his spikes thundering on the hard floor. 'I'm sure they'd tell me they heard the archangels singing Dixieland jazz if they thought it would get Fourcade off,' he shouted above the racket. 'It's a damn shame this has to come between us, Gus. You've got a bad apple in your barrel. Cut him out and be done with it.'

Gus squinted at him. 'Maybe the reason we don't have that tape is that Wily Tallant came and got it already. As exculpatory evidence.'

'What?' Pritchett squealed. 'You would just blithely hand something like that over to a *defense attorney*?'

Gus shrugged. 'I'm not saying it happened. I'm saying it might have.'

A.J. stepped in between them. 'If Tallant has it, he'll have to disclose it, Smith. And if the tape is gone, then they have nothing but biased hearsay that the call ever came in. It's no big deal.'

Other than the fact that Pritchett had just been embarrassed again.

'I don't know, Gus,' Pritchett lamented as they stepped out into the

943

warm spring sunshine. 'Maybe you've been at this too long. Your sense of objectivity has become warped. Just look at Johnny Earl: He's young, smart, untainted by the corruptions of time and familiarity. And he's black. A lot of people think it's time for a black sheriff in this parish – it's progressive.'

Gus blew a booger onto the sidewalk. 'You think I'm afraid of Johnny Earl? Might I remind you, I carried thirty-three percent of the black vote in the last election, and I was running against *two* blacks.'

'Don't bring it up, Gus,' Pritchett said. 'It just calls to mind those ugly vote-hauling allegations made against you.'

He started toward his Lincoln, where his caddy stood, waiting to drive him back to the country club. 'Doucet!' he barked. 'You come with me. We have charges to discuss. What all do you know about the statutes on conspiracy?'

Gus watched the lawyers climb into the Lincoln, then stomped back into the station, muttering, 'Dickhead college-boy prick. Threaten me, you little –'

'Sheriff?'

The bark came from Hooker. Gus rubbed a hand against his belly. Hell of a Saturday this was turning out to be. He stopped in front of Hooker's open door and stared inside.

'My office, Deputy Broussard.'

'You think someone put that snake in your Jeep.'

'Yes, sir. It couldn't have gotten there any other way.'

'And you think another deputy put it there?'

'Yes, sir, I –'

'Nobody else could have had access to the vehicle?'

'Well –'

'You keep it locked at home, do you?'

'No, sir, but –'

'You got proof another deputy did it? You got a witness?'

'No, sir, but –'

'You live over a goddamn convenience store, Deputy. You telling me no one stopped at the store last night? You telling me folks weren't in and out of that parking lot to do this deed or see it done?'

'The store closes at nine.'

'And after that, damn near anybody could have put that snake in your Jeep. Isn't that right?'

Annie blew out a breath. *Fourcade.* Fourcade could have done it, had motive to do it, was disturbed enough to do it. But she said nothing. The snake seemed an adolescent prank, and Fourcade was no adolescent.

'Hell, I've seen the inside of your Jeep, girl. That snake coulda hatched there, for all I know.'

'And you think it was a coincidence that York was patrolling that

944

stretch of road this morning,' Annie said. 'And that Mullen just happened along.'

Gus gave her a steady look. 'I'm saying you got no proof otherwise. York was on patrol. You ran off the road. He did his job.'

'And Mullen?'

'Mullen's off duty. What he does on his own time is no concern of mine.'

'Including interfering in the duty of another officer?'

'You're a fine one to talk on that score, Deputy,' he said. 'York ran you in 'cause he thought you mighta been drinking.'

'I wasn't drinking. They did it to humiliate me. And Mullen was the ringleader. York was just his stooge.'

'They found a half-empty pint of Wild Turkey under your driver's seat.'

Dread swirled in Annie's stomach. She could be suspended for this. 'I don't drink Wild Turkey and I don't drink in my vehicle, Sheriff. Mullen must have put it there.'

'You refused to go through the drill.'

'I'll take a Breathalyzer.' She realized she should have insisted on it at the scene. Now her career was crumbling beneath her feet because she'd been too proud and too stubborn. 'I'll take a blood test if you want.'

Noblier shook his head. 'That was an hour ago or better, and you weren't but five miles from home when you had the accident. If you had anything in your system, it's probably gone by now.'

'I *wasn't* drinking.'

Gus swiveled his big chair back and forth. He rubbed at the stubble on his chin. He never shaved on Saturday until his evening toilet before taking the missus out for dinner. He did love his Saturdays. This one was going to hell on a sled.

'You been under a lotta strain recently, Annie,' he said carefully.

'I *wasn't* drinking.'

'And you was kicking up dirt yesterday, saying someone keyed you out on the radio?'

'Yes, sir, that's true.' She decided to keep the muskrat incident to herself. She felt too much like a tattling child already.

A frown creased his mouth. 'This is all because of that business with Fourcade. Your chickens are coming home to roost, Deputy.'

'But I —' Annie cut herself off and waited, foreboding pressing down on her as the silence stretched.

'I don't like any of this,' Gus said. 'I'll give you the benefit of the doubt about the drinking. York should have given you the Breathalyzer and he didn't. But, as for the rest of the bullshit, I've had it. I'm pulling you off patrol, Annie.'

The pronouncement hit her with the force of a physical blow, stunning her. 'But, Sheriff —'

'It's the best decision I can make for all concerned. It's for your own

945

good, Annie. You come off patrol until this all blows over and settles down. You're out of harm's way, out of sight of the many people you have managed to piss off.'

'But I didn't do anything wrong!'

'Yeah, well, life's a bitch, ain't it?' he said sharply. 'I got people telling me you're trouble. You're sitting here telling me everybody's out to get you. I ain't got time for this bullshit. Every puffed-up muck-a-muck in the parish is on my case on account of Renard and this rapist, and the Mardi Gras carnival isn't but a week off. I'm telling you, I'm sick of the whole goddamn mess. I'm pulling you off patrol until this situation blows over. End of story. Are you on tomorrow?'

'No.'

'Fine, then take the rest of the day for yourself. Report to me Monday morning for your new assignment.'

Annie said nothing. She stared at Gus Noblier, disappointment and betrayal humming inside her like a power line.

'It's for the best, Annie.'

'But it's not what's right,' she answered. And before he could reply, she got up and walked out of the room.

16

It cost $52.75 to get the Jeep out of the impound lot. Financial insult added to ego injury. Steaming, Annie made the lot attendant dig through all the junk on the floor and check every inch of the interior for unpleasant surprises. He found none.

She drove down the block to the park and sat in the lot under the shade of a sprawling, moss-hung live oak, staring at the bayou.

How simple it had been for Mullen and his moron cohorts to get what they wanted – her off the job – and she had been powerless to stop it. A thumb on a radio mike switch, a planted pint of Wild Turkey, and she was off the street. The hypocrisy made her mad enough to spit. Gus Noblier was well known for ordering a little after dinner libation *to go*, yet he pulled her off the job on the lame and unsubstantiated suggestion that maybe she'd had a little something to spike her morning coffee.

Her instinctive response was to fight back, but how? Put a bigger snake in Mullen's truck? As tempting as that idea was, it was a stupid one. Retribution only invited an escalation of the war. Evidence was what she needed, but there wouldn't be any. Nobody knew better than a cop how to cover tracks. The only witnesses would be accessories. No one would come forward. No one would rat out a brother cop to save a cop who had turned on one of their own.

'You're getting down and dirty with Dean Monroe on KJUN. The hot topic this morning is still the big decision that went down in the Partout Parish Courthouse on Wednesday. A murder suspect walks on a technicality, and now two men sit in jail for violating *his* rights. Lindsay on line one, what's on your mind?'

'Injustice. Pam Bichon was my friend and business partner, and it infuriates me that the focus on her case has shifted to the rights of the man who terrorized and killed her. The court system did nothing to protect her rights when she was alive. I mean, wake up, South Lou'siana. This is the nineties. Women deserve better than to be patronized and pushed aside, and to have our rights be considered below the rights of murderers.'

'Amen to that,' Annie murmured.

A wedding party had come into the park for photographs. The bride stood in the center of the Rotary Club gazebo looking impatient while

947

the photographer's assistant fussed with the train of her white satin gown. Half a dozen bridesmaids in pale yellow organdy dotted the lawn around the gazebo like overgrown daffodils. The groomsmen had begun a game of catch near the tomb of the unknown Confederate war hero. Down on the bank of the bayou, two little boys in black tuxes busied themselves throwing stones as far as they could into the water.

Annie stared at the ripples radiating out from each splash. Cause and effect, a chain of events, one action the catalyst for another and another. The mess she found herself in hadn't begun with her arrest of Fourcade, or Fourcade's attack on Renard. It hadn't begun with Judge Monahan's dismissal of the evidence or the search that had uncovered that evidence. It had all begun with Marcus Renard and his obsession with Pam Bichon. Therein lay the dark heart of the matter: Marcus Renard and what the court system had inadvertently allowed him to do. Injustice.

Not allowing herself to consider the consequences, Annie started the Jeep and drove away from the park. She needed to take positive action rather than allow herself to be caught up in the wake of the actions of others.

She needed to do something – for Pam, for Josie, for herself. She needed to see this case closed, and who was going to do that, who was going to find the truth? A department that had turned on her? Chaz Stokes, whom Fourcade accused of betrayal? Fourcade, who had betrayed the law he was sworn to serve?

Turning north, she headed toward the building that housed Bayou Realty and the architectural firm of Bowen & Briggs.

The Bayou Realty offices were homey, catering to the tastes of women, offering an atmosphere that stirred the feminine instinct to nest. A pair of flowered chintz couches, plump with ruffled pillows, created a cozy L off to one side of the front room. Framed sales sheets with color photographs of homes being offered stood in groupings on the glass-topped wicker coffee table like family portraits. Potted ferns basked in the deep brick window wells. The scent of cinnamon rolls hung in the air.

The receptionist's station was unoccupied. A woman's voice could be heard coming from one of the offices down the hall. Annie waited. The bell on the front door had announced her entrance. Nerves rattled inside her.

'*Be bold*,' Fourcade had told her.

Fourcade was a lunatic.

The door to the second office on the right opened and Lindsay Faulkner stepped into the hall. Pam Bichon's partner looked like the kind of woman who was elected homecoming queen in high school and college and went on to marry money and raise beautiful, well-behaved children with perfect teeth. She came down the hall with the solid, sunny smile of a Junior League hospitality chairwoman.

'Good mornin'! How are you today?' She said this with enough familiarity and warmth that Annie nearly turned around to see if someone had come in behind her. 'I'm Lindsay Faulkner. How may I help you?'

'Annie Broussard. I'm with the sheriff's department.' A fact no longer readily apparent. She had changed out of her coffee-stained uniform into jeans and a polo shirt. She had tucked her badge into her hip pocket but couldn't bring herself to pull it out. She'd be in trouble enough as it was if Noblier caught wind of what she was up to.

Lindsay Faulkner's enthusiasm faded fast. Irritation flickered in the big green eyes. She stopped just behind the receptionist's desk and crossed her arms over the front of her emerald silk blouse.

'You know, you people just make me see red. This has been hell on us – Pam's friends, her family – and what have you done? Nothing. You know who the killer is and he walks around scot-free. The incompetence astounds me. My God, if you'd done your jobs in the first place, Pam might still be alive today.'

'I know it's been frustrating, Ms Faulkner. It's been frustrating for us as well.'

'You don't know what frustration is.'

'With all due respect, yes, I do,' Annie said plainly. 'I was the one who found Pam. I would like nothing better than to have this case closed.'

'Then go on upstairs and arrest him, and leave the rest of us alone.'

She marched back down the hall. Annie followed.

'Renard is upstairs right now?'

'Your powers of deduction are amazing, Detective.'

Annie didn't correct her presumption of rank. 'It must be like salt in the wound – having to work in the same building with him.'

'I hate it,' she said flatly, going into her office. 'Bayou Realty owns the building. If I could terminate their lease tomorrow, the whole lot of them would be out in the street, but once again the law is on *his* side.

'The gall of that man!' Her expression was a mix of horror and hatred. 'To come here and work as if he's done nothing wrong at all, while every day I have to walk past that empty office, Pam's office –'

She sat for a moment with a hand to her mouth, staring out the window at the parking lot.

'I know you and Pam were very close,' Annie said quietly, slipping into a chair in front of the desk. She extracted a small notebook and pen from her hip pocket and positioned the notebook on her thigh.

Lindsay Faulkner produced a small linen handkerchief seemingly from thin air and blotted delicately at the corners of her eyes. 'We were best friends from the day we met at college. I was Pam's maid of honor. I'm Josie's godmother. Pam and I were like sisters. Do you have a sister?'

'No.'

'Then you can't understand. When that animal murdered Pam, he murdered a part of me, a part that can't be buried in a tomb. I will carry that part inside me for the rest of my life. Deadweight, black with rot;

949

something that used to be so bright, so full of joy. He has to be made to pay for that.'

'If we can convict him, he'll get the death penalty.'

A little smile twisted at Faulkner's lips. 'We opposed capital punishment, Pam and I. Cruel and unusual, barbaric, we said. How naïve we were. Renard doesn't deserve compassion. No punishment could be cruel enough. I've tortured that man to death in my imagination more times than I can count. I've lain awake nights wishing I had the courage . . .'

She stared at Annie, the light of challenge in her eyes. 'Will you arrest me? The way they arrested Pam's father?'

'He did a sight more than imagine Renard dead.'

'Pam was Hunter's only daughter. He loved her so, and now he carries that dead piece inside him too.'

'Did you suspect Renard was the one harassing Pam?'

Guilt passed over the woman's face, and she looked down at her hands lying on the desktop. 'Pam said it was him.'

'And you thought . . . ?'

'I've been over this with the others,' she said. 'Don't you people talk to one another?'

'I'm trying to get a fresh perspective. Male detectives have a male point of view. I may pick up on something they didn't.' A good argument, Annie thought. She'd have to remember it when Noblier called her on the carpet for overstepping her bounds.

'He seemed so harmless,' Lindsay Faulkner whispered. 'You watch the movies, you think maniacs are supposed to look a certain way, act a certain way. You think a stalker is some lowlife with no job and a double-digit IQ. You never think, 'Oh, I bet that architect upstairs is a psychopath.' He's been here for years. I never – He hadn't . . .'

'We can't always see trouble coming,' Annie offered gently. 'If he'd given you no reason to suspect him –'

'Pam did, though. Not all along, but last summer, after she and Donnie split up. Renard started hanging around more, and it bothered her – the gifts he sent her, his manner around her. And when the harassment started, she didn't want to say anything at first, but she thought it was him.'

'Who did you think – ?'

'Donnie,' she said without hesitation. 'The harassment started not long after she told him she wanted the divorce. I thought he was trying to scare her. It seemed like the kind of thing he would think of. Donnie's emotional development arrested at about sixteen. I even called him on it, read him the riot act.'

'How did he react?'

She rolled her eyes. 'He accused me of poisoning Pam against him. I told him I'd tried that years ago, and she went and married him anyway.

Pam always looked at Donnie and saw his potential. She couldn't believe he wouldn't live up to it.'

'It must be very unpleasant for you now – trying to resolve the business issues.'

'It's a mess. The divorce would have cut Donnie cleanly away from the realty company. Pam would have worded her new will so her half of the business went to Josie in a trust. I would have had the option of buying it out with the partner insurance we were planning to buy. We'd never gotten around to that before – the partner insurance. We just never thought about it. I mean, we were both young and healthy.' She paused. 'Anyway, none of those changes happened before . . .'

Annie decided she liked this woman, liked her strength and her anger on her friend's behalf. She hadn't expected this kind of caring and conviction from a former debutante. She had expected hanky-wringing passive grief. *My prejudice*, she thought.

'Now what happens?' she asked.

'Now I have to deal with Donnie, who has the business acumen of a tick. He's being extra obnoxious because months before the marriage split up, Donnie's company was in a financial bind and Pam agreed to hide some land for him in the realty so the bank wouldn't take it.'

'Hide it?'

'Bichon Bayou Development "sold" these properties to Bayou Realty on paper. In reality, we were just holding them out of harm's way.'

'And you still have them?'

Her smile was slightly feral. 'Yes. But now Donnie holds Pam's half of the business, so technically the properties are partly his. However, before he can do anything with them, he has to have *my* approval. We're currently at a standoff. He wants his property back and I want full ownership of the business. The latest wrinkle is that Donnie suddenly thinks Pam's half of this business is worth double what it is. He's trying to play hardball, threatening me with some nebulous *other buyer* from New Orleans.'

Annie's pen went still on the paper. 'New Orleans?'

New Orleans. Real estate. Duval Marcotte.

Lindsay shook her head at the ridiculousness of the idea. 'What would anyone in New Orleans want with Bayou Breaux?'

'You think he's bluffing?'

'*He* thinks he's bluffing. I think he's an idiot.'

'What would you do if he sold his half to this buyer?'

'I don't know. Pam and I started this business together. It's important to me for that reason, you know, as something we built and shared as friends. And it's a strong little business; we do well enough. I enjoy it. I *will* sell this building if I get the chance,' she admitted, turning to look out at the parking lot. 'There are too many bad memories now. And that bastard upstairs. I keep picturing Detective Fourcade beating him to death. I –'

She stopped. Annie sat very still. Out in the front room the door opened and the bell announcing potential clients tinkled pleasantly.

'Broussard,' Faulkner murmured with accusation. 'You're the one who stopped him. My God. I thought you said you wanted this resolved.'

'I do.'

She rose with the poise and grace of old Southern breeding. 'Then why didn't you just walk away?'

'Because that would have been murder.'

Lindsay Faulkner shook her head. 'No, that would have been justice. Now, you'll excuse me,' she said, moving to the door. 'You will leave these offices. I have nothing further to say to you.'

Annie let herself out the rear exit of the realty office and stood in the hall. To her right was the door to the parking area where Fourcade had attacked Renard. Before her rose the stairs to the second floor and the offices of Bowen & Briggs. Renard was up there.

She thought of going up the stairs. The cop in her wanted to study Marcus Renard, try to pick him apart, figure him out, see how he would fit into the range of stalkers she had studied in books. A deeper instinct held her in place. He had called her his heroine, had sent her roses. She didn't like it.

The decision was taken away from her when the door at the top of the stairs swung open and Renard stepped out. He looked grotesque, like a monster from one of the Grimms' grimmer fairy tales. The troll under the bridge. Moderate swelling distorted features dotted with bruises the hues of rotten fruit. For a second, he didn't see Annie, and she thought of stepping back into the Bayou Realty office. Then the second was lost.

'Annie!' he exclaimed as best he could with his jaw wired shut. 'This is an unexpected pleasure!'

'It's not a social call,' Annie said flatly.

'Following up on my attack?'

'No. I came to see Ms Faulkner.'

He put a hand on the stair railing and leaned against it. Beneath the bruises he was pale. 'Lindsay is a hard, uncharitable woman.'

'Gee, and she says such nice things about you.'

'We used to be friends,' he claimed. 'In fact, we went out a time or two. Did she mention that?'

'No.' Lie or not, she wanted to hear more. The cop in her shoved the cautious woman aside. 'There's never been any mention of that anywhere.'

'I never brought it up,' he said. 'It seemed both irrelevant and indelicate.'

'How so?'

'It was years ago.'

'She's very vocal in accusing you of murder. I'd think you'd want to discredit her. Why haven't you said something?'

'I'm saying it now,' he said softly, his gaze beaming down on her. 'To you.'

It was an offer. He would give her things he wouldn't give anyone else. Because he thought she was his guardian angel.

'I was about to take my lunch break,' Renard said, easing his way down the steps. 'Would you join me?'

The offer struck her as so . . . ordinary. She believed this man to be a monster of the worst sort. The sight of Pam Bichon's body flashed in her mind. The brutality of the crime seemed bigger, stronger, more powerful than the man standing before her.

'I don't want to be seen with you,' she said bluntly. 'My life is difficult enough at the moment.'

'I'm not going out. I can't,' he admitted. 'My life is difficult, as well.'

The side door to the parking area opened, and a delivery boy stepped in with a white deli bag.

'Mr Briggs?' He looked up at Renard, his eyes widening. 'Man, that musta been some car wreck you was in.'

Renard pulled out his wallet without comment.

'I'll share my gumbo,' he offered Annie as the delivery boy left.

'I'm not hungry,' Annie said, but she didn't turn away. Marcus Renard was at the heart of everything, the rock in the pond that had set wave after wave rippling through life in Bayou Breaux.

'I'm not a monster,' Renard said. 'I'd like the chance to convince you of that, Annie.'

'You shouldn't talk to me without your lawyer.'

'Why not?'

Why not indeed? Annie thought. She was alone. She had no wire, no tape recorder. Even if he confessed, it wouldn't matter. Kudrow was the attorney of record; without his presence nothing Renard said would be admissible in court. He could confess to a dozen murders and not hang for one of them.

She weighed her options. They were in a place of business. She could still hear muffled voices coming from Bayou Realty. She was a cop. He wouldn't be stupid enough to try anything here, and he was in no condition to try. She wanted to know what drove him. What was it about Pam Bichon that had caught hold of this otherwise seemingly ordinary man and pulled him over the edge?

'All right.'

The offices of Bowen & Briggs encompassed a single, huge open space with a wood floor that had been sanded blond and varnished to a hard gloss. Gray upholstered modular walls set off various office and conference spaces on the west side. The east side was studded with half a dozen drafting tables and work centers. Renard took his bag to a table in the southeast corner, a space set aside for relaxing, drinking coffee, having lunch. A radio on the counter played classical music.

Annie followed him at a distance, taking her time to assess the place and wishing she had worn her backup weapon.

'You're in trouble.'

She jerked around toward Renard. He was busy lifting his lunch from the deli bag.

'You said your life is difficult now,' he prompted. 'You're in trouble because of Fourcade?'

'I'm in trouble because of you.'

'No.' He motioned her to the chair across from him and took his own seat. Fragrant steam billowed up as he pried the lid off the cup of gumbo, dark roux and sassafras filé. 'You would be in trouble because of me if I were Pam's murderer. I'm not. I should think you'd be convinced of that after that poor Nolan woman was attacked.'

'Unrelated cases. One thing has nothing to do with the other,' Annie said.

'Unless they're both the work of the Bayou Strangler.'

'Stephen Danjermond was the Bayou Strangler, and he's dead. The evidence against him was conclusive.'

'So was the evidence Fourcade planted in my desk. That doesn't make me a killer.'

Annie stared at him. She'd gone over the chronology of events. All the pieces fit. But he swore he was innocent. Was he just an accomplished liar or had he convinced himself of his innocence? She'd seen it happen. People embraced a persecution complex like a security blanket. Nothing was ever their fault. Someone else caused them to be selling dope. It was the fault of the rotten cops that they got busted. But she didn't think a persecution complex fit either Renard or Pam's murder. That was about something else entirely. Obsession.

'I want you to understand, Annie – May I call you Annie?' he asked politely. 'Deputy Broussard is a bit difficult for me, all things considered.'

'Yes,' Annie said, though she didn't like the idea of his using her first name. She didn't like the idea of it in his mouth, rolling over his tongue. She didn't like the idea of giving him anything, of acquiescing to any wish of his, no matter how small.

'I want you to understand, Annie,' he started again. 'I loved Pam like –'

'Like a friend. I know. We've been over this.'

'Are you working on her case now? Will you try to catch her killer?'

'I want her killer brought to justice,' she said, evading the specifics of her involvement with the case. 'You understand what that means, don't you?'

'Yes.' He lifted a spoon of gumbo to his stitched lip. 'I wonder if you do.'

Annie ignored the ominous import and pressed on. 'You said you went out with Lindsay Faulkner. Forgive me for saying so, but I have a hard time picturing that.'

'I don't always look this way.'

'You don't seem . . . compatible.'

'We weren't, as it happened. I believe Lindsay may have – How shall I suggest this? Other preferences.'

'You think she's a lesbian?'

He made a little shrug and looked down at his meal, seeming uncomfortable with the topic he had raised.

'Because she wouldn't sleep with you?' Annie said bluntly.

'Heavens, no. We had dinner. I never expected more. It was clear we wouldn't progress that far. It was her . . . her *way* with Pam. She was very protective. Jealous. She didn't like Pam's husband. She didn't like any man showing an interest in Pam.'

He took another spoon of gumbo and sipped it between his teeth.

'Are you gonna try to tell me you think Pam's partner killed her? In a jealous lesbian rage?'

'No. I don't know who killed her. I wish I did.'

'Then what's your point?'

'That Lindsay dislikes me. She wants to blame someone for Pam's death. She's chosen me.'

'*Everyone* has chosen you, Mr Renard. You *are* the primary suspect.'

'*Convenient* suspect,' he corrected her. 'Because I liked Pam. Because people think of me as a stranger here – they forget I was born here, lived here as a boy. They find it strange that I'm single and live with my mother and a brother who frightens people with his autism.'

'Because Pam believed you were stalking her,' Annie countered. 'Because you hung around her even after she told you to get lost. Because you had motive, means, opportunity, and no viable alibi for the night of the murder.'

'I was in Lafayette –'

'Going to a store that had already closed by the time you got to the Acadiana Mall. Bad luck, that. If the store had been open, you might have witnesses to corroborate your story.'

He looked at her steadily, and his voice was even when he spoke. 'I went there for supplies, not an alibi.'

'You can spare me the story,' Annie said. 'I've memorized the time line. At five-forty Lindsay Faulkner left the office and noted that your car was still in the parking lot. Pam was meeting with clients to write up an offer on a house. At eight-ten you stopped at Hebert's Hobby Shop and purchased a number of items, among them blades for an X-Acto knife.'

'A common tool for dollhouse builders.'

'Pam's clients left her office at eight-twenty. They were the last people to see Pam alive – with the exception of her killer. Meanwhile, Hebert's didn't have everything you needed –'

'French doors for my current project.'

'So you drove to Acadiana Mall in Lafayette, intending to visit the hobby store there, but it was closed,' she pressed on. 'And on your way

955

back you claim you developed car trouble – origin unknown – and sat along a back road for two hours before you got going again with the aid of an anonymous Good Samaritan no one has been able to track down in the three months since. You say you got home around midnight, but you have no one to confirm that because your mother was gone to Bogalusa to visit her sister. That's your story.'

'It's the truth.'

'Meanwhile, the medical examiner in Lafayette puts Pam's death around midnight, give or take, just a few miles from your home.'

'I *didn't* kill her.'

'You were obsessed with her.'

'I was infatuated,' he admitted, rising slowly from his chair. He went to a small refrigerator tucked into the lower cupboards and withdrew two bottles of iced tea. 'I wish she could have returned my feelings, but she didn't and I accepted that.'

He set the bottles on the table, pushing one in Annie's direction.

'Her husband had a far more compelling obsession than I.' He eased back into his chair, picked up a paper napkin, and dabbed at the spittle that had collected in the corners of his wired mouth as he struggled with speech. 'He didn't want to let her go. I think she was afraid of him. She told me she didn't dare see other men until the divorce was final.'

A convenient story to put off a man, Annie thought, though she couldn't dismiss the possibility it was true. It was common knowledge Donnie hadn't wanted the divorce. Lindsay Faulkner confessed to thinking Donnie had been the one harassing Pam. Rumors of a fight over Josie had been whispered around, though it seemed Donnie had no ground to stand on in that arena. He had been the cheat in the marriage. Pam had done nothing to threaten her standing as custodial parent.

'But then,' Renard murmured, staring down into his tea, 'maybe that was just an excuse. I think she was seeing someone for a short time.'

'Why would you think that?'

He couldn't answer her. The only way he would know was if he had watched her, followed her. He wouldn't admit to that, *couldn't* admit to it. The stalking was the basis for the whole case against him. If he admitted to stalking Pam Bichon, and if in that admission he revealed he had seen her with another man, that only added to his motive to kill her. Jealousy. She had spurned him for another.

Annie got up from the table. 'I've heard enough, thank you. Pam was tortured and murdered by her estranged husband, her secret lesbian partner, and/or a mystery lover you can't name or identify. Couldn't have been you that killed her. You're a victim of a malicious conspiracy. Never mind that you had motive, means, opportunity, and a crappy alibi. Never mind that the detectives found Pam's stolen ring in your house.'

Renard rose, too, and limped along beside her as she moved toward the door. 'There is more than one kind of obsession,' he said. 'Fourcade is obsessed with this case. He planted that ring. He's done that kind of thing before. He has a history.'

'I have no history. *I've* never hurt anyone. *I'd* never been arrested before this.'

'Maybe that just means you're good at it,' Annie said.

'I *didn't* do it.'

'Why should I believe you? More to the point: Why are you so bent on convincing me? You're a free man. The DA's got nothing on you.'

'For now. How long before Fourcade or Stokes manufactures something else? I'm an innocent man. My reputation has been ruined. They won't be satisfied until they have my life one way or another. Someone has to find the truth, Annie, and so far, you're the only one looking.'

'I'm looking,' she said in a cool voice. 'I don't guarantee you're gonna like what I find.'

Marcus held the door for her and watched as she descended the stairs and walked out of the building. She moved in a way that seemed unself-conscious, fresh. Freer than Pam in her physicality, in her gestures. Pam's free-spirit soul sister. He found comfort in the thought. Continuity.

He had pinned his heart on Pam, but Annie would set him free. He was sure of it.

17

The Bayou Realty office was closed and locked when Annie went around to the front of the building. Too bad. She wanted to see the look on Lindsay Faulkner's face when she told her Marcus Renard had her pegged for a lesbian.

Of course, there was the chance that it was true. Annie knew little about her. No one had ever looked that closely at Faulkner, as far as Annie knew. There had been no reason. With the business set up as it was at the time of Pam's death, Faulkner had no financial motive to kill her, and no other motive would have been considered. Women didn't kill other women in the manner Pam Bichon had died.

Annie crossed the street to the Jeep and glanced up at the building as she turned the key in the ignition. Renard was standing at a second-story window, looking out at her.

He swore he was innocent, that he loved Pam. He wanted Annie to find the truth.

Find the truth or muddy the waters? she wondered. She had just stepped into the investigation and already there were factors to consider she hadn't seen before. Fourcade had been down these twisted trails already. His offer hung in her mind like a seductive promise, something she should resist.

Turning away from Renard, she put the Jeep in gear and headed across town.

Donnie surveyed the scene from the seat of a backhoe, a bottle of Abita beer in hand. The Mardi Gras parade float taking shape before him was for Josie. She had talked him into it, those big brown eyes bright with excitement. Unable to deny her anything, he had organized a crew from the staff of Bichon Bayou Development and set them to work. He had envisioned Josie spending hours here with him as the flatbed became a crêpe-paper, fairy-tale kingdom, but Belle Davidson had taken her to Lake Charles for the day 'to get away from the atmosphere' in Bayou Breaux.

'To get away from me, more like,' he muttered.

He tipped his bottle up only to find it empty. He scowled and tossed it down into the bucket of the backhoe, where it shattered against the remains of several other brown bottles. The sound pierced through the country music blaring from the radio. Several heads turned in his direction from the float, but no one said anything.

People had grown wary of his moods since Pam's death. They walked around him on eggshells, hedging their bets in case the cops were wrong about Marcus Renard, in case Donnie was the resurrection of the Bayou Strangler. He was sick of it. He wanted it all behind him. It *should* have been behind him.

'Goddamn cops,' he grumbled.

'Sounds like maybe I should come back.'

Annie had let herself in a side door of the big shed where the construction company stored some of its heavy equipment.

Donnie glared down at her from his throne. 'Do I know you?'

'Annie Broussard, sheriff's office.' This time she flashed the badge. *Be bold.*

'Oh, Christ, now what? Did my check bounce? I don't care if it did. You can throw Fourcade back in the hoosegow, the ungrateful son of a bitch.'

'Why do you say that?'

He opened his mouth to complain, then swallowed it back. Fourcade was on suspension, off the case. No sense dredging up old suspicions with a new cop.

'The man is unstable, that's all,' he said as he climbed down from the backhoe. 'So, you're Fourcade's replacement. What happened to the other guy, that black guy – Stokes?'

'Nothing. He's still on the case.'

'Not that I care,' he said, bending to dig another bottle out of the old Coleman cooler that sat beside the backhoe's tire. 'You want my opinion: That guy is lazy. He was on the case when Renard started hassling Pam, and all he wanted to do was make time with her. Always looked to me like Fourcade was the brains of the pair. It's too damn bad he's off the case, except of course that he's nuts.'

He twisted the top off the bottle and tossed it into the backhoe bucket with the rest of the trash. 'Too damn bad he didn't get to close the case for good in that alley. You want a beer?'

'No, thanks.' Annie dipped her head a little, letting her bangs fall into her eyes, hoping recognition wouldn't dawn on Donnie as it had with Lindsay Faulkner.

'On duty?' He laughed. 'That never stopped any cop I ever knew – Gus Noblier included. What are you, new?'

'I need to ask you a couple questions.'

'I swear, that's all you people do – ask questions. You got more answers now than you know what to do with.'

'I spoke with Lindsay Faulkner this morning.'

His face twisted in distaste. 'Did she tell you I'm the Antichrist? The woman hates me. You would have thought she was Pam's big sister. They were that close. As close as women get without being lesbians.'

'She told me you're going to sell Pam's half of the business.'

'I've got my hands full with my own business. I have no desire to have Lindsay for a partner and she has no desire to have me.'

'She said you may have a buyer from New Orleans. Is that true?'

He slanted her a sly look. 'A good businessman doesn't tip his hand too far.'

'Are you telling me it's a bluff?' She smiled back, like a friend wanting in on the secret. 'Because a name came up and I could just make a couple phone calls . . .'

'What name?' She could feel him drawing back from her, raising his shields.

'Duval Marcotte.'

'It's a bluff,' he declared flatly. 'Make all the calls you want.'

He scratched at the stubble on the knob of his chin and gestured toward the float. 'What do you think of the masterpiece?'

Annie looked at the work in progress: a cheap pine framework covered with chicken wire. It could have been anything. Two women in cutoffs and tight T-shirts were stuffing chicken-wire holes with squares of blue crepe paper, talking, laughing, oblivious to the larger problems of the world.

'It's a castle,' Donnie explained. 'My daughter's idea. She picked a scene from *Much Ado About Nothing*. Can you believe that? Nine years old and she's into Shakespeare.'

'She's a very bright girl.'

'She wanted to help build it, but her grandmother had other ideas. Another Davidson woman conspiring against me.'

'Will Belle and Hunter challenge you for custody?'

He hunched his shoulders, still staring at the float. 'I don't know. Probably. I suppose it'll depend on whether Hunter goes to prison. I've got that in my favor: I haven't tried to kill anybody recently – or ever,' he amended, glancing down at Annie. 'That was a joke.'

'You want Josie to live with you full-time?'

'She's my daughter. I love her.'

As if it were as simple as that. As if he had managed to totally separate Donnie the Daddy from Donnie the Don Juan.

'Rumor had it, you would have fought Pam for her.'

'Oh, Christ, that again?' Impatience pulled at his features, making him look petulant. 'You've got your killer. Why don't you go hound him? I didn't do anything to Pam. I didn't kill her for the insurance or for the business or in a rage or anything else. I *couldn't* do anything to Pam. I was sure as hell in no condition that night to do anything to anybody. I drank too much, got a ride home from a friend, and passed out.'

'I know all that,' Annie said. 'I'm not looking at you as a suspect, Mr Bichon.' Though it had occurred to her more than once that drunkenness was easily faked and Donnie had as much motive as anyone – more than most.

According to the news reports, he had shown up at the Voodoo Lounge that night between nine and ten, and had been dropped off at home by his friend around eleven-thirty. Pam had last been seen at eight-twenty and had died around midnight. There were windows of opportunity on both ends of Donnie's story.

'I was just wondering what grounds you had to challenge Pam for custody.'

'Why? Pam is dead. What difference does it make now?'

'If Pam was involved with someone –'

'Renard killed her!' he roared suddenly. The cords in his neck stood out, as taut as guy wires. He spiked his bottle on the cement floor of the shed, shards of glass exploding outward, beer foaming like peroxide in a raw wound. 'He killed her! Now do your fucking job and put him away for it!'

He shoved past Annie and strode for the door. The float crew stared, mouths agape. Mary Chapin Carpenter shouted from the radio – 'I Take My Chances'.

Annie hustled after him. The brilliance of the afternoon nearly blinded her as she emerged from the shed. Squinting, she shaded her eyes with her hand. Donnie stood at the chain-link fence that corralled the possessions of his company, staring at the train tracks that ran behind the property.

'Look, I'm just trying to get at the whole truth,' she said, stepping up beside him. 'I wouldn't be doing my job if I didn't ask questions.'

'It's just – It's dragged on and on.' He swallowed and his Adam's apple bobbed like cork. His eyes stayed on the tracks. 'Why can't it just be over? Pam's gone. . . . I'm so tired of it. . . .'

He wanted the wounds to heal and disappear with no scars, no reminders. It was a good detective's job to keep picking and picking at those wounds. The trick was knowing when to dig and when to stand back. Annie had thought she would be able to read Donnie Bichon, know him for a liar if he was one. But the emotions that had caught him up were a tangled skein; she couldn't tell grief from remorse, fear from arrogance.

'I could have been a better husband,' he murmured. 'She could have been a better wife. You can think what you want of me for saying it.'

In the distance a train whistle blew. Donnie seemed not to have heard it. He was lost in memories.

'I just wanted what was mine,' he whispered, blinking against the threat of tears. 'I didn't want to lose her. I didn't want to lose Josie. I thought maybe if I scared her . . . threatened custody . . .'

If he scared her how? Was custody the only threat he'd made? Annie drew a breath to ask what he meant, but held it as he turned toward her.

'You look like her, you know,' he said, his voice strangely dreamy. 'The shape of your face . . . the hair . . . the mouth . . .'

He reached out as if to touch her cheek, but pulled back at the last instant. She wondered if it was sanity or the fear of breaking some inner spell that stopped him. Either way, it unnerved her. She didn't welcome comparison with a woman who had met such a brutal end.

'I miss her,' Donnie admitted. 'Always want what I can't have. I used to think that was ambition, but it's just . . . need.'

'What about Pam? What did she need?'

The train whistle blew again, louder, nearer.

'To be free of me,' he said simply, his expression bleak. 'And now she is.'

Annie watched him walk away, not back to the building but to a pearl white Lexus parked near the side gate. Behind her the Southern Pacific train whined past, wheels chattering over the connections in the track.

She had been working the case a matter of hours, and she felt as if she had stepped into a maze that appeared deceptively simple from the outside but was in reality a complex labyrinth, dark corridor full of mirrors. A small part of her wanted to turn back. A larger part of her wanted to go deeper, learn more. The mystery pulled at her, beckoned her. *Temptation*. The word came to her like a whispered secret from a hidden co-conspirator.

Fourcade. He was the guardian at the gate, her self-appointed guide if she would accept his offer. He held the map of the maze and the knowledge of the players. The trick would be deciding if he was friend or foe, if his offer was genuine or a trap. There seemed only one way to find out.

18

Even on a bright day the house had a sinister look. The brilliant spring sun failed to remove the shawl of shadows that fell down from the newly leafed trees. Shrouded in murky light and gray with neglect, it squatted amid the sprouting growth like a toothless crone, ugly and abandoned.

Nick stared at the house from the pirogue, fascinated by the possibility that evil could linger in a place like a scent. The house hadn't been bad off at the time of the murder. Recently vacated by renters at the time, and scheduled for some renovation work, the electricity had still been turned on. Since the murder, the place had been let go. Kids had thrown rocks through the windows. The stigma of death clung to it like grime.

Nick would not go inside. Some people would have called him superstitious, but they would have been people who had never stepped close to the boundary between good and evil; they didn't know the power or the possibilities. Still, it was telling that on a day as fine as this one, when other parts of Pony Bayou were thick with weekend fishermen, there were none within a quarter mile of this place.

He had set out in the pirogue intending to distance himself from thoughts of the case. But this place had drawn him like a magnet.

Another battle lost, and so he would give himself over to the obsession until a conclusion could be reached.

Would it be over now, he wondered, *had I killed Renard that night?*

Pony Bayou here was narrow, even this time of year, when the brown water was high and spilling into the forest. The banks were crowded with hackberry saplings and tangles of dewberry and poison ivy. The limbs of the black willow and water locust reached out over the column of water from both sides, like bony fingers stretching to touch one another.

The trees were alive with the sounds of birds excited by the early arrival of spring. The songs and shrieks and squawks blended into a cacophony that seemed to take on an especially discordant and unnerving quality. And on every available limb, log, and stump, water snakes had crawled out to sun themselves in an eerie ritual of spring. The forest along the banks seemed hung with reptiles, like dark, muscular ropes of live bunting.

Taking up the push-pole, Nick rose at the back of the pirogue and sent it gliding north and west. The route was twisted, his passing witnessed by no one. Nature claimed the land here for several miles and no man in recent history had challenged Her. Then the channel widened slightly and the forest came to an abrupt halt on the western bank, marking the edge of the first piece of domesticated property away from the murder scene. Marcus Renard's home.

The house stood a hundred yards or so away, elegant in its simplicity. Clean lines, plain columns. The modest home of a modest indigo planter in a past century. Tall French windows opened onto a brick veranda where Victor Renard sat at a patio table.

Victor was slightly bigger than Marcus, thicker bodied. While he had the social awareness of a small child, he had the physical strength of a thirty-seven-year-old man and had once been turned out of a group home for destroying a bed in a fit of temper. Emotions – his own or those of others – were difficult for him to comprehend or process. The autistic mind seemed unable to decode feelings. For the most part, he expressed none, though odd things would sometimes trigger agitation and occasionally anger. At the same time, Victor was mathematically gifted, able to easily work equations that could stump college students, and he could name the genus and species of thousands of animals and plants and describe each in textbook detail.

People around Bayou Breaux didn't understand Victor Renard's condition. They were frightened of him. They mistook him for being retarded or schizophrenic. He was neither.

Nick had considered it his duty to discover these things about Victor and his autism. An arsenal of information was far more useful to a detective than any other kind of weapon. The smallest, seemingly insignificant fact or detail could prove to be the one piece that made the rest of the puzzle work.

Victor Renard's mind was itself a complex mystery. If somewhere in the labyrinth he held a clue to his brother's guilt, Nick suspected they would never know. If they could ever bring Marcus to trial, Smith Pritchett would never attempt to use Victor as a witness. Aside from the familial connection, Victor's autism precluded him from appearing reliable or even coherent in court.

Nick leaned lightly against the push-pole, holding the pirogue against the slow current. He stood at the edge of his legal boundary. Kudrow had sought and been granted a temporary restraining order for his client, specifically outlining how near Nick could come to him. If he tested those limits too strongly or too often, he could be brought up on stalking charges. The irony both amused and disgusted him.

He watched as Victor became aware of him, sitting up straighter, then reaching for a pair of binoculars on the table. He came up out of his chair as if someone had set it on fire. He rushed twenty yards across the lawn, his gait strange, his arms straight down at his sides. He stopped and raised the binoculars again. Then he dropped the binoculars on the strap around his neck and began to rock himself from side to side in jerky, irregular movements, like a windup toy gone wrong.

'Not now!' Victor shouted, pointing at him. 'Red, red! Very red! Enter out!'

When Nick made no move to leave, Victor rushed forward another ten steps, wrapped his arms tight around his chest, and rocked himself around in a circle. Strange, piercing shrieks tore from him.

At the house, one of the French doors opened and Doll Renard rushed onto the veranda. Her agitation almost equaled her son's. She started toward Victor, then turned back toward the house. Marcus emerged, and limped across the lawn to his brother.

'Very red!' Victor screamed as Marcus took hold of his arm. 'Enter out!'

He screamed again as Marcus took the binoculars from him.

Nick expected shouting, then remembered Renard's fractured jaw and felt not remorse, but discomfort at the power of his own anger. Renard came toward the bank.

'You're violating the court order,' he said, hands curled into fists at his sides.

'I think not,' Nick said. 'I'm on a public waterway.'

'You're a criminal!'

Nick clucked his tongue. 'A matter of perspective, that.'

'We're calling the police, Fourcade!'

'This is the jurisdiction of the sheriff's office. You really think they'll come to your aid? You have no friends there, Marcus.'

'You're wrong,' Renard insisted. 'And you're breaking the law. You're harassing me.'

Yards behind him, Victor had fallen to his knees to rock himself. His banshee shrieks drove the birds from the trees.

Nick looked innocent. 'Who, me? I'm just fishing.' Lazily he straightened away from the push-pole, moving the pirogue from the bank. 'Ain't no law against fishing, no.'

He let the craft drift backward, following the curve of the land until his view of Renard's house and his brother was gone and only Renard himself remained in his line of vision. *Focus*, he thought. *Focus, calm, patience. Exist within the current, and the goal will be reached.*

Annie sat in an old ladder-back chair with a seat woven from the rawhide of some unfortunate long-dead cow. The view of the bayou was pretty from Fourcade's small gallery. She wondered if Fourcade ever idled his motor long enough to appreciate it. He didn't seem a man to care about such things, but then he had proven to be full of surprises, hadn't he?

It didn't surprise her that he lived in such a remote, inaccessible place. He was a remote, inaccessible man. It surprised her that his yard was neat, that he was obviously working on the house.

Her stomach growled. She'd been waiting an hour. Fourcade's truck was here, but Fourcade was not. God only knew where he'd gone. The sun was going down and her resolve was running out in direct proportion to her increasing need for a meal. To occupy her mind she tried to imagine a hiding spot in the Jeep where she might have tucked away an emergency Snickers and forgotten about it. She'd already been through the glove compartment and looked under the seats. She concluded that Mullen had stolen the candy, and was perfectly happy to waste another few moments hating him for it.

A pirogue came into view, skating through a patch of cypress deadheads. Nerves tightened in Annie's stomach, and she rose from the chair. Fourcade guided the boat in alongside the dock, took his time tying off the pirogue and walking up the bank. He wore a black T-shirt that fit him like a coat of paint and fatigue pants tucked into a pair of trooper boots. He didn't smile. He didn't blink.

'How did you find this place?' he asked.

'I'd be a poor candidate for detective if I couldn't manage to dig up an address.' Annie stepped behind the chair, resting her hands on its back.

'That you would, *chérie*. But no. You got initiative. You came to take the bull by the horns, *oui?*'

'I want to see what you have on the case.'

He nodded. 'Good.'

'But you have to know up front this doesn't change what happened Wednesday night. If that's what you're really after, then say so now and I'll just go on home.'

Nick studied her for a moment. She kept one hand close to the open flap of her faded denim jacket. She doubtless had the Sig Sauer handy. She didn't trust him. He didn't blame her.

He shrugged. 'You saw what you saw.'

'I'll have to testify. That doesn't make you angry? That doesn't make you want to – oh, say, plant a live snake in my Jeep?'

He leaned toward her and gently patted her cheek. 'If I wanted to hurt you, *chère*, I wouldn't leave it up to no snake.'

'Should I be relieved or afraid for my life?'

Fourcade said nothing.

'I don't trust you,' she admitted.

'I know.'

'If you pull any more of that crazy shit like you did last night, I'm gone,' she declared. 'And if I have to shoot you, I will.'

'I'm not your enemy, 'Toinette.'

'I hope that's true. I have enough of them right now. And I have them because of you,' Annie pointed out.

'Who ever said life was fair? Sure as hell wasn't me.'

He turned and walked away. He didn't invite her in; he expected her to follow him. No social niceties for Fourcade. They passed through the parlor, a room furnished with a toolbox and a sledgehammer. The floor was covered with a dirty canvas drop cloth. The kitchen was an absolute contrast – clean, bright, newly Sheetrocked, and painted the color of buttermilk. As tidy as a ship's galley. Nothing adorned the walls. Fresh herbs grew in a narrow tray on the windowsill above the sink.

Fourcade went to the sink to wash his hands.

'What changed your mind?' he asked.

'Noblier pulled me off patrol because the other deputies won't play nice. I gotta figure he won't promote me into your job anytime soon. So, if I want in on this case, you're my ticket.'

He expressed no sympathy, and asked for no details about her trouble with Mullen or the others. It was her problem, not his.

'Get yourself assigned to Records and Evidence,' he said, turning around, drying his hands on a plain white towel. 'You can read the files all day, study the reports.'

'I'll see what I can do. It's up to the sheriff.'

'Don't be passive,' he snapped. 'Ask for what you want.'

'And you think I'll just get it?' Annie laughed. 'You're really not from this planet, are you, Fourcade?'

His face grew hard. 'You won't get anything you don't ask for one way or another, sugar. You better learn that lesson fast, you want this job. People don't just give up their secrets. You gotta ask, you gotta pry, you gotta dig.'

'I know that.'

'Then do it.'

'I will. I *have*,' she insisted. 'I spoke with Donnie Bichon today.'

Fourcade looked surprised. 'And?'

'And he seems like a man with a conscience problem. But then maybe you don't wanna hear that – the two of you being so close and all.'

'I have no ties to Donnie Bichon.'

'He bailed you out of jail to the tune of a hundred thousand dollars.'

He rested his hands at the waist of his fatigue pants. 'As I said to Donnie, I will say to you: He bought my freedom, he did not buy me. No one buys me.'

'A refreshing policy for a New Orleans cop.'

'I'm no longer in New Orleans. I didn't assimilate well.'

'That's not what I've been reading,' Annie said. 'I spent the better part of the afternoon at the library. According to the *Times-Picayune*, you were the quintessential corrupt cop. You got a lotta ink down there. None of it good.'

'The press is easily manipulated by powerful people.'

Annie winced. 'Oooh, you know, it's remarks like that that lead people to draw unflattering conclusions about your sanity.'

'People think what they want. I know the truth. I lived the truth.'

'And your version of the truth would be what?' she pressed.

He simply stared at her, and she saw the bleakness of a soul who had lived a long, hard life and had seen too much that wasn't good.

'The truth is that I did my job too well,' he said at last. 'And I made the mistake of caring too deeply for justice in a place that has none, existentially speaking.'

'Did you beat that suspect?'

He said nothing.

'Did you plant that evidence?'

He bowed his head for a moment, then turned his back to her and pulled a cast-iron skillet from a lower cupboard.

She wanted to go to him, demand the truth, but she was afraid to get that near him. Afraid something might rub off on her – his intensity, his compulsion, the darkness that permeated his being. She was already involving herself in this case beyond the call of duty. She didn't want to go beyond reason, and she had a strong feeling Fourcade could take her there in a heartbeat.

'I need an answer, Detective.'

'It's irrelevant to the present case.'

'Prior bad acts inadmissible on the ground they may taint the opinion of the court? Bull. More often than not they establish a pattern of behavior,' Annie argued. 'Besides, we're not in court; we're in the real world. I have to know who I'm dealing with, Fourcade, and I already told you, I'm not long on trust at the moment.'

'Trust is of no use in an investigation,' he said, moving between stove, refrigerator, and butcher block. He set an assortment of vegetables on the chopping block and selected a knife of frightening proportions.

'It is with regards to partners,' Annie insisted. 'Did you plant that ring in Renard's desk?'

He looked up at her then, unblinking. 'No.'

'Why should I believe you? How do I know Donnie Bichon didn't pay you to plant it? He could have paid you to kill Renard the other night, for all I know.'

He sliced into a red bell pepper as if it were made of thin paper. 'Now who's paranoid?'

'There's a difference between healthy suspicion and delusion.'

'Why would I invite you into the investigation if I was dirty?'

'So you can use me like a puppet to achieve your own end.'

He smiled. 'You are far too smart for that, 'Toinette.'

'Don't waste your flattery.'

'I don't believe in flattery. Me, I say what's true.'

'When it suits you.'

She sighed as they came around the circle again. A conversation with Fourcade was like shadowboxing – all effort and no satisfaction.

'Why me?' she asked. 'Why not Quinlan or Perez?'

'It's a small division. We live in each other's pockets. One itches, another one scratches. You're outside the circle – that's an advantage.' He flashed the grin again, bright with a charm he never used. 'You're my secret weapon, 'Toinette.'

She tried one last time to talk herself out of this lunacy. But she didn't want to, and he knew it.

'You feel an obligation, a tie to Pam Bichon,' he said, 'and to those who've gone before her. You feel the shadows. That's why you're here. That and you know we want the same end, you and I: Renard in hell.'

'I want the case cleared,' Annie said. 'If Renard did it –'

'He did it.'

'– then fine. I'll dance in the street the day they send him from Angola to the next life. If he didn't do it –'

He jabbed the point of the knife into the butcher block. '*He did it.*'

Annie said nothing. She had to be out of her mind to come here to him.

'It's simple,' he said, calmer. He pulled the knife out of the block and began to dice an onion. 'I have what you need, 'Toinette. Facts, statements, answers to questions you have yet to ask. All of it can be checked if need be. You have an inquisitive mind, a free will, an appropriate skepticism. I have no power over you . . .' The knife stilled. He looked at her from under his brow. 'Do I?'

'No,' she said quietly, glancing away.

'Then we can proceed. But first, we eat.'

19

They ate. Stir-fried vegetables and brown rice. No meat. Odd that a man who chain-smoked would be a vegetarian, but Annie knew that she would have to become desensitized to Fourcade's contradictions. To expect the unexpected seemed a wise course, though one not easily settled into.

'You had two years at college. Why'd you quit?' he demanded, stabbing his fork into his dinner. He ate the way he did everything – with vehemence and no wasted movement.

'They wanted me to declare a major.' She felt uncomfortable with the idea that he had raided her personnel file. 'It seemed . . . restrictive. I was interested in lots of things.'

'Lack of focus.'

'Curiosity,' she retorted. 'I thought you liked my inquisitive nature.'

'You need discipline.'

'Look who's talking.' Annie frowned at him, pushing her rice around with her fork. 'What happened to your Taoist principles of nonresistant existence?'

'Often incompatible with police work. With regards to religions, I take what's useful to me and apply it where appropriate. Why did you become a cop?'

'I like helping people. It's different every day. I like solving mysteries. I get to drive a hot car. How about you?'

Words like *power* and *control* came to mind, but those were not the words he gave her.

'It's factual, logical, essential. I believe in justice. I believe in the struggle for the greater good. I believe the collective evil metastasizes with malignancies in the souls of individuals.'

'So it wasn't just the cool uniforms?'

Fourcade looked bemused.

'You enrolled in the academy in August '93,' he said. 'Just after the whole Bayou Strangler thing. Connection?'

'You know so much about me – you tell me.'

He ignored the suggestion of affront in her voice. He made no apologies for overstepping a boundary. 'You went to school with the fifth victim, Annick DelahoussayeGerrard. You were friends?'

'Yeah, we were friends,' she said.

She took her plate to the sink and stood looking out the window, seeing nothing. Night had wrapped itself around the house. Fourcade had no yard light. Of course he wouldn't. Fourcade would be one with the dark.

'We were best friends when we were little,' she said. 'The families called us the Two Annies. But, you know, we grew apart, ran with different crowds. Her folks ran a bar – it's the Voodoo Lounge now. They sold out after Annick was killed.

'I ran into her maybe a month before it happened. She was waitressing at the bar. She was getting divorced. I told her she should come up to Lafayette for a weekend, that we'd catch up and have some fun. But you know, that weekend never came. I suppose I didn't really mean for it to. We didn't have much in common anymore. Anyway, then came the news . . . and then the funeral.'

Nick watched her reflection in the window. 'Why do you think it hit you so hard if you'd grown so far apart?'

'I don't know.'

'Yes, you do.'

She was silent for a moment. He waited. The answer lay within her grasp. She didn't want to reach for it.

'We were two sides of the same coin once,' she said at last. 'A flip of the coin, a twist of fate . . .'

'It could have been you.'

'Sure, why not?' she said. 'You know, you read about a crime in the paper and you think how terrible for the victims, and then you turn the page and move on. It's so different when you know the people. The press called her by name for a week, then she became Victim Number Five and they were on to the next big headline. I saw what that crime did to her family, to her friends. I started thinking it would be good to try to make a difference for people like the Delahoussayes.'

Nick got up from the table and brought his plate to the sink to nest with hers. 'That's a good reason, 'Toinette. Honor, social responsibility.'

'Don't forget the hot car.'

'That's unnecessary.'

'The car?'

'The mask you wear,' he said. 'The effort you go to to hide the truth beneath layers of insignificant mannerisms and humor. It's a waste of energy.'

Annie shook her head. 'It's called having a personality. You oughta try it sometime. I'm betting it would improve your social life.'

The retort was made an instant before she realized what he had really said – that he lived with the protective pretenses stripped away from his soul; his needs, his thoughts, his feelings lay like raw and exposed nerve endings. She would never have thought of him as vulnerable, knew he

971

would never think of himself as such. How strange to see him that way. She wasn't sure it was something she wanted to see.

'A waste of time,' he said again, turning away. 'We've got a job to do. Let's get to it.'

He had turned the *grenier*, the loft that made up the second half-story of the house, into a study. The bed tucked into the far corner seemed like an afterthought, a grudging concession to the occasional need for sleep. A masculine place, with heavy wood furnishings, and an almost monkish quality in its sense of order. The bookcases were lined with titles, hundreds of books shelved by subject in alphabetical order. Criminology, philosophy, psychology, religion. Everything from aberrant behavior to the mysteries of Zen.

A ten-foot-long table held the reams of paperwork the Bichon homicide had generated. Photocopies of every statement, every lab report. Numbered binders filled with Fourcade's notes. A bulletin board behind the table held maps: one of a three-parish area, one of Partout Parish, one of the immediate Bayou Breaux area including the murder scene and Renard's home. Red pins marked significant sites. Fine red lines drawn between sites were annotated with exact mileage.

A second bulletin board held copies of the crime scene photos – stark, hard reality cast in the harsh light of a camera flash.

'Wow,' Annie murmured. 'I guess you believe in bringing your work home with you.'

'It's a duty, not a hobby.' He stood in front of one of the bookcases. 'You want a time clock and no worries, get a job at the lamp factory. You want to pass the buck on the tough stuff, stay in uniform.' He hit her with the Hard Stare. 'Is that what you want, 'Toinette? You wanna stay on the surface where everything is simple and safe, or do you want to go deeper?'

Once again she had the feeling he was the guardian at the gate of some secret world, that if she crossed the threshold, there would be no going back. She resented the idea.

'I want to be a detective,' she said. 'I want to help clear this case. I'm not pledging my allegiance to the Dark Lord or becoming a Jedi knight. I want to *do* the job, not *be* the job.'

That was Fourcade, the Zen detective. Disapproval hung on him like mist.

'It's a job, not a religion,' Annie said. 'You were born out of your time, Fourcade. You'd have made a hell of a Zealot.'

Her gaze shifted to the table, to the bulletin board and the pictures of Pam Bichon's grisly death. She wanted Fourcade's resources. She didn't have to embrace his doctrine of obsessive-compulsive behavior.

'I want this solved,' she said. 'End of story.'

She selected Donnie Bichon's file folder and opened it.

'Why did you go to him?' Fourcade asked. 'We looked at him and cleared him.'

'Because Lindsay Faulkner says he's fixing to sell Pam's half of the realty business.'

The news hit Nick like a rock to the chest. He had taunted Donnie with the idea just yesterday, never imagining the man would be fool enough to make such a move so soon after Pam's death. 'When did you hear this?'

'This morning. I stopped by the realty office.' She hesitated, weighing the pros and cons of telling the whole truth.

'You stopped by and what?' he demanded. 'If we're partners, we're partners, *chère*. No holding back.'

She took a deep breath as she set the file aside. 'She said Donnie claims he has a possible buyer on the hook . . . in New Orleans. Donnie told me it was a bluff.'

Nick had managed to all but banish the idea of Marcotte's involvement. It seemed too far-fetched. He couldn't imagine he had ever meant enough to Marcotte for him to inflict vengeance after all this time. Besides, Marcotte had gotten what he wanted back when, so what would be the point of dragging out the game?

Unless what he wanted now was Bayou Realty, and Nick's involvement was mere coincidence or karma. The question was: If Marcotte was involved, was the murder a result of that involvement or was his involvement a by-product of the crime?

'*C'est ein affaire à pus finir*,' Nick whispered.

'I figure it's a bluff,' Annie said. 'We – *you've* got Donnie's phone records from the period when Pam was being harassed. If the sale of the business was a motive for him to get rid of her, then he would have been in contact with his buyer during that time. Not from his home, if he had any sense, but no one would think twice about him calling New Orleans from the office. We can check it out.

'But I say if Donnie has this fat cat on the hook, why would he even bother to play games with Lindsay Faulkner?' she went on. 'And if he was afraid of having the sale raise a red flag with the cops, then why do anything out in the open? It's not that hard to hide deals. In fact, Donnie's done it before. He had Pam hiding property for him so he wouldn't lose it to the bank. Did you know about that?'

'Yes.'

Nick forced himself to move. *Forward* had become a mantra months ago. Move forward physically, psychologically, spiritually, metaphorically. Movement seemed to pull taut the lines upon which facts and ideas aligned themselves in his mind. Movement maintained order. So he moved forward and tried not to be spooked by the shadow that followed him.

'I'll go over the records,' he said. 'But I doubt the sale of the business has anything to do with the murder. It's more likely scavengers moving

973

in, taking advantage of an opportunity. A woman killed the way Pam was – that's no money murder. People killed for money reasons – they fall down steps, they drown, they disappear.'

He stopped in front of the table, his gaze on the photographs. 'This . . . this was personal. This was hate. Contempt. Control. Rage.'

'Or made to look so after the fact.'

'No,' he whispered. 'I can feel it.'

'Did you know her?' she asked quietly.

'She sold me this place. Nice lady. Hard to believe someone could have hated her this way.'

'Renard claims he loved her – like a friend. He insists he's being railroaded. He wants me to find the truth for him.' Her lips twisted. 'Gee, I'm a popular girl lately.'

He didn't pick up on the irony. He concentrated instead on Renard. 'You spoke with him? When? Where?'

'This morning. In his office. He invited me up. He's laboring under the misconception that I'm sympathetic toward him.'

'He trusts you?'

'I had the great luck to save his sorry ass – twice in one day. He seems to think just because I won't let individuals murder him, I won't want the state to do it, either.'

'You can get close to him, then,' Fourcade murmured. 'That's something Stokes and I could never do. He regarded us as the enemy from the first. Stokes had been riding him already for the harassment, before the murder. You come to him from a whole other direction.'

'I don't like the way your mind is bending,' Annie said. She went to one of the bookcases and stared at the titles. 'I told him flat out I think he did it.'

'But he wants to win you over, yes?'

'I don't know that I'd put it quite like that.'

Fourcade turned her around, his hands cupping her shoulders, and looked at her as if he was seeing her for the first time. '*Mais oui*. Oh, yeah. The hair, the eyes, 'bout the same size. You fit the victim profile.'

'So do half the women in South Lou'siana.'

'But *you* came into *his* life, *chère*. Like it was meant to be.'

'You're creeping me out, Fourcade.' She tried to wriggle away from his touch. 'You talk like he's a serial killer.'

'The potential is there. The psychopathology is there,' he said, and began pacing. 'Look at him: mid-thirties, white, single, intelligent, domineering mother, absent father, unsuccessful in maintaining relationships with women. It's classic.'

'But he doesn't have any criminal history. No pattern of escalating aberrant behavior.'

'Maybe, maybe not. Before he moved here, he had a girlfriend back in Baton Rouge. She died an untimely death.'

'The papers said she died in a car accident.'

'She was burned beyond recognition in a single-car crash on some back road not long after she told her mother she was going to break it off with Renard. She thought he was too possessive. "Smothering" was the word she used with her mother.'

He had obviously gone to the source for his information. The only thing the papers had gotten out of Elaine Ingram's mother was that she found Marcus Renard 'very pleasant and a gentleman' and that she wished her daughter had married him. If he'd been a monster then, no one had seen it . . . except perhaps Elaine.

'The mother doesn't think he killed her,' Annie said.

Fourcade looked impatient. 'It doesn't matter what she thinks. It matters what he did. It matters that he might have killed her. It matters that he might have had that kind of rage in him before and that he might have killed out of that rage.

'Look at this murder,' he said, gesturing to the photos. 'Rage, power, domination, sexual brutality. Not unlike your Bayou Strangler.'

'Are you saying you think maybe Renard did those women four years ago?' Annie asked. 'He moved back here in '93. You think he was the Bayou Strangler?'

Fourcade shook his head. 'No. I've been over those files. I've talked to the people who ended up pinning it on Danjermond: Laurel Chandler and Jack Boudreaux. They live up on the Carolina coast now. Too many bad memories 'round here, I guess, with her losing her sister to the Strangler and all. They tell a pretty convincing tale. The investigation backed them up.'

He stopped to stare at the crime scene photos. 'Besides, there are differences in the murders. Pam Bichon wasn't strangled to death.'

He touched a finger to one of the photos, a close-up of the bruising on the throat. 'She was choked manually – these bruises are thumbprints – and her hyoid bone was cracked. He probably choked her unconscious at some point. We can only hope so for her sake. But asphyxiation wasn't the cause of death. Loss of blood from the primary stab wounds was the cause of death.' He moved his finger to a shot of the woman's savaged bare chest. 'Because of the pattern of the blood splatters, I believe she was stabbed several times in the chest while she was standing, then fell to the floor. The choking happened sometime after she went down but before she was dead. Otherwise you wouldn't have this kind of bruising.

'The Strangler, he used a white silk scarf around the throat to kill his victims – that was his signature. And he tied them down with strips of white silk. See here? No ligature marks on Bichon's wrists or ankles.'

'But the sexual mutilation –'

He shook his head. 'Similar, but not the same by any means. Danjermond tortured his victims extensively before he killed them. The mutilation of Bichon was largely postmortem, suggesting it was about anger, hatred, disrespect, rather than any kind of erotic sadism – which was the case with the Strangler. That boy got off on it in a big way. Renard was pissed.

'And then there's the victim profile,' he said. 'The Strangler hunted women who were easily accessible: women who hung out in bars, looking for men, liked to pass a good time. That wasn't Pam Bichon.

'No,' he declared. 'The cases are unrelated. The way I see it, Renard fixated on Pam when he thought she might become available to him – when she separated from Donnie. He probably built a whole fantasy around her, and when she refused to cooperate in turning the fantasy into reality, he went over the line to the dark side.'

He turned and his gaze swept down over Annie. 'And now he's lookin' at you, *chère*.'

'Lucky me,' Annie muttered.

Fourcade ignored the sarcasm. 'Oh yeah,' he said, moving closer. 'You're being presented with a rare opportunity, 'Toinette. You can get close to him, open him up, see what's in his head. He lets you close enough, he'll give himself away.'

'Or kill me, if your theory holds true. I'd rather come across a nice piece of evidence, thanks anyway. The murder weapon. A witness who could put him at the scene. A trophy.'

'We found his trophy – the ring. Don't expect to find another. We never even found the gifts Pam gave back to him. We never found the other things he'd taken from her. He's too smart to make the same mistake twice – and that's what we need, sugar: for him to make a mistake. You could be it.' He brushed her bangs with his fingertips, caressed her cheek. The pad of his thumb skimmed the corner of her mouth. 'He could fall in love with you.'

She didn't like the way her pulse was pounding. She didn't like the way she saw Pam Bichon's corpse from every angle – torn, ragged, bloody; the feather mask a grotesque contrast.

'I'm not bait for your bear trap, Fourcade,' she said. 'If I can get something out of Renard, I will, but I'm not getting close enough for him to lay a finger on me. I don't want to get under his skin. I don't want to get inside his head – or yours, for that matter. I want justice, that's all.'

'Then go after it, *chère*,' he said, too seductively. 'Go after it . . . every way you can.'

20

'They should be made to pay for what they've put us through,' Doll Renard declared. She moved around the dining room like a humming-bird, flitting here, flitting there, resting nowhere.

'You've said that ten times,' Marcus grumbled.

'Eight.' Victor corrected him automatically and without smugness. 'Eight times. Repetition, multiplication. Two times four times, eight times. Even. Equal, *equals*. Equals sometime *equal*, sometime *odd*.'

He shook his head disapprovingly at the trick of the language.

Doll shot him a look of disgust. 'I'll say it 'til I'm blue. The Partout Parish Sheriff's Department has ruined our lives. I can't go anywhere without people staring and whispering. And most of the time they don't bother to whisper. 'There's that Doll Renard,' they say. 'How can she show her face after what her boy did?' It's even worse than after your father betrayed us. Of course, you wouldn't remember that. You were just a little boy. People are hateful, that's all.'

'I didn't do anything wrong,' Marcus reminded her. 'I'm innocent until proven guilty. Tell them that.'

She sniffed and flitted from the sideboard to the corner china cupboard. 'I wouldn't give them the satisfaction. Besides, they would just throw up to me how everyone knows you panted after that Bichon woman and she didn't want you.'

'Throw up,' Victor said, rocking from side to side on his chair.

It had taken an hour to calm him from the fit Fourcade had brought on, and he was still agitated. He was supposed to be helping polish the silver, but had decided tarnish was bacteria and refused to touch any of it. Bacteria, he believed, would run up his arms and gain access to his brain through his ear canals. 'Vomit. Puke. Spew. *Dis*gorge. *Re*gorge. Discharge – like excrement.'

'Victor, stop it!' Doll snapped, her bony hand fluttering over her heart. 'You're making us nauseous.'

'Talk – vomit words. Sound and sound alike,' he said, his eyes glazing over as he looked at something inside his scrambled brain.

Marcus tuned them both out, staring at his hands. He rubbed a jeweler's cloth up and down the stem of a marrow spoon and contemplated the uselessness of the thing. People didn't eat bone marrow anymore. The practice suggested a voraciousness that had gone out of vogue. To devour a creature's flesh, then crack its bones to suck out the very marrow of its life seemed a rapacious act. The hunger to consume a being whole was frowned upon, repressed.

He wondered if a need repressed deeply enough, long enough, eventually went into a person's marrow, reachable only if the bones were broken open. He wondered what would drain out of his own marrow. His mother's would be black as tar, he suspected.

'He beat you,' she reiterated, as if he needed reminding of Fourcade's sins. 'You could be permanently disfigured. You could be disabled. You could lose your job. It's a pure wonder they haven't fired you after everything that's gone on.'

'I'm a partner, Mother. They can't fire me.'

'Who will come to you with work? Your reputation is ruined – *and* mine. I've lost every single costume order I've gotten for Mardi Gras. And that man has the gall to come here, to harass us, and the sheriff's department does nothing! Nothing! I swear, we could all be murdered in our beds, and they would do nothing! They should be made to pay for what they've put us through.'

'Nine,' Victor said.

He rose abruptly from his chair as the hall clock struck eight, and hurried from the room.

'There he goes,' Doll muttered bitterly, her features pinching tight. 'He'll sleep like the dead. I can't remember the last time I had a decent night's sleep. Every night now I dream about my Mardi Gras masks. All the joy of them has been robbed from me. You know what people say. They say the mask found on that dead woman was from my collection, and, even though I know it wasn't, even though I can account for every single one of them, even though I know people are motivated by jealousy because my collection has won prizes year after year during Carnival, it's just robbed the joy from me.'

If his mother had ever had a moment's joy in her life, Marcus had never heard about it until after it had been 'robbed' from her, as if she were aware of the emotion only after the fact. He set the marrow spoon down and folded the jeweler's cloth.

'I called Annie Broussard,' he said. 'Perhaps she can do something about Fourcade.'

'What could *she* possibly do?' Doll asked sourly, annoyed at having the attention shifted from her own suffering.

'She stopped him from killing me,' he pointed out. 'I need to lie down. My head is pounding.'

Doll clucked her tongue. 'It's no wonder. You could have a brain injury. A blood vessel could burst in your head months from now, and then where would we be?'

I would be free of you, Marcus thought. But there were simpler ways to escape than death.

He went into his bedroom, pausing there only to take a Percodan from the drawer in the nightstand. Pills couldn't be left in the medicine chest where Victor would find them. Victor believed all pills to be both remedial and preventative. As a teenager he had twice had his stomach pumped to empty him of aspirin, stomach aids, vitamins and Midol.

Marcus broke the painkiller into pieces, worked them into his mouth, and washed them down with Coca-Cola – a practice his mother had harped against all his life. Doll believed Coca-Cola would react with drugs like alcohol and render a person comatose. He took an extra swig for spite and carried the can into his workroom.

Tension and anger kept him from going to his drawing table. He moved around the room hunched over because his ribs were especially sore. Everything hurt more tonight because of Fourcade. Because of Fourcade, he had hurried across the lawn, strained muscles, raised his blood pressure.

That bastard damn well would pay for what he'd done. Kudrow would see to that. Criminal charges, a civil suit. By the time the dust settled, what was left of Fourcade's career would be in shreds. The idea pleased Marcus enormously – using the very system his tormentors had tried to destroy him with to destroy his tormentors. He would ruin Stokes too if he could. Donnie Bichon had already destroyed Pam's trust and made her suspicious of all men. But Marcus would have eventually won her if she hadn't called the sheriff's department. Stokes had wasted no opportunity to turn Pam against him, planting doubts in her mind at every turn.

Marcus often wondered what might have been had Pam not misconstrued his interest and called the sheriff's office. They could have had something nice together. He had pictured it a thousand times: the two of them living a quiet, suburban kind of life. Friends and lovers. Husband and wife.

In the last few months Marcus had developed a strong dislike and disrespect for the sheriff's office and officers. Except Annie. Annie wasn't like the rest of them. Her heart was pure. The politics of the system had yet to corrupt her sense of fairness.

Annie would look for the truth, and when she found it he would make her his.

Victor rose at midnight, as he always did. He hadn't slept well. Fragmented dreams had driven into his brain like shards of stained glass. The colors disturbed him. Very red colors. *Red* like blood and *black* too. Dark *and* light. Light the color of urine.

The colors were too intense. Intensity was painful. Intensity could be very white or very red. White intensity came from soft and coolness; from certain feelings he couldn't name or describe; from specific visual images – semicolons and colons, phrases in parentheses, and horses. White intensity also came from a collection of precious words: *luminous, mystique, marble, running water*. He especially had to steel himself against the words. *Luminous* could produce such white intensity he would be rendered speechless and immobile.

And just a fine degree to the right of white intensity was red intensity. Like a circle with *Start* and *Stop* together. Very red intensity came from *heaviness*, pressure, the smell of cheddar cheese and of animal waste – but not human waste, even though humans were animals. *Homo sapiens.* Red words were *sluice* and *bunion* and sometimes *melon*, but not always. *Very* red words he couldn't verbalize, even in his own mind. He pictured them as objects he could allow himself only glimpses of. *Jagged, erect, slab, mucus.*

Very red intensity squeezed his brain and magnified his senses a hundredfold until the smallest sound was a piercing shriek and he could see and count each individual hair on a person's head and body. The sensory overload caused panic. Panic caused shutdown. Start and stop. Sound and silence.

His senses were full now, like water goblets lined up on a quivering, narrow ledge, the water moving, lapping at the rims and over them. *Mask*, he thought. Mask equaled *change* and sometimes *deception*, depending on red or white.

Victor stood in his room near the desk for a long time and listened to the fluorescent bulb in the lamp. Sizzle, hot *and* cold. An almost white sound. He felt time pass, felt the earth move in minute increments beneath his feet. His brain counted the passing moments by fractions until the Magic Number. At that precise instant, he broke from his stillness and let himself out of his room.

The house was silent. Victor preferred silence with darkness. He moved more freely without the burden of sound or light. He went down the hall and stood at the door to his mother's hobby room. Mother forbade him access to the room, but when Mother was asleep her thoughts and wishes ceased to exist – like television, On and Off. He counted by fractions in his mind to the Magic Number and let himself into the room, where he turned on the small yellow light of the sewing machine.

Dress forms stood here and there like headless women garbed in the elaborate costumes Mother had made for past Carnivals. The forms made Victor uneasy. He turned away from them, turned to the wall where the masks were displayed. There were twenty-three, some small, some of smooth shiny fabric, some large, some covered with sequins, some stitched like needlepoint faces with a protruding penis where the nose should have been.

Victor chose his favorite and put it on. He liked the sensation it gave him inside, though he couldn't name the feeling. Mask equaled change. Change, transformation, *transmutation*. Pleased, he let himself out of the room, went down the stairs and out into the night.

21

Kay Eisner had learned to hate men at an early age, courtesy of an uncle who had found her too tempting as a seven-year-old. No man she'd known in the thirty years since had caused her to change her opinion. She scoffed at the book that claimed men were from Mars. Men were from hell, and how every woman on the planet didn't see it was beyond her. War was a bloody game played by men. Politics was a power game played by men. Crime was a cancer in society, perpetrated and spread predominantly by men. The prisons were overflowing with men. Rapists and killers prowled the streets.

It pained her to have to work for a man, but men ran the world, so what were her choices? Arnold Bouvier was her foreman, but every hand doing the dirty work gutting catfish in his plant belonged to a woman. They were working extra shifts and overtime these days, on account of Lent coming up. Catholics all over America would be stocking up on frozen fish.

Kay had worked the Saturday second shift, thinking all the while that the overtime pay would bring her that much closer to her dream of going into business for herself. She wanted to sell collectible dolls by mail order, and deal with as few men face-to-face as she could.

She double-checked the locks on her doors – front and back – before going into the bathroom. Her work clothes went immediately into a diaper bucket with water, detergent, and bleach to combat the stink of fish. She turned the shower as hot as she could stand it and scrubbed her skin with Yardley lavender soap. The room was thick with steam by the time the hot water ran out.

Kay cracked open the window to cool things off. She dried her curly hair with a threadbare towel, never looking at herself in the mirror above the sink. She couldn't stand looking at the body that had betrayed her time and again throughout her life by attracting the attention of men.

Men were the scourge of the earth. She thought so no less than ten times a day. Thinking it now, she pulled on a shapeless nightshirt, went out of the bathroom and down the hall to her bedroom. She remembered the open bathroom window just as she lay down to sleep, her body aching with fatigue. She couldn't leave it. A rapist was prowling around the parish.

As if Kay had conjured him up from her nightmares, he emerged from the darkness of her closet as she started to rise. A demon in black, faceless, soundless. Terror cut through her like a spear. She screamed once before he struck her hard across the face and knocked her backward onto the bed. Twisting onto her stomach, she tried to pull herself across the mattress. But even as her instincts pushed her to escape, a fatalistic sense of inevitability filled her. The tears that came as he grabbed her by the hair were as much from hatred as from pain. Hate for the man about to rape her, and hate for herself. She wouldn't get away. She never had.

22

He remembered a woman. Or he had dreamed about a woman. Reality and its opposite floated around in his brain like the stuff in a Lava lamp. He groaned and shifted positions, sprawling on his belly. The rustling of the sheets was magnified to the sound of newspaper crumpling right next to his ear. That was when he remembered the booze – lots of it. He needed to pee.

A hand settled low on his back and a warm breath, stale with the smell of cigarettes, caressed his ear.

'Rise and whine, Donnie. You got some explaining to do.'

Fourcade.

Donnie bolted up and turned, twisting the sheet around his hips. He cracked his skull on the headboard and winced as pain bounced around inside his head.

'Jesus! Fuck! What the hell are you doing here?' he demanded. 'How'd you get in my house?'

Nick moved away from the bed, taking in the state of Donnie's bachelor habitat. Coming through the kitchen and living room he had surmised that Donnie had a cleaning woman, but not a cook. The kitchen garbage was full of frozen dinner cartons. A decorator had coordinated the town house so that it felt more like a hotel suite than a home. This had been a model to entice prospective buyers into the Quail Court condo development – until the unfortunate demise of Donnie's marital state. He had commandeered the model when he separated from Pam.

'That's nasty language for a Sunday morning, Tulane,' Nick said. 'What's the matter with you? You got no respect for the Sabbath?'

Donnie gaped at him, bug-eyed. 'You're a fucking lunatic! I'm calling the cops.'

He snatched the receiver off the phone on the nightstand. Nick stepped over and pressed the plunger down with his forefinger.

'Don't try my patience, Donnie. It ain't what it used to be.' He took the receiver away, recradled it, and sat down on the edge of the bed. 'Me, I wanna know what kind of game you're playing.'

'I don't know what the hell you're talking about.'

'I'm talking about you jerking Lindsay Faulkner's chain, telling her you gonna sell the realty. Telling her you got some big catfish on the hook down in New Orleans. That where you got the money to bail me out, Donnie?'

'No.'

''Cause that would have a very poetic irony about it. You kill your wife, collect the insurance, sell her business, use the money to bail out the cop that tried to kill the suspect.'

Donnie pressed the heels of his hands to his aching eyes. 'Jesus, I have told you and told you, I did *not* kill Pam. You know I didn't.'

'You're not wasting any time making a buck off her. Why didn't you tell me Friday about this pending deal?'

'Because it's none of your business. I have to take a piss.'

He threw back the covers and climbed out on the other side of the bed. He walked like a man who had fallen out of a moving car and rolled to a hard stop in the gutter. Black silk boxers hung low on his hips. He hadn't managed to take his socks off before succumbing to unconsciousness. They drooped around his ankles. The rest of his clothes lay where he'd dropped them as he'd peeled them off on his way to the bed.

Nick rose lazily and still beat him to the door of the master bath.

'You're dragging it low to the ground this morning, Tulane. Long night?'

'I had a few. I'm sure you can relate. Let me in the bathroom.'

'When we're through.'

'Fuck. Why'd I ever get hooked up with you?'

'That's what I wanna know,' Nick said. 'Who's your big money man, Donnie?'

He looked away and blew out a breath. He grimaced at the smell of himself as he inhaled – smoke, sweat, and sex. He wondered vaguely where the woman was. 'No one. I lied. It was a bluff. I told that little Cajun gal.'

'Uh-huh, and she's going over those phone records we pulled on you, Donnie,' he lied. 'She's gonna know ever'body you know by the time she's through.'

'I thought you were out of this, Fourcade. You're off the case. You're suspended. What do you care who I called or why?'

'I got my reasons.'

'You're insane.'

'So I hear people say. But, you know, it doesn't matter much to me, true or not. My existence is my perception, my perception is my reality. See how that works, Tulane? So, when I ask are you trying to swing a deal with Duval Marcotte, you need to answer me, because you're right here in my reality right now.'

Donnie closed his eyes again and shifted his weight from one foot to the other.

'We're gonna stand here 'til you wet yourself, Donnie. I want an answer.'

'I need cash,' he said with resignation. 'Lindsay wants to buy out Pam's share of the business. But Lindsay's a ball buster and she'd love nothing more than to screw me out of what she can. I want back the property Pam hid for me and I want every dime I can get out of Lindsay. I made up a little leverage, that's all.'

'You think she's stupid?' Nick said. 'You think she won't call your bluff?'

'I think she's a bitch and I'm not above doing something just to aggravate her.'

'You're just gonna piss her off, Donnie, same as you're pissing me off. You think *I'm* stupid? I'll find out if what you're telling me is a lie.'

'I gotta see if I can withdraw that bail,' Donnie muttered up to the ceiling.

Nick patted his cheek as he stepped away from the door. 'Sorry, *cher*. That check's been cashed and the cat is outta the bag. Hope you don't live to regret it.'

'I already have,' Donnie said, ducking into the bathroom, penis in hand.

Annie turned the Jeep in at the drive to Marcus Renard's home. It was a pretty spot . . . and a secluded one. She didn't like the second part, but she had made it clear to Renard over the phone that other people knew she was visiting him – a little insurance in case he was toying with the idea of dismembering her. She didn't tell him the person who knew she was coming here was Fourcade.

While she had been with Fourcade last night, forming their uneasy alliance, Renard had been calling her at home, leaving the message that Fourcade had paid him a visit earlier in the day. In calling, Renard had saved her from the job of formulating an excuse to see him.

'I couldn't think who else to turn to, Annie,' he'd said. 'The deputies wouldn't help. They'd sooner see that brute kill me. You're the only one I feel I can turn to.'

The idea, while it might have overjoyed Fourcade, gave Annie no comfort. She had told Fourcade she wouldn't play the role of bait, yet here she was. Assessing the suspect in his home environment, she told herself. She wanted to see Renard with his guard down. She wanted to see him interact with his family. But if Renard perceived this visit as a social call, then she was essentially bait whether she intended to be or not. Semantics. Perception was reality, Fourcade would say.

That son of a bitch. Why hadn't he told her he had come here? She didn't like the idea of him having a hidden agenda in all this.

The driveway broke free of the trees, and a lawn the size of a polo field stretched off to the left. The expanse was nothing fancy, just a close-cropped boundary meant to discourage wildlife from getting too near the house. She passed an old carriage shed that had been painted to match the house. Fifty yards farther into the property stood the home itself, graceful and simple, painted the color of old parchment with white trim and black shutters. She parked behind the Volvo and started toward the front gallery.

'Annie!'

Marcus came out, careful not to let the screen door slap shut behind him. More of the swelling had gone out of his face, but there was still no definition to his features. Most people would recoil from the sight of him, despite the fact that he was neatly dressed in crisp khakis and a green polo shirt.

'I'm so glad you've come.' He enunciated his words more clearly today, though it took an effort. He held his hands out toward her as if she were a dear distant cousin and might actually take hold of them. 'Of course, I was hoping you might have called me back last night. We were all so upset.'

'I got in late,' she said, noting the slight censure in his voice. 'By the sound of it, there was nothing to be done by that point.'

'I suppose not,' he conceded. 'The damage was done.'

'What damage?'

'The upset – to me, to my mother, most especially to my brother. It took hours to calm him. But we don't have to stand out here and discuss it. Please come in. I wish you could have accepted the invitation to dinner. It's been so long since we've entertained.'

'This isn't a social call, Mr Renard,' Annie reminded him, drawing the line clearly between them. She moved into the hall, took it in at a glance – forest green walls, a murky pastoral scene in a gilt frame, a brass umbrella stand. Victor Renard peered down at her between the white balusters of the second-floor landing, where he sat with his knees drawn up like a small child, as if he thought he could make himself invisible by compacting his frame.

Ignoring his brother, Marcus led the way through the dining room to the brick veranda that faced the bayou. 'It's such a lovely afternoon, I thought we could sit out.'

He pulled out a chair for her at the wrought iron table. Annie chose her own chair and settled herself, careful to adjust her jacket so that the tape recorder in the pocket didn't show. The recorder had been Fourcade's idea – order, actually. He wanted to know every word that was spoken between them, wanted to hear every nuance in Renard's voice. The tape would never be admissible in court, but if it gave them something to go on, it was worth the effort.

'So, you said Detective Fourcade violated the restraining order,' she began, taking out her notebook and pen.

'Well, not exactly.'

'Exactly what, then?'

'He was careful to stay back from the property line. But the fact that he came that near was upsetting to my family. We called the sheriff's office, but by the time the deputy arrived, Fourcade was gone and the man wouldn't so much as take a statement.' He dabbed at the corner of his mouth with a neatly folded handkerchief.

'If the detective didn't commit a crime, then there was no statement to take,' Annie said. 'Did Fourcade threaten you?'

'Not verbally.'

'Did he threaten you physically? Did he show a weapon?'

'No. But his presence was a perceived threat. Isn't that a part of the stalking law – perceived threats?'

The fact that he, of all people, would try to make use of the statute against stalking turned her stomach. It was all she could do to school her features into something like neutrality.

'That particular law leaves a great deal of room for interpretation,' she said. 'As you must be well aware by now, Mr Renard –'

'Marcus,' he corrected her. 'I'm aware that the authorities will bend any rule to suit them. These people have no respect for what's right. Except you, Annie. I was right about you, wasn't I? You're not like the others. You want the truth.'

'Everyone involved in the case wants the truth.'

'No. No, they don't,' he said, leaning forward. 'They had their minds made up from the first. Stokes and Fourcade came after me and no one else.'

'That's not true, Mr Renard. Other suspects were considered. You know they were. You were singled out by the process of elimination. We've been over this.'

'Yes, we have,' he said quietly, sitting back again. He studied her for a moment. His eyes were more visible today, like a pair of marbles set into dough. 'And you did state you believe in my guilt. If that's so, then why are you here, Annie? To try to trip me up? I don't think so. I don't think you'd bother, knowing nothing I say to you could be used against me. You have doubts. That's why you're here.'

'You claim you've been treated unfairly,' Annie said. 'If that's true, if the detectives have overlooked or ignored something that might exonerate you, why hasn't your own investigator – Mr Kudrow's investigator – cleared up these details for you?'

Marcus looked away. 'He's one man. My funds are limited.'

'What is it you think we should be looking at?'

'The husband, for one.'

'Mr Bichon has been thoroughly investigated.'

He changed tacks without argument. 'No real effort has been made to find the man who helped me get my car going that night.'

Annie consulted the notes she'd brought with her. 'The man whose name you didn't ask?'

'I wasn't thinking.'

'The man who was driving "some kind of dark truck" with a license plate that "may have" included the letters *F* and *J*?'

'It was night. The truck was dirty. I had no reason to take note of the tags, anyway.'

'What little you gave us to go on was liberally put forth by the media, Mr Renard. No one came forward.'

'But did the sheriff's office *try* to find him? I don't think so. Fourcade never believed anything I told him. Can you imagine him wasting his time to check it out?'

'Detective Fourcade is a very thorough man,' Annie said. Fourcade also had tunnel vision when it came to Renard. He had been thorough in his efforts to prove Renard's guilt. Had he been as thorough in trying to corroborate the man's claim of innocence? 'I'll look into it, but there isn't much to go on.'

Renard let out a sigh of relief that seemed out of proportion with her offer. 'Thank you, Annie. I can't tell you how much it means to me to have you do this.'

'I told you, I don't expect anything to come of it.'

'That's not the point. Tea?' He reached for the pitcher that sat in the center of the table beside a pair of glasses and a small vase sprouting daffodils.

Annie accepted the drink, taking a moment between sips to look around the yard. Pony Bayou was a stone's throw away. Downstream it branched around a muddy island of willows and dewberry. Somewhere to the south, beyond the dense growth of woods where the spring birds were singing, was the house where Pam had died. Annie wondered if the burly fisherman sitting in his boat down by the fork realized that or if he might have come here because of it. People were strange that way.

Panic surged through her. Could the fisherman have been someone from the SO? What if Noblier had reinstated the surveillance? What if Sergeant Hooker had come to this spot on his day off in search of bass and *sac-a-lait*? If someone saw her with Renard, she was going to be way up shit creek.

'Got anything in that boathouse?' Nodding to a small, low shed of rusting corrugated metal that jutted out over the bayou, she shifted the position of her chair, turning her back more squarely to the fisherman.

'An old bass boat. My brother likes to explore the bayou. He's something of a nature buff. Aren't you, Victor?'

Victor stepped out from behind a swath of drapery inside the French door Marcus had left cracked open. There was no guilt on his face, no embarrassment at having been caught spying. He stared at Annie, turning his body sideways, as if that might somehow fool her into thinking he wasn't looking at her.

'Victor,' Marcus said, rising gingerly, 'this is Annie Broussard. Annie saved my life.'

'I wish you wouldn't keep saying that,' Annie muttered.

'Why? Because you're modest or because you wish you hadn't?'

'I was doing my job.'

Victor sidled toward the table for a better look at her. He was dressed in pants an inch too short and a plaid sport shirt buttoned to the throat. He resembled Marcus in his normal, unremarkable state: plain features, fine brown hair neatly combed. Annie had seen him around town from time to time, always in the company of either Marcus or his mother. He held himself too carefully and stood too close to people in lines, as if his sense of space and the physical world were distorted.

'It's nice to meet you, Victor.'

He squinted in suspicion. 'Good day.' He glanced at Marcus. 'Mask, no mask. Sound and sound alike. *Mimus polyglottos.* Mockingbird. No. No.' He shook his head. '*Dumetella carolinensis. Suggest* the songs of other birds.'

'What does that mean?' Annie asked.

Marcus attempted a bland smile. 'Probably that you remind him of someone. Or more precisely, that you resemble someone you aren't.'

Victor rocked himself a little, muttering, 'Red *and* white. Now *and* then.'

'Victor, why don't you go get your binoculars?' Marcus suggested. 'The woods are full of birds today.'

Victor cast a nervous look over his shoulder at Annie. 'Change, *interchange*, mutate. One and one. Red *and* white.'

He held himself still for a moment, as if waiting for some silent signal, then hurried back into the house.

'I expect he sees a resemblance between you and Pam,' Marcus said.

'Did he know her?'

'They met at the office once or twice. Victor periodically expresses a curiosity in my work. And of course he saw her picture in the papers after . . . He reads three newspapers every day, cover to cover, every word. Impressive until you realize he'll be held in thrall by the sight of a semicolon while the bombing of the federal building in Oklahoma City meant nothing whatsoever to him.'

'It must be difficult to deal with his . . . condition,' Annie said.

Marcus looked to the open door and the empty dining room beyond. 'Our cross to bear, my mother says. Of course, she takes great satisfaction from having to shoulder the load.' He turned back toward Annie with another wan smile. 'Can't pick your relatives. Do you have family here, Annie?'

'In a manner of speaking,' she said evasively. 'It's a long story.'

'Family stories always are. Look at Pam's daughter. What a family story she'll have, poor little thing. What will become of her grandfather?'

'You'd have to ask the DA,' she said, though she thought she could give an accurate guess as to what would become of Hunter Davidson: nothing much. The outcry against his arrest had been considerable. Pritchett would never risk the wrath of his constituents by pressing for a trial. A deal would likely be cut quickly and quietly – maybe already had been – and Hunter Davidson would be doing community service for his attempted sin.

'He tried to kill me,' Renard said with indignation. 'The media is treating him like a celebrity.'

'Yeah. There's a lot of that going around. You're not a well-liked man, Mr Renard.'

'Marcus,' he corrected her. 'You're at least civil to me. I'd like to pretend we're friends, Annie.'

The emotion in his eyes was soft and vulnerable. Annie tried to imagine what had been in those eyes that black November night when he had plunged a knife into Pam Bichon.

'Considering what happened to your last "friend," I don't think that's a very good idea, Mr Renard.'

He turned his head as quickly as if she had slapped him, and blinked away tears, pretending to focus on the fisherman down the bayou.

'I would never have hurt Pam,' he said. 'I've told you that, Annie. That remark was deliberately hurtful to me. I expected better from you.'

He wanted her contrition. He wanted her to give him another inch of control, the way he had when he had asked to use her name. A little thing on the surface, but the psychological sleight of hand was smooth and sinister. Or she was blowing it out of proportion and giving this man more credit than he deserved.

'It's just healthy caution on my part,' she said. 'I don't know you.'

'I couldn't hurt you, Annie.' He looked at her once again with his watery hazel eyes. 'You saved my life. In certain Eastern cultures I would give you my life in return.'

'Yeah, well, this is South Lou'siana. A simple thanks is sufficient.'

'Hardly. I know you've been suffering because of what you did. I know what it is to be persecuted, Annie. We have that in common.'

'Can we move on?' Annie said. The intensity in his expression unnerved her, as if he had already determined that their lives would now be intertwined into eternity. Was this how a fixation began? As a misunderstanding of commitment? Had it been this way between him and Pam? Between him and his now-dead girlfriend from Baton Rouge?

'No offense,' she prefaced, 'but you have to admit you have a bad track record. You wanted to be involved with Pam, and now she's dead. You were involved with Elaine Ingram back in Baton Rouge, and she's dead.'

'Elaine's death was a terrible accident.'

'But you can see how it might give pause. There's a rumor that she was going to break off your relationship.'

'That's not true,' he insisted. 'Elaine could never leave me. She loved me.'

Could never, not *would* never. The choice of words was telling. Not: Elaine would never leave him of her own accord. But: Elaine *could* never leave him if he wouldn't allow it. Marcus Renard wouldn't have been the first man to use the 'if I can't have her, no one will' rationale. It was common thinking among simple obsessionals.

Doll Renard chose that moment to come onto the terrace. She wore a dotted polyester dress twenty years out of date and an enormous kitchen apron. The ties wrapped around her twice. She was thin in the same way Richard Kudrow was thin – as if her body had burned away from within, leaving bone and tough sinew. She offered no smile of welcome. Her mouth was a thin slash in her narrow face.

Annie thought she saw Marcus wince. She rose and extended her hand.

'Annie Broussard, sheriff's office. Sorry to disturb your Sunday, Mrs Renard.'

Doll sniffed, grudgingly offering a limp hand that collapsed in Annie's like a pouch of twigs. 'Our Sunday is the least of what you people have disturbed.'

Marcus rolled his eyes. 'Mother, please. Annie isn't like the others.'

'Well, *you* wouldn't think so,' Doll muttered.

'She's going to be looking into some things that could help prove my innocence. She saved my life, for heaven's sake. Twice.'

'I was just doing my job,' Annie pointed out. 'I *am* just doing my job.'

Doll arched a penciled-on brow and clucked her tongue. 'You've managed to misread the situation yet again, Marcus.'

He looked away from his mother, his color darkening, tension crackled in the air around him. Annie watched the exchange, thinking maybe she was better off not having any blood relatives. Her memories of her mother were soft and quiet. Better memories than a bitter reality.

'Well,' Doll Renard went on, 'it's about time the sheriff's office did *something* for us. Our lawyer will be filing suit, you know, for all the pain and anguish we've been caused.'

'Mother, perhaps you could try not to alienate the one person willing to help us.'

She looked at him as if he'd called her a filthy name. 'I have every right to state my feelings. We've been treated worse than common trash through all of this, while that Bichon woman is held up like some kind of saint. And now her father – all the world's calling him a martyred hero for trying to murder you. He belongs in jail. I certainly hope the district attorney keeps him there.'

'I really should be going,' Annie said, gathering her file and notebook. 'I'll see what I can find out on that truck.'

'I'll walk you to your car.' Marcus scraped his chair back and sent his mother a venomous look.

He waited until they were along the end of the house before he spoke again.

'I wish you could have stayed longer.'

'Did you have something more to say pertinent to the case?'

'Well – ah – I don't know,' he stammered. 'I don't know what questions you might have asked.'

'The truth isn't dependent on what questions I ask,' Annie said. 'The truth is what I'm after here, Mr. Renard. I'm not out to prove your innocence, and I certainly don't want you telling people that I am. In fact, I wish you wouldn't mention me at all. I've got trouble enough as it is.'

He made a show of drawing a fingertip across his mouth. 'My lips are sealed. It'll be our secret.' He seemed to like that idea too well. 'Thank you, Annie.'

'There's no need. Really.'

He opened the door of the Jeep, and she climbed in. As she backed up to turn around, he leaned against his Volvo. The successful young architect at leisure. *He's a murderer,* she thought, *and he wants to be my friend.*

A glint of reflected sunlight caught her eye and she looked up at the second story of the Renard home, where Victor stood in one window, looking down on her with binoculars.

'Man, y'all make the Addams family look like Ozzie and Harriet,' she said under her breath.

She thought about that as she drove north and west through the flat sugarcane country. Behind the face of every killer was the accumulated by-product of his upbringing, his history, his experiences. All of those things went to shape the individual and guide him onto a path. It wasn't a stretch to add up those factors in Renard's life and get the psychopathology Fourcade had spoken about. The portrait of a serial killer.

Marcus Renard wanted to be her friend. A shiver ran down her back.

She flicked on the radio and turned it up over the static of the scanner.

'. . . and I just think all these crimes, these rapes and all, are a backlash against the women's lib.'

'Are you saying women essentially ask to be raped by taking nontraditional roles?'

'I'm sayin' we should know our place. That's what I'm sayin'.'

'Okay, Ruth in Youngsville. You're on KJUN, all talk all the time. In light of last night's reported rape of a Luck woman, our topic is violence against women.'

Another rape. Since the Bichon murder and the resurrected tales of the Bayou Strangler, every woman in the parish was living in a heightened state of fear. Rich hunting grounds for a certain kind of sexual predator. That was the rush for a rapist – his victim's fear. He fed on it like a narcotic.

The questions came to Annie automatically. How old was the victim? Where and how was she attacked? Did she have anything in common with Jennifer Nolan? Had the rapist followed the same MO? Were they now looking at a serial rapist? Who had caught the case? Stokes, she supposed, because of the possible tie to the Nolan rape. That was what he needed — another hot case to distract him from the Bichon homicide investigation.

The countryside began to give way to small acreages interspersed with the odd dilapidated trailer house, then the new western developments outside of town. The only L. Faulkner listed in the phone book lived on Cheval Court in the Quail Run development. Annie slowed the Jeep to a crawl, checking numbers on mailboxes.

The neighborhood was maybe four years old, but had been strategically planned to include plenty of large trees that had stood on this land for a hundred years or more, giving the area a sense of tradition. Pam Bichon had lived just a stone's throw from here on Quail Drive. Faulkner's home was a neat redbrick Caribbean colonial with ivory trim and overflowing planters on the front step.

Annie pulled in the drive and parked alongside a red Miata convertible with expired tags. She hadn't called ahead, hadn't wanted to give Lindsay Faulkner the chance to say no. The woman had put her guard up. The best plan would be to duck under it.

No one answered the doorbell. A section of the home's interior was visible through the sidelights that flanked the door. The house looked open, airy, inviting. A huge fern squatted in a pot in the foyer. A cat tiptoed along the edge of the kitchen island. Beyond the island a sliding glass door offered access to a terrace.

The lingering aroma of grilled meat hooked Annie's nose before she turned the corner to the back side of the house. Whitney Houston's testimonial about all the man she'd ever need floated out the speakers of a boom box, punctuated by a woman's throaty laughter.

Lindsay Faulkner sat at a glass-topped patio table, her hair swept back in a ponytail. A striking redhead in tortoiseshell shades came out through the patio doors with a Diet Pepsi in each hand. The smile on Faulkner's face dropped as she caught sight of Annie.

'I'm sorry to interrupt, Ms Faulkner. I had a couple more questions, if you don't mind,' Annie said, trying to resist the urge to smooth the wrinkles from her blazer. Faulkner and her companion looked crisp and sporty, the kind of people who never perspired.

'I do mind, Detective. I thought I made myself clear yesterday. I'd rather not deal with you.'

'I'm sorry you feel that way, since we both want the same thing.'

'Detective?' the redhead said. She set the sodas on the table and settled herself in her chair with casual grace, a wry smile pulling at one corner of a perfectly painted mouth. 'What have you done now, Lindsay?'

'She's here about Pam,' Faulkner said, never taking her eyes off Annie. 'She's the one I was telling you about.'

'Oh.' The redhead frowned and gave Annie the once-over, a condescending glance intended to belittle.

'If I have to deal with you people at all,' Faulkner said, 'then I'd sooner deal with Detective Stokes. He's the one I've dealt with all along.'

'We're on the same side, Ms Faulkner,' Annie said, undaunted. 'I want to see Pam's murderer punished.'

'You could have let that happen the other night.'

'Within the system,' Annie specified. 'You can help make that happen.'

Faulkner looked away and sighed sharply through her slim patrician nose.

Annie helped herself to a chair, wanting to give the impression she was comfortable and in no hurry to leave. 'How well do you know Marcus Renard?'

'What kind of question is that?'

'Did you socialize?'

'Me, personally?'

'He claims you went out together a couple of times. Is that true?'

She gave a humorless laugh, obviously insulted. 'I don't believe this. Are you asking if I *dated* that sick worm?'

Annie blinked innocently and waited.

'We went out in a group from time to time – people from his office, people from mine.'

'But never one-on-one?'

Faulkner flicked a glance at the redhead. 'He's not my type. What's the point of this, Detective?'

'It's Deputy,' Annie clarified at last. 'I just want a clear picture of y'all's relationship.'

'I didn't have a "relationship" with Renard,' she said hotly. 'In his sick mind, maybe. What –'

She stopped suddenly. Annie could all but see the thought strike her – that Renard could have fixed on her as easily as on Pam. Judging by the shade of guilt that passed across her face, it wasn't the first time she had considered her good fortune at her friend's expense. She passed a hand across her forehead as if trying to wipe the thought away.

'Pam was too sweet,' she said softly. 'She didn't know how to discourage men. She never wanted to hurt anyone's feelings.'

'I'm curious about something else,' Annie said. 'Donnie was making noise about challenging Pam for custody of Josie, but I can't see that he had any grounds. Was there something? Another man, maybe?'

Faulkner looked down at her hands on the tabletop and picked at an imagined cuticle flaw. 'No.'

'She wasn't seeing anyone.'

'No.'

'Then why would Donnie think –'

'Donnie is a fool. If you haven't figured that out by now, then you must be one, too. He thought he could paint Pam as a bad mother because she sometimes worked nights and met with male clients for drinks and dinner, as if the realty was just a front for a personal dating service. The idiot. It was ridiculous. He was grasping at straws. He would have used the stalking against her if he could have.'

'Did Pam take him seriously?'

'We're talking about custody of her child. Of course she took him seriously. I don't see what this has to do with Renard.'

'He says Pam told him she didn't dare date until the divorce went through because she was afraid of what Donnie might do.'

'Yes, well, it turned out it wasn't Donnie she needed to be afraid of, was it?'

'You said she had a hard time discouraging men who were interested in her. Were there many sniffing around?'

Faulkner pressed two fingers against her right temple. 'I've been over all this with Detective Stokes. Pam had that girl-next-door quality. Men liked to flirt with her. It was reflexive. My God, even Stokes did it. It didn't mean anything.'

Annie wanted to ask if it hadn't meant anything because Pam was no longer interested in men. If Pam and Lindsay Faulkner had become partners beyond the office and Donnie found out, he certainly would have tried to use it in the divorce. That kind of discovery – the ultimate insult to masculinity – could have pushed a man on the edge *over* the edge. A motive that applied to Renard as easily as to Donnie.

She wanted to ask. Fourcade would have asked. Blunt, straight out. *Were you and Pam lovers?* But Annie held her tongue. She couldn't afford to piss off Lindsay Faulkner any more than she already had. If Faulkner complained about her to the sheriff or to Stokes, she'd be pulling the graveyard shift in detox for the rest of her broken career.

She pushed her chair back and rose slowly, pulling a business card from the pocket of her jacket. She had scratched out the phone number for the sheriff's office and replaced it with her home phone. She slid the card across the table toward Faulkner. 'If you think of anything else that might be helpful, I'd appreciate it if you'd call me. Thank you for your time.'

She turned to the redhead. 'I'd get those tags renewed on the Miata if I were you. It's a nasty fine.'

Out in the Jeep, Annie sat for a moment, staring at the house and trying to glean something useful from the conversation. More what-ifs. More maybes. Stokes and Fourcade had been over this ground enough to wear it smooth. What did she think she was going to find?

The truth, the key, the missing piece that would tie everything together. It was here in the maze somewhere, half hidden beneath some rock they hadn't quite overturned, lurking amid the lies and dead ends. Someone had to find it, and if she worked hard enough, looked long enough, dug a little deeper, she would be that someone.

23

The Voodoo Lounge had come into being as the indirect result of a gruesome murder, a fact that attracted the local cops in a way no other bar could. For years the place had been known as Frenchie's Landing, the hangout of farmhands and factory workers, blue-collars and rednecks. It was known for boiled crawfish, cold beer, loud Cajun music, and the occasional brawl. Still known for all of those things, the place had changed ownership in the fall of 1993, some months after the murder of Annick Delahoussaye-Gerrard at the hands of the Bayou Strangler. Worn-out with grief, Frenchie Delahoussaye and his wife had sold out to local musician and sometime bartender Leonce Comeau.

The cops had started hanging out there immediately after the murder, a show of respect and associated guilt that had quickly turned into routine. The habit lived on.

The parking lot was two-thirds full. The building stood on the bank of the bayou, raised off the ground on a sturdy set of stilts for times when the bayou rushed nearer. A new gallery was under construction around three sides of the building. Loud rocking zydeco music blasted through the walls, the volume rising as the screen door swung open and a pair of couples descended the steps, laughing.

Nick let himself in, walking past the framed photographs of celebrities and pseudocelebrities that had come here over the last four years to soak up the atmosphere. He took the place in at a glance. The house band, led by the bar's owner, belted out Zachary Richard's 'Ma Petite Fille Est Gone', Comeau contorting his face and body like a man with a neurological disorder. The dance floor was swarming with couples young and old bouncing and swinging to the infectious beat. Smoke hung in the air over the bar and tables. The smell of frying fish and gumbo was like a heavy perfume.

Stokes was in his usual spot, standing at the corner of the bar that afforded a view of the place and all the women in it. He wore a gray mechanic's shirt from a Texaco station with the name LYLE on a patch over the pocket. His porkpie hat perched on the back of his head like a mutant yarmulke. He caught sight of Nick and raised his glass.

'Hey, brothers, if it ain't our tarnished comrade!' he called, his square smile flashing bright in the center of his goatee. 'Nicky! Hey, man, you decide to go social or something?'

Nick wove his way between patrons, tolerating the slaps on the back that came from two different cops whose names he couldn't have said on pain of death. He stepped around a waitress with a tight T-shirt and inviting smile as if she were a post set into the floor.

Stokes shook his head at the wasted opportunity. He kissed the cheek of the bleached blonde on the stool next to him and gave her ass a farewell squeeze.

'Hey, sugar, how 'bout you go powder that pretty nose and let my man Nicky here take a load off. He's a legend, don'tcha know.'

The blonde slid down off the stool, letting her breasts graze Nick's arm. 'Hope you're back on the job soon, Detective.'

Stokes elbowed him as the woman walked away, her ass packed into a pair of jeans a size too small for comfort, just right for lust. 'That Valerie. Man, that girl's some piece of poontang, let me tell you. Got a pussy like a Vise-Grip. If I'm lyin', I'm dyin'. You ever done her?'

'I don't even know her,' Nick said with strained patience.

'She's Noblier's secretary, for Christ's sake. Hot for cops. Man, Nicky, sometimes I swear your hormones have gone dormant,' he declared with disgust. 'You could have your pick of the chicks in this joint, you know.'

Ignoring the vacant stool, Nick leaned against the bar, ordered a beer, and lit a cigarette. He didn't give a shit about Stokes's assessment of his sexual appetites. He didn't believe in sex as a casual pastime. There needed to be meaning, significance, intensity. But he made no effort to explain this to Stokes.

Up on the stage, the band had announced a break, dropping the decibel level in the bar to something slightly more conducive to conversation. Danny Collett and the Louisiana Swamp Cats blared out of the juke up front. Half the dancers didn't bother to leave the floor.

'You missing the job?' Stokes asked. He'd had a few. There was a vagueness in his pale eyes, an artificial glow on his cheeks.

'Some.'

'Gus say when he's bringing you back?'

'Depends on whether or not I take the big vacation to Angola.'

Stokes shook his head. 'That bitch Broussard. There's a chick more trouble than she's worth. I been thinking on that lesbian thing with her, and I don't see it. I think she just needs her pump primed, you know what I'm saying?'

Nick looked right at him. 'Quit ragging on Broussard. She stood up and did what she had to do. That took balls.'

Stokes's eyes popped. 'What's the matter with you, man? She put your dick in the wringer –'

'*I* put my dick in the wringer. She just happened to be there at the time.'

Stokes gave a snort. 'You're singing a new tune. What's up with that?'

A sly look swept across his face. He leaned closer, stroking his goatee. 'Maybe you got to looking and decided you wanna do the honors for her, huh? Give her an attitude adjustment with the old joystick? There's a challenge to rise to, if you know what I mean.'

'You know, Chaz, they say a mind is a terrible thing to waste,' Nick said. He pulled on his cigarette and exhaled twin jet streams through his nose. 'You been using yours at all lately or have you turned over all the duties to that piece of meat hanging between your legs?'

'I alternate between the two. Christ, who put the bug up your ass tonight?'

'Ah, this one's been there for a few days, *mon ami*, and I'm still not sure where it came from. Maybe you could help me with that, no?'

'Maybe. If I knew what the hell you're talking about.'

Nick leaned a little closer. 'Let's go take us a little walk in the night air, Chaz. We'll chat.'

Stokes forced an apologetic grin. 'Hey, Nicky, I got an agenda here tonight, man. I'll swing by tomorrow. We'll talk a blue streak. But tonight –'

Nick stepped in close and caught hold of his pride and joy in a crushing fist. 'Alternate, Chaz,' he ordered, his voice a low growl. 'You're getting on my nerves.'

As he let go, Stokes fell back a step, his face slack and pale with astonishment. He sucked in a gasp and shook himself like a wet cat, glancing around for witnesses. Life was moving on for everyone else in the bar. Fourcade's move had been too slick to draw notice.

'Fuckin' *A*!' he exclaimed in an outraged whisper. 'What the hell's wrong with you, man? You can't do that! You just grab my willy and give it a yank? What the fuck's wrong with you? You can't do that to a brother!'

Nick took a swig of Jax and wiped his mouth with the back of his hand. 'I just did it. Now that I got your attention, let's go get some air.'

He headed for a side door and Stokes moved with him, hesitant, wary, petulant. They stepped out onto the half-finished gallery where a sawhorse and a KEEP OUT! sign blocked the way to the bayou side of the building. Nick ignored the warning.

The gallery facing the bayou had no railing at this point in the construction. The drop was about twelve feet. Enough for the average drunk to fall and break his neck. Nick stepped to the edge of the platform and stood with his hands on his hips, thinking *calm, center*. Force was a tool of surprise in dealing with Stokes. Something to knock him off balance. A tool to be used sparingly, carefully. His goal was truth.

Still agitated, Stokes paced back and forth. 'Man, you are fuckin' crazy, grabbing my dick. What goes through that head of yours, Nick? Jesus!'

'Get over it.'

Nick lit another cigarette and stared out at the bayou. The moon shone down on half a dozen pontoon houseboats moored down the way, weekend retreats for people from town and from as far away as Lafayette. There were no lights in the windows tonight.

The music from inside the bar came through the wall in a muddled bass vibration. If he blocked it from his mind and focused, he could just hear the chorus of frog song and the slap and splash of a fish breaking the water. Lightning cracked the sky to the east – a storm sucking up along the Mississippi from the Gulf. A distant storm.

He thought of Marcotte. The distant storm.

'So why ain't you bending my ear, pard?' Stokes said, calming down. He propped a shoulder against a support post and crossed his arms over his chest. 'You're the one wanted to chat.'

'I heard there was another rape.'

'Yeah. So?'

'You catch it?'

'Yeah, I caught it. Looks like it's the same sicko did that Nolan woman the other night. Broke in about one A.M., knocked her around, tied her up, raped her, made her take a shower after. He's a smart son of a bitch, I'll give him that. We got diddly-squat to go on.'

'No semen?'

'Nope. He's taking it with him one way or another. Probably uses a condom. Maybe the lab'll find some latex residue on one of the swabs, but big fuckin' deal, you know? What'll that prove? He prefers Trojans?'

'He wear a mask?'

'Yeah. Spooked the shit out of these women, that mask did. Shades of the Bayou Strangler and all that crap.'

'And Pam Bichon.'

'And Bichon,' he conceded. 'Confuses the issue, you know what I'm saying? The mask was Renard's thing. So if Renard ain't this rapist, then is this rapist the one did Pam Bichon, folks wanna know. People are so fuckin' stupid. I mean, it's all over the news about that mask Renard left on Pam. This guy's an opportunist, that's all.'

'Who was the woman?'

'Kay Eisner. Mid-thirties, single, lives over near Devereaux, works at a catfish plant up in Henderson. What's your interest in all this?' he asked, fishing a cigarette out of the shirt pocket beneath the LYLE patch. 'I was you, Nicky, I'd be spending my free time a little better.'

'Just curious,' Nick said. He dropped his cigarette butt on the floorboards, ground it out with the toe of his boot.

Inside the bar, the band had come back onstage. Leonce Comeau wailed the intro to 'Snake Bite Love'. The drummer pounded the opening and the rest of the band jumped in at a run.

'The past overshadows the present foreshadows the future.'

Stokes blinked at him like a man nodding off in church. 'Nicky, man, I ain't drunk enough for philosophy.'

'We all got a past we drag around behind us,' Nick said. 'Sometimes it sneaks up and bites our ass.'

The shift in the tension between them was subtle, but there. A tightening of muscles. A heightened awareness. Nick watched Stokes's eyes like a poker player.

'What are you saying, Nicky?' Stokes said softly.

Nick let the silence hang, waited.

'I hear teeth snapping behind me,' he said. 'I feel that shadow on my back.' He stepped closer. 'All of a sudden a name is turning up again and again like a damn bad penny. Me, I find myself in a bad position and I keep on hearing that name. And I'm thinking there's no such thing as coincidence.'

'What name?'

'Duval Marcotte.'

Stokes didn't blink.

Anticipation tightened in Nick's belly like a knot. What did he want? The flash of recognition? For Stokes to be guilty? For another cop to have betrayed him? He wanted Marcotte. After all this time, after all the work to put it behind him, he wanted Marcotte – even at the cost of another man's honor. The realization was as heavy as stone, hard and abrasive against his conscience.

'Is he in this thing, Chaz?' he asked. 'It would have been a simple errand, piece a' cake. Get me to Laveau's, fill me up with liquor and ideas, point me in the right direction, see if I go off like a cocked pistol. Easy money, and hell, he's got plenty of it.'

The expression on Stokes's face softened and he laughed to himself. He looked out toward the bayou and beyond, where the storm was an eerie glow inside black clouds.

'Man, Nicky,' he whispered, shaking his head. 'You are one crazy motherfucker. Who the hell is Duval Marcotte?'

'Truth, Chaz,' Nick said. 'Truth, or this time I walk away with your cock in my pocket.'

'Never heard of him,' Stokes murmured. 'If I'm lyin', I'm dyin'.'

Annie's eyes crossed and her head bobbed. The autopsy report blurred and came back into focus. She rubbed a hand over her face, swept the straggling tendrils of hair behind her ears, and consulted her watch. Fourcade had no clocks. Fourcade was one with time, she supposed – or he didn't believe in the concept of time, or God knew what philosophy he embraced regarding the subject. It was after midnight.

She had been sitting at the big table in his study four hours. Fourcade had not made an appearance. He had entrusted her with a key to the house and ordered her to study everything he had on the case. She asked if there would be a quiz. He wasn't amused.

Where he was was anyone's guess. Annie told herself she was grateful for his absence. And still she kind of missed his blunt interrogation, his complex insights, and odd mystic philosophies.

'My Lord, you must be getting desperate for friends, girl,' she muttered at the thought.

It was probably true. She'd been shut out at work, cut off from A.J. by necessity. People she didn't even know were insulting her on her answering machine. She was a social creature – by necessity, she sometimes thought. There was a small sense of aloneness in her that dated back to childhood, a feeling she had always feared reflected her mother's detachment, and so she sought out the company of others in an attempt to keep the aloneness from growing and swallowing her whole.

She wondered if maybe that was what had happened to Fourcade.

Needing to move, Annie forced herself up from the chair and stretched. She made a circuit of the loft, checking out the bookcases, looking out the dormer windows, wandering into the small corner Fourcade had set aside for sleeping and changing clothes. There were no personal items on the dresser, not even the cast-off miscellany from pockets. Though the temptation was certainly there, she made no move to open a drawer. She would never have invaded someone's privacy without a warrant. Besides, she knew without looking that every sock, every T-shirt, would be folded neatly and arranged in an orderly manner. The bed was made military-style, the covers tight enough to bounce quarters on.

She wondered what he looked like sleeping. Did he attack sleep with the same ferocious focus as he attacked everything else in his life? Or did unconsciousness soften the hard edges?

'Thinking of spending the night, *chère*?'

Annie spun around at the sound of his voice. Fourcade stood well inside the room, hands on his hips, one leg cocked. She hadn't heard so much as the creak of a hinge or a step on the stairs.

'Don't you know better than to sneak up on a woman when there's a rapist out running around loose?' she demanded. 'I could have shot you.'

He discounted the possibility without comment.

'I was just stretching my legs,' she said, walking away from the bed, not wanting him to imagine she had been thinking about him in it. 'Where've you been? Renard's?'

'Why would I go there?' he said, his tone flat.

'Let's put that past tense,' Annie suggested. 'Why *did* you go there? My God, what were you thinking? He could have had you thrown back in jail.'

'How's that? You weren't on duty.'

Annie shook her head. 'Don't pull that attitude with me, thinking I'll back off. You already know I'm not repentant for running you in, other than that it's made my life a living hell. You must have come here straight from his house last night and you didn't say a word to me.'

'There was nothing to say. I was out in the boat. I ended up in the neighborhood. I didn't cross the property line. I didn't touch him. I didn't threaten him. In fact, *he* approached me.'

'And you didn't think any of this would be of interest to me, *partner*?'

'The encounter was irrelevant,' he said, moving away, dismissing Annie and her argument. She wanted to kick him.

'It's relevant in that you didn't share it with me.' She pursued him to the long table where she had been studying. 'If we're partners, we're partners. There's an expectation of trust, and you've already managed to break it.'

He sighed heavily. 'All right. Point taken. I should have told you. Can we move on?'

It was on the tip of Annie's tongue to demand an apology, but she knew Fourcade would somehow make her feel like a fool in the end.

He had turned his attention to the papers on the table. He picked up the discarded wrapper of a Butterfinger from among the files, frowned at it, and tossed it in the trash. 'What'd you learn tonight, 'Toinette?'

'That I probably need reading glasses, but I'm too vain to go to the eye doctor,' Annie said dryly.

He looked at her sideways.

'Joke,' she stated. 'A wry remark intended to lighten the moment.'

He turned back to the statements and lab reports.

She sighed and rubbed the small of her back with both hands. 'I learned that no fewer than a dozen people swore to Donnie's level of intoxication the night of the murder – some of them friends of his, some not. Doesn't necessarily let him off the hook.'

'I learned there was no semen found during the autopsy. The mutilation made it difficult to find out if she'd been raped, but then again, it just may not have been there. That makes me nervous.'

'Why is that?'

'This jerk running around out there now. I responded to the first call – Jennifer Nolan. No semen and the guy was wearing a Mardi Gras mask. Pam Bichon: no semen and a Mardi Gras mask left behind.'

'Copycat,' Fourcade said. 'The mask was common knowledge.'

'And he also knew not to come?'

'There's a certain rate of dysfunction among rapists. Maybe he couldn't come. Maybe he used a rubber. The cases are unrelated.'

'That's what I like about you, Nick,' Annie said sarcastically. 'You're so open-minded.'

'Don't become distracted by irrelevant external incidents.'

'Irrelevant? How is a serial rapist not relevant?'

'From what I've heard, there are more differences than similarities in the cases. One's a killer, one's a rapist. The rape victims were tied up. Pam was nailed down – thank Christ we managed to keep that out of the papers. The rape victims were attacked in their homes, Pam was not. Pam Bichon was stalked, harassed. Were the others? It's simple, sugar: Marcus Renard killed Pam Bichon, and someone else raped these women. You better make up your mind 'bout which is your focus.'

'My focus is the truth,' Annie said. 'It's not my job to draw conclusions – or yours, Detective.'

'You saw Renard today,' he said, dismissing her argument and her point once again.

Annie gritted her teeth in frustration. 'Yes. He left a message on my answering machine last night, asking for my assistance in dealing with your little chance encounter. It seems the deputy who answered the call yesterday was unsympathetic.'

'Where's the tape?'

She dug the cassette recorder out of her purse, turned the volume up, and set the machine on the table. Fourcade stared down at the plastic rectangle as if he could see Renard in it. He seemed to listen without breathing or blinking. When it was done, he nodded and turned toward her.

'Impressions?'

'He's convinced himself he's innocent.'

'Persecution complex. Nothing is his fault. Everybody's picking on him.'

'He's also convinced himself I'm his friend.'

'Good. That's what we want.'

'That's what *you* want,' she muttered behind his back. 'As a family they'd make great characters on *The Twilight Zone*.'

'He hates his mother, resents his brother. Feels shackled to the both of them. This guy's head is a psychological pressure cooker full of snakes.'

She couldn't argue with Fourcade's diagnosis. It was his vehemence that bothered her.

'What he said about that truck – the guy that supposedly helped him with his car that night,' she said. 'Did you check it out?'

'Ran the partial plate through DVM. Got a list of seventy-two dark-colored trucks. None of the owners helped a stranded motorist that night.' He gave her a sharp look. 'What you think, *chère* – you think I don't do my job?'

Annie chose her words carefully. 'I think your focus was proving Renard's guilt, not verifying his alibi.'

'I do the job,' he said tightly. 'I want my arrests to stand up in court. I do the job. I did it here. I don't just *think* Renard is guilty. He *is* guilty.'

'What about New Orleans?' The words were out before she could consider the folly of pushing him. The necessity of trusting him and the reluctance to trust him were issues too important to ignore, especially after his sin of omission regarding his visit to Renard.

'What about it?'

'You thought you knew who did the Candi Parmantel murder –'

'I did.'

'The charges against Allan Zander were dismissed.'

'That doesn't make him innocent, sugar.' He strode over to a neat stack of files on a corner of the table, digging down to pull one out.

'Here,' he said, thrusting it at her. 'The DMV list. Call 'em yourself if you think I'm a liar.'

'I never said I thought you were a liar,' Annie mumbled, peeking inside the cover. 'I just need to know you didn't run through this case with blinders on, that's all.'

'Renard, he winning you over, *chère*?' he asked sardonically. 'Maybe that's what this is all about, huh? He thinks you're pretty. He thinks you're cute. He thinks you'll help him. Good. That's just what I want him to think. Just don't *you* believe it.'

She *was* pretty, Nick thought, letting that simple truth penetrate his temper. Even with her hair a mess and a cardigan two sizes too big swallowing her up. There was an earnest quality to her that the job would eventually rub off. Not naïveté, but the next thing to it: idealism. The thing that made a good cop try harder. The thing that could drive a good cop toward the line so that obsession could pull her over it.

He skimmed his fingertips down the side of her face. 'I could tell you you're pretty. That's no lie. I could tell you I need you, take you to my bed even. Would you trust me then more than you trust a killer?' he asked, leaning close.

The edge of the table bit into the backs of Annie's thighs. His legs brushed against hers. His thumb touched the corner of her mouth and everything inside her turned hot and sensitive. She tried to catch a breath, tried to make sense of her response with a mind that felt suddenly numb.

'I don't trust Renard,' she said, her voice thready.

'Nor do you trust me.' His mouth was inches from hers, his eyes burning black. He traced his thumb down her throat to the hollow at the base of it where her pulse throbbed.

'You're the one who said trust is of no use in an investigation.'

He arched a brow. 'You investigating me, *chère*?'

'No. This isn't about you.' Even as she said it, she wondered. The case was about one woman's death and one man's guilt, but it was also about so much more.

'No,' Nick said, though he wasn't certain whether he was just repeating her answer or issuing a command to himself. He took half a step back to break contact, to distance his senses from the soft, clean scent of her.

'Don't you help him, 'Toinette,' he said, brushing back a stray lock of her hair. 'Don't let him use you. Control.' He curled his hand into a fist as he pulled it from her cheek. 'Control.'

I'm not the one in danger of losing it, Annie thought, ignoring the telltale shiver that ran through her. Fourcade dug a cigarette out of a stray pack on the table and walked away, trailing smoke. The truth was, she didn't feel she'd ever had control. The case had swept her up and swept her along, taking her places she hadn't expected to go. To this man, for instance.

'I should go,' she said, talking to his back as he stood at one of the dormer windows. 'It's late.'

'I'll walk you down.' His mouth twitched as he turned around. 'Check that Jeep for snakes.'

The night was soft with humidity, cool as a root cellar and rich with the fecund scent of earth and water. In the blackness beyond the fall of Fourcade's porch light, a pair of horned owls called in eerie harmony.

'Uncle Sos used to tell all the kids the stories about the *loup-garou*,' she said, looking off into the darkness. 'How they prowled the night looking for victims to cast their spells on. Scared the pee out of us.'

'There's worse things out there than werewolves, sugar.'

'Yeah. And it's our job to catch them. Somehow that seems a more daunting prospect in the dead of night.'

'Because the darkness is their dimension,' he said. 'You and I, we're supposed to walk the edge in between and pull them from their side to the other, where everyone can see what they are.'

It sounded like a mythic task that would require Herculean strength. Maybe this was why Fourcade had shoulders like a bull – because of the strain, the weight of the world.

She climbed up into the Jeep and tossed the DMV records on the passenger's seat.

'You watch yourself, 'Toinette,' he said, closing the door. 'Don't let the *loup-garou* get you.'

24

It wasn't a fictitious creature she had to worry about, Annie thought as she drove the road that cut through the dense woods. All the trouble she was facing had to do with mortal men: Mullen, Marcus Renard, Donnie Bichon — and Fourcade.

Fourcade.

He was as enigmatic as the *loup-garou*. A mysterious past, a nature as dark and compelling as his eyes. She told herself she didn't like that he had touched her, but she had allowed it and her body had responded in a way that wasn't smart. Her life was enough of a mess at the moment without getting involved with Fourcade.

'Don't go down there, Annie,' she muttered to herself.

She tuned in to the scanner to let the chatter distract her. Nothing much going on Sunday night. What bars were open at all closed early, and the usual troublemakers refrained out of token deference to the commandments. There was no traffic. The only life she encountered was a deer darting across the road and a stray dog eating the carcass of a dead armadillo. The world seemed a deserted place, except for the lonely souls who called in to the talk radio station to speculate about the possible return of the Bayou Strangler. No one had been strangled, but people seemed confident it was just a matter of time.

Annie listened with a mix of fascination and disgust. The level of fear in the population was rising, and the level of logic was falling in direct proportion. The Bayou Strangler had come back from the dead. The Bayou Strangler had killed Pam Bichon. Conspiracy theories were plentiful. Most centered on the cops having planted evidence four years ago to pin the murders on Stephen Danjermond after he was already dead, which tied in neatly with current theories about planted evidence implicating Renard and damning Fourcade.

Annie wondered if Marcus Renard was listening. She wondered if the rapist was out there somewhere soaking up the satisfaction of his infamy, smiling to himself as he listened. Or was he out there somewhere selecting his next victim?

Spooked, she pulled the Sig from her duffel bag when she turned into the lot at the Corners. She locked the Jeep and went up to her apartment, her senses tuned to catch the slightest noise, the slightest movement. She twisted sideways as she worked the lock with one hand, and looked out over the parking lot and past it. There were no lights on at Sos and Fanchon's house. There seemed to be nothing stirring, and yet she couldn't shake the feeling of eyes on her. Nerves strung too tight, she thought as she let herself into the house.

She had left a light on in the apartment and added more to it as she made a systematic check of the rooms, gun in hand. Only after that task was finished did she put the Sig Sauer away and let go the anxiety that had gathered in tight knots in her shoulders. She pulled a bottle of Abita from the refrigerator, toed off her sneakers, and went to the answering machine.

With all the angry calls since the Fourcade incident hit the airwaves, she had considered unplugging the thing. What was the sense of offering convenience to people who wanted only to abuse her? But there was always the chance of a call on the case, or so she hoped.

The tape spilled its secrets one at a time. Two reporters wanting interviews, two verbal-abuse calls, a breather, and three hang-ups. Each call was unnerving in its own way, but only one ran a shiver down her back.

'Annie? It's Marcus.' His voice was almost intimate, as if he had called from his bed. 'I just wanted to say how pleased I was that you stopped by today. You can't know what it means to me that you're willing to help. Everyone's been against me. I haven't had an ally except for my lawyer. Just to have you listen . . . to know you care about the truth . . . You can't know how special –'

'I don't want to know,' she said, but stopped herself from touching the reset button and pulled the cassette out instead. Fourcade would want to hear it. If things progressed with Renard, it could conceivably be deemed evidence. If he became infatuated with her . . . If the attraction evolved into obsession . . . Already he thought she was his friend.

'*Don't you help him, 'Toinette. . . . Don't let him use you.*'

'And just what do you think you're doing, Fourcade?' she murmured, slipping the tape into her sweater pocket.

The faint scent of smoke clung to her sweater. She let herself out the French doors onto the balcony for a breath of cool air.

Far out in the swamp an eerie green glow wobbled in the darkness – gases that had been ignited by nature and were burning off untended. Nearer, something splashed near the shore. Probably a coon washing his midnight snack, she told herself. But the explanation had the hollow ring of wishful thinking and the sense of a larger presence touched her like eyes.

Hair rising on the back of her neck, Annie did a slow scan of the yard – what she could see of it – from Sos and Fanchon's house, along the bank and past the dock where the swamp tour pontoons were tied up, to the south side of the building, where a pair of rusty Dumpsters stood. Only the finest grains of illumination from the parking-lot security light reached back here. Nothing moved. And still the sensation of a presence closed like a hand on her throat.

Slowly, Annie backed into the apartment, then dropped to her belly on the floor and crawled back onto the balcony to peer between the balusters. She did the scan again, following the same route, slowly, her pulse thumping in her ears.

The movement came at the Dumpsters. Faint, with a whisper of sound. The shape of a head. An arm reaching out. Black — all of it. A solid shadow. Moving toward the side of the building, toward the stairs to her apartment.

Annie scuttled backward into the apartment, pushed the doors shut, and scrambled to her bedroom, where she had left the Sig. Sitting on the floor, she checked the load in the gun as she called 911 and reported the prowler. Then she waited and listened. And waited. And waited. Five minutes ticked past.

She thought about the prowler, what his intentions might be. He could have been the rapist, but he could as easily have been a thief. A convenience store on the edge of nowhere would seem an easy target, and had been a target several times in the past. Uncle Sos had taken to keeping the cash box under his bed and a loaded shotgun in the closet — all against Annie's advice. If this was a burglar and he didn't find what he wanted in the store . . . if he went to the house in search of the money . . .

The potential for disaster turned Annie's stomach. She'd seen people shotgunned for fifty bucks in a liquor-store cash register. When she worked patrol in Lafayette, she'd seen a sixteen-year-old with his skull caved in because another kid wanted his starter jacket. She couldn't sit in her apartment and wait while some creep drew a bead on the only family she'd ever had.

She slipped her sneakers on and padded quietly to the bathroom and to the door behind the old claw-foot tub. The hinges groaned as she eased it open. She slipped through the door onto the seldom-used staircase that dropped steeply down into the stockroom of the store. Back pressed to the wall, gun in hand, raised and ready, she strained to listen for any sound of an intruder. Nothing. Slowly she descended one step at a time.

The light from the parking lot fell in the store's front windows like artificial moonlight. Annie moved down the short rows of goods like a prowling cat. Her hands were sweating against the Sig. She quickly dried one and then the other on the leg of her jeans.

The front door seemed the least risky place to exit. A thief would try to break in through the stockroom door on the south side, out of sight from the house and from the road. And if this wasn't a thief, if he was looking to gain access to the apartment, the only way up was the stairs on the south side of the building.

Annie let herself out quickly and slipped around the corner to the north side of the building. Where the hell was the radio car? It had to have been fifteen minutes since the call. They could have sent the cavalry from New Iberia in less time.

She made her way along the building, ducking beneath the gallery as soon as she could, hoping she was putting herself between the prowler and the house. She wanted to drive him away from it, not toward it. To scare him off toward the levee road seemed safest, though that was a likely spot for him to have hidden his vehicle.

The smell of dead fish was strong as she crept down the slope, holding herself steady against the foundation of the building with one hand and stepping with caution to keep from skidding on the crushed rock and clamshell. At the corner post of the gallery a cat hunched over scavenged fish entrails, growling low in its throat.

Annie could see no movement in the direction of the house. Adjusting her grip on the gun, she took a deep breath and stuck her head out around the corner. Nothing. Another deep breath and she turned the corner, leading with the Sig. The Dumpsters sat past the south end of the gallery.

She moved quickly toward them, still close to the building. Sweat beaded on her forehead and she resisted the urge to wipe it away. She was close now, she could feel it, could feel the presence of another being. Her senses sharpened, heightened. The sound of water dripping somewhere near seemed loud in her ears. The stench of gutted fish nearly made her gag. The scent seemed wrong somehow, but this wasn't the time to process that information.

She held up at the southeastern corner of the building, listening for the scrape of a foot on the ground or on the staircase to her apartment. She gathered herself to move around the corner, her mind racing ahead to visualize leading with the gun, focusing on her target, shouting out the warning to hold it. But as she drew breath to call out, a voice boomed behind her.

'Sheriff's deputy! Drop the gun!'

'I'm on the job!' Annie yelled, uncocking the Sig and tossing it to the side.

'On the ground! Now! Down on the ground!'

'I live here!' she called, dropping to her knees. 'The prowler's around the side!'

The cop didn't want to hear it. He rushed up like a charging bull and clocked her between the shoulders with his stick. 'I said, get down! Get the fuck down!'

Annie sprawled headlong on the ground, starbursts lighting up behind her eyes. The deputy yanked her left hand around behind her back and slapped on the cuff, twisted her right arm back and did the same.

'I'm Deputy Broussard! Annie Broussard.'

'Broussard? Really?' The surprise wasn't quite genuine. He rolled her onto her back and shone his flashlight in her face, blinding her. 'Well, what d'ya know? If it ain't our own little turncoat in the flesh.'

'Fuck yourself, Pitre,' Annie snapped. 'And get the cuffs off while you're at it.' She struggled to sit up. 'What the hell took you so long? I called this in twenty minutes ago.'

He shrugged, unconcerned, as he unlocked the handcuffs. 'You know how it is. We gotta prioritize calls.'

'And where did this rank? Somewhere below you paging through the latest *Penthouse*?'

'You really shouldn't insult your local patrol officer, Broussard,' he said, rising, dusting off the knees of his uniform. 'You never know when you might need him.'

'Yeah, right.'

Annie scooped up the Sig and pushed to her feet, biting back a groan.

She rolled her shoulders to try to dissipate the burning pain. 'Great job, Pitre. How many home owners do you normally assault in the course of a shift?'

'I thought you was a burglar. You didn't obey my commands to get down. You oughta know better.'

'Fine. It's my fault you whacked me. Now how about helping me look for the crook? Though I'm sure he's long gone after all your bellowing.'

Pitre ignored the gibe, sniffing the air as they walked up around the corner to the south side of the building. 'Jesus, what's that smell?' he said, shining the light ahead of them. 'You been killing hogs or something?'

Annie pulled her own flashlight from the back waistband of her jeans. *Dripping.* She could still hear dripping. It hit her as she walked beneath the staircase – a drop, and then another – falling from the stairs that led up to her apartment. She held her hand out and shone the beam of the flashlight on her palm as another drop hit, and another. Blood.

'Oh my God,' she breathed, bolting out from under the grisly shower.

'Christ Almighty,' Pitre muttered, backing up.

The crushed shell beneath the staircase was red with it, as if someone had rolled an open can of paint down the steps. And hanging down between the treads like ghoulish tinsel were animal entrails.

Annie wiped her hand on her T-shirt and moved to the end of the staircase. Shining her light up to the landing, she illuminated a trail of bloody carnage, intestines strung like a garland down the steps.

'Oh my God,' she said again.

A memory surfaced from a dark corner of her mind: Pam Bichon – stabbed and eviscerated. Then a possibility struck her like a bolt of lightning and the horror was magnified tenfold. *Sos. Fanchon.*

'Oh, God. Oh, no. No!' she screamed.

She wheeled away from Pitre and ran, feet slipping and skidding on the crushed shell, down the slope toward the dock. The beam of the flashlight waved erratically in front of her. *Sos. Fanchon. Her family.*

'Broussard!' Pitre shouted behind her.

Annie threw herself at the front door of the ranch house, pounding with the flashlight, twisting the doorknob with her bloody hand. The door swung open and she fell into Sos as a living room lamp went on.

'Oh God! Oh God!' she stammered, wrapping her arms around him in a frantic embrace. 'Oh, thank God!'

It's pig innards,' Pitre announced, poking at an intestine with his baton. 'Lotta pigs getting butchered this time of year.'

Annie was still shaking. She paced back and forth at the base of her steps, fuming. Pitre had found the five-gallon plastic bucket the stuff had come in and set it off to the side, in view by the light now coming from the front window of the store. Annie wanted to kick it. She wanted to pick it up and beat Pitre with it because he was handy and he was a jerk. He was probably in on the joke. If it was a joke.

'I wanna hear it from the lab,' she said.

'What? Why?'

'Because if a human body turns up two days from now missing its plumbing, someone's gonna want it back, Einstein.'

Pitre made a disgruntled sound. If it was evidence, he would have to deal with it, scrape it back into the bucket, and haul it away in his car.

'It's pig innards,' he insisted again.

Annie glared up into his face. 'Are you so sure because you don't wanna deal with it or because you *know*?'

'I don't know nothin',' he grumbled.

'If Mullen is behind this, you tell him I'll kick his ass all the way to Lafayette!'

'I don't know nothing about it!' Pitre griped. 'I answered your call. That's all I did!'

'Who's this Mullen, *chère*?' Sos demanded. 'Why for he'd do somethin' like dis to you?'

Annie rubbed a hand across her forehead. How could she possibly explain? Sos had never been happy with her choice of profession in the first place. He'd love to hear how deputies were trying to run her out of the department. And if it wasn't Mullen, then who?

'A bad joke, Uncle Sos.'

'A joke?' he huffed, incredulous. '*Mais non*. You didn' come laughin' to me, *chérie*. Ain' nothin' funny 'bout dis.'

'No, there isn't,' Annie agreed.

Fanchon looked up the stairs where half a dozen cats had come to feast on the entrails. 'Dat's some mess, dat's for sure.'

'Deputy Pitre and I will clean it up, Tante. It's evidence,' Annie said. 'You both go on back to bed. This is my mess. I'm sorry I woke you.'

It took another five minutes of arguing to convince them to go home and leave the mess. Annie didn't want them touched by this act any more than they had been. As they finally walked away, a residual wave of the panic she had felt for them washed through her. The world had gone mad. That she could have thought someone could have butchered Sos and Fanchon was proof of it. Deep inside, she was just as afraid as everyone else in the parish that evil had leached up from hell to contaminate their world and devour them all.

She wished for more reasons than one that she could pin this undeniably on Mullen. But the more she thought on it, the less certain she felt. Keying her out on the radio was simple, anonymous. The snake in her Jeep had been easily managed, but this . . . Too much chance of being caught red-handed, literally. And the correlation to Pam Bichon was unnerving.

At Annie's insistence, Pitre hiked up onto the levee road with her and shone his light around. Animal eyes glowed red as the beam cut across woods and brush. If there had ever been a car parked along here, it was long gone now. There were no bloody footprints. Tires made no useable impression on the rock road.

It was nearly three A.M. by the time Annie trudged back up to her apartment via the in-store stairs. Her muscles ached. The pain between her shoulder blades where Pitre had struck her had a knifelike quality. At the same time, she was too wired to sleep.

She pulled another Abita from the fridge, washed down some Tylenol, and plopped down in a chair at the kitchen table, where her own notes on Pam Bichon's homicide were still spread out.

She picked up the chronology and glanced over the entries.

10/9 1:45 A.M.: *Pam again reports a prowler. No suspect apprehended.*

10/10: On leaving house for school bus, Josie Bichon discovers the mutilated remains of a raccoon on the front step.

Marcus Renard wanted to be her friend. He had wanted to be Pam Bichon's friend, too. Pam had rejected him. Annie had called him a killer to his face. Pam was dead. And Annie was lining herself up to take Pam's place in his life. Because she wanted to play detective, because she needed to find justice for a woman trapped in the shadowland of victims.

She had never imagined she might run the risk of ending up there herself.

25

'I was thinking maybe I could go into Records and Evidence,' Annie said as she slid into the chair in front of Noblier's desk. She'd had all of three hours' sleep. She looked like hell already; lack of sleep wasn't going to alter the package noticeably.

The sheriff had apparently spent Sunday recuperating from the lousy past week. His cheeks and nose were sunburned, evidence of a day in his bass boat. He looked up at her as if she'd volunteered to clean toilets.

'Records? You *want* to go to Records?'

'No, sir. I *want* to stay on patrol. But if I can't do that, I'd like to go somewhere I haven't been. Learn something new.'

Annie struggled for visible enthusiasm. Sworn personnel were seldom wasted on jobs like records, but he was going to waste her no matter where he put her.

'I suppose you can't hardly cause any trouble there,' he muttered, petting his coffee mug.

'No, sir. I'll try not to, sir.'

He mulled it over while he took a bite out of his blueberry muffin, then nodded. 'All right, Annie, Records it is. But I've got something else I need you to do first today. Another learning experience, you might say. Go see my secretary. She'll lay it all out for you.'

McGruff the Crime Dog?'

Annie stared in horror at the costume hanging before her in the storage room: furry limbs and a trench coat. The giant dog head sat on top of the giant dog feet.

Valerie Comb smirked. 'Tony Antoine usually does it, but he called in sick.'

'Yeah, I bet he did.'

Noblier's secretary handed her a schedule. 'Two appearances this morning and two this afternoon. Deputy York will do the presentation. All you have to do is stand around.'

'Dressed up like a giant dog.'

Valerie sniffed and fussed with the chiffon scarf she had tied around her throat in a poor attempt to hide a hickey. 'You're lucky you got a job at all, you ask me.'

'I didn't.'

'You got ten minutes to get to Wee Tots,' she said, sauntering toward the door. 'Better shake a leg, Deputy. Or is that wag your tail?'

'You'd know more about that than I would,' Annie muttered under her breath as the door closed, leaving her with her new alter ego.

A learning experience.

She learned she would rather have worn the giant head out of the closet and down the halls of the station, thereby disguising herself completely and avoiding humiliation. But she also learned that she couldn't put the head on without help. It was as heavy and unwieldy as a Volkswagen bug. Her one attempt to get it on threw her off balance, and she staggered into a steel shelving unit, bounced off, and went dog headfirst into the paper recycling bin.

She learned she couldn't drive wearing giant dog feet. She learned there was no ventilation inside the suit, and the thing smelled worse than any real dog she'd ever encountered.

She learned York the Dork took his McGruff-detail duties far too seriously.

'Can you bark?' he asked as he adjusted her head. They stood in the small side parking lot at the Wee Tots Nursery School. His uniform was spotless, starched stiff. The creases in his pants looked sharp enough to slice cheese.

Annie glared out of the tiny eyeholes in McGruff's partly opened mouth. 'Can I what?' she asked, her voice muffled.

'Bark. Bark like a dog for me.'

'I'm going to pretend you didn't say that to me.'

York's little paintbrush mustache twitched with impatience. He moved around behind her and adjusted the brown tail that stuck out the back vent on the trench coat. 'This is important, Deputy Broussard. These children are depending on us. It's our job to teach them safety and to teach them that law enforcement personnel are their friends. Now say something the way McGruff might.'

'Get your hands off my tail or I'll bite you.'

'You can't say that! You'll frighten the children!'

'I was talking to you.'

'And your voice has to be much deeper, more growly. Like this.' He moved before her once again and prepared himself physically for the role, hunching his shoulders and making a face that looked like Nixon. 'Hello, boys and *girrrl*s,' he said in his best cartoon dog voice, which *sounded* like Nixon. 'I'm McG*rrr*uff the Crime Dog! Together we can all take a bite out of c*rrr*ime!'

'Yeah, you're a regular Scooby-Doo, York. You wanna wear this outfit?'

He straightened himself at the affront. 'No.'

'Then shut up and leave me alone. I'm in no mood.'

'You have an attitude problem, Deputy,' he declared, then turned on his heel and marched toward the side entrance of the school in his stick-up-the-butt gait.

Annie waddled along behind, tripped on the steps, landed on her giant dog snout. York heaved a long-suffering sigh, righted her, and guided her into the building.

A learning experience.

She learned that she had no mobility in a dog suit and no dexterity wearing paws. She learned that she was at a gross disadvantage being able to see only a small square of the world through McGruff's mouth. Toddlers existed entirely beneath that field of vision – and they knew it. They stomped on her feet and pulled her tail. One leapt from a desktop, yodeling like Tarzan and grabbed the big pink tongue lolling out of McGruff's mouth. Another sneaked in close and peed on her foot.

By the time they finished their program at Sacred Heart Elementary that afternoon, Annie felt like a pinata that had weathered the beating of one too many birthday revelers. York had stopped speaking to her altogether – but not before assuring her he would be reporting her uncooperative behavior to Sergeant Hooker and possibly even to the sheriff. According to him, she was a disgrace to crime dogs everywhere.

Annie stood on the sidewalk outside Sacred Heart with her McGruff head under her arm and watched York storm off to his cruiser. School was letting out. A herd of third graders dashed past her, barking. A bigger kid grabbed her tail and spun her around, never breaking stride on his way to the bus.

'This doesn't look good,' Josie said soberly. She stood on the steps with her arms around her backpack, her hair swept away from her face with a wide purple band.

'Hey, Jose, where y'at?' Annie said.

The girl shrugged, casting her gaze at the ground.

'You're gonna miss your bus.'

Josie shook her head. 'I'm supposed to go to the lawyer's office. Grandma and Grandpa Hunt are having a meeting. They let him out of jail yesterday, you know. We went to get him instead of going to church. I guess hardly anybody that breaks the law has to stay in jail, huh?'

'They let him out on bail?' Annie asked. Who would have thought Pritchett would move on Sunday? No one – that was the point. The offices were officially shut down, which made it a perfect day for clandestine maneuvers. The family didn't want the press making hay off them. Pritchett didn't want to upset the Davidsons any more than necessary. The Davidsons had a great many more friends among the voting constituency than Marcus Renard.

Josie shrugged again as she descended the steps and headed for the playground. 'I guess. I don't understand, but nobody wanted to talk about it. Grandpa Hunt especially. When he got home, he went fishing all alone, and when he came back he went into his study and didn't come out.'

Instead of going to the empty swing set, she sat down on a fat railroad tie that edged a patch of pansies beneath the shade of a live oak. Annie dropped the McGruff head on the asphalt and sat down beside her, rearranging her tail as best she could. On the other side of the school, the buses were roaring off.

'I know it's confusing for you, Jose. This is confusing for a lot of grown-ups, too.'

'Grandma says that detective tried to beat up the guy that killed my mom, but you stopped him.'

'He was breaking the law. Cops are supposed to enforce the law; they shouldn't ever break it. But just because I stopped Detective Fourcade doesn't mean I won't still try to get the guy that killed your mom. Do you understand?'

Josie turned sideways and reached out to touch a lavender pansy with her fingertip. A single tear slipped down her cheek and she whispered, 'No.'

She hung her head a little lower, her curtain of dark hair falling to hide her face. When she finally spoke, her voice was tiny and trembling. 'I . . . I really miss my mom.'

Annie reached out with a paw and gathered Josie close to her side. 'I know you miss her, sweetheart,' she said against the top of Josie's head. 'I know exactly how much you miss her. I'm so sorry any of this had to happen to you.'

'I want her back,' Josie sobbed out against the trench coat. 'I want her to come back and I know she's never going to and I hate it!'

'I know you do, honey. Life shouldn't have to hurt so much.'

'Sister Celeste says I sh-shouldn't be mad at G-God, but I am.'

'Don't you worry about God. He's got a lot to answer for. Who else are you mad at? Are you mad at me?'

The little girl nodded.

'That's okay. But I want you to know I'm doing my best to help, Jose,' she murmured. 'I promised you I would, and I am. But you have every right to be mad at whoever you want. Who else are you mad at? Your dad?'

She nodded again.

'And your grandma?'

Another nod.

'And Grandpa Hunt?'

'N-no.'

'Who else?'

Josie went still for a moment. Annie waited, anticipation born of hard experience thickening in her chest. A desultory breeze stirred the heads of the pansies. A painted bunting flitted down from an azalea bush to pluck at a crust of bread some child had peeled from a lunch sandwich and abandoned.

'Who else, Jose?'

The answer came in a small voice brimming with pain. 'Me.'

'Oh, Josie,' Annie whispered, hugging her tight. 'What happened to your mom wasn't your fault.'

'I-I w-was g-gone to Kristen's h-house. Maybe if if I h-had been home . . .'

Annie listened to the stammered confession, feeling nine years old inside, remembering the horrible burden of guilt no one had even suspected she carried. She had been with her mama always, had watched over her during the bad spells and prayed for God to make her happy. And the first time she'd gone away from home, Marie had ended her own life. The weight of that had pressed down on her until she thought it would crush her.

She remembered going down the levee road, the taste of bitter tears as she had thrown her stuffed Minnie Mouse into the water. The toy she had so cherished from her first-ever vacation trip, the trip that had marked the end of her mother's life. And she remembered Uncle Sos fishing the toy out of the reeds and sitting on the bank with her on his lap, both of them crying, the soggy Minnie Mouse squished between them.

'It wasn't your fault, Josie,' she murmured at last. 'I thought that, too, when my mom died. That maybe if I had been home I could have stopped it from happening. But we can't know when bad things are coming to our lives. We can't control what other people do.

'It's not your fault your mom died, honey. That's someone else's fault, and he's going to be made to pay. I promise. All I ask is for you to believe me when I tell you I'm your friend. I'll always be your friend, Josie. I'll always try to be here for you and I'll always try my hardest for you.'

Josie looked up at her. She tried to smile. 'Then how come you're dressed up like a dog?'

Annie made a face. 'A temporary setback. It won't last. I'm told I make a crummy crime dog.'

'You were pretty bad,' Josie admitted. She wrinkled her nose in distaste. 'You smell really gross, too.'

'Hey, watch the insults,' Annie teased. 'I'll sic all my fleas on you.'

'Yuck!'

'Come on, munchkin,' she said, standing slowly. 'I'll walk you downtown. You can help me carry my head.'

Lake Pontchartrain shone metallic aqua, as flat as a coin and stretching north as far as the eye could see, bisected by the Pontchartrain Causeway toll bridge. Several boats skimmed the surface in the middle distance, their pilots playing hooky from the usual Monday rigors of work. The view from this stretch of shore was expensive. Real estate along this part of the lake was in the category of 'if you have to ask, you can't afford it.' Duval Marcotte could afford it.

His mansion was Italianate in design, looking like something that would be more at home in Tuscany than Louisiana. Soft white stucco and a red tile roof. Straight, elegant lines and tall slim windows. An eight-foot-tall wall surrounded the property, but the iron gates stood open, affording passersby a view of emerald lawn and lavish flower gardens. A black Lincoln Town Car sat in the drive near the house. A surveillance camera peered down from atop a gatepost.

Nick drove past and circled around. The service entrance stood open, as well. A florist's van sat near the kitchen entrance of the house with its doors gaping wide. Nick parked his truck outside the gate and walked to the house, grabbing an enormous arrangement of spring flowers out of the van.

The kitchen was a hive of activity. A thin woman was overseeing two aproned assistants in the making of canapés. Two more women were unloading trays of champagne glasses onto the granite top of another work island. A brawny boy of twentysomething emerged from a door with a case of champagne and carried it to a table at the direction of a small effeminate blond man in gold-rimmed glasses, who then swung toward Nick. 'Take that to the red parlor. It goes on the round mahogany table near the fireplace.'

A maid swung the kitchen door open for him.

He had been in this house twice and had memorized the layout, could see in his mind's eye every stick of antique furniture and every painting that hung on the walls. The red parlor was on the left at the front of the house, a room that looked as if it might have hosted Napoleon, the decor Second Empire, ornate and ostentatious.

Nick set the arrangement on the round mahogany table and walked quickly down the hall of the east wing, his running shoes all but silent against the polished floor. He bypassed the main staircase in favor of the stairs at the far end of the hall. Marcotte's office was on the second floor of the east wing. A man of habit, he worked from home Mondays and Fridays. Business associates Marcotte wouldn't be seen with at his offices on Poydras Street in the central business district of New Orleans came to his home on a regular basis. Nick thought of the Town Car in the drive and frowned.

He would have been better off waiting, coming in late to surprise Marcotte in his bed, but that would have given Marcotte too good an excuse to shoot him or have him shot as an intruder. He was here for business, not revenge, he reminded himself as he ducked into a bathroom and shut the door behind him.

He stared at himself in the mirror above the pedestal sink. He wore a loose-fitting black sport coat over his white T-shirt, the cut of the jacket hiding the shoulder rig and the Ruger P.94 semiautomatic. His color was high along his cheekbones. His pulse was pounding a little too hard, and anticipation coated his mouth with a taste like copper. He hadn't seen Marcotte in more than a year, hadn't planned to see him ever again. He had done his best to close the door on that chapter of his life, and now he found himself sneaking back through it.

Closing his eyes, he breathed deeply, filled his lungs, and tried to still his mind. *Calm, center, focus.* Why was he here? Nothing visible tied Marcotte to the Bichon case. He had checked out every New Orleans number on Donnie's phone records from before the murder, finding no direct link to Marcotte. A relief. He didn't want to strengthen Donnie's motive for killing Pam when he knew in his gut Renard was the murderer. If Donnie had contacted Marcotte after Pam's death, Nick had no way of knowing. There was no cause to confiscate Bichon's phone records for that period of time. And if Donnie had contacted Marcotte after the fact, that took Marcotte out of the loop for the murder.

But even after reciting that logic, the uneasiness lingered. The spectre of Marcotte loomed in the shadows at the periphery of the case. Donnie needed Pam's case closed before he could move on plans to sell the realty. If Renard were taken out, the case would likely go away. If Nick was the one to take Renard out, and if he went down for doing the deed, he would then be removed from Marcotte's new playing field.

He let the air escape slowly between his lips. *Calm, center, focus.* He couldn't let the past press into this. He had to isolate the present, deal with the moment, think forward. *Control.* He stepped back into the hall and walked down to the lacquered cypress double doors.

Marcotte's young male secretary sat at a French desk in the small outer office. 'Can I help you?'

'I'm here to see Marcotte.'

The secretary took in Nick's appearance with suspicion and disapproval. 'I'm sorry, you don't have an appointment.'

'Don't be sorry. He'll see me.'

'Mr Marcotte is a very busy man. He's in a meeting.'

Nick leaned across the desk and grabbed hold of the man's necktie just below the knot, twisting it tight around his fist. The secretary's eyes went wide and a strangled sound of surprise leaked out of him.

'You're being very rude, college boy,' Nick said softly. They were nearly nose to nose. 'Lucky for you I'm such a patient guy. Me, I believe in giving people a second chance. Now why don't I unchoke you, and you can buzz Mr Marcotte? You tell him Nick Fourcade is here on business.'

Nick let him go and the secretary fell back in his chair, sucking in air. He reached for the phone and pressed the intercom button.

'I'm sorry to interrupt you, Mr. Marcotte.' He tried to clear his throat, but the raspy edge remained in his voice. 'There's a Nick Fourcade here to see you. He was adamant that I let you know.'

No reply issued from the machine. Nick tapped his toe impatiently. A moment later the double doors to Marcotte's inner sanctum swung open and four men stepped out.

Nick assessed the company quickly, stepping toward the nearest wall.

First came Vic 'The Plug' DiMonti, a mob boss of middling rank in greater New Orleans. He was built like a small cube with stubby legs and arms. In contrast, the muscle that flanked him was oversized, a matched set of steroid-pumped knee busters with crew cuts, no necks, and round Armani sunglasses.

Marcotte stayed in the open doorway as the wiseguys walked out. He looked like the most ordinary of men in dress trousers and a pin-striped shirt with the sleeves rolled up, his tie a neat blood red strip. Slim, sixty, bald on top. He was famous for his smile. His eyes were kindly. And inside his chest, his heart was a small black atrophied lump. He was lavishly benevolent, impressively humble, secretly vicious. He had bought and paid handsomely for a sterling image, and the few people in New Orleans's high circles who knew that gladly looked the other way.

'Well, if it isn't my old friend, Nick Fourcade!' he said, chuckling, jovial, flashing the kind of bonhomie reserved for old and dear acquaintances. 'This is a surprise!'

'Is it?'

'Come in, Nick,' he offered with a grand gesture. 'Evan, bring us coffee, will you?'

'I won't be staying,' Nick said as he stepped past his host into the office.

He was impressed against his will by the view of the lake through the Palladian window that centered the main wall. The room itself was no less impressive. The carpet was plush gray, a shade lighter than the walls. Objets d'art were displayed at intervals along the walls. The furnishings were museum quality.

'You've got a long drive back home,' Marcotte said, rounding his massive desk. 'I hear you've made quite a name for yourself out there in the Cajun nation.'

Nick made no comment. He positioned himself behind a Louis XIV armchair at one end of the desk, with the doors in view. He rested his hands on the back of the chair. Marcotte was the antithesis of everything he believed in: morality, justice, personal accountability. Nick had dreamed of punishing Marcotte for it, but there was no way of doing it without corrupting himself. The catch only fueled his anger.

'What brings you to my neck of the woods, Detective?' Marcotte asked. 'Aside from incredible nerve, that is.'

Elbows braced on the arms of his executive's chair, he pressed his fingertips into a pyramid and swiveled the chair slowly back and forth. 'I'd say it might be the party I'm throwing tonight, but I'm afraid your name is not on the guest list. Can't be official business: you are far out of your jurisdiction. Besides, I understand you've had a little professional setback recently.'

'What do you know about that?'

'What I read in the papers, Nick, my boy. Now what can I do for you?'

Marcotte's calm amazed him. The man had ruined him and he sat here as if there could be no hard feelings, as if it had meant nothing to him.

'Answer me a question,' he said. 'When did you first discuss the possible sale of Bayou Realty with Donnie Bichon?'

'Who is Donnie Bichon?'

'You're reading the papers, you know who he is.'

'You have some reason to believe I've spoken with him? Why would I be interested in some little backwater real estate company?'

'Oh, let me think.' Nick touched two fingers to his temple to emphasize the effort of concentration. 'Money? Making money. Hiding money. Laundering money. Take your pick. Maybe your friend Vic The Plug, he's looking for a little lightweight investment. Maybe you got some senators in your pocket, ready to bring riverboat gambling to the basin. Maybe you know something the rest of us don't.'

Marcotte's face went flat. 'You're offending me, Detective.'

'Am I? Well, hell, what else is new?'

'Nothing. You are as tedious as ever. I'm a well-respected business-man, Fourcade. My reputation is above reproach.'

'What kind of money does it take to buy a reputation like that? You pay extra depending on what crooks you wanna consort with?'

'Mr DiMonti owns a construction firm. We're developing a project together.'

'I'll bet you are. You gonna bring him and his goons out to Bayou Breaux with you?'

'You're mentally deranged, Fourcade. I have no interest in some snake-infested swamp town.'

Nick lifted a finger in warning. 'Ah. Watch what you say, Marcotte. That's *my* snake-infested swamp town – the one you drove me to. I don't wanna see your face there. I don't wanna smell the stink of your money.'

Marcotte shook his head. 'You don't learn, do you, swamp rat? I've been a perfect host to you, and you abuse me. I could have you arrested if I wanted to. How would that look in your file? Like you've lost your marbles, I'd say. Beating up suspects, driving all the way to New Orleans to harass a well-known businessman and philanthropist. You annoy me, Fourcade, like a mosquito. The last time I swatted you away. Don't pester me again.'

The door swung open, and the secretary carried in a silver tray set with a small coffee urn and bone china demitasse cups. The dark aroma of burned chicory filled the room.

'Never mind the coffee, Evan,' Marcotte said, never taking his eyes off Nick. 'Detective Fourcade has worn out his welcome.'

Nick winked at the secretary as he moved toward the door. 'You drink mine, *mon ami*. I hear it's good for a sore throat.'

He went back down the side stairs and let himself out through the solarium to avoid the crowd in the kitchen. The florist's van was gone. Vic DiMonti's thugs were not.

One stepped out from behind a potting shed to block the path to the gate. Nick pulled up ten feet from them and assessed his options. Stand his ground or run back the way he'd come, though he had the sinking feeling Meathead Number Two had already eliminated the second choice. The scuff of large feet on the brick path behind him confirmed the reality. Then DiMonti himself emerged from the potting shed with a hickory spade handle balanced in his thick paws.

'I got no quarrel with you, DiMonti,' Nick said. He kept his weight on the balls of his feet and his eyes on the thug in front of him. He could see the reflection of the twin in the man's sunglasses.

'I remember you, Fourcade,' DiMonti said. His accent was the near Brooklynese of the Irish Channel part of town, befitting a movie mobster. 'You're some kind of head case. They threw you off the force.' He barked a laugh. 'That's gotta take some doing – getting thrown off the NOPD.'

'It was nothing,' Nick said. 'Ask your friend Marcotte.'

'That's a good point you bring up, Fourcade,' DiMonti said, tapping the spade handle against his palm. 'Mr. Marcotte is a close personal friend of mine and a valued business associate. I don't want him upset. You see where I'm going with this?'

'Absolutely. So tell Tiny here to step aside and I'll be on my way.'

DiMonti shook his head sadly. 'I wish it were that simple, Nick. Can I call you Nick? You see, I think you got what they call a pattern of behavior here. You maybe need a little lesson from Bear and Brutus here to break you from that. Make you think twice before you come back here. You see what I'm saying?'

He saw Brutus behind him looming larger in Bear's sunglasses.

A spinning kick caught Brutus in the face, broke his nose and sunglasses, and sent him down on the brick path like a felled tree. Nick spun the other way, blocking a roundhouse right and popping Bear hard in the diaphragm. It was like hitting brick.

The thug caught him with a solid jab, and blood filled Nick's mouth. He brought his right foot up and hit Bear square in the knee, forcing the joint to bend in a way nature never intended. Howling, clutching at the knee, the thug doubled over, and Nick hit him with a combination that split his lip and sprayed a fountain of blood.

All he needed was Bear to go down and he could break for the gate. He didn't want to pull the Ruger. DiMonti hadn't come here to kill him and he wouldn't want the complications, but neither would he hesitate to do it. The Plug had dumped his share of bodies in the swamp. One more punch and Bear would be gone. But before Nick could draw back, DiMonti swung the spade handle like a baseball bat and caught him hard across the kidneys.

DiMonti swung again and Nick staggered forward, struggling to keep his feet under him, to keep moving. If he could run –

The thought was cut short as Brutus tackled him from behind and he went down face-first on the bricks. Then the world went black, and Nick's final thought was that it was probably just as well.

26

Annie blew out a sigh and dug through the stacks of paperwork, unearthing a packet of microcassette tapes labeled RENARD in Fourcade's bold caps. Interview tapes, no doubt made in his pocket. The official tapes would never have been allowed out of the sheriff's department, but Fourcade lived by his own set of rules – some of which she condoned, and others . . .

It made her uneasy thinking about it. Where would she draw the line? And where would he? She was breaking rules by involving herself in this case, but she felt it was justified, that she owed her allegiance to a higher authority. And was that what Fourcade had been thinking when he'd confronted Renard in that parking lot? That justice was a higher power than the law?

Where the hell was he? she wondered as she dug through her purse for her tape recorder. For a man who had been suspended and warned off the case, he certainly got around.

'Maybe he's out planting evidence for you to find, Annie,' she muttered, then chided herself for it.

She didn't believe he had planted the ring just because he'd been accused of doing it before. No one had proven the allegations made during the Parmantel murder investigation. Fourcade had resigned from the NOPD before anyone got the chance. The hoopla had died down and the case had gone away.

That right there made Annie think something was hinky about the charges. The case had gone away and no civil suit had been filed. Anybody with half a beef against the cops these days filed a civil suit. Allan Zander, the man Fourcade had accused of killing the hooker, Candi Parmantel, had just faded back into anonymity.

She told herself none of that mattered as she loaded tape number one into the player. Fourcade wanted to keep his past to himself, and all she wanted was to close this homicide. The rest was just baggage.

She hit the play button and set the machine on the table.

Fourcade titled the interview with Marcus Renard. He stated the date, time, and case number; his own name, rank, and badge number. Stokes stated his name, rank, and badge number. Chairs scraped against the floor, papers were shuffled.

Fourcade: 'What'd you think of that murder, Mr Renard?'

Renard: 'It's – it's horrible. I can't believe it. Pam . . . My God . . .'

Stokes: 'Can't believe what? That you could butcher a woman that way? Surprised yourself, did you?'

Renard: 'What? I don't know what – You can't think I could do that! Pam was – I would never –'

Stokes: 'Come on, Marcus. This is your ol' buddy Chaz you're talking to. I didn't fall off the turnip truck yesterday. You and me, we been having this same conversation now for what – six, eight weeks? Only this time you did something more than just look. Am I right? You got sick of looking. You got sick of her turning you down.'

Renard: 'No. It wasn't –'

Stokes: 'Come on, Marcus, get straight with this.'

Fourcade: 'Let's give him the benefit, Chaz. You tell us, Mr Renard. Where were you last Friday night?'

Renard: 'Am I being charged with something? Should I have a lawyer present?'

Fourcade: 'Me, I dunno, Mr Renard. Should you have a lawyer present? We just want you to set us straight, that's all.'

Renard: 'You have nothing to tie me to this. I'm an innocent man.'

Stokes: 'You wanted her, Marcus. I been here all along, remember? I know how you followed her around, sent her little notes, little presents. I know that was you calling her up, hanging around her house. I know what you did to that woman, and you might as well confess, Marcus, 'cause you can bet your ass we're gonna prove it, Nicky and me. If I'm lyin', I'm dyin'.'

The rumble of an engine broke Annie's concentration. She clicked the cassette player off and listened for a car door slamming. When the sound didn't come, she rose from her chair, sliding the Sig out of her purse.

The small window on the end of the house afforded a view of nothing. The night was black as pitch. Fourcade's retreat was stuck in the hip pocket of civilization, readily accessible to the animals that prowled the swamp – a fair number on two legs. Poachers and thieves and worse. Society's ragged fringe.

Last night came back to her in a rush. Who would be her enemy here?

No one could have followed her without her knowing it, which eliminated anyone from the department. A random attack by the roving rapist seemed unlikely. That predator knew the lifestyles and habits of his victims. He hadn't chosen them by accident.

Something thumped hard against the floor of the gallery. Leading with the Sig, Annie let herself out onto the landing.

'Nick? That you?'

She waited, debating, knowing she had already tipped her hand. Then came a low groan, the unmistakable sound of pain.

'Fourcade?' she called, easing down the stairs. 'Don't make me shoot you. I've got a big gun, you know.'

He lay on the gallery floor, the light spilling out the window illuminating his battered face.

'Oh my Lord!' Annie stuck the gun in her waistband and dropped down beside him. 'What happened? Who did this?'

Nick cracked open an eye and looked up at her. 'Never announce yourself until you know the situation, Broussard.'

'Man, even half dead you're bossy.'

'Help me up.'

'Help you up? I should call an ambulance! Or I suppose I could shoot you and put you out of your misery.'

He winced as he tried to push himself up onto his hands and knees. 'I'm fine.'

Annie made a rude sound. 'Oh, excuse me, I mistook you for someone who'd had the shit beat out of him.'

'*Mais* yeah,' he mumbled. 'That'd be me. It ain't the first time, sugar.'

'Why does that not surprise me?'

He straightened slowly, pain rippling through his body. 'Come on, Broussard, quit gawking and help me. If we're partners, we're partners.'

Annie moved around beside him and let him hook an arm around her shoulders. 'I don't mind saying you're more than I bargained for, Nick.'

He leaned heavily against her as she helped him into the house. They lurched past the front parlor like a pair of winos. Annie glanced at the blood that dyed the front of his T-shirt and muttered an expletive.

'Who did this?'

'Friend of a friend.'

'I think you need somebody to redefine that term for you. Where are we going?'

'Bathroom.'

She steered him down the hall and nearly fell into the tub as she lowered him to sit on the closed lid of the toilet.

'God, are you sure you're alive?' she said, squatting down in front of him.

'Looks worse than it is.'

'I suppose you're gonna tell me I should see the other guy.'

'They were ugly to start with.'

'They? Plural?'

'Nothing's broke,' Nick said, fighting off another groan as the muscles in his back seized up. 'I'll be pissing blood tomorrow, that's all.'

He leaned his forearms on his thighs and tried to concentrate on clearing away the dizziness. His head was banging like a ten-pound hammer on a cast-iron pot.

'Get me a whiskey,' he grumbled.

'Don't boss me around, Fourcade,' Annie said, digging through the small medicine cabinet. 'I have it on good authority you should never piss off your medical personnel.'

'Get me a whiskey, *please*, Nurse Ratched.'

She peered over her shoulder with a look of amazement. 'You *must* have a concussion. You just made a joke.'

'It's in the kitchen,' he ground out between his teeth, three of which felt loose. 'Third cupboard on the right.'

She went out and came back moments later with a tumbler of Jack Daniel's. She took the first shot herself.

'I want an explanation, Fourcade. And don't jerk me around. I've got a bottle of peroxide and I know how to use it.'

She set the whiskey on the sink and started to help him out of his jacket.

'I can do it,' he protested.

'Oh, God, don't be such a man. You can hardly move.'

Nick gave in and let her remove his jacket and his shoulder rig with the Ruger.

He was disgusted with himself. He should have anticipated DiMonti's attack, should have known better than to go out the same way he'd come in. He should have been fighting off the knuckle hangover with greater success. He shouldn't have needed someone to take care of him, and he couldn't allow himself to get used to it. He wasn't the kind of man who could expect that kind of comfort. His was a solitary existence by necessity. He had pared away the need for companionship to better focus on building the broken pieces of himself into something whole.

But the job was far from finished, and he was tired and battered, and Annie Broussard's touch felt too welcome.

He started to pull the bloodstained T-shirt off himself, until the pain cracked across his back again, as if DiMonti were right there with that damned spade handle.

'I thank God daily that I don't have testicles,' Annie grumbled. 'They obviously impair common sense.'

She began jerking the T-shirt up his back, but her hands stilled before she was halfway. Angry red welts lashed across the small of his back, blood pooling beneath them in bruises as dark as thunderheads.

'Jesus,' she breathed. She had to have hurt him just putting her arm around him to help him into the house, and he hadn't made a sound. Damned stubborn man, she thought. He'd probably gotten exactly what he deserved.

'It's nothing,' he snapped.

She didn't comment but moved more carefully as she peeled the T-shirt up. His skin was hot, the scent of him masculine with a feral undertone. Sweat and blood, she told herself. There was nothing sexual in it, nothing sexual in the act of undressing him.

Her knuckles grazed his collarbone. He was eye level with her breasts. The room suddenly seemed as small as a phone booth.

Fourcade leaned back as she stepped away, as if he may have felt it, too – the strange magnetic pull. He pulled the T-shirt off his arms and threw it on the tile floor. His chest was wide and hard-looking, covered with a mat of dark hair that trailed down the center of a six-pack of stomach muscles and disappeared into the waistband of his jeans.

Annie swallowed hard and moved to the sink.

'I'm waiting for that explanation,' she said. She waited another few minutes while she filled the sink with warm water and soaked a washcloth.

'I went to see Marcotte. A friend of his took exception to my visit.'

'Gosh, imagine that.' She dabbed gingerly at the blood that had crusted along a cut on his cheekbone. 'I'm sure you were your usual charming self – spouting paranoid delusions, accusing him of being the devil. What were you doing there in the first place? Did you find something in Donnie's phone records?'

'No, but I don't like Marcotte's smell hanging around this. I wanted to rattle his cage.'

'And you got your bell rung, instead. Careless.'

It was. He had said so himself countless times on the endless drive home. He was rusty, and beyond that, he didn't think straight when it came to Marcotte.

'So who were these "friends"?'

'A couple of knee busters belonging to Vic DiMonti.'

'Vic DiMonti. The wiseguy Vic DiMonti?'

'C'est *vrai*. You got it in one, angel. Didn't think a fine upstanding citizen like Marcotte would know anyone like that, did you? Well, you'll never see them on the society page together, that's for damn sure.'

He took a sip of the whiskey while she rinsed the blood out of the washcloth. The liquor stung the inside of his mouth where his teeth had cut into the soft tissue. It hit his empty stomach with an acidic hiss that was followed closely by a warm, numbing glow. He took another drink.

'This should have stitches,' Annie muttered, staring at the cut that sliced his left eyebrow.

She'd thought he was insane when he'd first brought up the subject of Marcotte. She'd thought Marcotte was just part of the baggage of his past that he dragged around behind him and wouldn't let anyone see inside of. But if Marcotte was Donnie's secret buyer, and if Marcotte consorted with mob types . . . maybe Fourcade wasn't so crazy after all.

'So what did Marcotte have to say?'

'Nothing. I didn't like the quality of his silence.'

'But if Donnie wasn't in contact with him before the murder, then he's not a motive. What Donnie does with his half of the company now is his own business.'

He took hold of her wrist and pulled her hand away from his split chin. 'The devil comes knocking at your door, 'Toinette, don'tcha turn your back on him just 'cause he's late for the first dance.'

Annie's breath caught at the leashed strength in his grip, at the dark fire in his eyes. This was what she had warned herself away – from his intensity, his obsessions.

'I'm in this to close the homicide,' she said. 'Marcotte is your demon, not mine. I don't even know what he did to win that exalted place in your heart.'

She had just finished telling herself she didn't want to know, and yet she found herself holding her breath as she waited for the explanation.

'If we're partners . . .' she whispered.

The silence, the moment, took on a strange density, as clear and thick as water. The air of expectation: too heavy to breathe, charged with electricity. The weight of it was more than he wanted, the import beyond what he would have allowed himself to consider. He wondered if she felt it, if she could recognize it for what it was. Then he took a deep breath and stepped off that inner ledge.

'I went looking for justice,' he said softly. 'Marcotte bent it over my head like a tire iron. He showed me a side to the system as tangled and oily as the innards of a snake.'

'You think Marcotte killed that hooker?'

'Oh, no.' He shook his head slightly. 'Allan Zander killed Candi Parmantel. Marcotte, he made it all go away – and my career along with it.'

'Why would he do that?'

'Zander is married to a cousin of Marcotte. He's nobody, no social climber, just another jerk-off white-collar working stiff. Frustrated with his job, disappointed in his marriage, looking to take it all out on somebody. He left that girl, that fourteen-year-old runaway who was selling her body so she could eat, dead in a back-alley Dumpster like she was so much refuse. And Duval Marcotte covered it up.'

'You know this?' Annie asked carefully. 'Or you think it?'

'I know. I can't prove it. I tried, and everything I tried turned back around on me. I wasn't the one who tampered with the evidence or lost the lab work.'

'Nobody else thought it was strange – all this stuff going wrong on one case?'

'Nobody cared. What's another dead hooker besides bad press? Besides, it didn't any of it look that big. A bad test here, a piece of evidence gone there. You know what they say: New Orleans is a marvelous place for coincidence.'

'But you weren't the only detective on the case. What about your partner?'

'He had a kid with leukemia. Big-time medical bills. Who do you think he cared more about – his child or some dead prostitute? I was the only player in the game who gave a damn about that girl. I didn't want Marcotte's money, I wanted Marcotte, and most of all I wanted Zander. Marcotte snapped me like a twig, and I couldn't prove a goddamn thing. The more noise I made, the crazier I looked. The chief wanted my ass on a platter. The captain wanted me out on a psych charge. My lieutenant stuck his neck out and let me resign. I hear he's working security for some oil company in Houston now.'

Wincing, he leaned over and dug his cigarettes and lighter out of his discarded jacket. He shook one out and lit up.

'Duval Marcotte, he does something like that for a little nothing/ nobody turd like Zander, what you think he'd do for someone like Vic DiMonti?'

Annie sat down on the edge of the tub and stared at her hands. Fourcade wasn't telling her he had crashed and burned in a big way. The rumors that had filtered out of New Orleans on the blue grapevine had whispered words like *crazy, paranoid, drunk, violent*. She thought of what he had said that night at Laveau's.

'You afraid of me? . . . You don't listen to gossip?'

'I take it for what it's worth. Half-truths, if that.'

'And how do you decide which half is true?'

'Do you believe me, 'Toinette?' he asked.

For a moment the only sound was the insect buzz of the fluorescent lights that flanked the medicine chest. It had been a long time since he'd cared if anyone believed him – not facts and evidence, *him*. He had put away that need, but now he felt the strange stirrings of hope in his chest, foreign fingers touching him in a way that was intrusive and seductive, and ultimately disturbing.

'It doesn't matter,' he said, stubbing his cigarette out on the rim of the sink.

'Yes, it does,' Annie corrected him. 'Of course it does.' She raked a hand back through her hair and exhaled. 'It must have been hell. I can't – No, I *can* imagine . . . a little bit. I've been learning lately about standing on the wrong side of an issue.'

'And I put you there, didn't I, *chère*?' He reached out to touch her chin. His smile was bitter and sad. 'What a helluva team we make, huh?'

She tried a smile to match his. 'Yeah. Who'd believe it?'

'No one. But it's right, you know. We want the same thing . . . need the same thing . . .'

His voice died to a whisper as he realized the conversation had shifted onto a new plane, that what was between them was attraction; that what he needed, what he wanted, was Annie. And she knew it. He could see it in her eyes – the surprise, apprehension, anticipation.

He slid his fingers into her hair, leaned forward, and touched his mouth to hers experimentally. A jolt went through him, a deep current that pulled at him, pulled him closer to her. He settled his mouth against hers and tasted her, whiskey warm and sweet with a kind of innocence he could barely remember. His hand cradled the back of her head and he kissed her deeply, without reserve, his tongue sliding against hers.

Annie sat frozen, paralyzed by the emotions and sensations unleashed by his kiss. Heat, fear, need, a dangerous excitement. It shocked her that she allowed him this intimacy, that she wanted it. That she wanted him. Her tongue moved against his and he groaned low in his throat.

The sense of power that rose within her, the passion that rose with it, terrified her. Fourcade was a man of dragons and deep secrets. If he wanted more than sex, he would want her soul.

She pulled away from the kiss, turned her face away, and felt his lips graze her cheek.

'I can't do this,' she whispered. 'You scare me, Nick.'

'What scares you? You think I'm crazy? You think I'm dangerous?'

'I don't know what to think.'

'Yes, you do,' he murmured. 'You're just afraid to admit it. I think, *chère*, you scare yourself.'

He touched her chin. 'Look at me. What do you see in me that scares you? You see in me what you're afraid to feel. You think if you go that deep you might drown, lose yourself . . . like me.'

A fine chill threaded through her. She pushed herself past it, pushed to her feet, kicked awake what wits hadn't gone entirely numb.

'You should be in bed – and not with me,' she said, letting the plug out of the sink. Her heart was beating too fast. She couldn't quite get her breath. She fumbled with the stopper and dropped it on the floor. 'Take some aspirin. Take a cold shower. You probably shouldn't drink too much in case you've got a –'

He caught hold of her wrist as if holding her physically could stop her from prattling on. Annie looked at him with suspicion. She had let him cross a barrier, and suddenly he could touch her. If he could touch her, he could pull her toward him, literally and figuratively. She told herself she didn't want that. She couldn't handle him, didn't know if she could trust him. She'd stood on the edge of a dark parking lot and watched him beat a suspect senseless.

'I need to go,' she said. 'After last night, God knows what might be on the agenda tonight.'

'What happened last night?' he asked, coming slowly to his feet.

Annie backed into the hall, trying to pass off a casual attitude she didn't feel. She told him in the briefest detail, the way she would write a report – without emotion. Nick propped himself up in the bathroom doorway, the near-empty glass of whiskey in his hand. He seemed to concentrate on every word she said.

'What did the lab say about the entrails?'

'Nothing yet. They'll call tomorrow. Pitre insisted it was pig intestines. It probably was. It was probably Mullen and his band of merry jerks just trying to rattle me, but . . .'

'But what?' Fourcade demanded. 'You got a feeling, 'Toinette, let's hear it. Speak your mind. Don't be shy.'

'Someone, presumably Renard, left a mutilated animal on Pam's doorstep back in October. Now I'm working the case and *this* happens.'

'You think it could have been Renard.'

'I don't know. Does that make sense? He didn't start harassing Pam until she'd rejected him. She rejected him, he punished her. He thinks I'm his champion. Why would he do something to jeopardize that?'

'Maybe punishment wasn't his goal with Pam,' Nick suggested. 'He was always quick enough to offer his concern after she had something bad happen.'

Annie nodded, considering. '*I know what it is to be persecuted,*' Renard had said to her just yesterday. '*We have that in common.*'

'Whoever did it – I'd like to wring their neck,' she muttered. 'It scared me. I hate being scared. It pisses me off.'

Nick almost smiled. She was working hard to be tough, to be a cop. But she'd never found herself involved in anything like this – not with the case, not with him. He'd seen the uncertainty in her eyes. He had to give her points for pushing past it.

'Call me when you get home,' he ordered. 'Partner.'

Annie looked up at his battered face and felt that strange pull toward him. It scared her. And it pissed her off. In ten days she would have to testify against him.

'I have to . . .' She moved her hand in the direction of the door.

He nodded slightly. 'I know.'

As she walked out of his house, she had the distinct feeling that their parting words hadn't been about leaving at all.

All she wanted was to do the job, to find some closure for Josie, for Pam. She had never meant to fall into this . . . this – God, what could she even call this thing with Fourcade? Attraction. It wasn't a relationship. She didn't want a relationship. She didn't want . . . to go that deep.

Shit.

There was still a light on in the store when she pulled in at the Corners, though closing had come and gone an hour ago. Sos had probably been regaling his cronies with the tale of the past night's adventure. But if he had had company, they'd gone home. There were no other cars in the lot. Down the way, the light burned low in the Doucets' living room. Tante Fanchon would be settling in for the news, soaking her bunions in the minispa foot bath Annie had given her for Christmas two years ago.

Annie turned the Jeep off and sat looking up at the apartment, her thoughts drifting back in time to her mother. Lovely Marie, so unto herself, so complicated, so mysterious . . . so deep. So deep she had drowned in herself, swamped by the intensity of her emotions.

There was nothing wrong in not wanting that. There was nothing wrong in staying safe on the ledge above that abyss.

She took a cleansing breath, feeling silly for having overreacted. She barely knew Fourcade. He'd stolen a kiss. Big deal.

She wanted him. *Big* deal.

She locked the Jeep, slung her duffel bag over her shoulder, and started toward the building as Sos came out onto the porch.

'Hey, *chère*, what you doin', draggin' in dis hour?' he asked, grinning. 'You on a hot date or what?'

'I could ask you the same,' Annie retorted, shuffling toward the edge of the gallery. Sos had left the security lights on, something he rarely did because he had a grudge against the electric company.

'*Mais non!*' He laughed. '*T'es en érreur.* Your *tante* Fanchon, she'd take a stick after me, *chère*. You know it.'

Annie managed a smile.

'You been out with Andre?'

'No.'

'Why not? How you ever gonna marry dat boy, you never see him?'

'Uncle Sos . . .' She couldn't bring herself to go into the speech, partly because of fatigue and partly because of a vague sense of guilt she had no desire to explore.

Sos stepped down off the porch, his boots scuffing on the rock. 'Hey, *'tite chatte,*' he said softly, his face creasing into lines of concern. He touched her cheek with callused fingers. 'You and Andre have another fight?'

'You've got A.J. on the brain,' Annie muttered. 'I'm just tired, that's all.'

He sniffed, indignant, and pulled her with him to the steps. 'Come on. You sit your pretty self down here with your uncle Sos and tell all about it.'

Annie sat down beside him and leaned her head against his shoulder, wishing she could just tell Uncle Sos and sort it all out, the way she had done when she was small. But life had grown so much more complicated than when she was ten and didn't have a mother to take her to the mother-daughter tea at school. Sos and Fanchon had been there for her then, always. She didn't want them touched by what was going on in her life now. She would protect them any way she could.

Sos clucked his tongue softly and hugged her against him. 'Like pullin' hen's teeth with a pliers, gettin' a story outta you. You all the time like dat, you know, even when you was just a tiny li'l thing. You don' wanna bother no one. How many times I gotta tell you, *chérie*, dat's what family is for, huh?'

Annie closed her eyes. 'It's just the job, Uncle Sos. Things are hard for me right now.'

'Because you stop that detective from killing that man what ever'one says is guilty?'

'Yeah.'

He hummed a note. 'Well, I'd like to see him dead, too, but that don' mean you did wrong. Somebody wanna say different, they can come to me.

'Dat horse's ass Noblier, he don' deserve you for a deputy, *chère*. You can always come work for your uncle Sos, you know. I'll give you a quarter you come seine the shiners out my bait tanks.'

1033

Annie found a chuckle for his teasing, then turned and hugged him fiercely. 'I love you.'

Sos patted her back and kissed the top of her head. '*Je t'aime, cherie.* You get some sleep tonight. Leave the rascals to me. I got fresh buckshot in the gun.'

'Oh, that's a comfort,' Annie muttered dryly.

She dragged herself up the stairs to the apartment. A small package waited for her on the landing, wrapped in paper sprigged with tiny violets and tied with a lavender bow. Automatically suspicious, she picked it up with care, listened to it, shook it a little, then carried it inside.

The light on the answering machine was blinking impatiently. She hit the message button and listened as she unwrapped the box.

'It's me,' A.J. said. 'Where you been? I thought maybe we could do that movie tonight, but . . . uh . . . I guess not, huh? Are you still pissed at me? Call me, will you?'

The confusion in his voice dragged at Annie's heart.

The machine beeped and a reporter came on asking for a few minutes of her time. He might as well have asked her to hit herself on the head with a hammer.

'This is Lindsay Faulkner.'

Annie's hands stilled on the white gift box.

'I've been thinking about some of the questions you asked the other day. I'm sorry if I've seemed uncooperative. That wasn't my intent. This has just dragged on, and I – Please call me when you get a chance.'

Annie looked at the cat clock on the kitchen wall. 10:27. Not too late. Abandoning the package on the table, she paged through the phone book, then dialed the number. The telephone on the other end rang four times before it picked up.

'Hello, Ms Faulkner, this is –'

'This is Lindsay Faulkner. I can't take your call right now, but if you'll leave your name, number, and a brief message at the tone, I'll get back to you as soon as I can.'

Annie blew out a breath in frustration, waited for the tone, and left her name and number. The expectation that had shot upward at the sound of Lindsay Faulkner's voice dropped like a rock, and she was left with nothing but questions that couldn't be answered.

She had felt all along that the woman was holding back on her. But when she'd read over the statements from the file, they seemed very straightforward. Stokes had not included any notes regarding concerns about Faulkner's candor or anything else. He, rather than Fourcade, had dealt with her during the murder investigation because he had already established a relationship with her during the stalking investigation. Asking him for his opinion was out of the question.

Resigning herself to waiting for Lindsay's revelations, she hit the message button on the answering machine again.

The next one began to play – a snickering, sniveling stream of profanity and lewd suggestions. Annie raised her eyes heavenward and made a mental note never to appear in front of a television camera again.

She turned her attention to the box, lifting the lid carefully, braced for the possibility of unpleasant surprise. Another dead muskrat, perhaps. Another live snake. But nothing sprang out at her. No aroma of death assaulted her senses. Nestled in layers of tissue was a sheer silk scarf, ivory printed with tiny blue flowers.

Frowning, she took it out and ran it through her hands, the cool, sensuous feel of it having the opposite of its desired effect. The card read: 'Something lovely for a lovely person. With thanks and gratitude – again. Marcus.'

Among the gifts he had given Pam Bichon was a silk scarf.

It appeared he had taken the bait Annie had never intended to dangle.

She set the scarf aside and picked up the phone to call Fourcade.

27

Our topic tonight: double standards in the justice system. You're tuned to KJUN, home of the giant jackpot giveaway. This is your *Devil's Advocate*, Owen Onofrio. We've learned today that Hunter Davidson of rural Partout Parish, the father of murder victim Pamela Bichon, was released from jail this weekend after an unprecedented private bond hearing. Sources in the DA's office say a deal was struck late today that will likely sentence Davidson to little more than community service for the attempted assault of murder suspect Marcus Renard.

'What do you think out there? Everyone with a TV saw it on the news last week: Mr. Davidson charging down the courthouse steps with a gun in his hand as the man accused of killing his daughter walked away on a technicality. Curtis from St Martinville, speak your mind.'

'Is it a double standard? I mean, they let Renard go. Why shouldn't they let Davidson go too?'

'But the court has yet to prove Renard guilty of a crime. Davidson committed his crime in front of a crowd of witnesses. Doesn't Davidson's obvious intent to kill deserve worse than a slap on the wrist and community service? Instead, we've been touting this man as a hero and turning him into a celebrity. He's reportedly had offers from Maury Povich, Larry King, and Sally Jessy to appear on their shows.'

Lindsay listened with disgust as she drove toward Bayou Breaux. She detested Owen Onofrio. The man's sole purpose in life seemed to be irritating people to the point of outburst. She disliked his devil's advocate game. She had no time for people without solid convictions, and yet she listened to the program more often than not on her drive home from the Association of Women Realtors meetings in Lafayette. The elevation in her blood pressure kept her from falling asleep at the wheel.

Without Pam for company, she had come to dread the monthly trip. They had always used the drive back for girl talk — True Confessions Time, Pam had called it — the kind of talks best held in the dimly lit interior of a car on a dark stretch of road. Soul-searching, souls-bared kinds of talks about life, love, motherhood, sisterhood.

She glanced at the empty passenger seat and felt a bottomless ache in her soul. She couldn't look at the night out here where houses were scarce and the only laws were nature's without thinking of Pam, alone with her killer where no one could see, no one could hear her cries for help.

Needing anger to fight off the despair, she hit the speed dial button on the car phone. As much as she hated Owen Onofrio, he had become a part of her self-therapy.

'You're on KJUN. All talk all the time.'

'This is Lindsay from Bayou Breaux.'

'Hey, Lindsay, it's Willy,' the assistant said, his voice a little too oily and intimate for her liking. 'If you don't win that jackpot soon, it won't be for lack of trying.'

'I'll donate it to Pam's daughter. Consider it payment for KJUN throwing her family into the public arena like the Christians to the lions.'

'Hey, you're on the line, aren't you?'

'Let me talk to Owen.'

'You're up next, Lindsay. That's just because I love the sound of your voice.'

Lindsay heaved a sigh into the receiver.

Onofrio's voice came on the line. 'Lindsay in Bayou Breaux, what's your opinion tonight?'

'I'd like to point out that there's a tremendous difference between a psychopath committing a brutal, sexual murder to satisfy some depraved personal appetite and a law-abiding, productive member of the human race being driven by the inadequacies of our justice system to commit a desperate act.'

'So you're condoning vigilante justice?'

'Of course not. I'm simply saying the crimes involved here are not interchangeable. It would be ridiculous, to say nothing of cruel, to send Hunter Davidson to jail. He did not, in fact, kill Marcus Renard. And hasn't he suffered enough? He's already been sentenced to the memory of his daughter's hideous death.'

'A thought-provoking point. Thank you, Lindsay.'

After confirming her address for the jackpot, Lindsay hung up and changed the station. She'd had her say, made her daily defense for Pam. She wondered when it would stop – the pain, the anger, the need to fight back.

The pain wasn't as intense as it had been at first. She couldn't maintain that level of fury and keep her own sanity. So it had found a more manageable level. She wondered how long she could get by calling it healthy, wondered how long she would be able to hold on to it. Her fear was that without the pain, without the outrage, there would be only emptiness. The prospect terrified her.

Maybe she should sell the business, move to New Orleans. Start fresh. Meet new people, renew old acquaintances from college. God knew Bayou Breaux offered little in the way of culture or a glitzy social life. What kept her there besides memories and spite?

Memories and friends. A simple way of life. Social obligations that meant hands-on involvement with the community. She loved it here. And then there was Josie, her goddaughter. She couldn't leave Josie.

The dashboard clock glowed 12:24 as she neared the turnoff to her home. She shouldn't have stayed so late after the meeting. She'd been in no mood for cheery chitchat and social niceties, and yet she had lingered, putting off the long, lonely drive home. Now it was too late to call Detective Broussard back. There was no real hurry. She could do it tomorrow. What she had was nothing, really. Just a thought, and one she didn't want to give credence to. Still, she felt guilty keeping it to herself.

She hit the garage door opener and parked the BMW beside the new bike she'd bought to force herself into a hobby. She dropped her briefcase on the dining room table and went straight to her bedroom, ignoring the blinking light on the answering machine. It was too late. She was too tired. Even the routine of washing her face and moisturizing her skin seemed too much effort, but she forced herself because, as her mother reminded her at regular intervals, she wasn't getting any younger. The strain of the past few months was showing beneath her eyes and in the lines around her mouth.

Exhausted, she climbed into bed, turned out the lights, and lay there, eyes open, a dull throb pounding in her temples. A weight hit the mattress beside her, curled into the crook behind her knees, and began purring. Taffy, the cat she had adopted from the Davidsons the year she and Pam had set up the business. The cat was asleep instantly, snoring softly.

Lindsay knew from too many nights of experience she wouldn't be so lucky. The headache wouldn't just go away, she wouldn't just go to sleep. She had tried meditation, relaxation tapes, reading a dull book. The only thing that worked was the sleeping pill her doctor had prescribed after Pam's murder. She was on her third refill, and he had made it clear there would be no more. She hated to think what she would do then.

The cat complained loudly as she threw the covers back.

'Yeah, well, be glad I never taught you how to fetch,' Lindsay mumbled.

She kept all her medications in a kitchen cupboard because she had read in *Cosmo* that the humidity in the bathroom was bad for the quality of pills and capsules. She didn't bother turning lights on as she went down the short hall to the kitchen. She had left the light in the range hood on, and it was plenty bright enough to see by. Bright enough, in fact, so that, as she turned the corner into the kitchen/dining area, she clearly saw the man coming in through the patio door.

He looked straight at her, and she saw the feathered mask. Time held fast for an instant as they recognized one another as predator and prey. Then the hold snapped, and the world was suddenly a blur of sound and motion.

Lindsay grabbed the first thing she could put her hands on and hurled it at him. He batted the pewter candlestick to the side and charged her, toppling a chair from its place at the table. She turned to run. If she could make it to the front door and onto the lawn – What? Who would look out and see her? It was after one in the morning. Her neighbors were tucked in bed, their houses were tucked back on the exclusive little properties she had sold them. If she screamed, would they even hear her?

A fleeting thought of Pam went through her mind like a lance, and she did scream for help.

He hit her from behind, knocking her to the floor. The Berber hall runner seared the skin of her knees and knuckles as she scrambled, trying to stand, trying to grab hold of something, anything to use as a weapon. Her fingers closed on the edge of the hall table that held the telephone and an array of framed family photos. Her attacker came down on her as she tried to pull herself up, and the table rocked sideways, dumping its contents with a crash.

Lindsay grabbed hold of the body of the telephone and swung back awkwardly at her assailant. He caught hold of her wrist and twisted her arm savagely. She surged up beneath him, her body bucking, legs kicking, free hand clawing at him, raking at the mask.

The word *No!* roared from her throat again and again as she fought. The sound of it wasn't even language to her own ears, but a cry of survival, of outrage.

He leaned back, dodging her hands, and grunted hard as her knee made contact with his groin. 'Fucking bitch!'

Lindsay shoved herself backward on the floor as his weight momentarily lifted. The door was only a few feet away. She twisted over onto her knees again and struggled to push to her feet. If she could get to the door –

Her arm stretched out toward the knob as something hit her as hard as a brick between the shoulder blades. She landed on her face, her chin bouncing on the hardwood. The next blow struck the back of her head with savage force. With the third she lost consciousness. Her last vague thought as she slipped toward the void was if she would see Pam on the other side.

28

The scarf wound around her wrists, the kiss of silk like cool breath against her fevered skin. It tightened and held her. It pulled her arms above her head. She was naked. Exposed, vulnerable. She couldn't escape, she couldn't fight.

Fourcade lowered his head to her breast, dragged his mouth slowly down across her belly. She groaned and twisted her body, feeling swept away on the racing tide of her pulse. She couldn't escape. It made no sense to fight.

His tongue touched her femininity, shooting heat through her veins. Then the head lifted, and Marcus Renard smiled at her.

Choking, Annie jerked awake. The sheets were tangled around her. The T-shirt she had slept in was soaked through with sweat. She knocked the alarm off the nightstand, silencing it, and sat up, fighting the urge to throw up. Dragging herself out of bed, she stumbled into the bathroom and splashed cold water in her face, trying to wash the images out of her memory – all of them.

Her workout lived up to its name. She felt every move in every muscle fiber. Live right, exercise, die anyway. She directed a few scathing thoughts at the Higher Power as she struggled for sit-up number forty. What was the point in following the rules, personally or professionally, if all that would bring her was pain and suffering? Then she thought of Fourcade, who broke the rules with impunity and would be lucky if he could crawl out of bed today. Maybe God was an equal-opportunity bully after all.

The time she'd spent tending Nick's wounds had become a surreal memory with the passing of the night. Maybe she hadn't really touched his naked chest. Maybe she hadn't let him play tonsil hockey. Maybe she hadn't dreamed about him. She tried to put it out of her head as she grabbed hold of the chin-up bar and dragged her body upward, straining every inch.

She thought instead of the story Fourcade had told her about New Orleans and Duval Marcotte. It didn't matter, she decided. Donnie Bichon had not contacted Marcotte before Pam's death, therefore Marcotte was not a motive for Donnie to have killed her. Unless *Marcotte* had contacted *him*. Unless their conversations had taken place over pay phones. Which made Donnie smarter than he let on. Who knew what his potential might be? She couldn't see him doing what had been done to Pam, but Fourcade's beating at the hands of DiMonti's men raised the unpleasant possibility of hired help.

She headed for the door, stopping as the scarf on the kitchen table caught the corner of her eye. What was she doing mapping out conspiracy scenarios when she had a suspected murderer leaving her tokens of his affection? Maybe she would have been better off with Fourcade's tunnel vision. Maybe whatever Lindsay Faulkner had to offer her would help put her on track.

She hit the trail at a slow jog. The ground fog was waist high, like something from an old horror movie. The sun was a huge fuchsia ball rising up through it in the east. Islands of trees seemed to float on it in the distance. Annie ran through it down the levee road. Fifty yards ahead a squadron of five blue herons leapt from the reeds and skimmed the top of the fog bank to a willow island, their spindly legs trailing behind them like fine streamers.

She ran two miles that seemed like ten, showered and dressed, then joined Fanchon and Sos for breakfast in the café.

'Someone left a package for me yesterday,' Annie said, stirring milk into her coffee. 'Did either of you happen to see him?'

'A secret lover?' Sos bobbed his eyebrows, mischief lighting his face. 'Dat's gotta be Andre, no? Sends you flowers, brings you presents. Dat boy's got it bad for you, *'tite chatte*. You listen to your Uncle Sos.'

Annie gave him a look. 'It wasn't A.J. I know who brought it. I was just wondering if either of you saw him.'

Sos scowled and muttered something under his breath.

Fanchon waved off the possibility. '*Mais non, chère*. We was so busy here, me, I thought I was chasin' myself. Two busloads of chil'run from Lafayette for the boat tours. Dat's like turnin' a hundred li'l raccoons loose in the store. Why for you wanna know?'

'No reason. It's not important.' Annie grabbed her coffee mug and pushed back from the table. She kissed them each on the cheek. 'I gotta go.'

'So who was he?' Sos called, his curiosity winning out over his pique.

Annie snatched a Snickers from the box as she passed down the candy aisle and waved goodbye with it. 'No one special.'

Just a likely stalker and murderer.

She didn't like the idea of Renard showing up here, trespassing on her private life, coming into contact with Sos and Fanchon. It seemed impossible Renard could have become fixated on her so quickly. She'd given him no encouragement, had in fact tried to *dis*courage him. Just as Pam had . . . and Pam Bichon had never saved his life.

She swung west at the edge of town, hoping to catch Lindsay Faulkner before she left for the office. Annie couldn't help but think her patience and persistence had paid off. She had appealed to Faulkner woman to woman and now she was going to get something Faulkner hadn't given the male detectives. She allowed herself a moment's smugness as she turned down Cheval Court.

Faulkner's garage door was closed. The front drapes were drawn. Annie walked up to the house and punched the doorbell as she leaned close to peer in the sidelight.

Lindsay Faulkner lay on the entry floor, her nightgown bunched up beneath her chin, her right arm reaching toward the portable handset of a phone that lay on the floor with an assortment of debris. Blood caked her golden hair at the roots. Her face was covered with it. Her ginger cat lay curled beside her, sleeping.

Swearing, Annie ran back to the Jeep and grabbed the radio mike.

'Partout Parish 911. Partout Parish 911. Requesting officers and an ambulance at 17 Cheval Court. Please hurry. And notify the detectives. This is a probable 261. Over.'

She confirmed the information as requested, giving her name and rank. Then, grabbing her gun out of her duffel in case the assailant was still on the premises, she ran back to the house to see if Lindsay Faulkner was alive.

The front door was locked, but the assailant had obligingly left the patio door standing wide open. Annie covered Lindsay's body with a blanket hastily dragged from the guest bedroom and knelt beside her, monitoring her weak pulse.

'Hang in there, Lindsay. The ambulance is on its way,' she said loudly. 'We'll have you to the hospital in no time. You've gotta hang tough. We'll need you to tell us who did this to you so we can catch the guy and make him pay. You've gotta hang on so you can help us with that.'

There was no response. Not a movement of eyelids or lips. Faulkner seemed to be clinging to the finest thread of life. The only good sign was that she had not gone into a fetal posture indicative of severe brain damage, but that didn't mean she couldn't die.

Annie stared at the face some animal had battered into unrecognizability. If this was the work of their serial rapist, why had he singled out Lindsay Faulkner? For the obvious reasons? That she was single, attractive, lived alone? She was also connected to a murder investigation. Just yesterday she'd found something relevant to say in regard to that murder. Had someone shut her up before she could tell it? The possibilities made Annie's nerves twitch.

The wail of approaching sirens penetrated the silence of the house. The EMTs stormed the place first, followed closely by Sticks Mullen. He scowled at Annie. She scowled at him.

'What the hell are you doing here, Broussard?'

'I could ask you the same thing,' Annie said, glancing at her watch. 'You're usually stuffing your face with doughnuts about this time. Lucky me, you picked today to be diligent instead of delinquent.'

She stepped back into the living room, out of the way of the EMTs, one eye on the paramedics as they worked.

'It looks to me like the attacker cracked her head with the base unit of the phone.' She pointed to where it lay bloody on the floor among scattered broken picture frames. 'She put up a fight.'

'For all the good it did her,' Mullen muttered.

'Hey, some jerk comes after me, I go down swinging,' Annie said. 'I'll make the guy wish he'd never set eyes on me.'

'There's plenty of that going around anyway.'

'Don't start with me,' Annie snapped.

She dared him with a glare, then started for the dining area. 'He came in here through the patio door. She must have heard him, came out of her bedroom, and confronted him.'

'Should have stayed put and called 911.'

'Wouldn't have done her any good. The phone's dead. You'll find the line cut, I imagine. Just like the others.'

The EMTs hefted up their stretcher and rolled it out the front door with Lindsay Faulkner motionless beneath the blanket. As they left, Stokes walked in, a gray fedora sitting back on the crown of his head, a slip of toilet paper glued to his left cheek with a dot of blood. His light eyes were shot through with red.

'Man, I hate these early calls,' he grumbled.

'Yeah, how inconsiderate of people to be attacked during your off-hours,' Annie said. 'At least she waited until morning to be found raped, beaten, and unconscious.'

Stokes scowled at her. 'What're you doing here, Broussard? Somebody call for McGruff?'

'I found her.'

He took a moment to digest that, his gaze sharpening. 'And I say again, what are you doing here? How'd you know her? You two playing "Bump the Doughnut" or something?'

Mullen snickered. Annie rolled her eyes.

'You know, Chaz, I hate to break it to you, but just because a woman won't have sex with you doesn't mean she's a lesbian. It just means she has standards.'

'Stop. You're spoiling my fantasies.' He nodded to Mullen. 'Go see if the phone line's cut. And see if there's any good footprints in the yard. Ground's soft. Maybe we can get a cast.'

Mullen went out the front. Stokes hiked up his baggy brown trousers and squatted down amid the junk that had toppled from the hall table.

'You gonna answer my question, Broussard?' he asked as he pulled on a pair of rubber gloves and picked up the bloody phone unit.

'She's my real estate agent,' Annie said automatically. 'I'm thinking of buying a house.'

'Is that right?' he said flatly. 'So why come all the way out here to see her when her office is – what? – all of four blocks from the department?'

1043

'She wanted to show me something out this way.'

'This neighborhood's a little out of your price range, isn't it, Deputy?'

'A girl can dream.'

'Uh-huh. And when did y'all set this up?'

'Lindsay called me last night and left a message on my machine.' Her eyes went to Faulkner's answering machine. Her own voice would be on the tape. Thank God she'd left nothing more than her name and number.

'I tried to call her back about ten-thirty, but the machine answered. Why all the questions?' she asked, turning it back around on him. 'You think I raped her and beat her head in?'

'Just doing my job, McGruff.' He narrowed his eyes as if he were visualizing Lindsay Faulkner's body on the floor. He rubbed his goatee and hummed a note. The puddle of blood that had leaked from her skull had dried dark on the honey-tone oak. Spatters and smears had soaked into the off-white Berber runner. 'He did her right here, huh?'

'Looked that way. Her nightgown was pulled up around her shoulders. There was a lot of bruising on her body.'

'So is this the work of our friendly neighborhood serial rapist?' Stokes said more to himself than to Annie. 'He did the other two in bed, tied them up.'

'It looks to me like she heard him coming,' Annie said. 'He didn't get the chance to surprise her in bed. And he didn't have to tie her up because he knocked her out with the phone.'

She squatted down beside the rug, her gaze zooming in on a patch of dark fibers embedded in the carpet runner where Faulkner's body had lain. She scratched at the spot gingerly with a fingernail and plucked at the loose end that came up, bringing it up close before her eyes.

'Looks to me like a piece of black feather,' she said, looking at Stokes as she held it out toward him. 'That answer your question for you?'

Don't you bend them papers shoving them in that way,' the records clerk snapped, his voice at a pitch that rivaled screeching chalk on a blackboard.

Annie twitched. 'Sorry, Myron.'

'That's *Mr* Myron. You on the other side of my counter, you call me Myron. You on *my* side of my counter, you call me *Mr* Myron. You are in *my* domain. You are *my* assistant.'

Myron jammed his hands at his belt and nodded sharply. A slight, prim black man, he wore a clip-on polyester tie every day and had his gray hair trimmed like a shrub every other Friday. He had worked records and evidence for twenty years and saw the presence of a uniform behind his counter as a direct threat to his kingdom.

'Don't let it go to your head,' Annie muttered. To Myron she gave her earnest face and said, 'I'll do my best.'

Myron gave her the skunk eye and went back to his desk.

Annie let his presence fade from mind as she concentrated on the facts of Lindsay Faulkner's attack. She was tempted to think this attacker was a copycat of their rapist, who was a copycat of sorts of Pam Bichon's killer, someone who had taken advantage of the first two rapes to silence Faulkner for his own reasons. Perhaps it had been his intent to murder her. He may well have believed she was dead when he left her.

But if that was the case, then who was this copycat? Renard would seem to be free from suspicion. Debilitated by the pounding Fourcade had given him, he couldn't have had the strength or the mobility to attack a strong, healthy woman like Lindsay. If not Renard, then who? Donnie? It was no secret he disliked Lindsay. If she was standing in the way of a deal for the real estate company . . .

Could he kill her? Make it look like rape? If it was Donnie, then did that mean he was involved in Pam's murder? If he had murdered Pam, killing Lindsay would have been easy by comparison.

The fragment of black feather was the sticking point for the copycat theory. That feather had been no plant left to implicate someone else. It appeared to be just the opposite, in fact. Something left behind by accident, hidden by his victim's unconscious body. Their boy had certainly left nothing else behind to incriminate himself.

Then again, the feather may not have come from a mask. It could have been part of a cat toy. It could have been tracked in by a visitor. They wouldn't know whether or not they had a match to the feather in the Nolan case until they heard back from the lab in New Iberia.

'Hey, Myron, what'd you do to deserve this, man?' Stokes asked, snickering as he set the rape kit on the counter. 'Who sicced the crime dog after you?'

Annie gladly abandoned her filing and went to the counter. 'Yeah, Chaz, we all got that joke the first ten times you made it. Is this Faulkner's? It took you long enough.'

'Hey, it takes how long it takes, you know what I'm sayin'. The doctors had to get her stabilized. Don't matter nohow. We got nothing from it. There was nothing under her nails. There's not gonna be anything on the swabs, and pubic hair all looks alike to me. This joker's good.'

'He sure seems to know what we'll look for,' Annie said. 'I'll bet he's got a record. Have you checked with the state for known offenders? Run the MO past NCIC?'

Stokes switched his attitude up a notch. 'I don't need you to tell me how to run an investigation, Broussard.'

'I believe my remark was in the form of a question, Detective,' she said with stinging sweetness. 'I know how swamped you are dealing with these rapes and the Bichon homicide, and what all. I might have offered to make those calls for you.'

Myron moved his head like an outraged banty rooster. 'That ain't your job!'

Annie shrugged. 'Just trying to be helpful.'

'Just trying to stick your nose in where it don't belong,' Stokes muttered. 'I told you before, Broussard, I don't need your kind of help. You stay the hell away from my cases.'

He turned to Myron. 'I need to get this stuff logged in and back out again. I'm taking it down to New Iberia myself, *personally*, so they can rush it through the lab and tell me I ain't got squat, just like I ain't got squat on those two other rapes.'

'Who's working them besides you?' Annie asked.

He glanced at her from under the brim of his fedora. 'I don't need this shit from you. These are my cases. Quinlan's helping with the background checks on the other two women – who they worked with and like that. Is that acceptable to you, *Deputy*?'

Annie raised her hands in surrender.

'I mean, I know you don't think *I'm* acceptable,' he went on with an edge in his voice. 'But hey, who's in plain clothes here and who's going around town in a goddamn dog suit?'

Myron looked up from the paperwork to glare at her, clearly unhappy with her for bringing the stigma of the dog suit into his realm.

Coming down the hall, Mullen let out a hound-dog howl. Annie tried not to grind her teeth.

'I always said you should be wearing a flea collar, Mullen,' she said, moving down the counter away from Stokes and Myron.

'You're moving down in the world, Broussard,' he said with glee as he set a plastic pee-cup on the counter, full to the lid with some drunk's donation to forensic science. 'Take a bite outta crime lately? You can wash it down with this.'

Annie yawned as she pulled out an evidence card and began to fill it out. 'Wake me up when you have something original to say. Does this urine belong to someone, or did you bring me this to impress me with your aim?'

Thwarted again, he momentarily stuck to facts. 'Ross Leighton. Another five-martini lunch at the Wisteria Club. But you got him beat, don't you, Broussard? Nipping Wild Turkey on the way to work.'

The pen stilled on the form. Annie raised her head. 'That's a lie and you know it.'

Mullen shrugged. 'I know what I saw in that Jeep Saturday morning.'

'You know what you *put* in my Jeep Saturday morning.'

'I know the sheriff pulled you off patrol and I'm still driving,' he said smugly, flashing his ugly yellow teeth. He put his hands on the counter and leaned in, the gleam in his eye as mean as a weasel's. 'Just what kind of witness are you gonna make against Fourcade?' he whispered. 'I hear you were drinking that night too.'

Annie held back her retort. She'd had a drink before dinner at Isabeau's that night. A glass of wine with the meal. The bartender at Laveau's could testify she had been in the bar. Maybe he wouldn't remember whether he'd served her or not. Maybe someone would make it worth his while to lose his memory. She had by no means been intoxicated that night, but

Fourcade's lawyer would have a field day insinuating that she may have been. What that would do for his case would be dubious; what it would do for her reputation would be obvious.

She gave a humorless half-laugh. 'I gotta say, Mullen, I wouldn't have given you credit for being that smart,' she murmured. 'I oughta shake your hand.'

As she reached out, she backhanded the specimen cup, knocked the lid askew, and sent Ross Leighton's urine spewing down the front of Mullen's pants.

Mullen jumped back like a scalded dog. 'You fuckin' bitch!'

'Oh, gee, look,' Annie said loudly, snatching the cup off the counter. 'Mullen wet his pants!'

Four people down the hall turned to stare. One of the secretaries from the business office stuck her head out the door. Mullen looked at them with horror. 'She did it!' he said.

'Well, that'd be a hell of a trick,' Annie said. 'I'd need a hose attachment. They know what they're looking at, Mullen.'

Fury contracted the muscles of his face. His thin lips tightened against his mouth, making his teeth look as big as a horse's. 'You'll pay for this, Broussard.'

'Yeah? What're you gonna do? Spill another bucket of pig guts down my steps?'

'What? I don't know what you're talking about. You done pickled your brain, Broussard.'

Hooker bulled his way through the gawkers. 'Mullen, what the fuck are you doing? You pissed yourself?'

'No!'

'Jesus Christ, clean up the mess and go change.'

'Don't forget the Depends!' someone called from down the hall.

'Broussard made the mess,' Mullen groused, bristling at the laughter. 'She ought to clean it up.'

Annie shook her head. 'That's not my job. The mess is on your side of the counter, Mr Patrol Deputy. I'm back here on my side of the counter, Myron's lowly assistant.'

The clerk looked up from his paperwork with the dignity of a king. '*Mr* Myron.'

It became quickly apparent to Annie that there were few advantages to working in records and evidence. Her one perk of the day came in the form of a fax from the regional lab in New Iberia: the preliminary results on the tests of the entrails that had been draped down her steps Sunday night. No detective had been assigned to the case, which meant the fax came into the machine in records and evidence to be passed on to the case deputy. By being right there when the message rolled out of the machine, Annie bypassed any contact with Pitre.

She held her breath as she read the report, as if the words had the

1047

power to bring back the smell. The scene flashed through her mind: the blood dripping, the gory garland of intestines, the fear for Fanchon and Sos.

Preliminary findings reported the internal organs to be from a hog. The news brought only a small measure of relief. The lab couldn't tell her where the stuff had come from. Hogs got butchered every day in South Louisiana. Butcher shops sold every part of them to people who made their own sausage. No one kept records of such things. Nor could the lab tell her who had dumped the viscera down her steps. If it hadn't been Mullen, then who? Why? Did it have anything to do with her investigation of Pam's murder?

Did Pam's murder have anything to do with Lindsay Faulkner's attack? The questions led one into another, into another, with no end in sight.

By late afternoon Lindsay Faulkner's status was listed as critical but stable. Suffering from a skull fracture, fractures to a number of facial bones, multiple contusions, and shock, she had not regained consciousness. The doctors were arguing over whether or not she should be transferred from Our Lady of Mercy to Our Lady of Lourdes in Lafayette. Until they could decide which apparition of the Virgin would prove more miraculous, Faulkner remained in Our Lady of Mercy's ICU.

News of the attack had hit the civilian airwaves. The sheriff scheduled a press conference for five. Scuttlebutt around the department was that a task force would be set up to appease the panicking public. With few leads to go on, there would be little for them to concentrate on, but all the ground would be covered again and again until they churned it to dust. If Stokes, who would head the task force, hadn't already checked with the state for recent releases of sex offenders or with the National Crime Information Center to cross-reference MOs of known sex offenders, that would happen now. Acquaintances of the victims would all be questioned again, with the aim of finding a clue, a connection between the women who had been raped.

As Annie sat at her temporary desk in the records room, she felt a pang of envy toward the people who would be working on the task force. It was the kind of job she had set her sights on, but unless she reversed her fortunes in the department, hell would freeze over before Noblier promoted her to detective.

Closing the Bichon homicide would go a long way toward improving her status. But if anyone found out she was conducting her own investigation – and with whom she was conducting that investigation – her career would be toast.

She thought about that as Myron reluctantly left his post for his afternoon constitutional in the men's room. What was she supposed to do if she came up with evidence? Who was she supposed to tell about Renard's apparent fixation on her? If Lindsay Faulkner had given her useful information, where would she have gone with it? Stokes didn't want her near his case, and if she gave him anything useful, he would doubtless claim the credit for himself. If she went to A.J., she would be jumping the food chain in a way that wouldn't win her points with anyone outside the DA's office. Should she go to the sheriff with any findings and risk his wrath for overstepping her boundaries? Or would Fourcade take the opportunity to put his own career back on track and leave her in the dust?

Maybe that was what that kiss had been all about. The closer he pulled her to him, the easier it would be to shove her behind him when he had what he needed.

She doodled on her notepad as her brain ran the slalom of possibilities. She had taken advantage of Myron's absence to pull some of the Bichon homicide file: Renard's initial statement, wherein he related the improbable story of his alibi, for which he had no corroborating witnesses. He had sent Fourcade on a wild-goose chase with his phantom Good Samaritan motorist, and he was trying to send her on the same pointless quest. A test of her loyalty, Annie supposed. Renard believed she was some kind of savior sent to deliver his life from the jaws of hell – or Angola penitentiary, not that there was a big difference between the two.

Mr Renard states motorist was driving a dark-colored pickup of undetermined make. Louisiana plates possibly bearing the letters FJ.

FJ. Annie traced the letters on her scratch pad over and over. Fourcade had run this piddling information through the DMV, had checked the resulting list and come up with nothing. *FJ.* She worked the *J* into a fish hook and drew a bug-eyed fish below it with the word *witness* incorporated into the scales. Renard didn't believe Fourcade had done anything with the information, and turned a blind eye to the fact that his own attorney hadn't come up with an alibi witness for him either. What did he think she would do that no one else had done for him?

She exaggerated the serifs on the F and added one at the bottom. E. *E.* She sat up a little straighter. Renard had said that it was night and the truck had been muddy.

A phone call to the DMV was simple enough. It was a morsel she could give Renard to buy another measure of his trust. She could put the request in Fourcade's name, have the list faxed directly to the machine in records, and no one would be the wiser.

She thought about the scarf lying on her table at home and the man in the shadows Sunday night, and reminded herself who she was playing games with. An accused and probable murderer. Donnie Bichon may have had motive, and the three rapes may have borne a chilling resemblance to Pam's death; the waters surrounding the case had become muddied, but Renard's fixation on Pam Bichon was a fact.

Marcus Renard had been fixated on Pam, Pam had rejected him, and Pam was dead.

She placed the call to the DMV, hanging up just seconds before Myron returned from his porcelain pilgrimage with the latest issue of *U.S. News & World Report*.

By the end of the shift Annie had half a dozen paper cuts and a headache from eyestrain. She also had two flat tires on the Jeep. The valve stems had been cut clean off. No one had seen anything. Translation: No one had seen Mullen exact his revenge. She called Meyette's Garage and was told it would be an hour before anyone could get away to help.

The afternoon was warm and muggy with the breath of a storm building out over the Gulf. Annie walked along the footpath on the bank of the bayou. The mob would be gathering for Noblier's press conference, she knew, but she wanted no part of that. She had to think the sheriff would omit her name from the story of the Faulkner attack. He wouldn't want the press taking any more interest in her than they already had. He would do what he thought was best for his department and his people, and if that meant bending or omitting the truth, then to hell with the truth.

And who am I to criticize? Annie thought as she stopped across the street from Bayou Realty. The end justified the means – as long as the end was for the good of human-kind, or yourself, or someone you loved, or some higher principle.

She had expected to see a CLOSED sign in the window of the realty office, but she could see the receptionist at her desk. The woman looked up expectantly as Annie walked in and the bell jingled, announcing her.

'It's not bad news, is it?' the woman asked, her cheeks paling. 'The hospital would have called. I just spoke with – Oh, mercy.'

The last words squeezed out of her like the final breath of air leaving a balloon. She looked fiftysomething with a matron's helmet of sprayed-hard gray-blond hair. Well dressed, nails done, real gold jewelry. The placard on her desk said GRACE IRVINE.

'No,' Annie said, realizing the uniform had spooked her. 'I don't have any news. The last I heard, there hadn't been any change.'

'No,' Grace said with a measure of relief. 'No change. That was what they just told me. Oh, my.' She patted her chest. 'You frightened me.'

'I'm sorry,' Annie said as she helped herself to the chair beside the desk. 'I was surprised to see the office open.'

'Well, I didn't find out what had happened until nearly noon. Of course, I was concerned when Lindsay didn't show up at her usual time, but I assumed she had made an impromptu meeting with a client. We do that, don't we? Rationalize. Even after Pam –'

She broke off and pressed a hand to her mouth as tears washed over her eyes. 'I can't believe this is happening,' she whispered. 'I tried calling her on her cellular phone. I tried the house. Finally I went out there, and there were deputies and that yellow tape across the door.'

She shook her head, at a loss for words. For an ordinary person, stumbling onto a crime scene had to be like stepping into an alternate reality.

'I kept the office open because I didn't know what else to do. I couldn't bear the thought of sitting at home, waiting, or sitting in that horrible waiting room at the hospital. The phone was ringing and ringing. There were appointments to cancel, and I had to call Lindsay's family. . . . I just felt I should stay.'

'You've known Lindsay a long time?'

'I knew Pam her whole life. Her mother is my second cousin once removed on the Chandler side. I've known Lindsay since the girls were in college. Dear, both of them, absolutely dear girls. They all but took me in after my husband passed away last year. They said I needed something to do with my time besides grieve, and they were right.' She made a motion to the books spread open across her desk. 'I'm studying to get my license. I've been thinking about trying to buy Pam's share of the business from Donnie.'

She turned her face away and took a moment to compose herself, dabbing at the corners of her eyes with a linen hankie.

'I'm sorry, Deputy,' she apologized. 'I'm rambling on. What can I do for you? Are you working on the case?'

'In a manner of speaking,' Annie said. 'I'm the one who found Lindsay this morning. She had left a message on my machine last night saying that she had something to tell me in relation to Pam's case. I was wondering if she might have told you what it was.'

'Oh. Oh, no, I'm afraid not. It was hectic here yesterday. Lindsay had several appointments in the morning. Then Donnie showed up unannounced, and they had a bit of a row over the business dealings and all. They never did get along, you know. Then the new listings arrived. I had an obligation in the afternoon at my grandson's school. He's in second grade at Sacred Heart. It was law enforcement day, oddly enough. McGruff the Crime Dog came with an officer. The grandparents were invited to attend.'

'I hear that's very popular,' Annie said flatly.

'I found it rather strange, to be perfectly frank. Anyway, Lindsay and I never had a chance to talk. I know she had something on her mind, but I assumed she told the detective. You may want to ask him.'

'The –' The words caught in Annie's throat. 'Who? Which detective?'

'Detective Stokes,' Grace Irvine said. 'She saw him over the lunch hour.'

29

Mouton's was the kind of place few men entered without a gun or a knife. Squatting on stilts on the bank of Bayou Noir south of Luck, it was the hangout of poachers and thieves and others living on the ragged hem of society. People looking for trouble looked at Mouton's, where just about anything could be had for the right price and no one asked any questions.

It was the latter truth that appealed to Nick on a Tuesday afternoon. He was in no mood for the Voodoo Lounge, wanted no one patting his back or expressing their useless sympathy for his situation. He wanted whiskey, settled for a beer, and waited for Stokes to show.

He had dragged himself out of bed at noon and forced himself through the Tai Chi forms, meditating on the movement of each aching muscle, trying to force the pain out with the power of his mind. The process had been excruciating and exhausting, but his sense of being was clearer for it. His mind was sharp, his nerves coiled tight as springs, as he nursed his beer, his back to a corner.

A couple of bikers were playing pool across the room with a barfly hooker hovering around them in a short skirt and push-up bra. Nearer, a pair of swamp rats sat at a table, trading stories and drinking Jax. John Lee Hooker was moaning on the juke, black delta blues in a redneck bar. There was an illegal card game going on in the back room, and horse racing on the color television mounted over the bar. The bartender looked like Paul Prudhomme's evil twin. He watched Nick with suspicion.

Nick took a slow pull on his beer and wondered if the guy had made him for a cop or for trouble. He knew he looked like the kind of trouble no one wanted on his doorstep, his face cut and bruised, the butt of the Ruger peeking out of his open jacket. He had left his mirrored sunglasses on, despite the gloom of the bar.

One of the swampers scraped his chair back and rose, scratching at the giant middle finger screened on the front of his black T-shirt. A filthy red ball cap was stuck down on his head, the brim bent into an inverted U to frame a pair of eyes too small for a bony face. Nick watched him approach, sitting forward a little on his chair, ready to move. If nothing else, the beating at the hands of DiMonti's thugs had knocked the rust off his survival instincts.

'My buddy and me, we got a bet,' the swamper said, weaving a little on his feet. 'I say you're that cop what beat the shit outta that killer, Renard.'

Nick said nothing, pulled a long drag on his cigarette, and exhaled through his nose.

'You are, ain't you? I seen you on TV. Let me shake your hand, man.' He stepped in close and popped Nick on the arm with his fist like an old buddy, as if seeing him on the news had somehow forged a bond between them. 'You're a fuckin' hero!'

'You're mistaken,' Nick said calmly.

'No way. You're him. Come on, man, shake my hand. I got ten bucks on it.' He cuffed Nick's arm again and flashed a bad set of teeth. 'I say they shoulda let you put that asshole's lights out in a permanent way. Li'l bayou justice. Save the taxpayers some money, right?'

He moved to make another friendly punch. Nick caught his fist and came up out of the chair, twisting the man's arm in a way that turned the swamper's face into the rough plank wall.

'I don't like people touching me,' he said softly, his mouth inches from his erstwhile friend's ear. 'Me, I don't believe in casual intimacy between strangers, and that's what we are – strangers. I am not your friend and I sure as hell am nobody's hero. See the mistake you've made here?'

The swamp rat tried to nod, rubbing his mashed cheek against the wall. 'Hey – hey, I'm sorry, all right? No offense,' he mumbled out the side of his mouth, spittle running down his chin.

'But you see, I've already taken offense, which is why I've always found apologies to be ineffectual and the products of false logic.'

Out of the corner of his eye Nick could see the bartender watching, one hand reaching down under the bar. The screen door slammed, the sound as sharp as gunfire. The swamp rat's buddy shot up from his chair, but he made no move to come any closer.

'Now you have to ask yourself,' Nick murmured, 'do you want your friend's ten dollars only to put it toward your doctor bills, or would you rather walk away a poorer but wiser man?'

'Jesus H., Nicky.' Stokes's voice came across the room, punctuated by the sound of his footfalls on the plank floor. 'I can't leave you alone ten minutes. You keep this up, you're gonna need a license to walk around in public.'

He came up alongside Nick, shaking his head. 'What'd he do? Touch you? Did you touch him?' he asked the swamp rat. 'Man, what were you thinking? Don't cross that line. The last guy that touched him is sucking his dinner through a straw.'

He tipped his fedora back and scratched his head. 'I'm telling you, Nicky, the inherent stupidity of humankind is enough to make me give up hope on the world as a whole. You want a drink? I need a drink.'

Nick stepped back from the swamper, his temper defused and dissipating, disappointment in himself coming in on the backwash. 'Sorry I lost my cool there,' he said. The corners of his mouth twitched at the joke. 'See? It doesn't mean shit.'

Rubbing a hand against his cheek, the swamp rat stumbled back to his buddy. The pair vacated their table and moved to the far end of the bar.

'You don't play well with others, Nicky,' Stokes complained, pulling a chair out from the table and turning it backward to straddle it. 'Where'd you learn your social skills – a reformatory?'

Nick ignored him. Shaking a cigarette out of the pack, he lit it on the move, needing to pace a bit to burn off the last of the energy spike. *Control. Center. Focus.* He'd had it there for a little while, and then it slipped away like rope through a sweaty hand.

'Long as I'm asking questions, what happened to your face? You run into the business end of a jealous husband?'

'I interrupted a business meeting. Mr DiMonti took exception.'

Stokes's brows lifted. '*Vic* "The Plug" DiMonti? The wiseguy?'

'You know him?' Nick asked.

'I know *of* him. Jesus, Nicky, you're a paranoid son of a bitch. First you think I set you up. Now you think I'm on the pad with the mob. And here I am – the best friend you got in this backwater. I could get a complex.' He shook his head sadly. 'You're the one lived in New Orleans, man, not me. What's DiMonti's beef with you?'

'I went to see Duval Marcotte. Marcotte is in real estate. DiMonti owns a construction company. Donnie Bichon is all of a sudden looking to sell his half of Bayou Realty. The realty company owns a fair amount of property 'purchased' by Pam from Bichon Bayou Development to keep Donnie's ass out of bankruptcy. And now I hear Lindsay Faulkner, of Bayou Realty, was attacked last night.'

'Raped. Probably the same guy did those other two,' Stokes said, motioning to catch the bartender's attention. 'This is some hard case with his pecker in overdrive. It wasn't no mob hit, for Christ's sake. You shoulda gone into the CIA, Nicky. They would love the way your mind works.'

'I don't make it for a mob hit. Me, I just don't like coincidence, that's all. You talk to Donnie?'

He nodded, glancing at the bar again. 'Christ, you scared the bartender off. I hope you're happy,' he muttered, casting a considering glance at Nick's half-empty bottle. 'You gonna drink that? I'm dying, man.'

'What'd he have to say for himself?'

'That he wishes he'd never heard of the Partout Parish Sheriff's Office. He tells me he was at his office 'til eleven doing paperwork, stopped off at the Voodoo for a couple, then went on home alone.' He drained the beer in two long gulps. 'I told him he oughta get himself a steady girlfriend. That boy is forever without corroboration. You know what I'm saying. But then he's short on brains for a college boy. Look what he blew off so he could chase tail. Pam was a fine lady and a meal ticket to boot, and he gave her nothing but a hard time.

'Why you chewing his bone anyway?' he asked, helping himself to a cigarette from the pack on the table. 'Guy bails you outta jail, the average man would show a little gratitude. You're trying to tie him to some big boogeyman conspiracy.'

'I don't like the connections, that's all.'

'Renard did Pam. You know it and I know it, my friend.'

'The rest is an unpleasant by-product,' Nick said, finally settling into his chair. 'What else have I got to do with my time?'

'Go fishing. Get laid. Take up golf. Get laid. I'd mainly get laid if I was you. You need it, pard. Your spring's wound too damn tight, and that's a fact. That's why you're always going off on people.'

He checked his watch and sat back. The place was filling up as day edged into evening. A waitress materialized from the back room. Dyed blond curls and a tight white tank top from Hooters in Miami. He flashed her the Dudley Do-Right smile.

'A pair of Jax, darlin', and a side order of what you got.'

With a sly smirk she leaned down close and reached across in front of him for the empty, treating him with the up-close and personal view of her cleavage. He gave a tiger growl as she walked away. Across the room, the biker with JUNIOR stitched on the breast pocket of his denim vest looked over from his pool game, scowling. Stokes kept one eye on the waitress.

'She wants me. If I'm lyin', I'm dyin'.'

'She wants a big tip.'

'You're a pessimist, Nicky. That's what happens when you look for the hidden meaning in every damn thing. You're doomed to disappointment – you know what I'm saying? Go for face value. Life's a whole hell of a lot simpler that way.'

'Like Faulkner's rape?' Nick said. 'You think it's part of the pattern because that's simpler, Chaz?'

Stokes scowled. 'I think it because it's a fact.'

'There's no change in the MO between this and the other two?'

'There's some, probably because she heard him coming. But everything else matches up. It was mean and clean, just like the others. Guy's probably got a sheet a mile long. I got a call in to the state to see what we might see.'

'Why her? Why Faulkner?'

'Why not? She's a looker, lives alone. He maybe didn't know she's a dyke.'

Nick arched a brow over the rim of his shades. 'She wouldn't sleep with you either, huh? This parish is just crawling with lesbians.'

'Hey. I call 'em like I see 'em.'

Someone had changed the channel on the television over the bar to a station out of Lafayette. The graphics said the broadcast was coming live from Bayou Breaux. Noblier's meaty face filled the screen. He stood behind a podium sprouting microphones, looking as unhappy as the proverbial cat in a room full of rocking chairs. Press conference. Every figurative rocker would be aiming for his tail.

Nick nodded toward the set. 'Why aren't you there? I hear you got the task force.'

'Hell, I *am* the task force,' Chaz muttered. 'Me and Quinlan and a few uniforms – Mullen and Compton from days, Degas and Fortier from nights. Big fuckin' deal. Quinlan tried to get the BBPD in on it – Z-Top and Riva. No way. Noblier and the chief are like dueling hard-ons on account of you. The official excuse is that the rapes have all been outside city limits. It's our turf, it's our case, it's our task force.' He shook his head and pulled on the cigarette. 'It's all for show anyway, man. We got zippo to go on. This is supposed to make the common folk feel safe.'

'So how come you're not up there reassuring all the single ladies, Hollywood?'

'Shit, I hate that media stuff,' he said. 'Bunch of hairdos asking stupid questions. I'll pass, thanks. I got a big enough headache as it is. Guess who called in on Faulkner?' he said with a pained expression. 'Broussard. Now what do you suppose she was doing there?'

Nick shrugged, the picture of disinterest. His attention had caught on the bikers. The one called Junior looked like a red-bearded upright freezer. An Aryan Brotherhood tattoo was etched into his right biceps. He stared at Stokes with reptilian eyes.

'Claims she's looking to buy a house. Yeah, right, I believe that,' Stokes sneered. 'It was just a coincidence. Like it was just a coincidence she came on you with Renard.' He shook his head as he helped himself to another smoke. 'I'm telling you, man, that chick is bad news. She's always where she hadn't oughta be. You want a conspiracy, you go see what she's up to. You know, rumor has it she's screwing the deputy DA – Doucet. There's your conspiracy.'

Junior came toward them from the pool table, intercepting the waitress and helping himself to one of the beers. Stokes swore under his breath and stood up.

'Hey, man, don't fuck with my drink.'

The biker curled his lip. 'You want a drink, go stick your head in a toilet.'

Stokes's eyes widened. 'You got a problem with me being here, Junior Dickhead? You think maybe I'm a little too brown for this bar?'

Junior took a swig of the Jax and belched. He glanced over his shoulder at his partner. 'This is the kind of trouble you get when niggers breed with white women.'

Stokes dropped a shoulder and hit him running, knocking Junior into the pool table. The biker sprawled on his back, his head banging hard on the slate. Balls bounced and scattered. The other biker stepped away, holding his cue stick like a baseball bat, as Chaz pulled his badge and shoved it in Junior's face.

'This make me any lighter, asshole?' he bellowed. 'How about this?' He pulled a Glock nine-millimeter from his belt holster and jammed the barrel into Junior's left nostril. 'You think you're the superior race, you Nazi cocksucker? What you thinkin' now?'

He slapped the biker hard on the cheek with the badge, then dropped it on the table and jammed his hand up under the man's chin. 'Don't you call me nigger! I ain't no nigger, you motherfucking cracker piece of shit! Call me a nigger and I'll blow your fuckin' head off and say you assaulted an officer!'

Junior made a strangled sound, his big face turning a shade redder than his beard.

Nick took in the wild rage in Stokes's eyes, knowing he was close to an edge, surprised by it, surprised to see it in someone else. Maybe they had something more in common than the job after all.

Nick braced his hands on the pool table, and leaned into Junior's bug-eyed field of vision. 'See what you get for being politically incorrect these days, Junior? People just don't take being abused like they used to.'

Stokes backed off and Junior rolled over, choking up phlegm on the green felt.

Stokes blew out a breath and forced a grin, twitching the tension out of his shoulders. 'Damn, Nicky, you spoiled my fun.'

Nick shook his head and started toward the door. 'And you say I'm the crazy one.'

Stokes shrugged off the responsibility. 'Hey, what can I say? He crossed my line.'

Annie sat at her kitchen table, a fork in a carton of kung pow chicken, Jann Arden singing in the background. The strange, voyeuristic lyrics of 'Living Under June' touched off thoughts of her own situation. The experiences of one person seeping into another's life, that person's life touching someone else.

Had she really believed she could become involved in this investigation and float from point to point in a bubble of invisibility? People talked to one another. The case was open and ongoing. Stokes was supposed to be working it; of course he would speak to Lindsay Faulkner. Lindsay had spoken with Annie. Why wouldn't she mention it to Stokes? She had no reason not to.

'Except that it could mean my ass,' Annie muttered.

If Stokes took this to the sheriff . . . It made her stomach hurt to imagine what Noblier would have to say about it. They'd have to bury her in that damn dog suit.

But Gus had said nothing outright when he'd called her into his office about the Faulkner attack, which could only mean Stokes hadn't brought it up . . . yet.

'Hooker was right,' Gus had growled, fixing her with his classic look of disgruntlement. 'It seems if there's a pile of shit around, you'll find one way or another to step in it. Just how did you come to be at Lindsay Faulkner's home, Deputy Broussard?'

She stuck with the lie she'd told Stokes, wondering too late if she'd trapped herself. There would be no paperwork at Bayou Realty to back her up. What if Stokes walked into the realty office and requested a file that didn't exist?

She would have to deal with that burning bridge when she came to it, she decided, setting her dinner aside. The question that nagged her more was this: If Stokes knew she was sniffing around his case and he didn't want her there, why hadn't he gone to the sheriff?

Maybe Faulkner *hadn't* told him about their meetings. There was no way of knowing until either Stokes made a move or Lindsay Faulkner regained consciousness.

'Why can't you just mind your own business, Annie?' she mused aloud.

Downstairs in the store, Stevie the night clerk was watching Speed again, deep in lust with Sandra Bullock. The sounds of crashes and explosions came up through the floor as if a small war were going on below. Ordinarily Annie was able to shut out the noise. Tonight she found herself wishing for the quiet of Fourcade's study, but she had no intention of seeking it out. She needed a night off, time to clear her head and take a hard look at what she'd gotten herself into. For all the good that would do her now.

Still, in spite of herself, she wondered how Fourcade was doing. She had called from a pay phone at noon and left a message on his machine about Lindsay Faulkner. He hadn't called her back. She occasionally lapsed into panicked thoughts of him lying on his floor dead from internal bleeding, but then talked herself out of them. It wasn't the first time he'd been on the receiving end of a pounding. He knew better than she did the extent of his own injuries.

He certainly hadn't kissed like a man on the brink of death.

No, he had kissed her like a blind man sensing light, like a man who needed to make a connection with another soul and wasn't quite sure how.

'Don't be stupid,' she muttered, turning her attention to the papers she had brought home with her from Nick's place the night before – the reports of the harassment Pam Bichon had endured before her murder, copies of reports from the Bayou Breaux PD on incidents that had occurred at her office.

Pam had feared for her safety and for Josie's. But her level of fear had seemed out of proportion to the officers who had taken the calls. While they had drawn no conclusions in the reports, it wasn't hard for another cop to read between the lines. They thought she was overreacting, being unreasonable, wasting their time. Why would she be afraid of Marcus

Renard? He seemed so normal, so harmless. Why should she think he was the one making the breather calls? What proof did she have he was stalking the shadows of her Quail Run property? How could it possibly frighten her to receive a silk scarf from an anonymous admirer?

Gooseflesh swept down Annie's arms. She knew Renard had given Pam a number of small gifts, but the only gift ever mentioned in detail in any of the paperwork or news reports had been a necklace with a heart-shaped pendant. He tried to give it to her on her birthday, shortly before her death.

Annie pulled her binder of news clippings and paged through the pockets, hunting for the one burning in her memory. It was a piece from the Lafayette *Daily Advertiser* that had run shortly after Renard's arrest, and it spoke specifically of Pam's birthday, when she had gone into the Bowen & Briggs office with a cardboard box containing the gifts he had given her during the preceding weeks. She had reportedly hurled the box at Renard, shouting angrily for him to leave her alone, that she wanted nothing to do with him.

She had given back to him everything he had ever given her, and among those gifts was a silk scarf. Annie could find no detailed description of it. The detectives had looked for the rejected gifts during a search of Renard's home but had never found them, and didn't consider them important. How would anyone consider a lovely silk scarf proof of harassment?

Nausea swirled through Annie as an idea hit. She reached across the table for the box, lifted the scarf and ran it through her fingers, her mind racing.

'*You look like her, you know,*' *Donnie said, his voice strangely dreamy.* '*The shape of your face . . . the hair . . . the mouth . . .*'

'*You fit the victim profile,*' *Fourcade said.* '*. . . you came into his life, chère. Like it was meant to be. . . . He could fall in love with you.*'

Had Pam Bichon held this very scarf in her hands, feeling the same strange sense of disquiet Annie felt right now?

The phone rang, sending her half a foot off her chair. She tossed the scarf aside and went into the living room.

The machine picked up on the fourth ring and she listened to herself advise the caller.

'If you're someone I'll actually want to talk to, leave a message after the tone. If you're a reporter, a salesman, a heavy breather, a crank, or someone with an opinion of me I don't want to hear, just don't bother. I'll only erase you.'

The warning hadn't seemed to deter anyone. The tape had been full by the time she'd gotten home. Word of her involvement in the Faulkner case had leaked out of the department like oil through a bad gasket. Three reporters had been lying in wait for her on the store gallery when she got home. But it wasn't a reporter who waited for the tone.

'Annie, this is Marcus.' His voice was tight. 'Could you please call me back? Someone took a shot at me tonight.'

Annie grabbed the receiver. 'I'm here. What happened?'

'Just what I said. Someone took a shot at me through a window.'

'Why are you calling me? Call 911.'

'We did. The deputies who came said it was a pity the guy was such a poor shot. They dug the bullet out of the wall and left. I'd like someone to look around, investigate.'

'And you'd like that someone to be me?'

'You're the only one who cares, Annie. You're the only one in that whole damn department who cares about justice being done. If it were up to the rest of them, I'd have been alligator bait weeks ago.'

He was silent for a moment. Annie waited, apprehension coiling around her stomach like a python.

'Please, Annie, say you'll come. I need you.'

Out over the Atchafalaya, thunder rumbled like distant cannon fire. He wanted her. He needed her. He was probably a killer. She had immersed herself in this case up to her chin. She took a breath and went deeper.

'I'll be right there.'

30

We were sitting here having coffee like civilized people,' Doll Renard said, gesturing to her dining room table like a tour guide, 'when suddenly the glass in that door shattered. I nearly had a heart attack! We're not the kind of people who have guns or know about guns! To think that someone would shoot into our home! What kind of world are we living in? To think I used to believe in the good of people!'

'Where were y'all sitting? Which chairs?'

Doll sniffed. 'The other officers didn't even bother to ask. I was right here, in my usual place,' she said, going to the chair at the end of the table.

'Victor was here in his usual seat.' Marcus claimed a chair that put his brother's back to the French doors.

At the mention of his name, Victor shook his head and slapped the palm of one hand on the table. He now sat at the head of the table, rocking himself, muttering incessantly. 'Not now. Not now. Very red. Enter out. Enter out *now*!'

'He'll be ranting for days,' Doll said bitterly.

Marcus cut her a look. 'Mother, please. We're all upset. Victor has as much reason as the rest of us. More than you – he could have been killed.'

Doll's jaw dropped as if he'd struck her. 'I never said he shouldn't be upset! How dare you talk to me that way in front of a guest!'

'I'm sorry, Mother. Forgive my short temper. My manners aren't what they should be. Someone meant to kill me earlier.'

Annie cleared her throat to draw his attention. 'Where were you sitting?'

He glanced toward the shattered door. Dozens of insects had flocked in through the hole and now swarmed around the light fixture. Gnats dotted the ceiling like flecks of black ink. 'I was out of the room.'

'You weren't sitting here when the shot was fired?'

'No. I had left the room several moments prior.'

'Why?'

'To use the bathroom. We'd been sitting here drinking coffee.'

'Do you own a handgun or a rifle?'

'Of course not,' he said, a flush creeping up his neck.

'I wouldn't have a gun in this house,' Doll said with great affront. 'I wouldn't even let Marcus have a BB gun as a boy. They're filthy instruments of violence and nothing more. His father had guns,' she said with accusation. 'I got rid of every one of them. Temptations to violence.'

'You can't think I staged this,' Marcus said, looking hard at Annie.

'Staged it?' Doll shrilled. 'What do you mean – "staged" it?'

Annie turned her back on them and went to the wall where the slug had buried itself in the thick horsehair plaster. It looked as if the call deputies had dug the thing out with a pickax. Plaster littered the floor in crumbled chunks and fine dust. The bullet had struck a good foot above the heads of anyone seated at the table. One of the things any marksman had to consider when aiming was the drop of the bullet as it traveled away from the barrel of the gun. To hit where this shot had hit, the triggerman had to have been aiming still higher.

'Either he was a piss-poor shot or he never meant to hit anyone,' she said.

'What do you mean?' Doll asked. 'Someone *shot at us*! We were sitting right here!'

'Had you noticed anyone hanging around earlier in the day?' Annie asked. 'Today or any other day recently?'

'Fishermen go past on the bayou,' she said, fluttering one bony hand in the direction of the waterway as she clutched the bodice of her baggy housedress with the other. 'And those horrible reporters come and go, though we have nothing to say to them. They do as they will. I've never seen such an ill-mannered lot in all my life. There was a time in this country when etiquette meant something –'

Marcus squeezed his eyes shut. 'Mother, could we please stick to the subject? Annie isn't interested in a discussion of the decline of formal manners and mores.'

Doll's complexion mottled pink and white. Her face went tight, pulling skin against bone and tendon. 'Well, excuse me if my views aren't important to you, Marcus,' she said tightly. 'Pardon me if you believe *Annie* doesn't want to hear what I think.'

'This has been traumatic for all of you, I'm sure,' Annie said diplomatically.

'Don't patronize me!' Doll snapped. Her entire body was trembling with anger. 'You think we're either criminals or fools. You're no better than any of the others.'

'Mother –'

'*Red! Red! No!*' Victor shrieked, rocking so hard the chair legs came up off the floor. He slapped the tabletop over and over.

'If you believe she cares about us, Marcus, you *are* a fool.' Doll turned away from him to her other son. 'Come along, Victor. You're going to bed. No one here needs our presence.'

'*Not now! Not now! Very red!*' Victor's voice screeched upward like metal rending. He curled himself into a ball as his mother clamped a white-knuckled hand on his shoulder.

'Come along, Victor!'

Sobbing, Victor Renard unfolded his body from the chair and allowed his mother to tow him from the room.

Marcus hung his head and stared at the floor, embarrassment and anger coloring his battered face. 'Well, wasn't that lovely? Another night in the life of the happy Renard family. I'm sorry, Annie. Sometimes I think my mother doesn't any more know what to do with her emotions than does Victor.'

Annie made no comment. It was more useful for her to see the Renards coming apart at the seams than to see them wrapped tightly in control. She moved toward the French doors, stepping around the broken glass. 'I'd like to look around outside.'

'Of course.'

Out on the terrace she filled her lungs with air that tasted of copper. Clouds appeared to sag to the treetops, bloated with rain that had yet to fall.

'Just to set things straight,' Marcus said, 'my mother has never believed in the good in people. She's been waiting for a lynch mob to show up on the front lawn, and never misses the opportunity to point out that it's all my fault. I'm sure she's secretly pleased by this in her own twisted way.'

'I didn't come here to discuss your mother, Mr Renard.'

'Please call me Marcus.' He turned toward her. The light that filtered out from the house softened and shadowed his bruises and stitches. With the swelling gone he was no longer grotesque, merely homely. He didn't look dangerous, he looked pathetic. 'Please, Annie. I need to at least pretend I have a friend in all this.'

'Your lawyer is your friend. I'm a cop.'

'But you're here and you don't have to be. You came for me.'

She wanted to tell him differently, had tried to set him straight, but either he didn't listen or he twisted the truth to suit himself.

It was the kind of thinking that applied to stalkers and other obsessive personalities. The unwillingness or inability to accept the truth. There was nothing overt in Renard's attitude. Nothing that could have been deemed crazy, and yet this subtle insistence to bend reality to his wishes was disturbing.

She wanted to distance herself from him. But the truth was the closer she got to him, the more likely she was to see something the detectives had missed. He might let down his guard, make a mistake. '*He could fall in love with you . . .*' and she'd be there to nail him.

'All right . . . Marcus,' she said, his name sticking in her mouth like a gob of peanut butter.

He let out a breath, as if in relief, and slid his hands into his pants pockets. 'Fourcade,' he said. 'You asked if anyone had come by recently. Fourcade was here on Saturday. On the bayou.'

'Do you have any reason to believe Detective Fourcade is the one who took that shot tonight?'

He made a choking laugh, pulled a handkerchief out of his pocket, and dabbed at the corners of his mouth. 'He tried to kill me last week, why not this week?'

'He wasn't himself that night. He'd lost a tough decision in court. He'd been drinking. He –'

'You're not going to make excuses for him at the hearing next week, are you?' he asked, looking at her with shock. 'You were there. You saw what he was doing to me. You said it yourself: he was trying to kill me.'

'We're not talking about last week. We're talking about tonight. Did you see him tonight? Have you seen him since Saturday? Has he called you? Has he threatened you?'

'No.'

'And of course you didn't see the shooter because you happened to be in the bathroom at the precise moment –'

'You don't believe me,' he said flatly.

'I believe if Detective Fourcade wanted you dead, you'd be meeting your maker right now,' Annie said. 'Nick Fourcade isn't going to mistake your brother for you or put a shot in the wall a foot above your head. He'd blow your skull apart like a rotten melon, and I don't doubt but that he could do it in the dark at a hundred yards.'

'He came here in a boat Saturday. He could have been on the bayou –'

'Everybody in this parish owns a boat, and about ninety percent of them think you should be drawn and quartered in public. Fourcade is hardly the only possibility here,' Annie argued. 'To be perfectly frank with you, Marcus, I *do* think you're a more likely candidate than Fourcade.'

He turned away from her then, staring out at the darkness. 'I didn't do this. Why would I?'

'To get attention. To get me over here. To sic the press on Fourcade.'

'You can test my hands for gunpowder residue, search the premises for the gun. I didn't do it.' He shook his head in disgust. 'That seems to be my motto these last months: I didn't do it. And while y'all are busy trying to prove me a liar, killers and would-be killers are running around loose.'

He blotted at his mouth again. Annie watched him, tried to read him, wondered how much of what he was letting her see was an act and how much of it he bought into himself.

'You know the worst part of all this?' he asked, his voice so soft Annie had to step closer to hear him. 'I never got to mourn Pam. I've not been allowed to express my grief, my outrage, my hurt, my loss. She was such a lovely person. So pretty.'

He looked down at Annie as lightning flashed and his expression was

1064

gilded in silver – a strange, glassy, dreamy look, as if he were looking at a memory that wasn't quite true.

'I miss her,' he whispered. 'I wish . . .'

What? That he hadn't killed her? That she had returned his affection instead of his gifts? Annie held her breath, waiting.

'I wish you believed me,' he murmured.

'It's not my job to believe you, Marcus,' she said. 'It's my job to find the truth.'

'I want you to know the truth,' he whispered.

The intimacy in his tone unnerved her, and she stepped back from him as the wind came in a great exhalation from the heavens, rattling the trees like giant pompons.

'I'll keep on top of this,' she said. 'See if the deputies come up with anything. But that's all I can do. I'm in enough hot water as it is. I'd appreciate it if you didn't tell anyone I'd been here.'

He drew his thumb and forefinger across his lips. 'Our secret. That makes two.' The idea seemed to please him.

Annie frowned. 'I'm checking on that truck – your Good Samaritan the night Pam died. I'm not making promises anything will come of it, but I want you to know I'm looking.'

He tried to smile. 'I knew you would. You wouldn't want to think you saved my life for no good reason.'

'I don't want it said the investigation wasn't thorough on all counts,' she corrected. 'For the record, Detective Fourcade looked into it, he just didn't find anything. Probably because there's nothing to find.'

'You'll find the truth, Annie,' he murmured, reaching out to touch her shoulder. His hand lingered a heartbeat too long. 'I promise you will.'

Annie's skin crawled. She shrugged off his touch. 'I'm gonna go get my flashlight. I want to have a look around the yard before the rain starts.'

The yard gave up no secrets. She searched for twenty minutes. Renard watched her from the terrace for a while, then disappeared into the house, returning some time later with his own flashlight, to help her look.

Annie didn't know what she had hoped to find. A shell casing, maybe. But she found none. The shooter could have disposed of it. It may well have been in the bayou if that was where the shooter had been – if the shooter had been anyone other than Renard himself.

She mulled the possibilities over in her mind as she drove out of the Renard driveway and headed for the main road. It wouldn't hurt to know where Hunter Davidson had been at the time of the shooting, though he was an old sportsman and she couldn't imagine him missing a target.

Maybe he had drawn a bead on the back of Victor Renard's head, having mistaken him for Marcus, and while staring through the crosshairs of the rifle's scope had been hit with the enormity of taking a human life, then popped the shot into the wall instead.

It seemed more likely that he would have looked at Renard in his sights and pulled the trigger on a tide of emotion. Remorse, if it came at all, would come after the revenge.

Nor did it make any sense to consider Fourcade as a suspect, for the very reasons she had given Marcus. Renard himself, on the other hand, had everything to gain by staging the incident. It gave him an excuse to call her. It cast suspicion on Fourcade, could be used to draw the media. The story could have rolled on the ten o'clock news, creating a full-fledged furor by morning. That's certainly what Renard's lawyer would have wanted.

Then where were the reporters? Renard hadn't called them; he had called her.

'*You're here and you don't have to be. You came for me.*'

The bayou road was empty and dark, a lonely trench between the dense walls of woods that ran on either side of it. The rain had finally begun to fall, an angry spitting that would, any second, become a deluge. Annie hit the switch for the wipers and glanced in the rearview mirror as lightning flashed – illuminating the silhouette of a car behind her. Big car. Too close. No lights.

She cursed herself for not paying attention. She had no idea how long the car had been behind her or where it had pulled onto the road.

As if the driver had sensed her notice, the headlights flared on – high beams glaring into the Jeep, blinding in their sudden intensity. At the same time, the heavens opened and the rain came down in a gush. Annie clicked the wipers up to high and punched the gas. The Jeep sprinted forward with the tail car right on its bumper.

Annie nudged the gas pedal again, the speedometer springing toward seventy. The car came with her like a dog on the heels of a rabbit. She grabbed the radio mike, then realized the cord had been severed cleanly from the base unit.

Premeditation. This was no random game. She had been chosen to play. But with whom?

There was no time to consider names. There was no time to do anything but act and react. She was outrunning her visibility, flying blind through sheets of rain. The road along here curved and bent back like a snake as it ran parallel to the bayou. Every corner tested the Jeep's traction and presented the threat of hydroplaning. Another mile and the road became a virtual land bridge between two areas of dense swamp.

The tail car swung into the left lane and roared up beside her. It was big – a Caddy, maybe – a tank of a car. Annie could sense the heft of it beside her. Too big for the curves, she thought, and hoped it would fall back. But it stayed with her, and she abandoned the distraction of hope, focusing on driving as the Jeep rocked into a turn and the wheels fought against her will.

The car had the inside of the curve and bore wide, hitting the Jeep, metal grinding on metal, trying to muscle her off the pavement. Her rear outside wheel hit the shoulder, and the Jeep jerked beneath her. Annie put her foot down and hung on, straining to hold the vehicle on course. The view through the windshield tilted, then slammed back hard onto a level plane.

'Son of a bitch!' she yelled.

She floored the accelerator as the road straightened out, and prayed there was nothing in the way. It was raining too hard for the water to run off the pavement, and plumes sprayed up from the wheels of the Jeep. The drag had to be pulling harder on the low-slung car, but it hung beside her, swerving in for another hit. Her side window shattered, chunks of it falling in on her.

Annie jerked the Jeep back into the car. The crash was like a burst of white noise. The car held its ground, repelling the Jeep like a rubber ball. For a heartbeat she had no control as the Jeep skidded toward the shoulder and the inky blackness of the swamp beyond. The right front tire hit the shoulder and dropped. Mud spewed up across the hood, across the windshield. The wipers smeared the mess across the glass.

Annie cranked the wheel to the left and prayed at the speed of sound as the Jeep bucked along, half on the road, half off, the swamp sucking at it like a hungry monster. From the corner of her eye, she could see the car swerving toward her again, and for a split second she saw the driver – a black apparition with gleaming eyes and a mouth tearing open on a scream she couldn't hear. Then the road curved hard to the right directly in front of her and the Jeep jumped back on the pavement, bumping noses with the car, sending a shower of sparks up into the rain.

Options streaked through Annie's mind like shooting stars. She couldn't out-muscle him and she couldn't outrun him, but she had four good all-terrain tires and a machine that was nimble for its size. If she could make the levee road, she would shake him.

She hit the brakes and went into a skid, downshifting. As the car shot past her, she bent the skid into a 180-degree turn and hit the gas. In the rearview, she could see the brake lights on the car glowing like red eyes in the night. By the time he got turned around, she would be halfway to the levee – if her luck held, if the trail out to Clarence Gauthier's camp wasn't under a foot of water.

Her headlights hit the sign. Nailed to the stump of a swamp oak that had been struck by lightning twenty years ago, the sign was a jagged piece of cypress plank, hand-lettered in blaze orange: KEEP OUT – TRESPASSER WILL BE ATE.

Behind her the car was lurching around. Annie swung the Jeep onto the dirt path and hit the brakes. Ahead of her, water lay across the trail in a glossy black sheet dimpled by rain. Too late, she thought she might have been wiser to sprint the miles back to Renard's house to take refuge with one killer in order to escape another. But the car was barreling toward her now, taking advantage of her hesitation.

If she couldn't make it across to higher ground, she was his, whoever the hell he was, for whatever the hell he wanted. She'd have to go for the Sig in the duffel bag on the passenger's seat, and hold the son of a bitch off until help came along.

She gunned the engine as she let out the clutch. The Jeep hit the water, engine roaring, wheels churning. Churning and catching. Churning and sinking.

'Come on, come on, come on!' Annie chanted.

The back end of the Jeep twisted to the right as the back tire slid toward the edge of the submerged trail. The engine was screaming. Annie was screaming. In the mirror she caught a glimpse of the car pulling up on the road behind her.

Then the front tires caught hold of firmer ground, and the Jeep scrambled to safety.

'Oh, Jesus. Oh, God. Oh, shit,' Annie muttered as she sped down the twisting trail, branches slapping at the windshield.

Someone ran out of the shack where Clarence Gauthier kept his fighting dogs. Annie took a right before she got to the camp, and flinched at the sound of a shotgun going off in warning. Another half mile on the trail that was rapidly disintegrating to bog and she was finally able to climb up onto the levee road.

Clear of the woods, the rain closed around her like a liquid curtain. Only the lightning allowed her nightmare glimpses of the world beyond the beam of her headlights. Black, dead, not a living thing in sight.

She felt ill. She was shaking.

Somebody had just tried to kill her.

The Corners store was closed. The light in Sos and Fanchon's living room glowed amber through the gloom across the parking lot. Annie pulled the Jeep in close to the staircase on the south side of the building and ran up to her landing. Her hands were trembling as she worked the lock. She struggled to mentally talk her nerves into calming down. She was a cop, after all. That someone tried to kill her probably shouldn't have bothered her so much. Maybe next time she would shrug it off entirely. Par for the course. Just another day on the job.

The hell it was.

Once inside the entry, she shed her sneakers, dropped her gear bag, and went straight to the kitchen. She pulled a chair across the floor. A dusty bottle of Jack Daniel's sat in the cupboard over the refrigerator.

She thought of Mullen as she pulled the whiskey down and set it on the counter. He would have liked this moment on videotape – evidence of her sudden alcoholism. Son of a bitch. If she found out he'd been behind the wheel of that car tonight . . . what? The consequences would go far beyond having him charged with a crime.

Life should have been so much simpler, Annie thought as she unscrewed the cap from the Jack and poured a double shot. She took a long sip, grimacing as the stuff slid down.

'You gonna offer me some of that?'

Heart in her throat, Annie bolted around. The glass hit the floor and shattered.

'I locked that door when I left,' she said.

Fourcade shrugged. 'And I told you before: It's not much of a lock.'

'Where's your truck?'

'Out of sight.'

Nick grabbed a dish towel and bent down to clean up the mess. 'You're a mite on the edge tonight, 'Toinette.'

He looked up at her standing beside the jaunty gator on her refrigerator. Her face was pale as death, her eyes shining like glass beads, her hair hanging in damp strings. He could feel the tension in her like the vibrations of a tuning fork.

'I suppose I am,' she said. 'Someone just tried to kill me.'

'What?' He jerked upright and looked her over as if he expected to see blood.

'Someone tried to run me off the bayou road into the swamp. And he damn near succeeded.'

Annie looked around her kitchen, at the old cupboards and the vintage fifties table, at the canisters on the counter and the ivy plant she had started from a sprig in Serena Doucet's bridal bouquet five years ago. She looked at the cat clock, watched its eyes and tail move with the passing seconds. Everything looked somehow different, as if she hadn't seen any of it in a very long time and now found none of it quite matched the images in her memory.

The whiskey boiled in her empty stomach like acid. She could still feel its path down the back of her throat.

'Somebody tried to kill me,' she murmured again, amazed. Dizziness swept through her like a wave. With as much cool and dignity as she could muster, she looked at Nick and said, 'Excuse me. I have to go throw up now.'

31

This is not one of my finer moments.'

Annie sat on her knees in front of the toilet, propped up on one side by the old claw-foot bathtub. She felt like a withering husk, too drained for anything deeper than cursory embarrassment. 'So much for my image as a lush.'

'Did you get a look at the driver?' Fourcade asked, leaning a shoulder against the door frame.

'Just a glimpse. I think he was wearing a ski mask. It was dark. It was raining. Everything happened so fast. God,' she complained in disgust. 'I sound like every vic I've ever rolled my eyes at.'

'Tags?'

She shook her head. 'I was too busy trying to keep my ass out of the swamp.

'I don't know,' she murmured. 'I thought Renard staged the shooting just to get me over there, but maybe not. Maybe whoever took that shot hung around, watched the cops, watched me come and go.'

'Why go after you? Why not wait 'til you're gone and take another crack at Renard?'

The answer might have made her throw up again if she hadn't already emptied her system. If the assailant was after Renard, it made no sense to go after her.

'You're probably right about the shooting,' he said. 'Renard, he wanted an excuse to call you. That story he gave you is lame as a three-legged dog.'

Annie pulled herself up to sit on the edge of the tub. 'If that's true, then Cadillac Man was there for one reason – me. He had to have followed me over there.'

She looked up at Fourcade as he came into the room, half hoping he would tell her no just to ease her worry. He didn't, wouldn't, wasn't that kind of man. The facts were the facts, he would see no purpose in padding the truth to soften the blows.

With a dubious look he pulled the towel away from the ceramic grasping hand that stuck out from the wall and soaked one end of it with cold tap water.

'You manage to piss people off, 'Toinette,' he said, taking a seat on the closed toilet.

'I don't mean to.'

'You have to realize that's a good thing. But you're not paying attention. You act first and think later.'

'Look who's talking.'

She pressed the cold cloth to one cheek, then the other. He looked concerned rather than contrite. She would have been better off with the latter. She was safer thinking of him as a mentor than pondering the meaning of these odd moments when he seemed to be something else.

'Me, I always think first, chère. My logic is occasionally flawed, that's all,' he said. 'How you doing? You okay?'

He leaned forward and pushed a strand of hair off her cheek. His knee brushed against her thigh, and in spite of everything Annie felt a subtle charge of electricity.

'Sure. I'm swell. Thanks.'

She pushed to her feet and went to the sink to brush her teeth.

'So, who wants you dead?'

'I don't know,' she mumbled through a mouthful of foam.

'Sure you do. You just haven't put the pieces together yet.'

She spat in the sink and glared at him out the corner of her eye. 'God, that's annoying.'

'Who might want you dead? Use your head.'

Annie wiped her mouth. 'You know, unlike you, I don't have a past chock-full of psychopaths and thugs.'

'Your past isn't the issue,' he said, following her to the living room. 'What about that deputy – Mullen?'

'Mullen wants me off the job. I can't believe he'd try to kill me.'

'Push any man far enough, you don't know what he might do.'

'Is that the voice of experience?' she said caustically, wanting to lash out at somebody. Maybe if she took a few swipes at him she would be able to reestablish the boundaries that had blurred last night.

She paced the length of the alligator coffee table, nervous energy rising in a new wave. 'What about you, Nick? I got you arrested. You could go down for a felony. Maybe you don't think you've got anything to lose getting rid of the only witness.'

'I don't own a Cadillac,' he said, his face stony.

'I gotta figure if you'd try to kill somebody, you probably wouldn't have any moral problem with stealing a car.'

'Stop it.'

'Why? You want me to use my head. You want me to be objective.'

'So use your head. I was here waiting for you.'

'I came up the levee. It's slower going. You could have ditched the Caddy and beat it over here in your truck.'

'You're pissing me off, Broussard.'

'Yeah? Well, I guess I do that to people. It's probably a wonder someone didn't kill me a long time ago.'

He caught hold of her arm, and Annie jerked out of his grasp, tears stinging her eyes.

'Don't touch me!' she snapped. 'I never said you could touch me! I don't know what you want from me. I don't know why you dragged me into this —'

'I didn't drag you. We're partners.'

'Oh, yeah? Well, *partner*, why don't you tell me again why you went to Renard's home Saturday? Were you scoping out a good sniper's vantage point?'

'You think I took that shot?' he said, incredulous. 'If I wanted Renard dead, sugar, he'd be in hell by now.'

'Yeah, I know. I kind of interrupted that send-off once already.'

'*C'est assez!*' he ordered, catching hold of her by both arms this time, hauling her up close.

'What're you gonna do, Nick? Beat me up?'

'What the hell's the matter with you?' he demanded. 'Why are you busting my balls here? I didn't touch Renard Saturday, I didn't take a shot at him tonight, and I sure as hell didn't try to kill you!'

He wanted to shake her, he wanted to kiss her, anger and sexual aggression bleeding together in a dangerous mix. He forced himself to stand her back from him and walk away.

'If we're partners, we're partners,' he said. 'That means trust. You have to trust me, 'Toinette. More than you trust a damn killer, for Christ's sake.'

He was amazed at the words that had come out of his mouth. He had never wanted a partner on the job, he didn't waste time trusting people. He wasn't even sure why he was angry with her. Her argument was logical. Of course she should consider him a suspect.

Annie blew out a breath. 'I don't know what to believe. I don't know who to believe. I never thought this would be so damn hard! I feel like I'm lost in a house of mirrors. I feel like I'm drowning. Someone tried to kill me! That doesn't happen to me every day. I'm sorry if I'm not reacting like an old pro.'

They stood across the length of the room from each other. Whether it was the distance or the moment, she looked small and fragile. Nick felt a strange stirring of compassion, and an unwelcome twinge of guilt. He had doubted her motives from the start, questioned the source of her interest in the Bichon case, when she was exactly what she appeared to be: a good cop who wanted to be better, who wanted to find justice for a victim. Simple and straightforward, no ulterior motives, no hidden agenda.

'It wasn't me, 'Toinette,' he murmured, closing the distance between them. 'I don't think you believe that it was. You just don't wanna think more than one person in this world might want you gone from it, *oui*? You don't wanna dig in that hole, do you, *chère*?'

'No,' she whispered as the fight drained out of her. She shut her eyes as if she could wish it all away. 'God, the things I get myself into.'

'You're in this case for good reason,' he said. 'It's your challenge, your obligation. You're in over your head, but you know how to swim – suck in a breath and start kicking.'

'Right now, I'd rather climb out of the water, thanks anyway.'

'No. Seek the truth, 'Toinette. In all things, seek the truth. In the case. In me. In yourself. You're not a child and you're nobody's pawn. You proved that when you stopped me from pounding Renard into the here-fucking-after. You're in this case because you want to be. You'll stick it out because you know you have to. Hang on. Hang tough.'

He raised a hand and touched her cheek, stroked his fingertips down her jaw. 'You're stronger than you know.'

'I'm scared, that's what I am,' she whispered. 'I hate being scared. It pisses me off.'

Annie told herself to turn away from his touch, but she couldn't make herself do it. His show of tenderness was too unexpected and too needed. He was too strong and too near.

'I'm sorry,' she murmured. 'I was scared I'd lose my job. That was bad enough. Now I have to be scared I'll lose my life.'

'And you're scared of me,' he said, his fingers curling beneath her chin.

She looked up at him, at the battered face, at the eyes bright with the intensity that burned inside him. She had told him just last night that he frightened her, but the fear wasn't of him.

'No,' she said softly. 'Not that way. I don't believe you were in that car. I don't believe you took that shot. I'm sorry. I'm sorry.'

She murmured the words again and again as the trembling came back.

His embrace seemed to swallow her up. He stroked a hand over her hair and down her back. He kissed the side of her neck, her cheek. Blindly, she turned her mouth into his, and he kissed her with the kind of heat that flared instantly out of control.

She opened her mouth beneath his and felt a wild rush as his tongue touched hers. She ached and trembled with the sensations of life, too aware she could have been dead. Heat blushed just beneath her skin and pooled thick and liquid between her legs. She could taste the need – his and her own. She could feel it, wanted to give in to it and obliterate everything else from her mind. She didn't want thought or reason or logic. She wanted Fourcade.

His hands slipped beneath her T-shirt and skimmed up her back. The shirt came off as they sank to their knees on the rug. He discarded his own between kisses. They came together, fevered skin to fevered skin, mouths and hands exploring. Annie pulled him down with her, arched into the touch of his lips on her breast, moaned at the feel of his tongue rasping against her nipple.

She allowed awareness of nothing but his touch, the strength of him, the masculine scent of his skin. She gave herself over entirely to sensation

– the texture of his chest hair, the smooth hardness of his stomach muscles, the feel of his erection in her hand.

He stroked his fingers down through the dark curls between her thighs and tested her readiness. And then he was inside her, filling her, stretching her. She dug her fingertips into his back, wrapped her legs around his hips, let the passion and the urgency of the act consume her. She let her orgasm blind her with a burst of intensity borne of fear and the need to reaffirm her own existence.

She cried out at the strength of it. She held tight to Nick as her body gripped his. His arms were banded around her. His voice was low and rough in her ear, a stream of hot, erotic French. He rode her harder, faster, bringing her to climax again and finding his own end as he drove deep within her. She felt him come, felt the sudden rigidity in the muscles of his back, heard him groan through his teeth. Then stillness . . . the only sound their ragged breathing. Neither of them moved.

Recriminations rose in Annie's mind like flotsam as the rush of physical sensation ebbed. Fourcade was the last man she should have allowed herself to want. Certainly one of the last she should have allowed herself to have. He was too complicated, too extreme. She had seen him commit a crime. She had questioned his motives, had questioned his sanity more than once. And yet she could find no genuine regret for crossing this particular line with him.

Maybe it was the stress of the situation. Maybe it was the inevitable eruption of the sexual tension that had pulled between them all along. Maybe she was losing her mind.

As she considered the last possibility, Nick raised his head and stared at her.

'Well, that took the edge off, *c'est vrai*,' he growled, his arms tightening around her. 'Now, let's go find a bed and get serious.'

Midnight had ticked past when Annie slipped from the bed. As she belted her old flannel robe, she studied Fourcade in the soft glow of the bedside hula-dancer lamp, surprised that he didn't open his eyes and demand an explanation for her sudden departure from between the sheets. He slept lightly, like a cat, but he didn't stir. His breathing was deep and regular. He looked too good in her bed.

'What have you gotten yourself into now, Annie?' she muttered as she padded down the hall.

She had no answers, didn't have the energy to search for them. But that didn't stop the questions from swarming in her mind. Questions about the case, about Lindsay Faulkner and Renard and whoever had been behind the wheel of that Cadillac. Questions about herself and her judgment and her capabilities.

Nick said she was stronger than she realized. He had also said she was too afraid to go deep within herself. She supposed he was right on both counts.

Flipping on the kitchen light, she walked slowly around the table, looking at everything she had laid out there. She reached for the scarf, needing to touch it, repulsed that a killer might have held it in his hands first, sickened that it might have been a gift to a woman who had died a horrible, brutal death.

'Renard, he sent you that, no?'

She jerked around at the sound of his voice. He stood in the doorway in jeans that were zipped but not buttoned, his chest and feet bare.

'I didn't mean to wake you.'

'You didn't.' He came forward, reaching for the strip of pale silk. 'He gave you this?'

'Yes.'

'Just like he did with Pam.'

'I have a creepy feeling it might be the same scarf,' Annie said. 'Do you know?'

He shook his head. 'I never saw the stuff. What he did with it after she gave it back to him is a mystery. Stokes might know if that's the one, but I doubt it. He'd have no reason to have taken note. It's not against the law to send a woman pretty things.'

'White silk,' she said. 'Like the Bayou Strangler. Do you think that's intentional?'

'If it was important to him that way, then I think he would have killed her with it.'

Shuddering a little at the thought, Annie hugged herself and wandered back into the living room. She hit the power button on her small stereo system in the bookcase, conjuring up a bluesy piano number. On the other side of the French doors the rain was still coming down. Softer, though. The bulk of the storm had moved on to Lafayette. Lightning ran across the northern sky in a neon web.

'Why did you go to Renard's Saturday, Nick?' she asked, watching his reflection in the glass. 'He could have had you arrested. Why risk that?'

'I don't know.'

'Sure you do.' She glanced at him over her shoulder, surprised as always by the brilliance of his sudden smile.

'You're learning, 'tite fille,' he said, wagging a finger at her as he came to stand beside her.

He pulled open one of the doors and breathed deeply of the cool air.

'I went to the house where Pam died,' he said, sobering. 'And then I went to see how her killer was living.

'Outrage is a voracious beast, you know. It needs to be fueled on a regular basis or eventually it dies out. I don't want it to die out. I want to hold it in my fist like a beating heart. I want to hate him. I want him punished.'

'What if he didn't do it?'

'He did. You know he did. *I* know he did.'

'I know he's guilty of something,' Annie said. 'I know he was obsessed with her. I believe he stalked her. His thought process frightens me – the way he justifies, rationalizes, turns things around. So subtle, so smooth most people would never even notice. I believe he could have killed her. I believe he probably killed her.

'On the other hand, someone tried to kill Lindsay Faulkner the very night she called to tell me something that might be pertinent to the case. And now someone's tried to kill me, and it wasn't Renard.'

'Keep the threads separate or you end up with a knot, 'Toinette,' Nick said sharply. 'One: You got a rapist running around loose. He chose Faulkner because she fit his pattern. Two: You've got a personal enemy in Mullen. He wants to scare you, maybe hurt you a little. Say he follows you over to Renard's and this gets him crazy – you not only turned on one of your own, you're consorting with the enemy. It pushed him over the line.'

'Maybe,' Annie conceded. 'Or maybe I'm making somebody nervous, poking around this case. Maybe Lindsay remembered something about Donnie and those land deals. You're the one who drew the possible connection between Donnie and Marcotte,' she reminded him. 'You're willing to look at that, but only in how it relates *after* the murder. Leave yourself open to possibilities, Detective, or you might shut the door on a killer.'

'I've considered the possibilities. I still believe Renard killed her.'

'Of course you do, because if Renard isn't the killer, then what does that make you? An avenging angel without motive is just a thug. Justice dispensed on an innocent man is injustice. If Renard isn't a criminal, then you are.'

The same line of thinking had drawn through Nick's mind as he drove back from New Orleans, aching from the beating DiMonti's goons had given him. What if the focus he had directed at Renard prevented him from seeing other possibilities? What did that make him, indeed?

'Is that what you think of me, 'Toinette? You think I'm a criminal?'

Annie sighed. 'I believe what you did to Renard was wrong. I've always wanted to believe in the rules, but I see them getting bent every day, and sometimes I think it's bad and sometimes I think it's fine – as long as I like the outcome. So what does that make me?'

'Human,' he said, staring out at the night. 'The rain's stopped.'

He went out onto the balcony. Annie followed, bare feet on the cool wet planks. To the north the sky was opaque with storm clouds. To the south, starlight studded the Gulf sky like diamonds.

'What are you gonna do about the Cadillac Man?' Nick asked. 'You didn't call it in.'

'I have a feeling I'd be wasting my time.' Annie swept water off the railing, pushed up the sleeves of her robe, and rested her forearms on the damp wood. 'No one in the department wants to rush to my aid these days. I'm not saying they're all against me, but I'd get apathy at best.

Besides, I don't have a tag number on the car. I'm not sure about the make. I can't describe the driver.

'I'll file a report in the morning and call around to the body shops myself, see if I can find a big car with half my paint job on the side. I could probably get better odds on the Saints winning the Super Bowl.'

'I'll check out Mullen's alibi,' Nick offered. 'It's time I had a little chat with him, anyhow.'

'Thanks.'

'I saw Stokes tonight. He says the Faulkner woman is stable but still unconscious.'

Annie nodded. 'She saw him over lunch yesterday. Did he say anything about that?'

'No.'

'Did he say anything about me?'

'That you're a pain in the ass. Same old, same old. Do you think she might have said something to him about you digging around?'

'I don't see why she wouldn't have. When I saw her Sunday, she told me she'd sooner deal with Stokes. She wasn't happy about me saving Renard's hide. So she sees Stokes over lunch, presumably to tell him something about Pam. Then she calls me that night: apologetic, wants to get together.'

'Why the change of heart?'

'I don't know. Maybe Stokes didn't think what she had to say was important. But if she *did* mention me, why didn't he call me on it?' she asked. 'I don't get that. This afternoon he told me to stay away from his cases, but why wouldn't he go to the sheriff? He knows I'm already in trouble. He might have a chance of getting me suspended. Why wouldn't he go for it?'

'But if he tells Noblier, that opens a can of worms for him too, sugar,' Nick said. 'If it looks like he's not working the case hard enough, maybe Gus takes it away from him – especially now that Stokes has the rape task force. He doesn't want to give up the Bichon homicide any more than I did.'

'Yeah ... I guess that makes sense.' She tried to shrug off her uneasiness. 'Maybe Lindsay didn't say anything. I guess I won't know 'til she comes around. *If* she comes around. I hope she comes around. I wish I knew what she wanted to tell me.'

The sounds of the night settled around them – wind in the trees, a splash in the water, the staccato *quock* of a black-crowned night heron out on one of the willow islands. The air was ripe with the smell of green growth and fish and mud.

Odd, Annie thought as she watched Fourcade watch the night, these brief stretches of calm quiet that sometimes lay between them, as if they were old partners, old friends. Other moments the air around them crackled with electricity, sexuality, temper, suspicion. Volatile, unstable, like the atmosphere in a newly forming world. The description fit both Fourcade and whatever was growing between them.

'This is where you grew up,' he said.

'Yeah. Once, when I was eight, I tied a rope to that corner post and tried to rappel down to the ground. I kicked in a screen down below and landed smack in the middle of a table of tourists from France.'

He chuckled. 'Destined for trouble from an early age.'

His words brought an unexpected image of her mother, coming here alone and pregnant, never revealing to anyone the father of her child. She had been trouble from conception, apparently. Every once in a while she felt a pinch of guilt for that, even though she'd had no say in the matter. The pain bloomed quick and bright, like a drop of blood from the prick of a thorn.

Nick watched as melancholy came over her like a veil and wondered at its source, wondered if that source was the reason she preferred the surface to the depths of life. He felt a sadness at the sudden absence of her usual spark. Was it that surface light in her that attracted him or the reserves of strength she had yet to tap?

'Me, I grew up out that way,' he said, pointing off to the southeast. 'The middle of nowhere was the center of my world. At least until I was twelve.'

Annie was surprised that he had offered the information. She tried to picture him as a carefree swamp kid, but couldn't.

'How did you go from there to here?' she asked.

The expression in his eyes turned remote and reflective. His voice sounded road-weary. 'The long way.'

'I actually thought you might have died last night,' she admitted belatedly.

'Disappointed?'

'No.'

'Some folks would be. Marcotte, Renard, Smith Pritchett.' He thought back to the comment Stokes had made that afternoon. 'What about Mr Doucet with the DA's office?'

'A.J.?' she said, looking puzzled. 'What's he got to do with you?'

'What's he got to do with *you*?' Nick asked. 'Rumor has it you're an item, you and Mr Deputy DA.'

'Oh, that,' Annie said, cringing inwardly. 'He'd blow a gasket if he knew you were here.'

'Because of what I did to Renard? Or because of what I did with you?'

'Both.'

'And on the second count: Does he have cause?'

'He would say yes.'

'I'm asking you,' Nick said, holding his breath as he waited for her answer.

'No,' she said softly. 'I'm not sleeping with him, if that's what you're asking.'

'That's what I'm asking, 'Toinette,' he said. 'Me, I don't like to share.'

'That's not to say I think this is such a great idea, Nick,' Annie admitted. 'I'm not saying I regret tonight. I don't. I *should*.' She sighed and tried again. 'It's just that . . . Look at the situation we're in. It's complicated enough, and – and – I don't just *do* this kind of thing, you know –'

'I know.' He stepped closer, settling his hands on her hips, wanting to touch her, to lay claim in a basic way. 'Neither do I.'

'I sure as hell shouldn't be doing it with you. I –'

He pressed a forefinger to her lips, silencing her. 'This isn't about the case. This has nothing to do with what happened with Renard. Understand?'

'But –'

'It's about attraction, need, desire. You felt it that night at Laveau's. So did I. Before any of the rest of this ever started. It's a separate issue. It has to make its own sense outside the context of the situation we're in. You can accept it or you can say no. What do you want, 'Toinette?'

Annie moved away from him. 'It must be nice to be so sure of everything,' she said. 'Who's guilty. Who's innocent. What you want. What I know. Aren't you ever confused, Nick? Aren't you ever uncertain? I am. You were right – I'm in over my head, and if one more thing weighs me down, I'll never come up for air.'

She looked for a reaction but his face was as impassive as granite.

'You want me to go?' he asked.

'I think what I want and what's best are two different things.'

'You want me to go.'

'No,' she said in exasperation. 'That's not what I *want*.'

He came toward her then, serious, purposeful, predatory. 'Then we'll deal with the rest later because I'm telling you, *chère*, I *know* what I want.'

Then he kissed her, and Annie let his certainty sweep them both away. He carried her back inside, back to bed, leaving the balcony an empty stage with an audience of one shrouded in shadows of midnight.

'I saw her with him.
    Touching him.
    Kissing him.
    THE WHORE.
    She has no loyalty. Just like before. It made me wish I had killed her.
    Love.
        Passion.
            Greed.
                Anger.
                    Hatred.
    Around and around the feelings spin, a red blur.
    You know, sometimes I can't tell one from the other. I have no power over them. They have all power over me. I wait for their verdict.
    Only time will tell.'

32

The black of the night sky was fading to navy in the east when Nick let himself out of Annie's apartment. He didn't want anyone finding him here come first light. Which was why he had parked his truck on a secluded boat landing off the levee road a quarter mile away. If word leaked of an association between the defendant and the key witness in the brutality case, there would be hell to pay for both of them.

He didn't wake Annie. He had no desire to wrestle with more questions. She had needed him, he had wanted her – it was as simple and as complex as that.

He didn't want to wonder where it would go from here. He didn't want to wonder why Antoinette, of all women, when he had allowed himself no woman in longer than he could remember. He had spent the last year trying to rebuild himself. There had been nothing left to give beyond what he gave to the job. He wouldn't have said he had anything to give now, when he was backed into yet another corner and in danger of losing not only his career but his identity. And yet, he found himself drawn to this woman. His accuser.

Antoinette, young, fresh, unspoiled. He was none of those things. Was that it? Did he simply want to touch something good and clean? Or was it about redemption or salvation or coercion?

'*Aren't you ever confused, Nick? Aren't you ever uncertain?*'

'All the time, *chère*,' he whispered as he drove away.

There was only one Mullen listed in the Bayou Breaux phone book. K. Mullen Jr lived a block north of the cane mill in a clapboard house built in the fifties and painted once since. Trees kept the lawn as sparse as an adolescent boy's beard. The garage sat back from the house; a bass boat and a Chevy truck were parked on the cracked concrete in front of it.

Nick walked back along the side of the building, peering into windows that hadn't been cleaned in this decade. The space was crammed with junk – old tires, a motorcycle, three lawn mowers, a mud-splattered all-terrain four-wheeler. No Cadillac. At the back of the building, a pair of speckled hunting dogs had worn two crescents of yard to dirt, pacing out to the ends of their chains to crap. The dogs lay tucked into balls between their two small shelters. They didn't crack an eye at Nick.

He went to the back door of the house and let himself in with no resistance from a lock. The kitchen was a depressing little room with dirty dishes on most of the available counter space. Junk mail was stacked up on the small table beside half a loaf of Evangeline Maid white bread, an opened sack of barbeque potato chips, and three empty long-neck bottles of Miller Genuine Draft. Mullen's Sig Sauer lay in its holster on top of the latest *Field & Stream*.

Nick searched through the cupboards and refrigerator, pulling out a cheap frying pan, eggs, butter. As the skillet was heating, he cracked eggs into a bowl, sniffed the milk to check it, then added a splash along with salt and pepper, and whipped it together with a fork. The pan gave a satisfying hiss as the liquid hit the surface.

'Hold it right there!'

Nick glanced over his shoulder. Mullen stood in the doorway in uniform trousers, a shotgun pressed into the hollow of his pasty white shoulder.

'You would hold a gun on me after you've presumed me to be your good friend?' Nick said, scraping a spatula through the bubbling eggs. 'That's bad manners, Deputy.'

'Fourcade?' Mullen lowered the gun and shuffled a little farther into the room, as if he didn't trust his eyes from a distance of five feet. 'What the hell are you doing here?'

'Me, I'm making a little breakfast,' Nick said. 'Your kitchen is a disgrace, Mullen. You know, the kitchen is the soul of the house. How you keep your kitchen is how you keep your life. Looking around here, I'd say you have no respect for yourself.'

Mullen made no comment. He laid the shotgun down on the table and scratched at his thin, greasy hair. 'Wha – ?'

'Got any coffee?'

'Why are you in my house? It's six o'clock in the goddamn morning!'

'Well, I figure we're such good friends, you won't mind. Isn't that right, Deputy?' Giving the eggs one last stir, he slid the pan from the burner, and turned around. 'Sorry, I don't have your first name down, but you know I didn't realize we were so close and so I forgot to ever give a shit about it.'

Mullen's expression was an ugly knot of perplexity. He looked like a man straining on the toilet. 'What are you talking about?'

'What'd you do last night' – Nick leaned over the table and scanned the mailing label on an envelope boasting YOUR NEW NRA STICKER ENCLOSED! – 'Keith?'

'Why?'

'It's called small talk. This is what buddies do, I'm told. Why you don't tell me all about what you did last night?'

'Went out to the gun club. Why?'

'Shot a few rounds, huh?' Nick said, dousing the eggs with Tabasco from the bottle sitting on the back of the stove. 'What'd you shoot? This handgun you've so carelessly left on your kitchen table?'

'Uh . . .'

'How about rifles? You shoot some clay?'

'Yeah.'

'You have no clean plates,' Nick announced with disapproval, picking up the frying pan by the handle. He tasted the eggs and forked up a second mouthful. 'You hear about someone taking a shot at Renard last night?'

'Yeah.' The uncertainty was still clear in his small mean eyes, but he had decided to pretend a bit of arrogance. They were *compadres* . . . maybe. He crossed his arms over his bare chest. A smirk twisted his lips, revealing crowded bad teeth. 'Too bad he missed, huh?'

'You might assume I would think that, knowing me like you do,' Nick said. 'That wasn't you trying to help justice along there, was it, Keith?'

Mullen forced a laugh. 'Hell no.'

''Cause that's against the law, don'tcha know. Now, you might say that didn't stop me the other night. Deputy Broussard stopped me.'

Mullen made a rude sound. 'That little bitch. She oughta mind her own goddamn business.'

'I hear you're trying to help her with that, no? Giving her a hard time and whatnot.'

'She don't know nothing about loyalty, turning on one of us. Cunt's got no business being in a uniform.'

Nick flinched at the obscenity, but held himself. His smile was sharp as he allowed himself to visualize swinging the frying pan like a tennis racket, Mullen's pointy head bouncing off the door frame, blood spraying from his nose and mouth.

'So, you've taken it upon yourself to avenge this wrong she committed against me,' Nick said. 'Because we're such good pals, you and me?'

'She hadn't oughta fuck with the Brotherhood.'

Nick sent the pan sailing across the kitchen like a Frisbee. It landed in the sink with a crash of glass breaking beneath it.

'Hey!' Mullen yelled.

Nick hit him hard in the chest with the heel of his hand, knocking him backward into the cupboards, and held him there, his knuckles digging into the soft hollow just below Mullen's sternum.

'I am *not* your brother,' he growled, staring into Mullen's eyes. 'The mere suggestion of a genetic tie is an insult to my family. Nor would I count you among my friends. I don't know you from something I would scrape off my shoe. And you've not impressed me here this morning, Keith, I have to say. So I think you'll understand when I tell you I take exception to you acting on my behalf.

'I fight my own battles. I take care of my own problems. I won't tolerate being used as an excuse by some redneck asshole who only wants to bully a woman. You got your own problem with Broussard – that's

1083

one thing. You drag my name into it, I'll have to hurt you. You'd be smart to just leave her alone so that I don't misinterpret. Have I made myself clear to you?'

Mullen nodded with vigor. Gasping for breath, he doubled over, rubbing his hand against his diaphragm as Nick stepped back.

'I might have guessed a man with no honor would keep his kitchen this way.' Nick shook his head as he took in the sorry state of the room one last time. 'Sad.'

Mullen looked up at him. 'Fuck you. You're just as fuckin' nuts as everyone says, Fourcade.'

Nick flashed a crocodile smile. 'Don't sell me short, Keith. I'm way crazier than people think. You'd do well to remember that.'

Annie had watched his truck go down the bayou road. A hollow feeling yawned in the middle of her. She didn't fall into bed with men she barely knew. She could count her lovers on one hand and have most of her fingers left over. Why Fourcade?

Because somewhere in the dark labyrinth that was Fourcade's personality there was a man worthy of more than what his past had dealt him. He believed in justice, a greater good, a higher power. He had destroyed his career for a fourteen-year-old dead girl no one else in the world cared about.

He had beaten a suspect bloody right before her very eyes. His hearing was little more than a week away.

'God, Broussard,' she groaned, 'the things you get into . . .'

Last night might have been about wanting and needing, but the future wasn't so simple. Fourcade could pretend to separate the attraction from the rest of it, but what would happen when she got up on the witness stand at his hearing and told the court she'd seen him commit a felony? And she *would* take the stand. Whatever feelings she had for him now didn't change what had happened or what would happen. She had a duty – to burn a cop on behalf of a killer.

Rubbing her temples, Annie went back into the apartment, pulled on a pair of shorts and a T-shirt, and went through her routine with the energy of a slug. She returned home from her run to the depressing sight of her half-trashed Jeep in the lot and A.J. sitting on the gallery.

He was already dressed for the office in a smart pin-striped suit and a crisp white shirt, his burgundy tie fluttering as he leaned forward with his forearms on his thighs. His eyes were on her, a ghost of a hopeful smile curved his mouth.

At that moment he'd never been more handsome to Annie, never more dear. It broke her heart to think she was going to hurt him.

'Glad to see you in one piece,' he said, rising as she came up the steps. 'That Jeep gave me a scare. What happened?'

'Sideswiped. No big deal. Looks worse than it was,' she lied.

He shook his head. 'Lou'siana drivers. We gotta stop giving away driver's licenses with Wheaties box tops.'

Annie found a smile for him and tugged on his tie. 'What are you doing out here at this hour?'

'This is what you get for never answering your phone messages.'

'I'm sorry. I've been busy.'

'With what? From what I hear, you've got time on your hands these days.'

She made a face. 'So you heard about my change in job description?'

'Heard you got stuck with crime dog duty.' He sobered just enough to make her nervous. 'Why didn't I hear it from you?'

'I wasn't exactly proud.'

'So? Since when do you not call me to whine and complain?' he said, his confusion plain, though he tried to smile.

Annie bit her lip and looked to the left of his shoulder. She would have given anything to wriggle out of this, but she couldn't and she knew it. Better to run through the minefield now and get it over with.

'A.J., we need to talk.'

He sucked in a breath. 'Yeah, I guess we do. Let's go upstairs.'

Images of her apartment flashed through Annie's head – the kitchen table spread with files from the Bichon case, her sheets rumpled from sex with Fourcade. She felt cheap and mean, a scarlet woman, a kicker of puppies.

'No,' she said, catching his hand. 'I need to cool off. Let's go sit on a boat.'

She chose the pontoon at the far end of the dock, grabbed a towel from the storage bin, and wiped the dew from the last aqua plastic bench seat. A.J. followed reluctantly, pausing to look at the tip box Sos had mounted near the gate – a white wooden cube with a window in front and a foot-long gator head fixed over the top hole, mouth open in a money-hungry pose. The hand-lettering on the side read: TIP'S (POURBOIRE) MERCI!

'Remember the time Uncle Sos pretended this gator bit his finger off and he had all us kids screaming?'

Annie smiled. ''Cause your cousin Sonny tried to sneak a dollar out.'

'Then old Benoit, he did the trick, only he really didn't have half his fingers. Sonny about wet himself.'

He slid onto the bench a few feet from her and reached out to touch her hand. 'We got a lotta good memories,' he said quietly. 'So why you shutting me out now, Annie? What's the deal here? You still mad at me about the Fourcade thing?'

'I'm not mad at you.'

'Then, what? We're going along fine, then all of a sudden I'm persona non grata. What –'

'What do you mean, 'going along fine'?'

'Well, you know –' A.J. struggled, clueless as to what he'd said wrong. He shrugged. 'I thought –'

'Thought what? That the last hundred times I told you we're just friends I was speaking in some kind of code?'

'Oh, come on,' he said, scowling. 'You know there's more between us –'

Annie pushed to her feet, gaping at him. 'What part of no do you not understand? You spent seven years in higher education and you can't grasp the meaning of a one-syllable word?'

'Of course I can, I just don't see that it applies to us.'

'Christ,' she muttered, shaking her head. 'You're as bad as Renard.'

'What's that supposed to mean? You're calling me a stalker?'

'I'm saying Pam Bichon told him *no* eight ways from Sunday and he just heard what he wanted to hear. How is that different from what you're doing?'

'Well, for starters, I'm not an accused murderer.'

'Don't be a smart-ass. I'm serious, A.J. I keep trying to tell you, you want something from me I can't give you! How much plainer can I make it?'

He looked away as if she'd slapped him, the muscles in his jaw flexing. 'I guess that's as plain as it gets.'

Annie sank back down on the bench. 'I don't want to hurt you, A.J.,' she said softly. 'That's the last thing I want to do. I love you –'

He barked a laugh.

'– just not in the way you need me to,' she finished.

'But see,' he said, 'we've been through this cycle before, and you come around or I come around, and then –'

Annie cut him off with a shake of her head. 'I can't do this, A.J. Not now. There's too much going on.'

'Which you won't tell me about.'

'I can't.'

'You can't tell me? Why? What's going on?'

'I can't do this,' she whispered, hating the need to keep things from him, to lie to him. Better to push him away so that he wouldn't want to know.

'I'm not the enemy, Annie!' he exploded. 'We're on the same side, for crying out loud! Why can't you tell me? *What* can't you tell me?'

She dropped her face into her hands. Allying herself with Fourcade, investigating on her own, trying to get Renard to fixate on her so she could trick him into showing the ugly truth that lay beneath his bland mask – she could no more tell A.J. any of it than she could tell Sheriff Noblier. They may all have wanted the same outcome, but they weren't all on the same side.

'Oh,' he said suddenly, as if an internal lightbulb just went on in his head, bright enough to hurt. 'Maybe you didn't mean the job. Jesus.' He huffed out a breath and looked at her sideways. 'Is there someone else? Is that where you've been lately – with some other guy?'

Annie held her breath. There was Nick, but one night did not a relationship make, and she couldn't see much hope in it lasting.

'Annie? Is that it? Is there someone else?'

'Maybe,' she hedged. 'But that's not it. That's not . . . I'm so sorry,' she said, weary of the fight. 'You can't know how much I wish I felt differently, how much I wish this could be what you want it to be, A.J. But wishing can't make it so.'

'Do I know him?'

'Oh, A.J., don't go there.'

He stood with his hands on his hips, looking away from her, his pride smarting, his logical mind working to make sense of feelings that seldom bent to the will of reason. He wasn't so different from Fourcade that way – too analytical, too rational, confounded by the vagaries of human nature. Annie wanted to put her arms around him, to offer him comfort as a friend, but knew he wouldn't allow it now. The feeling of loss was a physical pain in the center of her chest.

'I know what you want,' she murmured. 'You want a wife. You want a family. I want you to have those things, A.J., and I'm not ready to be the person to give them to you. I don't know that I'll ever be.'

He rubbed a hand across his jaw, blinked hard, checked his watch. 'You know –' He stopped to clear his throat. 'I don't have time for this conversation right now. I have to be in court this morning. I'll – ah – I'll call you later.'

'A.J. –'

'Oh – ah – Pritchett wants you in his office this afternoon. Maybe I'll see you there.'

Annie watched him walk away, stuffing a five in the alligator's mouth as he passed the tip box, her heart as heavy as a stone in her chest.

An old groundskeeper was scrubbing the toes of the Virgin Mary with a toothbrush when Annie wheeled into Our Lady of Mercy. Across the street, a woman smoking a pipe was selling cut flowers out of the back of a rusty Toyota pickup. Annie parked in the visitors' lot and climbed across the passenger's seat to let herself out of the Jeep. 'The Heap' she had decided to call it, trashed as it was. The impact of one of the collisions had jammed the driver's door shut.

'Dat ol' woman, she steal dem flowers,' the groundskeeper said, shaking the toothbrush at Annie as she passed. 'She steal 'em right out the garden at the Vet'rans Park. Me, I seen her do it. Why you don't arrest her?'

'You'll have to call the police, sir.'

His dark face squeezed tight, making his eyes pop out like Ping-Pong balls. 'You *is* the police!'

'No, sir, I'm with the sheriff's office.'

'Bah! Dogs is all dogs when you calls 'em for supper!'

'Yes, sir. Whatever that means,' Annie muttered as the doors whooshed open in front of her.

The ICU was quiet except for the sound of machines. A woman with cornrows and purple-framed glasses sat behind the desk, watching the monitors and talking on the phone. She barely glanced up as Annie passed. There was no guard at the door to Lindsay Faulkner's room. Good news, bad news, Annie thought. She didn't have to get past a uniform . . . and neither did anyone else.

Faulkner lay in her bed in the ICU looking like a science experiment gone wrong. Her head and face were swathed mummy-like in bandages. Tubes fed into her and out of her. Monitors and machines of mysterious purpose blinked and cheeped, their display screens filled with glowing medical hieroglyphics. The redhead with the expired license plates rose from her chair beside the bed as Annie approached.

'How's she doing?' Annie asked.

'Better, actually,' she said in a hushed tone. 'She's out of the coma. She's been in and out of consciousness. She's said a few words.'

'Does she know who did this to her?'

'No. She doesn't remember anything about the attack. Not yet, anyway. The other detective was already here and asked.'

Two miracles in one morning: Lindsay Faulkner conscious and Chaz Stokes out of bed before eight A.M. Maybe he was making an effort after all. Maybe the spotlight of the task force would bring out some ambition in him.

'Has she had many visitors?'

'They only allow family up here,' the redhead said. 'We haven't been able to reach her parents. They're traveling in China. Until we can get them here, the hospital has agreed to make exceptions to the rule. Belle Davidson has been in, Grace from the realty, me.'

'She'll need y'all to help her through this,' Annie said. 'She's got a long road ahead of her.'

'Don't talk . . . about me . . . like I'm not . . . here.'

At the sound of the weak voice, the redhead turned toward the bed, smiling. 'You weren't here a minute ago.'

'Ms Faulkner, it's Annie Broussard,' Annie said, leaning down. 'I came to see how you're doing.'

'You . . . found me . . . after . . .'

'Yes, I did.'

'Thank . . . you.'

'I wish I could have done more,' Annie said. 'There's a whole task force looking for the guy who did this to you.'

'You . . . on it?'

'No. I've been reassigned. Detective Stokes is in charge. I hear you had lunch with him the other day. Did you have something to tell him about Pam? Was that why you called me Monday?'

The silence stretched so long Annie thought perhaps consciousness had ebbed away from her again. The sounds of the monitors filled the cubicle. Annie started to draw back from the bed.

'Donnie,' Faulkner whispered.

'What about Donnie?'

'Jealous.'

'Jealous of who?' Annie asked, bending close.

'Stupid . . . It wasn't anything.'

She was slipping away. Annie touched Faulkner's arm in an attempt to maintain her connection to the waking world.

'Who was Donnie jealous of, Lindsay?'

The silence hung again, like a cold breath in the air.

'Detective Stokes.'

1089

33

Donnie was jealous of Stokes. Annie let her brain chew on that while she sorted through the faxes in the tray, pulling the one she'd requested from the DMV – a listing of trucks with Louisiana plates containing the partial sequence *EJ*.

It wasn't difficult to envision Stokes flirting with Pam. In fact, it would have been impossible not to. That was what Stokes did: spent his every spare moment honing his seduction skills. He considered it his duty to flirt with women. And, according to what Lindsay Faulkner had said Sunday, Pam brought out those qualities in men without even trying. Men were attracted to Pam, found her charming and sweet. Chaz Stokes would never be the exception to that rule.

With the stalking an ongoing thing, he would have had ample cause to see Pam on a fairly regular basis. Had Donnie gotten the wrong idea about the two of them? And what would he have done about it if he had? Confront Stokes? Confront Pam?

If Stokes knew Donnie was jealous, then he would certainly have examined that angle when Pam was murdered. She could check the statements tonight, ask Nick about it. Renard had alleged Pam was afraid of Donnie, was afraid to see another man socially because of what Donnie might do. Donnie had threatened a custody fight, as though he had grounds for challenging Pam's rights. But it wasn't as if Pam had been seeing Stokes in a social way.

Was it?

'*Stupid,*' Lindsay Faulkner had said. '*It wasn't anything.*'

But Donnie had thought otherwise. Had he heard what he wanted to hear, interpreted the situation to suit – or to rouse – his temper? Annie had seen a hundred examples in domestic abuse cases – the imagined slights, the phantom lovers, the contrived grounds for anger. Excuses to lash out, to hurt, to belittle, to punish.

No one had ever accused Donnie of abuse, but that didn't mean his mind didn't bend the same way. Pam had bruised his ego openly, publicly, kicking him out of their house, filing for divorce, trying to separate the companies. An imagined affair with Stokes might have pushed him over the edge.

He had said something derogatory about Stokes when she'd spoken with him Saturday, hadn't he? Something about Stokes being lazy. The remark had seemed almost racist, an attitude that would have yanked Stokes's chain, and rightly so. He would have been on Donnie like a pit bull. But Marcus Renard was the suspect Stokes had in his crosshairs.

She was giving herself an unnecessary headache. Nick was probably right. If she didn't keep the individual strands separate, she would end up with a knot – around her own neck. She had Renard on the hook, just the way Fourcade had predicted. If she kept her focus, she could reel him in. She decided she would swing by the hospital again at lunch and see if Lindsay could identify the scarf Renard had sent Pam.

'There is no time for dawdling, Deputy Broussard!' Myron pronounced, marching to his post with all the starch of a palace guard. 'We have our orders for the morning. Detective Stokes needs the arrest records for every man accused of a violent sexual crime in this parish dating back ten years. I will call up the list on the computer, you will then pull the files. I will log them out, you will deliver them to the task force in the detectives' building.'

'Yes, sir, Mr Myron,' Annie said with a plastic smile, sliding the fax from the DMV under her blotter.

They worked quickly, but interruptions of usual records division business dragged the task out – calls from the courthouse, calls from insurance companies, filling out the intake form on a newly arrested burglar, checking in evidence against the same burglar, checking out evidence for the trial of a suspected drug dealer.

All of it was tedious and Annie resented it mightily. She wanted to be the one receiving the files instead of the one digging for them through decades of filed-away crap. She wanted to be on the task force instead of in the paper trenches. Even working with Stokes would have been preferable to working with Myron the Monstrous.

Lunch was ten minutes with a Snickers bar and a telephone pressed to her ear, checking the local garages for any big sedans with passenger-side damage. She found none. Her adversary either had stashed the car or had taken it out of the parish for repairs. She checked the log sheet for recently stolen vehicles and found nothing to match. Expanding the parameters of her search, she started in on the list of garages in St Martin Parish.

'Hey, Broussard,' Mullen barked, leaning over the counter. 'Knock off the hen party and do your job, why don't you.'

Annie glared at him as she thanked another mechanic for nothing and hung up the phone.

'This task force is priority one,' Mullen said, puffing his bony chest out.

'Yeah? Well, how'd you get on it? You got pictures of the sheriff naked with a goat?'

He smirked, much too pleased with himself. 'I guess on account of my work on the Nolan rape.'

'Your work,' Annie said with disdain. 'I caught that call.'

'Yeah, well, you win some, you lose some.'

'You know, Mullen,' she muttered, 'I'd tell you to eat shit and die, but by the smell of your breath I guess it's already a staple of your diet.'

She expected him to snap at the bait, but he leaned back from her instead. 'Look, can I get the rest of those files now? As for our little feud, let's just let that go. No hard feelings.'

'No hard feelings?' Annie repeated. She leaned toward him, holding her voice low and taut. 'You terrorize me, threaten me, cost me a small fortune in damages, cost me my patrol. I'm standing back here playing a glorified goddamn secretary while you're making hay on a case that should have been mine, and you say *no hard feelings*?'

'You son of a bitch. Hard feelings are the only kind I've got right now. You'd better believe I find so much as a paint chip connecting you to that Cadillac or whatever the hell it was you tried to kill me with last night, I'll have your badge *and* your bony ass.'

'Cadillac?' Mullen looked confused. 'I don't know what you're talking about, Broussard. I don't know nothing about no Cadillac!'

'Yeah, right.'

'I didn't do nothing to you!'

'Oh, save the act,' Annie sneered. 'Take your files and get out of here.'

She gave the folders a shove and sent them over the edge of the counter, raining arrest reports all over the floor.

'Goddammit!' Mullen yelled, drawing Hooker out of his office.

'Jesus H., Mullen!' he shouted. 'You got a nerve condition or something? You got something wrong with your motor skills?'

'No, sir,' he said tightly, glaring at Annie. 'It was an accident.'

'South Lou'siana is traditionally a place of folk justice,' Smith Pritchett preached, strolling along the credenza in his office, his hands planted at his thick waist. 'The Cajuns had their own code here before organized law enforcement and judicial agencies provided a mitigating influence. The common mind here still makes a distinction between the law and justice. I am well aware that a great many people in this parish feel that Detective Fourcade's attack on Marcus Renard was an acceptable way to cure a particular social problem. However, they would be mistaken.'

Annie watched him with barely disguised impatience. This was likely the rough draft of his opening statement for Fourcade's trial, which would be weeks or months away if he was bound over. She sat in Pritchett's visitor's chair. A.J. stood across the room, arms crossed, back against the bookcase, ignoring the empty chair four feet away from her. His expression was closed tight. He hadn't spoken a word in the ten minutes she'd been here.

'People can't be allowed to take the law into their own hands,' Pritchett continued. 'We'd end up with chaos, anarchy, law*less*ness.'

The progression and conclusion pleased him enough that he paused to jot them down on a pad on his desk.

'The system is in place to mark boundaries, to draw a firm line and hold the people to it,' he said. 'There is no room for exceptions. You believe that, Deputy Broussard, or you would never have gone into law enforcement – isn't that right?'

'Yes, sir. I believe that's been established, and I've already given my statement to –'

'Yes, you have, and I have a copy right here.' He tapped his pen against a file folder. 'But I feel it's important for us to get to know each other, Annie. May I call you Annie?'

'Look, I have a job –'

'I understand you've been having some difficulties with other members of the department,' he said with fatherly concern as he perched a hip on a corner of his desk.

Annie shot a glance at A.J. 'Nothing I can't handle –'

'Is someone trying to coerce you? Dissuade you from testifying against Detective Fourcade?'

'Not in so many wor –'

'While a certain reticence on your part would be understandable here, Annie, I want to impress upon you the necessity and the importance of your testimony in this matter.'

'Yes, sir. I'm aware of that, sir. I –'

'Has Detective Fourcade himself approached you?'

'Detective Fourcade has made no attempt to keep me from testifying. I –'

'And Sheriff Noblier? Has he instructed you in any way?'

'I don't know what you mean,' Annie said, holding herself stiff against the urge to squirm.

'He's been less than cooperative in this matter. Which is a sad commentary on the effects of his tenure in office, I'm afraid. Gus thinks this parish is his little kingdom and he can make up the rules to suit himself, but that isn't so. The law is the law and it applies to everyone – detectives, sheriffs, deputies.'

'Yes, sir.'

He stepped around behind the desk and slid into his leather chair. Slipping on a pair of steel-rimmed reading glasses, he pulled her statement from the folder and glanced over it.

'Now, Annie, you were off duty that night, but A.J. tells me your personal vehicle is equipped with a police scanner and a radio, is that correct?'

'Yes, sir.'

'He tells me the two of you had a pleasant dinner at Isabeau's that evening.' He glanced up at her with another indulgent, fatherly smile. 'A very romantic setting. My wife's personal favorite.'

Annie said nothing. She thought she could feel A.J.'s stare burning into her. While it seemed he had told Pritchett everything else about their relationship, he hadn't told him it was over. Pritchett was trying to use it as leverage to shift her loyalties. Slimy lawyer.

'Where'd you go after dinner, Annie?'

She had managed to avoid this part of the story so far. It wasn't relevant to the incident – except that Fourcade had taken a phone call and then left the bar, which might have suggested premeditation to say nothing of collusion with someone. But no one else had been beating on Renard, and Fourcade couldn't be compelled to reveal the source or the content of the call, so what was the use of talking about it?

On the other hand, there were witnesses who could place her at Laveau's.

'I saw Detective Fourcade's truck across the street at Laveau's. I went to have a few words with him about what had happened at the courthouse.'

Pritchett looked at A.J., clearly unhappy at being taken by surprise. 'Why wasn't this in your statement, Deputy?'

'Because it preceded the incident and had no bearing on it.'

'What condition was Fourcade in?'

'He'd been drinking.'

'Was he aggressive, angry, antagonistic?'

'No, sir, he was . . . unhappy, morose, philosophical.'

'Did he speak about Renard? Threaten him?'

'No. He talked about justice and injustice.' And shadows and ghosts.

'Did he give any indication he was going to seek Renard out?'

'No.'

Pritchett pulled his glasses off and nibbled thoughtfully on an earpiece. 'What happened next?'

'We went our separate ways. I decided to stop at the Quik Pik for a few things. The rest is in my report and in the statement I gave Chief Earl.'

'Did you at any time pick up a call on your scanner regarding a suspected prowler in the vicinity of Bowen & Briggs?'

'No, sir, but I was out of the vehicle for several minutes, and then I had the regular radio on for a while and the scanner turned down. I was off duty, it was late.'

Silence hung like dust motes in the air. Annie picked at a broken cuticle and waited. Pritchett's chair squeaked as he rose.

'Do you believe there was a call, Deputy?'

If he asked her this question in court, Fourcade's attorney would object before the whole sentence was out of his mouth. *Calls for speculation.* But they weren't in court. The only person in the room who objected was Annie.

'I didn't hear the call,' she said. 'Other people did.'

'Other people *say* they did,' he corrected her. His voice rose with every syllable. He bent over and planted his hands on the arms of Annie's chair, his face inches from hers. 'Because Gus Noblier *told them* to say that they did. Because they want to protect a man who blew a major case, then took it upon himself to execute the suspect he couldn't outsmart!

'There was no call,' he said softly, pushing himself back. He sat against the desk again, his eyes on her every second. 'Did you arrest Fourcade that night and take him into custody?'

What difference did it make when the arrest had been made? What would it change? Fourcade was up on charges. Pritchett was simply looking for ammunition to use against Noblier, and Annie wanted no part of that feud.

She called up the words the sheriff himself had put in her mouth. 'I stumbled across a situation I didn't understand. I contained it. We went to the station to sort it out.'

'Why does Richard Kudrow claim he saw an arrest report that subsequently went missing?'

'Because he's a stinking weasel lawyer and he loves nothing better than to stir the pot.' She looked Pritchett in the eye. 'Why would you believe him? He lives to tie you up in knots in the courtroom. You can bet he's loving this – you and Noblier at each other's throats with cops in the middle.'

A small measure of satisfaction warmed her as she watched her strategy work. Pritchett pressed his lips together and moved away from the desk. The last thing he would want in the world would be having Richard Kudrow play him for a fool.

'How well do you know Nick Fourcade, Annie?' he asked, the driving force gone from his voice.

She thought of the night spent in Nick's arms, their bodies locked together. 'Not very.'

'He doesn't deserve your loyalty. And he sure as hell doesn't deserve a badge. You're a good officer, Annie. I've seen your record. And you did a good thing that night. I'm gonna trust you to do the right thing when you get up on the witness stand next week.'

'Yes, sir,' she murmured.

He checked his Rolex and turned to A.J. 'I'm needed elsewhere. A.J., would you show Annie out?'

'Of course.'

She started to get up, intending to leave on Pritchett's heels, but the door shut too quickly after him.

'He's late for his tee time,' A.J. said, not moving from the bookcase. 'Why are you lying to us, Annie?'

She flinched as if he'd spat the words in her face. 'I'm not –'

'Don't insult me,' he snapped. 'On top of everything else, don't insult me. I know you, Annie. I know everything about you. Everything. That scares you, doesn't it? That's why you're pushing me away.'

'I don't think this is the time or place for this conversation,' she muttered.

'You don't want anyone getting that deep in your soul, do you? 'Cause what if I leave or die like your mother –'

'Stop it!' Annie ordered, furious that he would use the most painful memories of her childhood against her.

'That hurts a hell of a lot more than losing someone who isn't a part of you,' he pressed on. 'Better to keep everyone at arm's length.'

'I want more than an arm's length away from you right now, A.J.,' Annie said tightly. She felt as if he had reached out unexpectedly and sliced her with a straight razor, cutting through flesh and bone.

'Why didn't you tell me you saw Fourcade earlier that night?' he asked.

'What difference does it make?'

'What difference does it make? I'm supposed to be your best friend! We had a date that night. You dumped me and went to see Fourcade –'

'That was not a date,' she argued. 'We had dinner. Period. You're my friend, not my lover. I don't have to clear my every move with you!'

'You don't get it, do you?' he said, incredulous. 'This is about trust –'

'*Whose* trust?' she demanded. 'You're giving me the goddamn third degree! One minute you claim to be my best friend and the next you're wondering why I didn't give you something you can use in court. You tell me we can separate who we are from what we do, but only when it's convenient for you. I've had it, A.J. I don't need this bullshit and I sure as hell don't need you taking potshots at my psyche!'

'Annie –'

He reached for her arm as she started for the door and she jerked away from him. The secretaries in the outer office watched with owl eyes as she stormed past.

The outer hall was dark and cool. Voices floated down from the third floor. The last of the day's court skirmishes had been fought, and the last of the warriors lingered in the hall, swapping stories and making deals. Annie headed for a side exit, letting herself out into sunshine that hurt her eyes. She fumbled with her sunglasses, then nearly ran into a man standing at the edge of the sidewalk.

'Deputy Broussard. This is serendipitous, I must say.'

Annie groaned aloud. *Kudrow*. He stood leaning against a *Times-Picayune* vending machine, his trench coat belted tightly around him despite the unseasonable heat and choking humidity of the afternoon. His posture suggested pain rather than laziness. His emaciated face was the color of a mushroom and glossed with perspiration. He looked as if he might die on the spot, draped over a headline heralding the approach of Mardi Gras.

'Are you all right?' Annie asked, torn between concern for him as a human and dislike of him as a person.

Kudrow tried to smile as he straightened. 'No, my dear, I am dying, but I won't be doing it here if that's what concerns you. I'm not quite ready to go just yet. There are still injustices to be corrected. You know all about that, don't you?'

'I'm not in the mood for your word games, lawyer. If you have something to say to me, then say it. I've got better things to do.'

'Like searching for Marcus's alibi witness? Marcus has told me you've taken an interest in his plight. How fascinating. This falls outside the scope of your duties, doesn't it?'

How much damage could he do with that knowledge? Sweat pooled between her shoulder blades and trickled down the valley of her spine. 'I'm looking into a couple of things out of curiosity, that's all.'

'A thirst for the truth. Too bad no one else in your department seems to share that quality. There's no evidence anyone is so much as looking into last night's shooting incident at the Renard home.'

'Maybe there's nothing to find.'

'Two people have openly tried to do Marcus harm in a week's time. Numerous others have threatened him. The list of suspects could read like the phone book, yet to my knowledge no one has been questioned.'

'The detectives are very busy these days, Mr Kudrow.'

'They'll have another homicide on their hands if they let this go,' he warned. 'This community is wound tighter than a watch spring. I can feel the air thickening with anger, with fear, with hate. That kind of pressure can only be contained to a point, then it explodes.'

A tight, rattling cough shook him and he leaned against the vending machine again, his energy spent, his eyes growing dull; an ill spectre of doom.

Annie walked away from him knowing he was right, feeling that same heaviness in the air, the same sense of anticipation. Even in the sunshine everything looked rimmed in black, like in a bad dream. Down the side street she could see city workers hanging pretty spring flags on the light poles, sprucing up the town for the Mardi Gras Carnival, but the sidewalks seemed strangely empty. There was no one in the park south of the law enforcement center.

Three women had been attacked in a span of a week. Cops were acting like criminals, and a suspected murderer had gone free. People were terrified.

Annie thought back to the summer the Bayou Strangler had hunted here, and remembered having the same uneasy feeling, the same irrational fear, the same sense of helplessness. But this time she was a cop, and all the other emotions were being compressed by the weight of responsibility.

Someone had to make it stop.

Myron welcomed her back to the records office with a pointed stare he directed from Annie to the clock.

'This gentleman from Allied Insurance needs a number of accident reports,' he said, nodding to a round mound of sweating flesh in rumpled seersucker on the opposite side of the counter. 'You will get him whatever he needs.'

On that order he took up his *Wall Street Journal* and marched off to the men's room.

'That's the best dang thing I've heard all day!' the insurance man chortled. He stuck out a hand that looked like a small balloon animal. 'Tom O'Connor. Easy to remember,' he said with a smarmy wink. 'Tomcat O'round the Corner. Get it?'

Annie passed on the handshake. 'I get it. What reports did you need?'

He pulled a crumpled list from his coat pocket and handed it to her. 'Hey, aren't you cute in that uniform! You look like a little lady deputy.'

'I *am* a deputy.'

His eyes popped and he let loose another volley of chuckles. 'Well, shoot me dead!'

'Don't tempt me,' Annie said. 'I'm armed and it's been a very bad day.'

She looked up to heaven as she took the list to the file cabinets. 'Purgatory is a clerical department, isn't it?'

As she sent Tom O'Connor on his way with his reports, the fax machine rang and kicked on. Annie watched the cover sheet roll out, her interest piquing at the letterhead – the regional crime lab in New Iberia. The transmission was addressed to Det. Stokes, but the fax number was for records instead of for the detectives' machine – one digit off.

She watched the sheets roll into the tray, plucking them up one at a time. Preliminary lab results on the meager physical evidence collected at Lindsay Faulkner's crime scene and from Lindsay Faulkner's person. Negative. Nothing from the rape kit – no semen, no hair, no skin from under her nails, though they knew she'd put up a fight. Blood samples from the carpet runner appeared to be hers. Same type, at least. More sophisticated tests for DNA would take weeks.

Just as Stokes had predicted, they had nothing, just as they had nothing from the Jennifer Nolan rape or the Kay Eisner rape. Lack of evidence was the one thing tying the cases together. And the black feather mask – if the fragment Annie had picked off Faulkner's rug matched the one she'd found at Nolan's trailer park. Nolan and Eisner had both seen their assailant, had both seen the mask. So far, Lindsay Faulkner remembered nothing. If that situation didn't improve, then the feather from the mask could be the only link to the other attacks.

She looked back through the transmission for mention of the feather, finding none. There should have been a note, at least.

Annie glanced at the clock. Myron would be another five minutes in men's room seclusion. The world's official timekeepers could have set their watches by Myron's bowels. She dialed the number for the lab from her desk and connected with the person she needed, rattling off the case number and what she was after.

She waited, scanning through the fax pages, frustrated by the lack of evidence. They had to be dealing with a pro, someone savvy enough and cold enough to force the women to wash away all trace evidence or, in the case of Lindsay Faulkner, to wash it away himself. He knew everything they would look for, down to pubic hairs and skin under the fingernails.

She wondered if the task force had gleaned anything from the old files, wondered if Stokes had heard back from the state pen, wondered if the NCIC or VICAP computers would come up with anything. She wished she was the person who would be finding out instead of the person waiting on sweaty insurance guys in the records department.

'Excuse me?' the woman's voice came back on the line. 'You said a black feather, didn't you?'

'Yes. There was one with the Nolan case, and what might have been a fragment of a black feather with the Faulkner case.'

'Not here, there isn't.'

'What do you mean?'

'I mean, I'm looking right at the inventories and I don't see any feathers. They were never logged in here. Sorry.'

Annie thanked the woman and hung up.

'No feathers,' she murmured as Myron marched back into the office.

'Deputy Broussard, what are you mumbling about?' he demanded.

Paying no attention to him, Annie went to the drawer at the counter and pulled the evidence card for the Faulkner case. She ran her finger down the inventory of items. The black feather-like fiber was listed fourth. The last name on the chain of custody list was Det. Chs. Stokes, who had signed out the entire list of items for the purpose of turning them over to the lab for examination.

She pulled the card for Nolan and ran her finger down the lines. The feather had been listed. The evidence had been checked out to Stokes for the purpose of turning it over to the lab. But the lab had no record of any feathers being checked in.

'What are you doing?' Myron asked, snatching the card from her fingers and squinting at it.

Annie grabbed the fax sheets from her desk and started for the door.

'Where do you think you're going?' the clerk demanded.

'To see Detective Stokes. He's got some explaining to do.'

34

The detectives had their own building across the alley from the main facility. Known affectionately as the Pizza Hut for the volume of pepperoni with extra cheese pies delivered there on a regular basis, it was a low, snot green cinder-block job that had once been office space for a road construction outfit. The sheriff's office had bought the property, converted the parking yard for the heavy equipment into an impound lot, and given the building to a detective division that had outgrown its allotted space in the aging law enforcement center.

Annie buzzed the door and was let in by the detective named Perez, his name spelled out in Magic Marker across the front of the Kevlar vest he wore over a T-shirt. His dark hair was scraped back into a short rattail. The mustache that covered his upper lip was bushy enough to hide small rodents. He gave Annie a sour once-over.

'I need to see Stokes.'

'You got a warrant?'

'Screw you, Perez.'

As she walked past him, he cupped a hand around his mouth and shouted, 'Hey, Chaz, you got the right to remain silent!'

The building was as cold as a walk-in freezer. Two window air conditioners groaned at the effort to maintain the temperature while electric fans blew the chilled air around the single front room. The room that had been given over to the rape task force was at the back. It had probably been the construction foreman's office at one time. A twelve-by-twelve cube paneled in cheap wood grain. Someone had started a soda can pyramid on the ledge of the barred window. The files Annie and Myron had gathered were strewn in haphazard piles over the long table that was the room's main piece of furniture. The hard-driving Cajun-spiced rock of Sonny Landreth's 'Shootin' for the Moon' was wailing out of a boom box on top of a corner file cabinet.

Mullen was on the phone. Stokes pranced behind the table, playing air guitar and mouthing lyrics, his crumpled porkpie hat tipped back on his head.

Annie rolled her eyes. 'Oh yeah, the women of this parish will sleep better knowing you're on the job, Stokes.'

He swung toward her. 'Broussard, you are a boil on the butt of my day. You know what I'm saying?'

'Like I care.' She held the faxes up. 'Your preliminary lab results on Faulkner. Where's the feather?'

He snatched the papers away from her and scanned them, frowning.

'Don't bother to pretend you're looking for it in there,' Annie said. 'The lab says they've never seen it or the one from the Nolan scene. I want to know why.'

Mullen still had the phone receiver pressed to his head, but his eyes were on them.

'Man, I need this like I need root canal,' Stokes muttered, turning for the back door.

Annie followed him out. The area behind the building was a wasteland of crushed shell, rock, and weeds with a view of the abandoned junkers in the impound lot.

'What'd you do with them, Chaz?' she demanded.

'I told you to keep your nose out of my cases,' he snapped, thrusting a finger at her.

'So you can feel free to fuck up with impunity?'

'Shut up!' he shouted, charging her. 'Shut the fuck up!'

Annie backpedaled into the side of the building.

'I'm just about half past sick of your shit, Broussard,' he snarled, his face inches from hers. His pale eyes were neon-bright with temper. The tendons in his neck stood out like iron rods. 'I know what I'm doing. How do you think I got this job? You think I got this job 'cause I'm browner than you? You think I skated in on my color?'

Annie glared right back at him. 'No. I think you got it because you're a man and you're full of bullshit. You talk a big game, and when somebody calls you on it, then they're suddenly a racist. I've had it up to my back teeth with that game. I don't hear Quinlan calling anybody a racist. I don't hear Ossie Compton calling anybody a racist. I don't hear anybody but you, and what you got is barely a suntan.'

She ducked under the arm he had braced against the building, and backed away from him. 'You're a jerk. You'd be a jerk if you were snow white. You'd be a jerk if you looked like Mel Gibson. End of topic. I want to know what you did with the evidence I collected. You can tell me or we can take it to the sheriff.'

Stokes paced, trying to school his temper or weigh his options or both. 'Don't you threaten me, Broussard,' he muttered. 'You're nothing but a little prick-teaser troublemaker.'

'Gus is still in his office,' Annie bluffed. 'I could have gone straight to him, you know.'

And run the risk of not only looking like a fool but renewing every hard feeling the men held toward her. Stokes would say the same thing to Gus he'd just said to her. He'd call her a troublemaker, and there wasn't a soul in the department who wouldn't believe him on some level.

'You dumped evidence,' she prodded, not wanting to give him time to think. 'What possible excuse do you have for that?'

'I didn't dump nothing,' he growled. 'The feathers went to the state lab.'

'Where's the receipt?'

'Fuck you! I don't have to answer to you, Broussard! Who the fuck do you think you are?'

'Maybe I'm the only person paying attention,' Annie shot back. 'Why would you send everything to New Iberia except the feathers?'

'Because I know a guy in the state lab and he owes me a favor. That's why. They got some brainiac fibers expert can look at a feather and tell if it came off a duck's ass in Outer Mongolia. So I sent him the goddamn feathers *and* the mask from the Bichon homicide. For all the good that'll do us.

'Those damn masks are a dime a dozen. What are we gonna do? Track down every manufacturer in Bumfuck, Thailand, and ask them what? Go to every five-and-dime and cheap-shit souvenir shop in South Lou'siana and ask them if they sold any masks to rapists? A hundred goddamn miles of legwork that'll get us jack shit.'

'Unless the feathers match up,' Annie said. 'Then you might be able to tie the first two rapes to Faulkner, at least. Even just by a thread would be more than you've got now. Faulkner doesn't remember anything about the attack. She may never.'

She knew instantly she'd made a mistake. Stokes's posture tightened, his gaze turned cold and hard.

'How do you know that?' he asked quietly.

Oh, shit. Annie jumped in with both feet. 'I went to see her this morning.'

'Fuckin' *A!*' Stokes shouted in disbelief. Then his voice dropped to a near whisper, and yet it skated sharply across Annie's nerves. 'You just do not listen, do you, bitch?

'This is *my* case,' he said, thumping a fist to his chest. 'I *will* make it. I don't have to answer to you. I find out you called the state lab to check my story, I'll haul your ass into Noblier's office – and if you think he isn't ready to cut you loose, you better think again, Broussard. You'll be working security at a gator farm by the time I'm through with you.

'Faulkner is *my* vic, *my* witness. You stay the hell away from her. You stay the hell away from my cases,' he warned, poking her sternum with a forefinger. 'You stay the hell away from me.'

He went back into the building, the barred storm door hissing shut behind him. Mullen stared out the window at her. A moment later, a car's engine roared to life on the other side of the building and tires squealed on pavement. She caught a glimpse of Stokes's black Camaro as it shot past toward the bayou.

What now? Annie couldn't imagine Stokes being so diligent as to send the feathers to a specialist, but if she called the state lab to check, he'd have her ass on a platter. If he had in fact taken the feathers to Shreveport, he would have kept the receipt with the case file, and the case file was in his possession. And if he hadn't sent the feathers to the state lab?

He admitted he didn't want to do the legwork, didn't want to chase down the source of the feathers. The chance of getting anything useful out of it was too big a long shot. He didn't want the feathers to match up with the mask from the Bichon homicide because that might mean someone other than Marcus Renard killed Pam Bichon. He didn't want the work. He didn't want the headache. He didn't want to be proved wrong.

A wanderer on the path of least resistance, that was Stokes. His problem had absolutely nothing to do with his color or anyone's perception of his color. It had to do with his own perception of the world and his priorities regarding it. He would rather have spent his time playing air guitar than seeing through the tedious business of tracking down a long-shot lead. He would rather have spent his time flirting with Pam Bichon than doing the grunt work that could have proved her stalking case. He hadn't perceived her to be in danger, so why follow up on anything?

Annie wondered what else he might have screwed up – on this case and on Pam's case. What might he have overlooked when Pam was being stalked? Something that could have been used against Renard when Pam filed for the restraining order? How differently might things have turned out if someone else had caught Pam's case in the beginning – Quinlan or Perez or Nick?

Now Stokes had charge of a task force that could affect the lives of any number of women. They were up against a criminal who knew the system, knew procedure, had left them virtually nothing at the scenes of three rapes. Only a pro would know what they needed –

Or a cop.

The idea swept a chill over her. Fear scratched at the back of her neck, and she turned her eyes on the Pizza Hut.

A cop would know exactly what went into building a rape case.

Stokes a rapist? It was crazy. He had more women than he could keep track of. But then, rape wasn't about sex. Plenty of rapists had wives or girlfriends. Rape was about anger and power. She thought of the way Stokes had looked as he charged her moments ago; the fury in his eyes. She thought of the way he had looked months ago when she had argued with him in the parking lot at the Voodoo Lounge, the hot blue flame of hate that had flared at her rejection of him.

But it was a long jump from anger to aggression to rape. It made more sense that Stokes was lazy than a sexual predator. It made more sense that their rapist was a career criminal than a career cop.

Still . . .

Stokes had control of all the evidence in three rapes that shared traits with Pam Bichon's homicide.

Stokes had investigated Pam's stalking complaints.

Donnie Bichon had been jealous of Pam's relationship with the detective. So said Lindsay Faulkner, who had met with Stokes over lunch on Monday and had her head bashed in that same night.

Donnie had been jealous of Stokes.

'*Stupid . . . It was nothing*,' Faulkner had said.

Annie wondered who might have broken that news to Stokes.

She finished her shift in clerical hell, changed clothes in her makeshift locker room, and went in search of estimates for the damage to the Heap, one eye peeled for a Cadillac with matching dents. The last of the three garages sat across the street from Po' Richard's sandwich shop.

Stomach growling, she contemplated supper. Going home this early would almost certainly mean a confrontation with Uncle Sos. She had avoided him and his questions this morning, but she wouldn't be that lucky again. He would want to know why A.J. had come and gone so quickly this morning. Going to Fourcade's place would mean what? Would they sit down and talk about what was going on between them or would they just end up in his bed, solving nothing, complicating everything?

She pulled up to the drive-through window and ordered a fried shrimp po'boy basket and a Pepsi. The kid at the window didn't recognize her. He didn't look like the type to watch the news. Shunning the picnic tables that sat out in front of the restaurant and the half-dozen people taking their suppers there, she drove down the block and parked in front of a vacant lot strewn with beer cans and broken glass. As she munched her dinner she stared out her broken window across the street to Bichon Bayou Development.

The office had been closed nearly two hours, but Donnie's Lexus sat alongside the building and a light shone in two of the windows. Why had Donnie been jealous of the time Pam spent with Stokes? Had he expected Pam to turn to him instead of to the cops during the stalking? Had that been his plan – to stalk Pam himself, frighten her anonymously, get her to turn to him, and win her back? It seemed like the kind of juvenile grand plan that would appeal to Donnie's arrested adolescent ego. And when the plan failed, he would have wanted to blame someone other than himself – Stokes, or Pam herself.

Annie picked the last shrimp from the cardboard tray and chewed it slowly, thinking of Lindsay. Faulkner disliked Donnie. *Hate* may not have been too strong a word. She may have come up with her latest revelation simply to make trouble for him. According to the receptionist at the realty, Donnie and Lindsay had argued Monday morning. Lindsay may have thought defaming Donnie would scare off his prospective buyer for the realty. And how would Donnie have reacted to that plan?

If he was capable of terrorizing the mother of his child, if he was capable of killing her, then what would stop him from beating Lindsay Faulkner's head in with a telephone?

She let herself out of the Jeep, crossed the street, and walked through the open side gate to Bichon Bayou Development. She chose a side door, near the window with the light shining through, rang the bell twice, and waited. A moment later Donnie pulled the door open and stared at her, a vague sheen glossing his eyes.

'Well, if it isn't the chick filler in my cop sandwich,' he drawled. He had shed his tie and left his shirt open at the throat, sleeves rolled up. The scent of whiskey hung on him like a faint cologne. 'I've got Fourcade on my ass, Stokes in my face, and you . . . What part of me do you want, Ms Broussard?'

'How much have you had to drink, Mr Bichon?'

'Why? Is there now some law against a man drowning his sorrows in the privacy of his own office?'

'No, sir,' Annie said. 'I'm just wondering if this conversation will be worth my while, that's all.'

He raked a hand through his brown hair, mussing it, and propped a shoulder on the door frame. The smile he flashed her seemed thin and forced. He looked tired, physically, spiritually. Sad, Annie decided, though she was careful not to let the assessment taint her feelings toward him. Donnie was the type of man a lot of women would want to mother the perpetual boy in a man's body, full of charm and mischief and confusion and potential. Had it been that boyish quality that had attracted Pam? Lindsay Faulkner had said Pam had always seen the potential in Donnie, but had never imagined he wouldn't live up to it.

'Are you always so straightforward, Detective?' he asked. 'Whatever happened to those coy games women learned while under their mothers' white-gloved tutelage?'

'It's Deputy,' Annie corrected. 'My mother died when I was nine.'

Donnie winced. 'God. I can't manage to do much of anything right these days. I'm sorry,' he said with genuine contrition. He stepped back from the door and motioned her in. 'I'm not so drunk to have lost all my manners or sense, though some would say I never had much of the latter to begin with. Come in. Have a seat. I just ordered a pizza.'

A gooseneck lamp was the only light on in his office, glowing gold on the polished oak desk and giving the place an intimate feel. A bottle of Glenlivet single malt scotch sat on the blotter beside a coffee mug that declared Donnie to be #1 DAD.

'Have you seen Josie this week?' Annie asked as she walked slowly around the office, taking in the wildlife art on the walls, the framed aerial photos of the Quail Run subdivision. A photo of Josie smiling like a pixie sat on the desk near the mug.

Donnie dropped into his chair. 'Hell, no. Every night's a school night. On the weekend Belle runs off with her. Let me tell you, the only thing worse than having an ex-wife is having an ex-mother-in-law. She lies when I call – tells me Josie's in the bathtub, she's gone to bed, she's doing homework.' He poured two fingers of scotch into the mug and drank half. 'I admit, I have dark thoughts about Belle Davidson.'

'Careful who you say that to, Mr Bichon.'

'That's right. Anything I say can and will be used against me. Well, I'm past caring at the moment. I miss my little girl.'

He sipped at the scotch, stroked his fingertips over the printing on the mug. There was an air of surprise about him, as if he had never expected to face any difficulty in his life and what he was going through now was a rude and unwelcome shock. Things had come too easily for him, Annie suspected. He was handsome. He was popular. He was an athlete. He expected love and adoration, instant forgiveness, no accountability. In many ways, he was as much a child as his daughter.

'Please have a seat so I can focus my eyes, Deputy. And please call me Donnie. I'm depressed enough without having to think attractive women feel compelled to call me "sir." ' He flashed the weary smile again.

Annie took a seat in the burgundy wing chair across the desk from him. He wanted to be friends, to pretend she was here for him instead of as a cop – the way Renard kept trying to do. But she felt less anxious about it with Donnie, which could prove to be a costly mistake, she reminded herself. He had as much reason to kill Pam as Renard. More. But he was handsome, and popular, and charming, and no one wanted to think he was guilty of anything other than cheating on his wife.

If she was going to play detective, it was her role to draw him out from behind his public facade. Get him to relax, get him to talk, see what he might reveal. She could once again play off the adversarial positions Stokes and Fourcade had taken with him. She could be his friend.

'Okay, Donnie,' she said. 'What's depressing you?'

'What isn't? I'm separated from my child. I'm being stalked by a psychopathic cop who *I* bailed out of jail. Now I've got Stokes coming in here asking me did I bash in Lindsay Faulkner's head – like I even thought anything could put a dent in it. Business is . . .' He let the statement trail off on a heavy sigh. 'And Pam . . .'

Tears filled his eyes and he looked away. 'This isn't what I wanted,' he whispered.

'It's not working out for the best for anyone,' Annie said. 'I saw Lindsay this morning. She's in pretty rough shape.'

'But that's got nothing to do with Pam,' he declared. 'It was that rapist.'

Annie didn't comment. In the brief silence she watched his expression of certainty slip. 'I suppose you heard about someone taking a shot at Renard last night.'

'It's the talk of the town,' Donnie said. 'I believe if he'd been killed, the Rotarians would have made the shooter grand marshal of the Mardi Gras parade. People are sick of waiting around for justice to be done.'

'Are you one of those people?'

'Hell, yes. Did I pull the trigger? Hell, no, and for once I've got half a dozen witnesses to back me up. I was here last night, working on the parade float.'

'And the crew is off tonight?'

'It's finished. I'm celebrating.' He lifted the bottle and raised his eyebrows. 'Want to help me?'

'No thanks.'

'That's the second time you've turned me down. If you're not careful, I'll get the feeling you don't like me.'

'And then what?'

He shrugged and grinned. 'I'll have to try harder. I dislike rejection.'

'What about competition? Lindsay told me you were jealous of Detective Stokes spending time with Pam.'

The grin flattened. He poured a little more scotch and took the mug with him as he unfolded his lanky body from the chair. 'The guy's a jerk, that's all. He was supposed to be investigating. All he really wanted was to get in her pants.'

'Do you think he ever succeeded?'

'Pam didn't sleep around.'

'And how would it be any of your business if she had?'

'She was still my wife,' he said, his expression tightening with suppressed anger.

'On paper.'

'It wasn't over.'

'Pam said it was.'

'She was wrong,' he insisted. 'I loved her. I screwed up. I know I screwed up, but I loved her. We would have worked things out.'

His determination amazed and unnerved Annie. 'Donnie, she had filed the papers.'

'She still had my name. She still wore my ring, for Christ's sake.' Tears welled in his eyes again and his hand trembled a little. 'And she's out with that –'

He wasn't drunk enough to finish the sentence. He shook his head at the temptation, turned away from it.

'What do you mean – out with him?' Annie prodded. 'You mean like on dates?'

'Lunch to discuss this aspect of the case. Dinner to go over that aspect of the case. I saw the way he looked at her. I know what he wanted. He didn't give a shit about the case. He didn't do anything to stop what was happening.'

'How do you know that?'

He blinked at her. 'Because I – I *know*. I was there.'

'Where?' Annie pressed, rising and stepping toward him, her instincts at attention. 'Did you follow him around? Did you talk to the sheriff? How would you know what he did or didn't do, Donnie?'

Unless you were involved.

He didn't answer for a moment, didn't look at her. 'You ask him,' he said at last. 'You ask him what he was doing. Ask him what he wanted. I can't believe he hasn't wanted the same thing from you.' His gaze moved over her face. 'Then again, maybe he has. Maybe you go for his type. What do I know?'

'His type?'

Sipping at his scotch, he moved away.

'Did you ever confront him about his interest in Pam?' Annie asked.

'He said if I had a problem with him, I should take it to the sheriff, but that I'd look like a jackass 'cause Pam sure as hell wasn't complaining.'

'How did that make you feel toward Pam?'

He didn't answer. He picked a small framed photograph off a shelf in the bookcase and looked at it as if he hadn't seen it in a very long time. A photograph of himself with Pam and Josie at about five. His family, intact.

'She was so pretty,' he whispered.

Setting the frame aside, he turned toward Annie again. 'Like you, Detective. Pretty brown eyes.' He reached up with a hesitant hand to brush her bangs to the side. 'Pretty smile.' He touched the corner of her mouth. 'Better watch out. I'll want to marry you.'

Annie held herself still, wondering how much of this talk was Donnie and how much was the liquor. Then the doorbell buzzed, and whatever had been in Donnie's head vanished.

'Pizza man,' he announced, walking out.

She wondered just how stable he was. His logic seemed perilously close to the classic pattern of the obsessive stalker everyone had pegged Renard to be. She wondered how angry he might have been seeing Pam with Stokes. She wondered how a man who reportedly chased every skirt in town could find any moral outrage at his estranged wife having lunch with another man. Even if Stokes had had designs on Pam, Pam had not reciprocated. 'It was nothing,' Lindsay had said; she had been reluctant even to raise the subject, it seemed so insignificant.

And yet she had raised the subject with Stokes the very day she had quarreled with Donnie ... and that same night someone had tried to silence her forever.

The pieces sifted through her mind: Donnie, desperate, losing a wife and a safety net for his business. Donnie, unable to cope with the idea of rejection. Donnie, in financial straits. Donnie, angry, driven to a dangerous limit by his problems and by the sight of his wife enjoying the company of another man – a man whose race might have added to the outrage in Donnie's mind. Pushed to that thin dark line, might he have crossed it in a moment of madness? Killed her in a fit of rage and covered the crime with atrocities no one would ever attribute to him?

The sudden ringing of the telephone broke Annie's concentration. She expected an answering machine to pick up, but none did. Who called a business line at this hour? A client? A girlfriend? A legitimate associate? A not-so-legitimate associate?

She picked up the receiver when the phone stopped ringing. Eyes on the door, she dialed star 69 and waited while the call chased itself back home.

On the fourth ring a man's voice answered. 'Marcotte.'

35

When will you paint that, Marcus? I want no reminders,' Doll said with drama. 'My nerves are still ragged tonight. They're worse, in fact. It's as if it's all coming back to me because of it being evening. My evenings will never be the same. The joy of my evenings has been robbed from me. I will never again be able to sit at this table and enjoy a cup of coffee after dinner. Certainly not with the wall looking that way. When will you paint it?'

'Tomorrow, Mother.'

Marcus scraped the last of the excess wet patching compound from the wall and into the can he had used to mix the concoction. He was no expert at repairing walls, let alone a bullet hole, but then no expert had been willing to do the job. Every call had been the same: They heard his name and hung up.

He had boarded up the broken French door himself. When the replacement glass arrived, he would have to learn about glazing, he supposed. Until then, the heavy drapes would be pulled across the door. Doll had closed every shade and drape in the house to block the view of any potential voyeur or sniper.

'The sheriff's office should have to pay for fixing that hole,' Doll said. 'It's their fault we have people shooting at us. The way they've railroaded you when you're guilty of nothing but making a fool of yourself over a woman. They're lazy and corrupt, and we'll all end up murdered in our beds because of them.'

'They're not all that way, Mother. Annie said she'd do her best to check into what happened last night.'

'Annie,' she said with disapproval. 'Don't delude yourself, Marcus. You think she's some kind of angel. She's no better than the rest.'

Tuning out his mother's droning, Marcus knelt to clean up his work area. He imagined what it would be like to move away from here and start fresh without the burden of his family or his reputation. He envisioned a house of his own design, perhaps on the Gulf Coast of Texas or Florida. Something open and bright, with a large deck facing the water.

He thought of coming home after work to cook dinner for Annie. She wasn't the domestic sort. He would take pleasure in teaching her. They would work side by side in the kitchen, and he would show her the proper way to fillet a fish. His hand would close over hers on the knife and guide her. He could almost feel the delicate bones of her hand beneath his, the smooth handle of the knife filling her palm. It would remind them both of the night before, when he had closed her hand around the shaft of his penis. Warmth flooded his groin.

'Marcus, are you listening to me?'

Doll's shrill tone tore through the fabric of his fantasy, ruining it. He briefly imagined surging to his feet with a roar, swinging the can of plaster mix, striking his mother across the face with it, plaster and blood spraying across the wall as she crumpled to the floor. But of course he didn't do that. It was only a moment's madness, there and gone. He wiped his hands on the damp towel and folded it neatly.

'What was that, Mother?'

'Will the paint match?' she asked with exasperation. 'I have a premonition that the spot will always stand out. That the color won't match no matter what we do, and every time I look at that wall I'll be taken with the fear.'

Marcus rose with the bucket in one hand and toolbox in the other. 'I'm sure it will match – so long as we allow the plaster to cure properly before we paint it.'

Doll drummed her fingertips against her sternum, frowning sourly. 'I wish you would paint it tonight.'

'If I paint it tonight, the spot will show.' He walked away as she clucked her tongue behind him.

He wanted out of the house, needed air, needed quiet. He wanted to see Annie. He had tried to call her, to thank her again for coming to his rescue, to ask her if she had made any progress on his case, but she wasn't home, which made him wonder what she was doing. As much as he didn't want to, he couldn't help but question if she was with a man tonight.

The thought aroused his jealousy. Men would want her. He did. And she might take a lover, not fully realizing yet what could be between them. He imagined tearing her from the arms of another man, striking her, punishing her, disciplining her for betraying him, taking her sexually with force and dominance. She would realize her mistake then. She would see the truth of his feelings for her. And in seeing that truth she would recognize her own feelings.

Strange, he thought as he washed the plaster residue from his hands, after Elaine had died, he hadn't wanted anyone to take her place for a long time. He hadn't expected to think of another woman after Pam's death. He still grieved for her. He still missed her. But the sharpness of that pain had faded and was being replaced by something else – hunger, need. Pam had ultimately rejected him. She had believed the lies of her husband and Stokes, and failed to see the truth of his devotion to her. He thought less and less of Pam, more and more of Annie, his angel.

He went through his bedroom to his sanctuary and turned on the lights and radio. A Haydn string quartet played softly as he took the portrait from its special place in the small secret storage cupboard hidden behind a panel of wainscoting. The cubbyhole had been there for more than a century. No telling what the original owners of the house had protected in it. Marcus lined the shelves with keepsakes he would share with no one. Treasured mementos of past loves. Things he wanted no one in his family to taint with so much as their mere knowledge of them. He touched several pieces now.

Closing the panel, he moved to his drawing table and arranged things to his satisfaction. The sketch was taking shape nicely. He stared at it for a long time, thinking, imagining. He concentrated first on her eyes with their slightly exotic shape. Then the slim, pert nose. Then the mouth – her incredibly sexy mouth with its full lower lip and quirking corners. He imagined touching her mouth with his, imagined her mouth moving over his naked body. He imagined her hands touching him. The arousal built until he finally went back to the secret cupboard and returned with a pair of women's black silk underpants. He opened his trousers and masturbated with the panties, his eyes on the portrait. He thought of what it would be like to be inside her, to press her body down beneath his and impale his shaft between her legs again and again and again, until she screamed with the ecstasy of it.

When it was over, he washed himself at the utility sink in the corner, rinsed out the panties, and put them away with his other treasures. He watched the clock and waited, too restless to work on the drawing. When the house was quiet and he knew his mother and Victor were likely both asleep, he let his restlessness drive him from the house into the night.

Nick paced his study as Annie recounted the events of the evening to him, culminating with Marcotte's call to Donnie. Things were starting to happen. The screws were turning.

Marcotte was in it now, and Nick couldn't help but wonder if that was his own doing. That Marcotte might never have taken an interest in Bayou Breaux if he hadn't drawn the man's attention to it didn't sit well. The possibility that Marcotte had been involved from the start pleased him even less.

The focus of the investigation was broadening rather than narrowing, suggesting he hadn't done the job right the first time around, and he didn't want to believe that. He had worked too hard to come back from the debacle of New Orleans and the Parmantel case.

'I feel like I'm balancing on the head of a pin, juggling bowling balls,' Annie muttered, starting to pace as Nick slowed, as if it were essential for one of them to keep in motion.

'If Marcotte was in contact with Donnie before Pam's murder, then that only adds to Donnie's motive,' she said. 'He was angry with Pam for leaving him. I think she was probably holding his property hostage in order to get him to drop the custody threat – which Lindsay Faulkner hinted might have been about Pam seeing male clients. I know Donnie was angry over the relationship he imagined between her and Stokes. If it was imagined.

'What do you know about that?' she asked. 'Was he talking about her around the office? Did he say anything to you?'

Nick shook his head. 'Not that I recall, but I don't listen to that crap, anyway. I don't care who's screwing who unless there's a felony involved. I sure as hell didn't listen to Stokes. He's got a new one every week, at least. I know he was friendly with her. He was quieter after her murder. He might have wanted to be the primary on the case, but he was tied up with the DA the morning you found her. I caught it instead, and Noblier left it that way, even though Stokes had worked the stalking angle. It was a matter of experience. I've worked more murders than the rest of them put together.'

'But Stokes never said anything personal about Pam, about the two of them?'

'Not in a sexual way, no. He admitted he wished he had done more for her during the harassment. He didn't take it seriously enough.'

'No kidding,' Annie said sarcastically. 'I've gone over those reports. He gave her pamphlets on domestic violence and told her to call the phone company to see if she couldn't get them to put a tap on her line. Lazy son of a bitch.'

She marched back toward him, her eyes bright with anger and adrenaline. She looked ready to wrestle tigers. Her anger pleased him.

'And what if Stokes is something worse than lazy?' Annie asked quietly, giving voice to the thought for the first time. She felt as if she had just let a poisonous snake loose in the room.

Fourcade looked at her with suspicion. 'What exactly are you saying, 'Toinette?'

'I had a little run-in with Stokes today over some of the evidence in those rapes. He claims he sent it in to the lab in Shreveport for analysis, but he threatened me not to check up on it. He says he'll go to Noblier and make a formal complaint about me digging around in his cases. But what's the big deal if I call – if the stuff is really there?'

'You think he didn't send it?' Nick said. 'Why wouldn't he?'

'This rapist knows everything we'll look for – hairs, fibers, fingerprints, body fluids. He goes so far as to make the victims clean under their fingernails after he's through with them. Who would know to be that careful? A pro . . . or a cop.'

'You think Stokes is the rapist? *Mais sa c'est fou!* That's crazy!' He actually laughed. Annie didn't see the humor.

'Why is that crazy?' she demanded. 'Because he's got all the women he wants? You know as well as I do it doesn't always work that way.'

'Come on, 'Toinette. Stokes is suddenly a rapist? Overnight he's a rapist? No way.'

'You think he's not capable of violence against a woman?' Annie said. 'Good ol' Chaz. Everybody's buddy. I can tell you from experience he doesn't like the word *no*.'

The import of her words struck Nick hard, awakening feelings of jealousy and protectiveness he would have said he didn't possess. 'He laid a hand on you?'

'He never got the chance,' Annie said. 'But that doesn't mean he didn't want to or that he hasn't thought about it a hundred times since. He's got an ugly temper with a touchy trigger.'

True enough, Nick thought. He'd seen Stokes's temper in action just yesterday.

'You thought he turned on you,' Annie reminded him.

And he wasn't entirely sure it wasn't true. But Nick couldn't decide if he suspected Stokes because Stokes was deserving of it or because Nick didn't want to accept 100 percent of the culpability for beating up Renard.

'There's a big jump from selling me out to being a rapist,' he said.

'But look at the connections to Stokes in all of this,' Annie said. 'Every time I turn around, there he is. He's got control of the rape task force, has access to all the evidence. Now he's checked out the feathers from the mask in two of the rapes *and* the mask from Pam Bichon's homicide, and he doesn't want me calling the lab to check on the stuff.'

Nick lifted his hands. 'Oh, hold on, 'Toinette. You're not gonna try to tie him to Bichon.'

'Why not?' Annie said. 'Stokes investigated Pam's stalking complaints. Donnie was jealous of the time Pam spent with him – so said Lindsay Faulkner, who met Stokes over lunch on Monday and had her head bashed in that same night.'

'You're way off the beam here,' Nick said, shaking his head. 'I was there, remember. Bichon was my case. You think I wouldn't have seen that?'

'Were you looking?' Annie challenged. 'Where did Stokes steer you? To Renard.'

'Nobody steers me. I went to Renard because the logic took me there. Stokes turns up in all of this because he's a cop, for God's sake. If you follow your line of thinking, you could tie *me* to the murder, I could tie you to the rapes.'

'I'm not the one trying to hide evidence,' Annie shot back.

'You don't know that he is, either. Maybe he just wants you out of his hair.'

'And maybe I'm right and you don't wanna hear it because it would make you look like a fool.'

'I don't wanna hear it because it's a waste of time,' he said stubbornly.

'Because it's my theory and not yours,' Annie argued. 'I told you at the start of this I wouldn't be your puppet, Nick. Don't blow me off now because I'm not stuck in the same tunnel with you. I think Stokes is a legitimate suspect.'

'He's a cop.'

'So are you!' she snapped. 'It didn't stop you from breaking the law.'

Her words slapped everything to a halt. She felt a sting of guilt that aggravated her. She wasn't the one who had something to feel guilty about. And yet, she couldn't let go of the feeling that she'd hurt him. Fourcade, the granite cop, the pillar of cold logic. No one else would have thought him capable of feeling hurt.

'I'm sorry,' she murmured. 'That was bitchy.'

'No. It's true enough. *C'est vrai.*'

He went to a dormer window and stared out at nothing.

'I just think it's another possibility,' Annie said. 'It's an angle no one's considered.'

An angle he didn't want to consider, Nick admitted. For exactly the reason she had said. Bichon had been his case. If he'd worked side by side with her killer and never seen it, what kind of cop did that make him?

He ran the possibility through his mind, trying to see it as if he'd never had anything to do with the case or with Stokes.

'I don't buy it,' he said. 'Stokes has been here four or five years, suddenly he butchers a woman and becomes a serial rapist? Uh-uh. That's not the way it works.'

He turned around and walked slowly back toward Annie. 'What other evidence was there in the rapes?'

'No blood, no semen, no skin. Nothing from the rape kits.' Then a memory surfaced. 'At the Nolan rape, I saw Stokes picking pubic hairs out of Jennifer Nolan's bathtub with a tweezers.'

'Check it out. Meanwhile, get me the case numbers on the rapes. I'll call Shreveport and tell them I'm Quinlan. See what they have to say.'

Annie nodded. 'Thanks,' she said, looking up at him. 'I'm sorry –'

'Don't be sorry, 'Toinette,' he ordered. 'It's a waste of energy. You had something on your mind, you laid it out. We'll see where it takes us, but I don't want you getting sidetracked. These rapes aren't your focus. The murder is your focus and Renard is your number one suspect. Pam Bichon herself, she told us that. You don't wanna listen to me, you listen to her.'

He was right. Pam had seen Renard for a monster and no one had listened to her. In turning away from Renard to look at other possibilities, was she also ignoring Pam's cries for help – or was she simply doing the job?

'Why couldn't I have been a cocktail waitress?' she asked on a weary sigh.

'If you weren't a cop, you wouldn't get to drive that hot car,' Nick murmured.

The humor was unexpected and welcome. Annie looked at his rugged face, the eyes that had seen too much. Logic told her to stay away from him, but the temptation to feel something other than uncertainty and apprehension was strong. He had the power to sweep it all away for a few hours, to blind her to everything but passion and raw need. A brief interlude of oblivion and obsession.

Obsession didn't seem like such a good thing to succumb to, considering where it had gotten Fourcade. But was it obsession she was afraid of or Fourcade or herself?

Annie forced herself to go to the board of crime scene photos and look at what had been left of Pam Bichon. A shudder of revulsion went through her, as sobering as a dousing of ice water.

Could Stokes have done this? With what motive? Lindsay Faulkner said he had flirted with Pam, that Donnie had been jealous. She never said that Pam had objected to Stokes's attentions. If Pam had put him off because she feared repercussions from Donnie, he had only to bide his time until the divorce went through. But Chaz Stokes was not a patient man, and not always a rational one. In a moment of blind fury could he have crossed the line?

It sounded weak to her. Maybe she wanted to look at Stokes only because he yanked her chain or because she knew he was a lazy cop.

Could Donnie have done this? In her mind's eye she could see him in the intimate light of his office, standing too close to her, that strange look of false remembrance and regret hanging crooked on his face. In a fit of anger, jealousy pushing him far beyond his limits, could he have butchered the mother of his child?

He had been drinking the night of the murder, as he had been tonight. Liquor was the key that opened the floodgates on ugly emotions. She'd seen it happen time and again. But to this level of brutality?

'You were in it from the start,' she said to Nick. 'Did you ever think Donnie could have done it?'

He joined her at the table. 'I've seen people driven to all manner of atrocities. I've seen parents kill their children, children kill their parents, husbands kill their wives, wives set their husbands on fire while they're passed out drunk. But this? I never believed he had the stomach for it. Motive, maybe, but the rest . . . no, I never believed it.

'I talked to the bartender who served Donnie at the Voodoo Lounge that night.' He shook a cigarette out of the pack on the table and played with it between his fingers. 'He swore Donnie had more than his share.'

'I know. I read the statement. But it was Friday night,' Annie reminded him. 'They were busy. Can he be sure Donnie drank everything he was served? And even if he drank it, how do we know he didn't just go in the men's room and puke it all up? If he's capable of doing this to a woman, then he's clever enough to build himself an alibi.'

'There's one big stumbling block, chère. Il a pas d'ésprit. Donnie, he's not clever at all,' he said. 'He's a whiner not a doer, and a screwup to boot. There's no way in hell Donnie Bichon commits a crime like this and he doesn't fuck up somewhere along the way. Fingerprints, fibers, skin under her fingernails, semen, *something*. There was damn near nothing at that crime scene – on or around the body. He consented to a search of his town house – nothing. No bloody clothes, no bloody towels, no bloody footprints in the garage, no traces of blood anywhere in the house.'

'What about this possible connection to Marcotte and Marcotte's connection to DiMonti?'

'That's no mob hit,' he said. 'Mob wants somebody dead, they take 'em out in the swamp and shoot 'em. They wrap eighty pounds of chain around the body and throw it in the Atchafalaya. Bump 'em and dump 'em. No boss would have this kind of psycho on his payroll. Killer like this, he's too unpredictable, he's a risk. I've said it all along and I say it again: This was personal.'

Annie turned her back to the photos and rubbed her hands over her face. 'My brain hurts.'

'Keep your eyes on the prize, 'Toinette. Don't turn your back on Renard just because you see other possibilities. He's calling you, sending you presents – same as he did with Pam. Same as he did with that gal up in Baton Rouge. There's two dead women in his wake. You leave Donnie and Marcotte to me. Renard is your focus. You got him on the hook, *'tite fille*. Reel him in.'

And then what? she thought, but she didn't ask the question. She simply let the silence settle between them, too hot and too tired to go any further with it tonight. The loft was warm and stuffy, the unexpected heat of the day having risen up into the rafters. The ceiling fans only stirred it around.

'Had enough for one day?' Nick asked. He brought the cigarette to his lips, then pulled it away and tossed it on the table beside the pack.

Annie nodded, following the move with her eyes. She wondered if he had changed his mind or if he had set it aside because he knew she didn't like it. Dangerous thinking. Foolish thinking. Fourcade did what he wanted.

'Stay the night,' he said. As if he had flipped a switch, the energy he radiated became instantly sexual. She felt it touch her, felt her own body stir in response.

'I can't,' she said softly. 'With everything that's gone on lately, Sos and Fanchon worry. I need to be home.'

'Then stay awhile,' he said, tilting her chin up. 'I want you, 'Toinette,' he murmured, lowering his head. 'I want you in my bed.'

'I wish it were that simple.'

'No, you don't. Because then it would be only sex, and you'd feel cheap and cheated and used. That's not what you want.'

'What is it, then, if it's not just sex?' Annie asked, surprised at his allusion to something more. He struck her as the kind of man who would want uncomplicated affairs, straightforward sex, no gray areas, no untidy emotions.

He stroked her cheekbone with his thumb, his expression pensive. 'It is what it is,' he whispered, touching his mouth to hers. If the answer was there, he didn't want to see it or wasn't ready to see it any more than she was ready to put a label on it.

'Stay and we can explore the possibilities,' he said against her lips.

He opened her mouth with his, touched his tongue to hers. A shiver ran through her like quicksilver.

'I want you,' he murmured, moving his hands down her back. 'You want me, yes?'

'Yes,' she admitted.

His gaze held hers. 'Don't be afraid of it, 'Toinette. Come deeper with me, *chère*.'

Deeper. Into the black water, the unknown. Sink or swim. She thought of A.J.'s accusation that she was pushing him away because he knew her too well, and Nick's assertion that she was afraid to know herself, afraid of what might lie beneath the surface. She thought of the sense of expectation she'd been feeling for weeks, the sense that she was treading water, waiting for something.

Fourcade was reaching out to her. The unknown was whether she would buoy him or he would pull her down into his darkness so deep she would drown.

He waited. Silent. Still and as taut as a clenched fist.

'I'll stay awhile,' she said.

He swept her off her feet and carried her to the bed. They stood beside it and undressed each other, fingers hurrying, fumbling at buttons. The heat of the room pressed in on them. Skin went slick with the heat of desire. Their bodies kissed, hot and wet, flesh to flesh, man to woman. His hands explored her: the soft fullness of a breast, the pearled tip of a nipple, the moist lips of femininity. She touched everything male about him: the hard-ridged muscles of his belly, the crisp dark hair that matted his chest, the shaft of his erection, as smooth and hard as a column of marble.

They fell across the crisp sheets, a tangle of limbs, her dark hair spilling across the pillow. She arched her body into the touch of his mouth as he kissed the beads of sweat from between her breasts and followed the trail down her belly to the point of her hip, the crease of her thigh, the back of her knee. She opened herself to the touch of his hand. He took her to the brink of fulfilment and left her hanging there, aching with the need to join her body with his.

He pulled a foil packet from the drawer of the nightstand. Annie took it from his fingers. Nick sat back against the headboard and held himself still against the exquisite torture of her small hands fitting the condom over his shaft. She looked up at him, her eyes wide, her mouth swollen and cherry red from his kisses. She looked both wanton and hesitant. He had never wanted a woman more – this woman who held sway over the fate of his career. This woman – sweet, normal Annie, who had never seen the dark side and probably never wanted to. He should have left her to her nice life, but she had wandered into his realm, and his need to touch her, to hold her to him, far outweighed his capacity for nobility.

He held his hand out to her. '*Viens ici, chérie,*' he murmured, pulling her toward him. 'Come take what you want.'

Hands at her waist, he guided her astride him. She eased herself down, taking him deep, her fingertips biting into his shoulders. They moved together. He held her tight. Their kisses tasted dark and salty-sweet.

Annie felt suspended in the rhythm of it, consumed by the intensity of it. She fell back in the support of his arms and floated while he sucked at her breast. She banded her arms around his shoulders and held tight as the urgency built.

'Open your eyes, *chère,*' he commanded. 'Open your eyes and look at me.'

Her gaze locked on his as the end came for both of them. One and then the other. Powerful. Intimate. More than sex.

In a week she would testify against him.

The thought trailed through her mind like a slug as she lay beside him. She wanted to know if his lawyer would try to cut a deal, but she didn't ask. She tried to imagine visiting him in prison. The image turned her stomach.

She supposed no jury in South Louisiana would convict him, given the false testimony any number of other officers were willing to give about the bogus 10–70 call that night, and the fact that almost everyone in Partout Parish believed Renard should have gotten worse than a beating. And so she was hoping that the justice system she had sworn to serve would corrupt itself to suit her wishes, and somehow that would be okay when Fourcade going after Renard in the first place was not.

Shades of gray, Noblier had told her. Like layers of soot and dirt. She felt it rubbing off on her.

'I have to go,' she said, a mix of reluctance and urgency struggling within her. She swung her legs over the side of the bed and sat up, reaching for her T-shirt.

Nick said nothing. He didn't expect her to stay – tonight or for the long haul. Why would she? A relationship between them would be difficult, and she had a nice tame lawyer waiting in the wings to give her a simple, normal life. Why would she not take that? He told himself it didn't matter. He was the kind of man meant to be alone. He was used to it. Solitude allowed him concentration for the job.

The job that would be taken from him forever if he was convicted of beating Marcus Renard. The hearing was a week away. The key witness stood with her back to him, scraping her dark hair into a messy ponytail. His accuser, his partner, his lover. He'd have been a hell of a lot better off hating her. But he didn't.

He climbed out of bed and picked up his jeans. 'I'll follow you home. In case Cadillac Man comes back for an encore.'

He stayed well back on the drive to the Corners. There were times when Annie thought he must have left off with the tail, and then she would catch a glimpse of his lights. He wasn't following her to prevent Cadillac Man from making another run at her, he was letting her run ahead, a rabbit to lure their predator. If her assailant took the bait, Fourcade would be there to bust the jerk.

Not exactly the way most lovers topped off a romantic interlude. But then, Fourcade was by no means typical. And they weren't exactly most lovers. Most lovers never had to face each other across a courtroom.

She turned in at the Corners and parked in front of the store. Moments later, Fourcade drove past, flashing his headlights once. He didn't stop.

She sat in the Jeep for a time, half listening to the radio – an argument about whether or not women should carry handguns in these dangerous times.

'You think a rapist is just gonna stand back when y'all say, 'Oh, wait, let me get my gun out my pocketbook so I can shoot you'?' the male caller said in a high falsetto. 'Marital arts – that's what women need.'

'You mean *martial* arts?'

'That's what I said.'

Annie shook her head and pulled her keys. She climbed to the passenger seat and gathered her stuff, slinging the strap of her duffel over one shoulder and scooping the files Fourcade had sent with her into her other arm. She added the detritus of her dinner and a sandal that had worked its way out from under the seat.

Overburdened, the duffel strap slipping on her shoulder, she climbed out of the Jeep and bumped the door shut with her hip. The load in her arm shifted precariously. As she came around the back of the Jeep, the shoe slipped off the pile and took the dinner garbage with it. The duffel strap fell, the weight of the bag jerking her right arm so that the files and other junk spilled to the ground.

'Shit,' she muttered, dropping to her knees.

The sound of the rifle shot registered in her mind a split second before the bullet hit.

36

The bullet ripped through the plastic back window of the Jeep, destroyed the windshield, and shattered the front window of the store. All in less time than it took to draw a breath – not that Annie was breathing.

She dropped flat on the ground, the crushed shell biting into her bare arms as she scooted under the Jeep, dragging her duffel bag with her. She couldn't hear a damn thing for the pounding of her pulse in her ears. The heat from the Jeep pressed down on her. Hands fumbling, she dug her Sig Sauer out of the bag, twitched the safety off and waited.

She couldn't see anything but the ground. If she crawled out from under the Jeep at the front, she could make it up onto the gallery. Using the Jeep for cover, she could climb through the broken front window, get to the phone, and call 911.

A screen door slapped in the distance.

'Who's there?' Sos called, racking the shotgun. 'Me, I shoot trespassers! And survivors – I shoot them twice!'

'Uncle Sos!' Annie yelled. 'Go back inside! Call 911!'

'I'd rather unload this buckshot in some rascal's ass! Where y'at, *chère*?'

'Go back in the house! Call 911!'

'The hell I will! Your *tante*, she already called! Cops are on the way!'

And if they were lucky, Annie thought, a deputy might arrive in half an hour – unless there already was a deputy right across the road with a rifle in his hands. She thought of Mullen. She thought of Stokes. Donnie Bichon came to mind. She considered the possibility of Renard. She had accused him of shooting into his own home. Maybe this was retribution.

She adjusted her grip on the Sig and scuttled toward the front end of the Jeep. The shot had to have come from the road or the woods beyond. She hadn't heard or seen a car. A shooter in the woods at night would lose himself in a hurry. It would take a dog to track him, and by the time a K-9 unit arrived, he would be long gone.

In the distance she could hear the radio car coming, siren wailing, giving all criminals in the vicinity ample warning of its imminent arrival.

Pitre was the deputy. To Sos and Fanchon, he showed a modicum of respect. To Annie he remarked that he hadn't realized there were so many poor shots in the parish. He made a laconic call back to dispatch to advise everyone of the situation, which was nothing – they had no suspect description, no vehicle description, nothing. At Annie's insistence he called for the K-9 unit and was told the officer was unavailable. A detective would be assigned the case in the morning – *if* she wanted to pursue the matter, Pitre said.

'Someone tried to kill me,' she snapped. 'Yeah, I think I don't wanna just drop that.'

Pitre shrugged, as if to say, 'suit yourself.'

The slug had passed through the front window of the store, shattered a display case of jewelry made from nutria teeth, and slammed into the old steel cash register that sat on the tour ticket counter. The cash register had sustained an impressive wound, but still worked. The slug had been mangled beyond recognition. Even if anyone ever went to the trouble of finding a suspect, they would have nothing to match for ballistics.

'Yeah, well, thanks for nothing, *again*,' Annie said, walking Pitre to his car.

He feigned innocence. 'Hey, I came with lights and siren!'

Annie scowled at him. 'Don't even get me started. Suffice it to say you're just about as big an asshole as Mullen.'

'Ooooh! You gonna go after me now?' he said. 'I heard you went after Stokes today. What is it with you, Broussard? You think the only way you'll get up the ladder is by knocking everybody else off? What ever happened to women who slept their way to the top?'

'I'd rather give bone marrow. Go piss up a rope, Pitre.' She flipped him off as he drove away.

After walking Fanchon back to the house, she used the phone in the store to call Fourcade. She chewed at a broken fingernail as she listened to the phone ring on the other end. On the sixth ring his machine picked up. He had asked her to stay the night, now the night was half gone and so was Fourcade. Where was he at one-thirty in the morning? Her mind worried at that question as she helped Sos board up the window to keep out looting raccoons.

It bothered her that she wanted Nick here for emotional reasons and not just as another cop. If she was going to get through this mess with Renard and the department and Fourcade's hearing, she had to be tougher. She needed to learn to separate the issues. She could almost hear him in her mind: *You're not dead. Suck it up and focus on your job, 'Toinette.*

And then he would put his arms around her and hold her safe against him.

As they worked on the window, she answered Sos's questions as best she could without revealing too much about the situation she had become embroiled in. But he knew she was holding things back from him, and she knew he knew.

He gave her a hard look as they walked out, his temper still up and bubbling. 'Look what you got yourself in now, *'tite fille*. Why you can't do things no way but the hard way? Why you don't just marry Andre and settle? Give your *tante* and me some grandbabies? *Mais non*, you gotta run off and do a man's job! You all the time beatin' on a hornet's nest with a stick! And now you gonna get stung. *Sa c'est de la couyonade!*'

'It'll work out, Uncle Sos,' Annie promised, feeling like a worm for lying to him. She could have been dead.

He made a strangled sound in his throat, but cupped her face in his callused hands. 'We worry 'bout you, *chérie*, your *tante* and me. You're like our own, you know dat! Why you gotta make life so hard?'

'I don't mean to look for trouble.'

Sos heaved a sigh and patted her cheek. 'But when trouble comes lookin' for you, you ain't hard to find, *c'est vrai*.'

Annie watched him walk away. She hated that this mess had touched him and Fanchon. If her life was going to stay this complicated, maybe she would have to think about moving away from the Corners.

'If my life is going to stay this complicated, maybe I'll have to think about moving into an asylum,' she muttered as she stepped down off the gallery and turned the corner to her stairs.

A small box wrapped in flowered paper with a white bow sat on the third step from the bottom. Renard. Annie recognized the paper. It was the same as what had been wrapped around the box with the scarf in it. A too-familiar sense of unease rippled through her at the idea of him coming here as if he felt entitled to touch her private life.

She stuffed the box into her duffel bag and went up to the apartment.

The sense of violation struck her immediately. The feeling that someone had invaded her home. From her vantage point in the front entry she could see across the living room, could see that the French doors were shut, the bolt turned. The air in the apartment was stifling and stale from an unexpectedly hot day with closed windows. A faint undertone of something earthy and rotten lingered. The swamp, Annie thought. Or maybe she needed to take the garbage out. She set her duffel bag on the bench and pulled out the Sig. With the gun raised and ready, she moved into the living room and hit the message button on the answering machine. If there was someone here, and he thought she was occupied listening to the machine, he might think to take advantage and attack her from behind.

Images of Lindsay Faulkner flashed through her mind – lying on the floor like a broken doll; head swathed in bandages like a mummy.

The messages rolled out of the machine. A Mary Kay lady who had seen her on the news and wanted to compliment her on her complexion. A distant Doucet 'cousin' who had seen her on the news and wondered if she could help him get a job as a deputy.

She moved out of the living room and around the perimeter of the kitchen. Nothing seemed out of order. The old refrigerator hummed and groaned. The alligator on the door grinned at her. The table was clean. She had swept her notes and files together before leaving this morning and stashed them in an old steamer trunk that sat in her living room – just in case.

The answering machine continued chattering. A.J.'s psychologist sister-in-law, Serena, wanted to offer a friendly ear if Annie needed to talk. Two hang-ups.

Back in the living room, Annie made the same slow, quiet circuit, looking for anything out of place, pausing at the French doors to double-check the lock. The gator coffee table seemed to watch her as she skirted past it.

'What's the deal, Alphonse?' Annie murmured.

Silence. Then Marcus Renard's voice spoke to her.

'Annie? This is Marcus. I wish you were home. I wanted to thank you again for coming over last night.' The voice was too sincere, too familiar. 'It means so much to know you care.' More silence, and then he said, 'Goodnight, Annie. I hope you're having a pleasant evening.'

The skin crawled on the back of her neck. She crossed the room and started down the hall as the machine reported two more hang-up calls.

The bathroom was clear. Her workout room appeared undisturbed. The tension ebbed a bit. Maybe she was still just reacting to the shooting. Maybe she was just projecting her feelings of violation at Renard having left another gift for her. He should never have been able to get into her home. The doors had been locked.

Then she turned the corner and opened the door to her bedroom.

The stench of decay hit her full in the face and turned her stomach inside out.

Nailed to the wall above her bed in a position of crucifixion, its legs broken and bent, hung a dead black cat. Its skull had been crushed, its entrails spilled out of the body cavity onto the pillows below. And above it one word was painted in blood – CUNT.

'People should get what they deserve, don't you think? Good or bad.

   She deserves to be confronted with the consequences of her sins. She deserves to be punished. Like the others.

   Betrayal is the least of her crimes.

   Terror is the least of mine.'

37

He lay in wait like a panther in the night, anger and anticipation contained by forced patience. The glowing blue numbers on the VCR clicked the minutes. 1:43.1:44. The low purr of an engine approached, passed one end of the house, and slipped into the garage.

The rattle of keys. The kitchen door swung open. He waited.

Footfalls on tile. Footfalls muffled by carpet. He waited.

The footsteps passed by his hiding place.

'Quite the night owl, aren't you, Tulane?'

Donnie bolted at the sound of the voice, but in a heartbeat, Fourcade materialized from the gloom of the living room and slammed him into the wall.

'You lied to me, Donnie,' he growled. 'That's not a wise thing to do.'

'I don't know what you're talking about!' Donnie blubbered, spittle collecting at the corners of his mouth. His breath reeked of scotch. The smell of sweat and fear penetrated his clothing.

Nick gave him a shake, banging his head back against the wall. 'In case you haven't noticed, Donnie, me, I'm not a patient man. And you, you're not too bright. This is bad combination, no?'

Donnie shivered. His voice took on a whine. 'What do you want from me, Fourcade?'

'Truth. You tell me you don't know Duval Marcotte. But Marcotte, he called you on the telephone tonight, didn't he?'

'I don't know him. I know *of* him,' he stressed. 'What if he called me? I can't control what other people do! Jesus, this is the perfect example – I did you a good turn and look how you treat me!'

'You don't like the way I treat you, Tulane?' Nick said, easing his weight back. 'The way you lie to me, I was tempted to beat the shit out of you a long time ago. Put in the proper perspective, my restraint has been commendable. Perspective is the key to balance in life, *c'est vrai?*'

Donnie edged away from the wall. Fourcade blocked the route to the kitchen and garage. He glanced across the living room. The furniture was an obstacle course of black shadows against a dark background; the only illumination, silver streetlight leaching in through the sheer front curtains.

Nick smiled. 'Don't you run away from me, Donnie. You'll only piss me off.'

'I've already managed to do that.'

'Yeah, but you ain't never seen me *mad, mon ami*. You don't wanna open that door, let the tiger out.'

'You know, this is it, Fourcade,' Donnie said. 'I'm calling the cops this time. You can't just break into people's homes and harass them.'

Nick leaned into the back of a tall recliner and turned the lamp beside it on low. Donnie had traded the Young Businessman look for Uptown Casual: jeans and a polo shirt with a small red crawfish embroidered on the left chest.

'Why are you wearing sunglasses?' Donnie asked. 'It's the middle of the damn night.'

Nick just smiled slowly.

'You sure you wanna do that, Donnie?' he said. 'You wanna call the SO? Because, you know, you do that, then we're all gonna have to have this conversation downtown – about how you lied to me and what all about Marcotte sniffing around the realty, wanting that land what's tied up there.

'Me,' – he shrugged – 'I'm just a friend who dropped by to chat. But you . . .' He shook his head sadly. 'Tulane, you just got more and more explaining to do. You see how this looks – you dealing with Marcotte? I'll tell you: It looks like you had one hell of a motive to kill your wife.'

'I never talked to Marcotte –'

'And now your wife's partner is attacked, left for dead –'

'I never laid a hand on Lindsay! I told Stokes, that son of a bitch –'

'It's just not looking good for you, Donnie.' Nick moved away from the chair, hands resting at the waist of his jeans. 'So, you gonna do something about that or what?'

'Do *what*?' Donnie said in exasperation.

'Did Marcotte contact you or the other way around?'

Donnie's Adam's apple bobbed in his throat. 'He called me.'

'When?'

'Yesterday.'

Nick silently cursed his own stupidity. 'That's the truth?' he demanded.

Donnie raised his right hand like a Boy Scout and closed his eyes, flinching. 'My hand to God.'

Nick grabbed his face with one big hand and squeezed as he backed him into another wall. 'Look at me,' he ordered. 'Look at me! You lie to God all you want, Tulane. God, He's not gonna kick your ass. You look at me and answer. Did you *ever* have contact with Duval Marcotte before Pam was killed?'

Donnie met his gaze. 'No. Never.'

And if that was the truth, then Nick had drawn Marcotte onto the scene himself. The obsession had blinded him to the possibilities. The possibility that Marcotte's interest would be piqued by Nick's ill-fated visit, and that Marcotte would be drawn to the scene like a lion to the smell of blood.

'He's the devil,' he whispered, letting Donnie go. Marcotte was the devil, and he had all but invited the devil to play in his own backyard. 'Don'tcha do business with the devil, Donnie,' he murmured. 'You'll end up in hell. One way or another.'

He dropped his gaze to the floor, reflecting on his own stupidity. There was no changing what he'd done, nothing to do but deal with it. Slowly Donnie's muddy work boots came into focus.

'Where you been tonight, Tulane?'

'Around,' Donnie said, straightening his shirt with one hand and rubbing his cheek with the other. 'I went to the cemetery for a while. I go there sometimes to talk to God, you know. And to see Pam. Then I went and checked a site.'

'In the dead of night?'

He shrugged. 'Hey, you like to go around in sunglasses. I like to get drunk and wander around half-finished construction sites. There's always the chance I'll fall in a hole and kill myself. It's kind of like Russian roulette. I don't have much of a social life since Pam was killed.'

'I suppose an unsolved murder in your past puts the ladies off.'

'Some.'

'Well . . . you watch your step, *cher*,' Nick said, backing toward the kitchen. 'We don't want you to meet an untimely end – unless you deserve it.'

He was gone as quickly and quietly as he had appeared. Donnie didn't even hear the door shut. But then, that may have been due to the pounding in his head. The shakes swept over him on a wave of weakness, and he stumbled into the bathroom with a hand pressed to his burning stomach. Bruising his knees on the tile, he dropped to the floor and puked into the toilet, then started to cry.

All he wanted was a simple, cushy life. Money. Success. No worries. The adoration of his daughter. He hadn't realized how close he had come to that ideal until he'd blown it all away. Now all he had was trouble, and every time he turned around he screwed himself deeper into the hole.

Hugging the toilet, he put his head down on his arms and sobbed.

'Pam . . . Pam . . . I'm so sorry!'

Annie dreamed she caught a bullet in her teeth. Tied to the bullet was a string. Pulling herself hand over hand along the string, she flew through the night, through the woods, and came to a halt with a rifle barrel pressed into the center of her forehead. At the stock end of the gun stood a shimmering apparition with an elaborate feather mask covering its face. With one hand the apparition removed the mask to reveal the face of Donnie Bichon. Another hand peeled away the face of Donnie Bichon to reveal Marcus Renard. Then Renard's face was peeled away to reveal Pam Bichon's death mask – the eyes partially gone, skin discolored and decomposing, tongue swollen and purple. Nailed to her chest was the dead black cat, its intestines hanging down like a bloody necklace.

'You are me,' Pam said, and fired the rifle. *Bang! Bang! Bang!*

Annie hurled herself upright on the sofa, gasping for breath, feeling as if her heart had leapt out of her chest.

The banging came again. A fist on wood. Bleary-eyed, she grabbed for the Sig on the coffee table.

''Toinette! It's me!' Fourcade called.

He stood at the French doors, scowling in at her.

Annie went to the doors and let him in. She didn't bother to ask the obvious question. Of course Fourcade wouldn't come to the front door. Her tormentor might have been watching from the woods, returning to the scene of his crimes. She asked the second-most obvious question instead.

'Where the hell were you?'

After slamming the door shut on the atrocity in her bedroom, she had gone back to the living room and sat down, trying to think what she should do. Call the SO? Bring Pitre back here and let him soak up the gory details to spread around the department at the shift change? What good would he do? None. She had called Fourcade instead, cursing him silently as his machine picked up again.

'Taking care of some business,' he said.

He stared at her as she paced back and forth along the coffee table with her arms banded around her. He took in everything about her – the disheveled hair, the dirty jeans and T-shirt. Reaching out as she came toward him, he plucked the Sig from her fingers and set it aside.

'Are you all right?'

'No!' she snapped. 'Someone tried to kill me. I think we've already established that I don't take that well. Then I find out someone came into my house, wrote on my wall in blood, and nailed a dead cat above my bed. I'm not okay with that either!'

From the corner of her eye she could see Fourcade watching her. He didn't seem to know what to do except fall back on the job, the routine. She was a victim – God, but she hated that label – and he was a detective.

'Tell me what happened from the time you parked the Jeep.'

She went through the story point by point, fact by fact, the way she had been trained to testify. The process calmed her somewhat, distanced her from the violation. In her mind, she tried to separate the victim in her from the cop. For the first time she told him about the skinned muskrat that had been left in her locker room, though she didn't put the two incidents on the same plane. It was one thing to play a nasty joke at work; breaking and entering was another matter. And what had been done in her bedroom seemed more threatening, more vile, more personal. Then again, if a deputy had been behind that rifle tonight, why not this too?

Nick listened, then headed toward the bedroom. Annie followed, reluctant to face it again.

'Did you touch anything?' he asked out of habit.

'No. God, I couldn't even bring myself to go in.'

He pushed the door open and stood there with his hands on his hips, a grimace twisting his lips. '*Mon Dieu.*'

He left Annie at the door and went into the room, taking in the details with a clinical eye.

The blood had been brushed on the wall. No visible fingerprints. The word *cunt* had been chosen for what reason? As an opinion? To shock? Out of disrespect? Out of anger?

In his mind's eye he could see Keith Mullen, skinny and ugly, standing in his filthy kitchen just that morning. '*She don't know nothing about loyalty, turning on one of us. Cunt's got no business being in a uniform.*'

Was the animal symbolic? An alley cat – sexually indiscriminate. Its guts spilled down onto the bed where Annie had made love with him just the night before.

And the positioning of its body, the nails through its forepaws, the evisceration – an obvious allusion to Pam Bichon. Meant to frighten or as a warning?

He thought of how close she had come to being shot and he wanted to hit something – *someone* – hard and repeatedly.

He worked to contain the rage even as he remembered Donnie Bichon's muddy boots. He set the thought aside for the moment.

'This cat – was she yours, 'Toinette?'

'No.'

'You talked to your *tante* and uncle 'bout did they see anyone around today?'

'We had that conversation when we were talking about who might want to shoot me. They were busy today. Tourists coming in early for Mardi Gras. They had to call in extra tour guides. They didn't have time to notice anyone special.'

'How'd anyone get in here? Were your doors locked when you came up?'

'Everything was locked up tight. You might be able to pick a lock to break in, but there's no locking these doors from the outside without a key.'

'So how did this creep get in?'

'There's only one other way.' She led him into the bathroom, to the door behind the old claw-foot tub. 'The stairs go down into the stockroom of the store.'

'Was it locked?'

'I don't know. I thought so. I usually keep it locked, but I went down this way Sunday night when the prowler was here. Maybe I forgot to lock it after.'

Nick stood in the tub and examined the locking mechanism in the doorknob, frowning disapproval. 'Ain't nothing but a button. Anybody could slip it with a credit card. How would anyone but family or employees know about these stairs?'

Annie shook her head. 'By luck. By chance. The rest rooms are across the hall at the bottom of the stairs. Someone going to use them might look through the stockroom and notice.'

He flicked on the light switch and descended the steep stairs, looking for any sign another person had been there – a footprint, a thread, a stray hair. There was nothing. The stockroom door stood open. Across the hall, he could see part of the door to the men's room.

'I'd say someone went out of their way to notice,' he murmured.

He went back up the steps and followed Annie to the living room. She curled herself into one corner of the sofa and rubbed her bare foot slowly back and forth under the jaw of her gator table. She looked small and forlorn.

'What d' you think, 'Toinette? You think the shooter and the cat killer are the same person?'

'I don't know,' Annie said. 'And don't try to tell me I do. Are the shooter and the cat killer one and the same? Is Renard's shooter my shooter too, or is Renard the shooter? Who hates me more: half the people I work *with* or half the people I work *for*? And what do they hate me for more: trying to solve this murder or preventing you from committing one?

'I'm so tired I can't see straight. I'm scared. I'm sick that someone would do that to that poor animal –'

Somehow, that was the last straw. Bad enough to have violence directed at her, but to have an innocent little animal, killed and mutilated for the sole purpose of frightening her was too much. She pressed her fingertips against her lips and tried to will the moment to pass. Then Fourcade was beside her and she was in his arms, her face against his chest. The tears she had fought so hard to choke back soaked into his shirt.

Nick held her close, whispering softly to her in French, brushing his lips against her forehead. For a few moments he allowed the feelings free inside him – the need to protect her, to comfort her, the blind rage against whoever had terrorized her. She had been so brave, such a fighter through all of this mess.

He pressed his cheek against the top of her head and held her tighter. It had been too long since he'd had anything of himself worth giving to another person. The idea that he wanted to was terrifying.

Annie held tight to him, knowing tenderness didn't come to him easily. This small gift from him meant more to her than she should have let it. As the tears passed, she wiped them from her cheeks with the back of her hand and studied his face as he met her stare, wondering . . . and afraid to wonder.

Her gaze shifted to the gift box she had left on her coffee table. Inside the box lay a small, finely detailed antique cameo brooch. The note enclosed read: 'To my guardian angel. Love, Marcus.'

Revulsion shuddered down her back.

Fourcade picked up the box and card and studied the brooch.

'He gave Pam gifts,' he said soberly. 'And he slashed her tires and left a dead snake in her pencil drawer at work.'

'Jekyll and Hyde,' Annie murmured.

If Renard had indeed been Pam's stalker, as Pam had insisted, then he had alternated between secretly terrifying her and giving her presents; showing his concern for her, claiming to be her friend. The contrast in those actions had kept the cops from taking seriously Pam's charge that Renard was the one stalking her.

Across the room the phone rang. Automatically, Annie looked at the clock. Half past three in the morning. Fourcade said nothing as she let the machine pick up.

'Annie? It's Marcus. I wish you were there. Please call me when you can. Someone just threw a rock through one of our windows. Mother is beside herself. And Victor – and I – I wish you could come over, Annie. You're the only one who cares. I need you.'

38

The flower woman was setting up at her station in the shade across the street from Our Lady, her pipe clenched between her teeth. The groundskeeper prowled the boulevard, a growling Weed Eater clutched in his hands.

'Here's the police gonna come arrest you, old witchy woman!' he screamed as Annie turned in the drive. He charged at the Jeep. 'Police girl! You gonna get her dis time or what?'

'Not me!' Annie called, driving past.

She parked the Jeep and, with the scarf and brooch in her pocketbook, headed for the building. If Pam had shown Renard's gifts to anyone, it would have been Lindsay. Annie hoped she was improved enough to tell her whether or not the things Renard had given her were the same tokens of affection being recycled to a new object of fixation.

The hospital was bustling with morning rounds for meals and medications. The strange plastic smell of antiseptics commingled with toast and oatmeal. The clang of meal trays and bedpans accented the hushed conversations and occasional moans as Annie walked down the halls.

The long, sleepless night hung heavy on her shoulders. The day stretched out in front of her like eighty miles of bad road. She would have to face an interview with the detective assigned to her shooting incident, and had already concocted a worst-case scenario in which Chaz Stokes caught the case and she would have to go to the sheriff and ask Stokes to be removed because she not only believed he was a suspect, but she also thought he could be a rapist and a murderer. She wouldn't have to worry about Stokes or anyone else killing her. She'd never make it out of Gus Noblier's office alive.

For a second or two she tried again to imagine Stokes sneaking up to her apartment to nail a dead cat to her wall, but she couldn't see it. He might have had the temperament for it, but she couldn't believe he would take the risk. She couldn't imagine anyone in the SO would.

Who then? Who could have slipped into the store, found those stairs, made it up to her apartment and down again unnoticed?

Renard had been to the Corners to leave gifts for her twice. Fanchon hadn't noticed him either time. If he had stalked Pam, he'd done so without detection.

Annie turned the corner to the ICU, and stepped directly into the path of Stokes.

His scowl was ferocious. He descended on her like a hawk, clamping a hand on her forearm and driving her away from the traffic flow in the hall.

'What the fuck are you doing here, Broussard?'

'Who put you in charge of visitors? I came to see my real estate agent.'

'Oh, really?' he sneered. 'Is she showing you something in a nice little two-bed room on the second floor?'

'She's an acquaintance and she's in the hospital. Why shouldn't I see her?' Annie challenged.

'Because I say so!' he barked. 'Because I know you ain't nothing but trouble, Broussard. I told you to stay the hell away from my cases.' His grip tightening on her arm, he pushed her another step toward the corner. 'You think I just like to hear myself talk? You think I won't come down on you like a ton of bricks?'

'Don't threaten me, Stokes,' Annie returned as she tried to wrench her arm free. 'You're in no position to –'

Alarms sounded at the ICU desk.

'Oh, shit!' someone yelled. 'She's seizing! Call Unser!'

Two nurses dashed for a room. Lindsay Faulkner's room.

Jerking free of Stokes, Annie rushed to the room and stared in horror at the scene. Faulkner's arms and legs were flailing, jerking like a marionette on the strings of a mad puppet master. A horrible, unearthly wail tore from her, accompanied by the shrieks of the monitors. Three nurses swarmed around her, trying to restrain her. One grabbed a padded tongue blade from the nurse server and worked to get it in Faulkner's mouth.

'Get an airway!'

'Got it!'

A doctor in blue scrubs burst past Annie into the room, calling, 'Diazepam: 10-milligram IV push!'

'Jesus H.,' Stokes breathed, pressing in close behind Annie. 'Jesus Fucking Christ.'

Annie glanced at him over her shoulder. His expression was likely no different from hers – shock, horror, anxious anticipation.

Another monitor began to bleat in warning and another round of expletives went up from the staff.

'She's in arrest!'

'Standard ACLS,' Unser snapped, thumping the woman on the chest. 'Phenytoin: 250 IV push. Phenobarbital: 55 IV push. I want a chem 7 and blood gases STAT! Tube and bag her!'

'She's in fine v-fib.'

'Shit!'

'Charge it up!'

One of the nurses spun around, a tube of blood in her hands. 'I'm sorry, we need you people out of here.' She herded Annie and Stokes from the door. 'Please go to the waiting area.'

Stokes's face was chalky. He rubbed his goatee. 'Jesus H.,' he said again, pulling his porkpie hat off and crumpling it with his fingers.

Annie hit him in the chest with both hands. 'What did you do to her?'

He looked as if she'd smacked him across the face with a dead carp. 'What? Nothing!'

'You come out of her room and two minutes later this happens!'

'Keep your voice down!' he ordered, reaching for her arm.

She jerked away from him. What if Stokes was the rapist? What if he was something worse?

'I went in to talk to her,' he said, as they entered the waiting area. 'She wasn't awake. Ask the nurse.'

'I will.'

'Christ, Broussard, what's the matter with you? You think I'm a killer?' he demanded, a flush creeping up his neck. 'Is that what you think? You think I'd walk into a hospital and kill a woman? You're out of your fucking mind!'

He sank down onto a chair and hung his long hands and the smashed hat between his knees.

'Maybe you oughta check yourself into this place,' he said. 'You need your damn head examined. First you go after Fourcade, now me. You're some kinda goddamn lunatic. You're like that crazy broad in *Fatal Attraction*. Obsessed – that's what you are.'

'She was better yesterday,' Annie insisted. 'I talked to her. Why would this happen?'

Stokes gave a helpless shrug. 'Do I look like George Fucking Clooney? I ain't no ER doc. It was some kind of seizure, that's all I know. Jesus, somebody bashed her head in with a telephone. What'd you expect?'

'If she dies, it's murder,' Annie declared.

Stokes pushed to his feet. 'I *told* you, Broussard –'

'It's murder,' she repeated. 'If she dies as a result of her injuries, the assault becomes a murder rap.'

'Well, yeah.' He dragged a jacket sleeve across his sweating forehead.

Annie stepped toward Faulkner's room again, trying to get a glimpse of her between the bodies of her rescue crew. The electric buzz and snap of the defibrillator was followed by another barrage of orders.

'Epinephrine and lidocaine! Dobutamine – run it wide open! Labs?'

'Not back.'

'Charging!'

'Clear!'

Buzz. Snap!

'Flat line!'

'We're losing her!'

They repeated the process so many times it seemed as if time, and hope, had become snagged in a continuous loop. Annie held herself rigid, directing her will at Lindsay Faulkner. *Live. Live. We need you.* But the loop broke. Motion in the room slowed to a stop.

'She's gone.'

'Damn.'

'Call it.'

Annie looked at the wall clock. Time of death: 7:49 A.M. Just like that, it was all over. Lindsay Faulkner was dead. A dynamic, capable, intelligent woman was gone. The suddenness of it stunned her. She had believed Faulkner would pull through, put her life back together, help solve the mysteries that had marred her life and taken her partner. But she was gone.

The staff trailed out of the room looking defeated, disgusted, blank. Annie wondered if any of them had known Lindsay Faulkner outside the walls of the hospital. She might have sold them a house or known them from the Junior League. It was a small-enough town.

The doctor came toward the waiting area, a frown digging deep into his long face. He looked fifty, his hair thick and the color of gunmetal. The name on his badge was FORBES UNSER. 'Are either of you family?'

'No,' Annie said. 'We're with the sheriff's office. I'm Deputy Broussard. I – ah – I knew her.'

'I'm sorry. She didn't make it,' he said succinctly.

'What happened? I thought she was doing better.'

'She was,' Unser said. 'The seizure was likely brought on by the trauma to her head. It led to cardiac arrest. These things happen. We did everything we could.'

Stokes stuck his hand out. 'Detective Stokes. I'm in charge of the Faulkner case.'

'Well, I hope you get the animal who attacked her,' Unser said. 'I've got a wife and two teenage daughters. I barely let them out of my sight these days. Madeline wants me to keep a gun under my pillow at night.'

'We're doing everything we can,' Stokes said. 'We'll want her body transported to Lafayette for an autopsy. Standard procedure. The sheriff's office will be in touch with your morgue.'

Unser nodded, then excused himself and went back to his normal duties for the day, the death of a woman in his care just a glitch in the schedule. *'These things happen.'*

Annie ducked into the ladies' room as Stokes started down the hall. She washed her hands and splashed cold water on her face, trying to clear away the images of Lindsay Faulkner seizing. How could it be a coincidence that the woman had gone into arrest not ten minutes after Stokes had been in the room with her? But there would be an autopsy. Stokes knew it. He was the one who had brought it up.

Unser was just coming out of another patient's room with a chart in his hand as Annie stepped back into the hall.

'Are you all right, Deputy?' he asked. 'You look a little pale.'

'I'll be fine. It was just a shock, that's all. That didn't look like a very pleasant way to die.'

'She fought it, but it was over before we could really do anything for her.'

'Is that the way it usually happens?'

'It's always a possibility with a head trauma.'

'I guess what I'm asking is: was there anything *unusual* about her death? Any strange readings, abnormal levels of . . . whatever?'

Unser shook his head. 'Not that I'm aware of. The blood test never came back. You can check with the lab.' He stepped up to the counter and handed the chart to the monitor technician. 'If they haven't lost it entirely, they might be able to answer your questions.'

Annie made her way to the lab and left the number for records with a woman who seemed as if she had just dropped in and offered to mind the place while everyone else went for coffee. Did she know if the Faulkner test results were in? No. Did she know when they might be? No. Did she know the name of the President of the United States? Probably not.

'Never get sick here,' Annie muttered as she walked away.

Outside the heat was already edging toward oppressive, an unwelcome joke from Mother Nature. Summer was long enough without adding an early preview. Sweat beaded immediately between her breasts and shoulder blades. The sun burned into her scalp.

'You gonna arrest me now?'

Stokes stood beside his Camaro in the red zone, smoking a cigarette. He had shed his jacket, leaving his lime green shirt free to blind anyone looking directly at it.

'I'm sorry,' Annie said without sincerity. 'I overreacted.'

'You accused me of being a goddamn killer.' He flung the cigarette butt down on the asphalt beside a crumpled Snickers wrapper and crushed it out with the toe of his brown and white spectators. 'Personally, I take umbrage at that. You know what I'm saying?'

'I said I was sorry.'

'Yeah, well, that don't cut it by half. I've had it with you, Broussard.'

'And what are you gonna do about it?' she asked quietly. 'Shoot me?'

'I hear I'd have to get in line. I've got better things to do.'

'Like screw around with the evidence on those rape cases?'

'Don't fuck with me, Broussard. I'll have your badge. I mean it.'

He slid behind the wheel of the Camaro and started the engine with a roar. Annie stood on the sidewalk and watched him drive away. He had just lost a victim and his primary concern was getting her fired. A charming, caring individual, that Chaz.

The groundskeeper emerged from behind the statue of Mary and made a beeline for Annie with his hedge clippers. 'Police girl! Hey! I pays my taxes! I'm a vet'ran! You go, you arrest dat ol' witchy woman! Stealin' dem flowers out the Vet'rans Park!'

'I'm sorry, sir,' Annie said, her eyes on Stokes's car as it turned the corner onto Dumas. 'Has she murdered anyone?'

'What?!' he squealed. 'No, she ain't killed nobody, but –'

'Then I can't help you.'

She walked away from him toward the Jeep, her mind on Stokes, while Donnie Bichon's pearl white Lexus turned out of the parking lot behind her and drove away down the backstreet.

Donnie was shaking like a man with DTs, though it hadn't been all that long since his last drink. He'd been allowing himself a shot every hour since Fourcade had left him, in an attempt to steady his nerves. All it seemed to be doing was acting as an accelerant for the stress eating a hole in the lining of his stomach. The flecks of blood in his vomit had confirmed that suspicion.

After Fourcade's first visit, he had passed out in the bathroom and dreamed of Pam. Dark hair and shining eyes. A sunny smile. A tongue like a pit viper. Hands tipped with claws that dug into him, closed around his balls, and choked his masculinity. He loved her and he hated her. She had grown up and he never wanted to. Life had seemed best when he was twenty, when he had the world by the tail and no responsibilities. Now the world had *him* by the tail.

Then suddenly Fourcade had him by the scruff of the neck, and Donnie found himself going down face-first into a swirling pool of vomit. Startled, he tried to grab a breath half a second too late, filled his mouth, and came up choking and retching.

'Yeah, you choke on it,' Fourcade growled. He bent his body over Donnie's, all but riding him into the porcelain. 'That's what your lies taste like the second time around.'

Donnie spat into the toilet bowl. The smell of fresh urine was strong as his bladder let go. 'Jesus! God!' he gasped and spat again, trying to clear the cold chunks of vomit from his mouth.

'Where were you tonight?' Fourcade demanded.

'You're crazy!'

Nick shoved his head back in the bowl. 'Wrong answer, Tulane! Where were you tonight? Where'd you get that mud on your boots?'

'I told you!'

'Don't fuck with me, Donnie. I'm in no mood. Where were you?'

'I told you!' Donnie cried. Tears streamed down his face through the puke on his cheeks. 'I don't know what you want from me!'

'You're gonna give me the keys to your car, Tulane. And I'm gonna look through every inch of it. And if I find a rifle, I'm gonna bring it back in here, stick it up your ass, and blow your brains out. Are we clear on this?'

Donnie dug his keys out of his jeans pocket and tossed them on the floor. 'I didn't do anything!'

'You better pray to God that's the truth, Donnie,' Fourcade said as he bent to scrape up the keys. ''Cause I don't think you'd know the truth if it bit your dick off.'

Terrified and sick, disgusted with himself, Donnie forced himself to his feet and followed Fourcade out to the garage, grabbing a kitchen towel as an afterthought to wipe the mess from his face. He watched from the doorway as Fourcade popped the trunk on the Lexus and dug through the junk — a bag of golf clubs, a nail gun, a filthy Igloo cooler, gloves, crumpled receipts, a toolbox, half a dozen baseball caps with the Bichon Bayou Development logo.

'You know, you're just as rotten as everybody says, Fourcade,' he declared. 'You don't have a warrant. You got no call to treat me like this. You're not a cop; you're a goddamn jackbooted thug. I shoulda let you rot in jail.'

'You gonna wish you had, Tulane, if I find anything in this car to hook you up with taking a shot at Annie Broussard last night.'

'I don't know what you're talking about. And why should you care about Broussard?'

'I got my reasons.' He closed the trunk and moved to the passenger's side doors. 'You know, you're right for once, Donnie. I'm not a cop, I'm on suspension. That makes me a private citizen, which means I don't need a warrant to seize incriminating evidence. Ain't that a kick in the head?'

'You're trespassing,' Donnie declared as Fourcade pulled open a back door.

'Me? Trespassing in the home of my good friend who bailed me outta jail? Who would believe that?'

'Is there any law you *won't* break?'

He shut the door and strolled back toward Donnie, shining the light in Donnie's face. 'Well, I'll tell you, Tulane, me, I believe life is a journey of self-exploration, and lately I'm discovering that I have a greater concern for justice than I have for the law. Can you appreciate the difference?'

He climbed the two steps to the kitchen door and snatched hold of Donnie's shirtfront before he could backpedal. 'The law would dictate that I would have somebody else run you in tonight and interview you with regards to this shooting incident —'

'I didn't shoot anybody —'

'While justice would bypass the formalities and cut to the heart of the matter.'

'It's not for you to be judge and jury.'

'You left out executioner.' He arched a brow. 'Was that purposeful or Freudian? Not that it matters. I find it amusing that you bring the point up now, Donnie. You seemed to think it would have been just fine if I'd dispatched Renard to hell the other night. Now it's you standing on that

1139

line, and you'd just as soon I keep to the proper side of it. I'd call you a hypocrite, but I have my own problems with the black and white of it all.'

He uncurled his fist from Donnie's shirt and took half a step back. 'I'm gonna let you off with a warning, Tulane. I didn't find what I thought I might, but if I so much as hear a whisper or come across a hair that might connect you to this, I'll find you, Donnie, and I won't be in a philosophical mood.'

The crazy son of a bitch.

Donnie had gone straight back into the bathroom after Fourcade left and puked again, then sat on the edge of the tub and stared at the streaks of blood in the bowl. Scotch, nerves, and imminent financial disaster were not a good mix.

He decided what he needed was a little something of the pharmaceutical variety to settle him down so he could think his way out of this mess. Old Dr Hollier had obliged, sympathetic to the tragedy in his life. He didn't know the half of it, Donnie thought.

Lindsay Faulkner was dead and Fourcade knew about Marcotte.

With the bitch queen of Bayou Breaux gone, the way was clear to make a deal for the realty – except for one obstacle: Fourcade.

How could Fourcade have possibly known about that phone call? Paranoia had driven Donnie to an assortment of wild conclusions involving phone taps, all of which he had subsequently dismissed in a more sober moment. Fourcade knew only about a single call, last night's call, nothing else, and he was in no position to be in on any phone tap. He was suspended, awaiting trial. Assault charges. He'd nearly beaten Renard to death.

That particular reminder had Donnie reaching for the open bottle of Mylanta he'd wedged into his cup holder. *Never should have paid that bail.* He had started hoping Fourcade would be bound over for trial next week, and would be thrown back in jail, but Donnie's lawyer had informed him the detective's bail would likely be continued and he would be a free man indefinitely, trial pending or no.

Pam had always told him he acted first and considered consequences too late. He wondered if she had ever realized just how right she'd been.

39

'You are late *again*.'

Myron stood at rigid attention in the middle of the room, his hands knotted together at the buckle of his skinny black belt, his expression sour with disapproval.

'I'm sorry, Myron,' Annie said, barely sparing him a glance as she entered his domain and went to the card drawer.

'*Mr* Myron,' he intoned. 'I'll have you know, I've spoken with the sheriff about your poor performance since you were assigned to me as *my* assistant. You are chronically tardy and run off at your own whim. This is a records department. Records are synonymous with stability. I cannot allow chaos in my records department.'

'I'm sorry,' she mumbled as she flicked through the evidence cards.

Myron's face pinched tight as he leaned over her shoulder. 'What are you doing, Deputy Broussard? Are you listening to me?'

Annie kept her eyes on her task. 'I'm a goof-off. You're pissed off. You want Gus to take me off this job, but I'll try to do better. Honest.'

She pulled the evidence card from the Nolan rape and ran a fingertip down the inventory. There, listed on the third line: HAIRS. The pubic hair Stokes had fished out of Jennifer Nolan's bathtub drain.

She tapped one foot impatiently. Myron moved into her field of vision again, looking a little uncertain at her lack of response to his tirade.

'What you looking at?' he asked. 'What you think you're doing?'

'My job,' she said simply, sliding the evidence card back in place.

Hairs had been logged in and checked back out to the lab. That didn't mean the hairs belonged to the rapist. Jennifer Nolan was a redhead. Her pubic hair would have stood out from any darker hair in the drain. Stokes could have picked out what he wanted and left the rest – left his own – to wash away.

Annie's stomach churned. She was on the verge of accusing a detective of being a serial rapist. If she was right, Chaz Stokes was not only a rapist but a murderer – either indirectly or directly. If she was wrong, he'd have her badge. She needed evidence, and he was in charge of every piece of it.

'Whatsa matter with you, Broussard?' Myron squawked. 'You sick or something? You been drinking?'

'Yeah, you know, I'm not feeling very well,' Annie mumbled, pushing the drawer shut. 'I might be sick. Excuse me.'

'I don't truck with drinkers,' Myron warned as she walked away. 'There ain't no place for that kind of thing in records. Alcohol is a tool of the devil.'

Annie wound her way through the halls to her locker room, went in, and sat down on her folding chair beneath the dull glow of the bare lightbulb. Someone had drilled a new hole in the wall – breast height. She would need to break out the spackling compound, but what she needed now was a few moments to untangle the threads in her mind.

'*Keep the threads separate or you end up with a knot,* 'Toinette.'

She had a knot all right, and she was trapped in the middle of it. Renard was sending her gifts. Donnie Bichon was in cahoots with Marcotte, who was in cahoots with the mob. Stokes was a bad cop at best and a killer at worst.

'You asked for it,' she muttered. 'You wanted to be a detective. You had to solve the mystery.'

One mystery at a time. Stokes seemed the most pressing problem. If her suspicions about him were right, then other women would be in danger.

'*I'll* be in danger,' she said, a flashback of last night coming to her in jarring black and white: the ink black of the night, the pale crushed shell of the parking lot, the white papers scattering at her feet as she dropped the files. The sharp crack of the rifle, the shattering of glass.

The memory bled back into another and another. The anger in Stokes's eyes as they had argued about the missing evidence. The fury on his face that night months ago when he had fought with her in the parking lot of the Voodoo Lounge because she wasn't interested in going out with him. The aggressive way he had moved toward her, as if he meant to strike her or grab her.

He was a man capable of instant, intense rage, which he covered with loose, easy charm. He was by turns irrational and coldly logical, depending on the subject. Unpredictable. A chameleon. These were traits that had formed over the course of his life, traits he had brought with him when he had come here from Mississippi four years ago. Coincidentally, not long before the Bayou Strangler had begun his reign of terror. He may have even worked one or both of the Partout Parish murders connected to the Strangler: Annie Delahoussaye and Savannah Chandler.

That could be easily checked out, though Annie didn't see the need. Despite the gossip that had run wild since Pam's death, she didn't believe the allegations that the cops had tampered with the evidence in the Strangler case. No, that evil had been burned out of Partout Parish . . . and a new one was taking root in the ashes.

What had brought Stokes here in the first place? she wondered. More important, what had he left behind? A good service record? Had his last supervisor been sad to lose him or glad to see the last of him? Had the city or county he worked in experienced a sudden drop in sex crimes after Stokes had gone? Had he left any victims in his wake?

It was rare for a man to become a sexual predator in his thirties. That kind of behavior generally started earlier – late teens or early twenties – and continued on throughout his life. Despite the claims of various tax-sponsored programs, true sexual predators were seldom if ever rehabilitated. Their heads were wired wrong, their malevolent attitudes toward women carved forever in stone hearts.

She needed to get into Stokes's personnel file, get the name of the last force he had served on in Mississippi. Personnel files were kept in the sheriff's offices under the ever-vitriolic, blue-shadowed glare of Valerie Comb.

A fist struck the door to the locker room with the force of a hurled rock, making Annie jump.

'Broussard? You in there?'

'Who wants to know?'

'Perez.' He pulled the door open and stuck his head in. 'Shit, I figured the least I could get out of this was to see you naked.'

'Get out of what?' she said peevishly.

'The case. Your shooter. I'm your detective. Lucky fucking me. Come on. I need your statement and I ain't got all day.'

Perez was as interested in her case as he was in the politics of Uruguay. He doodled on a yellow legal pad as Annie related not only the shooting incident but her run-in with the Cadillac Man the night before, since there was the possibility the two incidents were related.

'Did you get a tag number?'

'No.'

'Did you see the driver?'

'He was wearing a ski mask.'

'Know anybody with a big car like that?'

'No.'

'Why didn't you call it in that night?'

'Would you have done anything?'

He gave her a flat look.

'I wrote it up the next day,' she said. 'Called around to the body shops looking for the car. Nothing. Checked the log sheets for reports of a stolen Caddy, or something like a Caddy. Nothing.'

'And you didn't see the shooter last night?'

'No.'

'Didn't see his vehicle?'

'No.'

'Any ideas who it might have been?'

Annie looked at him for a long moment, knowing she couldn't name any of her prime suspects without revealing the mess she'd embroiled herself in, and certainly not without pissing Perez off by casting aspersions on two cops.

'I'm not very popular at the moment.'

'What a news flash.' He narrowed his eyes and stroked a finger across one side of his bushy mustache. 'I figured you'd point the finger at Fourcade. He's gotta hate you more than anyone else. We all know how you feel about him.'

'You don't know shit about me. It wasn't Fourcade.'

'How do you know?'

'Because Fourcade would be man enough to show his face, and if he wanted me dead, we wouldn't be having this conversation,' she said, rising from her chair. 'Are we finished, Detective? We both know this is pointless and I've got work to do.'

Perez shrugged. 'Yeah. I know where to find you . . . 'til somebody wises up and boots your tight little ass outta here.'

Annie left the interview room, glad she hadn't bothered to tell him about the crucified cat. Back in records, Myron seemed in danger of spontaneous combustion.

'Look at the time!' he ranted, scurrying around the office like a windup toy gone mad. 'Look at the time! You been gone half the day!'

Annie rolled her eyes. 'Well, excuse me for being the victim of a crime. You know, Myron, you are an extremely unsympathetic individual. I practically witnessed someone dying this morning. Someone took a shot at me last night. My life is basically in the toilet here, and all you do is rag on me.'

'Sympathy? Sympathy?' He chirped the word as if it were a questionable noun from another language. 'Why should I show you sympathy? You are *my* assistant. I'm the one needs sympathy.'

'Your wife has all my sympathy,' Annie said, pulling her chair back from her desk. 'You must have about ruined all the upholstery on her furniture by now with that stick up your ass.'

Myron gave an indignant sniff. Annie ignored him. She was past currying his favor. With everything that was happening or about to happen, she figured she would be either dead or fired inside a week. Where she wouldn't be was working in this clerical hell for the rest of her life.

Two minutes later she received the summons to Noblier's office.

Valerie Comb was not at her post when Annie arrived at the sheriff's office. The room was empty, the file cabinets with the personnel records unguarded. The door to Gus's inner office was closed. Annie went to it and pressed her ear against the blond wood. No conversation sounds. No chair creaks. Nothing.

She glanced longingly at the file cabinets again. It wouldn't take more than a minute – open the S drawer, find Stokes, one glance and she'd be done. There might not be another chance.

Swallowing at the hard lump of fear wedged in her throat like a chicken bone, she crossed the room to the cabinets, reached for the handle on the S drawer.

'May I help you?'

Annie swung around at the sound of the sharp voice, hastily crossing her arms over her chest. Valerie Comb stood with one hand on the doorknob, the other holding a steaming cup of coffee. Her overdone eyes were narrowed in suspicion, her mouth pressed into a thin painted line.

'I'm here to see the sheriff,' Annie said, beaming innocence.

Without comment, Valerie went to her desk, set the coffee down, and settled her fanny in her chair. Eyes on Annie, she pulled a pencil from her rat's nest of bleached hair and punched the intercom button with the eraser end of the pencil so as not to chip her slut red nails. Rumor had it she'd done half the guys in the department. She'd probably done Stokes.

'Sheriff, Deputy Broussard is here to see you.'

'Send her in!' Gus bellowed, his voice too big for the plastic box to contain.

Heart beating three steps too fast, Annie let herself into Noblier's inner sanctum. The shades were drawn. He sat back in his chair rubbing his eyes as if he might just have awakened from an afternoon nap.

'You must be out for some kind of record, Deputy,' he said, shaking his head.

'Sir?'

He waved at the chair across the desk from him. 'Sit down, Annie. Myron's been bending my ear. He says you're unreliable and you might be drinking on the job.'

'That's not true, sir.'

'That's the second time in a week I've heard your name and alcohol mentioned in the same breath.'

'I haven't been drinking, sir. I'll gladly take any test you want me to.'

'What I want is to know why two weeks ago I barely knew more than your name, now suddenly you're the burr up everybody's ass.' He leaned against his forearms on the desktop. To his right, paperwork was stacked like the Leaning Tower of Pisa. To his left lay a giant ceremonial ribbon-cutting scissors like something out of *Gulliver's Travels*.

'An unfortunate coincidence?' Annie suggested.

'Deputy, there are three things I do not believe in: UFOs, moderate Republicans, and coincidence. What the hell is going on with you? Every time I turn around you're in the middle of something you shouldn't be. You're working in records, for Christ's sake. How the hell can you get in trouble working in records?'

'Bad luck.'

'You're tripping over bodies, fighting with other deputies. Stokes was in here this morning telling me you were at the hospital when that Faulkner woman died. Why is that?'

Annie explained her absences from records as best she could, painting a picture of innocence that had been misinterpreted by Myron. She managed to depict herself as an unfortunate bystander regarding Lindsay Faulkner's attack and demise – in the wrong place at the wrong time. Noblier listened, his skepticism plain on his face.

'And this business about you getting shot at last night? What was that about?'

'I don't know, sir.'

'I sincerely doubt that,' Gus said, rising from his chair. He rubbed at a kink in his lower back as he walked away from the desk. 'Has Detective Fourcade made any effort to contact you since his release on bail?'

'Sir?'

'He's got a big ax to grind with you, Annie. As much as I respect Nick's abilities as a detective, you and I both know he's wrapped a little too tight.'

'With all due respect, sir, the harassment I've experienced since Detective Fourcade's arrest has come from other sources.'

'Yeah, you've managed to bring out the worst in a lot of people.'

Annie refrained from pointing out that blaming the victim was politically incorrect these days. The less she drew the sheriff into this mess at this time, the better. She had no proof of anything against anybody. He had already decided she was probably more trouble than she was worth. If she started making accusations against Stokes, it might just push him beyond tolerance.

'Maybe you should take some personal time, Annie,' he suggested, coming back to the desk. He pulled a file from the top of the stack and flipped it open. 'According to your record, you carried over all your sick days from last year. You could take yourself a little vacation.'

'I'd rather not, sir,' Annie said, holding herself stiff in her chair. 'I don't think that would send a very good message. It might look to the press like you're trying to force me out because of the Fourcade thing. Punishing your only female patrol officer for stopping a bad cop from killing a suspect – that's a pretty volatile story.'

Gus's head came up and he regarded her with a piercing stare. 'Are you threatening me, Deputy Broussard?'

She did her best to look doe-eyed. 'No, sir. Never. I'm just saying how it might look to some people.'

'People after my hide,' he muttered, talking aloud to himself. He scratched at his afternoon beard stubble. 'Smith Pritchett would love that, the ungrateful swine. He'll call me corrupt, a racist, *and* a sexist. Small-minded, that's what he is. Doesn't see the big picture. All he really wants is revenge on Fourcade for screwing that search at Renard's. He wanted to prosecute the big slam-dunk, media-circus case. Mr. Big Headlines.'

He snatched a folded newspaper off his blotter and snapped a big finger against a photograph of Pritchett at the Tuesday press conference, looking stern and authoritative. The headline read: 'Task Force Named in Mardi Gras Rapist Cases.'

'Look at that,' Gus complained. 'Like it was Pritchett's task force. Like he had squat to do with trying to solve these cases. You think you know a man . . .'

Annie tuned out the lament. She took the paper from the sheriff's hands as he walked away. The task force was page two news in the Wednesday *Daily Advertiser* from Lafayette. The article gave a brief encapsulation of the news conference and details of the three attacks that had taken place in Partout Parish over the last week's time. But it was the small sidebar that drew Annie's attention. Just two paragraphs with the headline 'Task Force Leader Experienced.'

Heading the Partout Parish task force in the investigation of what has come to be called the 'Mardi Gras Rapist' cases will be Detective Charles Stokes. Stokes, 32, has been with the Partout Parish Sheriff's Office since 1993 and is described by Sheriff August F. Noblier as 'a diligent and thorough investigator'.

Prior to joining the force in Partout Parish, Stokes served with the Hattiesburg (Mississippi) Police Department, where he also worked as a detective, and was part of the team credited with solving a series of sexual assaults against female students on the campus of William Carey College.

Chaz Stokes knew all about rape cases. He'd been there before. The question was: Had he solved the William Carey College rapes cases or had he committed them?

1147

40

The old Andrew Carnegie Library was open until nine on Thursdays. Annie hovered behind the three makeshift computer bays from about five-fifteen until the junior high geeks who used the machines to surf the Net for things they were too young to see had to go home for supper. Then she settled in at the computer farthest from prying eyes and went to work.

The computers had been a gift to the library from a well-known local author, Conroy Cooper. A new library would have been a better gift. The Carnegie had been old when Christ was in short pants. Dank and dimly lit, the place had always given Annie the creeps. The air was musty with the smell of moldering paper. Every wooden surface had either turned black with age or been worn pale from use. Even the librarian, Miss Stitch, seemed slightly mildewed.

But the computers were new and that was all that mattered. Annie was able to access the William Carey College Library, and once in that system, call up articles from the *Hattiesburg American* that related to the college rape cases in 1991 and 1992. She read them on the screen, scrutinizing for any similarities between those cases and the newly dubbed 'Mardi Gras' cases.

The victims — seven of them — had all been college students or had worked at the college. Physical characteristics of the women varied; ages hung in the late teens, early twenties. The assaults had taken place in their bedrooms late at night. Each woman lived in a ground-floor apartment. The attacks took place during warm weather, the rapist gaining entry through open windows. He used cut-off lengths of panty hose, which he brought with him, to tie his victims up. He spoke very little throughout the course of the rapes, his voice described as 'a harsh whisper'. Though none of the women had gotten a clean look at her rapist because he had worn a ski mask, several speculated from his voice that 'he may have been black'. The rapist used a condom, which he disposed of away from the scene of the crime, and no semen or pubic hairs had been recovered for evidence. Before leaving the last of his victims, the attacker helped himself to cash and credit cards.

Evander Darnell Flood, the man arrested for the crimes, had given that victim's Visa card to his girlfriend. According to an acquaintance hauled in on unrelated drug charges, Flood had bragged to him about the rapes. While his record was not admissible in court, Evander had previously been a guest of the Mississippi correctional facility in Parchman for seven years on a rape charge. Two previous charges had been dropped due to lack of evidence.

The prosecution built a circumstantial case against Flood with evidence discovered by the Hattiesburg Police Department detectives. And, while Evander swore to the last that he was being framed, that the police had planted the evidence, the jury convicted him and the judge sent him back to Parchman for the rest of his natural life.

Annie sat back from the computer screen and rubbed her eyes. There were differences in the cases and similarities, but then the same could be said for the majority of rape cases. A certain methodology was common to the crime. The differences tended to be personal: One rapist was a talker, using foul sexual language to help get him off; the next one was silent. One might prefer to cover his victim's face to depersonalize her; another would threaten her at knifepoint to keep her eyes open so he might see her fear.

She found more similarities here than differences, but it was the circumstances surrounding Flood's arrest and conviction that made Annie uneasy. Flood swore he was innocent, like 99.9 percent of the scumbags in prison. But the case against him hadn't been that strong. The acquaintance could easily have lied as part of a deal for leniency in his own case. Witnesses who claimed to have seen a man matching Flood's description in the vicinity of several of the rapes told weak, conflicting stories. Flood claimed to have found the last victim's credit card in the hallway of his apartment building. He claimed the cops had railroaded him because he had a record and lived in the area where the crimes had taken place.

He would have been an easy target for a frame. Because of his record, the cops would have known all about Evander early on. He lived in the area, had a part-time janitorial job at the college. His live-in girlfriend worked nights, robbing him of an alibi witness.

Annie closed her eyes and saw Stokes. As a detective assigned to the cases, planting evidence would have been a simple matter for him. He had been there in Renard's home the night Fourcade had found Pam's ring. Everyone had jumped on Nick with the accusation of tampering because he had been accused before. No one had looked twice at Chaz Stokes.

She went through the steps of instructing the computer to print the articles, then turned around in her chair while the dot-matrix printer chattered away. At the far end of one row of reference books, a face stared at her, then darted back into the shadows. Victor Renard.

Annie's heart gave a jolt. The library was nearly deserted. What action there was, was on the first floor: a blue-haired ladies' reading group trying to find satanic messages in The *Celestine Prophecy*. The second floor, where Annie was, was quiet as a church.

Victor peeked around the end of another bookcase, saw that she was looking right at him, and darted back.

'Victor?' Annie said. Abandoning the printer to its work, she eased out of her chair and moved carefully toward the bookcases. 'Mr. Renard? You don't have to hide from me.'

She made her way slowly down one row, muscles tensing, lungs aching against the held breath. The lighting back here was poor. Gooseflesh crawled down the back of her neck.

'It's Annie Broussard, Victor. Remember me? I'm trying to help Marcus,' she said, her conscience pinching her for lying to a mentally challenged person. Would she get another day in purgatory if her ultimate goal was good? *The end justifies the means.*

She started to turn right at the end of the human sciences row and caught a glimpse of him cowering in the corner to her left.

'How are you, Victor?' she asked, trying to sound pleasant, conversational. She turned toward him slowly, not wanting to spook him.

He didn't seem comfortable with her proximity. She was no more than a yard from him. He made a small uncertain keening sound in his throat and began to rock himself from side to side.

'It's all been very hard on you, hasn't it?' Annie said, her sympathy for him genuine.

According to what little she'd read about autistics in trying to understand more about Marcus Renard's brother, routine was sacred. Yet, Victor's life had to have been an endless series of upsets since the death of Pam Bichon. The press, the cops, disgruntled citizens had all focused their scrutiny and their speculation on the Renard family. Plenty of rumors had run around town that perhaps Victor himself was dangerous. His condition baffled and frightened people. His behavior seemed odd at best, and often inappropriate.

'Mask, mask. *No* mask,' he mumbled, looking at her out the corner of his eye.

Mask. Since Pam's death the word had taken on a menacing connotation that had only been compounded by the recent rapes. Coming from someone whose behavior was so strange, someone who happened to be the brother of a murder suspect, it added to the eeriness.

He raised the book in his hands, a collection of Audubon's prints, to cover his face and tapped a finger against the picture on the front, a finely detailed rendering of a mockingbird. '*Mimus polyglottos. Mimus, mimic.* Mask, no mask.'

Slowly he lowered the book to peer over it at her. His eyes had a glasslike quality, hard and clear and unblinking. 'Transformation, *transmutation*, alteration. *Mask.*'

'Do you think I look like someone I'm not? Is that it? Do I remind you of Pam?' Annie asked gently. How much of what had happened could be locked inside Victor Renard's mind? What secret, what clue, might be trapped in the strange labyrinth that was his brain?

He covered his face again. 'Red *and* white. Then *and* now.'

'I don't understand, Victor.'

'I think he's confused,' Marcus said.

Annie swung toward him, startled. She hadn't heard his approach at all. They were back in the farthest, dimmest corner of the library. She had Victor on one side, Marcus on another, a wall to her back.

'That you resemble Pam, but that you aren't Pam,' Marcus finished. 'He can't decide if it's good or bad, past or present.'

Victor rocked himself and bumped the Audubon book against his forehead over and over, muttering, 'Red, red, enter out.'

'How much of his language do you understand?' Annie asked.

'Some.' He was still speaking through gritted teeth, his jaw being wired shut, but with less difficulty. The swelling was gone from his face. The bruises looked yellow and black in the poor light. 'It's a code of sorts.'

'Very red,' Victor mumbled unhappily.

'*Red* is a watchword for things that upset him,' Marcus explained. 'It's all right, Victor. Annie is a friend.'

'Very white, very red,' Victor said, peering over the book at Annie. 'Very white, very red.'

'White is good, red is bad. Why he's putting the two together that way is beyond me. He's been very upset since the shooting the other night.'

'I can relate to that,' Annie said, turning her attention more squarely on Marcus. 'Someone took a shot at me last night.'

'My God.' She couldn't tell if his shock was genuine or not. He took a step toward her. 'Were you hurt?'

'No. I ducked, as it happened.'

'Do you know who did it? Was it because of me?'

'I don't know.' *Was it you*? she wondered.

'It's terrible someone would want to hurt you, Annie,' Marcus said, his gaze a little too intent. He inched closer to her by just shifting his weight. 'Especially when you know it was someone wanting to punish you for doing the right thing. That's the way of the world, I'm sad to say. Evil tries to eradicate good.

'Were you alone?' His voice softened. 'You must have been frightened.'

'That would be a mild understatement,' she said, resisting the urge to step away from him. 'I suppose I should be getting used to that kind of thing. I seem to be a favorite target all of a sudden.'

'I can empathize. I know exactly what you went through, Annie,' he said. 'Having a stranger reach into your life and commit an act of violence. It's a violation. It's rape. You feel so vulnerable, so powerless. So alone. Don't you?'

A shudder vibrated just under Annie's skin. He said nothing

threatening, nothing menacing. He offered her his understanding and concern ... in a way that was just a little too intense. He dabbed at the corners of his mouth with his handkerchief, as if the subject matter were making him salivate. Something about the light in his eyes seemed almost excitement, a secret. No one would have understood – except Pam Bichon. And possibly Elaine Ingram before her.

'I know what it's like,' he said. 'You know I do. You've been there for me so many times. I wish I could have been there for you. I feel so selfish now – calling you about someone throwing a rock through one of our parlor windows last night, wondering why you didn't call me back. And all the while you were in danger.'

'You called the sheriff's office, didn't you? About the rock?'

'I shouldn't have bothered,' he said bitterly. 'They're probably using the rock for a paperweight today. I'm sure they threw the note away.'

'What note?'

'The one bound to the rock with a rubber band. It said YOU DIE NEXT, KILLER.'

Victor made his strange squealing sound again and covered his face with his book.

'It was terribly upsetting,' Marcus went on. 'Someone is terrorizing my family, and the sheriff's office has done nothing. I'm being stalked just as surely as Pam was stalked by some deranged person, and the sheriff's office would be just as happy if someone killed me. You're the only one who cares, Annie.'

'Well, I'm afraid last night I was busy caring about not getting killed myself.'

'I'm so sorry. The last thing I want is to see you hurt, Annie – especially on my account.' He shifted closer, tilting his head down to an angle for sharing secrets. 'I care a great deal about you, Annie,' he murmured. 'You know that.'

'I hope you don't mean that in a personal way, Marcus,' she said, testing him. There were people just one floor down and his brother standing ten feet away, watching them over the edge of his picture book. He wouldn't risk anything here. 'I'm working on your case. That's all.'

He looked stunned for a split second, then smiled in relief. 'I understand. Conflict of interest. Your saving my life – twice – was merely in the line of duty.'

'That's right.'

'And your looking into my alibi and coming to the house the other night, even though it wasn't officially your case – that was just because you're a good cop.'

'That's right,' Annie said, another ripple of unease ribboning through her. Once again, he was reading something into her actions that simply wasn't true. And yet, his response was nothing she could even have related to someone else as being inappropriate.

'I'm just a deputy,' she said. 'That's all I can be to you, Marcus. Do you understand what I'm telling you? You shouldn't be sending me gifts.'

'A simple show of my gratitude,' he said.

'Your taxes pay my salary. That's all the gratitude I need.'

'But you've gone above and beyond the call. You deserve more than you're getting.'

Victor whimpered and rocked himself. 'Then *and* now. Enter out. Time and time *now*, Marcus. *Very* red.'

'It's not appropriate for you to give me gifts.'

'Do you have a boyfriend?' he asked, straightening, a fine thread of irritation tightening his voice. 'Did it make him angry – me sending you things?'

'That would be none of your business,' Annie said. She hardly dared blink for fear she would miss some small nuance of expression that would give him away.

'*Very red!*' Victor keened. He sounded on the verge of tears. 'Enter out now!'

Marcus glanced at his watch and frowned. 'Ah, we'd better go. It's getting on toward eight. Victor's bedtime. Can't disrupt the schedule, can we, Victor?'

Victor clutched his book to his chest and hurried toward the door to the hall.

Marcus made a stiff little bow to Annie, trying to be dashing. 'May I walk you out, Annie? Obviously, you need to be careful.'

She refrained from pointing out that having him escort her would hardly be considered a safe thing. He was either a killer or possibly the target of a killer. 'I'm not leaving just yet. I've got some work to do.'

He let it go as they started down the aisle toward the front of the room and better light. 'Have you made any progress on finding that driver who helped me?'

'No. I've been very busy.'

'But you're trying.'

The DMV list was still under the blotter on her desk. 'I'll do what I can.'

'I know you will, Annie,' he said as they reached the vacant desk area, where Victor stood in the doorway facing the hall, rocking himself from side to side. 'I know you'll do your best for me, Annie. You're very special.'

Before Annie could protest again, he said, 'Will you be going to the street dance with anyone Friday?'

As if he meant to ask her, Annie thought, amazed. She took another step away from him. 'I'll be going in uniform if they hold it at all. I'm scheduled to work.'

Marcus sighed. 'Too bad. You've been working so hard lately.'

Because of you, Annie thought, but she wasn't going to be the one to bring on another round of cloying gratitude.

She watched the Renard brothers go, Victor hugging the wall of the stairwell, his bird book raised to hide his face. *Mask.*

He wanted to hide who he was behind another façade. His brother may well have been hiding an alter ego beneath his bland, ordinary face. Annie turned toward the printer and the stack of articles that involved Chaz Stokes, who used his badge as a mask to cover God knew what. *Mask.*

'Yeah, Victor,' she murmured, collecting her things. 'There seems to be a lot of that going around.'

'It doesn't match,' Doll harped. 'I told you it wouldn't match. I had a premonition.'

'It's wet, Mother,' Marcus said, dabbing at the paint with a sponge in hopes of better blending it in with the rest of the wall. 'Paint always appears lighter when dry than when wet.'

Doll scrutinized the dining room wall, her thin face pinched tight with concentration. She crossed her arms and declared, 'I don't believe it's the same color. What's it called? Is it called *forest?*'

'I don't know, Mother. The can has a number, not a name.'

'Well, it had ought to say *forest*. I distinctly remember choosing the color *forest*. If it doesn't say *forest*, then how can you know it's the same shade?'

'Because I *know* that it is.'

He could feel his patience fraying like an old rope, and he resented her for it. He had come home from the library with his head full of Annie, a pleasant warmth glowing just under his skin. Shutting out Victor's incessant noise, he had spent the drive home replaying the encounter in his mind, from Annie's look of surprise when she'd first turned to face him to the subtle messages in her tone of voice. She couldn't publicly accept his attentions until she had cleared him of Pam's murder. He understood. He would have to be discreet. It would be like a game between them, another secret only they shared.

'It's not *forest*,' Doll muttered, moving to examine the spot from another angle. 'It's just as I saw it in my premonition. The color won't match no matter what we do, and every time I look at that wall I'll be taken with the fear of that night. Fear and shame – that's all my life has become. I can barely bring myself to leave the house these days.'

Marcus bit back the words that sprang instantly to his tongue. She had hounded him all morning to take her into town because she needed to go to the drugstore and the supermarket. She didn't trust him to get the brands she liked and she refused to write them down because she didn't necessarily go by names, but by the colors and graphics on the packages. And of course she couldn't take her own car and go herself on account of her nerves and the mysterious undiagnosed palsy that had been coming on her lately – because of him and the unwanted attention he'd drawn to the family.

'All because of your infatuation with that woman,' she said now, as if she was simply jumping back into the conversation they'd had nine hours ago. 'I don't know why you can't content yourself, Marcus.'

Content myself with what? With you? He looked at her out the corner of his eye as he climbed down from the step stool and began the process of cleaning up. He envisioned forcing her head into the paint can and drowning her in her damned *forest* paint, but of course he wouldn't do that any more than he would cram the paint-soaked sponge into her mouth and suffocate her, or stab her in the base of her throat with the screwdriver he'd used to open the can.

'Look what happened. Look what it's done to our lives.'

'What happened was not my fault, Mother,' he said, tapping the lid of the can down with a rubber mallet. If wielded with enough fury, would it do the same damage as a hammer?

'Of course it is,' Doll insisted. 'You were infatuated with that woman, and now she's dead and everyone naturally believes you did it. You should have left her alone.'

'It was a misunderstanding,' he said, gathering up his tools and the can. The spot would need a second application, but the paint couldn't be left out. Victor enjoyed the texture and viscosity of paint, and would put his hands into it and spill it out to watch it pool on the floor. 'Annie will clear it up for us. She's working on the case day and night.'

'Annie.' Doll shook her head, following him into the kitchen. 'She's no better than the rest of them, Marcus. You mark my words, she's not your friend.'

He stopped at the back door and stared at his mother, defiant. 'She saved my life. She's going out of her way to help me. I believe that would define the word *friend*.'

He pushed the door open with his elbow and went out to the small, locked shed where he kept things like paint and power tools. A single bulb illuminated the rough cypress walls. He put the paint and tools away and shut the light off. If he waited long enough, he knew his mother would go to bed and he wouldn't have to speak to her again until morning. It was nearly ten o'clock. She had to be in her room for the start of the news, though he could never imagine why. The news never failed to agitate and disgust her for one reason or another. Ritual. She was as bound to it as Victor.

She couldn't understand about Annie, he told himself as he waited for the kitchen light to go out. What did his mother know of friends? She'd never had one that he'd ever been aware of. He doubted even his father had been a friend to her. She would never understand about Annie.

The lights went out in the kitchen, then the dining room. Cutting across the terrace, Marcus went to his workroom and let himself in through one of the French doors with the key he kept under a flowerpot. He went first into his bedroom for a Percodan, to calm both his pains and his nerves, then came back into his studio and gathered his things from his private cupboard.

The drug began to work quickly, relaxing him, giving him a vaguely floaty feeling, insulating him from both physical pain and emotional unpleasantness. Staring at his sketch, he drove everything from his mind except Annie.

Of course he was taken with her. She was pretty. She was intelligent. She was fair-minded. She was his angel. That was what he called her when he imagined the two of them together – Angel. It would be his secret name for her, another little something they would share only with each other. He drew a finger across his lips like closing a zipper, then smiled to himself. That had already become a pet signal between them. They had to be careful. They had to be discreet. She was risking so much by helping him.

He lifted the small keepsake from the drafting table and let it swing from his fingertips, smiling at the whimsy of it. It was a silly thing, hardly appropriate for a grown woman with a serious profession, and yet it suited her. She was still a girl in many respects – fresh, unspoiled, fun, uncertain. He recalled in perfect detail the uncertainty on her face as she turned and saw him tonight in the library. It made him want to hold her. Instead, he held the comical little plastic alligator with the sunglasses and red beret that he had taken down from the rearview mirror in Annie's Jeep.

She wouldn't mind that he had taken it, he reasoned. It was just another small secret between them. He pressed a phantom kiss to the alligator's snout and smiled. The Percodan felt like warm wine flowing through his veins. He closed his eyes for a moment and felt as if his body were going to drift up out of the chair.

He had brought out several of his treasures. Setting the alligator down on the ledge of the drawing table, he picked up the small, ornate photo frame and ran a fingertip along the filigreed edge, smiling sadly at the woman in the picture. Pam. Pam and her darling daughter. The things that might have been if Stokes and Donnie Bichon hadn't poisoned her against him . . .

Regretfully, he set the photograph aside and picked up the locket. There would be a certain symbolism in passing it to Annie. A thread of continuity.

Holding the locket in one hand, he took up his pencil in the other and touched it to the paper.

'I knew it.'

Three words could not have held more accusation. Despite the melting effect of the drug, Marcus straightened his spine at the sound of the voice. His mother stood directly behind him. He hadn't heard her come in through the bedroom, he'd been so engrossed in his fantasies.

'Mother '

'I *knew* it,' Doll said again. She stared past him at the drawing on the tilt-top table. Tears rose in her eyes and she began to tremble. 'Oh, Marcus, not again.'

'You don't understand, Mother,' he said, sliding from his chair, the locket still dangling from his fist.

'I understand that you're pathetic,' she spat. 'You think that woman wants you? She wants you in jail! Do you belong there, Marcus?'

'No! Mama!'

Lunging past him, she grabbed the framed photograph from his table and held it so tightly in her hand that the metal cut into her fingers. She stared hard at the picture of Pam, her whole body trembling, then, sobbing, she threw the frame across the room.

'Why?' she cried. 'How could you do this?'

'I'm not a killer!' Marcus cried, his own tears burning his eyes. 'How can you think that, Mama?'

'Liar!' She slapped him hard on his chest with her open palm, staining his shirt with her blood. 'You're killing me now!'

Screaming, she turned and swept everything off the drawing table with a wild gesture.

'Mama, no!' Marcus cried, grabbing her arm as she reached for the portrait.

'Oh, Marcus!' Doll dragged her hand down her cheek, smearing her face with blood. 'I don't understand you.'

'No, you don't!' he shouted, pain tearing through his face as he strained against the wires in his jaw. 'I love Annie. You couldn't understand love. You don't know what love is. You know possession. You know manipulation. You don't know love. Get out. Get out of my room. I never asked you here. It's the one place I can be free of you. Get out! Get out!'

He screamed the words over and over while he staggered around the room, hitting things, smashing things blindly, knocking a dollhouse to the floor, where it splintered into kindling. Every blow he imagined landing on his mother's face, shattering the sour mask; striking her body and snapping bones.

Finally, he fell across his worktable, sobbing, pounding his fists, the fury running out of him. He lay there for a long time, his gaze blurry and unfocused, staring at nothing. After a while he realized his mother had gone. He straightened slowly and looked around the room. The destruction stunned him. His special things, his secrets, lay broken all around him. This was his sanctuary, and now it had been violated and ruined.

Without so much as righting the fallen chair, Marcus picked up his keys and walked out.

Victor sat among ruins and rocked himself, mewing. The house was dark and silent, which meant everyone else was asleep, which meant they had ceased to exist. Marcus forbade him to come into his Own Space, but

Marcus was asleep and therefore his wishes were Off like television. Victor usually liked to come in here and sit among the small houses. Also, he knew where Marcus kept his Secret Things, and sometimes Victor would open the Secret Door and take them out just to touch them. It made him feel strong to know about the Secret Door and to touch the Secret Things without anyone else knowing. It gave him a feeling of red *and* white intensity, and that was very exciting.

Tonight all Victor felt was *very* red. He hadn't been able to shut down his own mind at all – not even during his regular time. The red colors swirled around and around, cutting and poking at his brain. And his Controllers – the little faces he pictured inside his mind, the arbiters of emotion and etiquette only watched, their expressions disapproving. The Controllers were always angry when he couldn't stop the red colors. Red, *red, red*. Dark *and* light. Around and around. Cutting and cutting.

He had tried to soothe himself with the Audubon book, but the birds had looked at him angrily, as if they *knew* what was in his mind. As if they had heard the voices. Emotion filled him up like water, drowning him in intensity. He felt he couldn't breathe.

He had heard the voices earlier. They had come up through the floor into his room. *Very* red. Victor didn't like voices with no faces, especially red voices. He heard them from time to time, and what they said was never white, *always* red. He'd sat on his bed, keeping his feet off the floor, because he was afraid the voices might go up his pajama legs and get into his body through his rectum.

Victor waited for the voices to go away. Then he waited some more. He counted to the Magic Number three times by sixteenths before he left his room. He had come down to Marcus's Own Space, drawn by the need to see the face, even though it upset him. Sometimes he was like that. Sometimes he couldn't stop from hitting his fist against the wall, even though he knew it hurt him.

The disorder of the room upset him. He couldn't abide broken things. It hurt him in his brain to see broken glass or splintered wood. He felt he could see every torn molecule, and feel the pain of them. And yet he stayed in the room because of the face.

He closed his eyes and saw the face, opened them and saw the face again – the same, the same, the same, but different. Mask, no mask. The feeling it gave him was *very* red. He closed his eyes again and counted by fractions to the Magic Number.

Annie. She was The Other but *not* The Other. Pam, but *not* Pam. Elaine, but *not* Elaine. Mask, no mask. It was like before, and that was *very* red.

Victor rocked himself and whimpered *inside* his being, *not* outside. The intensity was building. His senses were too acute. Every part of him was hard with tension, even his penis. He worried that panic would strike and freeze him, trapping the red intensity inside where it would go on and on, and no one would be able to make it stop.

He lifted his hands and touched his favorite mask and rocked himself, tears running down his cheeks as he stared at his brother's pencil drawing of Annie Broussard, and the jagged, bloody tear that ran down the center of it.

41

Kim Young was a regular at the Voodoo Lounge. She worked three to eleven as an assistant manager at the Quik Pik on La Rue Dumas in Bayou Breaux and figured she deserved a beer or two after eight hours of clearing gas pumps, selling lottery tickets, and running teenagers off before they could shoplift the place into bankruptcy. Besides that, Icky Kebodeaux, the kid she supervised, was weird, smelled like a locker-room laundry basket, and had acne so bad she thought his whole face would explode one of these days and just ooze away. After eight hours of Icky's company, a beer was the least she deserved.

And so she always stopped off for a nightcap at the Lounge on her way home when Mike was out on the TriStar rig in the Gulf. They lived on the outskirts of Luck in a neat little brick house with a big yard. They had been married less than a year, and so far Kim found married life to be good news/bad news. Mike was a catch, but she was left alone for weeks at a time when he was on the rig. He was gone now and not due back for another week.

He was going to miss Carnival in Bayou Breaux, and Kim was feeling bitchy about that. At twenty-three she still liked to party, and she had decided she would damn well party without Mike if he wasn't willing to take the vacation days. He was always willing to take vacation days during hunting season, when *he* wanted to have some fun.

Screw him. She wasn't going to look good in tight jeans forever. She had already made arrangements to go to Carnival with Jeanne-Marie and Candace. Girls' night out. There were always plenty of guys to hook up with for fun at the street dance – if the town fathers allowed the street dance to go on this year.

Everyone was spooked about this rapist. One of the victims had died today. She'd heard it on the radio.

Kim would never have admitted it, but she hadn't been sleeping too well herself this last week. She had thought about moving in with her sister until Mike got home, but Becky had a month-old baby with colic and Kim wanted no part of that. Anyway, it wasn't as if she was helpless.

'What I want to know is if Baptists can't go to Disney World on account of the gays, can they go to Busch Gardens?' the caller on the radio asked. 'How do they know there ain't gays working at Busch

Gardens or Six Flags? My brother-in-law's cousin works at Six Flags, and he's so light in the loafers he floats. It's all just silly, if you ask me. What kind of good Christian people go around trying to figure out if perfect strangers are AC or DC?'

'Ah, there's a can of worms. Any Baptists out there care to comment? This is KJUN, all talk all the time. Home of the giant jackpot giveaway. We'll be right back after these messages.'

Kim wouldn't have minded winning that jackpot. She and Mike had been talking about putting away money toward a new boat. God knew she called into this stupid show often enough. She had called just tonight from the Quik Pik to give her opinion on canceling the street dance. Stupid, that's what that idea was. Nobody was going to get raped at the street dance. The worst that ever happened was fistfights.

She swung her old Caprice in under the carport beside the house as Zachary Richard sang a zydeco jingle for a casino downriver.

The house was safe and sound, just the way she'd left it. A basket of laundry sat on the kitchen table, ready for folding. She scooped it up, carried it with her to the bedroom, and did the job while she watched a rerun of *Cheers* on the tiny color set she'd bought to have on her dresser.

She went to bed at about one-thirty and lay awake for a long while, straining to listen for sounds in the house. The wind had picked up outside, and she grew frustrated trying to tell the difference between the rustle of tree branches and the scrape of footsteps outside the window. By one-fifty she had drifted off, a scowl on her face, her right hand jammed under Mike's pillow.

At 2:19 she woke with a start. He was here. She could feel his presence, dark and menacing. Her pulse raced out of control. She lay perfectly still, waiting.

She had left the night-light on in the bathroom down the hall, and a faint shaft of illumination spilled out the partly opened door into the hallway.

She saw him coming. The black figure of doom. No features, no face, as silent as death.

Death.

Why me? Kim wondered as he slipped into the bedroom. *Why did he pick me? What did I do to deserve this?*

She would know later, she thought, as he came toward the bed. She would find out after she killed him.

In one smooth motion, and without hesitation, Kim Young sat up, swung the gun out from under her husband's pillow, and pulled the trigger.

42

The dream was washed in filtered shades of red. Soft red light as grainy as dust. Deep red shadows as liquid as blood. She stood in front of what she thought was a mirror, but the face staring back was not her own. Lindsay Faulkner looked through the glass at her, her expression accusatory, scornful. Annie reached out a hand to touch the mirror. The apparition came through the glass and passed over her, passed *through* her.

She twisted around and tried to run, but her body was bound in place by raw red muscle growing up from the floor and reaching out of the walls. Across the room, the apparition suddenly fell backward onto the floor, screaming. Then the floor heaved upward and became a wall, and the apparition became Pam Bichon, blood running like wine from her gaping wounds, her dark eyes burning blankly into Annie's.

With a shout, Annie clawed her way out of the dream, out of sleep. The sheet was twisted around her body like a sarong. She struggled free of it and sat up on the couch with her knees drawn up and her head in her hands. Her hair was wild and damp with sweat. Her T-shirt was soaked through. The air conditioner kicked on and blew its cold breath over her, raising gooseflesh. The disturbing quality of the dream clung to her like body odor. Shadows and blood. *Shadowland*.

'I'm doing the best I can, Pam,' she whispered. 'I'm doing the best I can.'

Too edgy to lie back down, she went into her bedroom and changed T-shirts. Fourcade had cleaned up the mess for her, but she hadn't been able to bring herself to sleep in the bed. Maybe after the images had some time to fade from her mind. Maybe after this was all over and she had a chance to put a fresh coat of paint on the wall and buy some new pillows . . . Or maybe this was just one of the more obvious ways in which her life would never be the same.

She went to the kitchen for a drink, then pulled a Snickers bar from the freezer instead. Nibbling at the frozen chocolate, she wandered around her living room, using only the lights from the stereo system and the scanner to keep her from running into anything. Nick was outside somewhere. Stakeout duty. She didn't want to alarm him by turning on lights at two-thirty in the morning, even though it would have been nice to have some company. She was getting to like his company a little too much, she feared.

She sank down on the sofa and rubbed the taxidermized alligator's snout affectionately with her bare foot.

'Maybe I need to get a live pet, huh, Alphonse?' she muttered. The gator gave her his usual toothy grin.

Across the room the scanner scratched out a call.

'All units in the vicinity: We've got a possible 245 and a 261 at 759 Duff Road in Luck. Shots fired. Code 3.'

A possible assault and rape. All deputies were to come fast with lights and sirens.

'The caller says she shot him,' the dispatcher said. 'We've got an ambulance on the way.'

Luck was just down the road and across the bayou. And, if Annie's hunch was right, Chaz Stokes may just have been lying in a pool of blood at 759 Duff Road.

Two units made the scene ahead of her. The cars sat at flamboyant angles in the front yard of the little brick house, beacons rolling. One officer sat on the concrete front steps, either watching out for the ambulance or being sick. The latter, Annie guessed as she crossed the lawn.

He grabbed hold of the wrought iron railing to steady himself as he rose to his feet. The front-porch light gleamed off his red hair like the sun on a new copper penny and Annie thanked heaven for small favors. This cop was a Doucet. Blood was thicker than the Brotherhood. Blood was thicker than anything in South Louisiana.

'Hey, Annie, that you?'

'Hey, Tee-Rouge, where y'at?'

'Tossing my cookies. What you doing here, *chère*?'

'Caught it on the scanner. I thought the victim might appreciate having another woman here,' she lied.

Tee-Rouge gave a snort and waved a hand in dismissal. 'That's some victim. Somebody oughta lift that li'l gal's nightie and see what kind of hairy balls she's hiding under there. She shot this son of a bitch point-blank in the face with a cut-down shotgun.'

'Youch. Who is he?' Annie asked, trying for casual, feeling anything but. In her mind's eye she pictured Stokes creeping toward the woman's bed, the woman raising the shotgun, Stokes's face exploding.

Tee-Rouge shrugged. '*Chère*, his mama wouldn't know him if he sat up and called her name. He's got no ID, but he was wearing the mask. There's feathers all over the damn scene. This is our scumbag of the season right here.'

'You call the detectives?'

'Yeah, but Stokes, he's who-knows-where. In bed with some chick, probably – no offense.'

Annie's heartbeat quickened. 'He's not answering his page?'

'Not so far. Quinlan's on his way, but he lives clear up in Devereaux. It'll take him some time to get down here.'

'Who's inside?' she asked, starting for the door.

'Pitre.'

Groaning to herself, Annie went on into the house as a third cruiser came screaming down the road. Every patrol in the parish was being abandoned in favor of the excitement of a hot crime scene. Everybody wanted in on wrapping the Mardi Gras case.

The living room was empty. There was no immediate sign of the victim. The bedroom looked to be a straight shot down the hall to the left. Pitre stood just inside the doorway, at the feet of the fallen assailant. Annie took a deep breath and marched down the hall.

'I'm not gonna want pizza any time soon,' Pitre muttered, then looked up at the source of the footfalls. 'Broussard, what the hell are *you* doing here? You're not on tonight. Hell, you're barely on the force at all.'

Annie ignored him, turning to look at the dead man. He wasn't her first. He wasn't even her first by shotgun. But he was the first hit at close range, and the sight was by no means pretty.

The rapist lay on the floor, arms outflung. He was dressed in black, covering every inch of his body, including his hands. He could have been black, white, Indian – there was no telling. There was virtually nothing left of his face. The flesh-and-bone mask that set one human being apart from the next had been obliterated. The raw meat, shattered bone, and exposed brain matter could have belonged to anyone. The hair was saturated with blood, its color indistinguishable. A fragment of the black feather mask was stuck to a jagged piece of cranium. The stench of violent death was thick in the air.

'Oh my Lord,' Annie breathed, her knees wilting a bit. The Snickers bar threatened a return trip, and she had to steel herself against spewing it all over the crime scene.

Scraps and chunks of the assailant's face had been sprayed up onto the ceiling and on the pale yellow wall. The sawed-off shotgun lay abandoned on the bed.

'If you can't take it, leave, Broussard. Nobody asked you here,' Pitre said, moving around the bed to check out the shotgun. 'Stokes won't be amused to see you.'

'Yeah? Well, maybe the joke's on him,' Annie muttered, trying to think ahead. Should she pull Quinlan aside when he arrived and tell him about the possibility? Or should she just step back and let the thing unravel on its own? No one would thank her for having suspected Stokes.

'Hey,' Pitre said with the delighted surprise of a child finding the hidden prize in Cracker Jack. 'We know the guy had one blue eye.'

'How's that?'

A nasty grin lit his face as he leaned over the bed and stared at his find. ''Cause here it is. Would you look at that! That sucker musta popped

1164

clean out of his head when she shot him! It's just sitting here like a little egg!'

Stokes's turquoise blue orbs came clearly into focus in Annie's mind as she stepped around the body. But before she could get a look at Pitre's prize, a familiar voice sounded behind her.

'*Man Without a Face*. Anybody see that movie? This guy's uglier. If I'm lyin', I'm dyin'.'

Annie swung around, stunned. Stokes stood looking down at the body, chewing on a stick of boudin sausage, a Ragin' Cajuns ball cap backward on his head. He glanced over at her and made a face.

'Man, Broussard, you are like the goddamn clap – unwanted, unwelcome, and impossible to get rid of.'

'I'm sure you're the voice of experience,' Annie managed. She hadn't quite realized just how set she had been on Stokes's guilt until that moment. A mix of emotions swept over her as she watched him step around the body – disappointment, relief, guilt.

'Who asked you to the dance, anyway?' Stokes asked. 'We don't need any secretaries here, don't need any crime dogs.'

'I thought the victim might appreciate having another woman here.'

'Yeah, he probably would have if he wasn't dead.'

'I meant the woman.'

'Then go find her and get the hell outta my crime scene.' He looked right at her and said straight-faced, 'Can't have you messing up any evidence.'

As Annie went into the hall, Stokes leaned over the bed and looked at the shotgun. 'Man, that's what I call birth control. You know what I mean?'

Pitre laughed.

The victim, Kim Young, was in her neat little yellow kitchen, leaning back against the counter, trembling as if she had just walked out of a freezer. The pale blue baby-doll nightgown she wore barely cleared the tops of her thighs and was liberally flecked with blood and tissue. The mess had sprayed across her face and into her dishwater blond curls.

'I'm Deputy Broussard,' Annie said gently. 'Would you like to sit down? Are you feeling all right?'

She looked up, glassy-eyed. 'I – I shot that man.'

'Yes, you did.'

From where she stood, Annie could see the open patio door in the dining room, where the assailant had gained entry. A neat half-moon of glass had been cut out beside the handle.

'Did you get a look at him before you pulled the trigger?'

She shook her head, dislodging a bone fragment from her hair. It fell to the tile floor next to her bare foot. 'It was too dark. Something woke me up and and I was so *scared*. And then he was right there by the bed and I – I –'

1165

Tears choked her. Her face reddened. 'What if it had been Mike? It could have been Mike! I just shot —'

Ignoring the blood and gore, Annie put an arm around Kim Young's shoulders as the realization dawned in the woman's mind – that she might have killed a loved one by mistake. Then, instead of being a hero, as she would certainly be touted when the press caught up with the story, she would have been portrayed as stupid and hysterical, a misguided vigilante forced to pay a terrible price. The difference was the outcome, not the action. Just another one of life's little object lessons.

The assailant's name was Willard Roache, known affectionately by his old pals in the penal system as 'Cock' Roache. He had a long, ugly history of sexual assault charges and two convictions. He'd done his last jolt in Angola and had been released in June 1996. His last address listed with the state correctional system was in Shreveport, where he had dumped his parole officer and his identity.

Calling himself William Dunham, he had moved to Bayou Breaux in late December and secured a job as a technician at KJUN Radio, using a fake résumé no one had bothered to check. Working the evening shift with Owen Onofrio, Roache had answered the phones and recorded the names and addresses of callers for the giant jackpot giveaway. It was from this list he had chosen his victims.

Evidence obtained at Roache's home included photocopies of the lists with his personal notes scrawled in the margin. Next to Lindsay Faulkner's name he had written the words 'Sexy bitch'. Also found in his home was a box containing half a dozen black feather Mardi Gras masks that had come from a novelties wholesaler in New Orleans.

The information came in piece by piece throughout the day, starting with the discovery of Roache's car parked a short distance from Kim Young's home. At the sheriff's instruction, Roache's corpse was fingerprinted at the scene and the prints sent through the state automated fingerprint system with a rush order – the rush being a press conference set for four o'clock in the afternoon. Noblier wanted the case tied up with a ribbon before the start of Carnival for maximum PR benefit.

Annie prowled the records office all day like a caged animal, wanting to be a part of the team of deputies and detectives going through Roache's trailer, running evidence to the regional lab in New Iberia, making calls to map out the rapist's background. Myron barely allowed her to help catalog the evidence that was brought into their own lockup for safekeeping.

The frustration was almost unbearable. She wanted to see the proof for herself, go through the process of identifying the components of Roache's guilt, so that she could exorcise the last of the theory that had taken root in her own mind: that Chaz Stokes could have committed the crimes and that those crimes might have led them back to Pam's murder.

A theory was all it had been. As Fourcade had pointed out to her, she had no evidence, nothing but hunches, conjecture, speculation. A detective's job was to find irrefutable proof, to build the case solid and airtight – which Stokes might have done with Willard Roache before he had the chance to attack Kay Eisner and Lindsay Faulkner and Kim Young, had Stokes been inclined to work a little harder after Jennifer Nolan's attack.

Instead, Stokes did the research on Roache after the fact and readily accepted congratulations on his detective work. Because everyone was so happy to have the terror of this man stalking the parish over and done with, so far people were choosing to ignore the fact that Roache had lived in the same trailer park as Jennifer Nolan and had not been interviewed the day of her rape. He hadn't been home the morning the investigation had begun. Annie had knocked on his door herself and reported to Stokes that he wasn't home. Neither Stokes nor Mullen had bothered to go back. If they had, they might have recognized him later, when the state had faxed in descriptions and mug shots of sex offenders released from the system in the past year.

With all the bad things that had happened in recent weeks, the department needed something to celebrate. The death of Willard Roache was treated as a triumph, even though neither the department nor the task force had had any hand in ending Roache's crime spree. If anything, Annie thought, they should have considered it an embarrassment. It had taken a 120-pound clerk from the Quik Pik with a sawed-off shotgun to stop the predator. They could have as easily been mourning Kim Young's own death if Roache had wrestled the gun from her. But no one else seemed to see it that way.

At the end of the day the sheriff presented the conclusion of the case to the press like an elaborately wrapped present. Only Smith Pritchett seemed less than overjoyed, and only because the thunder was all Noblier's and there was no villain left to prosecute. Still, he took the opportunity to pontificate and state that the world was a better place without Willard Roache in it. No charges would be filed against Kim Young for protecting herself in her own home.

Everybody's a winner, Annie thought, standing toward the edge of the pack watching the press conference on the break-room set. Everyone except Jennifer Nolan, and Kay Eisner, and Lindsay Faulkner, and Kim Young – who, despite saving herself from a worse fate, had blown a man's head off and would have to live with that for the rest of her life.

Annie wandered back to records feeling at loose ends. *Focus*, Fourcade would say. The rape cases were closed, but the rapes were not her focus. Pam's murder was her focus. To that end she had Marcus Renard and Donnie Bichon to hold her attention.

'You have got no respect for this office,' Myron greeted her dourly. 'There is work to be done, and you're off watching television.'

Annie rolled her eyes as she scooped the afternoon mail off the counter. 'Oh, Jesus, Myron, go have a bowel movement, why don't you?

This is the records office. We're not guarding the ark of the covenant, for crying out loud.'

The clerk's eyes bugged out. His nostrils flared and his wiry frame quivered with outrage. 'That is *it*, Deputy Broussard! You are through in my office. I will *not* stand for any more.'

He stormed from the room, slamming the door behind him, and headed in the direction of Noblier's office. Annie leaned over the counter and shouted after him, 'Hey, ask for my old job back while you're at it!'

Guilt nipped her as he strode out of sight. She had always appreciated Myron for who he was – until she had to work with him. She had always had a respectful attitude toward her elders and her superiors, with few exceptions. Maybe Fourcade was a bad influence. Or maybe she just had more important things on her mind than kissing Myron's skinny ass.

She sorted through the mail, knowing Myron would go ballistic if she opened anything he deemed important. Most of it looked like insurance stuff: requests for accident reports and so on. One envelope bore the Our Lady of Mercy letterhead and was addressed to her.

Tearing the end open with her thumb, Annie extracted what looked to be a lab report. A copy of the chem 7 blood analysis on Lindsay Faulkner that Dr. Unser had requested during Faulkner's seizure. The test Annie had requested after Lindsay's death. The test the Our Lady lab had apparently lost.

She looked down the row of indecipherable symbols and corresponding numbers, none of it meaning anything to her. K+: 4.6 mEq/L. Cl-: 101 mEq/L. Na++: 139 mEq/L. BUN: 17 mg. Glucose: 120. It didn't matter much now. Willard Roache would likely be credited with both the attack and the death of Faulkner, unless the autopsy Stokes had requested turned up some anomaly.

'I have left my message with Sheriff Noblier's secretary,' Myron announced. 'I expect your position here will be terminated by the end of the day.'

Annie didn't bother to correct him, though she figured she had at least until Monday to be reassigned or suspended, depending on Gus's mood. Less than an hour shy of five o'clock on Friday, with a big win under his belt, the sheriff was doubtless off toasting himself with the town fathers.

'Then I might as well leave, hadn't I?' Annie said. 'As my last official act as your assistant, I'll take this report over to the detectives. Just to be kind to you, Myron.'

Annie walked into the Pizza Hut without bothering to ring the bell. On the phone, Perez looked up at her, dark eyes snapping impatience. She waved the report at him and gestured back to the task force war room.

The task force members had all been invited to the press conference so that Noblier could show them off and earn more praise for having the wisdom to select such a crack team. They had left their command center looking as if it had been ransacked by thieves. The radio on the file cabinet was blaring Wild Tchoupitoulas.

Moving along the table, Annie scanned file tabs until she came across the one marked FAULKNER, LINDSAY. It seemed pitifully thin for representing a woman's violent death. Not much would be added to it before the case was closed and it went into the drawers in Myron's domain. The autopsy report, Stokes's final report, that would be it.

She flipped the folder open and pulled the lab report Stokes had already collected, scanning the document to make certain it and the one she'd received were indeed the same item. K+: 4.6 mEq/L. CI-: 101 mEq/L. Na++: 139 mEq/L. BUN: 17 mg. Glucose: 120.

'What the hell is with you, Broussard?' Stokes demanded, striding into the room. 'Are you stalking me? Is that it? There's laws against that. You know what I'm saying?'

'Yeah? Well, who'd have thought you knew anything about it after the way you blew off Pam Bichon last fall?'

'I did not blow off Pam Bichon. Now why don't you tell me what you're doing in my face, then get out of it? I was having a damn fine day without you.'

'Our Lady sent over a dupe of the chem 7 blood test on Lindsay Faulkner. I thought it should be in the file, not that you care. Why bother following up when you barely did any work to begin with?'

'Fuck you, Broussard,' he said, snatching the report from her hand. 'It was just a matter of time before I woulda nailed Roache.'

'I'm sure that's a comfort to all the women he attacked after Jennifer Nolan.'

'Don't you have some paper clips to count?'

Mullen stepped into the doorway, cutting a glance from Annie to Stokes. 'You coming, Chaz? They can't start the party without us.'

Stokes flashed the Dudley Do-Right. 'I'm there, man. I am *there*.'

Annie shook her head. 'A party to celebrate the fact that a civilian closed your case for you. You ought to be so proud.'

Stokes settled his porkpie hat back on his head and straightened his purple tie. 'Yeah, Broussard, I am. My only regret is that Roache didn't get to you first.'

He herded her from the room and from the building. Annie went reluctantly on toward the law enforcement center, her eyes on Stokes and Mullen as they climbed into their respective vehicles and tore out of the parking lot, blasting their horns in celebration.

A civilian had cleared their hottest case and Pam Bichon's killer was still roaming free. She couldn't see much to be happy about.

'Or maybe I'm just a sore loser,' she muttered.

43

'You're listening to KJUN. All talk all the time. Our topic: safety versus civil rights should prospective employees be subjected to fingerprinting? Carl in Iota –'

Nick switched the radio off and sat up behind the wheel of the truck as Donnie left his office and climbed into the Lexus. He looked as pale as the car. His hunch-shouldered walk had a little extra bend in it. The pressure was getting to him. He would make a move soon, maybe tonight, and Nick wanted to be there when he did. He crushed out his cigarette with the half dozen butts in the ashtray, put the truck in gear, and waited until the Lexus had turned the corner at Dumas.

Patience was the key word here. Essential in surveillance. Essential in all aspects of life. A useful tool that was difficult to master. Men like Donnie never got the hang of it. He had moved too quickly to get rid of Pam's business. Haste attracted unwanted attention. But then had that been Donnie's doing or Marcotte's? Or mine? Nick wondered, the idea burning in his gut like an ulcer. He hadn't completely mastered patience himself.

La Rue Dumas was busy, the curbs lined with cars, the sidewalk full of people. The Lexus was four cars ahead and waiting at the green light to make a left turn. Friday night always drew people into town. Nick had heard Bayou Breaux's Carnival celebration attracted folks from all over South Louisiana for the street dance and various parties and pageants that went on from tonight through Fat Tuesday. With the demise of the serial rapist, the atmosphere of revelry would be cranked up an extra notch, relief adding wild euphoria to the mix.

All day the news had been full of 'late-breaking information' on the shooting of Willard Roache, who had been subsequently unmasked, so to speak, as the Mardi Gras rapist. So much for Annie's theory on Stokes as a sexual predator, though Nick had to give her grudging admiration for going after the tough angle. She had a passion for the work she was only just beginning to tap. With the rapist out of the way, she would be better able to focus on tripping up Renard.

Renard was still his number one bet. Donnie was up to no good, but it had the smell of dirty money rather than the smell of death. It was Renard who made Nick's hackles rise. Every time he went over the case in his mind, the trail, the logic, wound back to Renard. Every time. The story was there. He just hadn't managed to find the key to open the book. Until Annie.

A mixed blessing, that, he mused. His initial intent had been to use her as bait to draw Renard out. But the better that plan worked, the less he liked it. In his mind's eye he could still see the gruesome tableau in her bedroom. He had made the same connection he knew she had, recalling the sight of Pam Bichon nailed to the floor of that house out on Pony Bayou.

The idea of Renard terrorizing Annie that way, the idea of Renard thinking about Annie that way, the idea of Renard touching Annie in any way, brought a rush of emotion Nick wasn't quite sure how to handle. He knew it wasn't wise, but it was there and he was loath to walk away from it.

She would testify against him in six days.

He turned on Fifth as the Lexus took a right to drive south along the bayou road.

The parking lot at the Voodoo Lounge was nearly full. Nick spotted the Lexus and parked the truck on the berm up on the road. Zydeco music was blowing through the walls of the joint. Colorful Chinese lanterns had been strung around the building. Costumed party-goers were dancing on the half-finished gallery. A curvy blonde in a green sequined mask opened her top and shook her naked breasts like a pair of water balloons at Nick as he mounted the steps. He walked past her without reaction.

'Man, Nicky, you got ice water in those veins of yours! If I'm lyin', I'm dyin',' Stokes announced, clapping him on the back.

Nick shot him a look, taking in the incongruity of a Zorro mask and a porkpie hat.

Stokes shrugged. 'Hey, cut me some slack, pard. It's a special occasion!'

'So I hear.'

'Drinks are on the house for cops. You picked the right night to come out of your cave, Nicky.'

They wound their way through the throng toward the bar. The energy level was high, an almost palpable electricity that magnified the scents of fried shrimp, warm bodies, and cheap cologne. Chaz bulled his way to the bar and bellowed for shots. Nick moved toward the nearest corner, his gaze scanning the room for Donnie, who had found a spot midway down the long side of the bar. He didn't look like a man who had come to party. He sipped at his whiskey as if he were using it for medicinal purposes.

Stokes held a shot glass out to Nick and raised his own. 'To the timely end of another scumbag.'

'You can concentrate on Renard, now,' Nick said, leaning close to be heard without shouting over the noise.

'I intend to. There's nothing I want more than to put an end to that situation, believe me.' He tossed back his drink, grimaced at the kick in his gut, and shook himself like a wet dog. 'You ain't exactly a party animal, man. What you doing out and about on a crazy night like this?'

'Keeping an eye on something,' Nick said vaguely. 'A developing situation. Gotta do something to occupy my time.'

Stokes snorted. 'You need a hobby, man. I suggest Valerie out there on the veranda. That girl is a regular devil's playground for idle hands. You know what I'm saying?'

'What's the matter? You bored with her?'

He flashed a smile that was a little hard around the edges. 'My attentions are needed elsewhere tonight.'

'So are mine,' Nick said, as Donnie pushed himself back from the bar and headed for the door, a solitary ambassador of gloom among the sea of smiling faces.

Nick turned his back as Bichon passed, setting his glass on the bar.

'Have another,' Stokes offered, always magnanimous with the money of others.

'One's my limit tonight. Catch you later.'

He worked his way out onto the gallery and spotted the Lexus backing carefully out of the lineup of pickups and beaters. He waited until it was headed toward the southern exit of the lot, then jogged up onto the road at the north end, and jumped in the truck.

Traffic was enough to keep Donnie distracted as they headed out of town. Still, Nick hung well back. Patience. He wanted to see how this would play out, give Donnie a little bit of rope to see if he would hang himself with it.

Twilight had surrendered to evening. Fog hung over the water. The Lexus turned east, crossed the bayou, then went south again, and passed down the main street of Luck. At the edge of town it turned in at a supper club called Landry's.

Nick cruised past the restaurant, his eye catching on the sleek silver Lincoln that sat apart from the other cars in the lot, the driver a hulking black shadow behind the wheel. He turned the corner two blocks down, doubled back, and drove in the service entrance at the back of the property.

He entered the restaurant through the kitchen door that stood open, letting the rich aromas of beefsteak and good Cajun cooking roll out into the night. The kitchen help chose to ignore him as he moved through their domain.

Landry's dining room was large and dimly lit. A freestanding fireplace with fake logs glowing orange for ambiance stood in the center. Perhaps two-thirds of the white-draped tables were taken, mostly by older middle class couples dressed up for their big night out. The low hum of conversation was constant, the chink of flatware against china like the sound of small bells ringing across the room.

Donnie and Marcotte sat in the wraparound banquette of a round corner table. To Marcotte's left, one of DiMonti's twin thugs sat hunched over a table for two, making it look like something from a child's tea set. DiMonti was nowhere in sight.

Nick adjusted the lightweight jacket he wore to show just the butt of the Ruger in its shoulder rig, slipped his sunglasses on, and moved toward the table with casual ease. Donnie spotted him when he was still ten feet away, and his color washed from ashen to chalk.

'Starting the party without me, Tulane?' Nick said, sliding onto the banquette beside him.

Donnie bolted sideways, nearly spilling his drink. 'What the hell are you doing here, Fourcade?' he demanded in a harsh whisper.

Nick raised his eyebrows above the rims of his sunglasses. 'Why, seeing for myself what a lying weasel you are, Donnie. I'd say I'm disappointed in you, but it's no less than I expected.'

He reached inside his jacket for cigarettes and Donnie's eyes widened at the sight of the Ruger.

'This is a no-smoking table,' he said stupidly.

Nick stared straight at him through the mirrored lenses of the shades and lit up.

Marcotte watched the exchange with mild amusement, relaxed, his forearms resting on the tabletop. He didn't look the least out of place in the setting. In a simple white shirt and conservative tie, he couldn't have been pegged for a business tycoon. In contrast, even the simplest bumpkin would recognize the muscle for what he was. The loan-a-thug turned in his seat for a better view, revealing a smashed nose, held to his face with adhesive tape. Brutus. Nick smiled at him and nodded.

'This is a private meeting, Nick,' Marcotte said pleasantly. He glanced at Donnie. 'Nick here has a bit of a learning disability, Donnie. He needs to be taught all his lessons twice.'

Nick blew smoke out his nostrils. 'Oh, no. Me, I learned my lesson the first time. That's why I'm here tonight as adviser to my good friend Donnie, who bailed me out of jail not long ago.'

'A poor choice,' Marcotte said.

'Well, Donnie, he's none too bright for a college boy. Are you, Tulane? I keep telling him he doesn't want the devil playing in his backyard, but I don't know if he's hearing me. He's too preoccupied by the sound of money fanning in his ear.'

'I don't feel well,' Donnie muttered, starting to rise. Sweat beaded on his pasty forehead.

Nick put a hand on his shoulder. 'Sit down, Donnie. Last time I saw you near a toilet, you had your head in it. We don't want you to drown . . . just yet.'

'Adding coercion to your list of crimes now, Nick?' Marcotte said with an indulgent chuckle.

'Not at all. I'm just pointing out to my friend Donnie here the disadvantages of doing business with you. The scrutiny a deal with you would bring to bear on him and on the untimely death of his lovely wife.'

Tears welled in Donnie's eyes. 'I didn't kill Pam.'

His denial drew stares from two other tables.

Nick's gaze never wavered from Marcotte. He tapped the ash off his cigarette into Donnie's drink and took another long drag. 'You don't have to be guilty of something to have it ruin your life, Tulane. Nor do the guilty necessarily pay for their crimes. See how well I learn my lessons, Marcotte?

'It looks cold, Donnie – you trying to swing this deal,' he went on. 'Hell, that business ain't even yours to sell yet, technically speaking. This looks like something my friends in the sheriff's office would want to go over with a fine-tooth comb. They'll wanna dig through all your records and whatnot. You been wheeling and dealing for a while now. Who knows what else they might come up with?

'Folks catch wind of that kind of thing, they start thinking maybe you cheated them, and then they wanna sue. And, hey, you got all that money what Duval Marcotte paid you, so why shouldn't they try to get themselves a piece of it? Meanwhile, the Davidsons are talking to a lawyer about custody of your daughter.

'You see where this is going, Donnie?' he asked, still looking at Marcotte. 'Donnie, he doesn't always see the big picture. He fails to recognize the potential for disaster.'

'And you, Nick my boy, see that train coming and throw yourself in front of it anyway,' Marcotte said, shaking his head. 'You were born out of time, Fourcade. Chivalry went out a while back. It's called foolhardiness now.'

'Really?' The picture of disinterest, Nick crushed his smoke out and dropped the butt in Donnie's whiskey. 'I don't keep up with trends.'

'I have to go to the bathroom,' Donnie muttered, turning gray around the gills.

Nick slid out of the banquette. 'Take your time, Tulane. Do some thinking while you're in there.'

Donnie shuffled away from the table with one hand pressed to his stomach. Nick sat back down and stared at Marcotte. Marcotte sat back against the padded seat and crossed his arms. His dark eyes shone like polished stones.

'I believe you may have succeeded in ruining my chances for a deal, Nick.'

'I sincerely hope so. It's the least I can do, all things considered.'

'Yes, I suppose it is. And the least I can do is be gracious in defeat. For the moment.'

'You're giving up easily.'

Marcotte gave a shrug, pursing his lips. 'Que *sera sera*. It's been a diversion. I would never have come out here looking if it hadn't been for you rousing my interest, Nick. I'll draw some satisfaction from knowing you have that to dwell on. And you know what? Coming out here has just reminded me how much I like the country. Simple life, simple pleasures. I just may come back.'

Nick said nothing. He had thought he'd cut Marcotte out of his life like a cancer. But just enough of the old obsession had remained to pull him back across that line, and now Marcotte would be drooling at the edge of his sanctuary like a wolf biding his time.

The waitress edged toward the table, looking at Nick with suspicion. 'Can I get you a drink, sir?'

'No, thank you,' he said, easing himself up. 'I won't be staying. The company here turns my stomach.'

Donnie was bent over the sink, crying and gagging when Nick entered the men's room.

'You fit to drive home, Tulane?'

'I'm ruined, you son of a bitch!' he sobbed. 'I'm fucking broke! Marcotte would have advanced me money.'

'And you'd still be ruined – for all the reasons I just told you out there. You don't listen so good, Donnie,' Nick said, washing his hands. Every encounter with Marcotte left him feeling as if he'd been handling snakes. 'There's better ways out of trouble than selling your soul.'

'You don't understand. Pam's life insurance isn't coming through. I've lost two big jobs and I've got a loan coming due. I need money.'

'Quit your whining and be a man for once,' Nick snapped. 'You don't have your wife here to bail your ass out anymore. It's time to grow up, Donnie.'

He cranked a paper towel out of the machine on the wall, dried his hands carefully. 'Listen – you don't know it, but me, I'm the best friend you've got tonight, Tulane. But I'm telling you, cher, I find out you've turned on me in this, I find out you're trying to get back in bed with Marcotte, I find out you took that shot at Broussard the other night, you're sure as hell gonna wish I'd never been born.'

Donnie leaned his head against the mirror, too weak to stand unaided. 'I been wishing that for days now, Fourcade.'

Behind him, Nick heard the men's room door swish open. He could see the reflection of Brutus in a wedge of mirror. He shifted his weight to the balls of his feet and remained still.

'Everything all right in here, Mr. Bichon?' the thug asked.

'Hardly,' Donnie moaned.

'Everything's fine, Brutus,' Nick said. 'Mr. Bichon, he's just having some growing pains, that's all.'

'I didn't ask you, coonass.' Reaching inside his black jacket, Brutus pulled out a set of brass knuckles and slipped them over the thick fingers of his right hand. Nick watched in the mirror.

'I wouldn't go knocking family trees, King Kong,' he said. 'You're about to fall out of yours.'

He spun and kicked as Brutus stepped toward him, catching the big man on the side of the head. Brutus hit the paper towel machine face-first with a crash that reverberated off the tile walls. Blood gushed from his nose and mouth, and he dropped to the floor, out cold.

Nick shook his head as the manager rushed into the room to stare in horror, first at his broken towel dispenser, then at the mass of bleeding humanity lying on the tile.

'Floor's wet,' Nick said, moving casually for the door. 'He slipped.'

44

Big Dick Dugas and the Iota Playboys cranked up the volume on their battle-scarred guitars and launched into a fast and frantic rendition of 'C'est Chaud.' A cheer went up from the crowd and bodies began to move – young, old, drunk, sober, black, white, poor, and planter class.

There were easily a thousand people in the five-block length of La Rue France cordoned off for the annual event, all of them moving some part of their anatomy to the beat. Mouths smiling, faces shiny with the uncommon heat of the evening and the joy of liberation. The workweek was over, the five-day party was just starting, and the source of a collective fear had been obliterated from the planet.

The party atmosphere struck Annie as grotesque, a reaction she resented mightily. She had always loved the Mardi Gras festivities in Bayou Breaux. Unfettered pagan fun and frivolity before the dour days of Lent. The street dance, the food stands, the vendors selling balloons and cheap trinkets, the pageants and parade. It was a rite of spring and a thread of continuity that had run through her life from her earliest memories.

She remembered coming to the dance as a child, running around with her Doucet cousins while her mother stood off just to the side of the crowd, enjoying the music in her own quiet way, but never a part of the mass joy.

The memory brought an extra pang tonight. Annie felt she was in her own way apart from the rest of the revelers here. Not because of the uniform she was wearing, but because of the things she had experienced in the last ten days.

A burly bearded man tricked out in a pink dress and pearls, a cigar jammed into the corner of his mouth, tried to grab hold of her hand and drag her off the sidewalk into a two-step. Annie waved him off.

'I'm not that kind of girl!' she called, grinning.

'Neither am I, darlin'!' He flipped his skirt up, flashing a glimpse of baggy heart-covered boxer shorts.

The crowd around him roared and hooted. A woman dressed as a male construction worker gave a wolf whistle and tried to pinch his ass. He howled, grabbed her, and they danced off.

Annie managed a chuckle at the scene. As she started to turn away, she was detained by another costumed partyer, this one dressed in black with a white painted smiling mask, the classic theatrical portrayal of comedy. He held out a single rose to her and bowed stiffly when she accepted it.

'Thank you.' She tucked the stem of the rose through her duty belt, next to her baton as she walked away.

She loved the street dance less as a cop than as a civilian. Personnel from both the Bayou Breaux PD and the sheriff's office worked the Carnival events. A united front against hooliganism. The standing rule was to break up the fistfights, but arrest only the drunks stupid enough to swing at the cops. Anyone with a weapon went in the can for the night, and the DA's office had their pick of the litter come morning.

But even with the drunks and knife fights, the exuberant innocence of a small-town celebration usually outweighed the bad moments. Tonight it seemed that everyone was celebrating the shooting of Willard Roache more than they were celebrating Carnival. The air was crackling with the heady excitement of victorious vigilantism, and that struck Annie as a dangerous thing.

Crime in South Louisiana tended to be personal, confrontational. Folks here had their own sense of justice and an abundant supply of firearms. She thought of Marcus Renard and the incidents at his home in the past ten days. The shooting, the rock through the window. If he hadn't staged those incidents himself, if they had been the work of one of the many people who thought Fourcade should have been allowed to finish him off, then there was a real possibility that same someone might get carried away in the excitement of one criminal's demise and try for another's. And who in the SO, besides her, would even care?

God, maybe I am his guardian angel, after all.

The thought was not a comforting one, but neither could she let it go. The deeper she went into this case, the more complicated it became, the more options there seemed to be. It only became clearer to Annie that justice needed to be conducted through the proper channels, not doled out at random by the uninformed.

How popular that opinion would make her tonight, she thought, when everyone in the parish was heralding Kim Young as a heroine of the common folk.

She tried to look for a bright side to the shooting, thinking what a powder keg this street dance would have been if not for Kim Young and her trusty cut-down. The majority of revelers came to the dance in full Mardi Gras regalia: costumes, makeup, masks that ran the gamut from dead presidents to monsters to medieval fertility gods. Sequins and feather masks were in abundance. The celebration had its roots in ancient spring fertility rites and had retained a pervasive air of sexuality down through the centuries. Though it wasn't nearly so bawdy out here in the Cajun parishes as it was in the French Quarter of New Orleans, there would be plenty of flashes of bare skin before the night was through.

To think of a predator like Willard Roache running loose in this atmosphere was enough to make Annie's blood run cold. A rapist in a

Mardi Gras mask amid a sea of masks . . . and a heavily armed citizenry twitching at every shadow . . . They could certainly have ended up with a morgue full of bullet-ridden corpses instead of one dead Roache.

Annie edged her way along between the crowd and the storefronts, keeping her eyes open for anyone taking an undue interest in merchandise in the display windows. A knot of little boys of nine or ten stampeded past, blasting squirt guns. She fended off a stream with her hand, turning away and coming face-to-face again with the white painted mask.

He stood no more than a foot from her, near enough that she started at the sight of him.

'Do I know you?' she asked.

His painted face grinned at her as he handed her the string of a heart-shaped helium balloon. He pressed his hands to his chest dramatically then held them out to her, symbolically giving her his heart.

Puzzled, Annie sized up her masked admirer – his height, his build. Realization dawned with an eerie chill.

'Marcus?'

He raised a finger to his painted mouth and backed away, melting into the crowd, anonymous. But she knew who it was. It made perfect sense. The mask offered both freedom and secrecy. He hadn't been able to walk down the street in this town for months without drawing unwanted attention. Now he moved unnoticed past people who would have spat on him or worse had they known he was behind the smiling mask.

And what would the good townsfolk of Bayou Breaux do to her if they saw her taking romantic tokens from Marcus Renard? What would her fellow cops do? She would be further ridiculed and punished. They already had that in common, she and Marcus.

Annie looked at the balloon. He had given her his heart, and she had accepted it. God only knew how significant that would be in his mind. He wanted to believe she cared for him, just as he had wanted to believe Pam had cared for him. He believed the job was what kept her from him, just as he had believed Donnie had been the barrier between himself and Pam. Juliet and Romeo.

She handed the balloon to a little girl with a *Pocahontas* T-shirt and chocolate all over her face, and moved down the street.

A clown in a rainbow fright wig staggered toward her on the narrow band of sidewalk. The painted smile was lopsided beneath a rubber hog snout. Annie stepped right. The clown moved with her. She stepped left the same time he did. She turned to the side to motion him past. He swayed toward her instead, hitting her shoulder and spilling his beer down the front of her uniform.

'Hey, Bozo, watch it!' she snapped.

'Sorry, ociffer!' he declared, unrepentant.

From her left side a second drunk stumbled into her, this one wearing a

Reagan mask with a vacuous idiot grin. Another eight ounces of beer cascaded down her back.

'Shit!' she yelped. 'Watch where you're going!'

'Sorry, ociffer!' he said with singsong insincerity. He looked at the clown and the pair of them chuckled like Beavis and Butthead.

Annie glared at the rubber face, which sat atop a pair of bony shoulders. She looked down at the skinny stick legs in tight jeans.

'Son of a bitch!' she swore, grabbing hold of him by the shirtfront. 'Mullen, is that you inside that empty head?'

The clown hollered, 'Shit!'

Reagan stumbled back from her, pulling himself free. The two plunged into the gyrating crowd, laughing.

'Dammit!' Annie said, half under her breath, plucking at her saturated shirtfront.

The beer trickled down into the waistband of her pants, front and back. It ran down inside her body armor in front and soaked through the back. Anyone getting a whiff of her was going to think the stories about her recent sad decline into alcoholism were more than just rumors.

'Sarge, it's Broussard,' she said into the two-way as she started up the street. 'I just got doused. I'm 10 – 7 at the station. Back in a few. Out.'

'Hurry the hell up.'

She made her way north along the back side of the crowd, intending to cut east at the corner of Seventh, where she had parked her cruiser on the side street.

'Annie!'

A.J.'s voice caught her ear and she pulled up. He had left three messages on her machine at home and had tried to get her at work twice since she had been shot at, and she had avoided calling him back. She didn't want to explain. She didn't want to lie. She didn't want him trying to tie a knot in the connection she had severed between them.

He came toward her from the yellow light of a vendor's stand, a red-checked cardboard basket of fried oysters cradled in one hand, a bottle of Abita in the other. He was still in his suit from the day's business, though his tie was jerked loose.

'I thought you were off the street.'

Annie shrugged. 'I go where they tell me. I'm on my way to the station now. I just got a beer bath.'

'I'll walk you to your car.'

He fell in step beside her and she glanced up at him, trying to gauge his mood. His face was drawn and a deep line dug in between his brows. The noise of the band and the crowd faded as they turned the corner and walked away from the bright yellow light of the party.

'Why'd you work late?' Annie asked. 'Friday night. Big dance and all.'

'I ah sorta lost my standing date.'

She kicked herself mentally for opening that door.

'Task force moved at the speed of light to get the background on Roache, didn't they?'

'Yeah,' she said. 'Too bad they couldn't have found that enthusiasm earlier. Maybe they could have nailed his ass after Jennifer Nolan.'

'You would have,' he said, setting his supper on the hood of her cruiser.

'I would have tried, at least. That's the thing that galls me most about Stokes – he skates over everything and still comes out smelling like a rose. I wouldn't care how big a jerk he was if he did the job.'

A.J. shrugged. 'Some people do the job, some people live the job.'

'I don't live the job,' she snapped, not liking the correlation to Fourcade that A.J. couldn't possibly have known. 'But I hustle when I'm on it. That should count for something.'

'It should.'

But they both knew the thing that would count for her would be taking the witness stand on Thursday. Annie looked away and sighed.

'So, are you gonna tell me what that was all about the other night?' he asked. 'Someone taking a shot at you? My God, Annie.'

'Trying to scare me, that's all,' she said, still avoiding his gaze.

'That's *all*? You could have been killed!'

'It was a scare tactic. I'm not very popular as a witness for the prosecution.'

'You think it was Fourcade?' he demanded. 'That bastard! I'll get his bail revoked –'

'It wasn't Fourcade.'

'How do you know that?'

'It just wasn't,' she insisted. 'Leave it alone, A.J. You don't know anything about this.'

'Because you won't tell me! Christ, somebody tries to shoot you and I have to hear about it from Uncle Sos! You don't even bother to call me back when I try to check up on you –'

'Look,' she said, reining back her temper. 'Can we have this fight another time? I'm 10–7. Hooker's gonna chew me out if I don't go and get back.'

'I don't want to fight,' A.J. said wearily. He caught hold of her hand and hung on when she would have backed away. 'Just a minute, Annie. Please.'

'I'm on duty.'

'You're 10–7. Personal time. This is personal.'

She drew in a breath to protest and he pressed a finger against her lips. His expression was earnest in the filtered light of the streetlamp.

'I need to say this, Annie. I care about you. I don't want to see you hurt by anyone for any reason. I don't want to see you taking crazy chances. I want to take care of you. I want to protect you. I don't know who this other guy is –'

'A.J., don't –'

'And I don't know what he's got that I don't. But I love you, Annie. And I'm not gonna just walk away from this, from *us*. I love you.'

His admission stunned her silent. They hadn't been that close lately. There had been a time when she had expected him to say it, and he never had. Now he wanted her to say it and she couldn't – not with the meaning he wanted. The story of their lives. They were never quite in the same place at the same time. He wanted something from her she couldn't give, and she wanted a man she might just send on the road to prison in a week's time.

'I know you better than anyone, Annie,' he murmured. 'I won't give you up without a fight.'

He lowered his head and kissed her, slowly, sweetly, deeply. He pulled her against him, heedless of her beer-soaked shirt, and pressed her to him – breast to chest, belly to groin. Longing to regret.

'God, you think you mean it, don't you?' he whispered as he raised his head. 'That it's over.'

The hurt in his eyes brought tears to Annie's. 'I'm sorry, A.J.'

He shook his head. 'It's *not* over,' he pledged quietly. 'I won't let it be.'

Just like Donnie Bichon, Annie thought. Determined to hold on to Pam even after she'd served him with papers. Like Renard – seeing what he wanted to see, bending reality to open possibilities for the outcome he wanted. The difference was that she felt only frustration with A.J.'s bullheadedness, not fear. He hadn't crossed the line from tenacity to terror.

'Fair warning,' he said. Stepping back from her, he picked up his fried oysters and his beer. 'I'll see you around.'

Annie sat back against the car as he walked away. 'I need this like I need a hole in my head.'

She gave herself a moment to try to clear away the thought that she had somehow managed to become part of a romantic triangle, an idea that was too absurd for words. Instead, she tried to focus once again on the world around her: the noise of the band, the intermittent bang of firecrackers, the warm moist air, the silver light from the streetlamp, and the darkness beyond its reach.

The sensation of being watched crawled over her. The feeling that she suddenly wasn't alone on the deserted side street. She straightened slowly away from the car and strained to see into the shadows at the back of the paint store she had parked beside. At the mouth of the dark alley a white face seemed to float in the air.

'Marcus?' Annie said, straightening away from the cruiser, moving cautiously toward the building.

'You *kissed* him,' he said. 'That filthy lawyer. You *kissed* him!'

Anger vibrated in his voice. He took a step toward her.

'Yes, he kissed me,' Annie said. Pulse racing, she tried to settle her hands casually on her hips – the right one within reach of her baton, a can of Mace, the butt of her Sig. The tip of her middle finger pressed against the stem of the rose Renard had given her and a thorn bit deep into her skin, the pain sharp and surprising.

'Does that upset you, Marcus? That I let him kiss me?'

'He's – he's one of *them!*' he stammered, the words slurring as he forced them through his teeth. 'He's against me. Like Pritchett. Like Fourcade. How could you do this, Annie?'

'I'm one of "them" too, Marcus,' she said simply. 'I've told you that all along.'

He shook his head in denial, the grinning mask a macabre contrast to the shock and fury vibrating from him in waves. 'No. You're trying to help me. The work you've done. The way you've come to my aid. You saved my life – twice!'

'And I keep telling you, Marcus, I'm only doing my job.'

'I'm not your job,' he said. 'You came to help me time and again when you didn't have to. You didn't want anyone to know. I thought . . .'

He trailed off, unable to bring himself to say the words. Annie waited, marveling at the ease with which he had turned everything in his mind to fit his own wishes. It was crazy, and yet he sounded perfectly rational, as if any man would have made the same assumptions, as if he had every right to be angry with her for leading him on.

'You thought what?' she prodded.

'I thought you were special.'

'Like you thought Pam was special?'

'You're just like her after all,' he muttered, reaching into the deep pocket of his baggy black trousers.

Annie's hand moved to the butt of the Sig and slipped the lock strap free. A thousand people were having a party two hundred feet away, and she was standing alone with a probable murderer. The noise of the band seemed to fade to nothing.

'How do you mean?' she asked while her mind raced forward. Would he pull a knife? Would she have to take him down right here, right now? That wasn't how she thought it would go down. She didn't know what she had expected. A taped confession? The murder weapon surrendered without a fight?

'She took my friendship,' he said. 'She took my heart. And then she turned on me. And you're doing the same.'

'She was afraid of you, Marcus. That was you calling her, prowling around her house, slashing her tires – wasn't it?'

'I would never have hurt her,' he said, and Annie wondered if the answer was denial or guilt. 'She took my gifts. I thought she enjoyed my company.'

'And when she told you to get lost, you thought what – that maybe you could scare her anonymously and offer her comfort in person?'

'No. They turned her against me. She couldn't see how much I really cared. I tried to show her.'

'Who turned her against you?'

1183

'Her sorry excuse for a husband. And Stokes. They both wanted her and they turned her against me. What's your excuse, Annie?' he asked, bitterly. 'You want that lawyer? He's using you to do his dirty work for him. Can't you see that?'

'He's got nothing to do with this, Marcus. I want to solve Pam's murder. I told you that from the first.'

'You'll be sorry,' he said quietly. 'In the end, you'll be sorry.'

He started to pull his hand from his pocket. Heart pounding, Annie pulled the Sig and pointed it at his chest.

'Slowly, Marcus,' she ordered.

Slowly he drew his hand free, balled into a fist, and held it out to the side.

'Whatever it is, drop it.'

He opened his fingers, letting fall something small that hit the sidewalk with a soft rattle. With her left hand, Annie pulled her flashlight from her belt and took a step closer, the Sig still raised. Renard moved back toward the alley.

'Stand right there.'

She swept the beam of the flashlight down on the concrete and it reflected back off a strand of gold chain, a necklace lying like a length of discarded string with a heart-shaped locket attached.

'I thought you were special,' he said again.

Annie holstered the Sig and picked the necklace up.

'Is this the necklace you tried to give Pam?'

He stared at her through the empty eyes of the smiling mask and took another step back from her. 'I don't have to answer your questions, Deputy Broussard,' he said coldly. 'And I believe I'm free to go.'

With that, he turned and went back down the alley.

'Great,' Annie said under her breath, closing her fist on the locket.

Her edge with him had been her similarity to Pam, the woman he had fallen in love with. She had gained his trust, his respect, his attraction. In a heartbeat that was gone. Now she was more like Pam, the woman he may have butchered.

The two-way crackled against her hip and she jumped half a foot. 'Broussard? Where the fuck are you? Are you back on or what?'

Annie plucked at her wet shirt and bit back a groan. 'On my way, Sarge. Out.'

Sucking on the fingertip the thorn had lacerated, she wove her way through the crowd across France to the old Canal gas station. The place had been closed since the oil bust, and the old pumps had been taken out long ago, leaving weeds to sprout where they had once stood. The BUSINESS OPPORTUNITY FOR SALE sign had been propped in the front window so long it had turned yellow. A herd of teenage boys in baggy clothes and backward baseball caps milled around on the cracked concrete, drinking Mountain Dew and smoking cigarettes. Eyeing Annie with suspicion, they scattered like a pack of scruffy young dogs as she passed through their midst.

She went to the side of the building, where a pay phone was still in service. She dialed Fourcade and flapped her wet shirtfront as the phone on the other end rang. His machine clicked on with a curt 'Leave a message'.

'It's Annie. I just had a run-in with Renard. It's a long story, but the bottom line is I might have pushed him over the edge. He said some things that make me nervous. Um – I'm stuck working the dance, then I'm going home. I'm off tomorrow. I'll see you when I see you.'

She hung up feeling vaguely sick. She may have pushed a killer over the line from love to hate. Now what?

She watched the party from the corner of the vacant station, as removed from it as if she were standing behind a wall of glass. Inside her mind, she didn't hear the music of the band or the sounds from the crowd.

'*I would never have hurt her.*'

Not that he *hadn't* hurt Pam. He had made that verbal distinction before.

'*She couldn't see how much I really cared. I tried to show her.*'

How had he tried to show her? With his gifts or with the concern he had shown after he had scared her half to death? The same creepy, voyeuristic concern he had shown Annie when she'd told him about someone taking a shot at her.

'*Were you alone? You must have been frightened . . . Having a stranger reach into your life and commit an act of violence – it's a violation. It's rape. You feel so vulnerable, so powerless . . . so alone . . . Don't you?*'

Words of comfort that weren't comforting at all. He had made her feel vulnerable, made her feel violated, and he had done the same to Pam. She knew he had.

'*I thought you were special.*'

'*Like you thought Pam was special?*'

'*You're just like her, after all . . . You'll be sorry . . . In the end, you'll be sorry.*'

In the same way Pam must have been sorry? Sorry no one else could have seen the monster in him. Sorry no one had listened to her pleas for help. Sorry no one had heard her screams that night out on Pony Bayou.

Annie dug the necklace out of her pocket and held it up, watching the small gold locket sway back and forth. Renard had tried to give Pam a necklace for her birthday two weeks before she was killed.

'Officer Broussard?'

The soft voice broke Annie's concentration. She caught the locket in her fist and turned. Doll Renard stood beside her in a prison gray June Cleaver shirtwaist that had been intended for a woman with breasts and hips. In her hands she played nervously with the stem of a delicate butterfly-shaped mask covered in iridescent sequins. The elegant beauty of the mask seemed at odds with the woman holding it – plain, unadorned, her mouth a bitter knot.

'Mrs. Renard. Can I help you?'

Doll glanced away, anxious. 'I don't know if you can. I swear, I don't know what I'm doing here. It's a nightmare, that's what. A terrible nightmare.'

'What is?'

Tears glazed across the woman's eyes. One hand left the stem of her mask to pat at her heart. 'I don't know. I don't know what to do. All this time I thought we'd been wronged. All this time. My boys are all I have, you know. Their father betrayed us, and now they're all I have in the world.'

Annie waited. In her previous meetings with Doll she had found the woman melodramatic and shrill, but the stress stretched taut in Doll Renard's voice now had the ring of genuineness. Her small, sharp nose was red at the tip, her eyes rimmed in crimson from crying.

'I knew motherhood would be a joy and a trial,' she said, rubbing a hankie under her nose. 'But all the joy of it has been robbed from me. And now I fear it's become a nightmare.' Tears skimmed down her thin, pale cheeks. 'I'm so afraid.'

'Afraid of what, Mrs. Renard?'

'Of Marcus,' she confessed. 'I'm afraid my son has done something terribly wrong.'

45

'Could we go somewhere and talk?' Doll asked, glancing anxiously around at the masked revelers that moved up and down the street. She raised her own mask to partially hide her face. 'Marcus is here somewhere. I don't want him to see me speaking to you. We had a terrible quarrel last night. It was horrible. I never left my bed today, I was so distraught. I don't know what to do. You've been so kind, so fair to us, I thought . . .'

She paused, fighting the need to cry. Annie put a hand on her shoulder, torn between a woman's sympathy and a cop's excitement.

'I'm afraid I'm on duty –' she began.

'I wouldn't ask – I didn't want to – Oh, dear . . .' Doll raised a hand to her mouth and closed her eyes for a moment, working to compose herself. 'He's my son,' she said in a tortured whisper. 'I can't bear the thought that he might have –' Breaking off again, she shook her head. 'I shouldn't have come here. I'm sorry.'

She turned to go, shoulders hunched.

'Wait,' Annie said.

If Marcus Renard's mother had something, anything, that could connect him to the murder, she couldn't put off getting it. It was clear Doll's conscience had won the internal battle to bring her to this point, and just as clear that in a heartbeat she could back away in order to save her son.

'Where are you parked?'

'Down the street. Near Po' Richard's.'

'I'll meet you down there in five minutes. How's that?'

She shook her head a little. Her whole body seemed to be trembling. 'I don't know. I think this is a mistake. I shouldn't have –'

'Mrs Renard,' Annie said, touching her arm. 'Please don't back down now. If Marcus has done something bad, he needs to be stopped. It can't go on. You can't let it.'

She held her breath as Doll closed her eyes again, looking within herself for an answer that had to be tearing her mother's heart in two.

'No,' she whispered to herself. 'It can't go on. I can't let it go on.'

'I'll meet you at your car,' Annie said. 'We can have a cup of coffee. Talk. We'll sort it all out. What kind of car do you drive?'

Doll sniffed into her handkerchief. 'It's gray,' she said, sounding resigned. 'A Cadillac.'

Annie couldn't find Hooker in the sea of people, which was just as well. She didn't want him to see her going off in the opposite direction of the station. Ducking into a door well on the side street, she called him on the two-way to tell him she'd been stricken ill.

'What the hell's wrong with you, Broussard? You been drinking?'

'No, sir. Must be that stomach flu going around.' She paused to groan for effect. 'It's awful, Sarge. Out.'

Hooker swore his usual blue streak, but let her off. Deputies vomiting in public were bad for the image of the department. 'If I hear you been drinking, I'll suspend your ass! Out.'

Banishing the threat from her mind, she went to the cruiser and dumped the radio, afraid the chatter might frighten or distract Doll. Grabbing her minicassette recorder, she shoved it in a pants pocket and hustled down the dark side street toward Po' Richard's.

Doll Renard drove a gray Cadillac. If the passenger's side was damaged, then Marcus was the one who had terrorized her on the road that night. That would confirm Annie's Jekyll and Hyde theory. The adrenaline rush of finally catching a break was incredible. She felt almost light-headed with it. Renard's own mother was going to give him up. To her. Because of the work *she* had done on the case. Losing Marcus's trust wouldn't matter.

As she hurried down the sidewalk between closed businesses and parked cars, she tensed at every shadow, bolted past the openings to alleys. Marcus was lurking somewhere, hurt and angry over what he saw as her betrayal.

God only knew what he might do if he saw her with his mother. The relationship there was too twisted to fathom. The mother relying on the support of a son whom she never ceased to criticize and belittle; the grown man staying out of obligation to a woman he resented to the marrow of his bones. The line between their love and hate had to be a hairbreadth. What would it trigger in him to know his mother was about to commit the ultimate betrayal? The rage, the pain, would be incredible.

Annie had seen what his rage had done to Pam Bichon.

The car was parked at the curb, just east of Po' Richard's. Doll Renard paced beside it, one arm banded across her waist as if her stomach hurt, the other hand rubbing her sternum. Even in the poor light that reached over from the restaurant Annie could see the scars along the side of the Cadillac.

'Did you have an accident, Mrs. Renard?'

Doll looked blank, then glanced at the car. 'Oh, that,' she said, moving again. 'Marcus must have done that. I rarely drive. It's such a *big* car. I can't imagine why he bought me such a *big* car. So conspicuous. It's vulgar, really. And difficult to park. It preys on my nerves to drive it.

'I've developed a slight palsy from my nerves, you know. You can't imagine the strain it's been. Wondering, wanting to believe . . . Then last night . . . I can't stand it anymore.'

'Why don't we sit down and talk about it?' Annie suggested.

'Yes. Yes,' Doll repeated almost to herself, as if to reinforce the decision she had made. 'I took the liberty of getting coffee. It's just over here on this table.'

The cheap picnic tables that sat out in front of the restaurant were deserted and poorly lit. A hand-lettered sign in the front window announced: CLOSED for CARNIVAL. TAKE OUT ORDER'S ONLy.

Doll settled on the bench, fussing with her skirt like a debutante at a cotillion. Annie took her seat, stirred her coffee, and tested it. Dark and bitter, as always; hot but drinkable. She took a long sip, wanting the caffeine to burn off the fatigue of too many late nights. She needed to be sharp now, though it wouldn't do to appear overeager. She left her notebook in her shirt pocket. Under the table, she pressed the record button on the minicassette recorder.

'I'm not proud of this,' Doll began. She rested one hand on the table, her handkerchief clutched at the ready. 'He's my son. My loyalty should be to my family.'

'Letting this go on won't be in the interest of your family, Mrs. Renard. You're doing what's best.'

'That's what I keep telling myself. I have to do what's best.' She paused to sip at her coffee and compose herself.

Annie took a drink and waited, rubbing absently at the cut on her fingertip. She sat with her back to the restaurant and a view of the surrounding area. Without turning her head, she scanned the street, the sidewalk, the vacant lot beyond Po' Richard's property, trying to make out every shadow. No sign of Marcus, but then he was very good at staying just out of reach, just out of sight. She imagined him watching them now, his anger building toward the boiling point.

'It's been very difficult for me,' Doll said, 'raising the two boys on my own. Especially with Victor's difficulties. The state tried to take him away from me once and put him in a home. I wouldn't have it. He'll be with me 'til I die. He's my child, my burden to bear. I brought him into this world the way he is. I blamed myself for his condition, even though the doctors say it's no one's fault. How can we truly know what gets passed along from one generation to the next?'

Annie made no comment, but thought fleetingly of her own mother and the father she'd never known. 'What ever became of Mr Renard?'

Doll's face hardened. 'Claude betrayed us. Years ago. And now here I sit, about to betray my son.'

'You shouldn't think of it that way, Mrs. Renard. Why don't you tell me what it is you think Marcus has done wrong.'

'I don't know where to begin,' she said, looking down at her crumpled handkerchief.

'You said you had a fight with Marcus last night. What was that about?'

'You, I'm afraid.'

'Me?'

'I'm sure you realize Marcus has become quite taken with you. He does that, you see. He – he gets something in his head and there's no changing it. I can see it happening all over again with you. He's convinced there could be something . . . *personal* between the two of you.'

'I've told him that's not possible.'

'It won't matter. It never has.'

'This has happened before?'

'Yes. With the Bichon woman. And before her – when we lived in Baton Rouge –'

'Elaine Ingram?'

'Yes. Love at first sight, he called it. Within a week of meeting her, he was completely preoccupied. He followed her everywhere. Called her day and night. Lavished her with gifts. It was embarrassing.'

'I thought she returned his feelings.'

'For a time, but it became too much for her. He did the same with that Bichon woman. He suddenly decided he had to have her, even though she wanted no part of him. And I can see it starting again, with you. I confronted him about it.'

'What did he say?'

'He became irate and went into his workroom. No one is supposed to disturb him there, but I followed him,' she confessed. 'I never wanted to believe it was anything more than infatuation, what he felt for that woman, but I confess, I'd had a premonition. I'm very sensitive that way. I'd had these *feelings*, but I just wouldn't believe them.

'I watched Marcus from the door without him knowing. He went to a cupboard and got some things out of it, and I *knew*. I just *knew*.'

'What things?'

Doll bowed her head over the pocketbook in her lap. She reached into the bag and closed her hand around something, hesitating, withdrawing it slowly.

As she held the small picture frame out, Annie felt a strange rush shoot up her arms and into her head. She gripped one arm of the chair as the rush became a wave of dizziness. The picture frame that had gone missing from Pam Bichon's office. One of the items the detectives had searched for in order to at least tie Renard to the stalking charges. None of the items had ever been found.

Annie took it now and looked at it in the artificial light draining out the restaurant's front window. The frame was a delicate antique silver filigree, the glass inside it cracked. The photo was no more than two inches by three inches, but portrayed in that small space was a wealth of emotion – the love between a mother and child. Josie couldn't have been more than five, sitting on her mother's lap, gazing up at her with an angelic smile. Pam, her arms wrapped around her baby, smiling down at her with absolute adoration.

Marcus Renard had stolen this photograph and destroyed the relationship portrayed within it. He had taken a mother from her child. He had extinguished the spirit of a woman who had loved and had been loved by so many people.

The dizziness swooped through her again. A reaction to the photograph, Annie supposed. Or to the caffeine. She felt vaguely ill . . . at the sure knowledge that the man who had become infatuated with her was in fact the man who had committed unspeakable acts against the woman in this photograph. Fourcade had been right all along: the trail, the logic, led back to Renard.

'Marcus stole that, didn't he?' Doll said.

'Yes.'

'There were other things too, but I was afraid to take them. I believe he's stolen things from me,' she admitted. 'A cameo that was in my mother's family. A locket I'd had for years – since Victor was born. God only knows what he did with them.'

God and me, Annie thought, shuddering inwardly. And Pam Bichon. And probably Elaine Ingram before her. A clammy chill ran across her skin. She worked to pull in a deep breath of the humid night air, and stared down at the photograph that blurred a little before her eyes as the dizziness tipped through her again.

'I didn't want to believe he would do it again,' Doll said. 'The preoccupation and all.'

'Do you think he killed those women, Mrs. Renard?' Annie asked, the words sticking on her tongue. She took another drink of her coffee to clear the taste of the question. How awful for a mother to think her son was a murderer.

Doll pressed her hand over her face and began to weep, her body quivering. 'He's my son! He's all I have. I don't want to lose him!'

And yet she'd brought forward the evidence.

'I'm sorry,' Annie murmured. 'But we'll have to take this to the sheriff.'

She pushed her chair back and stood, swaying unsteadily on her feet, the dizziness swarming around her head like a cloud of bees. She felt as if she might just float off the ground, and had no control over whether she would or would not. As she stepped away from the table the ground seemed to dip beneath her feet, and she staggered.

'Oh, my goodness!' Doll Renard's voice sounded far away. 'Are you all right, Deputy Broussard?'

'Uh, I'm a little dizzy,' Annie mumbled.

'Perhaps you should sit back down?'

'No, I'll be fine. Too much caffeine, that's all. We need to get to the sheriff.'

She attempted another step and went down hard on one knee. The picture frame fell from her hand.

'Oh, dear!' Doll gasped. 'Let me help you!'

'This is embarrassing,' Annie said, steadying herself against the older woman as she rose. 'I'm so sorry.'

Doll sniffed and wrinkled her nose. 'Have you been drinking, Deputy?'

'No, no, that was an assident.' Alarm jumped through her at the sound of her own voice, the words slurred and indistinct. Her body felt heavy, as if she were moving through a vat of Jell-O. 'I'm just not feeling well. We'll go to the station. I'll be fine.'

They moved slowly toward the Cadillac, Doll Renard on Annie's right, supporting her. The woman was so much stronger than she looked, Annie thought. Or maybe it was just that she suddenly had no strength at all. An electric buzzing vibrated in her arms and legs. The fingertip she had pricked on the rose stem throbbed like a beating heart.

The rose thorn. The rose Marcus had given her.

Poisoned. God, she'd never expected that. But it was certainly poetic that a token of love would become an instrument of death when the love was spurned. He would think that way, the twisted, sick son of a bitch.

'Mizzuz Renard?' she said as she collapsed into the passenger's seat of the car. 'I think maybe we shhhould go to the hossspital. I think I might be dying.'

He wanted to kill her. He wanted to put his hands around Annie Broussard's throat and watch her face as he choked her. She had played him for a fool. The last joke would be on her. The violent fantasy splashed in vivid color through Marcus's mind as he pushed his way through the crowd.

The noise of the party was a discordant cacophony in his ears. The lights and colors were too bright, too garish against the black of night and the black of his mood. Faces loomed in at him, laughing mouths and hideous masks. He stumbled into a Ronald Reagan pretender, spilling the man's beer in a geyser onto the sidewalk.

'Fucking drunk!' Reagan shouted. 'Watch where you're going!'

In retaliation, the man shoved him hard, and Marcus careened into another reveler in a Zorro mask and a porkpie hat. Stokes.

Stokes stumbled backward, feet scrambling. Marcus fell with him, fell on him amid the forest of legs. He wished he had a knife. He imagined himself stabbing Stokes as they fell, then getting up and walking away before anyone realized.

'Stupid motherfucker!' Stokes yelled, getting up.

Before Marcus could right himself, Stokes booted him in the ribs. Holding himself, Marcus struggled to his feet and kept going, half doubled over, laughter ringing behind him. He pressed on through the crowd, then turned the corner and hurried down the side street toward Bowen & Briggs.

The thick, humid air burned in his lungs. His chest felt banded with steel, the pressure crushing against his cracked ribs. Small, sharp pains burst through him with every breath. His face was on fire. He tore off the painted mask and threw it in the gutter. It was no disguise compared to the mask Annie had worn. Betrayal with the lawyer was the least of her crimes. The slut. He had overlooked and rationalized and made excuses for her, sure that she would see in the end how right it could be between them. She deserved to be punished for what she'd put him through. He punished her in his mind as the emotions tore through him. Love, rage, hate. She would be sorry. In the end, she would be sorry.

He felt as if he'd been eviscerated. Why did this have to happen to him time and again? Why couldn't the women he loved love him in return? Why did his feelings grab hold so hard and refuse to let go? Love, passion, need, need, *need*. He was an otherwise normal man. He was intelligent. He had talents. He had a good job. Why did his need have to overwhelm him again and again?

As he let himself into the Volvo, tears rolled down his face, scalding with both pain and shame. His body was rigid and trembling with anger, the tension magnifying his various injuries, the physical pain further humiliating him. What kind of man was he? The kind other men kicked and scorned, the kind women sneered at, the kind women sought restraining orders against. He didn't think he could endure it any longer. The emotions were too much, too big, too painful. And in the back of his head he could hear his mother's mocking voice, telling him he was pathetic.

He *was* pathetic. That truth nearly crushed him with its weight.

He was sobbing as he passed the drive to the house where Pam had died. Her death would hang over him like a shadow for the rest of his life.

What kind of life was this to lead? A suspected murderer, a pathetic wretch living with his mother, spurned again and again by the women he loved. How many times had he wished himself away from here, envisioned a better life – with Elaine, with Pam, with Annie? But he would never go, and that better life would never happen. He would never live on the Gulf in a beach house and spend his evenings with Annie or any other woman. He would only become more pathetic, more isolated, be more loathed. What was the point?

He turned the Volvo down his driveway and gunned the engine. A sense of urgency had joined the other emotions writhing inside him like snakes. He slammed the car into park alongside the house and went inside.

Victor sat on the landing of the front stairs, wearing one of their mother's feather masks and rocking himself. He sprang to his feet and thundered down the steps, rushing to within inches of Marcus, shrieking, '*Red! Red! Red! Red!*'

1193

'Stop it!' Marcus snapped, shoving him back. 'You'll wake Mother.'

'Not now. Enter out, Mother. Red! *Very* red!'

'What are you talking about?' Marcus demanded, cutting through the dining room. Against his will, he glanced at the wall. Of course the paint didn't match. 'It's after midnight. Mother is in bed.'

Victor shook his head vigorously. 'Then *and* now. Enter out, Mother. *Red!*'

'I don't know what you mean,' Marcus said impatiently. 'Where would she have gone? You know Mother doesn't drive at night. You're being ridiculous.'

Frustration grabbed hold of Victor as they reached the door to Marcus's rooms, and he stopped beside the wall and banged his head against it, keening in his throat.

Marcus grabbed hold of him by the shoulders. 'Victor, stop it! Go to your room and calm down. Go look at one of your books.'

'*Then* and now. Then *and* now. Then and *now!*' he chanted.

Marcus heaved a sigh, feeling a deep sadness for his brother. Poor Victor, locked inside his own mind. Then again, maybe Victor was the lucky one.

'Come along,' he said, quietly.

Taking Victor by the hand, he led him upstairs to his room, shushing him the whole way.

'*Red! Red!*' Victor harped in a whisper, like a bird with laryngitis.

'Nothing is red, Victor,' Marcus said, turning on the lamp.

Victor sat down on the edge of the bed and rocked himself from side to side. The peacock plumes that arched up from the corners of his mask bobbed like antennae. He looked absurd.

'I want you to count to five thousand by sixteenths,' Marcus said. 'And when you're done, you let me know. Can you do that?'

Victor stared past him, his eyes glassy. Chances were good that by the time he reached five thousand he would have forgotten the source of his distress.

Marcus left the room and paused, looking at the door to his mother's room farther down the hall. Of course she would be in there, the spider in her nest. She would always be there – physically, psychologically, metaphorically. There was only one escape for any of them.

Purposeful, he went down to his bedroom, locked the door behind him, and went to the drawer where he kept his Percodan. The doctor had written the prescription for seventy-five pills, probably hoping he would take them all at once. He'd taken a number of them in the days and nights since his beating, but there were plenty left. More than enough. If he could find the bottle. It was gone from the drawer.

Victor? No. If Victor had taken an overdose of Percodan, agitation would not be the result. He would be lethargic or dead – and better off, either way.

Marcus turned away from the bed and continued on into his

workroom. He had cleaned up the mess his rage had created the night before. Everything was in its place once again, neat and tidy. The pencil portrait of Annie was on the drawing table. How fitting that it was torn, he thought, running his finger over the ragged edge of the paper. He imagined that the blood smeared across it was hers.

He turned to his worktable and the tools aligned with the precision of surgical instruments, contemplating the sharp razor's edge of the utility knife. Picking it up, he ran his thumb down the blade and watched his blood bloom along the cut, bright crimson. Tears came again, not at the physical pain, but at the enormous emotional burden of what he was about to do. He set the utility knife aside, disregarding it for his task. A butcher knife would serve the purpose, symbolically and literally. But first, he wanted the pills.

Going to the hidden panel in the wainscoting, he opened the cupboard, confronting his past and his perversion. That was what other people would call his love for women who didn't want him – perversion, obsession. They didn't know what obsession was.

The small tokens he had taken from Elaine and Pam and Annie sat in clusters on a shelf. Memories of things that might have been. A wave of bittersweet nostalgia washed over him as he chose a beautiful glass paperweight that had belonged to Pam. He held it in his hands and touched it to his face. It was cool against his tears.

'Drop it, you slimy, sick bastard.' The voice was low and thick with hate. 'That belonged to my daughter.'

The paperweight rolled from Marcus's hands and fell to the floor as he looked up into the face of Hunter Davidson.

'I hope you're ready to go to hell,' the old man said, cocking the hammer on the .45 he held. 'Because I've come to send you off.'

46

He'd been right from the start. The trail, the logic, led back to Renard. And if he had maintained his focus, if he hadn't allowed his past to leach into his present, Marcotte would have remained a bad distant memory.

Nick lit a cigarette and drew hard on it, trying to burn the bitter taste of the truth from his mouth. The damage was done. He would deal with the repercussions if and when they arose. His focus now had to be on the matter at hand: Renard.

Annie had apparently yanked his chain a little too hard. She needed backup, which was what Nick now felt he should have been doing all along instead of running off half-cocked at shadows. *Focus. Control.* He had let himself become distracted when he should have stayed true to his gut. The trail, the logic, led back to Renard.

He parked on a side street and entered the Carnival crowd, eyes scanning the mob for Broussard. If she had pushed Renard over the edge, then she could be in trouble, and he had no intention of waiting until morning or even waiting until she was off duty to find out. Whatever confrontation had taken place had been while she was working. That meant Renard was here, watching her.

The crowd was rowdy and drunk, the music loud. The street was filled with costumes and color and movement. Nick looked only for the slate blue uniforms of the SO deputies. He worked systematically down one side of La Rue France and up the other, barely pausing to accept the inane well wishes of his colleagues for the upcoming hearing. He saw no sign of Annie.

She could have been at the jail, booking in some drunk. He could have missed her in the crowd, she was so little. Or she could be in trouble. In the past ten days, she'd spent more time in trouble than out of it. And tonight she'd called to tell him she might have pushed a killer too far.

He could see Hooker loitering near a vendor selling fried shrimp, the fat sergeant scowling but tapping his toe to the music. Hooker would know where Annie was, but Nick doubted Hooker would give the information to him. He'd see too much potential for disaster.

'Nicky! My brother, my man. Where y'at?'

Stokes swayed toward him, his porkpie hat tipped rakishly over one masked eye. Each arm was occupied around a woman in a cut-to-the-ass miniskirt – a bottle blonde in leather and a brunette in denim. They appeared to be holding one another upright.

'This is my man, Nick,' Stokes said to the women. 'He don't no more know what to do with a party than he'd know what to do with a two-headed goat. You want one of these fine ladies to be your spirit guide into the party world, Nicky? We can go somewhere and have us a party of our own. You know what I mean?'

Nick scowled at him. 'You seen Broussard?'

'Broussard? What the hell you want with her?'

'Have you seen her?'

'No, and thank God for it. That chick ain't nothin' but grief, man. You oughta know. She – Oooohhh!' he cooed, as the possibilities dawned in his booze bumbled mind. 'Turnabout is fair play, huh? You wanna give her a little scare or somethin'?'

'Or something.'

'That's cool. I'm cool with that. Yeah. The bitch has it coming to her.'

'So go over there and ask Hooker where she's at. Make up a good excuse.'

The Dudley Do-Right flashed bright across Stokes's face. 'Mind my lady friends, Nicky. Girls, you be nice to Nicky. He's a monk.'

The blonde looked up at Nick as Stokes walked away. 'You're not *really* a monk, are you?'

Nick slipped his shades on, shutting the bimbo out, and said nothing, watching as Stokes approached the sergeant. The two exchanged words, then Stokes bought himself an order of shrimp and came back chewing.

'You're outta luck, friend. She done packed up her tight little ass and gone home.'

'What?'

'Hooker says she called in sick a while ago. He thinks maybe she was drinking.'

'Why would he think that?'

Stokes shrugged. 'I don't know, man. These rumors get around. You know what I mean? Anyhow, she ain't here.'

The anxiety in Nick's gut wound tighter. 'What's her unit number?'

'What's the difference? She's not in it.'

'I came past the station. Her Jeep's in the lot. What the hell is her unit number?' Nick demanded.

Stokes's confusion gave way to concern. He stopped chewing and swallowed. 'What're you planning, man?'

Nick's patience snapped. He grabbed Stokes by both shoulders and shook him, sending fried shrimp scattering on the sidewalk. 'What the hell is her unit number!'

'One Able Charlie!'

He wheeled and bolted through the crowd, Stokes's voice carrying after him.

'Hey! Don't do nothin' I wouldn't do!'

Nick barreled through the partyers, bouncing people out of his way with a lowered shoulder and a stiff forearm. Masks flashed by in his peripheral vision, giving the scene a surreal quality. When he finally reached his truck, his breath was sawing hot in and out of his lungs. The muscles in his ribs and back, still sore from DiMonti's beating, grabbed at him like talons.

He pulled the radio mike free of its holder, called dispatch, and, identifying himself as Stokes, asked to be patched through to One Able Charlie. The seconds ticked past, each one seeming longer than the last.

'Detective?' the dispatcher came back. 'One Able Charlie is not responding. According to the log that unit is off duty.'

Nick hung up the mike and started the truck. If Annie was off duty and her Jeep was still in the lot at the station, then where the hell was she?

And where the hell was Renard?

Leaning her head against the side window, Annie tried to fight off a wave of nausea as Doll put the Cadillac in gear and it lurched forward. As they passed the vacant lot adjacent to Po' Richard's, Annie thought she caught a glimpse of Marcus's smiling white mask in the darkness, laughing at her.

They crossed France a block above the party. The color and lights glared in the distance, then vanished. Annie groaned a little as the car turned right, the change of direction exacerbating her dizziness. She wondered what the poison was, wondered if there was an antidote, wondered if the blundering morons in the Our Lady lab would be able to figure any of it out before she died a horrible, agonizing death.

She told herself not to panic. Marcus couldn't have foreseen the events of the evening. He wouldn't have planned for her absolute rejection of him. If he followed his own pattern, he had probably intended only to make her ill so that he could then later offer her comfort. That was his pattern.

The business district gave way to residences. Blocks of small, neat ranch-style houses, many with a homemade shrine to the Virgin Mary in the front yard. Old claw-foot bathtubs had been cut in half and planted on end in the ground to form grottos for totems of Mary. The totems were mass-produced in a town not far from Bayou Breaux, and lay stacked like cordwood in the manufacturing yard beside the railroad tracks. Having seen that took away some of the mystique, Annie thought, her brain waves fracturing.

They should be at the hospital soon. The old groundskeeper would be scrubbing the toes of the giant Virgin Mary statue with a toothbrush.

'I appreciate this, Mizzuz Renard,' she said. 'I'll call the sheriff from the hospital. He'll come and pick yyyou up. Youuu did the right thing coming to mmme.'

'I know. I had to. I couldn't let it go on,' Doll said. 'I could see it happening all over again. Marcus becoming infatuated with you. You – a woman who would never have him. A woman who wants only to take

1198

my son from me and put him into prison – or worse. I can't let that happen. My boys are all I have.'

She turned and looked straight at Annie as they passed the turnoff for Our Lady of Mercy. The hate in her eyes seemed to glow red in the light of the dashboard.

'No one takes my boys away from me.'

47

'I'm on my way to hell.

Civilization passed behind them. The bayou country, ink black, vast and unwelcoming, stretched before them, a wilderness where violent death was the harsh reality of the day. Predator claimed prey here in an endless, bloody cycle, and no survivor mourned the demise of the less fortunate. Only the strong survived.

Annie had never felt weaker in her life. The nausea came in waves. The dizziness wouldn't abate. Her perceptions were beginning to distort. Sound seemed to come to her down a long tunnel. The world around her looked liquid and animated. Had to have been something in the coffee, she decided, something strong.

She tried to focus her eyes on the woman across the width of the big car. Doll Renard appeared elongated and so thin she could have been made of sticks. She didn't look as if she could have possessed the physical strength for violent rage. But Annie reminded herself that Doll Renard was younger than she looked, stronger than she looked. She was also a murderer. The frail, frumpy façade was as much a mask as the sequined domino that lay on the seat between them.

'Y*yyou* killed Pam? You di*iid* those things to Pam?' Annie said in disbelief, the gruesome images of the crime scene photos flashing through her mind, bright and bloody. She had dismissed the possibility of a woman perpetrator almost out of hand. Women didn't kill that way – with brutality, with cruelty, with hatred for their own gender.

'She got what she deserved, the whore,' Doll said bitterly. 'Men panting after her like dogs after a bitch in heat.'

'My God,' Annie breathed. 'But y*yyou* had to know M*mmarcus* would be a s*ssuspect.*'

'But Marcus didn't kill her,' Doll reasoned. 'He's innocent – of murder, at least. I watched him become obsessed with her,' she said with disgust. 'Just like with that Ingram woman. It didn't matter to him that she didn't want him. He gets these things in his head, and there's no getting them out. I tried. I tried to make *her* stop him, but he couldn't believe she would try to have him arrested. Her fear only seemed to draw him toward her.'

'Y*yyou* were the one . . . beh*iind* the stalking?'

'She would have taken him away from me – one way or the other.'

And so Doll had stabbed to death, crucified, and mutilated Pam Bichon. To end the obsession that had taken her son's attention away from her.

'I knew the police would question him, of course,' she went on. 'That was his punishment for trying to betray me. I thought it would teach him a lesson.'

Annie tried to swallow. Her reflexes had gone dull. Slowly she inched her right hand along the armrest, fingertips feeling for the butt of the Sig. The gun was gone. Doll had to have lifted it when she had been 'helping' Annie into the car, buckling her safely into the passenger's seat.

She glanced in the rearview, hoping against hope to see lights on their tail, but the night closed in behind them, and the swamp stretched out in front of them. Plenty of places to dump a body in the swamp.

The drug pulled at her, dragging her toward unconsciousness.

'Hhhow did yyou get Pam . . . to the house?' she asked, forcing her brain to stay engaged. She couldn't save herself if she wasn't conscious, and no one else was going to do it for her. Shifting her weight, she brought her right arm across her stomach and groaned, surreptitiously moving her fingertips onto the release button of her seat belt.

'It was pathetically easy. I called her under a false name and asked her to show the property to me,' Doll said, smiling at her own cleverness. 'Greedy little bitch. She wanted everything – money, beauty, men. She would have taken my son away from me, and she didn't even want him.'

It had been as simple as a phone call. Pam wouldn't have thought twice about meeting an older woman to show a rural property, even at night. Her problems had all been with men – or so she had thought. So they all had thought. Fourcade had been right all along: The trail, the logic, led back to Renard. He just hadn't realized which Renard. No one had given a second thought to Marcus Renard's flighty, strident mother.

And now that woman is going to kill me. The thought swept around inside Annie's mind like a cyclone. She thought she could see the letters of the sentence floating in the air. She had to do something. Soon. Before the drug pulled her all the way under.

'You're no better,' Doll said. 'Marcus wants you. He can't see you're an enemy. His desire for you takes him away from me. I tried to make you stop him from wanting you. Just like I did with that Bichon woman.'

'Youuu were in the carrr that night. You came tooo my house,' Annie said, the puzzle pieces floating up to the surface of her brain. She envisioned them rising up through the goo, sticky and wet with blood. 'How did youuu . . . get in? Hooow did you know . . . about the ssstairs?'

A smirk tugged at Renard's thin lips. 'I knew your mother. She did some piecework for me one season, sewing on my costumes. That was before Claude betrayed me, before I had to take the boys away from here. Everyone wanted my costumes then.'

Doll Renard had known her mother. The admission brought another wave of dizziness crashing through Annie. Doll Renard had been in her home when she was a child. She tried to search through her mind for some memory of her and Marcus coming face-to-face as children. Could that have been possible? Could either of them have had any inkling that their paths would cross this way in adulthood? That an acquaintance begun with an innocent encounter so long ago, then forgotten, would end in murder?

'She was whore, just like you,' Doll said. 'Blood will tell.'

Blood will tell. Annie saw the phrase flow from Doll's mouth in the form of a thick red snake.

She swallowed hard as the nausea came again, then pitched forward toward the dash and vomited on the floor. Doll made a sound of disgust. Annie hung there, free now of the seat belt, trying to get her breath, one hand braced against the dash. She had to do something. The drug was pulling her deeper into its embrace, the velvet blackness of unconsciousness seducing her.

Gathering what strength she could, she lunged across the width of the car, grabbing for the steering wheel. The Cadillac swerved hard to the right, tires screeching. Annie used the wheel to pull herself across the seat, one hand lying hard on the horn.

Doll screamed in outrage, slapping at Annie's face with one hand while she attempted to wrestle the wheel back to the left. The car dropped one front wheel off the shoulder of the road and bounced back, careening across the center line. The headlights shone on the glossy surface of black water.

Annie ducked her head to avoid the blows and clawed at the wheel again. She used her body to crowd Doll against the door, reaching across blindly with her left hand for the door handle. If she could get the door open, maybe she could push Doll out. She could see it happen in her mind's eye: Doll's brittle body hitting the asphalt like a crash-test dummy, bouncing, her head breaking open, her brain spilling out. She snagged the handle with the tips of two fingers.

The car went into a sudden, screeching skid as Doll jammed on the brakes. Annie flew into the dash, her head bouncing off the windshield, her shoulder slamming into the dashboard. The noise, the motion, the pain, the vertigo tumbled through her in an avalanche. She tried to push herself up from the floor as the car jolted onto the shoulder and stopped. She tried to get hold of something for support and orientation, tried to focus her eyes on something out in front of her – the barrel of a gun.

Her gun. In Doll Renard's hand. Three inches from her face.

Swinging wildly, she knocked the gun sideways, and the Sig went off with a deafening *pop!*, shattering a window somewhere in the car.

'Bitch!' Doll shrieked.

She grabbed Annie by the hair with her left hand and brought the gun down hard, slamming it against her temple and cheekbone once, twice.

Starbursts of color shot through Annie's head like a meteor shower.

Surrendering for the moment, she dropped to the floor, crumpled and limp, blood trickling in thin fingers down across her cheek. She could feel consciousness sliding away. She thought she could feel the world sliding beneath her, but it was only the car. They were moving again, off the main road. She could hear the soft swish of grass brushing against the sides of the Cadillac, the popping sound of tires crunching over rock.

She lay still on the floor, energy spent, knowing she had to find more, had to scrape together another burst or die. *Weapons*. The thought was a dim light in her mind. *Doll has the Sig. Doll has the Sig. Doll has the Sig.* She knew there had to be something more, another answer, stupid simple, but she couldn't think.

So tired.

Her limbs were as heavy as the branches of a live oak. Her hands felt the size of catcher's mitts. She tried to swallow around a tongue as thick as a copperhead. Maybe the red snake she had seen come out of Doll's mouth had gone into her own to choke her. A taste as bitter as acid filled her mouth.

Acid. That would be a weapon, she thought. She imagined throwing it in Doll Renard's face, imagined the face burning down to the skull bones while the rest of her body danced a mad jig of death.

Acid.

The car rolled to a stop. Doll popped the lock on the trunk, got out of the car, and slammed the door. Annie reached slowly down her right side to her duty belt, feeling back from her empty holster to the slim nylon case just behind it. She pried up the Velcro tab and slipped the small cylinder free with clumsy fingers.

Behind her, the car door opened. Annie's head snapped back as Doll grabbed her by the hair and pulled her backward.

'Get up! Get up!'

Annie fell onto the ground, wincing as Doll kicked her in the back and cursed her. Curling into a ball, she tried to protect her head. The fingers of her right hand wrapped tightly around the cylinder in her palm.

The door of the Cadillac swung shut, just missing Annie's head, then Doll had her by the hair again, dragging her into a sitting position. Annie opened her eyes, reaching out to steady herself against the side of the car as the dizziness spun her brain around and around. The car's headlights provided the only illumination, but it was enough. Tipping and spinning in front of her vision was a house, run-down, with broken windows gaping like toothless spots in an old crone's smile.

They were on Pony Bayou. This was the house where Pam Bichon had had her life cut out of her.

I didn't kill Pam,' Marcus said softly.

Hunter Davidson's broad face twisted with disgust. 'Don't stand there and lie to me. There's no judge here but God. There's no technicalities, no loopholes for you and your damn lawyer to jump through.'

'I loved her,' Marcus whispered, tears coming again to stream down his cheeks.

'*Loved her*?' Davidson's big body quivered with rage. Sweat ringed the underarms of his shirt. His thin hair was dark and shiny-wet. 'You don't know what love is. *I made her!* My wife bore her! She was our child! You don't know a damn thing about that kind of love. She was our baby, and you took her away from us!'

The irony, Marcus thought, was that he knew all about that kind of love. He had been caught in a sick mutation of it his whole life. Tonight he would have ended it. Now Pam's father would end it for him.

'You can't know how many times I've killed you,' Davidson said softly, moving forward. His eyes were glassy with the fever of hate. 'I dreamed of nailing you down and putting you through the hell my baby went through.'

'No,' Marcus whispered, crying harder now with fear. Spittle bubbled between his lips and dribbled down his chin. Against his will, his gaze darted to the big wooden table where his utility and X-Acto knives were laid out like surgical instruments. He shook his head. 'Please, no.'

'I wanted to hear you beg me for your life, the way Pam must have begged. Did she call for me when she was dying?' Davidson asked in a tortured voice. Tears as big as raindrops spilled down his ruddy cheeks. 'Did she call for her mama?'

'I don't know,' Marcus murmured.

'I hear her. *Every night.* I hear her calling for us, calling for me to save her, and there's not a damn thing I can do! She's gone. She's gone forever!'

He stood no more than two feet away now. The hand that held the gun was as big as a bear's paw, white-knuckled, trembling.

'You should die like that,' he whispered bitterly. 'But I didn't come here for revenge. I came for justice.'

The gun barked twice. Marcus's eyes widened in surprise as the force of the bullets knocked him backward. He felt nothing. Even as he fell into his drawing table, then to the floor, the back of his head bouncing off the hardwood, he felt nothing. His body jumped again and again as Davidson fired into him. Marcus felt as if he were watching the scene on a movie screen.

He was dying. Another irony. He would have taken his own life tonight. He would have ended his mother's quiet, twisted tyranny. He would have spared Victor a future without protection. Instead, he would die here on the floor, killed for a crime he didn't commit, a failure even in death.

They'll think Mmmmarrcus did it,' Annie said.

'No, they won't,' Doll corrected her. 'They'll know exactly who did it: you. Get up.'

Bracing herself against the Cadillac, Annie rose slowly, awkwardly.

Think. Try to think. Need a plan.

Thinking was as tiring and difficult as swimming upstream against a strong current. Thinking and walking simultaneously was nearly impossible. The ground rose and fell erratically beneath her feet. The house shimmered like a mirage in the glare of the headlights. Her breathing was becoming labored. She could feel her heartbeat slowing like the ticking of a clock winding down to a stop. It would be only a matter of time before the drugs pulled her under entirely, then Doll would stick the Sig in her mouth and pull the trigger. Suicide.

Her career had been in trouble. She'd been having difficulties with her co-workers. A number of people had reported she had recently developed a drinking problem. Would it be a stretch to believe she'd gone out to the house where she had found Pam Bichon's mutilated remains, taken a handful of downers, and blown her brains out with her service weapon?

'But hooow did I . . . get here?' she asked, pausing at the foot of the porch steps.

'Shut up!' Doll snapped, jabbing her in the back with the Sig. 'Get inside.'

The vehicle was just a minor snag, Annie supposed, as she staggered up the steps onto the porch. Doll Renard was an old hand at murder. She'd gotten away with it twice already.

The door stood open, as if someone had been expecting them. Annie stepped into the entry, her footfalls echoing in the empty hall. The beam of a portable lantern cut through the gloom, lighting the way to her death. The floor was thick with dust. Cobwebs festooned the doorways. The nose of the Sig jabbed into her back. Annie moved down the hall, her left hand against the wall, feeling her way like a blind person.

'How many . . . will youuu kill?' she mumbled. 'Hoow long before Marcus . . . knows? He'll hate you.'

'He's my son. My sons love me. My sons need me. No one will ever take them from me.' The vehemence in Doll's tone sounded practiced, as if she'd chanted those words over and over and over for years and years and years.

'Who tried to take them?' Annie asked. Her legs felt like rubber. Her body wanted to sink to the floor and succumb.

She stepped through a doorway and found herself in the dining room. The beam of the lantern swept across the floor as Doll set it down, illuminating the hasty retreat of a long black indigo snake across the dirty old cypress planks. For an instant she saw Pam lying there, arms outstretched, her body savaged. The head lifted and the decaying face turned toward her, mouth moving.

'*You are me. Help me. Help me. Help me!*' The words turned to a shriek that pierced through Annie's brain from ear to ear.

Help me, she thought, knowing no one would, knowing help was too much to hope for. Time was running out.

She bent over at the waist, leaning her right shoulder against the wall, trying to marshal what strength she had left. Doll stood two feet in front of her. The doorway to the hall was immediately to the right of Doll, with the stairs to the second floor right there, leading up into darkness. She needed a plan. She needed a weapon.

Doll has the Sig. Doll has the Sig.

Her baton was gone. Her fingers tightened on the slim canister in her palm. She tried to breathe, tried to think, stared at her black cop shoes.

Stupid simple.

'Claude would have,' Doll said. 'He betrayed us. He would have taken my boys away from me. I couldn't let that happen.'

'Your . . . husband?'

'He forced me to it. He betrayed us. He got what he deserved. I told him so,' she said. 'Right before I killed him.'

Doll came forward a step. 'It's time for you to lie down, Deputy.'

'Why the . . . mask on Pam?' Annie asked, ignoring the dictate. 'It led strraight . . . to youuu.'

'I don't know anything about that mask,' she said impatiently, gesturing with the gun for Annie to move. 'Over there, Deputy. Where that other cunt died.'

'I don't think I . . . can move,' Annie said, watching Doll's feet as the sensible matron shoes came another step closer.

'I told you to move,' she said with authority. 'Move!'

Annie took the command as her signal, calling on the last of her reserves. With her left hand, she batted the Sig to one side. The gun barked, spitting a shot into the ceiling. At the same time, Annie brought up her right hand with the can of Mace and sprayed.

Doll screamed as the pepper spray caught her in the right eye. She stumbled back, clawing at her face with her free hand, swinging the gun back into position with the other. The Sig cracked off another round, the bullet hitting Annie low in the chest, knocking her into the wall. The impact of the slug against her ballistic vest knocked the breath from her lungs, but there was no time to recover. She had to move. Now.

Doubled over, she rushed for the stairs and threw herself up into the darkness as the gun fired again. Arms and legs flailing clumsily, she scrambled for the second floor, slipping, falling, hitting her knee, cracking her elbow. The drug had destroyed her sense of equilibrium. She couldn't tell up from down from flat. When she hit the landing on the second floor, she sprawled on her face. The sound of her chin hitting the wood was almost as sharp as the sound of the shot Doll fired at her from below – but not nearly as sharp as the searing pain of the bullet tearing through the back of her left thigh and exiting through the front.

Scuttling on her belly like a gator, Annie propelled herself through the nearest doorway. Coughing at the dust she'd raised, fighting the sobs of pain, she tipped herself upright with her back against the wall behind the door. She felt for the entrance and exit wounds, her hand coming away wet with blood, but there was no arterial bleeding – a small favor. It would take her longer to die. The dizziness wobbled her like a top. The blackness added to the sense of vertigo. The only light in the room came through a single window, faint and gray.

Time was running out. She tore at the cuff of her uniform trousers. Her fingers felt as huge and unwieldy as sausages. She thought she could hear Doll coming up the steps, the sound of footfalls alternating with the pounding of her pulse in her ears.

She pushed herself to her feet with her back against the wall for balance and waited. Her left leg was deadweight, unable to support her at all. The rush of adrenaline and the drag of narcotics fought a tug-of-war within her. Her chest felt as if someone had hit her with a forty-pound hammer. She wondered if the force of the first bullet had cracked a rib and knew it wouldn't matter if she were dead.

The Sig reported a fraction of a second before the shot splintered through the door, six inches in front of Annie's face. Biting back the cry of surprise, she flattened herself against the wall and held her breath. Her hands were sweating, her grip unsure. She said a quick prayer and promised to go to confession more often. The inevitable bargain with God. But if God hadn't listened to Pam Bichon's cries while Doll Renard had tortured and killed her, then why would He listen now?

Somewhere across the hall she could hear the scratching of rats or coons or some other animal squatters. The Sig cracked off another round in that direction, away from the room where Annie stood. She held her position, hidden by the partially opened door, the window across the room giving her enough light to make out shapes, at least.

She would have one solid chance. She could hold herself together long enough for one chance. And if she didn't make good on it, she'd be dead.

Nick put his foot to the floor and ran the truck wide open down the straight sections of road. Woods and swamp flashed past in a blur. He was outrunning the reach of his headlights but not of his imagination.

Annie wasn't in her unit. Her Jeep sat in the parking lot behind the station. Her stuff was in her locker. She'd called in sick, Hooker had said. What the hell did that mean? Had Renard grabbed her and forced her to call in with a gun to her head? Had she wanted to get free of duty to check something out? Nick had no way of knowing. He knew only that he had a fist of apprehension in his gut and another one had him by the throat.

He hit the brakes and skidded past Renard's driveway, slammed the transmission into reverse and roared backward. Without a thought to the restraining order against him, he turned in the Renard drive and gunned it.

Lights glowed on the first floor toward the back of the house. Only one upstairs window was lit. Renard's Volvo sat at a cockeyed angle near the front veranda, the dome light on. It struck Nick as odd. Renard was as anal retentive as they came. To leave anything crooked or ajar was out of character.

He killed the truck's lights and engine, and climbed out. He had thought finding Renard at home would lessen his fears for Annie. Surely Renard would never bring her here. But the night air hung thick and heavy with tension around the old house. The quiet was the unnatural quiet of a world holding its breath.

And then came the shots.

The footsteps came nearer. Annie gulped a breath and wiped the sweat from her forehead with the back of her wrist. Dizzy. Sick. Weaker and weaker. Her vision was blurring. Time was running out.

'You'll die tonight one way or another.' Doll's voice sounded in the hall.

She was crying, cursing. The Mace had to be burning like a hot poker in her eye.

'You'll die, you'll die,' she promised over and over.

The footsteps shuffled nearer.

Annie could feel her on the other side of the door. And before her Pam suddenly appeared, her rotting corpse standing upright, glowing like a holy vision. Her mouth fell open and a single word spilled out on a tide of blood – *justice*.

Doll passed the door and turned, stepping into the vision. In that moment it seemed to Annie as if she had a spotlight turned on her. Doll's eyes bugged wide. Her mouth tore open. She raised the gun in slow motion.

And Annie pulled the trigger.

The nine-millimeter Kurz Back-Up bucked in her hands and Doll Renard's face shattered like glass. The force knocked her backward across the room. She was dead before she hit the floor.

Annie went limp against the wall, her head swimming, her vision fuzzing out. She blinked hard and watched as the apparition of Pam shot straight up through the ceiling and was gone.

Justice. She'd come into this looking for justice – for Pam, for Josie.

Let justice be done.

Too weak to return the Kurz to her ankle holster, she stuck the gun in the waistband of her pants, then tried to find within herself the strength to keep from dying.

48

He killed my baby girl,' Hunter Davidson mumbled. 'He killed my baby.'

He sat on his knees on the floor of Marcus Renard's studio, drenched in sweat, pale and trembling. He looked up at Nick, the pain in his eyes as wretched as anything Nick had ever seen.

'You understand, don't you?' Davidson said. 'I had to. He killed my girl.'

Nick kept his gun at his side, approaching the man cautious step by cautious step. A .45 hung limp in the big man's left hand, resting on his thigh. Marcus Renard lay on the floor, arms flung wide, his eyes half-open and sightless.

'Why you don't set that gun on the floor and slide it toward me, Mr. Davidson?' Nick said.

Hunter Davidson just sat there, his gaze on the man he had killed. Slowly, Nick bent down, took the .45 away from him, and stuck it in the back waistband of his jeans. He holstered his own weapon, then gently coaxed Davidson up from the floor and moved him away from the body.

'You have the right to remain silent, Mr. Davidson,' he began.

'I had to do it,' Davidson murmured more to himself than to Nick. 'He had to pay. We deserved justice.'

The system hadn't given it to him quickly enough. And now the justice meted out would be against him. The tragedy of Pam's death had just extended out another ring in the pond.

Nick looked from Renard's lifeless body to Pam's father and felt nothing but deep and profound sadness.

Victor held himself perfectly still outside the door to Marcus's Own Space. Marcus had given him a job to do. He tried always to please Marcus, even though Victor didn't fully understand what it meant to be pleased. *Pleased* was a white feeling – he knew that. But the sounds had driven him from his room before he could complete his counting task. The voices had come up through the floor – *very red*.

The house was quiet now, but the silence didn't give him a white feeling as it usually did. The Controllers in his head were frowning. *Red* seeped around the edges of his brain like bacteria. Then *and* now. Like before. Victor knew this feeling. He raised his hands to touch his special mask. The feel of the feathers against his fingertips was soft, *white*, like *running water*. And yet, he could feel the heavy *redness* all around. He could taste it in the air, feel it against his skin, pressing in on him, touching each individual hair on his body, reaching into his ears a sound that was not a sound. Tension. Sound *and* silence.

Mother was not asleep, as Marcus thought. Then *and* now. Like before. She was gone. Enter out. *Very* red. She was their mother, but *not* their mother sometimes. Mask, no mask. *Mask* equaled *change*, and sometimes *deception*. Victor had tried to tell, but Marcus didn't hear him. Marcus saw only one of Mother's faces, and he never heard The Voice. Sound and silence.

Victor stood just outside the door, staring in. He felt time pass, felt the earth move in minute increments beneath his feet. Marcus lay on the floor near the Secret Door. Asleep, but not asleep. Marcus had ceased to exist. His eyes were open, but he didn't see Victor. His shirt was red with blood. *Very red.*

Hesitant, Victor moved into the room, not looking at the other people. He kneeled down beside Marcus and touched the blood, though he didn't touch the holes. Holes were always bad. Bacteria and germs. Red holes were *very* bad.

'Not now, Marcus,' he said softly. 'Not now enter out.'

Marcus didn't move. Victor had tried to tell him about Mother and the Face Women – Elaine and Pam and Annie but Marcus didn't hear him. He had tried to tell him about the Waiting Man tonight, but Marcus didn't hear him. *Very, very* red.

Victor touched his brother's forehead with his bloody fingers and began to rock himself. He knew he wouldn't like for Marcus to not exist forever. He knew he didn't like the way his brother's face had changed. The Controllers frowned in his mind.

'Not now, Marcus,' he whispered. 'Not now enter out.'

Slowly he reached up and slipped the feather mask from his own face and placed it over his brother's.

Nick watched the strange, sad little ritual with a heavy heart. He wondered for the first time where Renard's mother was, why she hadn't come running at the sound of trouble. Then the roar of a big car engine cut into his thoughts, and he started for the front of the house, breaking into a run at the sound of metal hitting metal.

At the side of the house a Cadillac had broadsided Renard's Volvo. As Nick stepped out onto the veranda, the car's door opened and the driver fell out onto the lawn. Nick jumped down to the ground and jogged closer, that old hand of dread grabbing hold of him hard as he saw the uniform and the mop of dark hair.

''Toinette!' he shouted, sprinting the last few yards.

He dropped to the ground beside her, his trembling hands framing her face. He slid two fingers down the side of her throat to search for a pulse, praying, pleading.

Annie opened her eyes and looked up at him. Nick. It was nice to see him one last time, whether his image was real or not.

'Doll,' she murmured dreamily, a shudder quaking through her body. 'Doll killed Pam. And she killed me too.'

49

The edge of death was a place of darkness and light, sound and silence. She hovered there, slipping from one world into the next and back again.

The ambulance, the urgency of the EMTs, the lights, the sirens.

Utter stillness, a sense of calm and resignation.

The noise and motion of the ER.

The eerie peace of nonexistence.

Annie saw the landscape as bleak and still, a battlefield in the aftermath, bodies scattered across the ground, the sky hanging heavy and leaden, everything cast in the twilight colors of nightmares. Pam was there. And Doll Renard. And Marcus. Their souls rose from them like smoke from a dying fire and drifted just above the bloody ground. She stood on the sidelines and watched.

'*It's cold here, no?*' Fourcade whispered.

'*Where?*'

He raised his left hand, fingers spread, and reached out, not quite touching her. Slowly he passed his hand before her eyes, skimmed it around the side of her head, just brushing his fingertips against her hair.

'*In Shadowland.*'

He spoke as if he lived in this place. And yet, Annie felt herself being pulled away from him, deeper into the blackness.

'*Don't leave me here, 'Toinette,*' he murmured, his dark eyes filled with sadness. '*Me, I've been alone too long.*'

She stretched out her hand toward his, but couldn't quite reach. Then panic seized her as she felt herself being drawn backward, across the line between life and death. She didn't think she had the strength to break free. She was so tired, so weak. But she didn't want to die. She wasn't ready to die.

The darkness, as thick and liquid as oil, began to suck her under. Tapping into a reserve of strength she didn't know she possessed, Annie focused on the surface and tried to kick free.

The first thing she saw when she opened her eyes was Fourcade. He sat beside the bed, staring at her as if looking away would break her tenuous tie to the living world. She was aware of monitors beside her bed and the night beyond her window.

'Hi,' she whispered.

He leaned closer, still staring. 'I thought I lost you there, *chère*,' he said softly.

'Where?'

'In Shadowland.'

His eyes never leaving hers, he raised her hand to his lips and kissed the back of it. 'You scared me, 'Toinette. Me, I don't like to be scared. It pisses me off.' The corners of his mouth turned up a fraction of an inch.

Annie smiled dreamily. 'Well, we've got that in common.'

He leaned closer and touched his lips to hers, and Annie drifted off to sleep with a sigh of deep relief. When she woke again he was gone.

You're tuned to KJUN. All talk all the time. Our top story at the top of the hour: Local planter Hunter Davidson, father of murder victim Pamela Bichon, will be arraigned this afternoon in the Partout Parish Courthouse for the murder of Bayou Breaux architect Marcus Renard.

'Davidson's new attorney, Revon Tallant, has suggested an insanity defense will be employed, and expects that an alleged confession made by Davidson early Sunday morning will be ruled inadmissible by the court.

'Davidson had recently been released from Partout Parish Jail following a plea agreement on charges of attempted assault against Marcus Renard. District Attorney Smith Pritchett has been unavailable for comment. A formal statement is expected later this morning.'

Annie turned the radio off. During the two days she lay in the hospital bed, her senses had been bombarded with the story. On television, on the radio, in the newspapers. Accurate, inaccurate, twisted, and sensational- ized – she'd heard every version of Hunter Davidson's drama and her own. She had been besieged with requests for interviews, all of which she had declined. It was over. Time for everyone to try to repair the damage that had been done and move on.

Dr Van Allen had reluctantly agreed to let her go home. The drug Doll Renard had dosed her with had been effectively counteracted. The blood she had lost had been replaced. The pain in her thigh was constant, but tolerable. The bullet had passed through and through, missing both the bone and the vital femoral artery. She would limp for a while, but all things considered, she was damn lucky.

Lucky to be alive. Whether or not she would be lucky enough to have a job to go back to remained to be seen.

Gus had come to her bedside on Sunday to personally take her statement regarding Doll Renard. He listened without comment while Annie related the events of the last ten days, his face lined with a tense emotion she was afraid to name.

She thought about it now as she sat down on the edge of the bed to rest a moment from the effort of getting dressed. What had been gained and what had been lost in all of this? A murderer had been unmasked and stopped. Annie had gained insights into her own strengths and abilities.

But the losses seemed disproportionately heavy. She'd seen an ugly side to men she had to work with and rely upon. Lives had been altered, some damaged beyond repair.

She limped out of the hospital into a day that was cool and gray with the promise of rain, and eased herself awkwardly into the shotgun seat of the cruiser Noblier had sent for her. The deputy was Phil Prejean. He squirmed in the driver's seat like a five-year-old with a full bladder.

'I – ah – I'm sorry for what all that happened, Annie,' he said. 'I hope you can accept my apology.'

'Yeah, sure,' she said without conviction, and fixed her gaze out the window.

They drove out of the lot with an itchy silence thick in the air between them.

News vans from television stations all over Louisiana crowded the curbs out in front of the courthouse, even though the arraignment was still more than an hour away. The parking lot was clogged with cars. Annie wondered what those same reporters who had called Hunter Davidson a folk hero ten days ago would call him now that he'd killed an innocent man.

The story of a crime went so much deeper than what people read in the papers or saw on the nightly news. No reporter could cram into a column inch or a sixty-second sound bite how the repercussions rolled outward from a single violent epicenter to shake the lives of so many people – the victim's family and the perpetrator's, the cops and the community.

Josie Bichon had been left without a mother. Her grandfather would go to trial for murder. Belle Davidson had lost a daughter and stood to lose a husband. Victor Renard had lost the only people who could understand any part of the workings of his damaged mind. The people of Bayou Breaux had suffered irreparable damage to their sense of trust and safety.

Prejean pulled into a visitor's slot near the back entrance to the law enforcement center. Annie hoped it wasn't prophetic. Hooker scowled at her with suspicion as she limped past his desk, as if she had been revealed as an undercover spy on his shift. She received a variation on that same look from Myron as she passed the records counter. Valerie Comb in Noblier's outer office still looked at her as if she were a bad piece of meat.

The sheriff had put on his funeral suit for the day's media attentions, a charcoal pinstripe that didn't hang quite right on his big-boned frame. He'd already jerked his tie loose at the throat. He looked older than Annie remembered him a week ago.

'How you doing, Annie? You okay for this?'

Alarm struck a low, vibrating note in her gut. 'That depends on what *this* is, sir.'

'Have a seat,' he offered, pointing to one of his visitor's chairs. 'The doctor released you?'

'Yes, sir.'

'He signed a release? You'll forgive my skepticism, but you've developed a bad habit of defying orders recently.'

'They didn't give me a copy of it,' Annie said, sucking a breath in through clenched teeth as she settled herself down on the edge of the chair. 'They gave me a bill.'

His point about her insubordination made, Noblier didn't press for the documentation. He settled into his own chair and looked at her hard for a moment. Annie returned his stare evenly.

'We executed a search warrant on the Renard home over the weekend,' he began at last, opening the pencil drawer of his desk. 'Among possessions found in Marcus Renard's workroom were items known to belong to Pam Bichon. We also found this.'

He tossed the plastic dancing alligator across the desk. Annie picked it up, feeling a vague embarrassment at the silliness of the thing with its leering grin and red beret. Then feeling a creepy sense of violation. Renard had taken this innocent trinket from her as a token. He'd fondled it, held it, and thinking of her, tainted it.

'Deputy Prejean recognized it. Thought you might want it back.'

'Thank you, sir.' She slipped it into her jacket pocket, knowing she would throw it away the minute she left the room.

'Found in Doll Renard's bedroom was a nine-inch boning knife. Found it between her mattress and box spring,' he went on. 'Never found it before because the warrants never extended to Mrs. Renard's bedroom. The knife's been sent to the lab.'

'Was it clean?'

Noblier weighed his answer for a moment, then decided she'd earned it. 'No. It wasn't.'

The idea turned Annie's stomach. Doll Renard had kept a bloody knife beneath her mattress so that she could take it out and remind herself of the atrocities she had committed in the name of motherhood. But she appreciated the evidence for what it would provide. Closure – for Pam, for her family, for the cops who had worked the case. 'They'll be able to match blood and tissue.'

'I expect so.'

'Good.'

The sheriff went silent again, watching her, frowning. A bad sign, she thought.

'I been giving a lot of thought to this over the last couple of days, Annie,' he began. 'I can't condone my deputies going off on their own, investigating cases they ain't assigned to.'

'No, sir,' Annie murmured.

'You always have been one to stick your nose in where it don't belong.'

'Yes, sir.'

'Nothing but trouble. Creates dissension. Undermines command.'

Annie said nothing. She had a perverse need to relish the feel of her career slipping away.

'On the other hand, it shows initiative, guts, ambition,' he said, taking the pendulum back to the high side. 'Tell me this, Annie: Why'd you go after Fourcade that night?'

'Because it was the right thing to do.'

'And why'd you go after Renard on your own?'

It was Annie's turn to weigh her answer. She could have said she hadn't trusted Stokes to do the job, but that wasn't it, not really. Not on a gut level. Not in her soul, where it counted most.

'Because I felt I owed it to Pam. I was the first person to see what her killer had done to her. There was something very . . . personal about that. I felt like I owed her. I found her body, I wanted to find her justice too.'

Gus nodded his head, pursing his lips. 'You haven't talked to the press.'

'No, sir.'

'At the press conference this afternoon I'll be telling them how you were working undercover to help crack this case. Your next paycheck will reflect your overtime.'

Annie's eyes widened at what sounded for all intents and purposes to be a bribe.

Noblier read her face like a clock and narrowed his small eyes. 'I won't have my authority undermined, Annie. My deputies work *for* me, not around me. The OT is a bonus – consider it hazard pay. Understood?'

'Yes, sir.'

'You got a hell of a lot to learn about how the world works, Broussard.' He had already begun his dismissal of her, his attention going to the notes he had scribbled for the press conference. 'Report back to me when you come in off sick leave. We'll do the paperwork on your reassignment . . . Detective.'

Detective Broussard. Annie tried the sound of it in her mind as she hobbled back down the hall. It sounded good. She pulled the plastic alligator from her pocket and tossed it in the trash as she passed the sergeant's desk.

Fourcade was waiting for her outside the door. He stood leaning against the building, his ankles crossed, his hands in the pockets of his jacket, concern in his eyes.

'Noblier made me a detective,' she announced, hearing the ring of disbelief in her own voice.

'I know. I recommended you.'

'Oh.'

'It's where you belong, 'Toinette,' he said. 'You do good work. You dig hard. You believe in the job. You seek the truth, fight for justice – that's what it oughta be about.'

Annie made a little shrug and glanced away, uncomfortable with his praise. 'Yeah, well, I lose the cool uniform and the hot car.'

He didn't smile. Big surprise. He straightened away from the wall and touched her cheek with a gentle hand. 'How you doing, 'Toinette? You okay?'

The weight of it all pressed a sigh from her. 'Not exactly.'

She wanted to say she wasn't the same person she had been ten days ago, but she had the distinct feeling Nick would disagree with her. He would tell her she simply hadn't looked that deep inside before. She wondered what he saw when he looked that deeply within himself.

'Walk with me?' she said. 'Down to the bayou?'

Frowning, he looked across the parking lot to the strip of green boulevard fifty yards away. 'You sure?'

'I've been in bed for two days. I need to move. Slowly, but I need to move.'

She started without him. He fell in step beside her. Neither of them spoke as they crossed the distance. When they reached the bank, a small group of mallards started, then settled back onto the chocolate brown water, bobbing at the edge of the reeds like corks. Across the bayou, an old man was walking a dachshund.

Annie sat down gingerly on one end of a park bench, stretching her left leg carefully in front of her. Fourcade took the other end of the bench. The space between them was occupied by Marcus Renard.

'He was innocent, Nick,' she said softly.

He could have argued. Marcus Renard's obsession with Pam had acted as the catalyst for his mother's violence. But that wasn't the point here, and he knew it. He had followed the trail back to Marcus, stopped there, and meted out his own punishment.

'Would it have made a difference if he'd been guilty?'

Annie thought about it for a moment. 'It would have made it easier to rationalize, at least.'

'C'est vrai,' he murmured. 'True enough. But he wasn't guilty. I screwed up. I lost perspective. I lost control. Wrong is wrong, and a man is dead because of it. Because of me. I'll have to carry that the rest of my life.'

'You didn't pull the trigger.'

'But me, I loaded the gun, didn't I? Davidson believed so strongly that Marcus Renard killed his daughter in part because *I* believed so strongly that Marcus Renard killed his daughter. My focus became his focus. You should know how that works – I tried to force it on you too.'

'Only because it made sense. No one can fault your logic, Nick.'

He flashed the sudden smile, the edges of it hard with an inner bitterness. '*Mais* no. My faults lie deeper. I believe it's better to err on the side of passion rather than apathy.'

He cared too much, tried too hard. The job was his life, his mission. Everything else was secondary. Submerged in that obsession, he found it too easy to lose his perspective and his humanity. He needed an anchor, an alter ego, a voice to question his motives, a counterbalance to his single-mindedness.

He needed Annie.

'I hear Pritchett will drop the charges against you,' she said.

He leaned his forearms against his thighs and watched the dachshund man. '*Oui*. So, I not only indirectly caused Renard's death, I benefited from it.'

'So did I. I'm off the hook for testifying. That's no small relief,' she said, willing him to meet her eyes. He turned his head and looked at her. 'I didn't want to, Nick, but I would have.'

'I know. You're a woman of convictions, 'Toinette,' he said, offering her a smile that was softer, fond, almost sad. 'So where does that leave me?'

'I don't know.'

'Sure you do.'

Annie didn't bother to argue. He was right. He was a complex and difficult man. He would push her. He would test her. It would have been so much easier for her to turn to A.J., take what he wanted to give her, live a simple life. A nice simple life, just short of fulfilment. Maybe in time the restlessness would fade into contentment. Or maybe it was better to err on the side of passion.

'You're not an easy man, Nick.'

'No, I'm not,' he admitted, never taking his eyes off hers. 'So, you gonna help me with that, *chère*, or what? You gonna take a chance? Be bold?'

He held his breath and waited, stared at her and willed her to take the challenge.

'I don't know what I have in me to offer you, 'Toinette,' he confessed softly. 'But I'd like the chance to find out.'

Annie looked past his determination to his need. She looked at the hard face, the dark eyes burning on hers. He was too intense, too driven, too alone. But she had the distinct feeling he was what she had been waiting for. Her strongest instinct was to reach out to him.

'Me too,' she murmured, reaching across the space between them to lay her hand on his. 'If we're partners . . .'

He turned his hand over and twined his fingers with hers, the contact warm and right. '. . . we're partners.'

Epilogue

Victor sat at the small table in his room, cutting paper with a blunt-nosed scissors. The house was not his family house. Riverview was a group home for autistic adults. It was a strange place full of people he did not know. Some were kind to him. Some were not.

There was a large lawn with a tall brick wall around it and many trees around the perimeter, and a very nice garden. A good place for watching birds, though not nearly as many species as there had been at Victor's own house. And here he couldn't take a boat out on the bayou to search for more. Nor was he allowed to go outside in the night to listen for the night birds or observe the other creatures that preferred darkness to light. There were many that did. Some were predators. Some were not.

For the most part, Victor's life in this new place was quiet and calm. Somewhere between *red and white. Gray*, he had decided. Most days he felt very gray. Like sleeping, but awake. He often thought of Marcus and wished that he had not ceased to exist. He often thought of Mother.

Setting the scissors aside, he took up the small bottle of glue and set about putting the finishing touches on his creation. Mother had ceased to exist, Richard Kudrow had told him, though Victor had not seen her and did not know for a fact that this was true. Sometimes he dreamed that she came to him in the night, as she often had, and sat beside him on his bed and stroked his hair while she talked in the Night Voice.

A low hum of tension vibrated through him as he remembered the Night Voice. The Night Voice spoke of red things. The Night Voice spoke of *feelings*. Better not to have them.

Love.

> *Passion.*

>> *Greed.*

>>> *Anger.*

>>>> *Hatred.*

Their power was very red. The people they touched ceased to exist. Like Father. Like Mother. Like Marcus. Like Pam.

Sometimes Victor dreamed of the Dark Night and the things he had seen. *Very red.* Mother, but *not* Mother, doing things the Night Voice talked about. Even just remembering brought on a red intensity that paralyzed him, as it had that night. He had stood frozen outside the house for hours afterward, hidden in the darkness, unable to move or speak. Finally he had gone inside to see.

Pam, but *not* Pam. She had ceased to exist. Her cries remained locked inside Victor's mind, echoing and echoing. He didn't like the way her face had changed. Slowly, he took off his mask and laid it across her eyes.

Love.

　　Passion.

　　　　Greed.

　　　　　　Anger.

　　　　　　　　Hatred.

Emotions. Better not to have them. Better to wear a mask, he thought as he put his new one on and went to his small window to stare out at a world cast in the intense colors and soft shadows of twilight.

Hatred.

　　Anger.

　　　　Greed.

　　　　　　Passion.

　　　　　　　　Love.

The line between them is thin and dark.

Glossary of Cajun French

allons	let's go
arrète	stop
c'est assez	that's enough
c'est chaud	that's hot
c'est ein affaire à pus finir	it's a thing that has no end
c'est vrai	that's true
chère 'tite bête	poor little dear
chérie, chère, cher	cherished, beloved
coonass	a sometimes derogatory slang term for Cajun
éspèsces de tête dure	you hard-headed thing
fils de putain	son of a bitch
foute ton quant dici	get away
grenier	attic, loft
ici on parle français	French spoken here
Il a pas d'ésprit	he doesn't have any sense
je t'aime	I love you
jeune fille	young girl
le grand derangement	when the Cajuns were exiled from Canada
loup-garou	Cajun myth: werewolf
ma 'tite fille	my little girl
mais	but: often used for emphasis with yes or no
mais non	but no
mais sa c'est fou	but that's crazy
merde	shit
mon ami	my friend
mon Dieu	my God
pou	louse
pur Cajun	pure Cajun
que sera sera	what will be will be
sa c'est de la couyonade	that's foolishness
si vous plâit	please
t'es trop grand pour tes cullotes	you're too big for your britches

t'es en érreur	you're mistaken
tcheue poule	chicken ass
'tite chatte	little cat
'tite belle	little sweetheart
T- or Tee	preceding a name is short for *petite* or *'tite*, and denotes a nickname
viens ici	come here